Reviews for Rankin and Rebus

BEGGARS BANQUET

'There's not a dud in the pack, with each story perfectly judged and bearing all the hallmarks of a writer at the peak of his powers. Great summer reading.' *Time Out*

'Rankin forays into short stories, to exhilarating effect.' *Sunday Times*

'The short stories demonstrate in miniature the extraordinary extent and range of Rankin's output, his evocation of character and atmosphere as well as narrative pace.' *Scotland on Sunday*

'Masterfully plotted, clear and succinct.' *The Scotsman*

RESURRECTION MEN

'What is impressive in *Resurrection Men* is not just the deftness of the links between disparate crimes, but the fluency of the fugue-like counterpoint between investigations ... On this form, nothing is beyond him.' *Sunday Times*

'Rankin's Rebus novels should be required reading for anyone whose knowledge of Edinburgh has been derived from visits to the festival ... Rankin conveys the visceral fears and hatreds lurking just below the smart Georgian surface of the "you'll have your tea" New Town.'
 Sunday Telegraph

'Bears all the qualities that have established Rankin as one of Britain's leading novelists in any genre: a powerful sense of place; a redefinition of Scotland and its past; persuasive dialogue and a growing compassion among its characters.' *New Statesmen*

THE FALLS

'Rankin masterfully pulls his fascinating plot together, and his sense of place casts a powerful shadow over this subtle tale of the recurrence of evil.' *Guardian*

'*The Falls* pulses with vitality. Suspense vigorously propels you through its pages. Rankin's prose is crisp, laconic and witty. So is his tangy dialogue.' *Sunday Times*

'An extraordinarily rich addition to crime literature.'
 Independent on Sunday

'This is the work of a very good crime writer at his very best . . . whatever it is that makes a good crime writer, Ian Rankin has it in spades.'
 Irish Times

'*The Falls* is an inventive and absorbing book which lives up to the technical term of a rebus as an enigmatic puzzle.' *Scotsman*

'*The Falls*, the 12th full-length Inspector Rebus story, finds his creator, Ian Rankin, at his brilliant, mordant best, with the dark heart of the city featuring almost as strongly as Rebus himself.' *Sunday Telegraph*

'Few would disagree that Ian Rankin is making a contribution to crime fiction that will last. His novels are playing a significant part in redefining Scotland's image of itself in literature. He is one of a handful of British crime writers whose books are not only commercially success-ful but also build a strong case for why crime fiction at its best, can and should be considered as literature.' *Independent on Sunday*

SET IN DARKNESS

'Rankin is a master of his craft, handling each twist and turn of the plot with consummate skill as he takes us by the hand and leads us from the sparkling edifices of New Labour-controlled Scotland to the misty, mysterious Edinburgh alleyways, and from hip and trendy restaurants to dank pubs and bars without missing a step . . . Rankin is streets ahead in the British procedural writing field . . . our top crime writer.'

Independent on Sunday

'The book sets off at a cracking rate, with bodies piling up in the first few chapters . . . Running parallel to the excellently paced plot is the theme of Scotland's national identity, its past and future, its regeneration and re-evaluation . . . *Set in Darkness* sees Rankin in impeccable form and will undoubtedly please his legions of fans and increase his appeal even further.'

The List

'This is, astonishingly, the eleventh Inspector Rebus novel by a writer who is still not yet 40, but whose consistent level of excellence is unmatched in the field of British crime fiction.' Marcel Berlins,

The Times

'Rankin exhibits his customary pitch-perfect ear for dialogue, sense of place and eye for both the seamy and grand sides of Scottish life. His books demonstrate that it is possible to take familiar elements – murder, corruption, a beautiful city, an unconventional and oddly-named detective who likes a drink and is unlucky in love – and turn them into something more original and exciting than the standard Morse code. His books are powerful, fast-moving and compulsive. Rankin is without doubt Britain's best crime novelist.'

Express

'Rankin's particular skill is in producing a highly complex plot whose different strands cleverly come together at the end, a setting which brings to life the grim back streets of Edinburgh and a well-drawn cast of characters.'

Sunday Telegraph

Also by Ian Rankin

The Inspector Rebus Series

Knots & Crosses
Hide & Seek
Tooth & Nail (previously published as Wolfman)
Strip Jack
The Black Book
Mortal Causes
Let It Bleed
Black & Blue
The Hanging Garden
Death Is Not the End (a novella)
Dead Souls
Set in Darkness
The Falls
Resurrection Men
Beggars Banquet

Other Novels

The Flood
Watchman
Westwind

Writing as Jack Harvey

Witch Hunt
Bleeding Hearts
Blood Hunt

Rebus:
The Lost Years

Let It Bleed
Black & Blue
The Hanging Garden

Ian Rankin

ORION

This omnibus edition first published as *Rebus: The Lost Years*
in Great Britain in 2003 by Orion Books,
an imprint of The Orion Publishing Group
Orion House, 5 Upper St Martin's Lane, London WC2H 9EA

A CIP catalogue record for this book is
available from the British Library

ISBN (trade paperback) 0 75286 003 8

Typeset by Deltatype Ltd,
Birkenhead, Merseyside

Printed and bound in Great Britain by
Clays Ltd, St Ives plc

Contents

Let It Bleed

Acknowledgements

Grateful thanks to: Ronnie Mackintosh, for helping me with my inquiries; Councillor Devin Scobie, for steering me through local government; John Mathieson, Staff Training Officer, HM Prison Edinburgh, for his advice; The Scottish Office, especially the Publications Department, New St Andrew's House; staff of Edinburgh City Chambers; staff of LEEL and Scottish Enterprise; staff of Edinburgh Central Lending Library and the Scottish National Library; Jon for the sofa; and the usual nod to everyone at the Oxford Bar.

All inaccuracies are, of course, my own.

The lines quoted by Mrs Kennedy are from *The New Testament in Scots*, translated by W. L. Lorimer (Penguin, 1985).

3

Avarice, the spur of industry.

(David Hume, 'Of Civil Liberty')

The more sophisticated readers simply repeated the Italian proverb, 'If it isn't true, it's to the point.'

(Muriel Spark, *The Public Image*)

Without women, life is a pub.

(Martin Amis, *Money*)

One
Bridges

1

A winter night, screaming out of Edinburgh.

The front car was being chased by three others. In the chasing cars were police officers. Sleet was falling through the darkness, blowing horizontally. In the second of the police cars, Inspector John Rebus had his teeth bared. He gripped the doorhandle with one hand, and the front edge of his passenger seat with the other. In the driver's seat, Chief Inspector Frank Lauderdale seemed to have shed about thirty years. He was a youth again, enjoying the feeling of power which came from driving fast, driving a wee bit crazy. He sat well forward, peering through the windscreen.

'We'll get them!' he yelled for the umpteenth time. 'We'll get the bastards!'

Rebus couldn't unlock his jaw long enough to form a reply. It wasn't that Lauderdale was a bad driver . . . Well OK, it wasn't *just* that Lauderdale was a bad driver; the weather bothered Rebus too. When they'd taken the second roundabout at the Barnton Interchange, Rebus had felt the car's back wheels losing all grip on the slick road surface. The tyres weren't brand new to start with; probably retreads at that. The air temperature was near zero, the sleet lying treacherously in wait. They were out of the city now, leaving traffic lights and junctions behind. A car chase here should be safer. But Rebus didn't feel safe.

In the car in front were two young, keen uniforms, with a DS and a DC in the car behind. Rebus looked into the wing mirror and saw headlights. He looked out of the passenger-side window and saw nothing. Christ, it was dark out there.

Rebus thought: I don't want to die in the dark.

A telephone conversation the previous day.

'Ten grand and we let your daughter go.'

The father licked his lips. 'Ten? That's a lot of money.'

'Not to you.'

'Wait, let me think.' The father looked at the pad, where John Rebus had just scribbled something. 'It's short notice,' he told the caller. Rebus was listening on an earpiece, staring at the tape recorder's silently turning spools.

'That attitude could get her hurt.'

'No . . . please.'

'Then you'd better get the money.'

'You'll bring her with you?'

'We're not cheats, mister. She'll be there if the money is.'

'Where?'

'We'll phone tonight with details. One last thing, no police, understand? Any sign, even a distant siren, and next time you see her'll be the Co-op funeral parlour.'

'We'll get them!' Lauderdale shouted.

Rebus felt his jaw unlock. 'All right, we'll get them. So why not ease off?'

Lauderdale glanced at him and grinned. 'Lost your bottle, John?' Then he jerked the wheel and pulled out to overtake a transit van.

The phone caller had sounded young, working-class. In his mouth, 'understand' had become *unnerstaun*. He'd spoken of the Co-op. He'd used the word 'mister'. Young working class, maybe a bit naïve. Rebus just wasn't sure.

'Fife Police are waiting the other side of the bridge, right?' he persisted, shouting above the engine whine. Lauderdale had the poor gearbox pounding away in third.

'Right,' Lauderdale agreed.

'Then what's our hurry?'

'Don't be soft, John. They're *ours*.'

Rebus knew what his superior meant. If the front car made it over the Forth Road Bridge, then it was in Fife, and Fife Constabulary were waiting, a roadblock erected. It would be a Fife collar.

Lauderdale was on the radio, talking to the car ahead. His one-handed driving was only a little worse than his two-handed, shaking Rebus from side to side. Lauderdale put the radio down again.

'What do you reckon?' he said. 'Will they come off at Queensferry?'

'I don't know,' Rebus said.

'Well, those two L-plates in front think we'll catch them at the toll booths if they decide to go all the way.'

They probably would go all the way, too, driven by fear and adrenalin. The combination tended to put blinkers on your survival mechanism. You ran straight ahead, without thought or deviation. All you knew was flight.

'You could at least put on your seatbelt,' Rebus said.

'I could,' said Lauderdale. But he didn't. Boy racers didn't wear seatbelts.

The final slip-road was coming up. The front car sped past it. There was nowhere to go now but the bridge. The roadlighting high overhead grew thick again as they neared the toll booths. Rebus had a crazy notion of the fugitives stopping to pay their toll, just like everyone else. Winding down the window, fumbling for the coins . . .

'They're slowing.'

The road was spreading out, suddenly half a dozen lanes wide. Ahead of them stood the row of toll booths, and beyond that the bridge itself, curving up towards its midpoint as the steel coils held its carriageway in suspension, so that even on a clear, bright day you couldn't see the far end when you drove on to it.

'They're definitely slowing.'

Only yards separated the four cars now, and Rebus could see, for the first time in a while, the back of the car they were chasing. It was a Y-registration Ford Cortina. The overhead lighting allowed him to make out two heads, driver and passenger, both male.

'Maybe she's in the boot,' he said dubiously.

'Maybe,' Lauderdale agreed.

'If she's not in the car with them, they can't harm her.'

Lauderdale nodded, not really listening, then reached for the radio again. There was a lot of interference. 'If they go on to the bridge,' he said, 'that's it, dead end. There's no way off for them, unless the Fifers fuck up.'

'So we stay here?' Rebus suggested. Lauderdale just laughed. 'Thought not,' said Rebus.

But now something was happening. The suspects' car . . . red tail-lights. Were they braking? No, reversing, and at speed. They hit the front police car with force, sending it shunting into Lauderdale's.

'Bastards!'

Then the front car was off again, veering crazily. It headed for one of the closed booths, hitting the barrier, not snapping it off but bending it enough to squeeze through. The sound of metal sparking against metal, and then they were gone. Rebus couldn't believe it.

'They're on the wrong carriageway!'

And so they were, whether by accident or design. Picking up speed, the car was racing north along the southbound lanes, its headlights switched to full beam. The front police car hesitated, then followed. Lauderdale looked ready to do the same thing, but Rebus reached out a hand and tugged with all his might on the steering-wheel, bringing them back into the northbound lane.

'Stupid bastard!' Lauderdale spat, slamming the accelerator hard.

It was late night, not much traffic about. Even so, the driver of the front car was taking some risk.

'They'll only have this carriageway blocked, won't they?' Rebus pointed out. 'If those lunatics make it to the other side, they could get away.'

Lauderdale didn't say anything. He was looking across the central reservation, keeping the other two cars in sight. When he reached out for the radio, he all but lost control. The car jolted right, then harder to the left, slamming the metal side-rails. Rebus didn't want to think about the Firth of Forth, hundreds of feet below. But he thought of it anyway. He'd walked across the bridge a couple of times, using the footpaths either side of the roadways. That had been scary enough, the ever-present wind threatening to gust you over the side. He felt a charge in his toes: a fear of heights.

On the other carriageway, the inevitable was happening, the incredible just about to begin. An articulated lorry, up to speed after a crawl to the top of the rise, saw headlights ahead of it where no headlights should be. The suspects' car had already squeezed past two oncoming cars, and would have slipped into the outside lane to pass the artic, but the artic's driver panicked. He pulled into the outside lane and his hands froze, foot still hard on the accelerator. The truck hit metal and started to rise. It went up into the air, hanging over the central reservation, which was itself a network of steel lines. The trailer snagged and the cab snapped forward, breaking free of its container and sailing into the northbound lanes, sliding on sparks and a spray of water, directly into the path of the car in which Lauderdale and Rebus were travelling.

Lauderdale did his best to hit the brakes, but there was nowhere to go.

The cab was sliding diagonally, taking up both lanes. Nowhere to go. Rebus had a couple of seconds to take it in. He felt his whole being contract, everything trying to be where his scrotum was. He pulled his knees up, feet and hands against the dashboard, tucking his head against his legs . . .

Whump.

With his eyes screwed shut, all Rebus had to go on were noises and feeling. Something punched him in the cheekbone, then was gone. There was a shattering of glass, like ice cracking, and the sound of metal being tortured. His gut told him the car was travelling backwards. There were other sounds too, further away. More metal, more glass.

The artic cab had lost a lot of its momentum, and contact with the car stopped it dead. Rebus thought his spine would crack. Whiplash, did they call it? More like bricklash, slab-lash. The car stopped, and the first thing he realised was that his jaw hurt. He looked over to the driver's seat, reckoning Lauderdale had landed one on him for some unspecified reason, and saw that his superior wasn't there any more.

Well, his arse was there, staring Rebus in the face from its unpromising position where the windscreen used to be. Lauderdale's feet were tucked beneath the steering-wheel. One of his shoes had come off. His legs were draped over the steering-wheel itself. As for the rest of him, that was lying on what was left of the bonnet.

'Frank!' Rebus cried. 'Frank!' He knew better than to pull Lauderdale back into the car; knew better than to touch him at all. He tried opening his door, but it wasn't a door any more. So he undid his seatbelt and squeezed out through the windscreen. His hand touched metal, and he felt a sizzling sensation. Cursing and drawing his hand away, he saw he'd placed it on a section of uncovered engine-block.

Cars were pulling to a stop behind him. The DS and DC were running forwards.

'Frank,' Rebus said quietly. He looked at Lauderdale's face, bloody but still alive. Yes, he was sure Lauderdale was alive. There was just something . . . He wasn't moving, you couldn't even be sure he was breathing. But there was *some*thing, some unseen energy which hadn't departed. Not yet at any rate.

'You all right?' someone asked.

'Help him,' Rebus ordered. 'Get an ambulance. And check the lorry-cab, see how the driver is.'

Then he looked across to the other carriageway, and what he saw froze him. He couldn't be sure at first, not totally. So he climbed up on to the metal spars separating the two carriageways. And then he was sure.

The suspects' car had left the carriageway. Left it altogether. They'd somehow vaulted the crash-barrier, slid across the pedestrian walkway, and had enough velocity left to send them through the final set of railings, the ones separating the walkway from that drop to the Firth of Forth. A wind was whipping around Rebus, blowing the sleet into his eyes. He narrowed them and looked again. The Cortina was still there, hanging out into space, its front wheels through the rails but its back wheels and boot still on the walkway. He thought of what might be in the boot.

'Oh my God,' he said. Then he started to clamber over the thick metal tines.

'What are you doing?' someone yelled. 'Come back!'

But Rebus kept moving, only barely aware of the drop beneath him, the amounts of space between each metal bar and its neighbour. More space than metal. The cold metal felt good against his stinging palm. He passed the back of the lorry. It had come to rest on its side, half on the roadway, half resting on the central gap. There was a sign on its side: Byars Haulage. Jesus, it was cold. That wind, that damned eternal wind. Yet he could feel he was sweating. I should be wearing a coat, he thought. I'll catch my death.

Then he was on the carriageway, where a line of cars had come to an untidy stop. There was a proper gap between carriageway and walkway; a short distance, but all of it fresh air. Where the Cortina had made contact it had buckled the rails. Rebus stepped on to them, then made the short leap on to the walkway.

The two teenagers had stumbled from their car.

They'd had to climb over their seats and into the back in order to get out. The front doors led only to a fall. They were looking to left and right, seized by fright. There were sirens to the north. Fife Police were on their way.

Rebus held up his hands. The two uniformed officers were behind him. The youths weren't looking at Rebus; all they could see were uniforms. They understood simple things. They understood what uniforms meant. They looked around again, looking for an escape that wasn't there, then one of them – fair-haired, tall, slightly older-looking – gripped the younger one's hand and started leading him backwards.

'Don't do anything daft, sons,' said one of the uniforms. But they were just words. Nobody was listening. The two teenagers were against the rails now, only ten feet or so from the crashed car. Rebus walked slowly forwards, pointing with his finger, making it clear to them that he was going to the car. The impact had caused the boot to spring open an inch. Rebus carefully lifted it and looked in.

There was nobody inside.

As he closed the boot, the car rocked on its fulcrum then came to rest again. He looked towards the older of the boys.

'It's freezing out here,' he said. 'Let's get you into a car.'

Then things happened in slow motion. The fair-haired boy shook his head, almost smiling, and placed his arms around his friend in what looked like nothing less than an embrace. Then he leaned back against the rail and just kept leaning, taking his friend with him. There was no resistance. Their cheap trainers held against the road surface for a second, then slipped, legs flicking up and over as they fell into the darkness.

Maybe it was suicide, maybe flight, Rebus thought later. Whatever it was meant to be, it was death for sure. When you hit water from that height, it was like hitting concrete. A fall like that, through the dark, and they didn't scream, didn't utter a sound, and couldn't see the water rising to meet them.

Only they didn't hit water.

A Royal Navy frigate had just left Rosyth Dockyard and was gliding out towards the sea, and that's what they hit, embedding themselves in the metal deck.

Which, as everyone said back at the station, saved the police frogmen from a thankless sub-zero dip.

2

They took Rebus to the Royal Infirmary.

He travelled in the back of a police car. Frank Lauderdale was being brought by ambulance. Nobody knew yet how bad his injuries were. The frigate had been contacted by radio from Rosyth, but the crew had already found the bodies. Some had heard them hitting the deck. The frigate was returning to base. It would take a while to hammer the deck back into shape.

'I feel like I've been hit with a hammer myself,' Rebus told the nurse at the infirmary. He knew her; she'd treated him for burns a while back, rubbed lotion on and changed the dressings. She smiled as she left the little booth where he lay on an examining table. When she'd gone, Rebus took another account of himself. His jaw hurt where Lauderdale's fist had connected prior to flying through the windscreen. The pain seemed to be burrowing deep, like it was getting into the nerves of his teeth. Otherwise he didn't feel too bad; just shaken. He lifted his hands and held them in front of him. Yes, he could always blame the trembling on the crash, even if he knew he trembled a lot these days, smash or no smash. His palm was blistering nicely. Before putting on a dressing, the nurse had asked how he got the burn.

'Put my hand on a hot engine,' he'd explained.

'Figures.'

Rebus looked and saw what she meant: part of the engine's serial number had been branded on his flesh.

The doctor finally put in an appearance. It was a busy night. Rebus knew the doctor. His name was George Klasser and he was Polish or something, or at least his parents were. Rebus had always assumed Klasser was a bit too senior to do the night shift, yet here he was.

'Bitter outside, isn't it?' Dr Klasser said.

'Is that supposed to be funny?'

'Just making conversation, John. How do you feel?'

'I think I'm getting toothache.'

'Anything else?' Dr Klasser was fussing with the tools of his trade: penlight and stethoscope, a clipboard and non-working Biro. Eventually he was ready to examine the patient. Rebus didn't put up much of a fight. He was thinking of drinking: the creamy, almost gas-free head on a pint of eighty-bob. The warming aroma from a glass of malt.

'How's my chief inspector?' Rebus asked when the nurse returned.

'They're taking X-rays,' she told him.

'Car chases at your age,' Dr Klasser muttered. 'I blame television.'

Rebus took a good look at him, and realised he hadn't ever really looked at the man before, not properly. Klasser was in his early forties, steel-haired with a tanned and prematurely ageing face. If you only had head and shoulders to go on, you'd guess he was taller than was actually the case. He looked quite distinguished, which was why Rebus had pegged him for a senior consultant, something like that.

'I thought only lackeys and L-plates worked nights,' Rebus commented, while Klasser shone a light in his eyes.

Klasser put down the light and started to squeeze Rebus's back, prodding it like he was plumping up a cushion.

'Any pain there?'

'No.'

'What about there?'

'No more than usual.'

'Hmm ... In answer to your question, John, I notice *you're* working nights. Does that make you lackey or L-plate?'

'That hurts.'

Dr Klasser smiled.

'So,' Rebus said, easing his shirt back on, 'what've I got?'

Klasser found a pen that worked and scribbled something on his clipboard. 'By my estimate, the way you're going, you've got a year, maybe two.'

The two men stared at one another. Rebus knew precisely what the doctor was talking about.

'I'm serious, John. You smoke, you drink like a fish, and you don't exercise. Since Patience stopped feeding you, your diet's gone to hell. Starch and carbohydrate, saturated fat ...'

Rebus tried to stop listening. He knew his drinking was a problem these days precisely because he'd learned self-control. As a result, few people noticed that he *had* a problem. He was well dressed at work, alert when the occasion demanded, and even visited the gym some lunchtimes. He ate lazily, and maybe too much, and yes, he was back on the cigs. But then nobody was perfect.

'An uncanny prognosis, Doctor.' He finished buttoning his shirt, started tucking it into his waistband, then thought better of it. He felt more comfortable with the shirt outside his trousers. He knew he'd feel even more comfortable with his trouser button undone. 'And you can tell that just by prodding my back?'

Dr Klasser smiled again. He was folding up his stethoscope. 'You can't hide that sort of thing from a doctor, John.'

Rebus eased into his jacket. 'So,' he said, 'see you in the pub later?'

'I'll be there around six.'

'Fine.'

Rebus walked out of the hospital and took a deep breath. It was two-thirty in the morning, about as cold and dark as the night could get. He thought about checking on Lauderdale, but knew it could wait till morning. His flat was just across The Meadows, but he didn't fancy the walk. The sleet was

still falling, beginning to turn to snow, and there was that stabbing wind, like a thug you meet in a narrow lane, one who won't let you go.

Then a car horn sounded. Rebus saw a cherry-red Renault 5, and inside it DC Siobhan Clarke, waving towards him. He almost danced to the car.

'What are you doing here?'

'I heard,' she said.

'How come?' He opened the passenger-side door.

'I was curious. I wasn't on shift, but I kept in touch with the station, just to find out what happened at the meet. When I heard about the crash, I got dressed and came down here.'

'Well, you're a sight for sore teeth.'

'Teeth?'

Rebus rubbed his jaw. 'Sounds crazy, but I think that dunt has given me toothache.'

She started the car. It was lovely and warm. Rebus could feel himself drifting off.

'Bit of a disaster then?' she said.

'A bit.' They turned out of the gates, heading left towards Tollcross.

'How's the CI?'

'I don't know. They're X-raying him. Where are we going?'

'I'm taking you home.'

'I should go back to the station.'

She shook her head. 'I called in. They don't want you till morning.'

Rebus relaxed a little more. Maybe the painkillers were kicking in. 'When's the post-mortem?'

'Nine-thirty.' They were on Lauriston Place.

'There was a shortcut you could have taken back there,' Rebus told her.

'It was a one-way street.'

'Yes, but nobody uses it this time of night.' He realised what he'd said. 'Jesus,' he whispered, rubbing his eyes.

'So what was it?' Siobhan Clarke asked. 'I mean, was it an accident, or were they looking to escape?'

'Neither,' Rebus said quietly. 'If I'd to put money on it, I'd say suicide.'

She looked at him. 'Both of them?'

He shrugged, then shivered.

At the Tollcross lights they waited in silence until red turned to green. A couple of drunks were walking home, bodies tilted into the wind.

'Horrible night,' Clarke said, moving off. Rebus nodded, saying nothing. 'Will you attend the post-mortem?'

'Yes.'

'Can't say I'd fancy it.'

'Do we know who they were yet?'

'Not that I know of.'

'I keep forgetting, you're off-duty.'

'That's right, I'm off-duty.'

'What about the car, have we traced that?'

She turned towards him and laughed. It sounded odd to him, there in that stuffy overheated car, that time of night, with all that had gone before. Sudden laughter, as strange a sound as you'd ever hear. He rubbed his jaw and pushed an exploratory finger into his mouth. The teeth he touched seemed solid enough.

Then he saw feet suddenly sweeping out from under two young bodies, the bodies leaning back into space and disappearing. They hadn't made a sound. No accident, no escape attempt; something fatalistic, something agreed between them.

'Cold?'

'No,' he said, 'I'm not cold.'

She signalled to turn off Melville Drive. To the left, what he could see of The Meadows was covered in a fresh glaze of slow. To the right was Marchmont, and Rebus's flat.

'She wasn't in the car,' he said flatly.

'There was always that possibility,' Siobhan Clarke said. 'We don't even know she's missing, not for a fact.'

'No,' he agreed, 'we don't.'

'Just two daft laddies.' She'd picked up the expression, but it sounded awkward given her English accent. Rebus smiled in the dark.

And then he was home.

She dropped him outside his tenement door, and refused a half-hearted offer of coffee. Rebus didn't want her to see the dump he called home. The students had moved out in October, leaving the place not quite his. There were things not quite right, not quite the way he remembered. Cutlery was missing, and had been replaced with stuff he hadn't seen before. It was the same with the crockery. When he'd moved back here from Patience's, he'd brought his stuff back in boxes. Most of the boxes were in the hall, still waiting to be unpacked.

Exhausted, he climbed the stairs, opened his door, and walked past the boxes, making straight for the living room and his chair.

His chair was much the same as ever. It had remoulded itself quickly to his shape. He sat down, then got up again and checked the radiator. The thing was barely warm, and there was a racking noise from within. He needed a special key, some tool that would open the valve and let it bleed. The other radiators were the same.

He made himself a hot drink, put a tape into the cassette deck, and got the duvet off his bed. Back at his chair he took off some of his clothes and covered himself with the duvet. He reached down, unscrewed the top from a bottle of Macallan, and poured some into his coffee. He drank the first half of the mug, then added more whisky.

He could hear car engines, and metal twisting, and the wind whistling all around. He could see feet, the soles of cheap trainers, something close to a smile on the lips of a fair-haired teenager. But then the smile became darkness, and everything disappeared.

Slowly, he hugged himself to sleep.

3

Down at the City Mortuary in the Cowgate Dr Curt was nowhere to be seen, but Professor Gates was already at work.

'You know,' he said, 'you can fall from any height you want; it's just that last damned half-inch that's fatal.'

With him around the slab were Inspector John Rebus, Detective Sergeant Brian Holmes, another doctor, and a pathology assistant. The Preliminary Notification of Sudden Death had already been submitted to the Procurator Fiscal, and now the Sudden Death Report was being prepared on two deceased males, probable identities William David Coyle and James Dixon Taylor.

James Taylor – Rebus looked at the mess over which Professor Gates was fussing and remembered that final embrace. Ain't it good to know that you've got a friend.

The force of the impact of the bodies upon the steel deck of Her Majesty's naval frigate *Descant* had turned them from human beings into something more like hairy jam. There was some on the slab – the rest sat in gleaming steel buckets. No next of kin was going to be asked to participate in a formal identification. It was the sort of thing they could just about accomplish by DNA-testing, if such proved necessary.

'Flatpacks, we call them,' professor Gates said. 'Saw a lot at Lockerbie. Scraped them off the ground and took them to the local ice rink. Handy place, an ice rink, when you suddenly find yourself with two hundred and seventy bodies.'

Brian Holmes had seen bad deaths before, but he was not immune. He kept shuffling his feet and shifting his shoulders, and glaring with hard, judgemental eyes at Rebus, who was humming scraps of 'You're So Vain'.

Establishing time, date and place of death was straightforward. Certified cause of death was easy too, though Professor Gates wasn't sure of the precise wording.

'Blunt force trauma?'

'How about boating accident?' Rebus offered. There were some smiles at that. Like most pathologists, Professor Alexander Gates MD, FRC Path, DMJ (Path), FRCPE, MRCPG, was possessed of a sense of humour as wide as his letter-heading. A quite necessary sense of humour. He didn't look like a pathologist. He wasn't tall and cadaverously grey like Dr Curt, but was a bossy, shuffling figure, with the physique of a wrestler rather than an undertaker. He was broad-chested, bull-necked, and had pudgy hands, the fingers of which he delighted in cracking, one at a time or all together.

16

He liked people to call him Sandy.

'I'm the one issuing the death certificate,' he told Brian Holmes, who filled in the relevant box on the rough-up Sudden Death Report. 'My address care of Police Surgeoncy, Cowgate.'

Rebus and the others watched as Gates made his examination. He was able to confirm the existence of two separate corpses. Samples were taken of veinous blood for grouping, DNA, toxicology, and alcohol. Usually urine samples would be taken also, but that just wasn't possible, and Gates was even doubtful about the efficacy of blood testing. Vitreous humour and stomach contents were next, along with bile and liver.

Before their eyes, he started to reconstruct the bodies: not so they became identifiable as humans, not entirely, but just so he could be satisfied he had everything the bodies had once had. Nothing missing, and nothing extraneous.

'I used to love jigsaws when I was a youngster,' the pathologist said quietly, bent over his task.

Outside it was a dry, freezing day. Rebus remembered liking jigsaws too. He wondered if kids still played with them. The post-mortem over, he stood on the pavement and smoked a cigarette. There were pubs to left and right of him, but none were yet open. His breakfast tot of whisky had all but evaporated.

Brian Holmes came out of the mortuary stuffing a green cardboard file into his briefcase. He saw Rebus rubbing at his jaw.

'You all right?'

'Toothache, that's all.'

It was, too; it was definitely toothache, or at least gumache. He couldn't positively identify any one tooth as the culprit: the pain was just there, swelling below the surface.

'Give you a lift?'

'Thanks, Brian, but I've got my car.'

Holmes nodded and tugged up his collar. His chin was tucked into a blue lambswool scarf. 'The bridge is open again,' he said, 'one lane southbound.'

'What about the Cortina?'

'Howdenhall have it. They're fingerprinting, just in case she ever was in the car.'

Rebus nodded, saying nothing. Holmes said nothing back.

'Something I can do for you, Brian?'

'No, not really. I was just wondering . . . weren't you supposed to be at the station first thing?'

'So?'

'So why come here instead?'

It was a good question. Rebus looked back at the mortuary doors, remembering the scene all over again. The artic, assuming the crash position, Lauderdale spread across the bonnet, then seeing the other car . . . a final embrace . . . a fall.

He shrugged non-committally and made for his car.

Chief Inspector Frank Lauderdale was going to be all right.

That was the good news.

The bad news was that DI Alister Flower was looking for temporary promotion to fill Lauderdale's shoes.

'And with the funeral meats not yet cold,' said Chief Superintendent 'Farmer' Watson. He blushed, realising what he'd said. 'Not that there's . . . I mean, no funeral or . . .' He coughed into his bunched fist.

'Flower's got a point though, sir,' said Rebus, covering his boss's embarrassment. 'It's just that he's got the tact of a tomcat. I mean, somebody'll have to fill in. How long's Frank going to be out of the game?'

'We don't know.' The Farmer picked up a sheet of paper and read from it. 'Both legs broken, two broken ribs, broken wrist, concussion: there's half a page of diagnosis here.'

Rebus rubbed his bruised cheekbone, wondering if it was responsible for the broken wrist.

'We don't even know,' the Farmer went on quietly, 'whether he'll walk again. The breaks were pretty severe. Meantime, the last thing I need is Flower and you vying for any temporary promotion it may or may not be in my power to give.'

'Understood.'

'Good.' The Farmer paused. 'So what can you tell me about last night?'

'It'll be in my report, sir.'

'Of course it will, but I'd prefer the truth. What was Frank playing at?'

'How do you mean?'

'I mean driving around like the Dukes of Hazzard. We've got expend-ables for that sort of escapade.'

'We were just maintaining a pursuit, sir.'

'Of course you were.' Watson studied Rebus. 'Nothing you'd like to add to that?'

'Not much, sir. Except that it was no accident, and they'd no intention of getting away. It was a suicide pact: unspoken, but suicide all the same.'

'And why would they do that?'

'I've no idea, sir.'

The Farmer sighed and sat back in his chair. 'John, I think you should know my feelings on all of this.'

'Yes, sir?'

'It was an utter balls-up from start to finish.'

. . . And that was putting it mildly.

They were only there because of power, because of influence, because a favour was asked. That was how it had started: with a discreet call from the city's Lord Provost to the deputy chief constable of Lothian and Borders Police, requesting that his daughter's disappearance be investigated.

Not that anything unlawful was hinted at. It wasn't that she'd been abducted, assaulted, murdered, nothing like that. It was just that she'd walked out of the house one morning and not come back. Yes, she'd left a note. It was addressed to her father and the message was simple: 'Arseholes, I'm off.' It was unsigned, but was in the daughter's handwrit-ing.

Had there been a disagreement? An argument? Strong words? Well, it was impossible to have a teenager in the house without the occasional difference of view. And how old was the Lord Provost's daughter, little Kirstie Kennedy? There came the crux: she was seventeen, and a mature, well-educated seventeen at that, well able to look after herself and old

enough legally to leave home any time she wished. Which should have taken the matter out of the police's hands, except . . . except that it was the Lord Provost asking, the Right Honourable Cameron McLeod Kennedy, JP, Councillor for South Gyle.

So the message filtered down from the DCC: take a look for Kirstie Kennedy, but keep it quiet.

Which was, everyone agreed, next to impossible. You didn't ask questions on the street without rumours starting, people fearing the worst for the subject of your questions. This was the excuse given when the media got hold of the story.

There was a photograph of the daughter, a photo police had been given and which somehow the media got their paws on. The Lord Provost was furious about that. It proved to him that he had enemies within the force. As Rebus could have told him, if you went *demanding* a favour, someone down the line could come to resent it.

So there she was, on TV and in the papers: little Kirstie Kennedy. Not a very recent photo, maybe two or three years out of date; and the difference between fourteen or fifteen and seventeen was crucial. Rebus, father of a one-time teenage daughter, knew that. Kirstie was grown-up now, and the photo would be next to useless in helping trace her.

The Lord Provost quietened the media hubbub by giving a press conference. His wife was with him – his second wife, not Kirstie's mother; Kirstie's mother was dead – and she was asked what she'd like to say to the runaway.

'I'd just like her to know we're praying for her, that's all.'

And then came the first phone call.

It wasn't hard to phone the Lord Provost. He was in the phone book, plus his appointments number was listed alongside every other councillor in a useful pamphlet handed out to tens of thousands of Edinburgh residents.

The caller sounded young, a voice not long broken. He hadn't given a name. All he'd said was that he had Kirstie, and that he wanted money for her return. He'd even put a girl on the phone. She'd squealed a couple of words before being pulled away. The words had been 'Dad' and 'I'.

The Lord Provost couldn't be sure it was Kirstie, but he couldn't not be sure either. He wanted the police's help again, and they told him to set up a drop with the kidnappers; only there wouldn't be money waiting for them, there'd be police officers and plenty of them.

The intention wasn't to confront but to tail. A police helicopter was brought into play, along with four unmarked cars. It should have been easy.

It should have been. But the caller had selected as drop zone a bus stop on the busy Queensferry Road. Lots of fast-moving traffic, and nowhere to stop an unmarked car inconspicuously. The caller had been clever. When it came time for the pick-up, the Cortina had stopped on the other side of the road from the bus stop. The passenger had come hurtling across the road, dodging traffic, picked up the bag full of wads of newspaper, and taken it back to the waiting car.

Three of the police cars were facing the wrong way, and it took a devil of a time to turn them round. But the fourth had radioed back with the suspect car's whereabouts. The helicopter, of course, had been grounded

earlier, the weather being impossible. All of which left Lauderdale – officer in charge – furiously gunning his car to catch up with the race, and shedding years in the process.

Rebus hoped it had been worth it. He hoped Lauderdale, lying strapped up in hospital, would get a thrill from remembering the chase. All it had given Rebus were a sick feeling in the gut, a bad dream, and this damned sore face.

There was a collection going around to buy something for the chief inspector. Pointedly and all too quickly, DI Alister Flower put in a tenner. He was walking around with his chest stuck out and a greasepaint smile on his face. Rebus loathed him more than ever.

Everybody kept looking at Rebus, wondering if he'd be promoted over Flower. Wondering what Rebus would do if Flower suddenly became *his* boss. The rumours piled up faster than the collection money. It wasn't even close.

Rebus was not alone in reckoning the kidnapping for a hoax. They'd know for sure very soon, now that they had traced the car, located its owner, discovered that he'd loaned it to two friends and gone to those friends' shared house only to find nobody home.

The car owner was downstairs in an interview room. They were telling him that if he was straight with them, they'd forget about the car's lack of proper insurance. He was telling them story after story, the life and times of Willie Coyle and Dixie Taylor. Rebus went down to listen for a while. DS Macari and DC Allder were doing the interview.

'Detective Inspector Rebus enters, twelve-fifteen hours,' Macari said for the benefit of the tape recorder. 'So,' he said to the seated youth, 'how did they make out, Willie and Dixie? Both on the broo, but you can always supplement the broo, eh?'

Rebus stood against the wall, trying to appear casual. He even smiled towards the car owner, nodded to let him know everything was all right. The car owner was in his late teens, presentable enough, neatly dressed and groomed. He wore a discreet silver-loop earring in his right ear, but no other jewellery, not even a watch.

'They got along,' he said. 'Like, the dole money's no' bad, even social security, you can live on it if you're careful.'

'And they were careful?' Macari paused. 'Mr Duggan nods his head.' This again for the tape recorder. 'So why would they pull a stunt like this?'

Duggan shook his head. 'I wish I knew. I never got an inkling. Willie'd never asked for a loan of the car before. He said he had something to shift.'

'What sort of thing?'

'He didn't say.'

'But you loaned him the car anyway.'

'Like I say, Willie's the careful sort.'

'And Dixie?'

Duggan gave the hint of a smile. 'Well, Dixie's different. He needed looking after.'

'What? Was he soft in the head like?'

'No, he was just laid-back. He didn't ... it was hard to get him interested.' He looked up. 'It's hard to put into words.'

'Just try your best, Mr Duggan.'

'Ever since school, Willie and Dixie had been best pals. They liked the same music, same comics, same games. They understood one another.'

'And they shared digs ever since they left home?'

Rebus liked Macari's style. Around the station they called him 'Toni', after the character in *Our Wullie*. He'd managed to get Duggan relaxed and talkative; he'd forged a relationship. Rebus wasn't so sure of Allder; Allder was one of Flower's men.

'I think so,' Duggan was saying. 'They were right close. We had a book at school once. It had two characters like them in it, one daft and the other not.'

'*Of Mice and Men?*' Rebus offered.

'I thought that was Burns,' Allder said.

Rebus indicated to Macari that he was leaving.

'Inspector Rebus leaves room, twelve-thirty hours. So, Mr Duggan, to get back to the car . . .'

As ever, Rebus timed his exit just wrong. Alister Flower was walking along the corridor towards him, whistling 'Dixie'.

'There's a lad in there,' Rebus reminded him, 'has just lost two pals, one of them called Dixie.'

Flower stopped whistling and barked a short, unpleasant laugh. 'Must've been my, you know, subconscious.'

'You've got to be conscious to have one of those,' Rebus said, moving away. 'Which sort of disqualifies you.'

Flower wasn't letting him off so easily. He caught up with Rebus at the double doors. 'Things'll be different when I'm Chief Inspector,' he snarled.

'Yes, they will,' Rebus agreed. 'Because by then they'll have cured cancer and put a man on Mars.'

Then he pushed through the doors and was gone.

4

He drove out to Stenhouse. It was further out of town than he remembered, and nicer too. Quiet, once you came off Gorgie Road. Two-storey semis with tidy front gardens and swept pavements. Some of the doorsteps looked scrubbed; his mother had got down on her knees with all the other women in their cul-de-sac a couple of times a week to scrub the step with hot soapy water or bleach. A dirty front step reflected badly on the home within.

Rebus was more used to central Edinburgh, tenement city. The little suburbia managed to surprise him. Salt had been put down along the pavements and roads. In summer the neighbours would be out gossiping over fences, but this was winter and they were hibernating.

An Edinburgh winter could be a real stayer, starting early in October and lasting into April. The days were not constant: sometimes it was twilight all day; other times, with fresh snow on the ground, the sun's glare scoured your eyes. People walked everywhere squinting, either peering into the gloom or protecting themselves from the fierce light.

Today was a twilight day, the sky a dull maroon, threatening a fall. Rebus stuffed his hands into his pockets and felt the small paper bag. He'd found an ironmonger's on Gorgie Road, and had been directed to a specialist shop where he'd been sold a radiator key. Now he looked around, found the house he was looking for, and walked up to the front door.

'Afternoon, sir,' said Siobhan Clarke, answering his knock. 'How are you feeling?'

Rebus pushed his way inside. The house wasn't much warmer than outside. In the living room, Brian Holmes was flipping through a collection of CDs.

'Anything?' Rebus asked.

Holmes stood up. 'There are a few newspapers with items about the Kennedy case. Probably gave them the idea. No sign she's ever been here. Pretty unlikely she'd run about with dossers like those two. She's a Gillespie's girl; Willie and Dixie were strictly comprehensive.'

'Looks like a straightforward hoax, sir,' Clarke agreed.

Rebus was looking around. He turned to Clarke. 'Say you're a well brought-up wee lassie, good school, nice lifestyle. Say you want to run away from home and just disappear for a while, maybe for ever. Would you take up with people your own class, or would you head downmarket, where nobody'd know you and nobody'd care?'

'Down to guys like Willie and Dixie, you mean?'

22

Rebus shrugged. 'I'm only speculating. If you were to ask me, I'd say she's done what every runner from Scotland does – gone to London.'

'God help her,' Holmes said quietly.

'So, have you finished looking around?'

'No, sir.'

'Then don't let me stop you. In fact, plug that electric fire in and I might even lend a hand.'

Brian Holmes searched in his pockets for coins for the electric meter, then they got to work.

There were two bedrooms, one tidy, the bed made, the other a mess. The tidy room belonged to Willie Coyle, as a letter from the DSS lying by the bed confirmed. There were books on a bookshelf, most of them brand new. Rebus wondered which bookshop had been losing stock recently. He pulled out something called *Trainspotting*, and saw that there were some sheets of paper hidden behind the row of books. The sheets were stapled at one corner, professionally word-processed with charts and graphs. They seemed to comprise a business report, a plan of some kind.

Holmes looked over his superior's shoulder. 'Don't tell me Willie was an entrepreneur?'

Rebus shrugged, but rolled the report up and put it in his pocket.

'In here!' Siobhan Clarke called. By the time they reached her, she was pulling out her haul from beneath Dixie Taylor's bed. Three disposable syringes, still in their wrappers, a candle burnt to a nub, and a dessert spoon blackened on its bottom.

'No sign of any skag,' she said, standing up and straightening her hair.

'I'll check beneath the other bed,' Holmes said.

Rebus was smiling. ' "Skag"?' he said. 'What sort of books have *you* been reading?' then his face turned serious. 'Better call for back-up, give this place a thorough going over.'

'Right, sir.'

When Rebus was alone in the room, he examined the syringes. There was a fine layer of dust on the packets, and little balls of fluff lay in the spoon. Dixie obviously hadn't used his works in some time. Rebus went to the bathroom, checking for Methodone or whatever the doctors gave you these days to wean you off. But he found only flu powders, paracetamol, mouthwash. He checked the mail again, but found nothing from any hospital or rehab centre.

Then he phoned Professor Gates and asked about the blood samples.

'I haven't had the results yet. Is there a problem?'

'Possible heroin use,' Rebus said. 'At least by one of them.'

'I could check the bodies again. I wasn't really looking for puncture marks.'

'Would you find them if they were there?'

'Well, as you saw yourself, the bodies aren't exactly pristine, and IV users are good at hiding their wounds. They'll inject into the tongue, the penis –'

'Well, see what you can do, Professor.' Rebus put down the phone. He suddenly didn't feel comfortable indoors, so went to get some air. He lasted thirty seconds outside, then went next door and pushed the bell. A middle-aged woman opened the door, and Rebus started to show her his ID.

'I know who you are,' she said. 'It's a crying shame, those poor wee lads. Come in, come in.'

Her name was Mrs Tweedie, and she kept a warm house. Rebus sat down on the sofa and rubbed his hands, getting some feeling back into them while avoiding the burn on his palm.

'Did you know them well, Mrs Tweedie?'

She watched him take out his notebook and pen. 'You don't mind, do you?' he asked.

'Not at all, but I thought I might make us a cup of tea first. Is that all right?'

That was just fine with John Rebus.

He sat there for over half an hour. The room was so hot he thought he might nod off, but what Mrs Tweedie had to say brought him wide awake.

'Nice lads, the pair of them. Helped me home with my shopping once, and wouldn't stop for a cup of tea.'

'You saw them often?'

'Well, I saw them coming and going.'

'Did they keep regular hours? I mean, were they active at night?'

'I wouldn't know. I'm not late to bed. They sometimes played their music a bit loud, but all I did was turn up the telly. If they were having a party, they always warned us in advance.'

Rebus brought out the Kirstie photograph. 'Have you seen this girl before, Mrs Tweedie?'

'Gracious, yes!'

'Oh?'

'I saw her in the *Daily Record*.'

Rebus felt his hopes sink. 'But never round here?'

'No, never. I saw their landlord often though.'

Rebus frowned. 'I thought these houses were council-owned?'

Mrs Tweedie nodded. 'So they are.'

Rebus started to get it. 'But it's not Willie's and Dixie's names in the rent book?'

'They explained to me that they were . . . er, sub-something.'

'Sub-letting?'

'Aye, that's it. From the lad who had the house before them.'

'And what's his name, Mrs Tweedie?'

'Well, his first name's Paul. I don't know his second. Nice young lad, always smartly dressed. Only thing I didn't like, he wore one of those . . .' She tugged her ear and made a face. 'Doesn't look at all right on a man.'

'Paul Duggan?' Rebus suggested.

She tried the name out. 'You know,' she said, 'you could be right.'

As Rebus drove out on to Gorgie Road he had a song in his head. It was an old Neil Young number, 'The Needle and the Damage Done'. He stopped the car in front of the jail to collect his thoughts. An access road ran from Gorgie Road up to the gatehouse, the tall fence, and the solid building behind with its massive door and large clock. Though not yet five o'clock, it was dark, but the prison was well lit. Officially it was HM Prison Edinburgh; but everyone knew it as Saughton Jail. The main building looked like a Victorian workhouse.

They'd have ended up in jail, he thought to himself. They knew even a hoax kidnapping was a serious offence.

Willie Coyle, the taller, the fair-haired of the two. Rebus was imagining what had gone through Willie's mind in those final seconds before he took the plunge. Dixie and he would go to jail. They'd almost certainly be separated: different wings if not different jails. Dixie would have no one to look after him. Rebus thought of Lenny in *Of Mice and Men*. Dixie had been an injector, maybe he'd been helped off, helped by his friend Willie. But in Scotland's jails, there were plenty of drugs. Of course, you'd have to have something to trade, and a boy Dixie's age always had something to trade.

Had Willie weighed up the options? And had he then hugged his friend, hugged him to death? Rebus was beginning to like Willie Coyle. He was wishing he wasn't dead.

But he was, they both were. Cold and commingled on the slab, leaving not much behind except the fact that Paul Duggan was a very cool customer indeed. Rebus would be talking to Paul Duggan, sooner rather than later. But for now he had other people to see, another appointment. It was the one appointment he'd known all day he would keep, come hell or high water.

5

There was a gas-fire, the kind that gave out actual flames, burning in what looked like the original grate; and smoke too, though the smoke came from cigarettes and pipes. The TV was on, all but drowned out by the live music. As often happened on a winter's evening, Edinburgh's folk musicians managed to find themselves in the same pub at the same time. They were playing in a corner: three fiddles, a squeeze-box, a *bodhran*, and a flute. The flautist was the only woman. The men were bearded and ruddy-cheeked and wore thick-knit jumpers. The pints on their table were three-quarters full. The woman was thin and pale with long brown hair, but her cheeks were bright from firelight.

A few customers were up dancing, arms linked and birling in what space there was. Rebus liked to think they were just keeping warm, but in fact they looked like they were having fun.

'Three more halfs and a couple of nips,' he told the barman.

'And what are your friends drinking?'

'Ha ha,' said Rebus. He was flanked at the bar by his drinking companions, George Klasser and Donny Dougary. While Klasser was known as 'Doc', Dougary was called 'Salty'. Rebus didn't know either of them very well outside the confines of the pub, but most evenings between six and half-seven they were the best of pals. Salty Dougary was trying to be heard above the general confusion.

'So what I'm saying is, you can go anywhere on the superhighway, *any*where, and in future it'll be even bigger. You'll do your shopping by computer, you'll watch telly on it, play games, listen to music . . . and everything will be there. I can talk to the White House if I want: I can download stuff from all over the world. I sit there at my desk and I can travel anywhere.'

'Can you travel to the pub by computer, Salty?' a drinker further down the bar asked.

Salty ignored him and held his thumb and forefinger a couple of inches apart. 'Hard disks the size of credit cards, you'll have a whole PC in the palm of your hand.'

'You shouldn't say that to a policeman, Salty,' George Klasser offered, causing laughter. He turned to Rebus.

'How's that tooth?'

'The anaesthetic helps,' Rebus said, tipping the last of his whisky into his mouth.

'I hope you're not mixing alcohol and painkillers.'

'Would I do that? Salty, give the man some money.'

Salty stopped talking to himself. The barman was waiting, so he pulled out a ten-pound note, watching its sad ebbing as it flowed into the till. Salty was called Salty because of salt and sauce, which were what you put on your chip-shop supper. The connection being chips, since Salty worked in an electronics factory in South Gyle. He'd been a late arrival in 'Silicon Glen', and was hoping the industry would continue to prosper. Six factories before this one had closed on him, leaving long periods of jobless space between them. He still remembered the days when money was tight – 'I could have collected Social Security for Scotland' – and watched his money accordingly. He made microchips these days, feeding an assembly plant on Clydeside and another in Gyle Park West.

'Yé dancing?'

Rebus half turned to see a woman grinning toothlessly at him. He thought her name was Morag. She was married to the man with the tartan shoelaces.

'Not tonight,' he said, trying to look flattered. You could never tell with the man with the tartan shoelaces: dance with his wife and you were flirting; turn her down and you were, by implication, snubbing *him*. Rebus rested his foot on the polished brass bar-rail and drank his drinks.

By eight o'clock, both Doc and Salty had left, and an old guy in a shapeless bunnet was standing next to Rebus. The man had forgotten his false teeth, and his cheeks were sunken. He was telling Rebus about American history.

'I like it, ken. Just American, not any other kind.'

'Why's that?'

'Eh?'

'Why just American?'

The man licked his lips. He wasn't focusing on Rebus, or on anything in the bar. You couldn't be sure he was even focusing on the present day.

'Well,' he said at last, 'I suppose it's because of the Westerns. I love Westerns. Hopalong Cassidy, John Wayne ... I used to like Hopalong Cassidy.'

'*Could It Be Forever*,' said Rebus, 'that was one of his.'

Then he finished his drink and went home.

The telephone was ringing. Rebus considered not answering; resistance lasted all of ten seconds.

'Hello?'

'Hello, Dad.'

He flopped into his chair. 'Hello, Sammy. Where are you?' She paused too long. 'Still at Patience's, eh? How are you?'

'Fine.'

'How's work?'

'You really want to know?'

'Just being polite.' Fatherly, he thought suddenly: I should have said fatherly, not polite. Sometimes he wished life had a rewind function.

'Well, I won't bore you with the details then.'

'I take it Patience is out?' It stood to reason: Sammy never called when she was home.

'Yes, she's out with . . . I mean *at* something. She's out at something.'

Rebus smiled. 'What you really mean is that she's out *with* someone.'

'I'm not very good at this.'

'Don't blame yourself, blame your genes. Do you want to meet?'

'Not tonight, I'm dog-tired. Patience asked . . . she wondered if you'd like to come to tea some day. She thinks we should see more of one another.'

As usual, thought Rebus, Patience was right. 'I'd like that. When?'

'I'll ask Patience and get back to you. Deal?'

'Deal.'

'Well, I'm off for an early night. What about you?'

Rebus looked down at his chair. 'I'm already there. Sleep tight.'

'You too, Dad. Love you.'

'You too, pet,' Rebus said quietly, but only after he'd put down the phone.

He went over to the hi-fi. After a drink, he liked to listen to the Stones. Women, relationships, and colleagues had come and gone, but the Stones had always been there. He put the album on and poured himself a last drink. The guitar riff, one of easily half a dozen in Keith's tireless repertoire, kicked the album off. I don't have much, Rebus thought, but I have this. He thought of Lauderdale in his hospital bed; Patience out enjoying herself; Kirstie Kennedy in a Charing Cross cardboard-box. Then he saw cheap trainers, a final embrace, and Willie Coyle's face.

Rebus just couldn't seem to drink him off his mind.

He remembered the report he'd found hidden in Willie's bedroom. It was on the kitchen worktop, and he went to fetch it. It was a business plan, something to do with a computer software company called LABarum. The text explained that the dictionary definition of 'labarum' was 'moral standard or guide', and the reason the company would use upper case for the first three letters was to emphasise *Lothian And Borders*. The business plan discussed future development, coatings, projected balance sheet, employment range. It was dry, and it was couched in the conditional. Rebus got out the phone book but found no listing anywhere for LABarum.

Someone had been working on the text, underlining some phrases, circling words, doing jotted calculations beside the graphs and bar charts. Sentences had been deleted in red pen, words changed. Some points had been ticked. Rebus couldn't know if the handwriting was Willie Coyle's. He didn't know if Willie had owned such a thing as a red Biro. But he *did* wonder what such a document was doing hidden in Willie Coyle's bedroom. When he turned to the last sheet, there was a word scrawled diagonally across it and underlined heavily. The word was DALGETY. He flipped through the report again but found no other mention of Dalgety. Was it a person, a place, another company? The word was scored into the paper in blue ink. It was impossible to say if it was in the same hand as the amendments and marginalia.

He poured another drink – this would be his last – and flipped the album over. He was annoyed, more with himself than anyone. It was case closed after all: a couple of desperate hoaxers fell off a bridge and died. That was all. He should have cleared it from his mind by now. Yet he couldn't.

'Damn you, Willie,' he said out loud. He sat down again with his drink and picked up the business plan. There were a couple of letters in the top right-hand corner, written faintly in pencil. CK. He wondered if they were an abbreviation for 'check'.

'Who cares?' he said, trying to concentrate on the music. What a shambles the band were, yet sometimes they could get it so exactly right that it hurt.

'Here's to you, Willie,' Rebus said, raising his glass in the air.

6

It wasn't till he woke up in the morning freezing that he remembered the radiator key in his jacket pocket. The pipes were gurgling, the boiler roaring away, yet the radiators were barely warm.

He got coffee and a bacon roll from a café and had breakfast in his car on the way to work. There was a hard frost on the ground, and the sky was leaden, threatening worse. It had taken him five minutes to scrape the ice off his windscreen, and even so it was like driving a tank, peering through the one clear slit.

A message on his desk warned of a nine-thirty meeting in the Farmer's office. Rebus felt he deserved another coffee, and made for the canteen. A lone woman sat at a table, slowly stirring a beaker of tea.

'Gill?'

She looked up. It was Gill Templer. Rebus's face broke into its first grin of the year. He pulled out a chair and sat down.

'Hello, John.' Her eyes were on her drink.

'I thought you were in Fife.'

'Yes.'

'Sex Offences Unit, isn't it?'

'That's it.'

He nodded, trying to ignore the coolness in her tone. 'You look good.' He meant it too. Her short dark hair was feather-cut, long crescents sweeping over both ears to her cheeks. Her eyes were emerald green. She hadn't changed a bit. Gill Templer smiled an acknowledgement but didn't say anything.

Brian Holmes put a hand on Rebus's shoulder. 'Those pathology tests have come in.'

'Oh?'

Holmes went to fetch himself coffee and a dough-ring, Rebus following. 'So what's the news?' he asked.

Holmes took a bite out of his dough-ring and shrugged. 'Nothing,' he mumbled, swallowing. 'The professor can't confirm the presence of heroin or any other drug in the blood of either deceased. He thinks he may have a couple of jab marks on one corpse, but they're not recent.'

'Which body?'

'The shorter.'

'Dixie.' Rebus lifted his coffee and left Holmes to pay for it. When he turned, Gill Templer wasn't at the table any more. She had left the beaker of tea untouched.

'Who was she?' Holmes asked, tucking change back into his pocket.

'Someone I used to know.'

'Well, that narrows things down.'

Rebus picked a new table for them to sit at.

DI Alister Flower looked like he was on his way to a fashion shoot for one of the stores on Princes Street.

'Run out of dummies, have they?' Rebus asked, entering Farmer Watson's office.

Flower was wearing a light blue suit with blue shirt and a black and white tie with a zigzag motif. He'd set things off with polished brown loafers and what looked like white tennis socks. Rebus sat down next to him and realised his own shoes could do with a polish. There was a speck of grease from the bacon roll on his shirt.

'I've called this meeting,' the Farmer was saying, 'to put your minds at rest.'

'Inspector Flower's mind's always at rest, sir,' Rebus said.

Flower attempted an unselfconscious laugh, and Rebus realised how desperate the man was.

'See, John,' said the Farmer, 'you always have to make a joke of things.'

'Leave them laughing, sir.' But the Farmer wasn't laughing, and Rebus knew what that silence meant – as long as Rebus maintained 'an attitude', he'd find promotion impossible.

Which left Alister Flower.

'Aly,' the Farmer began. Flower sat to attention; Rebus had never seen the trick before. 'Aly, can I get you a refill?'

Flower looked at his cup, then gulped the contents down. 'Please, sir.'

The Farmer got up from his desk, took Flower's cup, and walked to the coffee machine. He had his back to both men when he spoke.

'The temporary replacement for Frank Lauderdale will start immediately.'

It hit Rebus then. It was like he'd assumed a new, much greater mass.

'Her name,' the Farmer went on, 'is Gill Templer.'

Flower made straight for the toilets, where he could conduct a swearing match with the mirror. Rebus walked thoughtfully back to the CID room. Gill was already there, reading a pathology report.

'Congratulations,' he said.

'Thank you.' She kept on reading. He didn't budge till she stopped and looked up at him. 'John?' she said quietly.

'Yes, boss?'

'My office.'

Lauderdale's name was still on the door; they wouldn't bother with a new plaque, not yet. But Rebus noticed she'd already changed a few things.

'Don't bother sitting,' she said. Rebus brought out a packet of cigarettes. 'Come on, you know the rules: no smoking.'

He put the cigarette in his mouth. 'I'll just suck on it then,' he said.

She closed the door, then went to Lauderdale's desk, resting against it, folding her arms.

'John, there's a lot of history here.' Rebus looked around the office. 'You know what I mean. I hear you and Dr Aitken have split up.'

Rebus took the cigarette out of his mouth. 'So?'

'So you're on the rebound, and I don't want you thinking *I* could be your springboard. Don't go thinking you can jump me a few times before you dive back in the pool.'

Rebus smiled. 'Did I catch you rehearsing in the canteen?'

'All I mean is, let's leave the past well alone, let's keep things professional.'

'Fine.' He put the cigarette back in his mouth.

She went behind the desk and sat down. 'So, what can you tell me about these two imbeciles who shut the Forth Bridge?'

'Hoaxers, maybe with debts or a habit to finance. Desperadoes. No sign that they ever knew the girl. Howdenhall checked the car; there are none of her prints inside.'

'So why were you so interested in the toxicology results?'

'Was I?'

'Someone came looking for you in the canteen to tell you they'd arrived.'

Rebus smiled again. 'I just wonder if maybe they were working for someone else.'

'Do you have a name?'

'Paul Duggan. He loaned the desperadoes his car. Plus they were sub-letting his council house.'

'That's illegal.'

'Yes, it is. We might want to ask him a few follow-up questions.'

She thought this over, then nodded. 'What else are you working on?'

He shrugged. 'Not a lot, it's always quiet this time of year.'

'Let's hope it stays that way. I know your reputation, John. It was bad enough when I knew you, but the story goes that it's even worse these days. I don't want trouble.'

Rebus looked out of the window. It had started snowing. 'Weather like this,' he said, 'there's never much trouble in Edinburgh, trust me.'

7

Hugh McAnally was universally known as Wee Shug. He didn't know why people called Hugh always ended up nicknamed Shug. There were a lot of things he didn't know, and never would know. He wished he'd spent his time in jail bettering himself. He supposed he'd bettered himself in some ways: he could use machine tools, and knew how a sofa was put together. But he knew he wasn't educated, not like his cell-mate. His cell-mate had been really clever, a man of substance. Not like Shug at all; chalk and cheese, if you came down to it. But he'd taught Shug a lot. And he'd been a friend. Surrounded by people, a jail could still be a lonely place without a friend.

Then again, what difference would it have made if he'd been brainier? None at all really, not a jot.

But he was going to make a difference to his life this evening.

It was another grievous night, a wind that was like walking through razor blades.

Councillor Tom Gillespie wasn't expecting many souls to make the trek to his surgery. He'd get a few complaints from the regulars about frozen and burst pipes, maybe a question about the cold weather allowance, and that would be about it. The constituents in his Warrender ward tended to be self-reliant – or easily cowed, depending on your point of view. Depending on your politics. He smiled across the room towards the extravagance he called a secretary, then studied the art on the classroom walls.

He always held his surgery in this school, third Thursday of every month during term-time. Between consultations he would catch up on correspondence, dictating letters into a hand-held recorder. The Central Members' Services Division at the City Chambers typed the letters up. For general political matters, matters relating to his party, there was a separate admin assistant.

Which was why, as Gillespie's wife had pointed out on numerous occasions, a private secretary was such an extravagance. But as the councillor had argued (and he was *very* good at argument), if he was going to get ahead of the crowd he needed to be busier than the other councillors, and above all he needed to *seem* to be busier. Short-term extravagance, long-term gain. You always had to be thinking in the long term.

He used the same rationale when he resigned his job. As he explained to

his wife Audrey, half the district councillors had other jobs beside the council, but this meant they could not concentrate all their energies on council or political business. He needed to seem so busy that he had no time for a day job. Council committee meetings took place during the day, and now he was free to attend them.

He had other arguments in his favour, too. By working on council business during the day, his evenings and weekends were relatively free. And besides (and here he would smile and squeeze Audrey's hand), it wasn't as if they needed the money. Which was just as well, since his district councillor's basic allowance was £4,700.

Finally, he would tell her, this was the most important time in local government for twenty years. In seven weeks' time there would be new elections and the change would begin, turning the City of Edinburgh into a single-tier authority to be called the City of Edinburgh Council. How could he afford not to be at the centre of these changes?

Audrey, though, had won one condition: his secretary should be an older woman, plain and bomely. Helena Profitt fitted that bill.

Thinking of it, he never really won an argument with Audrey, not outright. She just snarled and spat and started slamming doors. He didn't mind. He needed her money. Her money bought him time. If only it could save him the purgatory of these Thursday nights in the near-deserted school.

His secretary brought her knitting with her, and he could measure how quiet things had been by how much she got done in the hour. He watched her needles work, then went back to the letter he was writing. It wasn't an easy letter to write; he'd been trying for over a week now. It wasn't the sort of thing he could trust to dictation, and so far all he'd managed were his address at the top and the date beneath.

The school was quiet, the corridors well lit, the radiators burning away. The caretaker was busy somewhere, as were four cleaners. When the cleaners and the councillor had gone home, the caretaker would lock up for the night. One of the cleaners was a lot younger than the others, and had a tidy body on her. He wondered if she lived in his ward. He looked at the clock on the wall again. Twenty minutes to go.

He heard something slam, and looked over to the classroom door. A short man was standing there, looking deathly cold in a thin bomber-style jacket and shabby trousers. He had his hands deep in his jacket pockets and didn't look inclined to remove them.

'You the councillor?' the man asked.

Councillor Gillespie stood up and smiled. Then the man turned to Helena Profitt. 'So who are you?'

'My ward secretary,' Tom Gillespie explained. Helena Profitt and the man seemed to be studying one another. 'Can I help you?'

'Aye, you can,' the man said. Then he unzipped his jacket and drew out a sawn-off shotgun.

'You,' he said to Miss Profitt, 'get the fuck out.' He pointed the weapon at the councillor. 'You stay.'

Helena Profitt ran screaming from the classroom and nearly knocked over the cleaners. A pail of dirty water clattered to the wooden floor.

'I've just polished thon!'

'A gun, he's got a gun!'

The cleaners stared at her. A sound like a tyre exploding came from the classroom. Miss Profitt, who had fallen to her knees, was joined by the other women.

'What in Christ was that?'

'She said a gun.'

And now there was a figure in the doorway. It was the councillor, almost in control of his legs. He looked for all the world like one of the paintings on the classroom wall, only it wasn't paint that spattered his face and his hair.

Rebus stood in the classroom and looked at the paintings. Some of them were pretty good. The colours weren't always right, but the shapes were identifiable. Blue house, yellow sun, brown horse in a green field, and a red sky speckled with grey . . .

Oh.

The room had been cordoned off by the simple act of placing two chairs in the doorway. The body was still there, spreadeagled on the floor in front of the teacher's desk. Dr Curt was examining it.

'This seems to be your week for messy ones,' he told Rebus.

It was messy all right. There wasn't much left of the head except for the lower jaw and chin. Stick a shotgun in your gub and heave-ho with both barrels and you couldn't expect to win Mr Glamorous Suicide. You wouldn't even make the last sixteen.

Rebus stood beside the teacher's desk. There was a pad of lined paper on it. Scribbled on the top sheet was the message, 'Mr Hamilton – allotment allocation', alongside an address and telephone number. Blood had soaked through the paper. Rebus peeled off this first sheet. The sheet below was obviously the start of a letter. Gillespie had got as far as the word 'Dear'.

'Well,' Curt got to his feet, 'he's dead, and if you were to ask for my considered opinion, I'd say he used that.' He nodded towards the shotgun, which lay a couple of feet from the body. 'And now he's gone to the other place.'

'It's just a shot away,' said Rebus.

Curt looked at him. 'Is the photographer on his way?'

'Trouble getting his car to start.'

'Well, tell him I want plenty of head shots – pun unavoidable. I gather we've a witness?'

'Councillor Gillespie.'

'I don't know him.'

'He's councillor for my ward.'

Dr Curt was pulling on thin latex gloves. It was time to search the body. Initially, they were looking for ID. 'Cosy as this room is,' Dr Curt said, 'I'd prefer my own hearth.'

In the back pocket of the deceased's trousers, Rebus found an official-looking envelope, folded in two.

'Mr H. McAnally,' he read. 'An address in Tollcross.'

'Not five minutes away.'

Rebus eased the letter out of the envelope and read it. 'It's from the Prison Service,' he told Dr Curt. 'Details of assistance open to Mr H. McAnally on his release from Saughton Jail.'

*

Tom Gillespie had a wash in the school toilets. His hair was damp and lay in clumps against his skull. He kept rubbing a hand over his face and then checking the palm for blood. His eyes were red-rimmed from crying.

Rebus sat across from him in the headteacher's office. The office had been locked, but Rebus had commandeered it when the head arrived at the school. The cleaning ladies were being given mugs of tea in the staffroom. Siobhan Clarke was there with them, doing her best to calm down Miss Profitt.

'Did you know the man at all, Mr Gillespie?'

'Never seen him in my life.'

'You're sure of that?'

'Positive.'

Rebus reached into his pocket, then stopped. 'Do you mind if I smoke?' From the odour of stale tobacco in the room, he already knew the head wouldn't mind.

Gillespie shook his head. 'In fact,' he said, 'give me one while you're at it.' Gillespie lit the cigarette and inhaled deeply. 'Gave up three years ago.'

Rebus didn't say anything. He was studying the man. He'd seen his photo before, in election rubbish pushed through the letterbox. Gillespie was in his mid-forties. He wore red-rimmed glasses normally, but had left them on the desk. His hair was very thin and wispy on top, but curled thickly either side of his pate. His eyes had thick dark lashes, not just from the crying, and his chin was weak. Rebus couldn't have called him handsome. There was a simple gold band on his wedding finger.

'How long have you been a councillor, Mr Gillespie?'

'Six years, coming up for seven.'

'I live in your ward.'

Gillespie studied him. 'Have we met before?'

Rebus shook his head. 'So this man walks into the classroom . . . ?'

'Yes.'

'Looking for you in particular?'

'He asked if I was the councillor. Then he asked who Helena was.'

'Helena being Miss Profitt?'

Gillespie nodded. 'He told her to get out . . . Then he turned the shotgun around and stuck the end of it in his mouth.' He shivered, ash falling from his cigarette. 'I'll never forget that, never.'

'Did he say anything else?' Gillespie shook his head. 'He didn't say *anything*?'

'Not a word.'

'Do you have any idea why he did it?'

Gillespie looked at Rebus. 'That's your department, not mine.'

Rebus held the stare until Gillespie broke it by looking for somewhere to stub out the cigarette.

There's something in you, Rebus thought, something below the surface that's a lot cooler, a lot more deliberate.

'Just a few more questions, Mr Gillespie. How are your surgeries publicised?'

'There's a district council leaflet, most homes had one delivered. Plus I put up notices in doctors' surgeries, that sort of place.'

'They're no secret then?'

'What good would a councillor be if he kept his surgeries secret?'

'Mr McAnally lived at an address in Tollcross.'

'Who?'

'The man who killed himself.'

'Tollcross? That's not in my ward.'

'No,' Rebus said, getting to his feet. 'I didn't think it was.'

DC Siobhan Clarke sat in on the interview with Helena Profitt. Miss Profitt was still bawling, her few utterances barely decipherable. She was older than the councillor, maybe by as much as ten years. She clutched a large shopping-bag on her lap as if it was a lifebuoy keeping her afloat. Maybe it was. She was short, with fair hair which had been permed a while back, most of it lost now. A pair of knitting needles protruded from her bag.

'And then,' she wailed, 'he told me to get out.'

'His exact words?' Rebus asked.

She sniffed, calming a little. 'He swore. He told me to get the f-u-c-k out.'

'Did he say anything else?'

She shook her head.

'And you left the room?'

'I wasn't about to stay!'

'Of course not. What did you think he was going to do?'

She had not yet asked herself this. 'Well,' she said at last, 'I don't know what I thought. Maybe he was going to hold Tom hostage, or shoot him, something like that.'

'But why?'

Her voice rose. 'I don't know. Who knows why these days?' She collapsed into hysterical sobs again.

'Just a couple more questions, Miss Profitt.' She wasn't listening. Rebus looked to Siobhan Clarke, who shrugged. She was suggesting they leave it till morning. But Rebus knew better than that; he knew the tricks the memory could play if you left things too long.

'Just a couple more questions,' he persisted quietly.

She sniffed, blew her nose, wiped her eyes. Then she took a deep breath and nodded.

'Thank you, Miss Profitt. How long was there between you running out of the classroom and hearing the shots?'

'The classroom's at the end of the corridor,' she said. 'I pushed open the doors and bumped into the cleaning ladies. I fell to my knees and that's when I heard . . . that's when . . .'

'So we're talking about a matter of seconds?'

'Just a few seconds, yes.'

'And you didn't hear any conversation as you left the room?'

'Just the bang, that's all.'

Rebus rubbed the bridge of his nose. 'Thank you, Miss Profit, we'll get a car to take you home.'

Dr Curt was finished in the classroom. The Scene of Crime Unit had taken over, and the photographer, who had finally arrived, was changing film.

'We need to secure the locus,' Rebus told the headteacher. 'Can this room be locked?'

'Yes, there are keys in my desk. What about opening the school?'

'I wouldn't if I were you. We'll be in and out tomorrow . . . the door might be left open . . .'

'Say no more.'

'And you'll want to get the decorators in.'

'Right.'

Rebus turned to Dr Curt. 'Can we move him to the mortuary?'

Dr Curt nodded. 'I'll take a look at him in the morning. Has someone gone to that address?'

'I'll go myself. Like you say, it's only five minutes away.' Rebus looked to Siobhan Clarke. 'See that the Procurator Fiscal gets that Preliminary Notification.'

Curt looked back into the room. 'He'd only just been released from prison, maybe he was depressed.'

'That might explain a suicide, but not one like this: the amount of forethought, the setting . . .'

'Our American cousins have a phrase for it,' Curt said.

'What's that?' Rebus asked, feeling he was walking into another of the doctor's punchlines.

'In your face,' Dr Curt obliged.

8

Rebus walked to Tollcross.

He had a taste in his lungs and a scent in his nostrils, and he hoped the cold might deaden them. He could walk into a pub and deaden them that way, but he didn't. He remembered a winter years back, much colder than this. Minus twenty, Siberian weather. The pipes on the outside of the tenement had frozen solid, so that nobody's waste water could run away. The smell had been bad, but you could always open a window. Death wasn't like that; it didn't go away just because you opened a window, or took a walk.

There was ice underfoot, and he skited a couple of times. Another good reason for not having a drink: he needed his wits about him. He'd copied McAnally's address into his notebook. He knew the block anyway; it was a couple of streets up from the burnt-out shell of the Crazy Hose Saloon. There was an intercom at the main door. He flipped on his lighter and saw that MCANALLY was the third name up. His toes were going numb as he pressed the button. He'd been rehearsing what to say. No policeman liked to give bad news, certainly not news as bad as this. 'Your husband's lost the heid' just didn't fit the bill.

The intercom clattered to life. 'Don't tell me you've lost the keys, Shug? If you've been drinking and lost them, you can freeze your arse off, see if I care!'

'Mrs McAnally?'

'Who's that?'

'Detective Inspector Rebus. Can I come up?'

'Name of God, what's he done?'

'Can I come up, Mrs McAnally?'

'You better had.' The intercom buzzed, and Rebus pushed open the door.

The McAnallys lived one floor up: for once Rebus had been hoping for the top storey. He climbed slowly, trying to prepare his speech. She was waiting at the door for him. It was a nice new-looking door, dark-stained wood with a fan-shaped glass motif. New brass knocker and letterbox too.

'Mrs McAnally?'

'Come in.' She led him down a short hall into the living room. It was a tiny flat, but nicely furnished and carpeted. There was a kitchenette off the living room, both rooms adding up to about twenty feet by twelve. Estate agents would call it 'cosy' and 'compact'. All three bars of the electric fire were on, and the room was stifling. Mrs McAnally had been watching

television, a can of Sweetheart stout balanced on one wide arm of her chair, ashtray and cigarettes on the other.

She looked feisty; no other words would do. Cons' wives often got that look. The prison visits hardened their jawlines and turned their eyes into distrustful slits. Her hair was dyed blonde, and though she was spending the night in, she'd still polished her nails and stuck on some eyeliner and mascara.

'What's he done?' she said again. 'Sit down if you like.'

'I'll stand, thanks. The thing is, Mrs McAnally . . .' Rebus paused. That's what you did: you lowered your voice respectfully, said a few introductory words, and then you paused, hoping the widow or widower or mother or father or son or daughter would twig.

'The thing is what?' she snapped.

'Well, I'm sorry to have to tell you . . .'

Her eyes were on the television. It was a film, some noisy Hollywood adventure.

'Could we maybe have the sound down?' he suggested.

She shrugged and pressed the remote. The 'mute' sign came up on the screen. Rebus suddenly noticed how big the TV was; it filled a whole corner of the room. Don't make me say the words, he thought. Then he saw that her eyes were glinting. Tears, he thought. She's holding them back.

'You know, don't you?' he said quietly.

'Know what?' she snapped.

'Mrs McAnally, we think your husband may be dead.' She threw the remote across the room and got to her feet. 'A man committed suicide,' Rebus continued. 'He had a letter in his pocket addressed to your husband.'

She glared at him. 'What does that mean? It means nothing. Might have dropped it, somebody might've picked it up.'

'The deceased . . . the man, he was wearing a black nylon bomber jacket and some light-coloured trousers, a green jersey . . .'

She turned away from him. 'Where? Where was this?'

'Warrender Park.'

'Well then,' she said defiantly, 'Wee Shug went down Lothian Road, his usual haunts.'

'What time were you expecting him home?'

'Pubs are still open, if that answers your question.'

'Look, Mrs McAnally, I know this isn't easy, but I'd like you to come down to the mortuary and look at some clothing. Would that be all right?'

She had her arms folded and was rocking on the balls of her feet. 'No, it wouldn't be all right. What's the point? It's not Wee Shug. He's only been out a week, one miserable week. He can't be dead.' She paused. 'Was it a car run him over?'

'We think he took his own life.'

'Are you mad? Took his own . . . ? Get out of my house! Go on, out with you!'

'Mrs McAnally, we need to –'

But now she was swiping at him, catching him with her solid fists, propelling him before her, out of the room and down the hall.

'Keep away from him, do you hear? Keep away from both of us. This is nothing but harassment.'

'I know you're upset, Mrs McAnally, but an identification would clear things up, put your mind at rest.'

Her blows lost some of their power, then stopped altogether. Rebus's burnt palm stung where she'd caught it.

'I'm sorry,' she said, breathing hard.

'It's only natural, you're upset. Do you have a neighbour, a friend, someone who could be with you?'

'There's Maisie next door.'

'Fine. What if I get a car to pick you up? Maybe Maisie can go with you?'

'I'll ask her.' She opened the door and stepped out on to the landing, shuffling along to a door marked FINCH.

'I'll use your phone if that's all right,' Rebus called, retreating back into the flat.

He took a quick look around. Just the one bedroom and bathroom, plus a box room. He'd seen the rest of the place already. Again, the bedroom was very nicely furnished, pink ruched curtains and matching bedspread, a small dressing table covered in bottles of perfume. He went into the hall and made a couple of calls: one to order a car, the other to make sure someone from CID would be at the mortuary to help with the ID.

The door opened and two women came in. He'd been expecting Mrs Finch to be around Mrs McAnally's age, but she was in her early twenties, leggy with a short, tight skirt. She looked at him as if he might be some warped practical joker. He offered a smile in return which mixed compassion with interest. She didn't smile back, so he had to content himself with the sight of her long legs as she helped Mrs McAnally down the hall and into the living room.

'A wee Bacardi, Tresa,' Maisie Finch was saying, 'it'll calm your nerves. Before we do anything else, we'll have a wee Bacardi and Coke. Have you any Valium about the place? If you haven't, I think I've some in my bathroom cabinet.'

'He can't be dead, Maisie,' Tresa McAnally wailed.

'Let's not talk about him,' Maisie Finch replied.

Strange advice, Rebus thought, making ready to leave.

9

It wasn't much of a walk from Tollcross down to C Division HQ on Torphichen Place, but Rebus knew he was getting further and further away from his own flat. He didn't intend walking back, and hoped Torphichen would have a spare car he could use as a taxi.

There was a tall bald man in a thick shabby coat in reception. The man had his arms folded and was staring at his feet. There was no one behind the desk, so Rebus pressed the buzzer. He knew it would keep buzzing till someone arrived.

'Been here long?' he asked.

The man looked up and smiled. 'Evening, Mr Rebus.'

'Hello, Anthony.' Rebus knew the man. He was one of Edinburgh's homeless, one of the army who sold copies of the *Big Issue* every twenty yards or so along Princes Street. Rebus usually bought a copy from Anthony, whose sacred pitch was outside the St James Centre. 'Here to help us with our inquiries?'

Anthony gave a gap-toothed grin. 'Just keeping warm. I told the desk officer I was waiting for DC Reynolds, only I saw Mr Reynolds go into the Hopscotch Bar on Dalry Road.'

'Which means he's on for a sesh.'

'And I can sit here till somebody tumbles.'

A uniform was emerging into the reception booth. Rebus showed ID and the uniform came and unlocked the door for him.

'You know the way, sir?'

'I know the way. Who's on duty?'

'It's a bit of a graveyard up there.'

Rebus climbed the stairs anyway. Torphichen was an old station, and small, with plain stone walls and a slightly depressing air. Rebus liked it. Certainly he preferred it to the much newer and supposedly ergonomic St Leonard's, his home base. He looked into the CID room. The very man he wanted was sitting at a long, scarred wooden table, reading the evening paper.

'Mr Davidson,' Rebus said.

Davidson looked up, then groaned.

'I want a favour,' Rebus said, walking into the room.

'Now there's a surprise.'

'Have you heard about Warrender?'

'Shotgun suicide?' News got around. Davidson closed his paper.

'The man with the plan was called Hugh McAnally, lived in Tollcross.'

'I know Wee Shug. Wee Bastard's more like it. He'd only just come out of Saughton.'

'Maybe he was pining.'

'Want a drink?'

'Coffee maybe.'

But Davidson was reaching for his coat. 'I said a *drink*.'

'So long as you're not suggesting the Hopscotch. Rat-Arse Reynolds is in there.'

Davidson knotted his tartan scarf. 'All right, let's scotch the Hopscotch. And since you're buying, you get to choose.'

Rebus chose a big public house near Haymarket Station. The public bar was seething, but the saloon was quiet. They ordered doubles.

'Too cold outside to be drinking lager,' Davidson said. 'Your health.'

'And yours.' Rebus sipped and swallowed, feeling the liquid doing its immediate, no-nonsense business. It was almost too good sometimes. 'So,' he said, 'tell me about Wee Shug.'

'Ach, he was a small-timer, used to specialise in hopeless house-breakings.'

'Used to?'

'He moved on to reset, counterfeiting, this and that.'

'So how long had he been inside?'

'This stretch, you mean? Funny that, when I heard he was out I did a quick calculation. He's out early, served a bit under four years.'

'Well, if all we had him on was reset . . .'

Davidson was shaking his head. 'Sorry, you misunderstand. My fault. He wasn't sent down for any of his usual tricks.'

'What then?'

'Rape of a minor.'

'What?'

Davidson nodded. 'Thing is, we nailed him for it, but with hand on heart I don't know if it was a clean result.'

'Explain.' Rebus signalled for two more whiskies.

'Well, the lassie was fifteen, but everyone said the same thing – fifteen going on thirty-five. Not a shy lass at all, you should read the interview transcripts. But she was adamant he'd raped her. She was a minor, and the Procurator Fiscal went ahead with the prosecution. I wasn't too bothered; getting Wee Shug off the street was fine by me.'

'Was he living in Tollcross at that time?'

'That's always been his patch.'

Rebus paid for the second round of drinks. 'Was he the violent type?'

'Not that I ever saw. I mean, he had a temper when roused, but who doesn't? That was the thing about the rape, there were no physical injuries.'

'What about corroboration?'

'We had a bundle of circumstantial evidence. Neighbours heard raised voices, a scream, the girl herself was in a terrible state, crying and all. Plus Wee Shug admitted having sex with her, said he knew it was illegal and all but, as he put it, "only by a few months". The girl said it wasn't consensual, and we just about put together a case.'

'Say, for the sake of argument, that it *was* consensual.'

'Yes?'

'Then he's just come out of a four-year stretch for something he didn't do.'

Davidson shrugged. 'You're looking for a motive behind the suicide?'

Rebus was thoughtful for a moment. 'Suicides interest me right now.'

'And we're always looking for motives, eh, John?'

Rebus drank his drink. 'What about guns? Did he ever have anything to do with firearms?'

'Nothing. But he's probably still got cronies out there who know where to get them.'

'It was a sawn-off.'

'I can believe it. You couldn't get a full-length shotgun in your mouth and be able to pull the trigger. Far easier with something shorter.'

'Messy though.'

'No doubt, but it would do the job. You don't want to go off half-cocked, do you? With a sawn-off, there's less margin for error.'

'No margin at all,' said Rebus.

It was only when they were leaving that he thought to ask a question. 'McAnally's victim, what was her name again?'

Davidson had to think about it. 'Mary something. Mary Finlay. 'No . . .' He screwed shut his eyes. 'Mary Finch.'

Rebus stared at him. 'Maisie Finch?'

Davidson thought again. 'That's it, Maisie.'

'She lives next door to the McAnallys.'

'Did then, too. She'd known them for years.'

'Christ,' Rebus said quietly. 'I've just sent her down to the mortuary to help Tresa McAnally identify her husband.'

'What?'

'Do me a favour, will you? Lend me a car and a driver.'

'I'll do better than that, I'll drive you myself.'

But by the time they reached the mortuary, it was too late. The ID had been completed and everyone had gone home. Rebus stood on the Cowgate and looked longingly back towards the Grassmarket. Some of the pubs there would still be open, the Merchant's Bar for one. But he got back into the car instead and asked Davidson to take him home. He felt tired all of a sudden. God, he felt tired.

10

'He what?' Rebus said.

He was on the phone from St Leonard's to Dr Curt at the university's Pathology Department. They kept Curt and his colleagues busy, no mistake about that. On top of police work, Curt had a full teaching load in the Faculty of Medicine, and did crossover lectures to law students too.

But then Curt had an advantage over mere mortals: he never slept. You could call him out at any hour, and he was always alert. You could catch him in his office at eight in the morning.

It was actually eight-fifteen, and Rebus was nursing a large black decaf coffee from the early-opening deli on the Pleasance.

'Morning deafness, John?' Dr Curt said. 'I repeat, he was dying anyway.'

'Dying how?'

'Great big bloody tumours. Pancreas and large colon to start with. The man must have been in agony. I'm willing to bet the toxicology tests show the presence of powerful painkillers.'

'You mean he was out of his box?'

'He'd have to be to stand the pain.'

Rebus frowned. 'I don't get it.'

'Haven't you heard of voluntary euthanasia, self-inflicted in this case?'

'Yes, but with a sawn-off shotgun?'

'Well, that's not my department. I can give you effect, not cause.'

Rebus terminated the call and went to see his chief inspector.

Gill Templer had made more changes to Lauderdale's office. She'd brought in a few framed photographs of nieces and nephews, and a thriving yucca plant had appeared. There were also a couple of cards wishing her well in her new job.

'I hear you were at that suicide last night,' she said, motioning for him to sit.

He nodded distractedly. 'There's something not right about it.'

'Oh?'

So he set out what he knew. Gill Templer listened with her chin resting on both hands, a gesture he knew of old. He recognised the perfume she was wearing, too.

'Hmm,' she said when he'd finished, 'a lot of questions. But are they any of our concern?'

He shrugged. 'To be honest, I'm not sure. Give me a day or two, I might have an answer.'

'Those two lads on the bridge,' she said. 'Another suicide, another connection with the district council.'

'I know. It could just be coincidence.'

'I don't see how it could be anything else. OK, take a day or two, see what you come up with. But report back to me regularly – at least a couple of times a day.'

Rebus stood up. 'That's good,' he said. 'You're already managing to sound like a chief inspector.'

'John,' she said warningly, 'remember what I said.'

'Yes, ma'am. Will there be anything else?'

Gill Templer shook her head. She was already getting down to some paperwork.

Rebus left her office – it was hers now, no doubt about it – and walked straight into Siobhan Clarke.

'Any news on Paul Duggan?'

'He's coming in for a chat this afternoon.'

'Good,' said Rebus. 'Need me along?'

She shook her head. 'Brian and me have perfected our Jekyll and Hyde routine.'

'Which one of you plays Hyde?'

She ignored this. 'So what are you up to today?'

It was a good question. Rebus formed his answer. 'Chasing ghosts,' he said, making for his desk.

He phoned Tresa McAnally. She'd identified her husband's clothes, and had been able to identify his body, albeit with the face discreetly covered. Now all that was left for her were the funeral arrangements.

'Sorry to bother you again,' Rebus said, after introducing himself.

'What do you want?'

'Just wondered how you were coping.'

'Oh aye?' He should've known she wouldn't fall for that sort of patter.

'You knew your husband was ill, Mrs McAnally?'

'He told me he was.'

'Seriously ill though?'

'He never really said.'

'Well, what did he tell you was wrong with him?'

'Where do you want me to start? High blood pressure, kidney stones, ulcers, a heart murmur, emphysema ... see, Wee Shug was a bit of a hypochondriac.'

'But he *was* ill; he was on medication.'

'You know what doctors are like, they'll hand you a placebo and kiss you goodbye. I've read the stories, I know what goes on.' She paused. 'If you don't mind me asking, what's the point asking about his health now?'

'Well, I've reason to believe your husband was seriously ill. Terminally ill, Mrs McAnally.'

'I should've guessed,' she said finally, her tone chastened. 'He was different when he came out this time, quieter like. Was it the big C?'

'Yes.'

'Used to smoke rollies. I always told him, that's the way my own mother went.' Another pause as she dragged on her filter-tip. 'Is that why he did himself in?'

'What do you think?'

'Makes sense, eh? Poor wee bugger.'

Rebus cleared his throat. 'Mrs McAnally, have you any idea where he could have got the gun?'

'Not a clue.'

'Are you sure?'

'What's the difference where he got it? He only hurt himself.'

Thinking back to Councillor Gillespie and Miss Profitt, Rebus wondered about that. It seemed to him that Wee Shug McAnally had managed to hurt a lot of people . . . which brought him to thoughts of Maisie Finch.

'The funeral's next Tuesday, Inspector. You'd be welcome at the house.'

'Thanks, Mrs McAnally. I'll do my best.'

The sun was out, bathing the tired buildings in dazzling light. Edinburgh's architecture was best suited to winter, to sharp, cold light. You got the feeling of being a long way north of anywhere, some place reserved for only the hardiest and most foolhardy.

Rebus was glad to be out of the office. He knew he worked best on the street. Besides, the office was a battleground. He knew Flower would already be plotting against Gill Templer, marshalling his forces, waiting for her defences to slip. But she was tough – the way she was handling Rebus was proof of that. He knew she would keep him at arm's length and beyond. She was right, he did have a bad reputation. She wouldn't want any of his failures to rub off on her. So what if they'd known one another, had been an item? She was right – it was a long time ago. Now they were colleagues; more than that, she was his acting superior. He hadn't known many women make chief inspector. Good luck to her.

He drove past the Infirmary, chiding himself for not stopping to visit Lauderdale, and headed for Tollcross. He didn't want Tresa McAnally this time though.

He wanted her neighbour.

He pressed the buzzer marked FINCH and waited, shuffling his feet. His tooth was acting up. He'd made the mistake of opening his mouth to take a deep breath, and the frozen air had made straight for the nerve. He pressed the buzzer again, hoping he wouldn't have to visit a dentist.

The intercom came to life.

'Who is it?' The voice was neutral.

'Miss Finch? My name's Inspector Rebus, we sort of met last night.'

'What do you want?'

'Can I come up?'

The door buzzed and Rebus pushed it open. At the top of the stairs, he all but tiptoed past Tresa McAnally's door. Maisie Finch's door was ajar. He closed it after him.

'Miss Finch?'

She emerged suddenly from the bathroom, wearing a short towelling-robe and brushing her hair. He could smell soap and feel the warmth from her body.

'I was in the bath,' she said.

'Sorry to trouble you.'

He followed her into the living room. It wasn't what he'd expected. Half

the space was taken up with what looked like a hospital bed, with cast-iron frame, roller wheels, and a side-guard. Next to it was a liver-coloured commode. The mantelpiece was like a chemist's display, two dozen assorted boxes and bottles standing in a row.

Maisie Finch was moving magazines from the sofa. She motioned for him to sit, and took the commode for herself, tucking one leg under the other.

'What's the problem, Inspector?'

Her face was too angular to be good-looking, and she had slightly protruberant eyes, yet she was undeniably . . . the word that came to his mind was *charged*. He shifted on the sofa.

'Well, Miss Finch . . .'

'I suppose it's about Tresa?'

'In a way, yes.' He looked at the bed again.

'It's my mum's,' she explained. 'She's housebound, I have to look after her.' Rebus made show of looking around for the missing parent, and Maisie Finch laughed. 'She's in hospital.'

'I'm sorry.'

'Don't be. They take her every few months, just for a few days. It's to give me a break. This,' she said, opening her arms wide, 'is my winter holiday.'

Her movements had loosened her robe. She didn't seem to notice, and Rebus tried not to look. Men, he thought, are daft bastards.

'Want something to drink?' she asked. 'Or is it too early for you?'

'One person's early is someone else's late.'

She went into the kitchenette. Rebus walked over to the mantelpiece and examined the array of prescription drugs. He found a bottle of paracetamol and shook two into his hand.

'Heavy night?' she said, coming back with two bottles.

'Toothache,' he explained. He took the narrow bottle. It was chilled.

'San Miguel,' she told him. 'Spanish lager. Know what I do?' She sat down again, legs apart, resting her elbows on her knees. 'I stick the heater on as high as it'll go, shut my eyes and imagine I'm in Spain, poolside at some posh hotel.' She closed her eyes to prove the point, and angled her head towards an imaginary Mediterranean sun.

Rebus washed the pills down with lager. 'I'm sorry to hear about your mum though,' he said.

She opened her eyes, not pleased to have her reverie broken. 'Everyone tells me what a saint I am.' She mimicked a much older woman: ' "There's no' many like you, hen." Too right, there's not many as *daft* as me. You know how some people say life's passing them by? Well, in this case it's a fact. I sit on the commode between her bed and the window, and just stare out at the street for hours on end, listening to her breathing, waiting for it to stop.' She looked over at him. 'Have I shocked you?'

He shook his head. His own mother had been bedridden; he knew the feeling. But he hadn't come here for any of this.

'Sitting by the window all day,' he said, 'you must have seen Mr McAnally coming and going?'

'Yes, I saw him.'

'You don't like him, do you?'

'No, I don't.' She stood up abruptly.

'Mrs McAnally's all right though?'

She was moving towards the kitchenette, but stopped and turned on him. 'I'm not the saint; that woman's the saint! She's suffered, you wouldn't believe how she's suffered.'

'I think I would.'

She wasn't listening. 'Married to an animal like that.' She looked at him. 'You know what he did to me?' Rebus nodded, and she took a step back, recovering. 'You do?' she asked quietly. 'Is that why you're here?'

'I'm here because I'm curious, Miss Finch. I mean, you still live next door, you're friends with his wife.'

'What? You think mum and me were going to move out . . . because of *him*?'

'Something like that.'

'She's been offered sheltered accommodation, but in Granton. We've always lived in Tollcross. We always will.'

'This last week, it must have been awkward.'

'I kept out of his way. You can bet he kept out of *mine*.' She was by the window now, staring down on to the street, her back resting against the wall. It was as if she didn't want to be seen. 'He deserved what he got.'

Rebus frowned. 'You mean, what he did to himself?'

She looked at him, blinked. 'That's what I said.' Then she smiled and put the bottle to her lips.

11

The Ballistics facility at Howdenhall Forensic Science Lab wasn't Rebus's idea of a good time. There were too many guns around for his liking. He read the report and looked up at the white-coated scientist who'd prepared it. The other thing Rebus didn't like about Howdenhall, all the forensic boffins looked about nineteen years old. They'd been in their smart new building a year, and still looked pleased with themselves. The new facility had been financed by selling property, including police homes. Rebus didn't want to know how many homes the lab had cost.

'Not much, is there?' he said.

The white coat, who liked to be called Dave, laughed. 'You CID,' he said, plunging his hands into his pockets, 'you always want more. Who fired it? Where did he get it?'

'We know who fired it, smart-arse. But your second question's a good one. Where *did* he get it?'

'I'm Ballistics, not Intelligence. It's a common enough make of shotgun, the identifiers have been filed off. We've tried the usual processes, and there's no chance of recovering them. The cartridges were common stock, too.'

'What about the barrel?'

'What about it?'

'When was it filed off?'

Dave nodded. 'The edge the file left is still shiny; say in the last couple of months.'

'Have you checked the register?'

'Of course.' Dave led Rebus to a computer terminal and punched a couple of keys. 'There are over seventy thousand shotgun certificates on issue.'

Rebus blinked. 'Seventy *thousand*?'

'Compared to thirty-odd thousand for all other firearms combined. Nobody's really concerned about the amount of shotguns around.' He tapped another key. 'See? Ownership's highest in rural areas – Northern, Grampian, Dumfries and Galloway. It's not some brewhead from Gorgie that's buying these things, it's the establishment: farmers, landowners.'

'What about thefts?'

'They're on the computer, but I've checked. Nobody around Edinburgh has lost a shotgun recently.'

'Can I take a look anyway?'

'Sure.' Rebus sat down and Dave punched the keyboard again. The list of

recently reported thefts was not large; nearly all of them were south of the border. 'Want a print-out?'

'Yes.' Not that a print-out would help him.

'What's the big deal anyway?' Dave asked. 'It's a simple suicide, isn't it?'

'Suicide's still an offence.'

'The only one we don't prosecute after the fact. Is there something you're not telling me?'

'No,' Rebus said quietly. 'But there may be things some people aren't telling *me*.' He took the print-out and folded it into his pocket. 'One other thing.'

'What?'

'The prints on the gun, were they the deceased's?'

Dave seemed amused by the question. 'His and his alone. What are you up to, Inspector?'

But John Rebus wasn't about to answer that.

'Thank you for coming in, Councillor.'

Rebus had just come into the interview room. He'd been biding his time outside the door, letting Tom Gillespie get a bit nervous. An interview room could do that; it could destroy all your pre-planning. You walked in knowing what you were going to say, the line you were going to take with the police, but then the room started to work on you.

The thing was, it was just a room – crime prevention posters on the walls, a table, three chairs, four electrical sockets. There was a tin ashtray, commandeered from a local pub. The walls were creamy matt custard, institution yellow, and there was strip lighting on the ceiling. The lights burred continuously, an almost subliminal electric hum. Rebus wondered if it was that noise that got to people. He guessed there was a simpler truth: the interview room was in a police station, and if you were there, you were going to be interviewed by the police.

And when it came down to it, everyone had something to hide.

'Not at all,' Gillespie said, crossing one leg over the other to let Rebus know how relaxed he was. 'I hear the poor devil was an ex-prisoner.'

'He'd served just under four years for the rape of a minor.'

'Four years doesn't seem very long.'

'No, it doesn't.' They sat in silence for a moment, until Gillespie broke it.

'I had a friend once who committed suicide. He was still at university – this is going back a while. He was worried about exams, and his girlfriend had left him.' He paused. 'Left him for me, I should add.'

'Do you mind if I smoke?' Rebus asked.

'I thought smoking was forbidden in police stations.'

'If it bothers you, I won't light it.' He stuck the cigarette in the corner of his mouth and offered one to Gillespie. The councillor shook his head.

'I'd prefer it if you didn't light up.'

'Fair enough,' said Rebus, putting away cigarettes and lighter both. Well, he thought, this is interesting. The guy's been studying for *this* exam. Tells a personal story, one that doesn't paint him in the rosiest glow, and then asserts his authority. And all it was supposed to be was a few follow-up questions.

'How did he do it?' Rebus asked.

'Who?'

'Your friend.'

'Flung himself out of the halls of residence. Fifth floor. He was still alive, so they took him to hospital, checking for broken bones and internal bleeding. They were so busy, they didn't notice he'd taken an overdose before the jump.'

'Well,' Rebus said, 'both are fairly common roads out, aren't they? You leap or you sleep. Mr McAnally, on the other hand . . .'

'You were at the Forth Road Bridge, weren't you? When those two kids jumped? I saw your name in the paper.'

'We're here to talk about McAnally, Councillor.'

'Well, guns are a popular mode of suicide too, aren't they?'

'Maybe among gun owners, but McAnally didn't own a gun and probably had never used one before.'

Gillespie uncrossed his legs and crossed them the other way. 'But given his background, he'd find it easy enough to take possession of a gun.'

'I agree,' said Rebus. 'All the same . . .'

'What?'

'Why go to all the bother? I mean, even if you're determined to blow your head off, why walk from Tollcross to Warrender in the middle of a blizzard with this big heavy gun clutched beneath your jacket? And why walk into a school which would have been locked tight on every night of the month except one?' Rebus had risen to his feet. He rested his buttocks against the edge of the table and folded his arms. 'Why walk into a classroom and make sure Councillor Tom Gillespie is present? Why do that? Why did he specifically want to top himself in front of *you*? No other witnesses, no one else invited. It doesn't make sense to me.'

'Well, the man was obviously unhinged . . . maybe on drugs.'

'I've just seen the toxicology results. The police lab has all these smart machines –'

'At Howdenhall?' Rebus nodded. 'Yes, I know. I was there for the official opening.'

'Well, the results show that the deceased had had a couple of drinks, but no drugs, not one single painkiller.'

'What's your point, Inspector?'

Rebus turned around so that his hands were resting on the table. He was leaning over Gillespie, and Gillespie wasn't enjoying it.

'See, Councillor, Wee Shug McAnally was dying. He didn't have long to live at all. His insides were rotten, and he should have been doped to the eyeballs to stand the pain. Those drugs, though, they make your brain mushy, and Wee Shug didn't want that. He wanted to be *compos mentis* when he pulled the trigger.' Rebus stood up straight. 'Makes even less sense now, eh?' He popped the cigarette back into his mouth.

'Look, I don't see what any of this has to do with me.'

'Frankly neither do I. All I know is, it has *some*thing to do with you. Now what could that be?'

There was a line of perspiration on Gillespie's top lip. He took off his glasses and pinched the bridge of his nose. Rebus walked to the far wall and lit his cigarette. He didn't think the councillor would object.

'Look,' Gillespie said quietly, 'I really don't see any connection between

this man McAnally and me, none at all. I've never met him, never heard of him, and he didn't live in my ward.' He shrugged. 'Maybe he held some sort of mad grudge, something linked to his time in prison.'

Rebus walked slowly back to the table and sat down opposite Gillespie. 'That's it?' he said. 'That's your explanation?'

'I don't *have* an explanation! I just . . . give me a cigarette, please.'

Rebus lit the cigarette for him.

Gillespie studied the burning tip, then looked at Rebus. 'Why are you doing this?'

'I've already told you, Councillor, I've to prepare a report on a sudden, violent death, and there are inconsistencies.'

'You mean you don't know why he did it?'

'That's what I mean.'

'Well, I can't help you, I'm afraid.' Gillespie got to his feet, making ready to leave.

'Can't or won't?'

Gillespie glared at Rebus, then sat down again. 'What does that mean?'

'It means I think you're hiding something.'

'Such as?'

'That's what I have to find out . . . before I can finish my report.'

'Are all policemen like you?'

'No. Some of them you wouldn't want to meet.'

'I meet quite a few actually. A colleague of mine – regional councillor rather than district, but the same party – is chair of Lothian and Borders Joint Police Board.' Gillespie drew on his cigarette and blew the smoke out in a thin stream. 'He's quite a good friend.'

'It's always nice to have friends,' Rebus said.

Gillespie got to his feet again. 'Look,' he began. He swung his arms, as if he was deciding to say something he'd rather not say. 'I promised . . .' He sighed and sat down yet again. 'This may mean something or nothing, Inspector.' Rebus busied himself tidying the end of his cigarette against the ashtray. 'It's Helena, Helena Profitt.'

'Your ward secretary?'

'She . . . she told me she knew him.'

'McAnally?'

Gillespie nodded. 'When McAnally came into the room and saw her . . . there was a moment when he just stared. I asked her about it afterwards, and she told me she'd known him a long time ago. She wouldn't say any more than that.'

12

'What's wrong with your mouth?'

'Huh.'

'You keep poking it with your finger.'

'Nothing's wrong with it.' But Rebus knew something was wrong; he was just hoping it would go away. There was pressure inside his gum and top lip, a dull, unpleasant sensation that was now spreading either side of his nose. It felt as if his whole face should be swollen, but it was just a little red beneath the nose – and that could have been the drink or the weather.

'Whose idea was this?' he said, folding his arms around himself. They were walking on Portobello beach, the only souls mad enough in this seizure-inducing wind.

'Mine,' said Mairie Henderson.

Rebus had turned up at her flat expecting a hot drink and a soft couch, but instead she'd dragged him out for what she euphemistically called her 'constitutional'.

'You'd have to have the constitution of an ox to survive this,' Rebus muttered to himself. The blasts of air against his ears meant he could barely hear what Mairie was saying, and every time he opened his mouth to yell something back, the malevolent air flooded in and attacked his tooth again. Mairie ran to a wall and hunkered down with her back against it. Her cheeks looked as if they'd been sandblasted; which in a sense they had.

Rebus crouched beside her, thankful for the shelter. He liked to take an interest in Mairie, especially now she was a freelance journalist. He worried about that lack of salary, but she seemed to be doing all right.

'So,' he asked, 'what exactly did you come up with?'

She smiled. 'You forget, I used to cover local government, regional *and* district councils. It was my first job on the paper. I didn't have to do much digging.' She leaned forward and drew a circle in the sand. 'Where do you want me to start?'

'Give me some background.'

'District council, not regional?'

'That's right.'

'Well, about the only glamorous angle attached to district councildom is the fact of a big budget, which means only the four major cities are worth the candle.'

'From a journalist's perspective?'

'It's the only perspective I can give.' She pushed the hair out of her eyes.

'Therefore, being a district councillor is not an attractive proposition. You've got long, boring working hours, requiring you to take time off from your daytime job, plus eating into your evening hours, since a lot of the meetings are evening affairs, as are surgeries if they're not on a Saturday.'

'OK, so I won't be standing for councillor, unless the money compensates.'

Mairie shook her head. 'It's not great for such a thankless task. Of course, you can claim expenses, plus if you chair a committee there's a bonus, but even so ... For all these reasons and others, you find that councillors tend to fall into one of several groups: retired, unemployed, self-employed, or with an affluent spouse.'

'The first two because they've got lots of time, the last two because they can make time?'

She nodded. 'Result? A lot of councils are not what you'd call dynamic. Edinburgh's more interesting than most.'

'So tell me about Edinburgh.' Rebus stared out towards Inchkeith Island.

'Well, we've sixty-two wards, Labour holding most of them.'

'No surprise.'

'But there isn't much of a gap between Labour and the Tories, only about seven seats. The Lib-Dems have a few, and the SNP a couple. As to what the council does, if you'd ever had to sit in on their meetings and then write them up as even vaguely interesting prose, you'd know.'

'Boring?'

'Most councillors could bore for Britain at the World *Ennui* Cup.'

'So that's how you pronounce that word.' This got him a smile. She didn't smile much these days, not since she'd led Rebus to a horror above the Crazy Hose Saloon. Rebus looked out to sea. It seemed all whitecaps as far as the horizon.

'There are all sorts of committees and sub-committees,' she went on, 'and the full district council meets once a month. But despite all that, what the council basically does is house people. Glasgow District Council is the biggest landlord in Britain – one hundred and seventy thousand houses. It's rumoured the district councils were only given the housing portfolio after local government reorganisation so they'd have something to do.'

'You've lost me.'

'The Tories wanted to keep housing out of regional council control.' She sighed at his puzzled look. 'It's all to do with politics and it's all intensely dull.'

'And the councillors are dull too?'

'Almost of necessity. Maybe "worthy" would be a better word.' She looked at him. 'We're focusing in nicely on Councillor Tom Gillespie. He chairs an industrial planning committee, looking at economic and property development. The council has its own department – Economic Development and Estates – and mostly the committee would be checking to ensure that the department is working hard and not trying to fix anything.'

'Fix? You don't mean as in repair?'

'I don't. Land deals and building contracts can be worth millions. Even repairs to buildings can be worth hundreds of thousands. Suppose I handed you the contract to clean the windows of every council building in the city?'

'I'd have to buy a new chamois.'

'You could afford it. The only thing about Gillespie is that he's ambitious, but that's nothing new. Twenty years ago, just before the corporation became the district council, Malcolm Rifkind, George Foulkes, and Robin Cook wcrc all councillors. That's another thing: the district council is about to disappear with effect from April 1996. There are elections coming up so we can install a sort of shadow authority, if anyone bothers to vote.'

'Any news of crooked deals, bent councillors?'

'Nothing. Tom Gillespie is a diligent, hard-working councillor with no bad press, no apparent skeletons in his closet, not even any rumours. He's not a tippler, not a gambler, and he doesn't cheat on his wife with the secretary –'

'What makes you say that?'

She shrugged. 'It's just one of those things people sometimes do.' She touched the back of his hand. 'Do you know something I don't?'

Rebus stood up. 'That'd be the day. Which is he, by the way: self-employed? Unemployed?'

'Wealthy spouse. His wife runs her own business.'

Rebus looked around. 'Is there a café open somewhere?'

'We could try the Fun Park.' She wiped her hands clean of sand. 'Am I in for an exclusive?'

Rebus rubbed his shoe over the circle she'd made in the sand, obliterating it.

'Well?' she persisted.

'Are you still singing in that country and western band?'

'Now there's a subtle change of subject. You were about to answer my question.'

'What question?'

'About the exclusive.'

'No I wasn't.' They came off the beach on to the promenade. 'Can you check a couple of other things for me?'

'What?'

'A company name: LABarum.' He spelt it for her. 'That's all I've got on it. Plus another name. Dalgety.'

'A company?'

'I don't know. I've checked, and there are companies called Dalgety, plus it's a place name *and* a surname.'

'So what do you want me to do?'

He shrugged. 'If you find out anything about LABarum, maybe Dalgety will tie into it.'

'I'll see what I can do. Oh, I forgot to say, I'm talking to your daughter later on.'

Rebus stopped. 'You *forgot* to say?'

'OK, I wasn't going to tell you. I'm interviewing her on the McAnally suicide.' Rebus started walking again, Mairie hurrying to catch him up. 'Any comment you'd like to make at this point, Inspector, strictly *on* the record?'

'No comment, Miss Henderson,' Rebus growled.

He'd decided the interview room might prove just *too* much for Helena Profitt, so made an appointment to see her at her work. She worked part-

time in an office, on top of her post as Gillespie's ward secretary. But someone from her office phoned to say Miss Profitt had been taken ill with a migraine and had gone home. He tried her home number, but got no answer. It could wait. Meantime he made another appointment, this time with the Governor of HM Prison Edinburgh. He told the governor's secretary that it concerned the suicide of an ex-inmate. The secretary booked him in for Tuesday afternoon.

'Sooner would be better,' he told her.

'Sooner isn't possible,' she replied.

That night, after the usual session with Doc and Salty, he drove out to the Forth Road Bridge, parked, and walked on to the bridge itself. For once there was no howling gale, hardly even a breeze. There was no moon, and the temperature was still a degree or two above freezing. The bridge had been reopened, some temporary repairs completed. Initial structural surveys had shown no real damage to the fabric, though if the car had snapped one of the thick metal support cables, it would have been different.

He stood there shivering after the warmth of the pub and his car. He was a few yards from where the boys had jumped. The area was cordoned off with metal barriers, anchored by sandbags. Two yellow metal lamps marked off the danger area. Someone had climbed over the barriers and laid a small wreath next to the broken rail, weighing it down with a rock so it wouldn't be blown away. He looked up at the nearer of the two vast supports, red lights blinking at its summit as a warning to aircraft. He didn't really feel very much, except a bit lonely and sorry for himself. The Forth was down there, as judgemental as Pilate. It was funny the things that could kill you: water, a ship's hull, steel pellets from a plastic case. It was funny that some people actually *chose* to die.

'I could never do it,' Rebus said out loud. 'I couldn't kill myself.'

Which didn't mean he hadn't thought of it. It was funny the things you thought about some nights. It was all so funny, he felt a lump forming in his throat. It's only the drink, he thought. It's the drink makes me maudlin. It's only the drink.

13

Sometimes people who knew next to nothing about them called Edinburgh's drop-in centres drop-*out* centres. Rebus knew that the police weren't the most welcome guests, so he phoned ahead first.

He knew the person who ran the centre behind Waverley Station. Rebus had done him a favour once, bringing back a heroin addict who'd suffered sudden cold turkey on Nicolson Street. Some officers would have lifted the hapless wretch and taken him to the station for a knee in the groin and a long sweat. But Rebus had taken him where he wanted to go: the drop-in centre at Waverley. Turned out he was undergoing withdrawal, doing it all on his own.

'How is he?' Rebus asked Fraser Leitch, the centre's manager and guiding light.

Leitch was sitting in his mouldering office, surrounded by the usual mounds of paperwork. The shelves behind his desk were bowed under the weight of files, document boxes, magazines and books. Fraser Leitch scratched his grey-flecked beard.

'He was doing all right, last I heard. Retrained as a chippie and actually found a job. See, Inspector, sometimes the system works.'

'Or he's the exception that proves the rule.'

'The eternal pessimist.' Leitch got up and crouched in front of a tray on the floor. He checked there was water in the kettle and switched it on. 'I'll make a bet with you. I'll bet you're here to talk about Willie Coyle and Dixie Taylor.'

'I'd have to be daft to cover a bet like that.'

Leitch smiled. 'You know Dixie was a user?' Rebus nodded. 'Well, as far as I know, with Willie's help he'd been clean for a couple of months.'

'His works were still under his bed.'

Leitch shrugged as he tipped coffee into two mugs. 'The temptation's always there. I'll make another bet with you, I'll bet you've never tried heroin yourself.'

'You'd be right.'

'Me neither, but the way I've heard it described . . . Well, like I say, the temptation never goes away. You have to take it one day at a time.'

Rebus knew Fraser Leitch used to have a drink problem. What the man was saying was that once you had it, you had it for life, because even if you dried out, the cause of your problem was still there, never quite beyond reach.

'There's a joke I've heard,' Leitch said, as the kettle started to boil. 'Well, it's not much of a joke. Here it is: what kind of boat should Dixie have landed on?'

'I give up.'

'A sampan, because they're both close to junk. Like I say, bad joke.' He poured water and milk into the mugs, stirred them, and handed one to Rebus. 'Sorry, we don't stretch to pure Colombian.'

'Is that another joke?'

Leitch sat down again. 'I knew Dixie,' he said. 'I only met Willie a couple of times.'

'Willie wasn't a user?'

'He probably toked up, maybe dropped some E.'

'Pretty clean-living then. Were you surprised when you learned what they'd done?'

'Surprised? I don't know. How's your coffee?'

'Terrible.'

'Terrible or not, it's still twenty pence.' Leitch pointed to a box on the desk. Rebus found a one-pound coin and dropped it in.

'Keep the change.'

'Giving a quid qualifies you as a patron.' Leitch stuck his feet up on the edge of the desk, knees bent. He was wearing moccasins, their stitched seams coming undone. The bottoms of his denims were frayed too. He usually described himself as 'just another old hippy'.

'How's the centre doing?' Rebus asked.

'We're hanging on by the skin of our teeth.'

'You get district council funding?'

'Some.' Leitch frowned. 'Why do you ask?'

'What happens when the district council is replaced?'

'We pray the new authority keeps up our funding.'

Rebus nodded thoughtfully. 'I was asking if you were surprised about Willie and Dixie.'

Leitch thought for a moment. 'No,' he said, 'I don't suppose I was, except that it was a dafter stunt than I would have expected from them.'

'Because Willie was smarter than that?'

'He must have known they'd never get away with it. Dixie was a different proposition, crazy at times, a real heid-the-ba', but Willie could keep him under control.'

'Like Keitel and De Niro in *Mean Streets*.'

'That's not a bad comparison. Dixie would do something daft, and Willie would slap him about the head. Dixie wouldn't have taken it from anyone else. You realise a lot of what I'm telling you is second-hand? Like I said, I only met Willie a couple of times.' He paused. 'You were there, weren't you?'

'I was there,' Rebus said quietly. He shifted in his chair. 'They just . . . Willie put his arm around Dixie and then leaned back over the rail, and Dixie went with him. There was no resistance. They didn't jump, they just slipped away.'

'Christ.' Leitch took his feet off the desk.

'Why would they do that?'

Leitch got up and walked around the desk. 'I think you know the answer to that, or at least you have an inkling. They couldn't go to jail.'

'I know,' Rebus said. Two people die rather than go to jail; another dies rather than be out. Rebus touched his mouth with a finger, feeling the pain, the pressure, almost enjoying it.

Leitch landed a hand on his shoulder. 'Have you seen a counsellor?'

'What?'

'Don't the police have counselling?'

'Why would I want counselling?'

Leitch squeezed Rebus's shoulder and withdrew his hand. 'It's up to you,' he said, going back to his chair. They sat in silence for a while.

'Ever come across a guy called Paul Duggan?' Rebus asked at last.

'Name rings a bell. I can't put a face to it. Maybe I've just heard him mentioned around the centre.'

'He loaned Willie and Dixie his car. He was their landlord.'

'Oh, right, yes. A couple of guys who sometimes come in are tenants of his.'

'Any idea where they live?'

'Abbey Hill, somewhere round there.'

'What about the name Dalgety – does it mean anything to you?' Leitch thought about it and shook his head. Rebus dug into his pocket and brought out the photo of Kirstie Kennedy. 'I know it's a long shot,' he said, 'but have you seen her around the centre?'

'This is the Lord Provost's daughter. A couple of uniforms came asking about her just after she went missing.'

'The photo's a bit out of date, she'd look different now.'

'Then bring me a more recent photo. Don't tell me an out-of-date picture's the best her parents can do?'

Rebus thought about that as he left Fraser Leitch's office. The man had a point. Then again, how many photos did Rebus have of his own daughter? Precious few after age twelve. He was standing in the short dark hallway, half its walls taken up with noticeboards, the other half with marker-pen graffiti. Rebus studied the notices. One card was recent, its edges not yet dog-eared. It was printed, unlike its ballpoint neighbours. Altogether a very superior card.

ROOMS TO LET CHEAP.

There was a phone number and a name. The name was Paul. Rebus removed the card and put it in his pocket next to Kirstie Kennedy's photo.

He glanced into the two open rooms. In one, a couple of rows of plastic chairs were positioned in front of a TV. The TV was a twelve-inch black and white. One lad was in there, holding the indoor aerial above his head as he stared at the screen from a distance of about thirty inches. Another kid sat on one of the chairs, sleeping. In the other room, three more teenagers, two boys and a girl, were trying to play table tennis with one cracked ball, two rubberless bats, and a paperback book. Their net was a row of upended cigarette packets. They played quietly, without enthusiasm or hope.

On the steps outside, two more clients of the centre tried to bum first money and then cigarettes off him. He handed out a couple of ciggies, and even lit them.

'Shame about Dixie, eh?' he said.

'Fuck off, porker,' they said, moving back indoors.

Back at his flat, Rebus finally bled the central heating system, catching the water in empty coffee jars. One thing about the flat when he moved back in: plenty of empty coffee jars. He'd meant to ask the students why there were cupboards and boxes full of them.

He refilled the system, wondering what the pressure gauges on the front of the boiler should read. When he turned the system back on, there was a gushing, gurgling sound from the pipes, and the boiler shuddered as the gas jets burst into life.

He went through to the living room and stood with his hand on the radiator. It got warm, but stayed only warm, even with the thermostat all the way up. And there was a drip from the bleedcock. He twisted the key as hard as he could, but the drip remained. He tied a kitchen-cloth to it and let the cloth run down into one of the coffee jars. That would collect the drips, and stop them making a noise.

Yes, John Rebus had been here before.

He sat in his chair, lights out, and looked out of his window on to Arden Street, thinking of Maisie Finch, thinking of her mother and his own mother. There was frost on the roofs and bonnets of the parked cars. A group of students were laughing their way back to their digs. Rebus poured himself a whisky and told the students how lucky they were. Everybody out there was lucky. All the people sleeping rough, and bumming cigarettes, and plotting and scheming how to get ahead. Alister Flower, twisting and gnawing in his sleep; Gill Templer, still and unperturbed in hers; Frank Lauderdale, with an itch beneath his cast; Tresa McAnally, feet up in front of the TV; Kirstie Kennedy . . . wherever she was. They were all of them lucky.

Edinburgh was a lucky fucking town.

Two

Shreds

14

The following Tuesday, Rebus was at work uncharacteristically early.

But not so early as to be the first to arrive. Gill Templer was already there, her door ajar, fighting her way through paperwork. Rebus knocked and pushed the door open a little further.

'You're early,' she said, rubbing her eyes.

'What about you? Have you been here all night?'

'It feels like it. That coffee smells good.'

'Want me to fetch you one?'

'No, just give me half of yours.' She handed him a clean mug, and he poured half the contents of his beaker into it. Standing over the wastebasket, he was able to see what she'd been working on. She was trying to acquaint herself with every ongoing case, everything Frank Lauderdale had left behind.

'Tall order,' he said.

'You can help.'

'How's that, boss?'

'You're slow to type up your notes. The McBrane case and the Pettiford especially. I'd like to see them this morning.'

'Do you know how fast I type?'

'Just do it.'

'Would you settle for one out of two? I've a funeral on.'

'I want them both by lunchtime, Inspector.'

Rebus looked back at the open door. There was still no one else around. 'You know,' he said quietly, 'I'm going to start taking this personally.'

She looked up from her work. 'What's that?'

'The way you've been treating me ever since you got here. Frankly, it stinks. At first I thought it was just for show, but I'm not so sure. I know you've got something to prove to everybody, but that doesn't –'

'Tread carefully, Inspector.'

Rebus stared at her. Finally she looked down at the work in front of her. 'Thanks for the coffee,' she said quietly. 'I still want those case-notes by lunchtime.'

So he went to his desk and worked on them. He didn't like typing up case-notes, the hard slog of always using the right words, of getting everything right. No police officer liked it when a report which had been painstakingly prepared was sent back by the Procurator Fiscal because of some tiny flaw in the surface of the whole. You were waiting for news that

the precognition was being prepared, and instead the case came back to you with a note – 'unable to proceed as stands'.

The reporting officer – whose job was to liaise with the Crown – took most of the flak, and Rebus was RO on both the McBrane and Pettiford cases. It was his job to make a case that the Procurator-fiscal would accept. He supposed it was Gill Templer's job to make sure he did the work, but her attitude still rankled. As far as he could gather, she'd been a far from popular choice as Frank Lauderdale's replacement. If Lauderdale hadn't been universally respected, at least he'd been a *man*; and more than that, he'd been 'one of them'. Gill Templer had been brought in from Fife. And she was a woman. And she didn't even play golf.

The female officers seemed happy enough – the ill-feeling was among the males only. Siobhan Clarke, Rebus had noticed, had a new spring in her step, working under a woman. Maybe she saw in Gill Templer a future that could be hers. But Gill would have to step carefully. Traps would be laid for her. She'd have to be careful who she trusted. Rebus had so far given her the benefit of the doubt, reckoning she was being hard on him because she couldn't afford to be soft.

So far it looked like a one-way street.

He took his finished notes to her office, only to discover she was in conference with Farmer Watson. He left them prominently on her desk instead, and went to the washroom to change his tie, removing the blue one and replacing it with black. Brian Holmes came in as Rebus was checking himself in the mirror.

'Off to a party then?'

'In a manner of speaking, Brian. In a manner of speaking.'

Certainly, there was enough booze in the kitchenette to start a fair old hootenanny, but this was a wake rather than a celebration.

By the time Rebus got to Tresa McAnally's flat, the place was bursting at the seams with middle-aged men and women and their disgruntled offspring, plus a few older souls who had the honour of being given chairs to sit on. And in the middle of the living room, dressed top to toe in black but with red gloss fingernails, sat the widow. The curtains were closed, as were those of the neighbouring flats – a sign of solidarity. The Scots always rallied round for a send-off.

Rebus squeezed his way through the whispering throng, and held out his hand. 'Mrs McAnally,' he said.

She took his hand and exerted the minimum of pressure. 'Good of you to come.'

Then he was off again, backpedalling before she could turn to someone and say, 'This is the policeman who went to the school, he saw Wee Shug flat out on the floor and missing half his head.' Normally at these occasions the men retreated to the kitchen and got stuck into the whisky. But here there was only the kitchenette, separated from the living area by nothing more than a breakfast-bar. So the men had crammed themselves into the kitchenette, for all the world like a rush-hour busful. They passed around clean glasses, and then the whisky. Tumblers of sweet and dry sherry were passed out to the ladies. Soft drinks for the younger mourners, though you didn't have to be *too* old to qualify for a nip of the harder stuff.

Rebus took a glassful and toasted the small man next to him. The man was in his seventies, and wore a wartime charcoal-and-chalkine suit. He had a pinched face and kept moving his lips, pursing and puckering them. When he spoke, it was in an undertone.

'Here's to you then, son.'

'*Slàinte.*' They drank for a moment, savouring the cheap whisky. Savouring was better than having to talk, one reason why so much whisky was consumed at funerals.

'The hearse gets here in ten minutes,' the man informed Rebus.

'Right.' A closed casket of course; Tresa McAnally had been denied a final peek at her husband's blasted remains.

'Here's the minister.'

There was nothing wrong with the old guy's eyesight, despite the thick smeary lenses in his glasses. Rebus watched the minister as he moved through the room towards Tresa McAnally. He wore black, with the white dog-collar, and as he moved the crush of mourners parted before him. Ministers didn't make friends, not easily; they were like cops that way. People were always afraid they'd say the wrong thing in front of them. They had a skill though, these men of the cloth: they could conduct a conversation while remaining inaudible to all but the person they addressed.

The old man was unscrewing another whisky bottle, different brand. 'She's made the flat nice, hasn't she? I haven't been here for a couple of years.'

Rebus nodded, noticing that the huge TV set had been moved out to make more space. He guessed it was in the bedroom. He scanned the male mourners again, looking for old lags, known faces, looking for someone who could have procured a shotgun for Wee Shug.

'Oh aye,' the old man went on, 'it's lovely now. New carpets and wallpaper, really nice.'

And new TV, Rebus thought. New front door, and bedroom fittings that didn't exactly look superannuated. Money: where the hell had the money come from?

'New carpet in the hall, too,' the man was saying. He lowered his voice still further. 'I suppose she did it for Wee Shug. You know, to make his coming home a bit more welcome. I mean, after a jail cell you want something nice.'

Rebus looked at the man more closely. 'Served time yourself?'

'A long time ago, son. Back in the fifties. Saughton was a different place then, everything was different. And mind, I'm not saying it was worse.' Their drinks replenished, he screwed the top back on and passed the bottle to the next man along. Rebus wondered how many more old lags there were in the crush around him. Then he saw someone else coming into the room, and he stopped with his glass half an inch from his mouth.

She was dressed in black, a small woman with a pillbox hat and a short veil which covered her eyes but not her mouth. And behind her, much taller, a younger woman wearing a simple navy suit, low-cut and tight at the hips. It looked the sort of thing you would wear a blouse under, but Maisie Finch wasn't wearing a blouse, or anything else beneath it that Rebus could see.

For now, though, he was more interested in the woman with her. It was Helena Profitt. Rebus turned towards the draining-board, where a rubicund man, hot and jacketless and sporting bright red braces, was dispensing the drinks.

'Give us a couple of sherries,' Rebus murmured in the man's direction. The order was passed along and a few moments later Rebus had his sherries. He left his own whisky on the breakfast-bar and carried them into the living room.

Helena Profitt was having a muted conversation with Tresa McAnally, so Rebus tapped Maisie Finch on the shoulder. When she turned towards him, he handed her the glasses.

'Thanks.' She sniffed the contents before handing one glass on to Helena Profitt.

'Funny,' Rebus said, 'you never mentioned knowing Miss Profitt.'

She smiled, then took a sip of sherry and screwed up her face.

'Too sweet?'

'It's loupin'. Is there anything else?'

'Whisky, dark rum, soft drinks. Maybe some vodka.'

'A voddy would slip down.' She surveyed the scrum in the kitchenette and changed her mind, draining the glass.

'So,' Rebus said in an undertone, 'how *do* you know Helena Profitt?'

'Same way most folk in this room do.' She smiled again and turned to the widow. 'Tresa, hen, mind if I smoke?' The packet was already out of her pocket.

'Go ahead, Maisie.' A pause. 'It's what Wee Shug would have wanted. He liked a ciggie himself.'

Taking their signal from this, a lot of hands reached into pockets and handbags. Packs were opened, handed round. Rebus took one from Maisie, and she lit it for him.

'Nice lighter,' he said.

'It was a present.' She looked at the slim onyx and gold lighter before returning it to her pocket.

'So,' Rebus said, 'Miss Profitt used to live in the tenement?'

'Floor below this.'

As more people arrived and had to offer their condolences, or else needed to say goodbye before leaving, Rebus and Maisie found themselves moved away from the widow and Miss Profitt. They ended up by the mantelpiece. Rebus picked up a bereavement card. It was signed simply, 'From all Shug's pals in Saughton. We shall remember him.'

'Touching,' Maisie Finch said.

'Either that or a bit sick.'

'How's that, Inspector?' He noted she said 'Inspector' quite loudly. The nearest mourners looked him up and down, and he knew word would now go around.

'Depends why he killed himself,' he said. 'Maybe it had something to do with Saughton.'

'Tresa tells me he had the big C.'

'That's only one possible reason.' He found her eyes. 'I can think of others.'

She looked away, almost casual. 'Such as?'

'Guilt, shame, embarrassment.'

She smiled sourly. 'Not in Shug McAnally's vocabulary.'

'Self-pity?'

'That'd be more like it.'

Rebus saw a pillbox hat and veil moving towards the door. 'I'll be back,' he said.

Helena Profitt was at the front door when he caught her.

'Miss Profitt?' She turned to him. 'I think we'd better talk.'

He led her into the McAnallys' bedroom.

'Can't it wait?' she asked, looking around her, not liking the surroundings.

Rebus shook his head. The TV was in here sure enough, giving them a narrow aisle to move about in. 'You've been avoiding me,' he said.

She sighed. 'Tom told me he'd told you.'

'You recognised Mr McAnally that night?'

'Of course I did.'

'Did he recognise you?'

She nodded. 'I'm certain he did.'

'Did he know beforehand that you were close to the councillor?'

Now she stared at him through her veil. 'What do you mean "close"? I'm his ward secretary, that's all.'

'That's all I meant.'

'How could he have known? No, I don't think he knew.' She suddenly saw what he was getting at. 'His suicide had nothing to do with *me!*'

'We have to check these things. Why didn't you say anything at the time?'

'I . . .' She sat down on the edge of the bed, hands in her lap, then stood up again abruptly. Rebus watched the bedcover float, finding its level. It was a waterbed. Disconcerted, Helena Profitt patted her hat and tugged at her veil. It didn't make much of a hiding place.

'Is it to do with Maisie Finch?' Rebus asked.

She thought about it, then nodded solemnly before bursting into a fit of loud sobbing. Rebus touched her shoulder, but she spun away from him. A mourner opened the door and looked in. Rebus got the feeling there were others out there, all wanting to see the tears.

'She'll be all right,' he said, closing the door firmly. Helena Profitt had brought a hankie out of her sleeve and was blowing her nose. Rebus offered her his own handkerchief, and she used it to dab at her eyes. There was eyeshadow on the white cotton when she handed it back. The door was pushed open again. The man with the red braces stood there.

'What's going on?'

'Nothing,' Rebus said.

The man glowered. 'We know who you are. Maybe you'd better leave.'

'What are you going to do – throw me out?'

The sweaty face creased in a sneer. 'You lot are all the same.'

'And so are you lot.' Rebus pushed the door hard until it closed. He turned back to Helena Profitt.

'What is it you're not saying?' he asked solicitously. 'It'll come out eventually, you know.'

'I moved out of this tenement four years ago,' she said. 'I've only been back a couple of times since. I should come more often. Maisie's mother misses my little visits . . .'

Four years ago. 'After McAnally raped Maisie?' he guessed.

She breathed deeply a few times to calm herself. 'You know, we didn't do anything, none of us. We all heard a scream – I know *I* heard it – but nobody phoned for the police. Not until Maisie ran into Tresa's. It was Tresa herself who phoned, to say her own husband had just raped their next-door neighbour's girl. We heard the scream, but we just went on minding our own business.' She wiped her nose again. 'Isn't that typical of this bloody city?'

Rebus remembered the words he'd used so recently: guilt, shame, embarrassment.

'You felt ashamed?' he offered.

'You bet I did. I couldn't stand to live here any longer.'

He nodded. 'Are you surprised Maisie stayed on, knowing McAnally would be back?'

She shook her head. 'Maisie's mum would never move. Besides, Maisie and Tresa, they've always been close, especially so since the . . .'

Rebus tried to imagine walking out of prison and into a situation like that. How much closer had Tresa and the younger woman grown in McAnally's absence?

'Tell me what happened that night.'

'What?' She tucked the hankie back into her sleeve.

'The night of the assault.'

'What's it to you?' Her cheeks were reddening with anger. 'It's none of your business. It's long past, long forgotten.'

'Forgotten, Miss Profitt?' Rebus shook his head. 'I don't think so, not by a long chalk.'

Then he turned from her and left the room.

He looked into the living room. Smoke hung in the air like winter fog. He saw Maisie, perched on the arm of the widow's fat armchair, one slim leg crossed over the other. She was holding Tresa McAnally's hand and giving it a pat, and Tresa, head bowed, was listening to whatever Maisie was telling her. Listening to it, and managing to smile. Rebus would have called Tresa McAnally 'feisty'; maybe even 'brassy'. But neither description fitted her just now. Maybe it was just the circumstances, the funeral, but he didn't think so.

'Car's here,' someone at the window said, meaning that the hearse was arriving. The minister got to his feet to say a few words, a tumbler of whisky in one hand, cheeks redder than they had been. Rebus pushed his way back into the hall, slipped out of the open door, and made his way down the tenement stairs. The man in the braces leaned over the guard-rail.

'I hope we meet again, pal, some place where there are no witnesses.'

The threat echoed down the stairwell. Rebus kept walking. When he drove off, he left a space kerbside for the hearse.

15

Rebus wasn't the only one interested in Shug McAnally's suicide. He'd read the newspaper article, scanning it quickly first to see if he was mentioned. He wasn't, which was a relief. Mairie Henderson's was one of three names sharing the byline. It was impossible to see where her contribution started and ended except, of course, that she'd interviewed Rebus's daughter Sammy; and though Sammy wasn't mentioned by name, the outfit she worked for was: Scottish Welfare for Ex-Prisoners, or SWEEP as it preferred to be known.

The police called it Sooty.

SWEEP, like the other care agencies mentioned in the piece, was concerned that Hugh McAnally's suicide only a week after his release from prison was evidence of a problem of readjustment and a lack of real concern 'within the system' – Sammy's words to be sure. Police, prison staff, and Social Services were marked out for criticism. The governor of HM Prison Edinburgh could do no more than explain to the journalists how inmates were prepared for release back into society. A 'spokesman for SWEEP' insisted that ex-prisoners – SWEEP never called them 'offenders' – suffered the same psychological problems as released kidnap victims or hostages. Rebus could hear the words in Sammy's mouth; he'd heard them from her before.

He'd been surprised to get a letter from his daughter a couple of months back, saying she'd got a job in Edinburgh and was 'coming home'. He'd phoned her to check what this meant, and found it only meant she was returning to Edinburgh.

'Don't worry,' she told him, 'I don't expect you to put me up.'

The job she'd landed was with SWEEP. She'd been working for some time with inmates and ex-prisoners in London, ever since she'd visited a friend in jail and had seen the conditions and, as she put it, 'the loneliness'.

'This friend,' Rebus had unwisely said, 'what were they in for?'

After which their conversation had become stilted to say the least.

She didn't want to be met off the train, but he went to Waverley anyway. She didn't see him watching as she flung her army-style kitbag and scuffed red rucksack on to the platform. He wanted to walk forwards to greet her, maybe throw his arms around her, or more likely stand there in the hope that she'd throw her arms around *him*. But she hadn't wanted to be met, so he stood his ground, half hoping she'd see him anyway.

She didn't, she just looked around the concourse with a good deal of

pleasure, swung the rucksack on to her back, and picked up her kitbag. She was thin, dressed in clingy black leggings, Doc Marten shoes, a baggy grey T-shirt and black waistcoat. Her hair was long these days, ponytailed with pieces of bright cotton threaded through it. She sported several earrings in either ear, and a nose-stud. She was twenty years old, a woman, and her own woman at that, striding with confidence from the platform. He followed her up the ramp out of the station. A bright winter day was waiting for her. He didn't suppose she'd worry about the cold.

Later, she'd come to Patience's flat for a meal. Rebus had suggested vegetarian to Patience, just to be on the safe side.

'I always cook vegetarian for the teens and twenties,' she'd replied.

'I might have guessed you would.'

After that visit, there had been others, Sammy and Patience growing closer as Patience and Rebus moved even further apart. Until one day Rebus had left, giving the students who rented his flat their marching orders and moving himself back in.

Two days later, his set of keys to Patience's flat had been handed over to Sammy, and she'd moved her stuff into the guest bedroom. Not a permanent arrangement, as both women said; just something they wanted to do for now.

Sammy was still there.

That first evening, the evening of the stuffed red peppers, Rebus and Sammy had argued about prison and ex-prisoners, right and wrong, society versus the individual. Sammy kept using the words 'the system'; Rebus niggled her by using the term 'con'. Although he agreed with at least some of her points – well thought out, persuasively argued – he found himself setting up in opposition to her. It was something he did, not just with her. Glancing across the table at Patience, he'd seen a weary smile. She'd told him before: he liked to antagonise just to get a response.

'Know why?' she'd said. 'Because conflict is more *fun* for you than consensus.'

'No it isn't,' he'd told her. 'I'm just the devil's advocate, that's all.'

So he'd ignored the weary smile and continued his joust with his daughter . . .

He closed the paper, folded it, and tossed it into a wastepaper-bin. Gill Templer came into the office. He'd been waiting there for her for close to fifteen minutes. She didn't apologise.

'You forgot to tell me,' she said, 'that your daughter works for SWEEP.'

'It's not an issue.'

'You should have told me.'

He saw what she meant. 'You mean, before you gave an interview?'

'Some woman reporter, nice as ninepence until the end of the session, then: "and tell me, what is your feeling about one of your inspectors having a close relative so involved with SWEEP?" '

Mairie Henderson, thought Rebus. Probably not interested in the answer either, just trying to discomfit the interviewee, see if anything shook loose.

'What did you tell her?'

'I told her no comment. Then I went straight to Chief Superintendent Watson and asked him who the hell she'd meant.' She paused. 'It had to be you.'

'Is that my cue for a song?'

She slammed a hand down on her desk. 'It's your cue to get the hell out of my office!'

Rebus got the hell out.

Rebus's appointment with the governor of Saughton was in the late afternoon.

The guard-house phoned ahead, then let him through. He was met at the other side of the gate and taken to the governor's office. There was an ante-room where the secretary sat behind a computer. She was taking a phone call, but nodded for him to take a seat.

'You see,' she said into the receiver, 'control shift asterisk is supposed to clear that, but it's not doing it.' She listened, and tucked the receiver between cheek and shoulder so she could work on her keyboard with both hands. 'No, that's not working either. Hang on, that's got it. Thanks, bye.' She put the phone down and shook her head in exasperation. 'Sometimes they're more trouble than they're worth,' she confided to Rebus. 'The governor will be back in a couple of minutes.'

'Thanks,' Rebus said. 'Typewriters are about as high-tech as I can manage.'

'They keep sending me on courses, but after half an hour I'm completely bamboozled.'

The door Rebus had come through opened suddenly, and the governor came in. Rebus stood up, they shook hands, and the governor led him into the inner sanctum.

'Sit down, Inspector.'

'I appreciate you seeing me, sir.'

The governor dismissed this with a wave of his hand. 'It's not often a suicide on the *outside* brings me into the equation, but I've had reporters hounding me on this one. McAnally's death seems to have stirred up a bit of debate. They must be hard up for news.' He sat back, resting his hands on his stomach. 'And now,' he said, 'I've got you.'

The governor was a handsome man in his late fifties. He peered at Rebus over metal-framed glasses. He was bulky rather than fat, and his silvering hair was thick and healthy. His suit looked expensive, his shirt laundered, and his unfussy blue tie had a sheen that Rebus took for silk. He saw himself as a 'man-manager', and was a public voice in the drive to reform Scotland's penal system: an end to slopping-out and cell-sharing; brighter, better equipped halls; a strong emphasis on vocational training, education and counselling. Not every sight-impaired Open University student knew that their braille text was probably transcribed by Saughton's Braille Unit.

It wasn't all sunny though: Saughton had its drug problems, its share of HIV-positive inmates. But at least it had a full-time medical staff to cope, or to begin to try to cope.

Rebus had never met the governor before, though he'd seen him at functions, and come across him in the media. His name was Jim Flett or, more often, just 'Big Jim'.

'Well, you're right, sir,' Rebus said, 'I am here to talk to you about Hugh McAnally.'

'So I gather.' Flett tapped a manila file on his desk, the record of Prisoner

1117, C-Hall, HMP Edinburgh, McAnally, Hugh. Jim Flett opened the file. 'I've had a read of this, and I've been to talk to some of the warders and McAnally's fellow inmates.' He gave Rebus a grin. 'I *think* I'm prepared. By the way, something to drink?'

'I'm fine, thanks. This won't take long. Why was McAnally released so early?'

'Not *so* early. His good behaviour was taken into account, as was his illness.'

'You knew he was ill?'

'Inoperable cancer. Normally, the stage of sentence he was at, we'd be readying to transfer him to the TFF hostel.'

'What's that?'

'Training for Freedom. He'd have gone out unsupervised to a work placement. But Mr McAnally was a category C prisoner, and only category D's qualify for TFF. In any event, he was due parole.'

'What made him category C?'

Flett shrugged. 'A bust-up with a warder.'

'I thought you mentioned good behaviour?'

'The bust-up was a while back. The man was dying, Inspector. We knew we weren't going to see him in here again.'

'Did he seem suicidal?'

'Not as far as I'm aware. I'm just glad he did away with himself on the *out*side: it makes him your problem rather than mine.'

'What about aggro? Was he subject to threats or violence?'

'How do you mean?'

'He was a convicted rapist, his victim legally a child at the time of the offence. I hear the stories, same as everyone else: if you're a sex offender and you're not put in a separate wing, you get beaten up, people pish in your tea, you're an outcast. Can't exactly be good for the spirit.'

'Spirit?' Flett gave a wry smile. 'Let's just say I'm not aware of any incidents of that nature. If any occurred, they'd be dealt with.'

'I don't suppose the victims lodge complaints that often.'

'You think you know so much about us, Inspector, maybe you should be sitting *this* side of the desk?'

'No, thanks.'

'Look, there's nothing in his time here that made anyone think he was about to stick a shotgun in his gub.'

Rebus thought for a moment. 'Did you know him?'

'No, I didn't. He'd only been here eleven months.'

'Where was he before?'

'Glenochil.'

'Any problems while he was there?'

'Not according to the files. Look, Inspector, I know what you're thinking, what you're trying to put together. But he didn't commit harry-carry because of anything that happened to him in here. His cell-mate was as shocked as anyone when he heard what happened. McAnally had served two previous sentences; it's not as if incarceration was new or strange to him.'

Rebus thought again of Willie and Dixie, of what would have happened to them in prison.

'Surely,' Flett was saying, 'it's much more realistic to say that the illness wore him down and led him to kill himself.'

'With respect, sir, his previouses weren't for rape of a minor.'

Flett stared at Rebus, then glanced at his watch, letting him know the score.

'Just a couple of final questions, sir. How much money did he leave prison with?'

Flett had to check that in the file. 'There was eight pounds sixty among his effects when he came in.'

'And other than that?'

'Other than that, he was entitled to the same benefits as any other ex-prisoner. It seems an odd question to ask.'

'His flat shows signs of a recent overhaul; I'm wondering where the money came from.'

'Best ask his wife. Anything else?'

'Who was his contact on the outside?'

'You mean his supervising officer?' Flett looked this up too. 'Jennifer Benn at Social Services.' Rebus entered the name in his notebook. 'Well, if that's all, Inspector . . . ?' The governor was on his feet. He walked around the desk and smiled towards Rebus, and Rebus suddenly knew the man was hiding something. He'd been edgy during the conversation, as though expecting some awkward question to arise. It hadn't, and his relief was evident in that smile, in his complete change of attitude.

Rebus tried to think what the question could be. Out in the secretary's office, while Big Jim was shaking his hand a final time, he was still thinking about it. I've let him off the hook, he thought. He reran the meeting in his head as he walked back to his car.

'Buggered if I know,' he announced to himself. But as he sat in the idling car, he knew he was going to have to find out.

That evening, he visited one of only two drop-in centres available to ex-cons in Edinburgh. It reminded him most of Fraser Leitch's establishment, except that here there was a colour TV rather than black and white.

Nobody could help him. Hugh McAnally hadn't been near the place, not as far as anyone knew. He wasn't about to press the point or outstay his lukewarm welcome, but he took a quick look round before he left.

In a corner of the main room, a woman with a huge canvas bag slung over her shoulder was crouching down in conversation with a man who sat slumped in a chair. The man stared past her, not interested. Eventually the woman gave up, wrote something on a pad, closed it, and returned it to the canvas bag. The man leaned forward then and whispered something into her ear. She listened, her cheeks reddened, and she got to her feet, turning to walk away.

Rebus was right behind her. She brought herself up short to avoid a collision.

'You wouldn't be Jennifer Benn, would you?'

'That's me.'

'My lucky night.' Rebus looked past her, to where the seated man was rubbing his forehead, trying not to let Rebus see his face. 'Hiya, Pete.'

The man looked up and seemed to place Rebus. 'Evening, Mr Rebus.'

'How long have you been out?'

'Three weeks two days.'

'And you fancy another trip back already? Give the lady back her purse.'

The social worker stared in surprise as Pete slipped the bulging black leather purse out of his denim jacket. She snatched it back and checked the contents.

'Do you want to press charges?' Rebus asked. She shook her head. 'Fine, then let's have a little chat.'

By the time they reached the front door, Jennifer Benn had regained her composure.

'Where are we going?'

'Somewhere I'm a bit more welcome. There's a pub across the road.'

'I don't like pubs.'

'My car then?'

She turned to him. 'Can I see some ID?'

'I thought that scene back there would have been ID enough.' But she wasn't budging, so he dug out his warrant card, which she inspected slowly.

'All right,' she said, handing it back, 'we can talk here.'

'Here?' They were on the pavement. She wrapped a woollen scarf around her neck and pulled on sheepskin mitts. She was in her late-twenties and had frizzy blonde hair and outsized glasses. 'It's freezing here,' Rebus complained.

'Then best hurry up.'

He sighed. 'You were Shug McAnally's social worker?'

'That's right.'

'I'm investigating his suicide.'

She was shaking her head. 'I'm afraid I can't help. He never kept an appointment, we never met.'

'Did you report him?'

She nodded. 'But I didn't think anything would come of it. What punishment do you mete out to someone with terminal cancer?'

And with that she turned and walked quickly to her car. Rebus thought that she'd asked a very good question indeed.

16

Next morning, he found himself summoned to Chief Superintendent Watson's office.

Gill Templer was already there when he arrived. She was standing with her back to the filing cabinet, arms folded. There wasn't much room: three large cardboard boxes marked 'PanoTech' sat on the floor by the desk.

'My new computer,' the Farmer explained. 'Sit down, John.' The Farmer looked like a man with bad news: Rebus had been here before; same look, same tone of voice.

'I'd rather stand, sir.'

'Been up to anything we should know about, John?'

'No, sir.'

'Nothing at all?'

'Not that I know of, sir. Why?'

Watson glanced towards Gill Templer. 'I had a phone call yesterday evening from Allan Gunner.' Gunner: the deputy chief constable. 'He doesn't often call me at home.'

'Do I take it he had bad news?' Rebus decided to sit down after all.

'HM Inspectorate of Constabulary are thinking of investigating us.'

'Us?'

'B Division.'

'That's us all right.'

'It's no joking matter.'

Nor was it. HMIC was independent of the police service; it reported directly to the Secretary of State for Scotland.

HMIC's public remit encompassed examining police standards and indicating areas for improvement. It inspected all eight regional forces each year, but only four of these were full 'primary' inspections. They looked at rises in crime stats, falls in detection rates, and complaints from the public. No problem there: the recorded crime rate was steady when it wasn't falling, and recent clear-up rates were marginally improved. But HMIC could really screw up a station's working practices, just by being on the premises. There were long lists of questions to answer, an initial pre-inspection followed by the full inspection . . . and, as everyone in the room knew, HMIC could sometimes stumble upon something better left unqueried. Or, as the Farmer put it, 'You know those buggers, John. If they want to find dirt on us, there's dirt to be found. We don't exactly work in an antiseptic environment.'

'That's because we don't deal with people who wash behind their ears every morning. What are you getting at, sir? So what if we've been picked out? It's the luck of the draw.'

'Ah,' Watson said, holding up a prodigious forefinger. 'I only said they were *thinking* of picking us out.'

'I don't get it.'

The Farmer shifted – so far as he was able – in his chair. He was not a small man; it was not a large chair. 'To be honest, neither do I, the DCC was being bloody cagey. I think the gist was, we're doing something naughty, and if we stop doing it, another division might find itself under scrutiny instead of us.'

'Did he actually say that?' Gill Templer asked.

The Farmer shrugged. 'I'm giving my interpretation, that's all. Now, after his phone call, I did some thinking. I asked myself: who would be getting up people's noses? Well, I know one copper who's like cocaine in that respect.'

'Nobody sniffs coke these days, sir.' Watson just sat there, unblinking.

'OK,' Rebus said, standing again. 'I went to see Big Jim Flett yesterday, probably a couple of hours before Gunner called you.'

'Why?' Gill Templer asked. She looked furious that he hadn't told her beforehand.

'McAnally.'

'The suicide?' The Farmer frowned as Rebus nodded.

'The thing is, sir, there's something . . . I don't know, I just think there's something *there*. Why go all the way to Warrender School to blow your brains out in front of a councillor, a man who says he never even knew the deceased? And how come the widow's suddenly got money to spend? Those are two questions; I've got a wheen more.'

'Well,' the Farmer said, 'that might explain the second phone call. Also last night, and also at my home. It was from Derek Mantoni.'

'I don't know him.'

'*Councillor* Mantoni is chair of Lothian and Borders Joint Police Board.'

Rebus saw now: Gillespie had been complaining to his friend.

'He was asking about you, John.'

'Nice of him.'

'Apparently you've rubbed Councillor Gillespie up the wrong way. I should remind you that the councillor is a victim here, and one who's been through a terrible experience.' The Farmer sounded as if he was quoting Derek Mantoni.

'Inspector Rebus,' Gill Templer said, 'is there *any* reason to believe it wasn't a suicide?'

'No,' Rebus admitted. 'I'm sure it was suicide.'

'Then I don't see the problem.'

Rebus turned to her. 'Well, I *do*!' He jabbed his thumb into his chest to reinforce the point. 'And now everyone suddenly wants it covered up!' She turned her head away from him.

'John,' the Farmer warned, 'that's out of order. I've been looking at the hours you've been putting in. You're due some time off . . . a lot of time actually. It's a quiet time of year.'

Rebus held the Farmer's stare. 'You've got to back me up on this, sir.'

'I'm telling you to take some time off, that's all.'

'Who is it you're scared of: the DCC? Mantoni? HMIC?'

The Farmer ignored him. 'Take a week, ten days ... clear your head, Inspector.'

Rebus slammed both hands down on the desktop. A framed photo of the Farmer's family fell off and landed on a cardboard box. Gill Templer stooped to pick it up.

'You've got to back me up,' Rebus repeated. He knew Gill was a lost cause; he had eyes only for the Farmer, but the Farmer wasn't looking.

'I've given you an order, Inspector.'

Rebus gave one of the boxes a kick on his way out of the room.

When he thought it over later, Rebus didn't blame the Farmer. He was covering his arse; so was Gill, if it came down to it. Now Rebus was a free agent, or at least a loose one. He couldn't get anyone into trouble but himself, and that was fine with him. He'd cleared his desk, pushing everything into drawers and, when he ran out of space, the wastepaper-bin. He'd left St Leonard's without a word to anyone.

There were just the two problems – neither of them insignificant – and he pondered them as he sat in the back room of the Oxford Bar with a half of Caledonian Eighty and a double malt.

The first problem was, police routine gave his daily life its only shape and substance; it gave him a schedule to work to, a reason to get up in the morning. He loathed his free time, dreaded Sundays off. He lived to work, and in a very real sense he worked to live, too: the much-maligned Protestant work ethic. Subtract work from the equation, and the day became flabby, like releasing jelly from its mould. Besides, without work, what reason had he not to drink?

It worried him, because now there was nothing to stop him raising two fingers to the shade of Wee Shug McAnally, a man not exactly universally mourned, and get on with some serious bevvying instead. He could spend a seven-to-ten stretch in the Ox no problem, augmented by betting-shop gossip and nourished by pies and bridies. It would be wonderfully easy.

Then there was the second problem, not unconnected to the first.

For, now that he had so much time on his hands, what was to stop him booking a dentist's appointment?

The only thing to do was to keep working. Besides, there were some things he needed to do in a hurry, before word got around that he was on leave. The first of these involved another visit to C Division in Torphichen Place.

DI Davidson was again on duty, to Rebus's relief.

'I can smell it off you,' Davidson said, leading him to the CID room.

'What?'

'The drink. How can you torture me like that? There's another two hours before I finish my shift.'

Rebus saw that they were alone in the CID room. 'I need the case-notes on McAnally, the ones from the rape charge.'

'What for?'

Rebus shrugged. 'I just need to see them.'

Davidson went to a desk drawer and brought out a bunch of keys. 'You

know, John, there's enough to be getting on with in the here-and-now.' He went to a walk-in cupboard and opened it. 'I don't suppose there'll be a copy still here. Everything'll have been archived by now.'

There were reports packed tight along each shelf. On every spine, in fat felt-marker, was an officer's name, depending on whose copy the report was. The spines faced upwards, the base of each report facing out. On the base was the name of the accused. There was no McAnally.

So then they'd to traipse to another part of the building, locate another set of keys, and unlock a storeroom, inside which stood a dozen tall double-doored filing cupboards. Davidson stood in thought for a moment, then pointed at one.

'That's probably got the year we're after.' He unlocked the cabinet. There was a smell of musty paper, much stronger than in the cupboard they'd tried earlier. Davidson ran his finger along each row of spines. 'McAnally,' he said at last, pulling out two thick files of A4 paper and handing them to Rebus. Each was loose-bound, held together by two removable metal clips. The blue covers were faded at their edges. Davidson's surname was on the spine. Rebus read from one of the covers.

'The Case Against Hugh McAnally, Born 12.1.44.' He flipped through both files, not surprised to see their bulk consisted of witness statements.

'Enjoy,' said Davidson, relocking the cabinet.

Rebus stopped off on his way home and bought a jar of coffee, rolls, bacon, and two four-packs of Export. He was preparing for a long haul.

The flat was fairly warm. He emptied the jar beneath the leaking radiator and replaced it, then turned the hi-fi on. He washed three aspirin down with a swig of beer, then checked his face in the bathroom mirror. The skin around and below his nose was definitely inflamed. When he waggled one particular tooth it felt deadened, anaesthetised, while its neighbours jangled like they'd been wired to the mains. The blister on his palm had receded, and now sported only a thin strip of sticking-plaster. Beneath the plaster, the engine's serial number was still there.

I'm in great shape, he thought. I'm the perfect fucking specimen.

He took the beer through to the living room, sat down with the reports in his chair, and started to read.

He started with the Summary of Evidence, barely glanced down the List of Productions and List of Witnesses, skipped the Annual Leave of Officers, and got to work on the Statements and Tape Transcriptions. The witnesses comprised neighbours, the victim, the accused's wife, a couple of barmen, and the police doctor (Dr Curt, as it turned out), who had examined and taken samples from both victim and accused. Maisie Finch had been examined in hospital, where she spent the rest of the night under observation. It was noted that her mother – unaware of her daughter's presence – was in the same hospital at the time, just one floor up.

Hugh McAnally had been examined in the medical examination room at Torphichen. During the examination he kept protesting, 'I used a johnny, for fuck's sake, what's the problem?'

These words had endeared him to no one.

The story from the victim's point of view: Maisie had been alone in the flat, her mum being in hospital for a minor operation. At this time, her

mother was already all but housebound, looking after her a full-time occupation for Maisie. (Nobody had asked her how it felt to be cooped up all day with an invalid; or how it felt when her mum had been taken into hospital . . . Rebus remembered his own meeting with her – the bottles of strong lager, the 'holiday mood'.) Maisie knew Mr McAnally very well, had known him for years. She regarded him not just as a neighbour but as a family friend.

McAnally told her he had come to ask after her mother. Though he smelled of alcohol, she'd let him into the flat and offered to make a cup of tea. He asked if she had anything stronger. She knew there was a bottle of whisky in the bottom of her mother's wardrobe. It had been there since her father's death. Maisie went to fetch it, and McAnally followed. He pushed her on to the bed so she was face down, and held her head down with one hand . . .

Afterwards, he mumbled something. She thought it might have been an apology, but maybe not. He went out, leaving the door to the flat ajar. She could hear him tramping noisily down the stairwell. She ran to Mrs McAnally's door and thumped on it till she got an answer. Mrs McAnally herself called the police.

McAnally, by his own admission, left the tenement and headed for Lothian Road, drinking in a couple of pubs he frequented. This was backed up by the two barmen. Then he bought a fish supper, and was finishing it as he approached the main door of the tenement, where he was apprehended by two police officers who had been waiting in their car. He was taken to Torphichen Place police station and questioned, then charged.

McAnally's version was: he had indeed gone to Maisie Finch's flat to inquire about her mother, but also in the hope of having sex with Maisie. They'd had sex once before, while her mother was asleep in the other room. Both times, Maisie initiated proceedings. McAnally knew she was a 'good girl', but thought she got bored at home. He knew he was 'no spring chicken' nor yet 'Mr Universe', and her home life explained why Maisie wanted to have sex with him – 'I dare say I wasn't the only one.' Maisie herself had never said anything, never explained, and McAnally wasn't really bothered, 'so long as I was getting my hole.'

After a minute or so's conversation in the living room, Maisie suggested going through to her mother's bedroom, her reasoning being that her mother had a double bed, while Maisie only had a single. (Asked to describe Maisie's bedroom, McAnally was able to, though this proved nothing, since, as he later acknowledged, he'd been in there the previous month to change a faulty light-fitting.)

On the night in question, they progressed to the mother's bedroom, where – McAnally's version – intercourse took place, 'doggy style'. Asked why that particular position, McAnally said he thought maybe Maisie didn't like to look at his 'ugly old coupon'. (Rebus was glad *he* hadn't interviewed McAnally; he'd probably have taken a swing at him.) McAnally said he left the flat immediately afterwards, as Maisie didn't like him to hang about. One thing he said was that Maisie herself had provided the condom: 'I can't run around with johnnies in my pooch, Tresa'd be bound to find them.'

Yes, he was a choice article, Mr Hugh McAnally.

Rape cases could be difficult. Scottish law required corroboration, not just one person's word against another's. With allegations of rape, there was seldom absolute corroboration – rapists didn't work to an uninvited audience. But in this case there was the girl's cry, heard by some in the tenement (though not by all), and the fact that she made, as Davidson himself commented, a 'stonking good witness'. She would go into the witness box – not all rape victims would, for very good emotional reasons – and she would testify. She would 'put the old bastard behind bars'.

And she did.

Asked about the cry, McAnally at first said she was 'a screamer'–in other words, that she cried out at the point of climax. Davidson had added a pencilled comment in the margin, perhaps meaning to erase it later: 'What young girl would climax with the likes of you?' McAnally then changed his mind and said there was no scream, no cry at all. Which was excellent news for the prosecution, who had witnesses ready to testify that they had heard a cry.

Which point, Rebus mused, though tiny in the wider scheme of the case, was almost certainly what had swung the jury. Mostly it was his word against hers; but there were witnesses to the scream, witnesses like Helena Profitt.

Miss Profitt had given a statement, but had not been called to give evidence at the trial. That was probably the Procurator Fiscal's decision. The Fiscal's office would have precognosced Miss Profitt, and would have made a note for future reference that she was timid, nervy, and unlikely to perform well in court. Crown counsel had picked the best neighbours to show to the jury. It was part of their particular skill.

Rebus reached down for another tin of beer, and found they were all empty. He went to the fridge and found a solitary can, a couple of months past its expiry. It was freezing to the touch, but had plenty of gas when he opened it. He was drinking these days with one side of his mouth only, avoiding the painful side with anything too hot or cold. He put the can down and fried up some bacon, cutting open two rolls. He ate the rolls at the kitchen table.

It has to be serious, he thought. The governor of Saughton, the deputy chief constable . . . maybe even the Constabulary Inspectorate. They just didn't want him around. Why not? That was the question. It had to have something to do with McAnally. It looked to Rebus very much as though it had something to do with McAnally's time in Saughton.

He went back into the living room and got out McAnally's list of previous convictions. Small beer, he thought, taking a drink. He'd been lucky though, landing more than his fair share of fines and tickings-off when a custodial sentence might have been more usual. He'd served a year one time, eighteen months another – both for housebreaking – and that was about it. Otherwise it was just fines and admonitions.

Rebus sat back, forgetting to swallow the beer in his mouth. He was thinking something, something he didn't want to think. There was only one good reason he could think of why Wee Shug had been so lucky, one good reason why a judge might be so lenient time and time again.

Someone had put in a word.

And who was it usually put in a word with the judge? Answer: policemen.

And why did they do it . . . ?

Rebus swallowed the beer. 'He was a grass! Wee Shug McAnally was somebody's bloody snitch!'

Next morning, he woke up raring to go to work – then remembered he had no work to go to, no place he would be welcome. Just when he needed to ask some of his fellow officers a few very discreet questions.

He'd lain awake half the night, watching the amber street light on his bedroom ceiling, tumbling configurations in his mind. He couldn't get past the notion that McAnally had been somebody's eyes and ears on the street. All good policemen had them; anyone who wanted to get anywhere had them: grasses, stoolies, snitches, informers. They had a hundred titles and a hundred job descriptions.

It made sense; it explained those lenient sentences. But then McAnally had crossed the line – no judge was going to listen to too many pleas for leniency in a rape case. Four years off the street and a snitch lost his usefulness: there were new bandits around, people he didn't know and could never get to know. Four years was a long time on the street; the world moved fast down there.

Something else had occurred to Rebus in bed, around three a.m. by the blue-lit numerals on his clock. It – whatever 'it' was, whatever it was people were scared of – had to do with McAnally, yes, but the councillor was involved too. Rebus had let the councillor slip from the equation. He'd been busy on fractions on one half of the board, while the councillor sat untroubled on the other. And the councillor, unlike McAnally, was still alive to answer questions. Rebus was only going to get so far following the trail of the dead. It was time to concentrate on the living.

It was time to get concerned.

17

Councillor Tom Gillespie lived in a huge, bay-windowed semi not five minutes' walk from Rebus's flat. The house had been divided into two flats, one on the upper storey, one on the lower. Gillespie's was the ground-floor property. There was a trim lawn in front of the house, and a low stone wall topped with black glossy railings which ended in arrow-headed points. Rebus opened the gate and walked up to the front door. Clay-coloured road-salt crunched underfoot, spread up and down the path during the worst of the snow and ice. Now the ice had melted, apart from trimmings of sooty white in corners the sun never reached, and roads and paths throughout the city were blighted by salt, as treacherous underfoot as the ice it replaced.

Rebus could see movement behind the bay window as he rang the doorbell. It was an old-fashioned pull affair, the sprung bell chiming inside. Rebus heard an inner hallway door open, then a lock being pulled. The solid main door was opened by the councillor himself.

'Good morning, Mr Gillespie, mind if I have a word?'

'I'm up to my eyes in it, Inspector.'

From within, Rebus heard a motorised whine, then the sound of a woman sneezing. Gillespie's arm was across the doorway, blocking any attempt by Rebus to enter. It wasn't exactly Costa del Sol weather on the doorstep, but the councillor was sweating.

'I appreciate that, sir,' Rebus said, 'but this will only take a minute.'

'Did you speak to Helena Profitt?'

'I did, yes. And, by the way, thanks for setting the Joint Police Board on me.'

Gillespie wasn't about to apologise. 'I told you I had friends.'

There was a yip from within, like a Pekinese getting a deserved kick up the arse, and then a furious female voice.

'Tom! Tom!'

Gillespie pretended not to hear.

'I think you're wanted indoors,' Rebus remarked.

'Look, this really isn't the time for –'

'Tom, for Christ's sake!'

Gillespie snarled, turned on his heel and sprinted indoors. The front door was closing on Rebus with infinite slowness. He pushed it open and walked into the hall.

'Bloody thing's jammed again,' the woman was saying. 'Why the hell can't *you* do this?'

84

Then Gillespie, trying to keep his voice low. 'Just don't let him in! Go on then!'

A woman stumbled out of the front room like she'd been pushed from behind. She bumped into Rebus and some empty files clattered to the tile floor.

'Damnation,' she said. As the door closed behind her, Rebus could see that the bay-windowed room was some kind of office. He glimpsed a desk with a computer, chests of drawers with heaped documents slewed across their tops. He couldn't see whatever was making the noise, and he couldn't see Gillespie, but he heard a slap as the councillor either punched or kicked a piece of machinery.

He helped the woman retrieve the files. 'Nice colours,' he said.

'What?' She tucked some stray hairs back into place behind her ear. She was a tall, heavy-boned woman with a face full of strong features. Her thick dark hair was shoulder-length and parted to one side, a little lacking in life. Her eyes were full of life though; her eyes were blazing. She looked harassed, but was dressed with thoughtful elegance in a pearl-coloured silk blouse and a long skirt of Black Watch tartan.

'The files,' Rebus explained. 'The ones I always seem to buy are blue or grey or green. These are . . . well, they're more colourful.'

She looked at him like he was mad: they were only files.

'A stationer's on George Street,' she said.

Rebus nodded, trying not to look like he was memorising the letters on the front of the file he'd been studying. Not that the letters SDA/SE were difficult to remember.

'Something jammed?' Rebus asked.

She had been brought up a polite girl, taught manners at home and in school. She couldn't not answer a question so casually put, a harmless inquiry.

'The shredder,' she said.

Rebus nodded, confirming that he too had problems with his paper-shredder. 'You must be Mrs Gillespie?'

'That's right.'

'He's got you helping him, eh?'

She tried to laugh. 'Press-ganged.'

'I thought Councillor Gillespie had a secretary.'

Her smile vanished. She was thinking up some lie to tell him when the door opened and Gillespie emerged. This time, peering into the room, Rebus saw several cardboard boxes full of long thin strips of paper. Shredded documents.

Gillespie propelled his wife gently but firmly back into the office, closing the door after her. 'I don't recall inviting you in, Inspector.'

'Maybe you'll want to talk to your friend Councillor Mantoni again.'

Gillespie pulled out a handkerchief. 'Well, now you're here, come into the kitchen.' He wiped the handkerchief across his forehead. 'I'm parched.'

He led Rebus down the long hall, past a sitting room and dining room. They took a left past the blocked-in staircase and passed through a shorter, darker passage into the kitchen. There was pine everywhere: pine units, pine tongue-and-groove covering every surface except the floor, which boasted boards freshly sanded and varnished. A conservatory had been

added to the back, giving views on to the wide rear garden, mature rose bushes and laurel hedge; a small brick patio.

Gillespie busied himself with the kettle.

'I won't offer you a cup, Inspector. I know you'll be keen to be on your way.'

'I'm not that busy today actually, Mr Gillespie, but I won't stay for coffee.' Rebus paused. 'Thanks for the offer.'

Gillespie opened a cupboard and glowered at the mugs and glasses within. Reflected glare, thought Rebus.

'So what is it you want?' Gillespie reached for a mug.

'Dog shit,' said Rebus.

Gillespie fumbled the mug but retrieved it. 'What did you say?'

'Dog shit, Councillor: on the pavements, the grass . . . everywhere. It's a disgrace.'

'Are you trying to tell me you're not here in your official capacity?'

'Did I say I was? No, I'm here as a private individual, a constituent voicing a complaint to his elected representative.'

Gillespie opened a *cafetière* and poured ground coffee into it from a packet. By the time he finished he'd regained his composure.

'Well, Mr Rebus,' he said, 'people only usually complain in the summer. That's when the offending article is at its softest and smelliest. I've never received a complaint in the winter.'

'Then I'm speaking for the silent majority.'

Gillespie managed a smile. 'What do you really want? If I had a mind, I could construe this visit as harassment.'

After what Rebus had seen, he didn't really want anything else, but he was enjoying himself, and what were holidays for if you didn't enjoy yourself?

'Just what I say,' he replied.

Gillespie poured boiling water over the coffee grounds. 'Well, I'm surprised at you.'

'Why?'

'Because I'd have expected you of all people to know that dogs fouling the byways are a matter for the police. It's down to the police to trace the owners and bring a prosecution.'

'And the council doesn't do anything?'

'On the contrary, we've a Dog Warden Section whose job is to educate owners to act responsibly. The wardens also help the police in cases of prosecution. The Warden Section is part of the EHD.'

'Environmental Health Department?'

'Precisely. I can give you their number if you like. It's the least I can do . . . for a constituent.'

Rebus smiled and shook his head. He put his hands in his pockets and made as if to leave. But he stopped beside the councillor and lowered his voice.

'How scared are you?'

'What?'

'You look to me like you're shifting snowballs.'

The councillor started sweating again. He opened his mouth to say something, then changed his mind and concentrated on stirring the contents of the *cafetière*.

'All the shit that's about these days,' Rebus went on, 'you've got to watch you don't tread in it. You might end up on your arse, isn't that right, Councillor?'

'Just get out, will you?'

Rebus turned to leave. Gillespie put out a hand to stop him. 'Inspector, you're making a mistake.' Not a threat; a simple statement of fact.

'Talk to me.'

Gillespie thought about it, biting his bottom lip, then shook his head. Rebus stared at him, willing him to change his mind. But Gillespie was scared; it was in his eyes, in the sheen of his face.

The man was terrified.

'I'll let you out,' Gillespie said, leading Rebus back down the hall. He had the *cafetière* in one hand, two mugs in the other. Through the office door they could hear Mrs Gillespie cursing the machine again. She sounded like she was kicking it.

'Bit of a temper, your wife,' Rebus commented. He saw that Gillespie didn't have a free hand, so did the kindly thing and opened the office door for him.

'Has he gone yet?' Mrs Gillespie snarled.

'Just on my way, Mrs Gillespie,' Rebus told her, popping his head round the door, taking a good look round. 'Nice to have met you.'

Her face was flushed, anger turning quickly to embarrassment. 'I'm sorry,' she said.

'No need for that.'

And Rebus left them to it, whatever *it* was . . .

18

It took Rebus half the afternoon to decide that he was doing the right thing.

More accurately, it took him ten minutes to make up his mind, and a couple of hours to drink himself into a state where he was confident enough to follow through.

He wasn't just drinking though, he was hunting; eyes and ears open for news of Rico Briggs.

Rico was just about the best and worst housebreaker on the east coast. It wasn't that he was cack-handed: he could be in and out of most homes in minutes flat, be the occupants asleep, slumped in front of the TV, or making merry at a party. Rico's problem was that he was conspicuous, and fences didn't like that. Rico had been a big Hearts fan, not missing a fixture in seasons 1977–80, except when he'd served a wee stretch in Peterhead. One night in Leith Walk, dizzy after a trouncing of the Hibees, Rico had marched into a tattoo parlour and demanded the works.

Next morning, Rico had looked at his face in his bathroom mirror and seen that both tender cheeks now boasted the Hearts badge, a maroon heart with a cross in the middle. It took him only a day or two to start loathing his once-loved team; which was ironic, considering he was now a public poster-site for the men of Gorgie.

Not surprisingly, the tattoos were unique, and as good as fingerprints as far as the police were concerned. Realising this, Rico had started sporting a balaclava when working, which accentuated his other remarkable facial feature – a nose the dimensions of the Pyramid of Cheops. This, too, people tended to notice.

Rebus had tried talking Rico Briggs into retiring, and had been semi-successful. These days, Rico concentrated on passing his skills on to a series of apprentices; he'd even given Rebus a few clandestine lessons in lock-picking. They helped when the policeman mislaid his house-keys; and at other times too.

Rebus finally found Rico in a bar off Nicolson Street, a place whose sad-faced clients were usually in hiding after a haircut at the half-blind barber's next door. Surrounded by bad haircuts, it was surprising how Rico blended in.

'Hiya, Rico,' Rebus said, sliding on to the wooden stool next to him. 'How are you doing?'

Rico had the daily tabloid folded at the quick crossword, and was tapping

it with a half-size betting-shop pen, the kind with a ten-minute lifetime guarantee.

'Eight letters,' Rico said in a voice like road-salt, 'M-something-R-something-O. "On a desert island".' He looked to Rebus.

'Marooned.'

'Thanks, in that case I'll have a double,' Rico chuckled. 'Not heard that one before, Mr Rebus?'

'Not since *Double Barrel* was at the top of the charts.'

Rebus ordered the drinks while Rico rubbed both cheeks, the idea being that if he rubbed them often enough he'd sand the tattoos away.

'So, Mr Rebus, is it a job?'

Rebus nodded, wary of saying too much: he might be surrounded by bad haircuts, but nobody's ears had been severed.

'Tell you later.'

They drank their drinks in silence. The whole bar was quiet. Further down the bar, a customer nodded to the barman for a refill and the barman nodded back. A silent order, Rebus thought. Like monks. Which, given the tonsures, wasn't such a bad image.

They got out of the pub and walked towards the Pleasance. If they took a right, they'd come to St Leonard's, but they went left instead and headed to the Cowgate and Canongate. They talked as they walked, then entered a howff on the High Street to toast the mission.

At six o'clock, dark overhead except for an arc of moon looking like someone had pressed their thumbnail into the sky, Rebus and Rico sat in Rebus's parked car, engine running to keep the heater on. They were across the road from the Gillespie house, and Rebus was describing the layout. Rebus was more nervous than he would admit: if Rico were caught, if he talked, then Rebus could end up one of Big Jim Flett's clients. Rico asked a few questions, and Rebus supplied answers where he could.

'I'll go in through the conservatory,' Rico decided. 'You're sure about the alarm?'

'No alarm,' Rebus said.

People were hurrying along the pavement, faces down to avoid the icy wind which, Edinburgh fashion, was blowing horizontally just at head height. Rebus was having doubts about the whole enterprise, but could see no way round it. He thought of something else he'd wanted to ask Rico.

'Know anyone who's just come out of Saughton?'

'I don't mix with felons, Inspector.'

'Of course you don't, you've gone straight, we both know that.' Rebus's voice was quiet but insistent. 'Only, if you did know anyone, I'd like to talk to them. Nothing heavy or official, just a chat, a bit of info on Saughton itself.'

'There'd be a cash incentive?'

'There'd be a drink in it for both of you.'

'Well, wouldn't do any harm to ask around.'

'No harm at all,' Rebus agreed. He looked over to the Gillespie house. 'What time will you go in?'

'Two in the morning should do it. Best not stay here much longer though – we don't want to attract attention.'

Rico had a point: in Marchmont, you were always in somebody else's parking space. There were barely enough gaps for the residents, never mind visitors. Rebus put the gearstick into first.

'We'll get a bite to eat,' he said.

'Hiy, hold on.' Rico was pointing towards the house. The front door was standing open, and Mrs Gillespie suddenly appeared carrying two black binbags. Behind her, her husband carried two more. They opened their gate and deposited the bags on the pavement outside. Something wonderful dawned on Rebus. He looked up and down the street. Sure enough, a few bags were already out.

'Rubbish day the morn?' Rico suggested.

'Rico, it looks like I won't be needing you after all.'

In the end, Rico helped load the boot.

Rebus sat alone in his flat, having paid Rico off and dropped him back in the town centre. One of the binbags had contained nothing but empty tins, bags and boxes, and now it sat outside the main door of Rebus's tenement. But the other three sat open in the middle of Rebus's living room. He emptied the first bag on to the floor. Strands of white paper fell in a shivering heap. Rebus picked up one strand. It was the length of an A4 sheet and no more than two millimetres wide. He'd heard stories that shredded documents could be reconstructed. All it took was patience: colossal patience. He was sure there were clever ways of doing it – UV analysis or watermark-matching or batch-sorting – but all he had were his eyes. He couldn't just march into Howdenhall and drop the stuff off. Too many questions would be asked. He sat on the floor, picked up a few strands, and tried putting them together.

It took him about four minutes to realise the job was impossible.

He sat there smoking a cigarette, staring at the strands. They might tell him everything he needed to know. He finished the cigarette, poured himself a drink, and tried again. It took him a while to lose his temper. He dragged the kitchen table through and sat at it. Then he brought the anglepoise lamp through from his bedroom and plugged it in. The machine had jammed; there was a chance not all the strips had been separated completely.

He didn't find as many as two strips still joined at any one pont.

He swore for a while and walked around the flat, emptied the coffee jar and set it back under the radiator, then put his coat on and went to buy cigarettes and whisky. The corner shop was closed when he reached it. His watch said eleven-fifteen; he couldn't believe it was so late.

He walked on to the nearest pub and waded through the smoky, shouting throng. The barmaid gave him change for the cigarette machine but couldn't sell him a carry-out: it was after last orders. She told him about a licensed chip shop he could try, but it was a car-run away, so he walked briskly back to the flat and sought out untried bottles. There was a quarter of Bacardi for emergency dispensation should he ever manage to drag a woman as far as his bedroom. The thought of neat Bacardi repelled him only slightly more than the thought of mixing it with anything.

Which means, he thought, I can't be an alcoholic.

He unscrewed the top from the Bacardi anyway and sniffed it, then

screwed it back on. He'd have to be a lot more desperate . . . say, come four in the morning. Then he remembered the freezer. He opened it up and chipped away at the ice until he'd broken through to two trays of ice cubes, a single fish finger . . . and a small bottle. It was Polish vodka; a neighbour had given it to him after a trip home to Lodz; a present for feeding the cat for a week.

Rebus found a glass, filled it, and belatedly toasted Solidarity before draining it. The stuff was as smooth as anything he'd ever tried. A third of a litre of eighty-four proof. He took glass and bottle into the living room and put *Exile on Main Street* on the hi-fi. It sounded as good as ever.

He got back into the game, then decided to leave the first bag and start on the second. He filled the first bag back up, then dumped bag two on to the floor.

And his doorbell rang.

It was a little after midnight.

The main door was sometimes left unlocked. No need for visitors, welcome or not, to announce their presence until they were outside the door of the flat.

At this time on a Thursday night?

Rebus looked at the mess on the floor, then went out into the hall and tiptoed to the front door, just as the bell rang again. He could hear two voices at least, little more than murmurs. Suddenly, fingers pushed open his letterbox. Rebus stood to the side of the door, back pressed to the wall.

'Maybe he leaves the lights on when he's out.'

'Aye, and maybe he's half-shot and sleeping it off.'

Rebus turned the snib silently and yanked open the door. Siobhan Clarke, who'd been peering through the letterbox, stood up, but Rebus's eyes were on Brian Holmes.

'Half-shot, is it, Brian? I'm glad you hold me in such high regard.'

Holmes just shrugged. 'It's what I'd do on holiday.'

Rebus filled the doorway, his arms folded. 'So what are you doing: canvassing, polling, or maybe you were just passing?'

'We were working,' Brian Holmes explained. 'We went to get something to eat afterwards, and when we ran out of interesting topics, the conversation came round to you.'

'What about me?'

'We wondered,' Siobhan Clarke said, 'what the hell's going on.'

Rebus smiled. 'You and me both.' He stood back from the doorway. 'You better come in. You're the first to arrive; I haven't even got the party snacks out.' He noticed a brown carrier bag on the landing behind Brian Holmes.

'We brought our own party with us.' When Holmes picked up the bag, Rebus heard cans and bottles collide.

'You're always welcome here, Brian,' Rebus said, leading them indoors.

They sat in the living room, staring at the pile of paper strips. Siobhan Clarke took a gulp of coffee.

'You *stole* these?'

Rebus shook his head. 'A public service; I saved the binmen a job.'

Holmes looked to Siobhan. 'We did say we were coming here to help.'

'Yes, but this lot . . . ?' She flapped her arms. 'I doubt the "Blue Peter" appeal could sort this lot out. Talk about shreds of evidence.'

Rebus held up a pacifying hand. 'Look, this is my problem, not yours. I won't be disappointed if you scurry off home. In fact, it would be better for you if you did.'

'We know,' said Holmes.

Rebus looked at him. 'What do you mean?'

Siobhan Clarke explained. 'The Farmer spoke to us this afternoon. Basically, he warned us off. He said you were on leave, but he didn't think that would stop you sticking your nose in.' She looked up. 'His words, not mine.'

'We've been given new duties,' Brian Holmes added.

'Desk work, restructuring the filing system prior to full computerisation.'

'To keep you busy?'

'Yes.'

'And away from me?'

They both nodded.

'So naturally you come straight here?' Rebus got to his feet. 'You could be fucking up both your careers!'

'I'm not in CID to sort through a lot of old paperwork,' Siobhan Clarke retorted. Then she realised what she'd said, looked at the mound of shredded paper in front of her, and laughed.

They all did.

They hit lucky with the third bag.

'Look,' Siobhan Clarke said, 'it's not just white paper.'

Rebus took a strip from her: yellow card. 'Files,' he said. 'They shredded the folders as well!'

'Must be some machine,' Brian Holmes added.

'That's a bloody good point, Brian.'

The folders were a breakthrough. The problem with the paper was that there was so much of it. There wasn't nearly so much card, and what there was could be grouped by colour. The front of each file had a white printed label, and these were what Rebus wanted. He wanted the reconstructed labels.

But even knowing what they were looking for, it took time and effort. Rebus's eyes were stinging, and he kept rubbing them, which only blurred his vision.

'Get you two anything?' he kept saying. They would only shake their heads. Rebus demolished the cans on his own. He knew he'd had too much when he polished off a tin of Irn-Bru without realising it was non-alcoholic.

The streets grew quieter after the students had slouched home on the wings of blasphemy. Around two-thirty, the central heating clocked off and Rebus turned on the gas-fire. They each worked on a different colour of folder.

'I saw one of the folders when Mrs Gillespie dropped it,' Rebus said. 'It was marked SDA/SE. I presume the letters stand for Scottish Development Agency and Scottish Enterprise. Scottish Enterprise took over when the SDA was wound up. Councillor Gillespie, by the way, sits on an industrial planning committee.'

'So,' Holmes remarked, 'the SDA file could be completely innocent.'

'Certainly he had a genuine reason for having a file on the SDA. But why be in such a panic to shred it?'

Holmes conceded the point.

'I think I've got something,' Siobhan Clarke said. She'd all but completed a yellow file, the label intact save for a strip or two. 'Looks like the letters A C,' she said, 'then a name: Haldayne.'

Rebus fetched the phone book. There was no A. C. Haldayne in Edinburgh.

'Strange spelling,' Brian Holmes said. 'I've never come across Haldayne with a y.'

'Misspelt?' Siobhan Clarke said. 'The name of one of the councillor's constituents?'

Rebus shrugged. Half an hour later, it was Holmes's turn to complete a red file.

' "Gyle Park West",' he read out.

Rebus wasn't paying much attention; he was close to completing the last of the coloured folders, this one a lurid green.

' "Mensung",' he said, looking up. 'What the hell is Mensung?'

Siobhan Clarke yawned and rubbed at her eyes, then blinked a few times, looking around the room.

'You know,' she said, 'it's a good job this paper's lying everywhere. Without it, this place would look like a tip.'

It was six on Friday morning when Rebus's phone started ringing.

He fell off the chair, the duvet sliding with him. The phone was underneath one of the heaps of paper strips.

'Whoever you are,' he said, 'whatever you want . . . you're dead.'

'It's Siobhan, sir. I've been thinking about A. C. Haldayne.'

'Me, too,' Rebus lied.

'I've been thinking about that funny spelling. American names are sometimes spelt differently, aren't they?'

'Is that why you woke me up?'

'Well, it would tie in with AC.'

'Would it?'

'Christ, you're slow, sir.'

'It's six in the morning, Clarke.'

'All I mean is AC could stand for American Consulate. Haldayne could be a surname, and AC the consulate.'

Rebus sat up and opened his eyes. 'That's not bad.'

'I tried phoning the consulate, but got an answering machine. It offered me a lot of options, mostly to do with visa applications, then put me through to the consulate proper, but all I got was another answering machine message telling me the opening hours.'

'Try again in the morning.'

'Yes, sir. Sorry for waking you.'

'That's all right. Listen, Siobhan . . . thanks for helping me.'

'It's no problem, really.'

'Then you won't mind doing something else?' He could almost hear her smile.

'What?'

'That shredder. I'm wondering how long Gillespie's owned it.'

'You want me to check?'

'Yes.'

'Will do. Goodnight, sir.'

'Goodnight, Clarke.'

Rebus put down the receiver and decided to get up. Half a minute later, he was asleep on the living-room carpet.

19

On Sunday, Rebus was invited to Oxford Terrace for afternoon tea.

He was glad of the break, having spent much of the previous forty-eight hours trying to piece together some of the strands of A4 paper. He hadn't made any progress, but it had taken his mind off his swollen gum. By Saturday afternoon, he'd had enough and phoned a dentist, but of course by then all the dentists in Edinburgh were in the clubhouse, deciding over a second gin whether to bother with eighteen holes or, in this weather, just settle for nine.

On Sunday afternoon, dress smart but casual, he went to start his car and found it recalcitrant. Probably a loose connection. He looked under the bonnet, but was no mechanic. He was alone on the street, no one around to give him a jump-start, so he went back indoors and called for a cab, noticing too late that he had oil on his hands, a smudge of which had transferred itself to his trouser leg.

He was not in the best of moods as his driver took him north across the city.

Sammy answered the door. She was wearing thick black tights with a short jumble-sale dress falling over them. Under the dress she wore a white T-shirt.

'You're almost on time,' she said. 'We weren't expecting you so soon.'

'Did Patience teach you that one?'

He followed his daughter down the hall into the living room. Lucky the cat took one look at Rebus, seemed to remember him, and stalked off into the conservatory. Rebus heard the catflap rattle shut. Now it was only two against one; the odds were improving in Rebus's favour.

He knew there were things fathers said to their daughters, little criticisms they were expected to make to show they cared. But Rebus knew what his little criticisms would sound like: they'd sound like criticisms. So he kept his counsel. Patience came out of the kitchen wiping her hands on a dish-towel.

'John.'

'Hello, Patience.' They kissed the way friends did, a peck on the cheek, a hand on the shoulder.

'Be about two minutes,' she said, turning back into the kitchen. He didn't think she'd really looked at him. 'Go into the conservatory.'

Sammy again led the way. The table had a clean white cloth on it, with some dishes already laid. Patience had brought her potted plants indoors for the winter, leaving not much room for anything or anyone else. The

Sunday papers were heaped on the window-ledge. Rebus chose the chair nearest the garden door. Looking out of the conservatory window, he could see in through the kitchen window. Patience was busy at the sink, her face lacking emotion. She didn't look up.

'Liking it all right?' Rebus asked his daughter.

She nodded. 'It's great, and so's Patience.'

'How's the job?'

'Very stimulating; not easy, but stimulating.'

'What do you do exactly?'

'SWEEP's pretty small, we all muck in. I'm supposed to be developing communication skills in my clients.'

Rebus nodded. 'You mean so they can be a bit more polite next time they mug their granny?'

She glowered at him and he raised his hands. 'Just a joke,' he said.

'Maybe you need some communication skills yourself.'

'He's as blunt as a butt to the head,' Patience said, bringing in the teapot.

'Can I help?' Sammy offered.

'You sit there, I'll be back in a second.'

She was away far longer than a second; there was no conversation between times. Rebus watched Lucky the cat staring at him from the garden path. Patience returned with plates of cakes and biscuits. His mouth was imploring him: no hot drinks, no cakes or biscuits, no sugar, no crunching.

'I'll pour,' Sammy said. There was a clatter as Lucky came back in, seeking tidbits.

'Cake, John?' Patience said, offering him the pick from the plate. He took the smallest item he could find, a thin end-slice of madeira. Patience regarded his choice with suspicion: he'd always preferred ginger sponge, and she, who hated it, had bought one specially.

'Sammy,' Patience said, 'try the ginger.'

'It's a bit sweet for me,' Sammy replied. 'I'll just have a biscuit.'

'Fine.'

'This outfit of yours,' Rebus began.

'It's called SWEEP,' Sammy reminded him.

'Yes, SWEEP, who funds it?'

'We've charitable status. We get some donations, but spend more time than we ought to thinking up fund-raising schemes. The bulk of the money drips down from the Scottish Office.' She turned to Patience. 'We've this brilliant guy, he knows just how to word an application for funding, knows what grants are available . . .'

Patience looked interested. 'Is he nice?'

Sammy blushed. 'He's great.'

'And he deals with the Scottish Office?' Rebus asked.

'Yes.' Sammy couldn't see where this was leading. She worked with people who were mistrustful of police officers and other authority figures, mistrustful of their motives. Her colleagues were careful what they said in front of her. She'd been open with them from the start; she'd stated on the application form that her father was in Edinburgh CID. But there were some people who still didn't trust her entirely.

She knew one problem was the media. When the media learned who her

father was, they sought her out for a quote – her background made it more interesting. They called it 'personalising the issues'. There were some people in SWEEP who felt resentful of the attention she got.

She didn't really blame them. It was the system.

'More cake, John?'

The catflap clacked again as Lucky went back outside.

'No thanks, Patience,' Rebus said.

'I think maybe I'll try the madeira,' Sammy said. Which left an awful lot of ginger cake.

'You haven't touched your tea, John.'

'I'm waiting 'til it cools.' In the past, he'd always liked it scalding.

'Why are you so interested in SWEEP all of a sudden?' Sammy asked him.

'I'm not, but I might be interested in the Scottish Office.'

Sammy looked like she didn't believe him. She started to defend SWEEP, going on at length, her cheeks colouring with conviction. Rebus envied her that sense of conviction.

Then he said a couple of things, and an argument started. He couldn't help himself; he'd just had to take a contrary point of view. He tried drawing Patience into the debate, but she only shook her head slowly and sadly. Finally, when Sammy had collapsed into a sulk, Patience was ready with her summing-up.

'You see, Sammy, your father is the Old Testament type: retribution rather than rehabilitation. Isn't that right, John?'

Rebus just shrugged, drank some lukewarm tea, and absent-mindedly chewed on a slice of buttered ginger cake.

'And he's the classic Calvinist, too,' Patience went on. 'Let the punishment fit the crime, and then some.'

'That's not Calvinism,' Rebus said. 'It's Gilbert and Sullivan.' He sat forwards in his chair. 'Besides, the problem is that sometimes the punishment *doesn't* fit the crime. Sometimes there's punishment and no crime at all. Other times there's crime but no punishment; and worst of all –' he paused – 'nearly all of the time there's *unfairness*.' He looked at Sammy, wondering what SWEEP would have done for Willie Coyle and Dixie Taylor, wondering if anything at all, anything worth a candle, would have been left of them after prison.

Eventually, they found other things to talk about. Sammy didn't contribute much; she just kept staring at her father, as if seeing him afresh. The sky outside conceded defeat and collapsed from slate-grey to late-afternoon black. While Patience and Sammy were clearing the table, Rebus stared at Lucky through the window, then went over to the catflap and locked it shut. The cat saw what he had done. It miaowed at him once, registering its protest. Rebus waved it cheerio.

They sat in the living room, and Patience handed over a few things he'd left behind after the move: his second-best razor, some clean handker-chiefs, a pair of shoelaces, a tape of *Electric Ladyland*. He stuffed everything into his jacket pockets.

'Thanks,' he said.

'You're welcome.'

Sammy saw him back to the door and waved him off.

*

That evening, back at the flat, Rebus sat listening to Hendrix with a lined pad of paper in front of him. There were some words on it.

SDA/SE (Scottish Office?)

A. C. Haldayne (US Consulate?)

Mensung (?? – not in phone book)

Gyle Park West (industrial estate)

He knew about Gyle Park West because he'd driven out there that morning. It was a low-rise sprawl of smallish industrial and commercial units, sited next to the imposing PanoTech electronics company. At the entrance to the estate there was a sign listing the various companies on the site, including Deltona. He remembered that Salty Dougary worked for Deltona, and that Deltona provided microchips for PanoTech, the Pano-Tech factory being more of an assembly line, constructing computers from components sourced elsewhere.

None of which seemed to tie Councillor Gillespie to Wee Shug McAnally. None of which was in itself suspicious. The councillor was on an industrial planning committee, which was excuse enough for owning files on the SDA and Scottish Enterprise and on Gyle Park West. But then why the panic, the hurry to destroy those files? *That* was what interested Rebus.

As he drove out of Gyle, an area of the city he didn't really know, he realised something else. Gyle itself had boomed in the eighties, gaining new homes, industries, even its own railway station. Before then, it had just been a place near the airport. The airport had been its big advantage in the eighties, making for good fast communications. These days Gyle had an identity, and a lot of that was down to the injection of cash into the place. But there was something else in Gyle's favour.

Its district councillor just happened to be the Lord Provost, Cameron McLeod Kennedy.

The telephone rang, bringing him out of his reverie. He snatched the receiver. 'Hello?'

'Hello yourself.' It was Mairie Henderson.

'I was beginning to think you'd forgotten me,' Rebus said.

'I've only finally managed to track down LABarum.' Rebus picked up his pen and moved the pad closer. 'The reason I had trouble was, it doesn't exist.'

'What?'

'Not yet at any rate. It's a PanoTech project. Do you know who they are?'

'The computer company?'

'That's right. LABarum is something they've been toying with. See, the problem with Silicon Glen, with the whole Scottish electronics industry, is that it's a manufacturer. It puts bits and pieces together, but that's about all. Everything's sourced elsewhere.'

'Not everything, there's Deltona.'

'A *very* small cog in the machine. What we need in Scotland is a software giant, a Microsoft, somebody researching, developing and producing software to go *into* the machines.'

'LABarum?'

'That's right. But my source tells me it's not up and running yet. There's a question of funding. The talent's there, but to keep it in Scotland is going to cost money, lots and lots of money.' She paused. 'My source was curious, how did you hear about it?'

'I saw a business plan.'

'You did? Where? At PanoTech?'

'No.' What could he tell her? In a sub-let council house in Stenhouse? Hiding behind a teenager's paperback collection?

'Where then? The City Chambers?'

Rebus started. 'Why do you . . . ?' Then he thought about it. A plan to start up a computer software company, presumably in Gyle Park West . . . He looked at the writing on his pad. The district council would want to discuss it, they'd need to be aware of it. Tom Gillespie's committee would certainly know about it. And if it *was* to be sited in Gyle Park West, if it had anything to do with the district council at all, then the Lord Provost would know about it. Cameron McLeod Kennedy.

Rebus picked the business plan off the floor and looked at the initials on the front page. Mairie was telling him she'd drawn a blank with Dalgety, but he wasn't listening.

'CK,' he said quietly. Cameron Kennedy. 'Jesus, Mairie, those two kids did know Kirstie Kennedy after all!'

20

On Monday morning, Rebus went to the National Library on George IV Bridge. He passed through the security barrier and climbed the imposing staircase. At the main desk, he explained what he was looking for and was issued with a one-day reader's card. Then he found a spare computer console and sat down at it, reading the instructions for using the online system.

His search didn't take long. There was desperately little on the Scottish Development Agency; even less on Scottish Enterprise. He was sure that before its demise the SDA had been under the aegis of the Scottish Office, so tapped 'Scottish Office' into the computer. There were a lot of entries; he went through screen after screen of them: welfare, road-widening schemes, grants to the fishing industry, corporal punishment . . . But nothing new on either the SDA or Scottish Enterprise.

Across the road in the Central Library he met with similar results. The Edinburgh Room directed him to the Scottish Library downstairs, and the Scottish Library's microfiches were every bit as unhelpful as the high-tech facilities across the way. Finally, Rebus approached one of the librarians. She sat at a desk, sorting newspaper cuttings into five distinct piles.

'Yes?' she whispered.

'I'm looking for information on the Scottish Development Agency.'

'Have you checked the fiches?'

'Yes.'

'Well, those are our holdings.' She thought for a moment. 'You might try the Scottish Office direct.'

Yes, he might at that. He walked down the High Street and across North Bridge, then made down the side of the St James Centre – noting that Anthony wasn't on his usual pitch – to where the Scottish Office had hidden itself in a concrete box called New St Andrew's House. He told the guard on the door what he wanted, and was pointed in the direction of the reception desk. The woman there was very pleasant, but couldn't help. She phoned up to the Library and Publications Room, who couldn't help either. Rebus found it hard to believe that there was no history of the SDA available.

'They say nobody'd be interested,' she explained, putting down the telephone.

'Well, *I'm* interested.'

'You could ask at the HMSO bookshop.'

'On Lothian Road?'

'Yes.' She saw the look on his face. 'I've some other literature here you could take away with you.'

Desperate for something to show for his morning, Rebus picked out a few leaflets, one of which was an introduction to HM Inspectorate of Constabulary. Rebus wondered if it would mention anything about bribery.

'Thanks anyway,' he told the receptionist. There was a display in the reception area and he went over to look at it. New St Andrew's House was about to relocate to Leith. The move was costing millions. Rebus didn't feel any better for knowing where his taxes were headed. Sleet was coming down as he left the building.

Which gave him the excuse he needed to drop into the Café Royal. It was eleven-fifteen and he was the second customer of the day. He liked the place when it was empty. It was one of the few bars he knew which had less atmosphere the busier it got. His feet were tingling from the walk. He'd left his car at home, only expecting to walk as far as George IV Bridge.

The sleet had stopped by the time he left the bar. He walked along George Street, in order to avoid the shoppers on Princes Street, then headed up Lothian Road. A Lothian Road wind was one of nature's wonders; people were walking into it at an angle close to forty-five degrees. The headwind could exhaust you in minutes. Rebus kept his eyes to the pavement and concentrated on putting one foot after the other, like he was getting the hang of false legs.

The new Convention Centre was up. There was a lot of recent building work around the city: the Festival Theatre, Convention Centre, court annexe, National Library annexe, not to mention the new Scottish Office HQ. He stopped in a doorway to catch his breath and to consider the scale of the building programme: new roads, new developments . . . There was talk of building another road bridge across the Forth. But where was the money coming from? He walked on, deep in thought, and entered the HMSO shop. He'd been explaining his needs to the counter assistant for about thirty seconds when the man started to shake his head.

'I haven't finished yet,' Rebus snapped.

The man listened in silence, and when Rebus was finished he advised: 'You could try Scottish Enterprise direct.' He brought out the phone book to find its address. The HQ was in Glasgow, but there was a branch in Edinburgh: LEEL, Lothian and Edinburgh Enterprise Limited, had offices in Haymarket Terrace, which wasn't that far to walk, not compared to the distance he'd come.

The smart new building which housed LEEL boasted two very bored-looking receptionists and no guard at all on the door. He explained that he wanted general background information.

'Agatha will bring down what we've got,' he was told with a pleasant professional smile. 'If you'd like to take a seat . . . ?'

He sat down and read the bumf spread across the table in front of him. He noticed that his calves were aching. This, he thought, is called exercise. Some people did it every day.

The lift opened and a young woman walked towards him. She too had a Stepford-wifely smile for the public as she handed over a lavish folder, inside which was a set of glossy documents.

'This is all we've got at the moment,' she said.

'Thank you, Agatha, this is fine.'

Since he was so close, he dropped into Torphichen for a coffee. Davidson wasn't around, but DC Robert Burns was, so Rebus chewed the cud with him, enjoying the feel of being back inside a cop shop. Then he asked Burns for a favour.

'I need a lift home, Rab,' he said. 'Medical reasons.'

Back in his flat, Rebus read through what little he had. He hadn't found anything on Gyle Park West or anyone or anything called Mensung. The sum total of his recent discoveries had nothing to do with Councillor Gillespie at all. But what he did know was that Kirstie Kennedy had known Willie and Dixie in some capacity: how else to explain a document belonging to the Lord Provost turning up in Willie's bedroom? What he didn't yet know was why it was there. He assumed Kirstie had taken it from her parents' house, but why? Had it meant something to her? And why had Willie hidden it?

His phone was ringing. It was Siobhan Clarke. 'Where've you been?' she asked.

'Walking.'

'*Walking*?'

'How are things at St Leonard's?'

'The chief super is keeping tabs on Brian and me, and he keeps piling the work on.'

'So you haven't been able to do anything?'

'On the contrary, I've some interesting news. Councillor Gillespie's document shredder wasn't bought, it was rented. There's a business supply company in Stockbridge, they hire out all sorts of office equipment. Which reminds me, when you get back there's a little surprise for you.'

'What?'

'The new PCs have arrived.'

'Good, we could do with a few more men on the beat.'

'Gosh,' her voice dripped irony, 'I've not heard that one today. Anyway, there's one on your desk, plugged in and ready to run.'

'When did Gillespie rent the shredder?'

'Wednesday. He told the shop assistant he'd been trying to find one for a few days, but they were too expensive to buy.'

'Thank God he's mean with money, or we might never know he'd shredded anything.'

'Want to hear the rest? I finally got through to the consulate and asked to speak to Haldayne.' She paused. 'They told me Mr Haldayne was out of the office. His first name's Richard. I got them to spell his surname for me: it has a "y" in the middle.'

'You're a genius.'

'Want to hear the rest?'

Rebus forgot all about his sore calves, his weary feet. 'Go ahead.'

'I ran a check on Mr Richard Haldayne. Have you ever had dealings with the diplomats in town?'

'No.'

'Well, I have. I handed out a few parking tickets when I was in uniform.

My boss said I was wasting my time ticketing a diplomatic plate. They never pay their fines, because we're not allowed to prosecute them.'

'So you looked in the computer?'

'Eighteen unpaid parking tickets dating back to 1985. That's under two a year, which counts as law-abiding for a diplomat.'

'It's still a lot of tickets. An officer might want a quiet word with Mr Haldayne about them.'

'Just don't get caught, sir.'

'Same goes for you, Clarke, and thanks.'

He put the phone down and tapped his fingers on the receiver. It was a start, definitely a start. He lifted the receiver again and dialled Sammy's work number. She wasn't there. The woman who told him this sounded upset.

'I'm her father,' Rebus said, 'is anything wrong?'

'She was in a terrible state. Someone had to take her home.'

'Why was she in a state?'

'Her landlady.' The woman sniffed.

'What about her landlady?'

'Well, *she's* upset, and she got Sammy all upset.'

Rebus stopped pretending to be calm. 'Upset about what?'

'I love cats,' the woman said.

'What?'

'Cats. It's her landlady's cat. It was torn to bits last night by somebody's dog.'

Rebus finally plucked up the courage to phone Patience's flat, and was relieved that Sammy herself answered.

'I heard,' he said. 'How's Patience?'

'She's gone out. She was . . . it was horrible.'

Rebus swallowed. 'What happened?'

'Lucky was in the garden, and some dog must have come over the wall. Lucky ran to the catflap to get in, but the catflap was locked . . .' Her voice fell. 'And that was that.'

'Oh dear,' said Rebus.

'The thing is, Dad, Patience blames *me*.'

'I'm sure that's not –'

'She says I must have locked the flap. She's hardly spoken a word to me since I got back.'

'The lock must have fallen by itself.'

'I don't know. But I know *I* didn't do it.'

'Look, Sammy, the reason I'm phoning –'

'Yes?'

Rebus stared at the notes in front of him. 'SWEEP's contact at the Scottish Office: can you give me his name . . . ?'

He had an appointment that afternoon with the Lord Provost.

Rebus hadn't been specific on the telephone; he'd just told the secretary that it was part of an 'investigation' – he'd been careful not to preface the word with 'official police'. The secretary had taken his home number and called him back. The Lord Provost could see him for five minutes at four o'clock.

'Five minutes should do it,' Rebus had said.

As he walked through the main door of the City Chambers, he looked down at the floor, aware that directly beneath it was Mary King's Close, Edinburgh's buried plague street. They'd covered the street up and built on it anew: that was the Edinburgh way, to bury and forget.

The Lord Provost came out of his office to meet him. He looked tired, his pale face deeply lined, his square jaw slack. He had dark hair streaked with silver, and thick black eyebrows. It was a strongly defined face, the kind that might have been found, a generation back, at the coal-face.

'Inspector.' They shook hands. The Lord Provost turned to his secretary. 'My constitutional,' he said. 'I'll be five or ten minutes.' He turned back to Rebus. 'I like to get out of here for a few minutes in the afternoon, it clears my head. Do you mind?'

Rebus said he didn't.

No one on the street seemed to recognise Cameron Kennedy. He crossed the High Street and nodded towards St Giles's Cathedral. Rebus followed him into the huge old church. It was empty, save for a party of three tourists who huddled around their guidebook. Rebus and the Lord Provost walked the central aisle.

'How can I help you, Inspector?'

'Well, sir, it's about your daughter.'

The Lord Provost's face became more animated. 'Have you found her?'

'No, sir. But I know where she's been quite recently. You remember those two hoaxers?'

'Don't I just. You were in that terrible crash, weren't you?'

Rebus nodded. 'The thing is, it may not have been a hoax after all.'

'How do you mean?'

'Well, the girl you spoke to on the telephone . . .'

'Ach, I don't think it was Kirstie.'

'It could have been. There's evidence she knew the two boys who died.'

The Lord Provost looked at him. 'Evidence?'

'Something we found in a bedroom.' Rebus brought out the business plan and handed it to the Lord Provost. 'This *is* yours, isn't it, sir?'

The Lord Provost studied it. 'Where did you say you found it?'

'It was hidden in the bedroom belonging to one of the boys. Do you know when and where you lost it?'

'No, I . . . It was a while back. I thought I'd taken it home with me . . .'

'Kirstie probably took it with her when she left.'

The Lord Provost nodded slowly.

'The question is, why? I mean, did it have any significance for her?'

'I don't see how it could.'

'Me neither, I was hoping you might help. Take a look at the last page, please.'

The Lord Provost turned to the last page and looked startled.

'Did you write that, sir?'

'No.' He was staring wide-eyed at the name.

'Is it Kirstie's writing?'

'I don't know.'

'Well, do you know what it means?'

The Lord Provost shook his head slowly and closed the report. 'Inspector,

I . . . it seems to me maybe I'm making too much fuss over Kirstie. I'm sure she's managing fine.'

'What are you saying?'

'I'm saying I'm grateful to the police for trying to trace her, but maybe it's time to call a halt.'

Rebus narrowed his eyes. 'Why now?' He made to take the report back, but the Lord Provost was folding it into his pocket.

'Does there have to be a reason?'

'Is it something to do with that report?'

'You've read it?'

'Yes, sir.'

'It's just an initial report of a possible business venture.'

'In Gyle Park West?' The Lord Provost nodded. 'A new subsidiary of PanoTech?'

'You're well informed, Inspector.'

Rebus shrugged. 'I'm just curious why Kirstie would take it, and why it was kept hidden, like it had some importance.'

Kennedy smiled. 'It's of no importance, Inspector. It's a projection, it's just something that might happen. God knows we could do with it.'

'Why's that, sir?'

'The jobs, of course.'

'Tell me, is the LABarum plan before any committee at present?'

The Lord Provost sat in a pew. Rebus sat one pew in front of him. 'I don't see what that could have to do with my daughter.'

Rebus shrugged. 'I'm just curious.'

'It will be discussed soon, yes.'

'By Councillor Gillespie's industry committee?'

'Initially, yes. Look, I really don't see what this has to do with Kirstie. I accept that she could have taken the document from my office at home. I'd say if it was anything, it was an act of pure rebellion – she took it because she *could*.'

'Is she a rebel then, sir?'

'Aren't all teenagers?'

'Not all teenagers are drug-users, sir.'

Rebus watched the colour come back to the Lord Provost's cheeks. 'What did you say?'

'That's why you didn't have a more recent photo to give us. Junkies aren't exactly photogenic.'

The Lord Provost shot to his feet. 'How dare you!' The tourists stopped consulting their guidebook.

'Then tell me I'm a liar,' Rebus said quietly. The Lord Provost opened his mouth, then closed it again. 'Tell me I'm a liar and I'll take back what I said.'

Cameron Kennedy's eyes were glistening in the half-light. He looked all around him, at the frayed standards hanging limply from the walls, at the altar and the windows and the roof. Then he looked back to Rebus, shook his head, and walked away.

Rebus sat a few minutes by himself, hands clasped in his lap. He didn't exactly feel good about himself, but then that was nothing new.

21

The name of SWEEP's contact at the Scottish Office was Rory McAllister, and he agreed to meet Rebus for lunch the next day, suggesting an Italian restaurant at the top of Leith Walk.

When Rebus arrived at twelve-thirty, McAllister was already there. He'd just about completed the *Scotsman* crossword with an elegant chrome ballpoint pen. He stood up long enough to shake hands. Rebus noticed he was drinking mineral water.

'Stick to the businessman's lunch,' McAllister prompted, as a waiter handed Rebus an oversized menu. So Rebus stuck to the businessman's lunch.

Rory McAllister was in his late thirties with thinning, neatly cut hair and a face which still seemed to bear traces of both puppy-fat and acne. He peered at Rebus with eyes slightly narrowed, as if he might need spectacles but was too vain to wear them. His dark wool suit went well with a cream-coloured shirt and grey tie, knotted tightly at the throat.

Every inch the civil servant, Rebus thought. McAllister's voice was educated Edinburgh: nasal and lilting, not wanting to let go of the ends of syllables.

'So, Inspector,' he said, putting his newspaper out of sight under the table, 'your call was intriguing. What is it you want exactly?'

'I want you to tell me about the Scottish Office, Mr McAllister. I also need to know about the SDA and Scottish Enterprise.'

'Well,' McAllister started to unwrap a bread-stick, 'let's order while I collect my thoughts, shall we?' He spoke to the waiter in a quiet, firm voice. Rebus knew the type: loud only in agreement, never in denial; when roused to anger, he'd bet McAllister's voice would drop to a whisper.

'The tomato soup's not bad,' Rebus was informed. 'Ditto the veal, but the *pollo* is very good, too. And as for the wine . . .' Rebus shrugged assent with any suggestion McAllister might make. 'A half each of house white and red.' The civil servant snapped shut the wine list, another piece of business brought successfully to a close. He waved to two diners across the room. Their suits were like a uniform. The restaurant was filling quickly; half the diners looked like refugees from New St Andrew's House.

'So.' McAllister clapped his hands together and rubbed them. 'You want to know about the Scottish Office. Well, shall I start at the bottom or the top? You've met me, so that's the bottom taken care of.' He smiled to let Rebus know this was a joke. Sammy had said McAllister was a high-flier, clever and dedicated.

And helpful.

'So,' he went on, 'maybe I'll start at the top – the top, of course, being one of two men, depending on your situation. You can say that the Secretary of State for Scotland is the head of the Scottish Office, and as far as the public is concerned you'd be right. But politicians come and go, the Scottish Office remains.'

'You're saying the real head is the most senior civil servant?'

'Exactly, and that's the Permanent Under-Secretary, more usually known as the Permanent Secretary.'

'Why bother with two titles?'

McAllister laughed, a sound like a pig at the trough.

'Don't question; just accept.' A basket of bread rolls arrived, and he broke one into three. 'Now, the Scottish Office has responsibility for most functions of government in Scotland, excepting defence, foreign policy, and social security. We've a small outpost in Whitehall, but most of us are based here, either in St Andrew's House or New St Andrew's House.'

'St Andrew's House being . . . ?'

'It's on Regent Road. You know, it looks like the Reichstag.'

'Oh, the power station.'

McAllister conceded the image. 'That's where the Secretary of State and his advisors do their work. The rest of us are relegated to the neo-brutalism of New St Andrew's House – until Victoria Quay is ready.' Two bowls of thin-looking tomato soup arrived. 'The Secretary of State's retinue consists of the likes of the Lord Advocate and the Solicitor-General: they're both ministers of the Crown, of course.'

'Of course.'

'Plus a minister of State and three pusses.'

'Pusses?'

McAllister wiped the corners of his mouth with his napkin. 'Don't tell anyone I called them that: Parliamentary Under-Secretaries of State.'

'I thought you said there was only one?'

McAllister shook his head. 'Don't confuse Parliamentary with Permanent: the *Permanent* Under-Secretary is the only one who's a civil servant. He's the only one who is –'

'Permanent?'

McAllister nodded. He took some soup and chewed on his roll, preparing for another onslaught. The wine had arrived, and he poured a glass of white for himself. Rebus opted for red.

'Now,' McAllister said, 'we come to the departments.' He counted them off on his fingers: 'SOID, SOED, SOEnD, SOHHD, SOAFD, and – shamefully prosaic – Central Services.'

Rebus smiled. 'Mr McAllister, I think you're purposely trying to bamboozle me.'

McAllister looked shocked. 'No, I assure you . . .'

'Look, what I really want is a rundown on the SDA and Scottish Enterprise.'

'We'll get to them, don't worry.' The waiter came to take their bowls. 'Bit peppery today,' McAllister told him; not a complaint, a simple matter of interpretation.

The civil servant was halfway through his next dissertation before Rebus realised they'd moved on to the topics he was interested in.

'. . . so he was at SOHHD until the LECs came along. The SDA and HIDB became SE and HIE and the poor man, who'd been responsible for RDGs and RSA, found himself –'

'Keep going, you might just drift back into English.'

McAllister produced another snorted laugh. 'Maybe I don't have enough dealings with the public. I'm used to people who understand the codes.'

'Well, I don't understand the codes, so humour me.'

McAllister took a deep breath. 'The SDA,' he began, 'was set up by Wilson in 1975, some say to appease the rising nationalism of that time. It had a budget of £200 million – which was not inconsiderable for the time – and took over from three old existing bodies, including the SIEC–the Scottish Industrial Estates Corporation. The SIEC brought with it twenty-five *million* square metres of factory space.'

'Sounds like a lot.'

'A hellish lot, a lot to keep occupied. The SDA got busy. It's been estimated there were as many as five thousand projects under its aegis at any one time. And remember, the SDA didn't cover the whole of Scotland – there was the Highlands and Islands Development Board, too. In fact, HIDB was by far the elder of the two.' The pasta starters arrived. McAllister sprinkled parmesan cheese over his and got to work with his fork. 'Then someone had the bright idea of getting rid of the SDA.' He shook his head. 'Do you know the old saying, if it ain't broke, don't fix it? The SDA was in good fettle. It had been investigated by several bodies and committees and given a clean bill of health. It *did* get into trouble over the Glasgow Garden Festival, and over a deal with a building contractor called Quinlon, but by then the blueprint for Scottish Enterprise had already been set up.

'On the first of April – note the date – 1991, the SDA and HIDB became Scottish Enterprise and Highlands and Islands Enterprise. Basically, the changes were twofold: the new agencies took on the Scottish remit of the Training Agency and, more importantly, the central role of the SDA became more devolved.'

'How so?' Rebus wasn't touching the wine; he needed all his wits about him.

'Authority was devolved to a network of private-sector-led local enterprise companies, LECs for short.'

'Like Lothian and Edinburgh Enterprise Limited?'

'Yes, LEEL's one.'

'Is there any Scottish Office control?'

'Oh yes, Scottish Enterprise is sponsored by SOID.'

'The Scottish Office Industry Department?' McAllister gave a round of silent applause. 'Which leads us,' Rebus said, 'to funding.'

'Oh, I could talk all afternoon about funding, it's my specialty.'

'So what's Scottish Enterprise's annual budget?'

McAllister puffed out his cheeks. 'Around four hundred and fifty million.'

Rebus swallowed the last of his pasta. 'Forgive me, that sounds like a lot.'

'Well, the money has to be split: it covers enterprise, environment, youth and adult training, plus admin costs.'

'Well, put like that I can see it represents excellent value for money.'

McAllister nearly choked with laughter. 'You sound just like a civil servant!'

'I was being ironic. Tell me, Mr McAllister, why did you agree to meet me?'

The question took McAllister by surprise. He took time forming his answer. 'I've never met a police officer before,' he said. 'I suppose I was curious. Besides, it's nice to meet someone who's actually *interested* in what we do, no matter what his motives. You know, only about one in three voters in this country even *knows* there's such a thing as the Scottish Office. One in three!' He sat back and opened his arms. 'And we've got a budget of millions!'

'Tell me,' Rebus said quietly, 'any word of any . . . impropriety?'

'At Scottish Enterprise?'

Rebus nodded.

'No, none at all.'

'What about the SDA?'

One waiter removed their bowls, another set down the main course and accompanying vegetables. McAllister tucked in. He swallowed the first mouthful before answering Rebus's question.

'If there had been, Inspector, it would be dead and buried by now. When the SDA became Scottish Enterprise, the accounting procedures were changed: new set-up, new set of books. Like wiping the slate clean.'

'So what would have happened if any impropriety *had* been found?'

McAllister made a sweeping motion with his fork. 'Under the carpet with it.'

Rebus pondered this: wiping the slate clean, under the carpet . . . The district council was about to disappear, just as the SDA had done.

'You know, Mr McAllister, you don't seem very curious about *why* I want to know about the SDA and Scottish Enterprise.'

McAllister chewed on that. 'I suppose you'll tell me if and when you're ready. Until then, I don't see that it's any of my business. I'm not the curious sort, Inspector. In my line of work, that's seen as a strength.'

After a while Rebus asked: 'Who appoints the boards?'

'At SE and HIE, the Secretary of State.' McAllister poured the last of the wine into his glass. 'Not on his own, of course. He'd be advised by the Permanent Secretary. That, after all, is the job of the Permanent Secretary: to advise. Though he implements too, of course.' McAllister glanced at his watch, then signalled for the waiter. 'I don't know about you,' he said to Rebus, 'but I think I might skip pud.' And he patted his ample stomach. When the waiter approached, McAllister ordered espresso.

'Is that what you're investigating, Inspector – impropriety at the SDA?'

Rebus smiled. 'I thought you weren't curious. Tell me, does the word Mensung mean anything to you?'

McAllister tried it out. He'd torn open a plastic toothpick, and was working on his mouth. The sight made Rebus's teeth jangle. 'I *do* seem to know it . . . can't think why or what it is. Want me to check?'

'I'd be grateful, sir. One other thing, any connection between the SDA or Scottish Enterprise and the US Consulate?'

Again, McAllister seemed surprised by the question. 'Well, yes,' he said at last, as his coffee arrived. 'I mean, we do try to persuade American

companies to locate here, so contacts at a consular level are helpful – vital, even. They were especially so in the eighties.'

'Why was that?'

'Microelectronics was booming. Silicon Glen. Locate in Scotland was working superbly. Did I mention LiS? It was part-SDA, part-Scottish office, with a remit to get foreign companies to locate here. Most of its successes were American, mostly in the early to mid-eighties. Rumour had it that its successes had less to do with canny persuasion and economic argument than with a kind of informal freemasonry.'

'How do you mean?'

'Well, a lot of top executives in American companies were and are Scottish, either born here or with Scottish roots. LiS would target those individuals and work on them, trying to get them not only to open a factory here, but to persuade other Scots in positions of influence. Look at IBM. Actually, this isn't an example of LiS at work; IBM has had a presence in Scotland for forty years. They started in Greenock, and they're still there – the plant's massive, about a mile and a half long. But what took them to Greenock in the first place? I'll tell you. It wasn't economics or a skilled workforce – it was *sentimentality*. The head of IBM at that time was in love with the west coast of Scotland; and that's all it was.' McAllister shrugged and blew on his coffee.

Rebus wanted to go back a stage or two. 'Is that how a lot of it works? Who you know?'

'Oh, definitely.'

'And bribes?'

'Not for me to say.'

Why not? thought Rebus. You've said every bloody thing but. It was two-thirty, the restaurant empty save for their table.

'I mean,' McAllister said, 'one man's bribe is another's "financial incentive". Look at Pergau Dam. There's always room to bend the rules without necessarily breaking them. Regional Selective Assistance, for example, was and is discretionary. Who's to say it doesn't make a difference if the person applying for it went to school with the person who'll make the final decision? It's the way the world turns, Inspector.' He tried to find some dregs of coffee in his cup, then unwrapped the amaretto biscuit.

Rebus paid their bill, and the waiter locked the door after them. McAllister's face was flushed, his cheeks a network of broken blood vessels. Now that he'd asked his questions, Rebus was keen to be elsewhere. There was something about McAllister he didn't like. He knew how easy it was to cover something up by talking about it at length. One confession could be made to disguise another. He'd had cleverer men than McAllister in the interview room, but not very many . . .

The two men shook hands.

'I appreciate you taking the time and trouble, sir,' Rebus said.

'Not at all, Inspector. I appreciate you paying for lunch. Besides, who knows? Maybe one day I might need a favour from you.' McAllister winked.

'You might at that,' Rebus said.

After all, it was the way the world turned, the civil servant was right about that. Rebus turned and headed off in any direction that wasn't McAllister's.

22

'All I've got,' Rebus admitted, 'are questions and loose ends, and none of it is getting me any closer to why McAnally killed himself or why the councillor's so scared. Added to that, the Lord Provost sees the word Dalgety scrawled on a sheet of paper and suddenly doesn't want us looking for his daughter any more.'

He was on the phone to St Leonard's, speaking with Brian Holmes. The drip from the radiator was getting worse. His mouth was getting worse. Behind him in the living room were the binbags full of paper. All the answers, he felt, were there, just beyond his abilities.

'So?' said Holmes.

'Thanks for the vote of confidence.'

'What do you want me to say?'

Rebus pushed at the skin around his nose, feeling the pressure increase on his poor tooth. 'The reason I phoned,' he said, 'is to ask what the state of play is with friend Duggan.'

Holmes rustled some papers. 'Now there I can help you. Paul Duggan is Edinburgh's answer to Rachman. He's been cheating the council for years. Lives with his parents, doesn't pay them a penny rent, but he's applied for and been allotted four council properties . . . that's how many we've traced so far, there could be others. He doesn't mind hard-to-let flats, that's his secret.'

'How does he do it?'

'A series of pseudonyms, plus girls he drags along to Housing Office interviews with a few bambinos in tow. The girls are friends of his, the kids aren't his.'

'But he becomes their father for the duration of the interview?'

'And gets himself priority listed. Once he's been allocated a place, all he does is let it out. I'm amazed he can find anyone for some of them. That place in Saughton was a palace compared to the others in his portfolio.'

Rebus dug into his back pocket and brought out the card he'd taken from the Waverley drop-in. Paul. Cheap rooms.

'Why do you think,' Rebus asked, 'Willie and Dixie had the pick of Duggan's properties? House that size, he could have squeezed a few more bodies in.'

'Right enough, the flat I checked in Granton had sleeping-bags in the living room, kitchen, and bathroom.'

Rebus studied the telephone number on the card. 'Maybe I'll have a wee word with our friendly slum landlord. Is the Farmer keeping you busy?'

'He keeps asking if I know what you're up to.'

'And what do you tell him?'

'I can keep my mouth shut. I just hope you know what you're doing, sir.'

'Well, Brian, there's a first time for everything.'

Rebus broke the connection and called the number on the card.

'Hello?' It was a woman's voice, polite, not young.

'Eh, is Paul there?'

'I'll just get him for you.'

'Thanks.'

She put the receiver next to the phone, and he could hear her calling for her son, who was probably in his bedroom counting shillings into a sock. Finally, the receiver was picked up.

'Aye?'

'Paul?'

'Who's this?'

'My name's John, I saw your notice at the drop-in centre.'

'Which one? I've got half a dozen notices up.'

'The one behind Waverley.'

'Oh aye, right.'

'I need a room.'

'Are you claiming social security?'

Rebus winged it. 'I'd be paying cash, if that's what you're worried about.'

'No, it's just that you've caught me at a bad time, John. Bit of pressure on me at the moment, if you know what I mean.'

'I know all about pressure.'

'So I'm not really opening any new transactions right this minute.' There was a pause. 'Did you say cash? Would you need a rentbook?'

'Cash, no rentbook.'

'Tell you what, John, can we maybe meet?'

Rebus's smile didn't translate to his voice. 'What's the address?'

'No address. Do you know Leith cop shop?'

Rebus stopped smiling. He'd been rumbled. But Duggan misinterpreted his silence.

'Not keen, eh? Been in trouble, have you?'

'A little bit.'

'We're only meeting outside. I can take you to a flat near there, down by the Shore. And that area's coming up in the world, by the way.'

Rebus almost admired the cheek. 'What time?'

'Five on the dot.'

'I'll be there,' said Rebus.

He phoned Brian Holmes back. 'Rachman's portfolio, anything down near the Shore?'

'Leith? No,' said Holmes, 'nearest one to Leith's the place in Granton. Why?'

'Just that you haven't tracked them all down yet, that's all.'

At five minutes to five, he was across the road from the police station. He stood two steps up from the pavement in the doorway of a disused building. Leith was taking a few faltering steps towards respectability. Trendy cafés and restaurants had opened in hastily refurbished premises, usually

carved out of larger blocks of unrented space. There was a temporary feel to these new businesses; they always seemed to be 'under new management'. Leith's revival had begun down on the Shore and had all but stopped there, with warehouse conversions and a couple of upmarket bars. Now the revival had been given fresh momentum: the new Scottish Office HQ was under construction at Victoria Dock, and a sailors' home had been turned into a luxury hotel on Queen's Quay.

But Leith still retained its old, unique charm: it was still just about the only part of the city where you'd see prostitutes in daytime, freezing in short skirts and skimpy jackets. Rebus had passed some on his way down Bernard Street, readying themselves for the going-home trade: one quick leap for the homeward bound.

He stood in the doorway for quarter of an hour before Paul Duggan turned up. The young man was wearing an ankle-length black woollen coat, its collar turned up. On his feet were white trainers, so new they were almost luminous when caught in the headlamps of the passing traffic.

Duggan didn't pay any attention to Rebus as Rebus crossed the road; he was on the lookout for someone entirely different.

'Waiting for me?' Rebus asked.

It took Duggan a moment to place him. 'Christ, what do you want?'

'It was me that phoned. We didn't know you had another place on the Shore.'

'I don't know what you're talking about.'

'Come on, Paul, let's have a chat.'

'In there?'

Rebus looked towards the police station. 'No,' he said, 'not in there. This is just between us, understood?'

Rebus started walking, a hand on the sleeve of Duggan's coat.

'Where are we going?' Duggan asked.

'We're just walking, that's all. I've got a question for you. We know about four or five of your properties, and we know the Saughton let was the best of them by a fair old margin. So how come you only picked up two rents from it?'

Duggan stopped dead. 'Is this a trap? Are you miked up?'

Rebus laughed. 'For a tadpole like you? Behave, son, you're the council's problem, not mine.'

Rebus started walking again. Duggan caught him up. 'So what's the game?'

'I'm interested in Willie and Dixie, that's all. You told me you were their friend, so now I'm a wee bit interested in you, too.'

'That's why I gave them the house,' Duggan blurted out, thinking on his feet. 'They were my pals.'

'You *gave* them it? They didn't pay rent?'

'Oh . . . oh aye, they paid rent. What I meant was –'

'Don't bother, son, don't compound one lie with another, you'll never keep track. My guess is they worked for you. What did they do?'

Duggan bit his lip. 'They collected the rents,' he said at last.

'And got free rent in return? That makes more sense. When I look at you, I see a skinny young kid, a sap. The kind of tenants you must deal with, you'd need back-up, isn't that right? Just in case someone decided not to pay.' Duggan nodded.

'They'd've been perfect for that,' Rebus continued. 'Willie had brains, he could reason with the non-payers, and if that didn't work, crazy Dixie could go to work. Is that about the score?'

'That's it.'

Rebus sniffed, and seemed to be thinking. 'Whose idea was the kidnap ruse?' he said casually.

'I've told you, I didn't know anything about that! They just asked for my car!'

'Must have been Willie's idea,' Rebus went on, as if Duggan hadn't spoken. 'Dixie didn't have the brains.' He turned to Duggan. 'Unless it was your idea, of course.'

Duggan made to protest, but thought better of it. They walked on in silence. 'OK,' he said at last. 'OK, between you and me, right?'

Rebus shrugged. 'Like I said, I'm not after you particularly, Paul, unless you lie to me. Lying to me is not advisable.'

'I knew what they were up to.'

'Of course you did. A tight-fisted wee bastard like you wouldn't lend someone the steam from his breath without there being a pay-off.' Rebus produced the photo of Kirstie Kennedy. 'You saw her with Willie and Dixie, didn't you?'

'No.'

'What about Dalgety?'

'Eh?' The name clearly meant nothing to Duggan.

'Come on,' Rebus said, 'I *know* you've seen her. You spend a lot of time in drop-in centres –'

'No I don't.'

'You told me yourself your cards are up on half a dozen noticeboards. How do they get there: by magic?' Rebus pushed the photo towards Duggan. 'You've seen her.'

'No.'

'You're lying. What are you afraid of, Paul?'

They were down on the Shore, and Duggan was just realising it. They walked close to the water's edge, across the street from the bars. Soon they'd be up to the dock entrance. Rebus stopped and tugged on Duggan's arm. 'Look at her!' he spat. Duggan averted his face. 'Look at her!' Duggan glanced at the photo, then away again. His eyes were glinting in the streetlight.

'She knew Willie well enough to leave something in his bedroom. She *knew him* . . . and I know damned well you knew her!'

Duggan blinked. 'What did she leave in his bedroom?' he asked quietly.

'Just tell me where she is.'

Duggan started to shake his head, and Rebus hauled him by the coat-sleeve to the water's edge. The street was empty save for a line of cars whose owners were all in the howffs.

'Fancy a dip, Paul? It can be invigorating at this time of year, if the sewage and the rats don't get you.'

'This coat cost a fortune!' Duggan squealed.

'You won't need it in jail, son. You'll be tucked up in bed with some big bad bastard keeping you warm.'

'All right, all right!'

Rebus released his grip. Duggan looked up and down the street.

'Run if you like, Paul. I'll find you.'

'Jesus, calm down, will you? OK, I've seen her. She hung around for a while with Willie and Dixie.'

'How long?'

'A week, maybe a bit longer.'

'Is she still around?'

'I haven't seen her. I only saw her a couple of times.'

'At the house in Saughton?'

'No, no, at a couple of drop-in centres.'

'But you don't know where she is, or what she's doing?' Duggan shook his head. 'Right, here's what we're going to do. You're going to find her for me.'

'What?'

'Somebody like you, lots of contacts . . . should be easy.'

'You don't know what you're asking.'

Rebus pointed to the water. 'There's your alternative.' He held out the photo. 'Take this, it might help.'

'It won't.'

'Why not?'

'That's not what she looks like. We had a laugh when we saw that picture in all the papers. I mean, I can believe she might have looked like that before she started using.'

'Drugs?'

'And plenty of them by the look of her.'

Rebus frowned. 'You think she's been on them long?'

'Long enough. Maybe a year or so.'

'A *year*?'

Duggan shrugged. 'Only a guess; I'm not into that scene.'

'I'll bet you don't mind them as tenants though, eh?'

Duggan straightened his shoulders. 'How about looking at it this way – I'm doing the council's work for it, putting roofs over the heads of people who'd be on the street otherwise.'

'Mr Social Conscience. They'll be giving you the keys to the city next. Get out of my sight, and take the photo, it's got my phone number on the back. If I don't hear from you in a day or two, we'll have another chat. Maybe at your place this time, with your mum and dad listening. How would you like that?'

Duggan didn't answer. He rearranged his coat, which had fallen down over one shoulder, then pocketed the photograph. Rebus watched him shuffle away, back towards the traffic.

So, now he knew for certain why the Lord Provost hadn't had a more recent photo of his daughter. He wondered why Duggan had been so curious about whatever Kirstie had left in Willie Coyle's bedroom. But Rebus was beginning to get an idea about that, too.

23

He drove to the Ox, where Doc and Salty stood in their allotted places. Room was made for Rebus, and Doc ordered him a pint.

'Oh what blessed company,' Rebus said, lifting the glass. He turned to Salty Dougary. 'I was out at Gyle Park West the other day.'

'In your professional capacity?'

'Sort of. What can you tell me about the place?'

'It's an industrial estate. I work there. What else is there to know?'

'The businesses there, would they have dealings with Scottish Enterprise?'

Salty nodded. 'LEEL,' he said. 'Our boss at Deltona is mad keen on "worker participation", which means once a week we have to sit in the canteen for twenty minutes listening to him rattle on about client satisfaction, inward investment, productivity and the like. He's always on about LEEL.'

'So Deltona has had money from LEEL?'

'John, *everyone* on that estate has had help of some kind: relocation incentives, start-up incentives, retraining incentives, you name it.' He raised his glass. 'God bless Scottish Enterprise.'

'Why the interest?' Dr Klasser asked. This was not their usual level of conversation.

'It could be peripheral to a case I'm working on.' Except that there was no case and he wasn't supposed to be working.

'Well, keep your paws off Deltona,' Salty Dougary warned.

Rebus smiled. 'Ever heard of Mensung?' he asked.

'Don't they measure your intelligence?'

There was a snort from down the bar. 'They'd only need a six-inch ruler to measure yours, Salty.'

Salty laughed, so the speaker would know he wasn't amused. Rebus was still looking at him. 'To be honest,' Salty told him, 'it does ring a bell, way at the back of the old brainpan. I think it was a company.'

'On the estate?'

Dougary shrugged. The barman was taking a phone call. His eyes met Rebus's.

'For you, John.' He brought the telephone over. Rebus had another question for Salty.

'What about LABarum, ever heard of that?'

'What is this, *Mastermind*?'

Rebus took the receiver from the barman. 'Hello?'

'Is that you, John?'

Rebus recognised the voice – but it couldn't be, not calling him by his first name.

'Is that you, Flower?'

'Yes.'

DI Alister Flower – the Little Weed – calling Rebus 'John'. Something was wrong.

'What's up?'

'Just wondered if you could drop into the station for a chat.'

'A chat? Will you have the tea and biscuits ready?'

Flower laughed like he hadn't heard a better one all day. Rebus was more than curious.

'When?' he asked.

'Whenever you like.'

Rebus said he'd be there in half an hour.

The station was mid-evening quiet. To keep busy, most of the CID contingent had gone off to the scene of a car smash. The smash had taken place outside one of the neighbourhood's better Indian restaurants. So there was no one around the main office; no one but Alister Flower.

'John, how's the holiday?'

'I'm having a bit of trouble getting a tan.'

Rebus studied Alister Flower. There were a hundred reasons to dislike or even thoroughly loathe the man. The fact that he was a complete prick came pretty close to the top. Flower's eyes were always in movement, seeking out an angle or the main chance. The eyes were puffy, like the skin around them was constantly swollen. It could be genetic or to do with boozing, and it turned his eyes into slits. Rebus didn't like the fact that he couldn't always see those eyes.

Flower had friends around the station: spies, junior officers, who were a bit like him and would even like to *be* him. It scared Rebus. But there were no allies with him tonight. He sat on a desk, his feet on a chair. It wasn't his desk, wasn't his chair. Walking past his own desk, Rebus saw the new computer console. It didn't interest him at all.

'I was promised tea and biscuits,' he said.

'We can nip down the canteen after.'

'After what?'

'After I've shown you something. Come on.'

And he led Rebus down to the cells. There was a man in there, long-haired, unshaven, not happy.

'So who is he?'

'His name's Terry Shotts,' Flower explained. 'He's from Newcastle. We found him leaving a house in Prestonfield Avenue ... with half the contents under his arm.'

'So?' Rebus closed the viewing-flap in the cell door.

'So we went to his digs. There was some other stuff there, including some that we could trace immediately from the register. His scam is, he thieves here and sells in Newcastle, and what he thieves there he lays off *here*.'

'It's a tremendous feat of detection, Flower. I want to thank you for sharing it with me.'

Rebus started back upstairs, Flower following. He handed Rebus a folded sheet of paper.

'This is a list of the stuff the Geordies found in his flat. They traced some of it to a couple of break-ins, but the lists didn't match. Looks like he'd already sold some of the stuff on. Including a shotgun.' Rebus began to see the point. 'Shotts has been up here three weeks. I think he sold it to Shug McAnally.'

'Have you asked Mr Shotts?'

'He's as good as admitted it.'

Rebus stopped. 'Maybe I should talk to him.'

Flower blocked his path. 'I don't think that would do any good.' Rebus wasn't in the mood for a fight, so kept on walking. 'I thought you'd be pleased. I mean, it ties up the loose ends, doesn't it?'

'It might tie up one of them, but it just unravels a couple more. Want to know what they are? Number one, why are you interested? Number two, why would you want me to be "pleased"?'

They were back in the CID room.

'Well,' Flower said, making for his desk, 'I just thought you'd want to know.'

'That's just so much keech, Flower. What are you up to?'

Flower reached into a drawer and showed Rebus a bottle of whisky. Rebus shook his head, but Flower poured himself a measure into a broken-handled mug.

'What are you so damned paranoid about, Rebus?'

'You, for a start.' Flower took a gulp of whisky, then lit a cigarette.

'It's a fair point,' he conceded, through a wreath of smoke. 'OK, I'll tell you straight. Someone *asked* me to talk to you. You know I wouldn't do it otherwise.'

'That's more like it.' Rebus sat on the edge of a desk. 'So who's the someone?'

'Just someone important.'

'The Farmer?'

Flower smiled and exhaled noisily. Someone higher than the Farmer then, a lot higher.

'And just what,' Rebus asked, 'does this anonymous patron want me to know?'

Flower examined the tip of his cigarette. 'That you're on your way out, the way you're going.'

'Out?'

'Of the force.' Flower paused. 'At the very least.'

'Why?'

'You don't need to know that.'

Which meant, thought Rebus, that it was because of something he *might* do rather than something already done.

'So what should I do?' he asked.

'Stop being so bloody nosy.'

'About what?'

'McAnally, for Christ's sake.'

'What does –'

'Look, I'm just the message-boy, OK?'

'If the cap fits . . .'

Flower's eyes narrowed still further. 'Look,' he said at last, 'you know if it was up to me, I'd leave you to squat on the pan and send your career down the lavvy like the night before's kebab. All I'm doing is a favour for someone who wants you to have a final warning. Hear me? A final warning.' He stood up and flicked his butt into a waste-bin.

'Pretty convenient,' Rebus said, 'the source of the shotgun suddenly turning up . . . Who is it, Flower? The DCC? Big Jim Flett? What have they got to hide?' Rebus was standing inches from Flower. 'What's it got to do with *you*?' He jabbed Flower's chest with his finger.

'Touch me again, you're dead.'

'Tell your friend, if he wants to threaten me, he should do it himself. Nobody's scared of the message-boy.'

Then he turned and walked away. He was worried though. If they were serious – whoever *they* were – when he was so far from solving the puzzle, how would they react if he got any closer? He stopped at the door.

'By the way,' he said, 'your fag-end just set fire to that bin.'

Flower turned and saw that the contents of the waste-bin were indeed smouldering. He reached for some liquid to douse the fire.

He'd forgotten that it was whisky, not coffee, in his mug.

Rebus's phone was ringing as he got home. It was Rico Briggs.

'I had a word with a friend,' he told Rebus. Rico never liked to say too much on the phone.

'And?'

'Be in the bus station at eleven.'

'Tonight?'

'Tonight.'

'Whereabouts in the bus station?'

'Just be there. You'll pay him his share and mine.'

The line went dead.

24

At ten to eleven, Rebus was in the St Andrew's Square bus station. A few early drunks had assembled for the last bus home. There was a pub in the bus station; it sounded busy. A man sprinted out of it, slipped in a patch of oil, and fell like a sniper's bullet had got him. He got back to his feet in time to see his bus pull away, and started swearing. There was a gash in the knee of his trousers.

Exhaust fumes lay in heavy strata just above ground level. Rebus tried not to breathe too deeply as he walked up and down the ranks. A few teenagers were asleep on the precarious benches. An old man, looking dazed, crossed the concourse dressed in a duffel coat, pyjamas and slippers. The slippers looked brand new, maybe a Christmas present.

'Where are you?' Rebus hissed, stamping his feet. He pushed his hands deeper into his pockets and walked the ranks again.

'Sit down,' a voice said.

Rebus looked down at the figure. He'd thought the man was asleep, arms folded, head tucked into the front of his jacket. He was sitting at the last rank. There was a bus there, but with its lights off.

Rebus sat down, and the man looked up at him. He had greasy brown hair which fell over one eye, and he could have done with a shave. There was a small scar, no more than a nick, below his right eye. The eyes were piercing blue with long lashes. When he spoke, Rebus saw there was a tooth missing from the front of his mouth.

'Money.'

'You're Rico's friend?'

The man nodded. 'Money,' he repeated.

Rebus showed him two twenties, then handed them over. 'He said half for him.'

'He'll get half.' The voice was a lazy west coast drawl. 'You want to know about Saughton?'

'A man killed himself with a shotgun. He was fresh out of Saughton.'

'Which bit?'

'C Hall.'

The man shook his head. 'Can't help you then.'

A driver had come over to the bus, cashbox in hand. He opened the doors and went inside, closing them after him. Lights came on all the way up the bus.

'What do you mean?'

'Just what I say. I can't help.'

The engine started up, spewing fumes. A couple of people had joined the queue and were wondering whether to jump ahead of the two seated down-and-outs.

'Why not?'

'Never really knew anyone in C Hall.' The man stood up, Rebus rising with him. 'This is my bus.'

'Wait a minute.'

The man turned to him. The bus doors were opening, the people behind wanting to be in the warm. 'Ask Gerry Dip.'

'Gerry Dip?'

'He was in C Hall, came out a few weeks back.'

'Where can I find him?'

'Dipping fish, that's how he got the name.' The man climbed on to the platform. 'I hear he's working in a chip shop on Easter Road.'

Every chip shop in Scotland was at its busiest after the pubs had emptied. Even the bad ones, the ones with bony fish and rubber batter, had queues. Rebus took one look at the wares on display in the second chip shop he tried, and decided he would go without.

There was a queue almost out the door, but he walked to the front, ignoring the stares. A teenage girl was serving, mouth open in concentration.

'Salt and sauce?' she asked the customer.

'Is Gerry in?' Rebus asked.

She nodded further along the counter. There was a small man there dipping fish in a bucket of batter before tossing them into the fryer.

'Gerry?' Rebus asked. The man shook his head and pointed towards the back of the narrow shop, where a very tall, very skinny young man wearing a white cotton apron was playing the video machine.

It was one of those kick-and-chop games, the enemy bounding into view only long enough to be taken out again by the snarling cartoon hero.

'Gerry Dip?' Rebus said.

The player was in his mid-twenties, with cropped black hair and a nose-stud. His bare arms sported tattoos, and there were more on the backs of his hands. On his right wrist was a tattooed watch, the hands of which pointed to twelve. Rebus checked his own watch and saw that Gerry Dip's was dead-on.

Rebus saw that Dip was watching him in the screen's reflection. 'Not many people call me that,' he said.

'I'm a friend of a friend, someone you knew in Saughton. He said you could maybe help me. There'd be a drink in it.'

'How big a drink?'

Rebus had been to a cash machine. He laid a crisp twenty on the console. Maybe it affected Dip's concentration. A landmine tore the arms and legs off his man. The Game Over message flashed, and a digitised voice said, 'Feed . . . Money . . . Me . . . Hungry.'

Gerry Dip palmed the note. 'Let's retire to my office.'

He led Rebus behind the counter and told the fish batterer he'd swop places in five minutes. Then he pushed open a door and led Rebus into a

kitchen-cum-storeroom. Sacks of potatoes waited to be peeled, and two large freezers hummed.

'I hope you're not Environmental Health,' Gerry Dip said, getting a glass of water from the sink and gulping it. 'Actually, I know what you are, it gets so you can smell it after a while.'

Rebus let the remark go. 'A man was released from C Hall a couple of weeks back. He stuck a gun into his –'

'Wee Shug.' Dip nodded. 'I knew him, played cards a few times, talked about telly and the football.' Dip refilled his glass. 'You're up from six in the morning till nine at night, lights-out isn't till ten. You get to know people. Plus I worked with him in the upholstery workshop. He said he'd come down the chippie and see me – then I read about him in the papers.'

'Did you know he was ill?'

'He saw the doctor a lot, never talked about it though. I know he had some medicine: we wanted him to hand it round so we could get a buzz. What was wrong with him?'

'Cancer.'

'That why he topped himself?'

'Could be.'

'Well, if you want to know about Wee Shug, you should talk to his cell-mate. Now *there* was a fucking character. Hoity-toity, stayed in his cell even when he didn't need to.'

Big Jim Flett had mentioned a cell-mate; Rebus saw suddenly why Flett had been relieved at the end of their interview.

'Gerry, what was Wee Shug in for?'

'Housebreaking.'

'You sure about that?'

'That's what I heard.'

'Not rape?'

'What?'

No, thought Rebus, because rapists are usually kept away from the other prisoners. But the governor had let it slip that Wee Shug shared a cell.

'He wasn't inside for rape,' Gerry Dip said.

'How can you be sure?'

'We'd've known.'

'He's not likely to have told you himself.'

'No, but the screws would have, *somebody* would have. It's one secret you can't have in the nick.'

'Unless,' Rebus said quietly, 'nobody wanted you to know.'

25

Rebus called CID from a phone box near St Leonard's and, without identifying himself, asked to speak to either DS Holmes or DC Clarke.

It was a morning of heavy haar, floating across the city in a wet cloud from the coast. The kind of morning where you could imagine yourself back in time, a horse and coach cropping out of the mist rather than cars with their headlights on full. Rebus's skin and clothes were damp to the touch.

'DC Clarke speaking.'

'It's me. I want you to look up a name on the computer.'

'Well, it's a bit chaotic here just now. There was a small fire last night, a waste-bin went up. It's a bit of a mystery, nobody was here at the time.'

'Dear me.'

'The chief super's ordered an investigation. Meantime, half the office is off limits.'

'But the computer system's OK?'

'The only damage is the bin and the desk next to it. It was Inspector Flower found the blaze.'

'Really?'

'He threw a coat over the bin to snuff it out. It was Holmes's coat.'

'The one Nell gave him for Christmas?'

'That's the one. What's the name you want checking?'

'Charters.' He spelt it for her. 'I don't have a first name, but he's serving time in Saughton. I'd like his record. I'm in a callbox about a hundred yards away. There's a café across from the DIY store, I'll wait for you there.'

'I'll be as quick as I can.'

'The dough-rings are on me.'

But when Siobhan Clarke finally turned up at the café, she ordered a fried-egg sandwich instead, then handed Rebus a manila envelope.

'Did anyone see you at the computer?'

'I don't think so.'

'Watch your back. It's not just the Farmer – Flower's up to something, too.'

'What?'

'Fire-raising for a start.' Rebus opened the envelope and read through the contents. Clarke's food arrived and she bit into it, dripping yolk on to the plate.

'"Derwood Charters",' Rebus read aloud, '"age forty-six, divorced, ex-company director. Found guilty of fraud, serving three years of a six-year

sentence at HMP Edinburgh. Home address in Cramond till the place had to be sold. Date of birth . . . name of solicitor . . . no wife or next of kin".'

Rebus skipped through what little else there was. 'It's a bit bald, isn't it?'

'A bit.'

'Like somebody's been into the computer and shorn it. Which station dealt with him?' He looked through the notes again. 'Well, well: St Leonard's.'

'But before our time?'

Rebus nodded. 'I was still at Great London Road. But then so was Chief Inspector Lauderdale, yet his name's down here as part of the team.' He was thoughtful for a moment. 'Right, what I want you to do is –'

'Go back to the station and pull the case-notes out of the vault?'

'I know it's asking a lot.'

'Only my career.'

But he knew she'd do it anyway.

Rebus waited over an hour for Clarke to return. She carried a supermarket carrier bag with her, and laid it on the floor next to him. He ordered her a mug of tea; his own stomach was swilling with the stuff.

'It wasn't where it should have been,' she told him. 'It had been put back out of order.'

'Like someone wanted to hide it?'

'But without being too obvious. There are so many reports in the vault, it's easy for one to disappear if it's filed in the wrong place.'

'Did anyone see you?'

'Brian came to see what I was up to. I got him to keep an eye out for anyone else. Meantime, the sooner you read the case-notes, the sooner I can put them back.'

The woman who ran the café brought Siobhan Clarke's tea, and saw Rebus lift a heavy folder out of the carrier bag.

'Thinking of taking up residence?' she asked him.

'I'm doing you a favour,' he said, glancing at all the empty tables. 'Nobody comes into an empty café.'

'You did,' she replied.

Rebus just smiled and opened the case-notes, starting to read.

At lunchtime, Rebus made a dentist's appointment.

When he explained the problem, the receptionist asked him to hold the line. When she came back, she told him Dr Keene could squeeze him in at five.

The surgery was in a substantial semi-detached property on Inverleith Row, facing the entrance to the Botanic Gardens. Rebus was in a sweat as he sat in the waiting room. There was a woman in there with him, and he was relieved when she was called first. But that left only him. His ears seemed more receptive than usual. He could hear the whine of a drill, the clatter of metal probes being dropped on to trays. When the woman patient came out, she walked to the reception desk to make another appointment. The dentist was with her. Then the dentist turned and, smiling, came to the waiting-room doorway.

'Mr Rebus? Through here, please.'

He wore a white coat and half-moon glasses, and Rebus judged him to be in his late fifties.

'Sit down, please,' Dr Keene said, washing his hands. 'Some swelling around the mouth?'

Rebus sat on the chair and swung his legs up on to it, his hands gripping the armrests. Dr Keene came over.

'Now, just lie back and try to relax.' Rebus could hear his own hoarse breathing. 'That's it.' The dentist used an electric foot-switch to set the chair back so it was nearly flat, and to raise it up. He angled the lamp over the chair and switched it on. 'We'll just take a look.' He swivelled a tray of dental tools towards him and sat down on a high chair by Rebus's side.

'Open wide.'

There was music playing. Radio Two, the airwaves' answer to a placebo. Rebus opened his eyes and stared at the ceiling. There was a blown-up photograph there, a huge black and white aerial shot of Edinburgh, from Trinity in the north to as far south as the Braid Hills. He started to map out the streets in his mind.

'Looks like a wee abscess,' the dentist was saying. He put down one tool and reached for another, tapping it against one of Rebus's teeth. 'Feel anything?' Rebus shook his head. The assistant had joined them. Dr Keene said a few things to her in a language the patient wasn't supposed to understand, then started packing Rebus's mouth with cotton.

'What I'm going to do is drill into the tooth from behind, to try to drain off the poison. That'll release the pressure. The tooth is pretty well dead anyway, I'll do a root canal later. But for now the abscess needs to drain.'

Rebus could feel sweat on his forehead. A tube was being placed in his mouth, hoovering up what saliva there was.

'A little injection first. It'll take a minute or two to take.'

Rebus stared at the ceiling. There's Calton Hill, where Davey Soutar ended up. There's St Leonard's . . . and Great London Road. Hyde's Club was just down there. Ooyah! There's Stenhouse, where Willie and Dixie lived. You could see Saughton Jail quite clearly. And Warrender School, where McAnally blew his head off. He had a sense of the way the streets interconnected, and with them the lives of the people who lived and died there. Willie and Dixie had known Kirstie Kennedy, whose father was Lord Provost. McAnally had sought out a councillor as witness to his act of self-destruction. The city might cover a fair old area, its population might be half a million, but you couldn't deny how it all twisted together, all the criss-crossed lines which gave the structure its solidity . . .

'Now,' the dentist was saying, 'you might feel some discomfort at first . . .'

Rebus raced up and down the streets. Marchmont, where he lived; Tollcross, Tresa McAnally's home; South Gyle, only just taking off when the photograph was taken. There was no sign of the newer building work around the town. He saw holes in the ground and areas of wasteland where now there were structures and roads. And Jesus Christ Almighty it was hurting!

'Ah,' Dr Keene said at last, 'there we are.' Rebus could feel something nasty trickling down his throat. The pressure beneath his nose was easing. Like bleeding a radiator, he thought. 'Drill into the poison,' the dentist was saying, almost to himself, 'and you relieve the pressure.'

Yes, Rebus thought, that was absolutely right.

The dentist gave the rest of his mouth a once-over. The assistant had a card in her hand and was writing on it as Dr Keene recited a litany of decay.

'I won't do any of these fillings today,' he said to Rebus's relief.

Eventually he was allowed to rinse and spit, and the assistant removed the elasticated bib from around his neck. Rebus ran his tongue around his mouth. There was a gaping hole in the back of one of his front teeth.

'We've got to let that drain, give it a few days. Once it's drained, I can do the root canal. All right?' And he smiled at Rebus. 'Incidentally, when did you last have your teeth checked?'

'Eleven, twelve years ago.'

The dentist shook his head.

'I'll make up your appointments,' the assistant said, leaving the room. Dr Keene removed his latex gloves and went to wash his hands.

'Now that we all wear gloves,' he said, 'I don't really need to wash them. But I've done it for thirty years, hard to break the habit.'

'You wear the gloves because of HIV?'

'Yes. Well, goodbye then, Mr –'

'Inspector Rebus, actually.'

'Oh?'

'I wonder if I might have a word?' Rebus knew he was mumbling – the anaesthetic had frozen his mouth. But Dr Keene had no trouble understanding him.

'You mean officially?'

'Sort of. I believe you know a man called Derwood Charters?'

Dr Keene snorted and started rearranging his instruments.

'I'll take that as a yes,' Rebus said.

'Very much to my cost. Like you, he walked into my surgery one day requiring treatment. Then I bumped into him socially. We met a few more times, and he put a proposition to me.'

'A financial proposition?'

'He needed investors for a start-up. The man had a proven track record, he'd helped finance the PanoTech start-up for one thing, and you'd hardly call *that* a failure. Mind, I didn't just take his word for anything; I had my accountant look at the figures. The projections seemed sound, professionally done.'

'What was the company?'

'Derry was very persuasive, he always stipulated the downside of any project. Somehow, the more he talked them down, the more attractive he made them sound. He came across like he wasn't trying to sell you anything. The scheme I invested in, the company was going to profit from the downturn in the economy. That was the downside: other people's misery was going to make his investors money. He was offering retraining and counselling for employees who suddenly found themselves "reorganised" out of a job. He explained that once the company was up and running – it was to be called Albavise – he'd be able to draw on European Community grants, Scottish Office funding, all that. What he needed was start-up capital.' Dr Keene paused. 'Know what? I believed him then and I believe him now: if he'd used the money to start the company, it would have succeeded.'

'But he didn't set up a company, did he?'

Dr Keene sighed. 'He used it to pay off debts, and to finance his lifestyle. He'd picked out ten investors, each handing over five thou. Fifty thousand pounds, Inspector, and he blew the lot inside three months.'

Yes, and then tried to do a runner. Only, one of his investors had an accountant who was sharper than most. Charters was arrested as he made to board the shuttle to London.

'Once they started investigating his affairs – the Inland Revenue, Fraud Squad, what have you – they found a lot of discrepancies, none of which Derry was willing to discuss. He kept his peace all through the trial.' He looked at Rebus. 'Has something happened?'

Rebus shrugged. 'Early days yet, sir.' The stock response, but Dr Keene accepted it.

'It wasn't the cash that hurt, you know,' he told Rebus. 'It was that sense of betrayal.'

'I can imagine.'

The Charters case-notes had made for fascinating reading. For example, Rebus now knew that Frank Lauderdale had been attached to the Fraud Squad at the time they'd been investigating Albavise and Derwood Charters' other business interests. Thinking back on it, Rebus did recall a period when Lauderdale had been away from Great London Road. But Lauderdale was the least interesting part of it. For the man who had been head of the Fraud Squad back then, Chief Superintendent Allan Gunner, was now deputy chief constable of Lothian and Borders Police.

And that wasn't all . . .

'Dr Keene, do you know a man called Haldayne? Spelt with a "y".'

'I don't think so.'

'He's American, works at the consulate.'

Dr Keene was shaking his head. 'No, I don't know him. Is it important?'

'He's another of the investors ripped off over Albavise. I thought you might have met, that's all.'

'We might have met in court, had any witnesses been called. But Charters changed his mind at the last minute and pled guilty.'

'Really? Any idea why?'

'None. My solicitor was amazed. The case against him was by no means watertight and, as I say, he had a very good track record. It was possible he might have gone free, or at least got off with a heavy fine. But instead, he went to jail. I've often wondered why he did that.'

Rebus was wondering the same thing. 'Maybe,' he said, 'to protect someone or something that could have come to light at the trial.'

'But who or what?'

Rebus just smiled and winked. He collected his coat and put it on in the hallway. The assistant had already gone home. There was an appointment card on her desk. Dr Keene picked it up and handed it to Rebus.

'See you in a few days.'

Rebus looked at the card. There was a long column of appointments listed on its back. Six of them. Dates and times.

'Dr Keene,' he said, 'exactly how many fillings do I need?'

'Fifteen,' the dentist said matter-of-factly. Then he saw Rebus to the door.

26

That night, Rebus went to see Tresa McAnally.

The tenement door wasn't locked, so he climbed the stairs to her flat. He could hear music inside, good-time music, and the sounds of hands clapping in time. Rebus pressed the bell and waited, then pressed it again. The music was turned down. A voice came from behind the door. 'Who is it?'

'Inspector Rebus.'

'Wait a minute, will you?' She was a long time opening the door; even then she kept the chain on. 'What do you want?'

Behind her, the door to the living room was closed. There was a case of mixed spirits on the hall carpet. Tresa McAnally was dressed casually – baggy T-shirt, tight black slacks, looped gold earrings – and she was sweating from recent exertion.

'Can I come in?' Rebus asked.

'No, you can't. What is it?'

'It's about Wee Shug.'

'He's dead, end of story.' She made to close the door. Rebus pushed his hand against it.

'Where did the money come from, Tresa?'

'What money?'

'The money you spent on the flat.'

'You've no right to –'

'Maybe not, but I'll keep coming back till you tell me.'

'Then you'll be coming back till doomsday.'

Rebus smiled. 'That may be closer than you think.' He lifted his hand from the door, but she didn't shut it.

'What do you mean?'

'Who's in there with you?'

'Nobody.'

'Nobody?'

Not even Tresa McAnally was brass-necked enough to repeat the lie. She pushed the door closed.

Rebus stood for a moment, listening, then walked along to Maisie Finch's flat. He rang her bell, but she couldn't very well answer, not when she was busy hiding behind Tresa McAnally's living-room door.

Next morning, Rebus called the US Consulate.

'You're not another recording, are you?' Rebus asked.

'No, I'm not.'

'Good, can you put me through to Mr Haldayne, please?'

'Your name?'

'Detective Inspector John Rebus.'

'Hold the line, Inspector.'

He didn't have to hold long.

'Inspector? What can I do for you?' An American accent, smooth, urbane. Rebus wasn't exactly sure what 'Ivy League' meant, but Haldayne's voice brought to mind the image.

'Well, sir, for one thing you can start paying your parking tickets.'

A confident chuckle. 'Goodness, is that what this is all about? Well, certainly, if you insist. I wouldn't want to make a diplomatic incident out of it.'

'But you could, is that what you mean? The tickets aren't the main reason I'm ringing. I'd like to talk to you about Derwood Charters.'

'Jesus, what has he done this time?' A pause. 'Don't tell me I'm getting back my money?'

'Could we discuss it in person?'

'Yeah, I guess. You want to come here?' The US Consulate, where Haldayne would be at his most consular.

'The North British,' Rebus suggested, 'for morning coffee.'

'It's not called the North British any more, is it?'

'You've got a lot to learn about Scotland, Mr Haldayne. Ten-thirty?'

'That's fine, Inspector. I look forward to meeting you.'

Rebus's next call was to St Leonard's. He asked for Siobhan Clarke.

'How's life?'

'Ms Templer had me in her office first thing, wanting to know if you'd been in touch. She was asking a lot of questions.'

'Let her ask. As far as you know, I'm in Lanzarote.'

'Right.'

'Listen, Haldayne's parking tickets, what were the exact locations?'

'I think I jotted them down.' He could hear her searching her notebook.

'How goes the blaze inquiry?'

'A non-starter. It's down to an Act of God. They didn't find a cigarette or a match in the bin.'

'Of course not, Flower tidied up before he reported the fire.'

'Here we are: Princes Street, James Craig Walk, and Royal Circus. Those are all I've got, and no dates. The last two were multiples.'

Rebus thanked her and hung up. He found his *A–Z* and looked up James Craig Walk. It was hard by New St Andrew's House. So Haldayne *did* have dealings with the Scottish Office. Princes Street could just mean he was shopping. Rebus wasn't sure what or who Royal Circus represented. He remembered the councillor's files: SDA/SE; A. C. Haldayne; Gyle Park West; Mensung.

He still didn't know anything about Mensung. He was hoping Haldayne could help.

Rebus sat in the lounge of the Balmoral Forte Grand – formerly the North British – and told staff he was waiting for a guest but he'd order anyway: coffee for two – decaffeinated – and cakes or biscuits or something.

'Fruit scones, sir?'

'Fine, whatever.'

'Thank you, sir.'

Rebus was glad he was wearing one of his better suits. They'd made a good job of the hotel. Last time he'd had morning coffee here, it had been with Gill Templer, way back when they'd been 'an item'. The walls had had cracks in them, and the whole place had seemed faded and slightly seedy.

Rebus knew the American as soon as he walked in. He was tall and exceptionally well groomed and wearing a cream-coloured Burberry raincoat. Haldayne had fair hair, so fine and thin you could see pink scalp beneath it. He was around forty, and wore glasses with tortoiseshell circular frames. His face was thin, his forehead bulbous and shiny.

'Inspector Rebus?' He shook Rebus's hand, and Rebus motioned for him to sit.

'Cold enough for you over here?' Rebus asked.

'I was brought up in Illinois.' Haldayne slipped his coat off. 'We got winters you wouldn't believe.' He shivered at the memory and chuckled again; it was becoming an annoying habit.

Rebus had an annoying habit too: he kept poking the tip of his tongue into the hole in his tooth and trying to suck the poison out. He was getting to like that little bore-hole.

'Do you know a Dr Keene?' he asked the American.

Haldayne made a sceptical mouth. 'Care to give me a clue?'

'He's a dentist, and another of Derry Charters' victims.'

Haldayne sat back in his comfortable chair. 'Took me for five biggies. That still hurts; I'm a diplomat, not a millionaire.'

'What do you do at the consulate?'

'I have an industry remit. In some countries that would be a two-way process, but there aren't too many Scottish companies thinking of setting up plants in the US, so I tend to look after American companies who're thinking of setting up here. It's not as busy as it was.' He looked left and right. 'Waiting staff are slow.'

'I've already ordered. I hope you don't mind.' Haldayne shrugged. 'How did you come to know Derry Charters?'

'I was introduced to him at a party. Can't recall now who did the introducing . . .'

'Can you remember whose party?'

'Oh, it was some Scottish Office thing, that's why I was there.'

'And Mr Charters?'

'Well, he was a businessman. How much do you know about him before his bust?'

'Practically nothing,' Rebus lied, wondering what tack Haldayne might take.

'He ran a few companies, and ran them profitably. But he was always looking to expand. I think he just got bored, simple as that. He liked to set things up, get projects running, but after that he lost interest and started looking for something new. He was good at what he did, though; that's why I wasn't overcautious when he asked me to be a backer.'

'Did you know him well?'

'Not really. When he was talking deals he was fine, but he wasn't a social

animal. I got the feeling normal polite conversation bored the hell out of him. He was a genuine product of the eighties, one of Lady Thatcher's bulls.'

The tray arrived, with *cafetière* and a plate of fruit scones with butter, jam and clotted cream.

'Hey, this looks great, thank you,' Haldayne said to the waiter. He immediately took over, putting the cups out, serving the coffee. While he was pouring, Rebus asked a question.

'Ever heard of something or someone called Mensung?'

'Run it by me again.'

'Mensung.'

Haldayne shook his head, and handed Rebus a cup and saucer. He hadn't spilled a drop, hadn't even paused while pouring.

'If you help American companies, Mr Haldayne, does that mean you have dealings with Scottish Enterprise?'

'All the time.'

'And Locate in Scotland?'

'I've had dealings with them all, Inspector. Thing is, you're just beginning to establish a working relationship, then the government changes everything: changes the name, the rules, the players. SDA becomes Scottish Enterprise, HIDB becomes HIE, and I've got to start again from scratch, building up contacts, letting people know who I am.'

'It's a tough life.'

'But somebody's got to do it, right?' Haldayne spread cream on to half a scone. 'I love these pastries,' he confided, before taking a huge bite.

'You've been here a while?' Rebus asked.

'Nine years, on and off. They did send me back to the States for a couple of years in the middle, but I wangled my way back over again. I love Scotland – my ancestors came from here.'

'I heard a rumour once,' Rebus said, 'about a kind of Scottish mafia at the top of some US businesses, persuading people to locate in Scotland.'

Haldayne wiped cream from his mouth with a napkin. 'It happens,' he said. 'What can I say? It's not illegal.'

'What *would* be illegal, Mr Haldayne?'

'Bribes, money changing hands.'

'Companies can set up here very cheaply, can't they?'

'Some areas, some types of plant, sure. A lot of grant money swilling around, some from the European Community, some from British Government coffers.'

'There was the DeLorean scandal,' Rebus said.

'But the guy did have a sensational car.'

'And he took the British taxpayer for millions.'

'You'd still have paid those taxes, Inspector. If DeLorean hadn't taken them, some other guy would.' Haldayne shrugged again. His expressions, whether vocal or physical, were always slightly exaggerated, slightly more than you'd get from a Scot.

'So the Scottish mafia story is true?'

'I'd guess so. I'm being as open with you as I can.'

'I appreciate it, sir.'

'Hey, you're the one holding those parking tickets at my head.' Another chuckle. 'What kind of coffee is this?'

'Decaf.'

'It's not bad actually, but I do miss that caffeine rush. Waiter!' A teenager trotted over. 'Can I have a double espresso? Thank you.' Haldayne turned back to Rebus. 'So what's the story here, Inspector? We don't seem to be talking about Derry Charters any more.'

'Just part of an ongoing inquiry, sir. I'm not at liberty to –'

'Well, that's hardly fair, is it? Hardly *British*?'

'You're not in Britain now, Mr Haldayne.'

'But I've told you mine, now you should tell me yours.'

Rebus saw that Haldayne was having a good deal of fun at his expense. Suddenly he didn't know how much of Haldayne's story to believe. Lies usually came gift-wrapped in a thin tissue of truth. Rebus knew he would have to examine the wrappings later.

'Come on, Inspector,' Haldayne persisted. 'You're checking up on Derry, this much I know. But he's still serving time, right? So what has he done – set up some paper company from his cell?'

'Paper company?'

'You know, one that exists only on paper.' Haldayne came to an abrupt stop and reached into his pocket for a handkerchief.

He's stalling, thought Rebus. Why is he stalling? The espresso arrived, and Haldayne took a couple of appreciative mouthfuls, regaining his composure.

'I came here in good faith, Inspector,' he said at last. 'I didn't need to speak to a man who's not here in his official capacity.' Haldayne saw the look on Rebus's face, and smiled. 'I wanted to check that you were who you said you were. We US diplomats can't be too careful these days. Your chief inspector told me you're on official leave.'

Rebus took a bite from his scone, saying nothing.

'For a man on leave, Inspector, you sure as hell look busy to me.' Haldayne finished his cup of sludge. 'I'd like to say it's been a pleasure, but in fact it has been deeply frustrating.' He started to push his arms back into the sleeves of his coat. 'I don't expect to be troubled by you again, Inspector. I sent a cheque off today to cover those parking fines. As far as I'm concerned, there's no other reason for you to contact me.'

'Who do you know who lives in Royal Circus?'

Haldayne was disconcerted by the question. 'In the New Town?'

'That's the only Royal Circus I know.'

Haldayne made show of thinking about it. 'Not a soul,' he said brightly. 'My superior might move in those kinds of circles, but not me.'

'What kinds of circles?'

But Haldayne wasn't about to answer that. He got to his feet and made a little formal bow from the waist. 'I hope you don't mind picking up the tab, Inspector.' Then he turned and walked away.

Rebus let him go. He had plenty to think about, and plenty of coffee still to drink.

27

Rebus had two options: he could go home and wait for the Farmer or Gill to catch him; or he could go to St Leonard's and get it done with. He chose the latter route.

He'd been in the building less than three minutes before the Farmer spotted him.

'My office – *now*.'

Rebus noticed that the Farmer's computer was up and running. It had taken over his desk. The photo of his family had been moved to the top of the filing-cabinet.

'Getting to grips with it all right, sir?' Rebus asked. But the Farmer was not to be deflected.

'What the hell are you playing at? I ordered you to take a holiday!'

'And I'm enjoying every minute, sir.'

'Making a nuisance of yourself at a foreign consulate, that's your idea of fun?'

'I couldn't afford to go abroad.'

'The way you're going, maybe you can't afford not to.'

'It was just a bit of unfinished business, sir.'

'What sort of unfinished business?'

'It's not really a police matter, sir.'

The Farmer glowered at him. 'I hope to God that's the truth, Inspector.'

'Cross my heart and hope to die, sir.'

'You're one step from an official reprimand, two steps from suspension.'

And three steps from heaven, Rebus thought. He told the Farmer he understood.

In the main office, he checked for messages. There were half a dozen, stuck on to the screen of his new PanoTech computer. Around him he could hear the soft clack-clack of muffled keyboards. He stared at his own console as if it was an unfriendly visitor. His reflection stared back at him.

Three of the messages were from Rory McAllister at the Scottish Office. Rebus picked up the telephone.

'McAllister speaking.'

'Mr McAllister, it's John Rebus.'

'Inspector, thanks for getting back to me.' McAllister sounded relieved, but also edgy, not like himself.

'What's wrong?'

'Can we meet?'

'Sure, but give me some idea –'

'Calton Cemetery at one o'clock.' The phone went dead.

During the day, Calton Cemetery was more or less deserted. In summer, you'd get visitors looking for David Hume's grave. The more knowledgeable or curious might seek out the resting places of the publisher Constable and David Allan the painter. There was a statue of Abraham Lincoln, too, if it hadn't been sledgehammered by vandals.

At one o'clock on a crisp winter's day, nobody was interested in headstones. Such, at least, was Rebus's first impression as he walked through the cemetery gate. But then he saw that a gentleman was perusing the monuments, using a black rolled umbrella as a walking-cane. What hair he had mixed black with silver, and was slicked back from the forehead. His face and ears were red, maybe just from the cold, and he wore a black woollen overcoat, belted at the waist.

He saw Rebus, and gestured for him to join him. Rebus climbed the stone steps towards him.

'Haven't been here in years,' the man said. His voice had been Scots once, before the inflexions and elisions had been milked out of it. 'I take it you're Rebus?'

Rebus studied the man. 'That's right.'

'McAllister's not coming. I'm a colleague of his.'

Close up, the man's face was pockmarked and he had one slightly lazy eye. With his free hand, he played with the cashmere scarf tucked inside the collar of his coat.

'What's your name?' Rebus asked. The man seemed both surprised and amused by the question's bluntness.

'My name's Hunter.' Something about the way he said this, and his whole bearing, told Rebus he wasn't so much McAllister's colleague as his superior.

'Well, Mr Hunter, what can I do for you?'

'I'm interested in your line of inquiry, Inspector.'

'And what line is that, sir?'

'You were asking certain questions of McAllister.' A bus roared past, and Hunter raised his voice. 'The line of those questions intrigues me.'

'Why?'

'Why? Because the Scottish Office likes to take an interest.'

'In what exactly?'

The bus gone, Hunter lowered his voice again. 'I'll be succinct. I'd prefer it, Inspector, if you would discontinue your present line of inquiry. I don't believe it germane.'

'You'd *prefer* it?'

'There may be a conflict of interests.' Hunter lifted the walnut handle of his umbrella until it rested under his chin. 'Of course, I'm a civil servant and you are a policeman: it's not for me to interfere with your business.'

'Good of you, I'm sure.'

'But we are both, are we not, servants of the State?' Hunter swung the umbrella at some leaves on the ground. 'All I can say to you at this point, Inspector, is that your inquiries may well interfere with longstanding investigations *we* are pursuing.'

'I didn't know investigation was part of the Scottish Office's remit, Mr Hunter. Unless you're talking about an internal inquiry?'

'You are a clever man, Inspector, and I appeal to your intellect.'

'To be honest, sir, you don't appeal to me at all.'

Hunter's face darkened slightly. 'Let's not cross swords on this.' He swung at more leaves.

'Co-operation?'

Hunter considered this. 'Not yet, I'm afraid. The affair is confidential. But later, definitely. *Full* co-operation. What do you say?' He held out his hand. 'A gentleman's agreement.'

Rebus, knowing himself no gentleman, took the hand, just to put Hunter's mind at rest. The older man didn't look relieved, just quietly pleased that negotiations had been bloodless and – in his eyes – successful. He turned to leave.

'I'll call you when I've something I can say,' he told Rebus.

'Mr Hunter? Why did you get McAllister to phone me? Why not just call yourself?'

Hunter smiled with half his mouth. 'What's life without a little intrigue, Inspector?' He negotiated the steps carefully, with a slight limp. Too proud to carry a cane, he used a brolly instead. Rebus waited half a minute, then walked quickly to the gate and peered along the street to the right. Hunter was walking along Waterloo Place as if he owned it. Rebus kept well behind him as he followed.

It was a short walk, only as far as the Reichstag: St Andrew's House. Which, Rebus recalled, was where the most senior Scottish Office bureaucrats did their business. He recalled, too, that it was built on the site of the old Calton Gaol. Rebus walked past the sooty building and crossed the road. He stood outside the old Royal High School, putative HQ for any Scottish Assembly that might come along. It was mothballed, and a lone protector had taken up residence outside, his banners arguing for devolution and a Scottish Parliament.

Rebus stared at St Andrew's House for a couple of minutes, then walked back along Waterloo Place to where he'd illegally parked his car. It had received a ticket, but he could square that later. Over the years, he'd collected more tickets than Haldayne, a wheen more. Do as I say, he thought, not as I do. There had been other 'fringe benefits' along the way, too: cafés and restaurants where he ate for free, bars where his money was no good, a baker who'd slip him a dozen rolls. He wouldn't call himself corrupt, but there were some out there who'd say he'd been bribed, or greased for a future bribe. There were those who'd say he'd been bought.

Do as I say, not as I do. And with that he tore up the parking ticket.

Back at his flat, Rebus got out all the information he had on the Scottish Office. He didn't find the name Hunter anywhere. The documents were shy about naming names where civil servants were involved, though happy to trumpet the names of the incumbent Secretary of State, Minister of State, and Parliamentary Under-Secretaries, all of whom were either MPs or held seats in the House of Lords. As McAllister had explained, these were the temporary boys, the figureheads. When it came to the *permanent* force – the senior civil servants – Rebus found only silence and anonymity: modesty, he wondered, or discretion? Or maybe something else entirely.

He called Mairie Henderson at her home.

'Got a story for me?' she asked. 'I could do with one.'

'What do you know about the Scottish Office?'

'I know a bit.'

'Senior management?'

'There may have been changes since I last looked. Phone the paper, talk to – who'd be best? Home Affairs or Parliament? – yes, Roddy McGurk, talk to him, say I gave you his name.'

'Thanks, Mairie.'

'And I'm serious about the story, Inspector . . .'

Rebus called the newspaper office and asked for Roddy McGurk. He was put through immediately.

'Mr McGurk, I'm a friend of Mairie Henderson's. She said maybe you could help me clarify something.'

'Fire away.' The voice was West Highland.

'It's an identity, actually. A man called Hunter, Scottish Office, late-fifties, uses an umbrella when really he should have a stick . . .'

McGurk was laughing. 'Let me stop you there. You're describing Sir Iain Hunter.'

'And who's he when he's at home?'

McGurk laughed again. 'He *is* the Scottish Office. He's the Permanent Under-Secretary, usually known as –'

'The Permanent Secretary,' Rebus said, feeling queasy in his gut.

'Policy initiator for the whole country. You might call him "Mr Scotland".'

'Not a very public figure though?'

'He doesn't need to be. In the words of the old song, he's got the power.'

Rebus thanked McGurk and put the receiver down. He was trembling slightly. Mr Scotland . . . he's got the power. He wondered what he'd got himself into.

Then the telephone rang.

'I forgot to say . . .' Mairie Henderson began.

'Yes?'

'Remember you asked if there was any dirt on Councillor Gillespie?'

'Go on.'

'Well, there wasn't in my day, but I got talking yesterday to someone at BBC Scotland. You know I'm doing some radio stuff down at Queen Street? Anyway, it's not really Gillespie, it's about his wife.'

'What about her?'

'Word is, she's involved with someone else.'

'Having an affair, you mean?'

'Yes.'

Rebus remembered his visit to the councillor's home. There had seemed little love lost, but at the time he'd blamed other things.

'Who's her partner in crime?'

'That I don't know.'

'So how does your source at the Beeb know?'

'He didn't say, it's just some rumour he picked up when last in the City Chambers. The way it was told to him, he thinks maybe it's another councillor.'

'Well, let me know if you hear anything more. Bye, Mairie.'

Rebus put the phone down and tried to put his thoughts into some semblance of order. He stared at the bags of shredded paper, but they didn't help. He ended up repeating a question to himself.

What have I got myself into?

28

Chief Inspector Frank Lauderdale was in an open ward of the Royal Infirmary, but his bed was in a corner by a window, with a view over The Meadows. He'd drawn the curtain between his own bed and his neighbour's, affording some privacy. There was a vase of flowers on his bedside cabinet. They looked ready to expire in the hospital's infernal heat.

'You can almost see my flat from here,' Rebus said, looking out of the window.

'That's been a constant source of comfort to me,' Lauderdale said. 'It's taken you long enough to visit.'

'I don't like hospitals, Frank.'

'Neither do I. You think I'm in here for the good of my health?'

They shared a smile, and Rebus examined the patient. 'You look like shite, Frank.'

Lauderdale's face looked like an infant had tried shaving it with a safety razor. There were dozens of nicks and scars where the windscreen had cut him. His eyes were bruised and swollen, and there were black ugly stitches on his nose. With all the plaster and bandages he sported, he looked like the joke patient from a comedy sketch.

'How are the legs?' Rebus asked.

'Itchy.'

'That's supposed to be a good sign.'

'Oh, I'll walk again . . . so they say.' Lauderdale smiled nervously. 'Maybe I'll have a limp or two.'

'Two would be better,' said Rebus. 'They'd balance you up.'

'Want to sign my stookie?'

Rebus looked at the plastercasts on Launderdale's legs. They'd been signed by several visitors. 'Which one?'

'Take your pick.'

Rebus took a ballpoint pen from his pocket. It wasn't easy to write on the coarse surface, but he did his best.

'What does it say?' Lauderdale asked, craning his neck.

' "Clunk-click every trip." '

Lauderdale lay back again. 'What's happened about those two?'

He meant Willie and Dixie. 'Search me,' said Rebus. 'I'm on holiday.'

'So I'd heard.'

'Oh?'

'Your new boss told me. Frankly, I have my doubts: if I know you, while you're still in this city, you'll always be working. How is she shaping up?'

He meant Gill Templer. Rebus nodded. 'She's doing fine.' He wasn't sure this was what Frank Lauderdale wanted to hear. He pulled a chair over to the bed and sat down. 'I've got a problem actually, Frank.'

'Of course you have, that's why you're here.'

'It's not the Lord Provost's daughter . . .'

'You haven't found her yet?'

'I'm getting closer. She *did* know those two in the car.'

'I'd not heard that.'

Rebus shifted in the chair. 'I haven't exactly gone public with it.'

Lauderdale shook his head. 'Christ, John . . .'

'Like I say, *she's* not my immediate problem. My problem is a small-time loser called Wee Shug McAnally.'

'The one who gave himself a sawn-off haircut?'

'Yes.' Rebus ran his tongue over the hole in his tooth. 'See, he shared a cell in Saughton with a fraudster called Derwood Charters. Wee Shug was moved from another jail, and just happened to end up in that cell.' Rebus was staring hard at Lauderdale. 'It also just happened that none of the other cons knew what McAnally was in for. It was rape, by the way. Of a minor. Now, Frank, what does all that tell you?' Lauderdale said nothing. 'What it tells *me*,' Rebus went on, 'is that there was collusion at the top to stop the other cons getting to know.'

'Give me some water, will you?'

Rebus poured some for Lauderdale. 'Why would anyone do that?' Lauderdale asked, taking the beaker.

'There could be a multitude of reasons. Let me try one on you: say McAnally was in there as a plant.'

Lauderdale took his time drinking the water. 'A plant?' he said at last.

'Either to spy on Charters, or else to gain his trust. Now,' Rebus pulled his chair closer, not that Lauderdale was going anywhere, 'the reason Charters is inside is for fraud, and he was put inside by the Fraud Unit. Leading the investigation was Chief Superintendent Allan Gunner, now deputy chief constable. It so happens the DCC was the one who fixed me up with this lovely holiday. He threatened the Farmer with an HMIC inspection if I wasn't reined in.'

'He should have known better.' Lauderdale paused. 'But HMIC is an independent body, how could the DCC have control over their decisions?'

It was, Rebus conceded, a good point. The people who ran HMIC were civil servants rather than police officers.

'Well, anyway,' he said thoughtfully, 'it *was* Gunner who applied the pressure, I'm sure it was.'

'Other officers might have taken the hint, John.'

'Not me. Now, on that initial investigation of Charters were at least two officers of my acquaintance: yourself and Alister Flower. And Flower's been warning me off, too. Which makes for a nice little circle, don't you think, Frank?'

'Why come to me?'

'Maybe because you're the only person I can try. Maybe because, despite myself, I almost trust you. I mean, you're a schemer, a chancer, and you'd like the Farmer's office. But at heart you're a copper.' Rebus paused. 'Same as me. So come on, Frank, tell me about McAnally.'

'I can't.' Lauderdale saw the look on Rebus's face. 'I can't, because there's nothing to tell. You're right, I did work on the Albavise inquiry, but that's as far as it goes. I know this, though: if you're crossing not only Flower but the likes of the DCC and Big Jim Flett, then you'd better watch out.'

'I think it goes further than that even,' Rebus confided. 'The Scottish Office, maybe even MPs or ministers.'

'Christ, John,' Lauderdale whispered.

Rebus stood up. 'So maybe as you're packing your bags to go home, they'll be wheeling me in to take your place.'

'Don't joke about it.'

'Who said I was joking?'

'And don't tell me any more. The less I know the better.'

'For you or for me?'

Lauderdale sat up as best he could. 'Let it go,' he advised. 'For once in your dunder-headed life, just walk away.'

Rebus put the chair back where he'd found it. 'I can't do that, Frank.' He pushed his tongue into the hole again. The poison hadn't all drained yet.

'Take care of yourself,' he told Lauderdale.

'That should probably be my line.'

Rebus was halfway down the ward when he heard Lauderdale calling for him. He walked back to the bed. Lauderdale had propped himself up and was staring out of the wndow.

'Flower,' he said, not turning to look at Rebus.

'What about him, Frank?'

'McAnally was Flower's eyes and ears.'

'His snitch?'

Lauderdale nodded, eyes still on the window.

'I appreciate this,' said Rebus, turning away again.

'I hope you do, John,' Frank Lauderdale said quietly.

There was an envelope lying on the hall carpet. The post had already been; this had been delivered by hand: no stamp, just his name in blue ink. There was an embossed official crest on the sealed flap – the lion and the unicorn holding a shield between them. Rebus knew it was the Scottish Office crest. He flexed the envelope in his hands. It was thin and light, yet fairly solid. Leaving it on the arm of the chair, he went to the kitchen and added tap-water to a glass of whisky. He found a knife in the drawer, and took both glass and knife back through to the chair. He took a mouthful of whisky before slitting open the envelope.

It was a white card, an invitation, elaborate black embossed script with a gold border.

Sir Iain Hunter

requests the pleasure of your company

Saturday 4 March

Twelve Noon Ruthie Estate
 Perthshire

Rebus's name had been added in blue ink at the top of the card. There was no RSVP, just an address, and no telephone number. Rebus turned the card over and saw that it bore a printed map showing the location of the estate, about halfway between Perth and Auchterarder. Saturday was only two days off.

Rebus carried the invitation to his mantelpiece and leaned it against the otherwise bare wall. The only estate he'd ever been to before was the housing kind. He didn't suppose Ruthie Estate would be very like those at all.

Rebus was still wondering if he'd go or not when he set out for his evening session at the Ox.

Dr Klasser wasn't there. He'd telephoned to say he'd be very late, if he made it at all. The barman placed Rebus's pint in front of him, just as Salty Dougary walked in.

'It's bitter out there,' Dougary said.

'But it's called eighty-shilling in here. Go on, Jon, pour the man his poison.'

Dougary eased himself on to the barstool next to Rebus. 'I've got something for you.'

'What?'

'Remember you asked me about Mensung?'

Yes, Rebus remembered. He'd asked Rory McAllister too, only McAllister had been warned off; Rebus doubted he'd ever hear from him again.

'What about it?'

'I've remembered what it was,' Dougary said matter-of-factly. His drink had appeared, and he ordered some crisps.

'So what is it?' Rebus asked.

'Salt and vinegar, Jon,' Dougary told the barman. The volume on the TV was being turned up for some sports report. Dougary turned to Rebus. 'It was a company.' He took a mouthful of beer. 'And a packet of ready salted,' he told the barman.

'Did you say a company?'

'Eh?' Dougary's attention was already turning towards the TV. Rebus hauled him off the stool and out of the door, into the chill, dark street. Traffic rumbled past on Castle Street.

'It's freezing out here!' Dougary protested.

'Just tell me.' Dougary looked longingly towards the pub door. 'Tell me here,' Rebus persisted.

'Remember when I worked for that semiconductor company?'

'It was called Mensung?'

'It wasn't called any such thing. But it had this policy of trying to retrain workers it surfed out.'

'So?'

'So I was a turfee, and there was this agency, outplacement sort of thing. The agency ran seminars, or was supposed to. It was supposed to have all these fancy retraining schemes and programmes, half of which never materialised. *That* bunch of cowboys was called Mensung.'

'Is it still around?'

Dougary shrugged. 'I've been laid off twice since, and never come across it again.'

'Where was it based?'

'By the Playhouse, top of Leith Walk.'

'Do you still have any information on it, anything in writing?'

Dougary stared at him. 'I'd have to check with my secretary.' The irony was so heavy, you could hear it fall.

Rebus smiled. 'Stupid question, Donny. Sorry.'

'Can I go back in now?'

'Sure.'

'Is anything wrong?'

'How do you mean?'

'You called me Donny instead of Salty.'

'It's your name, isn't it?'

'I suppose it is,' said Dougary, pushing open the door.

29

One of the reasons Rebus drank was to put him to sleep.

He had trouble sleeping when sober. He'd stare into the darkness, willing it to form shapes so that he might better understand it. He'd try to make sense of life – his early disastrous Army years; his failed marriage; his failings as father, friend, lover – and end up in tears. And if he did eventually stumble into sober sleep, there would be troubled dreams, dreams about ageing and dying, decay and blight. The dark took on shapes in his dreams, but he daren't look at them. He'd run blindly instead, sometimes bumping into them, feeling the darkness mould itself around him.

Drunk, his sleep was dreamless, or seemed that way on waking. He might be drenched in sweat, but he wouldn't be shaking. So he always tried to have a few drinks last thing at night, usually in his chair – and since he was already comfortable, what was the point of getting up and going through to the bedroom?

He was in the chair, dead to the world, when the buzzer sounded. He sat up and switched on the lamp, then blinked his eyes open to check his watch. It was one-thirty. He staggered into the hall like he was learning to walk, and unhooked the intercom.

'Hello?'

'It's Patience.'

'Patience?' Without thinking, he buzzed her up, then went back into the living room to put on his trousers. When he got back to the door, she had almost reached his landing. She walked slowly, with purpose. Her head was bowed, eyes on the steps, not looking at him. Her hair was unbrushed.

'What's happened?'

She stood directly in front of him, and he could see how angry she was. She was so angry, she was preternaturally calm.

'I was lying in bed,' she said quietly, 'and I don't know what happened ... I suddenly saw it.'

'What?'

'You know Lucky's dead?'

'Yes, I'm sorry.'

She nodded to herself. 'Well, thanks for being there for me, I appreciate that. I was thinking, that's pretty cold-hearted, even for him. Sammy told me she'd told you. I wondered why you hadn't been in touch, and then I remembered. Stupid of me to forget. You were there on Sunday. You were

143

sitting right next to the conservatory door.' Her voice grew even quieter. 'You locked Lucky out.'

'Patience, I –'

'Didn't you?'

'Look, it's late, why don't –'

'Didn't you?'

'Christ, I don't know . . . all right, yes, if it makes you feel any better.' He rubbed a hand over his face. 'Yes, the racket he was making was driving me mental, so I locked the flap and then forgot. I'm sorry.'

She had opened the shoulder bag and was lifting out a smaller plastic bag. 'This is for you.' And as he put out a hand to take the bag, she slapped him hard on the left cheek. Then she turned and started downstairs.

'Patience!'

She didn't even pause. She just kept on going. He held up the bag, then opened it and looked inside.

It was just some bits and pieces, that was all.

Bits and pieces of Lucky the cat.

In the morning, he took the bag out to the back garden.

The garden was actually a shared drying-green, with a flower border tended by Mrs Cochrane on the floor below Rebus. Just inside the back door of the tenement was a padlocked walk-in cupboard. It was communal storage space, only Rebus didn't have anything he wanted communally stored. But he unlocked the door and lifted out the spade which had belonged to dear departed Mr Cochrane.

He sat the plastic bag down next to the flower border, looked around and up at the windows to see nobody was watching, then raised the shovel.

When it hit soil, he felt the collision all the way from his wrists to his spine. He tried again, and chipped away a sliver of frozen earth. He stooped to pick up his prize. It was like toffee, frozen toffee.

'Jesus,' he said, trying again. He could see his breath in the air. In the tenement across the back, someone making breakfast had come to their kitchen window. It wasn't daylight yet, but Rebus knew they could see him clearly enough.

It was all the exposure he needed to convince him he should give up.

Instead, he drove to the Cowgate, parked the car, and carried the bag with him into the City Mortuary.

'Inspector,' one of the staff said. 'What can we do for you today?'

Rebus handed over the bag, said thank you, and left.

He'd arranged to meet Holmes and Clarke in a trendy café near the university, but the place hadn't opened for the day, so they walked along to Nicolson Street and found a clean, well-lit coffee shop.

He asked them how things were at St Leonard's. They reckoned they were still under close scrutiny, but they could cope.

'Good,' he said, 'because I've got something else I want you to do for me. I want to know about a company. It probably no longer exists, but it was around in '86, '87.'

'A limited company?'

'No idea.'

'Directors?'

Rebus just shrugged. 'About all I can tell you is that it was called Mensung.'

Clarke and Holmes looked at one another. 'The councillor's file?' they said as one.

'It was a retraining company, not a very good one apparently. It had premises at the top of Leith Walk, next to the Playhouse. I want you to check Companies House, any registers you can find, any lists of retraining companies in Scotland.' He nodded to the waitress that they were ready to order. 'Now don't stint yourselves,' he told them. 'Believe me, you're going to earn this meal.'

He checked Leith Walk himself.

Next to the Playhouse was a pub, and then a newsagent's, but between them was a door, not quite shut. There were a couple of business plaques on the wall outside, and spaces where other plaques had been removed. Rebus pushed open the door, noting that it was none too steady on its hinges, and entered an unlit hallway smelling worse than many a bar's convenience. The stone steps up were deeply worn, the walls decorated with graffiti.

On the first floor, he was met by two solid doors, one with a card pinned to it saying Combined Knitwear, the other with a much older-looking nameplate: J. Joseph Simpson Associates. Rebus climbed to the second floor, but the doors here were anonymous and heavily padlocked. He went back down to the first floor and knocked on the door of Simpson Associates, then pushed the door open.

He was in a hallway much like his own flat's. Rooms led off, and there was a Reception sign pointing into one of them. The door was already open, so Rebus walked in. Seated behind desk and typewriter, an elderly man was on the telephone. Rebus was not totally surprised to see a male secretary, but he'd never come across such a superannuated one. Paperwork slewed across desk, chairs, and the carpet.

The man looked startled by Rebus's entry, and slammed the phone down.

'Sorry to interrupt,' Rebus said.

'Quite all right, quite all right.' The man made show of gathering up some of the sheets of paper. 'Now, what can I do for you, sir?'

The man reminded Rebus of Charles Laughton. He was rotund, with several chins, and had puffy, worried eyes with blotched shiny skin. He wore a suit which had been in fashion forty years before, including waistcoat and watch-chain. It struck Rebus for a moment that he would pass for Sir Iain Hunter's bloated and seedy elder brother.

Rebus showed his ID. 'Inspector Rebus, sir. I'm interested in a company that used to have its offices here.'

'Here?'

'In this building. About eight years ago, were you here then?'

'Most certainly.'

'The company was called Mensung.'

'Curious name.' The man repeated it silently a few times. 'No,' he said, 'I can't say I've heard of it.'

'Are you sure?'

'Completely sure.'

'Maybe if I could have a word with your employer?'

The man smiled. 'I *am* my employer. Joe Simpson at your service.'

'I'm sorry, Mr Simpson.'

'You thought I was the secretary?' Simpson looked amused. 'Well, I suppose I am at that. My last secretary left after only two days. Hopeless, these girls the agency sends. It's all hours with them, don't ever try to get them to stay a minute later than five o'clock.' He shook his head.

'You don't know who your secretary was eight years ago, Mr Simpson?'

Joe Simpson wagged a finger. 'You think her memory might be better than my own, but you'd be wrong. Besides, I've no idea. There have been so many women at this desk.' He shook his head again.

'So, Mr Simpson, eight years ago, what companies were there in this building?'

'Well, there was mine, of course, and then there was Capital Yarns.'

'Now Combined Knitwear?'

'The woman who ran Capital Yarns left in 1989. The place was empty the best part of a year, then a computer showroom opened – that lasted all of three months. The place was empty again until Mrs Burnett arrived. She's Combined Knitwear.'

'What about upstairs?'

'Oh, years back those were offices. Now they're just stockrooms, have been for a decade or more.'

Rebus was at a dead end, as surely as if he'd stayed on the floor above. He tried Simpson with the name Mensung again, spelt it for him, wrote it down, and all the old man did was twitch his head and say definitely and positively 'no'. So Rebus thanked him and went back out on to the landing, resting against the banister. These small tenement businesses, there were a lot of them in Edinburgh. Small, shifting and anonymous, he didn't see how they ever made money. It struck him that he didn't even know what J. Joseph Simpson Associates did. But he was willing to bet there were no associates, perhaps never had been.

He was about to leave when the door of Combined Knitwear opened and two women stepped out. They glanced towards him before continuing their conversation. One of the women wore a coat and carried two bulging plastic bags, which didn't seem heavy. Wool, Rebus surmised. The other woman wore a knitted two-piece, red and black check, and a string of pearls. A pair of glasses hung by a string around her neck. She was petite, trim, probably Rebus's age.

'Well, thanks again,' she said to the departing customer. Then to Rebus: 'Can I help?'

'Mrs Burnett?'

'Yes.' She sounded uneasy.

'Inspector Rebus.' Again he showed his ID.

'Is it a break-in? Those stockrooms could have steel doors, they'd still find a way in.'

'No, it's not a break-in.'

'Oh.' She looked at him. 'Look, I'm about to put the kettle on, do you fancy a cup?'

Rebus accepted her offer with pleasure.

Combined Knitwear's premises were laid out like Joe Simpson's: four

rooms leading off a narrow hallway. One room served as an office. Mrs Burnett was in there at the sink, filling a kettle. Rebus looked into the other rooms. Wool. Lots and lots of wool. Deep shelves had been installed to display the stuff. There were boxes of knitting patterns, a perspex case filled with pairs of needles. The walls and doors were decorated with blown-up photos from the fronts of various knitting patterns. Smiling, untroubled men. Women who looked like models from fifteen or twenty years ago. From a series of dowel-rods on one wall hung skeins of thick white wool. Rebus liked the smell of the place. It reminded him of his mother, and all his aunties and their friends. His mother used to tell him off for using her knitting needles as drumsticks.

He turned and saw that Mrs Burnett was standing in the doorway.

'You looked very peaceful there for a minute,' she said.

'I felt it.'

'Tea's about ready.'

'Do you happen to know what Mr Simpson next door does?'

She laughed lightly. 'I've been wondering that for years.'

'Years?'

'Did he tell you I was a newcomer? He doesn't remember me, but I used to work here when it was Capital Yarns. It wasn't my business, I was staff. But when I decided to set up for myself, and saw that this place was available – well, I couldn't help myself.' She sighed. 'Sentiment, Inspector. Nostalgia – never be swayed by it. Not too many customers are willing to make the trek from Princes Street. I'd be better off somewhere more central.'

Rebus recalled the story of how IBM had come to set up in Greenock: nostalgia again, but on a grand scale.

He followed Mrs Burnett through to the office. 'So were you working here eight years ago? Around 1986 or '87?'

She poured water into two mugs. 'Oh yes.'

'Was there an outfit here at that time called Mensung?'

'*Mensonge*?'

He spelt it for her.

'No,' she said, 'by that time there was just Mr Simpson and Capital Yarns. You're sure it was this address?' Rebus nodded, watching her dip the tea-bags. 'Milk and sugar?'

'Just milk, please.' She handed him the cup. 'Thanks. Why did you use that pronunciation just now?'

'*Mensonge*?'

'Yes. It sounds French.'

'It is French. It means lie.'

'What?'

'As in falsehood, fib, untruth. Is there something wrong with the tea, Inspector?'

'No, nothing at all, Mrs Burnett. The tea's fine. Just fine.'

To make absolutely sure, Rebus asked in the newsagent's. The owner, who had run the place eighteen years, shook his head. Then Rebus had a word with the letting agency, who confirmed that there was no record of any company called Mensung ever renting office space at the address.

'Can you tell me who owns the property?' Rebus asked. 'Just out of interest.'

The woman wasn't sure she could. Rebus stressed again that his inquiries were part of a police investigation, and she gave in.

'The owner's name,' she said, 'is a Mr J. Simpson. As an individual, Mr Simpson rents space to Simpson Associates, Combined Knitwear, and a Mr Albert Costello.'

'Costello?'

'The newsagent next door,' the letting agent said.

'Nothing so far,' Brian Holmes said over a lunchtime drink. 'No record the company ever existed.'

Rebus chewed on his last piece of bridie. 'I'm beginning to think it didn't. Where's Siobhan, by the way?'

'At the gym.'

'What's a gym?'

Brian Holmes smiled at that. He'd put on weight this past year or so, and now sported a dough-ring stomach and the beginnings of beer jowls. Perks of the job, some people said.

'I thought you worked-out some lunchtimes?' he said.

'Haven't done it for ages.'

But Rebus went swimming that afternoon, managing twenty thoughtful lengths, after which he had to sit in his cubicle for a while. That was the problem with exercise: it wasn't any fun. None of the fit and active people he saw around him seemed any happier than anyone else. No point exercising to elongate your life, when you weren't getting any more out of life than any other poor sod. He made up for the swimming by arriving early at the Ox, waiting to have a word with Salty Dougary, but Dougary didn't come, and Rebus decided to break the rules.

He'd visit Dougary at his home.

Dougary was divorced and rented the top floor of a sizeable house not a conversion-kick away from Murrayfield Stadium. He couldn't have looked more surprised to see Rebus if he'd found him servicing his ex-wife on the doorstep.

'What are you doing here?'

'I need a word, Salty.'

'I didn't feel like a drink tonight. Our boss is driving us like slaves, a big order with the deadline approaching, and Mathieson screaming down the telephone.'

'Mathieson?'

'Head honcho at PanoTech. You should see the way our boss –'

'Salty? Sorry to bring it up, but it's freezing out here.'

Dougary stepped aside to let Rebus in. 'I'll warn you,' he said, 'the place is a midden.'

Certainly, Rebus thought, it was no advert for the bachelor life.

'Have you run out of binbags or something?'

'I never seem to get time to clean up. Want a beer?'

'Thanks.' Rebus lifted pizza boxes, crisp bags and a couple of empty cans off the sofa and sat down. Salty came back with a couple of cans and handed one over.

'So what's the emergency?'

Rebus sipped froth from the top of the can. 'You said Mensung was at the top of Leith Walk.' Dougary nodded. 'Next to a newsagent's?' Another nod. 'Well, I took a look this morning, and nobody's heard of them.'

'So?'

'So, are you sure that's where they were?'

'That was the address on their letter-heading.'

'You're sure you wouldn't have any of their letters lying around?' Rebus scanned the room. His meaning was clear: you seem to hang on to everything else.

'Everything got chucked when Fiona and me split up. I mean *everything*. Letters, photos, I even lost my birth certificate. See, John, I never actually went to see Mensung at that address. The courses I did, they were held at a place on Corstorphine Road.'

'Do you remember the number?'

Dougary nodded. 'One-six-five Corstorphine Road. See, it's the date Fiona and me got married, sixteen-five, that's how I remember.' His face turned wistful. 'Two chips soldered together on the motherboard of life.'

Rebus tried to remember when he and Rhona had married. He thought it was probably June or July, but that was as much as he could recall.

First thing next morning, he drove along Corstorphine Road looking for number 165. Rebus didn't exactly know what a paper-chase was, but this was beginning to feel like one. The American, Haldayne, had mentioned paper companies, and Rebus felt he was chasing one now, something no more substantial than the sum of its letter-heading. His visit to Corstorphine Road seemed to confirm it.

The present occupants of the office suite told him that back in '86 and '87 the premises had been under a short let, sometimes for only days at a time. But there were no records of the actual occupants at that time. The suites had changed ownership several times since.

'Thanks for your help,' Rebus said.

Dead end, he thought. Dead company. He'd have to get Councillor Gillespie to talk to him, there was no other course left open. It was either that, or drop it altogether. That, after all, was what everyone wanted, but then he'd never been a crowd pleaser. He'd never played to the gallery.

He'd talk to Councillor Tom Gillespie. But after the weekend. And meantime, he had some fast shopping to do. New clothes. For some reason, he wanted new clothes to wear to Sir Iain's.

Three

Zugzwang

30

Two low-built stone pillars marked the start of the long, snaking driveway. Rebus turned off the main road on to the gravel track and stopped the car. There were no signs, nothing at all to tell him this was the right turning. He looked at the map on the back of his invitation and decided it was. The very anonymity of the track seemed to fit with Sir Iain Hunter. Either side of Rebus were open fields, but these soon gave way to dense woodland. Drystane dykes overgrown with moss separated the driveway from the trees.

Finally, after half a mile, he emerged from the shade into a bright expanse of tended lawn with greenhouses and a walled vegetable garden off. And directly in front of him stood a grey stone house in the Scots baronial style, boasting two turrets – probably ornamental – which started at the level of the first floor and tapered to slate-covered points above the roof-line. There were three cars – a Rover 800, Jaguar, and Maserati – parked on the clean pink gravel. Rebus stopped beside them and got out, trying not to be impressed. In the distance, a stream bisected the trim lawn, with a narrow humpbacked bridge across it. It reminded him of nothing so much as one of the fairways at St Andrews.

'It's a lovely view, isn't it?' The voice was Sir Iain's. He was walking towards Rebus, leaning lightly on a carved walking-stick. At home, it would appear the brolly wasn't necessary.

'Just thinking I should have brought my three-iron.'

'Ah, you play golf?'

'Only with a three-iron.'

Hunter laughed and placed a hand on Rebus's shoulder. 'Find the place all right?'

'No trouble.'

'Good.' Hunter was steering Rebus towards the house. 'I thought we'd have a drink first, then do a spot of shooting and just have a light lunch.'

'Shooting?'

'I take it you've handled a gun, Inspector?'

'I've handled a lot of things.'

'I did wonder if we might try for pheasant or winter hare, but decided on clay pigeon.'

'Well, it tastes nicer, doesn't it?'

Sir Iain Hunter shook his head, amused. 'There's no telling what you'll say next, Inspector.'

They entered a capacious hall with white marble floor and paintings on

the walls: modern art, which surprised Rebus. A lot of the stuff looked ill at ease in a setting of wood panelling and fluted columns. A staircase with a wrought-iron balustrade climbed up the middle of the hall and peeled off to left and right.

'In here,' Hunter said. 'Let me take your coat.'

Rebus slipped off his new raincoat and shrugged himself back into his sports jacket. He patted his tie flat and walked into the morning room.

A servant was dispensing drinks from a series of decanters on a trolley. So, Rebus thought, I was important enough to be met by the boss rather than the flunky. He stood there, not really looking at anyone, biding his time until Sir Iain came back into the room.

'Hello, John,' someone said, walking towards him, hand held out. The man held a heavy crystal tumbler in his other hand, and looked slightly embarrassed. It wasn't until Rebus had taken the man's hand that he recognised him.

It was Allan Gunner, the deputy chief constable.

'Do you know everyone?' Gunner said, leading Rebus to the drinks trolley. Rebus's first thought, after he'd recovered from the surprise, was: at least Gunner had the grace to look embarrassed. His second thought was: I've walked into this, fair and square.

The servant was waiting for Rebus's order. He was a little stooped from a lifetime's obsequiousness, and had a trying-to-please smile on his thin lips. He wore a tight little jacket of blue nylon, all its buttons done up. It probably helped with the stoop.

'I'll take a malt,' Rebus said.

'West Highland or Strathspey, sir?'

'Strathspey, and no water.'

Another guest laughed. 'Sir Iain won't allow water of any form near his whiskies.' He held his cigar and glass in one hand so he could extend the other towards Rebus.

'Colin Macrae,' he said.

'Sir Colin,' Gunner added, 'is Scottish Office Minister for Agriculture and the Environment.'

'John Rebus,' Rebus told the man.

Which left only two guests, both male, both involved in a muted discussion by the French windows. But Gunner was applying discreet pressure to Rebus's arm, manoeuvring him away from the drinks trolley, where Sir Colin was ordering a top-up. They ended up beside a massive stone fireplace.

Gunner spoke in a fierce whisper. 'I don't know what you're doing here –'

'Me neither.'

'But while we're in company, we'd better show a united front, especially in front of these characters.'

'Agreed.'

'So first-name terms, no formalities.'

'Fair enough, sir.'

'The name's Allan.'

'Allen.'

'Ah,' Hunter said, entering the room and pointing at them with his stick, 'the same old story, everyone's got a drink but the host.'

The servant poured without being asked. A telephone sounded in the hall, and he went to answer it, head bowed as he left the room.

'Cheers,' said Sir Iain. He motioned for Rebus to join him. 'Met everyone?'

The couple from the window were coming back to replenish their glasses. Rebus nodded towards them.

'Robbie,' Sir Iain said, 'come and meet Detective Inspector John Rebus. John, this is Robbie Mathieson.'

Mathieson shook Rebus's hand. He was tall, well built, and had thick black hair and a black beard. The glasses he wore sported blue tints.

'Pleased to meet you.' His accent was slightly American.

'PanoTech?' Rebus guessed.

Mathieson nodded, a bit put out by the recognition, and Sir Iain looked interested that Rebus should know Mathieson. Sir Iain turned to Allan Gunner.

'Chief Constable, is it a wonder the crime rate is falling and the detection rate rising when you can boast men of this calibre?' He looked back to Rebus. 'It's almost uncanny.'

A game was being played, and Rebus didn't know what it was. But he knew that his knowing who Mathieson was was part of it.

Gunner was correcting Sir Iain. 'It's *Deputy* Chief Constable.'

'A slip of the tongue,' Hunter said, with a wink to the general assembly. 'Perhaps I was merely looking into the future. That's what we civil servants are good at, you know. Dugald, your glass needs a top-up.'

Dugald held out his hand for a refill. Nobody had introduced him because nobody needed to. He was quiet, thoughtful, or maybe he just didn't waste words. Hardly surprising, when everything he said might be taken down and passed to the media, who might use it as evidence against him. He couldn't afford to trust those he did not know.

Certainly, he didn't know Rebus, but Rebus knew him. He was Dugald Niven, the Right Honourable Dugald Niven.

He was Secretary of State for Scotland.

'Let's take our drinks through to the gun room,' Sir Iain said, 'and get everyone kitted out.'

Rebus poured and drank another half glass before following everyone out of the room.

It was barely above zero outside – 'bracing' and 'fresh' according to Sir Iain – and they were going to have a picnic. The provisions would be waiting for them at the clay-pigeon site. To get to the site itself necessitated a walk through the woods. In the gun room, they'd been fitted with green sportsmen's jackets, sleeveless and thickly padded with cartridge-belt attached. They were handed a shotgun each, broken open for safety's sake.

Rebus stayed to the rear of the party, and Gunner slowed down to join him.

'So what *are* you doing here?' Gunner asked.

'I thought you'd know.'

'*Me?*'

'You've had me taken off an investigation.'

'I've done no such thing.'

'OK then, you *requested* I be taken off.'

Gunner tucked his shotgun more firmly under his arm. 'What's that got to do with you being here?'

'I wish I knew. If you're asking me to make an inspired guess . . . ?'

'Go on.'

'Well, I've been brought here so you can work on me.'

'What?'

'You're going to warn me off again, and I'll be so impressed by the surroundings and the company, I'll fall to my knees and plead forgiveness.'

Gunner gave him a blazing look. 'That's ridiculous.'

'In that case, what are *you* doing here?'

'I'm in the dark. First time I've been invited. Maybe Sir Iain wants to get to know me. He's a canny diplomat, as well as being a manipulator.' Gunner paused. 'The chief constable will be retiring soon.'

'Bit young for that, isn't he?'

'His wife's ill, she needs looking after.'

'So you'll be promoted?'

'I assume so.'

'Always supposing you're given a clean bill of health.'

'What?'

'By HMIC, for example. That kind of threat works both ways, Allan.'

Gunner narrowed his eyes. 'What do you mean?'

'Shug McAnally kills himself. I try to find out why. Turns out he's recently been sharing a cell with a man called Charters. This despite the fact McAnally's in for a sex attack. Only, none of the other inmates knows that.'

'I still don't see what you're getting at.'

'Yes you do. McAnally was Alister Flower's grass. Flower worked under you on the case against Charters. McAnally was put in Charters' cell to see what he could glean. Now, Flower hasn't got the weight to set up something like that; it'd need someone more senior to have a word with Big Jim Flett – someone like yourself, sir.' Gunner kept his eyes on the ground and said nothing. 'And now,' Rebus went on, 'I've got the likes of Hunter warning me off, too.'

Gunner looked up at the knot of men ahead. They were picking their way over fallen branches and through stunted undergrowth between mature trees.

'I want us to talk,' he said.

'Fine.'

'But not here.'

Sir Iain had stopped and was gesturing. 'Come on, slowcoaches! I've got one good leg and I'm still beating you.' He waited for them to join him.

'How much land have you got here, Sir Iain?' Gunner asked, suddenly the well-mannered guest.

'A hundred and seventy acres, but don't worry, we're not walking all of it.'

Soon they broke out of the woods into a rutted field of stubble. By the side of the field was a track just wide enough for the vehicle that sat there, a venerable Land-Rover the same olive green as their jackets. The servant was at the back of the vehicle, unpacking a large wicker hamper. There was another man halfway across the field, standing beside some apparatus Rebus took to be the clay-pigeon release.

Rebus ended up standing next to the Secretary of State. The man didn't seem inclined to speak. Rebus wondered what he'd been discussing with Robbie Mathieson in the morning room. Rebus turned to Mathieson.

'A friend of mine works for one of your suppliers.'

'Oh?' Mathieson didn't sound particularly interested.

'Deltona,' Rebus said.

Mathieson's beard moved in what might have been a smile. 'Then I hope he didn't have plans this weekend. I've been promised that plant will work all weekend. I'm due a big order from them by midweek. I wouldn't want to have to find a new supplier.'

'How's the work on LABarum progressing?'

Mathieson stared at him, then fed cartridges into the shotgun's double chamber. 'It's going pretty well,' he said. 'Can I ask how you know about it?'

Rebus shrugged. 'Word gets around.'

'Does it?' Mathieson snapped shut the gun.

'Actually, I came across a copy of your business plan in a council house in Stenhouse.'

'What was it doing there?' Mathieson seemed calm enough.

'I haven't the faintest idea,' Rebus told him. 'Someone had scrawled the word "Dalgety" on it.' Mathieson flinched and dropped a cartridge.

'Pull!' Sir Iain called. A clay disc sprang into the air. There was an explosion, then another, and the disc shattered. Sir Iain broke open his gun.

'Damned good shot,' commented Sir Colin Macrae.

'You know, it's unusual. Sir Iain's Saturdays are normally corporate affairs, but today we've got *two* policemen.' Mathieson looked like he wanted Rebus to tell him something, but Rebus didn't know what.

'Pull!' More gunshots filled the air.

'Not bad, Dugald, not bad!'

'Tell me,' Rebus asked Mathieson, 'do you know a man called Derwood Charters?'

'I don't think so.'

'I've heard he helped finance PanoTech in the early days.'

Mathieson laughed. 'You're misinformed.'

'Come on, Allan, you're next!'

When Robbie Mathieson's turn came, he missed the target with both barrels.

'Not like you, Robbie,' Sir Iain laughed, glancing towards Rebus. He looked uncommonly pleased. Rebus felt he was being used; he still didn't know why or how.

When his own turn came to shoot, he missed with both barrels. Sir Iain insisted he try again straight away.

'You're a tyro,' he said, 'you need the practice. I'm sure we all missed a few in the beginning.'

This time, Rebus chipped a bit off the disc with his second shot.

'See?' said Sir Iain. 'Now you're getting the hang of it!'

Maybe he was at that.

Ears still ringing, Rebus joined the others at the Land-Rover. There were flasks of Scotch broth, sandwiches in silver foil, hip-flasks of whisky and larger flasks of tea. Rebus's sandwich was brown bread and smoked

salmon. The salmon was sliced thick, and had been sprinkled with lemon juice and pepper. He took a small nip of whisky when the hip-flask came round, then drank two mugs of strong tea. With all the games he felt were going on, he wanted to clear his head. He wasn't sure if he was a player, a counter, or the die. He'd been shown one thing, though – the game was dangerous, at stake his professional career, which was everything he lived for. Practically every man present had it within his power to push Rebus off the playing-board and off the force. He started to get angry: angry with himself for coming; angry with Sir Iain Hunter – so smug, so manipulative – for bringing him here. Rebus knew now that he hadn't just been brought here so he could be warned off. He swallowed the anger down and held it in his gut. It was hotter than tea, stronger than whisky.

They were almost back at the house when Sir Iain gripped Rebus's elbow and led him towards the greenhouses.

'We'll catch you up!' he called to the others. Then, to Rebus, still holding him by the elbow: 'Have a nice chat with Robbie Mathieson?' Rebus shrugged off Sir Iain's hand. 'And with Allan Gunner too, I noticed.'

'Why am I here?'

'I admire your directness. You're here because I want to know if you've decided.'

'Decided what?'

'To stop your investigation.'

'Are you willing to tell me why you're so interested?'

Sir Iain's gaze hardened. 'I'm willing to tell you one thing, *if* you're willing to listen.'

They were standing in front of one of the long greenhouses. Looking through the misted windows, Rebus could see trestle tables and empty flower-pots and seed-trays, but there was nothing growing in there, nothing at all.

'I'm listening,' he said.

'Then I'll tell you that Scottish jobs are at risk.'

'At risk from what?'

'From *you*, Inspector, if you continue stumbling blindly around. Let it take its course, that's what I'm saying.'

Rebus turned to him. 'Let what take its course? You're not telling me anything, how am I supposed to know what to do and what not to do?'

'You know what to do,' Hunter said calmly: 'stop your little private investigation. If it goes any further, hundreds of jobs could disappear. Do you hear me? *Hundreds*. You wouldn't want that on your conscience, I'm sure.'

'I don't believe you,' Rebus said.

Hunter looked at him with something near pity. 'Yes you do, Inspector.'

He did, too. It was in Hunter's voice, in the way his frame shivered when he spoke. He believed what he was saying, believed it with a passion. *Hundreds of jobs.*

Sir Iain started to walk towards the house. Rebus followed, making sure he never caught up.

As agreed, Rebus and Gunner left the house separately but met up at a hotel in Auchterarder.

'I don't usually drink,' Gunner confided, washing down two aspirin with an orange juice. They sat in a corner of the quiet lounge bar. For a Saturday, the main street was quiet. The shoppers would all be in Perth, keeping warm in department stores and superstores. The TV was showing *Rio Bravo,* John Wayne doing his John Wayne walk.

'I don't usually shoot,' Rebus said.

'So now we've both seen how the other half lives.' Gunner put down his glass and took a deep breath. 'Let's get down to business. Whatever you think, Inspector, I wasn't there to "scare you off". I got my invite in the mail, same as you did. I've been thinking, and my conclusion is that Sir Iain wanted to play us off against one another. Or perhaps he thought that my presence would serve to unnerve you.'

Rebus nodded agreement. 'One other option,' he added. 'We were both there to scare someone else. Mathieson didn't like it that policemen were present.'

'What are they so worried about?'

'Hunter told me it has to do with jobs.'

'Jobs? What kind of jobs?'

Rebus shook his head. How far could he trust Gunner? The man was the first person who'd tried to take him out of the game. 'Are you going to own up about McAnally?'

Gunner examined his fingernails. 'You're right in just about every detail. I had McAnally moved to Saughton and into Charters' cell. Then he went and got cancer, and wasn't getting any information out of Charters, so I arranged for his early release.'

'And he went straight to Councillor Gillespie and blew his head off in front of him.'

'I don't know why he did that.'

'Why was McAnally in Charters' cell?'

'To see if he could talk himself into Charters' confidence. I wanted to see what Charters was hiding. I knew he was hiding something, but couldn't think what to do about it until Flower suggested McAnally.'

'And what is Charters hiding exactly?'

'Money, what else? I don't mean he's hiding it literally, though perhaps he is. But back in the mid-eighties he was coining it, and we weren't sure where the cash was coming from. He had about half a dozen companies – legit, as far as the Fraud Unit could tell – but they made more money than they should have.'

'I thought that's what Thatcherism was all about. Was one of his companies called Mensung?'

'Yes.'

'And were all his companies involved in retraining?'

'That sort of thing. Their paperwork was so convoluted – positively labyrinthine – that even our specialists couldn't find a clear path through it. They were all agreed on one thing. Derry Charters had a genius for muddying the water. You could track a company of his for months and not get to the bottom of its financial status.'

'I've heard he helped finance PanoTech at one time.'

'Who told you that?'

'Is it true?'

'I don't think so. Did one of Charters' investors tell you?' Rebus nodded. 'Probably a story he spun them. He could be very persuasive.'

'But all this was eight, nine years ago.'

'Yes, and since then he's cleaned up his act, or had done until he burnt people's fingers with Albavise.'

'So why are you still chasing him over a piece of ancient history?'

'A couple of reasons. One, I spent a lot of my time and effort in the Fraud Unit chasing him, without getting a result. It represents probably the only blot on my record. Two, our best guess when we investigated him was that he was fiddling millions.' He had Rebus's full attention. 'Millions,' he repeated. 'And for me, that makes him worth the chase.'

'Where did he fiddle these millions from?'

But Gunner just shrugged. Rebus was thoughtful for a moment. The bar was filling, and the TV had been switched over to show the football scores. Not that many games were being played: the pitches were dangerously hard.

'I've read the case against him on Albavise. Any chance that I can see the other paperwork?'

Gunner studied him. 'There's a hell of a lot, and it's in no particular order. You think you can spot something our financial gurus couldn't?'

Rebus shrugged. 'Just for my peace of mind. I'd like to talk to Charters, too.'

'What?'

'His cell-mate's committed suicide. It looks strange if nobody's been near to ask him about McAnally's state of mind prior to release. I mean, who'd know better than him?'

Gunner nodded. 'Fair point.'

'Speaking of McAnally, how much did you pay him?'

'What?'

'He was working for you, feeding you information, I'm assuming he was paid.'

'He didn't give us anything of relevance. We gave him a few pounds here and there, nothing more.'

Rebus was seeing Tresa McAnally's flat in his mind: new door, new décor, new TV.

'Does it matter?'

'It did to Wee Shug,' Rebus said quietly. Someone had given him the money, money he'd passed on to Tresa, almost like life insurance. Who did Wee Shug know with money apart from his cell-mate?

Gunner finished his drink. 'I wonder what Sir Iain will be up to tonight.'

'The way he was tucking into the hooch, sleeping it off, I'd imagine. Does he drive to Edinburgh and back every day?'

'He only uses Ruthie at weekends. When he's at work, he has a flat in the New Town.'

'Whereabouts exactly?'

'Royal Circus, I think.'

Royal Circus, thought Rebus, where Haldayne collected some of his parking tickets. Life was just full of coincidences, if you happened to believe, as Rebus himself did not, in coincidence.

31

Early Sunday morning, a sleepy-eyed detective sergeant from Lothian and Borders Police Headquarters turned up at Rebus's flat.

'You'd better give me a hand,' he said.

Rebus followed him down to where a patrol car idled kerbside. He peered in through the passenger-side window.

'Maybe we'd better hire a winch.'

It took them four trips to transfer the boxes from the car to Rebus's living room. Rebus put the binbags behind the sofa to make room on the floor.

'Sign here,' the DS said. He had a typed chitty: RECEIPT OF ALL CASE-NOTES (8 BOXES) CONCERNING DERWOOD CHARTERS. Rebus signed.

'Date and time, too,' said the DS.

'You'll be wanting a tip next,' Rebus muttered.

'If you're offering.'

'Well, here's one for you: when lifting, bend your knees, not your back.'

He phoned Siobhan Clarke.

'Why me?' she said.

'Because Brian Holmes has a home life.'

'That could be construed as discrimination. When do you want me there?'

'Say an hour.'

He tidied the living room a bit, depositing the binbags in the hall and setting the file boxes in a row on the floor. Then he collected up all the dirty mugs, glasses and dishes and took them through to the kitchen. He emptied the coffee-jar and put it back under the radiator, and opened the living-room window an inch to air the place. The sun was out, showing that the windows hadn't been cleaned since the autumn. Rebus decided enough was enough.

'She's coming here to work,' he told himself, 'not for a candlelit supper.'

They got two breaks, both late in the afternoon.

The first was a client's name: Quinlon.

'I've come across that name before,' Rebus said. It took him a while to place it. 'The civil servant, Rory McAllister, he mentioned someone called Quinlon; a building contractor. There'd been some shady business between the SDA and him – it was one of the things held against the SDA when they were deciding its fate.' Rebus flipped back a page in the notes. 'And Charters' client happened to be a building contractor.'

'So?'

'So, somehow the media got to hear about the SDA and Quinlon, and that story helped sink the SDA. Who was going to gain by the SDA's demise?'

'Charters?'

'Yes, because the financial slate was going to be wiped clean, and there'd be no possibility of a future investigation into where the SDA millions had gone.'

'You think Charters grassed on his client?'

'I wouldn't put anything past him.'

The second break came soon after.

It was clear from the case-notes that the Fraud Unit had been focusing on Charters. When his 'associates' were mentioned, they were dismissed as fronts or moneymen. Nobody thought the directors had anything to do with whatever swindles Charters was perpetrating.

Which was why they weren't mentioned often, and in the case of Mensung, not at all. But then Rebus picked up the photocopy of a letter sent by Charters to the SDA. The Mensung logo was at the top, together with the non-existent Leith Walk address – referred to as 'Mensung House'. At the foot of the letter was the company's registration number.

'You couldn't find Mensung in Companies House, right?'

'Right,' said Clarke. 'I had their archivist take a good look.'

'Well, either they were registered, or this is a phony number.'

'The records could have been mislaid.'

'Now wouldn't *that* be a coincidence.' The final line of the sheet was blurred. Rebus peered at the row of names, the names of Mensung's directors.

Because he knew what he was looking for, he could pick out the name Charters quite easily; the others were more difficult. It took real effort to decipher J Joseph Simpson's name.

'Figures,' Rebus said. He wanted another word with Simpson anyway, but this explained why he'd lied about Mensung's address: the company had been dodgy, under investigation, and Simpson had been a director. It wasn't the kind of thing you wanted to publicise when you were still in business.

As for the third and last name . . .

'Can you make that out?' Rebus asked, passing the sheet to Siobhan Clarke.

'Starts with an M,' she suggested. 'Murchieson?'

'Murchieson?'

'I don't know, maybe Matthews, something like that.'

Rebus took the sheet back from her. Matthews . . . Murchieson . . . 'Mathieson,' he said, staring at the slewed writing. 'Could it be Mathieson?'

She shrugged. 'As in . . .?'

'I met a man yesterday called Robbie Mathieson. He runs PanoTech.'

'Silicon Glen's homegrown success story?'

Rebus nodded. 'We've all just been supplied with PanoTech computers, haven't we?'

'Everybody from the chief constable down.'

Which meant that Allan Gunner would have one, too. 'Who do you suppose would decide something like that?'

'Like what?'

'Like which manufacturer was going to supply us?'

'It would be the director of Corporate Services, wouldn't it?'

'But the DCC would have a say.'

'Probably. Is it relevant?'

Rebus wondered. PanoTech put the computers together in Gyle Park West, and Gyle Part West was one of Councillor Gillespie's files. Mensung was another. There was the story that Derry Charters had something to do with the early financing of PanoTech. And PanoTech's boss just happened to be at Sir Iain Hunter's, looking worried about something. And Allan Gunner was there too . . .

Wheels within wheels, he thought. Scotland was a machine, a big machine if you looked at it from the outside. But from the inside, it assumed a new form – small, intimate, not that many moving parts, and all of them interconnected quite intricately. Rebus knew he was still outside the machine, but he knew now that one reason why he'd been invited to the shooting party was that Sir Iain Hunter was inviting him in. They could make him part of the machine, a chip on the motherboard. All it took was friends in the right places.

After that, anything could happen.

They worked solidly till five-thirty.

'I hope I'm being treated to dinner,' Clarke said, stretching her spine.

'Who's taking you?'

'You are,' she said.

Rebus shook his head. 'I've other plans tonight, sorry.'

'Well, thanks a lot. I give up my precious Sunday to help you, and then you boot me out.' She narrowed her eyes. 'Got a date?'

She was attempting a peculiarly Scottish tactic: being serious while pretending levity.

'I'm working,' Rebus said.

'Working?'

'I've got to talk to someone.'

'Anyone I know?'

Rebus shook his head. 'But don't think I don't appreciate your help.' He saw her to the door.

When the bell rang two minutes later, he thought she must have forgotten something. But it wasn't Siobhan Clarke standing on his doorstep. It was Gill Templer.

'Mind if I come in?' she said, walking past him.

'I was just on my way out.'

'This won't take long. I tried phoning, but it was engaged all afternoon.'

'I had it off the hook,' Rebus said, following her into the living room. She looked at the boxes of documents.

'I see you're really taking your furlough seriously.'

'Come on, Gill, it was foisted on me. You were there, remember.'

'I remember. The chief super had been getting incredible flak; in his shoes, I'd have done the same thing.'

'This isn't sounding like a social call.'

'That's because it isn't one. The Lord Provost is your latest victim. He called the chief super and said you'd been rude to him.'

'Did he mention specifics?'

'No.'

'I didn't think he would.'

'The Farmer will probably call you in the morning himself. I'd imagine it'll be an official reprimand, maybe even a suspension.' She turned to him, her eyes blazing. 'How could you do this to me?'

'What?'

'I'm your immediate superior! I'm in the post barely a week, and already you've caused the most unholy ructions. How do you think that makes me look?'

'It's got nothing to do with you.'

'Yes it bloody well has! It's got *everything* to do with me. You're one of my officers. How am I supposed to work, to get a feel for the job, when all the chief super does is fret about what grenade you're going to chuck next?'

Rebus nodded his understanding. 'That's what this is about. You're pissed off because the Farmer's not paying you enough attention. You want to create a good impression, and you're not making any impression at all.'

'Now you're just twisting my words.'

'Am I?' He grabbed her by the arms. 'Look me in the face and tell me that. Tell me I'm not right.'

She shrugged free of his grip. 'John,' she said, more calmly. 'I came here to warn you. Tomorrow morning could spell the end of your career.'

'You think I care about that?' He tried to sound casual.

She took a step towards him. 'Yes,' she said quietly, 'I think you do.' Her green eyes seemed to bore into him. 'I think, beneath it all, you're scared.'

'Scared?' He smiled. 'Of course I'm scared. I wouldn't mind if it was some big hard bastard who had me cornered in an alley, or if some kind of contract was out on me. But this is worse, this scares me to death.'

'Then drop it. Say you're sorry to a few people, and come back to work.'

He smiled again. 'It would be that easy, wouldn't it? You'd do it.'

'Yes, I would.'

'Well, I'll think about it.'

She tried to measure his sincerity, but it was like measuring haar.

32

Big Jim Flett was nowhere to be seen.

'Even the Big Man has to take a few hours off here and there,' his deputy said, leading Rebus down one of the corridors inside Saughton Jail.

'I'm sure,' Rebus said, even though he was sure the governor was avoiding him. He had lied to Rebus, and now Rebus knew it.

'Derry doesn't get many visitors,' the deputy said. He was a brisk, nervous man, ruddy-faced and jacketless with his shirt-sleeves rolled up.

'You know him then?'

'We've had conversations.'

'I was told he didn't mix.'

'That's true, but I've always found him pleasant enough.'

'He hasn't tried to sell you anything, has he?'

The deputy laughed. 'No, not yet. He'd make a damned good salesman though.'

'What's he like?'

'Quiet for the most part, never gives us any trouble.' They were nearing a metal door, beside which stood a warden. The warden unlocked the door and swung it open.

'You're sure you don't want me to stay?' the deputy asked Rebus. Rebus shook his head, but with a gracious smile. 'Well, Munro here will take Derry back to his cell when you're finished.'

'Thanks again,' Rebus said.

The door closed after him, the key rattling in its lock. Rebus was alone with Derwood Charters.

Charters was pacing the floor, arms folded, head bowed as if he was pondering some problem.

'Do you play chess?' Charters asked, without looking up.

'No.'

'Pity.'

Rebus looked around the room. There was a table, its legs bolted to the floor, and two chairs beside it. On one wall, a blackboard provided the room's only hint of decoration.

'Mind if I sit?' Rebus said.

'Make yourself comfortable.' Charters smiled at his little joke. He continued to pace the floor, and Rebus studied him. Charters was in his mid-forties, tall and broad-shouldered. He was immaculately groomed, his hair parted just so, his face shiny and clean-shaven. His fingernails looked manicured.

'Do you know what *zugzwang* means?'

'Sounds German,' Rebus said.

For the first time, Charters looked at him. 'Of course it's German. It's a chess position. It's when you've to play, only any move you make will spell disaster. Yet you've got to make a move. There was a chess puzzle in today's paper, and I'm damned if I can solve it.'

'The solution's easy,' Rebus said.

Charters stopped pacing. 'What?'

'Take up golf instead.'

Charters considered this, then smiled. He came and sat down opposite Rebus, folding his hands on the table. 'May I see some identification?'

Rebus took out his warrant card. Charters examined it against the light, as though it might represent a particularly brilliant forgery.

'On a Sunday night,' he said, handing it back.

'Pardon?'

'I don't get many visitors, let alone on a Sunday night. And a police officer at that.'

'I'm here to ask you a few questions about Wee Shug McAnally.'

'Ah yes, Hugh.' McAnally probably hadn't been called 'Hugh' by anyone apart from the minister at his christening and the judge who pronounced sentence on him. Charters seemed to read Rebus's mind. 'I respect a person's name, Inspector. It's all we bring into this world, and it's all we take out of it. My own name is sometimes abbreviated to Derry. In here, that has earned me the nickname "the apprentice boy".'

Charters' voice – quiet, atonal – had a mesmeric quality, and once his eyes had fixed on Rebus's, they never left them.

'You know he committed suicide, Mr Charters?'

'Very unfortunate.'

'Suicides have to be investigated.'

'I didn't know that.'

'Whether you know it or not, it happens to be the case. Tell me, did McAnally talk to you much?'

'All the time. To be frank, it annoyed me. Even when I was trying to read, he'd be blathering on about nothing of consequence, just filling the cell with noise. As though there wasn't enough noise in here already. At the start, I thought he'd been allotted my cell as some subtle form of punishment. You know, psychological torture.'

'So what did he talk about? I'm assuming these were fairly one-sided affairs?'

'They were soliloquys. As to the substance ... he talked about his background, his wife – interminably about his wife; I feel I know her as well as her gynaecologist must. He spoke of his affairs with other women, which I didn't believe for one second. And every time he finished a story, he'd ask me, *plead* with me, to tell him something about myself.' Charters paused. 'What do you make of that, Inspector? I mean, Hugh was obsessed with himself, and yet every now and then he'd suddenly stop and ask me something. Don't you think that's strange?'

Rebus ignored the question. 'What was he in for?'

'You see? You've avoided answering! That's what I had to do twenty times a day.'

'Are you going to answer?'

'He told me it was for housebreaking.'

'And I believe you're inside for fraud, is that correct?'

'Interesting,' Charters mused, patting his fingers against his mouth. 'Why would you ask me what Hugh was inside for?'

'I just wondered,' Rebus improvised, 'if the two of you ever talked about it. I'm trying to build up a picture of him.'

'To hazard a guess as to why he killed himself?'

'Yes.'

'Well, obviously he killed himself because he was dying of cancer.'

'Did he tell you that?'

Charters smiled again. 'I'm only guessing.'

'Well, you're probably right, that's probably why he did kill himself. What it doesn't explain is the manner.'

'You mean, why would he pick on a city councillor to witness his last rites?' Rebus nodded. 'Have you tried asking the councillor?'

'Yes.'

'And what did he say?' Charters was trying to sound casually curious. Rebus stared at him.

'Do you know the councillor?' he asked.

'Never met him.'

'That's not what I asked.'

Charters sat back and folded his arms. 'Now you're learning subtlety, Inspector. Our contest can only improve.'

'It's not a game of chess, Mr Charters.'

Charters looked penitent. 'Of course not, I'm sorry.'

'Do you know the councillor?' Rebus repeated.

'I read newspapers, Inspector, I keep up with events. So to a certain extent, yes, I *know* Councillor Gillespie.'

'And does he know you?'

'Why should he?'

It was Rebus's turn to smile. Charters had used the word 'subtlety'. Rebus was learning that he must needs be oblique.

'You ran a company called Mensung, didn't you?'

'A long time ago, yes.' Rebus noticed that though he was outwardly well groomed, Charters's teeth were the colour of dead fish. 'I like these tangents, Inspector. Your mind moves in mysterious ways. Difficult to *zugzwang* someone who plays so erratically. Why are you interested in a company I wound up seven years ago?'

'I told a friend of mine I was coming to speak to you. He said he attended some retraining seminars held by Mensung on Corstorphine Road.'

The response seemed to satisfy Charters. 'Which company did he work for?'

'He didn't say. He still works in electronics, for one of PanoTech's subcontractors.'

'Then maybe the seminars did him some good.'

Rebus nodded. 'I heard a story that you helped finance PanoTech when the company was in its infancy.'

Charters raised an eyebrow. 'Stories tend to become confused over time.'

'You'd nothing to do with it then?' Charters shook his head. 'By the way, why did Mensung go bust?'

'It didn't "go bust" – I wound it up. I was bored with it, and couldn't find anyone to buy me out.' He shrugged. 'I'm easily bored.' He got up and started pacing the room again. 'You know, Inspector, you told me you were here to ask a few questions about Hugh. We've strayed a long way from that particular topic, wouldn't you say?'

Rebus stood up.

'Going so soon?'

'You're enjoying yourself too much, *Derry*. This isn't supposed to be fun. A man's dead.'

Charters stopped pacing. 'A man who was dying anyway. A man who chose his own route out. Luckier than most of us, I'd wager. If the doctors told me I had only a few agonising months to live, I think I'd go find myself a gun, too. But the world would look so unfair to my eyes – all those people so alive and vibrant around me, all those ill people being cured in hospitals – maybe I'd want a witness to the injustice of it all, someone representing authority in my eyes and the eyes of those around me. Maybe I'd want him to *see* my agony, to share in my horror. It would have to be an easy target though ... and a councillor is such an easy target – accessible, public, approachable. I'd be making a point to the world. I would *refuse* to die in silence!'

The silence after Charters had finished was resonant. He had worked himself up to a pitch, and now calmed only slowly. There had been anger in his voice, and fervour, and conviction. His eyes were on Rebus's. *He'd make a damned good salesman.*

'I don't buy it,' Rebus said, going to the door.

'Inspector.' Rebus paused. 'You called me "Derry" – that was a cheap shot. Apart from that, you did pretty well.' He paced the floor again. 'Hugh didn't really talk about his wife that often. There was another woman ... he described her so accurately, I could probably paint her for you even now. Her name was Maisie. He talked about her all the time. I think he loved her more than anyone in the world. Perhaps you should talk to her.'

'I already have, Mr Charters.'

Rebus left the cell feeling that Charters had given a name to his own feelings about the investigation, Willie and Dixie, and life in general.

The word was *zugzwang*.

It was four a.m. when his phone rang. He came awake, but left it to ring. Four a.m., news just had to be bad. The caller persisted, and at last Rebus picked up the receiver.

'Mr Rebus?'

A young voice, insolent, a bit drunk. Loud music and voices in the background: a party.

'Yes?'

'It's Paul. Paul Duggan.'

'Paul, nice of you to call.'

'Is it late? I don't have my watch on.'

'It sounds like a great party, Paul. Give me the address and I'll drop by with a few uniforms.'

'Don't be like that, Mr Rebus. I bring glad tidings. I've found her.'

'Kirstie Kennedy?'

'Aye.'

'Is she all right?'

'Not bad for a junkie.'

'Can I speak to her?'

'Listen, she's adamant she's not going home. She says her stepmum's a lunatic.'

'I'd like to see her. There's no question of her having to go home.'

'I don't know.' Duggan sounded doubtful.

'Paul, don't hang up! Listen, would she talk to me if I paid her?'

'Look, I'll have a word with her. No promises, but I'll have a word, see what she says.'

'Just do me a favour. Phone in daylight next time.'

'If you're lucky, I might even phone when I'm sober.'

33

It was eight a.m. when his phone next rang.

'Yes?' he croaked, trying to find some saliva in his mouth.

'John?' It was the Farmer's voice.

Here it comes, thought Rebus. 'Morning, sir. What's it to be – reprimand, suspension, or dismissal?'

'Damn you, John. I had a hell of a weekend because of you.'

'I'm sorry, sir. I never meant to get you into trouble.'

'That's your problem, Inspector – you're selfish, no other word for it. I think you know damned well that these obsessions of yours end up damaging everyone around you, friend, foe and civilians alike.'

'Yes, sir.'

'But it doesn't bother you, does it?' Rebus didn't answer. The Farmer had obviously been preparing his speech for a while. 'As long as your own personal morality is satisfied, that's all that counts. Sod everybody else, isn't that right?'

'It feels that way sometimes, sir,' Rebus said quietly.

'Well, maybe you should consider that morality of yours, because it's no code *I'd* want to live with.'

'You don't have to live with it, sir. I do.'

'Well, you lead a charmed existence, that's all I can say.'

Rebus frowned. 'How do you mean?'

'I've discussed things with the DCC. He said he'd apologise to the Lord Provost on your behalf. He also said he thought HMIC would be investigating F Troop instead of us.'

F Troop: meaning F Division, Livingston. 'What are you saying, sir?'

'I'm saying I want you back here. The holiday's over. Report to my office this morning.'

'I've a dentist's appointment.'

'Well, this afternoon then.'

'Yes, sir.'

'Look, John, have you and the DCC had any contact?'

'I've been on holiday, sir.'

'Yes, but all the same?'

'Well, maybe I did bump into him by the pool . . .'

It was another grim day. No snow or ice, but a freezing wind and gusts of rain, the sky oppressively weighted with cloud. It was like the city was in a box, and someone had pushed the lid on too tightly.

Rebus's second visit to Dr Keene wasn't so traumatic. You could get used to anything. The tooth had drained nicely, and Keene did the root canal while Rebus concentrated on the photograph on the ceiling. He plotted Paul Duggan's property portfolio. Maybe Duggan had a point: nobody was suggesting he was overcharging his 'tenants' – he was making a profit out of each house and flat, but nothing outrageous. And meantime, he was putting roofs over heads. Rebus knew there might needs be a trade-off: if he wanted to see Kirstie, Duggan might want Rebus to put in a good word come trial time. Always supposing it came to trial. The district council was about to be replaced with another body. Who knew what would be written off?

Suddenly, something clicked in Rebus's brain. He saw something he should have seen before. He was so busy thinking that he didn't hear Dr Keene say that, while Rebus was there, he might as well start on the fillings . . .

There were no cheers, no banners or bunting as Rebus walked back into St Leonard's and poured himself a cup of coffee.

'A word to the wise,' Siobhan Clarke said.

'What?'

'You're pouring coffee down your tie.'

It was true: with his mouth still numb, he was dribbling. He went to the toilets and pulled out a clump of paper towels, soaked them in water and dabbed at his tie.

'Here he is,' said Flower, pushing open the door, 'the proverbial bad penny.'

'Don't be so hard on yourself,' Rebus retorted. Flower came to the sink and checked his hair in the mirror. 'I see you managed to start a fire, then take credit for putting it out.'

Flower chuckled. 'Word gets around, eh?'

'Speaking of words that get around, I had a chat with someone about your snitch.'

'Which one?'

'Shug McAnally. We could all have been spared some grief if you'd told me at the start he was working for you.'

'It's not the sort of thing you can publicise. I mean,' Flower looked around, 'planting a snitch in somebody's cell.'

'You don't mind telling me now though. Has the DCC had a word?'

'He said you'd been asking.' Flower looked unnaturally pleased with himself. Rebus could guess why.

'You think you're quids-in with the DCC, don't you?'

'Well, if it ever came out about McAnally, the DCC could get into trouble.' Flower winked. 'He needs to keep me sweet.'

'What you mean is, you've got him either way. If the plan succeeded, it'd be because of you. If it went badly, it would need covering up – which would take your help. Gunner would still owe you. That's why you've been blocking me: you didn't want me getting to the DCC – he's your little investment.'

Flower chuckled again, and tucked a stray hair back behind his ear. There was a sound of flushing from one of the two cubicles. Flower's head

jerked around, his mouth open, as the cubicle door opened and the Farmer came out.

This came as no surprise to Rebus: he'd seen the Farmer enter the toilets just before him.

'Morning, sir,' he said.

Flower didn't say anything. The Farmer pointed at him. 'My office, Inspector Flower, *now*!' Then he opened the door and was gone. Flower turned on Rebus.

'You knew! You bloody well knew!'

Rebus tossed the ball of sodden paper into the bin.

One-nil.

Someone was at the front desk asking for him, that was the message. But when Rebus got there, there was nobody about. Then he saw a figure outside, motioning to him. It was Paul Duggan. He was wearing his long black coat again, but it had a small tear in the sleeve, and a white smudge on one shoulder.

'Nothing personal like,' he said when Rebus joined him outside, 'but I hate police stations.'

'There's a café across –'

Duggan was shaking his head. 'She's waiting for us.'

'Kirstie?' Duggan nodded. 'Where?'

'Have you got a car?'

They went to Rebus's car.

Duggan directed him down the Pleasance and right on Holyrood Road. This was a dispiriting part of town; all empty sites and disused warehouses. The Younger Universe was under construction, and was going to make everything all right again, if you believed the publicity. Rebus hoped it would succeed; he liked the symbolism: the USA had Disneyland, and Scotland gets a theme park built by a brewery. The theme park would be a neighbour to Holyrood Palace, the monarch's Edinburgh residence. This, too, Rebus liked.

'Where are we going?'

'Just park by the palace gates.'

It was easy to park this time of year; in warmer seasons, the place was a log-jam of tourist coaches. A kid was at the locked gates, peering through them at the palace beyond.

'Toot your horn,' Duggan ordered. Rebus did so, to no effect.

'She's on another planet.' Duggan wound down his window. 'Hiy, Kirstie!'

Slowly the 'kid' turned, and Rebus saw a face older than the frame which supported it. Nobody had said Kirstie Kennedy would be so scrawny, so tiny. But as she walked towards the car her face was set like cement. Lipstick, eyeshadow and panstick provided her with a mask. She wore tight black jeans, accentuating her matchstick legs, and a long shapeless black jumper whose arms stretched down past her hands. Her hair was greasy, shoulder-length, tied back with a band. A spiky fringe, dyed blood-red, fell into her eyes. She was chewing gum. She pulled open the back door and climbed in.

'Hello, Kirstie,' Rebus said. 'Where do you want to go?'

'I want ice cream.'

Rebus thought of Luca's, but it was too far. 'Tollcross?' he suggested. Tollcross would do her.

They sat in the ice-cream parlour and she ordered the biggest concoction on the menu, plus a giant Coke. The place was quiet: an old couple, smoking and drinking frothy coffee; a harassed mother hissing at her two children who were arguing over bowls of garish ice cream.

Rebus had ordered coffee, Duggan orange juice and some apple pie with cream. Rebus remembered that he used to bring Sammy in here when she was a kid. He looked at the Lord Provost's daughter and tried to remember she was seventeen.

'Paul says you want a word.' Her voice was polite in a way no attitude could hide. Rebus knew that her street diction, her low-class language, had been only recently learned.

'How long have you been on the Bob Hope, Kirstie?'

'You mean the Merry?'

Duggan looked at Rebus. 'Merry Mac, crack,' he explained.

'Long enough,' Kirstie answered.

'Long enough to be tired of it?'

'Long enough to know you never get tired of it.' Her ice cream arrived: three different flavours with chocolate sauce, nuts, tinned peaches and wafers. The sight of it made Rebus's teeth crackle.

'Your dad's been worried,' he said.

'So what?'

'And your mum.'

Her sudden convulsion almost sent a mouthful of ice cream on to the table. 'My mum died when I was five. What you mean is, "that woman who lives with my dad".'

'OK.'

'Have you met her?'

'No.'

'She's off her trolley, praise the Lord.'

'So you don't get on with her. Is that why you ran away?'

'Does there have to be a reason?'

Rebus shrugged. 'Only, most teenagers I know who run away, they go a bit further.'

'You mean London? I didn't like it. My pals are all up here.'

'You mean pals like Willie and Dixie?'

She put the spoon back on her plate and started on the Coke. 'I liked Willie. Dixie was a nutter, you never knew what he'd do next, but Willie was all right.'

'You heard what they did?'

She nodded.

'You left that wreath for them on the bridge, didn't you?'

Another nod. She dipped her finger into the chocolate sauce. She was trying not to care, but there was still a core of sentiment buried in her brain, a precious nugget of guilt.

'Was it your idea, Kirstie?' She looked up at him. 'It was, wasn't it?'

She got to her feet. 'I have to go to the toilet.'

Rebus snatched her wrist. 'Why did you do it, Kirstie? Just for the money? Why did you take the LABarum plans from your father's office?'

She shook free of his grip. 'Let me go!' She stumbled away from the table and ran to the toilets. Rebus sat back and started to light a cigarette.

'No smoking,' the waitress told him.

'Can I get a beer?'

'We're not licensed.'

Rebus nicked his cigarette and put it back in the packet. He looked across the table at Paul Duggan.

'You like her, don't you?' Rebus said.

Duggan said nothing. He was making circles in the cream with his spoon.

'Remember I told you she'd left something in Willie's bedroom? It was some papers stolen from her father. Do you have any idea why she took them?'

Duggan shook his head slowly but determinedly. 'She's . . . go easy on her, OK?'

'Or what?'

'Or she'll run.' Duggan paused. 'Again.'

Eventually the toilet door opened and she walked back to the table, arms hanging in a lazy slouch. Rebus looked into her eyes and saw pupils shrunk to pinheads.

'That was stupid.'

'So what?' she said, starting back into her ice cream. After two mouthfuls, she pushed the plate away.

'The kidnap,' Rebus said, 'the ransom demand – it was all your idea, wasn't it?'

'Yes.'

'To get back at your stepmother?'

'My dad.'

'To get back at your dad?'

She nodded. 'And everything he represents, the old bastard.' She was much more together now, more confident. She didn't care what she told him.

'You know you committed an offence?' Rebus asked.

'I'd deny it in court. I'd deny it everywhere. Where's the proof that it wasn't just two wee boys with a daft scheme in their heads?'

'There's corroboration.' Rebus glanced towards Duggan.

'You think Paul would grass on me?' She leaned into Duggan's shoulder and stroked his face. 'He wouldn't do that.'

'Not even if I offered him a deal on his slum landlord scam?'

Kirstie shook her head. 'Paul wouldn't hurt me. His mum likes me too much.'

'Well, maybe I don't need Paul. Maybe all I need is that LABarum document. It links you to Willie.' He paused. 'Did you write "Dalgety" on the last page?' She nodded. 'Why?'

'It's something I heard my dad say on the phone . . . when I was listening in. Dalgety sounded important, someone he was worried about.'

'Dalgety's a person then?'

'Yes.'

'Kirstie, *why* did you steal the LABarum plan?'

Her face creased in a sneer. 'It's my dad, don't you see? If you look closely enough at it, if you read all the small print and between the lines, all you'll find there is my dad's face, smiling smugly back at you.'

'Why is he smug?'

'Because it's going to make him a hero. And it's all crooked. I heard him on the phone, they were talking about how to cover it all up. The whole fucking thing is just a lot of . . . a lot of . . . it's all just so much *shit*!'

'I can't have language like that,' the waitress warned. 'There are children in here.'

'Well, fuck them!' Kirstie screeched, jumping to her feet. 'Because they're all fucked anyway, just like everybody else!'

'I'll have to ask you to leave.'

Rebus and Duggan were on their feet too.

'Come on, Kirstie.'

'That girl's on drugs or something, I know it!'

Rebus threw money down on the table. Kirstie Kennedy's legs had buckled, and Duggan was holding her upright.

'Let's get her into the car,' Rebus said, knowing he should take her straight to St Leonard's, angry with himself because he knew that was the last thing he was going to do.

Instead, Duggan gave him directions back to where she was staying. It was a flat in Leith, in the maze of narrow roads behind Great Junction Street.

'One of yours, is it?' Rebus asked Duggan. But Duggan was busy stroking Kirstie's forehead, even though she was asleep.

They walked her up the stairs, one on either side, arms around her back, her arms over their shoulders. Rebus could feel the swell of a small breast, and the thin ribcage beneath.

'You did say you wanted to see her,' Duggan was saying, exculpating himself.

'And I'll want to see her again.' He knew there was more she could tell him, more he needed to hear from her.

He was trying to figure out who or what was responsible for the deaths of Willie and Dixie. This weightless creature he carried? The lads themselves? The police for giving chase? The Lord Provost for agreeing to it all? Maybe even the stepmother for driving Kirstie away? Except that it hadn't just been the stepmother, it had been some realisation about the Lord Provost himself . . .

Maybe it was the system, that same system Sammy so passionately attacked. A system that had failed Willie and Dixie as surely as it nurtured people like Sir Iain Hunter and Robbie Mathieson. In nature, there had to be balance; as some rose, others fell or were pushed or made the leap for themselves.

Or maybe . . . just maybe it had been Rebus himself, for crawling from the wreckage still with the need to confront them . . . standing there in front of them, forcing *them* to choose. My obsession, he thought. My private morality. Maybe the Farmer was right . . .

'Will you stay with her?' he asked Duggan when they reached the top of the stairs.

Duggan nodded. Rebus knew she'd be all right. She had someone who'd look after her.

'What about you?' Duggan asked. 'What are you going to do?'

But Rebus had released his hold on the body and was heading back downstairs.

*

He went into a dive he knew near the foot of Leith Walk. It had a burgundy linoleum floor and matching coloured walls, and was like staring into somebody's throat.

'Whisky,' Rebus said. 'A double.'

And when the whisky came, he drank it down in two gulps.

'Know something?' he said to the closest drinker. 'A couple of days ago, I was eating wild smoked salmon and shooting clay-pigeons.'

'Better that than the other way round, son,' the elderly drinker said, adjusting the cap on his head.

That night, Mrs Cochrane came upstairs to tell him there was a small dark patch on her living-room ceiling. Rebus had forgotten to empty the coffee-jar. Water had soaked the bare floorboard beneath.

'Wait till it's dried out,' he said by way of apology, 'and I'll touch up the paintwork.'

He'd been asleep in his chair, but now felt wide awake. It was half past eleven, too late to do anything. Then the telephone rang, and he picked it up.

'I'm not interested,' he said.

'You'll be interested in this.'

Rebus recognised the voice of DC Robert Burns. 'Don't tell me West End needs my help?'

'We're not that desperate. I just thought I'd do you a favour. Looks like we've got a murder.'

Rebus's grip tightened on the receiver. 'Anyone I know?'

'Identification near the body suggests the name's Thomas Gillespie.'

'*Councillor* Gillespie?'

'I haven't told you the best part yet. He was found in a lane connecting Dundee Street to Dalry Road.'

Rebus tried to fix the geography. 'Next to the cemetery?'

'Yes. The lane's called Coffin Walk.'

Coffin Walk climbed quite steeply from Dalry Road. It had the busy Western Approach Road on one side, Dalry Cemetery on the other. It was a narrow alley, well lit but long.

'If someone stopped you halfway,' Burns told Rebus, leading him down the lane, 'there'd be no escape.'

'But you'd see an attacker, wouldn't you? There's no place to hide.'

Burns nodded at the cemetery wall. 'You could stand behind there, listen for someone coming, then jump over when they got close. It's the perfect site for an ambush.'

'You think that's what this was?'

Burns shrugged. They were close to the body now. Police officers with torches were in the cemetery, looking for footprints and the murder weapon. The lane had been sealed off at both ends, and though there was a knot of policemen near the body, the only person actually next to it was the pathologist, Professor Gates. Gates was telling the photographer what to do, and DI Davidson was talking to the undertaker. Even in mufti – padded jacket and jeans rather than the black suit – an undertaker was recognisable.

'So what happened?' Rebus asked Burns.

'Somebody came out of the Diggers, walked up Angle Park Terrace,

looked down here, and saw the body. They thought it was a tramp sleeping rough. Well, there's a night shelter on Gorgie Road, so the guy came down here to say so.'

'Like a good citizen.'

'He saw the blood, knew fine well what had happened, and called us.'

Rebus pointed to a wallet, which lay a couple of feet from the body. 'That was lying there?'

'Yep, driver's licence, blood donor card . . .'

'But no cash or credit cards?'

'Cleaned out.'

'And nobody saw the attack?'

'My guess is, he hoofed it back over the wall.'

Professor Gates had finished his initial examination. 'We can wrap this one up,' he said.

But Rebus wanted a look first. Tom Gillespie lay in a protective foetal position. He hadn't been dead when he dropped. He'd curled himself around the pain in his gut.

'Stab wound,' Professor Gates said. 'The shock probably killed him.'

'Has his widow been notified?'

'Are you volunteering, John?' Davidson said.

'This isn't my patch, remember.'

'No, but you knew the deceased. Anything you want to tell us?'

Rebus shook his head. 'I will ask a question though: what was he doing here? He lives in Marchmont, chances are he'd never even heard of Coffin Walk. God knows I hadn't. So why was he here, where was he headed?'

'Maybe the Diggers.'

The Diggers was actually the Athletic Arms pub, but got its nickname from the gravediggers who'd used it in the past.

'Not much of a shortcut, is it?'

'Not much,' Davidson agreed. 'Lots of questions, John.'

'I know the way your mind works, Davidson. You think it's a simple mugging gone wrong – assailant: unknown; motive: robbery.'

'So let's hear your theory.'

Rebus smiled. His head was full of theories. Maybe too many for his own good. 'Give me a cigarette,' he said.

'Not at the locus, John,' Davidson warned. Rebus looked at the body again. It was being bagged. A trip to the mortuary first, and then the funeral parlour, your last journeys in the world as predictable as your first.

'I asked if you had a theory,' Davidson said.

'OK, OK.' Rebus put his hands up in surrender. 'Take me back to your nice warm police station, give me a cigarette, and I'll tell you a story. Just don't blame me if it doesn't make sense.'

He would tell Davidson what he knew, which wasn't half as much as he suspected.

Which itself wasn't half as much as he feared.

34

Next morning, when DI Davidson went to the widow's house, Rebus went with him.

The curtains were closed, reminding Rebus of the day of McAnally's funeral, inside Tresa's flat. The door was answered not by Mrs Gillespie but by Helena Profitt, dressed in circumspect black – skirt, tights and shoes – and a plain white blouse.

'I came as soon as I heard,' she said, leading them inside. She looked surprised to see Rebus. We must, he thought, stop meeting like this.

'Two policemen to see you, Audrey,' Miss Profitt said, opening the living-room door.

It was a big light room, with prominence given to the floor-to-ceiling bookcases which lined two walls. The TV didn't look much used, and though there was a video machine, Rebus couldn't see more than half a dozen tapes. At one end of the room was a huge desk covered in paperwork, and a small table supporting a telephone and fax machine. The room, it seemed to him, was little more than an extension of the office at the front of the house, making Rebus wonder about Gillespie's family life or, more pertinently, the lack of it.

His widow sat on the sofa, legs tucked beneath her. She'd started to rise, but Davidson had waved her back down. She looked as if she hadn't slept. There was an empty mug on the floor, and next to it a tiny brown bottle of tablets. Despite the central heating, Audrey Gillespie was trembling.

'Shall I make some tea?' Helena Profitt asked.

'Not for us, thanks,' Davidson said.

'Well, I'll leave you to it. Shall I pop back later, Audrey?'

'Only if it's not too much trouble.'

'Of course not.' Her eyes were red-rimmed from crying. Rebus saw through her act, saw she was as broken up as anyone. He followed her out of the room.

'Could you wait in the kitchen? I'd like a quick word.'

She nodded hesitantly. Rebus went back into the living room and sat down next to Davidson.

'Remember me, Mrs Gillespie?' Davidson was saying. 'We met last night.'

Davidson was good, better than a lot of coppers. It was a skill, handling other people's grief, gauging what to say and how to say it, knowing how much they could take.

Audrey Gillespie nodded, then looked at Rebus. 'And I know you, too, don't I?'

'I came to talk to your husband once.' Rebus strived for the same tone Davidson had used.

'Has the doctor seen you, Mrs Gillespie?' Davidson asked.

'He gave me pills to help me sleep. Ridiculous to think I could sleep.'

'But you're all right?'

'I'm . . .' She sought the words expected of her. 'I'm coping, thank you.'

'Do you feel up to answering a few more questions?'

She nodded, and Davidson relaxed a little. He brought out his notebook and consulted it.

'Now,' he said, 'you said last night that your husband had gone out to visit a constituent – that was what he told you?'

'Yes.'

'But he didn't say where he was meeting this constituent?'

'No.'

'Or the constituent's name?'

'No.'

'Or what they were going to discuss?'

She shrugged, remembering. 'We ate dinner at eight as usual – I'd done chicken casserole, Tom's favourite. He had two helpings. After that, I thought he'd either work in his office – he *always* has work to do – or else read the paper. Instead, he said he had to go out.'

'You're surprised he ended up in Dalry?'

'Very. We don't know anyone in that part of town. Why would he lie to me?'

'Well,' Rebus put in, 'he *was* hiding things from you, wasn't he?'

'What do you mean?'

Davidson gave Rebus a warning look, and Rebus softened his voice a little.

'I mean, the day I came here you were busy shredding documents – sackfuls of them – in a shredder your husband hired specially.'

'Yes, I remember. Tom said he was running out of space in the office. They were ancient history. As you can see, it's pretty cramped with all the paperwork.' She waved a hand around the room.

'Mrs Gillespie,' Rebus persisted, 'your husband headed the Industrial Planning Committee – did the documents have anything to do with that?'

'I've no idea.'

'If they were ancient history, why bother to shred them, why not just chuck them out?'

Audrey Gillespie got up and walked to the fireplace. Davidson gave Rebus an angry look.

'Tom said they could fall into the wrong hands. Journalists, people like that. He said it was to do with confidentiality.'

'Did you look at the files at all?'

'I . . . I don't remember.' She was frantic now, her wet eyes everywhere but on the two policemen.

'You weren't curious?'

'Look, I don't see what any of this has to do with *anything*.'

Rebus walked over to her and took her hands in his. 'It might have everything to do with your husband's murder, Mrs Gillespie.'

'Now, John,' Davidson complained, 'we don't know . . .'

But Audrey Gillespie looked into Rebus's eyes, and saw something there she could trust. She blinked away the tears. 'He was very secretive,' she said quietly, forcing herself to be calm. 'I mean, about whatever it was he'd been working on. He'd been at it for months – for the best part of a year, actually. I used to curse the hours he put in. He told me it would be worth it, he said we should always focus on the long view. By that he meant he would one day be an MP, it was what he lived for.'

'You've no inkling what this project of his was?'

She shook her head. 'It was something he'd discovered while serving on the committee, and I know it was to do with accounting. I could work that much out from the kinds of things he was reading – balance sheets, profit-and-loss accounts . . . I trained as an accountant, something Tom sometimes forgot. I run a string of shops now, but I still handle the books. I could have helped him, but he always had to do everything for himself.' She paused. 'You know, the only reason he really needed me was my money. I'm sorry if that sounds heartless.'

'Not at all,' Davidson said.

'Were these company accounts, Mrs Gillespie?' Rebus persisted.

'I think they must have been, the numbers involved: hundreds of millions of pounds.'

'*Hundreds* of millions?'

So it wasn't just Mensung, or even Charters' empire. It was much bigger. Rebus thought of PanoTech, and then recalled that someone else had used the phrase 'hundreds of millions' . . . Rory McAllister, or someone like him.

'Mrs Gillespie, could these figures have been to do with the SDA?'

'I don't know!' She slumped back on to the sofa.

'OK, John,' Davidson said, 'you've had your say.'

But Davidson might as well not have been there.

'You see, Mrs Gillespie,' Rebus said, sitting down beside her, 'the thing is, someone tried to scare your husband, and it worked. They paid a man called McAnally to put the fear of God into him. I don't know if they knew how far McAnally would go. McAnally confronted your husband, and I think gave him a message, a warning of some kind. Then McAnally killed himself, just to force the warning home. He was dying anyway, and he'd been paid handsomely. Your husband got scared, rightly so, and rented that shredder so he could destroy everything he'd been working on, all the evidence.'

'Evidence of what?' she asked.

'Of something very big. Now, McAnally slipped up, he died *too* spectacularly, and that got me curious. I don't think I've discovered even half what your husband knew, but that's not the point. The point is, these people suspect either that your husband was helping me – maybe he'd given me his notes – or that he would talk to me eventually. Either way, they decided he was beyond scaring. They had to go a bit further.'

'What you're saying is that, if you'd left well alone, Tom might still be alive.'

Rebus bowed his head. 'I accept what you're saying, but *I* didn't kill your husband.' He paused. 'I'd like to find out who did.'

'What can I do to help?'

Rebus glanced towards Davidson. 'You can start by telling us anything

you think might help. And you could go through your husband's papers; there might be some clue there.'

She thought for a moment. 'Will I be in danger, too?'

Rebus laid a hand on hers. 'Not at all, Mrs Gillespie. Look, is there no one Tom might have confided in?'

She started to shake her head. 'No, wait . . . there *is* someone.' Then she got up and left the room. Davidson was staring grimly at Rebus.

'See,' Rebus told him, 'you're great with the hearts and flowers, but weakness is there to be exploited.'

Davidson didn't say a word.

Audrey Gillespie carried a desk diary into the room. 'This is last year's,' she said, sitting down next to Rebus. 'Tom began all this cloak-and-dagger stuff back in May, but it only really took off in October and November.' She flipped to the pages for those months. Each day had its fill of meetings and engagements.

'See?' Mrs Gillespie said, pointing to a page. 'These meetings here. Two this week –' she flipped a couple of pages – 'two the next –' two more pages – 'then three more.'

The meetings were just a series of times, plus the same two letters – CK. 'Cameron Kennedy,' Rebus said.

'Yes.'

'Who?' Davidson asked. He'd come over to the sofa to look at the diary.

'The Lord Provost,' Mrs Gillespie explained. 'They kept meeting for lunch. I remember because Tom had to have his suits dry-cleaned; he had to look his smartest for the Lord Provost.'

'He didn't tell you why they were meeting so often?' Rebus had taken the diary from her and was flipping through it. There were no meetings with 'CK' until October, after which they took place once a week at least.

'Tom hinted there might be a good job in it come reorganisation. He's in the same political party as the Lord Provost.'

'This is interesting,' Rebus said, sitting back, the better to peruse the diary.

Davidson had some questions to ask – the usual ones – so Rebus excused himself. He found Helena Profitt seated at the kitchen table, tugging at a lace handkerchief.

'Terrible thing,' she said.

'Yes,' said Rebus, sitting down opposite her. He thought of Charters' 'subtlety', and the way Davidson had confronted the widow, and still he couldn't find an easy way to ask what he wanted to ask. 'Miss Profitt, this may not be the time . . .' She looked at him. 'But I was wondering if you knew . . . that is, if you had any suspicion that Mrs Gillespie and her husband . . .?'

'You mean,' she said softly, 'what was their marriage like?'

'Yes.'

Her face turned stony. 'That's despicable.'

'This is a *murder* inquiry, Miss Profitt. I'm sorry if I've disturbed your sensibilities, but questions must be asked. The sooner I ask them, the sooner we may catch the killer.'

She thought that over. 'You're right, I suppose. But it's still despicable.'

'Was Mrs Gillespie having an affair?'

Helena Profitt didn't say anything. She rose from the table and buttoned her coat.

'All right,' Rebus said, 'what about the Lord Provost? Did Councillor Gillespie tell you why they kept meeting?'

'Tom told me he had to brief him.'

'What about?'

'He didn't say. Something to do with the Industry Committee, I expect. Is that all, Inspector?'

Rebus nodded, and Helena Profitt walked out of the kitchen. He heard the front door open and close. I handled that beautifully, he thought.

He got back to the living room just as Davidson was closing his notebook and thanking Audrey Gillespie for her time.

'Not at all,' the widow replied, polite to the last.

Rebus and Davidson sat in the car outside, talking things over. They were pulling away when Rebus saw another car cruising the street, seeking a parking space. It was a sporty Toyota the colour of ashes.

'Stop for a second,' Rebus said. He adjusted the rearview mirror so he could watch the Toyota manoeuvre into a space. Its door opened and Rory McAllister got out, looking anxious. He locked the car, tidied his hair, and side-stepped puddles on his way to Audrey Gillespie's front door.

Rebus took Davidson to Arden Street and up the two flights to his flat.

'Got something for you,' he said, pointing to the binbags in the hall.

Davidson stared in amazement. 'The shredded documents?' Rebus nodded. 'I won't ask how you came by them.'

'Mrs Gillespie isn't going to kick up a fuss, especially if they help us find the killer.'

'I'm thinking what a defence lawyer could do with them.'

'I can think up a story between now and then.'

'So what am I supposed to do with them?'

'You're heading a murder investigation, Davidson. The identities of whoever planned Gillespie's murder are in there. So take them back to Torphichen Place and get a team working on reassembling the pages.'

'I can't see my boss going for it; we're short-handed as it is. Can't you take them to St Leonard's?'

Rebus shook his head. 'Know why? I don't know who I can trust, and the last thing I want is for these bags to be conveniently mislaid. So: you tell no one what all this paper is, and you tell no one where you got it. When you've put together the jigsaw, I'll bet you'll have names *and* motives. Come on, I'll help you load your car.'

'Generous to a fault,' said Davidson, picking up one of the bags.

They drove to the mortuary to talk with Professor Gates, but he was eating lunch in the university Staff Club, so they climbed up from the Cowgate to Chambers Street.

Rebus had been in the Staff Club before, and knew that if you looked like you belonged, you could breeze in. But the porter came out to stop them, so maybe they didn't look the academic type. Rebus showed his ID, and that made everything all right again.

Gates was dining alone, a newspaper folded on the table beside his plate. A half-bottle of wine and a bottle of water stood in front of him.

'What brings you here?' he said as they sat down. 'You're not eating?'

'No thanks,' Davidson said.

'A drink maybe,' Rebus prompted.

'I can recommend the water,' Gates said, protecting his wine.

They decided on beer, which the waitress would bring from the bar.

'What can I do for you?' the pathologist asked, dissecting a last floury potato.

'Just wondered if you'd anything for us.'

'On last night's stabbing? Give me a chance, will you? Have you located the murder weapon?'

'No,' Davidson admitted. 'We didn't find any footprints either. The ground in the cemetery was frozen.'

'Well, it was a long-bladed knife, serrated by the look of the skin around the wound. And that's about as much as I can say for now. The victim had tried to protect himself, there were defence nicks on the hands. Plus he'd been eating something greasy. There was grease on his fingers.'

Rebus looked at Davidson. 'Did you find any wrappings near the body?'

'Nothing fresh. What's your point?'

'Gillespie ate a big meal at eight – chicken casserole, two helpings. Do you think he ate it with his fingers?'

'Probably not.'

'So how come less than three hours later he decides to visit a chip shop?' Rebus turned to the pathologist. 'When you look at stomach contents, I'm willing to bet you won't find anything but chicken casserole.'

'I did think,' the pathologist said, 'that it was odd. I mean, most people would wipe their fingers afterwards. But this grease or lard, it was quite solid.'

Which told Rebus everything he needed to know.

35

It was still lunchtime when Rebus walked into the chip shop on Easter Road, and two men in jackets and ties queued behind a teenager in a thin parka with the stuffing bursting from its seams: Rebus waited at the back of the queue, and smiled and waved towards the server, who didn't return the greeting.

Finally it was Rebus's turn. 'Hello, Gerry.' Gerry Dip wiped the work surface where some sauce had spilt. 'Remember me?'

'What do you want?'

Rebus leaned over the counter. 'I want to know where you were last night between the hours of nine p.m. and eleven, and it better be the alibi to end them all.'

'What for?' Gerry Dip said.

Rebus just smiled. 'Come on, let's go for a ride.'

'I can't. I'm here on my own.'

'Then switch everything off and we'll lock the door after us, maybe put up a sign saying "Other fish to fry".'

Gerry Dip bent down as if reaching for a switch, and then flicked something across the counter at Rebus. It was a battered fish, straight out of the fat. Rebus ducked and it flew over his head, fat spattering him. Gerry Dip was on the move, shouldering open the door to the kitchen. Rebus ran around the counter and followed. In the kitchen, Dip had hauled a sack of potatoes on to its side and was already halfway out the back door. Rebus stumbled over the potatoes, dived and just missed Dip's ankles. He clambered to his feet and ran outside, finding himself in an alley. To his left was a dead end. To his right, Gerry Dip, running for it, the white apron flapping around his knees.

'Stop him!' Rebus yelled.

Davidson didn't need telling twice. He was waiting at the mouth of the alley, hands in pockets like a casual onlooker. But as Dip ran past, he flung out an arm and caught him in the throat. Dip flew back like he was attached by elastic to the ground. His hands went to his throat and he started gagging.

'You could have crushed his windpipe,' Rebus said, but not in a nasty sort of way.

At four p.m., with Gerry Dip still maintaining his vow of silence in the interview room, Rebus went for a drive.

Gerry was an old hand: he knew how to play the game called Helping Police With Their Inquiries. He'd keep quiet, with or without a solicitor. All he'd said so far was that this was harassment, and that he wanted to talk to someone from SWEEP. It would take more than Rebus's gut feeling to convict him of murder. There must needs be evidence. Rebus had explained to Davidson the complex series of connections which had brought Gerry Dip to mind. Now it was up to Davidson to convince his superiors that there was due cause for the granting of a search warrant for Gerry Dip's digs and the chip shop itself. The chip shop's owner had already explained that Gerry hadn't had a shift the previous night. Rebus saw it all clearly. A meeting arranged, Gillespie turning up, Gerry Dip surprising him, Gillespie trying to defend himself from the attack, grabbing at Dip's greasy shirt or jacket . . .

One thing nagged: Gerry Dip alone couldn't have lured Gillespie into the trap. There must have been someone else, someone he trusted, someone he wanted to meet . . .

The Right Honourable Cameron McLeod Kennedy, JP, had a detached bungalow in what would have tried calling itself Corstorphine had South Gyle not taken off. The houses were descendants of the boxy bungalows on Queensferry Road. There weren't many cars parked roadside; most of the bungalows boasted a garage, or at the very least a car-port. Rebus parked outside the Lord Provost's home. The door was open before he had reached the garden gate. The Lord Provost stood in the doorway, his wife a little behind him.

'You were so mysterious on the phone,' Kennedy said, shaking Rebus's hand. 'Is there any news?'

'The Lord will do as He sees fit,' his wife burst out, the voice booming from her heavy frame. The Lord Provost ushered her back indoors and led Rebus to the front sitting room.

'I've seen her,' Rebus said.

'Where is she?' Mrs Kennedy snapped. Rebus studied her. She had wide unblinking eyes and small pudgy hands which she'd rolled into fists. Her hair had been coaxed into an untidy bun, and her cheeks blazed. Rebus guessed at West Highland stock; it wasn't a wild stab in the dark to say she'd had a religious upbringing. For zeal, some of the Wee Frees could beat any Muslim Fundamentalists.

'She's safe, Mrs Kennedy.'

'I know that! I've prayed for her, of course she's safe. I've been praying for her soul.'

'Beth, please . . .'

'I've prayed harder than I've ever prayed in my life.'

Rebus looked around the room. The furniture had been positioned with exact precision on the carpet, and the ornaments looked like the distances between them had been calibrated by a professional. Net curtains covered the two small windows. There were photos of young children, but none of anyone aged twelve or over. Hard to imagine a teenager passing her evenings here.

'Inspector,' Cameron Kennedy said, 'I haven't asked you if you'd like something to drink.'

Rebus guessed that alcohol would not be on the list. 'No thanks.'

'We've ginger cordial left from New Year,' Mrs Kennedy barked.

'Thanks, but no. The thing is, sir, I'm not here primarily about your daughter. I'd like to talk to you about Tom Gillespie.'

'Terrible business,' the Lord Provost said.

'May the good Lord take his soul unto Him in heaven,' his wife added.

'I wonder,' Rebus said pointedly, 'if we might have a word in private.'

Kennedy looked to his wife, who didn't look like moving. Finally, with a sniff, she turned and left. Rebus heard a radio come on through the wall.

'A terrible business,' the Lord Provost repeated, sitting down and gesturing for Rebus to do the same.

'But it didn't come altogether as a surprise, did it?'

The Lord Provost looked up. 'Of course it did!'

'You knew the councillor was playing with fire.'

'Did I?'

'There'd already been that one attempt to scare him off,' Rebus smiled. 'I know what Gillespie was on to, and I know he approached you with the information, and made frequent progress reports thereafter.'

'That's not true.'

'Your little lunchtime meetings, we've records of them. He knew you'd be interested. For one thing, you're the Lord Provost. For another, his findings related directly to Gyle Park West, which is in *your* ward. I don't know what Gillespie's idea was. If I were being charitable, I'd say he was working in the public interest and would eventually have gone public with his findings. But really, I think he was trying to pressure you into helping further his career. It could be that his findings would never have come to light, but somebody couldn't be sure of that. Somebody tried scaring him, then decided to murder him instead.'

The Lord Provost sprang to his feet. 'You surely don't think *I* killed him?'

'I'm pretty sure I could convince my colleagues that you're a prime suspect. You'd have to explain the secret meetings and everything else.'

The Lord Provost's eyes narrowed, his eyebrows meeting in the middle. 'What is it you want?'

'I want you to tell me all about it.'

'You say you already know.'

'But I've yet to hear anyone say the words.'

The Lord Provost considered, then shook his head.

'Does that mean,' Rebus said, 'that your ward is more important than your own reputation?'

'I can't say anything.'

'Because PanoTech's involved?'

Kennedy's face contracted as if he'd been punched. 'It's got nothing to do with PanoTech. That company is one of the largest employers in Lothian. We *need* it, Inspector.'

'If it has nothing to do with PanoTech, does it still have to do with Robbie Mathieson?'

'I can't say anything.'

'Who's Dalgety? Why does he scare you so much? Kirstie told me she heard you talking about him with someone. And when you saw she'd written his name on the LABarum plan, you suddenly didn't want her found.'

'I've told you, I'm saying *nothing*!'

'In that case,' Rebus said, 'I won't trouble you any further.' He stood up. 'I'm sure you've got plenty to keep you busy, such as writing your speech of resignation.' He walked to the door.

'Inspector . . .' Rebus turned. 'About Kirstie . . . *is* she all right?'

Rebus walked back into the room. 'Would you like to see her?' The Lord Provost seemed in two minds. Weakness was there to be exploited. 'I could bring her here, but it would have to be a trade.'

'You don't "trade" with an innocent life!'

'Not so innocent, sir. I could think up half a dozen charges against your daughter, and between you and me I'd be failing in my duty if I didn't apprehend her and put her in a cell.'

The Lord Provost turned away and walked to the window. 'You know, Inspector, I'm no virgin, believe me. You want dirty tricks, underhand tactics, there's a lot you can learn from politics, even at district level . . . *especially* at district level.' Kennedy paused. 'You say you can bring her here?'

'I think so.'

'Then do it.'

'And we'll have a little chat, you and me? You'll tell me what I want to know?'

The Lord Provost turned to face him. 'I'll tell you,' he said, his face ashen.

They shook hands on it, and the Lord Provost saw him to the door. Somewhere behind them in the bungalow, Mrs Kennedy was singing a hymn.

So all Rebus had to do now was persuade Kirstie Kennedy that east or west, home was still the best.

Rebus went to her flat first, but there was no one home. He tried a couple of the drop-in centres, including the one behind Waverley – no joy – then started on the burger bars on Princes Street before driving back to Leith and visiting three pubs where pushers and users were known to meet. Nothing. He took a breather in a bar where he was less likely to get himself stabbed, then went to have a word with the few chilled prostitutes plying their trade near the Inner Harbour. One of them thought she recognised the description, but she could have been lying: it was warmer in his car than outside.

Then Rebus remembered something Kirstie had said, about how Paul's mum liked her. So he drove to Paul's parents' address. Duggan was embarrassed to see him, but his mother, a tiny, kindly woman, invited Rebus in.

'No night to be yacking on the doorstep.'

It was a tidy little flat just off Abbeyhill. Duggan gave Rebus a warning look as he led him, at his mother's insistence, into the living room. Duggan's dad was there, smoking a pipe and reading the paper. He stood up to shake Rebus's hand. He was small, like his wife. So here was the arch criminal, Paul Duggan, in his lair.

'Paul's not in any trouble, I hope,' the father asked, teeth grinning around the stem of his pipe.

'Not at all, Mr Duggan, I'm just looking for a friend of Paul's.'

'Well, Paul will help if he can, won't you, Paul?'

'Aye, sure,' Paul Duggan mumbled.

'It's Kirstie,' Rebus said.

'Kirstie?' Mr Duggan said. 'That name's familiar.'

'Maybe Paul's brought her back here once or twice, Mr Duggan.'

'Well, Inspector, he does sometimes bring a girlfriend back – but not for hanky-panky, mind you.' He winked. 'We keep an eye on him.'

The two men shared a laugh. Paul Duggan was shrinking almost visibly, bowed over on the sofa, hands between his legs. The years were peeling off him like paper from a damp wall.

'I haven't seen her,' he told Rebus.

'Since when?'

'Since the time we took her home.'

'Any idea where she could be?'

Mr Duggan removed the pipe from his mouth. 'I'm sure Paul would tell you if he could, Inspector.'

'Have you tried the flat?' Paul asked. Rebus nodded.

'She's not in your bedroom, is she, Paul?'

Duggan twitched, and his father sat forward in the chair. 'Now, Inspector,' he said, trying for another grin. Trying too hard.

'Where's your wife, Mr Duggan?'

Rebus got up and walked into the hall. Mrs Duggan was about to sneak Kirstie Kennedy out the front door.

'Bring her through here instead, Mrs Duggan,' Rebus said.

So they all sat in the living room, and the Duggans explained everything.

'See, we know who Kirstie is,' Mrs Duggan said, 'and she's told us why she ran away, and I can't say I blame her.' The Lord Provost's daughter sat next to her on the sofa, staring into the fire, and Mrs Duggan ran her hand through Kirstie's hair. 'Kirstie's got a problem with drugs, she accepts that and so do we. We thought if she was going to fight it, she better move in here for a wee while, get right away from all the . . . from the people who live that sort of life.'

'Is that right, Kirstie? Are you kicking it?'

She nodded, suppressing a shiver. Mrs Duggan put an arm around her. 'Sweats and shivers,' she said. 'Mr Leitch told us to expect them.' She turned to Rebus. 'He works at the Waverley drop-in.' Rebus nodded. 'He told us all about cold turkey.' She turned her attention back to the girl. 'Cold turkey, Kirstie, like on Boxing Day, eh?'

Kirstie snuggled deeper into Mrs Duggan's side, like she was a child again and Mrs Duggan her mother . . . Yes, thought Rebus, the mother she's been denied. And here was a willing substitute.

'See,' Mr Duggan said, 'we're afraid you've come to take her away. She doesn't want to go home.'

'She doesn't *have* to go home, Mr Duggan. The drugs apart, she's done nothing wrong.' Paul and Kirstie looked at him, and saw he wasn't going to mention the hoax kidnap. 'But the thing is,' Rebus said, his eyes holding Kirstie's, 'I need a favour. I've seen your stepmother, and I don't blame you for not wanting to see her . . . But what about your father? Would it hurt you to talk to him for five minutes, just to let him see you're all right?'

There was a long silence. Mrs Duggan whispered something in Kirstie's ear.

'I don't suppose so,' Kirstie said at last. 'Just now? Tonight?'

Rebus shook his head. 'Tomorrow will be fine.'

'I might be worse tomorrow.'

'I'll take that chance. Just one other thing: last time we met, you were telling me why you took that document from your dad's office.'

She nodded. 'I heard him talking on the telephone. He was talking about covering something up, some scandal. I heard him mention LABarum. He'd always told me I had to follow his example, but he turned out to be just like all the others – a liar, a cheat, a coward.' She was bursting into tears. 'He let me down again. So I grabbed that . . . whatever it was. I saw it was about LABarum.' She took a deep breath. 'Maybe I just wanted him to know I knew. It's all rotten, all of it.'

Mrs Duggan was still trying to quiet her as Rebus left the flat.

Back home, Rebus got the feeling the phone had just stopped ringing. Two minutes later, with the Stones softly on the hi-fi, it rang again. He'd been sitting with the whisky bottle in his lap, wondering if he could resist, wondering why he bothered.

'Yes?'

'It's Davidson.'

'Still at the station?'

'That I am. Gerry's still not talking.'

'Have you offered him a deal?'

'Not yet. We're holding him on a charge of assault, naming you as the injured party.'

'I'll never get the grease off that jacket. What about the search warrant?'

'We got it. I'm just waiting for Burns to get back. Hold on, here he comes.' Davidson put his hand over the mouthpiece. Rebus unscrewed the bottle with his free hand, but couldn't find a glass. Davidson came back on the line. 'It's a result. Two credit cards, Access and Visa, in the name of Thomas Gillespie, hidden under the mattress.'

'So now will you go for a deal?'

'I'll talk to his solicitor.'

'We don't just want Dip, remember. We want whoever ordered the hit.'

'Sure, John.' There wasn't what Rebus would call fervour in Davidson's voice. 'Now the bad news.'

'Listen, I'm serious – we want the paymaster!'

'And *I'm* serious about it being bad news.'

Rebus quietened. 'OK, what is it?'

'You told me to check if Charters had had any visitors since you saw him Sunday night. Well, he had one the next morning, and then again today. She's a regular apparently.'

'Yes?'

'Her name's Samantha Rebus. Now, John, it may be nothing at all. I mean, she's visited other prisoners too, and we know she works for SWEEP. It could just be that she –'

But John Rebus was already on his way.

'I don't see what the big deal is,' Sammy said.

'What?'

'I don't see what's the big deal.'

He'd been so steamed up, he'd rung Patience's doorbell twice before remembering the unpleasantness surrounding his last visit. But Sammy opened the door.

'Grab your coat,' he hissed, 'tell Patience it's a friend and you're going out.'

They'd gone to a hotel just around the corner from the flat. The bar was almost deserted, just the barmaid and one regular at the corner of the bar, the hatch open so there was no barrier between them. Rebus and Sammy took their drinks to the furthest corner.

'The big deal is,' he said, 'you smuggled something out of jail for him.'

'Just a letter.'

She calmly sipped her tequila and orange. Fathers and daughters, Rebus thought. He pictured the Lord Provost and Kirstie. You knew they had to make choices, and nobody in life made the right choices all the time. Daughters never grew up; in their fathers' eyes, all they did was become women.

'I've done it before,' Sammy was saying. 'You know the warders read all the mail before it goes out? They censor it and leer over it and . . . and I think it's revolting.' She paused. 'They can get very sniffy about gay love letters.'

'Charters told you he was gay?'

'He hinted at it: "a very special friend", he said.'

Rebus shook his head. 'Gerry Dip's special, all right. He's absolutely choice. Did you take the note to his flat?'

'The only address Derwood had was the chip shop.'

'And did you read the note?'

'Of course not.'

'A sealed envelope?' She nodded. 'Quite a fat envelope?' She thought about it. 'Yes,' she said.

'That's because it was full of money.'

'What have I done?' Her face was reddening, her voice rising. 'Broken some lousy prison rule, that's all.'

'I wish it were,' Rebus said quietly.

She quietened. 'What then?'

He couldn't tell her. He couldn't do *that* to her . . . But it would all come out eventually, wouldn't it?

'Sammy,' he said, 'I think Charters paid Gerry Dip to kill a man. That envelope you delivered contained instructions and payment.'

Her face lost all its lovely colour. '*What?*' The way she said it turned Rebus's gut liquid. She tried picking up her drink, but spilt it, then retched into her cupped hands. Rebus got a handerkerchief out of his pocket and handed it over.

'You're trying to scare me,' she said, 'that's all. You don't like my job and you're trying to scare me off!'

'Sammy, please . . .'

She got to her feet, spilling the rest of her drink over his trousers. He followed her to the door, watched by barmaid and customer, and called after her. But she was running: down the steps on to the pavement, and then along to the corner and around it, back into Oxford Terrace.

'Sammy!'

He watched her run, watched her until she'd disappeared.

'Shite!'

A drunk, walking past, wished him a belated happy new year. Rebus told the man where he could stick it.

36

As arranged, Rebus drove to South Gyle next morning. He parked his car around the corner from the Lord Provost's house, then went and rang the doorbell. The Lord Provost himself opened the door, and looked to left and right as if expecting her to be there.

'We'll have to go for a little drive,' Rebus informed him.

Then a figure came storming along the passage behind Cameron Kennedy and brushed him aside.

'Where is she?' Mrs Kennedy's voice trembled with emotion, her nostrils flaring. 'Where's the lost lamb?' She turned to her husband. 'You said he'd bring her!'

The Lord Provost looked at Rebus, who said nothing. 'I have to go with Inspector Rebus, Beth.'

'I'll fetch my coat,' Mrs Kennedy said.

'No, Beth.' The Lord Provost laid a hand on her arm. 'Best I go alone.'

An argument started. Rebus turned and walked back towards the gate. The Lord Provost came after him.

'Don't you want a coat?' Rebus asked.

'I'll be fine.'

His wife was calling to them from the door. ' "Thy will be blyther in heiven owre ae sinner at repents nor owre ninetie-nine saunts at need nae repentance." '

'She's learned the New Testament in Scots,' the Lord Provost explained. 'She knows it backwards.' It didn't sound like a boast.

Kirstie was sitting in the back seat of Rebus's car. Beside her was Paul Duggan. She'd had a bath, and her hair had been washed and rearranged. She was wearing clothes Mrs Duggan had bought for her – styles parents thought teenagers liked. You'd take her for a normal, sulky, shoulder-bechipped teenager, nothing more – if it wasn't for the vomiting fits and the muscle spasms, the bolts of lightning through her bones.

Kennedy gasped when he saw her.

'I said I'd bring her,' Rebus told him. 'Now get in.'

The Lord Provost's face was like chiselled stone as they drove towards the Forth Bridges, the same route Rebus had taken that night with Lauderdale. He told himself he'd chosen the meeting place because it was nearby, open and private. But he thought maybe he had a deeper motive.

They came off the A90 and went three-quarters round the roundabout, then headed towards the Moat House Hotel, whose huge, desolate car park

overlooked the Forth. At this time of day, this time of year, the car park was deserted save for a Ford Capri which looked as if it had been abandoned after a joyride. Rebus stopped the car and turned off the ignition.

'This is where we get out,' he told Paul Duggan.

Duggan squeezed Kirstie's hand. 'Will you be all right?' he asked her.

'I'll be fine,' she said coolly, watching her father in the rearview mirror, just as he was watching her.

So Rebus and Duggan got out.

Rebus walked across the tarmac and stood at the furthest edge. You got a great view of both bridges, and of the Fife coast beyond. You also took a beating from the wind, which blew from all directions. Rebus rode with it, swaying a little from the ankles. With his head tucked into his overcoat, he managed to light a cigarette at the sixth attempt. The smell of butane caused momentary nausea.

Paul Duggan was a little way off, resting one arm on a dull metal pay-view telescope. Rebus left him alone and just stared at the scenery. The clouds crawled past, looking as if they'd been hurt in too many bar-room brawls. Beneath them, Fife was a slab of grey-green pavement.

Paul Duggan had finally arrived beside him. 'Thinking about Willie and Dixie?' he suggested. Rebus glanced at him but said nothing.

'I'm not just a pretty face, Inspector.'

'I was thinking that they got me into this. Their suicide. They got me thinking about things . . . asking myself questions. When McAnally killed himself, I was interested enough to want to know why.' He smiled. 'You don't know what I'm talking about.'

Duggan just shrugged. 'I'm listening though.' There was silence between them for a while. Duggan scuffed his toes against the kerb. 'See this trouble I'm in, with the police and council and that . . .?'

'You think I can help?'

'I don't know.'

It was strange that Kirstie should have run away from one smothering household only to end up in another, but Rebus thought he knew the reason why. After the deaths of Willie and Dixie, she'd disintegrated. To her, they had represented 'real life', a life well away from her father and his political conspiracies. Willie and Dixie had been the other side of the coin, a side she'd come to like, maybe even admire. And she'd killed them, after which she'd spiralled downwards until she realised she needed shelter and comfort, or she too might die. Paul Duggan had been there for her, and so had his parents.

'You know,' Rebus said, thinking aloud, 'I think I know why she scrawled "Dalgety" on that document. If her father had paid the ransom – maybe even if he hadn't – she was planning to send the LABarum plan back to him. It was a warning, a message that she knew something, and that he should leave her alone if he didn't want her to reveal it to the world.'

'Never mind Kirstie for the moment, what about me?'

'Everybody's got to pay, Paul,' Rebus said, not looking at him. 'That's the way it works.'

'Aye, right,' Duggan said dismissively. 'And if I was some rich bastard that had been to Fettes, I'd have to pay too, is that right? I'd be treated the

same as an Oxgangs drop-out? Come *on*, Inspector, Kirstie's told me the way it works, the whole system.'

He turned and shuffled away.

He had a point, one Rebus would happily concede, only he had other things to think about right now. The wind had finished his cigarette in double-quick time, so he lit another. Duggan was over at the abandoned car, peering in. He tried a door, opened it, and got in. Shelter accomplished. Some people said the weather made the Scots: long drear periods punctuated by short bursts of enlightenment and cheer. There was almost certainly something to the theory. It was hard to believe this winter would end, yet he knew that it would: knew, but almost didn't believe. A matter of faith, as the old priest would say, or maybe the reverse of faith. Rebus hadn't been to church in a while, and missed his conversations with Father Leary. But he didn't miss the church, or even the Church. Leary would have no problem with suicide, in either concept or practice: it was a great sin, full stop. Assisted suicide, too, was a sin, every bit as heinous.

But when Rebus's mother had been ill that last time, she'd begged his father for release. And one day, young John had walked in and had seen his father on the edge of her bed. She was asleep, her chest making awful, liquid sounds, and his father sat there with a pillow in his hands ... looking at that pillow, then up at his son, asking to be told what to do.

Rebus knew if he hadn't walked in, his father might have done it, might have put her out of her misery.

Instead of which, she lingered for weeks.

He turned away from the Forth and found his vision blurred. He angled his head upwards, swallowing back the tears, and walked over to the abandoned car. Inside, Paul Duggan was crying.

'They were my friends, too,' he bawled. 'And her stupid plan killed them! And yet I can't hate her for it ... can't even get angry with her.'

Rebus put a hand on Duggan's shoulder.

'Nobody killed them,' he said quietly. 'They chose for themselves.'

The two of them sat there for a while, out of the wind, in shelter that wasn't theirs.

Afterwards, Rebus drove them back into town. The teenagers in the back were both pink-eyed from crying; the two men in the front were not. He didn't feel proud of the fact. He drove past the turn-off to Kennedy's estate, and the Lord Provost still said nothing. Eventually, Rebus pulled the car on to the kerb outside Duggan's Abbeyhill home.

'Where are we?' Kennedy asked.

'Kirstie's staying with some nice people,' Rebus explained.

The Lord Provost turned to his daughter. 'You're not coming home?'

'Not yet,' she said, as if each word was costing her something.

'You said you'd bring her back.'

'I didn't say she'd stay,' Rebus said. 'Kirstie's got to decide if and when.'

She was already getting out of the car, as was Duggan. On the pavement, she doubled over and dry-heaved, spitting up foamy saliva.

'Something's wrong with her,' Kennedy said. He made to open his door, but Rebus pulled the car abruptly off the kerb and into traffic.

'You know what's wrong with her,' he said. 'Now she's coming off, and I think she'll be all right.'

'You infer,' Kennedy said coldly, 'that she wouldn't be "all right" at home.'

'What do you think?' Rebus said, and he left it at that.

'Where are we going?'

'One good thing about Edinburgh, Lord Provost – there's always a quiet spot nearby. You and me are going to have a talk. At least, *you'll* be talking, I'll be listening.'

He directed them around the base of Salisbury Crags and up to a car park near the summit of Arthur's Seat. There were a few cars already there, parents and children out braving the gale. They would probably call it 'blowing away the cobwebs'.

But Rebus and the Lord Provost stayed in the car, and the Lord Provost did the talking – that had been their bargain, after all. And afterwards, with the silence between them like an extra seat, Rebus drove the Lord Provost home.

There was a man at the top of the hill. He was mending a wall.

Rebus followed the line of the dry-stane dyke, climbing slowly. He was between Edinburgh and Carlops, in the foothills of the Pentland range. There was no escape from the wind and the cold up here, but Rebus was sweating as he neared the top. The man saw him coming, but didn't stop working. He had three piles of stones close to him, varying in sizes and shapes. He would pick one up, feel it, study it, then either put it back in the pile or else add it to the wall. And with a fresh stone placed in the wall, a new challenge presented itself, and he had to study his mounds of stones all over again. Rebus stopped to catch his breath, and watched the man. It was the most painstaking work imaginable, and at the end of it the wall would be held together by nothing more than the artful arrangement of its constituent parts.

'It must be a dying craft,' Rebus said, having gained the summit.

'Why do you say that?' The man seemed amused.

Rebus shrugged. 'Electric fences, barbed wire; not many farmers depend on dry-stane dykes.' He paused. 'Or dry-stane dykers, come to that.'

The man turned to look at him. He was ruddy-cheeked with a thick red beard and fair hair turning grey at the temples. He wore a baggy Aran sweater and green combat jacket, cord trousers and black boots. He wasn't wearing gloves, and kept blowing on his hands.

'I need to keep them bare,' he explained. 'I feel the stones better that way.'

'Is your name Dalgety?'

'Aidan Dalgety, at your service.'

'Mr Dalgety, I'm Detective Inspector Rebus.'

'Is that right?'

'You don't sound surprised.'

'In a job like this, you don't get many visitors. That's one of the things I like about it. But since I started this wall, it's been like a main thoroughfare rather than a deserted hillside.'

'I know Councillor Gillespie visited you.'

'Several times.'

'He's dead.'

'I know.'

'And that's why you're not surprised to see a detective?'

Dalgety smiled to himself and judged another stone, turning it in his hand, weighing it in his palm, feeling for its centre of gravity. He placed it on the wall, then thought better of it and moved it to another spot. The process took a couple of minutes.

Rebus looked back the way he'd come, following the wall down to the by-road where he'd parked his car. 'Tell me, how many stones go into a wall like this?'

'Tens of thousands,' Dalgety said. 'You could spend years counting them. Men took years building them.'

'It's a far cry from computers.'

'Do you think so? Maybe it is. But then again, maybe there's *some* connection.'

'I understand you were Robbie Mathieson's partner, back in the early days of PanoTech.'

'It wasn't called PanoTech in my day. The name belongs to Robbie.'

'But the early designs . . . the early work was yours?'

'Maybe it was.' Dalgety tossed a stone from one pile to another.

'That's what I hear. He ran the company, but you designed the circuits. Your ideas made the company work.' Dalgety didn't say anything. 'And then he bought you out.'

'And then he bought me out,' Dalgety echoed.

'Is that the way it happened?'

'It happened just the way I told it to the councillor. I had a . . . I'd been working too hard for too long. I had a breakdown. And when I came out of it, the company wasn't mine any longer. Robbie had kissed me goodbye. And all the designs were his, too. The whole company was his. Dalmat, we were called – Dalgety and Mathieson. That was the first thing he changed.' Dalgety was weighing another stone.

'How did he find the money to buy you out? I take it you were bought out?'

'Oh yes, it was all above board. He had some money invested somewhere: it paid a handsome profit and he used it to buy my share.' He paused. 'That's what the lawyers told me afterwards. I didn't remember any of it – discussions, signing the papers, none of it.'

'You must have been bitter.'

Dalgety laughed. 'I had another breakdown. They put me in a private nursing home. That took care of a lot of the pay-off money. When I came out, I didn't want anything to do with the industry, or any industry like it. End of story.'

'PanoTech's grown since.'

'Robbie Mathieson is good at what he does. Do you know about him?' Rebus shook his head. 'His family moved to the States when Robbie was eighteen. He joined one of the big boys, IBM or Hewlett-Packard, someone like that. The company had operations in Europe, and Robbie was posted here. He liked Scotland. I was working on my own at the time, designing stuff, messing about with ideas, most of them impractical. We met, got to like one another, and he told me he was resigning and starting up his own computer business right here. He persuaded me along with him. We had a

couple of good years . . .' Dalgety seemed to have forgotten about the stone he was holding. The wind was hurting Rebus's ears, but he didn't let it show.

'I'm not telling you the whole truth,' Aidan Dalgety said at last. 'I was an alcoholic; or, at least, I was on the verge of becoming one. I think that's why Robbie wanted rid of me. Seemed to me afterwards that he must have been planning it for a while. I signed away the rights to a couple of components which went on to make PanoTech a lot of money.' He took a deep breath. 'But that was then and this is now.'

'This money Mathieson used to buy you out, where did it come from again?'

'There was a man called Derwood Charters. He got to know Robbie early on. I think he wanted to become company secretary, something like that. He had a lot of money-making schemes. Or should I say scams. Robbie told me about a couple of them. Charters would set up paper companies and then screw grants from all over the place – local authority, SDA, European Community. He had a genius for that sort of thing. I think he must have wangled development money for PanoTech somewhere down the line – the company grew so fast so quickly.'

'And you've never said anything about any of this?'

'Why should I? Good luck to them.'

'But Mathieson practically robbed you!'

'And now he keeps a lot of people in employment. I'm not such a high price to pay for an outcome like that.'

Rebus sat down on the cold earth, his back against the wall, and ran his hands over his head.

'You know,' Dalgety said, 'I still take an interest in the industry. I don't mean to, but I do. Thirty-five per cent of all the PCs manufactured in Europe are manufactured here, twenty-four per cent of all semiconductors. Two million computers a year come out of IBM's Greenock plant – that includes their *world* supply of screens and every IBM computer sold in Europe.' He was laughing. 'Fifty thousand people in the industry, and it's growing. The Japanese come here because productivity's so high – can you believe that?' He stopped laughing abruptly. 'But the root system's shallow, Inspector. We're big in hardware, but we need software, too, and we need to start sourcing – we source only fifteen per cent of all our components. We're an assembly line. Maybe PanoTech can change that.' He shrugged. 'Good luck to them.'

'So why did you talk to Gillespie?'

'Maybe to get it off my chest.' He examined the stone in his hand a final time, then threw it far into the distance. 'Maybe because nothing I say can make any difference. No investigation of PanoTech is going to get very far.'

'The councillor found that out.' Aidan Dalgety looked at him, but said nothing. 'You're not scared?'

'No,' Dalgety used both hands to lift a larger rock on to the wall. 'I'm not scared at all. This wall will be here after I'm gone, whether I live to be a hundred or drop dead tomorrow.' He patted the wall with his hands. 'I know what lasts.'

Rebus got to his feet. 'Well, thanks for talking to me.'

'No problem. I get bored sometimes just talking to the wall.' He was

laughing again as Rebus headed downhill. 'You know that old saying about walls having ears . . .?'

It was a day for open spaces. In the late afternoon, Rebus walked in the Botanic Gardens with Sir Iain Hunter.

'I like this place,' Sir Iain said, striding gamely with his rolled umbrella across the grass towards Inverleith House. 'Of course, it's lost something since they moved the Gallery of Modern Art. What do you think?'

'I think you're stalling.'

Sir Iain smiled. 'I've conducted meetings here before, Inspector. It's my open-air office. I choose the Botanics for some meetings precisely because they *are* so open. No chance of being overheard.' He stopped, looking around. The city centre was a panorama before them. 'Marvellous view,' he said.

'Nobody's listening in on us, if that's what you're worried about.'

'Well, the thought had crossed my mind. Nowhere is safe in this age of electronic eavesdropping.'

'I don't need to bug conversations,' Rebus said. 'I've got Gillespie's files.'

'Poor Councillor Gillespie.'

'Yes, poor Councillor Gillespie, lured to an alley and then stabbed in the guts by an ex-con hired by Derwood Charters, just as Charters paid McAnally to put a scare into Gillespie. I don't suppose he knew how far Wee Shug would go, what he'd do . . . He went too far.'

'And brought you scurrying to the scene, Inspector. Yes, perhaps that was a mistake. Well, I'm going to trust you. I'm going to assume you're not recording this little tête-à-tête.' Sir Iain tucked his cashmere scarf a little tighter around his neck. 'Now, why did you want to meet?'

'Because you're at the centre of it all.'

'Can you prove that?'

'Like I say, I've got –'

'Yes, yes, you've got Gillespie's files, but what do *they* prove?'

'You should know. The Lord Provost told you everything Gillespie told him. They prove that Charters' various companies existed only as shells for the most part. The front company was legit, but the others . . . well, if anyone decided to check, Charters would rent short-term office space, pay someone to take in mail addressed to Mensung House . . . that sort of thing. And I'm assuming he had someone at the Scottish Office tipping him off about any forthcoming investigations – he couldn't have run his scams so well for so long without help. How am I doing so far?'

Sir Iain was admiring the view. 'Wild inaccuracies compounded by conjecture.'

'Charters had sleeping partners. See, once the fake companies were running, he could apply for grants and other incentives, but to get the companies going in the first place required cash, working capital, and that's where the sleeping partners came in. He could guarantee a huge return on investment, provided the grant money came through. He was a wizard at playing the system, running rings around it. He made quick money for a lot of people, including Robbie Mathieson. I'm sure Mathieson wouldn't want anyone to know that the early money for PanoTech came from ripping off SDA and European Community schemes.

'Then there's Haldayne at the US Consulate. He'd met Charters socially, and was keen to make money. As an aside, I'd guess that once he was involved, you were able to pressure Haldayne into helping persuade American companies to move here. Same goes for Robbie Mathieson – he had US connections in the computer industry.'

'That's slanderous,' Sir Iain remarked, his smile unimpeachable.

'Well, Haldayne's been to your Royal Circus *pied-à-terre* plenty of times – we've got the parking tickets. You must have had *something* to talk about. Charters couldn't have got away with it, not to the same extent, without a network of friends and people he bribed. Civil servants predominantly. I've been asking around, Sir Iain. Eight years ago, you weren't nearly so high up the pecking order. But then you started a string of successes bringing new business into Scotland, and you started your ascent. And Ruthie Estate must have cost a bit. I wonder, did you buy that in the past eight years?

'The whole thing worked brilliantly for a long time. Companies came and went, and sometimes their registration documents disappeared with them. Then the SDA became Scottish Enterprise, accounting procedures changed, and nobody was going to be looking back at old projects financed by a dead organisation. But Charters couldn't stop, and one time he got sloppy, and was caught early on. He pled guilty, protecting his friends and making sure nothing would come out at a trial, and then Gillespie caught a glimpse of something, and it got him wondering. He started digging, and word got back to Charters.' Rebus paused. 'You told me once that you liked a bit of intrigue: how am I doing?'

Sir Iain just shrugged, looking bemused.

'Well,' said Rebus, 'I'm just getting to the best bit. Now, who passed the word back to Charters? Because whoever did is partly to blame for Gillespie's eventual murder. Gillespie had told his story to the Lord Provost – only natural that he'd tell somebody – but he never guessed the Lord Provost would go straight to Mathieson and tell *him*. But what else was he going to do? Mathieson is the biggest employer in his ward; the Lord Provost thought he'd warn him what was coming.'

'You think Mathieson told Charters?'

'Possibly. It could have been any of you.'

'*Us?*'

'You're in it up to your cashmere scarf.'

'Careful what you say, Inspector. Be *very* careful.'

'Why? So I don't get a knife in the guts?'

Hunter's cheeks coloured. 'That was . . .' He swallowed back the rest.

'Charters' doing?' Rebus guessed. 'Well, someone had to tell Charters in the first place, and they did so knowing *he'd* do something about it, something they were scared to do themselves.'

Sir Iain's eyes were watering, but it was from the breeze, not contrition. 'What are you going to do, Inspector?'

'I'm going to nail as many of you as I can.'

Finally Hunter turned to him. 'Do you recall what I said to you that day on my estate? Jobs are at risk, *lives* are at risk.' He sounded grotesquely sincere.

'It's all just policy to you, isn't it?' Rebus said. 'No right and wrong, legal and illegal, no fair and corrupt, just politics.'

'Listen to yourself, man,' Sir Iain Hunter spat. 'Who are you, some Old Testament prophet? What gives you the right to hold the scales?' He dug the tip of his umbrella into the ground, and waited for his breathing to ease. 'If you'd look into your heart, you'd see we're not on opposite sides.'

'But we are,' Rebus said determinedly.

'If this ever became public, there'd be more than a scandal – there'd be a crisis. Trust would be lost, overseas investors and corporations would turn away from Scotland. Don't tell me you want that.'

Rebus thought of Aidan Dalgety, busying himself with an endless wall – his only answer to frustration and anger. 'None of it's worth a single human life,' he said quietly.

'I think it is,' Hunter said. 'I really do think it is.'

Rebus turned to walk away.

'Inspector? I'd like you to talk with some people.'

It was the invitation Rebus had been waiting for. 'When?'

'Tonight if at all possible. I'll phone you with the details.'

'I'll be at St Leonard's till six,' Rebus said, leaving the old man to his view.

But Rebus couldn't face the police station, so went home instead.

And found, slowly but with growing confidence, that his flat had been broken into in his absence. It was a clean, meticulous job. There were no signs of forced entry, nothing had been taken, almost nothing looked out of place. But his books had been moved. He had them in what looked like unplanned towers, but were actually the order in which he'd bought them and intended to read them. One of the towers had been knocked over and put back up again out of order. His drawers had been closed, too, though he always left them open. And his record collection had been rifled – as if he could hide sacks of shredded paper inside album sleeves . . .

He sat down with a glass of whisky and tried not to think any thoughts. If he thought, he might not act. He might drop out, like Dalgety, and let them get on with it. He loathed Sir Iain Hunter for the way he used people. But then Paul Duggan used people too, if it came down to it. Kirstie, too, had used and abused her friends. Everybody used someone. The difference was, Sir Iain and his kind had everything – heart, soul, silver and gold – only nobody knew it, never even gave it a thought.

What was more, probably nobody cared.

His phone rang at seven.

'I did try St Leonard's,' Sir Iain said. 'They told me you'd not been back this afternoon.'

'Don't worry, your friends had left before I got back.'

'I beg your pardon?'

'Nothing, forget it. But hear this: Gillespie's files are in a safe place, and I mean *safe*.'

'You're not making much sense, Inspector.'

'Is that for the benefit of anyone listening in?'

'I only called to remind you of our meeting. Nine tonight, would that suit?'

'Let me just check my social calendar.'

'You know Gyle Park West?'

'I know it.'

'The PanoTech factory. You'll be expected at nine.'

37

PanoTech had won awards for the design of its Gyle Park West factory, with its automated shopfloor delivery system (a series of robot fork-lifts on a network of rails), and its bulbous shape with optimised interior light. The reception area was chrome and grey metal with a black rubberised floor.

There was a security guard on the desk, but Rebus was expected. As he walked through the automatic doors, an automatic voice telling him he was entering a 'Positively No Smoking Zone', he saw Sir Iain Hunter standing by a display case. There was a sheet over the case, but Sir Iain had lifted it, the better to inspect the model beneath.

'The new LABarum building,' he explained. 'They'll start construction in the spring.' He turned to Rebus. 'New jobs, Inspector.'

'And another feather in your cap. What'll it be this time – *Lord* Hunter of Ruthie?'

Sir Iain's smile evaporated. 'They're waiting for us in the boardroom.'

They took a bright elevator to the third and top floor, and emerged into a compact hallway with three doors off. Sir Iain pressed four numbers on a wall console, and pushed open one of the doors. Inside, three men were waiting, standing by the window. A light airplane was taking off from Turnhouse, so close you could almost see the exhausted executives inside.

Rebus looked at Haldayne first, then at J. Joseph Simpson, and finally at Robbie Mathieson. 'The gang's all here,' he commented.

'That's a cheap shot.' Mathieson came forward to take Rebus's hand. He was wearing an expensive suit, but showed he'd put aside the day's cares by having shed his tie and undone the top button of his shirt.

'Good of you to come,' he told Rebus, with what some people would have taken for sincerity.

'Good of you to ask me,' Rebus said, playing the game.

Mathieson waved a hand around the room. It had cream walls, some blown-up photos of computer chips, and a dozen framed awards for export, industry and achievement. There was a large oval table placed centrally, black like the floor. 'I have this place swept for bugs once a week, Inspector. Industrial espionage is a constant threat. Unfortunately, this meeting was arranged at short notice . . .'

'So?'

'So I don't have any of the relevant devices to hand. How can I be sure *you're* not bugged?'

'What do you want me to do?'

Mathieson tried to look embarrassed. It was just an act. 'I'd like you to remove your clothes.'

'Nobody said it was going to be that sort of party.'

Mathieson smiled, but angled his head, expecting compliance.

'Anyone want to join me?' Rebus said, removing his jacket.

Sir Iain Hunter laughed.

Rebus studied the four men as he stripped. Simpson looked the most ill at ease; probably because he was the least of the group. Haldayne had seated himself at the table and was toying with a fat chrome pen, as if already bored with proceedings. Mathieson stood by the window, averting his eyes from the disrobing. But Sir Iain stood fast and watched.

Rebus got down to underpants and socks.

'Thank you,' Mathieson said. 'Please get dressed again, and I apologise for putting you through that.' He was using his business voice, deep and confident, the American burr touched with Scots inflexions. 'Let's all sit down.'

Simpson hadn't even reached his chair before he started blurting out that he didn't know what he was doing here, it was all such a long time ago . . .

'You're here, Joe,' Mathieson reminded him firmly, 'because you broke the law of the land. We all did.'

Then he turned to Rebus.

'Inspector, a long time ago, almost in another age, we all profited from enterprises set up and run by Derwood Charters. Now, the question in court would be: did we know at the time that those profits were being made by fraudulent means?' He shrugged. 'That's a question for the lawyers, and you know how lawyers can be, especially with questions of corporate law. They might take years and several million pounds to come to their conclusions. A lot of time, a lot of money . . .' He opened his palms wide, a showman with his spiel. 'And for what? The fact of the matter is, some of those profits – illicitly gained – went to build this very factory, bringing jobs to hundreds, with spin-off benefits creating and sustaining hundreds, maybe thousands more. Including, as you told me yourself, a friend of yours. Now, in *law,* none of this would count for anything – quite rightly so. The law is a stern mistress, that's what they say.' A little smile. 'But the law, I would argue, isn't everything. There are considerations of a moral, ethical and economic order.' He raised a finger to stress the point, then touched it to his lips. 'Moral law, Inspector, is something else again. If bad money is used to good purpose, can it really be called bad money? If a child stole some apples, then went on to be a life-saving surgeon, would any court convict him of the original theft?'

Mathieson had prepared his lines well. Rebus tried not to listen, but his ears were working too well. Mathieson seemed to sense a change in him, and got up to walk around the table.

'Now, Inspector, if you want to drag up ancient history, you must do so, but the consequences will rest on *your* conscience. They sure as hell won't be on mine.'

Rebus wondered if it was possible that Mathieson had compiled a dossier on him, had people watch him, talk to acquaintances. No, those methods would not have told the essential truths, they wouldn't have revealed the

man to whom Mathieson was appealing so subtly and cleverly. It had to be more than that. It had to be instinct.

'A murder has been committed,' Rebus said.

Mathieson had been expecting this argument. 'Not with the knowledge of anyone in this room,' he said.

'You're saying it was Charters alone?'

Mathieson nodded, stroking his beard. Rebus wondered if he'd grown it in memory of Aidan Dalgety. 'Derwood has most to lose,' he was explaining. 'He's been in prison all these years, and if you make public what you know, he'll stay there.'

'But Gillespie was set up by someone he knew. He wouldn't have been in that alley otherwise.'

'Why not?'

'Because he was scared.'

'Then who was it?' Mathieson asked.

'I would guess Sir Iain,' Rebus said. Four pairs of eyes fixed the Permanent Secretary. 'Maybe Charters himself will tell us. As you say, he's got most to lose. He might be all too willing to bargain down any extension to his sentence.'

'This is preposterous,' Hunter said, thumping the floor with his cane.

'Is it?' Rebus said. 'You like guns, Sir Iain. You've got a whole room full of shotguns. What if I checked them against the records? Would they all be there, or would one be missing – the one you passed on to Shug McAnally?' Rebus turned to Mathieson. 'I want him. I want him tonight. The rest of you, maybe later.'

'Hold on,' Haldayne interrupted, 'what evidence do you have? We've told you we don't know any –'

'Save your defence, Mr Haldayne. I know Sir Iain's been controlling you all these years.'

Mathieson was shaking his head slowly. 'It would be very unfortunate indeed if *any* of this leaked out. If you arrest Sir Iain, you'll precipitate a media circus as well as political questions. Why can't you just charge Charters?'

'Because then you'd all be getting away with it.'

Mathieson looked frustrated. 'Inspector, understand one thing: I don't care about Sir Iain, I don't care about anyone here tonight – including myself, if it comes down to it.' His voice was rising the way it must have at other boardroom meetings, propelling him towards victory. 'What I care about – more deeply than you would ever understand or believe – is PanoTech.' Now the voice fell away. 'LABarum will be a major expansion, Inspector. A new factory, new R and D unit, meaning more suppliers, contractors, a huge injection of hard cash and confidence into the local economy. But more than that, LABarum will be Europe's Microsoft – Scotland will be producing its own software to install in the computers it manufactures.'

'No wonder everyone wants you kept sweet.'

'And you're going to put all that in jeopardy over something that happened eight years ago and hurt no one at the time; no one but the taxpayer, who wouldn't have known anyway how his or her money was being spent. A few million was a drop in the ocean, hardly even a ripple. Do

you have any idea of the scale of fraud being perpetrated in mainland Europe? A non-existent training scheme for airline pilots in Naples netted *seventeen* million pounds. Farm products and animals are shipped to and fro across borders, netting a subsidy every time. The EC has paid a *billion* pounds to have vineyards destroyed, yet there are more vines every year. The Greeks lop a branch off a vine and stick it in the ground so they'll be paid for *two*. I repeat, a few million hurt no one.'

'It hurt Aidan Dalgety.'

'Aidan hurt himself. You didn't know him then. He was becoming so erratic, he could have dragged the company down with him.'

'It's hurt other people since.' Rebus thought of Kirstie, finding out her father was no icon. He thought of her plan, a plan they all thought they could get away with because her father wasn't going to get his daughter back – they'd been bartering for the LABarum document, and for Kirstie's knowledge of the whole affair . . . And Willie and Dixie had died.

'I accept,' Mathieson was saying, 'that a man died. Derwood's gone crazy, that's what it comes down to.'

'There's one other consideration,' said Sir Iain, who'd had time to recover. 'As Mr Haldayne will acknowledge, two more US companies have seen the benefits of locating their European operations in Lothian. If my name, or Mr Haldayne's, were to be bandied about . . .' Hunter gave a modest shrug.

'Well,' Rebus said, 'this is turning into a harder sell than a Costa del Sol time-share.' He turned to Simpson. 'What about you, Joe?'

Simpson nearly slid from his chair. 'What about me?'

'Do you have any properties to bargain with in this little game of moral "Monopoly", or have you just picked up the Go-To-Jail card?'

'I can't go to jail! All I did was provide an accommodation address. It's not illegal!'

'Then why are you here?' Rebus looked to Mathieson, whose lips twitched.

'An offering,' he said.

'Hear that, Joe?'

Simpson had heard. He rose trembling to his feet.

'You could always testify against them,' Rebus told him.

'With what?' Haldayne said.

'Mr Haldayne has a point, Inspector.' Mathieson was sitting down again, in his big chief-executive chair at the end of the table. Tables without corners were supposed to make everyone equal, but Mathieson's chair was a leather throne. He looked and sounded completely unruffled by events thus far, while Rebus felt as if his head would explode.

Hundreds of jobs, spin-offs; happy, smiling faces. People like Salty Dougary, pride restored, given another chance. Did Rebus have the gall to think he could pronounce sentence on the future of people like that? People who wouldn't care who got away with what, so long as *they* had a pay-cheque at the end of the month?

Gillespie had died, but Rebus knew these men hadn't killed him, not directly. At the same time he hated them, hated their confidence and their indifference, hated their certainty that what they did was 'for the good'. *They* knew the way the world worked; *they* knew who – or, rather, *what* –

was in charge. It wasn't the police or the politicians, it wasn't anyone stupid enough to place themselves in the front line. It was secret, quiet men who got on with their work the world over, bribing where necessary, breaking the rules, but quietly, in the name of 'progress', in the name of the 'system'.

Shug McAnally was dead, but no one was grieving: Tresa was spending his money, and having a good time with Maisie Finch. Audrey Gillespie, too, might start enjoying life for the first time in years, maybe with her lover. A man had died – cruelly and in terror – but he was all there was on Rebus's side of the balance sheet. And on the other was everything else.

'Well, Inspector?' Mathieson could see something in Rebus's eyes – a red light that had changed to amber. He rose from the throne. 'Let's have a drink.'

Rebus hadn't noticed that the far wall was a series of recessed cupboards, their doors flush and handleless. Mathieson pushed the edge of one door and it opened automatically.

'I hope malt whisky's all right for everyone,' Mathieson said, as lightly as if they'd just finished a few rubbers of bridge.

'You don't have a drop of gin?' Joe Simpson squawked.

'You're right, Joe, I don't.'

'Then I'll take whisky.'

'Yes, Joe, you will.'

'Inspector,' Haldayne said in reasoned tones, 'we're in your hands. It's your decision now.'

'Let the man have a drink first,' Mathieson chided.

Sir Iain was staring levelly at Rebus, his mouth a moral pout. There was a line from a song stuck in Rebus's head, just when he least needed it: *'you can't always get what you want, but if you try some time, you'll find you get what you need'.*

I need a drink, he thought. And Robbie Mathieson – caring, smiling – brought him one.

'You're all right anyway,' Rebus told Haldayne. 'You'll have diplomatic immunity, the Get-Out-Of-Jail-Free card.'

Haldayne snorted his porcine laugh. 'I'm also the only one here who lost five grand to Derwood Charters over Albavise.'

'And you should have stayed out of it,' Sir Iain snarled.

'Hey,' Haldayne said, light glinting from his glasses, 'it worked in the past, didn't it?'

'You know, Inspector,' Mathieson said, rising above all this, 'any other policeman, any other public official, I might have been tempted to try offering a financial incentive.'

They all shut up to listen. Rebus sipped from his crystal tumbler.

'But with you,' Mathieson went on, 'I think that might have the opposite effect from the one intended.'

'And how much cash would I be worth to you, Mr Mathieson?'

'To me, nothing. But if it were a question of saving PanoTech . . . Well, it wouldn't be a matter of actual cash, of course. Cash is messy, and you wouldn't want any problems with the Inland Revenue.'

'Perish the thought.'

'But a new house with its own grounds, a trust fund for a daughter,

shares in a company which is going to do extraordinarily well in the next few years ... And then there are less tangible rewards – but no less valuable for that: friends in the right places, help when needed, a word in the right ear come promotion time ...' Mathieson's voice died away as he handed out the final drink – a very mean whisky for Joe Simpson – and took one for himself. He stood behind his throne, a plane droning in the night sky behind him.

'A little bit of bribery, eh?' Rebus commented.

Sir Iain Hunter sat forward. He looked like he was losing patience fast. He tapped his stick on the floor as he spoke. 'Is it wrong,' he said, 'to bribe rich foreign companies to come to a depressed region? I'd say, Inspector, that morally speaking, anyone who did that would be in the right.'

'Blackmail's blackmail,' Rebus said.

'I disagree.'

'And tell me, is nobody lining their own pockets?'

Sir Iain savoured his whisky. 'There must needs be incentives,' he said drily.

Rebus laughed. He felt a little looser after the drink. 'Exactly. And all this love of country and duty to the workers stuff is just so much shite. Tell me, why did you bring the DCC and me together that day?'

Sir Iain twisted in his chair. 'I saw how dangerous Charters had become. I wanted him stopped, but my position would not allow me to ... I felt it best to point you in the right direction rather than leading you there.'

Rebus laughed again. 'You old fraud. We were there to put the wind up Mathieson, to stop him even *thinking* about talking.' He turned to Mathieson. 'You were sweating like a pig in the killing pen.' Then back to Sir Iain. 'You used us the same way Charters used McAnally. *And* you've blackmailed Haldayne into helping bring firms here. What is it, is corruption part of the job description?'

Hunter said nothing. He was too angry to speak.

'Answer me this. Charters had a client called Quinlon, a building contractor who'd made money illicitly through a deal with someone in the SDA. Charters shopped Quinlon to the authorities so they'd think more seriously about closing down the SDA. Now, you all knew Charters back then, didn't you? You all knew that if the SDA disappeared, all accounts would be closed and the various frauds would remain undiscovered. So did you know about Quinlon?' He looked at Sir Iain. 'Did Charters maybe come to you with the story, and leave *you* to see that the right people heard about it?'

'This is sheer paranoia,' Sir Iain said. 'I refuse to discuss it.'

'OK, let's try this – Charters made a couple of million through his paper companies. Enough to make a stint in jail worthwhile. That's why he pled guilty. And when he gets out, the money's waiting for him. You all know that, and you're not going to do a thing about it. You know he's a murderer, too, but you've kept quiet about that as well.'

'Inspector,' Haldayne said, 'we're not leeches.'

'I know that – leeches are medicinal. You know something?' He was talking to all of them now. 'Tom Gillespie said something to me. He told me I was making a mistake. At the time, I took it as a threat, but it wasn't – it was the literal truth. I thought because he had something to hide it must

be something illicit. I was wrong about him all down the line; all he was was scared. He was terrified. Those last days of his life, all he felt was fear.' And dear God, Rebus knew what that felt like.

'Nobody's mourning him!' Sir Iain snapped.

Rebus turned to him. 'Now how do you know that?'

'What?'

'He's got a widow: you don't think she's in mourning?' Sir Iain studied the handle of his cane. 'I forgot,' he said. 'No, you didn't,' Rebus said quietly.

'So, what's it to be, Inspector?' Mathieson himself was beginning to look impatient. He knew he had won the argument, but might still lose the fight. He had his glass half raised, ready for a toast if Rebus gave the right answer, the answer everybody wanted. 'Just remember, if you want it, there's a place for you.'

Rebus was still staring at Sir Iain Hunter. He finished his whisky in one go and put the glass down. With his hands on the table, he pushed himself upright out of the chair.

'Here's my answer, Mr Mathieson,' he said.

He walked out without saying another word.

38

Because he hadn't decided.

His pride wouldn't let him kowtow to people like Hunter and Mathieson – they were men, not gods. And he hated people putting one over on him, which was exactly what would be happening if he gave in. But . . . but . . . He kept seeing those hundreds of faceless workers, driving to work in their new cars, or signing on in a sweltering dole office. One man's life against thousands . . . It wasn't fair, it shouldn't be down to him to decide.

Well, what was stopping him taking it elsewhere? He drove into town along Corstorphine Road, past the office suite used by Mensung, and decided to drop into Torphichen Place. Davidson probably wouldn't be there at this hour, but he could find out what was happening with Gillespie's files.

The duty desk officer let him through the door. Rebus walked along the silent hall and up the stairs. The only person in the CID room was Rab Burns.

'Hiya, John, what brings you here? The urbane conversation? The ersatz coffee?'

'Bags of rubbish, to be precise.'

'Eh?'

So Rebus explained, and Burns shook his head. 'I don't know anything about them.'

'Maybe they were locked away at close of play.'

'They'd be in the cupboard. Hold on, I'll fetch the key.' But there was nothing in the cupboard. 'You don't suppose they could have been thrown out by mistake?'

A shiver went across Rebus's shoulders. 'Mind if I use your phone?' He punched in Davidson's number and waited until the detective answered. 'It's me, where are the files?'

'John, I was going to call you.'

'Where are the files?'

'Orders, John.'

'What?'

'They were requisitioned. I was going to tell you in the morning.'

'Who was it?'

Davidson was a long time answering. 'The DCC's office.'

Rebus slammed down the receiver. Allan bloody Gunner! 'Any idea of the DCC's home number, Rab?'

'Oh aye, we're close friends like.'

Rebus's look shut him up. They found the number on the Emergency roster. Rebus rang and waited and waited. A woman picked up the receiver. There was laughter in the background. A party, maybe a dinner party.

'Mr Gunner, please.'

'Who shall I say?'

'Walt Disney.'

'Pardon?'

Rebus was shaking with anger. 'Just get him.'

A full minute later, Gunner lifted the receiver. 'Who is this?'

'It's Rebus. What the fuck are you playing at?'

'How dare you speak to me like that!' The words were hissed, Gunner not wanting his guests in the other room to hear.

'All right then. With respect, sir, what the fuck are you playing at?'

'What do you mean?'

'The Gillespie files, where are they?'

'In the incinerator.'

And Gunner cut the connection. Rebus tried again, but the line was busy – the receiver had been left off the hook. Rebus grabbed the Emergency roster from Burns and looked down it for Gunner's address.

'You can borrow my computer if you like,' Burns said.

'What for?'

'To write your letter of resignation.'

'Rab,' Rebus said to him, 'you stole that line from me.'

Rebus gave the bell a good long ring. Gunner didn't look surprised as he unlocked the door.

'Come into the study,' he said angrily.

As Rebus followed him, he heard the sounds of the dinner party. Instead of following Gunner into the study, he walked to a closed door and opened it.

'Evening,' he said. 'Sorry to drag the host away, we'll only be a minute.'

Then he smiled at the guests, closed the door again, and went into the study. Around the table had been seated the Lord Provost and his wife, the chief constable and his wife, and Gunner's wife. There were two other place settings, one for Gunner himself.

'Sir Iain couldn't make it then?' Rebus guessed.

Gunner closed the study door. 'He'll be joining us for coffee.'

'Cosy.'

'Look, Rebus –'

'I had a little think on the way here, and something occurred to me. Here it is. McAnally wasn't in Charters' cell to get to the bottom of anything; he was there so you could be sure Charters *was* keeping his mouth shut. And you got proof of that, because Charters paid McAnally to scare off the councillor. It was a cover-up from the beginning, whether Flower knew that's how you were playing it or not. You wanted the whole thing kept hidden, and now that you've burnt those papers, that's the way it'll stay.'

'That's up to you.'

Rebus shook his head. 'No, I'm worthless. It's up to people like *you*, and you're not going to do a damned thing. You're going to remain Hunter's puppet, all the way to chief constable.'

The doorbell rang again, and Gunner walked out, returning with Sir Iain Hunter.

'Well, Inspector,' Hunter said, removing his topcoat, 'you do seem to pop up everywhere.' He slipped a hand into his pocket and pulled out a cassette. 'It's all there,' he said, handing it to Gunner.

Rebus felt the floor move beneath him. 'You were bugged?' he said.

Hunter smiled. 'Thank God he didn't make us *all* strip.'

Rebus nodded. 'I begin to get it.'

'Sir Iain,' Gunner said, 'has been gathering evidence of an embarrassing scandal.'

'A scandal,' Rebus added, 'that will conveniently lack one important name. I should've known the Scottish Office was involved from the start. I can't see a prison governor, especially one like Big Jim Flett, covering up McAnally's record on the say-so of the police alone. But the DCC backed up by the Permanent Secretary . . . well, that would be a different story. After all, the Scottish Office pulls the purse-strings.' His eyes fixed on Hunter. 'And a lot of other strings besides.'

'Inspector Rebus,' Hunter said coolly, 'it is a fact of life that you simply *can't* have the Permanent Secretary mixed up in anything unsavoury. For the good of the country, he must be protected.'

'Even if he's in it up to his eyeballs?'

'Even then.'

'This stinks,' Rebus said. 'What's the tape? An insurance policy?'

'I'm preparing a file,' Gunner said. 'Unofficially, and to be kept under lock and key.'

'And if anything should happen to leak out in future . . .?'

'The file will show,' said Hunter, 'that Charters and others acted unlawfully.'

'To the extent of murder?' Hunter nodded. 'What about Mathieson? Will he be implicated?' Rebus smiled. 'Sorry, daft question. Of course he will. You'd sell everything to the court to save your own neck, you –'

'Hypocrite?' Hunter suggested. 'Hypocrisy is acceptable if it is for the public good.'

'You know,' Gunner added, 'I could have you booted off the force.'

'I'd fight you all the way.'

Gunner smiled. 'I know you would.'

Hunter touched Gunner's arm. 'We've kept your guests waiting long enough, Allan.'

Gunner's eyes were still on Rebus. 'Under normal circumstances, you'd be welcome to join us.'

'I wouldn't join you if you were coming apart at the seams.'

'The stories I hear,' Gunner said, 'it's *you* that's been coming apart at the seams.'

'Bear something in mind, Inspector,' Hunter said, examining his cane. '*You* were at that meeting, too. You're on the tape, listening to men confess their part in illegal acts. I didn't hear you caution them, I didn't hear you

do anything much. If questions should ever be asked, they'll be asked of you along with everyone else.'

'I'll see you to the door,' the chief constable-in-waiting told Rebus.

39

John Rebus did what he had to do – went on a forty-eight-hour bender.

It wasn't difficult in Edinburgh. Even in winter, without the benefit of extended summer opening hours, if you paced things right you could drink round the clock. It was all down to permutations of late-licence restaurants, casinos, and early-opening bars. You could always drink at home, of course, but that wasn't what a bender was about. You could hardly do your bender justice when the only person around to listen to your stories was your own sour self.

Rebus didn't worry about missing work. He'd been on benders before, after losing cases he'd tried desperately to win. Always he did it with the blessing of his superiors, who might even chip in towards expenses. He thought maybe he'd phoned the Farmer from some pub along the way, and maybe the Farmer had said something about Allan Gunner having OK'd things. Hard to tell though, hard to remember.

Still harder to forget.

He'd grab an hour's sleep, then be awake a couple of minutes at most before the knot was in his guts, reminding him of things he'd far rather forget.

Towards the close of the first day, he was in a bar on Lothian Road, and noticed Maisie and Tresa there, having a good time to themselves. They were at a table, and Rebus was at the bar. Pairs of men kept accosting them – to no avail. Then Maisie saw Rebus and got up, weaving towards him.

'I see the period of mourning's over,' Rebus said.

She smiled. 'Ach, Wee Shug was all right.'

'Why don't you tell me about it?'

Her eyes were only half open, heavy-lidded. 'See,' she began, 'it wasn't him I wanted, it was Tresa.' She lit a cigarette for herself, using the onyx and gold lighter. 'He came to see me the day he topped himself, told me what he was going to do. He gave me this lighter. Maybe he was looking for sympathy, or someone to talk him out of it. Daft bastard: he was doing just what I wanted. I wanted Tresa. I love her, really I do.'

Rebus remembered something she'd told him before, about Wee Shug: 'He deserved what he got.' He realised now that she hadn't meant it vindictively; she'd meant he deserved whatever he was paid. She'd stuck him in prison, and he'd still come back to her, telling his story . . .

'Was it rape?' Rebus asked.

She shrugged. 'Not really.'

He sucked on his cigarette. 'Did you scream?'

Now she laughed. 'The neighbours thought I did. They *wanted* to have heard it, otherwise there'd be no guilt. We Scots need a bit of guilt, don't we? It gets us through the day.'

Then she planted a kiss on his cheek, and stood back to gaze at him, before making her way back to where Tresa McAnally sat waiting for her.

She was right about the guilt, he thought. But there was more to it – the neighbours hadn't done anything at the time, and that was typically Edinburgh. People would rather not know, even if there was nothing there – they didn't want to be told that their body (or their country) was rotten with cancer, but nor did they want to be told that it wasn't. And in the end they just sat there, *zugzwanged,* while the likes of Charters and Sir Iain Hunter got on with another game entirely.

In the middle of the second day, in the same rancid clothes as the day before, wreathed in a fug of nicotine and whisky, and in possession of a hangover he was trying to drink away, he met Kirstie Kennedy. Maybe it was halfway down Leith Walk, or at the top of Easter Road. She was shorter than him, and wanted to whisper in his ear. She didn't need to stand on tiptoe to do it – he stooped under the weight of his skull and shoulders.

'You should get straight,' she told him. 'Killing yourself's no answer.'

He recalled her words later, when more or less seated on a bench in what purported to be a bar on Dalry Road. It had the dimensions and atmosphere of a bonded warehouse. He had just been speaking to the old thin man, the one who liked American history. Rebus had started to give him a history lesson which didn't have much to do with Hopalong Cassidy, and the man shuffled off to another part of the bar, where Tartan Shoelaces stood protectively close to his erring wife Morag. Rebus had stood them all a couple of drinks when he'd come in.

Some young turks were playing pool, and Rebus tried to concentrate on their game, but found himself yawning noisily.

'Not keeping you up, are we, pal?' one of the players snarled.

'Cut it out,' the barmaid called to them. 'He's polis.'

'He's guttered, that's what he is. Plain mortal.'

And then Kirstie's words came back to him. *You should get straight. Killing yourself's no answer.* Well, it depended what the question was. Get straight . . . straight, as in even. Someone sat down next to him. He tried turning his head to look at them.

'Found you at last.'

'Sammy?'

'I got a phone call from somebody called Kirstie. She said she was worried.'

'I'm fine. Nothing wrong with me.'

'You're a mess. What's happened?'

'The *system,* that's what's happened. You were right, Sammy. And I knew you were right, all the time I was saying you were wrong.'

She smiled at him. 'Well, you were right, too. I shouldn't have smuggled that note out for Derwood Charters.'

'Don't worry about it. Gerry Dip isn't talking. We'll pin him for the credit cards if nothing else. There'll be no mention of Charters at the trial. You won't be involved.'

'But I *am* involved.'

Rebus shook his head. 'Just keep your mouth quiet, that's what everyone else is doing. Nothing's going to happen.'

'Is that what this is about?'

Rebus straightened his back. He didn't like Sammy seeing him like this; that thought had only just struck him.

'Look,' he said, 'whether you can put this behind you or not is down to you and your conscience. That's what I'm saying.' He got to his feet. 'I'm going to clean up.'

He made it to the toilets. He didn't want the pool players coming in for a 'Dairy Discussion', so wedged the door shut with paper towels while he stuck his head under the cold tap. He dried himself off, then was copiously sick into the bowl. Unjamming the door, he walked back into the bar.

'Feeling better?' Sammy asked him.

'Ninety-five per cent to go,' Rebus told her, taking her hand in his.

Who could he go to?

The Lord Advocate? Hardly: he was probably on pheasant-shooting terms with Hunter. He was the *Establishment,* and the Establishment would be protected at all costs. The chief constable? But he was retiring, and wouldn't want anything to tarnish his last few months in office. The media perhaps, Mairie Henderson? It was the story of the year, except there was no proof. It would be the word of an embittered policeman against ... well, *everybody*.

He'd spent time steeping in the bath at home, then showering. Sammy had made him drink a couple of litres of orange juice, and about a packet of 'Resolve'.

'I can't forget what I did,' she told him quietly.

'Maybe you got my guilt complex along with my genes,' he told her.

After Sammy had gone back to Patience's, Rebus had called Gill Templer. He needed advice, he told her. They arranged to meet at her health club. She had a sauna and massage booked; they could talk in the bar after that.

There was a view from the bar's first-floor window down on to a quiet New Town street. All around Rebus sat healthy people, tanned and smiling with good teeth and trim confidence. He knew he fitted in like a paedophile in a classroom. He had trashed his bender clothes, just trashed them, and was wearing the gear he'd bought for the trip to Sir Iain's.

Gill came in and nodded towards him, then went to the bar and bought herself something non-alcoholic. Her skin glowed as she came over to his table. 'You look rough,' she said.

'You should have seen me earlier. You could have sanded doors with me.'

She picked a sliver of orange out of her glass and sucked on it. 'So what's the big mystery?'

He told her the whole story. She started to look uncomfortable halfway through, the look changing by degrees to simple bemusement.

'I'll take another orange juice, if you're buying,' she said when he'd finished.

She needed time to think, so Rebus didn't hurry the barman. But when he came back to the table, she still didn't have anything to say.

'See, Gill, what I need is the nod on a search warrant, so I can go into Gunner's house and seize the file and the tape. We could get one from a JP – there are enough councillors left to choose from.'

Her face darkened. 'Why me?' she said.

'Why not?'

'How good do you think *I'd* come out of this? Do you think anyone would forget that I was the one who'd helped you?'

'For Christ's sake, Gill.'

Her voice softened. She stared into her drink. 'Sorry, I'm letting you down, John.'

'They could crucify me if they wanted to.'

She stared at him. 'They don't want to. You don't know, do you? You really don't know.'

'Know what?'

'You're going to be promoted to chief inspector. There's an opening in Galashiels. It came down to the chief super from the DCC.' She smiled. 'You're trying to arrange a search warrant for his house, and he's busy giving you a hike up. How's *that* going to look in court?'

'It's true,' Chief Superintendent Watson confirmed.

Rebus was in the Farmer's office, but not sitting. He couldn't sit, couldn't even stand at ease.

'I don't want it, I won't accept it. That's allowed, isn't it?'

The Farmer made a pained face. 'If you refuse, it's a snub no one will forget. You might never get a second chance.'

'I don't mind snubbing Allan Gunner.'

'John, Gunner didn't recommend you for promotion, I did.'

'What?'

'Several months back.'

'You did?'

'Yes.'

'Well, it's a damned coincidence Gunner's held off making a decision until now. Whose idea was Galashiels?'

'It happens to be an opening.'

'It happens to be in the middle of nowhere. I can see they'd need a chief inspector down there, what with the farming vendettas and the Saturday night punch-up.'

'For once in your life, John, go easy on yourself, do yourself a favour. Stop beating yourself up like you're the Salvation Army drum. Just . . .' The Farmer shrugged.

'Drums don't beat themselves,' Rebus said. He was staring at the Farmer's computer, not listening any more. And then he started to smile, and looked at the Farmer. 'OK,' he said, 'tell Gunner I'll take it.'

'Good.'

But the Farmer wasn't as pleased as he'd expected he'd be. There was something going on, some motive he couldn't fathom. It was so bloody typical of Rebus to make him feel like a win was a draw, a draw a defeat.

'And, John,' he said, standing up, stretching out his hand, 'congratulations.'

Rebus stared at the hand but didn't take it. 'I didn't say I was accepting the promotion, sir, I just said to *tell* Gunner I was.'

And with that he left the Farmer's office.

Flower was on night-shift again.

Rebus didn't know why or how Flower got so many night-shifts. Maybe because at night he was more likely to see a spot of trouble. Rebus looked like trouble as he strode towards his adversary's desk, dragging a chair over and sitting astride it.

'Done any good fire-raising lately?'

Flower just sneered.

'Some good it did you,' Rebus went on.

'What?'

'I don't mean setting the bin on fire. I mean letting the DCC use your man McAnally like that. Whose idea was it to put him in Charters' cell?'

'What's it to you?'

'Humour me.' Rebus offered Flower a cigarette. Flower took it warily, and even then laid it to one side.

'All right,' he said, 'it was the DCC's.'

'That's what I figured. And you went along with it. I mean, who wouldn't? It meant the DCC owed you a favour – very handy that. But it didn't work out.'

'You've lost me.'

'I mean, the DCC had a hidden agenda. He wanted to use your man to make sure Charters *wasn't* talking, because some people on the outside were getting sweaty. Charters was protecting certain people, people like the head of PanoTech, and the Permanent Secretary at the Scottish Office. But a local councillor had started sniffing. Eventually, he would have talked to Charters – maybe he already had. That worried people, they needed to know how safe they were. As it turned out, Charters knew about the councillor and paid McAnally to give him a fright.'

'Shite.'

'Is it? Well, no matter.' Rebus sucked on his cigarette. He'd got Flower thinking, but that process might take weeks. 'Tell me,' he said, 'your friend the DCC, he didn't even get you Lauderdale's job. Didn't that make you think?'

'It was too soon. It would have looked suspicious.'

Rebus laughed, further discomfiting Flower. 'Is that what he told you?'

'Never you mind.'

'Well, bonny lad, I've got news for you – the DCC's just offered *me* promotion to chief inspector.'

'Away to hell.'

Rebus just shrugged. Flower picked up the cigarette he'd been given and lit it. Then he called the Farmer at home. They had a bruising conversation during which Flower brought up everything from his years in the force (three more than Rebus) to his charitable works. When he finally put the phone down, he was shaking.

'Know who you should phone now?' Rebus suggested. 'Your pal Allan Gunner. Ask him why me instead of you. Know what he'll say? Well, he might not say it, but it's the truth. He's promoting me because I'm

dangerous to him. I'm too dangerous for the usual demotion, so instead he's offering a bribe. And you're being left behind because he can afford to ignore you. That's a simple fact.'

'Why are you telling me this?' Flower hissed.

'Believe me, it's not just for the thrill of seeing you squirm.'

'Why then?'

Rebus leaned forward. 'How,' he asked confidentially, 'would you like my promotion?' Flower just sneered. It hurt Rebus to say what he was saying, but he tried not to let that show. He would sacrifice this and much more for a single, risky shot at his quarry. Above all, though, he wouldn't tell Flower about the move to Galashiels that went along with it . . . 'I mean it,' he said.

Flower saw with deep amazement that he did. 'What do I have to do?'

40

Winter mornings could sap you of good intentions and foolhardy schemes. Rebus and Flower wanted to be in their separate beds, tucked beneath a nice heavy woman, but instead were sitting in Rebus's car, across the street from Allan Gunner's house. It was still dark. A milk van passed, and a bread van, and a few bleak souls on their way to catch the first bus of the day.

'So this is morning,' Flower said.

'Not a pretty sight, is it?'

'You think this will work?'

'Have faith.' Rebus looked towards the house. 'He's up.'

Flower peered out through the windscreen. A light had come on upstairs in the Gunner household.

'We'll give him five minutes,' said Rebus.

But only two minutes later, the downstairs lights came on.

'Could be the wife,' Flower suggested, 'cooking a hearty breakfast for her deserving husband.'

'Have you ever heard the phrase "New Man"?'

'It's a shop, isn't it? What do you reckon, a couple more minutes? Let him get his feet under the breakfast table?'

'My legs are blocks of ice,' Rebus said, opening the car door. 'Let's do it now.'

They rang the doorbell, and heard Gunner's voice calling, 'I'll get it!' Then the door opened, revealing the deputy chief constable in shirt but not yet necktie or cufflinks, a mug of coffee in his hand. He took a step back into the hall.

'What the hell are you doing here?'

'Canvassing for the Natural Law Party,' Rebus said, stepping into the centrally heated house.

Gunner ran upstairs to have a word with his wife, and Rebus and Flower walked uninvited into the kitchen. Smoke was pouring from the electric grill. Flower lifted the grill-pan out and blew on the cremated bread. 'New Man, eh?'

Rebus switched the kettle back on and lifted two mugs from the draining-board. He was unscrewing the lid from the coffee-jar when Gunner returned. Gunner snatched the jar from him.

'Christ, you've got some gall.' He switched the kettle off. 'Why are you here?' He checked his watch, saw he hadn't put it on yet, and glanced instead at the wall-clock. 'Half a minute, then you're on your way.'

'We want the file you've compiled,' Rebus said, 'and the tape Sir Iain made. I think that'll do for now.'

Gunner looked to Flower. 'He's roped you in, eh? You must be mad. I could have you both up before the chief constable.'

'We'd like nothing better,' Flower said. He threw the remains of the toast into the bin. 'You lied to me.'

'If we don't get the file and the tape,' Rebus said, 'we take it further anyway. We're going to kick up such a stink, you'll think your drains have backed up. It'll be everywhere, believe me. There won't be enough clothes-pegs to go round.'

'You *are* mad. I'm not going to give you anything.'

'We'll start with the chief constable and the newspapers.'

Gunner folded his arms. 'Be my guests. You've just dug yourselves a very deep hole.'

'Holes have their uses,' Rebus said, 'when the bullets start to fly.'

'Get out!' Gunner snarled.

They got out.

'Think we were too obliging?' Flower muttered as they walked back down the path. 'We could have been harder on him.'

'It went fine. It's down to him now. Is he watching?'

Flower glanced back. 'Bedroom window.'

'Right.'

They walked to Rebus's car, got in and drove off.

A hundred yards along the road, Rebus stopped long enough to let Flower out. Flower's own car was parked there, and he got into it quickly. Rebus checked in his rearview, but Gunner hadn't come out of the house to check their departure, not on a morning like this. He drove on, went around the block, and ended up on the other side of Gunner's house.

They daren't trust to police frequencies, so had borrowed a couple of on-line cellular phones from a dealer who'd owed Rebus a favour. Rebus's phone rang, and he picked it up.

'Any sign of him?' Flower said.

'Not yet.'

'Maybe he's on the mark-two toast.'

'I don't think he'll have much of an appetite.'

It was five minutes more before Rebus heard a door bang shut. Then Gunner's gate opened. His Rover 800 was directly outside, and he unlocked it, got in, and started the engine.

'Bingo,' said Rebus.

'Has he anything with him?'

'A briefcase.'

'Well, here's hoping.'

Rebus had parked away from the street lighting, and was careful not to start his engine until Gunner was already on the move. Smoke billowed from his exhaust, hanging in the sub-zero air. Gunner's back windscreen was frosted over, and he hadn't taken time to scrape it.

'Fall in behind me,' Rebus told Flower, just before passing his stationary car.

Soon they joined a slow-moving stream of commuter traffic heading into town. The Rover's rear de-mister had taken care of the frost. When they came to a section of dual carriageway, Flower overtook Rebus.

'Where's he headed?'

'Not to work,' Rebus said. 'Not this way.'

They'd discussed routes he might take, places he might go. Princes Street hadn't figured in their calculations. There was light in the sky now, a deep bruise hanging over the Castle and the Old Town. Rebus's heater wasn't working properly – it only did that in the summer – and he curled his toes inside his shoes.

'He's signalling,' Flower said. 'Turning left on to Waverley Bridge. Maybe he's got a train to catch.'

Rebus thought he knew. 'No, but he's headed for the station.'

A long line of black taxis crept up from the subterranean concourse of Waverley Station, waiting their turn to take the commuters to business appointments and power breakfasts. They headed past the taxis, down the steep slope until they were underground. Gunner drove past the pick-up/drop-off point, and looked for a moment as if he was going to head up the exit ramp and back on to Waverley Bridge. But he took a left instead, and found a parking bay towards the back of the station.

'Find yourself a space,' Rebus told Flower, 'and follow on foot.'

'What if he sees me?'

'Get on to the platform, walk down it.'

'What if he goes on to the platform?'

'He hasn't come here for the trains. Hey, and take your phone with you.'

Rebus parked and headed round the other side of the concourse, anti clockwise to Gunner's clockwise. He managed a light jog, as if he was fighting a tight schedule. He walked down a platform towards the rear of the station, the telephone up to his face, as much for camouflage as anything.

'Oh, yes,' Flower said. And then Rebus was in position. In the distance, he could see Flower, and halfway between them Allan Gunner. He was where Rebus had guessed he'd be – at the Left Luggage counter. Rebus stood half-hidden by a billboard advertising industrial space to let. The irony wasn't lost on him as he watched Gunner hand over the briefcase and accept a ticket. When Gunner headed back the way he'd come, Rebus came from around the advertising hoarding and walked briskly towards Left Luggage, just in time to see the employee place the case on a rack right at the front.

'Well?' Flower said.

'Let him go.'

'Is it there?'

'Sweet as a nut, Flower. Sweet as a nut.'

Rico Briggs took some persuading.

Between them, in their many and various ways, Rebus and Flower were expert at the art of persuasion. Well, hadn't they panicked – persuaded – Gunner into getting rid of the evidence? If he'd had time to think, if it hadn't been early morning, he might have thought of a better hiding place. Left Luggage was a stop-gap – he just didn't want the stuff in his house. Rebus had read him just right, and in fact a Left Luggage office wasn't bad, not as a stop-gap.

Rebus and Flower took turns keeping the office under surveillance.

Surveillance was easy in a railway station: there were so many people just hanging around. They didn't want Gunner coming back and lifting the case without them knowing, though Rebus's guess was that it would stay there overnight. Gunner would work the day like any other, then go home and think about it, maybe make a few telephone calls – calls he wouldn't want to make from his own office. With the briefcase and its contents out of the way, he'd feel more confident. He'd want to use that time to think things through.

So the briefcase would be there overnight.

Rebus called Rico and got him to come down to the station. They met in the bar. Rebus had already consumed too much coffee and junk food, and the smell of stale alcohol in the bar almost did for him. The bar smelt the way bars always did at the start of a new day's business – of the previous day, of accumulation; too much smoke and spilt beer.

'Pint of lager,' Rico told the barman. The barman tried not to stare too hard at his customer's tattooed cheeks. Rico gave them a brisk rub while his drink was poured. When he saw there was a gaming machine in the bar, he walked over to it and fed in some coins. Rebus paid for the drink and carried it over to Rico. He had his cellphone in his free hand. I look like a businessman on the way down, he thought.

Maybe he was, at that.

Rebus explained the situation to Rico while Rico played the machine. When Rico ran out of coins, Rebus gave him more. Then his cellphone beeped.

'What does he say?' Flower asked.

'So far, he says no.'

'Let me talk to him.'

So Rebus relieved Flower. He let twenty minutes pass, then phoned the bar.

'Well?'

'He's just about cleaned me out of money,' Flower reported. And in the end it was the gaming machine that was the real persuader. It persuaded Rico to borrow money from Flower – real money – and suddenly Rico owed the policeman twenty pounds.

For the promise of more money, and a clean slate on his debt, Rico said he'd meet them at one in the morning.

Which was only thirteen hours away . . .

Rebus and Flower spent the rest of the day watching Left Luggage, reading newspapers and magazines purchased from the station stall, eating overpriced sandwiches, drinking weak coffee, and generally learning a lot about the life of a mainline railway station.

The security cameras bothered Rebus, so he paid a visit to ScotRail's security office and spoke to the staff, on the pretext of alerting them to a gang of pickpockets just up from Newcastle. It was warm in the security chief's office, and the man was ex-CID, friendly. They traded stories, Rebus asked for a tour. Which was how he saw everything would be all right. The camera trained on Left Luggage was hazy, distant: they'd see anyone going in, but they wouldn't get a good description. This was very much to Rico's advantage.

Besides, no one watched after midnight. The camera would record, but that was all.

The station was locked overnight, but still open at one o'clock. There were weird night trains to deal with, freight-haulers, a sleeper bound for London. Rebus thought he'd probably caught something, he kept shivering at his core. He didn't think it could just be nerves.

True to his word, but ten minutes late, Rico turned up.

'I brought some balaclavas,' he said.

'We won't need them.' Rebus explained about the cameras. They'd taken their cars into Cockburn Street, parked them there. They had a quick discussion as they walked down Platform One towards Left Luggage. Rico had checked the office out earlier, and now carried the tools he needed, tiny picklocks which reminded Rebus of dental instruments. Instinctively, his tongue sought the hole, but there was no hole there, Dr Keene had seen to that.

It took Rico a very long minute, but at last they were in.

With the shutters down, the place was in utter darkness, but Rebus had a couple of torches and handed one to Flower.

'Keep listening at the door, Rico,' he ordered. Then they went to work.

There wasn't much luggage to choose from, and the briefcase was just where Rebus knew it would be. Locked, but that didn't matter. He lifted it up and walked to the door.

'Here, Rico, see what you can do with this.'

He stood with his torch pointed at the case, while Rico brought out his picklocks. Flower, meantime, was moving luggage around, switching tags.

'What the hell are you doing?' Rebus hissed.

'Maximising confusion.'

'Well stop it. Put everything back. We don't want anyone knowing we've been in here.'

Rico made a clucking sound with his tongue. They switched the torches off and stood very still in the darkness, listening. Slow footsteps, coming nearer. A whistled pop tune. Rico rested his weight against the door. Someone tried the door, pushing it a couple of times. Then the shutters jumped a quarter-inch and fell back, then jumped again. If someone shone a torch through the crack, they'd see Flower standing not three feet from them like the last dummy in the shop window. The shutters clattered down again. The footsteps moved away.

Rebus started breathing again.

'I'm glad I thought to wear my brown underwear,' Rico whispered. Rebus shone the light back down on to the briefcase, and Rico tried the locks. They flipped open against his fingers.

Rebus lifted the lid of the case. Inside was a single fat document file and an audio cassette. Rebus lifted both out and instructed Rico to lock the case again.

'Is that it?' Flower said.

It took Rebus half a paragraph to be sure, then he smiled and nodded. He placed the evidence in a carrier bag, put the case back on its shelf, and wiped it clean with the sleeve of his jacket. Rico was looking around at the other bags and cases.

'No way,' Rebus said, coming to wipe the door where Rico had held it shut. 'And don't even *think* of coming back here on your own, understand?'

They relocked the door behind them, and walked up the slope just before the gates were closed for the night.

41

Rebus couldn't sleep.

He sat in his chair smoking a cigarette, reading the file the DCC had prepared – maybe 'crafted' was a better word. He'd done a good job of making it look so thorough while leaving so much out. He played part of the tape, using headphones so he could turn the volume up. Sir Iain was right about one thing – any lawyer listening to the tape would think that the police officer present hadn't done very much. Rebus found that his hand was shaking. He hadn't had a drink all day, and didn't especially want one now. He was just a bit scared, that was all. He wasn't sure he had enough, even now . . . especially now.

Then he thought of something, something he'd almost persuaded himself to forget, and reached for the phone book, finding the page, running his finger down the names, then along to a particular address. A flat on Dublin Street.

It was past three o'clock when Rebus got there, the streets dead, not even any taxis rippling over the setts. Rebus pressed the buzzer and waited, then pressed it again. Then a third time, keeping his finger on it this time.

The intercom crackled into life. 'What? What?'

'Mr McAllister?' Rebus inquired, as if it was the middle of the day.

'Yes?'

'It's Inspector Rebus. If you're alone, I'd like to come up for a word.'

Rory McAllister was half dressed and less than half awake. He was on his own.

Rebus walked around the spacious living room, admiring the ornaments and books, while McAllister made them both a cup of coffee.

Then they sat down opposite one another. McAllister rubbed at his eyes and yawned.

'So what is it, Inspector?'

Rebus put his mug down on the polished wooden floor. 'Well, it's just this, sir. That day we met for lunch, you were . . . well, how can I put it? It struck me afterwards that you were *too* enthusiastic, too willing to talk. Then I saw you going to see Audrey Gillespie and . . . well, I started thinking.'

McAllister tried to hide behind his steaming mug. 'About what?'

'You don't deny you went to see Mrs Gillespie?'

'Not at all. I know her, of course. I met her husband several times, professionally and socially. Mrs Gillespie accompanied her husband on those social occasions.'

Rebus nodded. 'And the other occasions – there's interaction between the district council and the Scottish Office?'

'Of course, and both Councillor Gillespie and myself worked on an industry remit.'

'Mmm,' Rebus said. 'And did the councillor know you were seeing his wife behind his back?'

'Now hang on –'

'Let me finish. You see, Mr McAllister, all this stuff Tom Gillespie found out, is it possible he could have gleaned so much unaided? Someone had to be passing him the information, perhaps anonymously.'

'You've lost me.'

'Never mind, you'll catch up. I think *you* found out about Mensung and PanoTech and Charters' other scams. Sir Iain trusted you, had you pegged as a possible successor. Maybe he had you go into Mensung to make sure there was nothing that could come to light.' Rebus stood up. 'Now, here's where it gets interesting. Because you either passed the information on so you could scupper Sir Iain – in other words, for the public good. Or you did it to keep Gillespie busy and out of the way while you enjoyed a fling with his wife – which might be called the private good. Either way, I think you did it.'

'And you were generous enough to drag me out of bed in the middle of the night to let me know your suspicions?' McAllister sat back in his chair, hands pressed to his chin as if in prayer.

'I came here,' Rebus said, 'because if you did it only to smooth your affair with Audrey Gillespie, then I'm sunk. Whereas, if you really *did* want to get at Sir Iain, then we could be of use to one another.'

McAllister looked up and frowned. 'How?'

So Rebus sat down again and told him.

It was Sir Iain he wanted. He'd cancelled out all the other numbers in the equation, except Charters and Sir Iain. And Sir Iain was one possible route to Derry Charters. Rebus wanted him. He wanted him because people like Sir Iain Hunter were always in the right, even when they were wrong. Sir Iain lived and worked by the same ground rules a lot of villains swore by. He was selfish without appearing to be, full of arguments and self-justifications. He espoused the public good, but lined his pockets with the public's money. He wasn't so very different from the likes of Paul Duggan. If Rebus tried hard enough, he found he could blame Sir Iain for the fates of Willie Coyle and Dixie Taylor. Kirstie had run away from home because her father had been shown the city's corrupt heart, and wasn't going to do anything about it. But the heart was artificial, and Sir Iain Hunter was working the bellows.

When Rebus climbed the stairs to his flat, he found someone huddled in his doorway. It was Sammy. His hand on her shoulder woke her up, and she sprang to her feet.

'What's happened?' he asked.

'I've been phoning you all day. I was worried about you.' There were dried tearstains down both her cheeks. 'I thought I'd wait for you here.'

He let her in. She looked around the living room and saw the duvet on the chair. 'Is this where you sleep?'

'Some nights,' Rebus said, lighting the fire.

'You can't get much rest there.'

'It's all right. Do you want anything to drink?' She shook her head.

'Are you all right?' she asked.

He puffed out his cheeks, then exhaled. 'I think so, just about.' He sank into his chair. 'I'm a bit scared, that's all. I'm going to do something tomorrow; it may not turn out the way I want.'

'One reason I wanted to see you,' she began. 'I can't get it out of my mind, that note . . . and what happened. I thought maybe if you could tell me the story, it would help.'

Rebus smiled. 'It's not exactly a bedtime story.'

His daughter had curled up in front of the fire, and held a cushion against her chest. 'Tell me anyway,' she said.

So Rebus told her, leaving nothing out – it was no less than she deserved. And afterwards, she fell asleep still clutching the cushion. Rebus placed the duvet over her, turned the fire down low, and sat down in his chair again, tears falling so softly that he knew he wouldn't wake her.

He was wearing his best suit.

Flower had phoned first thing to say he wasn't going. He didn't explain, didn't need to. Rebus didn't need any more from him. Flower was thinking tactically: if it all went wrong – as it well might – Flower would be in the foxhole. He still had Rebus's promise: chief inspector. *If* it all worked out.

Sammy had helped him with his grooming. He hadn't had much sleep, but he didn't look too bad considering, and the suit definitely helped.

'Patience chose it for me,' he told his daughter.

'She has good taste,' Sammy agreed.

He phoned first, stressing secrecy and urgency. There were problems, but finally he was given fifteen minutes in the mid-morning. Fifteen precious minutes. He had a bit of time to kill, so paced the flat, emptied the jar and put it back under the radiator, found his dental appointment card and tore it up.

Sammy gave him a good luck kiss as he left the flat.

'We're not so very different,' she told him.

'Like father and daughter,' he said, returning the kiss.

He parked at the front of St Andrew's House, and a guard came out and told him he couldn't do that. Rebus showed his warrant card, but the guard was adamant, and directed him to the visitors' parking.

'Tell me,' Rebus said, 'if I was Sir Iain Hunter, would I still have to move the car?'

'No,' said the guard, 'that would be different.'

And Rebus smiled, feeling a little of the tension leaving him. The man was right: that *would* be different.

He walked up the steps to the building. Close up, it didn't look so much like a power station or the Reichstag. He was signed in at the desk and given a visitor's pass. Security had to check the contents of his bag – just some papers and a cassette. Someone came down to escort him upstairs, where he was passed on to someone else who took him to a secretary's

office. On the way, in a short narrow corridor, his escort nearly bumped into Sir Iain Hunter. She apologised, but Sir Iain wasn't paying her any attention. Rebus winked at him and smiled as he passed. He didn't look back, but he could feel the eyes boring into him, right between the shoulder-blades.

This, he thought, is for Willie and Dixie, and for Tom Gillespie. And for everyone who doesn't know the way the system works, the way it makes room for lying and cheating and stealing.

But he knew, above all, that he was doing it for himself.

There was no secretary in the secretary's office, just Rory McAllister, looking very ill at ease but there, as he'd promised. Rebus found another wink to spare. Then the secretary came in and ushered them into an ante-chamber. She knocked on the door in front of them and opened it.

He'd joked with the security man about the contents of his bag – 'I'd hardly be carrying a bomb in a Spar carrier bag' – but now he walked into the room with the booby-trap tucked under his arm.

'Good of you to find time to see us, sir.'

He meant it, too. Dugald Niven, Secretary of State for Scotland, had a busy schedule. Rebus was sure it would go ahead as usual, no matter what.

Black & Blue

O would, ere I had seen the day
That treason thus could sell us,
My auld grey head had lien in clay,
Wi' Bruce and loyal Wallace!
But pith and power, till my last hour,
I'll mak' this declaration;
We're bought and sold for English gold –
Such a parcel of rogues in a nation.

Robert Burns,
'Fareweel to a' Our Scottish Fame'

If you have the Stones ... to say I can
rewrite history to my own specifications,
you can get away with it.

James Ellroy
(Capitalisation the author's own)

Empty Capital

Weary with centuries
This empty capital snorts like a great beast
Caged in its sleep, dreaming of freedom
But with nae belief . . .

<div align="right">

Sydney Goodsir Smith,
'Kynd Kittock's Land'

</div>

1

'Tell me again why you killed them.'

'I've told you, it's just this *urge*.'

Rebus looked back at his notes. 'The word you used was "compulsion".'

The slumped figure in the chair nodded. Bad smells came off him. 'Urge, compulsion, same thing.'

'Is it?' Rebus stubbed out his cigarette. There were so many butts in the tin ashtray, a couple spilled over on to the metal table. 'Let's talk about the first victim.'

The man opposite him groaned. His name was William Crawford Shand, known as 'Craw'. He was forty years old, single, and lived alone in a council block in Craigmillar. He had been unemployed six years. He ran twitching fingers through dark greasy hair, seeking out and covering a large bald spot at the crown of his head.

'The first victim,' Rebus said. 'Tell us.'

'Us' because there was another CID man in the biscuit-tin. His name was Maclay, and Rebus didn't know him very well. He didn't know anyone at Craigmillar very well, not yet. Maclay was leaning against the wall, arms folded, eyes reduced to slits. He looked like a piece of machinery at rest.

'I strangled her.'

'What with?'

'A length of rope.'

'Where did you get the rope?'

'Bought it at some shop, I can't remember where.'

Three-beat pause. 'Then what did you do?'

'After she was dead?' Shand moved a little in the chair. 'I took her clothes off and was intimate with her.'

'With a dead body?'

'She was still warm.'

Rebus got to his feet. The grating of his chair on the floor seemed to unnerve Shand. Not difficult.

'Where did you kill her?'

'A park.'

'And where was this park?'

'Near where she lived.'

'Where's that?'

'Polmuir Road, Aberdeen.'

'And what were you doing in Aberdeen, Mr Shand?'

He shrugged, running his fingers now along the rim of the table, leaving traces of sweat and grease.

'I wouldn't do that,' Rebus said. 'The edges are sharp, you might get cut.'

Maclay snorted. Rebus walked over towards the wall and stared at him. Maclay nodded briefly. Rebus turned back to the table.

'Describe the park.' He rested against the edge of the table, got himself another cigarette and lit it.

'It was just a park. You know, trees and grass, a play park for the kids.'

'Were the gates locked?'

'What?'

'It was late at night, were the gates locked?'

'I don't remember.'

'You don't remember.' Pause: two beats. 'Where did you meet her?'

Quickly: 'At a disco.'

'You don't seem the disco type, Mr Shand.' Another snort from the machine. 'Describe the place to me.'

Shand shrugged again. 'Like any other disco: dark, flashing lights, a bar.'

'What about victim number two?'

'Same procedure.' Shand's eyes were dark, face gaunt. But for all that he was beginning to enjoy himself, easing into his story again. 'Met her at a disco, offered to take her home, killed her and fucked her.'

'No intimacy then. Did you take a souvenir?'

'Eh?'

Rebus flicked ash on to the floor, flakes landed on his shoes. 'Did you remove anything from the scene?'

Shand thought it over, shook his head.

'And this was where exactly?'

'Warriston Cemetery.'

'Close to her home?'

'She lived on Inverleith Row.'

'What did you strangle her with?'

'The bit of rope.'

'The same piece?' Shand nodded. 'What did you do, keep it in your pocket?'

'That's right.'

'Do you have it with you now?'

'I chucked it.'

'You're not making it easy for us, are you?' Shand squirmed with pleasure. Four beats. 'And the third victim?'

'Glasgow,' Shand recited. 'Kelvingrove Park. Her name was Judith Cairns. She told me to call her Ju-Ju. I did her same as the others.' He sat back in the chair, drawing himself up and folding his arms. Rebus reached out a hand until it touched the man's forehead, faith-healer style. Then he pushed, not very hard. But there was no resistance. Shand and the chair toppled backwards on to the floor. Rebus was kneeling in front of him, hauling him up by the front of his shirt.

'You're a liar!' he hissed. 'Everything you know you got straight from the papers, and what you had to make up was pure dross!' He let go and got to his feet. His hands were damp where he'd been holding the shirt.

'I'm not lying,' Shand pleaded, still prone. 'That's gospel I'm telling you!'

Rebus stubbed out the half-smoked cigarette. The ashtray tipped more butts on to the table. Rebus picked one up and flicked it at Shand.

'Are you not going to charge me?'

'You'll be charged all right: wasting police time. A spell in Saughton with an arse-bandit for a roomie.'

'We usually just let him go,' Maclay said.

'Stick him in a cell,' Rebus ordered, leaving the room.

'But I'm him!' Shand persisted, even as Maclay was picking him off the floor. 'I'm Johnny Bible! I'm Johnny Bible!'

'Not even close, Craw,' Maclay said, quietening him with a punch.

Rebus needed to wash his hands, splash some water on his face. Two woolly suits were in the toilets, enjoying a story and a cigarette. They stopped laughing when Rebus came in.

'Sir,' one asked, 'who did you have in the biscuit-tin?'

'Another comedian,' Rebus said.

'This place is full of them,' the second constable commented. Rebus didn't know if he meant the station, Craigmillar itself, or the city as a whole. Not that there was much comedy in Craigmillar police station. It was Edinburgh's hardest posting; a stint of duty lasted two years max, no one could function longer than that. Craigmillar was about as tough an area as you could find in Scotland's capital city, and the station fully merited its nickname – Fort Apache, the Bronx. It lay up a cul-de-sac behind a row of shops, a low-built dour-faced building with even dourer-faced tenements behind. Being up an alley meant a mob could cut it off from civilisation with ease, and the place had been under siege numerous times. Yes, Craigmillar was a choice posting.

Rebus knew why he was there. He'd upset some people, people who mattered. They hadn't been able to deal him a death blow, so had instead consigned him to purgatory. It couldn't be hell because he knew it wasn't for ever. Call it a penance. The letter telling him of his move had explained that he would be covering for a hospitalised colleague. It had also stated that he would help oversee the shutting down of the old Craigmillar station. Everything was being wound down, transferred to a brand new station nearby. The place was already a shambles of packing cases and pillaged cupboards. Staff weren't exactly expending great energy solving ongoing cases. Nor had they put any energy into welcoming Detective Inspector John Rebus. The place felt more like a hospital ward than a cop-shop, and the patients were tranquillised to the hilt.

He wandered back to the CID room – the 'Shed'. On the way, he passed Maclay and Shand, the latter still protesting his guilt as he was dragged to the cells.

'I'm Johnny Bible! I fucking am and all!'

Not even close.

It was nine p.m. on a Tuesday in June and the only other person in the Shed was Detective Sergeant 'Dod' Bain. He glanced up from his magazine – *Offbeat*, the L&B newsletter – and Rebus shook his head.

'Thought not,' Bain said, turning a page. 'Craw's notorious for grassing himself up, that's why I left him to you.'

'You've as much heart as a carpet tack.'

'But I'm as sharp as one, too. Don't forget that.'

Rebus sat at his desk and considered writing his report of the interview. Another comedian, another waste of time. And still Johnny Bible was out there.

First there had been Bible John, terrorising Glasgow in the late 1960s. A well-dressed young man with reddish hair, who knew his Bible and frequented the Barrowland Ballroom. He picked up three women there, beat them, raped them, strangled them. Then he disappeared, right in the middle of Glasgow's biggest manhunt, and never resurfaced, the case open to this day. Police had a cast-iron description of Bible John from the sister of his last victim. She'd spent close on two hours in his company, shared a taxi with him even. They'd dropped her off; her sister had waved goodbye through the back window . . . Her description hadn't helped.

And now there was Johnny Bible. The media had been quick with the name. Three women: beaten, raped, strangled. That was all they'd needed to make the comparison. Two of the women had been picked up at nightclubs, discos. There were vague descriptions of a man who'd been seen dancing with the victims. Well-dressed, shy. It clicked with the original Bible John. Only Bible John, supposing he were still alive, would be in his fifties, while this new killer was described as mid-to-late twenties. Therefore: Johnny Bible, spiritual son of Bible John.

There were differences, of course, but the media didn't dwell on those. For one thing, Bible John's victims had all been dancing at the same dance hall; Johnny Bible ranged far and wide through Scotland in his hunt for victims. This had led to the usual theories: he was a long-distance lorry driver; a company rep. Police were ruling nothing out. It might even be Bible John himself, back after a quarter century away, the mid-to-late twenties description flawed − it had happened before with apparently watertight eyewitness testimony. They were also keeping a few things quiet about Johnny Bible − just as they had with Bible John. It helped rule out the dozens of fake confessions.

Rebus had barely started his report when Maclay swayed into the room. That was the way he walked, from side to side, not because he was drunk or drugged but because he was seriously overweight, a metabolism thing. There was something wrong with his sinuses too; his breathing often came in laboured wheezes, his voice a blunt plane against the grain of the wood. His station nickname was 'Heavy'.

'Escorted Craw from the premises?' Bain asked.

Maclay nodded towards Rebus's desk. 'Wants him charged for wasting our time.'

'Now that's what I call a waste of time.'

Maclay swayed in Rebus's direction. His hair was jet black, ringed with slick kiss-curls. He'd probably won Bonniest Bairn prizes, but not for a while.

'Come on,' he said.

Rebus shook his head and kept typing.

'Fuck's sake.'

'Fuck him,' Bain said, getting to his feet. He unhooked his jacket from the back of the chair. To Maclay: 'Drinkie?'

Maclay wheezed out a long sigh. 'Just the job.'

Rebus held his breath until they'd gone. Not that he'd been expecting to be asked along. That was their whole point. He stopped typing and reached into his bottom drawer for the Lucozade bottle, unscrewed the cap, sniffed forty-three per cent malt and poured in a mouthful. With the bottle back in its drawer, he popped a mint into his mouth.

Better. 'I can see clearly now': Marvin Gaye.

He yanked the report from the typewriter and crumpled it into a ball, then called the desk, told them to hold Craw Shand an hour, then release him. He'd just put down the phone when it started ringing.

'DI Rebus.'

'It's Brian.'

Brian Holmes, Detective Sergeant, still based at St Leonard's. They kept in touch. His voice tonight was toneless.

'Problem?'

Holmes laughed, no humour. 'I've got the world's supply.'

'So tell me the latest.' Rebus opened the packet one-handed, in mouth and lit.

'I don't know that I can, with you being in shit.'

'Craigmillar's not so bad.' Rebus looked around the stale office.

'I meant the other thing.'

'Oh.'

'See, I'm . . . I might have gotten myself into something . . .'

'What's happened?'

'A suspect, we had him in custody. He was giving me a shitload of grief.'

'You smacked him.'

'That's what he's saying.'

'Filed a complaint?'

'In the process. His solicitor wants to take it all the way.'

'Your word against his?'

'Right.'

'The rubber-heels will kick it out.'

'I suppose so.'

'Or get Siobhan to cover your arse.'

'She's on holiday. My partner for the interview was Glamis.'

'No good then, he's as yellow as a New York cab.'

A pause. 'Aren't you going to ask me if I did it?'

'I don't *ever* want to know, understood? Who was the suspect?'

'Mental Minto.'

'Christ, that brewhead knows more law than the Procurator Fiscal. OK, let's go talkies.'

It was good to be out of the station. He had the car windows rolled down. The breeze was almost warm. The station-issue Escort hadn't been cleaned in a while. There were chocolate wrappers, empty crisp bags, crushed bricks of orange juice and Ribena. The heart of the Scottish diet: sugar and salt. Add alcohol and you had heart *and* soul.

Minto lived in one of the tenement flats on South Clerk Street, first floor. Rebus had been there on occasions past, none of them savoury to the memory. Kerbside was solid with cars, so he double-parked. In the sky,

fading roseate was fighting a losing battle with encroaching dark. And below it all, halogen orange. The street was noisy. The cinema up the road was probably emptying, and the first casualties were tearing themselves away from still-serving pubs. Night-cooking in the air: hot batter, pizza topping, Indian spice. Brian Holmes was standing outside a charity shop, hands in pockets. No car: he'd probably walked from St Leonard's. The two men nodded a greeting.

Holmes looked tired. Just a few years ago he'd been young, fresh, keen. Rebus knew home life had taken its toll: he'd been there in his own marriage, annulled years back. Holmes's partner wanted him out of the force. She wanted someone who spent more time with her. Rebus knew all too well what she wanted. She wanted someone whose mind was on her when he was at home, who wasn't immersed in casework and speculation, mind games and promotion strategies. Often as a police officer you were closer to your working partner than your partner for life. When you joined CID they gave you a handshake and a piece of paper.

The piece of paper was your decree nisi.

'Do you know if he's up there?' Rebus asked.

'I phoned him. He picked up. Sounded halfway to sober.'

'Did you say anything?'

'Think I'm stupid?'

Rebus was looking up at the tenement windows. Ground level was shops; Minto lived above a locksmith's. There was irony there for those who wanted it.

'OK, you come up with me, but stay on the landing. Only come in if you hear trouble.'

'You sure?'

'I'm only going to speak to the man.' Rebus touched Holmes's shoulder. 'Relax.'

The main door was unlocked. They climbed the winding stairs without speaking. Rebus pushed at the bell and took a deep breath. Minto started to pull the door open, and Rebus shouldered it, propelling Minto and himself into the dimly lit hallway. He slammed the door shut behind him.

Minto was ready for violence until he saw who it was. Then he just snarled and strode back to the living room. It was a tiny room, half kitchenette, with a narrow floor-to-ceiling cupboard Rebus knew held a shower. There was one bedroom, and a toilet with a doll-house sink. They made igloos bigger.

'Fuck do you want?' Minto was reaching for a can of lager, high-alcohol. He drained it, standing.

'A word.' Rebus looked around the room, casually as it were. But his hands were by his sides, ready.

'This is unlawful entry.'

'Keep yapping, I'll show you unlawful entry.'

Minto's face creased: not impressed. He was mid-thirties but looked fifteen years older. He'd done most of the major drugs in his time: Billy Whizz, skag, Morningside speed. He was on a meth programme now. On dope, he was a small problem, an irritation; off dope, he was pure radge. He was Mental.

'Way I hear, you're fucked anyway,' he said now.

Rebus took a step closer. 'That's right, Mental. So ask yourself: what have I got to lose? If I'm fucked, might as well make it good and.'

Minto held up his hands. 'Easy, easy. What's your problem?'

Rebus let his face relax. 'You're my problem, Mental. Making a charge against a colleague of mine.'

'He laid into me.'

Rebus shook his head. 'I was there, didn't see a thing. I'd called in with a message for DS Holmes. I stuck around. So if he'd assaulted you, I'd've known, wouldn't I?'

They stood facing one another silently. Then Minto turned and slumped into the room's only armchair. He looked like he was going to sulk. Rebus bent down and picked something off the floor. It was the city's tourist accommodation brochure.

'Going somewhere nice?' He flicked through the lists of hotels, B&Bs, self-catering. Then he waved the magazine at Minto. 'If one single place in here gets turned, you'll be our first stop.'

'Harassment,' Minto said, but quietly.

Rebus dropped the brochure. Minto didn't look so mental now; he looked done in and done down, like life was sporting a horseshoe in one of its boxing gloves. Rebus turned to go. He walked down the hall and was reaching for the door when he heard Minto call his name. The small man was standing at the other end of the hall, only twelve feet away. He had pulled his baggy black T-shirt up to his shoulders. Having shown the front, he turned to give Rebus a view of the back. The lighting was poor – forty-watt bulb in a flyblown shade – but even so Rebus could see. Tattoos, he thought at first. But they were bruises: ribs, sides, kidneys. Self-inflicted? It was possible. It was always possible. Minto dropped the shirt and stared hard at Rebus, not blinking. Rebus let himself out of the flat.

'Everything all right?' Brian Holmes said nervously.

'The story is, I came by with a message. I sat in on the interview.'

Holmes exhaled noisily. 'That's it then?'

'That's it.'

Perhaps it was the tone of voice that alerted Holmes. He met John Rebus's stare, and was the first to break contact. Outside, he put out a hand and said, 'Thanks.'

But Rebus had turned and walked away.

He drove through the streets of the empty capital, six-figure housing huddled either side of the road. It cost a fortune to live in Edinburgh these days. It could cost you everything you had. He tried not to think about what he'd done, what Brian Holmes had done. The Pet Shop Boys inside his head: 'It's a Sin'. Segue to Miles Davis: 'So What?'

He headed in the vague direction of Craigmillar, then thought better of it. He'd go home instead, and pray there were no reporters camped outside. When he went home, he took the night home with him, and had to soak and scrub it away, feeling like an old paving slab, walked on daily. Sometimes it was easier to stay on the street, or sleep at the station. Sometimes he drove all night, not just through Edinburgh: down to Leith and past the working girls and hustlers, along the waterfront, South Queensferry sometimes, and then up on to the Forth Bridge, up the M90

through Fife, past Perth, all the way to Dundee, where he'd turn and head back, usually tired by then, pulling off the road if necessary and sleeping in his car. It all took time.

He remembered he was in a station car, not his own. If they needed it, they could come fetch it. When he reached Marchmont, he couldn't find a parking space on Arden Street, ended up on a double yellow. There were no reporters; they had to sleep sometime, too. He walked along Warrender Park Road to his favourite chip shop – huge portions, and they sold toothpaste and toilet-rolls too, if you needed them. He walked back slowly, nice night for it, and was halfway up the tenement stairs when his pager went off.

2

His name was Allan Mitchison and he was drinking in a hometown bar, not
ostentatiously, but with a look on his face that said he wasn't worried
about money. He got talking to these two guys. One of them told a joke. It
was a good joke. They bought the next round, and he bought one back. They
wiped tears from their eyes when he told his only gag. They ordered three
more. He was enjoying the company.

He didn't have many pals left in Edinburgh. Some of his one-time friends
resented him, the money he still made. He didn't have any family, hadn't
had for as long as he could remember. The two men were company. He
didn't quite know why he came home, or even why he called Edinburgh
'home'. He had a flat with a mortgage on it, but hadn't decorated it yet or
put in any furniture. It was just a shell, nothing worth coming back for.
But everyone went home, that was the thing. The sixteen days straight
that you worked, you were supposed to think about home. You talked about
it, spoke of all the things you'd do when you got there – the booze, the
minge, clubbing. Some of the men lived in or near Aberdeen, but a lot still
had homes further away. They couldn't wait for the sixteen days to end, the
fourteen-day break to begin.

This was the first night of his fourteen days.

They passed slowly at first, then more quickly towards the end, until you
were left wondering why you hadn't done more with your time. This, the
first night, this was the longest. This was the one you had to get through.

They moved on to another bar. One of his new friends was carrying an
old-style Adidas bag, red plastic with a side pocket and a broken strap.
He'd had one just like it at school, back when he was fourteen, fifteen.

'What have you got in there,' he joked, 'your games kit?'

They laughed and slapped him on the back.

At the new place, they moved to shorts. The pub was heaving, wall-to-
wall minge.

'You must think about it all the time,' one of his friends said, 'on the rigs.
Me, I'd go off my head.'

'Or blind,' said the other.

He grinned. 'I get my share.' Downed another Black Heart. He didn't
used to drink dark rum. A fisherman in Stonehaven had introduced him to
the stuff. OVD or Black Heart, but he liked Black Heart best. He liked the
name.

They needed a carry-out, keep the party going. He was tired. The train

from Aberdeen had taken three hours, and there'd been the paraffin budgie before that. His friends were ordering over the bar: a bottle of Bell's and one of Black Heart, a dozen cans, crisps and smokes. It cost a fortune, buying that way. They split it three ways even, so they weren't after his cash.

Outside, there was trouble finding a taxi. Plenty about, but already taken. They had to pull him out of the road when he tried to flag one down. He stumbled a bit and went down on one knee. They helped him back up.

'So what do you do exactly on the rigs?' one of them asked.

'Try to stop them falling down.'

A taxi had stopped to let a couple out.

'Is that your mother or are you just desperate?' he asked the male passenger. His friends told him to shut up, and pushed him into the back. 'Did you see her?' he asked them. 'Face like a bag of marbles.' They weren't going to his flat, there was nothing there.

'We'll go back to our place,' his friends had said. So there was nothing to do but sit back and watch all the lights. Edinburgh was like Aberdeen – small cities, not like Glasgow or London. Aberdeen had more money than style, and it was scary, too. Scarier than Edinburgh. The trip seemed to take for ever.

'Where are we?'

'Niddrie,' someone said. He couldn't remember their names, and was too embarrassed to ask. Eventually the taxi stopped. Outside, the street was dark, looked like the whole fucking estate had welshed on the lecky bill. He said as much.

More laughter, tears, hands on his back.

Three-storey tenements, pebble-dashed. Most of the windows were blocked with steel plates or had been infilled with breeze blocks.

'You live here?' he said.

'We can't all afford mortgages.'

True enough, true enough. He was lucky in so many ways. They pushed hard at the main door and it gave. They went in, one friend either side of him with a hand on his back. Inside, the place was damp and rotten, the stairs half-blocked with torn mattresses and lavatory seats, runs of piping and lengths of broken skirting-board.

'Very salubrious.'

'It's all right once you get up.'

They climbed two storeys. There were a couple of doors off the landing, both open.

'In here, Allan.'

So he walked in.

There was no electricity, but one of his friends had a torch. The place was a midden.

'I wouldn't have taken youse for down-and-outs, lads.'

'The kitchen's OK.'

So they took him through there. He saw a wooden chair which had once been padded. It sat on what was left of the linoleum floor. He was sobering up fast, but not fast enough.

They hauled him down on to the chair. He heard tape being ripped from a roll, binding him to the chair, around and around. Then around his head,

covering his mouth. His legs next, all the way down to the ankles. He was trying to cry out, gagging on the tape. A blow landed on the side of his head. His eyes and ears went fuzzy for a moment. The side of his head hurt, like it had just connected with a girder. Wild shadows flew across the walls.

'Looks like a mummy, doesn't he?'

'Aye, and he'll be crying for his daddy in a minute.'

The Adidas bag was on the floor in front of him, unzipped.

'Now,' one of them said, 'I'll just get out my games kit.'

Pliers, claw-hammer, staple-gun, electric screwdriver, and a saw.

Night sweat, salt stinging his eyes, trickling in, trickling out again. He knew what was happening, but still didn't believe it. The two men weren't saying anything. They were laying a sheet of heavy-duty polythene out on the floor. Then they carried him and the chair on to the sheet. He was wriggling, trying to scream, eyes screwed shut, straining against his bonds. When he opened his eyes, he saw a clear polythene bag. They pulled it down over his head and sealed it with tape around his neck. He breathed in through his nostrils and the bag contracted. One of them picked up the saw, then put it down and picked up the hammer instead.

Somehow, fuelled by sheer terror, Allan Mitchison got to his feet, still tied to the chair. The kitchen window was in front of him. It had been boarded up, but the boards had been torn away. The frame was still there, but only fragments of the actual window panes remained. The two men were busy with their tools. He stumbled between them and out of the window.

They didn't wait to watch him fall. They just gathered up the tools, folded the plastic sheet into an untidy bundle, put everything back in the Adidas bag, and zipped it shut.

'Why me?' Rebus had asked when he'd called in.

'Because,' his boss had said, 'you're new. You haven't been around long enough to make enemies on the estate.'

And besides, Rebus could have added, you can't find Maclay or Bain.

A resident walking his greyhound had called it in. 'A lot of stuff gets chucked on to the street, but not like this.'

When Rebus arrived, there were a couple of patrol cars on the scene, creating a sort of cordon, which hadn't stopped the locals gathering. Someone was making grunting noises in imitation of a pig. They didn't go much for originality around here; tradition stuck hard. The tenements were mostly abandoned, awaiting demolition. The families had been relocated. In some of the buildings, there were still a few occupied flats. Rebus wouldn't have wanted to stick around.

The body had been pronounced dead, the circumstances suspicious to say the least, and now the forensic and photography crews were gathering. A Fiscal Depute was in conversation with the pathologist, Dr Curt. Curt saw Rebus and nodded a greeting. But Rebus had eyes only for the body. An old-fashioned spike-tipped set of railings ran the length of the tenement, and the body was impaled on the fence, still dripping blood. At first, he thought the body grossly deformed, but as he stepped closer he saw what it was. A chair, half of it smashed in the fall. It was attached to the body by

runs of silver tape. There was a plastic bag over the corpse's head. The bag, once translucent, was now half-filled with blood.

Dr Curt walked over. 'I wonder if we'll find an orange in his mouth.'

'Is that supposed to be funny?'

'I've been meaning to phone. I was sorry to hear about your . . . well . . .'

'Craigmillar's not so bad.'

'I didn't mean that.'

'I know you didn't.' Rebus looked up. 'How many storeys did he fall?'

'Looks like a couple. That window there.'

There was a noise behind them. One of the woolly suits was vomiting on to the road. A colleague had an arm around his shoulders, encouraging the flow.

'Let's get him down,' Rebus said. 'Get the poor bastard into a body bag.'

'No electricity,' someone said, handing Rebus a torch.

'Are the floors safe to walk on?'

'Nobody's fallen through yet.'

Rebus moved through the flat. He'd been in dens like it a dozen times. Gangs had been in and sprayed their names and their urine around the place. Others had stripped out anything with even a whiff of monetary value: floor coverings, interior doors, wiring, ceiling roses. A table, missing one leg, had been turned upside down in the living room. There was a crumpled blanket lying on it, and some sheets of newspaper. A real home from home. There was nothing in the bathroom, just holes where the fittings had been. There was a large hole, too, in the bedroom wall. You could look right through into the adjoining flat, and see an identical scene.

The SOCOs were concentrating on the kitchen.

'What have we got?' Rebus asked. Someone shone their torch into a corner.

'Bag full of booze, sir. Whisky, rum, some tinnies and nibbles.'

'Party time.'

Rebus walked to the window. A woolly suit was standing there, looking down on to the street, where a team of four were trying to manoeuvre the body from the railings.

'That's just about as potted heid as you can get.' The young constable turned to Rebus. 'What's the odds, sir? Alky commits suicide?'

'Get used to that uniform, son.' Rebus turned back into the room. 'I want prints from the bag and its contents. If it's from an off-licence, you'll probably find price stickers. If not, could be from a pub. We're looking for one, more likely two people. Whoever sold them the hooch might give a description. How did they get here? Their own transport? Bus? Taxi? We need to know. How did they know about this place? Local knowledge? We need to ask the neighbours.' He was walking through the room now. He recognised a couple of junior CID from St Leonard's, plus Craigmillar uniforms. 'We'll split the tasks later. It could all be some hideous accident or joke gone wrong, but whatever it was the victim wasn't here on his tod. I want to know who was here with him. Thank you and goodnight.'

Outside, they were taking final photographs of the chair and the bonds around it, before separating chair from body. The chair would be bagged, too, along with any splinters they found. Funny how orderly it all became;

order out of chaos. Dr Curt said he'd do the post-mortem in the morning. That was fine by Rebus. He got back into the patrol car, wishing it were his own: the Saab had a half bottle of whisky tucked under the driver's seat. Many of the pubs would still be open: midnight licences. Instead, he drove back to the station. It was less than a mile away. Maclay and Bain looked like they'd just got in, but they'd already heard the news.

'Murder?'

'Something like it,' Rebus said. 'He was tied to a chair with a plastic bag over his head, mouth taped shut. Maybe he was pushed, maybe he jumped or fell. Whoever was with him left in a rush – forgot to take their carry-out.'

'Junkies? Dossers?'

Rebus shook his head. 'New jeans by the look of them, and new Nikes on his feet. Wallet with plenty of cash, bank card and credit card.'

'So we've got a name?'

Rebus nodded. 'Allan Mitchison, address off Morrison Street.' He shook a set of keys. 'Anybody want to tag along?'

Bain went with Rebus, leaving Maclay to 'hold the fort' – a phrase overused at Fort Apache. Bain said he didn't make a good passenger, so Rebus let him drive. DS 'Dod' Bain had a rep; it had followed him from Dundee to Falkirk and from there to Edinburgh. Dundee and Falkirk weren't exactly spa towns either. He sported a nick in the skin beneath his right eye, souvenir of a knife attack. Every so often, his finger strayed to the spot; it wasn't something he was conscious of. At five-eleven he was a couple of inches shorter than Rebus, maybe ten pounds lighter. He used to box middleweight amateur, southpaw, leaving him one ear which hung lower than the other and a nose which covered half his face. His shorn hair was salt-and-pepper. Married, three sons. Rebus hadn't seen much at Craigmillar to justify Bain's hardman rep; he was a regular soldier, a form-filler and by-the-book investigator. Rebus had just dispatched one nemesis – DI Alister Flower, promoted to some Borders outpost, chasing sheep-shaggers and tractor racers – and wasn't looking to fill the vacancy.

Allan Mitchison's flat was in a designer block in what wanted to be called 'the Financial District'. Scrapland off Lothian Road had been transformed into a conference centre and 'apartments'. A new hotel was in the offing, and an insurance company had grafted its new headquarters on to the Caledonian Hotel. There was room for more expansion, more road-building.

'Desperate,' Bain said, parking the car.

Rebus tried to remember the way the area had looked before. He only had to think back a year or two, but found the process difficult nonetheless. Was it just a big hole in the ground, or had they knocked things down? They were half a mile, maybe less, from Torphichen cop-shop; Rebus thought he knew this whole hunting-ground. But now he found that he didn't know it at all.

There were half a dozen keys on the chain. One of them opened the main door. In the well-lit lobby there was a whole wall of letterboxes. They found the name Mitchison – flat 312. Rebus used another key to open the box and remove the mail. There was some junk – 'Open Now! You Could Have Scooped Life's Jackpot!' – and a credit-card statement. He opened the

statement. Aberdeen HMV, an Edinburgh sports shop – £56.50, the Nikes – and a curry house, also in Aberdeen. A gap of just under two weeks, then the curry house again.

They took the narrow lift to the third floor, Bain shadow-boxing the full-length mirror, and found flat 12. Rebus unlocked the door, saw that an alarm panel was flashing on the wall in the small hallway, and used another key to disable it. Bain found the light-switch and closed the door. The flat smelled of paint and plaster, carpets and varnish – new, uninhabited. There wasn't a stick of furniture in the place, just a telephone on the floor beside an unrolled sleeping-bag.

'The simple life,' Bain said.

The kitchen was fully equipped – washing machine, cooker, dishwasher, fridge – but the seal was still across the door of the washer-drier and the fridge contained only its instruction manual, a spare lightbulb, and a set of risers. There was a swing-bin in the cupboard beneath the sink. When you opened the door, the lid of the bin opened automatically. Inside, Rebus saw two crushed beer cans and the red-stained wrappings from what smelled like a kebab. The flat's solitary bedroom was bare, no clothes in the built-in wardrobe, not even a coat-hanger. But Bain was dragging something out of the tiny bathroom. It was a blue rucksack, a Karrimor.

'Looks like he came in, had a wash, changed clothes and buggered off out again pronto.'

They started emptying the rucksack. Apart from clothing, they found a personal stereo and some tapes – Soundgarden, Crash Test Dummies, Dancing Pigs – and a copy of Iain Banks's *Whit*.

'I meant to buy that,' Rebus said.

'Take it now. Who's watching?'

Rebus looked at Bain. The eyes seemed innocent, but he shook his head anyway. He couldn't go handing anyone any more ammunition. He pulled a carrier bag out of one of the side pockets: new tapes – Neil Young, Pearl Jam, Dancing Pigs again. The receipt was from HMV in Aberdeen.

'My guess,' Rebus said: 'he worked in Furry Boot town.'

From the other side pocket, Bain produced a pamphlet, folded in four. He unfolded it, opened it, and let Rebus see what it was. There was a colour photograph of an oil platform on the front, beneath a headline: 'T-BIRD OIL – STRIKING THE BALANCE', and a sub-head: 'Decommissioning Offshore Installations – A Modest Proposal'. Inside, besides a few paragraphs of writing, there were colour charts, diagrams and statistics. Rebus read the opening sentence:

'"In the beginning there were microscopic organisms, living and dying in the rivers and seas many millions of years ago."' He looked up at Bain. 'And they gave their lives so that millions of years on we can tank around in cars.'

'I get the feeling Spike maybe worked for an oil company.'

'His name was Allan Mitchison,' Rebus said quietly.

It was getting light when Rebus finally arrived home. He turned the hi-fi on so that it was just audible, then rinsed a glass in the kitchen and poured an inch of Laphroaig, adding a dribble of water from the tap. Some malts demanded water. He sat down at the kitchen table and looked at the

newspapers laid out there, cuttings from the Johnny Bible case, photo-copies of old Bible John stuff. He'd spent a day in the National Library, fast-tracking the years 1968–70, winding a blur of microfilm through the machine. Stories had leapt out at him. Rosyth was to lose its Royal Navy Commander; plans were announced for a £50 million petrochemical complex at Invergordon; *Camelot* was showing at the ABC.

A booklet was advertised for sale – 'How Scotland Should be Governed' – and there were letters to the editor concerning Home Rule. A Sales and Marketing Manager was wanted, salary of £2,500 p.a. A new house in Strathalmond cost £7,995. Frogmen were searching for clues in Glasgow, while Jim Clark was winning the Australian Grand Prix. Meantime, members of the Steve Miller Band were being arrested in London on drug charges, and car parking in Edinburgh had reached saturation point . . .

1968.

Rebus had copies of the actual newspapers – purchased from a dealer for considerably more than their sixpenny cover price. They continued into '69. August. The weekend that Bible John claimed his second victim, the shit was hitting the fan in Ulster and 300,000 pop fans were turning up (and on) at Woodstock. A nice irony. The second victim was found by her own sister in an abandoned tenement . . . Rebus tried not to think of Allan Mitchison, concentrated on old news instead, smiled over an August 20 headline: 'Downing Street Declaration'. Trawler strikes in Aberdeen . . . an American film company seeking sixteen sets of bagpipes . . . dealings in Robert Maxwell's Pergamon suspended. Another headline: 'Big drop in Glasgow crimes of violence'. Tell that to the victims. By November, it was reported that the murder rate in Scotland was twice that of England and Wales – a record fifty-two indictments in the year. A debate on capital punishment was taking place. There were anti-war demos in Edinburgh, while Bob Hope entertained the troops in Vietnam. The Stones did two shows in Los Angeles – at £71,000 the most lucrative one-night stand in pop.

It was November 22 before an artist's impression of Bible John appeared in the press. By then he *was* Bible John: the media had come up with the name. Three weeks between the third murder and the artist's impression: the trail grown good and cold. There'd been an artist's drawing after the second victim too, but only after a delay of almost a month. Big, big delays. Rebus wondered about them . . .

He couldn't quite explain why Bible John was getting to him. Perhaps he was using one old case as a way of warding off another – the Spaven case. But he thought it went deeper than that. Bible John meant the end of the sixties for Scotland; he'd soured the end of one decade and the beginning of another. For a lot of people, he'd all but killed whatever dribble of peace and love had reached this far north. Rebus didn't want the twentieth century to end the same way. He wanted Johnny Bible caught. But somewhere along the road, his interest in the present case had taken a turning. He'd started to concentrate on Bible John, to the point where he was dusting off old theories and spending a small fortune on period newspapers. In 1968 and '69, Rebus had been in the Army. They'd trained him how to disable and kill, then sent him on tours – including, eventually, Northern Ireland. He felt he'd missed an important part of the times.

But at least he was still alive.

He took glass and bottle through to the living room and sank into his chair. He didn't know how many bodies he'd seen; he just knew it didn't get any easier. He'd heard gossip about Bain's first post-mortem, how the pathologist had been Naismith up in Dundee, a cruel bastard at the best of times. He'd probably known it was Bain's first, and had really done a job on the corpse, like a scrap merchant stripping a car, lifting out organs, sawing the skull open, hands cradling a glistening brain – you didn't do that so lightly these days, fear of hepatitis C. When Naismith had started unpeeling the genitals, Bain had dropped deadweight to the floor. But credit where due, he'd stuck around, hadn't bolted or hughied. Maybe Rebus and Bain could work together, once friction had smoothed their edges. Maybe.

He looked out of the bay window, down on to the street. He was still parked on a double yellow. There was a light on in one of the flats across the way. There was always a light on somewhere. He sipped his drink, not wanting to rush it, and listened to the Stones: *Black and Blue*. Black influences, blues influences; not great Stones, but maybe their mellowest album.

Allan Mitchison was in a fridge in the Cowgate. He'd died strapped to a chair. Rebus didn't know why. Pet Shop Boys: 'It's a Sin'. Segue to the Glimmer Twins: 'Fool to Cry'. Mitchison's flat hadn't been so different from Rebus's own in some respects: underused, more a base than a home. He downed the rest of his drink, poured another, downed that too, and pulled the duvet off the floor and up to his chin.

Another day down.

He awoke a few hours later, blinked, got up and went to the bathroom. A shower and shave, change of clothes. He'd been dreaming of Johnny Bible, getting it all mixed up with Bible John. Cops on the scene wearing tight suits and thin black ties, white bri-nylon shirts, pork-pie hats. 1968, Bible John's first victim. To Rebus it meant Van Morrison, *Astral Weeks*. 1969, victims two and three; the Stones, *Let It Bleed*. The hunt went on into 1970, John Rebus wanting to go to the Isle of Wight Festival, not managing it. But of course Bible John had disappeared by then . . . He hoped Johnny Bible would just sod off and die.

There was nothing in the kitchen to eat, nothing but newspapers. The nearest corner shop had closed down; it wasn't much more of a walk to the next grocer's along. No, he'd stop somewhere en route. He looked out of the window and saw a light-blue estate double parked outside, blocking three resident cars. Equipment in the back of the estate, two men and a woman standing on the pavement, supping coffee from takeaway beakers.

'Shit,' Rebus said, knotting his tie.

Jacketed, he walked outside and into questions. One of the men was hoisting a video camera up to his shoulder. The other man was speaking.

'Inspector, could we have a word? Redgauntlet Television, *The Justice Programme*.' Rebus knew him: Eamonn Breen. The woman was Kayleigh Burgess, the show's producer. Breen was writer/presenter, loved himself, RPIA: Royal Pain in Arse.

'The Spaven case, Inspector. A few minutes of your time, that's all we need really, help everybody get to the bottom—'

'I'm already there.' Rebus saw the camera wasn't ready yet. He turned quickly, his nose almost touching the reporter's. He thought of Mental Minto breathing the word 'harassment', not knowing what harassment was, not the way Rebus had grown to know.

'You'll think you're in childbirth,' he said.

Breen blinked. 'Sorry?'

'When the surgeons are taking that camera out of your arse.' Rebus tore a parking ticket from his windscreen, unlocked the car, and got in. The video camera was finally up and running, but all it got was a shot of a battered Saab 900 reversing at speed from the scene.

Rebus had a morning meeting with his boss, Chief Inspector Jim MacAskill. The boss's office looked as chaotic as any other part of the station: packing cases still waiting to be filled and labelled, half-empty shelves, ancient green filing-cabinets with their drawers open, displaying acre upon acre of paperwork, all of which would have to be shipped out in some semblance of order.

'The world's hardest jigsaw puzzle,' MacAskill said. 'If everything gets to the other end unscathed, it'll be a miracle on a par with Raith Rovers winning the UEFA Cup.'

The boss was a Fifer like Rebus, born and raised in Methil, back when the shipyard had been making boats rather than rigs for the oil industry. He was tall and well built and younger than Rebus. His handshake was not masonic, and he'd not yet married, which had caused the usual gossip that maybe the boss was a like-your-loafers. It didn't worry Rebus – he never wore loafers himself – but he hoped that if his boss was gay there was no guilt involved. It was when you wanted a secret kept that you fell prey to blackmailers and shame merchants, destructive forces both interior and exterior. Jesus, and didn't Rebus know about that.

Whatever, MacAskill was handsome, with plenty of thick black hair – no grey, no sign of dyeing – and a chiselled face, all angles, the geometry of eyes, nose and chin making it look like he was smiling even when he wasn't.

'So,' the boss said, 'how does it read to you?'

'I'm not sure yet. A party gone wrong, a falling out – literally in this case? They hadn't started on the booze.'

'Question one in my mind: did they come together? The victim could have come alone, surprised some people doing something they shouldn't—'

Rebus was shaking his head. 'Taxi driver confirms dropping off a party of three. Gave descriptions, one of which matches the deceased pretty well. The driver paid him most attention, he was behaving the worst. The other two were quiet, sober even. Physical descriptions aren't going to get us far. He picked up the fare outside Mal's Bar. We've had a word with the staff. They sold them the carry-out.'

The boss ran a hand down his tie. 'Do we know anything more about the deceased?'

'Only that he had Aberdeen connections, maybe worked in the oil business. He didn't use his Edinburgh flat much, makes me think he used to work heavy shifts, two weeks on, two off. Maybe he didn't always come home between times. He was earning enough to pay off a mortgage in the

Financial District, and there's a two-week gap between his latest credit-card transactions.'

'You think he could have been offshore during that time?'

Rebus shrugged. 'I don't know if that's the way it still works, but in the early days I had friends who went to seek their fortune on the rigs. The stints lasted two weeks, seven days a week.'

'Well, it's worth following up. We need to check family, too, next of kin. Priority for the paperwork and formal ID. Question one in my mind: motive. Are we sticking with an argument?'

Rebus shook his head. 'There was too much premeditation, way too much. Did they just happen to find sealing-tape and a polythene bag in that tip? I think they brought them. Do you remember how the Krays got to Jack "the Hat" McVitie? No, you're too young. They invited him to a party. He'd been paid to do a contract, but bottled it and couldn't pay them back. It was in a basement, so down he comes crying out for birds and booze. No birds, no booze, just Ronnie grabbing him and Reggie stabbing him to death.'

'So these two men lured Mitchison to the derelict flat?'

'Maybe.'

'To what end?'

'Well, first thing they did was tie him up and wrap a bag around his head, so they didn't have any questions to ask. They just wanted him crapping himself and then dead. I'd say it was straight assassination, with a bit of malicious cruelty thrown in.'

'So was he thrown or did he jump?'

'Does it matter?'

'Very much, John.' MacAskill stood up, leaned against the filing cabinet with his arms folded. 'If he jumped, that's tantamount to suicide, even if they *had* been planning to kill him. With the bag over his head and the way he was trussed up, we've got maybe culpable homicide. Their defence would be that they were trying to scare him, he got *too* scared and did something they hadn't been expecting – jumped through a window.'

'To do which he must have been scared out of his wits.'

MacAskill shrugged. 'Still not murder. The crux is, were they trying to scare him, or kill him?'

'I'll be sure to ask them.'

'It's got a gang feel to it: drugs maybe, or a loan he'd stopped repaying, somebody he'd ripped off.' MacAskill returned to his chair. He opened a drawer and took out a can of Irn-Bru, opened it and started to drink. He never went to the pub after work, didn't share the whisky when the team got a result. Soft drinks only: more ammo for the like-your-loafers brigade. He asked Rebus if he wanted a can.

'Not while I'm on duty, sir.'

MacAskill stifled a burp. 'Get a bit more background on the victim, John, let's see if it leads anywhere. Remember to chase forensics for fingerprint ID on the carry-out, and pathology for the PM results. Did he do drugs, that's question one in my mind. Make things easier for us if he did. Unsolved, and we don't even know how to frame it – not the sort of case I want to drag to the new station. Understood, John?'

'Unquestionably, sir.'

He turned to go, but the boss hadn't quite finished. 'That trouble over . . . what was the name again?'

'Spaven?' Rebus guessed.

'Spaven, yes. Quietened down yet, has it?'

'Quiet as the grave,' Rebus lied, making his exit.

3

That evening – a long-standing engagement – Rebus was at a rock concert at Ingliston Showground, an American headliner with a couple of biggish-name British acts supporting. Rebus was part of a team of eight, four different city stations represented, providing back-up (meaning protection) for Trading Standards sniffers. They were looking for bootleg gear – T-shirts and programmes, tapes and CDs – and had the full support of the bands' management. This meant backstage passes, liberal use of the hospitality marquee, a lucky-bag of official merchandising. The lackey passing out the bags smiled at Rebus.

'Maybe your kids or grandkids . . .' Thrusting the bag at him. He'd bitten back a remark, passed straight to the booze tent, where he couldn't decide between the dozens of hooch bottles, so settled for a beer, then wished he'd taken a nip of Black Bush, so eased the unopened bottle into his lucky-bag.

They had two vans parked outside the arena, way back behind the stage, filling with counterfeiters and their merchandise. Maclay weaved back to the vans nursing a set of knuckles.

'Who did you pop, Heavy?'

Maclay shook his head, wiping sweat from his brow, a Michelangelo cherub turned bad.

'Some choob was resisting,' he said. 'Had a suitcase with him. I punched a hole right through it. He didn't resist after that.'

Rebus looked into the back of a van, the one holding bodies. A couple of kids, hardening already to the system, and two regulars, old enough to know the score. They'd be fined a day's wages, the loss of their stock just another debit. The summer was young, plenty festivals to come.

'Fucking awful racket.'

Maclay meant the music. Rebus shrugged; he'd been getting into it, thought maybe he'd take home a couple of the bootleg CDs. He offered Maclay the bottle of Black Bush. Maclay drank from it like it was lemonade. Rebus offered him a mint afterwards, and he threw it into his mouth with a nod of thanks.

'Post-mortem results came in this afternoon,' the big man said.

Rebus had meant to phone, hadn't got round to it. 'And?'

Maclay crushed the mint to powder. 'The fall killed him. Apart from that, not much.'

The fall killed him: little chance of a straight murder conviction. 'Toxicology?'

'Still testing. Professor Gates said when they cut into the stomach, there was a strong whiff of dark rum.'

'There was a bottle in the bag.'

Maclay nodded. 'The decedent's tipple. Gates said no initial signs of drug use, but we'll have to wait for the tests. I went through the phone book for Mitchisons.'

Rebus smiled. 'So did I.'

'I know, one of the numbers I called, you'd already been on to them. No joy?'

Rebus shook his head. 'I got a number for T-Bird Oil in Aberdeen. Their personnel manager's going to call me back.'

A Trading Standards officer was coming towards them, arms laden with T-shirts and programmes. His face was red from exertion, his thin tie hanging loose at the neck. Behind him, an officer from 'F Troop' – Livingston Division – was escorting another prisoner.

'Nearly done, Mr Baxter?'

The Trading Standards officer dumped the T-shirts, lifted one and wiped his face with it.

'That should about do it,' he said. 'I'll round up my soldiers.'

Rebus turned to Maclay. 'I'm starving. Let's see what they've laid on for the superstars.'

There were fans trying to breach security, teenagers mostly, split half and half, boys and girls. A few had managed to inveigle their way in. They wandered around behind the barriers looking for faces they would recognise from the posters on their bedroom walls. Then when they did spot one, they'd be too awed or shy to talk.

'Any kids?' Rebus asked Maclay. They were in hospitality, nursing bottles of Beck's taken from a coolbox Rebus hadn't noticed first time round.

Maclay shook his head. 'Divorced before it became an issue, if you'll pardon the pun. You?'

'One daughter.'

'Grown-up?'

'Sometimes I think she's older than me.'

'Kids grow up faster than in our day.' Rebus smiled at that, Maclay a good ten years his junior.

A girl, squealing resistance, was being hauled back to the perimeter by two burly security men.

'Jimmy Cousins,' Maclay said, pointing out one of the security bears. 'Do you know him?'

'He was stationed at Leith for a while.'

'Retired last year, only forty-seven. Thirty years in. Now he's got his pension *and* a job. Makes you think.'

'Makes me think he misses the force.'

Maclay smiled. 'It can turn into a habit.'

'That why you divorced?'

'I dare say it played a part.'

Rebus thought of Brian Holmes, feared for him. Stress getting to the younger man, affecting work and personal life both. Rebus had been there.

'You know Ted Michie?'

Rebus nodded: the man he'd replaced at Fort Apache.

'Doctors think it's terminal. He won't let them cut, says knives are against his religion.'

'I hear he was handy with a truncheon in his day.'

One of the support bands entered the marquee to scattered applause. Five males, mid-twenties, stripped to the waist with towels around their shoulders, high on something – maybe just from performing. Hugs and kisses from a group of girls at a table, whoops and roars.

'We fucking killed them out there!'

Rebus and Maclay drank their drinks in silence, tried not to look like promoters, succeeded.

When they walked back outside, it was dark enough for the light-show to be worth watching. There were fireworks, too, reminding Rebus that it was the tourist season. Not long till the nightly Tattoo, fireworks you could hear from Marchmont, even with the windows closed. A camera crew, stalked by photographers, was itself stalking the main support band who were ready to go on. Maclay watched the procession.

'You're probably surprised they're not after you,' he said, mischief in his voice.

'Fuck off,' Rebus replied, making for the side of the stage. The passes were colour-coded. His was yellow, and it got him as far as the stage-wings, where he watched the entertainment. The sound system was a travesty, but there were monitors nearby and he concentrated on those. The crowd seemed to be having fun, bobbing up and down, a sea of disembodied heads. He thought of the Isle of Wight, of other festivals he'd missed, headliners who weren't around any more.

He thought of Lawson Geddes, his one-time mentor, boss, protector, his memory rippling back through two decades.

John Rebus, mid-twenties, a detective constable, looking to put Army years behind him, ghosts and nightmares. A wife and infant daughter trying to be his life. And Rebus maybe seeking out a surrogate father, finding one in Lawson Geddes, Detective Inspector, City of Edinburgh Police. Geddes was forty-five, ex-Army, served in the Borneo conflict, told stories of jungle war versus The Beatles, no one back in Britain very interested in a last spasm of colonial muscle. The two men found they shared common values, common night sweats and dreams of failure. Rebus was new to CID, Geddes knew everything there was to know. It was easy to recall the first year of growing friendship, easy now to forgive the few hiccups: Geddes making a pass at Rebus's young wife, almost succeeding; Rebus passing out at a Geddes party, waking in the dark and pissing into a dresser-drawer, thinking he'd found the toilet; a couple of fist-fights after last orders, the fists not connecting, turning into wrestling matches instead.

Easy to forgive so much. But then they landed a murder inquiry, Leonard Spaven Geddes' chief suspect. Geddes and Lenny Spaven had been playing cat-and-mouse for a couple of years – aggravated assault, pimping, the hijacking of a couple of cigarette lorries. Even whispers of a murder or two, gangster stuff, trimming the competition. Spaven had been in the Scots Guards same time as Geddes, maybe the bad blood started there, neither man ever said.

Christmas 1976, a gruesome find on farmland near Swanston: a woman's body, decapitated. The head turned up almost a week later, New Year's Day, in another field near Currie. The weather was sub-zero. From the rate of decay, the pathologist was able to say that the head had been kept indoors for some time after being severed from the body, while the body itself had been dumped fresh. Glasgow police semi-interested, the file on Bible John still open six years on. Identification from clothing initially, a member of the public coming forward to say the description sounded like a neighbour who hadn't been seen for a couple of weeks. The milkman had kept on delivering until he decided no one was home, that she had gone away for Christmas without telling him.

Police forced the front door. Unopened Christmas cards on the hall carpet; a pot of soup on the stove, speckled with mould; a radio playing quietly. Relatives were found, identified the body – Elizabeth Rhind, Elsie to her friends. Thirty-five years old, divorced from a sailor in the merchant navy. She'd worked for a brewery, shorthand and typing. She'd been well liked, the outgoing type. The ex-husband, suspect one, had a steel-toecapped alibi: his ship was in Gib at the time. Lists of the victim's friends, especially boyfriends, and a name came up: Lenny. No surname, someone Elsie had gone out with for a few weeks. Drinking companions provided a description, and Lawson Geddes recognised it: Lenny Spaven. Geddes formed his theory quickly: Lenny had zeroed in on Elsie when he learned she worked at the brewery. He was probably looking for inside gen, maybe thinking of a truck hijack or a simple break-in. Elsie refused to help, he got angry, and he killed her.

It sounded good to Geddes, but he found it hard to convince anyone else. There was no evidence either. They couldn't determine a time of death, leaving a twenty-four-hour margin of error, so Spaven didn't need to provide an alibi. A search of his home and those of his friends showed no bloodstains, nothing. There were other strands they should have been following, but Geddes couldn't stop thinking about Spaven. It nearly drove John Rebus demented. They argued loudly, more than once, stopped going for drinks together. The brass had a word with Geddes, told him he was becoming obsessed to the detriment of the inquiry. He was told to take a holiday. They even had a collection for him in the Murder Room.

Then one night he'd come to Rebus's door, begging a favour. He looked like he hadn't slept in a week, or changed his clothes over that time. He said he'd been following Spaven, and had tracked him to a lock-up in Stockbridge. He was probably still there if they hurried. Rebus knew it was wrong; there were procedures. But Geddes was shivering, wild-eyed. All idea of search warrants and the like evaporated. Rebus insisted on driving, Geddes giving directions.

Spaven was still in the garage. So were brown cardboard boxes, piled high: the proceeds from a South Queensferry warehouse break-in back in November. Digital clock-radios: Spaven was fitting plugs to them, preparing to hawk them around the pubs and clubs. Behind one pile of boxes, Geddes discovered a plastic carrier bag. Inside were a woman's hat and a cream shoulder-bag, both later identified as having belonged to Elsie Rhind.

Spaven protested his innocence from the moment Geddes lifted up the

carrier bag and asked what was inside. He protested all the way through the rest of the investigation, the trial, and as he was being hauled back to the cells after being handed down a life sentence. Geddes and Rebus were in court, Geddes back to normal, beaming satisfaction, Rebus just a little uneasy. They'd had to concoct a story: an anonymous tip-off on a consignment of stolen goods, a chance find . . . It felt right and wrong at the same time. Lawson Geddes hadn't wanted to talk about it afterwards, which was strange: usually they dissected their cases – successful or not – over a drink. Then, to everyone's surprise, Geddes had resigned from the force, with promotion only a year or two away. Instead, he'd gone to work in his father's off-sales business – there was always a discount waiting for serving officers – made some money, and retired at a youthful fifty-five. For the past ten years, he'd been living with his wife Etta in Lanzarote.

Ten years ago Rebus had received a postcard. Lanzarote had 'not much fresh water, but enough to temper a glass of whisky, and the Torres wines need no adulteration'. The landscape was almost lunar, 'black volcanic ash, so an excuse not to garden!', and that was about it. He hadn't heard anything since, and Geddes hadn't furnished his address on the island. That was OK, friendships came and went. Geddes had been a useful man to know at the time, he'd taught Rebus a lot.

Dylan: *Don't Look Back*.

The here and now: light-show stinging Rebus's eyes. He blinked back tears, stepped away from the stage, retreated to hospitality. Pop stars and entourage, loving the media interest. Flash-bulbs and questions. A spume of champagne. Rebus brushed flecks from his shoulder, decided it was time to find his car.

The Spaven case should have remained closed, no matter how loudly the prisoner himself protested. But in jail, Spaven had started writing, his writings smuggled out by friends or bribed jailers. Pieces had started to see publication – fiction at first, an early story picking up first prize in some newspaper competition. When the winner's true identity and whereabouts were revealed, the newspaper got itself a bigger news story. More writing, more publication. Then a TV drama, penned by Spaven. It won an award somewhere in Germany, another in France, it was shown in the USA, an estimated audience of twenty million worldwide. There was a follow-up. Then a novel, and then the non-fiction pieces started appearing – Spaven's early life at first, but Rebus knew where the story would lead.

By this time there was loud support in the media for an early release, nullified when Spaven assaulted another prisoner severely enough to cause brain damage. Spaven's pieces from jail became more eloquent than ever – the man had been jealous of all the attention, had attempted to murder Spaven in the corridor outside his cell. Self-defence. And the crunch: Spaven would not have been placed in this invidious position were it not for a gross miscarriage of justice. The second instalment of Spaven's autobiography ended with the Elsie Rhind case, and with mention of the two police officers who'd framed him – Lawson Geddes and John Rebus. Spaven reserved his real loathing for Geddes, Rebus just a bit-player, Geddes's lackey. More media interest. Rebus saw it as a revenge fantasy, planned over long incarcerated years, Spaven unhinged. But whenever he read

Spaven's work, he saw powerful manipulation of the reader, and he thought back to Lawson Geddes on his doorstep that night, to the lies they told afterwards . . .

And then Lenny Spaven died, committed suicide. Took a scalpel to his throat and opened it up, a gash you could fit your hand inside. More rumour: he'd been murdered by jailers before he could complete volume three of his autobiography, detailing his years and depredations in several Scottish prisons. Or jealous prisoners had been allowed access to his cell.

Or it was suicide. He left a note, three drafts crumpled on the floor, maintaining to the end his innocence in the Elsie Rhind killing. The media started sniffing their story, Spaven's life and death big news. And now . . . three things.

One: the incomplete third volume of autobiography had been published – 'heart-breaking' according to one critic, 'a massive achievement' for another. It was still on the best-seller list, Spaven's face staring out from bookshop windows all along Princes Street. Rebus tried to avoid the route.

Two: a prisoner was released, and told reporters he was the last person to see or speak to Spaven alive. According to him, Spaven's last words were: 'God knows I'm innocent, but I'm so tired of saying it over and over.' The story earned the ex-offender £750 from a newspaper; easy to see it as flannel waved at a gullible press.

Three: a new TV series was launched, *The Justice Programme*, a hard-hitting look at crime, the system, and miscarriages of justice. High ratings for its first series – attractive presenter Eamonn Breen scooping women viewers – so now a second series was on the blocks, and the Spaven case – severed head, accusations, and suicide of a media darling – was to be the showcase opener.

With Lawson Geddes out of the country, address unknown, leaving John Rebus to carry the film-can.

Alex Harvey: 'Framed'. Segue to Jethro Tull: 'Living in the Past'.

He went home by way of the Oxford Bar – a long detour, always worthwhile. The gantry and optics had a quietly hypnotic effect, the only possible explanation as to why the regulars could stand and stare at them for hours at a stretch. The barman waited for an order; Rebus did not have a 'usual' drink these days, variety the spice of life and all that.

'Dark rum, and a half of Best.'

He hadn't touched dark rum in years, didn't think of it as a young man's drink. Yet Allan Mitchison had drunk it. A seaman's drink, another reason to think he worked offshore. Rebus handed over money, downed the short in one sour swallow, rinsed his mouth with the beer, found himself finishing it too quickly. The barman turned with his change.

'Make it a pint this time, Jon.'

'And another rum?'

'Jesus, no.' Rebus rubbed his eyes, bummed a cigarette from his drowsy neighbour. The Spaven case . . . it had dragged Rebus backwards through time, forcing him to confront memory, then to wonder if his memory was playing tricks. It remained unfinished business, twenty years on. Like Bible John. He shook his head, tried to clear it of history, and found himself thinking of Allan Mitchison, of falling headlong on to spiked rails, watching

them rise towards you, arms held fast to a chair so there was only one choice left: did you confront doom open-eyed or closed? He walked around the bar to use the telephone, put money in and then couldn't think who to call.

'Forgotten the number?' a drinker asked as Rebus got his coin back.

'Aye,' he said, 'what's the Samaritans' again?'

The drinker surprised him, knew the number pat.

Four blinks from his answering machine meant four messages. He lifted the instruction manual. It was open at page six, the 'Playback' section boxed with red pen, paragraphs underlined. He followed the instructions. The machine decided to work.

'It's Brian.' Brian Holmes. Rebus opened the Black Bush and poured, listening. 'Just to say ... well, thanks. Minto's recanted, so I'm off the hook. Hope I can return the favour.' No energy in the voice, a mouth tired of words. End message. Rebus savoured the whisky.

Blip: message two.

'I was working late and thought I'd give you a call, Inspector. We spoke earlier, Stuart Minchell, personnel manager at T-Bird Oil. I can confirm that Allan Mitchison was in our employ. I can fax through the details if you have a number. Call me at the office tomorrow. Bye.'

Goodbye and bingo. A relief to know something about the deceased other than his taste in music. Rebus's ears were roaring: the concert and the alcohol, blood pounding.

Message three: 'It's Howdenhall here, thought you were in a hurry but I can't find you. Typical CID.' Rebus knew the voice: Pete Hewitt at the police lab, Howdenhall. Pete looked fifteen, but was probably early twenties, smart-mouthed with a brain to match. Fingerprints a speciality. 'I got mostly partials, but a couple of beauties, and guess what? Their owner's on the computer. Past convictions for violence. Phone me back if you want a name.'

Rebus checked his watch. Pete doing his usual tease. It was gone eleven, he'd be home or out on the ran-dan, and Rebus didn't have a home number for him. He kicked the sofa, wished he'd stayed home: carting off bootleggers a pure waste of time. Still, he had the Black Bush and a bagful of CDs, T-shirts he'd never wear, a poster of four tykes with acne close-ups. He'd seen their faces before, couldn't think where ...

One message to go.

'John?'

A woman's voice, one he recognised.

'If you're home, pick up, please. I hate these things.' Pause, waiting. A sigh. 'OK then, look, now that we're not ... I mean, now I'm not your boss, how about some socialising? Dinner or something. Give me a call at home or office, OK? While there's time. I mean, you won't be at Fort Apache for ever. Take care.'

Rebus sat down, staring at the machine as it clicked off. Gill Templer, Chief Inspector, one-time 'significant other'. She'd become his boss only recently, frost on the surface, no sign of anything but iceberg beneath. Rebus took another drink, toasted the machine. A woman had just asked him for a date: when had *that* last happened? He got up and went to the

bathroom, examined his reflection in the cabinet mirror, rubbed his chin and laughed. Twilit eyes, lank hair, hands that trembled when he lifted them level.

'Looking good, John.' Yes, and he could fib for Scotland. Gill Templer, looking as good these days as when they'd first met, *asking him out*? He shook his head, still laughing. No, there had to be something . . . A hidden agenda.

Back in the living room, he emptied his lucky-bag, found that the poster of the four tykes matched the cover of one of the CDs. He recognised it: The Dancing Pigs. One of Mitchison's tapes, their latest recording. He recalled a couple of the faces from the hospitality tent: *We fucking killed them out there!* Mitchison had owned at least two of their albums.

Funny he hadn't had a ticket to the gig . . .

His front door bell: short, two rings. He walked back down the hall, checking the time. Eleven-twenty-five. Put his eye to the spyhole, didn't believe what he saw, opened the door wide.

'Where's the rest of the crew?'

Kayleigh Burgess stood there, heavy bag hanging from her shoulder, hair tucked up under an oversized green beret, strands curling down past both ears. Cute and cynical at the same time: Don't-Muck-Me-About-Unless-I-Want-You-To. Rebus had seen the model and year before.

'In their beds, most likely.'

'You mean Eamonn Breen *doesn't* sleep in a coffin?'

A guarded smile; she adjusted the weight of the bag on her shoulder. 'You know,' not looking at him, fussing with the bag instead, 'you're doing yourself no favours refusing to even discuss this with us. It doesn't make you look good.'

'I was no pin up to start with.'

'We're not taking sides, that's not what *The Justice Programme*'s about.'

'Really? Well, much as I enjoy a blether on the doorstep last thing at night . . .'

'You haven't heard, have you?' Now she looked at him. 'No, I didn't think so. Too soon. We've had a unit out in Lanzarote, trying to interview Lawson Geddes. I got a phone call this evening . . .'

Rebus knew the face and tone of voice; he'd used them himself on many grim occasions, trying to break the news to family, to friends . . .

'What happened?'

'He committed suicide. Apparently he'd been suffering from depression since his wife died. He shot himself.'

'Aw, Christ.' Rebus swivelled from the door, legs heavy as he made for the living room, the whisky bottle. She followed him, placed her bag on the coffee table. He motioned with the bottle and she nodded. They chinked glasses.

'When did Etta die?'

'About a year ago. Heart attack, I think. There's a daughter, lives in London.'

Rebus remembered her: a cheeky-faced pre-teen with braces. Her name was Aileen.

'Did you hound Geddes the way you've hounded me?'

'We don't "hound", Inspector. We just want everyone to have their say. It's important to the programme.'

'The programme.' Rebus shook his head. 'Well, you've not got a programme now, have you?'

The drink had brought colour to her face. 'On the contrary, Mr Geddes's suicide could be construed as an admission of guilt. It makes a hell of a punch-line.' She'd recovered well; Rebus wondered how much of her earlier timidity had been an act. He realised she was standing in his living room: records, CDs, empty bottles, books piled high on the floor. He couldn't let her see the kitchen: Johnny Bible and Bible John spread across the table, evidence of an obsession. 'That's why I'm here . . . partly. I could have given you the news over the telephone, but I thought it was the sort of thing best done face to face. And now that you're alone, the only living witness so to speak . . .' She reached into the bag, produced a professional-looking tape deck and microphone. Rebus put down his glass and walked over to her, hands out.

'May I?'

She hesitated, then handed over the equipment. Rebus walked down the hall with it. The front door was still open. He stepped into the stairwell, reached a hand over the guard-rail, and let go the recorder. It fell two flights, case splintering on impact with the stone floor. She was right behind him.

'You'll pay for that!'

'Send me the bill and we'll see.'

He walked back inside and closed the door after him, put the chain on as a hint, and watched through the spyhole till she'd gone.

He sat in his chair by the window, thinking of Lawson Geddes. Typical Scot, he couldn't cry about it. Crying was for football defeats, animal bravery stories, 'Flower of Scotland' after closing time. He cried about stupid things, but tonight his eyes remained stubbornly dry.

He knew he was in shit. They only had *him* now, and they'd redouble their efforts to salvage a programme. Besides, Burgess was right: prisoner suicide, policeman suicide – it was a hell of a punchline. But Rebus didn't want to be the man to feed them it. Like them, he wanted to know the truth – but not for the same reasons. He couldn't even say *why* he wanted to know. One course of action: start his own investigation. The only problem was, the further he dug, the more he might be creating a pit for his own reputation – what was left of it – and, more importantly, that of his one-time mentor, partner, friend. Problem connected to the first: he wasn't objective enough; he *couldn't* investigate himself. He needed a stand-in, an understudy.

He picked up the telephone, pressed seven numbers. A sleepy response.

'Yeah, hello?'

'Brian, it's John. Sorry to phone so late, I need that favour repaid.'

They met in the car park at Newcraighall. Lights were on in the UCI cinema complex, some late showing. The Mega Bowl was closed; so was McDonald's. Holmes and Nell Stapleton had moved into a house just off Duddingston Park, looking across Portobello Golf Course and the Freightliner Terminal. Holmes said the freight traffic didn't keep him awake through the night. They could have met at the golf course, but it was too close to Nell for Rebus's liking. He hadn't seen her in a couple of years, not

even at social functions – each had a gift for knowing when the other would or wouldn't be in attendance. Old scrapes; Nell picking at the scabs, obsessive.

So they met a couple of miles away, in a gully, surrounded by closed shops – DIY store, shoe emporium, Toys 'R' Us – still cops, even off-duty. *Especially* off-duty.

Their eyes darted, using wing mirrors and rearview, looking for shadows. Nobody in sight, they still talked in an undertone. Rebus explained exactly what he wanted.

'This TV programme, I need some ammo before I talk to them. But it's too personal with me. I need you to go back over the Spaven case – case-notes, trial proceedings. Just read through them, see what you think.'

Holmes sat in the passenger seat of Rebus's Saab. He looked what he was: a man who'd got undressed and gone to bed, only to have to get up too shortly thereafter and put dayshift clothes on again. His hair was ruffled, shirt open two buttons, shoes but no socks. He stifled a yawn, shaking his head.

'I don't get it. What am I looking for?'

'Just see if anything jars. Just . . . I don't know.'

'You're taking this seriously then?'

'Lawson Geddes just killed himself.'

'Christ.' But Holmes didn't even blink; beyond compassion for men he didn't know, figures from history. He had too much on his own mind.

'Something else,' Rebus said. 'You might track down an ex-con who says he was the last person to talk to Spaven. I forget the name, but it was reported in all the papers at the time.'

'One question: do *you* think Geddes framed Lenny Spaven?'

Rebus made a show of thinking it over, then shrugged. 'Let me tell you the story. Not the story you'll find in my written notes on the case.'

Rebus began to talk: Geddes turning up at his door, the too-easy finding of the bag, Geddes frantic before, unnaturally calm after. The story they manufactured, anonymous tip-off. Holmes listened in silence. The cinema began to empty, young couples hugging, air-hopping towards their cars, walking like they'd rather be lying down. A gathering of engine-noise, exhaust fumes and headlights, tall shadows on the canyon walls, the car park emptying. Rebus finished his version.

'Another question.'

Rebus waited, but Holmes was having trouble forming the words. He gave up finally and shook his head. Rebus knew what he was thinking. He knew Rebus had put the squeeze on Minto, while believing Minto to have a case against Holmes. And now he knew that Rebus had lied to protect Lawson Geddes and to secure the conviction. The question in his mind a double strand – was Rebus's version the truth? How dirty was the copper sitting behind the steering-wheel?

How dirty would Holmes allow *himself* to get before he left the force?

Rebus knew Nell nagged him every day, quiet persuasion. He was young enough for another career, *any* career, something clean and risk-free. There was still time for him to get out. But maybe not much time.

'OK,' Holmes said, opening the car door. 'I'll start a.s.a.p.' He paused. 'But if I find any dirt, anything concealed in the margins . . .'

Rebus turned on his lights, high-beam. He started the car and drove off.

4

Rebus woke up early. There was a book open on his lap. He looked at the last paragraph he'd read before falling asleep, didn't recall any of it. Mail lying inside the door: who'd be a postman in Edinburgh, all those tenement stairs? His credit-card bill: two supermarkets, three off-licences, and Bob's Rare Vinyl. Impulse buys one Saturday afternoon, after a lunchtime sesh in the Ox – *Freak Out* on single vinyl, mint; *The Velvet Underground*, peel-off banana intact; *Sergeant Pepper* in mono with the sheet of cut-outs. He'd yet to play any of them, already had scratchy copies of the Velvets and Beatles.

He shopped on Marchmont Road, ate breakfast at the kitchen table with the Bible John/Johnny Bible material for a cloth. Johnny Bible headlines: 'Catch This Monster!'; 'Baby-Faced Killer Claims Third Victim'; 'Public Warned: Be Vigilant'. Much the same banners Bible John was earning a quarter-century before.

Johnny Bible's first victim: Duthie Park, Aberdeen. Michelle Strachan came from Pittenweem in Fife, so of course all her Furry Boot pals called her Michelle Fifer. She didn't look like her near-namesake: short and skinny, mousy shoulder-length hair, front teeth prominent. She was a student at Robert Gordon University. Raped, strangled, one shoe missing.

Victim two, six weeks later: Angela Riddell, Angie to her friends. In her time she'd worked at an escort agency, been arrested in a slapper sweep near Leith docks, and fronted a blues band, husky-voiced but trying too hard. A record company had now released the band's only demo as a CD single, making money from ghouls and the curious. Edinburgh CID had spent a lot of hours – thousands of man-hours – trawling through Angie Riddell's past, seeking out old clients, friends, fans of the band, looking for a prozzy punter turned killer, an obsessed blues fan, whatever. Warriston Cemetery, where the body was found, was a known haunt of Hell's Angels, amateur black magicians, perverts and loners. In the days following the discovery of the body, at dead of night you were more likely to trip over a snoozing surveillance team than a crucified cat.

A month-long gap, during which the first two murders had been connected – Angie Riddell not only raped and strangled, but missing a distinctive necklace, a row of two-inch metal crosses, bought in Cockburn Street – then a third killing, this time in Glasgow. Judith Cairns, 'Ju-Ju', was on the dole, which hadn't stopped her working in a chip shop late evenings, a pub some lunchtimes, and as a hotel chambermaid weekend

mornings. When she was found dead, there was no sign of her backpack, which friends swore she took everywhere, even to clubs and warehouse raves.

Three women, aged nineteen, twenty-four and twenty-one, murdered within three months. It was two weeks since Johnny Bible had struck. A six-week gap between victims one and two had been whittled to a calendar month between two and three. Everyone was waiting, waiting for the worst possible news. Rebus drank his coffee, ate his croissant, and examined photos of the three victims, culled from the newspapers, blown-up grainy, all the young women smiling, the way you only usually did for a photographer. The camera always lied.

Rebus knew so much about the victims, so little about Johnny Bible. Though no police officer would admit it in public, they were impotent, all but going through the motions. It was *his* play; they were waiting for *him* to slip up: overconfidence, or boredom, or a simple desire to be caught, the knowledge of what was right and wrong. They were waiting for a friend, a neighbour, a loved one to come forward, maybe an anonymous call – one that would prove not merely malicious. They were all waiting. Rebus ran a finger over the biggest photo of Angie Riddell. He'd known her, had been part of the team that had arrested her and a lot of other working girls that night in Leith. The atmosphere had been good, a lot of jokes, jibes at married officers. Most of the prostitutes knew the routine, those who did calming those who were new to the game. Angie Riddell had been stroking the hair of a hysterical teenager, a druggie. Rebus had liked her style, had interviewed her. She'd made him laugh. A couple of weeks later, he'd driven down Commercial Street, asked how she was doing. She'd told him time was money, and talk didn't come cheap, but offered him a discount if he wanted anything more substantial than hot air. He'd laughed again, bought her tea and a bridie at a late-opening café. A fortnight later, he found himself down in Leith again, but according to the girls she hadn't been around, so that was that.

Raped, beaten, strangled.

It all reminded him of the World's End killings, of other murders of young women, so many of them left unsolved. World's End: October '77, the year before Spaven, two teenagers drinking in the World's End pub on the High Street. Their bodies turned up next morning. Beaten, hands tied, strangled, bags and jewellery missing. Rebus hadn't worked the case, but knew men who had: they carried with them the frustration of a job left undone, and would carry it to the grave. The way a lot of them saw it, when you worked a murder investigation, your client was the deceased, mute and cold, but still screaming out for justice. It had to be true, because sometimes if you listened hard enough you could hear them screaming. Sitting in his chair by the window, Rebus had heard many a despairing cry. One night, he'd heard Angie Riddell and it had pierced his heart, because he'd known her, liked her. In that instant it became personal for him. He couldn't not be interested in Johnny Bible. He just didn't know what he could do to help. His curiosity about the original Bible John case was probably no help at all. It had sent him back in time, spending less and less time in the present. Sometimes it took all his strength to pull him back to the here and now.

Rebus had telephone calls to make. First: Pete Hewitt at Howdenhall.
'Morning, Inspector, and isn't she a beauty?'

Voice dripping irony. Rebus looked out at milky sunshine. 'Rough night,
Pete?'

'Rough? You could shave a yak with it. I take it you got my message?'
Rebus had pen and paper ready. 'I got a couple of decent prints off the
whisky bottle: thumb and forefinger. Tried lifting from the polythene bag
and the tape binding him to the chair, but only a few partials, nothing to
build a case on.'

'Come on, Pete, get to the ID.'

'Well, all that money you complain we spend on computers . . . I got a
match within quarter of an hour. The name is Anthony Ellis Kane. He has
a police record for attempted murder, assault, reset. Ring any bells?'

'Not a one.'

'Well, he used to operate out of Glasgow. No convictions these past seven
years.'

'I'll look him up when I get to the station. Thanks, Pete.'

Next call: the personnel office at T-Bird Oil. A long-distance call; he'd
wait and make it from Fort Apache. A glance out of the window: no sign of
the Redgauntlet crew. Rebus put his jacket on and made for the door.

He stopped in at the boss's office. MacAskill was guzzling Irn-Bru.

'We have a fingerprint ID, Anthony Ellis Kane, previous convictions for
violence.'

MacAskill tossed the empty can into his wastebasket. His desk was
stacked with old paperwork – drawer one of the filing cabinet. There was
an empty packing case on the floor.

'What about the decedent's family, friends?'

Rebus shook his head. 'Deceased worked for T-Bird Oil. I'm going to call
the personnel manager for details.'

'Make that job one, John.'

'Job one, sir.'

But when he got to the Shed and sat at his desk, he thought about
phoning Gill Templer first, decided against it. Bain was at his desk; Rebus
didn't want an audience.

'Dod,' he said, 'run a check on Anthony Ellis Kane. Howdenhall found his
prints on the carry-out.' Bain nodded and started typing. Rebus phoned
Aberdeen, gave his name and asked to be put through to Stuart Minchell.

'Good morning, Inspector.'

'Thanks for leaving a message, Mr Minchell. Do you have Allan
Mitchison's employment details?'

'Right in front of me. What do you want to know?'

'A next of kin.'

Minchell shuffled paper. 'There doesn't appear to be one. Let me check
his CV.' A long pause, Rebus happy not to be making the call from home.
'Inspector, it seems Allan Mitchison was an orphan. I have details of his
education, and there's a children's home mentioned.'

'No family?'

'No mention of a family.'

Rebus had written Mitchison's name on a sheet of paper. He underlined

it now, the rest of the page a blank. 'What was Mr Mitchison's position within the company?'

'He was . . . let's see, he worked for Platform Maintenance, specifically as a painter. We have a base in Shetland, maybe he worked there.' More paper shuffling. 'No, Mr Mitchison worked on the platforms themselves.'

'Painting them?'

'And general maintenance. Steel corrodes, Inspector. You've no idea how fast the North Sea can strip paint from steel.'

'Which rig did he work on?'

'Not a rig, a production platform. I'd have to check that.'

'Could you do that, please? And could you fax me through his personnel file?'

'You say he's dead?'

'Last time I looked.'

'Then there should be no problem. Give me your number there.'

Rebus did so, and terminated the call. Bain was waving him over. Rebus crossed the room and stood by Bain's side, the better to see the computer screen.

'This guy's pure mental,' Bain said. His phone rang. Bain picked up, started a conversation. Rebus read down the screen. Anthony Ellis Kane, known as 'Tony El', had a record going back to his youth. He was now forty-four years old, well known to Strathclyde police. The bulk of his adult life had been spent in the employ of Joseph Toal, a.k.a. 'Uncle Joe', who practically *ran* Glasgow with muscle provided by his son and by men like Tony El. Bain put down the receiver.

'Uncle Joe,' he mused. 'If Tony El is still working for him, we could have a very different case.'

Rebus was remembering what the boss had said: *it's got a gang feel to it*. Drugs or a default on a loan. Maybe MacAskill was right.

'You know what this means?' Bain said.

Rebus nodded. 'A trip to weegie-land.' Scotland's two main cities, separated by a fifty-minute motorway trip, were wary neighbours, as though years back one had accused the other of something and the accusation, unfounded or not, still rankled. Rebus had a couple of contacts in Glasgow CID, so went to his desk and made the calls.

'If you want info on Uncle Joe,' he was told during the second call, 'best talk to Chick Ancram. Wait, I'll give you his number.'

Charles Ancram, it turned out, was a Chief Inspector based in Govan. Rebus spent a fruitless half-hour trying to find him, then went for a walk. The shops in front of Fort Apache were the usual metal shutters and mesh grille affairs, Asian owners mostly, even if the shops were staffed with white faces. Men hung around on the street outside, T-shirted, sporting tattoos, smoking. Eyes as trustworthy as a weasel in a hen-house.

Eggs? Not me, pal, can't stand them.

Rebus bought cigarettes and a newspaper. Walking out of the shop, a baby buggy caught his ankles, a woman told him to mind where he was fucking going. She bustled away, hauling a toddler behind her. Twenty, maybe twenty-one, hair dyed blonde, two front teeth missing. Her bared forearms showed tattoos, too. Across the road, an advertising hoarding told him to spend £20k on a new car. Behind it, the discount supermarket was doing no business, kids using its car park as a skateboard rink.

Back in the Shed, Maclay was on the telephone. He held the receiver out to Rebus.

'Chief Inspector Ancram, returning your call.' Rebus rested against the desk.

'Hello?'

'Inspector Rebus? Ancram here, I believe you want a word.'

'Thanks for getting back to me, sir. Two words really: Joseph Toal.'

Ancram snorted. He had a west coast drawl, nasal, always managing to sound a little condescending. 'Uncle Joe Corleone? Our own dear Godfather? Has he done something I don't know about?'

'Do you know one of his men, a guy called Anthony Kane?'

'Tony El,' Ancram confirmed. 'Worked for Uncle Joe for years.'

'Past tense?'

'He hasn't been heard of in a while. Story is he crossed Uncle Joe, and Uncle Joe got Stanley to see to things. Tony El was all cut up about it.'

'Who's Stanley?'

'Uncle Joe's son. It's not his real name, but everyone calls him Stanley, on account of his hobby.'

'Which is?'

'Stanley knives, he collects them.'

'You think Stanley topped Tony El?'

'Well, the body hasn't turned up, which is usually proof enough in a perverse way.'

'Tony El's very much alive. He was through here a few days ago.'

'I see.' Ancram was quiet for a moment. In the background Rebus could hear busy voices, radio transmissions, police station sounds. 'Bag over the head?'

'How did you know?'

'Tony El's trademark. So he's back in circulation, eh? Inspector, I think you and me better have a talk. Monday morning, can you find Govan station? No, wait, make it Partick, 613 Dumbarton Road. I've a meeting there at nine. Can we say ten?'

'Ten's fine.'

'See you then.'

Rebus put down the telephone. 'Monday morning at ten,' he told Bain. 'I'm off to Partick.'

'You poor bastard,' Bain replied, sounding like he meant it.

'Want us to put out Tony El's description?' Maclay asked.

'Pronto. Let's see if we can lassoo him before Monday.'

Bible John flew back into Scotland on a fine Friday morning. The first thing he did at the airport was pick up some newspapers. In the kiosk, he saw that a new book had been published on World War Two, so bought that too. Sitting in the concourse, he flicked through the newspapers, finding no new stories concerning the Upstart. He left the papers on his seat and went to the carousel, where his luggage was waiting.

A taxi took him into Glasgow. He had already decided not to stay in the city. It wasn't that he had anything to fear from his old hunting-ground, but that a stay there would bring little profit. Of necessity, Glasgow brought back bittersweet memories. In the late sixties, it had been

reinventing itself: knocking down old slums, building their concrete equivalents on the outskirts. New roads, bridges, motorways – the place had been an enormous building site. He got the feeling the process was still ongoing, as if the city still hadn't acquired an identity it could be comfortable with.

A problem Bible John knew something about.

From Queen Street station, he took a train to Edinburgh, and used his cellphone to reserve a room at his usual hotel, placing it on his corporate account. He called his wife to tell her where he'd be. He had his laptop with him, and did some work on the train. Work soothed him; a busy brain was best. Go therefore now, and work; for there shall no straw be given you, yet shall ye deliver the tale of bricks. The Book of Exodus. The media back then had done him a favour, and so had the police. They'd issued a description saying his first name was John and he was 'fond of quoting from the Bible'. Neither was particularly true: his middle name was John, and he had only occasionally quoted aloud from the good book. In recent years, he'd started attending church again, but now regretted it, regretted thinking he was safe.

There was no safety in this world, just as there would be none in the next.

He left the train at Haymarket – in summer it was easier to catch a taxi there – but when he stepped out into sunshine, he decided to walk to the hotel: it was only five or ten minutes away. His case had wheels, and his shoulder-bag was not particularly heavy. He breathed deeply: traffic fumes and a hint of brewery hops. Tired of squinting, he paused to put on sunglasses, and immediately liked the world better. Catching his reflection in a shop window he saw just another businessman tired of travelling. There was nothing memorable about either face or figure, and the clothes were always conservative: a suit from Austin Reed, shirt by Double 2. A well-dressed and successful businessman. He checked the knot of his tie, and ran his tongue over the only two false teeth in his head – necessary surgery from a quarter-century before. Like everyone else, he crossed the road at the lights.

Check-in at his hotel took a matter of moments. He sat at the room's small circular table and opened his laptop, plugging it into the mains, changing the adaptor from 110v to 240. He used his password, then double-clicked on the file marked UPSTART. Inside were his notes on Johnny Bible so-called, his own psychological profile of the killer. It was building nicely.

Bible John reflected that he had something the authorities didn't have: inside knowledge of how a serial killer worked, thought and lived, the lies he had to tell, the guile and disguises, the secret life behind the everyday face. It put him ahead in the game. With any luck, he'd get to Johnny Bible before the police did.

He had avenues to follow. One: from his working habits, it was clear the Upstart had prior knowledge of the Bible John case. How did he gain this knowledge? The Upstart was in his twenties, too young to remember Bible John. Therefore he'd heard about it somewhere, or read about it, and then had gone on to research it in some detail. There were books – some of them recent, some not – about the Bible John killings or with chapters on them.

If Johnny Bible were being meticulous, he would have consulted all the available literature, but with some of the material long out of print he must have been searching second-hand bookshops, or else must have used libraries. The search was narrowing nicely.

Another connected avenue: newspapers. Again, it was unlikely the Upstart had open access to papers from a quarter-century ago. That meant libraries again, and very few libraries held newspapers for that length of time. Search narrowing nicely.

Then there was the Upstart himself. Many predators made errors early on, mistakes executed due to a lack either of proper planning or of simple nerve. Bible John himself was unusual: his real mistake had come with victim three, with sharing a taxi with her sister. Were there victims around who had escaped the Upstart? That meant looking through recent newspapers, seeking out attacks on women in Aberdeen, Glasgow, Edinburgh, tracking down the killer's false starts and early failures. It would be time-consuming work. But therapeutic, too.

He stripped and had a shower, then put on a more casual outfit: navy blazer and khaki trousers. He decided not to risk using the telephone in his room – the numbers would be logged by reception – so headed out into the sunshine. No phone boxes these days held directories, so he walked into a pub and ordered tonic water, then asked for the phone book. The barmaid – late teens, nose-stud, pink hair – handed it over with a smile. At his table, he took out notebook and pen and jotted down some numbers, then went to the back of the bar where the telephone was kept. It was next to the toilets – private enough for the purpose, especially just now with the pub all but empty. His calls were to a couple of antiquarian booksellers and three libraries. The results were, to his mind, satisfactory if by no means revelatory, but then he'd decided weeks back that this might be a drawn-out process. After all, he had self-knowledge on his side, but the police had hundreds of men and computers and a publicity machine. And they could investigate *openly*. He knew his own investigation into the Upstart had to be undertaken with more discretion. But he also knew he needed help, and that was risky. Involving others was always a risk. He'd considered the dilemma over long days and nights – on one side of the scales, his wish to track down the Upstart; on the other, the risk that in so doing, he would be putting himself – his identity – in danger.

So he'd asked himself a question: how badly did he want the Upstart? And had answered it: very badly. Very badly indeed.

He spent the afternoon on and around George IV Bridge – the National Library of Scotland and the Central Lending Library. He had a reader's card for the National Library, had done research there in the past – business; plus some reading on the Second World War, his main hobby these days. He browsed in local second-hand bookshops too, asking if they had any true-life crime. He told staff the Johnny Bible murders had kindled his interest.

'We only have half a shelf of true crime,' the assistant in the first shop said, showing him where it was. Bible John feigned interest in the books, then returned to the assistant's desk.

'No, nothing there. Do you also search for books?'

'Not as such,' the assistant said. 'But we keep requests . . .' She pulled out a heavy old-style ledger and opened it. 'If you put down what you're looking for, your name and address, if we happen across the book we'll get in touch.'

'That's fine.'

Bible John took out his pen, wrote slowly, checking recent requests. He flicked back a page, eyes running down the list of titles and subjects.

'Don't people have such varied interests?' he said, smiling at the assistant.

He tried the same ploy at three further shops, but found no evidence of the Upstart. He then walked to the National Library's annexe on Causewayside, where recent newspapers were kept, and browsed through a month's worth of *Scotsmans*, *Heralds* and *Press and Journals*, taking notes from certain stories: assaults, rapes. Of course, even if there *was* an early, failed victim, it didn't mean the attempt had gone reported. The Americans had a word for what he was doing. They called it shitwork.

Back in the National Library proper, he studied the librarians, looking for someone special. When he thought he'd found what he was looking for, he checked the library's opening hours, and decided to wait.

At closing time, he was standing outside the National Library, sunglasses on in the mid-evening light, crawling lines of traffic separating him from the Central Library. He saw some of the staff leave, singly and in groups. Then he spotted the young man he was looking for. When the man headed down Victoria Street, Bible John crossed the road and followed. There were a lot of pedestrians about, tourists, drinkers, a few people making their way home. He became just another of them, walking briskly, his eyes on his quarry. In the Grassmarket, the young man turned into the first available pub. Bible John stopped and considered: a quick drink before heading home? Or was the librarian going to meet friends, maybe make an evening of it? He decided to go inside.

The bar was dark, noisy with office workers: men with their suit jackets draped over their shoulders, women sipping from long glasses of tonic. The librarian was at the bar, alone. Bible John squeezed in beside him and ordered an orange juice. He nodded to the librarian's beer glass.

'Another?'

When the young man turned to look at him, Bible John leaned close, spoke quietly.

'Three things I want to tell you. One: I'm a journalist. Two: I want to give you £500. Three: there's absolutely nothing illegal involved.' He paused. 'Now, do you want that drink?'

The young man was still staring at him. Finally he nodded.

'Is that yes to the drink or yes to the cash?' Bible John was smiling too.

'The drink. You better tell me a little more about the other.'

'It's a boring job or I'd do it myself. Does the library keep a record of books consulted and borrowed?'

The librarian thought about it, then nodded. 'Some computerised, some still on cards.'

'Well, the computer will be quick, but the cards may take you a while. It'll still be easy money, believe me. What about if someone came in to consult old newspapers?'

'Should be on record. How long ago are we talking about?'

'It would be in the past three to six months. The papers they'd be looking at would be from 1968 to '70.'

He paid for two drinks with a twenty, opened his wallet so the librarian could see plenty more.

'It might take a while,' the young man said. 'I'll have to cross-reference between Causewayside and George IV Bridge.'

'There's another hundred if you can hurry things along.'

'I'll need details.' Bible John nodded, handed over a business card. It stated name and a phony address, but no phone number.

'Don't try to get in touch. I'll phone you. What's your name?'

'Mark Jenkins.'

'OK, Mark.' Bible John lifted out two fifties, tucked them into the young man's breast pocket. 'Here's something on account.'

'What's it all about anyway?'

Bible John shrugged. 'Johnny Bible. We're checking a possible connection with some old cases.'

The young man nodded. 'So what books are you interested in?'

Bible John handed him a printed list. 'Plus newspapers. *Scotsman*s and *Glasgow Herald*s, February '68 to December '69.'

'And what do you want to know?'

'People who've been looking at them. I'll need names and addresses. Can you do it?'

'Actual newspapers are held at Causewayside, we only stock microfilm.'

'What are you saying?'

'I may need to ask a colleague at Causewayside to help.'

Bible John smiled. 'My paper's not short of a bob or two, as long as we get results. How much would your friend want . . . ?'

273

The Whispering Rain

Mind me when mischief befalls me
from the cruel and the vain
 The Bathers,
 'Ave the Leopards'

5

The Scots language is especially rich in words to do with the weather: 'dreich' and 'smirr' are only two of them.

It had taken Rebus an hour to drive to Raintown, but another forty minutes to find Dumbarton Road. He hadn't been to the station before: Partick cop-shop had relocated in '93. The old station, the 'Marine', he'd been there, but not the new place. Driving in Glasgow could be a nightmare for the uninitiated, a maze of one-way streets and ill-signposted intersections. Rebus twice had to leave his car and call in for instructions, both times queuing outside phone boxes in the rain. Only it wasn't real rain, it was smirr, a fine spray-mist which drenched you before you knew it. It was blowing in from the west, moisture straight from the Atlantic Ocean. It was all Rebus needed first thing on a dreich Monday morning.

When he got to the station, he noticed a car in the car park, two figures inside, smoke billowing from an open window, radio playing. Reporters, had to be. They were the graveyard shift. At this point in a story, reporters divvied the hours into shifts, so they could go off and be somewhere else. Whoever was left on recce was on a promise to buzz any breaks in the story to the other journalists pronto.

When he finally pushed open the station door, there was scattered applause. He walked up to the desk.

'Finally made it, then?' the Duty Sergeant asked. 'Thought we were going to have to send out search parties.'

'Where's CI Ancram?'

'In a meeting. He said for you to go up and wait.'

So Rebus went upstairs, and found that the CID offices had become a sprawling Murder Room. There were photographs on the walls: Judith Cairns, Ju-Ju, in life and in death. More photos of the locus – Kelvingrove Park, a sheltered spot surrounded by bushes. A work rota had been posted – interview grind mostly, shoe-leather stuff, no big breaks expected but you had to make the effort. Officers clattered at keyboards, maybe using the SCRO computer, or even HOLMES – the major inquiry database. All murder cases – excluding those solved straight off – were put on the Home Office Large Major Enquiry System. There were dedicated teams – detectives and uniforms – who operated the system, typing in data, checking and cross-referencing. Even Rebus – no great fan of new technology – could see the advantages over the old card-index system. He stopped by a computer terminal and watched someone entering a

statement. Then, looking up, he saw a face he recognised, walked up to its owner.

'Hiya, Jack, thought you were still in Falkirk?'

DI Jack Morton turned, his eyes opening wide in disbelief. He rose from his desk, took Rebus's hand and pumped it.

'I am,' he said, 'but they're short-handed here.' He looked around the room. 'Understandably.'

Rebus looked Jack Morton up and down, couldn't believe what he saw. Last time they'd met, Jack had been a couple of stone overweight, a heavy smoker with a cough that could crack patrol-car windscreens. Now he'd shed the excess weight, and the perennial ciggie was missing from his mouth. More, his hair was professionally groomed and he was dressed in an expensive-looking suit, polished black shoes, crisp shirt and tie.

'What happened to you?' Rebus asked.

Morton smiled, patted his near-flat stomach. 'Just looked at myself one day and couldn't understand why the mirror didn't break. Got off the booze and the cigs, joined a health club.'

'Just like that?'

'Life and death decisions. You can't afford to hem and haw.'

'You look great.'

'Wish I could say the same, John.'

Rebus was thinking up a comeback when CI Ancram entered the room.

'DI Rebus?' They shook hands. The Chief Inspector didn't seem keen to let go. His eyes were soaking up Rebus. 'Sorry to keep you.'

Ancram was in his early fifties, and every bit as well dressed as Jack Morton. He was bald mostly, but with Sean Connery's style and a thick dark moustache to match.

'Has Jack been giving you the tour?'

'Not exactly, sir.'

'Well, this is the Glasgow end of the Johnny Bible operation.'

'Is this the nearest station to Kelvingrove?'

Ancram smiled. 'Proximity to the locus was just one consideration. Judith Cairns was his third victim, by then the media had already hit on the Bible John connection. And this is where all the Bible John files are stored.'

'Any chance I can see them?'

Ancram studied him, then shrugged. 'Come on, I'll show you.'

Rebus followed Ancram along the corridor to another suite of offices. There was a musty smell in the air, more library than cop-shop. Rebus saw why: the room was full of old cardboard boxes, box-files with spring hinges, packets of curl-edged paper bound with string. Four CID officers – two male, two female – were working their way through everything and anything to do with the original Bible John case.

'We had this lot stashed in a storeroom,' Ancram said. 'You should have seen the stoor that came off when we brought them out.' He blew on a folder, fine powder rising from it.

'You do think there's a connection then?'

It was a question every police officer in Scotland had asked every other police officer, for there was always the chance that the two cases, the two killers, had nothing in common, in which event hundreds of man-hours were being wasted.

'Oh yes,' Ancram said. Yes: it was what Rebus felt, too. 'I mean, the *modus operandi* is close enough to start with, then there are the souvenirs he takes from the scene. The description of Johnny Bible may be a fluke, but I'm sure he's copying his hero.' Ancram looked at Rebus. 'Aren't you?'

Rebus nodded. He was looking at all the material, thinking how he'd like to have a few weeks with it, how he might find something no one else had spotted ... It was a dream, of course, a fantasy, but on slow nights sometimes it was motivation enough. Rebus had his newspapers, but they told only as much of the story as the police had wanted made public. He walked over to a row of shelves, read the spines of the box-files: Door to Door; Taxi Firms; Hairdressers; Tailors' Shops; Hairpiece Suppliers.

'Hairpiece suppliers?'

Ancram smiled. 'His short hair, they thought maybe it was a wig. They talked to hairdressers to see if anyone recognised the cut.'

'And to tailors because of his Italian suit.'

Again Ancram stared at him.

Rebus shrugged. 'The case interests me. What's this?' He pointed to a wall chart.

'Similarities and dissimilarities between the two cases,' Ancram said. 'Dance halls versus the club scene. And the descriptions: tall, skinny, shy, auburn hair, well dressed ... I mean, Johnny could almost be Bible John's son.'

'That's something I've been asking myself. Supposing Johnny Bible *is* basing himself on his hero, and supposing Bible John's still out there somewhere ...'

'Bible John's dead.'

Rebus kept his eyes on the chart. 'But just supposing he isn't. I mean, is he flattered? Is he pissed off? What?'

'Don't ask me.'

'The Glasgow victim hadn't been to a club,' Rebus said.

'Well, she wasn't last *seen* in a club. But she'd been to one earlier that evening, he could have followed her from there to the concert.'

Victims one and two had been picked up by Johnny Bible in nightclubs, the nineties equivalent of a sixties dance hall: louder, darker, more dangerous. They'd been in parties, who were able to furnish only the vaguest descriptions of the man who had walked off into the night with their friend. But victim three, Judith Cairns, had been picked up at a rock concert in a room above a pub.

'We've had others too,' Ancram was saying. 'Three unsolveds in Glasgow in the late seventies, all three missing some personal item.'

'Like he never went away,' Rebus muttered.

'There's too much to go on, yet not nearly enough.' Ancram folded his arms. 'How well does Johnny know the three cities? Did he pick the clubs at random, or did he know them to start with? Was each locus chosen beforehand? Could he be a brewery delivery-man? A DJ? Music journalist? Maybe he writes fucking travel guides for all I know.' Ancram started a joyless laugh, and rubbed at his forehead.

'Could always be Bible John himself,' Rebus said.

'Bible John's dead and buried, Inspector.'

'You really think so?'

Ancram nodded. He wasn't alone. There were plenty of coppers who thought they knew who Bible John was, and knew him to be dead. But there were others more sceptical, and Rebus was among them. A DNA match probably wouldn't have been enough to change his mind. There was always the chance that Bible John was out there.

They had a description of a man in his late twenties, but witness evidence was notoriously uneven. As a result, the original photofits and artists' impressions of Bible John had been dusted off and put back into circulation with the media's help. The usual psychological ploys were being used too – pleas in the press for the killer to come forward: 'You obviously need help, and we'd like you to contact us.' Bluff, with silence the retort.

Ancram pointed to photos on one wall: a photofit from 1970, aged by computer, beard and glasses added, the hair receding at crown and temples. They'd been made public too.

'Could be anybody, couldn't it?' Ancram stated.

'Getting to you, sir?' Rebus was waiting for an invitation to call Ancram by his first name.

'Of course it's getting to me.' Ancram's face relaxed. 'Why the interest?'

'No real reason.'

'I mean, we're not here for Johnny Bible, are we? We're here to talk about Uncle Joe.'

'Ready when you are, sir.'

'Come on then, let's see if we can find two empty chairs in this fucking building.'

They ended up standing in the corridor, with coffee bought from a machine further along.

'Do we know what he strangles them with?' Rebus asked.

Ancram's eyes widened. 'More Johnny Bible?' He sighed. 'Whatever it is, it doesn't leave much of an impression. The latest theory is a length of washing-line; you know, the nylon stuff, plastic-coated. The forensic labs have tested about two hundred possibles, everything from rope to guitar strings.'

'What do you think about the souvenirs?'

'I think we should go public with them. I know keeping them hush-hush helps us rule out the nutters who walk in to confess, but I honestly think we'd be better off asking the public for help. That necklace, I mean, you couldn't get more distinctive. If someone out there has found it, or seen it . . . housey-housey.'

'You've got a psychic working the case, haven't you?'

Ancram looked nettled. 'Not me personally, some arsehole further up the ranks. It's a newspaper stunt, but the brass went for it.'

'He hasn't helped?'

'We told him we needed a demonstration, asked him to predict the winner of the two-fifteen at Ayr.'

Rebus laughed. 'And?'

'He said he could see the letters S and P, and a jockey dressed in pink with yellow spots.'

'That's impressive.'

'Thing is though, there *was* no two-fifteen at Ayr, or anywhere else for that matter. All this voodoo and profiling, a waste of time if you ask me.'

'So you've nothing to go on?'

'Not much. No saliva at the locus, not so much as a hair. Bastard uses a johnny, then takes it with him – wrapper included. My bet is, he wears gloves too. We've a few threads from a jacket or the like, forensics are still busy with them.' Ancram raised his cup to his lips, blew on it. 'So, Inspector, do you want to hear about Uncle Joe or not?'

'That's why I'm here.'

'I'm beginning to wonder.' Rebus just shrugged, so Ancram took a deep breath. 'OK, then listen. He controls a lot of the muscle-work – and I mean that literally; he has a share in a couple of bodybuilder gyms. In fact, he has a share in just about everything that's the least bit dodgy: money-lending, protection, prozzy pitches, betting.'

'Drugs?'

'Maybe. There are a lot of maybes with Uncle Joe. You'll see that when you read the files. He's as slippery as a Thai bath – he owns massage parlours too. Then he's got a lot of the taxi cabs, the ones that don't switch their meters on when you get in; or if they do, the rate-per-mile's been hiked. The cabbies are all on the broo, claiming benefit. We've approached several of them, but they won't say a word against Uncle Joe. Thing is, if the DSS start sniffing around for scroungers, the investigators receive a letter. It details where they live, spouse's name and daily movements, kids' names, the school they go to . . .'

'I get the picture.'

'So they start requesting a transfer to another department, and meantime go to their doctor because they're having trouble sleeping at night.'

'OK, Uncle Joe isn't Glasgow's Man of the Year. Where does he live?'

Ancram drained his cup. 'This is a beauty. He lives in a council house. But just remember: Robert Maxwell lived in a council house, too. You have to see this place.'

'I intend to.'

Ancram shook his head. 'He won't talk to you, you won't get past the door.'

'Want a bet?'

Ancram narrowed his eyes. 'You sound confident.'

Jack Morton walked past them, rolling his eyes: a general comment on life. He was searching his pockets for coins. As he waited for the machine to pour his drink, he turned to them.

'Chick, The Lobby?'

Ancram nodded. 'One o'clock?'

'Braw.'

'What about associates?' Rebus asked. He noticed Ancram hadn't yet said he could call him by his nickname.

'Oh, he has plenty of those. His guards are bodybuilders, hand-picked. Then he has some nutters, real headbangers. The bodybuilders might look the business, but these others *are* the business. There was Tony El, poly-bag merchant with a penchant for power tools. Uncle Joe still has one or two like him. Then there's Joe's son, Malky.'

'Mr Stanley knife?'

'Emergency rooms all over Glasgow can testify to *that* particular hobby.'

'But Tony El hasn't been around?'

Ancram shook his head. 'But I've had my grasses out sniffing on your behalf; I should hear back today.'

Three men pushed open the doors at the end of the hall.

'Aye, aye,' Ancram said in an undertone, 'it's the man with the crystal balls.'

Rebus recognised one of the men from a magazine photograph: Aldous Zane, the American psychic. He'd helped a US police force in their hunt for Merry Mac, so called because someone passing the scene of one of his murders – without realising what was happening on the other side of the wall – had heard deep gurgling laughter. Zane had given his impressions of where the killer lived. When police finally arrested Merry Mac, the media pointed out that the location bore a striking resemblance to the picture Zane had drawn.

For a few weeks, Aldous Zane was newsworthy all around the world. It was enough to tempt a Scottish tabloid to pay for him to offer his impressions in the Johnny Bible hunt. And the police brass were just desperate enough to offer their co-operation.

'Morning, Chick,' one of the other men said.

'Morning, Terry.'

'Terry' was looking at Rebus, awaiting an introduction.

'DI John Rebus,' Ancram said. 'DCS Thompson.'

The man stuck out his hand, which Rebus shook. He was a mason, like every second cop on the force. Rebus wasn't of the brotherhood, but had learned to mimic the handshake.

Thompson turned to Ancram. 'We're taking Mr Zane along to have another look at some of the physical evidence.'

'Not just a look,' Zane corrected. 'I need to touch it.'

Thompson's left eye twitched. Obviously he was as sceptical as Ancram. 'Right, well, this way, Mr Zane.'

The three men walked off.

'Who was the silent one?' Rebus asked.

Ancram shrugged. 'Zane's minder, he's from the news-paper. They want to be in on everything Zane does.'

Rebus nodded. 'I know him,' he said. 'Or I used to, years back.'

'I think his name's Stevens.'

'Jim Stevens,' Rebus said, still nodding. 'By the way, there's another difference between the two killers.'

'What?'

'Bible John's victims were all menstruating.'

Rebus was left alone at a desk with the available files on Joseph Toal. He didn't learn much more from them except that Uncle Joe seldom saw the inside of a court. Rebus wondered about that. Toal always seemed to know when police had him or his operations under surveillance, when the shit was heading fanwards. That way, they never found any evidence, or not enough to put him away. A couple of fines, that was about the sum total. Several big pushes had been made, but they'd always been abandoned for lack of hard evidence or because a surveillance was blown. As if Uncle Joe had a psychic of his own. But Rebus knew there was a more likely

explanation: someone in CID was feeding gen back to the gangster. Rebus thought of the fancy suits everyone seemed to be wearing, the good watches and shoes, the general air of prosperity and superiority.

It was west coast dirt, let them sweep it up or push it into the corner. There was a handwritten notation towards the end of the file; he guessed it was Ancram's writing:

'Uncle Joe doesn't need to kill people any more. His rep is weapon enough, and the bastard's getting stronger all the time.'

He found a spare telephone, made a call to Barlinnie Prison, then, no sign of Chick Ancram, went walkabout.

As he'd known he would, he ended up back in the musty-smelling room dominated by the old monster, Bible John. People in Glasgow still talked about him, had done even before Johnny Bible had come along. Bible John was the bedtime bogeyman made flesh, a generation's scare story. He was your creepy next-door neighbour; the quiet man who lived two flights up; he was the parcel courier with the windowless van. He was whoever you wanted him to be. Back in the early seventies, parents had warned their children, 'Behave, or Bible John will get you!'

Bogeyman made flesh. Now reproducing.

The shift of detectives looked to have taken a collective break. Rebus was alone in the room. He left the door open, not sure why, and pored over the documents. Fifty thousand statements had been taken. Rebus read a couple of the newspaper headlines: 'The Dance Hall Don Juan With Murder on his Mind'; '100 Day Hunt for Ladykiller'. In the first year of the hunt, over five thousand suspects had been interviewed and eliminated. When the third victim's sister gave her detailed description, police knew so much about the killer: blue-grey eyes; straight teeth except for one on the upper right which overlapped its neighbour; his preferred brand of cigarette was Embassy; he spoke of a strict upbringing, and he quoted passages from the Bible. But by then it was too late. Bible John was history.

Another difference between Bible John and Johnny Bible: the gaps between the killings. Johnny was killing every few weeks, while Bible John had killed to no pattern of weeks or even months. His first victim had been February '68. There followed a gap of nearly eighteen months – August '69, victim number two. And then two and a half months later, his third and final outing. Victims one and three had been killed on a Thursday night, the second victim on a Saturday. Eighteen months was a hell of a gap – Rebus knew the theories: that he'd been overseas, perhaps as a merchant seaman or navy sailor, or on some army or RAF posting; that he'd been in jail, serving time for some lesser offence. Theories, that's all they were. All three of his victims were mothers of children: so far, none of Johnny Bible's was. Was it important that Bible John's victims had been menstruating, or that they had children? He'd tucked a sanitary towel under his third victim's armpit – a ritual act. A lot had been read into that action by the various psychologists involved in the case. Their theory: the Bible told Bible John that women were harlots, and he was offered proof when married women left a dance hall with him. The fact that they were menstruating angered him somehow, fed his bloodlust, so he killed them.

Rebus knew there were those out there – always had been – who

believed there to be no connection, other than pure circumstance, between the three killings. They posited three murderers, and it was true that only strong coincidences connected the murders. Rebus, no great champion of coincidence, still believed in a single, driven killer.

Some great policemen had been involved: Tom Goodall, the man who'd gone after Jimmy Boyle, who'd been there when Peter Manuel confessed; then when Goodall died, there'd been Elphinstone Dalgliesh and Joe Beattie. Beattie had spent hours staring at photos of suspects, using a magnifying glass sometimes. He'd felt that if Bible John walked into a crowded room, he would know him. The case had obsessed some officers, sent them spiralling downwards. All that work, and no result. It made a mockery of them, their methods, their system. He thought of Lawson Geddes again . . .

Rebus looked up, saw he was being watched from the doorway. He got up as the two men walked into the room.

Aldous Zane, Jim Stevens.

'Any luck?' Rebus asked.

Stevens shrugged. 'Early days. Aldous came up with a couple of things.' He put out his hand. Rebus took it. Stevens smiled. 'You remember me, don't you?' Rebus nodded. 'I wasn't sure, back there in the hallway.'

'I thought you were in London.'

'I moved back three years ago. I'm mainly freelance now.'

'And doing guard duty, I see.'

Rebus glanced towards Aldous Zane, but the American wasn't listening. He was moving his palms over the paperwork on the nearest desk. He was short, slender, middle-aged. He wore steel-framed glasses with blue-tint lenses, and his lips were slightly parted, showing small, narrow teeth. He reminded Rebus a little of Peter Sellers playing Dr Strangelove. He wore a cagoule over his jacket, and made swishing sounds when he moved.

'What is this?' he said.

'Bible John. Johnny Bible's ancestor. They brought in a psychic on his case, too, Gerard Croiset.'

'The *paragnost*,' Zane said quietly. 'Was there any success?'

'He described a location, two shopkeepers, an old man who could help the inquiry.'

'And?'

'And,' Jim Stevens interrupted, 'a reporter found what looked like the location.'

'But no shopkeepers,' Rebus added, 'and no old man.'

Zane looked up. 'Cynicism is not helpful.'

'Call me par-agnostic.'

Zane smiled, held out his hand. Rebus took it, felt tremendous heat in the man's palm. A tingle ran up his arm.

'Creepy, isn't it?' Jim Stevens said, as though he could read Rebus's mind.

Rebus waved a hand over the material on all four desks. 'So, Mr Zane, do you *feel* anything?'

'Only sadness and suffering, an incredible amount of both.' He picked up one of the later photofits of Bible John. 'And I thought I could see flags.'

'Flags?'

'The Stars and Stripes, a swastika. And a trunk filled with objects . . .'
He had his eyes shut, the lids fluttering. 'In the attic of a modern house.'
The eyes opened. 'That's all. There's a lot of distance, a lot of distance.'

Stevens had his notebook out. He wrote quickly in shorthand. There was
someone else in the doorway, looking surprised at the assembly.

'Inspector,' Chick Ancram said, 'time for lunch.'

They took one of the duty cars into the west end, Ancram driving. There
was something different about him; he seemed at the same time more
interested in Rebus and warier of him. Their conversation collapsed into
point-scoring.

Eventually, Ancram pointed to a striped traffic-cone kerbside, protecting
the only space left on the street.

'Get out and move that, will you?'

Rebus obliged, placing the cone on the pavement. Ancram reversed the
car inch-perfect into the space.

'Looks like you've had practice.'

Ancram straightened his tie. 'Patrons' parking.'

They walked into The Lobby. It was a trendy-looking bar with too many
high uncomfortable-looking barstools, black and white tiled walls, electric
and acoustic guitars suspended from the ceiling.

There was a chalkboard menu behind the bar. Three staff were busy
with the lunchtime crush; more perfume than alcohol in the air. Office
girls, screeching over the slam of the music, nursing gaudy drinks;
sometimes one or two men with them, smiling, saying nothing, older. They
wore suits that said 'management': the banshees' bosses. There were more
cellphones and pagers on the tables than there were glasses; even the staff
seemed to carry them.

'What do you want?'

'Pint of eighty,' Rebus said.

'To eat?'

Rebus ran down the menu. 'Is there anything with meat?'

'Game pie.'

Rebus nodded. They were a row back from the bar, but Ancram had
caught a barman's attention. He stood on tiptoe and yelled the order over
the straw-perm heads of the teenagers in front. They turned, gave hostile
looks: he'd jumped the queue.

'All right, ladies?' Ancram leered. They turned away again.

He led Rebus through the bar to a far corner, where a table groaned with
green food: salads, quiche, guacamole. Rebus got himself a chair; there was
one already waiting for Ancram. Three CID officers sat there, not one with
a pint glass in front of him. Ancram made introductions.

'Jack you already know.' Jack Morton nodded, chewing pitta bread.
'That's DS Andy Lennox, and DI Billy Eggleston.' The two men gave curt
greetings, more interested in their food. Rebus looked around.

'What about the drinks?'

'Patience, man, patience. Here they come.'

The barman was approaching with a tray: Rebus's pint and game pie;
Ancram's smoked salmon salad and gin and tonic.

'Twelve pounds ten,' the barman said. Ancram handed over three fives,
told him to keep the change. He raised his glass to Rebus.

'Here's tae us.'

'Wha's like us,' Rebus added.

'Gey few, and they're a' deid,' Jack Morton said, raising his own glass of what looked suspiciously like water. They all drank, got down to eating, exchanging the day's gossip. There was a table of office girls nearby; Lennox and Eggleston tried intermittently to engage them in conversation. The girls got on with their own gossip. Clothes, Rebus reflected, did not necessarily make the man. He felt stifled, uncomfortable. There wasn't enough space on the table; his chair was too close to Ancram's; the music was using him as a punchbag.

'So what do you reckon to Uncle Joe?' Ancram asked at last.

Rebus chewed on a tough crescent of pastry. The others seemed to be waiting for his answer.

'I reckon I'll be visiting him sometime today.'

Ancram laughed. 'Let me know if you're serious, we'll lend you some armour.' The others laughed too, and started eating again. Rebus wondered just how much of Uncle Joe's money was floating around Glasgow CID.

'John and me,' Jack Morton was saying, 'worked the Knots and Crosses case together.'

'Is that right?' Ancram looked interested.

Rebus shook his head. 'Ancient history.'

Morton caught the tone of voice, lowered his head to his food, reached for the water.

Ancient history; and far, far too painful.

'Speaking of history,' Ancram said, 'sounds like you've got a bit of trouble with the Spaven case.' He smiled mischievously. 'I read about it in the papers.'

'It's all hype for the TV show,' was Rebus's only comment.

'We've got more problems with the DNAs, Chick,' Eggleston was saying. He was tall, skinny, starched. He reminded Rebus of an accountant; he'd bet he was good with paperwork, lousy on the street – every station needed at least one.

'They're an epidemic,' Lennox snarled.

'Society's problem, gentlemen,' Ancram said, 'which makes them our problem too.'

'DNAs?'

Ancram turned to Rebus. 'Do Not Accommodate. The council's been turfing out a lot of "problem clients", refusing to house them, even in the night shelters – druggies mostly, headers, the "psychologically disturbed" who've been returned to the community. Only the community's telling them to fuck right off again. So they're on the streets, making mischief, causing us grief. Kitting up in public, ODing on mainline Temazepam, you name it.'

'Fucking shocking,' Lennox offered. He had tight-curled ginger hair and crimson cheeks, his face heavily freckled, eyebrows and eyelashes fair. He was the only one smoking at the table. Rebus lit one up to join him; Jack Morton gave a reproachful look.

'So what can you do?' Rebus asked.

'I'll tell you,' Ancram said. 'We're going to round them up next weekend,

into a fleet of buses, and we're going to drop the whole lot of them off on Princes Street.'

More laughter at the table, directed at the visitor – Ancram waving the baton. Rebus checked his watch.

'Somewhere to be?'

'Yes, and I'd better get going.'

'Well, look,' Ancram said, 'if you *do* get an invite to Uncle Joe's abode, I want to know about it. I'll be here this evening, seven until ten. OK?'

Rebus nodded, waved a general goodbye, and got out.

Once outside, he felt better. He began to walk, not very sure in which direction he was headed. The city centre was laid out American-style, a grid system of one-way streets. Edinburgh might have its monuments, but Glasgow was built to monumental scale, making the capital seem like Toytown. Rebus walked until he saw something that looked more his kind of bar. He knew he needed shoring up for the trip he was about to take. A TV was playing quietly, but no music. And what conversation there was was muffled, low-key. He couldn't make out what the two men nearest him were saying, their accents were so thick. The only woman in the place was the barmaid.

'What'll it be today?'

'Grouse, make it a double. And a half-bottle to take out.'

He trickled water into the glass, reflected that if he'd eaten a couple of pies here and had a couple of whiskies, it wouldn't have been half as expensive as The Lobby. But then Ancram had paid at The Lobby; three crisp fivers from the pocket of a sleek suit.

'Just a Coke, please.'

Rebus turned to the new customer: Jack Morton.

'You following me?'

Morton smiled. 'You look rough, John.'

'And you and your cronies look *too* good.'

'I can't be bought.'

'No? Who can?'

'Come on, John, I was making a joke.' Morton sat down next to him. 'I heard about Lawson Geddes. Does that mean the stooshie'll die down?'

'Some hope.' Rebus drained his glass. 'Look at that,' he said, pointing out a machine on the corner of the bar. 'Jelly-bean dispenser, twenty pence a throw. Two things the Scots are famous for, Jack: our sweet tooth and alcohol consumption.'

'Two more things we're famous for,' Morton said.

'What?'

'Avoiding the issue and feeling guilty all the time.'

'You mean Calvinism?' Rebus chuckled. 'Christ, Jack, I thought the only Calvin you knew these days was Mr Klein.'

Jack Morton was staring at him, seeking eye-to-eye contact. 'Give me another reason why a man would let himself go.'

Rebus snorted. 'How long have you got?'

Morton to Rebus: 'As long as it takes.'

'Not nearly enough, Jack. Here, have a proper drink.'

'This is a proper drink. That stuff you're drinking, that's not really a drink.'

'What is it then?'
'An escape clause.'

Jack said he'd drive Rebus to Barlinnie, didn't ask why he wanted to go there. They took the M8 to Riddrie; Jack knew all the routes. They didn't say much during the trip, until Jack asked the question which had been hanging between them.

'How's Sammy?'

Rebus's daughter, now grown-up. Jack hadn't seen her in nearly ten years.

'She's fine.' Rebus had a change of subject ready. 'I'm not sure Chick Ancram likes me. He keeps . . . *studying* me.'

'He's a shrewd customer, be nice to him.'

'Any particular reason?'

Jack Morton bit back an answer, shook his head. They turned off Cumbernauld Road, approached the jail.

'Look,' Jack said, 'I can't hang around. Tell me how long you'll be and I'll send a patrol car for you.'

'An hour should do it.'

Jack Morton checked his watch. 'An hour it is.' He held out his hand. 'Good to see you again, John.'

Rebus took the hand, squeezed.

6

'Big Ger' Cafferty was waiting when he reached the Interview Room.

'Well, Strawman, this is an unexpected pleasure.'

Strawman: Cafferty's name for Rebus. The prison guard who had brought Rebus seemed disinclined to leave, and there were already two guards in the room keeping an eye on Cafferty. He'd already escaped once from Barlinnie, and now that they had him back, they were intent on keeping him.

'Hello, Cafferty.' Rebus sat down across from him. Cafferty had aged in prison, losing his tan and some musculature, putting on weight in all the wrong places. His hair was thin and greying quickly, and there was stubble on chin and cheekbones. 'I've brought you something.' He looked at the guards, eased the half-bottle out of his pocket.

'Not allowed,' one guard snapped.

'Don't worry, Strawman,' Cafferty said. 'I've plenty of hooch, this place is practically swimming in the stuff. It's the thought that counts, eh?'

Rebus dropped the bottle back into his pocket.

'I take it you've a favour to ask?'

'Yes.'

Cafferty crossed his legs, utterly at ease. 'What is it?'

'You know Joseph Toal?'

'Everyone and their dog knows Uncle Joe.'

'Yes, but you *know* him.'

'So?' There was an edge to Cafferty's smile.

'I want you to phone him, get him to speak to me.'

Cafferty considered the request. 'Why?'

'I want to ask him about Anthony Kane.'

'Tony El? I thought he was dead.'

'He left his prints at a murder scene in Niddrie.' Never mind what the boss said, Rebus was treating this as murder. And he knew the word would make more of an impression on Cafferty. It did. His lips rounded into an O, and he whistled.

'That was stupid of him. Tony El didn't used to be so stupid. And if he was still working for Uncle Joe . . . There could be fallout.' Rebus knew that connections were being made in Cafferty's mind, and they all led to Joseph Toal becoming his Barlinnie neighbour. There would be reasons for Cafferty to want Toal inside: old scores, debts unpaid, territory encroached. There were always old scores to be settled. Cafferty came to his decision.

'You'll need to get me a phone.'

Rebus got up, walked over to the guard who'd barked 'Not allowed', slipped the whisky into the man's pocket.

'We need to get him a phone,' he said.

They marched Cafferty left and right through corridors until they reached a payphone. They'd had to pass through three sets of gates.

'This is as near to the outside as I've been in a while,' Cafferty joked. The guards weren't laughing. Rebus provided the money for the call.

'Now,' said Cafferty, 'let's see if I remember . . .' He winked at Rebus, pressed seven digits, waited.

'Hello?' he said. 'Who's that?' He listened to the name. 'Never heard of you. Listen, tell Uncle Joe that Big Ger wants a word. Just tell him that.' He waited, glanced at Rebus, licked his lips. 'He says what? Tell him I'm phoning from the Bar-L and money's short.'

Rebus pushed another coin home.

'Well,' Cafferty growing angry, 'tell him he's got a tattoo on his back.' He covered the mouthpiece. 'Not something Uncle Joe goes blabbing about.'

Rebus got as close as he could to the earpiece, heard a dull rasp of a voice.

'Morris Gerald Cafferty, is that you? I thought someone was winding me up.'

'Hello, Uncle Joe. How's business?'

'Loupin'. Who's listening in?'

'At the last count, three monkeys and a dick.'

'You always liked an audience, that was your problem.'

'Sound advice, Uncle Joe, but years too late.'

'So what do they want?' They: Rebus the dick and the three monkey guards.

'The dick's from Edinburgh CID, he wants to come talk to you.'

'What about?'

'Tony El.'

'What's to tell? Tony hasn't worked for me in a twelve-month.'

'Then tell the nice policeman that. Seems Tony's been up to his old tricks. There's a cold one in Edinburgh, and Tony's prints on the scene.'

A low growl: human.

'You got a dog there, Uncle Joe?'

'Tell the cop I don't have anything to do with Tony.'

'I think he wants to hear it for himself.'

'Then put him on.'

Cafferty looked to Rebus, who shook his head.

'And he wants to look you in the eye while you're telling him.'

'Is he a poof or what?'

'He's old school, Uncle Joe. You'll like him.'

'Why did he come to you?'

'I'm his Last Chance Saloon.'

'And why the fuck did you agree?'

Cafferty didn't miss a beat. 'A half-bottle of *usquebaugh*.'

'Jesus, the Bar-L must be drier than I thought.' The voice not so rough.

'Send a whole bottle over and I'll tell him to go fuck himself.'

A croaky laugh. 'Christ, Cafferty, I miss you. How long to go?'

'Ask my lawyers.'

'Are you still keeping your hand in?'

'What do you think?'

'It's what I hear.'

'Nothing wrong with your hearing.'

'Send the bastard over, tell him he gets five minutes. Maybe I'll come see you one of these days.'

'Better not, Uncle Joe, when visiting time ends they might have misplaced the key.'

More laughter. The line went dead. Cafferty put down the receiver.

'You owe me, Strawman,' he growled, 'so here's my favour: put that old bastard away.'

But Rebus was already walking towards freedom.

The car was waiting for him, Morton keeping his word. Rebus gave the address he'd memorised from the Toal files. He was sitting in the back, two woolly suits in the front. The passenger turned in his seat.

'Isn't that where Uncle Joe lives?'

Rebus nodded. The woolly suits exchanged a look.

'Just get me there,' Rebus ordered.

The traffic was heavy, people heading home. Elastic Glasgow, stretching in four directions. The housing scheme, when they reached it, was much like any scheme its size in Edinburgh: grey pebbledash, barren play areas, tarmac and a smattering of fortified shops. Kids on bikes stopping to watch the car, eyes as keen as sentries'; brisk baby buggies, shapeless mothers with dyed blonde hair. Further into the estate, driving slowly: people watching from behind their windows, men at pavement corners, muttered confabs. A city within a city, uniform and enervating, energy sapped, nothing left but obstinacy: the words NO SURRENDER on a gable-end, a message from Ulster just as relevant here.

'Are you expected?' the driver asked.

'I'm expected.'

'Thank Christ for that at least.'

'Any other patrol cars around?'

The passenger laughed nervously. 'This is the frontier, sir. The frontier has a way of keeping its own law and order.'

'If you had his money,' the driver said, 'would you live here?'

'He was born here,' Rebus said. 'And I believe his house is a bit special.'

'Special?' The driver snorted. 'Well, judge for yourself.'

He brought the car to a stop at the entrance to a cul-de-sac. Rebus saw at the end of the cul-de-sac two houses which stood out from their neighbours for a single reason: they boasted stone cladding.

'One of those?' Rebus asked.

'Pick either door.'

Rebus got out of the car, leaned back in. 'Don't you dare drive away.' He slammed his door shut and walked up the cul-de-sac. He chose the left-hand of the two identical semi-detacheds. The door was opened from within, and an oversized man in a bulging T-shirt ushered him in.

'You the rozzer?' They were standing in a cramped hallway. Rebus nodded. 'Through there.'

Rebus opened the door to the living room, and did a double-take. The connecting wall between the two semis had been knocked through, providing a double-sized living space, open plan. The room also went further back than should have been feasible. Rebus was reminded of Dr Who's Tardis, and, alone in the room, walked towards the back of the house. A large extension had been added, including a sizeable conservatory. This should have minimised the space left for a garden, but the lawn outside was plentiful. There were playing-fields backing on to the house, and Rebus saw that Uncle Joe had taken a chunk out of these fields for his garden.

Planning permission, of course, was out of the question.

But then who needed planning permission?

'I hope your ears don't need cleaning,' a voice said. Rebus turned and saw that a small, stooped man had entered the room. He held a cigarette in one hand, while his other was busy with a walking-stick. He shuffled in carpet slippers towards a well-used armchair and fell into it, hands gripping the greasy anti-macassars, walking-stick lying across his lap.

Rebus had seen photographs of the man, but they hadn't prepared him for the reality. Joseph Toal really *did* look like someone's uncle. He was in his seventies, stocky, with the hands and face of a one-time coalminer. His forehead was all rippled flesh, and his thin grey hair was swept back and Brylcreemed. His jaw was square, eyes watery, and his glasses hung from a string around his neck. When he raised the cigarette to his lips, Rebus saw nicotine fingers, bruised ingrown nails. He was wearing a shapeless cardigan over an equally shapeless sports shirt. The cardigan was patched, loose threads hanging from it. His trousers were brown and baggy, stained at the knees.

'Nothing wrong with my ears,' Rebus said, coming forward.

'Good, because I'll say it only once.' He sniffed, controlling his breathing. 'Anthony Kane worked for me twelve, thirteen years, not all the time – short-term contracts. But then a year ago, maybe a little over, he told me he was walking, wanted to be his own boss. We parted on amicable terms, I haven't seen him since.'

Rebus gestured to a chair. Toal nodded to let him know he could sit. Rebus took his time getting comfortable.

'Mr Toal –'

'Everybody calls me Uncle Joe.'

'As in Stalin?'

'You think that's a new joke, son? Ask your question.'

Go: 'What was Tony planning to do when he left your employ?'

'He didn't go into specifics. Our parting conversation was . . . curt.'

Rebus nodded. He was thinking: I had an uncle who looked very much like you; I can't even remember his name.

'Well, if that's everything . . .' Toal made a show of starting to rise.

'Do you remember Bible John, Uncle Joe?'

Toal frowned, understanding the question but not its intent. He reached down to the floor for an ashtray, stubbed his cigarette into it. 'I remember fine. Hundreds of coppers on the street, it was bad for business. We co-operated a hundred per cent, I had men out hunting the bugger for months. *Months!* And now this new bastard turns up.'

'Johnny Bible?'

Pointing to himself: 'I'm a businessman. The slaughter of innocents sickens me. I've had all my taxi drivers –' he paused – 'I have interests in a local taxi firm – and I've instructed every single driver: keep your eyes peeled and your ears open.' He was breathing heavily. 'If anything comes to me, it'll go straight to the cops.'

'Very public-spirited.'

Toal shrugged. 'The public is my business.' Another pause, a frown. 'What's all this to do with Tony El?'

'Nothing.' Toal looked unconvinced. 'Call it tangential. Is it OK to smoke?'

'You're not staying long enough to enjoy it.'

Rebus lit up anyway, staying put. 'Where did Tony El go?'

'He didn't send a postcard.'

'You must have some idea.'

Toal thought about it, when he shouldn't have needed to. 'Somewhere south, I think. Maybe London. He had friends down there.'

'London?'

Toal wouldn't look at Rebus. He shook his head. 'I heard he headed south.'

Rebus stood up.

'Is it that time already?' Toal showed effort getting to his feet, steadying himself with the walking-stick. 'And here we were just getting to know one another. How's Edinburgh these days? Know what we used to say about it? Fur coat and nae knickers, that's Edinburgh.' A hacking laugh turned into a hacking cough. Toal gripped the walking-stick with both hands, knees almost buckling.

Rebus waited until he'd finished. The old man's face was puce, sweat breaking out. 'That may be true,' he said, 'but I don't see too many fur coats around here, never mind the knickers.'

Toal's face broke into a grin, showing yellow dentures. 'Cafferty said I'd like you, and you know what?'

'What?'

The grin turned to a scowl. 'He was wrong. And now I've seen you, I'm wondering more than ever why he sent you here. Not just for the price of a half-bottle, not even Cafferty's that cheap. You better get yourself back to Edinburgh, laddie. And take care of yourself, I hear it's not as safe as it used to be.'

Rebus walked to the far end of the living room, deciding to leave by the other front door. There was a staircase next to it, and someone came bounding down, nearly colliding with him. A big man in bad clothes, a face that said he wasn't too bright, arms tattooed with thistles and pipers. He'd be about twenty-five, and Rebus recognised him from the photos in the file: Mad Malky Toal, a.k.a. 'Stanley'. Joseph Toal's wife had died in childbirth, too old really to be having kids. But their first two had died, one in infancy, one in a car smash. So now there was only Stanley, heir apparent, and towards the back of the queue when the IQs were being divvied.

He gave Rebus a long look, full of grudge and threat, then loped towards his father. He was wearing the trousers from a pinstripe suit with T-shirt, white socks, trainers – Rebus had yet to meet a gangster with dress sense:

they spent money, but with no style – and his face sported half a dozen good-sized warts.

'Hey, Da, I've lost my keys to the beamer, where's the spare set?'

Rebus let himself out, relieved to see that the patrol car was still there. Boys were circling it on bikes, a cherokee party with scalps on their minds. Leaving the cul-de-sac, Rebus checked the cars: a nice new Rover; BMW 3 Series; an older Merc, one of the big ones, and a couple of less serious contenders. Had it been a used car lot, he'd have kept his money and looked elsewhere.

He squeezed between two bikes, opened the back door, got in. The driver started the engine. Rebus looked back to where Stanley was making for the BMW, bouncing on his heels.

'Now,' the passenger said, 'before we leave, have you counted that you still have all your fingers and toes?'

'West end,' Rebus said, leaning back in his seat and closing his eyes. He needed another drink.

The Horseshoe Bar first, a jolt of malt, and then outside for a taxi. He told the driver he wanted Langside Place in Battlefield. From the moment he'd walked into the Bible John room, he'd known he would make this trip. He could have had the patrol car take him, but didn't want to have to explain his interest.

Langside Place was where Bible John's first victim had lived. She'd worked as a nurse, lived with her parents. Her father looked after her small son while she went out dancing. Rebus knew her original destination had been the Majestic Ballroom in Hope Street, but somewhere along the way she'd decided on the Barrowland instead. If only she'd stuck to her first choice. What force had nudged her towards the Barrowland? Could you just call it fate and be done with it?

He told the driver to wait, got out of the cab and walked up and down the street. Her body had been found nearby, outside a garage in Carmichael Lane, clothing and handbag missing. Police had spent a lot of time and effort searching for them. They'd also done their best to interview people who'd been at the Barrowland that night, only there was a problem: Thursday night there was notorious. It was Over Twenty-Fives night, and a lot of married men and women went, leaving spouses and wedding rings behind. A lot of people shouldn't have been there, and made unwilling material as witnesses.

The taxi's engine was still running – and so was its meter. Rebus didn't know what he'd expected to find here, but he was still glad he'd come. It was hard to look at the street and see the year 1968, hard to get any feel for that era. Everything and everyone had changed.

He knew the second address: Mackeith Street, where the second victim had lived and died. Here was one thing about Bible John: he'd taken the victims so close to their homes, a sign either of confidence or indecision. By August 1969 police had all but given up the initial investigation, and the Barrowland was thriving again. It was a Saturday night, and the victim left her three children with her sister, who lived across the landing. In those days, Mackeith Street was tenements, but as the taxi reached its destination Rebus saw terraced housing, satellite dishes. The tenements

had long gone; in 1969 they'd been awaiting demolition, many of them empty. She'd been found in one of the derelict buildings, strangled with her tights. Some of her things were missing, including her handbag. Rebus didn't get out of the taxi, didn't see the point. His driver turned to him.

'Bible John, is it?'

Surprised, Rebus nodded. The driver lit a cigarette. He'd be about fifty, thick curling grey hair, his face ruddy, a boyish gleam to the blue eyes.

'See,' he said, 'I was a cabbie back then as well. Never really seem to have got out the rut.'

Rebus remembered the box-file with 'Taxi Firms' on its spine. 'Did the police question you?'

'Oh aye, but it was more that they wanted us to be on the lookout, you know, in case we ever got him in the back. But he looked like any other punter, there were dozens fit the description. We almost had a few lynchings. They had to give out cards to some of them: "This man is not Bible John", signed by the Chief Constable.'

'What do you think happened to him?'

'Ach, who knows? At least he stopped, that's the main thing, eh?'

'If he stopped,' Rebus said quietly. The third address was Earl Street in Scotstoun, the victim's body found on Hallowe'en. The sister, who had accompanied the victim all evening, had painted a very full picture of that night: the bus to Glasgow Cross, the walk up the Gallowgate . . . shops they stopped at . . . drinks in the Traders' Tavern . . . then the Barrowland. They both met men called John. The two men didn't seem to hit it off. One went to catch a bus, the other stayed, sharing their taxi. Talking. It gnawed at Rebus, as it had at so many before him: why would Bible John leave such a good witness behind? Why had he gone on to kill his third victim, knowing her sister would be able to draw such a vivid portrait of him: his clothes, what he'd talked about, his overlapping front teeth? Why had he been so reckless? Had he been taunting the police, or was there some other reason? Maybe he was heading away from Glasgow, so could afford this casual exit. But heading where? Somewhere his description would mean nothing – Australia, Canada, the USA?

Halfway to Earl Street, Rebus said he'd changed his mind and directed his driver to the 'Marine' instead. The old Partick station – which had been the heart of the Bible John inquiry – was empty and near-derelict. It was still possible to gain access to the building if you unlocked the padlocks, and no doubt kids had found they could get in without undoing any locks at all. But all Rebus did was sit outside and stare. A lot of men were taken to the Marine, questioned, and put in a line-up. There were five hundred formal identity parades, and many more informal ones. Joe Beattie and the third victim's sister would stand there and concentrate on faces, physiques, speech. Then there'd be a shake of the head, and Joe would be back to square one.

'You'll want to see the Barrowland next, eh?' his driver said. Rebus shook his head. He'd had enough. The Barrowland wouldn't tell him anything he didn't already know.

'Do you know a bar called The Lobby?' he said instead. The driver nodded. 'Let's go there then.'

He paid off the cabbie, adding a fiver as a tip, and asked for a receipt.

'No receipts, sorry, pal.'

'You don't happen to work for Joe Toal, do you?'

The man glared at him. 'Never heard of him.' Then he shifted into first and sped off.

Inside The Lobby, Ancram was standing at the bar, looking relaxed, the focus of a lot of attention: two men and two women in a huddle around him. The bar was full of after-work suits, careerists plotting furtively, women on the scent.

'Inspector, what'll it be?'

'My shout.' He pointed to Ancram's glass, then to the others, but Ancram laughed.

'You don't buy them drinks, they're journos.'

'It's my round anyway,' one of the women said. 'What'll you have?'

'My mother told me never to accept drinks from strangers.'

She smiled: lip gloss, eye-shadow, tired face trying for enthusiasm. 'Jennifer Drysdale.' Rebus knew why she was tired: it was hard work acting like 'one of the boys'. Mairie Henderson had told him about it – the pattern was changing only slowly; a lot of surface gloss about equality sloshed over the same old wallpaper.

Jeff Beck on the sound system: 'Hi-Ho Silver Lining'. Stupid lyric, and a hook that had lasted two decades and more. It comforted him that a place with The Lobby's pretensions should still cling to old hooks.

'Actually,' Ancram was saying, 'we should be making tracks. Right, John?'

'Right.' The use of his first name a hint: Ancram wanted out.

The reporters didn't look so happy any more. They flung questions at Ancram: Johnny Bible. They wanted a story, any story.

'I would if I could, but there's nothing to give.' Ancram had his hands up, trying to placate the foursome. Rebus saw that someone had placed a recording Walkman on top of the bar.

'Anything,' one of the men said. He even glanced towards Rebus, but Rebus was staying out of it.

'If you want a story,' Ancram said, pushing through the bodies, 'get yourselves a psychic detective. Thanks for the drinks.'

Outside, the smile fell from Ancram's face. An act, it had been no more than that. 'Bastards are worse than leeches.'

'And like leeches, they have their uses.'

'True, but who would you rather have a drink with? I've no car, do you mind walking?'

'Where to?'

'The next bar we find.'

But in fact they had to walk past three pubs – not places a policeman could drink in safely – until they hit one Ancram liked the look of. It was still raining, but mild. Rebus could feel sweat glueing his shirt to his back. Despite the rain, *Big Issue* sellers were out in force, not that anyone was buying: good-cause fatigue.

They shook themselves dry and settled on stools at the bar. Rebus ordered – malt, gin and tonic – and lit a cigarette, offering one to Ancram, who shook his head.

'So where have you been?'

'Uncle Joe's.' Among other places.

'How did you get on?'

'I spoke to the man.' And paid my respects . . .

'Face to face?' Rebus nodded; Ancram appraised him. 'Where?'

'At his house.'

'The Ponderosa? He let you in without a search warrant?'

'The place was immaculate.'

'He'd probably spent half an hour before you got there sticking all the booty upstairs.'

'His son was upstairs when I got there.'

'Standing guard on the bedroom door, no doubt. Did you see Eve?'

'Who's she?'

'Uncle Joe's clippie. Don't be fooled by the wheezing old pensioner routine. Eve's around fifty, still in good nick.'

'I didn't see her.'

'You'd've remembered. So, did anything rattle loose from the shaky old bugger?'

'Not much. He swore Tony El's been off the payroll for a year, and he hasn't seen him.'

A man came into the bar, saw Ancram, and was about to do a U-turn. But Ancram had already spotted him in the bar mirror, so the man walked up to him, brushing rain off his hair.

'Hiya, Chick.'

'Dusty, how's things?'

'No' bad.'

'You're doing away then?'

'You know me, Chick.' The man kept his head low, spoke in an undertone, shuffled off to the far end of the bar.

'Just someone I know,' Ancram explained: meaning, a snitch. The man was ordering a half and a 'hauf': whisky with a half-pint of beer to chase it down. He opened a packet of Embassy, made too much of a point of not looking along the bar.

'So was that all Uncle Joe gave you?' Ancram asked. 'I'm intrigued, how did you get to him?'

'A patrol car dropped me, I walked the rest of the way.'

'You know what I mean.'

'Uncle Joe and I have a mutual friend.' Rebus finished his malt.

'Same again?' Ancram asked. Rebus nodded. 'Well, I know you visited the Bar-L.' Jack Morton talking? 'And I can't think of *too* many people there who have Uncle Joe's ear . . . Big Ger Cafferty?' Rebus gave silent applause. Ancram laughed for real this time, not a show for reporters. 'And the old sod didn't tell you anything?'

'Just that he thought Tony El had moved south, maybe to London.'

Ancram picked the lemon out of his drink, discarded it. 'Really? That's interesting.'

'Why?'

'Because I've had my friends reporting in.' Ancram made the slightest movement with his head, and the snitch from the far end of the bar slid off his stool and came towards them. 'Tell Inspector Rebus what you told me, Dusty.'

Dusty licked non-existent lips. He looked the kind who snitched to feel important, not just for money or revenge.

'Word is,' he said, face still bowed so Rebus was looking at the top of his head, 'Tony El's been working up north.'

'North?'

'Dundee . . . north-east.'

'Aberdeen?'

'Up that way, aye.'

'Doing what?'

A fast shrug of the shoulders. 'Independent operator, who knows. He's just been seen around.'

'Thanks, Dusty,' Ancram said. Dusty sloped back to his end of the bar. Ancram signalled for the barmaid. 'Two more,' he said, 'and whatever Dusty's drinking.' He turned to Rebus. 'So who do you believe, Uncle Joe or Dusty?'

'You think he lied just to wind me up?'

'Or wind you down.'

Yes, down as far as London, a false trail that could have eaten into the investigation: wasted time, manpower, effort.

'The victim worked out of Aberdeen,' Rebus said.

'All roads leading to.' The drinks had arrived. Ancram handed over a twenty. 'Don't bother with change, keep it to pay for whatever else Dusty drinks, and give him what's left at the end. Plus one for yourself.'

She nodded, knew the routine. Rebus was thinking hard, routes leading north. Did he want to go to Aberdeen? It would keep him away from *The Justice Programme*, maybe keep him from thinking about Lawson Geddes. Today had been like a holiday in that respect. Edinburgh was too full of ghosts; but then so was Glasgow – Jim Stevens, Jack Morton, Bible John and his victims . . .

'Did Jack tell you I'd been to the Bar-L?'

'I pulled rank on him, don't blame Jack.'

'He's changed a lot.'

'Has he been nagging you? I wondered why he chased after you at lunchtime. The zeal of the converted.'

'I don't get it.' Rebus lifted the glass to his lips, poured it in smoothly.

'Didn't he say? He's joined AA, and I don't mean breakdown insurance.' Ancram paused. 'Come to think of it though, maybe I do.' He winked, smiled. There was something annoying about his smile; it was like he was party to secrets and motives – a patronising smile.

A very Glaswegian sort of smile.

'He was an alcoholic,' Ancram went on. 'I mean, he still is. Once an alky, always an alky, that's what they say. Something happened to him in Falkirk, he ended up in hospital, nearly in a coma. Sweats, spewing, slime dripping off the ceiling. Gave him a hell of a fright. First thing he did when he got out was look up the phone number for Samaritans, and they put him on to the Juice Church.' He looked at Rebus's glass. 'Christ, that was quick. Here, have another.' The barmaid already had a glass in her hand.

'Thanks, I will,' said Rebus, wishing he didn't feel so calm. 'Since you seem to be so loaded. Nice suit, too.'

The humour left Ancram's eyes. 'There's a tailor on Argyle Street, ten per cent discount for serving officers.' The eyes narrowed. 'Spit it out.'

'No, it's nothing really, just that when I was going through the files on Toal, I couldn't help noticing that he always seemed to have inside info.'

'Careful, laddie.'

The 'laddie' rankled; it was meant to.

'Well,' Rebus went on, 'everyone knows the west coast is open to bungs. Not always cash, you understand. Could be watches, ID bracelets, rings, maybe even a few suits . . .'

Ancram looked around the bar, as though begging for witnesses to Rebus's remarks.

'Would you care to name any names, *Inspector*, or is hearsay good enough for Edinburgh CID? The way I hear it, there's no cupboard-space left in Fettes, they're so jam-packed with skeletons.' He picked up his drink. 'And half those skeletons seem to have *your* fingerprints all over them.'

The smile again, sparkling eyes, laughter lines. *How did he know?* Rebus turned to go. Ancram's voice followed him out of the pub.

'We can't all go running to friends in Barlinnie! I'll see you around, Inspector . . .'

7

Aberdeen.

Aberdeen meant away from Edinburgh; no *Justice Programme*, no Fort Apache, no shite for him to skite in. Aberdeen looked good.

But Rebus had things to do in Edinburgh. He wanted to see the locus in daylight, so drove out there, not risking his own Saab; leaving it at Fort Apache and taking the spare Escort. Jim MacAskill wanted him on the case because he hadn't been around long enough to make enemies; Rebus was wondering how you ever made friends in Niddrie. The place was if anything bleaker by day: blocked-in windows, glass like shrapnel on the tarmac, kids playing in the sunshine with no real enthusiasm, eyes and mouths narrowing as his car cruised past.

They'd knocked a lot of the estate down; behind it was better housing, semi-detached. Satellite dishes a status symbol: the owners' status – unemployed. The estate boasted a derelict pub – insurance job blaze – and one all-purpose corner shop, its window full of video posters. The kids made this last their base. BMX bandits blowing bubble-gum. Rebus drove past slowly, his eyes on them. The death flat wasn't quite on the edge of the estate, not quite visible from Niddrie Mains Road. Rebus was thinking: Tony El didn't come from round here, and if he'd picked the spot by chance, there were other derelict flats nearer the main road.

Two men plus the victim. Tony El and an accomplice.

The accomplice had local knowledge.

Rebus climbed the stairs to the flat. The place had been sealed, but he had keys to both padlocks. The living room as before, upside-down table, blanket. He wondered who'd slept there, maybe they'd seen something. He reckoned his chances of finding them were one per cent; of getting them to talk, slightly less. Kitchen, bathroom, bedrooms, hallway. He kept close to the walls, so as not to fall through the floor. There was no one living in the block, but the next block along had glass in a couple of its windows: one on the first storey, one on the second. Rebus knocked on the first door. A dishevelled woman answered, an infant clinging round her neck. He didn't need to introduce himself.

'I don't know anything, and I didn't see or hear anything.' She made to close the door.

'You married?'

She opened the door again. 'What's it to you?'

Rebus shrugged; good question.

'He's down the boozer, most likely,' she said.

'How many kids have you got?'

'Three.'

'Must be pushed for space.'

'That's what we keep telling them. All they'll say is our name's on the list.'

'What age is your oldest?'

Eyes narrowing. 'Eleven.'

'Any chance he saw something?'

She shook her head. 'He'd've told me.'

'What about your man?'

She smiled. 'He'd have seen everything *twice.*'

Rebus smiled too. 'Well, if you hear anything . . . from the kids or your man . . .'

'Aye, right.' Slowly, so as not to cause offence, she shut the door on him.

Rebus climbed the next flight. Dog shit on the landing, a used condom: he tried not to connect the two. Felt-marker graffiti on the door – Wanker, HMFC, cartoon coitus. The occupier had given up trying to wipe it off. Rebus pushed the doorbell. No answer; he tried again.

A voice from within: 'Bugger off!'

'Could I have a word?'

'Who is it?'

'CID.'

A chain rattled, and the door opened two inches. Rebus saw half a face: an old woman, or maybe an old man. He showed his warrant card.

'You're not moving me out. I'll be here when they pull the place down.'

'I don't want to move you out.'

'Eh?'

Rebus raised his voice. 'Nobody wants to move you out.'

'Aye they do, but I'm not moving, you can tell them that.' Rebus caught foul breath, a meaty smell.

'Look, have you heard what happened next door?'

'Eh?'

Rebus peered through the gap. The hallway was littered with sheets of newspaper, empty cat-food tins. One more try.

'Someone was killed next door.'

'Don't try your tricks with me, boyo!' Anger in the voice.

'I'm not trying any . . . ach, to hell with it.' Rebus turned, started back downstairs. Suddenly the outside world looked good to him in the warm sunshine. It was all relative. He walked over to the corner shop, asked the kids a few questions, handed out mints to anyone who wanted one. He didn't learn anything, but ended up with an excuse to go inside. He bought a packet of extra-strong, put it in his pocket for later, asked the Asian behind the counter a couple of questions. She was fifteen, maybe sixteen, extraordinarily pretty. A video was playing on the TV, high up on one wall. Hong Kong gangsters shooting chunks out of each other. She didn't have anything to tell him.

'Do you like Niddrie?' he asked.

'It's all right.' Her voice was pure Edinburgh, eyes on the TV.

Rebus drove back to Fort Apache. The Shed was empty. He drank a cup

of coffee and smoked a cigarette. Niddrie, Craigmillar, Wester Hailes, Muirhouse, Pilton, Granton . . . They all seemed to him like some horrible experiment in social engineering: scientists in white coats sticking families down in this maze or that, seeing what would happen, how strong they'd have to become to cope, whether or not they'd find the exit . . . He lived in an area of Edinburgh where six figures bought you a three-bedroom flat. It amused him that he could sell up and be suddenly rich . . . except, of course, that he'd have nowhere to live, and couldn't afford to move anywhere nicer in the city. He realised he was just about as trapped as anyone in Niddrie or Craigmillar, nicer model of trap, that was all.

His phone rang. He picked it up and wished he hadn't.

'Inspector Rebus?' A woman's voice: administrative. 'Could you attend a meeting tomorrow at Fettes?'

Rebus felt a chill run the length of his spine. 'What sort of meeting?'

A cool smiling voice. 'I don't have that information. The request comes from the ACC's office.'

The Assistant Chief Constable, Colin Carswell. Rebus called him the 'CC Rider'. A Yorkshireman – as close to a Scot as the English got. He'd been with Lothian and Borders two and a half years, and so far nobody had a bad word to say about him, which should have put him in the *Guinness Book of Records*. There had been a hairy few months after the last Deputy Chief Constable resigned and before they appointed a new one, but Carswell had coped. Some were of the opinion that he was just *too* good, and therefore would never make it to Chief Constable. Lothian and Borders used to boast one DCC and two ACCs, but one of the ACC posts had now become 'Director of Corporate Services', about which no one on the force seemed to know anything at all.

'What time?'

'Two o'clock, it shouldn't take long.'

'Will there be tea and biccies? I'm not coming otherwise.'

A shocked pause, then a release of breath as she realised he was joking. 'We'll see what we can manage, Inspector.'

Rebus put down the phone. It rang again and he picked it up.

'John? It's Gill, did you get my message?'

'Yes, thanks.'

'Oh. I thought you might have tried to call me.'

'Mmm.'

'John? Is something wrong?'

He shook himself. 'I don't know. The CC Rider wants to see me.'

'Whatever for?'

'Nobody's saying.'

A sigh. 'What have you been up to this time?'

'Absolutely nothing, Gill, that's the God's honest truth.'

'Made any enemies yet at your new posting?' As she spoke, Bain and Maclay walked through the door. Rebus nodded a greeting.

'No enemies. Do you think I'm doing something wrong?' Maclay and Bain were shedding jackets, pretending not to be interested.

'Listen, about that message I left . . . ?'

'Yes, Chief Inspector?' Maclay and Bain dropped the pretence.

'Can we meet?'

'I don't see why not. Dinner tonight?'

'Tonight . . . yes, why not?'

She lived in Morningside, Rebus in Marchmont . . . make it a Tollcross rendezvous.

'Brougham Street,' Rebus said, 'that Indian place with the slat blinds. Half eight?'

'Sure.'

'See you there, Chief Inspector.'

Bain and Maclay went about their business, said nothing for a minute or two. Then Bain coughed, swallowed, spoke.

'How was Raintown?'

'I got out alive.'

'Find out anything about Uncle Joe and Tony El?' Bain's finger went to the nick below his eye.

Rebus shrugged. 'Maybe something, maybe nothing.'

'All right, don't tell us,' Maclay said. He looked funny, sitting at his desk. An inch had been sawn off each of the legs of his chair, so his thighs would fit under the lip of the desk. When Rebus had first arrived, he'd asked why Maclay hadn't just lifted the table legs up an inch. Until then, Maclay hadn't thought of it – sawing the chair legs had been Bain's idea.

'Nothing *to* tell,' Rebus argued. 'Except this – word is, Tony El's a free agent, working out of the north-east, so we need to contact Grampian CID and ask about him.'

'I'll fax them his details,' Maclay said.

'I take it there's been no sign?' Rebus asked.

Bain and Maclay shook their heads.

'I'll let you into the secret though,' Bain said.

'What?'

'There are at least *two* Indians on Brougham Street with slatted blinds.'

Rebus watched them have a good laugh about that, then asked what the background check on the decedent had produced.

'Not much,' Bain said, leaning back in his chair and waving a sheet of paper. Rebus got up, took the paper from him.

Allan Mitchison. Only child. Born in Grangemouth. His mother died in childbirth; his father went into decline, followed her two years later. Infant Allan was taken into care – no other kin found. Children's home, then a foster family. Put up for adoption, but was an unruly kid, a trouble-maker. Screaming fits, tantrums, then long sulks. He always ran away eventually, always found his way back to the children's home. Grew up into a quiet teenager, still prone to black sulks, the occasional outburst, but talented in some school subjects – English, geography, art, music – and mostly docile. Still preferred the children's home to foster life. Left school at seventeen. Having seen a documentary on life on a North Sea platform, decided he liked the look of it. Miles from anywhere, and an existence not unlike the children's home – regimented. He liked group life, dormitories, shared rooms. Painter. His work pattern was uneven – he'd spent time onshore as well as off – a spell of training at RGIT-OSC . . .

'What's RGIT-OSC?'

Maclay had been waiting for the question. 'Robert Gordon Institute of Technology's Offshore Survival Centre.'

'Is that the same as Robert Gordon's University?'

Maclay and Bain looked at one another, shrugged.

'Never mind,' Rebus said, thinking: Johnny Bible's first victim had attended RGU.

Mitchison had also worked at the Sullom Voe terminal on Shetland, a few other locations. Friends and workmates: plenty of the latter, precious few of the former. Edinburgh had proved a dead end: none of his neighbours had ever clapped eyes on him. And the word from Aberdeen and points north was only a little more encouraging. A couple of names: one on a production platform, one at Sullom Voe . . .

'Are these two willing to be interviewed?'

Bain: 'Christ, you're not thinking of going up *there*? First Glasgow, now teuchter-land – didn't you get a holiday this year?'

Maclay's high-pitched laughter.

Rebus: 'I seem to be a sitting target down here. I had a thought today – whoever picked out that flat knew the area. I'm thinking a local. Either of you have snitches in Niddrie?'

'Of course.'

'Then get talking to them, a man answering Tony El's description, he might've been hanging around the pubs and clubs, looking for local talent. Is there anything on decedent's employer?'

Bain lifted another sheet, waved it, smiling. Rebus had to get up again, go fetch it.

T-Bird Oil got its name from Thom Bird, who had been co-founder with 'Major' Randall Weir.

'Major?'

Bain shrugged. 'That's what they call him: Major Weir.'

Weir and Bird were both Americans, but with strong Scottish roots. Bird had died in 1986, leaving Weir in charge. It was one of the smaller companies hoovering up oil and gas from below the sea bed . . .

Rebus realised that he knew almost nothing about the oil industry. He had some pictures in his head, mostly disasters – Piper Alpha, the *Braer*.

T-Bird had its UK base in Aberdeen, near Dyce Airport, but the global HQ was in the US, and the company held other oil and gas interests in Alaska, Africa, and the Gulf of Mexico.

'Boring, eh?' Maclay offered.

'Is that meant to be a joke?'

'Just making conversation.'

Rebus got to his feet, put his jacket on. 'Well, much as I could listen to your dulcet tones all day . . .'

'Where are you going?'

'Station to station.'

No one seemed very interested in his return to St Leonard's; a couple of woolly suits stopped to say hello – it turned out they didn't even know he'd been transferred.

'I don't know who that says more about – me or you.'

In the CID offices he saw Siobhan Clarke at her desk. She was on the phone, and waved her pen at him as he passed. She wore a white short-

sleeved blouse, and her bare arms were deeply tanned, as were her neck and face.

Rebus kept looking, and acknowledged a few lukewarm greetings. Jings, but it was rare to be 'home'. He thought of Allan Mitchison and his empty flat: he'd come back to Edinburgh because it was as close to a home as he had.

Eventually he spotted Brian Holmes, chatting up a WPC, giving it plenty.

'Hello, Brian, how's the wife?'

The WPC turned red, mumbled some excuse and left.

'Ha fucking ha,' Holmes said. Now that the WPC had gone, he looked dead done in, shoulders slumped, skin grey, specks of stubble left behind by a too-casual razor.

'That favour . . .' Rebus prompted.

'I'm on it.'

'And?'

'*I'm on it!*'

'Go easy, son, we're all friends here.'

Holmes seemed to deflate. He rubbed his eyes, clawed fingers through his hair.

'Sorry,' he said. 'I'm beat, that's all it is.'

'Would coffee help?'

'Only if you can buy it by the vat.'

The canteen could stretch to an 'Extra Large'. They sat down, Holmes tearing open sachets of sugar and pouring them in.

'Look,' he said, 'about the other night, Mental Minto . . .'

'We don't talk about that,' Rebus said firmly. 'It's history.'

'Too much history around here.'

'What else have the Scots got?'

'You two look about as happy as nuns on a Club 18–30.' Siobhan Clarke pulled out a chair and sat down.

'Nice holiday?' Rebus asked.

'Relaxing.'

'I see the weather was lousy.'

She ran a hand up one arm. 'Took hours of work on the beach to get this.'

'You've always been conscientious.'

She sipped Diet Pepsi. 'So why's everyone so down in the dumps?'

'You don't want to know.'

She raised an eyebrow, but didn't say anything. Two tired, grey men; one young woman, tanned and brimming with life. Rebus knew he'd have to gee himself up for his evening date.

'So,' he asked Holmes casually, 'that thing I asked you to look into . . . ?'

'It's slow going. If you want my opinion,' he looked up at Rebus, 'whoever wrote up the notes was a master of circumlocution. There's a lot of circling around the subject. I'd guess most casual readers would give up rather than plough on.'

Rebus smiled. 'Why would the writer have done that?'

'To put people off reading it. He probably thought they'd flick to the summing-up, miss out all the rubbish in the middle. Thing is, you can lose things that way, bury them in the text.'

'Excuse me,' Siobhan said, 'have I walked into a masonic meeting by mistake? Is this some code I'm not supposed to get?'

'Not at all, Brother Clarke,' Rebus said, getting to his feet. 'Maybe Brother Holmes will tell you about it.'

Holmes looked to Siobhan. 'Only if you promise not to show me any holiday snaps.'

'I wasn't intending to.' Siobhan straightened her back. 'I know naturist beaches aren't your thing.'

Rebus was purposely early for the rendezvous. Bain hadn't been lying: there *were* two restaurants with wood-slatted blinds. They were eighty yards apart, and Rebus walked relays between the two. He saw Gill rounding the corner at Tollcross and waved to her. She hadn't overdressed for the occasion: new-looking denims, plain cream blouse, and a yellow cashmere jumper tied around her neck. Sunglasses, gold-chain necklace, and two-inch heels – she liked to make a noise when she walked.

'Hello, John.'

'Hiya, Gill.'

'Is this the place?'

He looked at the restaurant. 'There's another one just up the road if you'd prefer. Or there's French, Thai . . .'

'This is fine.' She pulled open the door, walked in ahead of him. 'Did you book a table?'

'Didn't think they'd be busy,' Rebus said. The restaurant wasn't empty, but there was a spare table for two by the window, directly beneath a distorting loudspeaker. Gill removed her brown leather shoulder-bag and laid it under her chair.

'Something to drink?' their waiter asked.

'Whisky and soda for me,' Gill said.

'Whisky, no additives,' Rebus ordered. As the first waiter left, another appeared with menus, popadums and pickles. After he'd gone, Rebus looked around, saw that no one at the other tables was paying attention, and reached up to tug at the speaker-cable, disconnecting it. The music above them stopped.

'Better,' Gill said, smiling.

'So,' Rebus said, laying his napkin across his thighs, 'is this business or social?'

'Both,' Gill admitted. She broke off as the drinks arrived. The waiter knew something was wrong, eventually placed it. He looked up at the silent speaker.

'It can be easily mended,' he told them. They shook their heads, then studied the menus. Having ordered, Rebus raised his glass.

'*Slàinte.*'

'Cheers.' Gill took a gulp of her drink, exhaled afterwards.

'So,' Rebus said, 'niceties taken care of . . . to business.'

'Do you know how many women make chief inspector in the Scottish force?'

'I know we're talking the fingers of a blind carpenter's hand.'

'Exactly.' She paused, realigned her cutlery. 'I don't want to screw up.'

'Who does?'

She glanced at him, smiled. Rebus: world's supply of fuck-ups, his life a warehouse filled to the rafters with them. Harder to shift than eight-track cartridges.

'OK,' he said, 'so I'm an authority.'

'And that's good.'

'No.' He shook his head. 'Because I'm *still* fucking up.'

She smiled. 'Five months, John, and I haven't made a good collar yet.'

'But that's about to change?'

'I don't know.' Another gulp of courage. 'Someone's passed me some information about a drug deal . . . a biggie.'

'Which protocol dictates you should pass on to the Scottish Crime Squad.'

She gave him a look. 'And hand those lazy bastards the glory? Come on, John.'

'I've never been a great believer in protocol myself. All the same . . .' All the same: he didn't want Gill fucking up. He could see this was important to her: maybe *too* important. She needed perspective, same as he needed on Spaven.

'So who passed you the info?'

'Fergus McLure.'

'Feardie Fergie?' Rebus pursed his lips. 'Wasn't he one of Flower's snitches?'

Gill nodded. 'I took over Flower's list when he moved.'

'Jesus, how much did he screw out of you?'

'Never you mind.'

'Most of Flower's grasses are worse than anyone they could possibly snitch on.'

'Nevertheless, he gave *me* his list.'

'Feardie Fergie, eh?'

Fergus McLure had been in and out of private hospitals half his life. A nervous wreck, he drank nothing stronger than Ovaltine, and couldn't watch anything more exciting than *Pets Win Prizes*. His constant supply of prescription drugs bolstered the profits of the British pharmaceutical industry. This said, he ran a nice little empire which just bordered on the legal: jeweller by trade, he also put on sales of Persian rugs, fire-damaged and water-damaged merchandise, receivership auctions. He lived in Ratho, a village on the edge of the city. Feardie Fergie was a known homosexual, but lived quietly – unlike some judges of Rebus's acquaintance.

Gill crunched on a popadum, dribbled chutney on the remaining piece.

'So what's the problem?' Rebus asked.

'How well do you know Fergus McLure?'

Rebus shrugged, lied. 'Reputation only. Why?'

'Because I want this watertight before I act on it.'

'Problem with snitches, Gill, you can't always have corroboration.'

'No, but I can have a second opinion.'

'You want me to talk to him?'

'John, for all your flaws –'

'For which I am famous.'

'– you're a good judge of character, and you know enough about informers.'

'My back-up subject for *Mastermind*.'

'I just want to know if you think he's on the level. I don't want to go to all the trouble and effort of opening an investigation, maybe setting up surveillance, taps, even a sting operation, only to have the carpet pulled out from under me.'

'Understood, but you know the Squaddies will be peeved if you keep them in the dark. They've got the manpower and experience for this sort of thing.'

She just stared at him. 'Since when did you start going by the book?'

'We're not talking about me. I'm the L&B bad apple – doubtless they think one's more than enough.'

Their food arrived, the table filling with platters and dishes, a nan bread big enough to be plotting world domination. They looked at one another, realising they didn't feel that hungry any more.

'A couple more of the same,' Rebus said, handing the waiter his empty glass. To Gill: 'So tell me Fergie's story.'

'It's sketchy. Some drugs are coming north in a consignment of antiques. They're going to be handed over to the dealers.'

'The dealers being. . . ?'

She shrugged. 'McLure thinks they're Americans.'

Rebus frowned. 'Who? The sellers?'

'No, the buyers. The sellers are German.'

Rebus went through the major Edinburgh dealers, couldn't think of a single American.

'I know,' Gill said, reading his thoughts.

'New boys trying to break in?'

'McLure thinks the stuff's headed further north.'

'Dundee?'

She nodded. 'And Aberdeen.'

Aberdeen again. Jesus. A town called malice. 'So how's Fergie involved?'

'One of his sales would be the perfect cover.'

'He's fronting?'

Another nod. She chewed on a piece of chicken, dipped nan bread into the sauce. Rebus watched her eat, remembering little things about her: the way her ears moved when she chewed, the way her eyes flicked over the different dishes, the way she rubbed her fingers together afterwards . . . There were rings around her neck that hadn't been there five years ago, and maybe when she visited her hairdresser they added some colour to her roots. But she looked good. She looked great.

'So?' she asked.

'Is that all he told you?'

'He's scared of these dealers, too scared to tell them to get lost. But the last thing he wants is us catching on and putting him in jail as an accessory. That's why he's grassing.'

'Even though he's scared?'

'Mm-hm.'

'When's all this supposed to happen?'

'When they phone him.'

'I don't know, Gill. If it were a peg, you couldn't hang a fucking hankie on it, never mind your coat.'

'Colourfully put.'

She was staring at his tie as she said it. It was a loud tie, purposely so: it was supposed to distract attention from his unironed shirt with the missing button.

'OK, I'll go talkies tomorrow, see if I can wring any more out of him.'

'But gently.'

'He'll be putty in my hands.'

They ate only half the food, still felt bloated. Coffee and mints came: Gill put both mints into her bag for later. Rebus had a third whisky. He was looking ahead, seeing them standing outside the restaurant. He could offer to walk her home. He could ask her back to his flat. Only she couldn't stay the night: there might be reporters outside in the morning.

John Rebus: presumptuous bastard.

'Why are you smiling?' she asked.

'Use it or lose it, they say.'

They split the bill, the drinks coming to as much as the food. And then they were outside. The night had grown cool.

'What are my chances of finding a taxi?' Gill was looking up and down the street.

'Pubs aren't out yet, you should be OK. My car's back at the flat . . .'

'Thanks, John, I'll be all right. Look, here's one.' She waved to it. The driver signalled and pulled over with a squeak of brakes. 'Tell me how you get on,' she said.

'I'll phone you straight after.'

'Thanks.' She pecked his cheek, a hand on his shoulder to steady herself. Then she got into the taxi and closed the door, giving her address to the driver. Rebus watched the cab execute a slow U-turn into the traffic heading for Tollcross.

Rebus stood there for a moment, looking at his shoes. She'd wanted a favour, that was all. Good to know he was still useful for some things. 'Feardie Fergie', Fergus McLure. A name from the past; one-time friend of a certain Lenny Spaven. Worth a morning trip to Ratho for definite.

He heard another taxi coming – unmistakable engine sound. Its yellow light was on. He waved it down, got in.

'The Oxford Bar,' he said.

The more Bible John thought about the Upstart . . . the more he learned about him . . . the surer he felt that Aberdeen was the key.

He sat in his study, door locked against the outside world, and stared at the UPSTART file on his laptop. The gap between victims one and two was six weeks, between victims two and three only four. Johnny Bible was a hungry little devil, but so far he hadn't killed again. Or if he had, he was still playing with the body. But that wasn't the Upstart's way. He killed them quick, then presented the bodies to the world. Bible John had worked back, and had found two newspaper stories – both in the Aberdeen *Press and Journal*. A woman attacked on her way home from a nightclub, a man attempting to drag her into an alley. She'd screamed, he'd panicked and fled. Bible John had driven out to the scene one night. He stood in the alley and thought of the Upstart standing there, biding his time till the nightclub emptied. There was a housing scheme nearby, and the route

home passed the mouth of the alley. Superficially, it was the perfect spot, but the Upstart had been nervous, ill-prepared. He'd probably been waiting there for an hour or two, standing back in the shadows, afraid someone would stumble upon him. His nerve had come and gone. When he'd finally picked a victim, he hadn't disabled it quickly enough. A scream was all it had taken to send him running.

Yes, it could well be the Upstart. He'd studied his failure, come up with a better plan: go *into* the nightclub, get talking to the victim . . . put the victim at its ease, then strike.

Second newspaper item: a woman complaining of a peeper in her back garden. When police were called, they found marks on her kitchen door, clumsy attempts at entering. Maybe connected to the first story, maybe not. Story one: eight weeks before the first murder. Story two: a further four weeks back. A pattern of months establishing itself. And another pattern on top of the first: peeper becoming attacker. Of course, there could be other stories he'd missed, ones from other cities, making for different theories, but Bible John was happy to go with Aberdeen. First victim: often the first victim was local. Once the killer's confidence was up, he would range further afield. But that first success was so very important.

A timid knock at the study door. 'I've made coffee.'

'I'll be out soon.'

Back to his computer. He knew the police would be busy compiling their own composites, their psychological profiles, remembered the one a psychiatrist had compiled of *him*. You knew he was 'an authority' because of all the letters after his name: BSc, BL, MA, MB, ChB, LLB, DPA, FRCPath. Meaningless in the wider scheme, as was his report. Bible John had read it in a book years back. The few things about him it got right, he attempted to remedy. The serial murderer was supposedly withdrawn, with few close friends, so he had forced himself to become gregarious. The type was known for a lack of drive and fear of adult contacts, so he took a job where drive and contacts were crucial. As for the rest of the thesis . . . rubbish, mostly.

Serial killers not infrequently had a history of homosexual activity – not guilty.

They were usually unmarried – tell that to the Yorkshire Ripper.

They often heard two voices inside their heads, one good and the other evil. They collected weapons, and gave them pet names. Many dressed up in women's clothes. Some showed an interest in black magic or in monsters, and collected sadistic pornography. Many had a 'private place' where objects such as hoods, dolls and rubber diving-suits would be kept.

He looked around his study and shook his head.

There were only a few points where the psychiatrist got it right. Yes, he would say he was egocentric – like half the population. Yes, he was neat and tidy. Yes, he had an interest in the Second World War (but not solely Nazism or concentration camps). Yes, he was a plausible liar – or rather, people were gullible listeners. And yes, he planned his culls well in advance, as it appeared the Upstart was now doing.

The librarian had not yet finished compiling his newspaper list. A check of requests for Bible John literature had drawn a blank. That was the bad news. But there was good news too. Thanks to the recent upsurge of

interest in the original Bible John case, he had newspaper details of other unsolved murders, seven of them. Five took place in 1977, one in '78, and one much more recently. These gave him a second thesis. The first had the Upstart just beginning his career; the second had him recommencing it after a long gap. He might have been out of the country, or in some institution, or even in a relationship where he did not feel it necessary to kill. If the police were being meticulous – which he doubted – they'd be looking at recent divorces of men who had married in '78 or '79. Bible John did not have the means at his disposal to do this, which was frustrating. He got up and stared at his shelves of books, not really seeing them. There was an opinion that the Upstart *was* Bible John, that the eyewitness descriptions were flawed. As a result, the police and the media had dusted off their photofits and artists' impressions.

Dangerous. He knew the only way to quash such speculation was to locate the Upstart. Imitation was *not* the sincerest form of flattery. It was potentially lethal. He had to find the Upstart. Either that or lead the police to him. One way or another, it would be done.

8

He was in a six a.m. opener, drinking off a good sleep.

He'd woken up way too early, got dressed, and decided to go for a walk. He crossed The Meadows, headed down George IV Bridge and the High Street, left on to Cockburn Street. Cockburn Street: shopping mecca to teenagers and hippies; Rebus remembered Cockburn Street market when it was a damned sight more disreputable than these days. Angie Riddell had bought her necklace in a shop on Cockburn Street. Maybe she'd worn it the day he'd taken her to the café, but he didn't think so. He switched off the thought, turned down a passageway, a steep flight of steps, and took another left on Market Street. He was opposite Waverley Station, and there was a pub open. It catered to night-shift workers, a drink or two before home and bed. But you saw businessmen in it too, bracing themselves for the day ahead.

With newspaper offices nearby, the regulars were printworkers and subs, and there were always first editions available, the ink just dry. Rebus was known here, and no one ever bothered him. Even if a reporter was having a drink, they didn't hassle him for stories or quotes – it was an unwritten rule, never breached.

This morning, three teenagers sat slumped at a table, barely touching their drinks. Their dishevelled and sleepy state told Rebus they'd just completed a 'twenty-four': round-the-clock drinking. The daytime was easy: you started at six in the morning – somewhere like this – and the pubs were licensed till midnight or one o'clock. After that, it had to be clubs, casinos, and you finished the marathon at a pizza parlour on Lothian Road, open till six a.m., at which point you returned here for the last drink of the session.

The bar was quiet, no TV or radio, the fruit machine not yet plugged in: another unwritten rule. At this time of day, what you did in this place was drink. And read the papers. Rebus poured a helping of water into his whisky, took it and a paper to a table. The sun outside the windows was skin-tone pink against a milky sky. It had been a good walk; he liked the city quiet: taxis and early risers, first dogs being exercised, clear, clean air. But the night before still clung to the place: a litter-bin upturned, a bench on the Meadows with a broken back, traffic cones hoisted on to bus shelter roofs. It was true of the bar too: last night's fug had not had time to dissipate. Rebus lit a cigarette and read his paper.

A story on the inside page caught his attention: Aberdeen was hosting an

312

international convention on offshore pollution and the role of the oil industry. Delegates from sixteen countries were expected to attend. There was a smaller story tacked on to the article: the Bannock oil and gas field, 100 miles north-east of Shetland, was coming to the end of its 'useful economic life', and was about to undergo decommissioning. Environmentalists were making an issue of Bannock's main production platform, a steel and concrete structure weighing 200,000 tonnes. They wanted to know what the owners, T-Bird Oil, planned to do with it. As required by law, the company had submitted an Abandonment Programme to the Oil and Gas Division of the Department of Trade and Industry, but its contents had not been made public.

The environmentalists were saying that there were over 200 oil and gas installations on the UK Continental Shelf, and they all had a finite production life. The government seemed to be backing an option which would leave the majority of the deep-water platforms in place, with only minimal maintenance. There was even talk of selling them off for alternative use – plans included prisons and casino/hotel complexes. The government and the oil companies were talking cost-effectiveness, and about striking a balance between cost, safety and the environment. The protesters' line was: the environment at *any* cost. Stoked up from their victory over Shell with the Brent Spar, the pressure groups were planning to make Bannock an issue too, and would be holding marches, rallies, and an open-air concert close to the site of the Aberdeen convention.

Aberdeen: fast becoming the centre of Rebus's universe.

He finished his whisky, decided against a second, then changed his mind. Flicked through the rest of the paper: nothing new on Johnny Bible. There was a property section; he checked the Marchmont/Sciennes prices, then laughed at some of the New Town specs: 'luxurious townhouse, elegant living on five floors . . .'; 'garage for sale separately, £20,000'. There were still a few places in Scotland where £20,000 would buy you a house, maybe with the garage thrown in. He looked down the 'Country Property' list, saw more wild prices, flattering photos attached. There was a place on the coast south-east of the city, picture windows and sea views, for the price of a Marchmont flat. Dream on, sailor . . .

He walked home, got in his car, and drove out to Craigmillar, one area of the city not yet represented in the property section, and not likely to be for some time to come.

The night shift was just about to come off. Rebus saw officers he hadn't seen before. He asked around: it had been a quiet night; the cells were empty, ditto the biscuit-tins. In the Shed, he sat at his desk and saw new paperwork staring up at him. He fetched himself a coffee and picked up the first sheet.

More dead ends on Allan Mitchison; the head of his children's home interviewed by local CID. A check of his bank account, nothing amiss. Nothing from Aberdeen CID on Tony El. A woolly suit came in with a package addressed to Rebus. Postmarked Aberdeen, a printed label: T-Bird Oil. Rebus opened it. Publicity material, a compliment slip from Stuart Minchell, Personnel Dept. Half a dozen A4 pamphlets, quality layout and paper, colour throughout, facts kept to a minimum. Rebus, author of five

thousand reports, knew waffle when he saw it. Minchell had enclosed a copy of 'T-BIRD OIL – STRIKING THE BALANCE', identical to the one in the side pocket of Mitchison's rucksack. Rebus opened it, saw a map of the Bannock field, laid out across a grid showing which blocks it occupied. A note explained that the North Sea had been divided into blocks of 100 square miles apiece, and oil companies initially made bids for exploration rights to these blocks. Bannock was slap-bang up against the international boundary – a few miles east and you came to more oil fields, but this time Norwegian rather than British.

'Bannock will be the first T-Bird field to undergo rigorous decommissioning,' Rebus read. There seemed to be seven options available, from Leave In Place to Total Removal. The company's 'modest proposal' was for mothballing: leaving the structure to be dealt with at a later date.

'Surprise, surprise,' Rebus muttered, noting that mothballing 'would leave funds available for future exploration and development'.

He put the pamphlets back in their envelope and shoved it in a drawer, returning to his paperwork. A sheet of fax paper was hidden near the bottom. He pulled it out. It was from Stuart Minchell, sent the previous day at seven in the evening: further details on Allan Mitchison's two workmates. The one who worked at the Sullom Voe terminal was called Jake Harley. He was on a walking/birdwatching holiday somewhere on Shetland, and probably hadn't yet heard of his friend's demise. The one who worked offshore was called Willie Ford. He was halfway through a sixteen-day stint, and 'of course' had learned about Allan Mitchison.

Rebus picked up his telephone, reached into the drawer for Minchell's compliment slip. He got the number from it and pushed the buttons. It was early; all the same . . .

'Personnel.'

'Stuart Minchell, please.'

'Speaking.' Bingo: Minchell a company man, early starter.

'Mr Minchell, it's Inspector Rebus again.'

'Inspector, you're lucky I picked up the phone. Usually I just let it ring, only way I can get some work done before the rush.'

'Your fax, Mr Minchell – why did you say "of course" Willie Ford had learned of Allan Mitchison's death?'

'Because they worked together, didn't I tell you?'

'Offshore?'

'Yes.'

'Which platform, Mr Minchell?'

'Didn't I tell you that either? Bannock.'

'The one that's being mothballed?'

'Yes. Our Public Relations team's got its work cut out there.' A pause. 'Is it important, Inspector?'

'Probably not, sir,' Rebus said. 'Thanks anyway.' Rebus put down the receiver, drummed his fingers against it.

He went out to the shops, bought a filled roll for breakfast – corned beef and onion. The roll was too floury, and stuck to the roof of his mouth. He bought himself a coffee to wash it down. When he got back to the Shed, Bain and Maclay were at their desks, feet up, tabloid reading. Bain was eating a dough-ring; Maclay burping sausage-meat.

'Snitch reports?' Rebus asked.

'Nothing so far,' Bain said, not taking his eyes from the paper.

'Tony El?'

Maclay's turn: 'Description's gone out to every Scottish force, nothing's come back.'

'I phoned Grampian CID myself,' Bain added, 'told them to check out Mitchison's Indian restaurant. Looks like he was a regular, they might know something.'

'Nice one, Dod,' Rebus said.

'Not just a pretty face, is he?' Maclay said.

The weather forecast was for sunshine and showers. It seemed to Rebus, as he drove out to Ratho, that they were coming at ten-minute intervals. Brisk black clouds, shafts of sunlight, blue skies, then clouds gathering again. At one point, it started raining when there didn't seem to be a cloud in the sky.

Ratho was surrounded by farmland, with the Union Canal bordering it to the north. It was popular in the summer: you could take a boat trip on the canal, or feed the ducks, or eat at a waterfront restaurant. Yet it was less than a mile from the M8, two miles from Turnhouse Airport. Rebus drove out along Calder Road, trusting to his sense of direction. Fergus McLure's house was on Hallcroft Park. He knew he could find it: there were only a dozen streets in the whole village. McLure was known to work from home. Rebus had decided against phoning ahead: he didn't want Fergie forewarned.

When he reached Ratho, it took him five minutes to locate Hallcroft Park. He found Fergie's address, stopped the car, and walked up to the door. There was no sign of life. He rang the bell a second time. Net curtains stopped him peering through the window.

'Should have phoned,' Rebus muttered.

A woman was walking past, terrier straining on its leash. The small dog made terrible choking sounds as it sniffed the pavement.

'Is he not in?' she asked.

'No.'

'Funny, his car's here.' She had time to nod in the direction of a parked Volvo before the dog hauled her away. It was a blue 940 estate. Rebus looked in through the windows, but all he saw was how clean the interior looked. He checked the mileage: low. A new car. The tyre-walls hadn't even had time to lose their shine.

Rebus got back into his own car – mileage to date fifty times the Volvo's – and decided to head back into town by the Glasgow Road. But as he made to drive over the canal bridge, he saw a police car at the far end of the restaurant car park, sitting on the slip-road down to the canal. There was an ambulance parked next to it. Rebus braked, reversed, and turned into the car park, crawling towards the scene. A woolly suit came to warn him off, but Rebus had his warrant card ready. He parked and got out.

'What is it?' he asked.

'Somebody went for a dip with their clothes on.'

The constable followed Rebus down to the jetty. There were cruise boats moored there, and a couple of tourist-types who looked like they'd come for

a trip on one of them. The rain had started again, pockmarking the surface of the canal. The ducks were keeping their distance. A body had been hauled out of the water, clothes sodden, and laid on the wooden slats that constituted the jetty. A man who looked like a doctor was checking for signs of life, no real hope in his face. The back door to the restaurant was open, staff members standing there, faces interested but full of horror.

The doctor shook his head. One of the tourists, a woman, began to cry. Her companion, a man, cradled his video camera and put an arm around her.

'He must've slipped and fallen in,' someone said, 'banged his head.'

The doctor checked the corpse's head, found a clean gash.

Rebus looked up towards the staff. 'Anyone see anything?' Headshakes. 'Who reported it?'

'I did.' The woman tourist, English accent.

Rebus turned to the doctor. 'How long has he been in the water?'

'I'm just a GP, not an expert. All the same, if you want a guess . . . not long. Certainly not overnight.' Something had rolled out of the drowned man's jacket pocket and wedged between two of the slats. A small brown bottle with white plastic top. Prescription pills. Rebus looked at the bloated face, fixed it to a much younger man, a man he'd interviewed in 1978 about his connection to Lenny Spaven.

'He's a local,' Rebus told the company. 'His name's Fergus McLure.'

He tried phoning Gill Templer, couldn't track her down, ended up leaving messages for her in half a dozen different places. Back home, he polished his shoes and changed into his best suit, picked out the shirt with the fewest creases, and found the most sober tie he had (excepting his funeral one).

He looked at himself in the mirror. He'd showered and shaved, dried his hair and combed it. The knot in his tie looked OK, and for once he'd found a matching pair of socks. He looked fine, felt anything but.

It was half past one, time to go to Fettes.

The traffic wasn't too bad, the lights with him, like they didn't want to hold up his appointment. He was early at L&B HQ, thought of driving around, but knew it would only make him more nervous. Instead, he went inside, and sought out the Murder Room. It was on the second floor, a large central office space with smaller compartments off for the senior officers. This was the Edinburgh side of the triangle Johnny Bible had created, the heart of the Angie Riddell investigation. Rebus knew some of the faces on duty, smiled, nodded. The walls were covered with maps, photographs, charts – an attempt at order. So much of police work was putting things in some kind of order: fixing chronology, getting the details right, tidying up after the mess of people's lives as well as their deaths.

Most of the people on duty this afternoon looked tired, lacking enthusiasm. They were waiting by telephones, waiting for the elusive tip-off, the missing link, a name or a sighting, waiting for the man . . . They'd been waiting a long time. Someone had mocked up a photofit of Johnny Bible: horns curling from the head, wisps of smoke from the flared nostrils, fangs and a serpent's forked tongue.

The Bogeyman.

Rebus looked closer. The photofit had been done on computer. The starting-point had been an old photofit of Bible John. With the horns and fangs, he bore a vague likeness to Alister Flower . . .

He examined the photographs of Angie Riddell in life, kept his eyes away from her autopsy pics. He remembered her the night he'd arrested her, remembered her sitting in his car talking, almost too full of life. Her hair seemed to be dyed a different colour in almost every picture, like she was never quite happy with herself. Maybe she'd just needed to keep changing, running from the person she'd been, laughing to stop herself crying. Circus clown, painted smile . . .

Rebus checked his watch. Fuck it: it was time.

9

There was just the CC Rider himself, Colin Carswell, waiting for Rebus in the comfortable and carpeted office.

'Take a seat, won't you?' Carswell had half-risen to welcome Rebus, now sat down again. Rebus sat opposite him, studying the desktop, looking for clues. The Yorkshireman was tall, with a body that sagged towards a beer-drinker's gut. His hair was brown, thinning, his nose small, almost flat like a pug's. He sniffed. 'Sorry, can't oblige with your request for biscuits, but there's tea or coffee if you want it.'

Rebus remembered the phone call: *Will there be tea and biccies? I'm not coming otherwise.* The remark had been passed along.

'I'm fine, thanks, sir.'

Carswell opened a folder, picked something up, a newspaper clipping. 'Damned shame about Lawson Geddes. I hear he was an exceptional officer in his day.'

The story concerned Geddes's suicide.

'Yes, sir,' Rebus said.

'They say it's a coward's way out, but I know *I* wouldn't have the guts.' He looked up. 'What about you?'

'I hope I never have to find out, sir.'

Carswell smiled, put the cutting back, closed the folder. 'John, we're getting flak from the media. At first it was just that TV crew, but now everyone seems to want to join the circus.' He stared at Rebus. 'Not good.'

'No sir.'

'So we've decided – the Chief Constable and myself – that *we* should make an effort.'

Rebus swallowed. 'You're reopening the Spaven case?'

Carswell brushed invisible dust off the folder. 'Not straight away. There's no new evidence, therefore no real need to.' He looked up quickly. 'Unless you know some reason why we should?'

'It was cut and dried, sir.'

'Try telling the media that.'

'I have, believe me.'

'We're going to open an internal inquiry, just to satisfy ourselves that nothing was overlooked or . . . untoward . . . at the time.'

'Putting *me* under suspicion.' Rebus could feel his hackles rising.

'Only if you've got something to hide.'

'Come on, sir, you reopen an investigation, *everyone* begins to look dirty. And with Spaven and Lawson Geddes dead, I'm left carrying the can.'

'Only if there's a can to carry.'

Rebus leapt to his feet.

'Sit down, Inspector, I've not finished with you yet!'

Rebus sat down, made his hands grip the sides of the chair. He felt if he let go, he might fly clean through the ceiling. Carswell was taking a second to regain his own composure.

'Now, to keep things objective, the inquiry will be headed by someone from outside Lothian and Borders, reporting directly to me. They'll go through the original files . . .'

Warn Holmes.

'. . . do any follow-up interviews deemed necessary, and compile their report.'

'Is this going to be made public?'

'Not until I have the finished report. It can't look like a whitewash, that's all I'll say. If any breach of the rules has taken place anywhere down the line, it'll be dealt with. Is that clear?'

'Yes, sir.'

'Now, is there anything you'd like to tell me?'

'Just between us, or do you want to bring the strongarm in?'

Carswell allowed this as a joke. 'I'm not sure you could call him that.'

Him.

'Who's in charge, sir?'

'An officer from Strathclyde, DCI Charles Ancram.'

Oh dear Jesus fucking Christ. His goodbye to Ancram: an accusation of graft. And Ancram had *known*, all that day he'd known this was coming, the way he'd smiled, like he had secrets, the way he'd studied Rebus, like they might well become adversaries.

'Sir, there may be some bad blood between CI Ancram and myself.'

Carswell stared at him. 'Care to elucidate?'

'No, sir, with respect.'

'Well, I suppose I could get Chief Inspector Flower instead. He's the bee's knees just now, nabbing that MP's son for cannabis growing . . .'

Rebus swallowed. 'I'd prefer CI Ancram, sir.'

Carswell glowered. 'It's not your bloody decision, is it, Inspector?'

'No, sir.'

Carswell sighed. 'Ancram's already been briefed. Let's stick with him . . . if that's all right with you?'

'Thank you, sir.' How did I get here, Rebus thought: thanking the man for putting Ancram on my tail . . . 'Can I go now, sir?'

'No.' Carswell was looking in the folder again, while Rebus tried to get his heart-rate down. Carswell read a note, spoke without looking up.

'What were you doing in Ratho this morning?'

'Sir?'

'A body was hauled out of the canal. I've had word you were there. Not exactly Craigmillar, is it?'

'I was just in the area.'

'Apparently you ID'd the body?'

'Yes, sir.'

'You're a handy man to have around.' Heavy with irony. 'How did you know him?'

Blurt it out or clam up? Neither. Dissemble. 'I recognised him as one of our snitches, sir.'

Carswell looked up. 'Whose in particular?'

'DI Flower's.'

'Were you looking to poach him?' Rebus kept his mouth shut, letting Carswell draw his own conclusions. 'On the very morning he took a tumble into the canal . . . strange coincidence?'

Rebus shrugged. 'These things happen, sir.' He fixed his eyes on Carswell's. They stared one another out.

'Dismissed, Inspector,' Carswell said.

Rebus didn't blink until he was back in the corridor.

He phoned St Leonard's from Fettes, his hand shaking. But Gill wasn't there, and nobody seemed to know where she was. Rebus asked the switchboard to page her, then asked to be put through to CID. Siobhan answered.

'Is Brian there?'

'I haven't seen him for a couple of hours. Are you two cooking something up?'

'The only thing cooking around here is my fucking goose. When you see him, tell him to call. And pass the same message along to Gill Templer.'

He broke the connection before she could say anything. Probably she'd have offered to help, and the one thing Rebus didn't want right now was anyone else involved. Lying to protect himself . . . lying to protect Gill Templer . . . Gill . . . he had questions for her, urgent questions. He tried her home number, left a message on the answering machine, then tried Holmes's home number: another machine, same message. Call me.

Wait. Think.

He'd asked Holmes to read up on the Spaven case, and that meant going through the files. When Great London Road police station had been burnt to the ground, a lot of files had gone up with it, but not the older stuff, because by then the older files had been shipped out to make space. They were stored with all the other ancient cases, all the clanking old skeletons, in a warehouse near Granton Harbour. Rebus had guessed Holmes would sign them out, but maybe not . . .

It was a ten-minute drive from Fettes to the warehouse. Rebus did it in seven. He allowed himself a grin when he saw Holmes's car in the car park. Rebus walked over to the main door, pulled it open, and was in a vast, dark, echoing space. Regimented rows of green metal shelves ran the length of the warehouse, filled with heavy-duty cardboard boxes, inside which lay the mouldering history of the Lothian and Borders force – and the City of Edinburgh force until its demise – from the 1950s to the 1970s. Documents were still arriving: tea-chests with labels hanging from them sat waiting to be unpacked, and it looked like a changeover was taking place – lidded plastic boxes replacing heavy-duty board. A small elderly man, very trim, with a black moustache and jam-jar glasses, was marching towards Rebus.

'Yes, can I help you?'

The man defined 'clerical'. When he wasn't looking at the floor, he was staring off somewhere past Rebus's right ear. He wore a grey nylon overall

over a white shirt with frayed collar and green tweed tie. Pens and pencils protruded from his top pocket.

Rebus showed his warrant card. 'I'm looking for a colleague, DS Holmes, I think he may be looking through some old case-notes.'

The man was studying the warrant card. He walked over to a clipboard and wrote down Rebus's name and rank, plus date and time of arrival.

'Is that necessary?' Rebus asked.

The man looked like he'd never in his life been asked such a thing. 'Paperwork,' he snapped, looking around at the warehouse's contents. 'It's *all* necessary, or I wouldn't be here.'

And he smiled, the overhead lighting glinting from his lenses. 'This way.'

He led Rebus down an alleyway of boxes, then took a right turn and finally, after a moment's hesitation, a left. They came into a clearing, where Brian Holmes sat at what looked like an old school desk, inkwell intact. There was no chair, so he was using an upturned box. His elbows rested on the desk, head in hands. There was a lamp on the desk, bathing the scene in light. The clerk coughed.

'Someone to see you.'

Holmes turned, stood up when he saw who it was. Rebus turned quickly to the clerk.

'Thanks for your help.'

'No trouble. I don't get many visitors.'

The little man shuffled away, footsteps receding into the distance.

'Don't worry,' Holmes said. 'I've laid a trail of breadcrumbs so we can find our way back.' He looked around. 'Isn't this the creepiest place you've ever been?'

'It's straight into the top five. Listen, Brian, there's a problem.' He held up his right hand. 'Fan.' Then his left. 'Shit.' He clapped both hands together. The sound reverberated through the warehouse.

'Tell me.'

'The CC Rider's opening an inquiry into the Spaven case, prior to reopening the case itself. And he's managed to put in charge someone I recently rubbed up the wrong way.'

'Silly you.'

'Silly me. So no doubt they'll be down here some day soon to lift the case-notes. And I don't want them lifting *you*.'

Holmes looked at the bulging files, the faded black ink on each cover. 'The files could get lost, couldn't they?'

'They could. Two problems. One, that would look highly suspicious. Two, I'm assuming Mr Clipboard knows which files you've been consulting.'

'That's true,' Holmes conceded. 'And it went down on his sheet.'

'Along with your name.'

'We could try slipping him some cash.'

'He doesn't look the type. He's not in this for money, is he?'

Holmes looked thoughtful. He also looked terrible: unevenly shaven, his hair uncombed and needing a trim. The bags under his eyes could have carried half a hundredweight of coal.

'Look,' he said at last, 'I'm halfway through . . . more than halfway. If I burn the candle tonight, maybe speed up my reading, I could have it finished by tomorrow.'

Rebus nodded slowly. 'What do you think so far?' He was almost scared to touch the files, to flip through them. It wasn't history, it was archaeology.

'I think your typing hasn't improved. Straight answer: there's something dodgy going on, that much I can read between the lines. I can see exactly where you're covering up, rewriting the true story to fit your version. You weren't quite so subtle in those days. Geddes's version reads better, more confident. He glosses over stuff, he's not afraid to understate. What I'd like to know is, what was the story with him and Spaven in the first place? I know you told me they served together in Burma or somewhere; how did they come to fall out? See, if we knew that, we'd know how valid the chip on Geddes's shoulder was, and maybe how far it would take him.'

Rebus clapped his hands again, this time in muffled applause.

'That's good going.'

'So give me another day, see what else I come up with. John, I *want* to do this for you.'

'And if they catch you?'

'I'll talk my way out, don't worry.'

Rebus's pager sounded. He looked to Holmes.

'Sooner you go,' Holmes said, 'sooner I can get back to it.'

Rebus patted him on the shoulder and headed back along the stacks. Brian Holmes: friend. Difficult to equate with the person who had roughed up Mental Minto. Schizophrenia, the policeman's ally: a dual personality came in handy . . .

He asked the clerk if he could use a telephone. There was one on the wall. He called in.

'DI Rebus.'

'Yes, Inspector, apparently you've been trying to reach DCI Templer.'

'Yes.'

'Well, I have a location for her. She's in Ratho, at some restaurant.'

Rebus slammed down the phone, cursing himself for not thinking of it sooner.

The wooden walkway where McLure's body had lain had been blown dry by the wind, leaving nothing to indicate that a death had occurred so recently. The ducks were skimming the water; one of the boats had just left with half a dozen passengers; diners in the restaurant chewed on their food and stared out at the two figures on the canal bank.

'I was in meetings half the day,' Gill said. 'I didn't hear about it until an hour ago. What happened?'

She had her hands deep in coat pockets, the coat a cream Burberry. She looked sad.

'Ask the pathologist. There was a cut on McLure's head, but that doesn't tell us a lot. He could have hit it when he slipped.'

'Or he could have been whacked and pushed in.'

'Or he could have jumped.' Rebus shivered; the death reminded him of the Mitchison options. 'My guess is, all the autopsy will tell us is whether he was alive when he hit the water. Right now I'll tell you he was probably alive, which still doesn't answer the question: accident, suicide, or a whack and a push?' He watched Gill turn away, begin to walk the towpath. He

322

caught up with her. It was starting to rain again, small drops, sparse. He watched them land on her coat, darkening it by degrees.

'Bang goes my big collar,' she said, an edge to her voice. Rebus turned up the collar of her coat, and she caught the joke, smiled.

'There'll be others,' he told her. 'Meantime, a man's dead – don't forget that.' She nodded. 'Listen,' he said, 'the ACC had me on the carpet this afternoon.'

'The Spaven case?'

He nodded. 'Plus he wanted to know what I was doing out here this morning.'

She glanced towards him. 'What did you say?'

'I didn't say anything. But the thing is . . . McLure ties in to Spaven.'

'What?' He had her full attention now.

'They palled around years back.'

'Jesus, why didn't you tell me?'

Rebus shrugged. 'It didn't seem an issue.'

Gill was thinking hard. 'But if Carswell links McLure to Spaven . . . ?'

'Then my being out here on the very morning Feardie Fergie met the big cheerio is going to look just a tad suspicious.'

'You have to tell him.'

'I don't think so.'

She turned to him, her hands gripping his lapels. 'You're protecting me from the fallout.'

The rain was growing heavier, drops sparkling in her hair. 'Let's just say I'm radiation-proof,' he said, leading her by the hand into the bar.

They ate a snack, neither of them bringing an appetite with them. Rebus's came with a whisky; Gill's with Highland Spring water. They sat facing one another at an alcove table. The place was a third full, nobody near enough to overhear.

'Who else knew?' Rebus said.

'You're the first person I've told.'

'Well, they could find out anyway. Maybe Fergie's nerve went, maybe he owned up. Maybe they just guessed.'

'Plenty of maybes.'

'What else have we got?' He paused, chewing. 'What about the other snitches you inherited?'

'What about them?'

'Snitches hear things, maybe Fergie wasn't the only one who knew about this drugs thing.'

Gill was shaking her head. 'I asked him at the time. He seemed confident it was being kept *very* quiet. You're assuming he was killed. Remember, he has a history of bad nerves, mental problems. Maybe the fear just got too much for him.'

'Do us both a favour, Gill, stick close to the investigation. See what the neighbours say: did he have any visitors this morning? Anyone out of the ordinary or suspicious? See if you can check his phone calls. My bet is it'll go down as an accident, which means no one's going to be working too hard on it. *Push them*, ask favours if you have to. Did he normally go for morning walks?'

She was nodding. 'Anything else?'

'Yes ... who's got the keys to his house?'

Gill made the calls, and they drank coffee until a DC turned up with the keys, fresh from the mortuary. Gill had asked about the Spaven case, Rebus giving only vague answers. Then they'd talked about Johnny Bible, Allan Mitchison ... all shop-talk, steering a wide berth around anything personal. But at one point they'd locked eyes, shared a smile, knowing the questions were there, whether they asked them or not.

'So,' Rebus said, 'what do you do now?'

'About the gen McLure gave me?' she sighed. 'There's nowhere to go with it, it was all so vague – no names or details, no date for the meeting ... it's gone.'

'Well, maybe.' Rebus lifted the keys, shook them. 'Depends whether you want to come snooping or not.'

The pavements in Ratho were narrow. To keep his distance from Gill, Rebus walked on the road. They didn't say anything, didn't need to. This was their second evening together; Rebus felt comfortable sharing everything but close proximity.

'That's his car.'

Gill walked around the Volvo, peered in through the windows. On the dashboard a small red light was blinking: the automatic alarm. 'Leather upholstery. Looks straight out of the showroom.'

'Typical Feardie Fergie car though: nice and safe.'

'I don't know,' Gill mused. 'It's the turbo version.'

Rebus hadn't noticed. He thought of his own aged Saab. 'Wonder what'll happen to it ...'

'Is this his house?'

They walked up to the door, used a mortise and a yale to open it. Rebus turned on the hall lights.

'Do you know if any of our lot has been in here?' Rebus asked.

'As far as I know, we're the first. Why?'

'Just trying out a scenario or two. Say someone came to see him here, and they frightened him. Say they told him to take a walk ...'

'Yes?'

'Well, he still had the presence of mind to double-lock the door. So either he wasn't that scared ...'

'Or whoever was with him double-locked the door, assuming that's what McLure would normally do.'

Rebus nodded. 'One more thing. Alarm system.' He pointed to a box on the wall, its light a steady green. 'It hasn't been switched on. If he was in a flap, he might forget. If he thought he wasn't coming back alive, he wouldn't bother.'

'He might not bother for a short stroll either though.'

Rebus conceded the point. 'Final scenario: whoever double-locked the door forgot or plain didn't know the alarm was there. See, door double-locked but alarm system off – it's not consistent. And someone like Fergie, Volvo driver, my guess is he'd *always* be consistent.'

'Well, let's see if he had anything worth nicking.'

They walked into the living room. It was crammed to bursting with furniture and nick-nacks, some modern, a lot looking like they'd been

handed down the generations. But though overfilled, the room was neat, dust-free, with expensive-looking rugs on the floor – far from fire-damaged stock.

'Supposing someone *did* come to see him,' Gill said. 'Maybe we should dust for prints.'

'Definitely maybe. Get forensics on to it first thing.'

'Yes, sir.'

Rebus smiled. 'Sorry, ma'am.'

They kept their hands in their pockets as they walked through the room: the reflex to touch things was always strong.

'No signs of a struggle, and nothing looks like it's been put back in the wrong place.'

'Agreed.'

Past the living room there was another, shorter hallway, leading to a guest bedroom and what had probably once been the lounge: only used when visitors called. Fergus McLure had turned it into an office. There was paperwork everywhere, and on a fold-out dining table sat a new-looking computer.

'I suppose someone's going to have to go through this lot,' Gill said, not relishing the task.

'I hate computers,' Rebus said. He had noticed a fat notepad beside the keyboard. He slipped a hand from his pocket and picked it up by its edges, angling it into the light. There were indents in the paper from the last written sheet. Gill came over to see.

'Don't tell me.'

'Can't make it out, and I don't think the pencil trick would help.'

They looked at one another, spoke their thoughts together.

'Howdenhall.'

'Check the bins next?' Gill said.

'You do it, I'll look upstairs.'

Rebus went back into the front hall, saw more doors, tried them: a small old-fashioned kitchen, family pictures on the walls; a toilet; a boxroom. He climbed the stairs, his feet sinking into deep-pile carpeting which muffled all sound. It was a quiet house; Rebus got the feeling it had been quiet even when McLure had been there. Another guest bedroom, large bathroom – unmodernised like the kitchen – and main bedroom. Rebus gave his attention to the usual places: beneath the bed, mattress and pillows; bedside cabinets, chest of drawers, wardrobe. Everything was obsessively arranged: cardigans folded just so and layered by colour; slippers and shoes in a row – all the browns together, then the blacks. There was a small bookcase boasting an uninspired collection: histories of carpets and Eastern art; a photographic tour of the vineyards of France.

A life without complications.

Either that or the dirt on Feardie Fergie was elsewhere.

'Found anything?' Gill called up the stairs. Rebus walked back along the corridor.

'No, but you might want to have someone check his business premises.'

'First thing tomorrow.'

Rebus came back down. 'What about you?'

'Nothing. Just what you'd expect to find in bins. Nothing saying, "Dope deal, two-thirty Friday at the carpet auction".'

'Pity,' Rebus said with a smile. He checked his watch. 'Fancy another drink?'

Gill shook her head, stretched. 'I'd better get home. It's been a long day.'

'*Another* long day.'

'Another long day.' She angled her head and looked at him. 'What about you? Are you heading off for another drink?'

'Meaning?'

'Meaning you drink more than you used to.'

'Meaning?'

Her look was intent. 'Meaning I wish you wouldn't.'

'So how much *should* I drink, doctor?'

'Don't take it like that.'

'How do you know how much I drink? Who's been squealing?'

'We went out last night, remember?'

'I only had two or three whiskies.'

'And after I left?'

Rebus swallowed. 'Straight home to bed.'

She smiled sadly. 'You liar. And you were back at it first thing: a patrol car saw you leaving that pub behind Waverley.'

'I'm under surveillance!'

'There are people out there who're worried about you, that's all.'

'I don't believe this.' Rebus threw open the door.

'Where are you going?'

'I need a fucking drink. You can come if you like.'

10

As he drove into Arden Street, he saw a group of people outside the main door to his tenement. They were shuffling their feet and cracking jokes, trying to keep morale up. One or two were eating chips from newspaper – a nice irony, since they had the look of reporters.

'Shit.'

Rebus drove past and kept going, watching in his rearview. There was nowhere to park anyway. He turned right at the junction, then next left, and ended up in a parking space outside Thirlestane Baths. He turned off the ignition and punched the steering-wheel a few times. He could always drive away, maybe head for the M90, race up to Dundee and back, but he didn't feel like it. He took a few deep breaths, feeling the blood pound through him, a rushing noise in his ears.

'Let's do it,' he said, getting out of the car. He walked down Marchmont Crescent to his chippie, then headed home, feeling the fried fat burning his palm through the layers of paper. He took his time walking up Arden Street itself. They weren't expecting him to be on foot, and he was almost on them before someone recognised him.

There was a camera crew, too: Redgauntlet – cameraman, Kayleigh Burgess, and Eamonn Breen. Caught on the hop, Breen flicked a cigarette on to the road and grabbed his microphone. The videocam had a spot attached. Spotlights always made you squint, which in turn made you look guilty, so Rebus kept his eyes nice and wide.

A journalist got in the first question.

'Inspector, any comment on the Spaven inquiry?'

'Is it true the case is being reopened?'

'How did you feel when you heard Lawson Geddes had killed himself?'

At that question, Rebus glanced towards Kayleigh Burgess, who had the grace to look down at the pavement. He was halfway up the path now, only feet from the tenement's main door, but surrounded by reporters. It was like wading through broth. He stopped and turned to face them.

'Ladies and gentlemen of the press, I have a short statement I'd like to make.'

They looked at each other, eyes registering surprise, then held out their tape recorders. A couple of older hacks near the back, who'd been here too often to raise any enthusiasm, were using pen and notepad.

The noise died down. Rebus held his wrapped package aloft.

'On behalf of the chip-eaters of Scotland, I'd like to thank you for providing our nightly wrappings.'

He was inside the door before they could think of anything to say.

In the flat, he left the lights off and walked over to the living-room window, peering down on to the scene outside. A few of the reporters were shaking their heads, calling in on mobile phones to see if they'd be allowed home. One or two were already making for their cars. Eamonn Breen was talking to camera, looking full of himself as usual. One of the younger journalists raised two fingers above Breen's head, turning them into rabbit's ears.

Looking across the road, Rebus saw a man standing against a parked car, arms folded. He was gazing up at Rebus's window, a smile on his face. He unfolded his arms long enough to give Rebus a silent round of applause, then got into his car and started the engine.

Jim Stevens.

Rebus turned back into the room, switched on an anglepoise lamp, sat down in his chair to eat the chips. But he still didn't have much of an appetite. He was wondering who had leaked the story to the vultures. The CC Rider had only told him this afternoon, and he'd told no one except Brian Holmes and Gill Templer. The answering machine was blinking furiously: four messages. He managed to work the machine without recourse to the manual, and was feeling pleased until he heard the Glaswegian accent.

'Inspector Rebus, it's CI Ancram here.' Brisk and businesslike. 'Just to let you know I'll probably arrive in Edinburgh tomorrow to get the inquiry under way, sooner we start, sooner it'll be over with. Best for all concerned, eh? I did leave a message at Craigmillar for you to phone me, but you don't seem to have been around to act on it.'

'Thank you and goodnight,' Rebus growled.

Beep. Message two.

'Inspector, it's me again. It would be very useful to know your planned movements for the next week or so, just to maximise my time effectively. If you could type out as full a breakdown as possible, I'd appreciate it.'

'I feel like I'm *having* a fucking breakdown.'

He went back to the window. They were clearing off. The Redgauntlet camera was being loaded into the estate car. Message three. At the sound of the voice, Rebus turned slack-jawed to watch the machine.

'Inspector, the inquiry will be based at Fettes. I'll probably bring one of my own men with me, but otherwise will utilise officers and civilian staff from Fettes. So as from tomorrow morning you can contact me there.'

Rebus walked over to the machine and stared down at it, daring it . . . daring it . . .

Beep. Message four.

'Two tomorrow afternoon for our first meeting, Inspector. Let me know if this—'

Rebus snatched up the machine and flung it at the wall. The lid flew open, ejecting the tape.

His doorbell rang.

He checked through the spyhole. Could *not* believe it. Opened the door wide.

Kayleigh Burgess took a step back. 'Christ, you look fierce.'

'I *feel* fierce. What the hell do you want?'

She brought a hand from behind her back, showing a bottle of Macallan. 'Peace offering,' she said.

Rebus looked at the bottle, then at her. 'Is this your idea of entrapment?'

'Absolutely not.'

'Any microphones or cameras about your person?'

She shook her head. Strands of curling brown hair came to rest against her cheeks and the sides of her eyes. Rebus stepped back into the hall.

'Lucky for you I've a drouth on me,' he said.

She walked ahead of him into the living room, giving him the chance to study her body. It was every bit as tidy as Feardie Fergie's house.

'Listen,' he said, 'I'm sorry about your tape machine. Send me the bill, I mean it.'

She shrugged, then saw the answering machine. 'What is it with you and technology?'

'Ten seconds, and already the questions have started. Wait here, I'll get the glasses.' He went into the kitchen and closed the door behind him, then gathered up the press cuttings and newspapers from the table, flinging them into a cupboard. He rinsed two glasses, and took his time drying them, staring at the wall above the sink. What was she after? Information, naturally. Gill's face came into his mind. She'd asked him for a favour, and a man had died. As for Kayleigh Burgess . . . maybe *she'd* been responsible for Geddes's suicide. He took the glasses through. She was crouched in front of the hi-fi, studying album spines.

'I've never owned a record player,' she said.

'I hear they're the next big thing.' He opened the Macallan and poured. 'I've no ice, though I could probably chip a block off the inside of the freezer.'

She stood up, took her glass from him. 'Neat's fine.'

She was wearing tight black denims, faded at bum and knees, and a denim jacket with fleece lining. Her eyes, he noticed, were slightly bulbous, her eyebrows arched – natural, he thought, not plucked. Sculpted cheekbones, too.

'Sit down,' he said.

She sat on the sofa, legs slightly apart, elbows on knees, holding the drink up to her face.

'It's not your first today, is it?' she asked him.

He sipped, put the glass on the arm of his chair. 'I can stop any time I want.' He held his arms wide. 'See?'

She smiled, drank, watching him above the rim of the glass. He tried to read the signals: coquette, minx, relaxed, sharp-eyed, calculating, amused . . .

'Who tipped you off about the inquiry?' he asked.

'You mean who tipped the media in general, or me personally?'

'Whichever.'

'I don't know who started the story, but one journalist told another and it spread from there. A friend of mine on *Scotland on Sunday* phoned me; she knew we were covering the Spaven case already.'

Rebus was thinking: Jim Stevens, standing on the sideline like the team manager. Stevens, Glasgow-based. Chick Ancram, Glasgow-based. Ancram knowing Rebus and Stevens went way back, spilling the story . . .

Bastard. No wonder he hadn't invited Rebus to call him Chick.

'I can almost hear the cogs turning.'

A thin smile. 'Pieces falling into place.' He reached for the bottle – had left it within grabbing distance. Kayleigh Burgess rested against the back of the sofa, sliding her legs under her, looking around.

'Nice room. Big.'

'It needs redecorating.'

She nodded. 'Cornices for definite, maybe around the window. I'd turf that out though.' She was referring to a painting above the fireplace: a fishing-boat in a harbour. 'Where's it supposed to be?'

Rebus shrugged. 'Somewhere that's never existed.' He didn't like the painting either, but couldn't conceive of throwing it out.

'You could strip the door,' she went on, 'it'd come up well from the look of it.' She saw his look. 'I've just bought my own place in Glasgow.'

'Nice for you.'

'The ceilings are too high for my liking, but –' His tone of voice caught her. She stopped.

'Sorry,' Rebus said, 'I'm a bit rusty on chit-chat.'

'But not on irony.'

'I get plenty of practice. How's the programme going?'

'I thought you didn't want to discuss it.'

Rebus shrugged. 'Got to be more interesting than DIY.' He got up to refill her glass.

'It's going OK.' She looked up at him; he kept his eyes on her glass. 'Be better if you agreed to be interviewed.'

'No.' He went back to his chair.

'No,' she echoed. 'Well, with you or without you, the programme will go out. It's already scheduled. Have you read Mr Spaven's book?'

'I'm not a great one for fiction.'

She turned to stare at the piles of books near the hi-fi. They called him a liar.

'I've seldom met a prisoner who didn't profess his or her innocence,' Rebus went on. 'It's a survival mechanism.'

'I don't suppose you've ever come across a miscarriage of justice either?'

'I've seen plenty. But the thing is, usually the "miscarriage" was that the criminal was getting away with it. The whole legal system is a miscarriage of justice.'

'Can I quote you on that?'

'This conversation is strictly *off* the record.'

'You're supposed to make that clear before you say anything.'

He wagged a finger at her. 'Off the record.'

She nodded, raised her glass in a toast. 'Here's to off-the-record remarks.'

Rebus put his glass to his lips, but didn't drink. The whisky was loosening him up, mixing with the exhaustion and a brain that seemed full to bursting. A dangerous cocktail. He knew he'd have to be more careful, starting straight away.

'Want some music?' he asked.

'Is that a subtle change of subject?'

'Questions, questions.' He went over to the hi-fi, slotted in a tape of *Meddle*.

'Who is it?' she asked.

'Pink Floyd.'

'Oh, I like them. Is it a new album?'

'Not exactly.'

He got her talking about her job, how she got into it, her life all the way back to childhood. Now and again she asked a question about *his* past, but he'd shake his head and lead her back into her own story.

She needs a break, he thought, as in a rest. But she was obsessed with her job, maybe this was as close as she could allow herself to come to a respite: she was with *him*, so it counted as work. It came down to guilt again, guilt and the work ethic. He thought of a story: World War One, Christmastime, the opposing sides emerging from their trenches to shake hands, play a game of football, then back into the trenches, picking up their guns again . . .

After an hour and four whiskies, she was lying on the sofa with one hand behind her head, the other resting on her stomach. She'd taken her jacket off, and was wearing a white sweatshirt beneath. She'd rolled the sleeves up. The lamplight made golden filaments of the hairs on her arms.

'Better get a taxi . . .' she said quietly, *Tubular Bells* in the background. 'Who's this again?'

Rebus didn't say anything. There was no need to: she was asleep. He could wake her, help her into a taxi. He could drive her home, Glasgow under an hour away at this time of night. But instead he covered her with his duvet, left the music on so low he could barely hear Viv Stanshall's intros. He sat in his chair by the window, a coat covering him. The gas fire was on, warming the room. He'd wait till she woke up in her own time. Then he'd offer a taxi or his services as driver. Let her choose.

He had a lot of thinking to do, a lot of planning. He had an idea about tomorrow and Ancram and the inquiry. He was turning it, shaping it, adding layers. A lot of thinking to do . . .

He awoke to street-lamp sodium and the feeling that he hadn't been asleep long, looked at the sofa and saw Kayleigh had gone. He was about to close his eyes again when he noticed her denim jacket still lying on the floor where she'd thrown it.

He got up from the chair, still groggy and suddenly not wanting to be. The hall light was on. The kitchen door was open. The light was on in there too . . .

She was standing by the table, paracetamol in one hand, a glass of water in the other. The newspaper clippings were spread in front of her. She started when she saw him, then looked at the table.

'I was looking for coffee, thought it might sober me up. I found these instead.'

'Casework,' Rebus said simply.

'I didn't know you were attached to the Johnny Bible inquiry.'

'I'm not.' He gathered up the sheets and put them back in the cupboard. 'There isn't any coffee, I've run out.'

'Water's fine.' She swallowed the tablets.

'Hangover?'

She gulped water, shook her head. 'I think maybe I can head it off.' She

looked at him. 'I wasn't snooping, it's important to me that you believe that.'

Rebus shrugged. 'If it finds its way into the programme, we'll both know.'

'Why the interest in Johnny Bible?'

'No reason.' He saw she couldn't accept that. 'It's hard to explain.'

'Try me.'

'I don't know ... call it the end of innocence.'

He drank a couple of glasses of water, let her wander back into the living room by herself. She came out again with her jacket on, pulling her hair out from behind the collar.

'I'd better go.'

'Do you want me to run you somewhere?' She shook her head. 'What about the bottle?'

'Maybe we can finish it another time.'

'I can't guarantee it'll still be here.'

'I can live with that.' She walked to the front door, opened it, turned back towards him.

'Did you hear about the drowning in Ratho?'

'Yes,' he said, face expressionless.

'Fergus McLure, I interviewed him recently.'

'Really?'

'He was a friend of Spaven.'

'I didn't know that.'

'No? Funny, he told me you pulled him in for questioning during the original case. Anything to say to that, Inspector?' She smiled coldly. 'Thought not.'

He locked the door and heard her walking downstairs, then went back into the living room and stood beside the window, looking down. She turned right, heading for The Meadows and a taxi. There was one light on across the road; no sign of Stevens' car. Rebus fixed his eyes on his own reflection. She knew about the Spaven-McLure connection, knew Rebus had interviewed McLure. It was just the kind of ammo Chick Ancram needed. Rebus's reflection stared back at him, mockingly calm. It took all his willpower to stop him punching out the glass.

11

Rebus was on the run – moving target and all that – morning hangover failing to slow him down. He'd packed first thing, a suitcase only half full, left his pager lying on the mantelpiece. The garage where he usually had his MOT done managed to give the Saab a once-over: tyre pressure, oil level. Fifteen minutes for fifteen quid. Only problem they found, the steering was slack.

'So's my driving,' Rebus told them.

He had calls to make, but avoiding his flat, Fort Apache, or any other cop-shop. He thought of the early-opening pubs, but they were like offices – he was known to work out of them. Too big a chance that Ancram would find him. So he used his local launderette, shaking his head at the offer of a service wash – ten per cent discount this week. A 'promotional offer'. Since when did launderettes need promotional offers?

He used the change machine to turn a five-pound note into coins, got coffee and a chocolate biscuit from another machine, and dragged a chair over to the wall-phone. First call: Brian Holmes at his house, a final red card on the 'investigation'. No answer. He didn't leave a message. Second call: Holmes at work. He disguised his voice and listened to a young DC tell him Brian was a no-show so far.

'Is there any message?'

Rebus put down the receiver without saying anything. Maybe Brian was working from home on the 'investigation', not answering the phone. It was possible. Third call: Gill Templer at her office.

'DCI Templer speaking.'

'It's John.' Rebus looked around the launderette. Two customers with their faces in magazines. Soft motor sound of washers and tumble-dryers. The smell of fabric conditioner. The manageress was loading powder into a machine. Radio on in the background: 'Double Barrel', Dave & Ansel Collins. Idiot lyric.

'You want an update?'

'Why else would I be phoning?'

'You're a smooth operator, DI Rebus.'

'Tell that to Sade. What have you done about Fergie?'

'The notepad's at Howdenhall, no result yet. A forensic team is going into the house today, checking for prints and anything else. They wondered why they were needed.'

'You didn't tell them?'

'I pulled rank. After all, that's what it's for.'

Rebus smiled. 'What about the computer?'

'I'm going back there this afternoon, look through the disks myself. I'll also question the neighbours about visitors, strange cars, all that.'

'And Fergie's business premises?'

'I'm off to his salesroom in half an hour. How am I doing?'

'So far, I can't complain.'

'Good.'

'I'll phone you later, see how it's going.'

'You sound funny.'

'Funny how?'

'Like you're up to something.'

'I'm not the type. Bye, Gill.'

Next call: Fort Apache, direct line to the Shed. Maclay picked up.

'Hello, Heavy,' Rebus said. 'Any messages for me?'

'Are you kidding? I need asbestos mitts for this phone.'

'DCI Ancram?'

'How did you guess?'

'ESP. I've been trying to reach him.'

'Where are you anyway?'

'Laid low, flu or something.'

'You don't sound too bad.'

'I'm putting on a brave face.'

'Are you at home?'

'At a friend's. She's nursing me.'

'Oh aye? Tell me more.'

'Not just now, Heavy. Look, if Ancram phones again . . .'

'Which he will.'

'Tell him I'm trying to reach him.'

'Does your Florence Nightingale have a number?'

But Rebus had hung up. He called his own flat, checking the answerphone was still working after the abuse he'd given it. There were two messages, both from Ancram.

'Give me a break,' Rebus said under his breath. Then he finished his coffee and ate the chocolate biscuit, and sat there staring at the windows of the tumble-dryers. His head felt like he was inside one, looking out.

He made two more calls – T-Bird Oil and Grampian CID – then decided to take a quick run out to Brian Holmes's, chancing that Nell wouldn't be there. It was a narrow terraced house, a nice size for two people. There was a tiny patch of garden out front, in desperate need of work. Hanging baskets were sited either side of the door, gasping for water. He'd thought Nell a keen gardener.

No one answered the door. He went to the window and looked in. They didn't have net curtains; some younger couples didn't bother these days. The living room was a bomb-site, the floor littered with newspapers and magazines, food wrappings, plates and mugs and empty pint glasses. The waste-paper bin was spilling beer cans. The TV played to an empty room: daytime soap, a tanned couple face to face. They looked more convincing when you couldn't hear them.

Rebus decided to ask next door. A toddler opened the door to him.

'Hiya, cowboy, is your mum in?'

A young woman was coming from the kitchen, wiping her hands on a dish-towel.

'Sorry to bother you,' Rebus said. 'I was looking for Mr Holmes, he lives next door.'

She looked out of the door. 'His car's gone, he always has the same spot.' She pointed to where Rebus's Saab was parked.

'You haven't seen his wife this morning, have you?'

'Not for ages,' the woman said. 'She used to drop by with sweets for Damon.' She rubbed the kid's hair. He shrugged her off and galloped back into the house.

'Well, thanks anyway,' Rebus said.

'He should be back this evening, he doesn't go out much.'

Rebus nodded. He was still nodding when he got to his car. He sat in the driver's seat, hands rubbing the wheel. She'd walked out on him. How long ago? Why hadn't the stubborn sod said anything? Oh sure, cops were famous for releasing their emotions, talking out their personal crises, Rebus himself a case in point.

He drove to the warehouse: no sign of Holmes, but the clerical clerk said he'd been working right up until closing time last night.

'Did he look like he was finished?'

The clerk shook his head. 'Said he'd see me today.'

Rebus thought about leaving a message, decided he couldn't risk it. He got back into the car and drove.

He drove through Pilton and Muirhouse, didn't want to cut too early on to the busy Queensferry Road. Traffic wasn't bad heading out of town – at least it was moving. He got change ready for the toll at the Forth Bridge.

He was going north. Not just to Dundee this trip. He was going to Aberdeen. He didn't know if he was running away, or heading for a confrontation.

No reason it couldn't be both. Cowards made good heroes sometimes. He stuck a tape into the cassette player. Robert Wyatt, *Rock Bottom*.

'Been there, Bob,' he said. And later: 'Cheer up, it might never happen.'

Saying which he switched tapes. Deep Purple playing 'Into the Fire'. The car accelerated just enough.

Furry Boot Town

12

It was a couple of years since Rebus had been in Aberdeen, and then only for an afternoon. He'd been visiting an aunt. She was dead now; he'd found out only after the funeral. She'd lived near Pittodrie Stadium, her old house surrounded by new developments. The house was probably gone now, flattened. For all the associations with granite, Aberdeen had a feeling of impermanence. These days it owed almost everything it had to oil, and the oil wouldn't be there for ever. Growing up in Fife, Rebus had seen the same thing with coal: no one planned for the day it would run out. When it did, hope ran out with it.

Linwood, Bathgate, the Clyde: nobody ever seemed to learn.

Rebus recalled the early oil years, the sound of Lowlanders scurrying north looking for hard work at high wages: unemployed shipbuilders and steelworkers, school-leavers and students. It was Scotland's Eldorado. You sat in Saturday afternoon pubs in Edinburgh and Glasgow, the racing pages folded open, dream horses circled, and spoke of the great escape you could make. There were jobs going spare, a mini-Dallas was being constructed from the husk of a fishing port. It was unbelievable, incredible. It was magic.

People watching J.R. scheme his way through another episode found it easy to fantasise that the same scenario was being played out on the north-east coast. There was an American invasion, and the Americans – roughnecks, bears, roustabouts – didn't want a quiet, self-contained coastal town; they wanted to raise hell, and started building from the ground up. So the initial stories of Eldorado turned into tales from the darkside: brothels, blood-baths, drunken brawls. Corruption was everywhere, the players spoke millions of dollars, and the locals resented the invasion at the same time as they took the cash and available work. For working-class males based south of Aberdeen, it seemed like the word made flesh, not just a man's world but a hardman's world, where respect was demanded and bought with money. It took only weeks for the switch: fit men came back shaking their heads, muttering about slavery, twelve-hour shifts, and the nightmare North Sea.

And somewhere in the middle, between hell and Eldorado, sat something approximating the truth, nothing like as interesting as the myths. Economically the north-east had profited from oil, and relatively painlessly at that. Like Edinburgh, commercial development had not been allowed to scar the city centre *too* deeply. But on the outskirts you saw the usual

industrial estates, the low-rise factory units, a lot of them with names connecting them to the offshore industry: On-Off; Grampian Oil; Plat-Tech . . .

However, before this there was the glory of the drive itself. Rebus stuck as far as possible to the coastal route, and wondered at the mind-set of a nation who would design a golf course along a clifftop. When he stopped at a petrol station for a break, he bought a map of Aberdeen and checked the location of Grampian Police HQ. It was on Queen Street, in the city centre. He hoped the one-way system wasn't going to be a problem. He'd been to Aberdeen maybe half a dozen times in his life, three of those for childhood holidays. Even though it was a modern city, he still joked about it the way a lot of Lowlanders did: it was full of teuchters, fish-gutters with funny accents. When they asked you where you were from, it sounded like they were saying 'Furry boot ye frae?' Thus, Furry Boot Town, while Aberdonians stuck to 'Granite City'. Rebus knew he was going to have to keep the jokes and jibes in check, at least until he had a feel for the place.

Traffic was bottle-necked heading into the centre, which was fine – it meant he had time to study both map and street names. He found Queen Street and parked, walked into Police HQ and told them who he was.

'I spoke to someone on the phone earlier, a DC Shanks.'

'I'll try CID for you,' the uniform on reception said. She told him to take a seat. He sat down and watched the movement of bodies in and out of the station. He could tell the plainclothes officers from ordinary punters – when you made eye contact, you knew. A couple of the men sported CID moustaches, bushy but neatly trimmed. They were young, trying to look older. Some kids were sitting across from him, looking subdued but with a gleam in their eyes. They were fresh-faced and freckly, with bloodless lips. Two of them were fair-haired, one red-headed.

'Inspector Rebus?'

The man was standing over to his right, could have been there a couple of minutes or more. Rebus stood up and they shook hands.

'I'm DS Lumsden, DC Shanks passed your message on. Something about an oil company?'

'Based up here. One of their employees took a flight out of an Edinburgh tenement.'

'Jumped?'

Rebus shrugged. 'There were others on the scene, one of them's a known villain called Anthony Ellis Kane. I've had word he's working up here.'

Lumsden nodded. 'Yes, I heard Edinburgh CID were asking about that name. Doesn't mean a thing to me, sorry. Normally, we'd assign the Oil Liaison Officer to look after you, but he's on holiday and I'm filling in, which makes me your guide for the duration.' Lumsden smiled. 'Welcome to Silver City.'

Silver for the River Dee which ran through it. Silver for the colour of the buildings in sunlight – grey granite transformed into shimmering light. Silver for the money the oil boom had brought. Lumsden explained as Rebus drove them back down on to Union Street.

'Another myth about Aberdeen,' he said, 'is that the folk are mean. Wait till you see Union Street on a Saturday afternoon. It must be the busiest shopping street in Britain.'

Lumsden wore a blue blazer with shiny brass buttons, grey trousers, black slip-on shoes. His shirt was an elegant blue and white stripe, his tie salmon-pink. The clothes made him look like the secretary of some exclusive golf club, but the face and body told another story. He was six feet two, wiry, with cropped fair hair emphasising a widow's peak. His eyes weren't so much red-rimmed as chlorinated, the irises a piercing blue. No wedding ring. He could have been anywhere between thirty and forty years old. Rebus couldn't quite place the accent.

'English?' he asked.

'From Gillingham originally,' Lumsden acknowledged. 'The family moved around a bit. My dad was in the forces. You did well to spot the accent, most people think I'm a Borderer.'

They were driving to a hotel, Rebus having declared that he'd probably be staying at least the one night, maybe more.

'No problem,' Lumsden had said. 'I know just the place.'

The hotel was on Union Terrace, overlooking the gardens, and Lumsden told him to park outside the entrance. He took a piece of card from his pocket and pressed it to the inside of the windscreen. It stated OFFICIAL GRAMPIAN POLICE BUSINESS. Rebus got his case out of the boot, but Lumsden insisted on carrying it. And Lumsden took care of the details at reception. A porter took the case upstairs, Rebus following.

'Just make sure you like the room,' Lumsden told him. 'And I'll see you in the bar.'

The room was on the first floor. It had the tallest windows Rebus had ever seen, and gave him a view down on to the gardens. The room was baking hot. The porter closed the curtains.

'It's always like this when we get the sun,' he explained. Rebus gave the rest of the room a once-over. It was probably the fanciest hotel room he'd ever been in. The porter was watching him.

'What, no champagne?'

The porter didn't get the joke, so Rebus shook his head and handed him a pound note. The porter explained how the in-house movies worked, told him about room service, the restaurant, and other facilities, then handed Rebus his key. Rebus followed the man back downstairs.

The bar was quiet, the lunchtime crowd having disappeared back to work, leaving their plates, bowls and glasses behind. Lumsden was perched on a stool at the bar, munching peanuts and watching MTV. There was a pint of beer in front of him.

'Forgot to ask your tipple,' he said as Rebus sat down next to him.

'A pint of the same,' Rebus told the barman.

'How's the room?'

'A bit rich for my taste, to be honest.'

'Don't worry, Grampian CID will pick up the tab.' He winked. 'It's a courtesy thing.'

'I must visit more often.'

Lumsden smiled. 'So tell me what you want to do while you're here.'

Rebus glanced at the TV screen, saw the Stones hamming it up in their latest production. Jesus, they looked old. Stonehenge with a blues riff.

'Talk to the oil company, maybe see if I can track down a couple of the deceased's friends. Find out if there's any sign of Tony El.'

'Tony El?'

'Anthony Ellis Kane.' Rebus reached into his pocket for his cigarettes. 'Do you mind?'

Lumsden shook his head twice: once to say he didn't mind, and again to refuse Rebus's offer of one.

'Cheers,' Rebus said, taking a mouthful of beer. He smacked his lips, it was OK. Beer was fine. But the row of optics kept trying to attract his attention. 'So how's the Johnny Bible case going?'

Lumsden scooped more peanuts into his mouth. 'It isn't. Dead slow to stop. Are you attached to the Edinburgh side?'

'Only by association. I've interviewed a few nutters.'

Lumsden nodded. 'Me too. I'd like to throttle some of them. I had to interview some of our RPOs, too.' He made a face. RPOs: Registered Potential Offenders. These were the 'usual suspects', a list of known perverts, sex attackers, flashers and peepers. In a case like Johnny Bible, they all had to be interviewed, alibis provided and checked.

'I hope you took a bath afterwards.'

'Half a dozen at least.'

'No new leads then?'

'Nothing.'

'You think he's local?'

Lumsden shrugged. 'I don't think anything: you need to keep an open mind. Why the interest?'

'What?'

'The interest in Johnny Bible.'

It was Rebus's turn to shrug. They sat in silence for a moment, until Rebus thought of a question. 'What does an Oil Liaison Officer do?'

'Blunt answer: liaises with the oil industry. It's a major player up here. The thing is, Grampian Police isn't just a dry-land force – our beat includes the offshore installations. If there's a theft on a platform, or a fight, or whatever, anything they bother to report, it's down to us to investigate. You can end up flying three hours out to the middle of hell on a paraffin budgie.'

'Paraffin budgie?'

'Helicopter. Three hours out, chucking your guts up along the way, so you can investigate some minor complaint. Thank Christ we don't usually get involved. It's a real frontier out there, with frontier policing.'

One of the Glasgow uniforms had said the same about Uncle Joe's estate. 'You mean they police themselves?'

'It's a bit naughty, but effective. And if it saves me a six-hour round trip I won't say I'm sorry.'

'What about Aberdeen itself?'

'Reasonably quiet, except at weekends. Union Street on a Saturday night can be like downtown Saigon. There are a lot of frustrated kids around. They've grown up with money and stories of money. Now they want their share, only it's not there any more. Christ, that was quick.' Rebus saw that he'd finished his pint; only the top inch was missing from Lumsden's. 'I like a man who's not afraid to bevvy.'

'I'll get this one,' Rebus said. The barman was standing ready. Lumsden didn't want another, so Rebus ordered an abstemious half. First impressions and all that.

'The room's yours for as long as you need it,' Lumsden said. 'Don't pay cash for that drink, charge it to the room. Meals aren't included, but I can let you have a few addresses. Tell them you're a cop, you'll find the bill pretty reasonable.'

'Tut tut,' Rebus said.

Lumsden smiled again. 'Some fellow officers I wouldn't tell that to, but somehow I think we're on the same wavelength. Am I right?'

'You could be.'

'I'm not often wrong. Who knows, my next posting could be Edinburgh. A friendly face is always an asset.'

'Speaking of which, I don't want my presence here broadcast.'

'Oh?'

'The media are after me. They're making a programme about a case, ancient history, and they want to talk to me.'

'I get the idea.'

'They may try tracking me down, phoning up pretending to be colleagues . . .'

'Well, no one knows you're here except me and DC Shanks. I'll try to keep it that way.'

'I'd appreciate it. They may try using the name Ancram. That's the reporter.'

Lumsden winked, finished the bowl of peanuts. 'Your secret's safe with me.'

They finished their drinks and Lumsden said he had to get back to the station. He gave Rebus his telephone numbers – office and home – and took note of Rebus's room number.

'Anything I can do, give me a call,' he said.

'Thanks.'

'You know how to get to T-Bird Oil?'

'I've got a map.'

Lumsden nodded. 'What about tonight? Fancy going for a meal?'

'Great.'

'I'll drop by about seven-thirty.'

They shook hands again. Rebus watched him leave, then headed back to the bar for a whisky. As advised, he charged it to the room, and took it upstairs. With the curtains closed, the room was cooler but still airless. He looked to see if he could open the windows, but couldn't. They had to be twelve feet high. With the curtains closed, he lay on the bed and slipped off his shoes, then replayed his conversation with Lumsden. It was something he did, usually finding things he could have said, better ways of saying them. Suddenly he sat up. Lumsden had mentioned T-Bird Oil, but Rebus couldn't recall telling him the name of the company. Maybe he had . . . or maybe he'd mentioned it to DC Shanks over the phone, and Shanks had told Lumsden.

He didn't feel relaxed any more, so prowled the room. In one of the drawers he found material about Aberdeen, tourist stuff, PR stuff. He sat down at the dressing table and started to go through it. The facts came with a zealot's force.

Fifty thousand people in the Grampian region worked in the oil and gas industry, twenty per cent of total employment. Since the early seventies,

the area's population had increased by sixty thousand, housing stock had increased by a third, creating major new suburbs around Aberdeen. A thousand acres of industrial land had been developed around the city. Aberdeen Airport had seen a tenfold increase in passenger numbers, and was now the world's busiest heliport. There wasn't a negative comment anywhere in the literature, except for the minor mention of a fishing village called Old Torry, which had been granted its charter three years after Columbus landed in America. When oil came to the north-east, Old Torry was flattened to make way for a Shell supply base. Rebus raised his glass and toasted the memory of the village.

He showered, changed his clothes, and headed back to the bar. A flustered-looking woman in long tartan skirt and white blouse came bustling up to him.

'Are you with the convention?'

He shook his head, and remembered reading about it: pollution in the North Sea or something. Eventually the woman shepherded three corpulent businessmen out of the hotel. Rebus went into the lobby and watched a limo take them away. He checked his watch. Time to go.

Finding Dyce was easy, he just followed signs to the airport. Sure enough, he saw helicopters in the sky. The area around the airport was a mix of farming land, new hotels, and industrial complexes. T-Bird Oil had its headquarters in a modest three-storey hexagon, most of it smoked glass. There was a car park at the front, and landscaped gardens with a path meandering through them to the building itself. In the distance, light aircraft were taking off and landing.

The reception area was spacious and light. Under glass there were models of the North Sea oilfields and of some of T-Bird's production platforms. Bannock was the biggest as well as the oldest. A scale-sized double-decker bus had been placed beside it, dwarfed by the rig. There were huge colour photos and diagrams on the walls, along with a slew of framed awards. The receptionist told him he was expected, and should take the lift to the first floor. The lift was mirrored, and Rebus examined himself. He remembered taking the lift up to Allan Mitchison's flat, Bain shadow-boxing his reflection. Rebus knew if he tried that just now, his reflection would probably win. He crunched down on another mint.

A pretty girl was waiting for him. She asked him to follow her, not exactly an onerous task. They moved through an open-plan office, only half the desks in current use. There were TVs switched on to Teletext news, share indices, CNN. They came out of the office into another corridor, much quieter, deep carpeting underfoot. At the second door, which was open, the girl gestured for Rebus to enter.

Stuart Minchell's name was on the door, so Rebus assumed the man rising to his feet to shake hands was Minchell.

'Inspector Rebus? Nice to meet you at last.'

It was true what they said about voices, you could seldom pin the right face and body to them. Minchell spoke with authority, but looked too young – mid-twenties tops, with a sheen to his face, red cheeks, short slicked-back hair. He wore round metal-framed glasses and had thick dark eyebrows, making the face seem mischievous. He still affected wide red braces with his trousers. When he half-turned, Rebus saw his hair at the back had been coaxed into the beginnings of a ponytail.

'Coffee or tea?' the girl was asking.

'No time, Sabrina,' Minchell said. He opened his arms wide to Rebus in apology. 'Change of plan, Inspector. I have to be at the North Sea Conference. I did try reaching you to warn you.'

'That's all right.' Rebus was thinking: shit. If he called Fort Apache, that means they'll know I'm up here.

'I thought we could take my car, talk on the way out there. I should only be half an hour or so. If you've any questions, we can talk afterwards.'

'That'll be fine.'

Minchell was shrugging into his jacket.

'Files,' Sabrina reminded him.

'Check.' He picked up half a dozen, stuffed them into a briefcase.

'Business cards.'

He opened his Filofax, saw he had a supply. 'Check.'

'Cellphone.'

He patted his pocket, nodded. 'Is the car ready?'

Sabrina said she'd check, and went to find her phone.

'We may as well wait downstairs,' Minchell said.

'Check,' said Rebus.

They waited for the lift. When it came, there were already two men inside, which still left room. Minchell hesitated. He looked like he was about to say they'd wait, but Rebus had already stepped into the lift, so he followed, with a slight bow to one of the men, the elder of the two.

Rebus watched in the mirror, saw the elder man staring back at him. He had long yellow-silver hair swept back from his forehead and behind both ears. He rested his hands on a silver-topped cane and wore a baggy linen suit. He looked like a character out of Tennessee Williams, his face chiselled and frowning, gait only slightly stooped despite his years. Rebus looked down and noticed the man was wearing a pair of well-worn trainers. The man brought a notepad out of his pocket, scribbled something on it while still holding his cane, tore the sheet off and handed it to the second man, who read it and nodded.

The lift opened at the ground floor. Minchell physically held Rebus back until the other two had got out. Rebus watched them march to the front door of the building, the man with the note veering off to make a call at reception. There was a red Jaguar parked directly outside. A liveried chauffeur held the back door open for Big Daddy.

Minchell was rubbing his brow with the fingers of one hand.

'Who was that?' Rebus asked.

'That was Major Weir.'

'Wish I'd known, I'd've asked him why I can't get Green Shield stamps with my petrol any more.'

Minchell wasn't in the mood for a joke.

'What was the note all about?' Rebus asked.

'The Major doesn't say much. He communicates better on paper.' Rebus laughed: communication breakdown. 'I'm serious,' Minchell said. 'I don't think I've heard him say more than a couple of dozen words all the time I've worked for him.'

'Something wrong with his voice?'

'No, he sounds fine, a little croaky, but that's to be expected. Thing is, his accent is American.'

'So?'

'So he wishes it was Scottish.'

With the Jag gone, they walked out to the car park. 'He's got this obsession with Scotland,' Minchell went on. 'His parents were Scots migrants, used to tell him stories about the "old country". He got hooked. He only spends maybe a third of the year here – T-Bird Oil stretches around the globe – but you can tell he hates to leave.'

'Anything else I should know?'

'He's a strict teetotaller, one whiff of alcohol from an employee and they're out.'

'Is he married?'

'Widower. His wife's buried on Islay or somewhere like that. This is my car.'

It was a midnight-blue Mazda racing model, low-slung with just enough room for two bucket seats. Minchell's briefcase all but filled the back. He hooked his phone up before turning the ignition.

'He had a son,' Minchell went on, 'but I think he died, too, or was disinherited. The Major won't talk about him. Do you want the good news or the bad?'

'Let's try the bad.'

'Still no sign of Jake Harley, he hasn't returned from his walking holiday. He's due back in a couple of days.'

'I'd like to head up to Sullom Voe anyway,' Rebus said. Especially if Ancram were going to be able to track him to Aberdeen.

'No problem with that. We'll get you up there on a chopper.'

'What's the good news?'

'Good news is, I've arranged for you to take another chopper out to Bannock to talk to Willie Ford. And as it's a day-trip, you won't need any survival training. Believe me, *that's* good news. Part of the training, they belt you into a simulator and tip you into a swimming pool.'

'You've been there?'

'Oh yes. Anyone making more than ten day-trips a year has to. Scared the hell out of me.'

'But the helicopters are safe enough?'

'Don't worry about that. And you're lucky just now: a nice window.' He saw Rebus's blank look. 'A window in the weather, no major storms brewing. See, oil is an all-year industry, but it's also seasonal. We can't always get to and from the platforms, it depends on the weather. If we want to tow a rig out to sea, we need to plot a window, then hope for the best. The weather out there . . .' Minchell shook his head. 'Sometimes it can make you believe in the Almighty.'

'Old Testament variety?' Rebus guessed. Minchell smiled and nodded, then made a call on his phone.

They came out of Dyce and into Bridge of Don, following signs to the Aberdeen Exhibition and Conference Centre. Rebus waited until Minchell had finished his call before asking a question.

'Where was Major Weir headed?'

'Same place we are. He's got to make a speech.'

'I thought you said he doesn't speak.'

'He doesn't. That man with him was his PR guru, Hayden Fletcher. He'll read the speech. The Major will sit beside him and listen.'

'Does that count as eccentric?'
'Not when you're worth a hundred million dollars.'

13

The Conference Centre car park was full of upper-tier management models: Mercs, Beamers, Jags, the occasional Bentley or Roller. A huddle of chauffeurs smoked cigarettes and swapped anecdotes.

'Might have been better PR if you'd all come on bikes,' Rebus said, getting his first view of a demo outside the prism-shaped dome which marked the entrance to the Centre. Someone had unfurled a huge banner from the roof, painted green on white: DON'T KILL OUR OCEANS! Security personnel were up there, trying to haul it in while still retaining their balance and dignity. Someone with a megaphone was leading the chant. There were demonstrators in full combat kit and radiation hoods, and others dressed up as mermaids and mermen, plus an inflatable whale which, gusted by the wind, was in danger of snapping its moorings. Uniformed police patrolled the demo, speaking into their shoulder radios. Rebus guessed there'd be a wagon nearby with the heavier artillery: riot shields, visors, US-style defence batons . . . It didn't look like that kind of demo, not yet.

'We're going to have to go through them,' Minchell said. 'I *hate* this. We're spending millions on environmental protection. I'm even a member of Greenpeace, Oxfam, you name it. But every bloody year it's the same.' He grabbed his briefcase and cellphone, remote-locked the car and set its alarm, then headed for the doors.

'You're supposed to have a delegate badge to get in,' he explained. 'But just show a warrant card or something. I'm sure it won't be a problem.'

They were close to the main demo now. There was background music through a portable PA, a song about whales, or maybe it was Wales. Rebus recognised the vocal style: The Dancing Pigs. People were shoving flyers at him. He took one of each and thanked them. A young woman was pacing in front of him like a caged leopard. She controlled the megaphone. Her voice was nasal and North American.

'Decisions made now will affect your children's grandchildren! You can't put a price on the future! Put the future first, for everybody's sake!'

She looked at Rebus as he passed her. Her face was blank, no hate, no recrimination, just working. Her bleached hair was rat-tailed, threaded with bright braids, one of which fell down the middle of her forehead.

'Kill the oceans and you kill the planet! Put Mother Earth before profits!'
Rebus was convinced even before he reached the door.

There was a bin inside, where the flyers were being dumped. But Rebus

folded his and put them in his pocket. Two guards wanted to see ID, but his warrant card, as predicted, was effective. There were more guards patrolling the concourse – private security, uniformed, wearing shiny caps which meant nothing. They'd probably had a one-day crash course in menacing pleasantry. The concourse itself was full of suits. Messages were being relayed over a PA system. There were static displays, tables piled high with literature, sales pitches for God knows what. Some of the booths looked to be doing good business. Minchell excused himself and said he'd meet Rebus at the main doors in about half an hour. He said he had to do some 'schmoozing'. This seemed to mean shaking hands with people, smiling, giving them a few words and in some cases his business card, then moving on. Rebus quickly lost him.

Rebus didn't see too many pictures of rigs, and those he did see were tension legs and semi-submersibles. The real excitement seemed to be FPSOs – Floating Production, Storage and Offloading Systems – which were like tankers, but did away with the need for a platform altogether. Flowlines connected straight to the FPSO, and it could store 300,000 barrels of oil.

'Impressive, isn't she?' a Scandinavian in a salesman's suit asked Rebus. Rebus nodded.

'No need for a platform.'

'And easier to scrap when the time comes. Cheap *and* environmental.' The man paused. 'Interested in leasing one?'

'Where would I park it?' He walked off before the salesman could translate.

Maybe it was his tracker's nose, but he found the bar with no difficulty and settled at the far end with a whisky and a bowl of nibbles. Lunch had been a petrol station sandwich, so he tucked in. A man came and stood next to him, wiped his face with a huge white handkerchief and asked for a soda water with lots of ice.

'Why do I still come to these things?' the man growled. His accent was pitched somewhere in mid-Atlantic. He was tall and thin, his reddish hair thinning. The flesh around his neck was slack, putting him in his early fifties, though he could have passed for five years younger. Rebus didn't have an answer for him, so said nothing. The drink arrived, and he downed it in one, then ordered another. 'Want one?' he asked.

'No thanks.'

The man noticed that Rebus's photocard was missing. 'Are you a delegate?'

Rebus shook his head. 'Observer.'

'The newspaper?'

Rebus shook his head again.

'Thought not. Oil's only news when something goes wrong. It's bigger than the nuclear industry, but gets half the coverage.'

'That's good, isn't it, if the news they're printing is all bad?'

The man thought about this, then laughed, showing perfect teeth. 'You've got me there.' He wiped his face again. 'So what exactly are you observing?'

'I'm off-duty right now.'

'Lucky you.'

'So what do you do?'

'I work my guts out. But I have to tell you, my company's just about given up trying to sell to the oil industry. They'd rather buy Yank or Scandinavian. Well, fuck them. No wonder Scotland's down the pan ... and we want independence.' The man shook his head, then leaned forwards over the bar. Rebus did likewise: co-conspirator. 'Mostly what I do is, I attend boring conventions like this. And I go home at night and wonder what it's all about. You sure about that drink?'

'Go on then.'

So Rebus let the man buy him a drink. The way he had said 'fuck them' made Rebus think he didn't swear that often. It was just something he did to break the ice, to show he was speaking man to man; off the record, as it were. Rebus offered a cigarette, but his friend shook his head.

'Gave them up years ago. Don't think I'm not still tempted.' He paused, looked around the bar. 'Know who I'd like to be?' Rebus shrugged. 'Go on, guess.'

'I wouldn't know where to start.'

'Sean Connery.' The man nodded. 'Think about it, with what he earns per film, he could give a pound to every man, woman and child in this country, and *still* have a couple of mill left over. Isn't that incredible?'

'So if you were Sean Connery, you'd give everyone a pound?'

'I'd be the world's sexiest man, what would I need money for?'

It was a good point, so they drank to it. Only thing was, talking about Sean reminded Rebus of Ancram, Sean's lookalike. He checked his watch, saw that he had to leave.

'Can I buy you one before I go?'

The man shook his head, then produced his business card, doing so in a slick movement, like a magician. 'In case you ever need it. My name's Ryan, by the way.' Rebus read the card: Ryan Slocum, Sales Manager, Engineering Division, and a company masthead: Eugene Construction.

'John Rebus,' he said, shaking Slocum's hand.

'John Rebus,' Slocum said, nodding. 'No business card, John?'

'I'm a police officer.'

Slocum's eyes widened. 'Did I say anything incriminating?'

'Wouldn't bother me if you did. I'm based in Edinburgh.'

'A long way from home. Is it Johnny Bible?'

'Why do you say that?'

'He's killed in both cities, hasn't he?'

Rebus nodded. 'No, it's not Johnny Bible. Take care, Ryan.'

'You too. It's a mad bad world out there.'

'Isn't it just?'

Stuart Minchell was waiting for him at the doors. 'Anything else you'd like to see, or shall we head back?'

'Let's go.'

Lumsden called up to his room, and Rebus came downstairs to meet him. Lumsden was well dressed, but casual – the blazer swapped for a cream jacket, yellow shirt open at the neck.

'So,' Rebus said, 'do I call you Lumsden all night?'

'First name's Ludovic.'

'Ludovic Lumsden?'

'My parents had a sense of humour. Friends call me Ludo.'

The evening was warm and still light. Birds were noisy in the gardens, and fat seagulls were picking their way along the pavements.

'It'll stay light till ten, maybe eleven,' Lumsden explained.

'Those are the fattest seagulls I've ever seen.'

'I hate them. Look at the state of the pavements.'

It was true, the slabs underfoot were speckled with birdshit. 'Where are we going?' Rebus asked.

'Call it a mystery tour. It's all within walking distance. You like mystery tours?'

'I like having a guide.'

Their first stop was an Italian restaurant, where Lumsden was well known. Everyone seemed to want to shake his hand, and the proprietor took him aside for a quiet word, apologising to Rebus beforehand.

'The Italians up here are docile,' Lumsden explained later. 'They never quite managed to run the town.'

'So who does?'

Lumsden considered the question. 'A mixture.'

'Any Americans?'

Lumsden looked at him, nodded. 'They run a lot of the clubs and some of the newer hotels. Service industry stuff. They arrived in the seventies, never moved away. Do you want to go to a club later?'

Rebus shrugged. 'It sounds almost respectable.'

Lumsden laughed. 'Oh, you want *sleaze*? That's supposed to be what Aberdeen's about, right? You've got the wrong idea. The city is strictly corporate. Later on, if you really want, I'll take you down by the docks: strippers and hard drinkers, but a tiny minority.'

'Living down south, you hear stories.'

'Of course you do: high-class brothels, dope and porn, gambling and alcohol. We hear the stories, too. But as for *seeing* the stuff . . .' Lumsden shook his head. 'The oil industry's pretty tame really. The roughnecks have all but disappeared. Oil's gone legit.'

Rebus was almost convinced, but Lumsden was trying too hard. He kept talking, and the more he talked the less Rebus believed. The owner came over for another word, drew Lumsden away to a corner of the restaurant. Lumsden kept a hand on the man's back, patting it. He flattened his tie as he sat down again.

'His son's running wild,' Lumsden explained. He shrugged, as if there were nothing more to say, and told Rebus to try the meatballs.

Afterwards, there was a nightclub, where businessmen vied with young turks for the attentions of the daytime shopworkers turned Lycra vixens. The music was loud and so were the clothes. Lumsden nodded his head to the pulse, but didn't look like he was enjoying himself. He looked like a tour guide. Ludo: player of games. Rebus knew he was being sold a line, the same line any tourists to the north would be sold – this was the country of Baxter's soups, men in skirts, and granny's hieland hame; oil was just another industry, the city and its people had risen above it. There was still a sense of Highland perspective.

There was no downside.

'I thought you might find this place interesting,' Lumsden yelled over the music.

'Why?'

'It's where Michelle Strachan met Johnny Bible.'

Rebus tried to swallow, couldn't. He hadn't noticed the name of the club. He looked with new eyes, saw dancers and drinkers, saw proprietorial arms around unwilling necks. Saw hungry eyes and money used for mating. He imagined Johnny Bible standing quietly by the bar, ticking off possibles in his mind, narrowing the options down to one. Then asking Michelle Fifer for a dance . . .

When Rebus suggested they move on, Lumsden didn't disagree. So far, they'd paid for one round of drinks: the restaurant meal had been 'taken care of', and the bouncer on the door of the club had nodded them through, bypassing the cash desk.

As they left, a man escorted a young woman past them. Rebus half-turned his head.

'Someone you know?' Lumsden asked.

Rebus shrugged. 'Thought I recognised the face.' He'd seen it only that afternoon: dark curly hair, glasses, olive complexion. Hayden Fletcher, Major Weir's 'PR guru'. He was looking like he'd had a good day. Fletcher's companion glanced back at Rebus and smiled.

Outside, there were still slants of purple light in the sky. In a cemetery across the road, starlings were mobbing a tree.

'Where now?' Lumsden said.

Rebus stretched his spine. 'Actually, Ludo, I think I'll just head back to the hotel. Sorry to wimp out like this.'

Lumsden tried not to look relieved. 'So what's your itinerary tomorrow?'

Suddenly Rebus didn't want him to know. 'Another meeting with the deceased's employer.' Lumsden seemed satisfied.

'And then home?'

'In a couple of days.'

Lumsden tried not to let his disappointment show. 'Well,' he said, 'get a good night's sleep. You know your way back?'

Rebus nodded and they shook hands. Lumsden headed off one way, Rebus the other. He kept walking in the direction of the hotel, taking his time, window-shopping, checking behind him. Then he stopped and consulted his map, saw that the harbour area was almost walking distance. But the first taxi that came along, he flagged it down.

'Where to?' the driver asked.

'Somewhere I can get a good drink. Somewhere down by the docks.' He thought: 'Down Where the Drunkards Roll.'

'How rough do you want?'

'As rough as it gets.'

The man nodded, started off. Rebus leaned forward in his seat. 'I thought the city would be livelier.'

'Ach, it's a bit early yet. And mind, the weekends are wild. Pay-packets coming off the rigs.'

'A lot of drinking.'

'A lot of *everything*.'

'I hear all the clubs are owned by Americans.'

'Yanks,' the driver said. 'They're everywhere.'

'Illegal as well as legal?'

The driver stared at him in his rearview. 'What were you after in particular?'

'Maybe something to get me high.'

'You don't look the type.'

'What does the type look like?'

'It doesn't look like a copper.'

Rebus laughed. 'Off-duty and playing away from home.'

'Where's home?'

'Edinburgh.'

The driver nodded thoughtfully. 'If *I* wanted to get high,' he said, 'I'd maybe think about Burke's Club on College Street. This is us.'

He pulled the cab to a stop. The meter read just over two pounds; Rebus handed over five and told him to keep the change. The driver leaned out of his window.

'You weren't a hundred yards from Burke's when I picked you up.'

'I know.' Of course he knew: Burke's was where Johnny Bible had met Michelle.

As the cab drew away, he took stock of his surroundings. Right across the road was the harbour, boats moored there, lights showing where men were still working – maintenance crews probably. This side of the road was a mix of tenements, shops and pubs. A couple of girls were working the street, but traffic was quiet. Rebus was outside a place called the Yardarm. It promised karaoke nights, exotic dancers, a happy hour, guest beers, satellite TV, and 'a warm welcome'.

As Rebus pushed open the door, he felt the warmth straight off. It was broiling inside. It took him a full minute to work his way to the bar, by which time the smoke was stinging even his hardened eyes. Some of the customers looked like fishermen – cherry faces, slick hair and thick jerseys. Others had hands blackened with oil – dockside mechanics. The women had eyes drooping from drunkenness, faces either too heavily made-up or else needing to be. At the bar, he ordered a double whisky. Now that the metric system had taken over, he could never remember whether thirty-five mils was less or more than a quarter-gill. Last time he'd seen so many drunks in the same place had been after a Hibs/Hearts match. He'd been drinking down Easter Road, and Hibs had won. Pandemonium.

It took him five minutes to engage in conversation with his neighbour, who used to work on the rigs. He was short and wiry, already completely bald in his thirties, and wore Buddy Holly glasses with jam-jar lenses. He had worked in the canteen.

'Best of fucking food every day. Three menus, two shifts. Top quality. The new arrivals always stuffed themselves, but they soon learned.'

'Did you work two weeks on, two off?'

'Everybody did. Seven-day weeks at that.' The man's face was pointing down at the bar as he spoke, like his head was too heavy to lift. 'You got hooked on it. The time I spent on land, I couldn't settle, couldn't wait to get back offshore.'

'So what happened?'

'Times got tougher. I was surplus to requirements.'

'I hear the rigs are hoaching with dope. Did you ever see any?'

'Fuck aye, all over the place. Just for relaxation, understand? Nobody was daft enough to go out to work wired up. One false move, a pipe can have your hand off – I know, I've seen it. Or if you lose your balance, I mean, it's a two-hundred-fucking-foot drop to the water. But there was plenty of dope, plenty of booze. And I'll tell you, there might not have been any women, but we had scud mags and films up to our ears. Never seen the like. All tastes catered for, and some of them were pretty disgusting. That's a man of the world talking, so you know what I mean.'

Rebus thought he did. He bought the wee man a drink. If his companion leaned any lower over the bar, his nose would be in the glass. When someone announced that the karaoke would start in five minutes, Rebus knew it was time to leave. Been there, done that. He used his map to guide him back towards Union Street. The night was growing livelier. Groups of teenagers were roaming, police wagons – plain blue transits – checking them out. There was a strong uniformed presence, but nobody seemed intimidated. People were roaring, singing, clapping their hands. Midweek Aberdeen was like Edinburgh on a bad Saturday night. A couple of woolly suits were discussing something with two young men, while girlfriends stood by chewing gum. A wagon was parked next to them, its back doors open.

I'm just a tourist here, Rebus told himself, walking past.

He took a wrong turn somewhere, ended up approaching his hotel from the opposite direction, passing a large statue of William Wallace brandishing a claymore.

'Evening, Mel,' Rebus said.

He climbed the hotel steps, decided on a nightcap, one to take up to his room. The bar was full of conventioneers, some of them still wearing their delegate badges. They sat at tables awash with empty glasses. A lone woman was perched at the bar, smoking a black cigarette, blowing the smoke ceilingwards. She had peroxide hair and wore a lot of gold. Her two-piece suit was crimson, her tights or stockings black. Rebus looked at her and decided they were stockings. Her face was hard, the hair pulled back and held with a large gold clasp. There was powder on her cheeks, and dark gloss lipstick on her lips. Maybe Rebus's age; maybe even a year or two older – the sort of woman men called 'handsome'. She'd had a couple of drinks, which was perhaps why she smiled.

'Are you with the convention?' she asked.

'No.'

'Thank Christ for that. I swear every one of them's tried chatting me up, but all they can talk about is crude.' She paused. 'As in crude oil – dead crude and live crude. Did you know there was a difference?'

Rebus smiled, shook his head and ordered his drink. 'Do you want another, or does that count as a chat-up line?'

'It does and I will.' She saw him looking at her cigarette. 'Sobranie.'

'Does the black paper make them taste any better?'

'The *tobacco* makes them taste better.'

Rebus got out his own pack. 'I'm a wood-shavings man myself.'

'So I see.'

The drinks arrived. Rebus signed the chit to charge them to his room.

'Are you here on business?' Her voice was deep, west coast or thereabouts, working-class educated.

'Sort of. What about you?'

'Business. So what do you do?'

World's worst reply to a chat-up: 'I'm a police officer.'

She raised one eyebrow, interested. 'CID?'

'Yes.'

'Are you working on the Johnny Bible case?'

'No.'

'The way the papers tell it, I thought every policeman in Scotland was.'

'I'm the exception.'

'I remember Bible John,' she said, sucking on the cigarette. 'I was brought up in Glasgow. For weeks my mum wouldn't let me out of the house. It was like being in the clink.'

'He did that to a lot of women.'

'And now it's all happening again.' She paused. 'When I said I remembered Bible John, your line should have been, "You don't look old enough".'

'Which proves I'm not chatting you up.'

She stared at him. 'Pity,' she said, reaching for her drink. Rebus used his own glass as a prop, too, buying time. She'd given him all the information he needed. He had to decide whether to act on it or not. Ask her up to his room? Or plead . . . what exactly? Guilt? Fear? Self-loathing?

Fear.

He saw the way the night could go, trying to extract beauty from need, passion from a certain despair.

'I'm flattered,' he said at last.

'Don't be,' she said quickly. His move again, an amateur chess player thrown against a pro.

'So what do *you* do?'

She turned to him. Her eyes said that she knew every tactic in this game. 'I'm in sales. Products for the oil industry.' She angled her head towards the rest of the men in the bar. 'I may have to work with them, but nobody says I have to share my time off with them.'

'You live in Aberdeen?'

She shook her head. 'Let me get you another.'

'I've an early start tomorrow.'

'One more won't hurt.'

'It might,' Rebus said, holding her gaze.

'Well,' she said, 'bang goes the perfect end to a perfectly shitty day.'

'Sorry.'

'Don't worry about it.'

He felt her eyes on him as he walked out of the bar towards reception. He had to force his feet up the stairs towards his room. Her pull was strong. He realised he didn't even know her name.

He switched on the TV while he got undressed. Some sub-Hollywood garbage: the women looked like skeletons with lipstick; the men acted with their necks – he'd seen barbers with more Method. He thought of the woman again. Was she on the game? Definitely not. But she'd hit on him

quick. He'd told her he was flattered; in truth, he was bemused. Rebus had always found relationships with the opposite sex difficult. He'd grown up in a mining village, a bit behind the times when it came to things like promiscuity. You stuck your hand in a girl's blouse and next thing her father was after you with a leather belt.

Then he'd joined the Army, where women were by turns fantasy figures and untouchables: slags and madonnas, there seemed no middle ground. Released from the Army, he'd joined the police. Married by then, but his job had proved more seductive, more all-consuming than the relationship – than *any* relationship. Since then, his affairs had lasted months, weeks, mere days sometimes. Too late now, he felt, for anything more permanent. Women seemed to like him – that wasn't the problem. The problem lay somewhere inside him, and it hadn't been eased by things like the Johnny Bible case, by women abused and then killed. Rape was all about power; killing, too, in its way. And wasn't power the ultimate male fantasy? And didn't he sometimes dream of it, too?

He'd seen the post-mortem photos of Angie Riddell, and the first thought that had come to him, the thought he'd had to push past, was: *good body*. It had bothered him, because in that instant she'd been just another object. Then the pathologist had got to work, and she had stopped being even that.

He was asleep as soon as his head touched the pillow. His prayer, as every night, was that there would be no dreams. He woke up in darkness, his back drenched in sweat, and to a ticking noise. It wasn't a clock, not even his watch. His watch was on the cabinet. This was closer, much more intimate. Was it coming from the wall? The headboard? He switched the light on, but the sound had stopped. Woodworm maybe? He couldn't find any holes in the headboard's wooden surround. He switched the lamp off and closed his eyes. There it was again: more geiger counter than metronome. He tried to ignore it, but it was too close. It was inescapable. It was the pillow, his feather pillow. There was something inside, something alive. Would it want to crawl into his ear? Lay its eggs there? Mutate or pupate or just enjoy a snack of wax and eardrum? Sweat cooled on his back and on the sheet beneath him. There was no air in the room. He was too tired to get up, too nervy to sleep. He did what he had to do – tossed the pillow towards the door.

No more ticking, but still he couldn't sleep. The ringing phone came as a relief. Maybe it was the woman from the bar. He'd tell her, I'm an alcoholic, a fuck-up, I'm no good for any other human being.

'Hello?'

'It's Ludo here, sorry to wake you.'

'I wasn't asleep. What's the problem?'

'A patrol car's coming to pick you up.' Rebus grimaced: had Ancram tracked him down already?

'What for?'

'A suicide in Stonehaven. Thought you might be interested. The name appears to be Anthony Ellis Kane.'

Rebus shot out of bed. 'Tony El? Suicide?'

'Looks like. The car should be there in five minutes.'

'I'll be ready.'

*

Now that John Rebus was in Aberdeen, things were more dangerous.
John Rebus.

The librarian's list had first thrown up the name, along with an address in Arden Street, Edinburgh EH9. With a short-term reader's ticket, Rebus had consulted editions of the *Scotsman* from February 1968 to December 1969. Four others had consulted the same sets of microfilm during the previous six months. Two were known to Bible John as journalists, the third was an author – he'd written a chapter on the case for a book on Scottish murderers. As for the fourth . . . the fourth had given his name as Peter Manuel. It would have meant nothing to the librarian writing out another short-term reader's ticket. But the real Peter Manuel had killed up to a dozen people in the 1950s, and been hanged for it at Barlinnie Prison. It became clear to Bible John: the Upstart had been reading up on famous murderers, and in the course of his studies had come across both Manuel and Bible John. Narrowing his search, he'd decided to concentrate his research on Bible John, learning more about the case by reading newspapers from the period. 'Peter Manuel' had requested not only *Scotsman*s from 1968–70, but *Glasgow Herald*s too.

His was to be thorough research. And the address on his reader's ticket was as fictitious as his name: Lanark Terrace, Aberdeen. The real Peter Manuel had carried out his killing spree in Lanarkshire.

But though the address was false, Bible John wondered about Aberdeen. His own investigations had already led him to site the Upstart in the Aberdeen area. This seemed a further connection. And now John Rebus was in Aberdeen, too . . . Bible John had been pondering John Rebus, even before he knew who he was. He was at first an enigma, and now a problem. Bible John had scanned some of the Upstart's most recent cuttings into the computer, and browsed through them while he wondered what to do about the policeman. He read another policeman's words: 'This person needs help, and we would ask him to come forward so that we can help him.' Followed by more speculation. They were whistling in the dark.

Except that one of them was in Aberdeen.

And Bible John had given him his business card.

He'd always known that it would be dangerous, tracking down the Upstart, but he could hardly have expected to bump into a policeman along the way. And not just any officer, but someone who'd been looking at the Bible John case. John Rebus, policeman, based in Edinburgh, address in Arden Street, currently in Aberdeen . . . He decided to open a new file on his computer, dedicated to Rebus. He had looked through some recent papers, and thought he'd found why Rebus was in Aberdeen: an oil-worker had fallen from a tenement window in Edinburgh, foul play suspected. Reasonable to conclude that Rebus was working that case rather than any other. But there was still the fact that Rebus had been reading up on the Bible John case. Why? What business was it of his?

And a second fact, more problematical still: Rebus now had his business card. It wouldn't mean anything to him, couldn't, not yet. But there might come a time . . . the closer he came to the Upstart, the more risks he would face. The card might mean something to the policeman sometime down the road. Could Bible John risk that? He seemed to have two options: quicken his hunt for the Upstart.

Or take the policeman out of the game.

He would think it over. Meantime, he had to concentrate on the Upstart.

His contact at the National Library had informed him that a reader's ticket required proof of identity: driver's licence, something like that. Maybe the Upstart had forged himself a whole new identity as 'Peter Manuel', but Bible John doubted it. More likely he had managed to talk himself past proving his identity. He would be good at talking. He'd be ingratiating, wheedling. He wouldn't look like a monster. His would be a face women – and men – could trust. He was able to walk out of nightclubs with women he'd met only an hour or two before. Getting round a security check would have posed him few problems.

He stood up and examined his face in the mirror. The police had issued a series of photofits, computer generated, ageing the original photofit of Bible John. One of them wasn't a bad likeness, but it was one amongst many. Nobody had so much as looked at him twice; none of his colleagues had remarked on any resemblance. Not even the policeman had seen anything. He rubbed his chin. The bristles showed through red where he hadn't shaved. The house was silent. His wife was elsewhere. He'd married her because it had seemed expedient, one more lie to the profile. He unlocked the study door, walked to the front door and made sure it was locked. Then he climbed the stairs to the upstairs hall, and pulled down the sliding ladder which led up into the attic. He liked it up here, a place only he visited. He looked at a trunk, on top of which sat a couple of old boxes – camouflage. They hadn't been moved. He lifted them off now and took a key from his pocket, unlocked the trunk and snapped open the two heavy brass clasps. He listened again, hearing only silence past the dull beat of his own heart, then lifted the lid of the trunk.

Inside, it was filled with treasure: handbags, shoes, scarves, trinkets, watches and purses – nothing with any means of identifying the previous owner. The bags and purses had been emptied, checked thoroughly for telltale initials or even blemishes and distinguishing marks. Any letters, anything with a name or address, had been incinerated. He settled on the floor in front of the open trunk, not touching anything. He didn't need to touch. He was remembering a girl who'd lived on his street when he'd been eight or nine – she'd been a year younger. They'd played a game. They would take it in turns to lie very still on the ground, eyes closed, while the other one tried to remove as much of their clothing as they could without the one being stripped feeling anything.

Bible John had been quick to feel the girl's fingers on him – he'd played by the rules. But when the girl had lain there, and he'd started working at buttons and zips . . . her eyelids had fluttered, a smile on her lips . . . and she'd lain there uncomplaining, even though he knew she must be able to feel his clumsy fingers.

She'd been cheating, of course.

Now his grandmother came to him, with her constant warnings: beware women who wear too much perfume; don't play cards with strangers on trains . . .

The police hadn't said anything about the Upstart taking souvenirs. No doubt they wanted to keep it quiet; they'd have their reasons. But the Upstart *would* be taking souvenirs. Three so far. And he'd be hoarding

them in Aberdeen. He'd slipped just a little, giving Aberdeen as his address on the reader's card . . . Bible John stood up suddenly. He saw it now, saw the transaction between the librarian and 'Peter Manuel'. The Upstart claiming that he needed the use of a reference library. The librarian asking for details, for proof of identity . . . The Upstart flustered, saying he'd left all that sort of thing at home. Could he go and fetch it? Impossible, he'd come down from Aberdeen for the day. A long way to travel, so the librarian had relented, issued the ticket. But now the Upstart was obliged to give Aberdeen as his address.

He *was* in Aberdeen.

Revived, Bible John locked the trunk, replaced the boxes exactly as they had been, and went back downstairs. It grieved him that with John Rebus so close, he might have to move the trunk . . . and himself with it. In his study, he sat at his desk. Have the Upstart based in Aberdeen but mobile. Have him learn from his first mistakes. So now he plans each cull well in advance. Are the victims chosen at random, or is there some pattern there? Easier to choose prey that wasn't random; but then easier, too, for the police to establish a pattern and eventually catch you. But the Upstart was young: maybe that was one lesson he *hadn't* yet learned. His choice of 'Peter Manuel' showed a certain cockiness, teasing anyone who was able to track him that far. He either knew his victims or he didn't. Two routes to follow. Route one: say he *did* know them, say there existed some pattern linking all three to the Upstart.

One profile: the Upstart was a travelling man – lorry driver, company rep, a job like that. Lots of travel throughout Scotland. Travelling men could be lonely men, sometimes they used the services of a prostitute. The Edinburgh victim had been a prostitute. Often they stayed in hotels. The Glasgow victim had worked as a chambermaid. The first victim – the Aberdeen cull – failed to fit that pattern.

Or did she? Was there something the police had missed, something *he* might find? He picked up his telephone, called Directory Enquiries.

'It's a Glasgow number,' he told the voice on the other end.

14

In the middle of the night, Stonehaven was only twenty minutes south of Aberdeen, especially with a maniac at the wheel.

'He'll still be dead when we get there, pal,' Rebus told the driver.

And so he was, dead in a bed & breakfast bathroom, one arm over the side of the bath Marat-style. He'd slashed his wrists by the book – up and down rather than across. The water in the bath looked cold. Rebus didn't get too close – the arm over the side had leaked blood all across the floor.

'The landlady didn't know who was in the bathroom,' Lumsden explained. 'She just knew whoever it was had been in there long enough. She got no answer, so went to fetch one of her "boys" – this place caters to oil-workers. She tells me she thought Mr Kane was an oil-worker. Anyway, one of her lodgers got the door open and they found this.'

'Nobody saw or heard anything?'

'Suicide tends to be a quiet affair. Follow me.'

They went along narrow passages and up two short flights of stairs to Tony El's bedroom. It was fairly tidy. 'The landlady vacuums and dusts twice a week, sheets and towels are changed twice a week too.' There was a bottle of cheap whisky with the top unscrewed, about a fifth of the bottle left. An empty glass stood beside it. 'Look over here.'

Rebus looked. On the dressing table sat a full set of works: syringe, spoon, cotton wool, lighter, and a tiny polythene bag of brown powder.

'I hear heroin's back in a big way,' Lumsden said.

'I didn't see marks on his arms,' Rebus said. Lumsden nodded that they were there, but Rebus went back to the bathroom to make sure. Yes, a couple of pinpricks on the inside left forearm. He went back to the bedroom. Lumsden was seated on the bed, flicking through a magazine.

'He hadn't been using long,' Rebus said. 'His arms are pretty clean. I didn't see the knife.'

'Look at this stuff,' Lumsden said. He wanted to show Rebus the magazine. A woman with a plastic bag over her head was being entered from behind. 'Some people have sick minds.'

Rebus took the magazine from him. It was called *Snuff Babes*. On the front inside page it stated that it was printed 'with pride' in the USA. It wasn't just illegal; it was the hardest core Rebus had ever seen. Pages and pages of mock-up deaths with sex attached.

Lumsden had reached into his pocket, drew out an evidence bag. Inside was a blood-stained knife. But no ordinary knife: a Stanley.

'I'm not so sure this was suicide,' Rebus said quietly.

So then he had to explain his reasons: the visit to Uncle Joe, how Uncle Joe's son came by his nickname, and the fact that Tony El used to be one of Uncle Joe's henchmen.

'The door was locked from the inside,' Lumsden said.

'And it hadn't been forced when I got here.'

'So?'

'So how did the landlady's "boy" get in?' He took Lumsden back to the bathroom and they examined the door: with the turn of a screwdriver, it could be locked and unlocked from the outside.

'You want us to treat this as murder?' Lumsden said. 'You think this guy Stanley walked in here, spiked Mr Kane, dragged him along to the bathroom, and sliced his wrists open? We just passed half a dozen bedroom doors and came up two flights of stairs – don't you think somebody might have noticed?'

'Have you asked them?'

'I'm telling you, John, no one saw anything.'

'And I'm telling you this has Joseph Toal written all over it.'

Lumsden was shaking his head. He'd rolled up the magazine. It was sticking out of his jacket pocket. 'All I see here is a suicide. And from what you've told me, I'm glad to see the back of the fucker, end of story.'

The same patrol car took Rebus back into the city, still keeping the wrong side of the speed limit.

Rebus felt wide awake. He paced his room, smoked three cigarettes. The city outside his cathedral windows was finally asleep. The adult pay-movie channel was still available. The only other thing on offer was beach vollcyball from California. For want of any other distraction he got out the flyers from the demo. They made depressing reading. Mackerel and other species of fish were now 'commercially extinct' in the North Sea, while others, including haddock – staple of the fish supper – wouldn't survive the millennium. Meantime, there were 400 oil installations out there which would one day become redundant, and if they were simply dumped along with their heavy metals and chemicals . . . bye-bye fishies.

Of course, it might be that the fish were for the crow road anyway: nitrates and phosphates from sewage, plus agricultural fertilisers . . . all drained into the seas. Rebus felt worse than ever, tossed the flyers into the bin. One of them didn't make it, and he picked it up. It told him there was going to be a march and rally on Saturday, with a benefit concert headlined by the Dancing Pigs. Rebus binned it and decided to check his answering machine at home. There were two calls from Ancram, agitated verging on furious, and one from Gill, telling him to call her whatever the hour. So he did.

'Hello?' She sounded like someone had gummed up her mouth.

'Sorry it's so late.'

'John.' She paused to check the time. 'It's so late it's practically early.'

'Your message said . . .'

'I know.' She sounded like she was struggling to sit up in bed, yawned mightily. 'Howdenhall worked on that message pad, used ESDA on it, electrostatics.'

'And?'

'Came up with a phone number.'

'Whereabouts?'

'Aberdeen code.'

Rebus felt his spine tingle. 'Where in Aberdeen?'

'It's the payphone in some discotheque. Hang on, I've got the name here . . . Burke's Club.'

Clickety-click.

'Does it mean anything to you?' she said.

Yes, he thought, it means I'm up here working at least two cases, maybe three.

'You said a payphone?'

'A public phone. I know because I called it. Not far from the bar by the sound of it.'

'Give me the number.' She did. 'Anything else?'

'The only fingerprints found belonged to Fergie himself. Nothing interesting on his home computer, except that he was trying a few tax dodges.'

'Hold the front page. And his business premises?'

'Nothing so far. John, are you OK?'

'Fine, why?'

'You sound . . . I don't know, sort of distant.'

Rebus allowed himself a smile. 'I'm right here. Get some sleep, Gill.'

'Night, John.'

'Night-night.'

He decided to try phoning Lumsden at the cop-shop. Conscientious: nearly three a.m. and he was there.

'You should be in the land of Nod,' Lumsden told him.

'Something I meant to ask earlier.'

'What?'

'That club we were in, the one where Michelle Strachan met Johnny Bible.'

'Burke's?'

'I just wondered,' Rebus said. 'Is it above board?'

'Moderately.'

'Meaning what?'

'It skates on thin ice sometimes. There's been a bit of drug dealing on the premises. The owners tried to clean it up, I think they've done a pretty good job.'

'Who owns it?'

'A couple of Yanks. John, what's this about?'

Rebus took less than a second constructing his lie. 'The Edinburgh jumper, he had a book of matches in his pocket. They were from Burke's.'

'It's a popular spot.'

Rebus made a sound of agreement. 'These owners, what were their names again?'

'I didn't say.' Cagey now.

'Is it a secret?'

A humourless laugh. 'No.'

'Maybe you don't want me bothering them?'

'Jesus, John . . .' A theatrical sigh. 'Erik-with-a-k Stemmons, Judd

Fuller. I don't see the point in talking to them.'

'Me neither, Ludo. I just wanted their names.' Rebus attempted an American accent. 'Ciao, baby.' He was smiling when he put down the receiver. He looked at his watch. Ten past three. It was a five-minute walk to College Street. But would the place still be open? He got out the phone book, looked up Burke's – the number listed was the same one Gill had given him. He tried it: no answer. He decided to leave it at that . . . for the moment.

Spinning in a narrowing gyre: Allan Mitchison . . . Johnny Bible . . . Uncle Joe . . . Fergus McLure's drug deal.

Beach Boys: 'God Only Knows'. Segue to Zappa and the Mothers: 'More Trouble Every Day'. Rebus picked his pillow off the floor, listened to it for a full minute, threw it back on to the bed, then lay him down to sleep.

He was awake early and didn't feel like breakfast, so went for a walk instead. It was a glorious morning. The seagulls were busy hoovering up the night before's leftovers, but the streets were otherwise uncrowded. He walked up to the Mercat Cross, then left along King Street. He knew he was heading in the vague direction of his aunt's house, but doubted he could find it on foot. Instead, he came to something looking like an old school building but calling itself RGIT Offshore. He knew RGIT was Robert Gordon's Institute of Technology, and that Allan Mitchison had studied for a time at RGIT-OSC. He knew Johnny Bible's first victim had studied at Robert Gordon's University, but not what she had studied. Had she taken classes here? He stared at the grey granite walls. The first murder was in Aberdeen. Only later did Johnny Bible move to Glasgow and Edinburgh. Meaning what? Did Aberdeen hold some particular significance for the killer? He'd walked the victim from a nightclub to Duthie Park, but that didn't mean he was local: Michelle herself could have shown him the way. Rebus got out his map again, found College Street, then traced a finger from Burke's Club to Duthie Park. A long walk, residential, nobody had seen them the whole length of the route. Had they taken especially quiet back roads? Rebus folded the map and put it away.

He headed past the City Hospital and ended up on the Esplanade: a long expanse of grass links with bowling green, tennis and putting. There were amusements, all closed this early. People were on the Esplanade – jogging, walking their dogs, morning constitutionals. Rebus joined them. Groynes divided the mostly sandy beach into neat compartments. It was as clean a part of the city as he'd seen, excepting the graffiti – an artist called Zero had been hard at work, making this his or her personal gallery.

Zero the Hero: a character from somewhere . . . Gong. Jesus, he hadn't thought of them for years. Pot-head pixies with stoned synths. Floating anarchy.

At the end of the Esplanade, next to the harbour, stood a couple of squares of housing, a village within the city. The squares themselves comprised drying greens and garden sheds. Dogs barked a warning as he passed. It reminded him of the east neuk of Fife, fishermen's cottages, brightly painted but unpretentious. A taxi was cruising the harbour. Rebus waved it down. The R&R was over.

*

There was a demo outside the headquarters of T-Bird Oil. The young woman with the braided hair who'd been so persuasive the previous day was sitting cross-legged on the grass, smoking a roll-up, looking like she was on her break. The young man currently on the megaphone didn't have half her anger or eloquence, but his friends cheered him on. Maybe he was new to the demonstrating game.

Two young woolly suits, no older than the activists, were in consultation with three or four environmentalists in red boiler-suits and gas masks. The policemen were saying that if they took the gas masks off, conversation might be less of a chore. They were also asking that the demonstration move off land owned by T-Bird Oil. Namely, the patch of grass in front of the main entrance. The demonstrators were saying something about the laws of trespass. Legal knowledge came with the territory these days. It was like rules of unarmed combat to a squaddie.

Rebus was offered the same literature as the day before.

'I already took,' he said with a smile. Braid-hair looked up at him and squinted, like she was taking a photograph.

In the reception area, someone was videoing the demo through the windows. Maybe for police intelligence; maybe for T-Bird's own files. Stuart Minchell was waiting for Rebus.

'Isn't it unbelievable?' he said. 'I hear there are groups like that one outside each of the Six Sisters, plus smaller operations like ours.'

'The Six Sisters?'

'The big North Sea players. Exxon, Shell, BP, Mobil . . . I forget the other two. So, ready for the trip?'

'I'm not sure. What are my chances of getting a kip?'

'It might be pretty bumpy. Good news is, we've a plane heading up, so you'll be spared a budgie – at least for today. You'll fly in to Scatsta. It used to be an RAF base. Saves the hassle of changing at Sumburgh.'

'And it's near Sullom Voe?'

'Right next door. Someone'll be there to meet you.'

'I appreciate this, Mr Minchell.'

Minchell shrugged. 'Ever been to Shetland?' Rebus shook his head. 'Well, you're probably not going to see much of it, except from the air. Just remember, when that plane takes off, you're not in Scotland any more. You're a "Sooth-Moother" heading for miles and miles of bugger all.'

15

Minchell drove Rebus to Dyce Airport. The plane was a twin-propeller model with seats for fourteen, but today carrying only half a dozen passengers, all men. Four of them wore suits, and were quick to open their briefcases, disgorging sheafs of paper, ring-bound reports, calculators, pens and laptops. One wore a sheepskin jacket and lacked what the others would probably call 'proper grooming'. He kept his hands in his pockets and stared out of the window. Rebus, who didn't mind an aisle seat, decided to sit beside him.

The man tried to stare him elsewhere. His eyes were bloodshot, grey stubble covering cheeks and chin. In reply, Rebus fastened his seatbelt. The man growled, but shifted upright, allowing Rebus half an armrest. Then he went back to window-watching. A car was drawing up outside.

The engine started up, propellers turning. There was a stewardess at the back of the cramped compartment. She hadn't closed the door yet. The man in the window-seat turned to the assembly of suits.

'Prepare to shite yourselves.' Then he started laughing. Whisky fumes from the night before wafted over Rebus, making him glad he'd skipped breakfast. Someone else was boarding the plane. Rebus peered down the aisle. It was Major Weir, dressed in a kilt, sporran attached. The suits froze. Sheepskin was still chuckling. The door slammed shut. Seconds later, the plane began to taxi.

Rebus, who hated flying, tried to think himself into a nice Intercity 125, speeding along terra firma, no intention of suddenly pushing skywards.

'Grab that armrest any harder,' his neighbour said, 'and you'll uproot the fucking thing.'

The ascent was like an unpaved road. Rebus thought he could feel fillings popping loose and hear the plane's various bolts and soldered joins snapping. But then they were levelling out, and things settled down. Rebus started breathing again, noticed sweat on his palms and brow. He adjusted the air-intake above him.

'Better?' the man said.

'Better,' Rebus agreed. The wheels retracted, covers closing. The sheepskin explained what the sounds were. Rebus nodded his thanks. He could hear the stewardess behind them.

'I'm sorry, Major, if we'd known you were coming we'd have arranged for coffee to be served.'

She got a grunt for her trouble. The suits were staring at their work, but

couldn't concentrate. The plane hit some turbulence, and Rebus's hands went to the armrests again.

'Fear of flying,' sheepskin said with a wink.

Rebus knew he had to get his mind off the flight. 'Do you work at Sullom Voe?'

'Practically *run* the place.' He nodded towards the suits. 'I don't work for this lot you know. I'm just cadging a lift. I work for the consortium.'

'The Six Sisters?'

'And the rest. Thirty-odd at the last count.'

'You know, I don't know a damned thing about Sullom Voe.'

Sheepskin gave him a sidelong look. 'You a reporter?'

'I'm a CID detective.'

'Just so long as you're not a reporter. I'm the relief Maintenance Manager. We're always getting grief in the press about cracked pipes and spills. I'll tell you, the only leaks around *my* terminal are the ones to the fucking papers!' He stared out of the window again, as if their conversation had reached a natural end. But a full minute later he turned to Rebus.

'There are two pipelines into the terminal – Brent and Ninian – plus we offload from tankers. Four jetties in near-constant use. I was here from the start, 1973. That's only four years after the first exploration ships chugged into Lerwick. By Christ, I'd have loved to've seen the looks on the fishermen's faces. They probably thought it was the start of bugger all. But oil came and oil stayed, we got to fuck with the islands, and they screwed every penny they could out of the consortium. Every last penny.'

As sheepskin talked, his mouth began to relax. Rebus thought he might still be drunk. He spoke quietly, mostly with his face to the window.

'You should have seen the place in the seventies, kiddo. It was like the Klondike – trailer parks, shanty towns, the roads churned to mud. We had power cuts, not enough fresh water, and the locals fucking hated us. I loved it. There was about one pub we could all drink in. The consortium were choppering in supplies like we were at war. Fuck, maybe we were.'

He turned to Rebus.

'And the weather . . . the wind'll strip the skin off your face.'

'So I needn't have brought a razor?'

The big man snorted. 'What takes you to Sullom Voe?'

'A suspicious death.'

'On Shetland?'

'In Edinburgh.'

'How suspicious?'

'Maybe not very, but we have to check.'

'I know all about that. It's like at the terminal, we run hundreds of checks every day, whether they're needed or not. The LPG chilldown area, we had a suspected problem there, and I stress *suspected*. I'll tell you, we had more men on standby than God knows what. See, it's not that far from the crude oil storage.'

Rebus nodded, not sure what the man was getting at. He seemed to be drifting off again. Time to reel him in.

'The man who died worked for a while at Sullom Voe. Allan Mitchison.'

'Mitchison?'

'He might've been on maintenance. I think that was his speciality.'

Sheepskin shook his head. 'Name doesn't . . . no.'

'What about Jake Harley? He works at Sullom Voe.'

'Oh aye, I've come across him. Don't much like him, but I know the face.'

'Why don't you like him?'

'He's one of those Green bastards. You know, *ecology*.' He almost spat the word. 'What the fuck's ecology ever done for us?'

'So you know him.'

'Who?'

'Jake Harley?'

'I said so, didn't I?'

'He's off on some walking holiday.'

'On Shetland?' Rebus nodded. 'Aye, sounds about right. He's always on about archaeology and whatsit, bird-watching. The only birds I'd spend all day watching don't have fucking feathers on them, let me tell you.'

Rebus to himself: *I thought I was bad, but this guy redefines all the terms.*

'So he's off walking and bird-watching: any idea where he'd go?'

'The usual places. There are a few bird-watchers at the terminal. It's like pollution control. We know we're doing all right as long as the birds don't suddenly start turning up their toes. Like with the *Negrita*.' He almost bit off the end of the word, swallowed hard. 'Thing is, the wind's so fierce, and the currents are fierce too. So you get dispersal, like with the *Braer*. Somebody told me Shetland has a complete change of air every quarter-hour. Perfect dispersal conditions. And fuck it, they're only birds. What are they good for, when it comes down to it?'

He rested his head against the window.

'When we get to the terminal, I'll get a map for you, mark some of the places he might go . . .' Seconds later, his eyes were closed. Rebus got up and went to the back of the cabin, where the toilet was. As he passed Major Weir, who was seated in the very back row, he saw he was deep in the *Financial Times*. The toilet was no smaller than a child's coffin. If Rebus had been any wider, they'd have had to starve him out. He flushed, thinking of his urine splashing into the North Sea – as far as pollution went, a mere drop in the ocean – and tugged open the accordion doors. He slid into the seat across the aisle from the Major. The stewardess had been sitting there, but he could see her up front in the cockpit.

'Any chance of a keek at the racing results?'

Major Weir lifted his eyes from the newsprint, swivelled his head to take in this strange new creature. The whole process couldn't have taken longer than half a minute. He didn't say anything.

'We met yesterday,' Rebus told him. 'My name's Detective Inspector Rebus. I know you don't say much . . .' he patted his jacket . . . 'I've a notepad in my pocket if you need one.'

'In your spare time, Inspector, are you some sort of comedian?' The voice was a cultured drawl; urbane just about summed it up. But it was also dry, a little rusty.

'Can I ask you something, Major? Why did you name your oilfield after an oatcake?'

Weir's face reddened with sudden rage. 'It's short for Bannockburn!'

Rebus nodded. 'Did we win that one?'

'Don't you know your history, laddie?' Rebus shrugged. 'I swear, sometimes I despair. You're a *Scot*.'

'So?'

'So your past is important! You need to know it so you can learn.'

'Learn what, sir?'

Weir sighed. 'To borrow a phrase from a poet – a Scots poet, he was talking about words – that we Scots are "creatures tamed by cruelty". Do you see?'

'I think I'm having trouble focusing.'

Weir frowned. 'Do you drink?'

'Teetotal is my middle name.' The Major grunted his satisfaction. 'Trouble is,' Rebus went on, 'my first name's Not-at-all.'

He got it eventually and grudged a frowning smile, the first time Rebus had seen the trick.

'The thing is, sir, I'm up here—'

'I know why you're up here, Inspector. When I saw you yesterday, I had Hayden Fletcher find out who you were.'

'Can I ask why?'

'Because you stared back at me in the elevator. I'm not used to that sort of behaviour. It meant you didn't work for me, and since you were with my personnel manager . . .'

'You thought I was after a job?'

'I meant to see to it you didn't get one.'

'I'm flattered.'

The Major looked at him again. 'So why is my company flying you to Sullom Voe?'

'I want to talk to a friend of Mitchison's.'

'Allan Mitchison.'

'You knew him?'

'Don't be ridiculous. I had Minchell report to me yesterday evening. I like to know everything that's going on in my company. I have a question for you.'

'Go ahead.'

'Could Mr Mitchison's death have anything to do with T-Bird Oil?'

'At the moment . . . I don't think so.'

Major Weir nodded, lifted his newspaper to eye level. The interview was over.

16

Welcome to the Mainland,' Rebus's guide said, meeting him on the tarmac.
Major Weir had already been installed in a Range Rover and was speeding from the airfield. A row of helicopters stood in repose nearby. The wind was . . . well, the wind was *serious*. It was flapping the helicopters' rotor blades, and it was singing in Rebus's ears. The Edinburgh wind was a pro; sometimes you walked out your front door and it was like being punched in the face. But the Shetland wind . . . it wanted to pick you up and shake you.

The descent had been rocky, but before that he'd had his first sighting of Shetland proper. 'Miles and miles of bugger all' didn't do it justice. Hardly any trees, plenty of sheep. And spectacular barren coastline with white breakers crashing into it. He wondered if erosion was a problem. The islands weren't exactly large. They'd crossed to the east of Lerwick, then passed some dormitory towns, which, according to Sheepskin's commentary, had been mere hamlets in the 1970s. He'd woken up by then, and had come armed with a few more facts and fancies.

'Know what we did? The oil industry, I mean? We kept Maggie Thatcher in power. Oil revenue paid for all those tax cuts. Oil revenue paid for the Falklands War. Oil was pumping through the veins of her whole fucking reign, and she never thanked us once. Not once, the bitch.' He laughed. 'You can't help liking her.'

'Apparently there are pills you can take.' But Sheepskin wasn't listening.

'You can't separate oil and politics. The sanctions against Iraq, whole point was to stop him flooding the market with cheap oil.' He paused. 'Norway, the bastards.'

Rebus felt he'd missed something. 'Norway?'

'They've got oil, too, only they've banked the money, used it to kickstart other industries. Maggie used it to pay for a war and a bloody election . . .'

As they swung out to sea past Lerwick, Sheepskin had pointed out some boats – bloody big boats.

'Klondikers,' he said. 'Factory ships. They're busy processing fish. Probably doing more environmental damage than the whole North Sea oil industry. But the locals just let them get on with it, they don't give a bugger. Fishing's a heritage thing with them . . . not like oil. Aah, fuck the lot of them.'

Rebus still hadn't learned the man's name when they parted on the runway. There was someone waiting for Rebus, a slight grinning man with

too many teeth in his head. And he said, 'Welcome to the Mainland.' Then explained what he meant in the car, during the short trip to the Sullom Voe terminal. 'That's what Shetlanders call the main island: Mainland, as opposed to mainland with a small m, which means . . . well, the mainland.' A snort for a laugh. He had to wipe his nose on the sleeve of his jacket. He drove the way a kid would when seated in its father's car: bent forward, hands overly busy on the steering-wheel.

His name was Walter Rowbotham, and he was a new recruit to the Sullom Voe Public Relations Department.

'I'd be happy to show you around, Inspector,' he said, still grinning, trying too hard to please.

'Maybe if there's time,' Rebus conceded.

'My pleasure entirely. You know, of course, that the terminal cost one thousand three hundred million just to construct. That's pounds, not dollars.'

'Interesting.'

Rowbotham's face practically lit up, encouraged now. 'The first oil flowed into Sullom Voe in 1978. It is a major employer and has helped contribute greatly to Shetland's low unemployment rate, currently around four per cent or half the Scottish average.'

'Tell me something, Mr Rowbotham.'

'Walter, please. Or Walt if you like.'

'Walt.' Rebus smiled. 'Had any more trouble with the LPG chilldown?'

Rowbotham's face turned pickled baby beet. Jesus, Rebus thought, the media were going to love him . . .

They ended up driving through half the installation to get to where Rebus wanted to be, so he heard most of the tour narration anyway and learned more than he hoped he'd ever have to know about debutanising, de-ethanising and depropanising, not to mention surge tanks and integrity meters. Wouldn't it be great, he thought, if you could fit integrity meters to human beings?

At the main administration building they'd been told that Jake Harley worked in the process control room, and that his colleagues were waiting there and knew a police officer was coming to talk to them. They passed the incoming crude lines, the pigging station, and the final holding basin, and at one point Walt thought they were lost, but he had a little orientation map with him.

Just as well: Sullom Voe was huge. It had taken seven years to build, breaking all sorts of records in the process (and Walt knew every one of them), and Rebus had to admit that it was an impressive monster. He'd been past Grangemouth and Mossmorran dozens of times, but they just weren't in the picture. And if you looked out past the crude oil tanks and the unloading jetties, you saw water – the Voe itself to the south; then Gluss Isle over to the west, doing a good impression of unspoilt wilderness. It was like a sci-fi city transported to prehistory.

For all of which, the process control room was about as peaceful a place as Rebus had ever been. Two men and a woman sat behind computer consoles in the centre of the room, while the walls were taken up with electronic charts, softly flashing lights indicating the oil and gas flows. The only sounds were those of fingers on keyboards, and the occasional muted

conversation. Walt had decided that it was his job to introduce Rebus. The atmosphere had quieted him, as if he'd walked into the middle of a church service. He went to the central console and spoke in an undertone to the trinity seated there.

The elder of the two men stood up and came to shake Rebus's hand.

'Inspector, my name's Milne. How can we help?'

'Mr Milne, I really wanted to speak to Jake Harley. But since he's made himself scarce, I thought maybe you could tell me a little about him. Specifically, about his friendship with Allan Mitchison.'

Milne wore a check shirt, its sleeves rolled up. He scratched at one arm while Rebus spoke. He was in his thirties, with tousled red hair and a face pitted from teenage acne. He nodded, half-turning to his two colleagues, assuming the role of spokesman.

'Well, we all work beside Jake, so we can tell you about him. Personally, I didn't know Allan very well, though Jake introduced us.'

'I don't think I've ever met him,' the woman said.

'I met him once,' the other man added.

'Allan only worked here for two or three months,' Milne went on. 'I know he struck up a friendship with Jake.' He shrugged. 'Really, that's about it.'

'If they were friends, they must have had something in common. Was it bird-watching?'

'I don't think so.'

'Green issues,' the woman said.

'That's true,' Milne said, nodding. 'Of course, in a place like this, we always end up talking about ecology sooner or later – sensitive subject.'

'Is it a big thing with Jake?'

'I wouldn't go that far.' Milne looked to his colleagues for support. They shook their heads. Rebus realised that nobody was talking much above a whisper.

'Jake works right here?' he asked.

'That's right. We alternate shifts.'

'So sometimes you're working together . . .'

'And sometimes we're not.'

Rebus nodded. He was learning nothing; wasn't sure he'd ever actually thought he *would* learn anything. So Mitchison had been into ecology – big deal. But it was pleasant here, relaxing. Edinburgh and all his troubles were a long way away, and felt it.

'This looks like a cushy job,' he said. 'Can anyone apply?'

Milne smiled. 'You'll have to hurry, who knows how long the oil will last?'

'A while yet surely?'

Milne shrugged. 'It's down to the economics of retrieval. Companies are beginning to look west – Atlantic oil. And oil from west of Shetland is being landed at Flotta.'

'On Orkney,' the woman explained.

'They won the contract from us,' Milne went on. 'Five or ten years from now, the profit margin may be bigger out there.'

'And they'll mothball the North Sea?'

All three nodded, like a single beast.

'Have you talked to Briony?' the woman asked suddenly.

'Who's Briony?'

'Jake's . . . I don't know, she's not his wife, is she?' She looked to Milne.
'Just a girlfriend, I think.'
'Where does she live?' Rebus asked.
'Jake and her share a house,' Milne said. 'In Brae. She works at the swimming pool.'
Rebus turned to Walt. 'How far is it?'
'Six or seven miles.'
'Take me.'

They tried the baths first, but she wasn't on shift, so they tracked down her house. Brae looked to be suffering a crisis of identity, like it had suddenly plopped into being and didn't know what to make of itself. The houses were new but anonymous; there was obviously money around, but it couldn't buy everything. It couldn't turn Brae back into the village it had been in the days before Sullom Voe.

They found the house. Rebus told Walt to wait in the car. A woman in her early twenties answered his knock. She was wearing jogging bottoms and a white singlet, her feet bare.
'Briony?' Rebus asked.
'Yes.'
'Sorry, I don't know your last name. Can I come in?'
'No. Who are you?'
'I'm Detective Inspector John Rebus.' Rebus showed his warrant card. 'I'm here about Allan Mitchison.'
'Mitch? What about him?'
There were a lot of answers to that question. Rebus picked one. 'He's dead.' Then he watched the colour drain from her face. She clung on to the door as if for support, but she still wasn't letting him in.
'Would you like to sit down?' Rebus hinted.
'What happened to him?'
'We're not sure, that's why I want to talk to Jake.'
'You're not sure?'
'Could be an accident. I'm trying to fill in some background.'
'Jake isn't here.'
'I know, I've been trying to reach him.'
'Somebody from personnel keeps phoning.'
'On my behalf.'
She nodded slowly. 'Well, he's still not here.' She hadn't taken her hand off the jamb.
'Can I get a message to him?'
'I don't know where he is.' As she spoke, the colour started to return to her cheeks. 'Poor Mitch.'
'You've no idea where Jake is?'
'He sometimes goes off on a walk. He doesn't know himself where he'll end up.'
'He doesn't phone you?'
'He needs his space. So do I, but I find mine when I swim. Jake walks.'
'He's due back tomorrow though, or the day after?'
She shrugged. 'Who knows?'
Rebus reached into a pocket, wrote on a page of his notebook, tore it out.

He held it out to her. 'It has a couple of phone numbers. Will you tell him to call me?'

'Sure.'

'Thanks.' She was staring dully at the piece of paper, her eyes just short of tears. 'Briony, is there anything you can tell me about Mitch? Anything that might help?'

She looked up from the card to him.

'No,' she said. Then, slowly, she closed the door on his face. In that final glimpse of her before the door separated them, Rebus had found her eyes, and seen something there. Not just bewilderment or grief.

Something more like fear. And behind it, a degree of calculation.

It struck him that he was hungry, and gasping for coffee. So they ate in the Sullom Voe canteen. It was a clean white space with potted plants and no smoking signs. Walt was rattling on about how Shetland remained more Norse than Scots; nearly all the place names were Norwegian. To Rebus, it was like the edge of the world, and he liked that. He told Walt about the man on the plane, the one in sheepskin.

'Oh, that sounds like Mike Sutcliffe.'

Rebus asked to be taken to him.

Mike Sutcliffe had changed out of his sheepskin and was dressed in crisp work clothes. They finally found him in heated conversation beside the ballast water tanks. Two underlings were listening to him complain that they could be replaced by gibbons and nobody would notice. He pointed up at the tanks, then out towards the jetties. There was a tanker moored at one of them, it couldn't have been any bigger than half a dozen football pitches. Sutcliffe saw Rebus and lost the thread of his argument. He dismissed the workers and began to move away, only he had to get past Rebus first.

Rebus had a smile ready. 'Mr Sutcliffe, did you get me that map?'

'What map?' Sutcliffe kept walking.

'You said you might have an idea where I could find Jake Harley.'

'Did I?'

Rebus was almost having to jog to keep up with him. He wasn't wearing the smile any more. 'Yes,' he said coldly, 'you did.'

Sutcliffe stopped so suddenly, Rebus ended up in front of him. 'Look, Inspector, I'm up to my gonads in thistles right now. I don't have time for this.'

And he walked, his eyes not meeting Rebus's. Rebus marched alongside, keeping silent. He kept it up for a hundred yards, then stopped. Sutcliffe kept going, looking like he might walk right along the jetty and across the water if he had to.

Rebus went back to where Walt was standing. He took his time, thoughtful. The bum's rush and then some. What or who had changed Sutcliffe's mind? Rebus pictured an old white-haired man in kilt and sporran. The picture seemed to fit.

Walt took Rebus back to his office in the main admin building. He showed Rebus where the phone was, and said he'd be back with two coffees. Rebus closed the office door, and sat down behind the desk. He was surrounded by

oil platforms, tankers, pipelines, and Sullom Voe itself – huge framed photos on the walls; PR literature stacked high; a scale model of a super tanker on the desk. Rebus got an outside line and telephoned Edinburgh, weighing up diplomacy against bullshit and deciding it might save time to just tell the truth.

Mairie Henderson was at home.

'Mairie, John Rebus.'

'Oh Christ,' she said.

'You're not working?'

'Haven't you heard of the portable office? Fax-modem and a telephone, that's all you need. Listen, you owe me.'

'How so?' Rebus tried to sound aggrieved.

'All that work I did for you, and no story at the end of it. That's not exactly *quid pro quo*, is it? And journalists have longer memories than elephants.'

'I gave you Sir Iain's resignation.'

'A full ninety minutes before every other hack knew. And it wasn't exactly the crime of the century to begin with. I *know* you held back on me.'

'Mairie, I'm hurt.'

'Good. Now tell me this is purely a social call.'

'Absolutely. So how are you keeping?'

A sigh. 'What do you want?'

Rebus swung ninety degrees in the chair. It was a comfortable chair, good enough to sleep in. 'I need some digging.'

'I am completely and utterly surprised.'

'The name's Weir. He calls himself Major Weir, but the rank may be spurious.'

'T-Bird Oil?'

Mairie was a *very* good journalist. 'That's the one.'

'He just made a speech at that convention.'

'Well, he had someone else read it out.'

A pause. Rebus flinched. 'John, you're in Aberdeen?'

'Sort of,' he confessed.

'Tell me.'

'Later.'

'And if there's a story . . . ?'

'You're in pole position.'

'With something longer than a ninety-minute lead time?'

'Absolutely.'

Silence on the line: she knew he could be lying. She was a journalist; she knew these things.

'OK, so what do you want to know about Weir?'

'I don't know. Everything. The interesting stuff.'

'Business or personal life?'

'Both, mainly business.'

'Do you have a number in Aberdeen?'

'Mairie, I'm not *in* Aberdeen. Especially if anyone asks. I'll get back to you.'

'I hear they're reopening the Spaven case.'

'An internal inquiry, that's all.'

'Preliminary to a reopening?'

Walt opened the door, brought in two beakers of coffee. Rebus stood up. 'Look, I have to go.'

'Cat got your tongue?'

'Bye, Mairie.'

'I checked,' Walt said, 'your plane leaves in an hour.' Rebus nodded and took the coffee. 'I hope you've enjoyed your visit.'

Christ, Rebus thought, he means it, too.

17

That evening, once he'd recovered from the flight back to Dyce, Rebus ate at the same Indian restaurant Allan Mitchison had frequented: no coincidence. He didn't know why he wanted to see the place for himself; he just did. The meal was decent, a chicken dopiaza neither better nor worse than he could find in Edinburgh. The diners were couples, young and middle-aged, their conversations quiet. It didn't look the sort of restaurant you'd raise hell in after sixteen days offshore. If anything, it was a place for contemplation, always supposing you were dining alone. When Rebus's bill came, he recalled the sums on Mitchison's credit-card statement – they were about double the present figure.

Rebus showed his warrant card and asked to speak to the manager. The man came bounding up to his table, nervous smile in place.

'Is there some problem, sir?'

'No problem,' Rebus said.

The manager lifted the bill from the table and was about to tear it up, but Rebus stopped him.

'I'd prefer to pay,' he said. 'I only want to ask a couple of questions.'

'Of course, sir.' The manager sat down opposite him. 'What can I do to help?'

'A young man called Allan Mitchison used to eat here regularly, about once a fortnight.'

The manager nodded. 'A policeman came in to ask me about him.'

Aberdeen CID: Bain had asked them to check up on Mitchison, their report back an almost total blank.

'Do you remember him? The customer, I mean?'

The manager nodded. 'Very nice man, very quiet. He came maybe ten times.'

'Alone?'

'Sometimes alone, sometimes with a lady.'

'Can you describe her?'

The manager shook his head. There was a clatter from the kitchen, distracting him. 'I just remember he was not always alone.'

'Why didn't you tell the other policeman this?'

The man didn't seem to understand the question. He got to his feet, the kitchen decidedly on his mind. 'But I did,' he said, moving away.

Something Aberdeen CID had conveniently left out of their report . . .

There was a different bouncer on the door at Burke's Club, and Rebus paid

his entrance money the same as everybody else. Inside, it was seventies
night, with prizes for the best period costume. Rebus watched the parade of
platform shoes, Oxford bags, midis and maxis, kipper ties. Nightmare
stuff: it all reminded him of his wedding photos. There was a *Saturday
Night Fever* John Travolta, and a girl who was doing a passable imitation
of Jodie Foster in *Taxi Driver*.

The music was a mix of kitsch disco and regressive rock: Chic, Donna
Summer, Mud, Showaddywaddy, Rubettes, interspersed with Rod Stew-
art, the Stones, Status Quo, a blast of Hawkwind and bloody 'Hi-Ho Silver
Lining'.

Jeff Beck: up against the wall *now*!

The odd song clicked with him, had the power to send him reeling in the
years. The DJ somehow still had a copy of Montrose's 'Connection', one of
the very best cover versions of a Stones song. Rebus in the Army listened to
it in his billet late at night, playing on an early Sanyo cassette player, an
earpiece plugged in so nobody else could hear. Next morning, he'd be deaf
in one ear. He switched the earpiece about each night so he wouldn't suffer
long-term damage.

He sat at the bar. That seemed to be where the single men congregated
in silent appraisal of the dance floor. The booths and tables were for
couples and office parties, squawks of women who genuinely looked to be
enjoying themselves. They wore low-cut tops and short tight skirts, and in
the shadowy half-light they *all* looked terrific. Rebus decided he was
drinking too quickly, poured more water into his whisky and asked the
barman for more ice, too. He was seated at the corner of the bar, less than
six feet from the payphone. Impossible to use it when the music was
pounding, and there hadn't been much of a let-up yet. Which made Rebus
think – the only sensible time to use the payphone would be out of hours,
when the place was quiet. But at that time there'd be no punters on the
premises, just staff . . .

Rebus slipped off his stool and circuited the dance floor. The toilets were
signposted down a passageway. He went inside and listened to someone in
one of the cubicles snorting something. Then he washed his hands and
waited. The toilet flushed, the lock clicked, and a young man in a suit came
out. Rebus had his warrant card ready.

'You're under arrest,' he said. 'Anything you say—'

'Hey, wait a minute!' The man still had flecks of white powder in his
nostrils. He was mid-twenties, lower management struggling to be middle.
His jacket wasn't expensive, but at least it was new. Rebus pushed him
against the wall, angled the hand-drier and pushed the button so the hot
air blew across his face.

'There,' he said, 'blow some of that talc away.'

The man turned his face away from the heat. He was shaking, his whole
body limp, beaten before they really got started.

'One question,' Rebus said, 'and then you walk out of here . . . how does
the song go? As free as a bird. One question.' The man nodded. 'Where did
you get it?'

'What?'

Rebus pushed a bit harder. 'The stuff.'

'I only do this on a Friday night!'

'Last time: where did you get it?'

'Just some guy. He's here sometimes.'

'Is he here tonight?'

'I haven't seen him.'

'What does he look like?'

'Nothing special. Mr Average. You said one question.'

Rebus let the man go. 'I lied.'

The man sniffed, straightened his jacket. 'Can I go?'

'You're gone.'

Rebus washed his hands, loosened the knot in his tie so he could undo his top button. The sniffer might go back to his booth. He might decide to leave. He might complain to the management. Maybe they paid their way so busts like this wouldn't happen. He left the toilet and went looking for the office, couldn't find one. Out in the foyer, there was a staircase. The bouncer was parked in front of it. Rebus told the tux he wanted to speak to the manager.

'No can do.'

'It's important.'

The bouncer shook his head slowly. His eyes didn't move from Rebus's face. Rebus knew what he saw: a middle-aged lush, a pathetic figure in a cheap suit. It was time to disabuse him. He opened his warrant card.

'CID,' he told the tux. 'People are selling drugs on these premises and I'm a heartbeat away from calling in the Drugs Squad. *Now* do I get to talk to the boss?'

He got to talk to the boss.

'My name's Erik Stemmons.' The man came around from his desk to shake Rebus's hand. It was a small office, but well furnished. Good sound-proofing too: the bass from the dance floor was as much as you could hear. But there were video screens, half a dozen of them. Three showing the main dance floor, two the bar, and one a general view of the booths.

'You want to put one in the bogs,' Rebus said, 'that's where the action is. You've got two on the bar: staff problems?'

'Not since we put the cameras in.' Stemmons was dressed in jeans and a white T-shirt, the arms of which he'd rolled up to his shoulders. He had long curling locks, maybe permed, but his hair was thinning and there were telltale lines down his face. He wasn't much younger than Rebus, and the younger he tried to look the older he seemed.

'Are you with Grampian CID?'

'No.'

'Thought not. We get most of them in here, good customers. Sit down, won't you?'

Rebus sat down. Stemmons got comfortable behind his desk. It was covered with paperwork.

'Frankly I'm surprised by your allegation,' he went on. 'We co-operate fully with the local police, and this club is as clean as any in the city. You know of course that it's impossible to rule narcotics out of the equation.'

'Someone was snooking up in the toilet.'

Stemmons shrugged. 'Exactly. What can we do? Strip search everyone as they enter? Have a sniffer dog roaming the premises?' He laughed a short laugh. 'You see the problem.'

'How long have you lived here, Mr Stemmons?'

'I came over in '78. Saw a good thing and stayed. That's nearly two decades. I'm practically integrated.' Another laugh; another no reaction from Rebus. Stemmons placed his palms on the desktop. 'Wherever Americans go in the world – Vietnam, Germany, Panama – entrepreneurs follow. And so long as the pickings stay good, why should we leave?' He looked down at his hands. 'What do you *really* want?'

'I want to know what you can tell me about Fergus McLure.'

'Fergus McLure?'

'You know, dead person, lived near Edinburgh.'

Stemmons shook his head. 'I'm sorry, that name means nothing to me.'

Oh, Vienna, Rebus nearly sang. 'You don't seem to have a phone in here.'

'Excuse me?'

'A phone.'

'I carry a mobile.'

'The portable office.'

'Open twenty-four hours. Look, if you've a beef, take it up with the local cops. I don't need this grief.'

'You haven't seen grief yet, Mr Stemmons.'

'Hey.' Stemmons pointed a finger. 'If you've got something to say, say it. Otherwise, the door's the thing behind you with the brass handle.'

'And you're the thing in front of me with the brass neck.' Rebus stood up and leaned across the desk. 'Fergus McLure had information on a drug ring. He died suddenly. Your club's phone number was lying on his desk. McLure wasn't exactly the clubbing type.'

'So?'

Rebus could see Stemmons in a court of law, saying the exact same thing. He could see a jury asking itself the question too.

'Look,' Stemmons said, relenting. 'If I was setting up a drug deal, would I give this guy McLure the number of the club's payphone, which *anyone* might pick up, or would I give him my mobile number? You're a detective, what do you think?'

Rebus saw a judge tossing the case out.

'Johnny Bible met his first victim here, didn't he?'

'Jesus, don't drag that up. What are you, a ghoul or something? We had CID hassling us for weeks.'

'You didn't recognise his description?'

'Nobody did, not even the bouncers, and I pay them to remember faces. I told your colleagues, maybe he met her after she left the club. Who's to say?'

Rebus went to the door, paused.

'Where's your partner?'

'Judd? He's not in tonight.'

'Does he have an office?'

'Next door.'

'Can I see it?'

'I don't have a key.'

Rebus opened the door. 'Does he have a mobile phone too?'

He'd caught Stemmons off-guard. The American coughed a response.

'Didn't you hear the question?'

'Judd doesn't have a mobile. He hates telephones.'

'So what does he do in an emergency? Send up smoke signals?'

But Rebus knew damned well what Judd Fuller would do.

He'd use a payphone.

He thought he'd earned a last drink before home, but froze halfway to the bar. There was a new couple in one of the booths, and Rebus recognised both of them. The woman was the blonde from his hotel bar. The man sitting beside her, arms draped along the back of the booth, was her junior by about twenty years. He wore an open-necked shirt and a lot of gold chains around his neck. He'd probably seen someone dressed that way in a film once. Or maybe he was going in for the fancy-dress contest: seventies villain. Rebus knew the warty face straight away.

Mad Malky Toal.

Stanley.

Rebus made the connection, made almost too many of them. He felt dizzy, and found himself leaning against the wall-phone. So he picked up the receiver and slammed home a coin. He had the phone number in his notebook. Partick police station. He asked for DI Jack Morton, waited an age. He pushed more money home, only to have someone come on and tell him Morton had left the office.

'This is urgent,' Rebus said. 'My name's DI John Rebus. Do you have his home number?'

'I can get him to call you,' the voice said. 'Would that do, Inspector?'

Would it? Glasgow was Ancram's home turf. If Rebus handed over his number, Ancram could get to hear of it, and would know where he was . . . Fuck it, he was only here another day. He reeled the number off and put down the receiver, thanking God the DJ had been playing a slow number: Python Lee Jackson, 'In a Broken Dream'.

Rebus had those to spare.

He sat at the bar, his back to Stanley and his woman. But he could see them distorted in the mirror behind the optics. Dark distant figures, coiling and uncoiling. Of course Stanley was in town: hadn't he killed Tony El? But why? And two bigger questions: was he here in Burke's Club by coincidence?

And what was he doing with the blonde from the hotel?

Rebus was starting to get inklings. He kept an ear out for the telephone, prayed for another slow record. Bowie, 'John, I'm Only Dancing'. A guitar like sawing through metal. It didn't matter: the phone didn't ring.

'Here's one we'd all rather forget,' the DJ drawled. 'But I want to see you up dancing to it anyway, otherwise I might just have to play it again.'

Lieutenant Pigeon: 'Mouldy Old Dough'. The telephone rang. Rebus leapt to it.

'Hello?'

'John? Got the hi-fi loud enough?'

'I'm at a disco.'

'At your age? Is this the emergency – you want me to talk you out of there?'

'No, I want you to describe Eve to me.'

'Eve?'

'Uncle Joe Toal's woman.'

'I've only seen her in photos.' Jack Morton thought about it. 'Blonde out of a bottle, face that could bend nails. Twenty or thirty years ago she *might* have looked like Madonna, but I'm probably being generous.'

Eve, Uncle Joe's lady – chatting Rebus up in an Aberdeen hotel. Coincidence? Hardly. Readying to pump him for information? Nap hand. And up here with Stanley, the two of them looking pretty cosy . . . He remembered her words: *'I'm in sales. Products for the oil industry.'* Yes, Rebus could guess now what kind of products . . .

'John?'

'Yes, Jack?'

'This phone number, is that an Aberdeen code?'

'Keep it to yourself. No grassing me up to Ancram.'

'Just one question . . . ?'

'What?'

'Can I really hear "Mouldy Old Dough"?'

Rebus closed the conversation, finished his drink and left. There was a car parked on the other side of the road. The driver lowered his window so Rebus could see him. It was DS Ludovic Lumsden.

Rebus smiled, waved, started to cross the road. He was thinking: I don't trust you.

'Hiya, Ludo,' he said. Just a man who'd been out for a drink and a dance. 'What brings you here?'

'You weren't in your room. I guessed you might be here.'

'Some guess.'

'You lied to me, John. You told me about a book of matches from Burke's Club.'

'Right.'

'They don't do books of matches.'

'Oh.'

'Can I give you a lift?'

'The hotel's only two minutes away.'

'John.' Lumsden's eyes were cold. 'Can I give you a lift?'

'Sure, Ludo.' Rebus walked around the car and got into the passenger seat.

They drove down to the harbour, parked on an empty street. Lumsden turned off the ignition and turned in his seat.

'So?'

'So what?'

'So you went to Sullom Voe today and didn't bother to tell me. So why has my patch suddenly become *your* patch? How would you like it if I started creeping around Edinburgh behind your back?'

'Am I a prisoner here? I thought I was one of the good guys.'

'It's not your town.'

'I'm beginning to see that. But maybe it's not *your* town either.'

'What do you mean?'

'I mean who really runs the place, behind the scenes? You've got kids going mad with frustration, you've got a ready audience for dope and anything else that might give their life a kick. In that club tonight, I saw the lunatic I told you about, Stanley.'

'Toal's son?'

'That's him. Tell me, is he up here for the floral displays?'

'Did you ask him?'

Rebus lit a cigarette, wound down the window so he could flick the ash out. 'He didn't see me.'

'You think we should question him about Tony El.' A statement of fact, no answer required. 'What would he tell us – "sure, I did it"? Come on, John.'

A woman was knocking on the window. Lumsden lowered it, and she was into her spiel.

'Two of you, well, I don't normally do threesomes but you look like nice . . . Oh, hello Mr Lumsden.'

'Evening, Cleo.'

She looked at Rebus, then Lumsden again. 'I see your tastes have changed.'

'Lose yourself, Cleo.' Lumsden wound the window back up. The woman disappeared into the darkness.

Rebus turned to face Lumsden. 'Look, I don't know just how bent you are. I don't know whose money will be paying for my stay at the hotel. There's a lot I don't know, but I'm beginning to get the feeling I *know* this city. I know it because it's much the same as Edinburgh. I know you could live here for years without glimpsing what's beneath the surface.'

Lumsden started to laugh. 'You've been here – what? – a day and a half? You're a tourist here, don't presume to *know* the place. I've been here a hell of a lot longer, and even I couldn't claim that.'

'All the same, Ludo . . .' Rebus said quietly.

'Is this leading somewhere?'

'I thought you were the one who wanted to talk.'

'And you're the one who's talking.'

Rebus sighed, spoke slowly as to a child. 'Uncle Joe controls Glasgow, including – my guess – a fair bit of the drug trade. Now his son's up here, drinking in Burke's Club. An Edinburgh snitch had some gen on a consignment headed north. He also had the phone number of Burke's. He ended up dead.' Rebus held up a finger. 'That's one strand. Tony El tortured an oil-worker, who consequently died. Tony El scurried back up here but neatly passed away. That's three deaths so far, every one of them suspicious, and nobody's doing much about it.' A second finger. 'Strand two. Are the two connected? I don't know. At the moment, all that connects them is Aberdeen itself. But that's a start. You don't know me, Ludo, a start is all I need.'

'Can I change the subject slightly?'

'Go ahead.'

'Did you get anything on Shetland?'

'Just a bad feeling. A little hobby of mine, I collect them.'

'And tomorrow you're going out to Bannock?'

'You've been busy.'

'A few phone calls, that's all it took. Know something?' Lumsden started the car. 'I'll be glad to see the back of you. My life was simple until you came along.'

'Never a dull moment,' Rebus said, opening the door.

'Where are you going?'

'I'll walk. Nice night for it.'

'Suit yourself.'

'I always do.'

Rebus watched the car move off, turn a corner. He listened to the engine fade, flicked his cigarette on to the tarmac and started to walk. The first place he passed was the Yardarm. It was Exotic Dancer night, with a scarecrow on the door charging admission. Rebus had been there, done that. The heyday of the exotic dancer had been the late seventies, every pub in Edinburgh seemed to have them: men watching from behind pint glasses, the stripper selecting her three records from the jukebox, a collection afterwards if you wanted her to go a bit further.

'Only two quid, pal,' the scarecrow called, but Rebus shook his head and kept walking.

The same night-time sounds were around him: drunken whoops, whistles, and the birds who didn't know how late it was. A prowl of woolly suits was questioning two teenagers. Rebus passed by, just another tourist. Maybe Lumsden was right, but Rebus didn't think so. Aberdeen felt so much like Edinburgh. Sometimes, you visited a town or city and couldn't get a handle on it, but this wasn't one of those.

On Union Terrace a low stone wall separated him from the gardens, which were in a gully below. He saw his car still parked across the road, directly outside the hotel. He was about to cross when hands grabbed at his arms and hauled him backwards. He felt the small of his back hit the wall, felt himself tipping backwards, up and over.

Falling, rolling . . . Skidding down the steep slope into the gardens, not able to stop himself, so going with the roll. He hit bushes, felt them tear at his shirt. His nose gouged the earth, tears springing into his eyes. Then he was on the flat. Clipped grass. Lying winded on his back, adrenalin masking any immediate damage. More sounds: crashing through bushes. They were following him down. He half rose to his knees, but a foot caught him, sent him sprawling on to his front. The foot came down hard on his head, held it there, so he was sucking grass, his nose feeling ready to break. Someone wrenched his hands behind his back and up, the pressure just right: excruciating pain couldn't overcome the knowledge that if he moved, he'd pop an arm out of its socket.

Two men, at least two. One with the foot. One working the arms. The alcoholic streets seemed a long way off, traffic a distant drone. Now something cold against his temple. He knew the feeling – a handgun, colder than dry ice.

A voice hissing, close to his ear. Blood pounding there, so he had to strain to hear it. A hiss close to a whisper, hard to identify.

'There's a message, so I hope you're listening.'

Rebus couldn't speak. His mouth was full of dirt.

He waited for the message, but it didn't come. Then it did.

Pistol-whipped to the side of his head, just above the ear. An explosion of light behind his eyes. Then darkness.

He woke up and it was still night. Sat up and looked around. His eyes hurt when he moved them. He touched his head – no blood. It hadn't been that

kind of thwack. Blunt, not sharp. Just the one by the feel of things. After he'd lost consciousness they'd left him. He searched his pockets, found money, car keys, warrant card and all his other cards. But of course it hadn't been a robbery. It had been a message, hadn't they told him so themselves?

He tried standing. His side hurt. He checked, saw that he'd grazed it coming down the slope. A graze on his forehead too, and his nose had bled a little. He checked the ground around him, but they hadn't left anything. It wouldn't have been professional. All the same, he tried as best he could to trace the route they'd come down, just in case something had been left behind.

Nothing. He hauled himself back over the wall. A taxi driver looked at him in disgust and pressed harder on the accelerator. He'd seen a drunk, a tramp, a loser.

Last year's man.

Rebus limped across the road into the hotel. The woman behind the reception desk was reaching for the phone, ready to summon back-up, but then recognised him from earlier.

'Whatever happened to you?'

'Fell down some steps.'

'Do you want a doctor?'

'Just my key, please.'

'We've a first aid kit.'

Rebus nodded. 'Have it sent up to my room.'

He took a bath, a good long soak, then towelled off and examined the damage. His temple was swollen where the butt had connected, and he had a headache worse than half a dozen hangovers. Some thorns had lodged in his side, but he was able to pick them out with his fingernails. He cleaned the graze, no need for plasters. He might ache in the morning, but he'd probably sleep, so long as the ticking noise didn't come back. A double brandy had arrived with the first aid; he sipped it, hand trembling. He lay on his bed and phoned home, checking the machine. Ancram, Ancram, Ancram. It was too late to phone Mairie, but he tried Brian Holmes's number. A lot of rings later, Holmes picked up.

'Aye?'

'Brian, it's me.'

'What can I do you for?'

Rebus had his eyes screwed shut; difficult to think past the pain. 'Why didn't you tell me Nell had walked out?'

'How do you know?'

'I came by your house. I know a batch pad when I see one. Do you want to talk about it?'

'No.'

'Is it the same problem as before?'

'She wants me to leave the force.'

'And?'

'And maybe she's right. But I've tried before, and it's hard.'

'I know.'

'Well, there's more than one way of leaving.'

'How do you mean?'

'Nothing.' And he wouldn't say any more about it. He wanted to talk about the Spaven case. The bottom line from his reading of the notes: Ancram would smell collusion, a certain economy with the truth; which wasn't to say there was anything he could do about it.

'I also notice you interviewed one of Spaven's friends at the time, Fergus McLure. He's just died, you know.'

'Dearie me.'

'Drowned in the canal, out Ratho way.'

'What did the post-mortem say?'

'He received a nasty bump to the head some time before entering the water. It's being treated as suspicious, so . . .'

'So?'

'So if I were you, I'd steer clear. Don't want to hand Ancram any more ammo.'

'Speaking of Ancram . . .'

'He's looking for you.'

'I sort of missed our first interview.'

'Where are you?'

'Laying low.' With his eyes closed and three paracetamol in his stomach.

'I don't think he went for your flu story.'

'That's his problem.'

'Maybe.'

'So you're finished on Spaven?'

'Looks like.'

'What about that prisoner? The one who was the last to speak to Spaven?'

'I'm on it, but I think he's no fixed abode, could take a while.'

'I really appreciate it, Brian. Do you have a story ready if Ancram finds out?'

'No problem. Take care, John.'

'You too, son.' *Son?* Where had *that* come from? Rebus put down the phone, picked up the TV remote. Beach volleyball would just about do him for tonight . . .

Dead Crude

18

Oil: black gold. The North Sea's exploration and exploitation rights had been divvied up long ago. The oil companies spent a lot of money on that initial exploration. A block might yield no oil or gas at all. Vessels were sent out laden with scientific equipment, their data studied and discussed – all this before a single test well was sunk. The reserves might lie three thousand metres beneath the sea bed – Mother Nature not keen to give up the hidden trove. But the plunderers had ever more technical expertise; water depths of two hundred metres no longer bothered them. In fact, the latest discoveries – Atlantic oil, two hundred kilometres west of Shetland – involved a water depth of between four and six hundred metres.

If the test drilling proved successful, showing reserves worth the game, a production platform would be built, along with all the various modules to accompany it. In some parts of the North Sea the weather was too unpredictable for tanker loading, so pipelines would have to be installed – the Brent and Ninian pipelines took crude directly to Sullom Voe, while other pipelines carried gas to Aberdeenshire. All this, and still the oil proved stubborn. In many fields, you could expect to recover only forty or fifty per cent of the available reserve, but then the reserve might consist of one and a half billion barrels.

Then there was the platform itself, sometimes three hundred metres high, a jacket weighing forty thousand tonnes, covered in eight hundred tonnes of paint, and with additional weight of modules and equipment totalling thirty thousand tonnes. The figures were staggering. Rebus tried to take them in, but gave up after a while and decided just to be awestruck. He'd only ever once seen a rig, when he'd been visiting relatives in Methil. The street of prefab bungalows led down to the construction yard, where a three-dimensional steel grid lay on its side, towering into the sky. From a distance of a mile, it had been spectacular enough. He recalled it now, staring at the glossy photographs in the brochure, a brochure all about Bannock. The platform, he read, carried fifteen hundred kilometres of electrical cable, and could accommodate nearly two hundred workers. Once the jacket had been towed out to the oilfield and anchored there, over a dozen modules were placed atop it, everything from accommodation to oil and gas separation. The whole structure had been designed to withstand winds of one hundred knots, and storms with hundred-foot waves.

Rebus was hoping for calm seas today.

He was sitting in a lounge at Dyce Airport, only a little nervous about the

flight he was about to take. The brochure assured him that safety was paramount in 'such a potentially hazardous environment', and showed him photos of fire-fighting teams, a safety and support vessel on constant standby, and fully equipped lifeboats. 'The lessons of Piper Alpha have been learned.' The Piper Alpha platform, north-east of Aberdeen: over a hundred and sixty fatalities on a summer's night in 1988.

Very reassuring.

The flunkey who'd handed him the brochure had said he hoped Rebus had brought something to read.

'Why?'

'Because the flight can take three hours total, and most of the time it's too noisy for chit-chat.'

Three hours. Rebus had gone into the terminal's shop and bought himself a book. He knew the journey comprised two stages – Sumburgh first, and then a Super Puma helicopter out to Bannock. Three hours out, three hours back. He yawned, checked his watch. It wasn't quite eight o'clock yet. He'd skipped breakfast – didn't like the idea of boaking it back up on the flight. His total consumption this morning: four paracetamol, one glass of orange juice. He held his hands out in front of him: tremors he could put down to aftershock.

There were two anecdotes he liked in the brochure: he learned that a 'derrick' was named after a seventeenth-century hangman; and that the first oil had come ashore at Cruden Bay, where Bram Stoker once took his holidays. From one kind of vampirism to another . . . only the brochure didn't put it like that.

There was a television on in front of him, playing a safety video. It told you what to do if your helicopter went down into the North Sea. It all looked very slick on the video: nobody panicked. They slid out of their seats, located the inflatable life-rafts and launched them on to the calm waters of an indoor pool.

'Holy God, what happened to you?'

He looked up. Ludovic Lumsden was standing there, newspaper folded in his jacket pocket, a beaker of coffee in his hand.

'Mugged,' Rebus said. 'You wouldn't know anything about it, would you?'

'Mugged?'

'Two men were waiting for me last night outside the hotel. Threw me over the wall into the gardens, then stuck a gun against my head.' Rebus rubbed the lump on his temple. It felt worse than it looked.

Lumsden sat down a couple of seats away, looked aghast. 'Did you get a look at them?'

'No.'

Lumsden put his coffee on the floor. 'Did they take anything?'

'They weren't *after* anything. They just had a message for me.'

'What?'

Rebus tapped his temple. 'A thumping.'

Lumsden frowned. 'That was the message?'

'I think I was supposed to read between the lines. You wouldn't be any good at translating, would you?'

'What do you mean?'

'Nothing.' Rebus stared at him hard. 'What are you doing here?'

Lumsden was staring at the tiled floor, mind elsewhere. 'I'm coming with you.'

'Why?'

'Oil Liaison. You're visiting a rig. I should be there.'

'Keeping an eye on me?'

'It's procedure.' He looked towards the television. 'Don't worry about ditching, I've had the training. What it boils down to is, you've got about five minutes from the time you hit the water.'

'And after five minutes?'

'Hypothermia.' Lumsden lifted his coffee cup, drank from it. 'So pray we don't hit a storm out there.'

After Sumburgh Airport, there was nothing but sea and a sky wider than any Rebus had seen before, thin clouds strung across it. The twin-engined Puma flew low and loud. The interior was cramped, and so were the survival suits they'd been made to put on. Rebus's was a bright orange one-piece with a hood, and he'd been ordered to keep it zipped up to his chin. The pilot wanted him to keep his hood up, too, but Rebus found that sitting down with the hood tight across his head, the legs of the suit threatened to dissect his scrotum. He'd been in choppers before – back in Army days – but for short hops only. Designs might have changed over the years, but the Puma didn't sound any quieter than the old buckets the Army had used. Everyone, however, wore ear-protectors, through which the pilot could talk to them. Two other men, contract engineers, flew with them. From flying height, the North Sea looked tranquil, a gentle rise and fall showing the currents. The water looked black, but that was just cloud cover. The brochure had gone into great detail concerning anti-pollution measures. Rebus tried to read his book, but couldn't. It juddered on his knees, blurring the words, and he couldn't keep his mind on the story anyway. Lumsden was looking out of the window, squinting into the light. Rebus knew Lumsden was keeping an eye on him, and he was doing so because Rebus had touched a nerve last night. Lumsden tapped his shoulder, pointed through the window.

There were three rigs below them, off to the east. A tanker was moving away from one of them. Tall flares sent bright yellow flames licking into the sky. The pilot told them they would pass to the west of the Ninian and Brent fields before reaching Bannock. Later, he came back on the radio.

'This is Bannock coming up now.'

Rebus looked past Lumsden's shoulder, saw the single platform coming into view. The tallest structure on it was the flare, but there were no flames. That was because Bannock was coming to the end of its useful life. Very little gas and oil were left to exploit. Next to the flare was a tower, like a cross between an industrial chimney and a space rocket. It was painted with red and white stripes, like the flare. It was probably the drilling tower. Rebus made out the words T-Bird Oil on the jacket below it, along with the block number – 211/7. Three large cranes stood against one edge of the platform, while a whole corner was given over to a helipad, painted green with a yellow circle surrounding the letter H. Rebus thought: one gust could have us over the side. There was a two-hundred-foot drop to the waiting sea. Orange lifeboats clung to the underside of the jacket, and

in another corner sat layers of white Portakabins, like bulk containers. A ship sat alongside the platform – the safety and support vessel.

'Hello,' said the pilot, 'what's this?'

He'd spotted another boat, circling the platform at a distance of maybe half a mile.

'Protesters,' he said. 'Bloody idiots.'

Lumsden looked out of his window, pointing. Rebus saw it: a narrow boat painted orange, its sails down. It looked to be very close to the safety ship.

'They could get themselves killed,' Lumsden said. 'And good riddance.'

'I do like a copper with a balanced view.'

They swept out to sea again and banked sharply, then headed for the heliport. Rebus was deep in prayer as they seemed to weave wildly, only fifty feet or so above the deck. He could see the helipad, then white-capped water, then the helipad again. And then they were down, landing on what looked like a fishing net covering the white capital H. The doors opened and Rebus removed his ear-protectors. The last words he heard were, 'Keep your head down when you get out.'

He kept his head down when he got out. Two men in orange overalls, wearing yellow hard hats and ear-protectors, led them off the helipad and handed out hard hats. The engineers were led one way, Rebus and Lumsden another.

'You'll probably want a mug of tea after that,' their guide said. He saw that Rebus was having trouble with the hat. 'You can adjust the strap.' He showed him how. There was a fierce wind blowing, and Rebus said as much. The man laughed.

'This is dead calm,' he yelled into the wind.

Rebus felt like he wanted to hang on to something. It wasn't just the wind, it was the feeling of how fragile this whole enterprise was. He'd expected to see and smell oil, but the most obvious product around here wasn't oil – it was seawater. The North Sea surrounded him, massive compared to this speck of welded metal. It insinuated itself into his lungs; the salt gusts stung his cheeks. It rose in vast waves as if to engulf him. It seemed bigger than the sky above it, a force as threatening as any in nature. The guide was smiling.

'I know just what you're thinking. I thought the same thing myself first time I came out here.'

Rebus nodded. The Nationalists said it was Scotland's oil, the oil companies had the exploitation rights, but the picture out here told a different story: oil belonged to the sea, and the sea wouldn't give it up without a fight.

Their guide led them to the relative safety of the canteen. It was clean and quiet, with brick troughs filled with plants, and long white tables ready for the next shift. A couple of orange overalls sat drinking tea at one table, while at another three men in checked shirts ate chocolate bars and yoghurt.

'This place is mad at mealtimes,' the guide said, grabbing a tray. 'Tea all right for you?'

Lumsden and Rebus agreed that tea was fine. There was a long serving-hatch, and a woman at the far end smiling at them.

'Hello, Thelma,' their guide said. 'Three teas. Lunch smells good.'

'Ratatouille, steak and chips, or chilli.' Thelma poured tea from a huge pot.

'Canteen's open twenty-four hours,' the guide told Rebus. 'Most guys, when they first arrive, they overeat. The puddings are lethal.' He slapped his stomach and laughed. 'Isn't that right, Thelma?' Rebus recalled the man in the Yardarm telling him much the same thing.

Even seated, Rebus's legs felt shaky. He put it down to the flight. Their guide introduced himself as Eric, and said that seeing how they were police officers, they could skip the introductory safety video.

'Though by rights I'm supposed to show you it.'

Lumsden and Rebus shook their heads, and Lumsden asked how close the platform was to decommissioning.

'Last oil's already been pumped out,' Eric said. 'Pump a final load of seawater into the reservoir and most of us will ship out. Maintenance crew only, until they decide what to do with her. They'd better make up their minds soon, manning this even just with maintenance shifts is an expensive business. You still have to get the supplies out here, the shift changeovers, and you still need the safety ship. It all costs money.'

'Which is all right so long as Bannock is producing oil?'

'Exactly,' said Eric. 'But when it's not producing . . . well, the accountants start having palpitations. We lost a couple of days' worth last month, some problem with the heat exchangers. They were out here, waving their calculators about . . .' Eric laughed.

He was nothing like the roustabout of legend, the myth of the roughneck. He was a skinny five and a half feet and wore steel-rimmed glasses above a sharp nose and pointed chin. Rebus looked at the other men in the canteen and tried to equate them with the picture of the oil 'bear', face blackened with crude, biceps expanding as he fought to contain a gusher. Eric saw him looking.

'The three over there,' meaning the checked shirts, 'work in the Control Room. Nearly everything these days is computerised: logic circuits, computer monitoring . . . You should ask for a look round, it's like NASA or something, and it only takes three or four people to work the whole system. We've come a long way from "Texas Tea".'

'We saw some protesters in a boat,' Lumsden said, scooping sugar into his mug.

'They're off their noggins. These are dangerous waters for a craft that size. Plus they circle too close, all it'd take is a gust to blow them into the platform.'

Rebus turned to Lumsden. 'You're the Grampian Police presence here, maybe you should do something.'

Lumsden snorted and turned to Eric. 'They haven't done anything illegal yet, have they?'

'All they're breaking so far are the unwritten maritime rules. When you've finished your tea, you'll want to see Willie Ford, is that right?'

'Right,' Rebus said.

'I told him we'd meet him in the recky room.'

'I'd like to see Allan Mitchison's room, too.'

Eric nodded. 'Willie's room: the cabins here are twin berths.'

'Tell me,' Rebus said, 'the decommissioning – any idea what T-Bird are going to do with the platform?'

'Might still end up sinking it.'

'After the trouble with Brent Spar?'

Eric shrugged. 'The accountants are in favour. They only need two things: the government on their side, and a good public relations campaign. The latter's already well under way.'

'With Hayden Fletcher in charge?' Rebus guessed.

'That's the man.' Eric picked up his hard hat. 'All finished?'

Rebus drained his mug. 'Lead the way.'

Outside, it was now 'blustery' – Eric's description. Rebus held on to a rail as he walked. Some workers were leaning over the side of the platform. Beyond them, Rebus could see a huge spume of water. He went up to the rail. The support ship was sending jets of water in the direction of the protest boat.

'Trying to scare them off,' Eric explained. 'Keep them from getting too close to the legs.'

Christ, thought Rebus, why today? He could just see the protest boat ramming the platform, forcing an evacuation . . . The jets continued their work, all four of them. Someone passed him a pair of binoculars and he trained them on the protest vessel. Orange oilskins – half a dozen figures on the deck. Banners tied to the rails. NO DUMPING. SAVE OUR OCEANS.

'That boat doesn't look too healthy to me,' someone said.

Figures were going below, reappearing, waving their arms as they explained something.

'Stupid buggers, they've probably let the engine flood.'

'She can't be left to drift.'

'Could be a Trojan horse, lads.'

They all laughed at that. Eric moved off, Rebus and Lumsden following. They climbed up and down ladders. At certain points, Rebus could see clear through the latticework of steel flooring to the churning sea below. There were cables and pipes everywhere, but nowhere you could trip over them. Eventually, Eric opened a door and led them down a corridor. It was a relief to be out of the wind; Rebus realised they'd been outdoors for all of eight minutes.

They passed rooms with pool tables in them, and table-tennis tables, dart boards, video games. The video games seemed popular. Nobody was playing table-tennis.

'Some platforms have swimming pools,' Eric said, 'but not us.'

'Is it my imagination,' Rebus asked, 'or did I just feel the floor move?'

'Oh aye,' Eric said, 'there's a bit of give, has to be. In a swell, you'd swear she was going to break free.' And he laughed again. They kept walking along the corridor, passing a library – no one in it – and a TV room.

'We've three TV rooms,' Eric explained. 'Satellite telly only, but mostly the lads prefer videos. Willie should be in here.'

They entered a large room with a couple of dozen stiff-backed chairs and a large-screen TV. There were no windows, and the lights had been dimmed. Eight or nine men sat, arms folded, in front of the screen. They were complaining about something. A man was standing at the video recorder, holding a tape in his hand, turning it over. He shrugged.

'Sorry about this,' he said.

'That's Willie,' Eric said.

Willie Ford was in his early forties, well built but slightly hunched, with a regulation number one haircut: down to the wood. His nose covered a quarter of his face, a beard protected most of the rest. With more of a tan, he might have passed for a Muslim Fundamentalist. Rebus walked up to him.

'Are you the policeman?' Willie Ford asked. Rebus nodded.

'The natives look restless.'

'It's this video. It was supposed to be *Black Rain*, you know, Michael Douglas. But instead it's some Jap flick with the same name, all about Hiroshima. Close but no cigar.' He turned to the audience. 'Some you win, guys. You'll have to settle for something else.' Then shrugged and moved away, Rebus following. The four of them went back along the corridor and into the library.

'So you're in charge of entertainment, Mr Ford?'

'No, I just like videos. There's a place in Aberdeen does fortnight rentals. I usually bring some out with me.' He was still holding the video. 'I can't believe this. The last foreign language film that lot watched was probably *Emmanuelle*.'

'You get porn films?' Rebus asked, like he was just making conversation.

'Dozens of them.'

'How strong?'

'It varies.' An amused look. 'Inspector, did you fly out here to ask me about dirty videos?'

'No, sir, I came to ask you about Allan Mitchison.'

Ford's face clouded like the sky outside. Lumsden was watching from the window, maybe wondering if they'd have to stay the night . . .

'Poor Mitch,' Ford said. 'I still can't believe it.'

'You shared a room?'

'These past six months.'

'Mr Ford, we don't have too much time, so you'll forgive me if I'm blunt.' Rebus paused to let him digest this. His mind was half on Lumsden. 'Mitch was killed by a man called Anthony Kane, a thug for hire. Kane used to work for a Glasgow ganglord, but recently he's apparently been operating freelance out of Aberdeen. The night before last, Mr Kane turned up dead, too. Do you know *why* Kane would kill Mitch?'

Ford looked stunned, blinked a few times and let his jaw drop open. Eric was looking disbelieving, too, while Lumsden affected a look of merely professional interest. Finally Ford was able to speak.

'I've . . . I've no idea,' he said. 'Could it be a mistake?'

Rebus shrugged. 'It could be anything. That's why I'm trying to compose a picture of Mitch's life. For that, I need his friends' help. Will you help me?'

Ford nodded. Rebus sat down on a chair. 'Then you can start,' he said, 'by telling me about him, tell me anything and everything you can.'

At some point, Eric and Lumsden wandered off for lunch. Lumsden brought sandwiches back for Rebus and Willie Ford. Ford talked, pausing only to take drinks of water. He told Rebus what Allan Mitchison had told him of his background – the parents who weren't his real parents; the

special school with its dorms. That was why Mitch liked the rigs – the sense of fellowship, and the shared accommodation. Rebus began to see why his flat in Edinburgh had remained unloved. Ford knew a lot about Mitch, knew that his hobbies included hill-walking and ecology.

'Is that how he came to be friends with Jake Harley?'

'Is he the one at Sullom Voe?' Rebus nodded. Ford nodded with him. 'Yes, Mitch told me about him. They were both keen on ecology.'

Rebus thought of the demo boat outside . . . thought of Allan Mitchison working in an industry that was a target for Green protest.

'How involved was he?'

'He was pretty active. I mean, the work schedule here, you can't be active all the time. Sixteen days out of every month, he was offshore. We get TV news, but not much in the way of newspapers – not the kind Mitch liked to read. But that didn't stop him organising that concert. Poor sod was looking forward to it.'

Rebus frowned. 'What concert?'

'In Duthie Park. Tonight, I think, if the weather holds.'

'The protest concert?' Ford nodded. 'Allan Mitchison *organised* it?'

'Well, he did his bit. Contacted a couple of the bands to see if they'd play.'

Rebus's head birled. The Dancing Pigs were playing that gig. Mitchison was a big fan of theirs. Yet he hadn't had a ticket for their Edinburgh gig . . . No, because he hadn't needed one – *he would be on the guest list*! Which meant what exactly?

Answer: bugger all.

Except that Michelle Strachan had been murdered in Duthie Park . . .

'Mr Ford, weren't Mitch's employers worried about his . . . loyalty?'

'You don't *have* to be in favour of raping the world to get a job in this industry. In fact, as industries go it's a lot cleaner than some.'

Rebus mulled this over. 'Mr Ford, can I take a look at your cabin?'

'Sure.'

The cabin was small. You wouldn't want to suffer claustrophobia of a night. There were two narrow single beds. Above Ford's bed were pinned pictures; nothing above the other bed but holes where the drawing-pins had been.

'I packed away all his stuff,' Ford explained. 'Do you know if there's anyone . . . ?'

'There's no one.'

'Oxfam then, maybe.'

'Whatever you like, Mr Ford. Let's call you the unofficial executor.'

That did it. Ford slumped on his bed, head in hands. 'Oh Jesus,' he said, rocking. 'Jesus, Jesus.'

Tactful, John. The silver-tongued clarion of bad news. With tears in his eyes, Ford excused himself and left the room.

Rebus got to work.

He opened drawers and the small built-in wardrobe, but eventually found what he wanted beneath Mitchison's bed. A binbag and a series of carrier bags: the deceased's worldly goods.

They didn't amount to much. Maybe Mitchison's background had something to do with it. If you didn't burden yourself with stuff, you could

high-tail it out of anywhere, any time. There were some clothes, some books – sci-fi, political economics, *The Dancing Wu-Li Masters*. The last one sounded to Rebus like a ballroom competition. He found a couple of envelopes of photographs, went through them. The platform. Workmates. The budgie and its crew. Other groups, onshore this time: trees in the background. Only these didn't look like workmates – long hair, tie-dye T-shirts, reggae hats. Friends? Friends of the Earth? The second packet seemed light. Rebus counted the photos: fourteen. Then he pulled out the negatives: a count of twenty-five. Eleven short. He held the negs up to the light, but couldn't make out much. The missing photos seemed more of the same; group portraits, a couple of them with only three or four figures. Rebus put the negs in his pocket, just as Willie Ford came back into the room.

'Sorry about that.'

'My fault, Mr Ford. I spoke without thinking. You know earlier I asked you about porn?'

'Yes.'

'What about drugs?'

'I don't use them.'

'But if you did . . .'

'It's a closed circle, Inspector. I don't use, and no one's offered me any. As far as I'm concerned, people could be shooting up round the corner and I'd never know, because I'm not in the loop.'

'But there is a loop?'

Ford smiled. 'Maybe. But on R&R time only. I'd *know* if I was working beside someone who was wired. They know better than to do that. Working on a platform, you need all the wits you've got and any you can borrow.'

'Have there been accidents?'

'One or two, but our safety record's good. They weren't drug-related.'

Rebus looked thoughtful. Ford seemed to remember something.

'You should see what's happening outside.'

'What?'

'They're bringing the protesters aboard.'

So they were. Rebus and Ford went out to take a look. Ford donned his hard hat, but Rebus carried his: he couldn't get it to sit right, and the only thing threatening to fall from the skies was rain. Lumsden and Eric were already there, along with a few other men. They watched the bedraggled figures climb the last few steps. Despite their oilskins, they looked soaked – courtesy of the power hoses. Rebus recognised one of them: it was braid-hair again. She looked glum verging on furious. He moved towards her, until she was looking at him.

'We must stop meeting like this,' he said.

But she wasn't paying him any attention. Instead, she yelled 'NOW!' and snaked to her right, bringing her hand out of her pocket. She already had one half of the handcuffs clamped around her wrist, and now attached the other firmly around the top rail. Two of her companions did likewise, and started yelling protests at the tops of their voices. Two others were hauled back before they could complete the process. The cuffs were snapped shut on themselves.

'Who's got the keys?' an oil-worker was yelling.

'We left them on the mainland!'

'Christ.' The oilman turned to a colleague. 'Go fetch the oxy-acetylene.' He turned to braid-hair. 'Don't worry, the sparks may burn, but we'll have you out of there in a jiffy.'

She ignored him, kept on chanting with the others. Rebus smiled: you had to admire it. Trojan horse with knobs on.

The torch arrived. Rebus couldn't believe they were really going to do it. He turned to Lumsden.

'Don't say a word,' the policeman warned. 'Remember what I said about frontier justice. We're well out of it.'

The torch was lit, a little flare of its own. There was a helicopter overhead. Rebus had half a mind – maybe more than half – to throw the torch over the side.

'Christ, it's the telly!'

They all looked up. The helicopter was hovering low, a video camera pointed straight at them.

'Fucking TV news.'

Oh great, Rebus thought. That's just spot on. Really low-key, John. National television news. Maybe he should just send Ancram a post-card . . .

19

Back in Aberdeen, he thought he could still feel the deck moving beneath him. Lumsden had headed off home, carrying with him a promise from Rebus that he'd be packed and off the following morning.

Rebus hadn't mentioned he might be back.

It was early evening, cool but bright, the streets busy with last shoppers trudging home and Saturday night revellers starting early. He walked down to Burke's Club. A different bouncer again, so no grief there. Rebus paid his money like a good boy, waded through the music until he reached the bar. The place hadn't been open long, only a few punters in, looking like they'd be moving on if things didn't start happening. Rebus bought an overpriced short loaded with ice, gave the place a once-over in the mirror. No sign of Eve and Stanley. No sign of any obvious dealers. But Willie Ford was right about that: what did dealers look like? Leave aside the junkies and they looked much like anyone else. Their trade was in eye contact, in a shared knowledge with the person whose eyes they were meeting. A cross between a transaction and a chat-up.

Rebus imagined Michelle Strachan dancing in here, beginning the last movements of her life. As he sloshed the ice around his glass, he decided to walk a route from the club to Duthie Park. It might not be the route *she* took, and he doubted it would throw up anything like a clue, but he wanted to do it, same as he'd driven down to Leith to pay his respects to Angie Riddell's patch. He started off down South College Street, saw from his map that if he kept to this route he'd be walking a main thoroughfare alongside the Dee. Lots of traffic: he decided Michelle would have cut through Ferryhill, so did likewise. Here the streets were narrower and quieter; big houses, leafy. A comfortable middle-class enclave. A couple of corner shops were still doing business – milk, ice-lollies, evening papers. He could hear children playing in back gardens. Michelle and Johnny Bible had walked down here at two a.m. It would have been deserted. If they'd been making any noise, it would have been noted behind the net curtains. But no one had reported anything. Michelle couldn't have been drunk. Drunk, her student friends said, she got loud. Maybe she was a bit merry; just enough to have lost her survival instinct. And Johnny Bible . . . he'd been quiet, sober, his smile failing to betray his thoughts.

Rebus turned on to Polmuir Road. Michelle's digs were halfway down. But Johnny Bible had persuaded her to keep walking down to the park. How had he managed it? Rebus shook his head, trying to clear it of jumble.

Maybe her digs were strict, she couldn't invite him in. She liked it there, didn't want to be kicked out for an infraction of the rules. Or maybe Johnny had commented on the nice mild night, how he didn't want it to end, he liked her so much. Couldn't they just walk down to the park and back? Maybe walk through the park, just the two of them. Wouldn't that be perfect?

Did Johnny Bible *know* Duthie Park?

Rebus could hear something approximating music, then silence, then applause. Yes: the protest concert. The Dancing Pigs and friends. Rebus went into the park, passed a children's play area. Michelle and her beau had come this way. Her body had been found near here, not far from the Winter Gardens and the tea-room . . . There was a huge open space at the heart of the park, and a stage had been erected. Several hundred kids comprised the audience. Bootleggers had spread out their merchandise on the grass, alongside tarot readers, hairbraiders, and herbalists. Rebus forced a smile: it was the Ingliston concert in miniature. People were passing through the crowd, rattling collecting tins. The banner which had adorned the roof of the Conference Centre – DON'T KILL OUR OCEANS! – was now flapping atop the stage. Even the inflatable whale was there. A girl in her mid-teens approached Rebus.

'Souvenir T-shirts? Programmes?'

Rebus shook his head, then changed his mind. 'Give me a programme.'

'Three pounds.'

It was a stapled Xerox with a colour cover. The paper was recycled, and so was the text. Rebus flicked through it. Right at the back there was a list of Thank Yous. His eye caught a name a third of the way down: Mitch, 'with love and gratitude'. Allan Mitchison had played his part organising the gig, and here was his reward – and memorial.

'I'll see if I can do better,' Rebus said, rolling the programme into his pocket.

He made for the area behind the stage, which had been cordoned off by means of arranging lorries and vans into a semi-circle, inside which the bands and their entourages moved like zoo exhibits. His warrant card got him where he wanted to be, as well as a few dirty looks.

'You in charge?' he asked the overweight man in front of him. The man was in his fifties, Jerry Garcia with red hair and a kilt, sweat showing through a stained white vest. Beads of perspiration dripped from his overhanging brow.

'Nobody's in charge,' he told Rebus.

'But you helped organise—'

'Look, what's your problem, man? The concert's licensed, the last thing we need is grief.'

'I'm not giving any. I just have a question about the organisation.'

'What about it?'

'Allan Mitchison – Mitch.'

'Yes?'

'Did you know him?'

'No.'

'I hear he was responsible for getting the Dancing Pigs to play.'

The man thought about it, nodded. 'Mitch, right. I don't know him, I mean, I've seen him around.'

'Anyone I could ask about him?'

'Why, man, what's he done?'

'He's dead.'

'Bad number.' He shrugged. 'Wish I could help.'

Rebus made his way back to front-of-stage. The sound system was the usual travesty, and the band didn't sound nearly as good as on their studio album. Notch one up for the producer. The music stopped suddenly, the momentary silence sweeter than any tune. The singer stepped up to the mike.

'We've got some friends we'd like to bring on. A few hours back they were fighting the good fight, trying to save our seas. Put your hands together for them.'

Applause, cheering. Rebus watched two figures walk onstage, still dressed in orange oilskins: he recognised their faces from Bannock. He waited, but there was no sign of braid-hair. When they started their speeches, he turned to go. There was one last collecting tin to be avoided, but he thought better of it, folded a fiver in through the slot. And decided to treat himself to dinner in his hotel: putting it on the room, of course.

Insistent noise.

Rebus folded it into his dream, then gave up. One eye open: chinks of light through the heavy curtains. What fucking time was it? Bedside lamp: on. He clawed at his watch, blinked. Six a.m. What? Did Lumsden want rid of him *that* badly?

He swung out of bed, walked stiff-legged to the door, working his muscles. He'd washed a great dinner down with a bottle of wine. In itself the wine would have posed no problem, but as a *digestif* he'd put away four malts, in flagrant disregard of the drinker's rule: never mix the grape and the grain.

Thump, thump, thump.

Rebus pulled open the door. Two woolly suits stood there, looking like they'd been up for hours.

'Inspector Rebus?'

'Last time I looked.'

'Will you get dressed, please, sir?'

'You don't like the outfit?' Y-fronts and a T-shirt.

'Just get dressed.'

Rebus looked at them, decided to comply. When he walked back into the room, they followed, looked around the way cops always do.

'What have I done?'

'Tell them at the station.'

Rebus looked at him. 'Tell me you're fucking joking.'

'Language, sir,' the other uniform said.

Rebus sat on the bed, pulled on clean socks. 'I'd still like to know what this is all about. You know, on the q.t., officer to officer.'

'Just a few questions, sir. Quick as you can.'

The second uniform tugged open the curtains, light stabbing Rebus's eyeballs. He seemed impressed by the view.

'We had a brawl in the gardens a few nights ago. Remember, Bill?'

His colleague joined him at the window. 'And someone jumped off the bridge a fortnight back. Whee, smack on to Denburn Road.'

'Woman in the car got an awful fright.'

They smiled at the memory.

Rebus stood up, looked around him, wondering what to take.

'Shouldn't be too long, sir.'

They were smiling at *him* now. Rebus's stomach did a back-flip. He tried not to think about timbale of haggis . . . cranachan with a fruit coulis . . . wine and whisky . . .

'Feeling a bit rough, sir?'

The uniform looked about as solicitous as a razor blade.

20

'My name's Chief Inspector Edward Grogan. We've a few questions for you, Inspector Rebus.'

So everyone keeps telling me, Rebus thought. But he didn't say anything, just sat there with arms folded and a wronged man's smouldering look. Ted Grogan: Rebus had heard of him. Hard bastard. He looked it, too: bull-necked and bald, his physique more Frazier than Ali. Thin eyes and thick lips; a street-taught fighter. Jutting forehead; simian.

'You already know DS Lumsden.' Sitting over by the door, head bowed, legs apart. He looked exhausted, embarrassed. Grogan sat down opposite Rebus at the table. They were in a biscuit-tin, though they probably had another name for it in Furry Boot Town.

'No point beating around the bush,' Grogan said. He looked about as comfortable on the chair as a prize Aberdeen Angus. 'How did you get the bruises?'

'I told Lumsden.'

'Tell me.'

'I was mugged by a couple of message-boys. Their message was a pistol-whipping.'

'Any other scars?'

'They pushed me over a wall, I hit a thorn-bush on the way down. My side's scratched.'

'Is that it?'

'That's it. Look, I appreciate your concern, but—'

'But that's not our concern, Inspector. DS Lumsden says he dropped you off down by the docks, night before last.'

'That's right.'

'I believe he offered you a lift to your hotel.'

'Probably.'

'But you didn't want that.'

Rebus looked over at Lumsden. *What the fuck is going on?* But Lumsden's gaze was still concentrated floorwards. 'I felt like a walk.'

'Back to your hotel?'

'Right.'

'And on the way, you were beaten up?'

'With a pistol.'

A smile, mixing sympathy with disbelief. 'In Aberdeen, Inspector?'

'There's more than one Aberdeen. I don't see what this has to do with anything.'

'Bear with me. So you walked home?'

'To the very expensive hotel Grampian Police provided for me.'

'Ah, the hotel. We'd pre-booked for a visiting Chief Constable, only he cancelled at the last minute. We'd have ended up paying anyway. I believe DS Lumsden used his initiative and decided you might as well stay there. Highland courtesy, Inspector.'

Highland fabrication more like.

'If that's your story.'

'It's not *my* story that's important here. On this walk home of yours, did you see anyone, speak to anyone?'

'No.' Rebus paused. 'I saw a crew of your finest in discussion with a couple of teenagers.'

'You spoke to them?'

Rebus shook his head. 'Didn't want to interfere. This isn't my patch.'

'From what DS Lumsden tells me, you've been acting like it was.'

Rebus caught Lumsden's eyes. They stared right through him.

'Did a doctor look at your injuries?'

'I fixed myself up. Hotel reception had a first aid kit.'

'They asked you if you wanted a doctor.' A statement.

'I said it wasn't necessary. Lowland self-reliance.'

A cool smile from Grogan. 'You spent yesterday on an oil rig, I believe.'

'With DS Lumsden at my heels.'

'And last night?'

'I had a drink, went for a walk, ate dinner at the hotel. I put it on the tab, by the way.'

'Where did you drink?'

'Burke's Club, a dope-dealer's paradise on College Street. My bet is, my attackers started life there. What's the going rate up here for hiring hardmen? Fifty for a duffing? Seventy-five per broken limb?'

Grogan sniffed, rose to his feet. 'Those prices might be a wee bit on the high side.'

'Look, with respect, I'm about two hours from out of here. If this is some kind of warning, it's too much too late.'

Grogan spoke very quietly. 'It's not a warning, Inspector.'

'What is it then?'

'You say when you left Burke's you went for a walk?'

'Yes.'

'Where?'

'Duthie Park.'

'A fair hike.'

'I'm a big Dancing Pigs fan.'

'Dancing Pigs?'

'A band, sir,' Lumsden said, 'they were playing a concert last night.'

'It talks.'

'No need for that, Inspector.' Grogan was standing behind Rebus. The invisible interrogator: did you turn to face him, or did you stare at the wall? Rebus had played the trick himself many a time. Objective: unnerve the prisoner.

Prisoner – Jesus.

'You'll remember, sir,' Lumsden said, voice almost atonal, 'that's the route Michelle Strachan took.'

'That's true, isn't it, Inspector? I expect you knew that.'

'How do you mean?'

'Well, you've been taking a great interest in the Johnny Bible case, haven't you?'

'I've been involved tangentially, sir.'

'Oh, tangentially?' Grogan came back into view, showing yellow teeth that looked like they'd been filed short. 'Well, that's one way of putting it. DS Lumsden says you seemed very interested in the Aberdeen side of the case, kept asking him questions.'

'With respect, that's DS Lumsden's interpretation.'

'And what's yours?' Leaning over the desk, fists resting on it. Getting in close. Objective: cow the suspect, show him who's boss.

'Mind if I smoke?'

'Answer the question!'

'*Stop treating me like a fucking suspect!*'

Rebus regretted the outburst immediately – sign of weakness, sign he was rattled. In army training, he'd survived days on end of interrogation techniques. Yes, but back then his head had been emptier; there'd been less to feel guilty about.

'But, Inspector,' Grogan sounding hurt by the flare-up, 'that's precisely what you are.'

Rebus grabbed at the edge of the table, feeling its rough metal edge. He tried to stand, but his legs failed him. He probably looked like he was crapping himself, forced his hands to release the table.

'Yesterday evening,' Grogan said coolly, 'a woman's body was found in a crate on the dockside. Pathologist reckons she was killed sometime the previous night. Strangled. Raped. One of her shoes is missing.'

Rebus was shaking his head. Sweet Jesus, he was thinking, not another one.

'There's no sign that she fought back, no skin beneath the fingernails, but she could have lashed out with her fists. She had the look of a strong woman, tenacious.'

Involuntarily, Rebus touched the bruise on his temple.

'You were down near the docks, Inspector, and in a foul mood according to DS Lumsden.'

Rebus was on his feet. 'He's trying to stitch me up!' Attack, they said, was the best form of defence. Not necessarily true, but if Lumsden wanted to play dirty, Rebus would give as good as he got.

'Sit down, Inspector.'

'He's trying to protect his fucking clients! How much do you take a week, Lumsden? How much do they slip you?'

'*I said sit down!*'

'Sod you,' said Rebus. It was like a boil had burst; he couldn't halt the outpour. 'You're trying to tell me I'm Johnny Bible! I'm nearer Bible John's age, for Christ's sake.'

'You were at the docks around the time she was murdered. You arrived back at your hotel cut and bruised, your clothes a mess.'

'This is bullshit! I don't have to listen to this!'

'Yes you do.'

'Charge me then.'

'We've a few more questions, Inspector. This can be as painless as you like, or it can be absolute bastarding agony. You choose, but before you do that – *sit down!*'

Rebus stood there. His mouth was open, and he wiped saliva from his chin. He looked over at Lumsden, who was still seated, albeit tensed, ready to jump if words became deeds. Rebus wouldn't give him the satisfaction. He sat down.

Grogan took a deep breath. The air in the room – what was left of it – was beginning to smell bad. It wasn't even half past seven.

'Bovril and oranges at half time?' Rebus asked.

'That might be a long way off.' Grogan walked to the door, opened it and stuck his head out. Then he held the door wide open so someone outside could come in.

Chief Inspector Chick Ancram.

'Saw you on the news, John. Not exactly telegenic, are you?' Ancram slipped off his jacket and placed it carefully over the back of a chair. He looked like he was about to enjoy himself. 'You weren't wearing your hard hat, mightn't have recognised you otherwise.' Grogan walked over to where Lumsden was sitting, like a tag-team wrestler leaving the ring. Ancram started rolling up his sleeves.

'Going to be a hot one, John, eh?'

'A scorcher,' Rebus muttered. Now he knew why CID liked dawn raids: he felt exhausted already. Exhaustion played tricks with your mind; it made you make mistakes. 'Any chance of a coffee?'

Ancram looked to Grogan. 'I don't see why not. How about you, Ted?'

'I could do with a cup myself.' He turned to Lumsden. 'On you go, son.'

'Fucking message-boy,' Rebus couldn't help saying.

Lumsden sprang to his feet, but Grogan had a restraining hand out.

'Easy, son, just go get those coffees, eh?'

'And DS Lumsden?' Ancram called. 'Make sure Inspector Rebus gets decaf, we don't want him getting all jumpy.'

'Any jumpier and I'd be a kangaroo. Lumsden? I like hundred per cent decaf, no pissing or howking into it, OK?'

Lumsden left the room in silence.

'Now then.' Ancram sat down across from Rebus. 'You're a hard man to catch.'

'You've gone to a lot of trouble.'

'I think you're worth it, don't you? Tell me something about Johnny Bible.'

'Like what?'

'Anything. His methods, background, profile.'

'That could take all day.'

'We've got all day.'

'Maybe you have, but my room's got to be vacated by eleven, or else it's another day's rate.'

'Your room's already empty,' Grogan said. 'Your stuff's in my office.'

'Inadmissible as evidence: you should have had a search warrant.'

Ancram shared a laugh with Grogan. Rebus knew why they were laughing, he'd've been doing it too if he'd been where they were. But he

wasn't. He was where a lot of men and women, some of them barely adult, had been before him. Same chair, same sweaty room, same set-up. Hundreds and thousands of them, suspects. In the eyes of the law, innocent until proven guilty. In the eyes of the interrogator, the other way round. Sometimes to prove to yourself that a suspect was innocent you had to break them. Sometimes you had to go that far before you were sure in your mind. Rebus didn't know how many sessions like this he'd sat in on . . . hundreds, certainly. He'd broken maybe a dozen suspects only to find they were innocent. He knew where he was, knew why he was there, but that didn't make it any easier.

'I'll tell *you* something about Johnny Bible,' Ancram said. 'His profile can fit several professions, and one of those is serving or retired police officer, someone who knows our methods and is careful not to leave trace evidence.'

'We've a physical description of him. I'm too old.'

Ancram screwed up his face. 'IDs, John, we all know their failings.'

'I'm not Johnny Bible.'

'Doesn't mean you're not a copycat. Mind, we're not saying you are. All we're saying is, there are questions that have to be asked.'

'So ask them.'

'You came to Partick.'

'Correct.'

'Ostensibly to talk to me about Uncle Joe Toal.'

'Uncannily astute.'

'Yet if memory serves, you ended up asking me a lot of questions about Johnny Bible. And you seemed to know a lot about the Bible John case.' Ancram waited to see if Rebus had a smart comeback. None came. 'While in Partick, you spent a lot of time in the room where the original Bible John files were being checked.' Ancram paused again. 'And now a TV reporter tells me you have cuttings and notes about Bible John and Johnny Bible stashed in your kitchen cupboards.'

Bitch!

'Now wait a minute,' Rebus said.

Ancram sat back. 'I'm waiting.'

'Everything you've said is true. I *am* interested in the two cases. Bible John . . . that takes a bit of explaining. And Johnny Bible . . . well, for one thing, I knew one of the victims.'

Ancram sat forward. 'Which one?'

'Angie Riddell.'

'In Edinburgh?' Ancram and Grogan exchanged a look. Rebus knew what they were thinking: another connection.

'I was part of the team that picked her up once. I saw her again after that.'

'Saw her?'

'Drove down to Leith, passed the time of day.'

Grogan snorted. 'There's a euphemism I've not heard before.'

'We talked, that's all. I bought her a cup of tea and a bridie.'

'And you didn't tell anyone? Do you know how that looks?'

'Another black mark against me. I've got so many, I could play Al Jolson on stage.'

Ancram got up. He wanted to pace the room, but it wasn't big enough. 'This is bad,' he said.

'How can the truth be bad?' But Rebus knew Ancram was right. He didn't want to agree with Ancram about *anything* – that would be to fall into the interrogator's trap: empathy – but he couldn't make himself disagree on this one point. This *was* bad. His life was turning into a Kinks song: 'Dead End Street'.

'You're up to your oxters, pal,' Ancram said.

'Thanks for reminding me.'

Grogan lit a cigarette for himself, offered one to Rebus, who refused the ploy with a smile. He had his own if he wanted one.

He wanted one – but not enough yet. Instead, he scratched at his palms, clawing his nails across them, a wake-up call to his nerve-endings. There was silence in the room for a minute or so. Ancram rested his backside against the table.

'Christ, is he waiting for the coffee beans to grow or what?'

Grogan shrugged. 'Shift changeover, the canteen'll be busy.'

'You just can't get the staff these days,' Rebus said. Head down, Ancram smiled into his chest. Then he gave a sideways look at the seated figure.

Here we go, thought Rebus: the sympathy routine. Maybe Ancram read his mind, changed his own accordingly.

'Let's talk a bit more about Bible John,' he said.

'Fine with me.'

'I've started on the Spaven case-notes.'

'Oh aye?' Had he got to Brian Holmes?

'Fascinating reading.'

'We had a few publishers interested at the time.'

No smile for that one. 'I didn't know,' the inquisitor said quietly, 'that Lawson Geddes worked on Bible John.'

'No?'

'Or that he was kicked off the inquiry. Any idea why that was?'

Rebus didn't say anything. Ancram spotted the flaw in the armour, stood up and leaned over him.

'You didn't know?'

'I knew he'd worked the case.'

'But you didn't know he'd been ordered off it. No, because he didn't tell you. I found that particular nugget in the Bible John files. But no mention of why.'

'Is this going anywhere other than up the garden path?'

'Did he talk to you about Bible John?'

'Maybe once or twice. He talked a lot about his old cases.'

'I'm sure he did, the two of you were close. And from what I hear, Geddes liked to shoot his mouth off.'

Rebus glared at him. 'He was a good copper.'

'Was he?'

'Believe it.'

'But even good coppers make mistakes, John. Even good coppers can cross the line *once* in their lives. Little birdies tell me you've crossed that line more than a few times yourself.'

'Little birdies shouldn't shit in their own nests.'

Ancram shook his head. 'Your past conduct isn't an issue here.' He straightened up and turned away, letting that remark sink in. He still had his back to Rebus when he spoke. 'You know something? This media interest in the Spaven case, it coincided with the first Johnny Bible killing. Know what that might make people think?' Now he turned round, held up a finger. 'A copper obsessed with Bible John, remembering stories his old sparring partner told him about the case.' Second finger. 'The dirt on the Spaven case is about to be uncovered, years after said copper thought it was buried.' Third finger. 'Copper snaps. There's been this time bomb in his brain, and now it's activated . . .'

Rebus got to his feet. 'You know it's not true,' he said quietly.

'Convince me.'

'I'm not sure I need to.'

Ancram looked disappointed in him. 'We'll want to take samples – saliva, blood, prints.'

'What for? Johnny Bible hasn't left any clues.'

'I also want a forensic lab to look at your clothes, and a team to give your flat the once-over. If you haven't done anything, there should be nothing to object to.' He waited for a reply, got none. The door opened. 'About fucking time,' he said.

Lumsden bearing a tray swimming with spilled coffee.

Break-time. Ancram and Grogan went into the corridor for a chat. Lumsden stood by the door, arms folded, thinking he was on guard duty, thinking Rebus wasn't pumped-up enough to rip his head off.

But Rebus just sat there drinking what was left of his coffee. It tasted disgusting, so probably *was* unleaded. He took out his cigarettes, lit one, inhaled like it might be his last. He held the cigarette vertical, wondered how something so small and brittle could have taken such a hold over him. Not so very different from this case . . . The cigarette wavered: his hands were shaking.

'This is you,' he told Lumsden. 'You've sold your boss a story. I can live with that, but don't think I'll forget.'

Lumsden stared at him. 'Do I look scared?'

Rebus stared back, smoked his cigarette, said nothing. Ancram and Grogan came back into the room, all businesslike.

'John,' Ancram said, 'CI Grogan and I have decided this would be best dealt with in Edinburgh.'

Meaning they couldn't prove a thing against him. If there was the slightest possibility, then Grogan would want a home collar.

'There are disciplinary matters here,' Ancram went on. 'But they can be dealt with as part of my inquiry into the Spaven case.' He paused. 'Shame about DS Holmes.'

Rebus went for it, had to. 'What about him?'

'When we went to pick up the Spaven case-notes, some clerk told us there'd been a lot of interest in them recently. Holmes had consulted them three days in a row, apparently for hours at a time – when he should have been on regular duties.' Another pause. 'Your name was down, too. Apparently you visited him. Going to tell me what he was up to?'

Silence.

'Removing evidence?'

'Fuck off.'

'That's the way it looks. Stupid move, whatever it was. He's refusing to talk, facing disciplinary action. He could be out on his ear.'

Rebus kept his face a blank; not so easy to blank his heart.

'Come on,' Ancram said, 'let's get you out of here. My driver can take your car, we'll take mine, maybe have a wee chat on the road.'

Rebus stood up, walked over to Grogan, who straightened his shoulders as if expecting physical assault. Lumsden clenched his fists, ready. Rebus stopped with his face inches from Grogan's.

'Are you on the take, sir?' It was fun to watch the balloon fill with blood, highlighting burst veins and ageing lines.

'John . . .' Ancram warned.

'It's an honest question,' Rebus went on. 'See, if you're not, you could do a lot worse than put a surveillance on two Glasgow hoods who seem to be holidaying up here – Eve and Stanley Toal, only his real name's Malky. His dad's called Joseph Toal, Uncle Joe, and he runs Glasgow, where CI Ancram works, lives, splashes out money and buys his suits. Eve and Stanley drink at Burke's Club, where coke isn't something in a long glass with ice. DS Lumsden took me there, looked like he'd been before. DS Lumsden reminded me that Johnny Bible had picked out his first victim there. DS Lumsden drove me down to the harbour that night, I didn't *ask* to be taken there.' Rebus looked over at Lumsden. 'He's a canny operator, DS Lumsden. The games he plays, no wonder he's called Ludo.'

'I won't have malicious comments made about my men.'

'Surveillance on Eve and Stanley,' Rebus stressed. 'And if it's blown, you know where to look.' Same place he was looking now.

Lumsden flew at him, hands at his throat. Rebus threw him off.

'You're as dirty as bilge-water, Lumsden, and don't think I don't know it!'

Lumsden swung a punch; it didn't connect. Ancram and Grogan pulled the two of them apart. Grogan pointed to Rebus, but spoke to Ancram.

'Maybe we'd better keep him here after all.'

'I'm taking him back with me.'

'I'm not so sure about that.'

'I said I'm taking him back, Ted.'

'Long time since I had two men fighting over me,' Rebus said with a smile.

The two Aberdeen officers were looking ready to plough a field with him. Ancram slapped a proprietorial hand on to his shoulder.

'Inspector Rebus,' he said, 'I think we'd best be going, don't you?'

'Do me one favour,' Rebus said.

'What?' They were in the back of Ancram's car, heading for Rebus's hotel, where they'd pick up his car.

'A quick detour down to the docks.'

Ancram glanced at him. 'Why?'

'I want to see where she died.'

Ancram looked at him again. 'What for?'

Rebus shrugged. 'To pay my respects,' he said.

Ancram had only a vague idea where the body had been found, but it didn't take long to find the runs of bright police tape which were there to

secure the scene. The docks were quiet, no sign of the crate in which the body had been discovered. It would be in a police lab somewhere. Rebus kept the right side of the cordon, looked around him. Huge white gulls strutted at a safe distance. The wind was fresh. He couldn't tell how close this was to the spot where Lumsden had dropped him off.

'What do you know about her?' he asked Ancram, who stood, hands in pockets, studying him.

'Name's Holden, I think. Twenty-seven, twenty-eight.'

'Did he take a souvenir?'

'Just one of her shoes. Listen, Rebus . . . all this interest is because you once bought a prostitute a cup of tea?'

'Her name was Angie Riddell.' Rebus paused. 'She had beautiful eyes.' He gazed towards a rusting hulk chained dockside. 'There's a question I've been asking myself. Do we let it happen, or do we make it happen?' He looked at Ancram. 'Any idea?'

Ancram frowned. 'I'm not sure I understand.'

'Me neither,' Rebus admitted. 'Tell your driver to be careful with my car. The steering's a bit loose.'

The Panic of Dreams

21

They were chasing him up and down monkey-puzzle ladders, the tumorous sea raging beneath, buckling weakened metal. Rebus lost his grip, tumbled down steel steps, gashed his side and dabbed a hand there, finding oil instead of blood. They were twenty feet above him and laughing, taking their time: where was there for him to go? Maybe he could fly, flap his arms and leap into space. The only thing to fear was the drop.

Like landing on concrete.

Was that better or worse than landing on spikes? He had decisions to make; his pursuers weren't far behind. They were never far behind, yet he always stayed in front of them, even wounded. I could get out of this, he thought.

I could get out of this!

A voice directly behind him: 'In your dreams.' Then a push out into space.

Rebus started awake so suddenly his head hit the car roof. His body surged with fear and adrenalin.

'Christ,' Ancram said from the driver's seat, regaining control of the steering-wheel, 'what happened?'

'How long was I asleep?'

'I didn't realise you were.'

Rebus looked at his watch: maybe only a couple of minutes. He rubbed his face, told his heart it could stop hammering any time it liked. He could tell Ancram it was a bad dream; he could tell him it was a panic attack. But he didn't want to tell him anything. Until proven otherwise, Ancram was the enemy as surely as any gun-toting thug.

'What were you saying?' he said instead.

'I was outlining the deal.'

'The deal, right.' The Sunday papers had slid from Rebus's lap. He picked them off the floor. Johnny Bible's latest outrage had made only one front page; the others had been printed too early.

'Right now, I've enough against you to have you suspended,' Ancram said. 'Not such an unusual situation for you, Inspector.'

'I've been there before.'

'Even if I overlook the Johnny Bible questions, there's still the matter of your distinct lack of co-operation with my inquiries into the Spaven case.'

'I had flu.'

Ancram ignored this. 'We both know two things. First, a good cop is going to get into trouble from time to time. I've had complaints made against *me*

in the past. Second, these TV programmes almost never uncover new evidence. It's all speculation and maybes, whereas a police investigation is meticulous, and the gen we gather is passed to the Crown Office and pored over by what are supposed to be some of the finest criminal lawyers in the country.'

Rebus turned in his seat to study Ancram, wondering where this was leading. In the mirror, he could see his own car being driven with due care and attention by Ancram's lackey. Ancram kept his eyes on the road.

'See, John, what I'm saying is, why run when you've nothing to fear?'

'Who says I've nothing to fear?'

Ancram smiled. The old pals routine was just that – a routine. Rebus trusted Ancram the way he'd trust a paedophile in a play park. All the same, when Uncle Joe had lied about Tony El, it was Ancram who'd come up with the Aberdeen info . . . Whose side was the man on? Was he playing a double game? Or had he just thought Rebus wouldn't get anywhere, info or no info? Was it a way of covering up that he was in Uncle Joe's pocket?

'If I'm hearing you right,' Rebus said, 'you're saying I've nothing to fear from the Spaven case?'

'This could be true.'

'You'd make it true?' Ancram shrugged. 'In return for what?'

'John, you've ruffled more feathers than a puma in a parrot-house, and you've been about as subtle.'

'You want me to be more subtle?'

Ancram's voice tightened. 'I want you to sit on your arse for once.'

'Drop the Mitchison inquiry?' Ancram didn't say anything. Rebus repeated the question.

'You might find it does you the world of good.'

'And you'd have done Uncle Joe Toal another good turn, eh, Ancram?'

'Wake up to reality. This isn't a linoleum floor, big squares of black and white.'

'No, it's grey silk suits and crisp green cash.'

'It's give and take. People like Uncle Joe don't go away: you get rid of him and a young pretender starts making claims.'

'Better the devil you know?'

'Not a bad motto.'

John Martyn: 'I'd Rather Be the Devil'.

'Here's another,' Rebus said, 'don't rock the boat. Sounds like that's what you're telling me.'

'I'm *advising* you for your own good.'

'Don't think I don't appreciate it.'

'Christ, Rebus, I begin to see why you're always out on a limb: you're not easy to like, are you?'

'Mr Personality six years running.'

'I don't think so.'

'I even cried on the catwalk.' A pause. 'Did you ask Jack Morton about me?'

'Jack has a bizarrely high opinion of you, something I put down to sentiment.'

'Big of you.'

'This is getting us nowhere.'

'No, but it's passing the time.' Rebus saw signs for a service area. 'Are we stopping for lunch?'

Ancram shook his head.

'You know, there's one question you haven't asked me.'

Ancram considered not asking, then caved in. 'What?'

'You haven't asked what Stanley and Eve were doing in Aberdeen.'

Ancram signalled to pull into the service area, braking hard. The driver in Rebus's Saab nearly missed the slip-road, tyres squealing on tarmac.

'Trying to lose him?' Rebus enjoyed seeing Ancram rattled.

'Coffee break,' Ancram snarled, opening his door.

Rebus sat with the tabloid on the table in front of him, reading about Johnny Bible. The victim this time was Vanessa Holden, twenty-seven and married – none of the others had been married. She was director of a company which put on 'corporate presentations': Rebus wasn't entirely sure what that meant. The photo in the paper was the usual smile-for-the-camera job, taken by a friend. She had shoulder-length wavy hair, nice teeth, probably hadn't thought about dying much short of her eightieth birthday.

'We've got to catch this monster,' Rebus said, echoing the last sentence of the story. Then he crumpled the paper and reached for his coffee. Glancing down at the table, he caught a sideways glimpse of Vanessa Holden, and got the feeling he'd seen her before somewhere, just a fleeting glance. He covered her hair with his hand. Old photo; maybe she'd changed hairstyle. He tried to see her face with a few more miles on its clock. Ancram wasn't watching, was talking to the lackey, so he didn't see the shock of recognition hit Rebus's face.

'I have to make a phone call,' Rebus said, rising. The public phone was beside the front door; he'd be in view of the table. Ancram nodded.

'What's the problem?' he said.

'Today's Sunday, I should've been at church. The minister will be worried.'

'This bacon's easier to swallow than that.' Ancram stabbed his fork at the offending article. But he let Rebus go.

Rebus made the call, hoped he'd have enough change: Sunday, cheap rate. Someone at Grampian Police HQ picked up.

'DCI Grogan, please,' Rebus said, his eyes on Ancram. The restaurant was busy with Sunday drivers and their families; no chance of Ancram hearing him.

'I'm afraid he's busy at the moment.'

'This is about Johnny Bible's latest victim. I'm in a phone box and money's tight.'

'Hold on, please.'

Thirty seconds. Ancram watching him, frowning. Then: 'DCI Grogan speaking.'

'It's Rebus.'

Grogan sucked in breath. 'What the hell do you want?'

'I want to do you a favour.'

'Oh aye?'

'It could make your career.'

'Is this your idea of a joke? Because let me tell you—'

'No joke. Did you hear what I said about Eve and Stanley Toal?'

'I heard.'

'Are you going to do anything?'

'Maybe.'

'Make it a definite . . . as a favour to me.'

'And then you'll do me this premier-league favour of yours?'

'That's right.'

Grogan coughed, cleared his throat. 'All right,' he said.

'For real?'

'I keep my promises.'

'Then listen. I've just seen a photo of Johnny's latest victim.'

'And?'

'And I've seen her before.'

A moment's silence. 'Where?'

'She was walking into Burke's Club one night as Lumsden and I were leaving.'

'So?'

'So she was on the arm of someone I knew.'

'You know a lot of people, Inspector.'

'Which doesn't mean I'm connected to Johnny Bible. But maybe the man on her arm is.'

'Do you have a name for him?'

'Hayden Fletcher, works for T-Bird Oil. Public relations.'

Grogan was writing it down. 'I'll look into it,' he said.

'Don't forget your promise.'

'Did I make a promise? I don't recall.' The line went dead. Rebus wanted to hammer the receiver, but Ancram was watching, and besides there were children nearby, drooling over a toy display and devising plans of attack on their parents' pockets. So he replaced the receiver just like any other human being and walked back to the table. The driver got up and went outside, didn't once look at Rebus, so Rebus knew he was under orders.

'Everything OK?' Ancram asked.

'Hunky-dory.' Rebus sat down opposite Ancram. 'So when does the inquisition begin?'

'As soon as we can find a vacant torture chamber.' They both ended up smiling. 'Look, Rebus, personally I don't give a midge's IQ what happened twenty years ago between your pal Geddes and this Lenny Spaven. I've seen villains stitched up before: you can't nail them for the thing you *know* they did, so you nail them for something else, something they didn't do.' He shrugged. 'It happens.'

'There were rumours it happened to Bible John.'

Ancram shook his head. 'I don't think so. But see, here's the crux of the matter. *If* your chum Geddes became obsessed with Spaven, and stitched him up – with your help, wittingly or unwittingly . . . Well, you know what that means?'

Rebus nodded, but couldn't say the words: they'd been choking him for weeks. They'd choked him back then for a few weeks, too.

'It means,' Ancram went on, 'the real killer got away with it. Nobody's ever tried looking for him, he's scot-free.' He smiled at this last phrase,

then sat back in his chair. 'Now I'm going to tell you something about Uncle Joe.' He had Rebus's attention. 'He's probably involved in drug dealing. Big profits, unlikely he wouldn't want some. But Glasgow was sewn up years ago, and rather than get into a war we think he's been casting his net wider.'

'As far as Aberdeen?'

Ancram nodded. 'We're compiling a file prior to setting up a surveillance op in conjunction with the Squaddies.'

'And every surveillance you've tried in the past has failed.'

'There's a double loop to this one: if someone leaks word to Uncle Joe, *we'll* know where the leak started.'

'So you end up with either Uncle Joe or the grass? It might work . . . if you don't go around telling everyone about it.'

'I'm trusting you.'

'Why?'

'Because you could fuck things up, pure and simple.'

'You know, I've been here before, people telling me to lay off, leave everything to them.'

'And?'

'And they've usually had something to hide.'

Ancram shook his head. 'Not this time. But I *do* have something to offer. Like I say, *personally* I've no interest in the Spaven case, but professionally I'm duty-bound to do my job. Thing is, there are ways and ways of presenting a report. I could minimise your part in the whole thing, I could leave you out altogether. I'm not telling you to drop any investigation; I'm just asking you to freeze it for a week or so.'

'And let the trail grow cold, maybe enough time for a few more suicides and accidental deaths?'

Ancram looked exasperated.

'Just do your job, Chief Inspector,' Rebus said. 'And I'll do mine.' Rebus got to his feet, looked for the paper with the Johnny Bible story, stuffed it in his pocket.

'Here's the deal,' Ancram said, smouldering. 'I'm going to have a man with you at all times, reporting back to me. It's either that or a suspension.'

Rebus jerked his thumb towards the window. 'Him out there?' The driver was enjoying a smoke in the sunshine. Ancram shook his head.

'Someone who knows you better.'

Rebus came up with the answer a second before Ancram spoke.

'Jack Morton.'

He was waiting for Rebus outside the flat. Water was dribbling down the dishels from where neighbours were cleaning their cars. Jack had been sitting in his own car, windows rolled down, his paper open at the crossword. Now he was out of the car and had his arms folded, head inclined to the sun's rays. He was dressed in a short-sleeved shirt and faded jeans, newish white trainers on his feet.

'Sorry to muck up your weekend,' Rebus told him, as he got out of Ancram's car.

'Remember,' Ancram called to Jack, 'don't let him out of your sight. If he goes for a dump, I want you keeking through the keyhole. If he says he's putting the rubbish out, I want you inside one of the bags. Understood?'

'Yes, sir,' Jack said.

The police driver was asking Rebus where he should park the Saab. Rebus pointed to the double-yellow line at the bottom of the street. The windscreen still boasted its Grampian Police Business sign. Rebus was in no hurry to tear it off. Ancram got out of his driving seat and opened the rear door. His driver handed Rebus the keys to the Saab and his suitcase out of the boot, and got into his boss's car, adjusting the seat and the rearview. Rebus and Jack watched Ancram being driven away.

'So,' Rebus said, 'I hear you're with the Juice Church these days.'

Jack wrinkled his nose. 'I can take or leave the holy roller stuff, but it's helped me give up the hooch.'

'That's great.'

'How come I never know when you're being serious?'

'Years of practice.'

'Nice holiday?'

'Nice doesn't begin to describe it.'

'I see your face took a dunt.'

Rebus touched his temple. The swelling was going down. 'Some people get temperamental when you beat them to the sunbeds.'

They climbed the stairwell, Jack a couple of steps behind Rebus.

'Are you seriously not going to let me out of your sight?'

'That's what the boss wants.'

'And what he wants he gets?'

'If I know what's good for me. It's taken me a lot of years to come to the conclusion that I *do* want what's good for me.'

'So speaks the philosopher.' Rebus put his key in the lock, pushed the door open. There was some mail on the hall carpet, but not much. 'You realise this is probably against a couple of dozen laws. I mean, you can't just follow me around if I don't want you to.'

'So take it to the Court of Human Rights.' Jack followed Rebus into the living room. The suitcase stayed out in the hall.

'Fancy a drink?' Rebus asked.

'Ha ha.'

Rebus shrugged, found a clean glass and poured himself some of Kayleigh Burgess's whisky. It went down without touching the sides. He exhaled noisily. 'You must miss it though?'

'All the time,' Jack admitted, slumping on to the sofa.

Rebus poured another. 'I know I would.'

'That's half the battle.'

'What?'

'Admitting you'd have a problem without it.'

'I didn't say that.'

Jack shrugged, got to his feet again. 'Mind if I make a phone call?'

'My home is your home.'

Jack walked over to the telephone. 'Looks like you've got some messages. Want to play them?'

'They'll all be from Ancram.'

Jack lifted the receiver, pressed seven digits. 'It's me,' he said at last. 'We're here.' Then he put the telephone down.

Rebus looked at him above the rim of the glass.

'There's a team on its way,' Jack explained. 'To look the place over. Chick said he'd tell you.'

'He told me. No search warrant, I suppose?'

'If you want it, we can get one. But if I were you, I'd just sit back and let it happen – quick and painless. Plus . . . if anything ever comes to court, you'll have the prosecution on a technicality.'

Rebus smiled. 'Are you on my side, Jack?' Jack sat down again, but didn't say anything. 'You told Ancram I'd phoned you, didn't you?'

Jack shook his head. 'I kept my trap shut when maybe I shouldn't.' He sat forward. 'Chick knows we go back, you and me, that's why I'm here.'

'I don't get it.'

'It's a loyalty thing, he's testing my loyalty to him, pitting the past – that's you and me – against *my* future.'

'And how loyal are you, Jack?'

'Don't push it.'

Rebus drained his glass. 'This is going to be an interesting few days. What happens if I get lucky winching? Are you going to want to hide beneath the bed, like a piss-pot or the fucking bogeyman?'

'John, don't get—'

But Rebus was on his feet. 'This is my home, for Christ's sake! The one place I can hide from all the shite flying around out there! Am I supposed to just sit here and take it? You standing guard, forensics sniffing around like mongrels at a lamp-post – am I supposed to sit here and let you get on with it?'

'Yes.'

'Well fuck that, Jack, and fuck you, too.' The doorbell rang. 'You get it,' Rebus said. 'They're your dogs.'

Jack looked hurt as he made for the door. Rebus went into the hall, grabbed his case and took it into his bedroom. He threw it on the bed and opened it. Whoever had packed it had just stuffed everything in, clean and dirty. The whole lot would have to go to the launderette. He lifted out his wash-bag. There was a note folded below it. It told him that 'certain items of clothing' had been held back by Grampian Police for forensic 'exploration'. Rebus looked: his grass-stained trousers and torn shirt from the night he'd been attacked, they were missing. Grogan was having them tested, just in case Rebus *had* killed Vanessa Holden. Fuck him, fuck them all. Fuck the whole fucking lot of them. Rebus threw the open case across the room, just as Jack came to the doorway.

'John, they say they won't be long.'

'Tell them to take as long as they like.'

'And tomorrow morning there'll be blood tests and a saliva sample.'

'I'll have no trouble with the latter. Just stand Ancram in front of me.'

'He didn't ask for this job, you know.'

'Fuck off, Jack.'

'I wish I could.'

Rebus pushed past him into the hall. He glanced into the living room. There were men in there, some of them he knew, all dressed in white boiler-suits and polythene gloves. They were lifting the cushions from his sofa, ruffling the pages of his books. They didn't look like they were enjoying it: small consolation. It made sense that Ancram would use local

people: easier than hauling a consignment from weegie-land. The one crouching in front of the corner cupboard got up, turned. Their eyes met.

'*Et tu*, Siobhan?'

'Afternoon, sir,' Siobhan Clarke said, ears and cheeks reddening. It was about all Rebus needed. He grabbed his jacket, headed for the door.

'John?' Jack Morton called after him.

'Catch me if you can,' Rebus said. Halfway down the stairs, Jack did just that.

'Where are we going?'

'We're going to a pub,' Rebus told him. 'We'll take my car. You won't be drinking, so you can drive me home afterwards. That way we stay the right side of the law.' Rebus pulled the door open. 'Now let's see just how strong your Juice Church really is.'

Outside, Rebus almost collided with a tall man with black curly hair, turning grey. He saw the microphone, heard the man rattle off a question. Eamonn Breen. Rebus ducked his head just enough to catch Breen on the bridge of his nose: no power in the 'Glasgow kiss', just enough to let Rebus past.

'Bastard!' Breen spluttered, dropping the mike and cupping both hands over his nose. 'Did you catch that? Did you?'

Rebus glanced back, saw blood dripping between Breen's fingers, saw the cameraman nodding, saw Kayleigh Burgess over to one side, a pen in her mouth, looking at Rebus with half a smile.

'She probably thought you'd prefer to have a friendly face around,' Jack Morton said.

They were standing in the Oxford Bar, and Rebus had just told him about Siobhan.

'Given the circumstances, I know I would.' Jack was halfway down a pint of fresh orange and lemonade. Ice rattled in the glass when he tipped it. Rebus was on his second pint of Belhaven Best, motoring in fifth: nice and smooth. Sunday evening in the Ox, only twenty minutes after opening time, the place was quiet. Three regulars stood beside them at the bar, heads angled up towards the television, some quiz programme. The quizmaster had topiary where his haircut should have been and teeth transplanted from a Steinway. His job was to hold a card up to just below his face, read out the question, stare at the camera, then repeat the question as though nuclear disarmament depended on the answer.

'So, Barry,' he intoned, 'for two hundred points: which character plays the Wall in Shakespeare's *A Midsummer Night's Dream*?'

'Pink Floyd,' said the first regular.

'Snout,' said the second.

'Cheerio, Barry,' said the third, waving his fingers at the television, where Barry was clearly in trouble. A buzzer sounded. The quizmaster opened the question to the other two contestants.

'No?' he said. 'No takers?' He seemed surprised, but had to refer to his card to find the answer. 'Snout,' he said, looking at the hapless trio, then repeating the name just so they'd remember next time. Another card. 'Jasmine, for a hundred and fifty points: in which American state would you find the town of Akron?'

'Ohio,' said the second regular.

'Isn't he a character in *Star Trek*?' asked the first.

'Cheerio, Jasmine,' said the third.

'So,' Jack asked, 'are we talking?'

'It takes more than my home being raided, my clothes confiscated, and a suspicion of multiple murder hanging over my head to put *me* in the huff. Of course we're fucking talking.'

'Well, that's all-fucking-right then.'

Rebus snorted into his drink, then had to wipe foam off his nose. 'I can't tell you how much I enjoyed nutting that wanker.'

'He probably enjoyed the fact that the whole thing was being filmed.'

Rebus shrugged, reached into his pocket for cigarettes and lighter.

'Go on then,' Jack said, 'give me one.'

'You've stopped, remember?'

'Aye, but there's no AA for smokers. Come on.'

But Rebus shook his head. 'I appreciate the gesture, Jack, but you're right.'

'About what?'

'About looking out for your future. You're dead right. So don't cave in, stick to it. No booze, no cigs, and report my doings back to Chick Ancram.'

Jack looked at him. 'You mean that?'

'Every word of it,' Rebus drained his glass. 'Except the bit about Ancram, of course.'

Then he ordered another round.

'The answer's Ohio,' the quizmaster said, no surprise to anyone in the bar.

'I think,' Jack said a little later on, halfway down his second pint of juice, 'we're about to hit our first crisis of faith.'

'You need a piss?' Jack nodded. 'Well forget it,' Rebus said, 'I'm not going in there with you.'

'Give me your word you'll stay put.'

'Where would I go?'

'John . . .'

'OK, OK. Would I get you into trouble, Jack?'

'I don't know, would you?'

Rebus winked at him. 'Off you go to the bog and find out.'

Jack stood his ground as long as he could, then turned and fled. Rebus leaned his elbows on the bar, smoking his cigarette. He was wondering what Jack would do if he ran out on him right now: would he report it to Ancram, or would he keep quiet? Would he be doing himself any favours by reporting it? After all, it showed him in a bad light, and he wouldn't want that. So maybe he'd keep quiet. Rebus could go about his business without Ancram knowing.

Except that Ancram had ways of knowing. The man wasn't solely dependent on Jack Morton. It was an interesting point, nevertheless: a point of faith, apt enough on a Sunday night. Maybe Rebus would drag Jack along to see Father Conor Leary later on. Jack used to be a real hun, a blue-nose, maybe still was. A drink with a Catholic priest might send him scurrying into the night. He looked round and saw Jack at the top of the steps, looking relieved – in both senses of the word.

Poor bastard, Rebus thought. Ancram wasn't being fair on him. You could see the strain around Jack's mouth. Rebus felt tired suddenly, remembered he'd been up since six, and had been on the rack ever since. He drained his glass and gestured towards the door. Jack seemed only too glad to be leaving.

When they got outside, Rebus asked him, 'How close were you in there?'

'To what?'

'Ordering a *real* drink.'

'As close as I ever get.'

Rebus leaned on the roof of the car, waiting for Jack to unlock it. 'Sorry I did that to you,' he said quietly.

'What?'

'Brought you here.'

'I should have the willpower to go into a pub without drinking.'

Rebus nodded. 'Thanks,' he said.

And he had a little smile to himself. Jack would be OK. Jack wouldn't shop him. The man had lost too much self-respect already.

'There's a spare room,' Rebus said, getting into the car, 'but no sheets or anything. We'll make up the sofa if that's OK.'

'That'll be fine,' Jack said.

Fine for Jack, yes, but not so fine for Rebus. It meant he'd have to sleep in his bed. No more nights half-dressed on the chair by the window. No more Stones at two a.m. He knew he had to get busy, had to finish this as fast as he could, one way or another.

Beginning tomorrow.

As they left the Ox, Rebus decided on a detour, directed Jack down towards Leith, let him drive them around for a bit, then pointed to a darkened shop doorway.

'That was her pitch,' he said.

'Whose?' Jack stopped the car. The street was lifeless, the working girls busy elsewhere.

'Angie Riddell's. I knew her, Jack. I mean, I'd met her a couple of times. First time, it was business, I was pulling her in. But then I came down here looking for her.' He looked at Jack, expecting a jokey comment, but Jack's face was serious. He was listening. 'We sat and talked. Next thing I knew, she was dead. It's different when you know someone. You remember their eyes. I don't mean the colour or anything, I mean all the things their eyes told you about them.' He sat in silence for a moment. 'Whoever killed her, he couldn't have been looking at her eyes.'

'John, we're not priests, you know. I mean, this is a *job*, right? You have to be able to lay it aside sometimes.'

'Is that what you do, Jack? Home after a shift, and suddenly everything's OK? Doesn't matter what you've seen out there, your home is your castle, eh?'

Jack shrugged, hands rubbing the steering-wheel. 'It's not my life, John.'

'Good for you, pal.' He looked towards the doorway again, expecting to see something of her there, the trace of a shadow, something left behind. But all he saw was darkness.

'Get me home,' he told Jack, closing his eyes with both thumbs.

The Fairmount Hotel was situated in Glasgow's west end, just off the main

traffic routes. From the outside, it was an unassuming slab of concrete. Inside, it was a middle-management sort of place, its main business taking place during the week. Bible John booked for the Sunday night only.

News of the Upstart's latest victim had broken on Sunday morning, too late for coverage in the quality press. Instead, he caught the hourly news bulletins on the radio in his room, tuning between half a dozen stations, and watched what TV news he could, making notes between times. The Teletext flashes were brief paragraphs. Almost all he knew was that the victim, a married woman in her late twenties, had been found near the harbour in Aberdeen.

Aberdeen again. It was all fitting together. At the same time, if it was the Upstart, he was breaking his pattern – his first married victim, and perhaps his oldest. Which might mean that the pattern had never been there in the first place. It didn't of necessity negate an existing pattern; it just meant that that pattern had yet to be established.

Which was what Bible John was counting on.

Meantime, he opened the UPSTART file on his laptop and read the notes on the third victim. Judith Cairns, known to her friends as Ju-Ju. Twenty-one years old, shared a rented flat in Hillhead, just across Kelvingrove Park – he could almost see Hillhead from his window. Although she was registered unemployed, Judith Cairns had worked the black economy – some bar work at lunchtimes; a chip shop in the evenings; and weekend mornings as a chambermaid at the Fairmount Hotel. Which was, Bible John was guessing, how the Upstart had come to meet her. A travelling man frequented hotels: he should know. He wondered how close he was to the Upstart – not physically, but mentally. He didn't want to feel close in any way to this brash pretender, this usurper. He wanted to feel unique.

He paced his room, wanting to be back in Aberdeen while the latest inquiry unfolded, but he had work here in Glasgow, work he could not accomplish until the middle of the night. He stared out of the window, imagining Judith Cairns crossing Kelvingrove Park: she must have done it dozens of times. And one time she did it with the Upstart. Once was all he needed.

During the course of the afternoon and evening, more news filtered down of the latest victim. She was now being described as a 'successful twenty-seven-year-old company director'. The word *businessman* was like a shriek in Bible John's head. Not a lorry driver or any other profession; a simple businessman. The Upstart. He sat down at his computer and scrolled back to his notes on the first victim, the student at Robert Gordon's University, studying geology. He needed to know more about her, but couldn't think which route to take. And now there was a fourth victim to occupy him. Perhaps study of number four would mean he wouldn't need the first cull to complete his picture. Tonight might point the way.

He went out late for a walk. It was very pleasant, balmy night air, not much traffic about. Glasgow wasn't such a bad place: he'd been to cities in the States that could eat it for brunch. He remembered the city of his youth, stories of razor gangs and bare-knuckle bouts. Glasgow had a violent history, but that didn't tell the full story. It could be a beautiful city, too, a city for photographers and artists. A place for lovers . . .

I didn't want to kill them. He would like to be able to tell Glasgow that, but of course it would be a lie. At the time . . . at the last moment . . . all he'd wanted in the world was their death. He had read interviews with killers, sat through trial testimony a couple of times, too, wanting someone to explain his feelings to him. No one came close. It was impossible either to describe or to understand.

There were many who especially didn't understand his choice of third victim. It felt preordained, he could have told them. It didn't matter about the witness in the taxi. Nothing mattered, it had all been decided by some higher power.

Or some lower one.

Or merely by some collision of chemicals in his brain, by a genetic mismatch.

And afterwards, there'd been his uncle's offer of a job in the States, so he could afford to leave Glasgow. Leave the whole life behind him and create a new one, a new identity . . . as if marriage and a career could ever take the place of what he'd left behind . . .

He bought the next morning's edition of the *Herald* at a street corner and retired to a bar to devour it. He drank orange juice and sat in a corner. No one paid him any attention. There were more details about the Upstart's latest victim. She worked in corporate presentations, which meant putting together packages for industry: videos, displays, speech-writing, trade stands . . . He studied the photo again. She'd worked in Aberdeen, and there was really only one industry in Aberdeen. Oil. He didn't recognise her, felt sure they'd never met. All the same, he wondered why the Upstart had chosen *her*: could he be sending Bible John a message? Impossible: it would mean he knew who Bible John was. Nobody knew. Nobody.

It was midnight when he returned to the hotel. Reception was deserted. He went up to his room, dozed for a couple of hours, and had the alarm wake him at half past two. He took the carpeted stairs down to reception, which was still deserted. Breaking into the office took thirty seconds. He closed the door after him and sat down in darkness at the computer. It was switched on and in screen-saver mode. He nudged the mouse to activate the screen, then got to work. He searched back six weeks from the date of Judith Cairns's murder, checking room registrations and payment methods. He was looking for accounts charged to companies based in or near Aberdeen. His feeling was that the Upstart hadn't come to this hotel looking for a victim, but had been here on business, and had found her by chance. He was looking for the elusive pattern to start emerging.

Fifteen minutes later, he had a list of twenty companies, and of the individuals who had paid with a company credit card. For now, that was all he needed, but he was left with a dilemma: delete the files from the computer, or leave them? With the information deleted, he would have every chance of beating the police to the Upstart. Yes, but someone from the hotel staff would notice, and would be curious. They might contact the police. There would probably be back-ups on floppy. He would actually be helping the police, alerting them to his presence . . . No, leave well alone. Do no more than is necessary. The maxim had served him well in the past.

Back in his room, he pored over the list in his notebook. It would be easy to check where each company was based, what it did – work for later. He

had a meeting in Edinburgh tomorrow, and would use the trip to do something about John Rebus. He checked Teletext one last time before retiring for the night. After turning off the lights, he opened the curtains, then lay down on the bed. There were stars in the sky, a few of them bright enough to be visible through the street light. Dead, a lot of them, or so the astronomers said. So many dead things around, what difference would another one make?

None at all. Not one jot.

22

They took Jack's car to Howdenhall, Rebus sitting in the back, calling Jack his 'chauffeur'. It was a gloss-black Peugeot 405, three years old, turbo version; Rebus disregarded the No Smoking sticker and lit up, but kept the window open beside him. Jack didn't say anything, didn't even look in the rearview. Rebus hadn't slept well in the bed; night sweats, the sheets like a straitjacket. Chase dreams waking him every hour or so, sending him shooting out of bed to stand naked and trembling in the middle of the floor.

Jack for his part had complained first thing of a stiff neck. His second complaint: the kitchen, bare fridge and all. He couldn't go out to the shops, not without Rebus, so they'd made straight for the car.

'I'm gutting,' he complained.

'So stop and we'll eat something.'

They stopped at a bakery in Liberton: sausage rolls, beakers of coffee, a couple of macaroon cakes. Sat eating them in the car, parked double yellow by a bus stop. Buses rattled them as they passed, hinting they should shift. There were messages on the backs of some of them: Please Give Way to This Bus.

'I don't mind the buses,' Jack said. 'It's their drivers I object to. Half of them couldn't pass the time of day, never mind a PSV test.'

Rebus's comment: 'It's not buses that have the choke-hold on this place.'

'You're cheery this morning.'

'Jack, just shut your gub and drive.'

They were ready for him at Howdenhall. The team last night at his flat had taken away all his shoes, so the forensic bods could check for footprints and fail to match them against any left at the scene of Johnny Bible's murders. First thing Rebus had to do this morning was remove the shoes he was wearing. They gave him plastic overshoes to wear, and said his own would be returned to him before he left. The overshoes were too big, uncomfortable – his feet slid around inside them, and he had to curl his toes to keep them from slipping off.

They decided against a saliva test – it was the least reliable – but plucked hairs from his head.

'Could you graft them on to my temples when you're finished?'

The woman with the tweezers smiled, went about her business. She explained that she had to get the roots – PCR analysis wouldn't work on shed hair. There was a test available in some places, but . . .

'But?'

She didn't answer, but Rebus knew what she'd meant: but they were just going through the motions with him. Neither Ancram nor anyone else was expecting the expensive tests to yield any positive result. The only result would be a nettled, unsettled Rebus. That's what the whole thing was about. Forensics knew it; Rebus knew it.

Blood sample – the need for a warrant had been waived – and fingerprints next, plus they wanted some strands and threads from his clothes. I'm going on the computer, Rebus thought. For all that I'm not guilty, I'll still be a suspect in the eyes of history. Anyone digging the files out in twenty years' time will see that a policeman was interviewed, and gave samples . . . It was a grim feeling. And once they had his DNA on record . . . well, that was him on the register. The Scottish DNA database was just beginning to be compiled. Rebus started to wish he'd insisted on a warrant.

Throughout each process Jack Morton stood by, averting his face. And afterwards, Rebus got his shoes back. It felt like the forensic science staff were staring at him; maybe they were, maybe they weren't. Pete Hewitt wandered past – he hadn't been present at the fingerprinting – and made a crack about the biter bit. Jack grabbed Rebus's arm, stopped him from swinging. Hewitt shuffled off double-quick.

'We're due at Fettes,' Jack reminded Rebus.

'I'm ready.'

Jack looked at him. 'Maybe we'll stop off somewhere first, get another coffee.'

Rebus smiled. 'Afraid I'll take a swing at Ancram?'

'If you do, bear in mind he's a southpaw.'

'Inspector, do you have any objections to this interview being recorded?'

'What happens to the recording?'

'It'll be dated and timed, copies made: one for you. Transcripts ditto.'

'No objections.'

Ancram nodded to Jack Morton, who set the machine running. They were in an office on the third floor of Fettes. It was cramped, and looked like it had hastily been vacated by a disgruntled tenant. There was a waste paper bin by the desk, waiting to be emptied. Paper-clips littered the floor. The walls still bore marks where Sellotaped pictures had been yanked down. Ancram sat behind the scratched desk, the Spaven case-notes piled to one side. He was wearing a formal dark-blue pinstripe with pale blue shirt and tie, and looked like he'd been for a haircut first thing. There were two pens in front of him on the desk – a blue fine-nib Bic with yellow casing, and an expensive-looking lacquered rollerball. His buffed and filed nails tapped against a clean pad of A4 paper. A typed list of notes, queries and points to be raised sat to the right of the pad.

'So, doctor,' Rebus said, 'what are my chances?'

Ancram merely smiled. When he spoke, it was for the benefit of the tape machine.

'DCI Charles Ancram, Strathclyde CID. It's –' he consulted a thin wristwatch – 'ten forty-five on Monday the twenty-fourth of June. Preliminary interview with Detective Inspector John Rebus, Lothian and Borders Police. This interview is taking place in office C25, Lothian Police Headquarters, Fettes Avenue, Edinburgh. Also present is—'

'You forgot the postcode,' Rebus said, folding his arms.

'That was the voice of DI Rebus. Also present is DI Jack Morton, Falkirk CID, currently on secondment to Strathclyde Police, Glasgow.'

Ancram glanced at his notes, picked up the Bic and ran through the first couple of lines. Then he picked up a plastic beaker of water and sipped from it, watching Rebus over the rim.

'Any time you're ready,' Rebus told him.

Ancram was ready. Jack sat by the table on which the tape machine sat. Two mikes ran from it to the desk, one pointing towards Ancram, one towards Rebus. From where he was sitting, Rebus couldn't quite see Jack. It was just him and Ancram, the chessboard set for play.

'Inspector,' Ancram said, 'you know why you're here?'

'Yes, sir. I'm here because I've refused to give up an investigation into possible links between Glaswegian gangster Joseph Toal, the Aberdeen drug market, and the murder of an oil-worker in Edinburgh.'

Ancram flicked through the case-notes, looking bored.

'Inspector, you know that interest in the Leonard Spaven case has been revived?'

'I know the TV sharks have been circling. They think they can smell blood.'

'And can they?'

'Just a leaky old ketchup bottle, sir.'

Ancram smiled; it wouldn't come over on the recording.

'CI Ancram smiles,' Rebus said, for the record.

'Inspector,' referring to his notes, 'what started this media interest?'

'Leonard Spaven's suicide, added to his public notoriety.'

'Notoriety?'

Rebus shrugged. 'The media get a vicarious thrill from reformed thugs and murderers, especially when they show some artistic leaning. The media often aspire to art themselves.'

Ancram seemed to expect more. They sat in silence for a moment. Cassette whirr; motor noise. Someone along the corridor sneezed. No sunshine today: iron-clad skies forecasting rain; a bitter wind off the North Sea.

Ancram sat back in his chair. His message to Rebus: I don't need the notes, I *know* this case. 'How did you feel when you heard Lawson Geddes had killed himself?'

'Gutted. He was a good officer, and a good friend to me.'

'You had your differences though?'

Rebus tried to hold the stare; ended up blinking first. Thought: of such accumulated setbacks were battles lost.

'Did we?' Old trick, answer a question with a question. Ancram's look said it was a tired move.

'I've had my men talk to some serving officers from the time.' A glance towards Jack, not even lasting a second. Drawing Jack in. Good tactics, sowing doubt.

'We had minor disagreements, same as everybody else.'

'You still respected him?'

'Present tense.'

Ancram bowed his head, acknowledging this. Fingered his notes, like

stroking a woman's arm. Possessive. But doing it for comfort too, for reassurance.

'So, you worked well together?'

'Pretty well. Mind if I smoke?'

'We'll have a break at . . .' checking his watch, 'eleven-forty-five. Fair enough?'

'I'll try to survive.'

'You're a survivor, Inspector. Your record speaks for itself.'

'So talk to my record.'

A quick smile. 'When did you find out that Lawson Geddes had it in for Leonard Spaven?'

'I don't understand the question.'

'I think you do.'

'Think again.'

'Do you know why Geddes was kicked off the Bible John inquiry?'

'No.' It was the one question that had power, real power: it could *get* to Rebus.

Because he wanted to know the answer.

'You don't? He never told you?'

'Never.'

'But he talked about Bible John?'

'Yes.'

'See, it's all a bit vague . . .' Ancram went into a drawer, hefted two more bulging files on to the desk. 'I've got Geddes's personnel file and reports here. Plus some stuff from the Bible John inquiry, bits and pieces he was involved in. Seems he grew obsessed.' Ancram opened one file, turned pages idly, then looked at Rebus. 'Does that sound familiar?'

'You're saying he was obsessed with Lenny Spaven?'

'I know he was.' Ancram let that sink in, nodding his head. 'I know it from interviews with officers from the time, but more importantly I know it because of Bible John.'

The bastard had hooked Rebus. They were only twenty minutes into the interview. Rebus crossed his legs, tried to look unconcerned. His face was so taut, he knew the muscles were probably visible beneath the skin.

'See,' Ancram went on, 'Geddes tried to tie Spaven to the Bible John case. Now, the notes aren't complete. Either they were destroyed or lost, or else Geddes and his superior didn't write down everything. But Geddes was going after Spaven, no doubt about that. Tucked away in one of the files I found some old photographs. Spaven's in them.' Ancram held the photos up. 'They're from the Borneo campaign. Geddes and Spaven were in the Scots Guards together. My feeling is that something happened out there, and from then on Geddes was out for Spaven's blood. How am I doing so far?'

'Filling the time nicely till the ciggie break. Can I see those photos?'

Ancram shrugged, handed them over. Rebus looked. Old black and whites with crimped edges, a couple of them no bigger than two inches by an inch and a half, the rest four-by-sixes. Rebus picked Spaven out straight away, the raptor grin hauling him into history. There was a minister in the photos, army uniform and dog collar. Other men posing, dressed in baggy shorts and long socks, faces sweat-shiny, eyes almost scared. Some of the

faces were blurred; Rebus couldn't make out Lawson Geddes in any of them. The photos were exteriors, bamboo huts in the background, an old jeep nosing into one shot. He turned them over, read an inscription – Borneo, 1965 – and some names.

'Did these come from Lawson Geddes?' Rebus asked, handing them back.

'I've no idea. They were just in with all the other Bible John junk.' Ancram slipped them back into the file, counting them as he did so.

'They're all there,' Rebus said. Jack Morton's chair scraped the floor: he was checking how long till the tape had to be switched.

'So,' Ancram said, 'we've got Geddes and Spaven serving together in the Scots Guards; we've got Geddes chasing Spaven during the Bible John inquiry – and getting booted off the case; then we wind forwards a few years and what do we have? Geddes still chasing Spaven, but this time for the murder of Elizabeth Rhind. And getting booted off the case again.'

'Spaven definitely knew the victim.'

'No argument there, Inspector.' Pause: four beats. '*You* knew one of the Johnny Bible victims – does it mean you killed her?'

'Come up with her necklace in my flat and ask me again.'

'Ah, well this is where it gets interesting, isn't it?'

'Oh good.'

'You know the word serendipity?'

'I pepper my speech with it.'

'Dictionary definition: the ability to make happy chance finds. Useful word.'

'Absolutely.'

'And Lawson Geddes had the gift, didn't he? I mean, you get an anonymous tip-off about a consignment of stolen clock-radios. So you hoof it over to a garage, no search warrant, no nothing, and what do you find? Leonard Spaven, the clock-radios, and a hat and shoulder-bag – both belonging to the murder victim. I'd call that a *very* happy chance find. Except it wasn't chance, was it?'

'We had a warrant.'

'Signed retrospectively by a tame JP.' Ancram smiled again. 'You think you're doing all right, don't you? You think *I'm* doing all the talking, which means you're saying nothing incriminating. Well listen, I'm talking because I want you to know where we stand. Afterwards, you'll have every opportunity for rebuttal.'

'I'll look forward to that.'

Ancram referred to his notes. Rebus's mind was still half on Borneo and those photographs: what the hell could they have to do with Bible John? He wished he'd looked at them a bit harder.

'I've been reading your own version of events, Inspector,' Ancram went on, 'and I begin to see why you had your pal Holmes take a good look at them.' He looked up. 'That *was* the idea, wasn't it?'

Rebus said nothing.

'See, you weren't quite a seasoned officer back then, for all Geddes had taught you. You wrote a good report, but you were too conscious of the lies you were telling and the gaps you were having to create. I'm good at reading between the lines, practical criticism if you like.'

Rebus had a picture in his mind: Lawson Geddes shivering and wild-eyed on his doorstep.

'So here's how I think it went. Geddes was following Spaven – out on a limb by this time; he'd been ordered off the case. He tracked him to the lock-up one day, waited until Spaven was gone and then broke in. Liked the look of what he saw, and decided to plant some evidence.'

'No.'

'So he breaks in again, only this time he has some of the victim's stuff with him. Now, he didn't get it from an evidence locker, because according to the records nobody removed a hat or a bag from the victim's abode. So how did he get it? Two possibilities. One, he waltzed back into her home and took it. Two, he already had it on him, because right from the start he had the idea of fitting up Spaven.'

'No.'

'To the first or to the second?'

'To both.'

'You'll stand by that?'

'Yes.'

Ancram had been leaning further over the desk as he'd made each point. Slowly he sat back again, glanced at his watch.

'Cigarette break?' Rebus asked.

Ancram shook his head. 'No, I think that's enough for today. You made so many cock-ups in the course of that false report, it's going to take me time to list them all. We'll go through them next meeting.'

'I'm excited already.' Rebus got up and reached into a pocket for his cigarettes. Jack had switched off the recorder and ejected the tape. He handed it to Ancram.

'I'll have a copy made immediately and sent to you for verification,' Ancram told Rebus.

'Thanks.' Rebus inhaled, wished he could hold his breath for ever. Some people, when they exhaled no smoke came out. He wasn't that selfish. 'One question.'

'Yes?'

'What am I supposed to tell my colleagues when I drag Jack here into the office with me?'

'You'll think of something. You're a more practised liar these days.'

'I wasn't fishing for a compliment, but thanks anyway.' He made to leave.

'A little birdie tells me you put the nut on a TV reporter.'

'I tripped, fell into him.'

Ancram almost smiled. 'Tripped?' Waited till Rebus had nodded. 'Well, it's going to look good, isn't it? They got the whole thing on video.'

Rebus shrugged. 'This little birdie of yours . . . anyone in particular?'

'Why do you ask?'

'Well, you have your sources, don't you? In the press, I mean. Jim Stevens for one. Nice little friendship the two of you have got.'

'No comment, Inspector.' Rebus laughed, turned away. 'One more thing,' Ancram said.

'What?'

'When Geddes was trying to pin the murder on Spaven, you interviewed some of Spaven's friends and associates, including . . .' Ancram made show of looking for the name in his notes. 'Fergus McLure.'

'What of it?'

'Mr McLure's recently deceased. I believe you went to see him the morning he died?'

Who'd been talking?

'So?'

Ancram shrugged, looked satisfied. 'Just another . . . coincidence. By the way, DCI Grogan called me this morning.'

'It must be love.'

'Do you know a pub in Aberdeen called the Yardarm?'

'It's down by the docks.'

'Yes, it is. Ever been inside?'

'Maybe.'

'A drinker in there says definitely. You bought him a drink, talked about the rigs.'

The wee man with the heavy cranium. 'So?'

'So it shows you were at the docks the night *before* Vanessa Holden was murdered. Two nights in a row, Inspector. Grogan's beginning to sound *very* edgy. I think he wants you back in his custody.'

'Are you going to hand me over?' Ancram shook his head. 'No, you wouldn't want that, would you?'

Rebus almost blew some smoke in Ancram's face. Almost. Maybe he was more selfish than he thought . . .

'That went as well as could be expected,' Jack Morton said. He was in the driver's seat, Rebus electing to sit in the front with him.

'Only because you thought there'd be a bloodbath.'

'I was trying to remember my first aid training.'

Rebus laughed, releasing tension. He had a headache.

'Aspirin in the glove compartment,' Jack told him. Rebus opened it. There was a little plastic bottle of Vittel there, too. He washed down three tablets.

'Were you ever in the Scouts, Jack?'

'I was a sixer in the Cubs, never made the transfer to Scouts. I had other hobbies by then. Are the Scouts still going?'

'Last I heard.'

'Remember Bob-a-Job week? You had to go round the neighbours, washing windows, digging their gardens. Then at the end, you handed all the cash over to Akela.'

'Who promptly stuck half in his pocket.'

Jack looked at him. 'There's a touch of the cynic in you, isn't there?'

'Maybe just a touch.'

'So where to now? Fort Apache?'

'After what I've just been through?'

'The Ox?'

'You're learning.'

Jack opted for tomato juice – watching his weight, he said – while Rebus had a half-pint and, after a moment's thought, a nip. The lunchtime trade wasn't in yet, but the pies and bridies were heating in preparation. Maybe the barmaid had been in the Girl Guides. They took their drinks through to the back room, settled at a corner table.

'It's funny being back in Edinburgh,' Jack said. 'Never used to drink here, did we? What was the name of the local along Great London Road?'

'I don't remember.' It was true; he couldn't even recall the pub's interior, yet must have been in there two or three hundred times. It was just a place for drink and discussion; what life it had the drinkers brought with them.

'Jesus, the money we wasted in there.'

'There speaks the reformed drinker.'

Jack forced a smile, lifted his glass. 'John, tell me though, why do you drink?'

'It kills my dreams.'

'It'll kill *you* in the end, too.'

'Something's got to.'

'Know what someone said to me? They said you were the world's longest surviving suicide victim.'

'Who said that?'

'Never mind.'

Rebus was laughing. 'Maybe I should apply to the *Guinness Book of Records*.'

Jack drained his glass. 'So what's the itinerary?'

'There's someone I'm supposed to call, a journalist.' He looked at his watch. 'I suppose she might be home. I'm going back to the bar to use the phone. Are you coming?'

'No, I'll trust you.'

'You sure?'

'Fairly.'

So Rebus went to call Mairie, but all he got was her answering machine. He left a brief message, and asked the barmaid if there was a photographer's within walking distance. She nodded, gave him directions, then went back to wiping glasses. Rebus summoned Jack, and they drifted out of the pub into a day that was growing warmer. There was still a blanket of cloud overhead, oppressive, almost thundery. But you just knew the sun was pummelling it, like a child with its pillow. Rebus took his jacket off, slung it over his shoulder. The photographer's was one street further along, so they cut through Hill Street.

The shop carried a window display of portraits – wedding couples seeming to radiate light, young children beaming smiles. Frozen moments of happiness – the great deception – to frame and put in pride of place in your cabinet or on top of the television.

'Holiday snaps, is it?' Jack asked.

'Just don't ask how I got them,' Rebus warned. He explained to the assistant that he wanted reprints made of each negative. She jotted down the instructions and told him it would be next day.

'No chance of one-hour?'

'Not with reprints, sorry.'

Rebus took the receipt from her and folded it into his pocket. Outside again, the sun had given up. It was raining. Rebus kept his jacket off, sweating enough as it was.

'Look,' Jack said, 'you don't have to tell me anything you don't want to, but I wouldn't mind knowing a bit about all this.'

'All what?'

'Your trip to Aberdeen, all the little coded messages between Chick and you, just, well, *everything*.'

'Probably best you don't know.'

'Why? Because I'm working for Ancram?'

'Maybe.'

'Come on, John.'

But Rebus wasn't listening. Two shops down from the photographer's was a small DIY store: paint and brushes and wallpaper rolls. It gave Rebus an idea. Back at the car, he gave directions, telling Jack they were on a mystery tour – remembering Lumsden saying the same thing to him his first night in Furry Boot Town. Near St Leonard's Rebus told Jack to make a left.

'Here?'

'Here.'

It was a do-it-yourself superstore. The car park was almost empty, so they parked close to the doors. Then Rebus hopped out and found a trolley with four working wheels.

'You'd think in a place like this they'd have someone who could fix them.'

'What are we doing here?'

'I need a few things.'

'You need provisions, not bags of plaster.'

Rebus turned to him. 'That's just where you're wrong.'

He bought paint, rollers and brushes, turps, a couple of ground-sheets, plaster, a hot-air gun, sandpaper (coarse and fine), and varnish, sticking it all on his credit card. Then he treated Jack to lunch at a nearby café, a haunt of his from St Leonard's days.

And afterwards: home. Jack helped him carry everything upstairs.

'Brought any old clothes with you?' Rebus asked.

'I've a boiler-suit in the boot.'

'Better bring it up.' Rebus stopped, stared at his open door, dropped the paint and ran into the flat. A quick check told him there was no one there. Jack was examining the jamb.

'Looks like someone took a crowbar to it,' he said. 'What's missing?'

'The hi-fi and telly are still there.'

Jack walked in, checked the rooms. 'Looks much the same as when we left it. Want to call it in?'

'Why? We both know this is Ancram trying to rattle me.'

'I don't see that.'

'No? Funny I get a break-in when I'm being interrogated by him.'

'We should call it in, that way the insurance will cover you for a new door-frame.' Jack looked around him. 'Surprised nobody heard it.'

'Deaf neighbours,' Rebus said. 'Edinburgh's famous for them. All right, we'll call it in. You go back to the store and fetch another lock or something.'

'And what will you be doing?'

'Sitting here, minding the fort. I promise.'

The minute Jack was out of the door, Rebus headed for the telephone. He asked to be put through to DCI Ancram. Then he waited, looking around the room. Somebody breaks in, then leaves without taking the hi-fi. It was almost an insult.

'Ancram.'

'It's me.'

'Something on your mind, Inspector?'

'My flat's been broken into.'

'I'm sorry to hear it. What did they take?'

'Nothing. That's where they slipped up. I thought you should tell them.'

Ancram laughed. 'You think I had something to do with it?'

'Yes.'

'Why?'

'I was hoping you'd tell me. The word "harassment" springs to mind.' As soon as he said it, he thought of *The Justice Programme*: how desperate were they? Desperate enough for a spot of housebreaking? He couldn't see it, not Kayleigh Burgess. Eamonn Breen, however, was another matter entirely . . .

'Look, this is a pretty serious allegation. I'm not sure I want to listen to it. Why not calm down and think it over?'

Rebus was doing just that. He hung up on Ancram, got his wallet out of his jacket pocket. It was full of scraps of paper, receipts, business cards. He plucked out Kayleigh Burgess's, phoned her office.

'I'm afraid she's not here this afternoon,' a secretary told him. 'Can I take a message?'

'What about Eamonn?' Trying to sound like a friend. 'Is he in by any chance?'

'I'll just check. What's the name?'

'John Rebus.'

'Hold the line.' Rebus held. 'No, sorry, Eamonn's out as well. Shall I tell him you called?'

'No, it's all right, I'll catch up with him later. Thanks anyway.'

Rebus went through the flat again, more carefully this time. His first thought had been a straight break-in; his second some sort of ruse to wind him up. But now he was thinking of other things someone could have been looking for. It wasn't easy to tell: Siobhan and her friends hadn't exactly left the place as they'd found it. But nor had they been particularly thorough. For instance, they hadn't spent time in the kitchen, hadn't opened the cupboard where he kept all his cuttings and newspapers.

But someone had. Rebus knew which cutting he'd last read, and it was no longer on top of the pile. Instead, it had migrated south three or four layers. Maybe Jack . . . no, he didn't think Jack had been snooping.

But someone had. Someone most definitely had.

By the time Jack got back, Rebus had changed into jeans and a gaudy T-shirt bearing the legend DANCING PIGS. A couple of woolly suits had been round to inspect the damage and scribble some notes. They gave Rebus a reference number. His insurers would want it.

Rebus had already moved some of the furniture out of the living room into the hall, and placed a ground-sheet over everything else. The other sheet went on the carpet. He lifted the fishing-boat painting off the wall.

'I like that,' Jack said.

'Rhona gave it to me, the first birthday I had after we were married. Bought it at a craft fair, thought it'd remind me of Fife.' He was studying the painting and shaking his head.

'I take it it didn't?'

'I come from west Fife – mining villages, rough – not the East Neuk.' All fishing creels, tourists and retirement homes. 'I don't think she ever understood.' He took the painting through to the hall.

'I can't believe we're doing this,' Jack said.

'And on police time. Which would you rather do, paint the walls, strip the door, or fit the lock?'

'Paint.' With his blue boiler-suit on, Jack looked the part. Rebus handed him the roller, then reached under the sheet to put the hi-fi on. Stones, *Exile on Main Street*. Just right. The two of them got to work.

23

They took a break and walked up Marchmont Road, buying groceries. Jack kept his boiler-suit on, said he felt like he was undercover. He had a smudge of paint on his face, but didn't bother wiping it off. He was enjoying himself. He'd sung along to the music, even though he didn't always know the words. They bought junk food mostly, carbohydrate, but added four apples and a couple of bananas. Jack asked if Rebus was going to buy any beer. Rebus shook his head, chose Irn-Bru and bricks of orange juice instead.

'What's all this in aid of?' Jack asked as they sauntered home.

'Clearing the mind,' Rebus answered, 'giving me time to think . . . I don't know. Maybe I'm thinking of selling.'

'Selling the flat?'

Rebus nodded.

'And doing what exactly?'

'Well, I could buy a round-the-world ticket, couldn't I? Take off for six months. Or stick the money in the bank and live off the interest.' He paused. 'Or maybe buy myself a place outside town.'

'Whereabouts?'

'Somewhere by the sea.'

'That'd be nice.'

'Nice?' Rebus shrugged. 'Yes, I suppose so. I just fancy a change.'

'Right next to the beach?'

'Could be a clifftop, who knows?'

'What's brought this on?'

Rebus thought about it. 'My home doesn't feel like my castle any longer.'

'Yes, but we bought all the painting stuff before the break-in.'

Rebus didn't have an answer to that.

They worked the rest of the afternoon, windows open to let out the paint fumes.

'Am I supposed to sleep in here tonight?' Jack asked.

'The spare room,' Rebus told him.

The phone rang at half past five. Rebus got to it just as the answering machine cut in.

'Hello?'

'John, it's Brian. Siobhan told me you were back.'

'Well, she should know. How are you?'

'Shouldn't I be asking *you* that?'

'I'm fine.'

'Me too.'

'You're not pick of the week with DCI Ancram.'

Jack Morton started to take an interest in the call.

'Maybe not, but he's not my boss.'

'He has pull, though.'

'So let him pull.'

'Brian, I know what you're up to. I want to talk to you about it. Can we come round there?'

'We?'

'It's a long story.'

'Maybe I could come see you.'

'This place is a building site. We'll be there in about an hour, all right?'

Holmes hesitated, then said that would be fine.

'Brian, this is Jack Morton, an old friend of mine. He's with Falkirk CID, currently seconded to DI John Rebus.'

Jack winked at Brian. He'd washed the paint off his face and hands. 'What he means is, I'm supposed to keep him out of trouble.'

'UN Peacekeeper, eh? Well, come in.'

Brian Holmes had spent the hour tidying the living room. He saw Rebus's appraisal.

'Just don't go into the kitchen – looks like an Apache raiding party's ridden through.'

Rebus smiled and sat on the sofa, Jack next to him. Brian asked if they wanted anything to drink. Rebus shook his head.

'Brian, I've told Jack a wee bit about what's happened. He's a good man, we can speak in front of him. OK?'

Rebus was taking a calculated risk, hoping the afternoon's bonding had worked. If not, at least they'd made progress on the room: three walls with first coats, and half of one side of the door stripped. Plus a new lock on the door.

Brian Holmes nodded and sat down on a chair. There were photos of Nell on top of the gas fire. It looked like they'd been newly framed and placed there: a makeshift shrine.

'Is she at her mum's?' Rebus asked.

Brian nodded. 'But mostly working late shifts at the library.'

'Any chance she's coming back?'

'I don't know.' Brian made to bite a fingernail, discovered there was nothing there to bite.

'I'm not sure this is the answer.'

'What?'

'You can't make yourself resign, so you're going to let Ancram kick you out: not co-operating, acting the mule.'

'I had a good teacher.'

Rebus smiled. It was true, after all. He'd had Lawson Geddes; and Brian had had him.

'This happened to me once before,' Brian went on. 'At school, I had this really good friend, and we were going to go to university together, only he'd decided to go to Stirling, so I said I'd go there, too. But my first choice had been Edinburgh, and to knock Edinburgh's offer on the head I had to fail Higher German.'

'And?'

'And I sat in the exam hall . . . knowing if I just sat there and didn't answer any of the questions, that would be it.'

'But you answered them?'

Brian smiled. 'Couldn't help myself. I got a C pass.'

'Same problem now,' Rebus said. 'If you go this way, you'll always regret it, because in your heart you don't *want* to leave. You like what you're doing. And beating yourself up about it . . .'

'What about beating other people up?' Brian looked straight at him as he asked the question. Mental Minto, sporting bruises.

'You lost the head once.' Rebus held up a finger for emphasis. 'It was once too often, but you got away with it. I don't think you'll do that to anyone ever again.'

'I hope you're right.' Holmes turned to Jack Morton. 'I had this suspect in the biscuit-tin, I gave him a smack.'

Jack nodded: Rebus had told him all about it. 'I've been there myself, Brian,' Jack said. 'I mean, it's never come to blows, but I've been close. I've skinned my knuckles on a few walls.'

Holmes held up ten fingers: scrapes all across them.

'See,' Rebus said, 'like I say, you're beating *yourself* up. Mental's got a few marks, but they'll fade.' He tapped his head. 'But when the bruises are in here . . .'

'I want Nell back.'

'Of course you do.'

'But I want to be a copper.'

'You've got to make both those clear to her.'

'Christ.' Brian rubbed his face. 'I've tried explaining it . . .'

'You've always written a good, clear report, Brian.'

'What do you mean?'

'If the words aren't coming out right, try writing them down.'

'Send her a letter?'

'Call it that if you like. Just put down what it is you want to say, maybe try explaining why you feel that way.'

'Have you been reading *Cosmopolitan* or something?'

'Only the problem page.'

They had a laugh at that, though it didn't really merit one. Brian stretched in his chair. 'I need a sleep,' he said.

'Get an early night, write the letter first thing tomorrow.'

'Maybe I will, aye.'

Rebus started to get to his feet. Brian watched him rise.

'Don't you want to hear about Mick Hine?'

'Who he?'

'Ex-con, the last man to speak to Lenny Spaven.'

Rebus sat down again.

'I had a job tracking him down. Turns out he was here in town all the time, sleeping rough.'

'And?'

'And I had a word with him.' Brian paused. 'And I think you should, too. You'll get a very different picture of Lenny Spaven, believe me.'

Rebus believed him, whatever he meant. He didn't want to, but he did.

*

441

Jack was utterly opposed to the idea.

'Look, John, my boss is going to want to talk to this guy Hine, right?'

'Right.'

'How's it going to look when he finds out not just that your pal Brian's been there first, but that *you've* followed up?'

'It's going to look bad, but he hasn't told me not to.'

Jack growled his frustration. They'd dropped his car back at the flat, and were now walking down on to Melville Drive. One side of the road was Bruntsfield Links, the other the Meadows, a flat grassy stretch which could be wonderful on a hot summer's afternoon – a place to relax, to play football or cricket – but scary at night. The paths were lamp-lit, but it was like the wattage had been turned down. Some nights, the walk was positively Victorian. But this was summer, the sky still pink. There were squares of light shining from the Royal Infirmary and a couple of the tall university buildings huddled around George Square. Female students crossed the Meadows in packs, a lesson learned from the animal world. Maybe there were no predators out there tonight, but the fear was just as real. The government had pledged to combat 'the fear of crime'. It was reported on the TV news just before the latest Hollywood shoot-'em-up.

Rebus turned to Jack. 'You going to grass me up?'

'I should.'

'Yes, you should. But will you?'

'I don't know, John.'

'Well, don't let our friendship stand in your way.'

'That helps me a lot.'

'Look, Jack, the water I'm in is so deep, I'd probably die of the bends coming back up. So I might just as well stay down here.'

'Ever heard of the Marianas Trench? Ancram probably has one just like it waiting for you.'

'You're slipping.'

'What?'

'He was Chick before, now he's "Ancram". You better watch yourself.'

'You're sober, aren't you?'

'As a judge.'

'Can't be Dutch courage then, which means it's plain insanity.'

'Welcome to my world, Jack.'

They were headed for the back of the Infirmary. There were benches provided just this side of the perimeter wall. Dossers, travellers, down-and-outs . . . whatever you wanted to call them . . . they used these benches as beds in the summer. There used to be one old guy, Frank, who Rebus saw every summer, and at the end of every summer he disappeared like a migrating bird, only to reappear the next year. But this year . . . this year Frank hadn't appeared. The homeless people Rebus saw were a lot younger than Frank, his spiritual children, if not grandchildren; only they were different – tougher and more frightened, wired and tired. Different game, different rules. Edinburgh's 'gentlemen of the road': twenty years ago you could have measured them in mere dozens. But not these days. Not these days . . .

They woke up a couple of sleepers, who denied being Mick Hine and said they didn't know who he was, and then hit lucky with the third bench. He

was sitting upright, a pile of newspapers beside him. He had a tiny transistor radio, which he held hard to his ear.

'Are you deaf or does it just need new batteries?' Rebus asked.

'Not deaf, not dumb, not blind. He said another copper might want to talk to me. Do you want a seat?'

Rebus sat down on the bench. Jack Morton rested against the wall behind it, like he'd rather be somewhere out of earshot. Rebus drew out a fiver.

'Here, get some batteries.'

Mick Hine took the money. 'So you're Rebus?' He gave Rebus a long look. Hine was early forties, balding, with a slight squint. He wore a decent enough suit, only it had holes in both knees. Beneath the jacket was a baggy red T-shirt. Two supermarket carrier bags sat on the ground beside him, bulging with worldly goods. 'Lenny talked about you. I thought you'd be different.'

'Different?'

'Younger.'

'I was younger when Lenny knew me.'

'Aye, that's true. Only film stars get younger, have you noticed that? The rest of us get wrinkled and grey.' Not that Hine was either. His face was lightly tanned, like polished brass, and what hair he had was jet black and worn long. He had grazes on his cheeks and chin, forehead, knuckles. Either a stumble or a beating.

'Did you fall over, Mick?'

'I get dizzy sometimes.'

'What does the doctor say?'

'Eh?'

No doctor consulted. 'You know there are hostels, you don't need to be out here.'

'Full up. I hate queueing, so I'm always at the back. Your concern has been noted by Michael Edward Hine. Now, do you want to hear the story?'

'In your own time.'

'I knew Lenny in prison, we shared a cell for maybe four months. He was the quiet type, thoughtful. I knew he'd been in trouble before, and yet he didn't fit with prison life. He taught me how to do crosswords, sort out all the jumbled letters. He was patient with me.' Hine seemed to be drifting off, but pulled himself back. 'The man he wrote about is the man he was. He told me himself, he'd done wickedness and never been punished for it. But that didn't make it any easier on his soul, being punished for a crime he didn't commit. Time and again he told me, "I didn't do it, Mick, I swear to God and anybody else who's up there." It was an obsession with him. I think if he hadn't had his writing, he might have done away with himself sooner.'

'You don't think he was got at?'

Hine thought it over before shaking his head firmly. 'I believe he took his own life. That last day, it was like he'd come to a decision, made peace with himself. He was calmer, almost serene. But his eyes . . . he wouldn't look at me. It was like he couldn't deal with people any more. He talked, but he was conversing with himself. I liked him such a lot. And his writing was beautiful . . .'

'The last day?' Rebus prompted. Jack was peering through the railings at the hospital.

'The last day,' Hine repeated. 'That last day was the most spiritual of my life. I really felt touched by . . . grace.'

'Lovely girl,' Jack muttered. Hine didn't hear him.

'You know what his last words were?' Hine closed his eyes, remembering. ' "God knows I'm innocent, Mick, but I'm so tired of saying it over and over." '

Rebus was fidgeting. He wanted to be flippant, ironic, his usual self – but now he found he could identify all too easily with Spaven's epitaph; even perhaps – just a little – with the man himself. Had Lawson Geddes really blinded him? Rebus hardly knew Spaven at all, yet had helped put him in jail for murder, breaching rules and regulations in the process, aiding a man who was feverish with hatred, spellbound by revenge.

But revenge for what?

'When I heard he'd cut his throat, it didn't surprise me. He'd been stroking his neck all day.' Hine leaned forward suddenly, his voice rising. 'And to his dying day he insisted *you* set him up! You and your friend!'

Jack turned towards the bench, ready for trouble. But Rebus wasn't worried.

'Look at me and tell me you didn't!' Hine spat. 'He was the best friend I ever had, the kindest, gentlest man. All gone now, all gone . . .' Hine held his head in his hands and wept.

Of all the options open to him, Rebus knew which he favoured – flight. And that's exactly the option he took, Jack working hard to keep up with him as he fled across the grass, back towards Melville Drive.

'Wait up!' Jack called. 'Hold on there!' They were halfway across the playing-field, in the twilit centre of a triangle bordered by footpaths. Jack tugged at Rebus's arm, tried to slow him. Rebus turned and threw the arm off, then swung a punch. It caught Jack on the cheek, spinning him. There was shock on his face, but he was ready for the second blow, blocked it with a forearm, then threw a right of his own – no southpaw. He feinted, made Rebus think he was aiming for the head, then landed one hard into yielding gut. Rebus grunted, felt the pain but rode with it, took two steps back before launching himself. The two men hit the ground in a roll, their blows lacking force, wrestling for supremacy. Rebus could hear Jack saying his name, over and over. He pushed him off, and came up into a crouch. A couple of cyclists had stopped on one of the paths and were watching.

'John, what the fuck are you doing?'

Teeth bared, Rebus swung again, even more wildly, giving his friend plenty of time to dodge and launch a punch of his own. Rebus almost defended himself, but thought better of it. Instead, he waited for the impact. Jack hit him low, the sort of blow that could wind a man without doing damage. Rebus doubled over, fell to hands and knees, and spewed on to the ground, spitting out mostly liquid. He went on trying to cough everything out, even when there was nothing left to expel. And then he started crying. Crying for himself and for Lawson Geddes, and maybe even for Lenny Spaven. And most of all for Elsie Rhind and all her sisters, all the victims he couldn't help and would never ever be able to help.

Jack was sitting a yard or so away, forearms resting on his knees. He

was breathing hard and sweating, pulling off his jacket. The crying seemed to take for ever, bubbles of snot escaping from Rebus's nose, fine lines of saliva from his mouth. Then he felt the shuddering lessen, stop altogether. He rolled on to his back, his chest rising and falling, an arm across his brow.

'Christ,' he said, 'I needed that.'

'I haven't had a fight like that since I was a teenager,' Jack said. 'Feel better?'

'Much.' Rebus got a handkerchief out, wiped eyes and mouth, then blew his nose. 'Sorry it had to be you.'

'Rather me than some innocent bystander.'

'That's pretty accurate.'

'Is that why you drink? To stop this happening?'

'Christ, Jack, I don't know. I drink because I've always done it. I like it; I like the taste and the sensation, I like standing in pubs.'

'And you like sleep without dreams?'

Rebus nodded. 'That most of all.'

'There are other ways, John.'

'Is this where you try to sell me the Juice Church?'

'You're a big boy, make up your own mind.' Jack got to his feet, pulled Rebus to his.

'I bet we look like a couple of dossers.'

'Well, you do. I don't know about me.'

'Elegant, Jack, you look cool and elegant.'

Jack touched a hand to Rebus's shoulder. 'OK now?'

Rebus nodded. 'It's daft, but I feel better than for ages. Come on, let's go for a walk.'

They turned and headed back towards the Infirmary. Jack didn't ask where they were going. But Rebus had a destination in mind: the university library in George Square. It was just closing as they walked in, the departing students, folders huddled to chests, giving them plenty of room as they walked up to the main desk.

'Can I help you?' a man asked, looking them up and down. But Rebus was walking around the desk to where a young woman was bowed over a pile of books.

'Hello, Nell.'

She looked up, couldn't place him at first. Then the blood left her face. 'What's happened?'

Rebus held up a hand. 'Brian's fine. Jack here and me ... well, we ...'

'Tripped and fell,' Jack said.

'You shouldn't drink in pubs with stairs.' Now she knew Brian was all right, she was regaining her composure fast, and with it her wariness. 'What do you want?'

'A word,' Rebus said. 'Maybe outside?'

'I'll be finished here in five minutes.'

Rebus nodded. 'We'll wait.'

They went outside. Rebus went to light a cigarette but found the packet crushed, its contents useless.

'Christ, just when I could do with one.'

'Now you know how it feels to give up.'

They sat on the steps and stared at George Square Gardens and the buildings surrounding it, a mishmash of old and new.

'You can almost feel all that brain power in the air,' Jack commented.

'Half the force has been to university these days.'

'And I bet they don't go swinging punches at their friends.'

'I've said I'm sorry.'

'Did Sammy ever go to uni?'

'College. I think she did something secretarial. She works for a charity now.'

'Which one?'

'SWEEP.'

'Working with ex-cons?'

'That's it.'

'Did she do it to have a dig at you?'

Rebus had asked himself the same question many times. He shrugged. 'Fathers and daughters, eh?'

The door swung open behind them. It was Nell Stapleton. She was tall, with short dark hair and a defiant face. No earrings or jewellery.

'You can walk me to the bus stop,' she told them.

'Look, Nell,' Rebus started, realising that he should have thought this through, should have rehearsed, 'all I want to say is, I'm sorry about you and Brian.'

'Thanks.' She was walking quickly. Rebus's knee hurt as he kept up.

'I know I'm unlikely material as marriage guidance, but there's something you have to know: Brian's a born copper. He doesn't want to lose you – it's killing him – but leaving the force would be a slow death in itself. He can't *make* himself leave, so instead he's trying to get into trouble, so the high hiedyins will have no alternative but to boot him out. That's no way to sort a problem.'

Nell didn't say anything for a while. They headed for Potterrow, crossed the road at the lights. They were headed for Greyfriars, plenty of bus stops there.

'I know what you're saying,' she said at last. 'You're saying it's a no-win situation.'

'Not at all.'

'Please, just listen to me.' Her eyes were glistening in the sodium light. 'I don't want to spend the rest of my life waiting for the phone call, the one that tells me there's bad news. I don't want to plan weekends off and holidays away only to have them cancelled because some case or court appearance takes precedence. That's asking too much.'

'It's asking a hell of a lot,' Rebus conceded. 'It's a high-wire act without the safety net. But all the same . . .'

'What?'

'You can make it work. A lot of people do. Maybe you can't plan things too far in advance, maybe there'll be cancellations and tears. When the chances come, you take them.'

'Have I wandered into a Dr Ruth show by mistake?' Rebus sighed, and she stopped walking, took his hand. 'Look, John, I know why you're doing this. Brian's hurting, and you don't like to see it. I don't like it either.' A

distant siren wailed, down towards the High Street, and Nell shivered. Rebus saw it, looked into her eyes, and found himself nodding. He knew she was right; his own wife had said the same things. And the way Jack was standing, the look on his face, he'd been here before, too. Nell started walking again.

'He'll leave the force, Nell. He'll make them dump him. But for the rest of his life . . .' He shook his head. 'It won't be the same. *He* won't be the same.'

She nodded. 'I can live with that.'

'You don't know for sure.'

'No, I don't.'

'You'll take that risk, but you won't risk him staying put?' Her face hardened, but Rebus didn't give her time for a comeback. 'Here's your bus. Just think about it, Nell.'

He turned and walked back towards the Meadows.

They'd made up a bed for Jack in the spare room – Sammy's old bedroom, complete with Duran Duran and Michael Jackson posters. They'd washed themselves and shared a pot of tea – no alcohol, no ciggies. Rebus lay in bed and stared at the ceiling, knew sleep wouldn't come for ages, and that when it did his dreams would be fierce. He got up and tiptoed through to the living room, keeping the lights off. The room was cool, they'd kept the windows open late, but the fresh paint and the old scorched paint from the door left a nice smell. Rebus uncovered his chair and dragged it over to the bay window. He sat down and pulled his blanket over him, felt himself relax. There were lights on across the way and he concentrated on them. I'm a peeper, he thought, a voyeur. All cops are. But he knew he was more than that: he liked to get involved in the lives around him. He had a need to *know* which went beyond voyeurism. It was a drug. And the thing was, when he had all this knowledge, he then had to use booze to blank it out. He saw his reflection in the window, two-dimensional, ghostly.

I'm almost not here at all, he thought.

24

Rebus woke up and knew something was wrong. He showered and dressed and still couldn't put a name to it. Then Jack came slouching through to the kitchen and asked if he'd slept well.

And he had. *That* was what was different. He'd slept very well indeed, and he'd been sober.

'Any word from Ancram?' Jack asked, staring into the fridge.

'No.'

'Then you're probably clear for today.'

'He must be in training for the next bout.'

'So do we crack on with the decorating, or actually go to work?'

'Let's do an hour's painting,' Rebus said. So that's what they did, Rebus keeping half an eye on the street outside. No reporters, no *Justice Programme*. Maybe he'd scared them off; maybe they were biding their time. He hadn't heard anything about an assault charge: Breen was probably too happy with the video footage to consider any further action. Plenty of time to file a complaint after the programme went out . . .

After the painting, they took Jack's car to Fort Apache. Jack's initial response did not disappoint Rebus.

'What a shit-hole.'

Inside, the station was a frenzy of packing and moving. Vans were already taking crates and boxes to the new station. The desk sergeant had become a shirt-sleeved foreman, making sure the cases were labelled and the moving crew knew where they were to go once they reached their destination.

'It'll be a miracle if it goes to plan,' he said. 'And I notice CID aren't giving a hand.'

Jack and Rebus gave him a round of applause: an old joke, but well intentioned. Then they went to the Shed.

Maclay and Bain were in situ.

'The prodigal son!' Bain exclaimed. 'Where the hell have you been?'

'Helping CI Ancram with his inquiries.'

'You should have called in. MacAskill wants a word, toot-sweet.'

'I thought I told you never to call me that.'

Bain smirked. Rebus introduced Jack Morton. There were nods, handshakes, grunts: the usual procedure.

'You better go see the Boss,' Maclay said. 'He's been fretting.'

'I've been missing him, too.'

'Did you bring us back anything from Aberdeen?'

Rebus searched his pockets. 'Must have slipped my mind.'

'Well,' Bain said, 'you were probably busy.'

'Busier than you two, but that wouldn't be hard.'

'Go see the Boss,' Maclay told him.

Bain was wagging a finger. 'And you should be nice to us, otherwise we might not tell you what our snitches came up with.'

'What?' Local snitches: word out for Tony El's accomplice.

'After you've talked to MacAskill.'

So Rebus went to see his boss, leaving Jack Morton outside the door.

'John,' Jim MacAskill said, 'what have you been playing at?'

'Different games, sir.'

'So I hear, and you've not proved proficient at any of them, eh?'

MacAskill's office was emptying, but there was some way to go. His filing cabinet stood with its drawers gutted, the files themselves spread across the floor.

'Nightmare,' he said, noticing Rebus's look. 'How's your own packing coming?'

'I travel light, sir.'

'I forget, you've not been with us long. Sometimes it seems like for ever.'

'I have that effect on people.'

MacAskill smiled. 'Question one in my mind, this reopening of the Spaven case: is it going to go anywhere?'

'Not if I have my way.'

'Well, Chick Ancram's pretty persistent . . . and thorough. Don't depend on him overlooking something.'

'Yes, sir.'

'I've had a word with your boss at St Leonard's. He tells me this is par for the course.'

'I don't know, sir, seems like I'm playing under a handicap.'

'Well, anything I can do, John . . .'

'Thank you, sir.'

'I know the way Chick will play it: attrition. He'll sweat the arse off you, run you in circles. He makes it easier for you to lie and say you're guilty than to keep telling the truth. Watch out for that.'

'Will do.'

'Meantime, question one: how are you feeling?'

'I'm all right, sir.'

'Well, there's not much happening around here that we can't handle. So any time off you need, take it.'

'I appreciate that.'

'Chick's west coast, John. He shouldn't be over here.' MacAskill shook his head, went to his drawer for a can of Irn-Bru. 'Bugger,' he said.

'Problem, sir?'

'I've gone and bought the diet stuff.' He opened it anyway. Rebus left him to his packing.

Jack was right outside the door.

'Did you catch any of that?'

'I wasn't listening.'

'My boss just told me I can bunk off whenever I like.'

'Which means we can finish doing up the living room.'

Rebus nodded, but he was thinking of finishing something else instead. He went into the Shed and stood in front of Bain's desk.

'Well?'

'Well,' Bain said, sitting back, 'we did what you asked, put word out with our snitches. And they came up with a name.'

'Hank Shankley,' Maclay added.

'He's not got much of a record, but he's game to make a few quid where he can, no scruples attached. And he gets around. Word is, he's had a windfall and after a couple of drinks he was boasting about his "Glasgow connection".'

'Have you talked to him?'

Bain shook his head. 'Bided our time.'

'Waiting for you to turn up,' Maclay added.

'Have you been rehearsing this routine? Where can I find him?'

'He's a keen swimmer.'

'Anywhere in particular?'

'The Commie Pool.'

'Description?'

'Big building at the top of Dalkeith Road.'

'I meant Shankley.'

'You can't miss him,' Maclay said. 'Late thirties, six feet tall and skinny as a pole, short fair hair. Nordic looking.'

'The description we got,' Bain corrected, 'was albino.'

Rebus nodded. 'I owe you for this, gents.'

'You haven't heard who it was spilled the beans.'

'Who?'

Bain grinned. 'Remember Craw Shand?'

'Claimed to be Johnny Bible?' Bain and Maclay nodded. 'Why didn't you tell me he was a snitch of yours?'

Bain shrugged. 'Didn't want it broadcast. But Craw's a big fan of yours. See, he likes it rough now and then . . .'

Outside, Jack made for the car, but Rebus had other plans. He went into a shop and came out with six cans of Irn-Bru, *not* diet, then marched back into the station. The desk sergeant was sweating. Rebus handed him the carrier bag.

'You shouldn't have,' the sergeant said.

'They're for Jim MacAskill,' Rebus said. 'I want at least five to reach him.'

Now he was ready to go.

The Commonwealth Pool, which had been built for the Commonwealth Games in 1970, was sited at the top of Dalkeith Road, at the foot of Arthur's Seat, and just over quarter of a mile from St Leonard's police station. In the days when he swam, Rebus used the Commie Pool at lunchtimes. You found yourself a lane – never an empty lane, it was like easing out of a slip-road on to a motorway – and you swam, pacing yourself so you didn't catch up with the person in front, or let the person behind gain on you. It was OK, but a bit too regimented. The other option was to

swim breadths in the open pool, but then you were in with the kids and their parents. There was a separate pool for infants, plus three flumes Rebus had never been down, and elsewhere in the building were saunas, gym, and a café.

They found a space in the overflow car park and went in by the main entrance. Rebus showed ID at the kiosk and gave a description of Shankley.

'He's a regular,' the woman told him.

'Is he here just now?'

'I don't know. I've only just come on.' She turned to ask the other woman in the booth, who was counting coins into polythene bank-bags. Jack Morton tapped Rebus's arm and nodded.

Beyond the kiosk there was a wide open space, with windows looking down on to the main pool. And standing there, glugging Coke from the can, stood a very tall, very thin man with damp, bleached hair. He had a rolled-up towel under one arm. When he turned, Rebus saw that his eyebrows and lashes were fair. Shankley saw two men examining him, placed them immediately. When Rebus and Morton started towards him, he ran.

He turned a corner into the open-plan café, but couldn't see an exit from there, so kept running, ended up beside the children's play area. This was a large netted enclosure totalling three storeys, with slides and walkways and other challenges – a toddler assault course. Rebus liked sometimes to sit with a post-swim coffee watching the kids playing, wondering which would make the best soldier.

Shankley was cornered and knew it. He turned to face them: Rebus and Jack were smiling. The impulse to flee was still too strong: Shankley pushed past the attendant, opened the door to the play area, ducked and went in. Two huge padded rollers stood directly in front of him, like a giant mangle. He was thin enough to squeeze between them.

Jack Morton laughed. 'Where's he going to go from there?'

'I don't know.'

'Let's grab a cup of tea and wait for him to get fed up.'

Rebus shook his head. He'd heard a noise from the top storey. 'There's a kid in there.' He turned to the attendant. 'Isn't there?'

She nodded. Rebus turned to Jack. 'Possible hostage. I'm going in. Stay out here, tell me where Shankley is.'

Rebus took off his jacket and went in.

The rollers were the first obstacle. He was too big to squeeze through, but managed to push his way through the gap between them and the side netting. He remembered his SAS training: assault courses you wouldn't believe. Kept going. A pool of coloured plastic balls to wade through, and then a tube curving upwards, leading to the first floor. A slide nearby – he climbed that. Through the netting he could see Jack, pointing up and towards the far corner. Rebus stayed in a crouch, looked around. Punch-bags, a net across a yawning gap, a cylinder to crawl through . . . more slides and climbing-ropes. There: far corner, wondering what to do next. Hank Shankley. People in the café were watching, no longer interested in swimming. One floor further up was the kid. Rebus had to get there before Shankley; either that or grab Shankley first. Shankley didn't know anyone was in here with him. Jack was shouting up, distracting him.

'Hey, Hank, we can wait here all day! All night too if we have to! Come on out, we only want a chat! Hank, you look ridiculous in there. Maybe we'll just padlock it shut and keep you for an exhibit.'

'Shut up!' Flecks of foam from Shankley's mouth. Skinny, gaunt ... Rebus knew it was crazy to worry about HIV, but found himself worrying anyway. Edinburgh was still HIV city. He was about fifteen feet from Shankley when he heard a swooshing sound coming towards him fast. He was passing the exit to one of the tubes when a pair of feet hit him, toppling him on to his side. A boy about eight years old stared at him.

'You're too big for in here, mister.'

Rebus got up, saw Shankley coming for them, and started dragging the kid by the scruff of his neck. He backed up to the slide, then dropped the boy down it. He was turning to confront Shankley when another foot hit him – the albino's. He bounced off the mesh wall and tumbled down the padded slide. The boy was making his way to the entrance, where the attendant gestured for him to hurry. Shankley slid down, both fists out, and clubbed Rebus on the neck. He was sprinting for the kid, but the boy was already through the rollers. Rebus dived at Shankley, brought him down into the plastic balls, caught him with a decent punch. Shankley's arms were tired from swimming; he pummelled Rebus's sides, but it was like being hit by a rag doll. Rebus grabbed a ball, stuffed it into Shankley's mouth, where it wedged, the lips taut and bloodless. Then he hit Shankley in the groin, twice, and that just about did it.

Jack came to help him drag the unresisting figure out. 'You all right?' he asked.

'The kid hurt me more than he did.'

The boy's mother was hugging her son, checking he was all right. She gave Rebus a dirty look. The boy was complaining he still had ten minutes left. The attendant came after Rebus.

'Excuse me,' she said, 'could I have our ball back?'

St Leonard's being so close, they took Shankley there, asked for and were given an empty biscuit-tin, only recently vacated by the smell of it.

'Sit there,' Rebus told Shankley. Then he took Jack outside, spoke in an undertone.

'To fill you in, Tony El killed Allan Mitchison – I still don't know why exactly. Tony had local help.' He tilted his head towards the door. 'I want to know what Hank knows.'

Jack nodded. 'Do I stay dumb, or is there a part for me?'

'You're the good guy, Jack.' Rebus patted his shoulder. 'Always have been.'

They went back into the room as a team, like in the old days.

'Well, Mr Shankley,' Rebus opened, 'so far we've got resisting arrest and assaulting a police officer. Plenty of witnesses, too.'

'I haven't done nothing.'

'Double negative.'

'Eh?'

'If you haven't done nothing, you must have done *something*.'

Shankley just looked glum. Rebus had him pegged already: Bain's 'no scruples attached' had given him the clue. Shankley lived to no code

whatsoever, except perhaps 'Look after number one'. He didn't give a toss for anything or anyone. There was no intelligence other than a root instinct to survive. Rebus knew he could play on that.

'You don't owe Tony El anything, Hank. Who do you think grassed you up?'

'Tony who?'

'Anthony Ellis Kane. Glasgow hardman relocated to Aberdeen. He was down here to do a job. He needed an associate. Somehow he ended up with you.'

'Not your fault,' Jack chipped in, hands in pockets, 'you're an accessory. We're not doing you for murder.'

'Murder?'

'That young guy Tony El was after,' Rebus explained. 'You scouted out somewhere to take him. That was about the sum of your part, wasn't it? The rest was down to Tony.'

Shankley bit his top lip, showing a bottom row of narrow uneven teeth. His eyes were pale blue with dark flecks in them, his pupils contracted to pencil dots.

'Of course,' Rebus said, 'there's another way we can play it. We could say *you* tossed him out that window.'

'I don't know nothing.'

'Don't know *anything*,' Rebus reminded him. Shankley folded his arms, spread his long legs.

'I want a lawyer.'

'Been watching the *Kojak* repeats, Hank?' Jack asked. He looked to Rebus, who nodded: no more Mr Nice Guy.

'I'm bored with this, Hank. Know what? We're going to take you for fingerprinting now. You left prints all over that squat. You even left behind the carry-out. Prints all over it. You remember touching the bottles? The cans? The bag they were in?' Shankley was trying hard to remember. Rebus's voice grew quieter. 'We've got you, Hank. You're fucked. I'll give you ten seconds to start talking, and that's it – promise. Don't think you can talk to us later, we won't be listening. The judge will have his hearing-aid switched off. You'll be on your own. Know why?' He waited till he had Shankley's attention. 'Because Tony El croaked. Someone sliced him open in a bathtub. Could be you next.' Rebus nodded. 'You need friends, Hank.'

'Listen . . .' The Tony El story had woken Shankley up. He sat forward in his chair. 'Look, I'm . . . I . . .'

'Take your time, Hank.'

Jack asked him if he wanted something to drink. Shankley nodded. 'Cola or something.'

'Fetch me one, too, Jack,' Rebus said. Jack went down the hall to the machine. Rebus bided his time, pacing the room, giving Shankley time to decide how much he was going to tell and with how much gloss. Jack came back, tossed one can at Shankley, handed the other to Rebus, who pulled it open and drank. It wasn't a real drink. It was cold and way too sweet, and the only kick it would give him was from caffeine rather than alcohol. He saw Jack watching him, screwed up his face in reply. He wanted a cigarette, too. Jack read the look, shrugged.

'Now then,' Rebus said. 'Do you have a story for us, Hank?'

Shankley burped, nodded. 'It's like you said. He told me he was here to do a job. Said he had Glasgow connections.'

'What did he mean by that?'

Shankley shrugged. 'Never asked.'

'Did he mention Aberdeen at all?'

Shankley shook his head. 'Glasgow was what he said.'

'Continue.'

'He offered me fifty notes to find him a place where he could take someone. I asked him what he was going to do, and he said ask a few questions, maybe give them a doing. That was all. We waited outside this block of flats, quite posh.'

'The Financial District?'

Another shrug. 'Between Lothian Road and Haymarket.' That was it. 'Saw this young guy come out, and we followed him. For a while, we just watched, then Tony said it was time to strike up his acquaintance.'

'And?'

'Well, we got chatting to him, like. I got to enjoying myself, forgot what was happening. Tony looked like he'd forgotten, too. I thought maybe he was going to call it off. Then we went outside for a taxi, and when the young guy couldn't see us, he gave me a look, and I knew it was still on. But I swear, I only thought the kid was for a kicking.'

'Not so.'

'No.' Shankley's voice dropped. 'Tony had a bag with him. When we got to the flat, he brought out tape and stuff. Tied the kid to the chair. He had a plastic sheet, put a bag over the kid's head.' Shankley's voice cracked. He cleared his throat, took another swallow of cola. 'Then he started taking stuff out of the bag, tools, you know, like a joiner would use. Saws and screwdrivers and that.'

Rebus looked to Jack Morton.

'And that's when I realised the plastic sheet was to catch the blood, the kid wasn't just getting a kicking.'

'Tony planned to torture him?'

'I suppose so. I don't know . . . maybe I'd've tried to stop him. I've never done anything like that before. I mean, I've doled it out in my time, but never . . .'

The next question used to be the one that counted; Rebus wasn't so sure any more. 'Did Allan Mitchison jump, or what?'

Shankley nodded. 'We had our backs turned. Tony was taking the tools out, and I was just staring at them. The kid had a bag over his head, but I think he saw them. He got between us and went out the window. Must've been scared to death.'

Looking at Shankley, and remembering Anthony Kane, Rebus sensed again how bland monstrosity could be. Faces and voices didn't give any clue; no one sported horns and fangs, dripping blood and all slouching malevolence. Evil was almost . . . it was almost childlike: naïve, simplistic. A game you played and then woke up from, only to find it wasn't pretend. The real-life monsters weren't grotesques: they were quiet men and women, people you passed on the street and didn't notice. Rebus was glad he couldn't read people's minds. It would be pure hell.

'What did you do?' he asked.

'Packed up and shipped out. We went back to my place first, had a couple of drinks. I was shaking. Tony kept saying it was a mess, but he didn't seem worried. We realised we'd left the hooch – couldn't remember if our dabs were on it. I thought they were. That's when Tony took off. He left me my share, I'll give him that.'

'How far do you live from the flat, Hank?'

'About two minutes' walk. I'm not there much; the kids call me names.'

Life can be cruel, Rebus thought. Two minutes: when he'd arrived at the scene, Tony El might have been only two minutes away. But they'd ended up meeting in Stonehaven . . .

'Didn't Tony give you any idea *why* he was after Allan Mitchison?' Shankley shook his head. 'And when did he first approach you?'

'Couple of days before.'

Therefore premeditated. Well, of course it was premeditated, but more than that it meant Tony El had been in Edinburgh, preparing the scheme, while Allan Mitchison had still been in Aberdeen. The night of his death had been his first day of leave. So Tony El hadn't followed him south from Aberdeen . . . yet he knew what Allan Mitchison looked like, knew where he lived – there was a telephone in the flat, but unlisted.

Allan Mitchison had been set up by someone who'd known him.

It was Jack Morton's turn. 'Hank, think carefully now, didn't Tony say *anything* about the job, about who was paying him?'

Shankley thought, then nodded slowly. He looked pleased with himself: he'd remembered something.

'Mr H.,' he said. 'Tony said something about Mr H. He clammed up afterwards, like he hadn't meant to.' Shankley almost danced in his seat. He wanted Rebus and Morton to like him. Their smiles told him they did. But Rebus was thinking furiously; the only Mr H. he came up with was Jake Harley. It didn't fit.

'Good man,' Jack cajoled. 'Now think again, tell us something else.'

But Rebus had a question. 'Did you see Tony El jacking up?'

'No, but I knew he was doing it. When we were following the kid, first bar we went in, Tony went to the bog. He came out, and I knew he was on something. Living where I do, it gets so you can tell.'

Tony El a shooter. It didn't mean he wasn't killed. All it meant was, maybe he'd made Stanley's job easier. Tony El sky-high easier to murder than Tony El with defences up. Drugs to Aberdeen . . . Burke's Club a magnet for them . . . Tony El using – and selling? He wished he'd asked Erik Stemmons about Tony El.

'I need the toilet,' Shankley said.

'We'll get a uniform to take you. Stay here.' Rebus and Morton left the room.

'Jack, I want you to trust me.'

'How far?'

'I want you to stay here and take Shankley's statement.'

'While you do what?'

'Take someone to lunch.' Rebus checked his watch. 'I'll be back here by three.'

'Look, John . . .'

'Call it parole. I go to lunch, I come back. Two hours.' Rebus held up two fingers. 'Two hours, Jack.'

'Which restaurant?'

'What?'

'Tell me where you're going. I'll phone every quarter of an hour, you better be there.' Rebus looked disgusted. 'And I want to know who your guest is.'

'It's a woman.'

'Name?'

Rebus sighed. 'I've heard of driving a hard bargain, but you've got your HGV.'

'Name?' Jack was smiling.

'Gill Templer. Chief Inspector Gill Templer. OK?'

'OK. Now the restaurant.'

'I don't know. I'll tell you when I get there.'

'Phone me. If you don't, Chick gets to know, OK?'

'It's back to "Chick", is it?'

'He gets to know.'

'All right, I'll phone.'

'With the restaurant's number?'

'With the number. Know what, Jack? You've put me right off eating.'

'Order plenty and bring me a doggy bag.'

Rebus went in search of Gill, found her in her office. She told him she'd already eaten.

'So come and watch me.'

'An offer I can't refuse.'

There was an Italian restaurant on Clerk Street. Rebus ordered a pizza: he could take anything he couldn't eat back to Jack. Then he phoned St Leonard's and left the pizzeria's number, told them to pass it on.

'So,' Gill said when he was seated again, 'been busy?'

'Plenty busy. I went to Aberdeen.'

'What for?'

'That phone number on Feardie Fergie's pad. Plus a few other things.'

'What other things?'

'Not necessarily connected.'

'Tell me, did the trip pass without incident?' She picked up a piece of the garlic bread which had just arrived.

'Not exactly.'

'You surprise me.'

'They say it keeps a relationship on its toes.'

Gill took a bite of bread. 'So what did you find out?'

'Burke's Club is dirty. It's also where Johnny Bible's first victim was last seen alive. The place is run by two Yanks; I only spoke with one of them. I think probably his partner's the grubbier of the two.'

'And?'

'And, also in Burke's I saw a couple of members of a Glaswegian crime family. You know Uncle Joe Toal?'

'I've heard of him.'

'I think he's delivering dope to Aberdeen. From there, I'd guess some of it goes to the rigs – a captive market; a lot of boredom on a rig.'

'You'd know, of course?' she joked. Then she saw the look on his face, and her eyes narrowed. 'You went on a rig?'

'Most terrifying experience of my life, but cathartic with it.'

'Cathartic?'

'An old girlfriend used to use words like that; they rub off on you after a while. The club's owner, Erik Stemmons, denied knowing Fergie McLure. I almost believe him.'

'Which puts his partner in the frame?'

'To my mind.'

'And that's as far as it's got – your mind? I mean, there's no evidence?'

'Not a shred.'

His pizza arrived. Chorizo, mushroom and anchovy. Gill had to look away. The pizza was pre-cut into six fat slices. Rebus lifted one on to his plate.

'I don't know how you can face that.'

'Me neither,' said Rebus, sniffing the surface. 'But it'll make a hell of a doggie bag.'

There was a cigarette machine. If he looked over Gill's right shoulder he could see it there on the wall. Five brands, any of which would suffice. There was a book of matches waiting in the ashtray. He'd ordered a glass of house white, Gill spring water. The wine – 'delicately bouqueted' as the menu put it – arrived, and he gave it the nose test before sipping. It was chilled and sour.

'How's the bouquet?' Gill asked.

'Any more delicate and it'd need Prozac.' The drinks card was in front of him, standing erect in its little holder, listing aperitifs and cocktails and digestifs, plus wines, beers, lagers, spirits. It was the most reading Rebus had done in a couple of days. As soon as he'd finished, he read it again. He wanted to shake the author's hand.

One segment of pizza was enough.

'Not hungry?' Gill asked.

'I'm dieting.'

'You?'

'I want to be fit for my walks along the beach.'

She wasn't following him, shook her head clear of seeming non-sequiturs.

'The thing is, Gill,' he said after another sip of wine, 'I think you were on to something big. And I think it can be salvaged. I just want to be sure it's *your* collar.'

She looked at him. 'Why?'

'Because of all the Christmas presents I've never given you. Because you deserve it. Because it'll be your *first*.'

'It doesn't count if you've done all the work.'

'It'll count all right, all I'm doing is reconnaissance.'

'You mean you're not finished?'

Rebus shook his head, asked the waiter to put the rest of the pizza in a box. He lifted the last piece of garlic bread.

'I'm not nearly finished,' he told her. 'But I might need your help.'

'Oh-oh. Here it comes.'

Rebus spoke quickly. 'Chick Ancram's got me set up for a series of grillings. I've already had one, and between ourselves he didn't cook me more than medium rare. But they take up time, and I might want to head north again.'

'John . . .'

'All I need you to do . . . *might* need you to do, is telephone Ancram some day and tell him I'm working for you on something urgent, so we'll have to reschedule the interview. Just charm the socks off him and give me some time. That's all I need. I'll try to keep you out of it if I can.'

'So, to recap, all you need is for me to lie to a fellow officer who is carrying out an internal investigation? And meantime, lacking any physical or verbal evidence, you'll be solving the drug-running case?'

'Nicely summarised. I can see why you're the CI instead of me.' He shot to his feet, ran to the payphone. He'd heard it ringing before anyone in the restaurant. It was Jack, checking on him. He reminded Rebus about the doggy bag.

'Being brought to the table as I speak.'

When he got to the table, Gill was checking the bill.

'This is on me,' Rebus said.

'At least let me leave the tip. I ate most of the bread. And besides, my water cost more than your wine.'

'You got the better deal. What's it to be, Gill?'

She nodded. 'I'll tell him anything you like.'

25

Jack still had the power to surprise his old friend: wolfed the pizza. His only comment: 'You didn't eat much.'

'Bit bland for me, Jack.'

Rebus was itching now: for a cigarette and Aberdeen both. There was something up there he wanted; he just didn't know quite what it was.

The truth maybe.

He should have been itching for a drink too, but the wine had put him off. It slopped in his stomach, liquid heartburn. He sat at a desk and read through Shankley's statement. The big man was in a cell downstairs. Jack had worked fast; Rebus couldn't see anything missing.

'So,' he said, 'I'm back from parole. How did I do?'

'Let's not make it a regular date, my heart couldn't take it.'

Rebus smiled, picked up a phone. He wanted to check his machine at home, see if Ancram had plans for him. He did: nine tomorrow morning. There was another message. It was from Kayleigh Burgess. She needed to talk with him.

'I'm seeing someone in Morningside at three, so how about four at that big hotel in Bruntsfield? We can have afternoon tea.' She said it was important. Rebus decided to go out there and wait. He'd have preferred to leave Jack behind . . .

'Know what, Jack? You're severely cramping my style.'

'How do you mean?'

'With women. There's one I want to see, but I bet you're going to tag along, aren't you?'

Jack shrugged. 'I'll wait outside the door if you like.'

'It'll be a comfort to know you're there.'

'It could be worse,' stuffing his face with the last of the pizza, 'just think, how do Siamese twins arrange their love lives?'

'Some questions are best left unanswered,' Rebus said.

He thought: Good question though.

It was a nice hotel, quietly upmarket. Rebus worked out a possible dialogue in his head. Ancram knew about the clippings in his kitchen, and Kayleigh was the only possible source. He'd been furious at the time, less angry now. It was her job after all: information, and using that information to elicit other information. It still rankled. Then there was the Spaven-McLure connection: Ancram had picked up on it; Kayleigh knew about it. And finally, above all, there was the break-in.

They waited for her in the lounge. Jack flicked through *Scottish Field* and kept reading out descriptions of estates for sale: 'seven thousand acres in Caithness, with hunting lodge, stabling, and working farm'. He looked up at Rebus.

'Some country this, eh? Where else could you lay your hands on seven thousand acres at knockdown prices?'

'There's a theatre group called 7:84 – know what it means?'

'What?'

'Seven per cent of the population controls eighty-four per cent of the wealth.'

'Are we in the seven?'

Rebus snorted. 'Not even close, Jack.'

'I wouldn't mind a taste of the high life, though.'

'At what cost?'

'Eh?'

'What would you be willing to trade?'

'No, I mean like winning the lottery or something.'

'So you wouldn't take back-handers to drop a charge?'

Jack's eyes narrowed. 'What are you getting at?'

'Come on, Jack. I was in Glasgow, remember? I saw good suits and jewellery, I saw something approaching the smug.'

'They just like to dress nice, makes them feel important.'

'Uncle Joe's not doling out freebies?'

'I wouldn't know if he was.' Jack lifted the magazine to shield his face: matter closed. And then Kayleigh Burgess walked in through the door.

She saw Rebus immediately, and a blush started creeping up her neck. By the time she'd walked over to where he was rising from his chair, it had climbed as far as her cheeks.

'Inspector, you got my message.' Rebus nodded, eyes unblinking. 'Well, thanks for coming.' She turned to Jack Morton.

'DI Morton,' Jack said, shaking her hand.

'Do you want some tea?'

Rebus shook his head, gestured towards the free chair. She sat down. 'So?' he said, determined to make nothing easy for her, not ever again.

She sat with her shoulder-bag in her lap, twisting the strap. 'Look,' she said, 'I owe you an apology.' She glanced up at him, then away, took a deep breath. 'I didn't tell CI Ancram about those cuttings. Or about Fergus McLure knowing Spaven, come to that.'

'But you know he knows?'

She nodded. 'Eamonn told him.'

'And who told Eamonn?'

'I did. I didn't know what to make of it . . . I wanted to bounce it off someone. We're a team, so I told Eamonn. I made him promise it'd go no further.'

'But it did.'

She nodded. 'He was straight on the phone to Ancram. See, Eamonn . . . he's got a thing about police brass. If we're investigating someone at Inspector level, Eamonn always wants to go over their heads, talk to their superiors, see what gets stirred up. Besides, you haven't exactly made a favourable impression with my presenter.'

'It was an accident,' Rebus said. 'I tripped.'

'If that's your story.'

'What does the footage say?'

She thought about it. 'We were shooting from behind Eamonn. Mostly, what we've got is his back.'

'I'm off the hook then?'

'I didn't say that. Just stick to your story.'

Rebus nodded, getting her drift. 'Thanks. But why did Breen go to Ancram? Why not *my* boss?'

'Because Eamonn knew Ancram was to lead the inquiry.'

'And how did he know *that*?'

'The grapevine.'

A grapevine with few grapes attached. He saw Jim Stevens again, staring up at the window of his flat . . . Stirring it . . .

Rebus sighed. 'One last thing. Do you know anything about a break-in at my flat?'

Her eyebrows rose. 'Should I?'

'Remember the Bible John stuff in the cupboard? Someone took a crowbar to my front door, and all they wanted was to rifle through it.'

She was shaking her head. 'Not us.'

'No?'

'Housebreaking? We're journalists, for Christ's sake.'

Rebus had his hands up in a gesture of appeasement, but he wanted to push it a little further. 'Any chance Breen would go out on a limb?'

Now she laughed. 'Not even for a story the size of Watergate. Eamonn fronts the programme, he doesn't do any digging.'

'You and your researchers do?'

'Yes, and neither of them seems the crowbar type. Does that leave me in the frame?'

As she crossed one leg over the other, Jack studied them. His eyes had been running all over her like a kid's over a Scalextric set.

'Consider the matter closed,' Rebus said.

'But it's true? Your flat was broken into?'

'Matter closed,' he repeated.

She almost pouted. 'How's the inquiry going anyway?' She held up a hand. 'I'm not snooping, call it personal interest.'

'Depends which inquiry you mean,' Rebus said.

'The Spaven case.'

'Oh, that.' Rebus sniffed, considering his response. 'Well, CI Ancram is the trusting sort. He has real faith in his officers. If you plead innocent, he'll take it at face value. It's a comfort to have superiors like that. For instance, he trusts me so much he's got a minder on me like a limpet on a rock.' He nodded towards Jack. 'Inspector Morton here is supposed to not let me out of his sight. He even sleeps at my flat.' He held Kayleigh's gaze. 'How's that sound?'

She could hardly form the words. 'It's scandalous.'

Rebus shrugged, but she was reaching into her bag, bringing out notebook and pen. Jack glowered at Rebus, who winked back. Kayleigh had to flick through a lot of pages to find a fresh sheet.

'When did this start?' she said.

'Let's see . . .' Rebus pretended to be thinking. 'Sunday afternoon, I think. After I'd been interrogated in Aberdeen and dragged back here.'

She looked up. 'Interrogated?'

'John . . .' Jack Morton warned.

'Didn't you know?' Rebus's eyes widened. 'I'm a suspect in the Johnny Bible case.'

On the drive back to the flat, Jack was furious.

'What did you think you were up to?'

'Keeping her mind off Spaven.'

'I don't get it.'

'She's trying to make a programme about Spaven, Jack. She's not doing one on policemen being nasty to other policemen, and she's not doing one on Johnny Bible.'

'So?'

'So now her head's swimming with everything I told her – and not a jot of it has to do with Spaven. It'll keep her . . . what's the word?'

'Preoccupied?'

'Good enough.' Rebus nodded, looked at his watch. Five-twenty. 'Shit,' he said. 'Those pictures!'

Traffic was at a crawl as they detoured into the centre of town. Rush-hour Edinburgh was a nightmare these days. Red lights and chugging exhausts, frayed nerves and drumming fingers. By the time they reached the shop it had closed for the night. Rebus checked the opening hours: nine tomorrow. He could pick up the photos on his way to Fettes and only be a little late for Ancram. Ancram: the very thought of the man was like voltage passing through him.

'Let's go home,' he told Jack. Then he remembered the traffic. 'No, second thoughts: we'll stop off at the Ox.' Jack smiled. 'Did you think you'd cured me?' Rebus shook his head. 'I sometimes come off for a couple of days at a stretch, it's no big thing.'

'It could be though.'

'Another sermon, Jack?'

Jack shook his head. 'What about the ciggies?'

'I'll buy a packet from the machine.'

He stood at the bar, resting one shoe on the foot-rail, one elbow on the polished wood. In front of him sat four objects: a packet of cigarettes with seal unbroken; a box of Scottish Bluebell matches; a thirty-five millilitre measure of Teacher's whisky; and a pint of Belhaven Best. He was staring at them with the concentration of a psychic willing them to move.

'Three minutes dead,' a regular commented from along the bar, like he'd been timing Rebus's resistance. A profound question was running through Rebus's mind: did he want them, or did *they* want *him*? He wondered how David Hume would have got on with that. He picked the beer up. No wonder you called it 'heavy': that's just what it was. He sniffed it. It didn't smell too enticing; he knew it would taste OK, but other things tasted better. The aroma of the whisky was fine though – smoky, filling nostrils and lungs. It would sear his mouth, burn going down, and melt through him, the effect lasting not long.

And the nicotine? He knew himself that when he took a few days off the ciggies, he could sense how bad they made you smell – your skin, clothes, hair. Disgusting habit really: if you didn't give yourself cancer, chances were you were giving it to some poor bastard whose only misfortune was in getting too close to you. Harry the barman was waiting for Rebus to act. The whole bar was. They knew something was happening; it was written on Rebus's face – there was almost pain there. Jack stood beside him, holding his breath.

'Harry,' Rebus said, 'take those away.' Harry lifted the two drinks, shaking his head.

'I wish we could get a picture of this,' he said.

Rebus slid the cigarettes along the bar towards the smoker. 'Here, take them. And don't leave them lying too close to me, I might change my mind.'

The smoker lifted the packet, amazed. 'Payback for the singles you've nicked off me in the past.'

'With interest,' Rebus said, watching Harry pour the beer down the sink. 'Does it go straight back into the barrel, Harry?'

'So, do you want anything else, or did you just come in for a seat?'

'Coke and crisps.' He turned to Jack. 'I'm allowed crisps, right?'

Jack was resting a hand on his back, patting him softly. And he was smiling.

They stopped in at a shop on the way to the flat, came out again with the makings of a meal.

'Can you remember the last time you cooked?' Jack asked.

'I'm not that cack-handed.' The answer to the question was 'no'.

Jack, it turned out, enjoyed cooking, but he found Rebus's kitchen lacking the finer tools of his craft. No lemon zester, no garlic crusher.

'Give the garlic here,' Rebus offered, 'I'll stamp on it.'

'I used to be lazy,' Jack said. 'When Audrey left, I tried cooking bacon in the toaster. But cooking's a doddle once you get your head round it.'

'What's it going to be anyway?'

'Low-fat spagbog, with salad if you'll get your arse in gear.'

Rebus got his arse in gear, but found he had to nip out to the deli for the makings of the dressing. He didn't bother with a jacket: it was mild out.

'Sure you can trust me?' he said.

Jack tasted the sauce, nodded. So Rebus went out on his own, and thought about not going back. There was a pub on the next corner, its doors open. But of course he was going back: he hadn't eaten yet. The way Jack slept, if Rebus ever wanted to high-tail it that would be the time.

They set the table in the living room – the first time it had been used for a meal since Rebus's wife had left. Could that be true? Rebus paused, a fork and spoon in his hand. Yes, it was true. His flat, his refuge, suddenly seemed emptier than ever.

Maudlin again: another reason he drank.

They shared a bottle of Highland Spring water, chinked glasses.

'Shame it's not fresh pasta,' Jack said.

'It's fresh *food*,' Rebus replied, filling his mouth. 'Rare enough in this flat.'

They ate the salad afterwards – French-style, Jack said. Rebus was reaching for seconds when the phone rang. He picked it up.

'John Rebus.'

'Rebus, it's CI Grogan here.'

'CI Grogan,' Rebus looked to Jack, 'what can I do for you, sir?' Jack came to the phone to listen.

'We've run preliminary tests on your shoes and clothing. Thought you'd like to know you're in the clear.'

'Was there ever any doubt?'

'You're a copper, Rebus, you know there are procedures.'

'Of course, sir. I appreciate you phoning.'

'Something else. I had a word with Mr Fletcher.' Hayden Fletcher: PR at T-Bird. 'He admitted knowing the latest victim. Gave us a detailed breakdown of his movements the night she was killed. He even offered blood for DNA analysis if we thought it would help.'

'He sounds cocky.'

'That just about sums him up. I took an instant dislike to the man, something I don't often do.'

'Not even with me?' Rebus smiled at Jack. Jack mouthed the words 'Go easy'.

'Not even with you,' Grogan said.

'So that's two suspects eliminated. Doesn't get you much further, does it?'

'No.' Grogan sighed. Rebus could imagine him wiping tired eyes.

'What about Eve and Stanley, sir? Did you heed my advice?'

'I did. Mindful of your mistrust of DS Lumsden – an excellent officer, by the way – I set two men on it off my own bat, reporting directly to me.'

'Thank you, sir.'

Grogan coughed. 'They were staying in a hotel near the airport. Five-star, usually an oil company hang-out. Driving a BMW.' The one from Uncle Joe's cul-de-sac no doubt. 'I've a description of the car and licence details.'

'Not needed, sir.'

'Well, my men followed them to a couple of nightclubs.'

'During business hours?'

'Daylight hours, Inspector. They went in carrying nothing, and came out the same way. However, they also paid visits to several banks in the city centre. One of my men got close enough in one bank to see that they were making a cash deposit.'

'In a bank?' Rebus frowned. Was Uncle Joe the type to trust to banks? Would he let strangers get within a mile of his ill-gained assets?

'That's about it, Inspector. They ate a few meals together, went for a drive down to the docks, then left town.'

'They've gone?'

'Left tonight. My men followed them as far as Banchory. I'd say they were headed for Perth.' And after that, Glasgow. 'The hotel confirms they've checked out.'

'Did you ask the hotel if they're regulars?'

'We did and they are. They started using it about six months ago.'

'How many rooms?'

'They always book two.' There was a smile in Grogan's voice. 'But the story is, the maids only ever had to clean one of them. Seems they were sharing one room, and leaving the other untouched.'

Bingo, Rebus thought. Housey-housey and fucking clickety-click.
'Thanks, sir.'
'Does this help you in something?'
'It might help a lot, I'll be in touch. Oh, something I meant to ask . . .'
'Yes?'
'Hayden Fletcher: did he say how he came to know the victim?'
'A business acquaintance. She organised the stand for T-Bird Oil at the North Sea Convention.'
'Is that what "corporate presentations" means?'
'Apparently. Ms Holden designed a lot of the stands, then her company did the actual construction and setting-up. Fletcher met her as part of that process.'
'Sir, I appreciate all of this.'
'Inspector . . . if you're coming north again any time, call to let me know, understood?'
Rebus understood that it wasn't an invitation to afternoon tea.
'Yes, sir,' he said, 'goodnight.'
He put the phone down. Aberdeen beckoned, and he was damned if he'd give anyone prior notice. But Aberdeen could wait another day. Vanessa Holden connected to the oil industry . . .
'What is it, John?'
Rebus looked up at his friend. 'It's Johnny Bible, Jack. I just got a strange feeling about him.'
'What?'
'That he's an oilman . . .'

They tidied everything away and washed up, then made mugs of coffee and decided to go back to the decorating. Jack wanted to know more about Johnny Bible, and about Eve and Stanley, but Rebus didn't know where to start. His head felt clogged. He kept filling it with new information, and nothing drained away. Johnny Bible's first victim had been a geology student at a university with close ties to the oil industry. Now his fourth victim made stands for conventions, and working in Aberdeen, he could guess who her best clients had been. If there was a connection between victims one and four, was there something he was missing, something linking two and three? A prostitute and a barmaid, one in Edinburgh, the other Glasgow . . .
When the telephone rang, he put down his sandpaper – the door was looking good – and picked it up. Jack was using a ladder to reach the cornices.
'Hello?'
'John? It's Mairie.'
'I've been trying to reach you.'
'Sorry, another assignment – a *paying* one.'
'Did you find out anything about Major Weir?'
'A fair bit. How was Aberdeen?'
'Bracing.'
'It'll do that to you. These notes . . . probably too much to read over the phone.'
'So let's meet.'

'Which pub?'

'Not a pub.'

'There must be something wrong with the line. Did you just say "not a pub"?'

'How about Duddingston Village? That's about halfway. I'll park by the loch.'

'When?'

'Half an hour?'

'Half an hour it is.'

'We'll never get this room finished,' Jack said, stepping down off the ladder. He had traces of white paint in his hair.

'Grey suits you,' Rebus told him.

Jack rubbed at his head. 'Is it another woman?' Rebus nodded. 'How do you manage to keep them apart?'

'The flat has a lot of doors.'

Mairie was waiting when they got there. Jack hadn't been around Arthur's Seat in years, so they took the scenic route; not that there was much to see at night. The huge hump of a hill, looking like nothing so much as – even kids could see it – a crouched elephant, was a great place to blow off the cobwebs – and anything else you might have on you. At night, though, it was poorly lit and a long way from anywhere. Edinburgh had lots of these glorious empty spaces. They were fine and private places right up until the moment you met your first junkie, mugger, rapist or gay-basher.

Duddingston Village was just that – a village in the midst of a city, sheltering beneath Arthur's Seat. Duddingston Loch – more outsize pond than true loch – looked down on to a bird sanctuary and a path known as the Innocent Railway: Rebus wished he knew where it got the name.

Jack stopped the car and flashed his lights. Mairie switched hers off, unlocked her door, and came loping towards them. Rebus leaned into the back to open the door, and she got in. He introduced her to Jack Morton.

'Oh,' she said, 'you worked the Knots and Crosses case with John.'

Rebus blinked. 'How do you know that? It was before your time.'

She winked at him. 'I've done my research.'

He wondered what else she might know, but hadn't time to speculate. She handed him a brown A4 envelope.

'Thank God for e-mail. I've a contact on the *Washington Post* and he got me most of what's there.'

Rebus switched on the interior light. There was a spot-lamp specially for reading by.

'Usually he wants to meet me in pubs,' Mairie told Jack, 'right seedy ones at that.'

Jack smiled at her, turned in his seat with his arm hanging down over the headrest. Rebus knew Jack liked her. Everyone liked Mairie from the off. He wished he knew her secret.

'Seedy pubs suit his personality,' Jack said.

'Look,' Rebus interrupted, 'will you two bugger off and go look at the ducks or something?'

Jack shrugged, checked it was OK with Mairie, and opened his door. Alone, Rebus settled deeper into his seat and started to read.

Number one: Major Weir was not a Major. It was a nickname, earned in adolescence. Two, his parents had handed on to him their love of all things Scottish – up to and including a craving for national independence. There were a lot of facts about his early years in industry, latterly the oil industry, and reports of Thom Bird's demise – nothing suspicious about it. A journalist in the States had started writing an unauthorised biography of Weir, but had given up – rumour had it he was paid not to finish the book. A couple of stories, unsubstantiated: Weir left his wife amid much acrimony – and later, much alimony. Then something about Weir's son, either deceased or disinherited. Maybe off in some ashram or feeding the African hungry, maybe working in a burger parlour or Wall Street futures. Rebus turned to the next sheet, only to find there wasn't one. The story had finished mid-sentence. He got out of the car, walked to where Mairie and Jack were in huddled conversation.

'It's not all here,' he said, waving what sheets he had.

'Oh, yes.' Mairie reached into her jacket, brought out a single folded sheet and handed it over. Rebus stared at her, demanding an explanation. She shrugged. 'Call me a tease.'

Jack started laughing.

Rebus stood in the glare of the headlights and read. His eyes widened and his mouth fell open. He read it again, then for a third time, and had to run a hand through his hair to make sure the top of his head hadn't just blown off.

'Everything all right?' Mairie asked him.

He stared at her for a moment, not really seeing anything, then pulled her to him and planted a kiss on her cheek.

'Mairie, you're perfect.'

She turned to Jack Morton.

'I second that,' he said.

Sitting in his car, Bible John had watched Rebus and friend drive out of Arden Street. His business had kept him an extra day in Edinburgh. Frustrating, but at least he'd been able to take another look at the policeman. It was hard to tell from a distance, but Rebus seemed to sport bruises on his face, and his clothes were dishevelled. Bible John couldn't help but feel a little disappointed: he'd been hoping for a more worthy adversary. The man looked dead done in.

Not that he thought them adversaries, not really. Rebus's flat had not thrown up much, but it *had* revealed that Rebus's interest in Bible John was connected to the Upstart. Which went some way towards explaining it. He hadn't stayed as long in the flat as he would have liked. Being unable to pick the lock, he'd been forced to break the door. He couldn't know how long it would take for neighbours to spot something. So he had been swift, but then there'd been so little in the flat worth his attention. It told him something about the policeman. He felt now that he *knew* Rebus, at least to a degree – he felt the loneliness of his life, the gaps where sentiment and warmth and love should have been. There was music, and there were books, but neither in great quantity nor of great quality. The clothes were utilitarian, one jacket much like another. No shoes. He found that bizarre in the extreme. Did the man possess only one pair?

And the kitchen: lacking in utensils and produce. And the bathroom: needing redecorating.

But back in the kitchen, a small surprise. Newspapers and cuttings hastily hidden, easily found. Bible John, Johnny Bible. And evidence that Rebus had gone to some trouble: the original papers must have been bought from a dealer. An investigation within the official investigation, that was what it looked like. Which made Rebus more interesting in Bible John's eyes.

Paperwork in the bedroom: boxes of old correspondence, bank statements, very few photographs – but enough to show that Rebus had once been married, and had a daughter. Nothing recent though: no photos of the daughter grown-up, no recent photos at all.

But the one thing he'd come here for . . . his business card . . . no sign of it at all. Which meant either that Rebus had thrown it away, or that he carried it with him still, in a jacket pocket or wallet.

In the living room, he noted Rebus's telephone number, then closed his eyes, making sure he had committed the flat's layout to memory. Yes, easy. He could come back here at dead of night and walk through the place without disturbing anything or anyone. He could take John Rebus any time he wanted to. Any time at all.

He wondered about Rebus's friend though. The policeman didn't seem the gregarious type. They'd been painting the living room together. He couldn't know if it was connected to the break-in; probably not. A man Rebus's age, maybe a little younger, quite a tough-looking individual. Another policeman? Perhaps. The man's face had lacked Rebus's intensity. There was something in Rebus – he had noticed it during their first meeting, and it had been reinforced this evening – a singleness of purpose, a sense of determination. Physically, Rebus's friend seemed the superior, but that wouldn't make Rebus a pushover. Physical strength could take a person only so far.

After that, it was down to attitude.

26

They were waiting outside the photo shop when it opened next morning. Jack looked at his watch for only the fifteenth time.

'He'll kill us,' he said for the ninth or tenth. 'No, I mean it, really he will.'

'Relax.'

Jack looked about as relaxed as a headless chicken. When the manager started unlocking the shop, they sprinted from the car. Rebus had the stub ready in his hand.

'Give me a minute,' the manager said.

'We're late for something.'

Coat still on, the manager browsed through a box of photograph packets. Rebus imagined family days out, holidays abroad, red-eyed birthdays and blurred wedding receptions. There was something faintly desperate and yet touching about collections of photographs. He'd looked through a lot of photo albums in his time – usually seeking clues to a murder, a victim's acquaintances.

'You'll have to wait anyway while I unlock the till.' The manager handed over the packet. Jack glanced at the price, slapped down more than enough to cover it, and dragged Rebus out of the shop.

He drove to Fettes like there was a murder scene waiting there. Traffic honked and squealed as he did his stunt-driver routine. They were still twenty minutes late for the meeting. But Rebus didn't mind. He had his reprints, the missing photos from Allan Mitchison's cabin. They were similar to the other pictures: group shots, but with fewer figures. And in all of them, braid-hair, standing right next to Mitchison. In one, she had an arm around him; in another, they were kissing, grinning as their lips met.

Rebus wasn't surprised, not now.

'I hope they were bloody well worth it,' Jack said.

'Every penny, Jack.'

'That's not what I meant.'

Chick Ancram sat with hands clasped, his face the colour of rhubarb crumble. The files were in front of him, as though they hadn't been moved since the previous meeting. His voice had a slight vibrato. He was in control, but only just.

'I had a phone call,' he said, 'from someone called Kayleigh Burgess.'

'Oh yes?'

'She wanted to ask me a few questions.' He paused. 'About you. About the role DI Morton is currently playing in your life.'

'It's gossip, sir. Jack and myself are just good friends.'

Ancram slapped both hands down on the desk. 'I thought we had a deal.'

'Can't say I remember.'

'Well, let's hope your long-term memory's better.' He opened a file. 'Because now the fun really begins.' He nodded for a sheepish Jack to switch on the tape recorder, then started off by giving date and time, officers present . . . Rebus felt as if he'd explode. He really thought if he sat there a second longer, his eyeballs would fly from their sockets like those jokeshop glasses with spring-loaded eyes. He'd felt like this before, just before a panic attack. But he wasn't panicking now; he was just *charged*. He stood up. Ancram broke off what he'd been saying.

'Something the matter, Inspector?'

'Look,' Rebus rubbed at his forehead, 'I can't think straight . . . not about Spaven. Not today.'

'That's for me to decide, not you. If you're feeling ill, we can call for a doctor, but otherwise . . .'

'I'm not ill. I just . . .'

'Then sit down.' Rebus sat down, and Ancram went back to his notes. 'Now, Inspector, on the night referred to, your report states that you were at Inspector Geddes's house, and there was a telephone call?'

'Yes.'

'You didn't actually hear the conversation?'

'No.' Braid-hair and Mitchison . . . Mitch the organiser, protester. Mitch the oil-worker. Killed by Tony El, henchman to Uncle Joe. Eve and Stanley, working Aberdeen, sharing a room . . .

'But DI Geddes told you it was to do with Mr Spaven? A tip-off?'

'Yes.' Burke's Club, police hang-out, maybe an oil-workers' hang-out too. Hayden Fletcher drinking there. Ludovic Lumsden drinking there. Michelle Strachan meets Johnny Bible there . . .

'And Geddes didn't say who the call was from?'

'Yes.' Ancram looked up, and Rebus knew he'd given the wrong answer. 'I mean, no.'

'No?'

'No.'

Ancram stared at him, sniffed, concentrated on his notes again. There were pages and pages of them, specially prepared for this session: questions to be asked, 'facts' double-checked, the whole case stripped down and rebuilt.

'Anonymous tip-offs are pretty rare in my experience,' Ancram said.

'Yes.'

'And they're almost always made to a police station's general desk. Would you agree?'

'Yes, sir.' Was Aberdeen the key then, or did the answers lie further north? What did Jake Harley have to do with it? And Mike Sutcliffe – Mr Sheepskin – hadn't Major Weir warned him off? What was it Sutcliffe had said? He'd said something on the plane, then stopped suddenly . . . Something about a boat . . .

And did any of it connect to Johnny Bible? *Was* Johnny Bible an oilman?

'So it would be rational to deduce that DI Geddes knew the caller, wouldn't it?'

'Or they knew him.'

Ancram shrugged this aside. 'And this tip-off just happened to concern Mr Spaven. Didn't that strike you at the time as a bit of a coincidence, Inspector? Seeing as Geddes had been warned off Spaven already? I mean, it must have been clear to you that your boss was *obsessed* with Spaven?'

Rebus got up again and started pacing the small room as best he could. 'Sit down!'

'With respect, sir, I can't. If I sit there any longer, I'm going to stick my fist in your face.'

Jack Morton covered his eyes with one hand.

'What did you say?'

'Wind the tape back and take a listen. And that's why I'm up and walking: crisis management if you like.'

'Inspector, I'd caution you—'

Rebus laughed. 'Would you? That's big of you, sir.' Ancram was rising to his feet. Rebus turned away and walked to the far wall, turned round again and stopped.

'Look,' he said, 'a simple question: do you want to see Uncle Joe fucked?'

'We're not here to—'

'We're here to put on a show – you know that as well as I do. The brass are sweaty about the media; they want the force to look good if that programme ever gets made. This way, everyone sits back and says there was an inquiry. TV seems to be about the only thing brass are afraid of. Villains don't scare them, but ten minutes of negative coverage, dearie me, no. Can't have that. All for a programme which will be stared at by a few million, half of them with the sound down, the other half not taking it in, then forgotten about the very next day. So,' he took a deep breath, 'simple yes or no.' Ancram didn't say anything, so Rebus repeated the question.

Ancram signalled for Jack to turn off the machine. Then he sat back down.

'Yes,' he said quietly.

'I can see that it happens.' Rebus kept his voice level. 'But I don't want *you* getting sole credit. If it's anyone's, the collar belongs to CI Templer.' Rebus went back to his chair, propped himself on the edge of it. 'Now *I* have a couple of questions.'

'Was there a phone call?' Ancram asked, surprising Rebus. They stared at one another. 'Tape's off, this is between the three of us. Was there ever a phone call?'

'I answer yours and you answer mine?' Ancram nodded. 'Of course there was a phone call.'

Ancram almost smiled. 'You liar. He came to your house, didn't he? What did he tell you? Did he say you wouldn't need a search warrant? You must've known he was lying.'

'He was a good cop.'

'Every time you come out with that line, it sounds thinner. What's the matter: stopped finding it convincing?'

'He was.'

'But he had a problem, a little personal demon called Lenny Spaven. You were his friend, Rebus, you should have stopped him.'

'Stopped him?'

Ancram nodded, eyes gleaming like moons. 'You should have helped him.'

'I tried,' Rebus said, his voice a whisper. It was another lie: Lawson by that time had been a junkie with a craving, and only one thing would help – the taste itself.

Ancram sat back, trying not to look satisfied. He thought Rebus was cracking. The inner doubts had been sown – not for the first time. Ancram could now water them with sympathy.

'You know,' he said, 'I'm not blaming you. I think I know what you were going through. But there was a cover-up. There was that one central lie: the tip-off.' He lifted his notes an inch off the desk. 'It's written all over these, and it throws everything else into the pot, because if Geddes had been following Spaven, what was to stop him planting a little evidence along the way?'

'It wasn't his style.'

'Not even when pushed to the limit? Had you seen him there before?'

Rebus couldn't think of a thing to say. Ancram had been leaning forward in his seat again, palms against the desk. He sat back. 'What did you want to ask?'

When Rebus was a child, they'd lived in a semi-detached with a close separating it from the next house along. The close had led to both back gardens. Rebus played football there with his dad. Sometimes he placed a foot against either wall and pushed his way up towards the roof of the close. And sometimes he'd just stand in the middle and throw a small hard rubber ball as hard as he could against the stone floor. The ball would bounce like anything, zipping back and forth, floor to roof to wall to floor to roof . . .

His head felt like that now.

'What?' he said.

'You said you had a couple of questions.'

Slowly, Rebus's head came back to the here and now. He rubbed his eyes. 'Yes,' he said. 'First off, Eve and Stanley.'

'What about them?'

'Are they close?'

'You mean how do they get on? All right.'

'Just all right?'

'No flare-ups to report.'

'I was thinking more of jealousy.'

Ancram cottoned on. 'Uncle Joe and Stanley?'

Rebus nodded. 'Is she clever enough to play one off against the other?' He'd met her, thought he already knew the answer. Ancram just shrugged. The conversation had obviously taken an unexpected turn.

'Only,' Rebus said, 'in Aberdeen they were sharing a hotel room.'

Ancram narrowed his eyes. 'You're sure of this?' Rebus nodded. 'They must be mad. Uncle Joe'll kill them both.'

'Maybe they don't think he can.'

'How do you mean?'

'Maybe they think they're stronger than him. Maybe they reckon in a war the muscle-men would change sides. Stanley's the one people are scared of these days, you said as much yourself. Especially with Tony El gone.'

'Tony was history anyway.'

'I'm not so sure.'

'Explain.'

Rebus shook his head. 'I need to talk to a couple of people first. Have you heard of Eve and Stanley working together in the past?'

'No.'

'So this Aberdeen jaunt . . . ?'

'I'd say it's a newish excursion.'

'Hotel records say the past six months.'

'So the question is, what's Uncle Joe setting up?'

Rebus smiled. 'I think you know the answer to that: drugs. He's lost the market in Glasgow, it's already been divvied up. So he can fight for a piece, or he can play away from home. Burke's will take the stuff and sell it on, especially with someone from CID in their pocket. Aberdeen's still a nice market, not the hotbed of fifteen or twenty years ago, but a market nonetheless.'

'So tell me, what are you going to do that the rest of us can't?'

Rebus shook his head. 'I still don't know if you're on the level; I mean, you might be see-sawing.'

This time Ancram really did smile. 'I could say the same about you and the Spaven case.'

'Probably.'

'I won't be satisfied until I know. I think maybe that makes us similar.'

'Look, Ancram, we walked into that lock-up and the bag was *there*. Does it matter how *we* came to be there?'

'It could have been planted.'

'Not with my knowledge.'

'Geddes never confided? I thought the two of you were close?'

Rebus was on his feet. 'I may not be around for a day or two. All right?'

'No, it's not all right. I'll expect you here tomorrow, same time.'

'For Christ's sake . . .'

'Or we can turn the machine back on right now and you can tell me what you know. That way, you'll have all the time in the world. And I think you'll find it easier to live with yourself, too.'

'Living with myself has never been the problem. Breathing the same air as people like you – *that's* my problem.'

'I've already told you, Strathclyde Police and the Squaddies are planning an operation . . .'

'One that'll get nowhere, because for all we know half the Glasgow force is in Uncle Joe's pocket.'

'I'm not the one who goes visiting him at home, with a word put in by a certain Morris Cafferty.'

There was a sudden tightening around Rebus's chest. Coronary, he thought. But it was only Jack Morton, arms holding him, stopping him moving in on Ancram.

'Tomorrow morning, gentlemen,' Ancram said, like they'd had a useful session.

'Yes, sir,' Jack said, hustling Rebus out of the room.

Rebus told his friend to get them on to the M8.

'No way, José.'

'Then park near Waverley, we'll take the train.'

Jack didn't like the way Rebus looked: like his wiring was shorting out. You could almost see the sparks behind his eyes.

'What are you going to do in Glasgow? Walk up to Uncle Joe and say, "Oh, by the way, your woman's shagging your son"? Even you can't be *that* stupid.'

'Of course I'm not that stupid.'

'Glasgow, John,' Jack pleaded. 'It's not our territory. I'll be back in Falkirk in a few weeks, and you . . .'

Rebus smiled. 'Where'll I be, Jack?'

'God and the Devil know.'

Rebus was still smiling; thought to himself: I'd rather be the Devil.

'You've always got to be the hero, haven't you?' Jack asked.

'Time loves a hero, Jack,' Rebus told him.

On the M8, halfway between Edinburgh and Glasgow, slowed by syrupy traffic, Jack tried again.

'This is crazy. I mean *really* crazy.'

'Trust me, Jack.'

'Trust you? The guy who tried to lay me out two nights back? With friends like you . . .'

'. . . you'll never be short of enemies.'

'There's still time.'

'Not really, you just think there is.'

'You're talking out your arse.'

'Maybe you're just not listening.' Rebus felt calmer now they were on the road. To Jack, he looked like someone had pulled the plug on him: no more sparks. He almost preferred the model with the faulty wiring. The lack of emotion in his friend's voice was chilling, even in the overheated car. Jack slid his window down a little further. The speedometer was steady on forty, and that was them in the outside lane. Traffic to their left was *really* crawling. If he could find a space, he'd move to the inside – anything to delay their arrival.

He'd oftentimes admired John Rebus – and heard him praised by other officers – for his tenacity, the way he worried at a case terrier-style, more often than not tearing it open, spilling out secret motives and hidden bodies. But that same tenacity could also be a weakness, blinding him to danger, making him impatient and reckless. Jack knew why they were headed for Glasgow, thought he knew pretty well what Rebus would want to do there. And, as ordered by Ancram, Jack would be close by when the crap came tumbling down.

It was a long time since Rebus and Jack had worked together. They'd been an effective team, but Jack had been glad enough of the posting out of Edinburgh. Too claustrophobic – the town and his partner both. Rebus had seemed even then to spend more time living in his own head than in the company of others. Even the pub he chose to haunt was one with fewer than usual distractions: TV, one fruit machine, one cigarette machine. And when group activities were arranged – fishing trips, golf competitions, bus runs – Rebus never signed up. He was an irregular regular, a loner even in company, his brain and heart only fully engaged when he was working a

case. Jack knew the score only too well. Work had a way of wrapping itself around you, so you were cut off from the rest of the world. People you met socially tended to treat you with suspicion or outright hostility – so you ended up mixing only with other cops, which bored your wife or girlfriend. *They* began to feel isolated too. It was a bastard.

There were plenty of people on the force who coped, of course. They had understanding partners; or they could shut work out whenever they went home; or it was just a job to them, a way of keeping up with the mortgage. Jack would guess CID was split fifty-fifty between those for whom it was a vocation, and those who could fit into any other type of office life, anywhere, any time.

He didn't know what else John Rebus could do. If they kicked him off the force . . . he'd probably drink his pension dry, become just another old ex-cop hanging on to a fund of stories, telling them too often to the same people, trading one form of isolation for another.

It was important that John should stay on the force. It was therefore important to keep him off Shit Street. Jack wondered why nothing in life was ever easy. When he'd been told by Chick Ancram that he'd be 'keeping an eye' on Rebus, he'd been pleased. He'd seen them going out together, reminiscing about cases and characters, haunts and high points. He should have known better. *He* might have changed – become a 'yes-man', a pencil-pusher, a careerist – but John was the same as always . . . only worse. Time had seasoned his cynicism. He wasn't a terrier now: he was a fighting dog with locking jaws. You just knew that no matter how bloody he got, how much pain there was behind the eyes, the grip was there to the death . . .

'Traffic's beginning to shift,' Rebus said.

It was true; whatever the problem had been, it was clearing. The speedo was up to fifty-five. They'd be in Glasgow in no time at all. Jack glanced over at Rebus, who winked without moving his eyes from the road ahead. Jack had a sudden image of himself propping up a bar, dipping into his pension for another drink. Fuck that. For his friend's sake, he'd go the ninety minutes, but no more: no extra time, no penalties. Definitely no penalties.

They made for Partick police station, since their faces were known there. Govan had been another possibility, but Govan was Ancram's HQ and not a place they could do business on the q.t. The Johnny Bible investigation had picked up some momentum from the most recent murder, but all the Glasgow squad were really doing was reading through and filing material sent from Aberdeen. It made Rebus shiver to think he'd walked past Vanessa Holden in Burke's Club. For all that Lumsden had been trying to stitch him up, Aberdeen CID had one thing right: quite a string of coincidences tied Rebus to the Johnny Bible inquiry. So much so that Rebus was beginning to doubt coincidence had much to do with it. Somehow, he couldn't yet say how exactly, Johnny was connected to one of Rebus's other investigations. At present it was no more than a hunch, nothing he could do anything about. But it was there, niggling him. It made him wonder if he knew more about Johnny Bible than he thought . . .

Partick, new and bright and comfortable – basically your state-of-the-art cop-shop – was still enemy territory. Rebus couldn't know how many friendly ears Uncle Joe might have on-site, but he thought he might know a quiet spot, a place they could make their own. As they wandered through the building, a few officers nodded or greeted Jack by name.

'Base camp,' Rebus said at last, turning into the deserted office which was temporary home to Bible John. Here he was, spread out across tables and the floor, pinned and taped to the walls. It was like standing in the middle of an exhibition. The last photofit of Bible John, the one compiled by his third victim's sister, was repeated around the room, along with her description of him. It was as if by repetition, by piling image upon image, they could will him into physical being, turn wood pulp and ink into flesh and blood.

'I hate this room,' Jack said as Rebus closed the door.

'So does everyone else by the look of things. Long tea-breaks and other business to attend to.'

'Half the force weren't alive when Bible John was on the go. He's lost any sort of meaning.'

'They'll be telling their grandkids about Johnny Bible though.'

'True enough.' Jack paused. 'Are you going to do it?'

Rebus saw that his hand was lying on the receiver. He picked it up, punched in the numbers. 'Did you doubt me?' he asked.

'Not for a minute.'

The voice that answered was gruff, unwelcoming. Not Uncle Joe, not Stanley. One of the bodybuilders. Rebus gave as good as he got.

'Malky there?'

Hesitation: only his close friends called him Malky. 'Who wants to know?'

'Tell him it's Johnny.' Rebus paused. 'From Aberdeen.'

'Haud on.' Clatter as the receiver was dropped on to a hard surface. Rebus listened closely, heard television voices, game-show applause. Watching: Uncle Joe maybe, or Eve. Stanley wouldn't like game shows; he'd never get a question right.

'Phone!' the bodybuilder called.

A long wait. Then a distant voice: 'Who is it?'

'Johnny.'

'Johnny? Johnny who?' The voice closer.

'From Aberdeen.'

The receiver was picked up. 'Hello?'

Rebus took a deep breath. 'For your own sake you better sound natural. I know about you and Eve, know what you've been up to in Aberdeen. So if you want to keep it quiet, sound natural. Don't want Muscle Man to get even the slightest suspicion.'

A rustling sound, Stanley turning away for privacy, tucking the phone into his chin.

'So what's the story?'

'You've got a nice scam going, and I don't want to fuck it up unless I have to, so don't do anything that would make me do that. Understood?'

'No bother.' The voice was not used to attempting levity when its brain demanded bloody restitution.

'You're doing all right, Stanley. Eve'll be proud of you. Now we need to talk, not just you and me, the three of us.'

'My dad?'

'Eve.'

'Oh, right.' Calming again. 'Eh . . . no problem with that.'

'Tonight?'

'Eh . . . OK.'

'Partick police station.'

'Wait a minute . . .'

That's the deal. Just to talk. You're not walking into anything. If you're worried, keep your gob shut until you hear the deal. If you don't like it, you can walk. You won't have said anything, so there's nothing to fear. No charges, no tricks. It's not you I'm interested in. Are we still on?'

'I'm not sure. Can I call you back?'

'I need a yes or no right now. If it's no, you might as well pass me across to your dad.'

Condemned men laughed with more humour. 'Look, for myself, there's no problem. But there are other parties involved.'

'Just tell Eve what I've told you. If she won't come, that doesn't mean you shouldn't. I'll get some visitors' passes for you. False names.' Rebus looked down at a book open in front of him, found two straight off. 'William Pritchard and Madeleine Smith. Can you remember that?'

'I think so.'

'Repeat them.'

'William . . . something.'

'Pritchard.'

'And Maggie Smith.'

'Close enough. I know you can't just sneak off, so we'll leave the time open. Get here when you can. And if you start thinking of bottling it, just remember all those bank accounts and how lonely they'll be without you.'

Rebus put down the phone. His hand was hardly trembling.

27

They notified the front desk and got visitors' passes made up, and after that there was nothing to do but wait. Jack said the room felt cold and musty at the same time; he had to get out. He suggested the canteen or a corridor or anywhere, but Rebus shook his head.

'You go. I think I'll stay here, see if I can decide what to say to Bonnie and Clyde. Bring me back a coffee and maybe a filled roll.' Jack nodded. 'Oh, and a bottle of whisky.' Jack looked at him. Rebus smiled.

He tried to remember his last drink. He recalled standing in the Ox with two glasses and a packet of cigs. But before that . . . Wine with Gill?

Jack had said the room was cold; it felt stifling to Rebus. He took off his jacket, loosened his tie and undid the top button of his shirt. Then he wandered around the office, peering into desk drawers and grey cardboard boxes.

He saw: interview transcripts, their covers faded and curling at the edges; handwritten reports; typed reports; evidence summaries; maps, mostly hand-drawn; duty logs; ream after ream of witness statements – descriptions of the man seen in the Barrowland Ballroom. Then there were the photographs, matt black and whites, ten by eight and smaller. The Ballroom itself, interior and exterior. It looked more modern than the word 'ballroom' conjured up, reminded Rebus a bit of his old school – flat building panels with the occasional window. Three spots sat atop a concrete canopy, pointing up towards the windows and the sky. And on the canopy itself – a useful shelter from the rain while you were waiting either to be admitted or, afterwards, for your lift – the words 'Barrowland Ballroom' and 'Dancing'. Most of the exterior pictures had been taken on a wet afternoon, women caught on the periphery with plastic rain-mates, men in bunnets and long coats. More photographs: police frogmen searching the river; the loci, CID in their trademark pork-pie hats and raincoats – a back lane, the back court of a tenement, another back court. Typical locations for a cuddle and a feel-up, maybe going a wee bit further. Too far for the victims. There was a photo of Superintendent Joe Beattie, holding out an artist's impression of Bible John. Looking between the portrait and Beattie, the men's expressions seemed similar. Several members of the public had commented on it. Mackeith Street and Earl Street – victims two and three were killed on the streets where they lived. He'd taken them so close to their homes: why? So they'd relax their defences? Or had he been vacillating, putting off the attacks? Nervous to ask for a kiss and a cuddle,

478

or just plain scared and with his conscience battling his deep desire? The files were full of such aimless speculation, and more structured theories from professional psychologists and psychiatrists. In the end they'd been as helpful as Croiset the psychic detective.

Rebus thought of meeting Aldous Zane in this very room. Zane had been in the papers again – he'd inspected the latest locus, given the same rambling spiel, and been flown home. Rebus wondered what Jim Stevens was up to now. He remembered Zane's handshake, the way it had tingled. And Zane's impressions of Bible John – though Stevens had been present, the paper hadn't bothered printing them. A trunk in the attic of a modern house. Well, Rebus could have come up with better than that himself, if some paper had put him up in a posh hotel.

Lumsden had put him up in a posh hotel, probably thinking CID would never know. Lumsden had tried to get pally with him, telling him they were alike, showing Rebus that he had stature in the city – free meals and drinks, free entrance to Burke's Club. He'd been testing Rebus, seeing how open he'd be to a bung. But at whose behest? The club's owners? Or Uncle Joe himself . . . ?

More photos. There seemed no end to them. It was the onlookers who interested Rebus, the people who didn't know they'd been snapped for posterity. A woman in high heels, good legs – all you could see of her were heels and legs, the rest hidden behind a WPC taking part in a reconstruction. Woolly suits searching the back courts off Mackeith Street, looking for the victim's handbag. The courts looked like bomb-sites – drying-poles poking up out of stunted grass and rubble. Roadside motor cars: Zephyrs, Hillman Imps, Zodiacs. A world ago. A bundle of posters sat in one box, the rubber band long ago perished. Photofits of Bible John along with varying descriptions: 'Speaks with a polite Glasgow accent and has an erect posture'. Very helpful. The phone number of the inquiry HQ. They'd received thousands of phone calls, boxes of them. Brief details of every one, with more detailed back-up notes if the call seemed worth checking.

Rebus's eyes moved over the remaining boxes. He chose one at random – a big flat cardboard box, inside which were newspapers from the time, intact and unread for quarter of a century. He examined front pages, then turned to the back to look at the sports. A few of the crosswords had been half-done, probably by a bored detective. Slips of paper stapled to each banner-head gave page numbers with Bible John coverage. But Rebus wasn't going to find anything there. He looked at the other stories instead and smiled at some of the adverts. Some seemed artless by today's standards; others hadn't aged at all. In the personal ads, people were selling lawnmowers, washing machines, and record players at knockdown prices. In a couple of papers, Rebus found the same ad, framed like a public notice: 'Find a New Life and a Good Job in America – Booklet Tells You How'. You had to send off a couple of stamps to an address in Manchester. Rebus sat back, wondering if Bible John had got that far.

In October '69, Paddy Meehan had been sentenced at the High Court in Edinburgh and had shouted out, 'You've made a terrible mistake – I'm innocent!' That made Rebus think of Lenny Spaven; he shook the thought away and turned to a new paper. November 8: gales forced the evacuation of the Staflo oil rig; November 12: a report that the owners of the *Torrey*

Canyon had paid out £3 million in compensation after losing 5,000 tons of Kuwaiti crude into the English Channel. Elsewhere, Dunfermline had decided to allow *The Killing of Sister George* to be shown in the town, and a brand new Rover three-and-a-half-litre would cost you £1,700. Rebus turned to late December. The SNP chairman was predicting that Scotland stood 'on the threshold of a decade of destiny'. Nice one, sir. December 31: Hogmanay. The *Herald* wished its readers a happy and prosperous 1970, and led with the story of a shootout in Govanhill: one constable dead, three wounded. He put the paper down, the gust blowing some photos off the desk. He picked them up: the three victims, so full of life. Victims one and three shared some facial similarities. All three looked hopeful, like the future just might bring them everything they were dreaming of. It was good to have hope, and never to give up. But Rebus doubted many people managed that. They might smile for the camera, but if caught unawares they'd more likely look bedraggled and exhausted, like the bystanders in the photos.

How many victims were there? Not just Bible John or Johnny Bible, but all the killers, the punished and the never found. The World's End murders, Cromwell Street, Nilsen, the Yorkshire Ripper . . . And Elsie Rhind . . . If Spaven hadn't killed her, then the murderer must have been hooting with laughter all through the trial. And he was still out there, maybe with other scalps added to his tally, other unsolveds. Elsie Rhind lay in her grave unavenged, a forgotten victim. Spaven had committed suicide because he couldn't bear the weight of his innocence. And Lawson Geddes . . . had he killed himself over grief for his wife, or because of Spaven? Had cold realisation finally crept over him?

The bastards were all gone; only John Rebus was left. They wanted to shift their burdens on to him. But he was refusing, and he'd go on refusing, denying. He didn't know what else he could do. Except drink. He wanted a drink, wanted one desperately. But he wasn't going to have one, not yet. Maybe later, maybe sometime. People died and you couldn't bring them back. Some of them died violently, cruelly young, without knowing why they'd been chosen. Rebus felt surrounded by loss. All the ghosts . . . yelling at him . . . begging him . . . shrieking . . .

'John?'

He looked up from the desk. Jack was standing there with a mug in one hand and a roll in the other. Rebus blinked, his vision was going: it was like he was looking at Jack through a heat haze.

'Christ, man, are you all right?'

His nose and lips were wet. He wiped at them. The photos on the desk were wet too. He knew he'd been crying and pulled out a handkerchief. Jack put the mug and roll down and rested an arm along his shoulders, squeezing gently.

'Don't know what's up with me,' Rebus said, blowing his nose.

'Yes you do,' Jack said quietly.

'Yes, I do,' Rebus acknowledged. He gathered up the photographs and newspapers and stuffed them all back into their boxes. 'Stop looking at me like that.'

'Like what?'

'I wasn't talking to you.'

Jack lifted his backside on to a desk. 'Not many defences left, have you?'

'Doesn't look like it.'

'Time to get your act together.'

'Ach, Stanley and Eve won't be here for a while yet.'

'You know that's not—'

'I know, I know. And you're right: time to get my act together. Where do I start? No, don't tell me – the Juice Church?'

Jack just shrugged. 'Your decision.'

Rebus picked up the roll and bit into it. A mistake: the block in his throat made it hard to swallow. He gulped at the coffee, managed to finish the roll – bland ham and wet tomato. Then remembered he had to make another call: a Shetland number.

'I'll be back in a minute,' he told Jack.

In the toilets he washed his face. Tiny red veins had burst in the whites of his eyes; he looked like he'd been on a bender.

'Stone cold sober,' he told himself, heading back to the telephone.

Briony, Jake Harley's girlfriend, picked up.

'Is Jake there?' Rebus asked.

'No, sorry.'

'Briony, we met the other day, DI Rebus.'

'Oh, yes.'

'Has he been in touch?'

A long pause. 'Sorry, I missed that. The line's not great.'

It sounded just fine to Rebus. 'I said, has he been in touch?'

'No.'

'No?'

'That's what I said.' Edgy now.

'OK, OK. Aren't you a bit worried?'

'What about?'

'Jake.'

'Why should I be?'

'Well, he's been off on his own longer than intended. Maybe something's happened.'

'He's all right.'

'How do you know?'

'I just do!' Almost shouting now.

'Calm down. Look, why don't I get—'

'Just leave us alone!' The phone died on him.

Us. Leave *us* alone. Rebus stared at the receiver.

'I could hear her from over here,' Jack said. 'Sounds like she's cracking up.'

'I think she is.'

'Boyfriend trouble?'

'Boyfriend *in* trouble.' He put the receiver down. There was an incoming call.

'DI Rebus.'

It was the front desk, telling him the first of his visitors had arrived.

Eve looked much as she had that night in the bar of Rebus's hotel – dressed for business in a two-piece suit, conservative blue rather than vamp red,

and with the gold jewellery on wrists, fingers and neck, and the same gold clasp pulling back her peroxide hair. She had a handbag with her, and tucked it under her arm as she clipped on her visitor's pass.

'Who's Madeleine Smith?' she asked as they climbed the stairs.

'I got her name out of a book, I think she was a murderess.'

She gave Rebus a look which managed to be hard and amused at the same time.

'This way,' Rebus said. He led her to the Bible John room, where Jack was waiting. 'Jack Morton,' Rebus said, 'Eve . . . I don't know your last name. It's not Toal, is it?'

'Cudden,' she said coldly.

'Sit down, Ms Cudden.'

She sat down, reached into her bag for the black cigarettes. 'Do you mind?'

'Actually, there's no smoking allowed,' Jack said, sounding apologetic. 'And neither Inspector Rebus nor myself are smokers.'

She looked at Rebus. 'Since when?'

Rebus shrugged. 'Where's Stanley?'

'He'll be here. We thought it wise to leave separately.'

'Uncle Joe won't suspect?'

'Well, that's *our* problem, not yours. As far as Joe knows, Malky's going out on the ran-dan, and I'm visiting a friend. She's a good friend, she'll not let on.'

Her tone told Rebus she'd used the friend before – other times, other assignations.

'Well,' he said, 'I'm glad you arrived first. I wanted to have a private word.' He rested against a desk, folded his arms to stop his hands shaking. 'That night in the hotel, you were setting me up, yes?'

'Tell me what you know.'

'About you and Stanley?'

'Malky.' Her face creased. 'I hate that nickname.'

'OK then, *Malky*. What do I know? I know just about everything. The two of you head north every now and then on business for Uncle Joe. I'd guess you're go-betweens. He needs people he can trust.' He gave a twist to the last word. 'People who won't share their hotel bedroom, leaving the other one vacant. People who won't rip him off.'

'Are we ripping him off?' Disregarding Jack, she'd lit up. There were no ashtrays in sight, so Rebus placed a wastepaper-bin beside her, inhaling the smoke as he did so. Wonderful smoke. Almost a contact high.

'Yes,' he said, retreating to the desk. They'd placed Eve's chair in the middle of the floor, Rebus to one side of her, Jack the other. She looked comfortable enough with the arrangement. 'I don't see Uncle Joe as a bank account kind of villain. I mean, he probably wouldn't trust the banks in Glasgow, never mind Aberdeen. Yet there you are, you and Malky, dumping wads of cash into several accounts. I have dates, times, bank details.' An exaggeration, but he reckoned he could wing it. 'I've got statements from hotel employees, including maids who never need to clean Malky's room. Funny, he doesn't strike me as the tidy sort.'

Eve exhaled smoke down her nostrils, managed a smile. 'All right,' she said.

'Now,' Rebus went on, wanting to rid her of the confident smile, 'what would Uncle Joe say to all this? I mean, Malky's blood, but you're not, Eve. I'd say you were expendable.' Pause. 'And I'd say you know it, have done for a while.'

'Meaning?'

'Meaning I don't see you and Malky as an item, not long term. He's too thick for you, and he'll never be rich enough to make up for that. I can see what he sees in *you*: you're an accomplished seducer.'

'Not that accomplished.' Her eyes found his.

'Pretty good though. Good enough to hook Malky. Good enough to talk him into skimming from the Aberdeen money. Let me guess: your story was that the two of you would bugger off together when there was enough set by?'

'My language may not have matched yours.' Her eyes were calculating slits, but the smile had gone. She knew Rebus was going to deal; she wouldn't be here otherwise. She was wondering what she could get away with.

'But you wouldn't, right? Just between us, you were planning to clear off by yourself.'

'Was I?'

'I'm banking on it.' He stood up, walked towards her. 'I don't want you, Eve. Good fucking luck to you, I say. Take the money and run.' He lowered his voice. 'But I want Malky. I want him for Tony El. And I want the answers to some questions. When he gets here, you're going to talk to him. You're going to persuade him to co-operate. Then we'll talk, and it'll go down on tape.' Her eyes widened. 'The story is, it's my insurance in case you decide to stick around.'

'But in reality?'

'It'll take Malky down, and Uncle Joe with him.'

'And I walk away?'

'Promise.'

'How do I know I can trust you?'

'I'm a gentleman, remember? You said as much in the bar.'

She smiled again, her eyes not moving from his. She looked like a cat: same morals, same instinct. Then she nodded her head.

Malcolm Toal arrived at the station fifteen minutes later, and Rebus left him with Eve in an Interview Room. The station was evening quiet, not yet late enough for pub rowdies, knife fights, blow-ups before bed. Jack asked Rebus how he wanted to play it.

'Just sit there and look like everything I say is the word of God, that'll be good enough for me.'

'And if Stanley makes a move?'

'We can handle him.' He'd already told Eve to find out if Malky was carrying. If he was, Rebus wanted the weaponry on the table by the time he returned. He went into the toilets again, just to steady his breathing and look at himself in the mirror. He tried to relax his jaw muscles. In the past, he'd have been reaching for the quarter-bottle of whisky in his pocket. But tonight there was no quarter-bottle, no Dutch courage. Which meant for once he'd be relying on the real thing.

Back in the Interview Room, Malky looked at him with eyes like lasers, proof that Eve had said her piece. Two Stanley knives lay on the table. Rebus nodded, satisfied. Jack was busy setting up the recorder and breaking the seals on a couple of tapes.

'Has Ms Cudden explained the situation, Mr Toal?' Malky nodded. 'I'm not interested in the pair of you, but I *am* interested in everything else. You slipped up, but you can still get out of this, same as you've been planning all along.' Rebus tried not to look at Eve, who was looking anywhere but at lovelorn Stanley. Christ, she was a tough one. Rebus really had taken a liking to her; he almost liked her better now than he had that night in the bar. Jack nodded that the recorder was running.

'OK, now we're recording I'd like to make it clear that this is for my own personal insurance, and won't be used against the pair of you at any time, so long as you clear off afterwards. I'd like you to introduce yourselves.' They did, Jack checking the levels and adjusting them.

'I'm Detective Inspector John Rebus,' Rebus said, 'and with me is Detective Inspector Jack Morton.' He paused, pulled out the third chair at the table and sat down, Eve to his right, Toal to his left. 'Let's start with that night in the hotel bar, Ms Cudden. I'm not a great believer in coincidence.'

Eve blinked. She'd expected the questions to relate to Malky alone. Now she saw that Rebus really *was* going to have some insurance.

'It wasn't coincidence,' she said, fumbling for another Sobranie. The packet slipped, and Toal picked it up, taking out a cigarette, lighting it for her, then handing it over. She could hardly bear to take it – or else wanted Rebus to think that. But Rebus was looking at Toal, surprised by the gesture. There was unexpected affection in 'Mad Malky', a real joy at being close to his lover, even in the present situation. He seemed very different from the scowling complainer Rebus had met at the Ponderosa: younger now, face shining, eyes wide. Hard to believe he could kill in cold blood – but not impossible. He was dressed in the same awful non-style of their previous meeting – the trousers from a shell-suit with an orange leather jacket and a blue patterned shirt, set off with scuffed black slip-on shoes. His mouth moved like he was chewing gum, even though he wasn't. He sat low in the chair, legs open, hands resting between his thighs, high up near the crotch.

'It was planned,' Eve went on. 'Well, sort of. I thought there was a good chance you'd hit the bar before you went to bed.'

'How come?'

'The word is, you like to drink.'

'Says who?'

She shrugged.

'How did you know which hotel I'd be in?'

'I was told.'

'Who by?'

'The Yanks.'

'Tell me their names.' By the book, John.

'Judd Fuller, Erik Stemmons.'

'They both told you?'

'Stemmons specifically.' She smiled. 'Coward that he is.'

'Go on.'

'I think he thought handing you to us was a better option than putting Fuller on to you.'

'Because Fuller would have been harder on me?'

She shook her head. 'He was thinking of himself. If *we* went after you, the two of them were in the clear. Judd's difficult to control sometimes.' Toal snorted at that. 'Erik would rather he didn't get worked up.'

Probably Stemmons had reined in Fuller, so all Fuller's men had done was pistol-whip Rebus rather than put him out of the game. One yellow card: he couldn't see Fuller giving a second. Rebus wanted to ask her more. He wanted to know how far she'd have gone to find out what he knew . . . But somehow he thought that line of questioning might blow *all* Malky's fuses.

'Who told the Yanks where I was staying?'

He already knew the answer – Ludovic Lumsden – but wanted it on tape if possible. But Eve shrugged, and Toal shook his head.

'Tell me what you were doing in Aberdeen.'

Eve busied herself with her cigarette, so Toal cleared his throat.

'Working for my dad.'

'Doing what specifically?'

'Selling an' that.'

'Selling?'

'Dope – speed, skag, anything and everything.'

'You sound very relaxed, Mr Toal.'

'Mibbe resigned would be nearer the mark.' Toal sat up in his chair. 'Eve says we can trust you. I wouldn't know about that, but I know what my dad'll do when he finds out we've been skimming.'

'So I'm the lesser of two evils?'

'You said it, not me.'

'All right, let's get back to Aberdeen. You were supplying drugs?'

'Aye.'

'Who to?'

'Burke's Club.'

'The individuals' names?'

'Erik Stemmons and Judd Fuller. Specifically Judd, though Erik knows the score, too.' He smiled at Eve. 'Score,' he repeated. She nodded, letting him know she got the joke.

'Why specifically Judd Fuller?'

'Erik runs the club, does the business side of things. Doesnae' like getting his hands dirty, you know, pretends everything's above board.'

Rebus remembered Stemmons' office – paperwork everywhere. Mr Businessman.

'Can you give me a description of Fuller?'

'You've met him: he gave you that beating.' Toal grinned. The man with the pistol: had he sounded American? Had Rebus been listening that hard?

'I didn't see him though.'

'Well, he's six feet, black hair, it always looks wet. Brylcreem or something. Back-combs it, long, like that *Saturday Night Fever* guy.'

'Travolta?'

'Aye, in that other film. You know.' Toal made like he was spraying the room with bullets.

'*Pulp Fiction?*'

Toal clicked his fingers.

'Except Judd's face is thinner,' Eve added. 'In fact, he's thinner all round. He does like wearing dark suits though. And there's a scar on the back of one of his hands, looks like it was sewn together too tight.'

Rebus nodded. 'Does Fuller deal only drugs?'

Toal shook his head. 'Naw, he's got fingers in every pie: prozzies, porn, casinos, a bit of reset, fake designer stuff – watches and shirts an' that.'

'All-round entrepreneur,' Eve added, flicking ash into the wastebin. She was being careful to say nothing that would incriminate her.

'And Judd and Erik aren't the only ones. There are some Yanks in Aberdeen worse than they are: Eddie Segal, Moose Maloney . . .' Toal saw the look on Eve's face and ground to a halt.

'Malcolm,' she said sweetly, 'we do want to get out of this alive, don't we?'

Toal's face reddened. 'Forget I said that,' he told Rebus. Rebus nodded, but the machine wouldn't forget.

'So,' Rebus said, 'why did you kill Tony El?'

'Me?' Toal said, going into his act. Rebus sighed and looked at the tips of his shoes.

'I think,' Eve prodded, 'that means the Inspector wants *everything*. We don't talk to him, he has a word with your dad.'

Toal stared at her, but she held it; he broke off first. His hands went back to his crotch. 'Yeah,' he said, 'well, I was under orders.'

'Who from?'

'Dad, of course. See, Tony was still working for us. He was day-to-day running of the Aberdeen end. All that stuff about him leaving, that was just a story. But after you came and spoke to Dad . . . he went through the fucking roof, because Tony had been doing outside hits, endangering the operation. And now you were on to him, so . . .'

'So Tony had to go?' Rebus was remembering that Tony El had bragged to Hank Shankley about his 'Glasgow connections' – he hadn't been lying.

'That's right.'

'And I don't suppose you were too upset to see the back of him?'

Eve smiled. 'Not particularly upset, no.'

'Because to save his own neck, Tony might have grassed the two of you?'

'He didn't know we were skimming, but he found out about the hotel arrangements.'

'Biggest mistake he ever made,' Toal said, grinning again. He was getting cockier by the minute, enjoying telling the story, basking in the knowledge that everything was going to be fine. As he grew cockier, so Eve seemed to regard him with less and less good grace. She'd be relieved to be free of him, Rebus could see that. The poor little bastard.

'You had CID fooled, they thought it was suicide.'

'Well, when you've a cop or two in your pocket . . .'

Rebus looked at Toal. 'Say that again.'

'A cop or two on the payroll.'

'Names?'

'Lumsden,' Toal said. 'Jenkins.'

'Jenkins?'

'He's something to do with the oil industry,' Eve explained.

'Oil Liaison Officer?'

She nodded.

Who'd been on holiday when Rebus had arrived, Lumsden standing in for him. With those two on your side, you'd have no trouble supplying the production platforms with whatever they needed – a real captive market. And when the workers came ashore, you had further delights for them: clubs, prozzies, booze and gambling. The legit and the illicit working side by side, each feeding the other. No wonder Lumsden had tagged along on the trip out to Bannock; he was protecting his investment.

'What do you know about Fergus McLure?'

Toal looked to Eve, ready to talk but seeking permission. She nodded, keeping her own mouth shut.

'He had a little accident, got too close to Judd.'

'Fuller killed him?'

'Hands on, that's what Judd said.' There was a hint of hero worship in Toal's voice. 'Told McLure they had to talk somewhere private, said walls had ears. Moseyed down to the canal with him, a dunt to the head with his gun, and into the water.' Toal shrugged. 'He was back in Aberdeen in time for a late breakfast.' He smiled at Eve. 'Late.' Presumably another joke, but she was beyond smiling back. She just wanted out of there.

Rebus had other questions, but he was beginning to tire. He decided to leave it at that. He got up and nodded for Jack to switch off the machine, then told Eve she could go.

'What about me?' Toal asked.

'You don't leave together,' Rebus reminded him. Toal seemed to accept this. Rebus saw Eve along the corridor and down the stairs. Neither of them said a word, not even goodbye. But he watched her leave before asking the desk officer for a couple of uniforms a.s.a.p. at the Interview Room.

When he got back, Jack had just finished rewinding the tapes, and Toal was on his feet, doing some stretching exercises. There was a knock, and the two uniforms came in. Toal stood up straight, sensing something was wrong.

'Malcolm Toal,' Rebus said, 'I am charging you with the murder of Anthony Ellis Kane on the night of—'

With a roar, Mad Malky flew at Rebus, hands scrabbling at his neck.

The woolly suits eventually got him into a cell, and Rebus sat on a chair in the Interview Room, watching his hands shaking.

'You OK?' Jack asked.

'Know what, Jack? You're like a broken record.'

'Know what, John? You're always needing it asked.'

Rebus smiled and rubbed his neck. 'I'm fine.'

As Toal had run at him, Rebus had kneed the young man in the groin with enough force to lift him off his feet. After that, the uniforms had found him just about manageable, especially with a Vulcan death grip to his carotid.

'What do you want to do?' Jack asked.

'One copy of the tape goes to CID here. It'll give them enough to go on until we get back.'

'From Aberdeen?' Jack guessed.

'And points north.' Rebus pointed to the machine. 'Stick the copy back in and turn it on.' Jack did so. 'Gill, here's a little present for you. I hope you'll know what to do with it.' He nodded, and Jack stopped recording and ejected the tape.

'We'll drop it off at St Leonard's.'

'So we *are* going back to Edinburgh?' Jack was thinking of tomorrow's meeting with Ancram.

'Only long enough for a change of clothes and a doctor's line.'

Outside in the car park, a solitary figure was waiting: Eve.

'Going my way?' she asked.

'How did you know?'

She smiled her most feline smile. 'Because you're like me – you've got unfinished business in Aberdeen. I'm only going to be there as long as it takes to visit a few banks and close a few accounts, but there are those two hotel rooms . . .'

A good point: they'd need a base, preferably one Lumsden didn't know about.

'He's in a cell?' she asked.

'Yes.'

'How many men did you need?'

'Just the two.'

'I'm surprised.'

'We all surprise ourselves sometime,' Rebus said, opening the back door of Jack's car for her.

Rebus wasn't surprised to find Gill Templer's office locked up for the night. He looked around the night-shift and saw Siobhan Clarke trying to make herself inconspicuous, dreading their first meeting since she'd been part of the search team at his flat. He walked up to her, the yellow padded envelope in his hand.

'It's OK,' he said, 'I know why you were there. I think I should thank you.'

'I just thought . . .'

He nodded. The relief on her face made him wonder what she'd been going through.

'Working on anything?' he asked, figuring she was owed a minute's conversation. Jack and Eve were downstairs in the car, getting to know one another.

'I've been on Johnny Bible background: deadly dull.' She perked up. 'One thing though. I was going through the old newspapers in the National.'

'Yes?' Rebus had been there, too: he wondered if that was her story.

'One of the librarians told me someone was looking at recent newspapers and asking about people calling up ones from 1968 to '70. I thought the combination was a bit odd. The recent papers were all from just before the first Johnny Bible murder.'

'And the others were the years Bible John was operating?'

'Yes.'

'A journalist?'

'That's what the librarian says. Only, the card he handed over was a fake. He contacted the librarian by telephone.'

'Did the librarian have anything?'

'A few names. I took them down, on the off-chance. A couple of them *are* journalists. One is you. The others, God knows.'

Yes, Rebus had spent a long day poring over the old stories, arranging for photocopies to be made of the relevant pages . . . building his collection.

'And the mysterious journalist?'

'No idea. I got a physical description, but it doesn't help much. Early fifties, tall, fair-haired . . .'

'Doesn't rule too many people out, does it? Why the interest in recent papers? No, wait . . . Looking for cock-ups.'

Siobhan nodded. 'That's what I thought. And at the same time asking about people who'd shown an interest in the original Bible John case. It might sound crazy, but maybe Bible John's out there looking for his offspring. Thing is, whoever he was . . . he's got your name now, *and* your address.'

'Nice to have a fan.' Rebus thought for a moment. 'Those other names . . . can I see?'

She found the relevant page in her notebook. One name leapt out: Peter Manuel.

'Something?' she asked.

Rebus pointed. 'Not his real name. Manuel was a killer back in the fifties.'

'Then who . . . ?'

Reading up on Bible John, using a killer's name as an alias. 'Johnny Bible,' Rebus said quietly.

'I'd better have another word with that librarian.'

'First thing in the morning,' Rebus advised. 'Speaking of which . . .' He handed her the envelope. 'Can you see to it that Gill Templer gets this?'

'Sure.' She shook it. The cassette rattled. 'Anything I should know about?'

'Definitely not.'

She smiled. 'Now you've whetted my curiosity.'

'Then unwhet it.' He turned to leave. He didn't want her to see how shaken he was. Someone else was hunting Johnny Bible, someone who now had Rebus's name and address. Siobhan's words: *Bible John . . . looking for his offspring.* Description: tall, fair-haired, early fifties. The age was right for Bible John. Whoever it was knew Rebus's address . . . and his flat had been broken into, nothing stolen, but his newspapers and cuttings disturbed.

Bible John . . . looking for his offspring.

'How's the inquiry?' Siobhan called.

'Which one?'

'Spaven.'

'A doddle.' He stopped, turned back to her. 'By the way, if you're really bored . . . ?'

'Yes?'

'Johnny Bible: there could just be an oil connection. The last victim worked for oil companies and drank with oilmen. First victim studied at

RGIT, geology, I think. Find out if there's any connection to oil, see if there's something we can link to victims two and three.'

'You think he lives in Aberdeen?'

'Right now, I think I'd lay money on it.'

Then he was gone. One more stop to make before the long haul north.

Bible John was driving through the streets of Aberdeen.

The town was quiet. He liked it that way. The trip to Glasgow had been useful, but the fourth victim had proved more useful still.

From the hotel computer, he had his list of twenty companies. Twenty guests of the Fairmount Hotel who had paid by corporate credit card in the weeks before Judith Cairns's murder. Twenty companies based in the north-east. Twenty individuals he needed to check, any one of whom could be the Upstart.

He'd played with the connection between the victims, and numbers one and four had given him his answer: oil. Oil was at the heart of it. Victim one had studied geology at Robert Gordon's, and in the north-east the study of geology was in so many ways connected to the subject of oil exploration. Victim four's company numbered oil companies and their ancillaries among its best clients. He was looking for someone connected to the oil industry, someone so very like himself. The realisation had shaken him. On the one hand, it made it even more imperative he track down the Upstart; on the other, it made the game that much more dangerous. It wasn't physical danger – he had long since conquered that particular fear. It was the danger of losing his hard-fought-for identity as Ryan Slocum. He almost felt he *was* Ryan Slocum. But Ryan Slocum was just a dead man, a newspaper obituary he'd come across. So he'd applied for a duplicate birth certificate, pleading the original's loss in a house fire. This had been in pre-computer days, easy to get away with.

So his own past ceased to exist . . . for a time, at least. The trunk in the attic told a different story, of course. It gave the lie to his change of identity: you couldn't change the man you were. His trunk full of souvenirs, most of them American . . . He had made arrangements for the trunk to be moved soon, when his wife was out of the house. A moving company would send a transit. The trunk would be taken to a self-storage warehouse. It made sense as a precaution, but he still regretted it; it was like saying the Upstart had won.

No matter what the outcome.

Twenty companies to check. So far he had dismissed four possible suspects as being too old. A further seven companies were not involved in the oil industry in any way that he could see – they went to the bottom of the list. Leaving nine names. It was a slow business. He'd used guile during telephone calls to the companies' offices, but guile would only go so far. He'd also had recourse to the telephone book, finding addresses for the names, watching their homes, waiting for a glimpse of a face. Would he know the Upstart when he saw him? He felt he would; at least, he'd recognise the type. But then Joe Beattie had said the same about Bible John – that he'd recognise him in a crowded room. As if a man's heart showed in the creases and contours of his face, a sort of phrenology of sin.

He parked the car outside another house, called his office to check for

messages. In his line of work, they expected him to be out of the office for long periods of the day, if not for days and weeks at a time. It was the perfect career, really. No messages, nothing for him to think about but the Upstart . . . and himself.

In the early days, he had lacked patience. This was no longer the case. This slow stalking of the Upstart would only make the final confrontation sweeter. But this thought was tempered with another: that the police could be closing in, too. After all, the information was there for them to find: it was just a matter of making the connections. So far only the Edinburgh prostitute failed to fit the pattern, but if he could connect three out of four, he'd be satisfied. He could bet, too, that once he knew the Upstart's identity he could place him in Edinburgh at the time she was killed: hotel records maybe; or a receipt for petrol from an Edinburgh filling station . . . Four victims. One more already than the Bible John of the sixties. It was galling, he had to say it. It rankled.

And someone would pay for it. Very soon.

North of Hell

'Scotland will be reborn the day
the last minister is strangled with
the last copy of the *Sunday Post*.'

Tom Nairn

28

It was after midnight when they reached the hotel. It was situated near the airport, one of the shiny new constructions Rebus had passed on his way to T-Bird Oil. There was too much glare in the lobby, too many mirrors reflecting full-length portraits of three weary figures with meagre luggage. Maybe they would have provoked suspicion, but Eve was a regular and had a business account, so that was that.

'It all goes through the taxi firm,' she explained, 'so this is my treat. Just sign out of the rooms when you're finished, they'll send the bill to Joe's Cabs.'

'Your usual rooms, Ms Cudden,' the clerk said, handing over the keys, 'plus one a few doors further along.'

Jack had been looking through the hotel directory. 'Sauna, health club, weight gym. We should fit right in, John.'

'It's all oil execs,' Eve said, leading them to the lifts. 'They like that kind of thing. Keeps them fit enough to handle the hokey-cokey. And I don't mean the dance.'

'Do you sell everything direct to Fuller and Stemmons?' Rebus asked.

Eve stifled a yawn. 'You mean, do I deal myself?'

'Yes.'

'Would I be that stupid?'

'What about the punters – any names?'

She shook her head, smiled tiredly. 'You never stop, do you?'

'It takes my mind off things.' Specifically: Bible John, Johnny Bible . . . out there somewhere, and maybe not so very far away . . .

She handed their room keys to Rebus and Jack. 'Sleep well, boys. I'll probably be long gone when you wake up . . . and I won't be coming back.'

Rebus nodded. 'How much will you be taking with you?'

'About thirty-eight thou.'

'A decent skim.'

'Decent profits all round.'

'How soon till Uncle Joe finds out about Stanley?'

'Well, Malcolm won't be in a hurry to tell him, and Joe's used to him disappearing for a day or two on the trot . . . With any luck, I won't even be in the country when the bomb goes off.'

'You look the lucky type to me.'

They left the lift at the third floor and checked the numbers on their keys. Rebus ended up next door to Eve: Stanley's old room. Jack was two doors further down.

Stanley's old room was a good size and boasted what Rebus guessed were the usual corporate embellishments: mini-bar, trouser press, a little saucer of chocolates on the pillow, a bathrobe laid out on the turned-down bed. There was a notice clipped to the robe. It asked him not to take it home with him. If he wanted to, he could purchase one from the health club. 'Thank you for being a considerate guest.'

The considerate guest made himself a cup of Café Hag. There was a price list on top of the mini-bar, detailing the delights within. He stuck it in a drawer. The wardrobe boasted a mini-safe, so he took the mini-bar key and locked it inside. Another barrier for him to get past, another chance to change his mind if he *really* wanted that drink.

Meantime, the coffee tasted fine. He had a shower, wrapped himself in the bathrobe, then sat on his bed and stared at the connecting door. Of course, there would have to be a connecting door: couldn't have Stanley hopping around the corridor at all hours. There was a simple lock his side, as there would be on the other. He wondered what he would find if he unlocked the door: would Eve's be standing open? If he knocked, would she let him in? What about if *she* knocked? He turned his eyes from the door, and they settled on the mini-bar. He felt peckish – there would be nuts and crisps inside. Maybe he could . . . ? No, no, no. He turned his attention back to the connecting door, listened hard, couldn't hear any movement from Eve's room. Maybe she was already asleep – early start and all that. He found he wasn't feeling tired any more. Now he was here, he wanted to get to work. He pulled open his curtains. It had started to rain, the tarmac glistening and black like the back of a huge fat beetle. Rebus pulled a chair over to the window. Wind was driving the rain, making shifting patterns in the sodium light. As he stared, the rain began to resemble smoke, billowing out of the darkness. The car park below was half full, the cars huddled like cattle while their owners stayed snug and dry.

Johnny Bible was out there, probably in Aberdeen, probably connected to the oil industry. He thought about the people he'd met these past days, everyone from Major Weir to Walt the tour guide. It was ironic that the person whose case had brought him here – Allan Mitchison – was not only connected to oil but was also the only candidate he could rule out, being long dead by the time Vanessa Holden met her killer. Rebus felt guilty about Mitchison. His case was becoming swamped by the serial killings. It was a job, something Rebus had to do. But it wasn't wedged in his throat the way the Johnny Bible case was, something he had either to cough up or choke on.

But he wasn't the only one with an interest in Johnny. Someone had broken into his flat. Someone had been checking library records. Someone using a false identity. Someone with something to hide. Not a reporter, not another policeman. Could Bible John really be out there still? Dormant somewhere until brought to life by Johnny Bible? Enraged by the act of imitation, by its temerity and the cold fact that it brought the original case back up into the light? Not only enraged, but feeling endangered, too – externally and internally: fear of being recognised and caught; fear of not being the bogeyman any longer.

A new bogeyman for the nineties, someone to be scared of again. One mythology erased and replaced by another.

Yes, Rebus could feel it. He could sense Bible John's hostility to the young pretender. No flattery in imitation, none at all . . .

And he knows where I live, Rebus thought. He's been there, touched my obsession, and wondered how far I'm willing to take it. But why? Why would he place himself in danger like that, breaking into a flat in the middle of the day? Looking for what exactly? Looking for something in particular? But *what*? Rebus turned the question over in his mind, wondered if a drink would help, got as far as the safe before turning back, standing there in the middle of the room, his whole body crackling with need.

The hotel felt asleep; easy to imagine the whole country asleep and dreaming blameless dreams. Stemmons and Fuller, Uncle Joe, Major Weir, Johnny Bible . . . everyone was innocent in sleep. Rebus walked over to the connecting door and unlocked it. Eve's door was slightly ajar. Silently, he pushed it wide open. Her room was in darkness, curtains closed. Light from his own room lay like an arrow along the floor, pointing towards the king-size bed. She lay on her side, one arm on top of the covers. Her eyes were closed. He took one step into her room, not merely a voyeur now but an intruder. Then he just stood there, watching her. Maybe he'd have stayed that way for long minutes.

'Wondered how long it would take you,' she said.

Rebus walked across to her bed. She reached both arms up to him. She was naked beneath the covers, warm and sweet-smelling. He sat down on the bed, took her hands in his.

'Eve,' he said quietly, 'I need one favour from you before you go.'

She sat up. 'Not counting this?'

'Not counting this.'

'What?'

'I want you to phone Judd Fuller. Tell him you need to see him.'

'You should stay away from him.'

'I know.'

She sighed. 'But you can't?' He nodded, and she touched his cheek with the back of her hand. 'OK, but now I want a favour in return.'

'What?'

'Take the rest of the night off,' she said, pulling him towards her.

He woke up alone in her bed, and it was morning. He checked to see if she'd left a note or anything, but of course she hadn't: she wasn't the type.

He walked through the open doorway and locked his door after him, then switched off the lights in his room. There was a knock at his door: Jack. Rebus pulled on pants and trousers and was halfway to the door when he remembered something. He walked back to the bed and removed the chocolates from the pillow, then pulled the covers down, messing them up. He surveyed the scene, punched a head-shaped dent in one pillow, then answered the door.

And it wasn't Jack at all. It was one of the hotel staff, carrying a tray.

'Morning, sir.' Rebus stood aside to let him in. 'Sorry if I woke you. Miss Cudden specified the time.'

'That's OK.' Rebus watched the young man slide the tray on to the table by the window.

'Would you like me to open it?' Meaning the half-bottle of champagne

resting in an ice-bucket. There was a jug of fresh orange juice, a crystal glass, and a folded copy of the morning's *Press & Journal*. In a slim porcelain vase stood a single red carnation.

'No.' Rebus lifted the bucket. 'This, you can take away. The rest is fine.'

'Yes, sir. If you'll just sign . . . ?'

Rebus took the proffered pen, and added a hefty tip to the bill. Fuck it, Uncle Joe was paying. The young man broke into a big grin, making Rebus wish he was this generous every morning.

'Thank *you*, sir.'

When he'd gone, Rebus poured a glass of juice. The fresh-squeezed stuff, cost a fortune in the supermarket. Outside, the roads were still damp, and there was plenty of cloud overhead, but the sky looked like it might break into a grin of its own before the morning was out. A light aircraft took off from Dyce, probably Shetland-bound. Rebus looked at his watch, then called Jack's room. Jack answered with a noise somewhere between an inquiry and an oath.

'Your morning alarm call,' Rebus trilled.

'Fuck off.'

'Come by for orange juice and coffee.'

'Give me five minutes.'

Rebus said that was the least he could do. Next he tried phoning Siobhan at home – got her machine. Tried her at St Leonard's, but she wasn't there. He knew she wouldn't be slow in going about the work he'd given her, but he wanted to stick close to her, needed to know when she got a result. He put down the phone and looked at the tray again, then smiled.

Eve had left him a message after all.

The dining room was quiet, most tables taken by single men, some of them already at work on portable phones and laptops. Rebus and Jack got stuck in – juice and cornflakes, then the Full Highland Breakfast with a big pot of tea.

Jack tapped his watch. 'Quarter of an hour from now, Ancram's going to hit the roof.'

'Might knock some sense into him.' Rebus scraped a pat of butter on to his toast. Five-star hotel, but the toast was still cold.

'So what's our plan of attack?'

'I'm looking for a girl, she's in photos with Allan Mitchison, an environmental protester.'

'Where do we start?'

'You sure you want in on this?' Rebus looked around the dining room. 'You could spend the day here, try the health club, watch a film . . . It's all on Uncle Joe.'

'John, I'm sticking by you.' Jack paused. 'As a friend, not Ancram's dogsbody.'

'In that case, our first port of call's the Exhibition Centre. Now eat up, it's going to be a long day, believe me.'

'One question.'

'What?'

'How come *you* got the orange juice this morning?'

*

The Exhibition Centre was almost deserted. The various stalls and stands – many of them, as Rebus now knew, designed by Johnny Bible's fourth victim – had been dismantled and taken away, the floors hoovered and polished. There were no demonstrators outside, no inflatable whale. They asked to speak to someone in charge, and were eventually taken to an office where a brisk, bespectacled woman introduced herself as 'the Deputy' and asked them how she could help.

'The North Sea Conference,' Rebus explained, 'you had a bit of trouble with protesters.'

She smiled, her mind on other things. 'Bit late to do anything about that, isn't it?' She moved some papers around her desk, looking for something.

'I'm interested in one particular protester. What was the name of the group?'

'It wasn't that organised, Inspector. They came from all over: Friends of the Earth, Greenpeace, Save the Whale, God alone knows.'

'Did they cause any trouble?'

'Nothing we couldn't handle.' Another frozen smile. But she was looking harassed: she really had misplaced something. Rebus got to his feet.

'Well, sorry to trouble you.'

'No trouble. Sorry I can't help.'

'Don't worry about it.'

Rebus turned to go. Jack bent down and retrieved a sheet of paper from the floor, handed it to her.

'Thanks,' she said. Then she followed them out of her office. 'Look, a local pressure group was responsible for the march on the Saturday.'

'What march?'

'It ended at Duthie Park, there was some music afterwards.'

Rebus nodded: Dancing Pigs. The day he'd visited Bannock.

'I can give you their phone number,' she said. The smile was human now.

Rebus telephoned the group's headquarters.

'I'm looking for a friend of Allan Mitchison's. I don't know her name, but she's got short fair hair, with some of it braided, you know, with beads and stuff. One braid hangs down past her forehead to her nose. Sort of an American accent, I think.'

'And who might you be?' The voice was cultured; for some reason, Rebus visualised the speaker sporting a beard, but it wasn't the kilted Jerry Garcia, different accent.

'My name's Detective Inspector John Rebus. You know Allan Mitchison is dead?'

A pause, then an exhalation: cigarette smoke. 'I heard. Bloody shame.'

'Did you know him well?' Rebus was trying to recall the faces in the photographs.

'He was the shy type. Only met him a couple of times. Big fan of Dancing Pigs, that's why he tried so bloody hard to get them to top the bill. I was amazed when it worked. He bombarded them with letters, you know. Maybe a hundred or more, probably wore down their resistance.'

'And his girlfriend's name?'

'Not given out to strangers, I'm afraid. I mean, I've only your word for it you're a police officer.'

'I could come over—'

'I don't think so.'

'Look, I'd really like to talk to you . . .'

But the telephone was dead.

'Want to take a run down there?' Jack suggested.

Rebus shook his head. 'He won't tell us anything he doesn't want to. Besides, I've got the feeling by the time we got there he'd have gone out for the day. Can't afford to waste time.'

Rebus tapped his pen against his teeth. They were back in his bedroom. The telephone had a speaker, and he'd kept it on so Jack could hear. Jack was helping himself to last night's chocolates.

'Local cops,' Rebus said, picking up the receiver. 'That gig was probably licensed, maybe Queen Street will have records of other organisers.'

'Worth a go,' Jack agreed, plugging in the kettle.

So Rebus spent twenty minutes knowing how a pinball feels, as he was shunted from one office to another. He was pretending to be a Trading Standards Officer, interested in bootleggers, following up on an operation at an earlier Dancing Pigs concert. Jack nodded his approval: not a bad story.

'Yes, John Baxter here, City of Edinburgh Trading Standards. I was just explaining to your colleague . . .' And off he went again. When he was passed on to yet another voice, and recognised it as belonging to the first person he'd spoken to, he slammed down the phone.

'They couldn't organise the proverbial piss-up.'

Jack handed him a cup of tea. 'End of the road?'

'No chance.' Rebus consulted his notebook, picked up the phone again and was put through to Stuart Minchell at T-Bird Oil.

'Inspector, what a pleasant surprise.'

'Sorry to keep pestering you, Mr Minchell.'

'How's your investigation?'

'To be honest, I could use a bit of help.'

'Fire away.'

'It's about Bannock. The day I went out there, some protesters were brought aboard.'

'Yes, I heard. Handcuffed themselves to the rails.' Minchell sounded amused. Rebus remembered the platform, the strong gusts, the way his hard hat wouldn't stay on, and the helicopter overhead, filming everything . . .

'I was wondering what happened to the protesters. I mean, were they placed under arrest?' He knew they weren't: a couple of them had been at the concert.

'Best person to ask would be Hayden Fletcher.'

'Do you think you could ask for me, sir? On the quiet, as it were.'

'I suppose so. Give me your number in Edinburgh.'

'That's all right, I'll call you back . . . say, twenty minutes?' Rebus glanced towards the window: he could almost see the T-Bird headquarters from here.

'Depends if I can find anyone.'

'I'll try again in twenty minutes. Oh, and Mr Minchell?'

'Yes?'

'If you should need to speak to Bannock, could you put a question from me to Willie Ford?'

'What's the question?'

'I want to know if he knew Allan Mitchison had a girlfriend, blonde with braided hair.'

'Braided hair.' Minchell was writing it down. 'Can do.'

'If so, I'd like her name, and an address if possible.' Rebus thought of something else. 'When the protesters came to your headquarters, you had them videoed, didn't you?'

'I don't remember.'

'Could you find out? It would be security, wouldn't it?'

'Do I still have twenty minutes for all this?'

Rebus smiled. 'No, sir. Let's make it half an hour.'

Rebus put down the phone and drained his tea.

'How about another phone call now?' Jack asked.

'Who to?'

'Chick Ancram.'

'Jack, look at me.' Rebus pointed to his face. 'Could a man this ill possibly pick up the telephone?'

'You'll swing.'

'Like a pendulum do.'

Rebus gave Stuart Minchell forty minutes.

'You know, Inspector, you make working for the Major seem like a picnic by comparison.'

'Glad to be of service, sir. What have you got?'

'Just about everything.' A rustle of paper. 'No, the protesters weren't arrested.'

'Isn't that a bit generous, under the circumstances?'

'It would only have generated more bad publicity.'

'Something you don't need right now?'

'The company did get names out of the protesters, but they were false. At least, I'm assuming Yuri Gagarin and Judy Garland are aliases.'

'Sound reasoning.' Judy Garland: Braid-Hair. Interesting choice.

'So they were detained, given something hot to drink, and flown back to the mainland.'

'Very decent of T-Bird.'

'Yes, isn't it?'

'And the video recording?'

'That was, as you guessed, our security staff. Precautionary, I'm told. If there's trouble, we have physical evidence.'

'They don't use the film to identify the protesters?'

'We're not the CIA, Inspector. We're an oil company.'

'Sorry, sir, go on.'

'Willie Ford says he knew Mitch *had* been seeing someone in Aberdeen – past tense. But they never discussed her. Mitch was – quote – "a dark horse on the question of his love life" – unquote.'

Dead ends everywhere.

'Is that everything?'

'That's it.'

'Well, thank you, sir, I really appreciate this.'

'My pleasure, Inspector. But next time you want a favour, try not to make it on a day when I'm due to sack a dozen of our workforce.'

'Hard times, Mr Minchell?'

'A book by Dickens, Inspector Rebus. Goodbye.'

Jack was laughing. 'Good line,' he said approvingly.

'So it should be,' Rebus said, 'he was less than a mile away.' He walked over to the window, watched another plane taking off in the near-distance, the roar of its jets fading as it headed north.

'Had enough for one morning?'

Rebus didn't say anything. He'd been expecting Eve to call. There was that favour. He wondered if she'd do it. She owed him, but crossing Judd Fuller didn't sound like the wisest move on the dance floor. She'd been dancing her own little steps for years: why trip up now?

Jack repeated his question.

'One option left,' Rebus said, turning to face him.

'What's that?'

'Flight.'

At Dyce Airport, Rebus showed his warrant card and asked if there were any flights out to Sullom Voe.

'Not for a while,' he was told. 'Maybe in four or five hours.'

'We're not fussy who we fly with.'

Shrugs, shakes of the head.

'It's important.'

'You could always hitch a ride to Sumburgh.'

'That's miles from Sullom Voe.'

'Only trying to be helpful. You could rent a car.'

Rebus thought about it, then had a better idea. 'How soon could we be out of here?'

'To Sumburgh? Half an hour, forty minutes. There's a helicopter stopping there on its way out to Ninian.'

'Fine.'

'Let me talk to them.' She picked up her telephone.

'We'll be back in five minutes.'

Jack followed Rebus over to the public telephones, where Rebus made a call to St Leonard's. He was put through to Gill Templer.

'I'm halfway through listening to the tape,' she said.

'Better than *Saturday Night Theatre*, isn't it?'

'I'm going through to Glasgow later on. I want to talk to him myself.'

'Good idea, I've left a copy of the tape with Partick CID. Have you seen Siobhan this morning?'

'I don't think so. Which shift is she working? If you like, I can try to find her.'

'Don't bother, Gill, long distance doesn't come cheap.'

'Oh hell, where are you now?'

'Ill in bed, if Ancram comes asking.'

'And looking for that favour?'

'A phone number, actually. Lerwick police station. I'm assuming such a thing exists.'

'It does,' she said. 'Under the auspices of Northern Division. There was a conference in Inverness last year, they were complaining about keeping tabs on Orkney and Shetland.'

'Gill . . .'

'I've been looking it up while I talk.' She reeled the number off; it went into his notebook.

'Thanks, Gill. Bye.'

'John!'

But he'd cut her off. 'How are you for change, Jack?' Jack showed him some coins. Rebus took most of them, then called Lerwick and asked if they could lend a car for half a day. He explained it was a murder inquiry, Lothian and Borders. Nothing to get het up about, they'd only be interviewing a friend of the victim.

'Well now, a car . . .' the voice drawled, like Rebus had asked for a spaceship. 'When would you be arriving?'

'We're on a chopper out of here in about half an hour.'

'Two of you?'

'Two of us,' Rebus said, 'which rules out a motorbike.'

His reward: a deep gurgling laugh. 'Not necessarily.'

'Can you do it?'

'Well, I can do *some*thing. Only problem might be if the cars are out elsewhere. Some of our calls are to the back of beyond.'

'If there's no one to meet us at Sumburgh, I'll phone again.'

'You do that now. Cheerio.'

Back at the desk, they found they were on the flight in thirty-five minutes.

'I've never been on a helicopter,' Jack said.

'An experience you'll never forget.'

Jack frowned. 'Can you try that again with a bit more enthusiasm?'

29

There were half a dozen planes on the ground at Sumburgh Airport, and the same number of helicopters, most of them connected as if by umbilical cords to neighbouring fuel tankers. Rebus walked into the Wilsness Terminal, unzipping his survival suit as he went, then saw that Jack was still outside, taking in the coastal scenery and bleak inland plain. There was a fierce wind rising, and Jack had his chin tucked into his suit. Post-flight, he looked pale and slightly queasy. Rebus for one had spent the entire time trying not to remember his outsized breakfast. Jack eventually saw him signalling, and came in from the cold.

'Doesn't the sea look blue?'

'Same colour you'd turn after two more minutes out there.'

'And the sky . . . incredible.'

'Don't go New Age on me, Jack. Let's get these suits off. I think our escort with the Escort has just arrived.'

Only it was an Astra, snug with three of them inside, especially when the uniformed driver was built like a rock formation. His head – minus the diced cap – brushed the roof of the car. The voice was the same as on the telephone. He'd shaken Rebus's hand as though greeting some foreign emissary.

'Have you been to Shetland before?'

Jack shook his head; Rebus admitted he'd been once, but added no further details.

'And where would you like me to take you?'

'Back to your base,' Rebus said from the cramped back seat. 'We'll drop you off and turn the car in when we're finished.'

The woolly suit – whose name was Alexander Forres – boomed his disappointment. 'But I've been two decades on the force.'

'Yes?'

'This would be my first murder inquiry!'

'Look, Sergeant Forres, we're only here to talk to a friend of the victim. It's background – routine and boring as hell.'

'Ach, all the same . . . I was quite looking forward to it.'

They were heading up the A970 to Lerwick, twenty-odd miles north of Sumburgh. The wind buffeted them, Forres' huge hands tight on the steering-wheel, like an ogre choking an infant. Rebus decided to change the subject.

'Nice road.'

'Paid for with oil money,' Forres said.

'How do you like being ruled from Inverness?'

'Who says we are? You think they come checking up on us every week of the year?'

'I'd guess not.'

'You'd guess right, Inspector. It's like Lothian and Borders – how often does someone from Fettes bother travelling down to Hawick?' Forres looked at Rebus in the rearview. 'Don't go thinking we're all idiots up here, with just enough sense to set light to the boat come Up-Helly-Aa.'

'Up-Helly what?'

Jack turned towards him. 'You know, John, where they burn a longboat.'

'Last Tuesday in January,' Forres said.

'Odd form of central heating,' Rebus muttered.

'He's a born cynic,' Jack told the sergeant.

'Well, it'd be sad for him if he died one.' Forres's eyes were still on the rearview.

On the outskirts of Lerwick, they passed ugly prefabricated buildings which Rebus guessed were connected to the oil industry. The police station itself was in the New Town. They dropped Forres off, and he went in to fetch them a map of Mainland.

'Not that you could get very lost,' he'd told them. 'There are only the three big roads to worry about.'

Rebus looked at the map and saw what he meant. Mainland comprised a shape in the vague form of a cross, the A970 its spine, the 971 and 968 its arms. Brae was as far north again as they'd just come. Rebus was going to be driving, Jack navigating – Jack's decision; he said it would give him a chance to sightsee.

The drive was by turns awe-inspiring and bleak: coastal vistas giving way to interior moorland, scattered settlements, a lot of sheep – many of them on the road – and few trees. Jack was right though, the sky *was* amazing. Forres had told them this season was 'simmer dim' – a time of year without true darkness. But in winter, daylight became a precious commodity. You had to respect people who chose to live miles from everything you took for granted. Easy enough to be a hunter-gatherer in a city, but out here . . . It wasn't the sort of scenery to inspire conversation. They found their dialogues crumbling into grunts and nods. As close as they were in the speeding car, they were in isolation each from the other. No, Rebus was damned sure he couldn't survive out here.

They took a left fork towards Brae, and found themselves suddenly on the island's west coast. It was still hard to know what to make of the place – Forres was the only born and bred Shetlander they'd met. What architecture they'd seen in Lerwick had been a mix of Scottish and Scandinavian styles, a sort of Ikea baronial. Out in the country, the crofts were the same as any in the Western Isles, but the names of the settlements showed Scandinavian influence. As they drove through Burravoe and into Brae, Rebus realised he felt just about as foreign as he ever had in his life.

'Where to now?' Jack asked.

'Give me a minute. When I was here before, we came into town the other way . . .' Rebus got a fix on where they were, and eventually led them to the

house Jake Harley shared with Briony. Neighbours looked out at the police car like they'd never seen one before; maybe they hadn't. Rebus tried Briony's door – no answer. He knocked harder, the sound echoing emptily. A look in through the living-room window: untidy, but not a mess. A woman's untidiness, not quite professional enough. Rebus went back to the car.

'She works at the swimming pool, let's give it a shot.'

The pool, with its blue metal roof, was hard to miss. Briony was pacing the edge of the pool, watching children at play. She wore the same uniform of singlet and jogging bottoms as when they'd last met, but now had tennis shoes on her feet. Her ankles were bare: lifesavers didn't bother with socks. She had a referee's tin whistle strung around her neck, but the kids were behaving themselves. Briony saw Rebus and recognised him. She put the whistle in her mouth and gave three short blasts: a recognised signal – another staff member took her place poolside. She walked up to Rebus and Jack. The temperature was getting on for tropical, with humidity to match.

'I told you,' she said, 'Jake's still not shown up.'

'I know, and you said you weren't worried about him.'

She shrugged. She had short dark hair which fell straight most of the way before ending in kiss-curls. The style took half a dozen years off her, turning her into a teenager, but her face was older – slightly hardened, whether by climate or circumstance Rebus couldn't say. Her eyes were small, as were nose and mouth. He tried not to think of a hamster, but then she twitched her nose and the picture was complete.

'He's a free agent,' she said.

'But you were worried last week.'

'Was I?'

'When you closed the door on me. I've seen the look enough times to know.'

She folded her arms. 'So?'

'So one of two things, Briony. Either Jake's in hiding because he's in fear of his life.'

'Or?'

'Or he's already dead. Either way, you can help.'

She swallowed. 'Mitch . . .'

'Did Jake tell you why Mitch was killed?'

She shook her head. Rebus tried not to smile: so Jake had been in touch since they'd last spoken.

'He's alive, isn't he?'

She bit her lip, then nodded.

'I'd like to talk to him. I think I can get him out of this mess.'

She tried to gauge the truth of this, but Rebus's face was a mask. 'Is he in trouble?' she asked.

'Yes, but not with us.'

She looked back at the pool, saw everything was under control. 'I'll take you,' she said.

They drove back through the moorland and down past Lerwick, heading for a place called Sandwick on the eastern side of Mainland, just ten miles north of where their helicopter had originally landed.

Briony didn't want to talk during the drive, and Rebus guessed she didn't know much anyway. Sandwick turned out to be a spread of land taking in older settlements and oil-era housing. She directed them to Leebotten, a nestling of sea-front cottages.

'Is this where he is?' Rebus asked as they got out of the car. She shook her head and pointed out to sea. There was an island out there, no sign of habitation. Cliffs and rocky approaches. Rebus looked to Briony.

'Mousa,' she said.

'How do we get there?'

'Boat, always supposing somebody's willing to take us.' She knocked on a cottage door. It was opened by a middle-aged woman.

'Briony,' the woman said simply, more statement of fact than greeting.

'Hello, Mrs Munroe. Is Scott in?'

'He is.' The door opened a little wider. 'Come in, won't you?'

They entered one decent-sized room which seemed kitchen and living room both. A large wooden table took up most of the space. By the fireplace were two armchairs. A man was rising from one of them, unhooking wire reading-glasses from his ears. He folded them and put them in his waistcoat pocket. The book he'd been reading lay open on the floor: it was a family-sized Bible, black leather cover and brass clasps.

'Well now, Briony,' the man said. He was middle-aged or a little after, but his weatherbeaten face was that of an old man. His hair was silver, cut short with the careful simplicity of a home barber. His wife had gone to the sink to fill the kettle.

'No thanks, Mrs Munroe,' Briony said, before turning back to the man. 'Have you seen Jake lately, Scott?'

'I was over there a couple of days back, he seemed fine.'

'Could you take us across?'

Scott Munroe looked to Rebus, who stuck out a hand.

'Detective Inspector Rebus, Mr Munroe. This is DI Morton.'

Munroe shook both hands, putting no power into it: what had he to prove?

'Well, the wind's dropped a bit,' Munroe said, rubbing the grey stubble on his chin. 'So I suppose that's all right.' He turned to his wife. 'Meg, what about some bread and ham for the lad?'

Mrs Munroe nodded and silently set about her work, while her husband readied himself. He found oilskins for all of them and waterproof boots for himself, by which time a parcel of sandwiches and flask of tea sat waiting. Rebus stared at the flask, knowing Jack was doing the same, both gasping for a drink.

But there was no time for that. They were off.

It was a small boat, freshly painted and with an outboard motor. Rebus had had visions of them rowing across.

'There's a jetty,' Briony said when they were under way, rising and falling against the choppy water. 'A ferry usually takes visitors across. We'll have a bit of a hike, not much.'

'It's a bleak spot to choose,' Rebus yelled above the wind.

'Not that bleak,' she said with the ghost of a smile.

'What's that?' Jack said, pointing.

It stood on the edge of the island, next to where sloping strata of rock

eased down into the dark water. Sheep grazed on the grass around the structure. To Rebus, it looked like some gigantic sandcastle or upturned flower-pot. As they got closer he saw it had to be over forty feet high, maybe fifty feet in diameter at its base, and was constructed from large flat stones, thousands of them.

'Mousa Broch,' Briony said.

'What is it?'

'Like a fort. They lived there, it was easy to defend.'

'Who lived there?'

She shrugged. 'Settlers. Maybe a hundred years BC.' There was a low-walled area behind the broch. 'That was the Haa; it's just a shell now.'

'And where's Jake?'

She turned to him. 'Inside the broch, of course.'

They landed, Munroe saying he'd circle the island and be back for them in an hour. Briony carried the bag of provisions, and struck out towards the broch, watched by the slow-chewing sheep and a few strutting birds.

'You live in a country all your life,' Jack was saying, the hood of his oilskin up to protect him from the wind, 'and you never even *know* stuff like this is out there.'

Rebus nodded. It *was* an extraordinary place. The feel of his feet on the grass wasn't like walking across lawn or field; it was like he was the first person ever to walk there. They followed Briony through a passageway and into the heart of the broch itself, sheltered from the wind but with no roof to protect them from threatening rain. Munroe's 'one hour' was a warning: any later and they'd be in for a rough if not dangerous crossing.

The blue nylon one-man tent looked incongruous pitched in the broch's central court. A man had risen out of it to hug Briony. Rebus bided his time. Briony handed over the bag of tea and sandwiches.

'God,' Jake Harley said, 'I've got too much food here as it is.'

He didn't look surprised to see Rebus. 'I thought she'd crack under pressure,' he said.

'No pressure necessary, Mr Harley. She's worried about you, that's all. I was worried too for a while there – thought you might have had an accident.'

Harley managed a smile. 'By which you don't really mean "accident"?' Rebus nodded. He was staring at Harley, trying to see him as 'Mr H.', the person who had ordered Allan Mitchison's execution. But that seemed way off the mark.

'I don't blame you for going into hiding,' Rebus said. 'Probably the safest thing you could have done.'

'Poor Mitch.' Harley looked down at the ground. He was tall, well built, with short, thinning black hair and metal-rimmed glasses. His face had retained a touch of the schoolboy, but he was badly needing a shave and to wash his hair. The tent's flaps were open, showing ground-mat, sleeping-bag, a radio and some books. Leaning against the interior wall of the broch was a red rucksack, and nearby a camping-stove and carrier bag filled with rubbish.

'Can we talk about it?' Rebus asked.

Jake Harley nodded. He saw that Jack Morton was more interested in the broch itself than in their conversation. 'Isn't it incredible?'

'Bloody right,' Jack said. 'Did it ever have a roof?'

Harley shrugged. 'They built lean-tos in here, so maybe they didn't need a roof up there. The walls are hollow, double-thick. One of the galleries still leads to the top.' He looked around. 'There's a lot we don't know.' Then he looked at Rebus. 'It's been here two thousand years. It'll be here long after the oil's gone.'

'I don't doubt that.'

'Some people can't see it. Money's made them short-sighted.'

'You think this is all about money, Jake?'

'Not all of it, no. Come on, I'll show you the Haa.'

So they walked back out into the wind, crossing the grazing land and coming to the low wall around what had been a good-sized stone-built house, only the shell of which remained. They circuited the boundary, Briony walking with them, Jack further back, reluctant to leave the broch.

'Mousa Broch has always been lucky for the hunted. There's a story in the *Orkneyinga Saga*, an eloping couple took shelter here . . .' He smiled at Briony.

'You found out Mitch was dead?' Rebus asked.

'Yes.'

'How?'

'I phoned Jo.'

'Jo?'

'Joanna Bruce. Mitch and her had been seeing one another.' So at last Braid-hair had a name.

'How did she know?'

'It was in the Edinburgh paper. Jo's a media checker – she reads all the papers first thing every morning to see if there's anything the various pressure groups should know.'

'You didn't tell Briony?'

Jake took his girlfriend's hand and kissed it. 'You'd only have worried,' he told her.

'Two questions, Mr Harley: why do you think Mitch was killed, and who was responsible?'

Harley shrugged. 'As to who did it . . . I'd never be able to prove anything. But I know why he was killed – it was my fault.'

'Your fault?'

'I told him what I suspected about the *Negrita*.'

The ship Sheepskin had mentioned on the flight to Sullom Voe; afterwards clamming up.

'What happened?'

'It was a few months back. You know Sullom Voe has some of the strictest procedures going? I mean, time was tankers would swill out their dirty bilges as they approached the coast – it saved pumping them ashore at the terminal . . . saved time, which meant *money*. We used to lose black guillemots, great northern divers, shags, eider ducks, even the otters. That doesn't happen now – they tightened up. But mistakes still happen. That's all the *Negrita* was, a mistake.'

'An oil spill?'

Harley nodded. 'Not a big one, not by the standards we've managed to set with *Braer* and *Sea Empress*. The first mate, who should have been in

charge, was in the sick bay – bad hangover apparently. A crew member who hadn't done the job before hit the wrong sequence of levers. The thing was, the crew member didn't have any English. That's not unusual these days: the officers might be British, but the hired help is the cheapest the company can get, which usually means Portuguese, Filipino, a hundred other nationalities. My guess is, the poor sod just didn't understand the instructions.'

'It was hushed up?'

Harley shrugged. 'Never really news in the first place, not a big enough spill.'

Rebus frowned. 'So what's the problem?'

'Like I say, I told Mitch the story . . .'

'How did you know?'

'The crew landed at the terminal. They were in the canteen. I got talking to one of them, he looked awful – I can speak a bit of Spanish. He told me he did it.'

Rebus nodded. 'And Mitch?'

'Well, Mitch found out something that *had* been covered up. Namely the tanker's real owners. It's not easy with these boats – they're registered here, there and everywhere, leaving a real paper trail in their wake. Not always easy to get details from some of the registration ports. And sometimes the name on the papers doesn't mean much – companies own other companies, more countries are involved . . .'

'A real maze.'

'Purposely so: a lot of the tankers out there are in shocking condition. But maritime law is international – even if we wanted to stop them landing, we couldn't, not without the say-so of all the other signatories.'

'Mitch found out that T-Bird Oil owned the tanker?'

'How did you know?'

'An educated guess.'

'Well, that's what he told me.'

'And you think someone at T-Bird had him killed? But why? Like you say, it wasn't a newsworthy spill.'

'It would be with T-Bird in the frame. They're going all out to persuade the government to let them dump their platforms at sea. They're talking up the environment and their record in that area. We're Mr Clean, so let us do what we want.' Harley showed bright white teeth as he spoke, the words almost a sneer. 'So tell me, Inspector, am I being paranoid? Just because Mitch gets thrown out of a window doesn't mean he was assassinated, right?'

'Oh, he was assassinated all right. But I'm not sure the *Negrita* had much to do with it.' Harley stopped walking and looked at him. 'I think you'd be quite safe going back home, Jake,' Rebus said. 'In fact, I'm sure of it. But first, there's something I need.'

'What?'

'An address for Joanna Bruce.'

30

The trip back was a real follicle transplant – hairier even than the trip out. They'd taken Jake and Briony back to Brae, then dropped the car off at Lerwick and begged a lift to Sumburgh. Forres was still in the huff, but relented eventually and checked the flights back, one of which gave them enough time for a Cup-a-Soup at the station.

At Dyce, they climbed back into Jack's car and sat there for a couple of minutes, adjusting to being back on the ground. Then they headed south on the A92, using the directions Jake Harley had given them. It was the same road Rebus had been taken on the night Tony El had been killed. They had Stanley for that – no matter what. Rebus wondered what else the young psychopath might spill, especially now he'd lost Eve. He'd know she'd flown; he'd know she wouldn't have left the loot behind. Maybe Gill would have twisted more stories out of him.

It could be the making of her.

They saw signposts to Cove Bay, followed Harley's instructions and came to a lay-by, behind which were parked a dozen vans, caravans, buses and campers. Bumping over ineffectual earth mounds, they came into a clearing in front of a forest. Dogs were barking, kids out playing with a punctured football. Clothes-lines hung between branches, and someone had lit a bonfire. A few adults had parked themselves around the fire, passing joints, one woman strumming a guitar. Rebus had been to travellers' camps before. They came in two designs. There was the old-style gypsy camp, with smart caravans and builders' lorries, the inhabitants – Romanies – olive-skinned and lapsing into a tongue Rebus couldn't understand. Then there were the 'New Age travellers': usually with buses which had passed their last MOT on a wing and a prayer. They were young and savvy, cut dead wood for fuel, and worked the social security system, despite government attempts to render it unworkable. They gave their kids names the kids would kill them for when they grew up.

Nobody paid Rebus and Jack any heed as they walked towards the campfire. Rebus kept his hands in his pockets, and tried not to make fists of them.

'Looking for Jo,' he said. He recognised the guitar chords: 'Time of the Preacher'. He tried again. 'Joanna Bruce.'

'Bummer,' someone said.

'That could be arranged,' Jack cautioned.

The joint went from hand to hand. 'Decade from now,' someone else said, 'this won't be illegal. It might even be on prescription.'

Smoke billowed from grinning mouths.

'Joanna,' Rebus reminded them.

'Warrant?' the guitarist asked.

'You know better than that,' Rebus told her. 'I only need a warrant if I want to bust this place. Want me to fetch one?'

'Macho Man!' someone sang.

'What do you want?'

There was a small white caravan hooked up to an antiquated Land-Rover. She'd opened the caravan door – just the top half – and was leaning out.

'Can you smell the bacon, Jo?' the guitarist asked.

'Need to talk to you, Joanna,' Rebus said, walking towards the caravan, 'about Mitch.'

'What about him?'

'Why he died.'

Joanna Bruce looked at her fellow travellers, saw that Rebus had their attention, and unlocked the bottom half of her door. 'Better come in,' she said.

The caravan was cramped and unheated. There was no TV, but untidy stacks of magazines and newspapers, some of them with articles clipped out, and on the small folding table – benches either side, the whole thing convertible into a bed – a laptop computer. Standing, Rebus's head touched the caravan roof. Joanna shut down the computer, then gestured for Rebus and Jack to take the bench seats, while she balanced atop a pile of magazines.

'So,' she said, folding her arms, 'what's the story?'

'My question exactly,' Rebus replied. He nodded towards the wall behind her, where some photos had been pinned for decoration. 'Snap.' She looked round at the pictures. 'I've just had another lot of those developed,' Rebus explained: they were the originals missing from Mitch's envelope. She sat there with a face like stone, giving nothing away. There was kohl around her eyes and her hair was white fire in the glow from the gas lighting. For a full half-minute, the soft roar of igniting gas was the only sound in the caravan. Rebus was giving her time to change her mind, but she was using that time to erect further barricades, her eyes closing to slits, mouth pressed shut.

'Joanna Bruce,' Rebus mused. 'Interesting choice of name.' She half-opened her mouth, closed it again.

'Is Joanna your real first name, or did you change that too?'

'What do you mean?'

Rebus looked at Jack, who was sitting back, trying to look the part of the relaxed visitor, telling her it wasn't two against one, that she'd no need to be afraid. When Rebus spoke, he spoke to Jack's face.

'Your real surname's Weir.'

'How ... who told you that?' Trying to laugh it off.

'Nobody needed to. Major Weir had a daughter; they fell out; he disowned her.' And changed her sex to a son, maybe to muddy the water. Mairie's source had said as much.

'He didn't disown her! *She* disowned *him!*'

Rebus turned to her. Her face and body were animated now, clay come to life. Her fists gouged at her knees.

'Two things put me on track,' he said quietly. 'One, that surname: Bruce, as in Robert the . . . as any student of Scottish history would know. Major Weir is daft on Scots history, he even named his oilfield after Bannockburn, which as we know was won by Robert the Bruce. Bruce and Bannock. I'm guessing you picked the name because you thought it would rile him?'

'It riles him all right.' Half a smile.

'The second thing was Mitch himself, once I knew you two were friends. Jake Harley tells me Mitch had gleaned some gen on *Negrita*, top-secret stuff. Well, Mitch might have been resourceful in some areas, but I couldn't see how he'd manage to work his way back through a paper trail. He travelled light, no sign of any notes or anything like that, either in his flat or in his cabin. I'm assuming he got the gen from you?' She nodded. 'And you'd have to seriously have it in for T-Bird Oil to bother with that sort of labyrinth in the first place. But we already know you've got something against T-Bird – the demo outside their HQ; chaining yourself to Bannock in full view of the TV cameras. I thought maybe it was something personal . . .'

'It is.'

'Major Weir's your father?'

Her face turned sour and strangely childlike. 'Only in the biological sense. Even then, if you could get a gene transplant I'd be at the front of the queue.' Her voice sounded more American than ever. 'Did he kill Mitch?'

'Do *you* think he did?'

'I'd like to think so.' She stared at Rebus. 'I mean, I'd like to think he'd sink that low.'

'But?'

'But nothing. Maybe he did, maybe he didn't.'

'You reckon he had the motive?'

'Sure.' Not aware she was doing it, she picked at a nail and then bit it, before starting on another. 'I mean, *Negrita* and the way T-Bird's culpability was hushed up . . . and now the dumping. He had plenty of economic reasons.'

'Was Mitch threatening to go to the media with the story?'

She removed a sliver of nail from her tongue. 'No, I think he was trying blackmail first. Keep quiet about everything, so long as T-Bird went for ecological scrapping of Bannock.'

'Everything?'

'What?'

'You said "everything", like there was more.'

She shook her head. 'No.' But she wasn't looking at him.

'Joanna, let me ask you something: why didn't *you* go to the media, or try blackmail on your father? Why did it have to be Mitch?'

She shrugged. 'He had the *chutzpah*.'

'Did he?'

Another shrug. 'What else?'

'See, the way it looks to me . . . you don't mind tormenting your father – as publicly as possible. You're at the front of every demo, you make sure your picture's on TV . . . but if you actually came forward and let the world know who you *are*, that would be even more effective. Why the secrecy?'

Her face turned childlike again, her mouth busy with fingers, knees together. The single braid fell between her eyes, like she wanted to hide from the world but be caught at the same time – a child's game.

'Why the secrecy?' Rebus repeated. 'Seems to me it's precisely because this is so personal between you and your father, like some sort of private game. You like the idea of torturing him, letting him wonder when you'll go public with any of this.' He paused. 'Seems to me maybe you were using Mitch.'

'No!'

'Using him to get at your father.'

'No!'

'Which means he had something you found useful. What could that be?' She got up. 'Get out!'

'Something that drew the two of you together.'

She clamped her hands over her ears, shaking her head.

'Something from your past . . . your childhoods. Something like blood between you. How far back does it go, Jo? Between you and your father – how far into the past does it stretch?'

She swung around and slapped his face. Hard. Rebus rode it, but it still stung.

'So much for non-violent protest,' he said, rubbing the spot.

She slumped down on the magazines again, ran a hand over her head. It came to rest on one of her braids, which she twirled nervously. 'You're right,' she said, so quietly Rebus almost didn't hear.

'Mitch?'

'Mitch,' she said, remembering him at last. Allowing herself that pain. Behind her, lighting flickered over the photographs. 'He was so uptight when we met. Nobody could believe it when we started seeing one another – chalk and cheese they said. They were wrong. It took a while, but one night he opened up to me.' She looked up. 'You know his background?'

'Orphaned,' Rebus said.

She nodded. 'Then institutionalised.' She paused. 'Then abused. He said there were times he'd thought of coming forward, telling people, but after all this time . . . he wondered what good it would do.' She shook her head, tears forming. 'He was the most unselfish person I've ever met. But inside, it was like he was eaten away, and Jesus, I know *that* feeling.'

Rebus got it. 'Your father?'

She sniffed. 'They call him "an institution" in the oil world. Me, I was institutionalised . . .' A deep breath, nothing theatrical about it: a necessity. 'And then abused.'

'Christ,' Jack said quietly. Rebus's heart was racing; he had to fight to keep his voice level.

'For how long, Jo?'

She looked up angrily. 'You think I'd let the prick get away with it *twice*? I ran as soon as I could. Kept running for years, then thought: fuck it, *I'm* not to blame. I'm not the one who should be doing this.'

Rebus nodded understanding. 'So you saw a bond between Mitch and you?'

'That's right.'

'And you told him your own story?'

'Quid pro quo.'

'Including your father's identity?' She started to nod, but stopped, swallowed instead. 'That's what he was blackmailing your father with – the incest story?'

'I don't know. Mitch was dead before I could find out.'

'But that was his intention?'

She shrugged. 'I guess.'

'Jo, I think we'll need a statement from you. Not now, later. All right?'

'I'll think about it.' She paused. 'We can't prove anything, can we?'

'Not yet.' Maybe not ever, he was thinking. He slid out of the seat, Jack following.

Outside, there were more songs around the camp-fire. Candles danced inside Chinese lanterns strung from the trees. Faces had turned shiny orange, like pumpkins. Joanna Bruce watched from her doorway, leaning against the bottom half of the door as before. Rebus turned to say goodbye.

'Will you be camped here a while?'

She shrugged. 'The way we live, who knows?'

'You like what you're doing?'

She gave the question serious thought. 'It's a life.'

Rebus smiled, moved away.

'Inspector!' she called. He turned back to her. Kohl was dribbling down her cheeks. 'If everything's so wonderful, how come everything's so fucked up?'

Rebus didn't have an answer to that. 'Don't let the sun catch you crying,' he told her instead.

On the drive back, he tried answering her question for himself, found he couldn't. Maybe it all had to do with balance, cause and effect. Where there was light, there must needs be dark. It sounded like the start of a sermon, and he hated sermons. He tried out his own personal mantra instead: Miles Davis, 'So What?' Only it didn't sound so clever now.

It didn't sound clever at all.

Jack was frowning. 'Why didn't she come forward with any of this?' he asked.

'Because as far as she's concerned, it's got nothing to do with us. It didn't even have anything to do with Mitch, he just blundered in.'

'Sounded more like he was invited.'

'An invitation he should have refused.'

'You think Major Weir did it?'

'I'm not sure. I'm not even sure it matters. He's not going anywhere.'

'How do you mean?'

'He's in this little private hell she's constructed for the two of them. As long as he knows she's out there, demonstrating against everything he holds dear ... that's his punishment and her revenge. No getting away from it for either of them.'

'Fathers and daughters, eh?'

'Fathers and daughters,' Rebus agreed. And past misdemeanours. And the way they refused to go away ...

They were beat when they got back to the hotel.

'Round of golf?' Jack suggested.

Rebus laughed. 'I could just about manage coffee and a round of sarnies.'

'Sounds good to me. My room in ten minutes.'

Their rooms had been made up, fresh chocolates on the pillows, clean bathrobes laid out. Rebus changed quickly, then phoned reception to ask if there were any messages. He hadn't checked before – hadn't wanted Jack to know he was expecting one.

'Yes, sir,' the receptionist trilled. 'I've a phone message for you here.' Rebus's heart rose: she hadn't just upped and run. 'Shall I read it to you?'

'Please.'

'It says, "Burke's, half an hour after closing. Tried another time, another place, but he wasn't having any." There's no name.'

'That's fine, thanks.'

'You're welcome, sir.'

Of course he was welcome: business account. The whole world sucked up to you if you were corporate. He got the outside line, tried Siobhan at home, got her machine again. Tried St Leonard's, was told she wasn't there. Tried her at home again, deciding this time to leave his telephone number on her machine. Halfway through, she picked up.

'What's the use of an answering machine when you're home?' he asked.

'Call filtering,' she said. 'I get to check if you're a heavy breather or not before I talk to you.'

'My breathing's under control, so talk to me.'

'First victim,' she said. 'I spoke to someone at Robert Gordon's. Deceased was studying geology, and it included time spent offshore. People who study geology up there almost always get a job in the oil industry, the whole course is geared towards it. Because she spent time offshore, deceased did a survival module.'

Rebus was thinking: chopper simulator, ducked in a swimming pool.

'So,' Siobhan went on, 'she spent time at OSC.'

'The Offshore Survival Centre.'

'Which deals with nothing but oil people. I got them to fax me staff and student rolls. So much for the first victim.' She paused. 'Victim two seemed completely different: older, different set of friends, different city. But she was a prostitute, and we know that a lot of businessmen use that sort of service when they're away from home.'

'I wouldn't know.'

'Victim four worked closely with the oil industry, which left Judith Cairns, the Glasgow victim. Variously employed, including part-time cleaning at a city-centre hotel.'

'Businessmen again.'

'So tomorrow they begin faxing me names. They weren't keen, client confidentiality and all that.'

'But you can be persuasive.'

'Yes.'

'So what are we hoping for? A guest at the Fairmount who's got a connection with Robert Gordon's?'

'It'll be in my prayers.'

'How soon tomorrow will you know?'

'That's down to the hotel. I may have to drive over there and gee them up.'

'I'll phone you.'

'If you get the machine, leave a number where I can reach you.'

'Will do. Cheers, Siobhan.' He put the telephone down, went along to Jack's room. Jack was wearing his robe.

'I might have to splash out on one of these,' he said. 'Sarnies are on their way up, ditto a big pot of coffee. I'm just going to take a shower.'

'Fine. Listen, Siobhan might be on to something.' He filled Jack in.

'Sounds promising. Then again . . .' Jack shrugged.

'Christ, and I thought I was cynical.'

Jack winked, went into the bathroom. Rebus waited till he could hear the shower running, and Jack humming what sounded like 'Puppy Love'. Jack's clothes were on a chair. Rebus fished in the jacket pockets, came up with car keys, pocketed them for himself.

He wondered what time Burke's closed on a Thursday night. He wondered what he was going to say to Judd Fuller. He wondered how badly Fuller would take it, whatever it was.

The shower stopped. 'Puppy Love' segued into 'What Made Milwaukee Famous'. Rebus liked a man with catholic tastes. Jack emerged, wrapped in his robe and doing prizefighter impressions.

'Back to Edinburgh tomorrow?'

'First thing,' Rebus agreed.

'To face the music.'

Rebus didn't say he might well be facing the music long before that. But when the sandwiches arrived, he found he'd lost his appetite. Thirsty though: four cups of coffee. He needed to stay awake. Long night coming, no moon in the sky.

Darkness on the short drive in, thin rain falling. Rebus felt jolted by coffee, loose wires sparking where his nerves should be. One-fifteen in the morning: he'd rung Burke's, the bar-side payphone, asked a punter what time the place shut.

'Party's nearly finished, ya radge!' Phone slammed home. Background music: 'Albatross', so it was moon-dance time. Two or three slows, your last chance to grab a breakfast partner. Desperate times on the dance floor; as desperate in your forties as in your teens.

Albatross.

Rebus tried the radio – vacuous pop, pounding disco, telephone chat. Then jazz. Jazz was OK. Jazz was fine, even on Radio Two. He parked near Burke's, watched a dumb-show as two bouncers took on three farm-boys whose girlfriends were trying to pull them away.

'Listen to the ladies,' Rebus muttered. 'You've proved yourselves for tonight.'

The fight dissolved into pointed fingers and swearing, the bouncers, arms not touching their sides, waddling back inside. A final kick at the doors, saliva hitting the porthole-styled windows, then hauled away and up the road. Opening curtain on another north-east weekend. Rebus got out and locked the car, breathed the city air. Shouts and sirens up on Union Street. He crossed the road and headed for Burke's.

The doors were locked. He kicked at them, but nobody answered: probably thinking the farm-boys were back. Rebus kept kicking. Someone

poked a head round the interior doors, saw he didn't look like a punter, shouted something back into the club. Now a bouncer came out, jangling a chain of keys. He looked like he wanted to go to bed, day's work done. The door rattled, and he opened it an inch.

'What?' he growled.

'I've an appointment with Mr Fuller.'

The bouncer stared at him, pulled the door wide. The lights were on in the main bar, staff emptying ashtrays and wiping down tables, collecting an enormous number of glasses. With the lights up, the interior looked as bleak as any moorland vista. Two men who looked like DJs – ponytails, black sleeveless T-shirts – sat smoking at the bar, sinking bottles of beer. Rebus turned to the bouncer.

'Mr Stemmons around?'

'I thought your appointment was with Mr Fuller.'

Rebus nodded. 'Just wondered if Mr Stemmons was available.' Talk to him first – the sane member of the cast; businessman, therefore a listener.

'He might be upstairs.' They went back into the foyer, climbed to where Stemmons and Fuller had their offices. The bouncer opened a door. 'In you go.'

In Rebus went, ducking too late. The hand hit his neck like a side of beef, flooring him. Fingers sought his throat, probing for the carotid artery, applying pressure. No brain damage, Rebus thought, as the edges of his vision darkened. Please, God, let there be no damage . . .

31

He woke up drowning.

Sucking foam and water in through his nose, his mouth. Fizzing taste – not water, beer. He shook his head wildly, opened his eyes. Lager trickled down his throat. He tried coughing it out. Someone was standing behind him, holding the now-empty bottle, chuckling. Rebus tried turning and found his arms were on fire. Literally. He could smell whisky, see a shattered bottle on the floor. His arms had been doused in the stuff and set alight. He cried out, wriggled. A bar towel flapped at the flames and they died. The smouldering towel fell with a slap on to the floor. Laughter echoing around the walls.

The place reeked of alcohol. It was a cellar. Bare lightbulbs and aluminium kegs, boxes of bottles and glasses. Half a dozen brick pillars supporting the ceiling. They hadn't tied Rebus to one of these. Instead, he hung suspended from a hook, the rope fraying his wrists, arms readying to pop from sockets. Rebus shifted more weight on to his feet. The figure from behind tossed the beer-bottle into a crate and came round to stand in front of him. Slick black hair with a kiss-curl at the front, and a large hooked nose in the centre of a face lush with corruption. A diamond glinted in one of the teeth. Dark suit, white T-shirt. Rebus took a wild guess – Judd Fuller – but reckoned the time for introductions was past.

'Sorry I don't have Tony El's ingenuity with power tools,' Fuller said. 'But I do what I can.'

'From where I'm standing, you're doing fine.'

'Thanks.'

Rebus looked around. They were alone in the cellar, and nobody'd thought to tie his legs together. He could kick Fuller in the balls and . . .

The punch came low, hitting him just above the groin. It would have doubled him up, if his arms had been free. As it was, he instinctively raised his knees, lifting his feet off the floor. His shoulder-joints told him this was not the brightest move.

Fuller was walking away, flexing the fingers of his right hand. 'So, cop,' he said, his back to Rebus, 'how do you like it so far?'

'I'm ready for a break if you are.'

'Only break you're going to get is your goddamn neck.' Fuller turned to him, grinned, then picked up another beer-bottle, smacked it open against a wall and gulped half the contents.

The smell of the alcohol was overpowering, and the few mouthfuls Rebus

had swallowed seemed already to be having an effect. His eyes stung; so did his hands where the flames had licked them. His wrists were already blistering.

'We have a nice club here,' Fuller was saying. 'Everybody has fun. You can ask around, it's a popular spot. What gives you the right to spoil the party?'

'I don't know.'

'You made Erik upset the night you talked to him.'

'Does he know about this?'

'He'll *never* get to know about this. Erik's happier not knowing. He has an ulcer, you know. He *worries*.'

'Can't think why that is.' Rebus stared at Fuller. If you caught his face in the right kind of shadow, he resembled a young Leonard Cohen, the Travolta comparison *way* off.

'You're a nuisance, that's all you are, an itch that needs to be scratched.'

'You don't get it, Judd. You're not in America. You can't just hide a body here and hope nobody stumbles across it.'

'Why not?' Fuller opened his arms wide. 'Boats head out of Aberdeen all the time. Weight you down and tip you into the North Sea. Know how hungry the fish are out there?'

'I know it's *over*fished – do you want some trawler netting me?'

'Option two,' Fuller said, raising two fingers, 'the mountains. Let the fucking sheep find you, nibble you clean to the bone. Plenty of options, don't think we haven't used them before.' He paused. 'Why did you come here tonight? What did you *ever* hope you were going to do?'

'I don't know.'

'When Eve phoned . . . she couldn't hide it, it was in her voice – I knew she was shitting me, setting me up. But I have to admit, I was expecting something a little more challenging.'

'Sorry to disappoint you.'

'I'm glad it's you, though, I've been wanting to see you again.'

'Well, here I am.'

'What did Eve tell you?'

'Eve? She didn't tell me anything.'

A roundhouse kick took time: Rebus did what he could, turned sideways on to it, caught it in the ribs. Fuller followed up with a punch to the face, his hand moving so slowly Rebus could see the scar on its back – a long ugly welt. A tooth split in half, one of his root-canal jobs. Rebus spat the tooth and some blood at Fuller, who backed off a little, impressed at the damage.

Rebus knew he was dealing with someone who at best could be termed unpredictable, at worst psychotic. Without Stemmons to keep him in check, Judd Fuller looked capable of anything.

'All I did,' Rebus lisped, 'was do a deal with her. She set up the meeting with you, and I let her go.'

'She must have told you *something*.'

'She's a hard nut to crack. I got even less from Stanley.' Rebus tried to sound defeated: not difficult. He wanted Fuller to go for the whole story.

'Stanley and her have gone off together?' Fuller chuckled again. 'Uncle Joe's going to shit monkeys.'

'Putting it mildly.'

'So tell me, cop, how much do you know? Make it good, maybe we can work something out.'

'I'm open to offers.'

Fuller shook his head. 'I don't think so. Ludo already sniffed you out about that.'

'He didn't exactly have the cards you've got.'

'Well, that's true.' Fuller took a swipe at Rebus's face with the jagged neck of his bottle. Instead of connecting, Rebus felt air brush his cheek. 'Next time,' Fuller said, 'I might get careless. You could lose your looks.'

As if the condemned man cared for beauty. But Rebus was shaking.

'Do I look like martyr material? All I was doing was my job. It's what they pay me for, I'm not married to it!'

'But you're persistent.'

'Blame fucking Lumsden, he got right up my back!' A memory came to him unbeckoned: closing time at the Ox, nights when they'd stumbled out into the cold, joking about getting locked in the cellar and drinking the place dry. Now all Rebus wanted was out.

'How much do you know?' The jagged glass was an inch from his nose. Fuller stretched his arm until the bottle was beneath Rebus's nostrils. Lager fumes, the cold touch of glass, pressing upwards. 'Remember the old joke?' Fuller asked. 'Ask yourself how you'd smell without a nose.'

Rebus sniffed. 'I know the lot,' he spat.

'And how much is that?'

'The dope comes up from Glasgow, straight to here. You sell it, and ship it out to the rigs. Eve and Stanley collected the cash, Tony El was Uncle Joe's man on the spot.'

'Proof?'

'Almost non-existent, especially with Tony El dead and Eve and Stanley on the run. But—' Rebus swallowed.

'But what?'

Rebus kept his mouth shut. Fuller flicked the bottle up and pulled it away. Rebus's nose dribbled fresh blood.

'Maybe I'll just bleed you dry! "But what?"'

'But it doesn't matter,' Rebus said, trying to wipe his nose on his shirt. His eyes were watering. He blinked, tears streaking both cheeks.

'Why not?' Fuller interested.

'Because people are blabbing.'

'Who?'

'You know I can't—'

The bottle flew to his right eye. Rebus screwed his eyes shut. 'All right, all right!' The bottle stayed where it was, so close he had to focus past it. He took a deep breath. Time to stir the shit. His big plan. 'How many cops on your payroll?'

Fuller frowned. 'Lumsden?'

'He's been talking . . . and someone's been talking to him.'

Rebus could almost hear the cogs creaking inside Fuller's head, but even he had to work it out eventually.

'Mr H?' Fuller's eyes widened. 'Mr H. talked to Lumsden, I heard about that. But it was supposed to be about the woman who got herself killed . . .' Fuller busied himself thinking.

Mr H. – the man who'd paid Tony El. And now Rebus knew who Mr H. was – Hayden Fletcher, interviewed by Lumsden about Vanessa Holden. Fletcher had paid Tony El to take care of Allan Mitchison – the two men had probably met right here. Maybe Fuller himself had introduced them.

'It's not just you. They've been grassing up Eddie Segal, Moose Maloney . . .' Rebus pulling out the names Stanley had mentioned.

'Fletcher and Lumsden?' Fuller said to himself. He shook his head, but Rebus could see he was halfway convinced. He stared at Rebus, who tried to look as beaten as a man could be – no great acting required.

'There's a Scottish Crime Squad operation coming,' Rebus said. 'Lumsden and Fletcher are in their pockets.'

'They're dead men,' Fuller said at last.

'Why stop when you're having fun?'

A cold, wicked smile. Fletcher and Lumsden were for the future: but Rebus was right here.

'We'll go for a little ride,' Fuller said. 'Don't worry, you did all right. I'll make it quick. One bullet to the back of the head. You won't go out screaming.' He let the bottle drop to the floor and crunched glass on his way to the stairs. Rebus looked around fast, no way of knowing how long he had. The hook looked pretty solid – it had held his weight so far, no problem. If he could stand on a box, get some height, then he could unhook the ropes. There was the empties' crate, not three feet away. Rebus stretched, his arms in agony, felt with his shoe, just touched the rim of the crate and started to drag it. Fuller had climbed up through a trapdoor, but left it open. Rebus could hear a voice echoing in the bar. Maybe Fuller wanted a bouncer, someone to witness the policeman's demise. The crate caught in a dip in the floor, wouldn't budge. Rebus tried to lift it with the toe of his shoe, couldn't. He was soaked: blood, booze and sweat. The box gave, and he hauled it beneath him, climbed on to it and pushed with his knees. He freed the rope from the hook and brought his arms down slowly, trying to enjoy the pain, feeling blood tingle its way back along them. His fingers stayed numb and cold. He chewed at the knots in the rope, couldn't budge them. There was plenty of broken glass around, but sawing through would take too long. He bent down, picked up a broken bottle, then saw something even better.

A cheap pink plastic lighter. Fuller had probably used it to ignite the whisky on Rebus's arms, dropped it afterwards. Rebus picked it up, looked around. There was a lot of booze down here. No way out except the ladder. He found a rag, opened a bottle of whisky and stuffed it into the neck. Not quite a petrol bomb, but a weapon at any rate. One option: ignite it and toss it into the club, get the fire alarm going and wait for the cavalry. Supposing they came. Supposing that would stop Judd Fuller . . .

Option two: think again.

He looked around. CO_2 cylinders; plastic crates; runs of rubber tubing. Hanging on the wall: a small fire extinguisher. He grabbed the fire extinguisher, primed it, got it under one arm so he could carry the whisky bottle up the steps.

The club looked dead, dimly lit. Someone had left a glitterball turning, throwing glass jewels across walls and ceiling. He was halfway across the dance floor when the door flew open, Fuller standing there, lit from behind

by the foyer. He had a set of car keys between his teeth, dropped them as his mouth opened. He was reaching into his jacket pocket when Rebus got the rag lit, tossed the bottle two-handed. It turned in the air, shattered in front of Fuller. A pool of blue flame spread across the floor. Rebus was still coming, fire extinguisher ready. The gun was in Fuller's hand as the spray caught him full in the face. Rebus followed it up with a head-butt to the bridge of Fuller's nose and a knee hard into the groin. Not exactly textbook stuff, but powerfully effective. The American sank to his knees. Rebus kicked him in the face and ran, pulled open the door to the outside world and almost fell into Jack Morton.

'Christ Almighty, man, what have they done to you?'

'He's got a gun, Jack, let's get the fuck out of here.'

They sprinted for the car. Jack got the keys from Rebus's pocket. Into the car and accelerating away, Rebus feeling a bewildering mix of emotions, chief among them elation.

'You smell like a brewery,' Jack said.

'Jesus, Jack, how did you get here?'

'Took a taxi.'

'No, I mean . . .'

'You can thank Shetland.' Jack sniffed. 'That wind up there, I've got a cold coming. Went to get the hankie out of my trouser pocket . . . no car keys. No car in the car park, and no John Rebus tucked up in bed.'

'And?'

'And reception repeated the message they gave you, so I phoned for a taxi. What the hell happened?'

'I took a beating.'

'I'd say that was an understatement. Who's got the gun?'

'Judd Fuller, the American.'

'We'll stop at the nearest phone, get an armed response unit over there.'

'No.'

Jack turned. 'No?' Rebus was shaking his head. 'Why not?'

'I was taking a calculated risk, Jack.'

'Time to buy a new calculator.'

'I think it worked. Now all we need to do is give it a bit of time.'

Jack thought about it. 'You want them turning on each other?' He nodded. 'Never were one to play by the book, were you? The note was from Eve?' Rebus nodded. 'And you thought you'd leave me out. Know something? When I saw the keys were gone, I was so angry, I almost said "Stuff it, let him do what he wants, it's his neck".'

'It almost was.'

'You're a stupid bastard.'

'Years of dedicated practice, Jack. Can you stop and untie me?'

'I like you better tied up. Casualty or a doctor call-out?'

'I'll be fine.' The nosebleed had already stopped; there was no pain from the dead tooth.

'So what *did* you do there?'

'I fed Fuller a line, and I found out Hayden Fletcher hired Allan Mitchison's killer.'

'And you're telling me there wasn't an easier way?' Jack shook his head slowly. 'If I live to be a hundred, I swear I'll never understand you.'

'I'll take that as a compliment,' Rebus said, leaning his head back against the seat.

Back at the hotel, they decided it was time to leave Aberdeen. Rebus had a bath first, and Jack checked his injuries.

'Strictly an amateur sadist, our Mr Fuller.'

'He did apologise at the start.' Rebus checked his gap-toothed smile in the mirror.

Every bit of his body ached, but he'd live, and he didn't need a doctor to agree with him. They loaded the car, signed out without fuss, and got back on the road.

'What an end to our holidays,' Jack commented. But his audience of one was already asleep.

When he had narrowed the list to four individuals, four companies, it was time to use the 'key' – Vanessa Holden herself.

More of the suspects had turned out to be too old, or not right in some other way: one, first name Alex, had turned out to be a woman.

Bible John made the call from his own office, door closed. He had his notepad in front of him. Four companies, four individuals.

Eskflo	James Mackinley
LancerTech	Martin Davidson
Gribbin's	Steven Jackobs
Yetland	Oliver Howison

The call was to Vanessa Holden's company. A receptionist answered.

'Hello,' he told her, 'Queen Street CID here, Detective Sergeant Collier. General question: I was wondering if you'd ever undertaken any work for Eskflo Fabrication?'

'Eskflo?' The receptionist sounded dubious. 'Let me put you through to Mr Westerman.'

Bible John wrote the name on his notepad, circled it. When Westerman answered, he repeated his question.

'Is this to do with Vanessa?' the man asked.

'No, sir, though I was sorry to hear about Ms Holden. You have my deepest sympathies – same goes for everyone here.' He looked around the walls of his office. 'And I'm sorry to have to call at such a distressing time.'

'Thank you, Detective Sergeant. It's been a great shock.'

'Of course, and rest assured, we're following up several lines of inquiry concerning Ms Holden. But my present request concerns a suspected fraud.'

'Fraud?'

'Nothing to do with yourselves, Mr Westerman, but we're investigating several companies.'

'Including Eskflo?'

'Indeed.' Bible John paused. 'You'll appreciate that I'm telling you this in the strictest confidence?'

'Oh, of course.'

'Now, the companies I'm concerned with are . . .' He made show of shuffling some papers, eyes on the notepad. 'Here we are: Eskflo, LancerTech, Gribbin's, and Yetland.'

'Yetland,' said Westerman, 'we did some work for them recently. No, wait . . . We pitched for a contract, didn't get it.'

'And the others?'

'Look, can I get back to you? I'm going to have to go to the files. I seem to be having trouble concentrating.'

'I understand, sir. I'm due out on a call . . . how about if I phone again in an hour?'

'Perhaps if I call you when I'm ready?'

'I'll phone again in an hour, Mr Westerman. I do appreciate this.'

He put the phone down, bit a fingernail. Would Westerman try phoning Queen Street CID, asking for a DS Collier? He'd give him forty minutes.

But in the end, he gave him thirty-five.

'Mr Westerman? That call didn't take as long as I thought. I wonder if you've come up with anything for me?'

'Yes, I think I've got what you need.'

Bible John concentrated on the tone of voice, listening for any doubt or suspicion, any inkling Westerman might have that he was not talking to a policeman. He found none.

'As I said,' Westerman continued, 'we pitched for a Yetland contract but didn't get it. That was in March this year. Lancer . . . we did a panel display for them in February. They had a stand at the Safety at Sea conference.'

Bible John consulted his list. 'Do you happen to know who your contact was?'

'I'm sorry, Vanessa handled it. She was very good with clients.'

'The name Martin Davidson doesn't ring any bells?'

'I'm afraid not.'

'Not to worry, sir. And the other two companies . . . ?'

'Well, we've worked for Eskflo in the past, but not for a couple of years. And Gribbin's . . . well, to be honest, I've never heard of them.'

Bible John ringed Martin Davidson's name. Put a question mark beside James Mackinley: a lag-time of a couple of years? Doubtful, but possible. Decided that Yetland was a distant third, but just to be sure . . .

'Would Yetland have dealt with yourself or Ms Holden?'

'Vanessa was on holiday around then. It was just after Safety at Sea, she was exhausted.'

Bible John scored both Yetland and Gribbin's off his list.

'Mr Westerman, you've been a big help. I appreciate it.'

'Glad to help. Just one thing, Detective Sergeant?'

'Yes, sir?'

'If you ever find the bastard who killed Vanessa, give him one from me.'

Two M. Davidsons in the phone book, one James Mackinley and two J. Mackinleys. Addresses noted.

Then another phone call, this time to Lancer Technical Support.

'Hello, it's the Chamber of Commerce here, just a general question. We're compiling a database on local companies connected to the oil business. That would include LancerTech, wouldn't it?'

'Oh yes,' the receptionist said. 'Definitely.' She sounded a bit frazzled. Background noise: staff talking, a photocopier, another phone ringing.

'Can you give me a thumbnail sketch?'

'Well . . . we, erm, we design safety aspects into oil platforms, support vessels . . .' She sounded like she was reading from a crib-sheet. 'That sort of thing.' Her voice trailed off.

'I'm just writing that down,' Bible John told her. 'If you work in safety design, can I take it you have links to RGIT?'

'Oh yes, close links. We co-operate on half a dozen projects. A couple of our staff are partly based there.'

Bible John underlined the name Martin Davidson. Twice.

'Thank you,' he said. 'Goodbye.'

Two M. Davidsons in the phone book. One might be a woman. He could telephone, but that would be to give the Upstart advance warning . . . What would he do with him? What did he want to do with him? He had begun his task in anger, but was now composed . . . and more than a little curious. He could call the police, an anonymous tip-off, that's what they were waiting for. But he knew now that he wasn't going to do that. At one point, he'd assumed he could simply dispatch the wretch and resume his life as before, but that just wasn't possible. The Upstart had changed everything. His fingers went to his tie, checked the knot. He ripped the sheet from his notepad and tore it into tiny pieces, letting them flutter into the wastebin.

He wondered if he should have stayed in the States. No, there would always have been the craving for home. He remembered one of the early theories about him – that he had been a member of the 'Exclusive Brethren'. And in a sense, he had been and still was. And intended to remain a member.

Good understanding giveth favour, but the way of transgressors is hard.

Hard it was, hard would always be. He wondered if he had 'good understanding' of the Upstart? He doubted it, and wasn't sure he wanted to understand.

The truth was, now he was here, he didn't know what he wanted.

But he knew what he needed.

32

They crash-landed in Arden Street at breakfast time, neither of them feeling much like breakfast. Rebus had taken over the driving at Dundee, so Jack could crawl into the back seat for an hour. It was like driving back after one of his all-nighters, the roads quiet, rabbits and pheasant in the fields. The cleanest time of day, before everyone got busy messing it up again.

There was mail behind the door of the flat, and so many messages on his machine the red indicator was almost solid.

'Don't you dare leave,' Jack said, before shuffling into the guest room, leaving the door open. Rebus made a mug of coffee, then slumped into his chair by the window. The blisters on his wrists looked like nettle-rash. His nostrils were crusted with blood.

'Well,' he said to the waking world, 'that went as well as could be expected.' He closed his eyes for five minutes. The coffee was cold when he opened them again.

His phone was ringing. He got to it before the machine.

'Hello?'

'CID awakes. It's like a Ray Harryhausen film.' Pete Hewitt from Howdenhall. 'Look, I shouldn't be doing this, but strictly off the record . . .'

'What?'

'All those forensic checks we ran on you – nothing. I expect they'll get round to telling you officially, but I thought I'd put your mind at rest.'

'If only you could, Pete.'

'Hard night?'

'Another one for the record books. Thanks, Pete.'

'Bye, Inspector.'

Rebus didn't put down the receiver; called Siobhan instead. Got her answering machine. Told her he was at home. Another home number, this time answered.

'What?' The voice groggy.

'Morning, Gill.'

'John?'

'Alive and kicking. How did it go?'

'I talked with Malcolm Toal, I think he's good as gold – that is, when he's not hitting his head against the cell wall – but . . .'

'But?'

'But I've passed everything on to the Squaddies. They're the experts, after all.' Silence. 'John? Look, I'm sorry if you think I bottled out . . .'

527

'You can't see me smiling. You played it just right, Gill. You'll get your share of the glory, but let them do the dirty work. You've learned.'

'Maybe I had a good teacher.'

He laughed quietly. 'No, I don't think so.'

'John . . . thanks . . . for everything.'

'Want to know a secret?'

'What?'

'I'm on the wagon.'

'Good for you. I'm really impressed. What happened?'

Jack slouched into the room, yawning and scratching his head.

'I had a good teacher,' Rebus said, replacing the receiver.

'I heard the phone,' Jack said. 'Any coffee on the go?'

'In the kettle.'

'Want one?'

'Go on then.' Rebus went into the hall and picked up his mail. One envelope was fatter than the others. London postmark. He tore it open as he walked through to the kitchen. There was another envelope inside, fat, with his name and address printed on it. There was also a single sheet of notepaper. Rebus sat down at the table to read it.

It was from Lawson Geddes's daughter.

My father left the enclosed envelope with instructions that it should be sent on to you. I'm just back from Lanzarote, having had to arrange not only the funeral but the sale of my parents' house and the sorting out and removal of all their things. As you may remember, Dad was a bit of a magpie. Apologies for the slight delay in sending this on, which I trust you will understand. Hoping all is well with you and your family.

She'd signed it Aileen Jarrold (*née* Geddes).

'What is it?' Jack asked as Rebus tore open the second envelope. He read the first couple of lines, then looked up at Jack.

'It's a very long suicide note,' he said. 'From Lawson Geddes.'

Jack sat down and they read it together.

John, I'm sitting here writing this in the full and certain knowledge that I'm about to top myself: we always called it the coward's way out, remember? I'm not so sure about that now, but I get the feeling I'm maybe being more selfish than cowardly exactly, selfish because I know the telly are looking at Spaven again – they've even sent a team to the island. This isn't about Spaven, it's about Etta. I miss her, and I want to be with her, even if all the afterlife consists of is my bones lying next to hers somewhere.

As Rebus read, the years melted away again. He could hear Lawson's voice, and see him swaggering into the station, or marching into a pub like he was the landlord, a word for everybody whether he knew them or not . . . Jack got up for a minute and returned with two mugs of coffee. They read on.

With Spaven dead and me out of the way, there'll only be you left for the telly people to hassle. I don't like to think of that – I know you'd nothing to do with any of it. So here's this letter, after all these years, and maybe it'll explain things. Show it to whoever you need to. They say dying men tell no lies, and maybe they'll accept that the following is the truth as I know it.

I knew Lenny Spaven back in the Scots Guards. He was always getting into trouble, finding himself consigned to jankers or even on occasion the glasshouse. He was a skiver, too, and that's how he came to be involved with the minister. Spaven used to attend the Sunday church service (I say 'church' – in Borneo it was a tent, back home it was a Nissen hut). But I suppose a lot of places can be churches in the sight of God. Maybe I'll ask him when I see him. It's ninety-odd degrees outside, and I'm drinking firewater – the old usquebaugh. It tastes better than ever.

Rebus caught the sudden tang of whisky at the back of his mouth: memory playing tricks. Lawson used to drink Cutty Sark.

Spaven helped the minister out, laying hymnaries on the chairs, then counting them back in at the end. You know yourself there are some buggers in the Army would steal a hymnary as soon as anything else. There weren't many regular attenders. If things got hairy, a few more souls would turn up, praying it wouldn't be them being nailed into a box at the end of play. Well, like I say, Spaven had it cushy. I didn't have much to do with him, or with any of the church types.

The thing is, John, there was a murder – a prostitute near our camp. A native girl from the kampong. The villagers blamed it on us, and even the Gurkhas knew it was probably a British soldier. There was an investigation – civil and military. Funny really, I mean, there we were going hell for leather killing people – it was what we got paid for – and there they were looking into a single murder. Anyway, they never found anyone for it. Thing is though, that prozzy was strangled, and one of her sandals was never recovered.

Rebus turned a page.

Well, all that was behind me. I was a bobby, back in Scotland and happy with my lot. Then I got roped into the Bible John case. You've got to remember, we didn't know him as 'Bible John' until very late on. It was after the third victim that we got the description of him quoting from the Bible. That's when the papers came up with the name. Well, when I thought about someone quoting from the Bible, a strangler and rapist, I remembered Borneo. I went to my boss and told him all about it. He said it was a long shot of Olympic standards, but that I could chase it up in my own time if I liked. You know me, John, never one to resist a challenge. Besides, I had a shortcut planned – Lenny Spaven. I knew he was back in Scotland, and he'd have info on all the church-goers. So I got in touch with him, but he'd gone from bad to rotten, didn't want anything to do with it. I'm the persistent type, and he complained about me to my boss. That got me a warning to ease off, but I wasn't about to ease off. I knew what I wanted: I reckoned Lenny might have photos from his days in Borneo, maybe with him and the rest of the flock. I wanted to show them to the woman who'd shared the taxi with Bible John. I wanted to see if she recognised anyone. But bloody Spaven kept standing in my way. Eventually, I did manage to get some photos – going the long way round, talking to the Army first, then tracking down the minister from the time. It took weeks.

Rebus looked at Jack. 'The photos Ancram showed us.' Jack nodded.

We showed the photos to the eyewitness. Mind, they were eight or nine years out of date, and not very good to start with, water damaged some of them. She said she couldn't be sure, she thought one of them 'was like him' – her words. But as my

boss said, there were hundreds of men out there in the big wide world who bore a physical resemblance to the killer: we'd interviewed most of them. That wasn't good enough for me. I got the man's name, he was called Ray Sloane – an unusual enough name, and it wasn't hard to track him down. Only he'd cleared out. He'd been living in a bedsit in Ayr, working as a toolmaker. But he'd recently given notice and moved on, nobody knew where. I was convinced in my mind that he could be the man we were looking for, but I couldn't convince my boss to go all-out on finding him.

See, John, that delay while I was dealing with the Army, it was all down to Spaven. If he'd helped, I'd have been on to Sloane before he'd had a chance to pack up and ship out. I know it, I can feel it. I might have had him. Instead of which, I had nothing but my anger and frustration, both of which I vented too publicly. The boss kicked me off the inquiry, and that was that.

'Your coffee's getting cold,' Jack said. Rebus took a gulp, turned another page.

Or at least it was until Spaven came back into my life, moving to Edinburgh much the same time I did. It was like he was haunting me, and I couldn't forgive him for what he'd done. If anything, as time passed I grew to despise him even more. That's why I wanted him for the Elsie Rhind killing. I admit it, to you and to anyone else reading this, I wanted him so badly it was like a hard ball in my stomach, something only surgery would remove. When I was told to ease off on him, I didn't. When I was told to steer clear, I steered closer. I followed him – on my own time – I tracked him every day and every night. I went without sleep for the best part of three days. But it was worth it when I saw him make for that lock-up, somewhere we didn't know about. I was elated, ecstatic. I didn't know what we'd find inside, but I had the feeling we'd find something. That's why I came rushing over to your house, why I dragged you back there with me. You asked me about a search warrant, and I told you not to be so stupid. I put a lot of pressure on you, using our long friendship as blackmail – I was feverish, I'd have done anything, and that surely included breaking rules I now saw as being there to punish the police and protect the villains. So in we went, and found the heaps of boxes, all that knock-off from the factory job in Queensferry. Plus the bag. Elsie Rhind's, as it turned out. I nearly dropped to my knees to thank God for finding it.

I know what a lot of people thought – yourself included. They thought I'd planted it there. Well, I swear on my deathbed (except I'm writing this at the table) that I did not. I found it fair and square, even though I made us break the rules to accomplish it. But you see, that one crucial piece of evidence would have been ruled inadmissible because of the way we'd come to find it, which is why I persuaded you – against your better judgement – to stick to the story I invented. Am I sorry I did it? Yes and no. It can't be very comfortable for you just now, John, and it can't have been a nice thing to have lived with all these years. But we got the murderer, and in my mind – and I've spent God knows how long thinking about it, reliving it, running through the way I played it – that's what really counts.

John, I hope all this fuss dies down. Spaven's not worth it. Nobody's giving much thought to Elsie Rhind, are they? The victim can never win. Chalk this one up to Elsie Rhind. Just because a villain can write doesn't make him less of a villain. I read that the commandants at the concentration camps used to put their feet up at night and read the classics while listening to a bit of Beethoven. Monsters can do that. I know this now. I know because of Lenny Spaven.

Your friend, Lawson.

Jack patted Rebus's back. 'He's just cleared you, John. Wave this in Ancram's face and that's the end of that.'

Rebus nodded, wishing he could feel relief, or any other sensible emotion.

'What's wrong?' Jack asked.

Rebus tapped the paper. 'This is,' he said. 'I mean, most of it is probably right, but it's still a lie.'

'What?'

Rebus looked at him. 'The stuff we found in the lock-up . . . I saw it in Elsie Rhind's house the first time we went round there. Lawson must have lifted it later.'

Jack looked uncomprehending. 'Are you sure?'

Rebus flew to his feet. 'No, I'm not sure, and that's the real bastard of it! I'll never be sure.'

'I mean, it was twenty years ago, your mind plays tricks.'

'I know. Even at the time, I wasn't a hundred per cent sure I'd seen them before – maybe I saw a different bag, different hat. I went round to her place, took another look. This was when we had Spaven in custody. I looked for the hat and the bag I'd seen there . . . and they were gone. Ah, shit, maybe I didn't see them at all, only thought I did. It doesn't change the fact that I *think* I saw them. I *think* Lenny Spaven was set up, and I've always thought it . . . and I've never done a thing about it.' He sat down again. 'Never even told anyone till now.' He tried to pick up his mug but his hand was shaking. 'DTs,' he said, forcing a smile.

Jack was thoughtful. 'Does it matter?' he said at last.

'You mean whether I'm right or not? Jesus, Jack, I don't know.' Rebus rubbed his eyes. 'It was all so long ago. Does it matter if the killer got away? Even if I'd come forward at the time, it would have maybe cleared Spaven but it wouldn't have got us the real killer, would it?' He let out a breath. 'I've been spinning it in my head all these years, the grooves are worn almost to nothing.'

'Time to buy a new record?'

Rebus smiled for real this time. 'Maybe you're right.'

'One thing I don't understand . . . why didn't Spaven himself explain any of this? I mean, he never touches on it in his book. He could have just said why Geddes had it in for him.'

Rebus shrugged. 'Look at Weir and his daughter.'

'You mean it was personal?'

'I don't know, Jack.'

Jack picked up the letter, turning its pages. 'Interesting about the Borneo pics though. Ancram thought they were relevant because they showed Spaven. Now we find it was this guy Sloane that Geddes was after.' Jack checked his watch. 'We should nip over to Fettes, show this to Ancram.'

Rebus nodded. 'Let's do it. But first, I want a photocopy of Lawson's letter. Like you say, Jack, I might not believe it, but it's here in black and white.' He looked up at his friend. 'Which should be good enough for *The Justice Programme.*'

Ancram looked like he should have been fitted with a pressure valve. He

was so angry he'd almost swung all the way round to calm. His voice was the first wisp of smoke from a sleeping volcano.

'What is it?'

Rebus was trying to hand him a sheet of paper, folded in half. They were in Ancram's office. Ancram was seated, Rebus and Jack standing.

'Look and see,' Rebus said.

Ancram stared at him, then unfolded the headed note.

'It's a doctor's line,' Rebus explained. 'Forty-eight-hour stomach bug. Dr Curt was very clear that I should isolate myself. He said it could be catching.'

When he spoke, Ancram's voice was little more than a whisper. 'Since when do pathologists hand out sick notes?'

'You haven't seen the queues at my health centre.'

Ancram crunched the note into a ball.

'It's dated and everything,' Rebus said. Of course it was: Dr Curt had been their last call before heading north with Eve.

'Shut up, sit down, and listen to me while I tell you why you're on an official reprimand. And don't think a reprimand's going to be the end of the affair.'

'Maybe you should read this first, sir,' Jack said, handing over Geddes's letter.

'What is it?'

'Not so much the end of the affair, sir,' Rebus told him, 'more like the heart of the matter. While you're digesting it, maybe I could have a browse through the files.'

'Why?'

'Those Borneo pics, I'd like another look.'

After the first few sentences of Lawson Geddes's confession, Ancram was hooked. Rebus could have walked out unnoticed with the files under his arm. But instead he slipped the photos out of their packet and went through them, checking the back of each for identifying names.

In one photo, third from the left was marked as Pvt. Sloane, R. Rebus stared at the face. Slightly blurred, with some water damage and fading. A fresh-faced young man, not long out of teens, his smile slightly crooked, maybe the fault of his teeth.

Bible John had one tooth which overlapped another, according to the eye-witness.

Rebus shook his head. That really was stretching the evidence, and Lawson Geddes had done enough of that in his time for both of them. Without knowing exactly why, and checking first that Ancram was still immersed in the letter, Rebus slid the photo into his pocket.

'Well,' Ancram said at last, 'this will obviously have to be discussed.'

'Obviously, sir. No interview today then?'

'Just a couple of questions. Number one, what the devil happened to your nose and tooth?'

'I got too close to a fist. Anything else, sir?'

'Yes, what the hell have you been doing with Jack?'

Rebus turned, saw what Ancram meant: Jack fast asleep on a chair by the wall.

'So,' Jack said, 'this is the big challenge.'

They'd come to the Oxford Bar, just for somewhere to be. Rebus ordered two orange juices, then turned to Jack. 'You want some breakfast?' Jack nodded. 'And four packets of crisps, any flavour,' Rebus told the barmaid.

They raised their glasses, said 'Cheers', and drank.

'Fancy a smoke?' Jack asked.

'I'd kill for one,' Rebus said, laughing.

'So,' Jack said, 'what's been achieved?'

'Depends on your point of view,' Rebus said. He'd been asking himself the same question. Maybe the Squaddies would nab all the drug players: Uncle Joe, Fuller, Stemmons. Maybe before that happened, Fuller would have done something with Ludovic Lumsden and Hayden Fletcher. Maybe. Hayden Fletcher was a regular at Burke's. He met Tony El there, maybe even scored nose-talc from him. Maybe Fletcher was the type who liked to hang out with gangsters – some people were like that. Seeing the Major was worried, and learning that Allan Mitchison was the problem . . . it would have been easy to talk it over with Tony El, and for Tony to see the chance of some easy cash . . . Maybe Major Weir himself ordered Mitch's death. Well, his was the one certain punishment, his daughter would make sure of that. And had Tony El ever actually intended to kill Mitch? Rebus couldn't even be sure of that. Maybe he'd have torn the bag from Mitch's head at the last minute. Then maybe he'd have warned him to forget all about T-Bird Oil.

It seemed part of some larger pattern, accidents forming themselves into a dance of association. Fathers and daughters, fathers and sons, infidelities, the illusions we sometimes call memory. Past errors harped on, or made good by spurious confession. Bodies littered down the years, mostly forgotten except by the perpetrators. History turning sour, or fading away like old photographs. Endings . . . no rhyme or reason to them. They just happened. You died, or disappeared, or were forgotten. You became nothing more than a name on the back of an old photo, and sometimes not even that.

Jethro Tull: 'Living in the Past'. Rebus had been a slave to that rhythm for far too long. It was the work that did it. As a detective, he lived in people's pasts: crimes committed before he arrived on the scene; witnesses' memories ransacked. He had become a historian, and the role had bled into his personal life. Ghosts, bad dreams, echoes.

But maybe now he had a chance. Look at Jack: he'd reinvented himself. Good news week.

The phone rang, was answered by the barmaid, who nodded towards Rebus. He took the receiver.

'Hello?'

'I tried your first home, decided to try your second home.'

Siobhan. Rebus straightened up.

'What did you get?'

'A name: Martin Davidson. Stayed at the Fairmount three weeks before the Judith Cairns murder. The room was charged to his employer, a firm called LancerTech, as in technical support. Based in Altens, just outside Aberdeen. They design the safety elements into platform equipment, that sort of thing.'

'You've talked to them?'

'Soon as I got his name. Don't worry, I didn't mention him. I just asked a couple of general questions. Receptionist said I was the second person in two days to ask her the same thing.'

'Who was the other person?'

'Chamber of Commerce, she said.' They were quiet for a moment.

'And Davidson fits with Robert Gordon's?'

'He hosted some seminars earlier this year. His name was down on the staff roll.'

A solid connection. Rebus could feel it like a punch. His knuckles were white on the receiver.

'There's more,' Siobhan said. 'You know how businesses sometimes stay faithful to one hotel chain? Well, the Fairmount has a sister establishment here. Martin Davidson of LancerTech was in town the night Angie Riddell was killed.'

Rebus saw her picture again: Angie. Hoped she was getting ready to rest.

'Siobhan, you're a genius. Have you told anyone else?'

'You're the first. After all, you gave me the tip.'

'I gave you a hunch, that's all. It might not have paid off. This is down to you. Now take it to Gill Templer – she's your boss – tell her what you've just told me, let her pass it on to the Johnny Bible team. Stick to procedure.'

'It's him, isn't it?'

'Pass the news along, and make sure you get the credit. Then we'll wait and see. All right?'

'Yes, sir.'

He put down the receiver, told Jack what she'd just told him. Then they just stood there, drinking their drinks, staring at the mirror behind the bar. Calmly at first, then with more agitation. Rebus was the first to say what they both knew.

'We need to be there, Jack. *I* need to be there.'

Jack looked at him, nodded. 'Your turn to drive or mine?'

33

British Telecom had listings for two Martin Davidsons in Aberdeen. But Friday afternoon, he was most likely still at work.

'Doesn't mean we'll find him at Altens,' Jack said.

'Let's go there anyway.' Practically Rebus's only thought the whole drive: he *needed* to see Martin Davidson, not necessarily speak to him, just clap eyes on him. Eye contact: Rebus wanted *that* memory.

'He could be working at OSC, or anywhere else for that matter,' Jack went on. 'He might not even be in Aberdeen.'

'Let's go there anyway,' Rebus repeated.

Altens Industrial Estate was south of the city, signposted off the A92. They found a map at the entrance to the estate, and used it to wind their way in towards LTS – Lancer Technical Support. There was what looked like a jam at one point, cars blocking the road, nobody going anywhere. Rebus got out to take a look, and almost wished he hadn't. They were police cars, unmarked but with telltale static coming from their radios. Siobhan had passed on the info, and someone had been fast to act.

A man was bearing down on Rebus. 'What the hell are you doing here?'

Rebus shrugged, hands in pockets. 'Informal observer?'

DCI Grogan narrowed his eyes. But his mind was elsewhere; he'd no time or inclination for argument.

'Is he inside?' Rebus asked, nodding towards the LTS building, a typical industrial unit of windowless white corrugation.

Grogan shook his head. 'We came steaming down here, now it seems he hasn't come in today.'

Rebus frowned. 'Day off?'

'Not officially. The switchboard tried his home, no answer.'

'Is that where you're headed?'

Grogan nodded.

Rebus didn't ask if they could tag along; Grogan would only say no. But once the convoy was moving, no one would notice an extra car at the tail.

He got back into the Peugeot and told Jack about it, while Jack reversed and found a parking spot out of the way. They watched the police cars execute three-point turns and head back out of the estate, then eased their way in behind the last of them.

They headed north over the Dee and along Anderson Drive, passing more buildings belonging to Robert Gordon's University, and several oil company HQs. At last they headed off Anderson Drive, past Summerhill

Academy, and into a tight maze of suburban streets with green-field sites beyond.

A couple of the cars left the convoy, probably to circle around and come at Davidson's house from the other direction, blocking him in. Brake lights came on, the cars stopping in the middle of the road. Doors opened, officers appearing. Quick confabs, Grogan issuing orders, pointing to left and right. Most eyes were on a single house, its curtains closed.

'Reckon he's flown?' Jack asked.

'Let's find out.' Rebus undid his seatbelt and opened the door.

Grogan was sending men to the neighbouring houses, some to ask questions, some to nip out the back door and work their way round the back of the suspect's house.

'Hope this isn't a wild goose chase,' Grogan muttered. He saw Rebus, but still barely registered his presence.

'Men in position, sir.'

People had come out of their houses, wondering what was going on. Rebus could hear the distant chimes of an ice-cream van.

'Armed Response Unit standing by, sir.'

'I don't think we'll need them.'

'Right you are, sir.'

Grogan sniffed, ran a finger under his nose, then selected two men to go with him to the suspect's door. He pressed the bell, and there was a collective holding of breath while they waited. Grogan rang again.

'What can they see round the back?'

One of Grogan's men radioed to ask. 'Curtains are closed upstairs and down, no sign of life.'

Just like at the front.

'Buzz a JP, say we need a warrant.'

'Right, sir.'

'And meantime, take a sledgehammer to that bloody door.'

The officer nodded, gave a signal, and a car boot was opened. Inside was like the back of a builder's van. Out came the sledgehammer. Three blows and the door was open. Ten seconds later there were cries for an ambulance. Ten seconds after that, someone suggested a hearse instead.

Jack was a good copper: the boot of *his* car held Scene of Crime equipment, including overshoes and gloves, and the all-over plastic boiler-suits which made you look like a walking condom. Officers were being kept out of the house so as not to contaminate the scene. They stood crammed in the doorway, trying to see what they could. When Rebus and Jack stepped forward, no one recognised them, so took them for forensics. The crowd parted for a moment, and both men were inside.

The rules on contamination didn't seem to extend to senior officers and their flunkeys: Grogan stood in the living room, hands in pockets, examining the scene. The body of a young man lay on the black leather sofa. His fair hair was matted over a deep cut. More blood had dried on his face and neck. There were signs of a struggle: the glass and chrome coffee table overturned, magazines crumpled underfoot. A black leather jacket had been thrown over the man's chest, a gentle act after the bloodshed. Stepping closer, Rebus saw marks on the neck, visible below the blood-

lines. On the floor in front of the body sat a large green holdall, the sort you took to the gym or for a weekend trip. Rebus peered inside, saw a backpack, a single shoe, Angie Riddell's necklace ... and a length of plastic-covered clothes-line.

'I think we can rule out suicide,' Grogan muttered.

'Knocked unconscious, then strangled,' Rebus guessed.

'You reckon it's him?'

'That bag isn't just sitting there for fun. Whoever did this, they knew who he was, and wanted us to know, too.'

'An accomplice?' Grogan asked. 'A mate, someone he blabbed to?'

Rebus shrugged again. He was intent on the corpse's face, felt cheated by it: the closed eyes, the repose. *I've come all this way, thanks to you, you bastard* ... He stepped closer, lifted the jacket a couple of inches and peered beneath. A black slip-on shoe had been stuffed into Martin Davidson's left armpit.

'Oh Christ,' Rebus said, turning to Grogan and Jack. 'Bible John did this.' He saw disbelief mingled with horror in their faces. Rebus lifted the jacket a little higher so they could see the shoe. 'He's been here all the time,' he said. 'He never went away ...'

The Scene of Crime team did their business, photographing and videoing, bagging and taping potential evidence. The pathologist examined the body, then said it could be removed and taken to the mortuary. There were reporters outside, kept at a distance by police cordons. Once the SOC team had finished upstairs, Grogan took Rebus and Jack up for a look. He didn't seem to mind them being there, probably wouldn't have minded if he'd had Jack the Ripper himself for an audience: Grogan was the man who'd be on TV tonight, the man who tracked down Johnny Bible. Only he hadn't, of course – someone had beaten them to it.

'Tell me again,' Grogan said, as they climbed the stairs.

'Bible John took souvenirs – shoes, clothes, handbags. But he also placed a sanitary towel in the left armpit. Downstairs ... that was him letting us know who did this.'

Grogan shook his head. He would take some convincing. Meantime, he had things to show them. The main bedroom was just that, but beneath the bed were boxes of magazines and videos – hard core S&M, similar to the stuff in Tony El's bedroom, text in English and several other languages. Rebus wondered if one of the American gangs had brought it to Aberdeen.

There was a small guest bedroom with a padlock on it. Crowbarred open, it gave the lie to one area of speculation. A couple of the CID men had been wondering if Johnny Bible were tricking them – killing an innocent man and setting him up to look like the killer. The guest bedroom said Martin Davidson was Johnny Bible. It had been turned into a shrine to Bible John and other killers: dozens of scrapbooks, cuttings and photos pinned to the cork boards which lined the walls, videos of documentaries about serial killers, paperback books, heavily annotated, and at the centre of it all a blow-up of one of the Bible John flyers: the face almost smiling, a kindly face, and above it the same basic question: Have You Seen This Man?

Rebus almost answered yes; there was something about the shape of the face, he'd seen it before somewhere ... somewhere recently. He took the

Borneo photo from his pocket, looked at Ray Sloane, then back at the poster. They were very alike, but that wasn't the similarity that was niggling Rebus. There was something else, *someone* else . . .

Then Jack asked him something from the doorway, and Rebus lost it.

They followed everyone back to Queen Street. Rebus and Jack had, by association, become part of the team. There was quiet jubilation, tempered with the knowledge that another murderer was in their midst. But as at least one officer put it, 'If he did for that bastard, good luck to him.'

Which, Rebus guessed, would be the reaction Bible John would be hoping for. He'd be hoping they wouldn't try too hard to find him. *If* he'd come out of retirement, then it had been to one end only – the killing of his impersonator. Johnny Bible had taken the glory, the achievement away from his predecessor; now there'd come the revenge.

Rebus sat in the CID office, staring into space, thinking. When someone handed him a cup, he raised it to his lips. But then Jack's hand stopped him.

'It's whisky,' he warned. Rebus looked down, saw sweet liquid the colour of honey, gazed at it for a moment, then put the cup down on the desk. There was laughter in the office, cheering and singing, like a football crowd after a result: same songs, same chants.

'John,' Jack said, 'remember Lawson.' It sounded like a warning.

'What about him?'

'He became obsessed.'

Rebus shook his head. 'This is different. I *know* it was Bible John.'

'What if it was?'

Rebus shook his head slowly. 'Come on, Jack, after everything I told you? After Spaven and everything else? You know better than to ask that.'

Grogan was waving Rebus over to a telephone. Smiling, with whisky breath, he handed Rebus the receiver.

'Someone wants a word.'

'Hello?'

'What in God's name are *you* doing there?'

'Oh, hello, Gill. Congratulations, looks like everything's coming right for once.'

She melted a little. 'Siobhan's doing, not mine. I only passed the info along.'

'Make sure that goes on record.'

'I will.'

'I'll talk to you later.'

'John . . . when are you coming back?' Not what she'd wanted to ask.

'Tonight, maybe tomorrow.'

'OK.' She paused. 'See you then.'

'Fancy doing something on Sunday?'

She sounded surprised by the question. 'What sort of thing?'

'I don't know. A drive, a walk, somewhere down the coast?'

'Yes, OK.'

'I'll call you. Bye, Gill.'

'Bye.'

Grogan was refilling a cup. There were at least a couple of crates of whisky, and three of bottled beer.

'Where do you get this stuff?' Rebus asked.

Grogan smiled. 'Oh, you know.'

'Pubs? Clubs? Places you're owed a favour?'

Grogan just winked. More officers were arriving all the time – uniforms, civilian staff, even people who looked to be off-duty: all had heard, and all wanted to be part of it. The top brass looked stiff but smiling, declining refills.

'Maybe Ludovic Lumsden gets it for you?'

Grogan's face creased. 'I know you think he shafted you, but Ludo's a good copper.'

'Where is he?'

Grogan looked around. 'No idea.'

In fact, no one knew where Lumsden was; he hadn't been seen all day. Someone had called him at home, but only got an answering machine. His bleeper was turned on, but he wasn't responding. A patrol car, detouring past his house, reported no sign of him, though his car was outside. Rebus got an idea, and went downstairs to the comms room. There were people at work here – taking incoming calls, keeping communications open with patrol cars and beat officers. But they had a bottle of whisky of their own, and plastic cups to go round. Rebus asked if he could see the day's sheets.

He only had to look back an hour. A call from a Mrs Fletcher, reporting her husband missing. He'd gone to work that morning as usual, but hadn't arrived, and hadn't come home since. The sheet listed details of his car and a brief description. Patrols had been requested to keep a lookout. In another twelve hours or so, they'd start to deal with it more seriously.

Christian name of missing spouse: Hayden.

Rebus recalled Judd Fuller talking about dumping bodies at sea, or inland, places they'd never be found because no one ever went there. He wondered if that would be the fate of Lumsden and Fletcher ... No, he couldn't do it. He wrote a message on the back of one of the sheets and handed it to the duty officer, who read it silently before reaching for the mike.

'Any patrol in the vicinity of the city centre, to College Street, Burke's Club. Apprehend Judd Fuller, co-owner, and bring to Queen Street for questioning.' The comms officer turned to Rebus, who nodded. 'And check the cellar,' he continued, 'persons possibly being held there against their will.'

'Please repeat,' one patrol car said. The message was repeated. Rebus went back upstairs.

In spite of the party, some work was still being done. Rebus saw Jack manoeuvring one of the secretaries into a corner, chatting her up twenty to the dozen. Near them, a couple of desk-bound officers were making phone calls. Rebus picked up a spare receiver, called Gill.

'It's me.'

'What's happened?'

'Nothing. Listen, you passed all the stuff about Toal and Aberdeen on to the Scottish Crime Squad?'

'Yes.'

'Who's your contact there?'

'Why?'

'Because whoever it is, I've a message for them. I think Judd Fuller has picked up DS Ludovic Lumsden and a man called Hayden Fletcher, and intends to make sure they're not seen again.'

'What?'

'A patrol car's gone out to the club, God knows what they'll find, but the Squaddies should keep an eye on it. If they're found, they'll be brought back to Queen Street. The Squaddies might want someone on the scene.'

'I'll get on it. Thanks, John.'

'Any time.'

I'm getting soft in my old age, he thought. Or maybe I've just relocated my conscience.

He went walkabout, asked a few drinkers the same question, and eventually had the Oil Liaison Officer, DI Jenkins, pointed out to him. Rebus just wanted to look at him. His name was mentioned in Stanley's confession, along with Lumsden. The Squaddies would be wanting a word with him. He was smiling, looking unconcerned, tanned and rested after his holiday. It gave Rebus a warm glow to realise the man would soon be sweating under an internal inquiry.

Maybe he wasn't getting so soft after all.

He walked over to the working officers, looked down over their shoulders. They were doing the preliminary work on the murder of Martin Davidson, collating information from neighbours and employer, trying to track down a next of kin, and all the time keeping the media at bay.

One of them slammed his phone down and suddenly had a big grin on his face. He reached for his mug of whisky and drained it.

'Something?' Rebus asked.

A balled-up piece of paper hit the officer on the head. Laughing, he threw it back.

'Neighbour came off the night-shift,' he said, 'found a car blocking his drive. Had to park on the street. Says he hadn't seen the car before, and took a good look so he'd know it again. Woke up around lunchtime, and it was gone. Metallic blue BMW, 5 Series. He even got part of the licence plate.'

'Hell's bells.'

The officer was reaching for his phone. 'Shouldn't take too long.'

'It better not,' Rebus replied, 'or DCI Grogan may not be sober enough to take it in.'

34

Grogan caught Rebus in the hallway, slapped an arm around him. He was missing his tie, and the top two buttons of his shirt were open, showing tufts of wiry grey hair. He'd danced a jig with a couple of WPCs and was sweating profusely. The shift had changed; or rather, a new shift had come on, while the old shift stayed put, not wanting to break the spell. There was occasional talk of pubs and restaurants, nightclubs and bowling alleys, but nobody seemed to leave, and there was communal applause when an Indian restaurant nearby delivered boxes and bags full of food – courtesy of the brass, who by then actually *had* left the scene. Rebus had helped himself to pakora, keema nan, and chicken tikka, while one CID officer tried to explain to another why his saying 'Bhajis, we don' need no steenking bhajis' was a joke.

Judging by Grogan's breath, he hadn't taken a meal break. 'My wee Lowland laddie,' he said. 'How are you doing? Enjoying our Highland hospitality?'

'It's a great party.'

'So why the face like a thistle?'

Rebus shrugged. 'It's been a long day.' And a long night before it, he could have added.

Grogan patted his back. 'You're welcome back here any time, any time at all.' Grogan made towards the toilets, paused and turned. 'Any sign of Ludo?'

'He's in the City Hospital, next bed along from a man called Hayden Fletcher.'

'What?'

'There's a Crime Squad officer on the ward, too, waiting for them to wake up and give their statements. *That's* how clean Lumsden is. About time you woke up to the fact.'

Rebus went downstairs to the interview rooms, opened the door of the one *he'd* been interviewed in. There were two more Squaddies inside. And smoking a cigarette at the table, Judd Fuller. Rebus had come down earlier, just for a look, and to explain to the officers what had happened, referring them back to Gill's tapes and notes.

'Evening, Judd,' Rebus said now.

'Do I know you?'

Rebus walked up to him. 'You stupid bastard, you let me get away but you still went on using the cellar.' He shook his head. 'Erik will be disappointed.'

'Screw Erik.'

Rebus nodded. 'Every man for himself now, eh?'

'Let's get it over with.'

'What?'

'Why you're here.' Fuller looked up at him. 'You want a free hit at me, this is the only chance you're ever going to get. So make it good.'

'I don't need to hit you, Judd.' Rebus grinned, showing the stunted tooth.

'Then you're yellow.'

Rebus shook his head slowly. 'I used to be, but not any more.'

He turned his back and walked.

Back in CID, the party was in full swing. A cassette player had been wired up, accordion reels at distorted volume. Only two couples were dancing, and then not very well: there was barely room between the desks for professional ceilidh enthusiasts. Three or four bodies lay slumped at their desks, heads on arms. Someone else lay prone on the floor. Rebus counted nine empty whisky bottles, and someone had been sent out for more cases of beer. Jack was still talking with the secretary, his cheeks red from the heat in the room. The place was beginning to smell like a changing room at full-time.

Rebus walked around the room. The walls were still covered with material pertaining to Johnny Bible's local victims: maps, diagrams, duty rosters, photographs. He studied the photos, as if memorising the smiling faces. He saw that the fax machine had just finished spewing something out. Car ownership details, metallic blue BMWs. Four in Aberdeen, but only one with the same sequence of letters the witness recalled. Registered to a company called Eugene Construction with a Peterhead address.

Eugene Construction? *Eugene Construction?*

Rebus emptied his pockets on to a desktop, finding petrol receipts, notebook, scraps of paper with telephone numbers, Rennies, a book of matches . . . there: business card. Given to him by the man he'd met at the convention. Rebus studied the card. Ryan Slocum, Sales Manager, Engineering Division. The parent company: Eugene Construction, with a Peterhead address. Trembling, Rebus lifted the Borneo photo and looked at it, remembering the man he'd met that day in the bar.

'No wonder Scotland's down the pan. And we want independence.'

He'd handed over his business card, then Rebus had announced that he was a policeman.

'Did I say anything incriminating . . . ? Is it Johnny Bible?'

The face, the eyes, the height . . . close to the man in the photograph. Close. Ray Sloane . . . Ryan Slocum. Someone had broken into Rebus's flat, looking for something, taking nothing. Looking for something that might incriminate them? He looked again at the business card, then reached for a phone, eventually tracked Siobhan down at home.

'Siobhan, the guy you talked to at the National Library . . . ?'

'Yes?'

'He gave you a description of the so-called journalist?'

'Yes.'

'Give it to me again.'

'Hang on.' She went to fetch her notebook. 'What's this about anyway?'

'I'll tell you later. Read it out.'

' "Tall, fair-haired, early fifties, longish face, no distinguishing featur-
es." '

'Anything about the accent?'

'Nothing down here.' She paused. 'Oh, yes, he *did* say something. He said
it was twangy.'

'Like American?'

'But Scottish.'

'It's him.'

'Who?'

'Bible John, just like you said.'

'*What?*'

'Stalking his offspring . . .' Rebus rubbed his forehead, pinched the bridge
of his nose. He had his eyes screwed shut. Was it or wasn't it? *Was* he
obsessed? How different was Johnny Bible's shrine from the scene in his
own kitchen, the table covered in cuttings?

'I don't know,' he said. But he did know. He did. 'Talk to you later,' he
told Siobhan.

'Wait!'

But that was the one thing he couldn't do. He needed to know. He needed
to know right now. He looked round the room, saw dissolution and reverie,
nobody who could drive, no back-up.

Except Jack.

Who had one arm around the secretary now, and was whispering in her
ear. She was smiling, holding her cup with a steady hand. Maybe she was
drinking the same thing Jack was: cola. Would Jack give him the keys? Not
without an explanation, and Rebus wanted to do this alone, needed to. His
motive: confrontation, and maybe exorcism. Besides, Bible John had
cheated him out of Johnny Bible.

Rebus called downstairs. 'Any cars going begging?'

'Not if you've been drinking.'

'Try me with a breath test.'

'There's an Escort parked outside.'

Rebus searched desk drawers, found a phone book. Peterhead . . . Slocum
R. No listing. He could try BT, but an unlisted check would take time.
Another option: get on the road. It was what he wanted anyway.

The city streets were wild: another Friday night, young souls at play.
Rebus was singing 'All Right Now'. Segue into: 'Been Down So Long'.
Thirty miles north to Peterhead, deep-water port. Tankers and platforms
went there for servicing. Rebus wound the motor up, not much traffic
heading out of the city. Sky glowing dull pink. Simmer dim, as the
Shetlanders called it. Rebus tried not to think about what he was doing.
Breaking rules he'd advised others not to break. No back-up. No real
authority up here, a long way from home.

He had the address for Eugene Construction, got it from Ryan Slocum's
business card. *I stood next to Bible John in a bar. He bought me a drink.*
Rebus shook his head. Probably a lot of other people could say the same, if
only they knew; Rebus wasn't so special. The company's phone number was
on the card, but all he'd got was an answering machine. It didn't mean no
one was there: security wouldn't necessarily answer the phones. The card
also had a pager number for Slocum, but Rebus wasn't about to use that.

The company was housed behind a tall mesh fence. It took twenty minutes of driving around and asking questions before he found it. It wasn't dockside, which was where he'd expected it to be. There was a country business park on the edge of town, and Eugene Construction bordered that. Rebus drove up to the gates. They were locked. He sounded his horn. There was a gatehouse, its lights on, but nobody in. Past the gates were barriers, painted red and white. His headlamps picked them out, and then behind them, coming forwards, a sauntering figure in guard's uniform. Rebus left the car running, walked up to the gate.

'What is it?' the guard asked.

He pressed his warrant card to the mesh. 'Police. I need a home address for one of your employees.'

'Can't it wait till morning?'

Gritted teeth. 'Afraid not.'

The guard – sixties, retirement age, low-slung paunch – rasped at his chin. 'I don't know,' he said.

'Look, who do you contact in an emergency?'

'My office.'

'And they contact someone from the company?'

'I suppose so. Haven't had to test it. Some kids tried to scale the fence a few months back, but they –'

'Could you phone in?'

'– heard me coming and ran away sharpish. What?'

'Could you phone in?'

'I suppose so, if it's an emergency.' The guard walked towards his hut.

'And could you let me in while you're at it? I'll need to use your phone afterwards.'

The guard scratched his head, muttered something, but shook a chain of keys from his pocket and walked up to the gate.

'Thanks,' Rebus told him.

The hut was sparsely furnished. Kettle, mug, coffee and a little jar of milk sat on a rusted tray. There was a one-bar electric heater, two chairs, and a paperback novel on the desk: a western. Rebus took the telephone and explained the situation to the guard's supervisor, who asked to speak to the guard again.

'Yes, sir,' the guard said, 'ID and everything.' Staring at Rebus like he might be leader of a heist gang. He put Rebus back on, and the supervisor handed him the name and phone number he needed. Rebus made the call, waited.

'Hello?'

'Is that Mr Sturges?'

'Speaking.'

'Sir, I'm sorry to disturb you at this hour. My name's Detective Inspector John Rebus. I'm calling from your company's gatehouse.'

'Not a break-in or something?' The man sighed. A break-in meant he'd have to get dressed and go down there.

'No, sir, I just need some information on one of your employees.'

'Can't it wait till morning?'

'Afraid not.'

'Who is it anyway?'

'Ryan Slocum.'

'Ryan? What's wrong?'

'A serious illness, sir.' Rebus had used the lie before. 'An elderly relative. They need Mr Slocum's permission to operate.'

'Good God.'

'That's why it's urgent.'

'Yes, I see, I see.' It always worked: grandmas in peril. 'Well, it's not every employee whose address I know off the top of my head.'

'But you know Mr Slocum's?'

'Been to dinner there a few times.'

'He's married?' Enter a spouse into the equation. Rebus hadn't imagined Bible John married.

'Wife's name's Una, lovely couple.'

'And the address, sir?'

'Well, it's the phone number you'll be wanting?'

'Both actually. That way, if no one's home, we can send someone round to wait.'

Rebus copied the details into his notebook, thanked the man and put down the phone.

'Any idea how to get to Springview?' he asked the guard.

35

Springview was a modern development on the coast road south of town. Rebus parked outside Three Rankeillor Close, shut off the engine, and took a good long look at the house. There was a landscaped garden to the front – clipped lawn, rockery, shrubs and flower beds. No fence or hedge separated the garden from the pavement in front. The other properties were the same.

The house itself was a newish two-storey with gabled roof. To the right of the house was an integral garage. There was an alarm box above one of the bedroom windows. A light was on behind the living-room curtains. The car parked on the gravel driveway was a white Peugeot 106.

'Now or never, John,' Rebus told himself, taking a deep breath as he got out of the car. He walked up to the front door and rang the bell, then stepped back off the doorstep. If Ryan Slocum himself answered, Rebus wanted a bit of distance. He remembered his army training – unarmed combat – and an old maxim: shoot first, ask questions later. Something he should have remembered when he'd gone to Burke's Club.

A woman's voice came through the door. 'Yes? What is it?'

Rebus realised he was being watched through a spyhole. He stepped back up on to the doorstep, so she could get a close look. 'Mrs Slocum?' Holding his warrant card up in front of him. 'CID, madam.'

The door was flung open. A small, slender woman stood there, black cusps beneath her eyes, her hair short and dark and untidy.

'Oh my God,' she said, 'what's happened?' Her accent was American.

'Nothing, madam.' Relief washed over her face. 'Why should there be?'

'Ryan,' she said, sniffing back tears. 'I don't know where he is.' She sought a handkerchief, realised the box was back in the living room, and told Rebus he'd better come in. He followed her into the large, well-furnished room, and while she was pulling out paper hankies took the opportunity to open the curtains a little. If a blue BMW turned up, he wanted to know about it.

'Working late maybe?' he said, already knowing the answer.

'I tried his office.'

'Yes, but he's a sales manager, could he be entertaining a client?'

'He always phones, he's very dutiful that way.'

Dutiful: odd choice of word. The room looked the sort that got cleaned before it was ever dirty; Una Slocum looked like the cleaner. Her hands twitched with the bundle of tissues, her whole face drawn with tension.

'Try to calm down, Mrs Slocum. Is there anything you could take?' He'd bet she had a doctor's prescription somewhere in the house.

'In the bathroom, but I don't want any. They make me dopey.'

Towards the far end of the room, a large mahogany dining table and six straight-backed chairs sat in front of a trio of wall units. China dolls behind glass, bathed by recessed lighting. Some silverware. No family photographs . . .

'Maybe a friend who could . . . ?'

Una Slocum sat down, got up again, remembering she had a guest. 'Some tea, Mr . . . ?'

'Rebus, Inspector Rebus. Tea would be great.'

Give her something to do, keep her mind busy. The kitchen was only slightly smaller than the living room. Rebus peered out into the back garden. It looked enclosed, no easy way for Ryan Slocum to sneak up on the house. Rebus's ears were primed for car noises . . .

'He's gone,' she said, stopping suddenly in the middle of the floor with the kettle in one hand, teapot in the other.

'What makes you say that, Mrs Slocum?'

'A suitcase, some clothes . . . they're gone.'

'Business, maybe? Something at the last minute?'

She shook her head. 'He'd have left a note or something, a message on the machine.'

'You've checked?'

She nodded. 'I was in Aberdeen all day, shopping, walking around. When I got back, the house felt different somehow, emptier. I think I knew right off.'

'Has he said anything about leaving?'

'No.' The ghost of a smile. 'But a wife gets to know, Inspector. Another woman.'

'A woman?'

Una Slocum nodded. 'Isn't it always? He's been so . . . I don't know, just *different* lately. Short-tempered, distracted . . . spending time away from home when I knew he'd no business meetings.' She was still nodding, confirming it to herself. 'He's gone.'

'And you've no idea where he could be?'

She shook her head. 'Wherever *she* is, that's all.'

Rebus walked back through to the living room, checked the window: no BMW. A hand touched his arm, and he spun. It was Una Slocum.

'Jesus,' he said. 'I nearly died.'

'Ryan always complains I never make any noise. It's the carpet.'

Half-inch Wilton, yards of it.

'Have you any children, Mrs Slocum?'

She shook her head. 'I think Ryan would have liked a son. Maybe that was the problem . . .'

'How long have you been married?'

'A long time, fifteen years, nearer sixteen.'

'Where did you meet?'

She smiled, drifting back. 'Galveston, Texas. Ryan was an engineer, I was a secretary in the same company. He'd emigrated from Scotland some time before. I could tell he missed home, I always knew we'd end up coming back.'

'How long have you been here?'

'Four and a half years.' And no killings during that time, so maybe Bible John *had* come out of retirement for this one job . . . 'Of course,' Una Slocum said, 'we go back now and then to see my folks. They're in Miami. And Ryan goes over three or four times a year on business.'

Business. Rebus added a rider to his previous thought: *or maybe not*.

'Is he a church-goer, Mrs Slocum?'

She stared at him. 'He was when we met. It tailed off, but he's been attending again.'

Rebus nodded. 'Any chance I could look around? He may have left a clue where he was headed.'

'Well . . . I suppose that would be all right.' The kettle came to the boil and clicked off. 'I'll make the tea.' She turned to go, paused, turned back. 'Inspector, what are you doing here?'

Rebus smiled. 'A routine inquiry, Mrs Slocum, to do with your husband's work.'

She nodded as though this explained everything, then walked silently back to the kitchen.

'Ryan's study's to the left,' she called. So Rebus started there.

It was a small room, made smaller by the furniture and book-shelves. There were dozens of books about the Second World War, a whole wall covered with them. Papers were laid out neatly on the desk – stuff from Slocum's work. In the drawers were more work files, plus others for tax, house and life insurance, pension. A life put into compartments. There was a small radio, and Rebus turned it on. Radio Three. He turned it off again, just as Una Slocum put her head round the door.

'Tea's in the living room.'

'Thank you.'

'Oh, another thing, he's taken his computer.'

'Computer?'

'You know, a laptop. He used it a lot. He kept this door locked while he worked, but I could hear the clatter of keys.'

There was a key on the inside of the door. When she'd gone, Rebus closed the door and locked himself in, then turned and tried to imagine this as the den of a murderer. He couldn't. It was a workspace, nothing more. No trophies, and no place to hide them. No bag filled with souvenirs, like Johnny Bible had collected. And no shrine, no scrapbooks of horror. No indication at all that this person lived a double life . . .

Rebus unlocked the door, went through to the living room, checked the window again.

'Find anything?' Una Slocum was pouring tea into fine china cups. A Battenberg cake had been sliced on a matching plate.

'No,' Rebus admitted. He took a cup and a slice of cake from her. 'Thank you.' Then retreated to the window again.

'When your husband's a salesman,' she went on, 'you get used to seeing him irregularly, to having to attend boring parties and gatherings, to being hostess at dinner parties where the guests are not ones you'd have chosen for yourself.'

'Can't be easy,' Rebus agreed.

'But I never complained. Maybe Ryan would have paid me more attention if I had.' She looked at him. 'You're sure he's not in trouble?'

Rebus put on his most sincere face. 'I'm positive, Mrs Slocum.'

'I suffer from nerves, you know. I've tried everything – pills, potions, hypnosis . . . But if something's in you, there's not much they can do, is there? I mean, if it's there from the time you're born, a little ticking time bomb . . .' She looked around. 'Maybe it's this house, so new and all, nothing for me to do.'

Aldous Zane had predicted a house like this, a modern house . . .

'Mrs Slocum,' Rebus said, eyes on the window, 'this might sound like a daft request, and I've no way to explain it, but do you think I could take a look at your attic?'

A chain on the first-floor landing. You tugged at it and the trapdoor opened, the wooden steps sliding down to meet you.

'Clever,' Rebus said. He began to climb, Una Slocum staying on the landing.

'The light switch is just to your right when you get up,' she called.

Rebus poked his head into space, half-expecting a shovel to come crashing down on it, and fumbled for the switch. A single bare bulb illuminated the floored attic.

'We talked about converting it,' Una Slocum called. 'But why bother? The house is too big for us as it is.'

The attic was a few degrees cooler than the rest of the house, testament to modern insulation. Rebus looked around, not sure what he might find. What had Zane said? Flags: the Stars and Stripes and a swastika. Slocum had lived in the US, and seemed fascinated by the Third Reich. But Zane had also seen a trunk in the attic of a large, modern house. Well, Rebus couldn't see anything like that. Packing cases, boxes of Christmas decorations, a couple of broken chairs, a spare door, a couple of hollow-sounding suitcases . . .

'I haven't been up here since last Christmas,' Una Slocum said. Rebus helped her up the last couple of steps.

'It's big,' Rebus said. 'I can see why you thought of converting it.'

'Planning permission would have been the problem. All the houses here are supposed to stay the same. You spend a fortune on a place, then you aren't allowed to do anything with it.' She lifted a folded piece of red cloth from one of the suitcases, brushed dust from it. It looked like a tablecloth, maybe a curtain. But when she shook it, it unfurled into a large flag, black on a white circle with red border. A swastika. She saw the shock on Rebus's face.

'He used to collect this sort of stuff.' She looked around, her face creasing into a frown. 'That's odd.'

Rebus swallowed. 'What?'

'The trunk's gone.' She pointed to a space on the floor. 'Ryan must have moved it.' She looked around, but it obviously wasn't anywhere in the attic.

'Trunk?'

'A big old thing, he's had it for ever. Why would he move it? Come to that, *how* would he move it?'

'What do you mean?'

'It was heavy. He kept it locked, said it was full of old stuff, mementoes of his life before we met. He promised he'd show me some day . . . Do you think he took it with him?'

Rebus swallowed again. 'A possibility,' he said, making for the stairs. Johnny Bible had a holdall, but Bible John needed a whole trunk. Rebus began to feel queasy.

'There's more tea in the pot,' Mrs Slocum said as they went back down to the living room.

'Thanks, but I really must be going.' He saw her try to hide a look of disappointment. It was a cruel life when the only company you had was a policeman chasing your husband.

'I'm sorry,' he said, 'about Ryan.' Then he glanced out of the window one last time.

And there was a blue BMW parked by the kerb.

Rebus's heart kicked at his chest. He couldn't see anyone in the car, no one moving towards the house . . .

Then the doorbell rang.

'Ryan?' Mrs Slocum was making for the door. Rebus caught her and pulled her back. She squealed.

He put a finger to his lips, motioned for her to stay where she was. His gorge was rising, as if he might bring up the curry from earlier. His whole body felt electric. The bell went again. Rebus took a deep breath, ran to the door and hauled it open.

A young man stood there, denim jacket and jeans, spiky gelled hair, acne. He was holding out a set of car keys.

'Where did you get it?' Rebus roared. The youth took a step back, stumbled off the step. 'Where did you get the car?' Rebus was out of the door now and looming over him.

'Work,' the youth said. 'P-part of the s-service.'

'What is?'

'Returning your c-car. From the airport.' Rebus stared at him, demanding more. 'We do valet cleaning, all that. And if you drop your car off and want it taking back to your house, we do that, too. Sinclair Car Rentals . . . you can check!'

Rebus held out a hand, pulled the youth to his feet.

'I was only going to ask if you wanted it put away,' the youth said, ashen-faced.

'Leave it where it is.' Rebus tried to control his trembling. Another car had drawn up, a horn sounded.

'My lift,' the youth explained, the terror still not completely gone from his face.

'Where was Mr Slocum headed?'

'Who?'

'The car's owner.'

The youth shrugged. 'How should I know?' He put the keys in Rebus's hand, headed back down the drive. 'We're not the gestapo,' his parting shot.

Rebus handed the keys to Mrs Slocum, who was staring at him like she had questions, like she wanted to start again from the beginning. Rebus shook his head, marched off. She looked at the keys in her hand.

'What am I going to do with two cars?'
But Rebus was gone.

He told his story to Grogan.

The Chief Inspector was almost sober – and very ready to go home. He'd already been talked to by the Crime Squad. They'd said they'd have more questions for him tomorrow, all to do with Ludovic Lumsden. Grogan listened with growing impatience, then asked what evidence there was. Rebus shrugged. They could place Slocum's car near the scene of the murder, and at a curious hour of the morning. But they couldn't do more than that. Maybe forensics would throw up some connection, but they both guessed Bible John was too smart to allow that to happen. Then there was the story outlined in Lawson Geddes's letter – a dead man's tale – and the photo from Borneo. But that meant nothing without a confession from Ryan Slocum that he'd once been Ray Sloane, had lived in Glasgow in the late sixties and had been – and still was – Bible John.

But Ryan Slocum had disappeared.

They contacted Dyce Airport, but there was no record of his having taken a plane out of there, and no taxi or car rental company would admit seeing him. Had he already left the country? What had he done with the trunk? Was he lying low in some hotel nearby, waiting for the fuss to die?

Grogan said they'd make inquiries, put out an alert to ports and airports. He didn't see what else they could do. They'd send someone out to talk with Mrs Slocum, maybe go through the house with a fine-toothed comb ... Tomorrow maybe, or the day after. Grogan didn't sound too enthusiastic. He'd found his serial killer for today, and had little inclination to go chasing ghosts.

Rebus found Jack in the canteen, drinking tea and eating chips and beans.

'Where did you get to?'

Rebus sat down beside him. 'Thought maybe I was cramping your style.'

Jack shook his head. 'Tell you what though, I nearly asked her back to that hotel.'

'Why didn't you?'

Jack shrugged. 'She told me she could never trust a man who didn't drink. Do you feel like heading back?'

'Why not?'

'John, where *did* you get to?'

'I'll tell you on the way back. It might help keep you awake ...'

36

Next morning, after a few hours' sleep on the chair, Rebus telephoned Brian Holmes. He wanted to know how he was doing, and whether Ancram's threats had evaporated in the light of Lawson Geddes's letter. The call was answered quickly.

'Hello?' A woman's voice: Nell's. Softly, Rebus put the receiver down. So she was back. Did that mean she'd come to terms with Brian's work? Or had he promised to give it up? Rebus was sure to find out later.

Jack wandered through. He reckoned his job of 'minder' was finished, but had stayed the night anyway – too tired to contemplate the miles home to Falkirk.

'Thank God it's the weekend,' he said, rubbing both hands through his hair. 'Any plans?'

'I thought I might nip down to Fettes, see what the score is with Ancram.'

'Good idea, I'll come with you.'

'You don't need to.'

'But I want to.'

They took Rebus's car for a change. But when they got to Fettes, Ancram's office was bare, no sign of it ever having been occupied. Rebus telephoned Govan, and was put through.

'Is that it finished?' he asked.

'I'll write up my report,' Ancram said. 'No doubt your boss will want to discuss it with you.'

'What about Brian Holmes?'

'It'll all be in the report.'

Rebus waited. 'All of it?'

'Tell me something, Rebus, are you clever or just spawny?'

'Is there a difference?'

'You've really mucked things up. If we'd gone ahead against Uncle Joe, we could have had the mole.'

'You'll have Uncle Joe instead.' Ancram grunted a response. 'You *know* who the mole is?'

'I have a hunch. Lennox, you met him that day in The Lobby.' DS Andy Lennox: freckles and ginger curls. 'Thing is, I've no hard evidence.'

Same old problem. In law, *knowing* was not enough. Scots law was stricter still: there must needs be corroboration.

'Maybe next time, eh?' Rebus offered, putting down the phone.

They drove back to the flat so Jack could pick up his car, but then he had to climb the stairs with Rebus, having forgotten some of his kit.

'Are you ever going to leave me alone?' Rebus asked.

Jack laughed. 'Starting any minute.'

'Well, while you're here you can help me shift the stuff back into the living room.'

It didn't take long. The last thing Rebus did was hook the fishing-boat back on the wall.

'So what now?' Jack asked.

'I suppose I could see about getting this tooth fixed. And I said I'd meet up with Gill.'

'Business or pleasure?'

'Strictly off-duty.'

'A fiver says you end up talking shop.'

Rebus smiled. 'Five says you're on. What about you?'

'Ach, I thought while I'm in town I might check out the local AA, see if there's a meeting. It's been too long.' Rebus nodded. 'Want to tag along?'

Rebus looked up, nodded. 'Why not?' he said.

'The other thing we could do is keep on with the decorating.'

Rebus wrinkled his nose. 'The mood's passed.'

'You're not going to sell?' Rebus shook his head. 'No cottage by the sea?'

'I think I'll settle for where I am, Jack. It seems to suit me.'

'And where's that exactly?'

Rebus considered his answer. 'Somewhere north of hell.'

He got back from his Sunday walk with Gill Templer and stuck a fiver in an envelope, addressed it to Jack Morton. Gill and he had talked about the Toals and the Americans, about how they'd go down on the strength of the tape. Rebus's word might not be enough to convict Hayden Fletcher of conspiracy to murder, but he'd have a damned good go. Fletcher was being brought south for questioning. Rebus had a busy week ahead. His telephone rang as he was tidying the living room.

'John?' the voice said. 'It's Brian.'

'Everything all right?'

'Fine.' But Brian's voice was hollow. 'I just thought I'd . . . the thing is . . . I'm putting in my papers.' A pause. 'Isn't that what they say?'

'Jesus, Brian . . .'

'Thing is, I've tried to learn from you, but I'm not sure you were the right choice. A bit too intense maybe, eh? See, whatever it is you've got, John, I just don't have it.' A longer pause. 'And I'm not sure I even want it, to be honest.'

'You don't have to be like me to be a good copper, Brian. Some would say you should strive to be what I'm not.'

'Well . . . I've tried both sides of the fence, hell, I've even tried sitting *on* the fence. No good, any of it.'

'I'm sorry, Brian.'

'Catch you later, eh?'

'Sure thing, son. Take care.'

He sat down in his chair, stared out of the window. A bright summer's afternoon, a good time to go for a walk through the Meadows. Only Rebus

had just come back from a walk. Did he really want another? His phone rang again and he let the machine take it. He waited for a message, but all he could hear was static crackle, background hiss. There was someone there; they hadn't broken the connection. But they weren't about to leave a message. Rebus placed a hand on the receiver, paused, then lifted it.

'Hello?'

He heard the other receiver being dropped into its cradle, then the hum of the open line. He stood for a moment, then replaced the receiver and walked into the kitchen, pulled open the cupboard and lifted out the newspapers and cuttings. Dumped the whole lot of them into the bin. Grabbed his jacket and took that walk.

Afterword

The genesis of this book was a story I heard very early in 1995, and I worked on the book all through that year, finishing a satisfactory draft just before Christmas. Then on Sunday January 29 1996, just as my editor was settling down to read the manuscript, the *Sunday Times* ran a story headlined 'Bible John "living quietly in Glasgow"', based on information contained in a book to be published by Mainstream in April. The book was *Power in the Blood* by Donald Simpson. Simpson claimed that he had met a man and befriended him, and that eventually this man had confessed to being Bible John. Simpson also claimed that the man had tried to kill him at one point, and that there was evidence the killer had struck outside Glasgow. Indeed, there remain many unsolved west-coast murders, plus two unsolveds from Dundee in 1979 and 1980 – both victims were found stripped and strangled.

It may be coincidence, of course, but the same day's *Scotland on Sunday* broke the story that Strathclyde Police had new evidence in the ongoing Bible John investigation. Recent developments in DNA analysis had given them a genetic fingerprint from a trace of semen left on the third victim's tights, and police had been asking as many of the original suspects as they could find to come forward to have a blood sample taken and analysed. One such suspect, John Irvine McInnes, had committed suicide in 1980, so a member of his family had given a blood sample instead. This seems to have proved a close enough match to warrant exhuming McInnes's body so as to carry out further tests. In early February, the body was exhumed (along with that of McInnes' mother, whose coffin had been placed atop her son's). For those interested in the case, the long wait began.

As I write (June 1996), the wait is still going on. But the feeling now is that police and their scientists will fail – indeed, already have failed – to find incontrovertible proof. For some, the seed has been sown anyway – John Irvine McInnes will remain the chief suspect in their minds – and it is true that his personal history, compared alongside the psychological profile of Bible John compiled at the time, makes for fascinating reading.

But there is real doubt, too – some of it also based on offender profiling. Would a serial killer simply cease to kill, then wait eleven years to commit suicide? One newspaper posits that Bible John 'got a fright' because of the investigation, and this stopped him killing again, but according to at least one expert in the field, this simply fails to fit the recognised pattern. Then there's the eyewitness, in whom chief investigator Joe Beattie had so

much faith. Irvine McInnes took part in an identity parade a matter of days after the third murder. Helen Puttock's sister failed to pick him out. She had shared a taxi with the killer, had watched her sister dance with him, had spent hours in and out of his company. In 1996, faced with photos of John Irvine McInnes, she says the same thing – the man who killed her sister did not have McInnes's prominent ears.

There are other questions – would the killer have given his real first name? Would the stories he told the two sisters during the taxi ride be true or false? Would he have gone ahead and killed his third victim, knowing he was leaving a witness behind? There are many out there, including police officers and numbering people like myself, who would refuse to be convinced even by a DNA match. For us, he's still out there, and – as the Robert Black and Frederick West cases have shown – by no means alone.

Acknowledgements

Thanks to: Chris Thomson, for permission to quote from one of his songs; Dr Jonathan Wills for his views on Shetland life and the oil industry; Don and Susan Nichol, for serendipitous help with the research; the Energy Division of the Scottish Office Industry Department; Keith Webster, Senior Public Affairs Officer, Conoco UK; Richard Grant, Senior Public Affairs Officer, BP Exploration; Andy Mitchell, Public Affairs Advisor, Amerada Hess; Mobil North Sea; Bill Kirton, for his offshore safety expertise; Andrew O'Hagan, author of *The Missing*; Jerry Sykes, who found the book for me; Mike Ripley, for the video material; the inebriated oil-worker Lindsey Davis and I met on a train south of Aberdeen; Colin Baxter, Trading Standards Officer *extraordinaire*; my researchers Linda and Iain; staff of the Caledonian Thistle Hotel, Aberdeen; Grampian Regional Council; Ronnie Mackintosh; Ian Docherty; Patrick Stoddart; and Eva Schegulla for the e-mail. Grateful thanks as ever to the staffs of the National Library of Scotland (especially the South Reading Room) and Edinburgh Central Library. I'd also like to thank the many friends and authors who got in touch when the Bible John case hit the headlines again early in 1996, either to commiserate or to offer suggestions for tweaks to the plot. My editor, Caroline Oakley, had faith throughout, and referred me to the James Ellroy quote at the start of my own book . . . Finally, a special thank you to Lorna Hepburn, who told me a story in the first place . . .

Any 'implags' will be from the following: *Fool's Gold* by Christopher Harvie; *A Place in the Sun* by Jonathan Wills; *Innocent Passage: The Wreck of the Tanker* Braer by Jonathan Wills and Karen Warner; *Blood on the Thistle* by Douglas Skelton; *Bible John: Search for a Sadist* by Patrick Stoddart; *The Missing* by Andrew O'Hagan.

Major Weir's quote – 'creatures tamed by cruelty' – is actually the title of Ron Butlin's first poetry collection.

The Hanging Garden

For Miranda

'If all time is eternally present
All time is unredeemable.'

T.S. Eliot, 'Burnt Norton'

'I went to Scotland and found nothing there that looks
like Scotland'

Arthur Freed, Producer Brigadoon

Book One

'In a Hanging Garden/Change the past'

They were arguing in the living room.

'Look, if your bloody job's so precious . . .'

'What do you want from me?'

'You know bloody well!'

'I'm working my arse off for the three of us!'

'Don't give me that crap.'

And then they saw her. She was holding her teddy bear, Pa Broon, by one well-chewed ear. She was peering round the doorway, thumb in her mouth. They turned to her.

'What is it, sweetie?'

'I had a bad dream.'

'Come here.' The mother crouched down, opening her arms. But the girl ran to her father, wrapped herself around his legs.

'Come on, pet, I'll take you back to bed.'

He tucked her in, started to read her a story.

'Daddy,' she said, 'what if I fall asleep and don't wake up? Like Snow White or Sleeping Beauty?'

'Nobody sleeps for ever, Sammy. All it takes to wake them up is a kiss. There's nothing the witches and evil queens can do about that.'

He kissed her forehead.

'Dead people don't wake up,' she said, hugging Pa Broon. 'Not even when you kiss them.'

1

John Rebus kissed his daughter.

'Sure you don't want a lift?'

Samantha shook her head. 'I need to walk off that pizza.'

Rebus put his hands in his pockets, felt folded banknotes beneath his handkerchief. He thought of offering her some money – wasn't that what fathers did? – but she'd only laugh. She was twenty-four and independent; didn't need the gesture and certainly wouldn't take the money. She'd even tried to pay for the pizza, arguing that she'd eaten half while he'd chewed on a single slice. The remains were in a box under her arm.

'Bye, Dad.' She pecked him on the cheek.

'Next week?'

'I'll phone you. Maybe the three of us . . .?' By which she meant Ned Farlowe, her boyfriend. She was walking backwards as she spoke. One final wave, and she turned away from him, head moving as she checked the evening traffic, crossing the road without looking back. But on the opposite pavement she half-turned, saw him watching her, waved her hand in acknowledgement. A young man almost collided with her. He was staring at the pavement, the thin black cord from a pair of earphones dribbling down his neck. Turn round and look at her, Rebus commanded. Isn't she incredible? But the youth kept shuffling along the pavement, oblivious to her world.

And then she'd turned a corner and was gone. Rebus could only imagine her now: making sure the pizza box was secure beneath her left arm; walking with eyes fixed firmly ahead of her; rubbing a thumb behind her right ear, which she'd recently had pierced for the third time. He knew that her nose would twitch when she thought of something funny. He knew that if she wanted to concentrate, she might tuck the corner of one jacket-lapel into her mouth. He knew that she wore a bracelet of braided leather, three silver rings, a cheap watch with black plastic strap and indigo face. He knew that the brown of her hair was its natural colour. He knew she was headed for a Guy Fawkes party, but didn't intend staying long.

He didn't know nearly enough about her, which was why he'd wanted them to meet for dinner. It had been a tortuous process: dates rejigged, last-minute cancellations. Sometimes it was her fault, more often his. Even tonight he should have been elsewhere. He ran his hands down the front of his jacket, feeling the bulge in his inside breast pocket, his own little time bomb. Checking his watch, he saw it was nearly nine o'clock. He could drive or he could walk – he wasn't going far.

He decided to drive.

Edinburgh on firework night, leaves blown into thick lines down the pavement. One morning soon he would find himself scraping frost from his car windscreen, feeling the cold like jabs to his kidneys. The south side of the city seemed to get the first frost earlier than the north. Rebus, of course, lived and worked on the south side. After a stint in Craigmillar, he was back at St Leonard's. He could make for there now – he was still on shift after all – but he had other plans. He passed three pubs on his way to his car. Chat at the bar, cigarettes and laughter, a fug of heat and alcohol: he knew these things better than he knew his own daughter. Two out of the three bars boasted 'doormen'. They didn't seem to be called bouncers these days. They were doormen or front-of-house managers, big guys with short hair and shorter fuses. One of them wore a kilt. His face was all scar tissue and scowl, the scalp shaved to abrasion. Rebus thought his name was Wattie or Wallie. He belonged to Telford. Maybe they all did. Graffiti on the wall further along: Won't Anyone Help? Three words spreading across the city.

Rebus parked around the corner from Flint Street and started walking. The street was in darkness at ground level, except for a café and amusement arcade. There was one lamppost, its bulb dead. The council had been asked by police not to replace it in a hurry – the surveillance needed all the help it could get. A few lights were shining in the tenement flats. There were three cars parked kerbside, but only one of them with people in it. Rebus opened the back door and got in.

A man sat in the driver's seat, a woman next to him. They looked cold and bored. The woman was Detective Constable Siobhan Clarke, who had worked with Rebus at St Leonard's until a recent posting to the Scottish Crime Squad. The man, a Detective Sergeant called Claverhouse, was a Crime Squad regular. They were part of a team keeping twenty-four-hour tabs on Tommy Telford and all his deeds. Their slumped shoulders and pale faces bespoke not only tedium but the sure knowledge that surveillance was futile.

It was futile because Telford owned the street. Nobody parked here without him knowing who and why. The other two cars parked just now were Range Rovers belonging to Telford's gang. Anything but a Range Rover stuck out. The Crime Squad had a specially adapted van which they usually used for surveillance, but that wouldn't work in Flint Street. Any van parked here for longer than five minutes received close and personal attention from a couple of Telford's men. They were trained to be courteous and menacing at the same time.

'Undercover bloody surveillance,' Claverhouse growled. 'Only we're not undercover and there's nothing to survey.' He tore at a Snickers wrapper with his teeth and offered the first bite to Siobhan Clarke, who shook her head.

'Shame about those flats,' she said, peering up through the windscreen. 'They'd be perfect.'

'Except Telford owns them all,' Claverhouse said through a mouthful of chocolate.

'Are they all occupied?' Rebus asked. He'd been in the car a minute and already his toes were cold.

'Some of them are empty,' Clarke said. 'Telford uses them for storage.'

'But every bugger in and out of the main door gets spotted,' Claverhouse added. 'We've had meter readers and plumbers try to wangle their way in.'

'Who was acting the plumber?' Rebus asked.

'Ormiston. Why?'

Rebus shrugged. 'Just need someone to fix a tap in my bathroom.'

Claverhouse smiled. He was tall and skinny, with huge dark bags under his eyes and thinning fair hair. Slow-moving and slow-talking, people often underestimated him. Those who did sometimes discovered that his nickname of 'Bloody' Claverhouse was merited.

Clarke checked her watch. 'Ninety minutes till the changeover.'

'You could do with the heating on,' Rebus offered. Claverhouse turned in his seat.

'That's what I keep telling her, but she won't have it.'

'Why not?' He caught Clarke's eyes in the rearview. She was smiling.

'Because,' Claverhouse said, 'it means running the engine, and running the engine when we're not going anywhere is wasteful. Global warming or something.'

'It's true,' Clarke said.

Rebus winked at her reflection. It looked like she'd been accepted by Claverhouse, which meant acceptance by the whole team at Fettes. Rebus, the perennial outsider, envied her the ability to conform.

'Bloody useless anyway,' Claverhouse continued. 'The bugger knows we're here. The van was blown after twenty minutes, the plumber routine didn't even get Ormiston over the threshhold, and now here we are, the only sods on the whole street. We couldn't blend in less if we were doing panto.'

'Visible presence as a deterrent,' Rebus said.

'Aye, right, a few more nights of this and I'm sure Tommy'll be back on the straight and narrow.' Claverhouse shifted in his seat, trying to get comfortable. 'Any word of Candice?'

Sammy had asked her father the same thing. Rebus shook his head.

'You still think Tarawicz snatched her? No chance she did a runner?' Rebus snorted.

'Just because you want it to be them doesn't mean it was. My advice: leave it to us. Forget about her. You've got that Adolf thing to keep you busy.'

'Don't remind me.'

'Did you ever track down Colquhoun?'

'Sudden holiday. His office got a doctor's line.'

'I think we did for him.'

Rebus realised one of his hands was caressing his breast pocket. 'So is Telford in the café or what?'

'Went in about an hour ago,' Clarke said. 'There's a room at the back, he uses that. He seems to like the arcade, too. Those games where you sit on a motorbike and do the circuit.'

'We need someone on the inside,' Claverhouse said. 'Either that or wire the place.'

'We couldn't even get a plumber in there,' Rebus said. 'You think someone with a fistful of radio mikes is going to fare any better?'

'Couldn't do any worse.' Claverhouse switched on the radio, seeking music.

'Please,' Clarke pleaded, 'no country and western.'

Rebus stared out at the café. It was well lit with a net curtain covering the bottom half of its window. On the top half was written 'Big Bites For Small Change'. There was a menu taped to the window, and a sandwich board on the pavement outside, which gave the café's hours as 6.30 a.m. – 8.30 p.m. The place should have been closed for an hour.

'How are his licences?'

'He has lawyers,' Clarke said.

'First thing we tried,' Claverhouse added. 'He's applied for a late-night extension. I can't see the neighbours complaining.'

'Well,' Rebus said, 'much as I'd love to sit around here chatting . . .'

'End of liaison?' Clarke asked. She was keeping her humour, but Rebus could see she was tired. Disrupted sleep pattern, body chill, plus the boredom of a surveillance you know is going nowhere. It was never easy partnering Claverhouse: no great fund of stories, just constant reminding that they had to do everything 'the right way', meaning by the book.

'Do us a favour,' Claverhouse said.

'What?'

'There's a chippy across from the Odeon.'

'What do you want?'

'Just a poke of chips.'

'Siobhan?'

'Irn-Bru.'

'Oh, and John?' Claverhouse added as Rebus stepped out of the car. 'Ask them for a hot-water bottle while you're at it.'

A car turned into the street, speeding up then screeching to a halt outside the café. The back door nearest the kerb opened, but nobody got out. The car accelerated away, door still hanging open, but there was something on the pavement now, something crawling, trying to push itself upright.

'Get after them!' Rebus shouted. Claverhouse had already turned the ignition, slammed the gear-shift into first. Clarke was on the radio as the car pulled away. As Rebus crossed the street, the man got to his feet. He stood with one hand against the café window, the other held to his head. As Rebus approached, the man seemed to sense his presence, staggered away from the café into the road.

'Christ!' he yelled. 'Help me!' He fell to his knees again, both hands scrabbling at his scalp. His face was a mask of blood. Rebus crouched in front of him.

'We'll get you an ambulance,' he said. A crowd had gathered at the window of the café. The door had been pulled open, and two young men were watching, like they were onlookers at a piece of street theatre. Rebus recognised them: Kenny Houston and Pretty-Boy. 'Don't just stand there!' he yelled. Houston looked to Pretty-Boy, but Pretty-Boy wasn't moving. Rebus took out his mobile, called in the emergency, his eyes fixing on Pretty-Boy: black wavy hair, eyeliner. Black leather jacket, black polo-neck, black jeans. Stones: 'Paint it Black'. But the face chalk-white, like it had been powdered. Rebus walked up to the door. Behind him, the man was beginning to wail, a roar of pain echoing into the night sky.

'We don't know him,' Pretty-Boy said.

'I didn't ask if you knew him, I asked for help.'

Pretty-Boy didn't blink. 'The magic word.'

Rebus got right up into his face. Pretty-Boy smiled and nodded towards Houston, who went to fetch towels.

Most of the customers had returned to their tables. One was studying the bloody palmprint on the window. Rebus saw another group of people, watching from the doorway of a room to the back of the café. At their centre stood Tommy Telford: tall, shoulders straight, legs apart. He looked almost soldierly.

'I thought you took care of your lads, Tommy!' Rebus called to him. Telford looked straight through him, then turned back into the room. The door closed. More screams from outside. Rebus grabbed the dish-towels from Houston and ran. The bleeder was on his feet again, weaving like a boxer in defeat.

'Take your hands down for a sec.' The man lifted both hands from his matted hair, and Rebus saw a section of scalp rise with them, like it was attached to the skull by a hinge. A thin jet of blood hit Rebus in the face. He turned away and felt it against his ear, his neck. Blindly he stuck the towel on to the man's head.

'Hold this.' Rebus grabbing the hands, forcing them on to the towel. Headlights: the unmarked police car. Claverhouse had his window down.

'Lost them in Causewayside. Stolen car, I'll bet. They'll be hoofing it.'

'We need to get this one to Emergency.' Rebus pulled open the back door. Clarke had found a box of paper hankies and was pulling out a wad.

'I think he's beyond Kleenex,' Rebus said as she handed them over.

'They're for you,' she said.

2

It was a three-minute drive to the Royal Infirmary. Accident & Emergency was gearing up for firework casualties. Rebus went to the toilets, stripped, and rinsed himself off as best he could. His shirt was damp and cold to the touch. A line of blood had dried down the front of his chest. He turned to look in the mirror, saw more blood on his back. He had wet a clump of blue paper towels. There was a change of clothes in his car, but his car was back near Flint Street. The door of the toilets opened and Claverhouse came in.

'Best I could do,' he said, holding out a black T-shirt. There was a garish print on the front, a zombie with demon's eyes, wielding a scythe. 'Belongs to one of the junior doctors, made me promise to get it back to him.'

Rebus dried himself off with another wad of towels. He asked Claverhouse how he looked.

'There's still some on your brow.' Claverhouse wiped the bits Rebus had missed.

'How is he?' Rebus asked.

'They reckon he'll be okay, if he doesn't get an infection on the brain.'

'What do you think?'

'Message to Tommy from Big Ger.'

'Is he one of Tommy's men?'

'He's not saying.'

'So what's his story?'

'Fell down a flight of steps, cracked his head at the bottom.'

'And the drop-off?'

'Says he can't remember.' Claverhouse paused. 'Eh, John . . .?'

'What?'

'One of the nurses wanted me to ask you something.'

His tone told Rebus all he needed to know. 'AIDS test?'

'They just wondered.'

Rebus thought about it. Blood in his eyes, his ears, running down his neck. He looked himself over: no scratches or cuts. 'Let's wait and see,' he said.

'Maybe we should pull the surveillance,' Claverhouse said, 'leave them to get on with it.'

'And have a fleet of ambulances standing by to pick up the bodies?'

Claverhouse snorted. 'Is this sort of thing Big Ger's style?'

'Very much so,' Rebus said, reaching for his jacket.

'But not that nightclub stabbing?'

'No.'

Claverhouse started laughing, but there was no humour to the sound. He rubbed his eyes. 'Never got those chips, did we? Christ, I could use a drink.'

Rebus reached into his jacket for the quarter-bottle of Bell's.

Claverhouse didn't seem surprised as he broke the seal. He took a gulp, chased it down with another, and handed the bottle back. 'Just what the doctor ordered.'

Rebus started screwing the top back on.

'Not having one?'

'I'm on the wagon.' Rebus rubbed a thumb over the label.

'Since when?'

'The summer.'

'So why carry a bottle around?'

Rebus looked at it. 'Because that's not what it is.'

Claverhouse looked puzzled. 'Then what is it?'

'A bomb.' Rebus tucked the bottle back into his pocket. 'A little suicide bomb.'

They walked back to A&E. Siobhan Clarke was waiting for them outside a closed door.

'They've had to sedate him,' she said. 'He was up on his feet again, reeling all over the place.' She pointed to marks on the floor – airbrushed blood, smudged by footprints.

'Do we have a name?'

'He's not offered one. Nothing in his pockets to identify him. Over two hundred in cash, so we can rule out a mugging. What do you reckon for a weapon? Hammer?'

Rebus shrugged. 'A hammer would dent the skull. That flap looked too neat. I think they went for him with a cleaver.'

'Or a machete,' Claverhouse added. 'Something like that.'

Clarke stared at him. 'I smell whisky.'

Claverhouse put a finger to his lips.

'Anything else?' Rebus asked. It was Clarke's turn to shrug.

'Just one observation.'

'What's that?'

'I like the T-shirt.'

Claverhouse put money in the machine, got out three coffees. He'd called his office, told them the surveillance was suspended. Orders now were to stay at the hospital, see if the victim would say anything. The very least they wanted was an ID. Claverhouse handed a coffee to Rebus.

'White, no sugar.'

Rebus took the coffee with one hand. In the other he held a polythene laundry-bag, inside which was his shirt. He'd have a go at cleaning it. It was a good shirt.

'You know, John,' Claverhouse said, 'there's no point you hanging around.'

Rebus knew. His flat was a short walk away across The Meadows. His large, empty flat. There were students through the wall. They played music a lot, stuff he didn't recognise.

'You know Telford's gang,' Rebus said. 'Didn't you recognise the face?'

Claverhouse shrugged. 'I thought he looked a bit like Danny Simpson.'

'But you're not sure?'

'If it's Danny, a name's about all we can hope to get out of him. Telford picks his boys with care.'

Clarke came towards them along the corridor. She took the coffee from Claverhouse.

'It's Danny Simpson,' she confirmed. 'I just got another look, now the blood's been cleaned off.' She took a swallow of coffee, frowned. 'Where's the sugar?'

'You're sweet enough already,' Claverhouse told her.

'Why did they pick on Simpson?' Rebus asked.

'Wrong place, wrong time?' Claverhouse suggested.

'Plus he's pretty low down the pecking order,' Clarke added, 'making it a gentle hint.'

Rebus looked at her. Short dark hair, shrewd face with a gleam to the eyes. He knew she worked well with suspects, kept them calm, listened carefully. Good on the street, too: fast on her feet as well as in her head.

'Like I say, John,' Claverhouse said, finishing his coffee, 'any time you want to head off . . .'

Rebus looked up and down the empty corridor. 'Am I in the way or something?'

'It's not that. But your job's *liaison* – period. I know the way you work: you get attached to cases, maybe even overattached. Look at Candice. I'm just saying . . .'

'You're saying, don't butt in?' Colour rose to Rebus's cheeks: *Look at Candice*.

'I'm saying it's our case, not yours. That's all.'

Rebus's eyes narrowed. 'I don't get it.'

Clarke stepped in. 'John, I think all he means is –'

'Whoah! It's OK, Siobhan. Let the man speak for himself.'

Claverhouse sighed, screwed up his empty cup and looked around for a bin. 'John, investigating Telford means keeping half an eye on Big Ger Cafferty and his crew.'

'And?'

Claverhouse stared at him. 'Okay, you want it spelling out? You went to Barlinnie yesterday – news travels in our business. You met Cafferty. The two of you had a chinwag.'

'He asked me to go,' Rebus lied.

Claverhouse held up his hands. 'Fact is, as you've just said, he asked you and you went.' Claverhouse shrugged.

'Are you saying I'm in his pocket?' Rebus's voice had risen.

'Boys, boys,' Clarke said.

The doors at the end of the corridor had swung open. A young man in a dark business suit, briefcase swinging, was coming towards the drinks machine. He was humming some tune. He stopped humming as he reached them, put down his case and searched his pockets for change. He smiled when he looked at them.

'Good evening.'

Early-thirties, black hair slicked back from his forehead. One kiss-curl looped down between his eyebrows.

'Anyone got change of a pound?'

They looked in their pockets, couldn't find enough coins.

'Never mind.' Though the machine was flashing EXACT MONEY ONLY he stuck in the pound coin and selected tea, black, no sugar. He stooped down to retrieve the cup, but didn't seem in a hurry to leave.

'You're police officers,' he said. His voice was a drawl, slightly nasal: Scottish upper-class. He smiled. 'I don't think I know any of you professionally, but one can always tell.'

'And you're a lawyer,' Rebus guessed. The man bowed his head in acknowledgement. 'Here to represent the interests of a certain Mr Thomas Telford.'

'I'm Daniel Simpson's legal advisor.'

'Which adds up to the same thing.'

'I believe Daniel's just been admitted.' The man blew on his tea, sipped it.

'Who told you he was here?'

'Again, I don't believe that's any of your business, Detective . . .?'

'DI Rebus.'

The man transferred his cup to his left hand so he could hold out his right. 'Charles Groal.' He glanced at Rebus's T-shirt. 'Is that what you call "plain clothes", Inspector?'

Claverhouse and Clarke introduced themselves in turn. Groal made great show of handing out business cards.

'I take it,' he said, 'you're loitering here in the hope of interviewing my client?'

'That's right,' Claverhouse said.

'Might I ask why, DS Claverhouse? Or should I address that question to your superior?'

'He's not my –' Claverhouse caught Rebus's look.

Groal raised an eyebrow. 'Not your superior? And yet he manifestly is, being an Inspector to your Sergeant.' He looked towards the ceiling, tapped a finger against his cup. 'You're not strictly colleagues,' he said at last, bringing his gaze back down to focus on Claverhouse.

'DS Claverhouse and myself are attached to the Scottish Crime Squad,' Clarke said.

'And Inspector Rebus isn't,' Groal observed. 'Fascinating.'

'I'm at St Leonard's.'

'Then this is quite rightly part of your division. But as for the Crime Squad . . .'

'We just want to know what happened,' Rebus went on.

'A fall of some kind, wasn't it? How is he, by the way?'

'Nice of you to show concern,' Claverhouse muttered.

'He's unconscious,' Clarke said.

'And likely to be in an operating theatre fairly soon. Or will they want to X-ray him first? I'm not very up on the procedures.'

'You could always ask a nurse,' Claverhouse said.

'DS Claverhouse, I detect a certain hostility.'

'Just his normal tone,' Rebus said. 'Look, you're here to make sure Danny Simpson keeps his trap shut. We're here to listen to whatever bunch of shite the two of you eventually concoct for our delectation. I think that's a pretty fair summary, don't you?'

Groal cocked his head slightly to one side. 'I've heard about you, Inspector. Occasionally stories can become exaggerated but not, I'm pleased to say, in your case.'

'He's a living legend,' Clarke offered. Rebus snorted and headed back into A&E.

There was a woolly suit in there, seated on a chair, his cap on his lap and a paperback book resting on the cap. Rebus had seen him half an hour before. The constable was sitting outside a room with its door closed tight. Quiet voices came from the other side. The woolly suit was called Redpath and he worked out of St Leonard's. He'd been in the force a bit under a year. Graduate recruit. They called him 'The Professor'. He was tall and spotty and had a shy look about him. He closed the book as Rebus approached, but kept a finger in his page.

'Science fiction,' he explained. 'Always thought I'd grow out of it.'

'There are a lot of things we don't grow out of, son. What's it about?'

'The usual: threats to the stability of the time continuum, parallel universes.' Redpath looked up. 'What do you think of parallel universes, sir?'

Rebus nodded towards the door. 'Who's in there?'

'Hit and run.'

'Bad?' The Professor shrugged. 'Where did it happen?'

'Top of Minto Street.'

'Did you get the car?'

Redpath shook his head. 'Waiting to see if she can tell us anything. What about you, sir?'

'Similar story, son. Parallel universe, you could call it.'

Siobhan Clarke appeared, nursing a fresh cup of coffee. She nodded a greeting towards Redpath, who stood up: a courtesy which gained him a sly smile.

'Telford doesn't want Danny talking,' she said to Rebus.

'Obviously.'

'And meantime he'll want to even the score.'

'Definitely.'

She caught Rebus's eyes. 'I thought he was a bit out of order back there.' Meaning Claverhouse, but not wanting to name names in front of a uniform.

Rebus nodded. 'Thanks.' Meaning: you did right not to say as much at the time. Claverhouse and Clarke were partners now. It wouldn't do for her to upset him.

A door slid open and a doctor appeared. She was young, and looked exhausted. Behind her in the room, Rebus could see a bed, a figure on the bed, staff milling around the various machines. Then the door slid closed.

'We're going to do a brain scan,' the doctor was telling Redpath. 'Have you contacted her family?'

'I don't have a name.'

'Her effects are inside.' The doctor slid open the door again and walked in. There was clothing folded on a chair, a bag beneath it. As the doctor pulled out the bag, Rebus saw something. A flat white cardboard box.

A white cardboard pizza box. Clothes: black denims, black bra, red satin shirt. A black duffel-coat.

'John?'

And black shoes with two-inch heels, square-toed, new-looking except for the scuff marks, like they'd been dragged along the road.

He was in the room now. They had a mask over her face, feeding her oxygen. Her forehead was cut and bruised, the hair pushed away from it. Her fingers were blistered, the palms scraped raw. The bed she lay on wasn't really a bed but a wide steel trolley.

'Excuse me, sir, you shouldn't be in here.'

'What's wrong?'

'It's this gentleman –'

'John? John, what is it?'

Her earrings had been removed. Three tiny pin-pricks, one of them redder than its neighbours. The face above the sheet: puffy blackened eyes, a broken nose, abrasions on both cheeks. Split lip, a graze on the chin, eyelids which didn't even flutter. He saw a hit-and-run victim. And beneath it all, he saw his daughter.

And he screamed.

Clarke and Redpath had to drag him out, helped by Claverhouse who'd heard the noise.

'Leave the door open! I'll kill you if you close that door!'

They tried to sit him down. Redpath rescued his book from the chair. Rebus tore it from him and threw it down the hall.

'How could you read a fucking book?' he spat. 'That's Sammy in there! And you're out here reading a book!'

Clarke's cup of coffee had been kicked over, the floor slippy, Redpath going down as Rebus pushed at him.

'Can you jam that door open?' Claverhouse was asking the doctor. 'And what about a sedative?'

Rebus was clawing his hands through his hair, bawling dry-eyed, his voice hoarse and uncomprehending. Staring down at himself, he saw the ludicrous T-shirt and knew that's what he'd take away from this night: the image of an Iron Maiden T-shirt and its grinning bright-eyed demon. He hauled off his jacket and started tearing at the shirt.

She was behind that door, he thought, and I was out here chatting as casual as you like. She'd been in there all the time he'd been here. Two things clicked: a hit and run; the car speeding away from Flint Street.

He grabbed at Redpath. 'Top of Minto Street. You're sure?'

'What?'

'Sammy . . . top of Minto Street?'

Redpath nodded. Clarke knew straight away what Rebus was thinking. 'I don't think so, John. They were headed the opposite way.'

'Could have doubled back.'

Claverhouse had caught some of the exchange. 'I just got off the phone. The guys who did Danny Simpson, we picked up the car. White Escort abandoned in Argyle Place.'

Rebus looked at Redpath. 'White Escort?'

Redpath was shaking his head. 'Witnesses say dark-coloured.'

Rebus turned to the wall, stood there with his palms pressed to it. Staring at the paintwork, it was like he could see *inside* the paint.

Claverhouse put a hand on his shoulder. 'John, I'm sure she's going to be fine. The doctor's gone to fetch you a couple of tablets, but meantime what about one of these?'

Claverhouse with Rebus's jacket folded in the crook of his arm, the quarter-bottle in his hand.

The little suicide bomb.

He took the bottle from Claverhouse. Unscrewed its top, his eyes on the open doorway. Lifted the bottle to his lips.

Drank.

Book Two

'In the Hanging Garden/No one sleeps'

A seaside holiday: caravan park, long walks and sandcastles. He sat in a deck-chair, trying to read. Cold wind blowing, despite the sun. Rhona rubbed suntan lotion on Sammy, said you couldn't be too careful. Told him to keep an eye open, she was going back to the caravan for her book. Sammy was burying her father's feet in the sand.

He was trying to read, but thinking about work. Every day of the holiday, he sneaked off to a phone box and called the station. They kept telling him to go and enjoy himself, forget about everything. He was halfway through a spy thriller. The plot had already lost him.

Rhona was doing her best. She'd wanted somewhere foreign, a bit of glamour and heat to go with the sunshine. Finances, however, were on his side. So here they were on the Fife coast, where he'd first met her. Was he hoping for something? Some memory rekindled? He'd come here with his own parents, played with Mickey, met other kids, then lost them again at the end of the fortnight.

He tried the spy novel again, but casework got in the way. And then a shadow fell over him.

'Where is she?'

'What?' He looked down. His feet were buried in sand, but Sammy wasn't there. How long had she been gone? He stood up, scanned the seashore. A few tentative bathers, going in no further than their knees.

'Christ, John, where is she?'

He turned round, looked at the sand dunes in the distance.

'The dunes . . .?'

They warned her. There were hollows in the dunes where the sand was eroding. Small dens had been created – a magnet for kids. Only they were prone to collapse. Earlier in the season, a ten-year-old boy had been dug out by frantic parents. He hadn't quite choked on the sand . . .

They were running now. The dunes, the grass, no sign of her.

'Sammy!'

'Maybe she went into the water.'

'You were supposed to be keeping an eye on her!'

'I'm sorry. I . . .'

'Sammy!'

A small shape in one of the dens. Hopping on its hands and knees. Rhona reached in, pulled her out, hugged her.

'Sweetie, we told you not to!'

'I was a rabbit.'

Rebus looked at the fragile roof: sand meshed with the roots of plants and grasses. Punched it with a fist. The roof collapsed. Rhona was looking at him.

End of holiday.

3

John Rebus kissed his daughter.

'See you later,' he said, watching her as she left the coffee shop. Espresso and a slice of caramel shortbread – that's all she'd had time for – but they'd fixed another date for dinner. Nothing fancy, just a pizza.

It was October 30th. By mid-November, if Nature were feeling bloody, it would be winter. Rebus had been taught at school that there were four distinct seasons, had painted pictures of them in bright and sombre colours, but his native country seemed not to know this. Winters were long, outstaying their welcome. The warm weather came suddenly, people stripping to T-shirts as the first buds appeared, so that spring and summer seemed entwined into a single season. And no sooner had the leaves started turning brown than the first frost came again.

Sammy waved at him through the café window then was gone. She seemed to have grown up all right. He'd always been on the lookout for evidence of instability, hints of childhood traumas or a genetic predisposition towards self-destruction. Maybe he should phone Rhona some day and thank her, thank her for bringing Samantha up on her own. It couldn't have been easy: that was what people always said. He knew it would be nice if he could feel some responsibility for the success, but he wasn't *that* hypocritical. The truth was, while she'd been growing up, he'd been elsewhere. It was the same with his marriage: even when in the same room as his wife, even out at the pictures or around the table at a dinner party . . . the best part of him had been elsewhere, fixed on some case or other, some question that needed answering before he could rest.

Rebus lifted his coat from the back of his chair. Nothing left for it but to go back to the office. Sammy was headed back to her own office; she worked with ex-convicts. She had refused his offer of a lift. Now that it was out in the open, she'd wanted to talk about her man, Ned Farlowe. Rebus had tried to look interested, but found that his mind was half on Joseph Lintz – in other words, same problem as always. When he'd been given the Lintz case, he'd been told he was well suited to it: his Army background for one thing; and his seeming affinity for historical cases – by which Farmer Watson, Rebus's chief superintendent, had meant Bible John – for another.

'With respect, sir,' Rebus had said, 'that sounds like a load of balls. Two reasons for me getting lumbered with this: one, no other bugger will touch it with a bargepole; two, it'll keep me out of the way for a while.'

'Your remit,' the Farmer had said, unwilling to let Rebus rile him, 'is to

sift through what there is, see if any of it amounts to evidence. You can interview Mr Lintz if it'll help. Do whatever you think necessary, and if you find enough to warrant a charge . . .'

'I won't. You know I won't.' Rebus sighed. 'Sir, we've been through this before. It's the whole reason the War Crimes section was shut down. That case a few years back – lot of hoo-ha about bugger all.' He was shaking his head. 'Who wants it all dragged up, apart from the papers?'

'I'm taking you off the Mr Taystee case. Let Bill Pryde handle that.'

So it was settled: Lintz belonged to Rebus.

It had started with a news story, with documents handed over to a Sunday broadsheet. The documents had come from the Holocaust Investigation Bureau based in Tel Aviv. They had passed on to the newspaper the name of Joseph Lintz, who had, they said, been living quietly in Scotland under an alias since the end of the war, and who was, in fact, Josef Linzstek, a native of Alsace. In June 1944, Lieutenant Linzstek had led the 3rd Company of an SS regiment, part of the 2nd Panzer Division, into the town of Villefranche d'Albarede in the Corrèze region of France. 3rd Company had rounded up everyone in the town – men, women, children. The sick were carried from their beds, the elderly pulled from their armchairs, babies hoisted from their cots.

A teenage girl – an evacuee from Lorraine – had seen what the Germans were capable of. She climbed into the attic of her house and hid there, watching from a small window in the roof-tiles. Everyone was marched into the village square. The teenager saw her schoolfriends find their families. She hadn't been in school that day: a throat infection. She wondered if anyone would tell the Germans . . .

There was a commotion as the mayor and other dignitaries remonstrated with the officer in charge. While machine guns were aimed at the crowd, these men – among them the priest, lawyer, and doctor – were set upon with rifle butts. Then ropes were produced, and strung over half a dozen of the trees which lined the square. The men were hauled to their feet, their heads pushed through the nooses. An order was given, a hand raised then dropped, and soldiers pulled on each rope, until six men were hanging from the trees, bodies writhing, legs kicking uselessly, the movements slowing by degrees.

As the teenager remembered it, it took an age for them to die. Stunned silence in the square, as if the whole village knew now, knew that this was no mere check of identity papers. More orders were barked. The men, separated from the women and children, were marched off to Prudhomme's barn, everyone else shepherded into the church. The square grew empty, except for a dozen or so soldiers, rifles slung over their shoulders. They chatted, kicked up dust and stones, shared jokes and cigarettes. One of them went into the bar and switched the radio on. Jazz music filled the air, competing with the rustle of leaves as a breeze twisted the corpses in the trees.

'It was strange,' the girl later said. 'I stopped seeing them as dead bodies. It was as if they'd become something else, parts of the trees themselves.'

Then the explosion, smoke and dust billowing from the church. A moment's silence, as though a vacuum had been created in the world, then screams, followed immediately by machine-gun fire. And when it finally

stopped, she could still hear it. Because it wasn't just inside the church: it was in the distance, too.

Prudhomme's barn.

When she was finally found – by people from surrounding villages – she was naked except for a shawl she had found in a trunk. The shawl had belonged to her grandmother, dead the previous year. But she was not alone in escaping the massacre. When the soldiers had opened fire in Prudhomme's barn, they'd aimed low. The first row of men to fall had been wounded in the lower body, and the bodies which fell on them shielded them from further fire. When straw was strewn over the mound and set alight, they'd waited as long as they could before starting to claw their way out from beneath, expecting at any moment to be shot. Four of them made it, two with their hair and clothes on fire, one dying later from his wounds.

Three men, one teenage girl: the only survivors.

The death toll was never finalised. No one knew how many visitors had been in Villefranche that day, how many refugees could be added to the count. A list was compiled of over seven hundred names, people who had most likely been killed.

Rebus sat at his desk and rubbed his eyes with his knuckles. The teenage girl was still alive, a pensioner now. The male survivors were all dead. But they'd been alive for the Bordeaux trial in 1953. He had summaries of their evidence. The summaries were in French. A lot of the material sitting on his desk was French, and Rebus didn't speak French. That was why he'd gone to the Modern Languages department at the university and found someone who could. Her name was Kirstin Mede, and she lectured in French, but also had a working knowledge of German, which was handy: the documents which weren't in French were in German. He had a one-page English summary of the trial proceedings, passed on from the Nazi hunters. The trial had opened in February 1953 and lasted just under a month. Of seventy-five men identified as having been part of the German force at Villefranche, only fifteen were present – six Germans and nine French Alsatians. Not one of them was an officer. One German received the death sentence, the others jail terms of between four and twelve years, but they were all released as soon as the trial finished. Alsace hadn't been enjoying the trial, and in a bid to unite the nation, the government had passed an amnesty. The Germans, meantime, were said to have already served their sentences.

The survivors of Villefranche had been horrified.

Even more extraordinary to Rebus's mind, the British had apprehended a couple of German officers involved in the massacre, but had refused to hand them over to the French authorities, returning them to Germany instead, where they lived long and prosperous lives. If Linzstek had been captured then, there would have been none of the present commotion.

Politics: it was all down to politics. Rebus looked up and Kirstin Mede was standing there. She was tall, deftly constructed, and immaculately dressed. She wore make-up the way women usually did only in fashion adverts. Today she was wearing a check two-piece, the skirt just touching her knees, and long gold-coloured earrings. She had already opened her briefcase and was pulling out a sheaf of papers.

'Latest translations,' she said.

'Thanks.'

Rebus looked down at a note he'd made to himself: 'Corrèze trip necessary??' Well, the Farmer had said he could have whatever he wanted. He looked up at Kirstin Mede and wondered if the budget would stretch to a tour guide. She was sitting opposite him, putting on half-moon reading glasses.

'Can I get you a coffee?' he asked.

'I'm a bit pushed today. I just wanted you to see these.' She laid two sheets of paper on his desk so that they faced him. One sheet was the photocopy of a typed report, in German. The second sheet was her translation. Rebus looked at the German.

'– Der Beginn der Vergeltungsmassnahmen hat ein merkbares Aufatmen hervorgerufen und die Stimmung sehr günstig beeinflusst.'

'The beginning of reprisals,' he read, 'has brought about a marked improvement in morale, with the men now noticeably more relaxed.'

'It's supposed to be from Linzstek to his commander,' she explained.

'But no signature?'

'Just the typed name, underlined.'

'So it doesn't help us identify Linzstek.'

'No, but remember what we were talking about? It gives a reason for the assault.'

'A touch of R&R for the lads?'

Her look froze him. 'Sorry,' he said, raising his hands. 'Far too glib. And you're right, it's almost like the Lieutenant is trying to justify the whole thing in print.'

'For posterity?'

'Maybe. After all, they'd just started being the losing side.' He looked at the other papers. 'Anything else?'

'Some further reports, nothing too exciting. And some of the eyewitness testimony.' She looked at him with pale grey eyes. 'It gets to you after a while, doesn't it?'

Rebus looked at her and nodded.

The female survivor of the massacre lived in Juillac, and had been questioned recently by local police about the man in charge of the German troops. Her story hadn't changed from the one she'd told at the trial: she'd seen his face only for a few seconds, and looking down from the attic of a three-storey house. She'd been shown a recent photo of Joseph Lintz, and had shrugged.

'Maybe,' she'd said. 'Yes, maybe.'

Which would, Rebus knew, be turfed out by the Procurator Fiscal, who knew damned well what any defence lawyer with half a brain would do with it.

'How's the case coming?' Kirstin Mede asked. Maybe she'd seen some look cross his face.

'Slowly. The problem is all this stuff.' He waved towards the strewn desk. 'On the one hand I've got all this, and on the other I've got a wee old man from the New Town. The two don't seem to go together.'

'Have you met him?'

'Once or twice.'

'What's he like?'

What was Joseph Lintz like? He was cultured, a linguist. He'd even been a Professor at the university, back in the early '70s. Only for a year or two. His own explanation: 'I was filling a vacuum until they could find someone of greater standing'. He'd been Professor of German. He'd lived in Scotland since 1945 or '46 – he was vague about exact dates, blaming his memory. His early life was vague, too. He said papers had been destroyed. The Allies had had to create a duplicate set for him. There was only Lintz's word that these new papers were anything but an official record of lies he'd told and which had been believed. Lintz's story – birth in Alsace; parents and relatives all dead; forced enlistment in the SS. Rebus liked the touch about joining the SS. It was the sort of admission that would make officials decide: he's been honest about his involvement with that, so he's probably being honest about the other details. There was no actual record of a Joseph Lintz serving with any SS regiment, but then the SS had destroyed a lot of their own records once they'd seen the way the war was headed. Lintz's war record was vague, too. He mentioned shell-shock to explain the gaps in his memory. But he was vehement that he had never been called Linzstek and had never served in the Corrèze region of France.

'I was in the east,' he would say. 'That's where the Allies found me, in the east.'

The problem was that there was no convincing explanation as to how Lintz had found himself in the United Kingdom. He said he'd asked if he could go there and start a new life. He didn't want to return to Alsace, wanted to be as far away from the Germans as possible. He wanted water between him and them. Again, there was no documentation to back this up, and meantime the Holocaust investigators had come up with their own 'evidence', which pointed to Lintz's involvement in the 'Rat Line'.

'Have you ever heard of something called the Rat Line?' Rebus had asked at their first meeting.

'Of course,' Joseph Lintz had said. 'But I never had anything to do with it.'

Lintz: in the drawing room of his Heriot Row home. An elegant four-storey Georgian edifice. A huge house for a man who'd never married. Rebus had said as much. Lintz had merely shrugged, as was his privilege. Where had the money come from?

'I've worked hard, Inspector.'

Maybe so, but Lintz had purchased the house in the late-1950s on a lecturer's salary. A colleague from the time had told Rebus everyone in the department suspected Lintz of having a private income. Lintz denied this.

'Houses were cheaper back then, Inspector. The fashion was for country properties and bungalows.'

Joseph Lintz: barely five foot tall, bespectacled. Parchment hands with liver spots. One wrist sported a pre-war Ingersoll watch. Glass-fronted bookcases lining his drawing room. Charcoal-coloured suits. An elegant way about him, almost feminine: the way he lifted a cup to his lips; the way he flicked specks from his trousers.

'I don't blame the Jews,' he'd said. 'They'd implicate everyone if they could. They want the whole world feeling guilty. Maybe they're right.'

'In what way, sir?'

'Don't we all have little secrets, things we're ashamed of?' Lintz had smiled. 'You're playing their game, and you don't even know it.'

589

Rebus had pressed on. 'The two names are very similar, aren't they? Lintz, Linzstek.'

'Naturally, or they'd have absolutely no grounds for their accusations. Think, Inspector: wouldn't I have changed my name more radically? Do you credit me with a modicum of intelligence?'

'More than a modicum.' Framed diplomas on the walls, honorary degrees, photos taken with university chancellors, politicians. When the Farmer had learned a little more about Joseph Lintz, he'd cautioned Rebus to 'ca' canny'. Lintz was a patron of the arts – opera, museums, galleries – and a great giver to charities. He was a man with *friends*. But also a solitary man, someone who was happiest when tending graves in Warriston Cemetery. Dark bags under his eyes, pushing down upon the angular cheeks. Did he sleep well?

'Like a lamb, Inspector.' Another smile. 'Of the sacrificial kind. You know, I don't blame you, you're only doing your job.'

'You seem to have no end of forgiveness, Mr Lintz.'

A careful shrug. 'Do you know Blake's words, Inspector? "And through all eternity/ I forgive you, you forgive me." I'm not so sure I can forgive the media.' This last word voiced with a distaste which manifested itself as a twist of facial muscles.

'Is that why you've set your lawyer on them?'

' "Set" makes me sound like a hunter, Inspector. This is a *newspaper*, with a team of expensive lawyers at its beck and call. Can an individual hope to win against such odds?'

'Then why bother trying?'

Lintz thumped both arms of his chair with clenched fists. 'For the principle, man!' Such outbursts were rare and short-lived, but Rebus had experienced enough of them to know that Lintz had a temper . . .

'Hello?' Kirstin Mede said, angling her head to catch his gaze.

'What?'

She smiled. 'You were miles away.'

'Just across town,' he replied.

She pointed to the papers. 'I'll leave these here, OK? If you've any questions . . .'

'Great, thanks.' Rebus got to his feet.

'It's OK, I know my way out.'

But Rebus was insistent. 'Sorry, I'm a bit . . .' He waved his hands around his head.

'As I said, it gets to you after a while.'

As they walked back through the CID office, Rebus could feel eyes following them. Bill Pryde came up, preening, wanting to be introduced. He had curly fair hair and thick blond eyelashes, his nose large and freckled, mouth small and topped with a ginger moustache – a fashion accessory he could well afford to lose.

'A pleasure,' he said, taking Kirstin Mede's hand. Then, to Rebus: 'Makes me wish we'd swopped.'

Pryde was working on the Mr Taystee case: an ice-cream man found dead in his van. Engine left running in a lock-up, looking initially like suicide.

Rebus steered Kirstin Mede past Pryde, kept them moving. He wanted

to ask her out. He knew she wasn't married, but thought there might be a boyfriend in the frame. Rebus was thinking: what would she like to eat – French or Italian? She spoke both those languages. Maybe stick to something neutral: Indian or Chinese. Maybe she was vegetarian. Maybe she didn't like restaurants. A drink then? But Rebus didn't drink these days.

'. . . So what do you think?'

Rebus started. Kirstin Mede had asked him something.

'Sorry?'

She laughed, realising he hadn't been listening. He began to apologise, but she shook it off. 'I know,' she said, 'you're a bit . . .' And she waved her hands around her head. He smiled. They'd stopped walking. They were facing one another. Her briefcase was tucked under one arm. It was the moment to ask her for a date, any kind of date – let *her* choose.

'What's that?' she said suddenly. It was a shriek, Rebus had heard it, too. It had come from behind the door nearest them, the door to the women's toilets. They heard it again. This time it was followed by some words they understood.

'Help me, somebody!'

Rebus pushed open the door and ran in. A WPC was pushing at a cubicle door, trying to force it with her shoulder. From behind the door, Rebus could hear choking noises.

'What is it?' he said.

'Picked her up twenty minutes ago, she said she needed the loo.' The policewoman's cheeks wore a flush of anger and embarrassment.

Rebus grabbed the top of the door and hauled himself up, peering over and down on to a figure seated on the pan. The woman there was young, heavily made-up. She sat with her back against the cistern, so that she was staring up at him, but glassily. And her hands were busy. They were busy pulling a streamer of toilet-paper from the roll, stuffing it into her mouth.

'She's gagging,' Rebus said, sliding back down. 'Stand back'. He shouldered the door, tried again. Stood back and hit the lock with the heel of his shoe. The door flew open, catching the seated woman on the knees. He pushed his way in. Her face was turning purple.

'Grab her hands,' he told the WPC. Then he started pulling the stream of white paper from her mouth, feeling like nothing so much as a cheap stage-show magician. There seemed to be half a roll in there, and as Rebus caught the WPC's eye, both of them let out a near-involuntary laugh. The woman had stopped struggling. Her hair was mousy-brown, lank and greasy. She wore a black skiing jacket and a tight black skirt. Her bare legs were mottled pink, bruising at one knee where the door had connected. Her bright red lipstick was coming off on Rebus's fingers. She had been crying, was crying still. Rebus, feeling guilty about the sudden laughter, crouched down so that he could look into her make-up-streaked eyes. She blinked, then held his gaze, coughing as the last of the paper was extracted.

'She's foreign,' the policewoman was explaining. 'Doesn't seem to speak English.'

'So how come she told you she needed the toilet?'

'There are ways, aren't there?'

'Where did you find her?'

'Down the Pleasance, brazen as you like.'

'That's a new patch on me.'

'Me, too.'

'Nobody with her?'

'Not that I saw.'

Rebus took the woman's hands. He was still crouching in front of her, aware of her knees brushing his chest.

'Are you all right?' She just blinked. He made his face show polite concern. 'OK now?'

She nodded slightly. 'OK,' she said, her voice husky. Rebus felt her fingers. They were cold. He was thinking: junkie? A lot of the working girls were. But he'd never come across one who couldn't speak English. Then he turned her hands, saw her wrists. Recent zigzag scar tissue. She didn't resist as he pushed up one sleeve of her jacket. The arm was a mass of similar inflictions.

'She's a cutter.'

The woman was talking now, babbling incoherently. Kirstin Mede, who had been standing back from proceedings, stepped forward. Rebus looked to her.

'It's not anything I understand . . . not quite. Eastern European.'

'Try her with something.'

So Mede asked a question in French, repeating it in three or four other languages. The woman seemed to understand what they were trying to do.

'There's probably someone at the uni who could help,' Mede said.

Rebus started to stand up. The woman grabbed him by the knees, pulled him to her so that he nearly lost his balance. Her grip was tight, her face resting against his legs. She was still crying and babbling.

'I think she likes you, sir,' the policewoman said. They wrested her hands free, and Rebus stepped back, but she was after him at once, throwing herself forwards, like she was begging, her voice rising. There was an audience now, half a dozen officers in the doorway. Every time Rebus moved, she came after him on all fours. Rebus looked to where his exit was blocked by bodies. The cheap magician had become straight man in a comedy routine. The WPC grabbed her, pulled her back on to her feet, one arm twisted behind her back.

'Come on,' she said through gritted teeth. 'Back to the cell. Show's over, folks.'

There was scattered applause as the prisoner was marched away. She looked back once, seeking Rebus, her eyes pleading. For what, he did not know. He turned towards Kirstin Mede instead.

'Fancy a curry some time?'

She looked at him like he was mad.

'Two things: one, she's a Bosnian Muslim. Two, she wants to see you again.'

Rebus stared at the man from the Slavic Studies department, who'd come here at Kirstin Mede's request. They were talking in the corridor at St Leonard's.

'Bosnian?'

Dr Colquhoun nodded. He was short and almost spherical, with long black hair which was swept back either side of a bald dome. His puffy face

was pockmarked, his brown suit worn and stained. He wore suede Hush Puppies – same colour as the suit. *This*, Rebus couldn't help feeling, was how dons were supposed to look. Colquhoun was a mass of nervous twitches, and had yet to make eye contact with Rebus.

'I'm not an expert on Bosnia,' he went on, 'but she says she's from Sarajevo.'

'Does she say how she ended up in Edinburgh?'

'I didn't ask.'

'Would you mind asking her now?' Rebus gestured back along the corridor. The two men walked together, Colquhoun's eyes on the floor.

'Sarajevo was hit hard in the war,' he said. 'She's twenty-two, by the way, she told me that.'

She'd looked older. Maybe she was; maybe she was lying. But as the door to the Interview Room opened and Rebus saw her again, he was struck by how unformed her face was, and he revised her age downwards. She stood up abruptly as he came in, looked like she might rush forward to him, but he held up a hand in warning, and pointed to the chair. She sat down again, hands cradling the mug of sweetened black tea. She never took her eyes off him.

'She's a big fan,' the WPC said. The policewoman – same one as the toilet incident – was called Ellen Sharpe. She was sitting on the room's other chair. There wasn't much space in the Interview Room: a table and two chairs just about filled it. On the table were twin video recorders and a twin cassette machine. The video camera pointed down from one wall. Rebus gestured for Sharpe to give her seat to Colquhoun.

'Did she give you a name?' he asked the academic.

'She told me Candice,' Colquhoun said.

'You don't believe her?'

'It's not exactly ethnic, Inspector.' Candice said something. 'She's calling you her protector.'

'And what am I protecting her from?'

The dialogue between Colquhoun and Candice was gruff, guttural.

'She says firstly you protected her from herself. And now she says you have to continue.'

'Continue protecting her?'

'She says you own her now.'

Rebus looked at the academic, whose eyes were on Candice's arms. She had removed her skiing jacket. Underneath she wore a ribbed, short-sleeved shirt through which her small breasts were visible. She had folded her bare arms, but the scratches and slashes were all too apparent.

'Ask her if those are self-inflicted.'

Colquhoun struggled with the translation. 'I'm more used to literature and film than . . . um . . .'

'What does she say?'

'She says she did them herself.'

Rebus looked at her for confirmation, and she nodded slowly, looking slightly ashamed.

'Who put her on the street?'

'You mean . . .?'

'Who's running her? Who's her manager?'

Another short dialogue.

'She says she doesn't understand.'

'Does she deny working as a prostitute?'

'She says she doesn't understand.'

Rebus turned to WPC Sharpe. 'Well?'

'A couple of cars stopped. She leaned in the window to talk with the drivers. They drove off again. Didn't like the look of the goods, I suppose.'

'If she can't speak English, how did she manage to "talk" to the drivers?'

'There are ways.'

Rebus looked at Candice. He began to speak to her, very softly. 'Straight fuck, fifteen, twenty for a blow job. Unprotected is an extra fiver.' He paused. 'How much is anal, Candice?'

Colour flooded her cheeks. Rebus smiled.

'Maybe not university tuition, Dr Colquhoun, but someone's taught her a few words of English. Just enough to get her working. Ask her again how she got here.'

Colquhoun mopped his face first. Candice spoke with her head lowered.

'She says she left Sarajevo as a refugee. Went to Amsterdam, then came to Britain. The first thing she remembers is a place with lots of bridges.'

'Bridges?'

'She stayed there for some time.' Colquhoun seemed shaken by the story. He handed her a handkerchief so she could wipe her eyes. She rewarded him with a smile. Then she looked at Rebus.

'Burger chips, yes?'

'Are you hungry?' Rebus rubbed his stomach. She nodded and smiled. He turned to Sharpe. 'See what the canteen can come up with, will you?'

The WPC gave him a hard stare, not wanting to leave. 'Would you like anything, Dr Colquhoun?'

He shook his head. Rebus asked for another coffee. As Sharpe left, Rebus crouched down by the table and looked at Candice. 'Ask her how she got to Edinburgh.'

Colquhoun asked, then listened to what sounded like a long tale. He scratched some notes on a folded sheet of paper.

'The city with the bridges, she says she didn't see much of it. She was kept inside. Sometimes she was driven to some rendezvous . . . You'll have to forgive me, Inspector. I may be a linguist, but I'm no expert on colloquialisms.'

'You're doing fine, sir.'

'Well, she was used as a prostitute, that much I can infer. And one day they put her in the back of a car, and she thought she was going to another hotel or office.'

'Office?'

'From her descriptions, I'd say some of her . . . work . . . was done in offices. Also private apartments and houses. But mostly hotel rooms.'

'Where was she kept?'

'In a house. She had a bedroom, they kept it locked.' Colquhoun pinched the bridge of his nose. 'They put her in the car one day, and next thing she knew she was in Edinburgh.'

'How long was the trip?'

'She's not sure. She slept part of the way.'

'Tell her everything's going to be all right.' Rebus paused. 'And ask her who she works for now.'

The fear returned to Candice's face. She stammered, shaking her head. Her voice sounded more guttural than ever. Colquhoun looked like he was having trouble with the translation.

'She can't tell you,' he said.

'Tell her she's safe.' Colquhoun did so. 'Tell her again,' Rebus said. He made sure she was looking at him while Colquhoun spoke. His face was set, a face she could trust. She reached a hand out to him. He took it, squeezed.

'Ask her again who she works for.'

'She can't tell you, Inspector. They'd kill her. She's heard stories.'

Rebus decided to try the name he'd been thinking of, the man who ran half the city's working girls.

'Cafferty,' he said, watching for a reaction. There was none. 'Big Ger. Big Ger Cafferty.' Her face remained blank. Rebus squeezed her hand again. There was another name . . . one he'd been hearing recently.

'Telford,' he said. 'Tommy Telford.'

Candice pulled her hand away and broke into hysterics, just as WPC Sharpe pushed open the door.

Rebus walked Dr Colquhoun out of the station, recalling that just such a walk had got him into this in the first place.

'Thanks again, sir. If I need you, I hope you won't mind if I call?'

'If you must, you must,' Colquhoun said grudgingly.

'Not too many Slavic specialists around,' Rebus said. He had Colquhoun's business card in his hand, a home phone number written on its back. 'Well,' Rebus put out his free hand, 'thanks again.' As they shook, Rebus thought of something.

'Were you at the university when Joseph Lintz was Professor of German?'

The question surprised Colquhoun. 'Yes,' he said at last.

'Did you know him?'

'Our departments weren't that close. I met him at a few social functions, the occasional lecture.'

'What did you think of him?'

Colquhoun blinked. He still wasn't looking at Rebus. 'They're saying he was a Nazi.'

'Yes, but back then . . .?'

'As I say, we weren't close. Are you investigating him?'

'Just curious, sir. Thanks for your time.'

Back in the station, Rebus found Ellen Sharpe outside the Interview Room door.

'So what do we do with her?' she asked.

'Keep her here.'

'You mean charge her?'

Rebus shook his head. 'Let's call it protective custody.'

'Does *she* know that?'

'Who's she going to complain to? There's only one bugger in the whole city can make out what she's saying, and I've just packed him off home.'

'What if her man comes to get her?'

'Think he will?'

She thought about it. 'Probably not.'

'No, because as far as he's concerned, all he has to do is wait, and we'll release her eventually. Meantime, she doesn't speak English, so what can she give us? And she's here illegally no doubt, so if she talks, all *we'd* probably do is kick her out of the country. Telford's clever . . . I hadn't realised it, but he is. Using illegal aliens as prossies. It's sweet.'

'How long do we keep her?'

Rebus shrugged.

'And what do I tell my boss?'

'Direct all inquiries to DI Rebus,' he said, going to open the door.

'I thought it was exemplary, sir.'

He stopped. 'What?'

'Your knowledge of the charge-scale for prostitutes.'

'Just doing my job,' he said, smiling.

'One last question, sir . . . ?'

'Yes, Sharpe?'

'Why? What's the big deal?'

Rebus considered this, twitched his nose. 'Good question,' he said finally, opening the door and going in.

And he knew. He knew straight away. She looked like Sammy. Wipe away the make-up and the tears, get some sensible clothes on her, and she was the spitting image.

And she was scared.

And maybe he could help her.

'What can I call you, Candice? What's your real name?'

She took hold of his hand, put her face to it. He pointed to himself.

'John,' he said.

'Don.'

'John.'

'Shaun.'

'John.' He was smiling; so was she. 'John.'

'John.'

He nodded. 'That's it. And you?' He pointed at her now. 'Who are you?'

She paused. 'Candice,' she said, as a little light died behind her eyes.

4

Rebus didn't know Tommy Telford by sight, but he knew where to find him.

Flint Street was a passageway between Clerk Street and Buccleuch Street, near the university. The shops had mostly closed down, but the games arcade always did good business, and from Flint Street Telford leased gaming machines to pubs and clubs across the city. Flint Street was the centre of his eastern empire.

The franchise had until recently belonged to a man called Davie Donaldson, but he'd suddenly retired on 'health grounds'. Maybe he'd been right at that: if Tommy Telford wanted something from you and you weren't forthcoming, predictions of your future health could suddenly change. Donaldson was now in hiding somewhere: hiding not from Telford but from Big Ger Cafferty, for whom he had been holding the franchise 'in trust' while Cafferty bided his time in Barlinnie jail. There were some who said Cafferty ran Edinburgh as effectively from inside as he ever had done outside, but the reality was that gangsters, like Nature, abhorred a vacuum, and now Tommy Telford was in town.

Telford was a product of Ferguslie Park in Paisley. At eleven he'd joined the local gang; at twelve a couple of woolly suits had visited him to ask about a spate of tyre slashings. They'd found him surrounded by other gang members, nearly all of them older than him, but he was at the centre, no doubt about it.

His gang had grown with him, taking over a sizeable chunk of Paisley, selling drugs and running prostitutes, doing a bit of extortion. These days he had shares in casinos and video shops, restaurants and a haulage firm, plus a property portfolio which made him landlord to several hundred people. He'd tried to make his mark in Glasgow, but had found it sealed down tight, so had gone exploring elsewhere. There were stories he'd become friendly with some big villain in Newcastle. Nobody could remember anything like it since the days when London's Krays had rented their muscle from 'Big Arthur' in Glasgow.

He'd arrived in Edinburgh a year ago, moving softly at first, buying a casino and hotel. Then suddenly he was inescapably *there*, like the shadow from a raincloud. With the chasing out of Davie Donaldson he'd given Cafferty a calculated punch to the gut. Cafferty could either fight or give up. Everyone was waiting for it to get messy . . .

The games arcade called itself Fascination Street. The machines were all flashing insistence, in stark contrast to the dead facial stares of the

players. Then there were shoot-'em-ups with huge video screens and digital imprecations.

'Think you're tough enough, punk?' one of them challenged as Rebus walked past. They had names like Harbinger and NecroCop, this latter reminding Rebus of how old he felt. He looked at the faces around him, saw a few he recognised, kids who'd been pulled into St Leonard's. They'd be on the fringes of Telford's gang, awaiting the call-up, hanging around like foster children, hoping The Family would take them. Most of them came from families who weren't families, latchkey kids grown old before their time.

One of the staff came in from the café.

'Who ordered the bacon sarnie?'

Rebus smiled as the faces turned to him. Bacon meant pig meant him. A moment's examination was all he warranted. There were more pressing demands on their attention. At the far end of the arcade were the really big machines: half-size motorbikes you sat astride as you negotiated the circuit on the screen in front of you. A small appreciative coterie stood around one bike, on which sat a young man dressed in a leather jacket. Not a market-stall jacket, something altogether more special. Quality goods. Shiny sharp-toed boots. Tight black denims. White polo neck. Surrounded by fawning courtiers. Steely Dan: 'Kid Charlemagne'. Rebus found a space for himself in the midst of the glaring onlookers.

'No takers for that bacon sarnie?' he asked.

'Who are you?' the man on the machine demanded.

'DI Rebus.'

'Cafferty's man.' Said with conviction.

'What?'

'I hear you and him go back.'

'I put him inside.'

'Not every cop gets visiting rights though.' Rebus realised that though Telford's gaze was fixed on the screen, he was watching Rebus in its reflection. Watching him, talking to him, yet still managing to control the bike through hairpin bends.

'So is there some problem, Inspector?'

'Yes, there's a problem. We picked up one of your girls.'

'My what?'

'She calls herself Candice. That's about as much as we know. But foreign lassies are a new one on me. And you're fairly new around here, too.'

'I'm not getting your drift, Inspector. I supply goods and services to the entertainment sector. Are you accusing me of being a pimp?'

Rebus stuck out a foot and pushed the bike sideways. On the screen, it spun and hit a crash barrier. A moment later, the screen changed. Back to the start of the race.

'See, Inspector,' Telford said, still not turning round. 'That's the beauty of games. You can always start again after an accident. Not so easy in real life.'

'What if I cut the power? Game over.'

Slowly, Telford swivelled from the hips. Now he was looking at Rebus. Close up, he looked so young. Most of the gangsters Rebus had known, they'd had a worn look, undernourished but overfed. Telford had the look of some new strain of bacteria, not yet tested or understood.

'So what is it, Rebus? Some message from Cafferty?'

'Candice,' Rebus said quietly, the slight tremor in his voice betraying his anger. With a couple of drinks in him, he'd have had Telford on the floor by now. 'From tonight, she's off the game, understood?'

'I don't know any Candice.'

'Understood?'

'Hang on, let's see if I've got this. You want me to agree with you that a woman I've never met should stop touting her hole?'

Smiles from the spectators. Telford turned back to his game. 'Where's this woman from anyway?' he asked, almost casually.

'We're not sure,' Rebus lied. He didn't want Telford knowing any more than was necessary.

'Must have been a great little chat the two of you had.'

'She's scared shitless.'

'Me, too, Rebus. I'm scared you're going to bore me to death. This Candice, did she give you a taste of the goods? I'm betting it's not every scrubber would get you this het up.'

Laughter, Rebus its brunt.

'She's off the game, Telford. Don't think about touching her.'

'Not with a bargepole, pal. Myself, I'm a clean-living sort of individual. I say my prayers last thing at night.'

'And kiss your cuddly bear?'

Telford looked at him again. 'Don't believe all the stories, Inspector. Here, grab a bacon sarnie on your way out, I think there's one going spare.' Rebus stood his ground a few moments longer, then turned away. 'And tell the mugs out front I said hello.'

Rebus walked back through the arcade and out into the night, heading for Nicolson Street. He was wondering what he was going to do with Candice. Simple answer: let her go, and hope she had the sense to keep moving. As he made to pass a parked car, its window slid down.

'Fucking well get in,' a voice ordered from the passenger seat. Rebus stopped, looked at the man who'd spoken, recognised the face.

'Ormiston,' he said, opening the back door of the Orion. 'Now I know what he meant.'

'Who?'

'Tommy Telford. I'm to tell you he said hello.'

The driver stared at Ormiston. 'Rumbled again.' He didn't sound surprised. Rebus recognised the voice.

'Hello, Claverhouse.'

DS Claverhouse, DC Ormiston: Scottish Crime Squad, Fettes's finest. On surveillance. Claverhouse: as thin as 'twa ply o' reek', as Rebus's father would have said. Ormiston: freckle-faced and with Mick McManus's hair – slick, pudding-bowl cut, unfeasibly black.

'You were blown before I walked in there, if that's any consolation.'

'What the fuck were you doing?'

'Paying my respects. What about you?'

'Wasting our time,' Ormiston muttered.

The Crime Squad were out for Telford: good news for Rebus.

'I've got someone,' he said. 'She works for Telford. She's frightened. You could help her.'

'The frightened ones don't talk.'

'This one might.'

Claverhouse stared at him. 'And all we'd have to do is . . .?'

'Get her out of here, set her up somewhere.'

'Witness relocation?'

'If it comes to that.'

'What does she know?'

'I'm not sure. Her English isn't great.'

Claverhouse knew when he was being sold something. 'Tell us,' he said.

Rebus told them. They tried not to look interested.

'We'll talk to her,' Claverhouse said.

Rebus nodded. 'So how long has this been going on?'

'Ever since Telford and Cafferty squared off.'

'And whose side are we on?'

'We're the UN, same as always,' Claverhouse said. He spoke slowly, measuring each word and phrase. A careful man, DS Claverhouse. 'Meantime, you go charging in like some bloody mercenary.'

'I've never been a great one for tactics. Besides, I wanted to see the bastard close up.'

'And?'

'He looks like a kid.'

'And he's as clean as a whistle,' Claverhouse said. 'He's got a dozen lieutenants who'd take the fall for him.'

At the word 'lieutenants', Rebus's mind flashed to Joseph Lintz. Some men gave orders, some carried them out: which group was the more culpable?

'Tell me something,' he said, 'the teddy bear story . . . is it true?'

Claverhouse nodded. 'In the passenger seat of his Range Rover. A fucking huge yellow thing, sort they raffle in the pub Sunday lunchtime.'

'So what's the story?'

Ormiston turned in his seat. 'Ever hear of Teddy Willocks? Glasgow hardman. Carpentry nails and a claw-hammer.'

Rebus nodded. 'You welched on someone, Willocks came to see you with the carpentry bag.'

'But then,' Claverhouse took over, 'Teddy got on the wrong side of some Geordie bastard. Telford was young, making a name for himself, and he very badly wanted an in with this Geordie, so he took care of Teddy.'

'And that's why he carries a teddy around with him,' Ormiston said. 'A reminder to everyone.'

Rebus was thinking. Geordie meant someone from Newcastle. Newcastle, with its bridges over the Tyne . . .

'Newcastle,' he said softly, leaning forward in his seat.

'What about it?'

'Maybe Candice was there. Her city of bridges. She might link Telford to this Geordie gangster.'

Ormiston and Claverhouse looked at one another.

'She'll need a safe place to stay,' Rebus told them. 'Money, somewhere to go afterwards.'

'A first-class flight home if she helps us nail Telford.'

'I'm not sure she'll want to go home.'

'That's for later,' Claverhouse said. 'First thing is to talk to her.'

'You'll need a translator.'

Claverhouse looked at him. 'And of course you know just the man . . . ?'

She was asleep in her cell, curled under the blanket, only her hair visible. The Mothers of Invention: 'Lonely Little Girl'. The cell was in the women's block. Painted pink and blue, a slab to sleep on, graffiti scratched into the walls.

'Candice,' Rebus said quietly, squeezing her shoulder. She started awake, as if he'd administered an electric shock. 'It's OK, it's me, John.'

She looked round blindly, focused on him slowly. 'John,' she said. Then she smiled.

Claverhouse was off making phone calls, squaring things. Ormiston stood in the doorway, appraising Candice. Not that Ormiston was known to be choosy. Rebus had tried Colquhoun at home, but there'd been no answer. So now Rebus was gesturing, letting her know they wanted to take her somewhere.

'A hotel,' he said.

She didn't like that word. She looked from him to Ormiston and back again.

'It's OK,' Rebus said. 'It's just a place for you to sleep, that's all, somewhere safe. No Telford, nothing like that.'

She seemed to soften, came off the bed and stood in front of him. Her eyes seemed to say, I'll trust you, and if you let me down I won't be surprised.

Claverhouse came back. 'All fixed,' he said, his examination falling on Candice. 'She doesn't speak any English?'

'Not as practised in polite society.'

'In that case,' Ormiston said, 'she should be fine with us.'

Three men and a young woman in a dark blue Ford Orion, heading south out of the city. It was late now, past midnight, black taxis cruising. Students were spilling from pubs.

'They get younger every year.' Claverhouse was never short of a cliché.

'And more of them end up joining the force,' Rebus commented.

Claverhouse smiled. 'I meant prossies, not students. We pulled one in last week, said she was fifteen. Turned out she was twelve, on the run. All grown-up about it.'

Rebus tried to remember Sammy at twelve. He saw her scared, in the clutches of a madman with a grievance against Rebus. She'd had lots of nightmares afterwards, till her mother had taken her to London. Rhona had phoned Rebus a few years later. She just wanted to let him know he'd robbed Sammy of her childhood.

'I phoned ahead,' Claverhouse said. 'Don't worry, we've used this place before. It's perfect.'

'She'll need some clothes,' Rebus said.

'Siobhan can fetch her some in the morning.'

'How is Siobhan?'

'Seems fine. Hasn't half cut into the jokes and the language though.'

'Ach, she can take a joke,' Ormiston said. 'Likes a drink, too.'

This last was news to Rebus. He wondered how much Siobhan Clarke would change in order to blend with her new surroundings.

'It's just off the bypass,' Claverhouse said, meaning their destination. 'Not far now.'

The city ended suddenly. Green belt, plus the Pentland Hills. The bypass was quiet, Ormiston doing the ton between exits. They came off at Colinton and signalled into the hotel. It was a motorist's stop, one of a nationwide chain: same prices, same rooms. The cars which crowded the parking area were salesmen's specials, cigarette packets littering the passenger seats. The reps would be sleeping, or lying in a daze with the TV remote to hand.

Candice seemed reluctant to get out of the car, until she saw that Rebus was coming, too.

'You light up her life,' Ormiston offered.

At reception, they signed her in as one half of a couple – Mrs Angus Campbell. The two Crime Squad cops had the routine off pat. Rebus watched the hotel clerk, but a wink from Claverhouse told him the man was OK.

'Make it the first floor, Malcolm,' Ormiston said. 'Don't want anyone peeking in the windows.'

Room number 20. 'Will someone be with her?' Rebus asked as they climbed the stairs.

'Right there in the room,' Claverhouse said. 'The landing's too obvious, and we'd freeze our bums off in the car. Did you give me Colquhoun's number?'

'Ormiston has it.'

Ormiston was unlocking the door. 'Who's on first watch?'

Claverhouse shrugged. Candice was looking towards Rebus, seeming to sense what was being discussed. She snatched at his arm, jabbering in her native tongue, looking first to Claverhouse and then to Ormiston, all the time waving Rebus's arm.

'It's OK, Candice, really. They'll take care of you.'

She kept shaking her head, holding him with one hand and pointing at him with the other, prodding his chest to make her meaning clear.

'What do you say, John?' Claverhouse asked. 'A happy witness is a willing witness.'

'What time's Siobhan expected?'

'I'll hurry her up.'

Rebus looked at Candice again, sighed, nodded. 'OK.' He pointed to himself, then to the room. 'Just for a little while, OK?'

Candice seemed satisfied with this, and went inside. Ormiston handed Rebus the key.

'I don't want you young things waking the neighbours now . . .'

Rebus closed the door on his face.

The room was exactly as expected. Rebus filled the kettle and switched it on, dumped a tea-bag into a cup. Candice pointed to the bathroom, made turning motions with her hands.

'A bath?' He gestured with his arm. 'Go ahead.'

The curtain over the window was closed. He parted it and looked out. A grassy slope, occasional lights from the bypass. He made sure the curtains were closed tight, then tried adjusting the heating. The room was stifling. There didn't seem to be a thermostat, so he went back to the window and opened it a fraction. Cold night air, and the swish of nearby traffic. He

opened the pack of custard creams, two small biscuits. Suddenly he felt ravenous. He'd seen a snack machine in the lobby. Plenty of change in his pockets. He made the tea, added milk, sat down on the sofa. For want of any other distractions, he turned the TV on. The tea was fine. The tea was absolutely fine, no complaints there. He picked up the phone and called Jack Morton.

'Did I wake you?'

'Not really. How's it going?'

'I wanted a drink today.'

'So what's new?'

Rebus could hear his friend making himself comfortable. Jack had helped Rebus get off the booze. Jack had said he could phone any time he liked.

'I had to talk to this scumbag, Tommy Telford.'

'I know the name.'

Rebus lit a cigarette. 'I think a drink would have helped.'

'Before or after?'

'Both.' Rebus smiled. 'Guess where I am now?'

Jack couldn't, so Rebus told him the story.

'What's your angle?' Jack asked.

'I don't know.' Rebus thought about it. 'She seems to need me. It's been a long time since anyone's felt like that.' As he said the words, he feared they didn't tell the whole story. He remembered another argument with Rhona, her screaming that he'd exploited every relationship he'd ever had.

'Do you still want that drink?' Jack was asking.

'I'm a long way from one.' Rebus stubbed out his cigarette. 'Sweet dreams, Jack.'

He was on his second cup of tea when she came back in, wearing the same clothes, her hair wet and hanging in rat's-tails.

'Better?' he asked, making the thumbs-up sign. She nodded, smiling. 'Do you want some tea?' He pointed to the kettle. She nodded again, so he made her a cup. Then he suggested a trip to the snack machine. Their haul included crisps, nuts, chocolate, and a couple of cans of Coke. Another cup of tea finished off the tiny cartons of milk. Rebus lay along the sofa, shoes off, watching soundless television. Candice lay on the bed, fully-clothed, sliding the occasional crisp from its packet, flicking channels. She seemed to have forgotten he was there. He took this as a compliment.

He must have fallen asleep. The touch of her fingers on his knee brought him awake. She was standing in front of him, wearing the T-shirt and nothing else. She stared at him, fingers still resting on his knee. He smiled, shook his head, led her back to bed. Made her lie down. She lay on her back, arms stretched. He shook his head again and pulled the duvet over her.

'That's not you any more,' he told her. 'Goodnight, Candice.'

Rebus retreated to the sofa, lay down again, and wished she would stop saying his name.

The Doors: 'Wishful Sinful' . . .

A tapping at the door brought him awake. Still dark outside. He'd forgotten to close the window, and the room was cold. The TV was still playing, but Candice was asleep, duvet kicked off, chocolate wrappers

strewn around her bare legs and thighs. Rebus covered her up, then tiptoed to the door, peered through the spyhole, and opened up.

'For this relief, much thanks,' he whispered to Siobhan Clarke.

She was carrying a bulging polythene bag. 'Thank God for the twenty-four-hour shop.' They went inside. Clarke looked at the sleeping woman, then went over to the sofa and started unpacking the bag.

'For you,' she whispered, 'a couple of sandwiches.'

'God bless the child.'

'For sleeping beauty, some of my clothes. They'll do till the shops open.'

Rebus was already biting into the first sandwich. Cheese salad on white bread had never tasted finer.

'How am I getting home?' he asked.

'I called you a cab.' She checked her watch. 'It'll be here in two minutes.'

'What would I do without you?'

'It's a toss-up: either freeze to death or starve.' She closed the window. 'Now go on, get out of here.'

He looked at Candice one last time, almost wanting to wake her to let her know he wasn't leaving for good. But she was sleeping so soundly, and Siobhan could take care of everything.

So he tucked the second sandwich into his pocket, tossed the room-key on to the sofa, and left.

Four-thirty. The taxi was idling outside. Rebus felt hungover. He went through a mental list of all the places he could get a drink at this time of night. He didn't know how many days it had been since he'd had a drink. He wasn't counting.

He gave his address to the cabbie, and settled back, thinking again of Candice, so soundly asleep, and protected for now. And of Sammy, too old now to need anything from her father. She'd be asleep too, snuggling into Ned Farlowe. Sleep was innocence. Even the city looked innocent in sleep. He looked at the city sometimes and saw a beauty his cynicism couldn't touch. Someone in a bar – recently? years back? – had challenged him to define romance. How could he do that? He'd seen too much of love's obverse: people killed for passion and from lack of it. So that now when he saw beauty, he could do little but respond to it with the realisation that it would fade or be brutalised. He saw lovers in Princes Street Gardens and imagined them further down the road, at the crossroads where betrayal and conflict met. He saw valentines in the shops and imagined puncture wounds, real hearts bleeding.

Not that he'd voiced any of this to his public bar inquisitor.

'Define romance,' had been the challenge. And Rebus's response? He'd picked up a fresh pint of beer and kissed the glass.

He slept till nine, showered and made some coffee. Then he phoned the hotel, and Siobhan assured him all was well.

'She was a bit startled when she woke up and saw me instead of you. Kept saying your name. I told her she'd see you again.'

'So what's the plan?'

'Shopping – one quick swoop on The Gyle. After that, Fettes. Dr Colquhoun's coming in at noon for an hour. We'll see what we get.'

Rebus was at his window, looking down on a damp Arden Street. 'Take care of her, Siobhan.'

'No problem.'

Rebus knew there'd be no problem, not with Siobhan. This was her first real action with the Crime Squad, she'd be doing her damnedest to make it a success. He was in the kitchen when the phone rang.

'Is that Inspector Rebus?'

'Who's speaking?' A voice he didn't recognise.

'Inspector, my name is David Levy. We've never met. I apologise for calling you at home. I was given this number by Matthew Vanderhyde.'

Old man Vanderhyde: Rebus hadn't seen him in a while.

'Yes?'

'I must say, I was astonished when it transpired he knew you.' The voice was tinged with a dry humour. 'But by now nothing about Matthew should surprise me. I went to him because he knows Edinburgh.'

'Yes?'

Laughter on the line. 'I'm sorry, Inspector. I can't blame you for being suspicious when I've made such a mess of the introductions. I am a historian by profession. I've been contacted by Solomon Mayerlink to see if I might offer assistance.'

Mayerlink . . . Rebus knew the name. Placed it: Mayerlink ran the Holocaust Investigation Bureau.

'And exactly what "assistance" does Mr Mayerlink think I need?'

'Perhaps we could discuss it in person, Inspector. I'm staying in a hotel on Charlotte Square.'

'The Roxburghe?'

'Could we meet there? This morning, ideally.'

Rebus looked at his watch. 'An hour?' he suggested.

'Perfect. Goodbye, Inspector.'

Rebus called into the office, told them where he'd be.

5

They sat in the Roxburghe's lounge, Levy pouring coffee. An elderly couple in the far corner, beside the window, pored over sections of newspaper. David Levy was elderly, too. He wore black-rimmed glasses and had a small silver beard. His hair was a silver halo around a scalp the colour of tanned leather. His eyes seemed constantly moist, as if he'd just chewed on an onion. He sported a dun-coloured safari suit with blue shirt and tie beneath. His walking-stick rested against his chair. Now retired, he'd worked in Oxford, New York State, Tel Aviv itself, and several other locations around the globe.

'I never came into contact with Joseph Lintz, however. No reason why I should, our interests being different.'

'So why does Mr Mayerlink think you can help me?'

Levy put the coffee pot back on its tray. 'Milk? Sugar?' Rebus shook his head to both, then repeated his question.

'Well, Inspector,' Levy said, tipping two spoonfuls of sugar into his own cup, 'it's more a matter of moral support.'

'Moral support?'

'You see, many people before you have been in the same position in which you now find yourself. I'm talking about objective people, professionals with no axe to grind, and no real stake in the investigation.'

Rebus bristled. 'If you're suggesting I'm not doing my job . . .'

A pained look crossed Levy's face. 'Please, Inspector, I'm not making a very good job of this, am I? What I mean is that there will be times when you will doubt the validity of what you are doing. You'll doubt its worth.' His eyes gleamed. 'Perhaps you've already had doubts?'

Rebus said nothing. He had a drawerful of doubts, especially now that he had a real, living, breathing case – Candice. Candice, who might lead to Tommy Telford.

'You could say I'm here as your conscience, Inspector.' Levy winced again. 'No, I didn't put that right, either. You already have a conscience, that's not under debate.' He sighed. 'The question you've no doubt been pondering is the same one I've asked myself on occasions: can time wash away responsibility? For me, the answer would have to be no. The thing is this, Inspector.' Levy leaned forward. 'You are not investigating the crimes of an old man, but those of a young man who now happens to be old. Focus your mind on that. There have been investigations before, half-hearted affairs. Governments wait for these men to die rather than have to try

them. But each investigation is an act of remembrance, and remembrance is never wasted. Remembrance is the only way we learn.'

'Like we've learned with Bosnia?'

'You're right, Inspector, as a species we've always been slow to take in lessons. Sometimes they have to be hammered home.'

'And you think I'm your carpenter? Were there Jews in Villefranche?' Rebus couldn't remember reading of any.

'Does it matter?'

'I'm just wondering, why the interest?'

'To be honest, Inspector, there is a slight ulterior motive.' Levy sipped coffee, considering his words. 'The Rat Line. We'd like to show that it existed, that it operated to save Nazis from possible tormentors.' He paused. 'That it worked with the tacit approval – the *more* than tacit approval – of several western governments and even the Vatican. It's a question of general complicity.'

'What you want is for everyone to feel guilty?'

'We want recognition, Inspector. We want the truth. Isn't that what you want? Matthew Vanderhyde would have me believe it is your guiding principle.'

'He doesn't know me very well.'

'I wouldn't be so sure of that. Meantime, there are people out there who want the truth to stay hidden.'

'The truth being . . .?'

'That known war criminals were brought back to Britain – and elsewhere – and offered new lives, new identities.'

'In exchange for what?'

'The Cold War was starting, Inspector. You know the old saying: My enemy's enemy is my friend. These murderers were protected by the secret services. Military Intelligence offered them jobs. There are people who would rather this did not become general knowledge.'

'So?'

'So a trial, an open trial, would expose them.'

'You're warning me about spooks?'

Levy put his hands together, almost in an attitude of prayer. 'Look, I'm not sure this has been a completely satisfactory meeting, and for that I apologise. I'll be staying here for a few days, maybe longer if necessary. Could we try this again?'

'I don't know.'

'Well, think about it, won't you?' Levy extended his right hand. Rebus took it. 'I'll be right here, Inspector. Thank you for seeing me.'

'Take care, Mr Levy.'

'*Shalom*, Inspector.'

At his desk, Rebus could still feel Levy's handshake. Surrounded by the Villefranche files, he felt like the curator of some museum visited only by specialists and cranks. Evil had been done in Villefranche, but had Joseph Lintz been responsible? And even if he had, had he perhaps atoned during the past half-century? Rebus phoned the Procurator Fiscal's office to let them know how little progress he was making. They thanked him for calling. Then he went to see the Farmer.

'Come in, John, what can I do for you?'

'Sir, did you know the Crime Squad had set up a surveillance on our patch?'

'You mean Flint Street?'

'So you know about it?'

'They keep me informed.'

'Who's acting as liaison?'

The Farmer frowned. 'As I say, John, they keep me informed.'

'So there's no liaison at street level?' The Farmer stayed silent. 'By rights there should be, sir.'

'What are you getting at, John?'

'I want the job.'

The Farmer stared at his desk. 'You're busy on Villefranche.'

'I want the job, sir.'

'John, liaison means diplomacy. It's never been your strongest suit.'

So Rebus explained about Candice, and how he was already tied into the case. 'And since I'm already in, sir,' he concluded, 'I might as well act as liaison.'

'What about Villefranche?'

'That remains a priority, sir.'

The Farmer looked into his eyes. Rebus didn't blink. 'All right then,' he said at last.

'You'll let Fettes know?'

'I'll let them know.'

'Thank you, sir.' Rebus turned to leave.

'John . . .?' The Farmer was standing behind his desk. 'You know what I'm going to say.'

'You're going to tell me not to tread on too many toes, not to go off on my own little crusade, to keep in regular contact with you, and not betray your trust in me. Does that just about do it, sir?'

The Farmer shook his head, smiling. 'Bugger off,' he said.

Rebus buggered off.

When he walked into the room, Candice rose so quickly from her chair that it fell to the floor. She came forward and gave him a hug, while Rebus looked at the faces around them – Ormiston, Claverhouse, Dr Colquhoun, and a WPC.

They were in an Interview Room at Fettes, Lothian and Borders Police HQ. Colquhoun was wearing the same suit as the previous day and the same nervous look. Ormiston was picking up Candice's chair. He'd been standing against one wall. Claverhouse was seated at the table beside Colquhoun, a pad of paper in front of him, pen poised above it.

'She says she's happy to see you,' Colquhoun translated.

'I'd never have guessed.' Candice was wearing new clothes: denims too long for her and turned up four inches at the ankle; a black woollen V-neck jumper. Her skiing jacket was hanging over the back of her chair.

'Get her to sit down again, will you?' Claverhouse said. 'We're pushed for time.'

There was no chair for Rebus, so he stood next to Ormiston and the WPC. Candice went back to the story she'd been telling, but glanced

regularly towards him. He noticed that beside Claverhouse's pad of paper sat a brown folder and an A4-sized envelope. On top of the envelope sat a black and white surveillance shot of Tommy Telford.

'This man,' Claverhouse asked, tapping the photo, 'she knows him?'

Colquhoun asked, then listened to her answer. 'She . . .' He cleared his throat. 'She hasn't had any direct dealings with him.' Her two-minute commentary reduced to this. Claverhouse dipped into the envelope, spread more photos before her. Candice tapped one of them.

'Pretty-Boy,' Claverhouse said. He picked up the photo of Telford again. 'But she's had dealings with this man, too?'

'She's . . .' Colquhoun mopped his face. 'She's saying something about Japanese people . . . Oriental businessmen.'

Rebus shared a look with Ormiston, who shrugged.

'Where was this?' Claverhouse asked.

'In a car . . . more than one car. You know, a sort of convoy.'

'She was in one of the cars?'

'Yes.'

'Where did they go?'

'They headed out of town, stopping once or twice.'

'Juniper Green,' Candice said, quite clearly.

'Juniper Green,' Colquhoun repeated.

'They stopped there?'

'No, they stopped before that.'

'To do what?'

Colquhoun spoke with Candice again. 'She doesn't know. She thinks one of the drivers went into a shop for some cigarettes. The others all seemed to be looking at a building, as if they were interested in it, but not saying anything.'

'What building?'

'She doesn't know.'

Claverhouse looked exasperated. She wasn't giving him much of anything, and Rebus knew that if there was nothing she could trade, Crime Squad would dump her straight back on the street. Colquhoun was all wrong for this job, completely out of his depth.

'Where did they go after Juniper Green?'

'Just drove around the countryside. For two or three hours, she thinks. They would stop sometimes and get out, but just to look at the scenery. Lots of hills and . . .' Colquhoun checked something. 'Hills and flags.'

'Flags? Flying from buildings?'

'No, stuck into the ground.'

Claverhouse gave Ormiston a look of hopelessness.

'Golf courses,' Rebus said. 'Try describing a golf course to her, Dr Colquhoun.'

Colquhoun did so, and she nodded agreement, beaming at Rebus. Claverhouse was looking at him, too.

'Just a guess,' Rebus said with a shrug. 'Japanese businessmen, it's what they like about Scotland.'

Claverhouse turned back to Candice. 'Ask her if she . . . accommodated any of these men.'

Colquhoun cleared his throat again, colour flooding his cheeks as he

spoke. Candice looked down at the table, moved her head in the affirmative, started to speak.

'She says that's why she was there. She was fooled at first. She thought maybe they just wanted a pretty woman to look at. They had a nice lunch . . . the beautiful drive . . . But then they came back into town, dropped the Japanese off at a hotel, and she was taken up to one of the hotel rooms. Three of them . . . she, as you put it yourself, DS Claverhouse, she "accommodated" three of them.'

'Does she remember the name of the hotel?'

She didn't.

'Where did they have lunch?'

'A restaurant next to flags and . . .' Colquhoun corrected himself. 'Next to a golf course.'

'How long ago was this?'

'Two or three weeks.'

'And how many of them were there?'

Colquhoun checked. 'The three Japanese, and maybe four other men.'

'Ask her how long she's been in Edinburgh,' Rebus asked.

Colquhoun did so. 'She thinks maybe a month.'

'A month working the street . . . funny we haven't picked her up.'

'She was put there as a punishment.'

'For what?' Claverhouse asked. Rebus had the answer.

'For making herself ugly.' He turned to Candice. 'Ask her why she cuts herself.'

Candice looked at him and shrugged.

'What's your point?' Ormiston asked.

'She thinks the scars will deter punters. Which means she doesn't like the life she's been leading.'

'And helping us is her only sure ticket out?'

'Something like that.'

So Colquhoun asked her again, then said: 'They don't like that she does it. That's why she does it.'

'Tell her if she helps us, she won't ever have to do anything like that again.'

Colquhoun translated, glancing at his watch.

'Does the name Newcastle mean anything to her?' Claverhouse asked.

Colquhoun tried the name. 'I've explained to her that it's a town in England, built on a river.'

'Don't forget the bridges,' Rebus said.

Colquhoun added a few words, but Candice only shrugged. She looked upset that she was failing them. Rebus gave her another smile.

'What about the man she worked for?' Claverhouse asked. 'The one before she came to Edinburgh.'

She seemed to have plenty to say about this, and kept touching her face with her fingers while she talked. Colquhoun nodded, made her stop from time to time so he could translate.

'A big man . . . fat. He was the boss. Something about his skin . . . a birthmark maybe, certainly something distinctive. And glasses, like sunglasses but not quite.'

Rebus saw Claverhouse and Ormiston exchange another look. It was all

too vague to be much use. Colquhoun checked his watch again. 'And cars, a lot of cars. This man crashed them.'

'Maybe he got a scar on his face,' Ormiston offered.

'Glasses and a scar aren't going to get us very far,' Claverhouse added.

'Gentlemen,' Colquhoun said, while Candice looked towards Rebus, 'I'm afraid I'm going to have to leave.'

'Any chance of coming back in later, sir?' Claverhouse asked.

'You mean today?'

'I thought maybe this evening . . .?'

'Look, I do have other commitments.'

'We appreciate that, sir. Meantime, DC Ormiston will run you back into town.'

'My pleasure,' Ormiston said, all charm. They needed Colquhoun, after all. They had to keep him sweet.

'One thing,' Colquhoun said. 'There's a refugee family in Fife. From Sarajevo. They'd probably take her in. I could ask.'

'Thank you, sir,' Claverhouse said. 'Maybe later on, eh?'

Colquhoun seemed disappointed as Ormiston led him away.

Rebus walked over to Claverhouse, who was shuffling his photos together.

'Bit of an oddball,' Claverhouse commented.

'Not used to the real world.'

'Not much help either.'

Rebus looked towards Candice. 'Mind if I take her out?'

'What?'

'Just for an hour.' Claverhouse stared at him. 'She's been cooped up here, and only her hotel room to look forward to. I'll drop her back there in an hour, hour and a half.'

'Bring her back in one piece, preferably with a smile on her face.'

Rebus motioned for Candice to join him.

'Japanese and golf courses,' Claverhouse mused. 'What do you think?'

'Telford's a businessman, we know that. Businessmen do deals with other businessmen.'

'He runs bouncers and slot machines: what's the Japanese connection?'

Rebus shrugged. 'I leave the hard questions to the likes of you.' He opened the door.

'And John?' Claverhouse warned, nodding towards Candice. 'She's Crime Squad property, OK? And remember, *you* came to *us*.'

'No bother, Claverhouse. And by the way, I'm your B Division liaison.'

'Since when?'

'With immediate effect. If you don't believe me, ask your boss. This might be your case, but Telford works out of *my* territory.'

He took Candice by the arm and marched her from the room.

He stopped the car on the corner of Flint Street.

'It's OK, Candice,' he said, seeing her agitation. 'We're staying in the car. Everything's all right.' Her eyes were darting around, looking for faces she didn't want to see. Rebus started the car again and drove off. 'Look,' he told her, 'we're leaving.' Knowing she couldn't understand. 'I'm guessing this is where you started from that day.' He looked at her. 'The day you

went to Juniper Green. The Japanese would be staying in a central hotel, somewhere pricey. You picked them up, then headed east. Along Dalry Road maybe?' He was speaking for his own benefit. 'Christ, I don't know. Look, Candice, anything you see, anything that looks familiar, just let me know, OK?'

'OK.'

Had she understood? No, she was smiling. All she'd heard was that final word. All she knew was that they were heading away from Flint Street. He took her down on to Princes Street first.

'Was it a hotel here, Candice? The Japanese? Was it here?' She gazed from the window with a blank look.

He headed up Lothian Road. 'Usher Hall,' he said. 'Sheraton . . . Any of it ring a bell?' Nothing did. Out along the Western Approach Road, Slateford Road, and on to Lanark Road. Most of the lights were against them, giving her plenty of time to study the buildings. Each newsagent's they passed, Rebus pointed it out, just in case the convoy had paused there to buy cigarettes. Soon they were out of town and entering Juniper Green.

'Juniper Green!' she said, pointing at the signpost, delighted to have something to show him. Rebus attempted a smile. There were plenty of golf courses around the city. He couldn't hope to take her to every one of them, not in a week never mind an hour. He stopped for a few moments by the side of a field. Candice got out, so he followed, lit a cigarette. There were two stone gateposts next to the road, but no sign of a gate between them, or any sort of path behind them. Once there might have been a track, and a house at the end of it. Atop one of the pillars sat the badly worn representation of a bull. Candice pointed towards the ground behind the other pillar, where another lump of carved stone lay, half-covered by weeds and grass.

'Looks like a serpent,' Rebus said. 'Maybe a dragon.' He looked at her. 'It'll all mean something to somebody.' She looked back at him blankly. He saw Sammy's features, reminded himself that he wanted to help her. He was in danger of letting that slip, of focusing on how she might help them get to Telford.

Back in the car, he branched off towards Livingston, intending to head for Ratho and from there back into town. Then he noticed that Candice had turned to look out of the back window.

'What is it?'

She came out with a stream of words, her tone uncertain. Rebus turned the car anyway, and drove slowly back the way they'd just come. He stopped at the side of the road, opposite a low dry-stone wall, beyond which lay the undulations of a golf course.

'Recognise it?' She mumbled more words. Rebus pointed. 'Here? Yes?' She turned to him, said something which sounded apologetic.

'It's OK,' he told her. 'Let's take a closer look anyway.' He drove to where a vast iron double-gate stood open. A sign to one side read POYNTING-HAME GOLF AND COUNTRY CLUB. Beneath it: 'Bar Lunches and A La Carte, Visitors Welcome'. As Rebus drove through the gates, Candice started nodding again, and when an oversized Georgian house came into view she almost bounced in her seat, slapping her hands against her thighs.

'I think I get the picture,' Rebus said.

He parked outside the main entrance, squeezing between a Volvo estate and a low-slung Toyota. Out on the course, three men were finishing their round. As the final putt went in, hands went to wallets and money changed hands.

Two things Rebus knew about golf: one, to some people it was a religion; two, a lot of players liked a bet. They'd bet on final tally, each hole, even every shot if they could.

And didn't the Japanese have a passion for gambling?

He took Candice's arm as he escorted her into the main building. Piano music from the bar. Panatella smoke and oak-panelling. Huge portraits of self-important unknowns. A few old wooden putters, framed behind glass. A poster advertised a Halloween dinner-dance for that evening. Rebus walked up to reception, explained who he was and what he wanted. The receptionist made a phone call, then led them to the Chief Executive's office.

Hugh Malahide, bald and thin, mid-forties, already had a slight stammer, which intensified when Rebus asked his first question. By throwing it back at the questioner, he seemed to be playing for time.

'Have we had any Japanese visitors recently? Well, we do get a few golfers.'

'These men came to lunch. Maybe a fortnight, three weeks back. There were three of them, plus three or four Scottish men. Probably driving Range Rovers. The table may have been reserved in the name of Telford.'

'Telford?'

'Thomas Telford.'

'Ah, yes . . .' Malahide wasn't enjoying this at all.

'You know Mr Telford?'

'In a manner of speaking.'

Rebus leaned forward in his chair. 'Go on.'

'Well, he's . . . look, the reason I seem so reticent is because we don't want this made common knowledge.'

'I understand, sir.'

'Mr Telford is acting as go-between.'

'Go-between?'

'In the negotiations.'

Rebus saw what Malahide was getting at. 'The Japanese want to buy Poyntinghame?'

'You understand, Inspector, I'm just the manager here. I mean, I run the day-to-day business.'

'But you're the Chief Executive.'

'With no personal share in the club. The actual owners were set against selling at first. But an offer has been made, and I believe it's a very good one. And the potential buyers . . . well, they're persistent.'

'Have there been any threats, Mr Malahide?'

He looked horrified. 'What sort of threats?'

'Forget it.'

'The negotiations haven't been *hostile*, if that's what you mean.'

'So these Japanese, the ones who had lunch here . . . ?'

'They were representing the consortium.'

'The consortium being . . . ?'

'I don't know. The Japanese are always very secretive. Some big company or corporation, I'd guess.'

'Any idea why they want Poyntinghame?'

'I've wondered that myself.'

'And?'

'Everyone knows the Japanese love golf. It might be a prestige thing. Or it could be that they're opening a plant of some kind in Livingston.'

'And Poyntinghame would become the factory social club?'

Malahide shivered at the thought. Rebus got to his feet.

'You've been very helpful, sir. Anything else you can tell me?'

'Look, this has been off the record, Inspector.'

'I've no problem with that. I don't suppose you've got any names?'

'Names?'

'Of the diners that day.'

Malahide shook his head. 'I'm sorry, not even credit card details. Mr Telford paid cash as usual.'

'Did he leave a big tip?'

'Inspector,' smiling, 'some secrets are sacrosanct.'

'Let's keep this conversation that way, too, sir, all right?'

Malahide looked at Candice. 'She's a prostitute, isn't she? I thought as much the day they were here.' There was revulsion in his voice. 'Tarty little thing, aren't you?'

Candice stared at him, looked to Rebus for help, said a few words neither man understood.

'What's she saying?' Malahide asked.

'She says she once had a punter who looked just like you. He dressed in plus-fours and made her whack him with a mashie-niblick.'

Malahide showed them out.

6

Rebus telephoned Claverhouse from Candice's room.

'Could be something or nothing,' Claverhouse said, but Rebus could tell he was interested, which was good: the longer he stayed interested, the longer he'd want to hang on to Candice. Ormiston was on his way to the hotel to resume babysitting duties.

'What I want to know is, how the hell did Telford land something like this?'

'Good question,' Claverhouse said.

'It's way out of his previous sphere, isn't it?'

'As far as we know.'

'A chauffeur service for Jap companies . . .'

'Maybe he's after the contract to supply their gaming machines.'

Rebus shook his head. 'I still don't get it.'

'Not your problem, John, remember that.'

'I suppose so.' There was a knock at the door. 'Sounds like Ormiston.'

'I doubt it. He's just left.'

Rebus stared at the door. 'Claverhouse, wait on the line.'

He left the receiver on the bedside table. The knock was repeated. Rebus motioned for Candice, who'd been flicking through a magazine on the sofa, to move into the bathroom. Then he crept up to the door and put his eye to the spyhole. A woman: the day-shift receptionist. He unlocked the door.

'Yes?'

'Letter for your wife.'

He stared at the small white envelope which she was trying to hand him.

'Letter,' she repeated.

There was no name or address on the envelope, no stamp. Rebus took it and held it to the light. A single sheet of paper inside, and something flat and square, like a photograph.

'A man handed it in at reception.'

'How long ago?'

'Two, three minutes.'

'What did he look like?'

She shrugged. 'Tallish, short brown hair. He was wearing a suit, took the letter out of a briefcase.'

'How do you know who it's for?'

'He said it was for the foreign woman. He described her to a T.'

Rebus was staring at the envelope. 'OK, thanks,' he mumbled. He closed the door, went back to the telephone.

'What is it?' Claverhouse asked.

'Someone's just dropped off a letter for Candice.' Rebus tore open the envelope, holding the receiver between shoulder and chin. There was a Polaroid photo and a single sheet, handwritten in small capitals. Foreign words.

'What does it say?' Claverhouse asked.

'I don't know.' Rebus tried a couple of words aloud. Candice had emerged from the bathroom. She snatched the paper from him and read it quickly, then fled back into the bathroom.

'It means something to Candice,' Rebus said. 'There's a photo, too.' He looked at it. 'She's on her knees gamming some fat bloke.'

'Description?'

'The camera's not exactly interested in his face. Claverhouse, we've got to get her away from here.'

'Hang on till Ormiston arrives. They might be trying to panic you. If they want to snatch her, one cop in a car isn't going to cause much of a problem. Two cops just might.'

'How did they know?'

'We'll think about that later.'

Rebus was staring at the bathroom door, remembering the locked cubicle at St Leonard's. 'I've got to go.'

'Be careful.'

Rebus put down the receiver.

'Candice?' He tried the door. It was locked. 'Candice?' He stood back and kicked. The door wasn't as strong as the one in St Leonard's; he nearly took it off its hinges. She was seated on the toilet, a plastic safety razor in her hand, slashing it across her arms. There was blood on her T-shirt, blood spraying the white tiled floor. She started screaming at him, the words collapsing into monosyllables. Rebus grabbed the razor, nicked his thumb in the process. He pulled her off the toilet, flushed the razor, and started wrapping towels around her arms. The note was lying in the bath. He waved it in her face.

'They're trying to scare you, that's all.' Not even half-believing it himself. If Telford could find her this quickly, if he had the means of writing to her in her own language, then he was much stronger, much cleverer than Rebus had suspected.

'It's going to be OK,' he went on. 'I promise. It's all OK. We'll look after you. We'll get you out of here, take you somewhere he can't get to you. I promise, Candice. Look, this is me talking.'

But she was bawling, tears dripping from her cheeks, head shaking from side to side. For a time, she'd actually believed in knights on white chargers. Now, she was realising how stupid she'd been . . .

The coast seemed to be clear.

Rebus took her in his car, Ormiston tucked in behind. No other way to play it. It was a trade-off: a speedy exit versus hanging around for a cavalry escort. And the way Candice was bleeding, they couldn't afford to wait. The drive to the hospital was nerve-tingling, then there was the wait while her wounds were checked and some of them sewn up. Rebus and Ormiston waited in A&E, drinking coffee from beakers, asking one another questions they couldn't answer.

'How did he know?'

'Who did he get to write the note?'

'Why give us a warning? Why not just grab her?'

'What does the note say?'

It struck Rebus that they were near the university. He took Dr Colquhoun's card from his pocket and phoned his office. Colquhoun was in. Rebus read the message out to him, spelling some of the words.

'They sound like addresses,' Colquhoun said. 'Untranslatable.'

'Addresses? Are any towns named?'

'I don't think so.'

'Sir, we'll be taking her to Fettes if she's well enough . . . any chance you could meet us there? It's important.'

'Everything with you chaps is important.'

'Yes, sir, but this is *important*. Candice's life may be in danger.'

Colquhoun took time answering. 'I suppose in that case . . .'

'I'll send a car for you.'

After an hour, she was well enough to leave. 'The cuts weren't too deep,' the doctor said. 'Not life-threatening.'

'They weren't meant to be.' Rebus turned to Ormiston. 'She thinks she's going back to Telford, that's why she did it. She *knows* she's going back to him.'

Candice looked as though all the blood had been drained from her. Her face seemed more skeletal than before, and her eyes darker. Rebus tried to recall what her smile looked like. He doubted he'd be seeing one for a while. She kept her arms folded protectively in front of her, and wouldn't meet his eyes. Rebus had seen suspects act that way in custody: people for whom the world had become a trap.

At Fettes, Claverhouse and Colquhoun were already waiting. Rebus handed over the note and photo.

'As I said, Inspector,' Colquhoun stated, 'addresses.'

'Ask her what they mean,' Claverhouse demanded. They were in the same room as before. Candice knew her place, and was already seated, her arms still folded, showing cream-coloured bandages and pink plasters. Colquhoun asked, but it was as though he'd ceased to exist. Candice stared at the wall in front of her, unblinking, her only motion a slight rocking to and fro.

'Ask her again,' Claverhouse said. But Rebus interrupted before Colquhoun could start.

'Ask her if people she knows live there, people who are important to her.'

As Colquhoun formed the question, the rocking grew slightly in intensity. There were fresh tears in her eyes.

'Her mother and father? Brothers and sisters?'

Colquhoun translated. Candice tried to stop her mouth trembling.

'Maybe she left a kid behind . . .'

As Colquhoun asked, Candice flew from her chair, shouting and screaming. Ormiston tried to grab her, but she kicked out at him. When she'd calmed, she subsided in a corner of the room, arms over her head.

'She's not going to tell us anything,' Colquhoun translated. 'She was stupid to believe us. She just wants to go now. There's nothing she can help us with.'

Rebus and Claverhouse shared a look.

'We can't hold her, John, not if she wants to leave. It's been dodgy enough keeping her away from a lawyer. Once she starts asking to go . . .' He shrugged.

'Come on, man,' Rebus hissed, 'she's shit-scared, and with good reason. And now you've got all you're going to get out of her, you're just going to hand her back to Telford?'

'Look, it's not a question of –'

'He'll kill her, you know he will.'

'If he was going to kill her, she'd be dead.' Claverhouse paused. 'He's cleverer than that. He knows damned well all he had to do was give her a fright. He *knows* her. It sticks in my craw, too, but what can we do?'

'Just keep her a few days, see if we can't . . .'

'Can't what? You want to hand her over to Immigration?'

'It's an idea. Get her the hell away from here.'

Claverhouse pondered this, then turned to Colquhoun. 'Ask her if she wants to go back to Sarajevo.'

Colquhoun asked. She slurred some answer, choking back tears.

'She says if she goes back, they'll kill everyone.'

Silence in the room. They were all looking at her. Four men, men with jobs, family ties, men with lives of their own. In the scheme of things, they seldom realised how well off they were. And now they realised something else: how helpless they were.

'Tell her,' Claverhouse said quietly, 'she's free to walk out of here at any time, if that's what she really wants. If she stays, we'll do our damnedest to help her . . .'

So Colquhoun spoke to her, and she listened, and when he'd finished she pushed herself back on to her feet and looked at them. Then she wiped her nose on her bandages, pushed the hair out of her eyes, and walked to the door.

'Don't go, Candice,' Rebus said.

She half-turned towards him. 'OK,' she said.

Then she opened the door and was gone.

Rebus grabbed Claverhouse's arm. 'We've got to pull Telford in, warn him not to touch her.'

'You think he needs telling?'

'You think he'd listen?' Ormiston added.

'I can't believe this. He scared her half to death, and as a result we let her walk? I really can't get my head round this.'

'She could always have gone to Fife,' Colquhoun said. With Candice out of the room, he seemed to have perked up a bit.

'Bit late now,' Ormiston said.

'He beat us this time, that's all,' Claverhouse said, his eyes on Rebus. 'But we'll take him down, don't worry.' He managed a thin, humourless smile. 'Don't think we're giving up, John. It's not our style. Early days yet, pal. Early days . . .'

She was waiting for him out in the car park, standing by the passenger-door of his battered Saab 900.

'OK?' she said.

'OK,' he agreed, smiling with relief as he unlocked the car. He could think of only one place to take her. As he drove through The Meadows, she nodded, recognising the tree-lined playing fields.

'You've been here before?'

She said a few words, nodded again as Rebus turned into Arden Street. He parked the car and turned to her.

'You've been *here*?'

She pointed upwards, fingers curled into the shape of binoculars.

'With Telford?'

'Telford,' she said. She made a show of writing something down, and Rebus took out his notebook and pen, handed them over. She drew a teddy bear.

'You came in Telford's car?' Rebus interpreted. 'And he watched one of the flats up there?' He pointed to his own flat.

'Yes, yes.'

'When was this?' She didn't understand the question. 'I need a phrasebook,' he muttered. Then he opened his door, got out and looked around. The cars around him were all empty. No Range Rovers. He signalled for Candice to get out and follow him.

She seemed to like his living room, went straight to the record collection but couldn't find anything she recognised. Rebus went into the kitchen to make coffee and to think. He couldn't keep her here, not if Telford knew about the place. Telford . . . why had he been watching Rebus's flat? The answer was obvious: he knew the detective was linked to Cafferty, and therefore a potential threat. He thought Rebus was in Cafferty's pocket. Know your enemy: it was another rule Telford had learned.

Rebus phoned a contact from the *Scotland on Sunday* business section.

'Japanese companies,' Rebus said. 'Rumours pertaining to.'

'Can you narrow that down?'

'New sites around Edinburgh, maybe Livingston.'

Rebus could hear the reporter shuffling papers on his desk. 'There's a whisper going round about a microprocessor plant.'

'In Livingston?'

'That's one possibility.'

'Anything else?'

'Nope. Why the interest?'

'Cheers, Tony.' Rebus put down the receiver, looked across at Candice. He couldn't think where else to take her. Hotels weren't safe. One place came to mind, but it would be risky . . . Well, not so very risky. He made the call.

'Sammy?' he said. 'Any chance you could do me a favour . . . ?'

Sammy lived in a 'colonies' flat in Shandon. Parking was almost impossible on the narrow street outside. Rebus got as close as he could.

Sammy was waiting for them in the narrow hallway, and led them into the cramped living room. There was a guitar on a wicker chair and Candice lifted it, setting herself on the chair and strumming a chord.

'Sammy,' Rebus said, 'this is Candice.'

'Hello there,' Sammy said. 'Happy Halloween.' Candice was putting chords together now. 'Hey, that's Oasis.'

Candice looked up, smiled. 'Oasis,' she echoed.

'I've got the CD somewhere . . .' Sammy examined a tower of CDs next to the hi-fi. 'Here it is. Shall I put it on?'

'Yes, yes.'

Sammy switched the hi-fi on, told Candice she was going to make some coffee, and beckoned for Rebus to follow her into the kitchen.

'So who is she?' The kitchen was tiny. Rebus stayed in the doorway.

'She's a prostitute. Against her will. I don't want her pimp getting her.'

'Where's she from again?'

'Sarajevo.'

'And she doesn't have much English?'

'How's your Serbo-Croat?'

'Rusty.'

Rebus looked around. 'Where's your boyfriend?'

'Out working.'

'On the book?' Rebus didn't like Ned Farlowe. Partly it was that name: 'Neds' were what the *Sunday Post* called hooligans. They robbed old ladies of their pension books and walking-frames. Those were the Neds of this world. And Farlowe meant Chris Farlowe: 'Out of Time', a number one that should have belonged to the Stones. Farlowe was researching a history of organised crime in Scotland.

'Sod's law,' Sammy said. 'He needs money to buy the time to write the thing.'

'So what's he doing?'

'Just some freelance stuff. How long am I babysitting?'

'A couple of days at most. Just till I find somewhere else.'

'What will he do if he finds her?'

'I'm not that keen to find out.'

Sammy finished rinsing the mugs. 'She looks like me, doesn't she?'

'Yes, she does.'

'I've got some time off coming. Maybe I'll phone in, see if I can stay here with her. What's her real name?'

'She hasn't told me.'

'Has she any clothes?'

'At a hotel. I'll get a patrol car to bring them.'

'She's really in danger?'

'She might be.'

Sammy looked at him. 'But I'm not?'

'No,' her father said. 'Because it'll be our secret.'

'And what do I tell Ned?'

'Keep it short, just say you're doing your dad a favour.'

'You think a journalist's going to be content with that?'

'If he loves you.'

The kettle boiled, clicked off. Sammy poured water into three mugs. Through in the living room, Candice's interest had shifted to a pile of American comic books.

Rebus drank his coffee, then left them to their music and their comics. Instead of going home, he made for Young Street and the Ox, ordering a mug of instant. Fifty pee. Pretty good deal, when you thought about it. Fifty pence for . . . what, half a pint? A pound a pint? Cheap at twice the

price. Well, one-point-seven times the price, which would take it to the price of a beer . . . give or take.

Not that Rebus was counting.

The back room was quiet, just somebody scribbling away at the table nearest the fire. He was a regular, a journalist of some kind. Rebus thought of Ned Farlowe, who would want to know about Candice, but if anyone could keep him at bay, Sammy could. Rebus took out his mobile, phoned Colquhoun's office.

'Sorry to bother you again,' he said.

'What is it now?' The lecturer sounded thoroughly exasperated.

'Those refugees you mentioned. Any chance you could have a word with them?'

'Well, I . . .' Colquhoun cleared his throat. 'Yes, I suppose I could talk to them. Does that mean . . .?'

'Candice is safe.'

'I don't have their number here.' Colquhoun sounded fuddled again. 'Can it wait till I go home?'

'Phone me when you've talked to them. And thanks.'

Rebus rang off, finished his coffee, and called Siobhan Clarke at home.

'I need a favour,' he said, feeling like a broken record.

'How much trouble will it get me in?'

'Almost none.'

'Can I have that in writing?'

'Think I'm stupid?' Rebus smiled. 'I want to see the files on Telford.'

'Why not just ask Claverhouse?'

'I'd rather ask you.'

'It's a lot of stuff. Do you want photocopies?'

'Whatever.'

'I'll see what I can do.' Voices were raised in the front bar. 'You're not in the Ox, are you?'

'As it happens, yes.'

'Drinking?'

'A mug of coffee.'

She laughed in disbelief and told him to take care. Rebus ended the call and stared at his mug. People like Siobhan Clarke, they could drive a man to drink.

7

It was 7 a.m. when the buzzer sounded, telling him there was someone at his tenement's main door. He staggered along the hall to the intercom, and asked who the bloody hell it was.

'The croissant man,' a rough English voice replied.

'The what?'

'Come on, dick-brain, wakey-wakey. Memory's not so hot these days, eh?'

A name tilted into Rebus's head. 'Abernethy?'

'Now open up, it's perishing down here.'

Rebus pushed the buzzer to let Abernethy in, then jogged back to the bedroom to put on some clothes. His mind felt numb. Abernethy was a DI in Special Branch, London. The last time he'd been in Edinburgh had been to chase terrorists. Rebus wondered what the hell he was doing here now.

When the doorbell sounded, Rebus tucked in his shirt and walked back down the hall. True to his word, Abernethy was carrying a bag of croissants. He hadn't changed much: same faded denims and black leather bomber, same cropped brown hair spiked with gel. His face was heavy, pockmarked, and his eyes an unnerving, psychopath's blue.

'How've you been, mate?' Abernethy slapped Rebus's shoulder and marched past him into the kitchen. 'Get the kettle on then.' Like they did this every day of the week. Like they didn't live four hundred miles apart.

'Abernethy, what the hell are you doing here?'

'Feeding you, of course, same thing the English have always done for the Jocks. Got any butter?'

'Try the butter-dish.'

'Plates?'

Rebus pointed to a cupboard.

'Bet you drink instant: am I right?'

'Abernethy . . .'

'Let's get this ready first, then talk, OK?'

'The kettle boils quicker if you switch it on at the plug.'

'Right.'

'And I think there's some jam.'

'Any honey?'

'Do I look like a bee?'

Abernethy smirked. 'Old Georgie Flight sends his love, by the way. Word is, he'll be retiring soon.'

George Flight: another ghost from Rebus's past. Abernethy had unscrewed the top from the coffee jar and was sniffing the granules.

'How fresh is this?' He wrinkled his nose. 'No class, John.'

'Unlike you, you mean? When did you get here?'

'Hit town half an hour ago.'

'From London?'

'Stopped a couple of hours in a lay-by, got my head down. That A1 is murder though. North of Newcastle, it's like coming into a third-world country.'

'Did you drive four hundred miles just to insult me?'

They took everything through to the table in the living room, Rebus shoving aside books and notepads, stuff about the Second World War.

'So,' he said, as they sat down, 'I'm assuming this isn't a social call?'

'Actually it is, in a way. I could have just telephoned, but I suddenly thought: wonder how the old devil's getting on? Next thing I knew, I was in the car and heading for the North Circular.'

'I'm touched.'

'I've always tried to keep track of what you're up to.'

'Why?'

'Because last time we met . . . well, you're different, aren't you?'

'Am I?'

'I mean, you're not a team player. You're a loner, bit like me. Loners can be useful.'

'Useful?'

'For undercover, jobs that are a bit out of the ordinary.'

'You think I'm Special Branch material?'

'Ever fancied moving to London? It's where the action is.'

'I get action enough up here.'

Abernethy looked out of the window. 'You couldn't wake this place with a fifty-megaton warhead.'

'Look, Abernethy, not that I'm not enjoying your company or anything, but why *are* you here?'

Abernethy brushed crumbs from his hands. 'So much for the social niceties.' He took a gulp of coffee, squirmed at its awfulness. 'War Crimes,' he said. Rebus stopped chewing. 'There's a new list of names. You know that, because you've got one of them living on your doorstep.'

'So?'

'So I'm heading up the London HQ. We've established a temporary War Crimes Unit. My job's to collate gen on the various investigations, create a central register.'

'You want to know what I know?'

'That's about it.'

'And you drove through the night to find out? There's got to be more to it.'

Abernethy laughed. 'Why's that?'

'There just has. A collator's job is for someone good at office work. That's not you, you're only happy in the field.'

'What about you? I'd never have taken you for a historian.' Abernethy tapped one of the books on the table.

'It's a penance.'

'What makes you think it's any different with me? So, what's the score with Herr Lintz?'

'There's no score. So far all the darts have missed the board. How many cases are there?'

'Twenty-seven originally, but eight of those are deceased.'

'Any progress?'

Abernethy shook his head. 'We got one to court, trial collapsed first day. Can't prosecute if they're ga-ga.'

'Well, for your information, here's where the Lintz case stands. I can't prove he was and is Josef Linzstek. I can't disprove his story of his participation in the war, or how he came to Britain.' Rebus shrugged.

'Same tale I've been hearing up and down the country.'

'What did you expect?' Rebus was picking at a croissant.

'Shame about this coffee,' Abernethy said. 'Any decent caffs in the neighbourhood?'

So they went to a café, where Abernethy ordered a double espresso, Rebus a decaf. There was a story on the front of the *Record* about a fatal stabbing outside a nightclub. The man reading the paper folded it up when he'd finished his breakfast and took it away with him.

'Any chance you'll be talking to Lintz today?' Abernethy asked suddenly.

'Why?'

'Thought I might tag along. It's not often you get to meet someone who might have killed seven hundred Frenchies.'

'Morbid attraction?'

'We're all a bit that way inclined, aren't we?'

'I've nothing new to ask him,' Rebus said, 'and he's already been muttering to his lawyer about harassment.'

'He's well connected?'

Rebus stared across the table. 'You've done your reading.'

'Abernethy the Conscientious Cop.'

'Well, you're right. He has friends in high places, only a lot of them have been hiding behind the curtains since this all started.'

'Sounds like you think he's innocent.'

'Until proven guilty.'

Abernethy smiled, lifted his cup. 'There's a Jewish historian been going around. Has he contacted you?'

'What's his name?'

Another smile. 'How many Jewish historians have you been in touch with? His name's David Levy.'

'You say he's been going around?'

'A week here, a week there, asking how the cases are going.'

'He's in Edinburgh just now.'

Abernethy blew on his coffee. 'So you've spoken with him?'

'Yes, as it happens.'

'And?'

'And what?'

'Did he try his "Rat Line" story?'

'Again, why the interest?'

'He's tried it with everyone else.'

'What if he has?'

'Jesus, do you always answer a question with a question? Look, as collator, this guy Levy's name has popped up on my computer screen more than once. That's why I'm interested.'

'Abernethy the Conscientious Cop.'

'That's right. So shall we go see Lintz?'

'Well, seeing you've come all this way . . .'

On the way back to the flat, Rebus stopped at a newsagent's and bought the *Record*. The stabbing had taken place outside Megan's Nightclub, a new establishment in Portobello. The fatality had been a 'doorman', William Tennant, aged 25. The story had made the front page because a Premier League footballer had been on the periphery of the incident. A friend who'd been with him had received minor cuts. The attacker had fled on a motorbike. The footballer had offered no comment to reporters. Rebus knew him. He lived in Linlithgow and a year or so back had been caught speeding in Edinburgh, with – in his own words – a 'wee bitty Charlie', meaning cocaine, on his person.

'Anything interesting?' Abernethy asked.

'Someone killed a bouncer. Quiet little backwater, eh?'

'A story like that, in London it wouldn't rate a column inch.'

'How long are you staying here?'

'I'll be off today, want to drop in on Carlisle. They're supposed to have another old Nazi. After that, it's Blackpool and Wolverhampton before home.'

'A sucker for punishment.'

Rebus drove them the tourist route: down The Mound and across Princes Street. He double-parked in Heriot Row, but Joseph Lintz wasn't home.

'Never mind,' he said. 'I know where he'll probably be.' He took them down Inverleith Row and turned right into Warriston Gardens, stopping at the cemetery gates.

'What is he, a gravedigger?' Abernethy got out of the car and zipped his jacket.

'He plants flowers.'

'Flowers? What for?'

'I'm not sure.'

A cemetery should have been about death, but Warriston didn't feel that way to Rebus. Much of it resembled a rambling park into which some statuary had been dropped. The newer section, with stone driveway, soon gave way to an earthen path between fading inscriptions. There were obelisks and Celtic crosses, lots of trees and birds, and the electric movements of squirrels. A tunnel beneath a walkway took you to the oldest part of the cemetery, but between tunnel and driveway sat the heart of the place, with its roll-call of Edinburgh's past. Names like Ovenstone, Cleugh, and Flockhart, and professions such as actuary, silk merchant, iron-monger. There were people who'd died in India, and some who'd died in infancy. A sign at the gate informed visitors that the place had been the subject of a compulsory purchase by the City of Edinburgh, because previous private owners had let it fall into neglect. But that same neglect was at least part of its charm. People walked their dogs here, or came to practise photography, or just mused among the tombstones. Gays came looking for company, others for solitude.

After dark, of course, the place had another reputation entirely. A Leith prostitute – a woman Rebus had known and liked – had been found murdered here earlier in the year. Rebus wondered if Joseph Lintz knew about that . . .

'Mr Lintz?'

He was trimming the grass around a headstone, doing so with a half-sized pair of garden shears. There was a sheen of sweat on his face as he forced himself upright.

'Ah, Inspector Rebus. You have brought a colleague?'

'This is DI Abernethy.'

Abernethy was examining the headstone, which belonged to a teacher called Cosmo Merriman.

'They let you do this?' he asked, his eyes finally finding Lintz's.

'No one has tried to stop me.'

'Inspector Rebus tells me you plant flowers, too.'

'People assume I am a relative.'

'But you're not, are you?'

'Only in so far as we are the family of man, Inspector Abernethy.'

'You're a Christian then?'

'Yes, I am.'

'Born and bred?'

Lintz took out a handkerchief and wiped his nose. 'You're wondering if a Christian could commit an atrocity like Villefranche. It's perhaps not in my interest to say this, but I think it entirely possible. I've been explaining this to Inspector Rebus.'

Rebus nodded. 'We've had a couple of talks.'

'Religious belief is no defence, you see. Look at Bosnia, plenty of Catholics involved in the fighting, plenty of good Muslims, too. "Good" in that they are believers. And what they believe is that their faith gives them the right to kill.'

Bosnia: Rebus saw a sharp image of Candice escaping the terror, only to end up more terrified still, and more trapped than ever.

Lintz was stuffing the large white handkerchief into the pocket of his baggy brown cord trousers. In the outfit – green rubber overshoes, green woollen jersey, tweed jacket – he did look like a gardener. Little wonder he attracted so little attention in the cemetery. He blended in. Rebus wondered how artful it was, how deeply he'd learned the skill of invisibility.

'You look impatient, Inspector Abernethy. You're not a man for theories, am I right?'

'I wouldn't know about that, sir.'

'In that case, you must not know very much. Now Inspector Rebus, he listens to what I have to say. More than that, he looks *interested*. Whether he is or not, I can't judge, but his performance – if performance it be – is exemplary.' Lintz always spoke like this, like he'd been rehearsing each line. 'Last time he visited my home, we discussed human duality. Would you have any opinion on *that*, Inspector Abernethy?'

The look on Abernethy's face was cold. 'No, sir.'

Lintz shrugged: case against the Londoner proven. 'Atrocities, Inspector, occur by an effort of the collective will.' Spelling it out; sounding like the lecturer he had once been. 'Because sometimes all it takes to turn us into devils is the fear of being an outsider.'

Abernethy sniffed, hands in pockets. 'Sounds like you're justifying war crimes, sir. Sounds to me like you might even have been there yourself.'

'Do I need to be a spaceman to imagine Mars?' He turned to Rebus, gave him the fraction of a smile.

'Well, maybe I'm just a bit too simple, sir,' Abernethy said. 'I'm also a bit parky. Let's walk back to the car and carry on our discussion there, all right?'

While Lintz packed his few small tools into a canvas bag, Rebus looked around, saw movement in the distance, between headstones. The crouched figure of a man. Split-second glimpse of a face he recognised.

'What is it?' Abernethy asked.

Rebus shook his head. 'Nothing.'

The three men walked in silence back to the Saab. Rebus opened the back door for Lintz. To his surprise, Abernethy got into the back, too. Rebus took the driver's seat, felt warmth returning slowly to his toes. Abernethy had his arm along the back of the seat, his body twisted towards Lintz.

'Now, Herr Lintz, my role in all this is quite straightforward. I'm collating all the information on this latest outbreak of alleged old Nazis. You understand that with allegations such as these, very serious allegations, we have a duty to investigate?'

'Spurious allegations rather than "serious" ones.'

'In which case you've nothing to worry about.'

'Except my reputation.'

'When you're exonerated, we'll take care of that.'

Rebus was listening closely. None of this sounded like Abernethy. The hostile graveside tone had been replaced by something much more ambiguous.

'And meantime?' Lintz seemed to be picking up whatever the Londoner was saying between the lines. Rebus felt deliberately excluded from the conversation, which was why Abernethy had got into the back seat in the first place. He'd placed a physical barrier between himself and the officer investigating Joseph Lintz. There was something going on.

'Meantime,' Abernethy said, 'co-operate as fully as you can with my colleague. The sooner he's able to reach his conclusions, the sooner this will all be over.'

'The problem with conclusions is that they should be conclusive, and I have so little proof. This was wartime, Inspector Abernethy, a lot of records destroyed . . .'

'Without proof either way, there's no case to answer.'

Lintz was nodding. 'I see,' he said.

Abernethy hadn't voiced anything Rebus himself didn't feel; the problem was, he'd voiced it to the suspect.

'It would help if your memory improved,' Rebus felt obliged to add.

'Well, Mr Lintz,' Abernethy was saying, 'thanks for your time.' His hand was on the elderly man's shoulder: protective, comforting. 'Can we drop you somewhere?'

'I'll stay here a little longer,' Lintz said, opening the door and easing himself out. Abernethy handed the bag of tools to him.

'Take care now,' he said.

Lintz nodded, gave a small bow to Rebus, and shuffled back towards the gate. Abernethy climbed into the passenger seat.

'Rum little bugger, isn't he?'

'You as good as told him he was off the hook.'

'Bollocks,' Abernethy said. 'I told him where he stands, let him know the score. That's all.' He saw the look on Rebus's face. 'Come on, do you really want to see him in court? An old professor who keeps cemeteries tidy?'

'It doesn't make it any easier if you sound like you're on his side.'

'Even supposing he *did* order that massacre – you think a trial and a couple of years in clink till he snuffs it is the answer? Better to just give them all a bloody good scare, stuff the trial, and save the taxpayer millions.'

'That's not our job,' Rebus said, starting the engine.

He took Abernethy back to Arden Street. They shook hands, Abernethy trying to sound like he wanted to stay a little longer.

'One of these days,' he said. And then he was gone. As his Sierra drew away, another car pulled into the space he'd just vacated. Siobhan Clarke got out, bringing with her a supermarket carrier bag.

'For you,' she said. 'And I think I'm owed a coffee.'

She wasn't as fussy as Abernethy, accepted the mug of instant with thanks and ate a spare croissant. There was a message on the answering machine, Dr Colquhoun telling him the refugee family could take Candice tomorrow. Rebus jotted down the details, then turned his attention to the contents of Siobhan's carrier bag. Maybe two hundred sheets of paper, photocopies.

'Don't get them out of order,' she warned. 'I didn't have time to staple them.'

'Fast work.'

'I went back into the office last night. Thought I'd get it done while no one was about. I can summarise, if you like.'

'Just tell me who the main players are.'

She came to the table and pulled a chair over beside him, found a sequence of surveillance shots. Put names to the faces.

'Brian Summers,' she said, 'better known as "Pretty-Boy". He runs most of the working girls.' Pale, angular face, thick black lashes, a pouting mouth. Candice's pimp.

'He's not very pretty.'

Clarke found another picture. 'Kenny Houston.'

'From Pretty-Boy to Plug-Ugly.'

'I'm sure his mother loves him.' Prominent teeth, jaundiced skin.

'What does he do?'

'He runs the doormen. Kenny, Pretty-Boy and Tommy Telford grew up on the same street. They're at the heart of The Family.' She sifted through more photos. 'Malky Jordan . . . he keeps the drugs flowing. Sean Haddow . . . bit of a brainbox, runs the finances. Ally Cornwell . . . he's muscle. Deek McGrain . . . There's no religious divide in The Family, Prods and Papes working together.'

'A model society.'

'No women though. Telford's philosophy: relationships get in the way.'

Rebus picked up a sheaf of paper. 'So what have we got?'

'Everything but the evidence.'

'And surveillance is supposed to provide that?'

She smiled over the top of her mug. 'You don't agree?'

'It's not my problem.'

'And yet you're interested.' She paused. 'Candice?'

'I don't like what happened to her.'

'Well, just remember: you didn't get this stuff from me.'

'Thanks, Siobhan.' He paused. 'Everything going all right?'

'Fine. I like Crime Squad.'

'Bit livelier than St Leonard's.'

'I miss Brian.' Meaning her one-time partner, now out of the force.

'You ever see him?'

'No, do you?'

Rebus shook his head, got up to show her out.

He spent about an hour sifting through the paperwork, learning more about The Family and its convoluted workings. Nothing about Newcastle. Nothing about Japan. The core of The Family – eight or nine of them – had been at school together. Three of them were still based in Paisley, taking care of the established business. The rest were now in Edinburgh, and busy prying the city away from Big Ger Cafferty.

He went through lists of nightclubs and bars in which Telford had an interest. There were incident reports attached: arrests in the vicinity. Drunken brawls, swings taken at bouncers, cars and property damaged. Something caught Rebus's eye: mention of a hot-dog van, parked outside a couple of the clubs. The owner questioned: possible witness. But he'd never seen anything worth the recall. Name: Gavin Tay.

Mr Taystee.

Recent dodgy suicide. Rebus gave Bill Pryde a bell, asked how that investigation was going.

'Dead-end street, pal,' Pryde said, not sounding too concerned. Pryde: too long the same rank, and not going anywhere. Beginning the long descent into retirement.

'Did you know he ran a hot-dog stall on the side?'

'Might explain where he got the cash from.'

Gavin Tay was an ex-con. He'd been in the ice cream business a little over a year. Successful, too: new Merc parked outside his house. His financial records hadn't hinted at money to spare. His widow couldn't account for the Merc. And now: evidence of a job on the side, selling food and drink to punters stumbling out of nightclubs.

Tommy Telford's nightclubs.

Gavin Tay: previous convictions for assault and reset. A persistent offender who'd finally gone straight ... The room began to feel stuffy, Rebus's head clotted and aching. He decided to get out.

Walked through The Meadows and down George IV Bridge, took the Playfair Steps down to Princes Street. A group was sitting on the stone steps of the Scottish Academy: unshaven, dyed hair, torn clothes. The city's dispossessed, trying their best not to be ignored. Rebus knew he had things in common with them. In the course of his life, he'd failed to fit several niches: husband, father, lover. He hadn't fitted in with the Army's ideas of what he should be, and wasn't exactly 'one of the lads' in the police. When one of the group held out a hand, Rebus offered a fiver, before crossing Princes Street and heading for the Oxford Bar.

He settled into a corner with a mug of coffee, got out his mobile, and called Sammy's flat. She was home, all was well with Candice. Rebus told her he had a place for Candice, she could move out tomorrow.

'That's fine,' Sammy said. 'Hold on a second.' There was a rustling sound as the receiver was passed along.

'Hello, John, how are you?'

Rebus smiled. 'Hello, Candice. That's very good.'

'Thank you. Sammy is . . . uh . . . I am teaching how to . . .' She broke into laughter, handed the receiver back.

'I'm teaching her English,' Sammy said.

'I can tell.'

'We started with some Oasis lyrics, just went from there.'

'I'll try to come round later. What did Ned say?'

'He was so shattered when he came home, I think he barely noticed.'

'Is he there? I'd like to talk to him.'

'He's out working.'

'What did you say he was doing again?'

'I didn't.'

'Right. Thanks again, Sammy. See you later.'

He took a swig of coffee, washed it around his mouth. Abernethy: he couldn't just let it go. He swallowed the coffee and called the Roxburghe, asked for David Levy's room.

'Levy speaking.'

'It's John Rebus.'

'Inspector, how good to hear from you. Is there something I can do?'

'I'd like to talk to you.'

'Are you in your office?'

Rebus looked around. 'In a manner of speaking. It's a two-minute walk from your hotel. Turn right out of the door, cross George Street, and walk down to Young Street. Far end, the Oxford Bar. I'm in the back room.'

When Levy arrived, Rebus bought him a half of eighty-bob. Levy eased himself into a chair, hanging his walking-stick on the back of it. 'So what can I do for you?'

'I'm not the only policeman you've spoken to.'

'No, you're not.'

'Someone from Special Branch in London came to see me today.'

'And he told you I'd been travelling around?'

'Yes.'

'Did he warn you against speaking to me?'

'Not in so many words.'

Levy took off his glasses, began polishing them. 'I told you, there are people who'd rather this was all relegated to history. This man, he came all the way from London just to tell you about me?'

'He wanted to see Joseph Lintz.'

'Ah.' Levy was thoughtful. 'Your interpretation, Inspector?'

'I was hoping for yours.'

'My utterly subjective interpretation?' Rebus nodded. 'He wants to be sure of Lintz. This man works for Special Branch, and as everyone knows Special Branch is the public arm of the secret services.'

'He wanted to be confident I wasn't going to get anything out of Lintz?'

Levy nodded, staring at the smoke from Rebus's cigarette. This case was like that: one minute you could see it, the next you couldn't. Like smoke.

'I have a little book with me,' Levy said, reaching into his pocket. 'I'd like you to read it. It's in English, translated from the Hebrew. It's about the Rat Line.'

Rebus took the book. 'Does it prove anything?'

'That depends on your terms.'

'Concrete proof.'

'Concrete proof exists, Inspector.'

'In this book?'

Levy shook his head. 'Under lock and key in Whitehall, kept from scrutiny by the Hundred Year Rule.'

'So there's no way to prove anything.'

'There's one way . . .'

'What?'

'If someone talks. If we can get just *one* of them to talk . . .'

'That's what this is all about: wearing down their resistance? Looking for the weakest link?'

Levy smiled again. 'We have learned patience, Inspector.' He finished his drink. 'I'm so grateful you called. This has been a much more satisfactory meeting.'

'Will you send your bosses a progress report?'

Levy chose to ignore this. 'We'll talk again, when you've read the book.' He stood up. 'The Special Branch officer . . . I've forgotten his name?'

'I didn't give it.'

Levy waited a moment, then said, 'Ah, that explains it then. Is he still in Edinburgh?' He watched Rebus shake his head. 'Then he's probably on his way to Carlisle, yes?'

Rebus sipped coffee, offered no comment.

'My thanks again, Inspector,' Levy said, undeterred.

'Thanks for dropping by.'

Levy took a final look around. 'Your office,' he said, shaking his head.

8

The Rat Line was an 'underground railway', delivering Nazis – sometimes with the help of the Vatican – from their Soviet persecutors. The end of the Second World War meant the start of the Cold War. Intelligence was necessary, as were intelligent, ruthless individuals who could provide a certain level of expertise. It was said that Klaus Barbie, the 'Butcher of Lyons', had been offered a job with British Intelligence. It was rumoured that high-profile Nazis had been spirited away to America. It wasn't until 1987 that the United Nations released its full list of fugitive Nazi and Japanese war criminals, forty thousand of them.

Why so late in releasing the list? Rebus thought he could understand. Modern politics had decreed that Germany and Japan were part of the global brotherhood of capitalism. In whose interests would it be to reopen old wounds? And besides, how many atrocities had the Allies themselves hidden? Who fought a war with clean hands? Rebus, who'd grown to adulthood in the Army, could comprehend this. He'd done things . . . He'd served time in Northern Ireland, seen trust disfigured, hatred replace fear.

Part of him could well believe in the existence of a Rat Line.

The book Levy had given him went into the mechanics of how such an operation might have worked. Rebus wondered: was it really possible to disappear completely, to change identity? And again, the recurring question: did any of it matter? There did exist sources of identification, and there *had* been court cases – Eichmann, Barbie, Demjanjuk – with others ongoing. He read about war criminals who, rather than being tried or extradited, were allowed to return home, running businesses, growing rich, dying of old age. But he also read of criminals who served their sentences and became 'good people', people who *had* changed. These men said war itself was the real culprit. Rebus recalled one of his first conversations with Joseph Lintz, in the drawing room of Lintz's home. The old man's voice was hoarse, a scarf around his throat.

'At my age, Inspector, a simple throat infection can feel like death.'

There didn't seem to be many photographs around. Lintz had explained that a lot had gone missing during the war.

'Along with other mementoes. I do have these photos though.'

He'd shown Rebus half a dozen framed shots, dating back to the 1930s. As he'd explained who the subjects were, Rebus had suddenly thought: what if he's making it up? What if these are just a bunch of old photos he picked up somewhere and had framed? And the names, the identities he

now gave to the faces – had he invented them? He'd seen in that instant, for the first time, how easy it might be to construct another life.

And then, later in their conversation that day, Lintz, sipping honeyed tea, had started discussing Villefranche.

'I've been thinking a lot about it, Inspector, as you might imagine. This Lieutenant Linzstek, he was in charge on the day?'

'Yes.'

'But presumably under orders from above. A lieutenant is not so very far up the pecking order.'

'Perhaps.'

'You see, if a soldier is under orders . . . then they must carry out those orders, no?'

'Even if the order is insane?'

'Nevertheless, I'd say the person was at the very least *coerced* into committing the crime, and a crime that very many of us would have carried out under similar circumstances. Can't you see the hypocrisy of trying someone, when you'd probably have done the same thing yourself? One soldier standing out from the crowd . . . saying no to the massacre: would you have made that stand yourself?'

'I hope so.' Rebus thinking back to Ulster and the 'Mean Machine' . . .

Levy's book didn't prove anything. All Rebus knew was that Josef Linzstek's name was on a list as having used the Rat Line, posing as a Pole. But where had the list originated? In Israel. Again, it was highly speculative. It wasn't *proof*.

And if Rebus's instincts told him Lintz and Linzstek were one and the same, they were still failing to tell him whether it mattered.

He dropped the book back to the Roxburghe, asked the receptionist to see that Mr Levy got it.

'I think he's in his room, if you'd like to . . .'

Rebus shook his head. He hadn't left any message with the book, knowing Levy might interpret this as a message in itself. He went home for his car, drove down to Haymarket and along to Shandon. As usual, parking near Sammy's flat was a problem. Everyone was home from work and tucked in front of their televisions. He climbed the stone steps, wondering how treacherous they'd get when the frosts came, and rang the bell. Sammy herself led him into the living room, where Candice was watching a game show.

'Hello, John,' she said. 'Are you my wonderwall?'

'I'm nobody's wonderwall, Candice.' He turned to Sammy. 'Everything all right?'

'Just fine.'

At that moment, Ned Farlowe walked in from the kitchen. He was eating soup from a bowl, dunking a folded slice of brown bread into it.

'Mind if I have a word?' Rebus said.

Farlowe shook his head, then jerked it in the direction of the kitchen.

'Can I eat while we talk? I'm starving.' He sat down at the foldaway table, got another slice of bread from the packet and spread margarine on it. Sammy put her head round the doorway, saw the look on her father's face, and made a tactical retreat. The kitchen was about seven foot square

and too full of pots and appliances. Swinging a cat, you could have done a lot of damage.

'I saw you today,' Rebus said, 'skulking in Warriston Cemetery. Coincidence?'

'What do you think?'

'I'm asking you.' Rebus leaned his back against the sink unit, folded his arms.

'I'm watching Lintz.'

'Why?'

'Because I'm being paid to.'

'By a newspaper?'

'Lintz's lawyer has interim interdicts flying around. Nobody can afford to be seen near him.'

'But they still want him watched?'

'If there's a court case coming, they want to know as much as possible, stands to reason.'

By court case, Farlowe didn't mean any trial of Lintz, but rather of the newspapers themselves, for libel.

'If he catches you . . .'

'He doesn't know me from Adam. Besides, there'd always be somebody to take my place. Now do I get to ask a question?'

'Let me say something first. You know I'm investigating Lintz?' Farlowe nodded. 'That means we're too close. If you find out anything, people might think it came from me.'

'I haven't told Sammy what I'm doing, *specifically* so there's no conflict of interests.'

'I'm just saying others might not believe it.'

'A few more days, I'll have enough money to fund the book for another month.' Farlowe had finished his soup. He carried the empty bowl over to the sink, stood next to Rebus.

'I don't want this to be a problem, but the bottom line is: what can you do about it?'

Rebus stared at him. His instinct was to stuff Farlowe's head into the sink, but how would that look with Sammy?

'Now,' Farlowe said, 'do I get to ask my question?'

'What is it?'

'Who's Candice?'

'A friend of mine.'

'So what's wrong with *your* flat?'

Rebus realised he was no longer dealing with his daughter's boyfriend. He was confronted with a journalist, someone with a nose for a story.

'Tell you what,' said Rebus, 'say I didn't see you in the cemetery. Say we didn't just have this little chat.'

'And I don't ask about Candice?' Rebus stayed quiet. Farlowe considered the deal. 'Say I get to ask you a few questions for my book.'

'What sort of questions?'

'About Cafferty.'

Rebus shook his head. 'I could talk about Tommy Telford though.'

'When?'

'When we've got him behind bars.'

Farlowe smiled. 'I could be on the pension by then.' He waited, saw Rebus was going to give him nothing.

'She's only here till tomorrow anyway,' Rebus said.

'Where's she off to?'

Rebus just winked. Left the kitchen, returned to the living room. Talked to Sammy while Candice's game show reached its climax. Whenever she heard audience laughter, she joined in. Rebus made arrangements for the following day, then left. There was no sign of Farlowe. He'd either hidden himself in the bedroom or else gone back out. It took Rebus a few moments to remember where he'd parked his car. He drove home carefully; stopped for all the lights.

The parking spaces were all taken in Arden Street. He left the Saab on a yellow line. As he approached his tenement door, he heard a car door open and spun towards the sound.

It was Claverhouse. He was on his own. 'Mind if I come in?'

Rebus thought of a dozen reasons for saying yes. But he shrugged and made for the door. 'Any news of the stabbing at Megan's?' he asked.

'How did you know we'd be interested?'

'A bouncer gets stabbed, the attacker flees on a waiting motorbike. It was premeditated. And the majority of the bouncers work for Tommy Telford.'

They were climbing the stairs. Rebus's flat was on the second floor.

'Well, you're right,' Claverhouse said. 'Billy Tennant worked for Telford. He controlled the traffic in and out of Megan's.'

'Traffic as in dope?'

'The footballer's friend, the one who got wounded, he's a known dealer. Works out of Paisley.'

'Therefore connected to Telford, too.'

'We're speculating he was the target, Tennant just got in the way.'

'Leaving only one question: who was behind it?'

'Come on, John. It was Cafferty, obviously.'

'Not Cafferty's style,' Rebus said, unlocking his door.

'Maybe he's learned a thing or two from the Young Pretender.'

'Make yourself at home,' Rebus said, walking down the hall. The breakfast things were still on the dining table. Siobhan's bag of goodies was down the side of a chair.

'A guest.' Claverhouse had noticed the two mugs, two plates. He looked around. 'She's not here now though?'

'She wasn't here for breakfast either.'

'Because she's at your daughter's.'

Rebus froze.

'I went to settle up with the hotel. They said a police car had come and taken all her things away. So then I asked around, and the driver gave me Samantha's address as the drop-off.' Claverhouse sat down on the sofa, crossed one leg over the other. 'So what's the game, John, and how come you've seen fit to leave me on the bench?' He sounded calm now, but Rebus could tell there'd been a storm.

'Do you want a drink?'

'I want an answer.'

'When she walked out ... she waited beside my car. I couldn't think where to take her, so I brought her here. But she recognised the street. Telford had been watching my flat.'

Claverhouse looked interested. 'Why?'

'Maybe because I know Cafferty. I couldn't let Candice stay here, so I took her to Sammy's.'

'Is she still there?' Rebus nodded. 'So what happens now?'

'There's a place she can go, the refugee family.'

'For how long?'

'What do you mean?'

Claverhouse sighed. 'John, she's . . . the only life she's known here is prostitution.'

Rebus went over to the hi-fi for something to do, looked through his tapes. He needed to do *some*thing.

'What's she going to do for money? Are you going to provide? What does that make you?'

Rebus dropped a CD, turned on his heels. 'Nothing like that,' he spat.

Claverhouse had his hands up, palms showing. 'Come on, John, you know yourself there's –'

'I don't know anything.'

'John . . .'

'Look, get out, will you?' It wasn't just that it had been a long day, more that it felt like the day would never end. He could feel the evening stretch to infinity, no rest available to him. In his head, bodies were swaying gently from trees while smoke engulfed a church. Telford was on his arcade motorbike, cannoning off spectators. Abernethy was touching an old man's shoulder. Soldiers were rifle-butting civilians. And John Rebus . . . John Rebus was in every frame, trying hard to remain an onlooker.

He put Van Morrison on the hi-fi: *Hardnose the Highway*. He'd played this music on East Neuk beaches and tenement stakeouts. It always seemed to heal him, or at least patch the wounds. When he turned back into the room, Claverhouse was gone. He looked out of his window. Two kids lived in the second-floor flat across from his. He'd watched them often from this window, and they never once saw him, for the simple reason that they never so much as glanced outside. Their world was complete and all-absorbing, anything outside their window an irrelevance. They were in bed now, their mother closing the shutters. Quiet city. Abernethy was right about that. There were large chunks of Edinburgh where you could live your whole life and never encounter a spot of bother. Yet the murder rate in Scotland was double that of its southern neighbour, and half those murders took place in the two main cities.

Not that the statistics mattered. A death was a death. Something unique had disappeared from the world. One murder or several hundred . . . they all meant something to the survivors. Rebus thought of Villefranche's sole existing survivor. He hadn't met her, probably never would. Another reason it was hard to get passionate about a historical case. In a contemporary one, you had many of the facts to hand, and could talk to witnesses. You could gather forensic evidence, question people's stories. You could measure guilt and grief. You became part of the whole story. This was what interested Rebus. The people interested him; their stories fascinated him. When part of their lives, he could forget his own.

He noticed the answering machine was flashing: one message.

'Oh, hello there. I'm . . . um, I don't know how to put this . . .' Placed the

voice: Kirstin Mede. She sighed. 'Look, I can't do this any more. So please don't . . . I'm sorry, I just can't. There are other people who can help you. I'm sure one of them . . .'

End of message. Rebus stared down at the machine. He didn't blame her. *I can't do this any more*. That makes two of us, Rebus thought. The only thing was, *he* had to keep going. He sat down at his table and pulled the Villefranche paperwork towards him: lists of names and occupations, ages and dates of birth. Picat, Mesplede, Rousseau, Deschamps. Wine merchant, china painter, cartwright, housemaid. What did any of it mean to a middle-aged Scot? He pushed it aside and lifted Siobhan's paperwork on to the table.

Off with Van the Man; on with side one of *Wish You Were Here*. Scratched to hell. He remembered it had come in a black polythene wrapper. When opened, there'd been this smell, which afterwards he'd learned was supposed to be burning flesh . . .

'I need a drink,' he said to himself, sitting forward in his chair. 'I want a drink. A few beers, maybe with whiskies attached.' Something to smooth the edges . . .

He looked at his watch; not even near to closing time. Not that it mattered much in Edinburgh, the land that closing time forgot. Could he make it to the Ox before they shut up shop? Yes, too easily. It was nicer to have a challenge. Wait an hour or so and then repeat the debate.

Or call Jack Morton.

Or go out, right now.

The telephone rang. He picked it up.

'Hello?'

'John?' Making it sound like 'Sean'.

'Hello, Candice. What's up?'

'Up?'

'Is there a problem?'

'Problem, no. I just wanting . . . I say to you, see you tomorrow.'

He smiled. 'Yes, see you tomorrow. You speak very good English.'

'I was chained to a razor blade.'

'What?'

'Line from song.'

'Oh, right. But you're not chained to it now?'

She didn't seem to understand. 'I'm . . . uh . . .'

'It's OK, Candice. See you tomorrow.'

'Yes, see you.'

Rebus put down the receiver. Chained to a razor blade . . . Suddenly he didn't want a drink any more.

9

He picked Candice up the next afternoon. She had two carrier bags, her worldly belongings. She gave Sammy as much of a hug as her bandaged arms would allow.

'See you again, Candice,' Sammy said.

'Yes, see you. Thanks . . .' Lost for an ending to the sentence, Candice opened her arms wide, bags swinging.

They stopped off at McDonald's (her choice) for something to eat. Zappa and the Mothers: 'Cruising for Burgers'. The day was bright and crisp, just right for crossing the Forth Bridge. Rebus took it slowly, so Candice could take in the view. He was heading towards Fife's East Neuk, a cluster of fishing villages popular with artists and holidaymakers. Out of season, Anstruther seemed practically deserted. Though Rebus had an address, he stopped to ask directions. Finally, he parked in front of a small terraced house. Candice stared at the red door until he gestured for her to follow him. He hadn't been able to make her understand what they were doing here. Hoped Mr and Mrs Drinic would make a better job of it.

The door was opened by a woman in her early forties. She had long black hair, and peered at him over half-moon glasses. Then her attention shifted to Candice, and she said something in a language both women understood. Candice replied, looking a little shy, not sure what was going on.

'Come in, please,' Mrs Drinic said. 'My husband is in the kitchen.'

They sat around the kitchen table. Mr Drinic was heavily built, with a thick brown moustache and wavy brown and silver hair. A pot of tea was produced, and Mrs Drinic drew her chair beside Candice's and began talking again.

'She's explaining to the girl,' Mr Drinic said.

Rebus nodded, sipped the strong tea, listened to a conversation he could not understand. Candice, cautious at first, grew more animated as she told her story, and Mrs Drinic was a skilled listener, sympathising, showing shared horror and exasperation.

'She was taken to Amsterdam, told there would be a job there for her,' Mr Drinic explained. 'I know this has happened to other young women.'

'I think she left a child behind.'

'A son, yes. She's telling my wife about him.'

'What about you?' Rebus asked. 'How did you end up here?'

'I was an architect in Sarajevo. No easy decision, leaving your whole life behind.' He paused. 'We went to Belgrade first. A refugee bus brought us to

Scotland.' He shrugged. 'That was nearly five years ago. Now I am a carpenter.' A smile. 'Distance no object.'

Rebus looked at Candice, who had started crying, Mrs Drinic comforting her.

'We will look after her,' Mrs Drinic said, staring at her husband.

Later, at the door, Rebus tried to give them some money, but they wouldn't take it.

'Is it all right if I come and see her sometime?'

'But of course.'

He stood in front of Candice.

'Her real name is Karina,' Mrs Drinic said quietly.

'Karina.' Rebus tried out the word. She smiled, her eyes softer than Rebus remembered them, as if some transformation were beginning. She bent forward.

'Kiss the girl,' she said.

A peck on both cheeks. Her eyes filling with tears again. Rebus nodded, to let her know he understood everything.

At his car, he waved once, and she blew him another kiss. Then he drove around the corner and stopped, gripping the steering-wheel hard. He wondered if she'd cope. If she'd learn to forget. He thought again of his ex-wife's words. What would she think of him now? Had he exploited Karina? No, but he wondered if that was only because she hadn't been able to give him anything on Telford. He felt he had somehow failed to do the right thing. So far, the only choice she'd had to make was when she'd waited for him by his car rather than going back to Telford. Before then and after, all the decisions had been taken for her. In a sense, she was still as trapped as ever, because the locks and chains were in her mind; they were what she expected from life. It would take time for her to change, to begin trusting the world again. The Drinics would help her.

Heading south down the coast, thinking about families, he decided to visit his brother.

Mickey lived on an estate in Kirkcaldy, his red BMW parked in the driveway. He was just home from work and suitably surprised to see Rebus.

'Chrissie and the kids are at her mum's,' he said. 'I was going to grab a curry for dinner. How about a beer?'

'Maybe just a coffee,' Rebus said. He sat in the lounge until Mickey returned, toting a couple of old shoe-boxes.

'Look what I dug out of the attic last weekend. Thought you might like a look. Milk and sugar?'

'A spot of milk.'

While Mickey went to the kitchen to fetch the coffee, Rebus examined the boxes. They were filled with packets of photographs. The packets had dates on them, some with questionmarks. Rebus opened one at random. Holiday snaps. A fancy-dress parade. A picnic. Rebus didn't have any pictures of his parents, and the photos startled him. His mother had thicker legs than he remembered, but a tidy body, too. His father used the same grin in every shot, a grin Rebus shared with Mickey. Digging further into the box, he found one of himself with Rhona and Sammy. They were on a beach somewhere, the wind playing havoc. Peter Gabriel: 'Family Snapshot'.

Rebus couldn't place it at all. Mickey came back through with a mug of coffee and a bottle of beer.

'There are some,' he said, 'I don't know who the people are. Relatives maybe? Grandma and Grandad?'

'I'm not sure I'd be much help.'

Mickey handed over a menu. 'Here,' he said, 'best Indian in town. Pick what you want.'

So Rebus chose, and Mickey phoned the order in. Twenty minutes till delivery. Rebus was on to another packet. These photos were older still, the 1940s. His father in uniform. The soldiers wore hats like McDonald's counter staff. They also wore long khaki shorts. 'Malaya' written on the backs of some, 'India' on the others.

'Remember, the old man got himself wounded in Malaya?' Mickey said.

'No, he didn't.'

'He showed us the wound. It was in his knee.'

Rebus was shaking his head. 'Uncle Jimmy told me it was a cut Dad got playing football. He kept picking the scab off, ended with a scar.'

'He told us it was a war wound.'

'He was fibbing.'

Mickey had started on the other box. 'Here, look at these . . .' Handing over an inch-thick collection of postcards and photographs, secured with an elastic band. Rebus pulled the band off, turned the cards over, saw his own writing. The photos were of him, too: posed snaps, badly taken.

'Where did you get these?'

'You always used to send me a card or a photo, don't you remember?'

They were all from Rebus's own Army days. 'I'd forgotten,' he said.

'Once a fortnight, usually. A letter to Dad, a card for me.'

Rebus sat back in his chair and started to go through them. Judging by the postmarks, they were in chronological sequence. Training, then service in Germany and Ulster, more exercises in Cyprus, Malta, Finland, and the desert of Saudi Arabia. The tone of each postcard was breezy, so that Rebus failed to recognise his own voice. The cards from Belfast consisted of almost nothing but jokes, yet Rebus remembered that as one of the most nightmarish periods of his life.

'I used to love getting them,' Mickey said, smiling. 'I'll tell you, you almost had me joining up.'

Rebus was still thinking of Belfast: the closed barracks, the whole compound a fortress. After a shift out on the streets, there was no way to let off steam. Booze, gambling and fights – all taking place within the same four walls. All culminating in the Mean Machine . . . And here were these postcards, here was the image of Rebus's past life that Mickey had lived with these past twenty-odd years.

And it was all a lie.

Or was it? Where did the reality lie, other than in Rebus's own head? The postcards were fake documents, but they were also the only ones in existence. There was nothing to contradict them, nothing except Rebus's word. It was the same with the Rat Line, the same with Joseph Lintz's story. Rebus looked at his brother and knew he could break the spell right now. All he had to do was tell him the truth.

'What's the matter?' Mickey asked.

'Nothing.'

'Ready for that beer yet? The food'll be here any second.'

Rebus stared at the cooling mug of coffee. 'More than ready,' he said, putting the rubber band back around his past. 'But I'll stick to this.' He lifted the mug, toasted his brother.

10

Next morning, Rebus went to St Leonard's, telephoned the NCIS centre at Prestwick and asked if they had anything connecting British criminals to European prostitution. His reasoning: *someone* had brought Candice – she was still Candice to him – from Amsterdam to Britain, and he didn't think it was Telford. Whoever it was, Rebus would get to them somehow. He wanted to show Candice her chains could be broken.

He got NCIS to fax him what information they had. Most of it concerned the 'Tippelzone', a licensed car park where drivers went for sex. It was worked by foreign prostitutes mainly, most of them lacking work permits, many smuggled in from Eastern Europe. The main gangs seemed to be from former Yugoslavia. NCIS had no names for any of these kidnappers-cum-pimps. There was nothing about prostitutes making the trip from Amsterdam to Britain.

Rebus went into the car park to smoke his second cigarette of the day. There were a couple of other smokers out there, a small brotherhood of social pariahs. Back in the office, the Farmer wanted to know if there was any progress on Lintz.

'Maybe if I brought him in and slapped him around a bit,' Rebus suggested.

'Be serious, will you?' the Farmer growled, stalking back to his office.

Rebus sat down at his desk and pulled forward a file.

'Your problem, Inspector,' Lintz had said to him once, 'is that you're afraid of being taken seriously. You want to give people what you think they expect. I mention the Ishtar gate, and you talk of some Hollywood movie. At first I thought this was meant to rouse me to some indiscretion, but now it seems more a game you are playing against *yourself.*'

Rebus: seated in his usual chair in Lintz's drawing room. The view from the window was of Queen Street Gardens. They were kept locked: you had to pay for a key.

'Do educated people frighten you?'

Rebus looked at the old man. 'No.'

'Are you sure? Don't you perhaps wish you were more like them?' Lintz grinned, showing small, discoloured teeth. 'Intellectuals like to see themselves as history's victims, prejudiced against, arrested for their beliefs, even tortured and murdered. But Karadzic thinks himself an intellectual. The Nazi hierarchy had its thinkers and philosophers. And even in Babylon . . .' Lintz got up, poured himself more tea. Rebus declined a refill.

'Even in Babylon, Inspector,' Lintz continued, getting comfortable again, 'with its opulence and its artistry, with its enlightened king ... do you know what they did? Nebuchadnezzar held the Jews captive for seventy years. This splendid, awe-inspiring civilisation ... Do you begin to see the madness, Inspector, the flaws that run so deep in us?'

'Maybe I need glasses.'

Lintz threw his cup across the room. 'You need to listen and to learn! You need to understand!'

The cup and saucer lay on the carpet, still intact. Tea was soaking into the elaborate design, where it would become all but invisible ...

He parked on Buccleuch Place. The Slavic Studies department was housed in one of the tenements. He tried the secretary's office first, asked if Dr Colquhoun was around.

'I haven't seen him today.'

When Rebus explained what he wanted, the secretary tried a couple of numbers but didn't find anyone. Then she suggested he take a look in their library, which was one floor up and kept locked. She handed him a key.

The room was about sixteen feet by twelve, and smelled stuffy. The shutters across the windows were closed, giving the place no natural light. A No Smoking sign sat on one of four desks. On another sat an ashtray with three butts in it. One entire wall was shelved, filled with books, pamphlets, magazines. There were boxes of press cuttings, and maps on the walls showing Yugoslavia's changing demarcation lines. Rebus lifted down the most recent box of cuttings.

Like a lot of people he knew, Rebus didn't know much about the war in ex-Yugoslavia. He'd seen some of the news reports, been shocked by the pictures, then had got on with his life. But if the cuttings were to be believed, the whole region was being run by war criminals. The Implementation Force seemed to have done its damnedest to avoid confrontation. There had been a few arrests recently, but nothing substantial: out of a meagre seventy-four suspects charged, only *seven* had been apprehended.

He found nothing about slave traders, so thanked the secretary and gave her back her key, then crawled through the city traffic. When the call came on his mobile, he nearly went off the road.

Candice had disappeared.

Mrs Drinic was distraught. They'd had dinner last night, breakfast this morning, and Karina had seemed fine.

'There was a lot she said she couldn't tell us,' Mr Drinic said, standing behind his seated wife, hands stroking her shoulders. 'She said she wanted to forget.'

And then she'd gone out for a walk down to the harbour, and hadn't returned. Lost maybe, though the village was small. Mr Drinic had been working; his wife had gone out, asking people if they'd seen her.

'And Mrs Muir's son,' she said, 'he told me she'd been taken away in a car.'

'Where was this?' Rebus asked.

'Just a couple of streets away,' Mr Drinic said.

'Show me.'

Outside his home on Seaford Road, Eddie Muir, aged eleven, told Rebus what he'd seen. A car stopping beside a woman. A bit of chat, though he couldn't hear it. The door opening, the woman getting in.

'Which door, Eddie?'

'One of the back ones. Had to be, there were two of them in the car already.'

'Men?'

Eddie nodded.

'And the woman got in by herself? I mean, they didn't grab her or anything?'

Eddie shook his head. He was straddling his bike, keen to be going. One foot kept testing a pedal.

'Can you describe the car?'

'Big, a bit flash. Not from round here.'

'And the men?'

'Didn't really get a good look. Driver was wearing a Pars shirt.'

Meaning a football shirt, Dunfermline Athletic. Which would mean he was from Fife. Rebus frowned. A pick-up? Could that be it? Candice back to her old ways so soon? Not likely, not in a place like this, on a street like this. It was no chance encounter. Mrs Drinic was right: she'd been snatched. Which meant someone had known where to find her. Had Rebus been followed yesterday? If he had, they'd been invisible. Some device on his car? It seemed unlikely, but he checked wheel-arches and the underbody: nothing. Mrs Drinic had calmed a little, her husband having administered medicinal vodka. Rebus could use a shot himself, but turned down the offer.

'Did she make any phone calls?' he asked. Drinic shook his head. 'What about strangers hanging around the street?'

'I would have noticed. After Sarajevo, it's hard to feel safe, Inspector.' He opened his arms. 'And here's the proof – nowhere's safe.'

'Did you tell anyone about Karina?'

'Who would we tell?'

Who knew? That was the question. Rebus did. And Claverhouse and Ormiston knew about the place, because Colquhoun had mentioned it.

Colquhoun knew. The nervy old Slavic Studies specialist knew . . . On the way back to Edinburgh, Rebus tried phoning him at office and home: no reply. He'd told the Drinics to let him know if Candice came back, but he didn't think she'd be coming back. He remembered the look she'd given him early on when he'd asked her to trust him. *I won't be surprised if you let me down.* Like she'd known back then that he'd fail. And she'd given him a second chance, waiting for him beside his car. And he'd let her down. He got back on his mobile and called Jack Morton.

'Jack,' he said, 'for Christ's sake, talk me out of having a drink.'

He tried Colquhoun's home address and the Slavic Studies office: both locked up tight. Then he drove to Flint Street and looked for Tommy Telford in the arcade. But Telford wasn't there. He was in the café's back office, surrounded as usual by his men.

'I want to talk to you,' Rebus said.

'So talk.'

'Without the audience.' Rebus pointed to Pretty-Boy. 'That one can stay.'

Telford took his time, but finally nodded, and the room began to empty. Pretty-Boy stood against a wall, hands behind his back. Telford had his feet up on his desk, leaning back in his chair. They were relaxed, confident. Rebus knew what *he* looked like: a caged bear.

'I want to know where she is.'

'Who?'

'Candice.'

Telford smiled. 'Still on about her, Inspector? How should I know where she is?'

'Because a couple of your boys grabbed her.' But as he spoke, Rebus realised he was making a mistake. Telford's gang was a *family*: they'd grown up together in Paisley. Not many Dunfermline supporters that distant from Fife. He stared at Pretty-Boy, who ran Telford's prostitutes. Candice had arrived in Edinburgh from a city of bridges, maybe Newcastle. Telford had Newcastle connections. And the Newcastle United strip – vertical black and white lines – was damned close to Dunfermline's. Probably only a kid in Fife could make the mistake.

A Newcastle strip. A Newcastle car.

Telford was talking, but Rebus wasn't listening. He walked straight out of the office and back to the Saab. Drove to Fettes – the Crime Squad offices – and started looking. He found a contact number for a DS Miriam Kenworthy. Tried the number but she wasn't there.

'Fuck it,' he told himself, getting back into his car.

The A1 was hardly the country's fastest road – Abernethy was right about that. Still, without the daytime traffic Rebus made decent time on his way south. It was late evening when he arrived in Newcastle, pubs emptying, queues forming outside clubs, a few United shirts on display, looking like prison bars. He didn't know the city. Drove around it in circles, passing the same signs and landmarks, heading further out, just cruising.

Looking for Candice. Or for girls who might know her.

After a couple of hours, he gave up, headed back into the centre. He'd had the idea of sleeping in his car, but when he found a hotel with an empty room, the thought of en-suite facilities suddenly seemed too good to miss.

He made sure there was no mini-bar.

A long soak with his eyes closed, mind and body still racing from the drive. He sat in a chair by his window and listened to the night: taxis and yells, delivery lorries. He couldn't sleep. He lay on the bed, watching soundless TV, remembering Candice in the hotel room, asleep under sweet wrappers. Deacon Blue: 'Chocolate Girl.'

He woke up to breakfast TV. Checked out of the hotel and had breakfast in a café, then called Miriam Kenworthy's office, relieved to find she was an early starter.

'Come right round,' she said, sounding bemused. 'You're only a couple of minutes away.'

She was younger than her telephone voice, face softer than her attitude. It was a milkmaid's face, rounded, the cheeks pink and plump. She studied him, swivelling slightly in her chair as he told her the story.

'Tarawicz,' she said when he'd finished. 'Jake Tarawicz. Real name Joachim, probably.' Kenworthy smiled. 'Some of us around here call him Mr Pink Eyes. He's had dealings – meetings anyway – with this guy Telford.' She opened the brown folder in front of her. 'Mr Pink Eyes has a lot of European connections. You know Chechnia?'

'In Russia?'

'It's Russia's Sicily, if you know what I mean.'

'Is that where Tarawicz comes from?'

'It's one theory. The other is that he's Serbian. Might explain why he set up the convoy.'

'What convoy?'

'Running aid lorries to former Yugoslavia. A real humanitarian, our Mr Pink.'

'But also a way of smuggling people out?'

Kenworthy looked at him. 'You've been doing your homework.'

'Call it an educated guess.'

'Well, it gets him noticed. He got a papal blessing six months ago. Married to an Englishwoman – not for love. She was one of his girls.'

'But it gives him residency here.'

She nodded. 'He hasn't been around that long, five or six years . . .'

Like Telford, Rebus thought.

'But he's built himself a rep, muscled in where there used to be Asians, Turks . . . Story is, he started with a nice line in stolen icons. A ton of stuff has been lifted out of the Soviet bloc. And when that operation started drying, he moved into prossies. Cheap girls, and he could keep them docile with a bit of crack. The crack comes up from London – the Yardies control that particular scene. Mr Pink spreads their goods around the north-east. He also deals heroin for the Turks and sells some girls to Triad brothels.' She looked at Rebus, saw she had his attention. 'No racial barriers when it comes to business.'

'So I see.'

'Probably also sells drugs to your friend Telford, who distributes them through his nightclubs.'

' "Probably"?'

'We've no hard proof. There was even a story going around that Pink wasn't selling to Telford, he was *buying*.'

Rebus blinked. 'Telford's not that big.'

She shrugged.

'Where would he get the stuff?'

'It was a story, that's all.'

But it had Rebus thinking, because it might help explain the relationship between Tarawicz and Telford . . .

'What does Tarawicz get out of it?' he asked, making his thoughts flesh.

'You mean apart from money? Well, Telford trains a good bouncer. Jock bouncers get respect down here. Then, of course, Telford has shares in a couple of casinos.'

'A way for Tarawicz to launder his cash?' Rebus thought about this. 'Is there anything Tarawicz *doesn't* have a finger in?'

'Plenty. He likes businesses which are fluid. And he's still a relative newcomer.'

Eagles: 'New Kid in Town'.

'We think he's been dealing arms: a lot of stuff crossing into Western Europe. The Chechens seem to have weaponry to spare.' She sniffed, gathered her thoughts.

'Sounds like he's one step ahead of Tommy Telford.' Which would explain why Telford was so keen to do business with him. He was on a learning curve, learning how to fit into the bigger picture. Yardies and Asians, Turks and Chechens, and all the others. Rebus saw them as spokes on a huge wheel which was trundling mercilessly across the world, breaking bones as it went.

'Why "Mr Pink Eyes"?' he asked.

She'd been awaiting the question, slid a colour photo towards him.

It was the close-up of a face, the skin pink and blistered, white lesions running through it. The face was puffy, bloated, and in its midst sat eyes hidden by blue-tinted glasses. There were no eyebrows. The hair above the jutting forehead was thin and yellow. The man looked like some monstrous shaved pig.

'What happened to him?' he asked.

'We don't know. That's the way he looked when he arrived.'

Rebus remembered the description Candice had given: sunglasses, looks like a car-crash victim. Dead ringer.

'I want to talk to him,' Rebus said.

But first, Kenworthy gave him a guided tour. They took her car, and she showed him where the street girls worked. It was mid-morning, no action to speak of. He gave her a description of Candice, and she promised she'd put the word out. They spoke with the few women they met. They all seemed to know Kenworthy, weren't hostile towards her.

'They're the same as you or me,' she told him, driving away. 'Working to feed their kids.'

'Or their habit.'

'That too, of course.'

'In Amsterdam, they've got a union.'

'Doesn't help the poor sods who're shipped there.' Kenworthy signalled at a junction. 'You're sure he has her?'

'I don't think Telford does. Someone knew addresses back in Sarajevo, addresses that were important to her. Someone shipped her out of there.'

'Sounds like Mr Pink all right.'

'And he's the only one who can send her back.'

She looked at him. 'Why would he do a thing like that?'

Just as Rebus was thinking their surroundings couldn't get any grimmer – all industrial decay, gutted buildings and pot-holes – Kenworthy signalled to turn in at the gates of a scrapyard.

'You're kidding?' he said.

Three Alsatians, tethered by thirty-foot chains, barked and bounded towards the car. Kenworthy ignored them, kept driving. It was like being in a ravine. Either side of them stood precarious canyon walls of car wrecks.

'Hear that?'

Rebus heard it: the sound of a collision. The car entered a wide clearing, and he saw a yellow crane, dangling a huge grab from its arm, pluck up the car it had dropped and lift it high, before dropping it again on to the carcass of another. A few men were standing at a safe distance, smoking cigarettes and looking bored. The grab dropped on to the roof of the top car, denting it badly. Glass shimmered on the oily ground, diamonds against black velvet.

Jake Tarawicz – Mr Pink Eyes – was in the crane, laughing and roaring as he picked up the car again, worrying it the way a cat might play with a mouse without noticing it was dead. If he'd seen the new additions to his audience, it didn't show. Kenworthy hadn't got out of her car immediately. First, she'd fixed on a face from her repertoire. When finally she was ready, she nodded to Rebus and they opened their doors simultaneously.

As Rebus stood upright, he saw that the grab had dropped the car and was swinging towards them. Kenworthy folded her arms and stood her ground. Rebus was reminded of those arcade games where you had to pick up a prize. He could see Tarawicz in the cab, manipulating the controls like a kid with a toy. He remembered Tommy Telford on his arcade bike, and saw at once something the two men had in common: neither had ever really grown up.

The motorised hum stopped suddenly, and Tarawicz dropped from the cab. He was wearing a cream suit and emerald shirt, open at the neck. He'd borrowed a pair of green wellies from somewhere, so as to keep his trousers clean. As he walked towards the two detectives, his men stepped into line behind him.

'Miriam,' he said, 'always a pleasure.' He paused. 'Or so the rumour goes.' A couple of his men grinned. Rebus recognised one face: 'The Crab', that's what he'd been called in central Scotland. His grip could crush bones. Rebus hadn't seen him in a long time, and had never seen him so smartly groomed and dressed.

'All right, Crab?' Rebus said.

This seemed to disconcert Tarawicz, who half-turned towards his minion. The Crab stayed quiet, but colour had risen to his neck.

Up close, it was hard not to stare at Mr Pink Eyes's face. His eyes demanded that you meet them, but you really wanted to study the flesh in which they sat.

He was looking at Rebus now.

'Have we met?'

'No.'

'This is Detective Inspector Rebus,' Kenworthy explained. 'He's come all the way from Scotland to see you.'

'I'm flattered.' Tarawicz's grin showed small sharp teeth with gaps between them.

'I think you know why I'm here,' Rebus said.

Tarawicz made a show of astonishment. 'Do I?'

'Telford needed your help. He needed a home address for Candice, a note to her in Serbo-Croat . . .'

'Is this some sort of riddle?'

'And now you've taken her back.'

'Have I?'

Rebus took a half-step forward. Tarawicz's men fanned out either side of

their boss. There was a sheen on Tarawicz's face which could have been sweat or some medical cream.

'She wanted out,' Rebus told him. 'I promised I'd help her. I never break a promise.'

'She wanted out? She told you that?' Tarawicz's voice was teasing.

One of the men behind cleared his throat. Rebus had been wondering about this man, so much smaller and more reticent than the others, better dressed and with sad drooping eyes and sallow skin. Now he knew: lawyer. And the cough was his way of warning Tarawicz that he was saying too much.

'I'm going to take Tommy Telford down,' Rebus said quietly. 'That's my promise to you. Once he's in custody, who knows what he'll say?'

'I'm sure Mr Telford can look after himself, Inspector. Which is more than can be said for Candice.' The lawyer coughed again.

'I want her kept off the streets,' Rebus said.

Tarawicz stared at him, tiny black pupils like spots of absolute darkness.

'Can Thomas Telford go about his daily business unfettered?' he said at last. Behind him, the lawyer almost choked.

'You know I can't promise that,' Rebus said. 'It's not me he has to worry about.'

'Take a message to your friend,' Tarawicz said. 'And afterwards, stop being his friend.'

Rebus realised then: Tarawicz was talking about *Cafferty*. Telford had told him that Rebus was Cafferty's man.

'I think I can do that,' Rebus said quietly.

'Then do it.' Tarawicz turned away.

'And Candice?'

'I'll see what I can do.' He stopped, slid his hands into his jacket pockets. 'Hey, Miriam,' he said, his back still to them, 'I like you better in that red two-piece.'

Laughing, he walked away.

'Get in the car,' Kenworthy said through gritted teeth. Rebus got into the car. She looked nervous, dropped her keys, bent to retrieve them.

'What's wrong?'

'Nothing's wrong,' she snapped.

'The red two-piece?'

She glared at him. 'I don't have a red two-piece.' She did a three-point turn, hitting brakes and accelerator with a little more force than necessary.

'I don't get it.'

'Last week,' she said, 'I bought some red underwear . . . bra and pants.' She revved the engine. 'Part of his little game.'

'So how does he know?'

'That's what I'm wondering.' She shot past the dogs and out of the gate. Rebus thought of Tommy Telford, and how he'd been watching Rebus's flat.

'Surveillance isn't always one-way,' he said, knowing now who'd taught Telford the skill. A little later he asked about the scrapyard.

'He owns it. He's got a compacter, but before the cars get squashed he likes to play with them. And if you cross him, he welds your seatbelt shut.' She looked at him. 'You become part of his game.'

Never get personally involved: it was *the* golden rule. And practically every

case he worked, Rebus broke it. He sometimes felt that the reason he became so involved in his cases was that he had no life of his own. He could only live *through* other people.

Why had he become so involved with Candice? Was it down to her physical resemblance to Sammy? Or was it that she had seemed to need *him*? The way she'd clung to his leg that first day . . . Had he wanted – just for a little while – to be someone's knight in shining armour, the real thing, not some mockery?

John Rebus: complete bloody sham.

He phoned Claverhouse from his car, filled him in. Claverhouse told him not to worry.

'Thanks for that,' Rebus said. 'I feel a whole lot better now. Listen, who's Telford's supplier?'

'For what? Dope?'

'Yes.'

'That's the real joker in the pack. I mean, he does business with Newcastle, but we can't be certain who's dealing and who's buying.'

'What if Telford's selling?'

'Then he's got a line from the continent.'

'What do Drugs Squad say?'

'They say not. If he's landing the stuff from a boat, it means transporting it from the coast. Much more likely he's buying from Newcastle. Tarawicz has the contacts in Europe.'

'Makes you wonder why he needs Tommy Telford at all . . .'

'John, do yourself a favour, switch off for five minutes.'

'Colquhoun seems to be keeping his head down . . .'

'Did you hear me?'

'I'll talk to you soon.'

'Are you heading back?'

'In a manner of speaking.' Rebus cut the call and drove.

11

'Strawman,' said Morris Gerald Cafferty, as he was escorted into the room by two prison guards.

Earlier in the year, Rebus had promised Cafferty he would put a Glasgow gangster, Uncle Joe Toal, behind bars. It hadn't worked, despite Rebus's best efforts. Toal, pleading old age and illness, was still a free man, like a war criminal excused for senility. Ever since then, Cafferty had felt Rebus owed him.

Cafferty sat down, rolled his neck a few times, loosening it.

'So?' he asked.

Rebus nodded for the guards to leave, waited in silence until they'd gone. Then he slipped a quarter-bottle of Bell's from his pocket.

'Keep it,' Cafferty told him. 'From the look of you, I'd say your need was greater than mine.'

Rebus put the bottle back in his pocket. 'I've brought a message from Newcastle.'

Cafferty folded his arms. 'Jake Tarawicz?'

Rebus nodded. 'He wants you to lay off Tommy Telford.'

'What does he mean?'

'Come on, Cafferty. That bouncer who got stabbed, the dealer wounded . . . There's war breaking out.'

Cafferty stared at the detective. 'Not my doing.'

Rebus snorted, but looking into Cafferty's eyes, he found himself almost believing.

'So who was it?' he asked quietly.

'How do I know?'

'Nevertheless, war is breaking out.'

'That's as may be. What's in it for Tarawicz?'

'He does business with Tommy.'

'And to protect that, he needs to have *me* warned off by a cop?' Cafferty was shaking his head. 'You really buy that?'

'I don't know,' Rebus said.

'One way to finish this.' Cafferty paused. 'Take Telford out of the game.' He saw the look on Rebus's face. 'I don't mean top him, I mean put him away. That should be *your* job, Strawman.'

'I only came to deliver a message.'

'And what's in it for you? Something in Newcastle?'

'Maybe.'

'Are you Tarawicz's man now?'

'You know me better than that.'

'Do I?' Cafferty sat back in his chair, stretched out his legs. 'I wonder about that sometimes. I mean, it doesn't keep me awake at night, but I wonder all the same.'

Rebus leaned on the table. 'You must have a bit salted away. Why can't you just be content with that?'

Cafferty laughed. The air felt charged; there might have been only the two of them left in the world. 'You want me to retire?'

'A good boxer knows when to stop.'

'Then neither of us would be much cop in the ring, would we? Got any plans to retire, Strawman?'

Despite himself, Rebus smiled.

'Thought not. Do I have to say something for you to take back to Tarawicz?'

Rebus shook his head. 'That wasn't the deal.'

'Well, if he does come asking, tell him to get some life insurance, the kind with death benefits.'

Rebus looked at Cafferty. Prison might have softened him, but only physically.

'I'd be a happy man if someone took Telford out of the game,' Cafferty went on. 'Know what I mean, Strawman? It'd be worth a lot to me.'

Rebus stood up. 'No deal,' he said. 'Personally, I'd be happy if you wiped one another out. I'd be jumping for joy at ring-side.'

'Know what happens at ring-side?' Cafferty rubbed at his temples. 'You tend to get spattered with blood.'

'As long as it's someone else's.'

The laughter came from deep within Cafferty's chest. 'You're not a spectator, Strawman. It's not in your nature.'

'And you're some kind of psychologist?'

'Maybe not,' said Cafferty. 'But I know what gets people excited.'

Book Three

'Cover my face as the animals cry.'

Running through the hospital, stopping nurses to ask directions. Sweat dripping off him, tie hanging loose around his neck. Taking right turns, left turns, looking for signs. Whose fault? He kept asking himself that. A message which failed to reach him. Because he was on a surveillance. Because he wasn't in radio contact. Because the station didn't know how important the message was.

Now running, a stitch in his side. He'd run all the way from the car. Up two flights of stairs, down corridors. The place was quiet. Middle of the night.

'Maternity!' he called to a man pushing a trolley. The man pointed to a set of doors. He pushed through them. Three nurses in a glass cubicle. One of them came out.

'Can I help?'

'I'm John Rebus. My wife . . .'

She gave him a hard look. 'Third bed along.' Pointing . . . Third bed along, curtains closed around it. He pulled the curtains open. Rhona lay on her side, face still flushed, hair sticking to her brow. And beside her, nuzzling into her, a tiny perfection with wisps of brown hair and black, unfocused eyes.

He touched the nose, ran a finger round the curves of an ear. The face twitched. He bent past it to kiss his wife.

'Rhona . . . I'm really sorry. They didn't get the message to me until ten minutes ago. How did it . . . ? I mean . . . he's beautiful.'

'He's a she,' his wife said, turning away from him.

12

Rebus was sitting in his boss's office. It was nine-fifteen and he had slept for probably forty-five minutes the previous night. There'd been the hospital vigil and Sammy's operation: something about a blood clot. She was still unconscious, still 'critical'. He'd called Rhona in London. She'd told him she'd catch the first train she could. He'd given her his mobile number, so she could let him know when she arrived. She'd started to ask . . . her voice had cracked. She'd put down the receiver. He'd tried to find some feeling for her. Richard and Linda Thompson: 'Withered and Died'.

He'd called Mickey, who said he'd drop by the hospital sometime today. And that was it for the family. There were other people he could call, people like Patience, who had been his lover for a time, and Sammy's landlady until far more recently. But he didn't. He knew in the morning he'd call the office where Sammy worked. He wrote it in his notebook so he wouldn't forget. And then he'd called Sammy's flat and given Ned Farlowe the news.

Farlowe had asked a question nobody else had: 'How about you? Are you all right?'

Rebus had looked around the hospital corridor. 'Not exactly.'

'I'll be right there.'

So they'd spent a couple of hours in one another's company, not really saying very much at first. Farlowe smoked, and Rebus helped him empty the pack. He couldn't reciprocate with whisky – there was nothing in the bottle – but he'd bought the young man several cups of coffee, since Farlowe had spent nearly all his money on the taxi from Shandon . . .

'Wakey-wakey, John.'

Rebus's boss was shaking him gently. Rebus blinked, straightened in his chair.

'Sorry, sir.'

Chief Superintendent Watson went around the desk and sat down. 'Hellish sorry to hear about Sammy. I don't really know what to say, except that she's in my prayers.'

'Thank you, sir.'

'Do you want some coffee?' The Farmer's coffee had a reputation throughout the station, but Rebus accepted a mug gladly. 'How is she anyway?'

'Still unconscious.'

'No sign of the car?'

'Not the last I heard.'

'Who's handling it?'

'Bill Pryde started the ball rolling last night. I don't know who's taken it from him.'

'I'll find out.' The Farmer made an internal call, Rebus watching him over the rim of his mug. The Farmer was a big man, imposing behind a desk. His cheeks were a mass of tiny red veins and his thin hair lay across the dome of his head like the lines of a well-furrowed field. There were photos on his desk: grandchildren. The photos had been taken in a garden. There was a swing in the background. One of the children was holding a teddy bear. Rebus felt his throat start to ache, tried to choke it back.

The Farmer put down the receiver. 'Bill's still on it,' he said. 'Felt if he worked straight through we might get a quicker result.'

'That's good of him.'

'Look, we'll let you know the minute we get something, but meantime you'll probably want to go home . . .'

'No, sir.'

'Or to the hospital.'

Rebus nodded slowly. Yes, the hospital. But not right this minute. He had to talk to Bill Pryde first.

'And meantime, I'll reassign your cases.' The Farmer started writing. 'There's this War Crimes thing, and your liaison on Telford. Are you working on anything else?'

'Sir, I'd prefer it if you . . . I mean, I want to keep working.'

The Farmer looked at him, then leaned back in his chair, pen balanced between his fingers.

'Why?'

Rebus shrugged. 'I want to keep busy.' Yes, there was that. And he didn't want anyone else taking his work. It was *his*. He owned it; it owned him.

'Look, John, you're going to want some time off, right?'

'I can handle things, sir.' His gaze met the Farmer's. 'Please.'

Across the hall in the CID room he nodded as everyone came up to say how sorry they were. One person stayed at their desk – Bill Pryde knew Rebus was coming to see him.

'Morning, Bill.'

Pryde nodded. They'd met in the wee small hours at the Infirmary. Ned Farlowe had been napping in a chair, so they'd stepped into the corridor to talk. Pryde looked tireder now. He had loosened the top button of his dark green shirt. His brown suit looked lived-in.

'Thanks for sticking with it,' Rebus said, drawing over a chair. Thinking: *I'd rather have had someone else, someone sharper* . . .

'No problem.'

'Any news?'

'A couple of good eyewitnesses. They were waiting to cross at the lights.'

'What's their story?'

Pryde considered his reply. He knew he was dealing with a father as well as a cop. 'She was crossing the road. Looked like she was heading down Minto Street, maybe making for the bus stop.'

Rebus shook his head. 'She was walking, Bill. Going to a friend's in Gilmour Road.'

She'd said as much over the pizza, apologising that she couldn't stay longer. Just one more coffee at the end of the meal . . . one more coffee and she wouldn't have been there at that moment. Or if she'd accepted his offer of a lift . . . When you thought about life, you thought of it as chunks of time, but really all it was was a series of connected moments, any one of which could change you completely.

'The car was heading south out of town,' Pryde went on. 'Looks like he ran a red light. Motorist sitting behind him seemed to think so.'

'Reckon he was drunk?'

Pryde nodded. 'Way he was driving. I mean, could be he just lost control, but in that case why didn't he stop?'

'Description?'

Pryde shook his head. 'We've got a dark car, a bit sporty. Nobody caught the licence plate.'

'It's a busy enough street, must've been other cars around.'

'A couple of people have called in.' Pryde flicked through his notes. 'Nothing helpful, but I'm going to interview them, see if I can jog a memory or two.'

'Could the car have been nicked? Maybe that's why he was in a hurry.'

'I can check.'

'I'll help you.'

Pryde considered this. 'You sure?'

'Try and stop me, Bill.'

'No skid marks,' Pryde said, 'no sign that he tried braking, either before or after.'

They were standing at the junction of Minto Street and Newington Road. The cross-streets were Salisbury Place and Salisbury Road. Cars, vans and buses queued at the traffic lights as pedestrians crossed the road.

It could have been any one of you, Rebus thought. Any one of them could have taken Sammy's place . . .

'She was about here,' Pryde went on, pointing to a spot where, just past the lights, a bus lane started. The carriageway was wide, a four-lane road. She hadn't crossed at the lights. She'd been lazy, carrying on down Minto Street a few strides, then crossing in a diagonal. When she'd been a child, they'd taught her about crossing the road. Green Cross Code, all of that. Drummed it into her. Rebus looked around. At the top of Minto Street were some private houses and bed & breakfasts. On one corner stood a bank, on another a branch of Remnant Kings, with a takeaway next door.

'The takeaway would have been open,' Rebus said, pointing. On the third corner stood a Spar. 'That place, too. Where did you say she was?'

'The bus lane.' She'd crossed three lanes, been only a yard or two from safety. 'Witnesses say she was nearly at the kerb when he hit her. I think he was drunk, lost it for a second.' Pryde nodded towards the bank. There were two phone boxes in front of it. 'Witness called from there.' The wall behind the phone boxes had a poster glued to it. Grinning maniac behind a steering-wheel, and some writing: 'So many pedestrians, so little time'. A computer game . . .

'It would have been so easy to avoid her,' Rebus said quietly.

'Sure you're OK? There's a café up the road.'

'I'm fine, Bill.' He looked around, took a deep breath. 'Looks like offices behind the Spar, doubtful anyone would have been there. But there are flats above Remnant Kings and the bank.'

'Want to talk to them?'

'And the Spar and the kebab shop. You take the B&Bs and the houses, meet back here in half an hour.'

Rebus talked to everyone he could find. In the Spar, there was a new shift on, but he got home phone numbers from the manager and called up the workers from the previous night. They hadn't seen or heard anything. First they'd known had been the flashing lights of the ambulance. The kebab shop was closed, but when Rebus banged on the door a woman came through from the back, wiping her hands on a tea-towel. He pressed his warrant card to the glass door, and she let him in. The shop had been busy last night. She didn't see the accident – she called it that, 'the accident'. And that's what it was: the word really hadn't sunk in until she said it. Elvis Costello: 'Accidents Will Happen'. Was the next line really 'It's only hit and run'?

'No,' the woman said, 'the first thing that caught my attention was the crowd. I mean, only three or four people, but I could see they were standing around something. And then the ambulance came. Will she be all right?'

The look in her eyes was one Rebus had encountered before. It almost wanted the victim dead, because then there was a story to be told.

'She's in hospital,' he said, unable to look at the woman any longer.

'Yes, but the paper said she's in a coma.'

'What paper?'

She brought him the first edition of the day's *Evening News*. There was a paragraph on one of the inside pages – 'Hit and Run Coma Victim'.

It wasn't a coma. She was unconscious, that was all. But Rebus was thankful for the story. Maybe someone would read it and come forward. Maybe guilt would begin to press down on the driver. Maybe there'd been a passenger . . . It was hard to keep secrets, usually you told *some*one.

He tried Remnant Kings, but of course they had been closed last night, so he climbed to the flats above. There was no one home at the first flat. He wrote a brief message on the back of a business card and pushed it through the letterbox, then jotted down the surname on the door. If they didn't call him, he'd call them. A young man answered the second door. He was just out of his teens and pushed a thick lock of black hair away from his eyes. He wore Buddy Holly glasses and had acne scars around his mouth. Rebus introduced himself. The hand went to the hair again, a backward glance into the flat.

'Do you live here?' Rebus asked.

'Mm, yeah. Like, I'm not the owner. We rent it.'

There were no names on the door. 'Anyone else in at the moment?'

'Nope.'

'Are you all students?'

The young man nodded. Rebus asked his name.

'Rob. Robert Renton. What's this about?'

'There was an accident last night, Rob. A hit and run.' So many times he'd been in this situation, passing on the bland news of another changed life. It was a whole hour since he'd telephoned the hospital. In the end,

they'd taken his mobile number, said it might be easier if they phoned him whenever there was news. They meant easier for them, not him.

'Oh, yes,' Renton was saying, 'I saw it.'

Rebus blinked. 'You saw it?'

Renton was nodding, hair bobbing in front of his eyes. 'From the window. I was up changing a CD, and –'

'Is it OK if I come in for a minute? I want to see what kind of view you had.'

Renton puffed out his cheeks, exhaled. 'Well, I suppose . . .'

And Rebus was in.

The living room was fairly tidy. Renton went ahead of him, crossed to where a hi-fi rack sat between two windows. 'I was putting on a new CD, and I looked out of the window. You can see the bus stop, and I wondered if I might catch Jane coming off a bus.' He paused. 'Jane's Eric's girlfriend.'

The words washed over Rebus. He was looking down on the street, where Sammy had been walking. 'Tell me what you saw.'

'This girl was crossing the road. She was nice-looking . . . I thought so anyway. Then this car came through the lights, swerved and sent her flying.'

Rebus closed his eyes for a second.

'She must have gone ten feet in the air, hit that hedge, bounced back on to the pavement. She didn't move after that.'

Rebus opened his eyes. He was at the window, Renton standing just behind his left shoulder. Down on the street, people were crossing the road, walking over the spot where Sammy had been hit, the spot where she'd landed. Flicking ash on to the pavement where she'd lain.

'I don't suppose you saw the driver?'

'Not from this angle.'

'Any passengers?'

'Couldn't tell.'

He wears glasses, Rebus thought. How reliable is he?

'When you saw it happen, you didn't go down?'

'I'm not a medical student or anything.' He nodded towards an easel in the corner, and Rebus noticed a shelf of paints and brushes. 'Someone ran to the phone box, so I knew help was coming.'

Rebus nodded. 'Anyone else see it?'

'They were in the kitchen.' Renton paused. 'I know what you're thinking.' Rebus doubted it. 'You're thinking I wear specs, so maybe I didn't see it right. But he definitely swerved. You know . . . deliberately. I mean, like he was aiming for her.' He nodded to himself.

'*Aiming* for her?'

Renton made a movement with his hand, imitating a car gliding off one course and on to another. 'He steered straight for her.'

'The car didn't lose control?'

'That would have been jerkier, wouldn't it?'

'What colour was the car?'

'Dark green.'

'And the make?'

Renton shrugged. 'I'm hopeless with cars. Tell you what though . . .'

'What?'

Renton took off his glasses, started polishing them. 'Why don't I try sketching it for you?'

He moved the easel over to the window and got to work. Rebus went into the hall and called the hospital. The person he got through to didn't sound too surprised.

'No change, I'm afraid. She's got a couple of visitors with her.'

Mickey and Rhona. Rebus terminated the call, made another to Pryde's mobile.

'I'm in one of the flats over Remnant Kings. I've got an eyewitness.'

'Yes?'

'He saw the whole thing. And he's an art student.'

'Yes?'

'Come on, Bill. Do you want me to draw it for you?'

There was silence for a moment, then Pryde said 'Ah'.

13

Rebus held the mobile to his ear as he walked through the hospital.

'Joe Herdman's put together a list,' Bill Pryde was saying. 'Rover 600 series, the newer Ford Mondeos, Toyota Celica, plus a couple of Nissans. Rank outsider is the BMW 5-series.'

'It narrows things down a bit, I suppose.'

'Joe says the Rover, Mondeo and Celica are favourites. He's given me a few more details – chrome around the number-plates, stuff like that. I'm going to call our artist friend, see if anything clicks.'

A nurse was glaring at Rebus as he walked towards her.

'Let me know what he says. Talk to you later, Bill.' Rebus slipped the phone back into his pocket.

'You're not supposed to use those things in here,' the nurse snapped.

'Look, I'm in a bit of a hurry . . .'

'They can interfere with the machines.'

Rebus pulled up, colour leaving his face. 'I forgot,' he said. He put a shaking hand to his forehead.

'Are you all right?'

'Fine, fine. Look, I won't do it again, OK?' He started to move off. 'You can rely on that.'

Rebus took a photocopy of Renton's drawing from his pocket. Joe Herdman was a desk sergeant who knew everything about cars. He'd been useful before, turning a vague description into something more concrete. Rebus looked at the drawing as he walked. All the details were there: buildings in the background, the hedge, the onlookers. And Sammy, caught at the point of impact. She'd half-turned, was stretching out her hands as if she could push the car to a stop. But Renton had drawn fine lines issuing from the back of the car, representing the air being pushed, representing speed. Where there should have been a face, he had left a blank oval. The back half of the car was very clearly defined, the front a blur of disappearing perspective. Renton said he'd left out anything he couldn't be sure of. He promised he hadn't let his imagination fill in the blanks.

It was the face, or the lack of it . . . it disturbed Rebus more than anything else in the picture. He drew himself into the scene, wondered what he'd have done. Would he have concentrated on the car, caught its licence plate? Or would his attention have been focused on Sammy? Which would have prevailed: cop instincts or fatherhood? Someone at the station had said, 'Don't worry, we'll get him.' Not, 'Don't worry, she'll be all right.'

Which brought it all down to two things: him – meaning the driver – and retribution, rather than her – the victim – and recovery.

'I'd just have been another witness,' Rebus said quietly. Then he folded the drawing and put it away.

Sammy had a room to herself, all tubes and machinery, the way he'd seen it in films and on TV. Only here the room was dingier, paint flaking from the walls and around the window-frames. The chairs had metal legs and rubber feet and moulded plastic seats. A woman rose as he came in. They embraced. He kissed the side of her forehead.

Aiming for her. Didn't anyone say that?

'Hello, Rhona.'

'Hello, John.'

She looked tired, of course, but her hair was stylishly cut and dyed the colour of a dull golden harvest. Her clothes were smart and she wore jewellery. He studied her eyes. Their colour was wrong. Coloured contacts. Not even her eyes were going to betray her past.

'Christ, Rhona, I'm sorry.'

He was whispering, not wanting to disturb Sammy. Which was ludicrous, because right now all he wanted in the world was for her to wake up.

'How is she?' he asked.

'Much the same.'

Mickey stood up. There were three chairs arranged in a sort of semi-circle. Mickey and Rhona had been sitting with an empty chair between them. As Rhona broke from Rebus's embrace, his brother took her place.

'This is so fucking awful,' Mickey said, his voice low. He looked the same as ever: a party animal who'd stopped getting the invites.

Niceties dispensed with, Rebus went to Sammy's bedside. Her face was still bruised, and now he could place the probable cause of each abrasion: hedge, wall, pavement. One leg was broken, both arms heavily bandaged. A teddy bear, missing one ear, lay by her head. Rebus smiled.

'You brought Pa Broon.'

'Yes.'

'Do they know yet if there's any . . . ?' His eyes were on Sammy as he spoke.

'What?' Rhona wanted him to spell it out. No hiding place.

'Brain damage,' he said.

'Nobody's told us anything,' she said, sounding snubbed.

Aiming for her. Didn't anyone say that? No, none of the other onlookers had even hinted as much, but then they hadn't had Renton's grandstand view.

'Has nobody been in?'

'Not since I got here.'

'And I was here before Rhona,' Mickey added. 'Haven't seen a soul.'

It was enough. Rebus strode from the room. A doctor and two nurses were standing chatting at the end of the corridor. One of the nurses was leaning against a wall.

'What's going on?' Rebus exploded. 'Nobody's been near my daughter all morning!'

The doctor was young, male. Blond hair cut short with a parting.

'We're doing everything we can.'

'What does that mean?'

'I can appreciate that you're –'

'Fuck you, pal. Why hasn't the big man been to look at her? Why's she just lying there like a –' Rebus choked back the words.

'Your daughter was seen by two specialists this morning,' the doctor said quietly. 'We're waiting for some test results to determine whether to operate again. There's some brain swelling. The tests take a little time to process, there's nothing we can do about it.'

Rebus felt cheated: still angry, but nothing to feel angry *about*, not here. He nodded, turned away.

Back in the room, he explained the situation to Rhona. A suitcase and large holdall were sitting behind one of the machines.

'Listen,' he told her, 'it'd make sense if you stayed at the flat. It's only ten minutes away, and I could let you have the car.'

She was shaking her head. 'We're booked into the Sheraton.'

'The flat's nearer, and I tend not to charge . . .' *We?* Rebus looked at Mickey, whose eyes were on the bed. Then the door opened and a man came in. Short, thickly built, breathing hard. He was rubbing his hands to let everyone know he'd been to the toilet. Loose folds of flesh furrowed his brow and bulged from his shirt collar. His hair was thick and black, like an oil-slick. He stopped when he saw Rebus.

'John,' Rhona said, 'this is a friend of mine, Jackie.'

'Jackie Platt,' the man said, reaching out a plump hand.

'When Jackie heard, he insisted on driving me up.'

Platt shrugged, his head almost disappearing into his shoulders. 'Couldn't have her training it up on her ownio.'

'Hell of a drive,' Mickey said, his tone hinting at repetition.

'Could have done without the roadworks,' Jackie Platt agreed. Rebus's eyes caught Rhona's; she looked away quickly, dodging reproach.

To Rebus, this bulk didn't belong. It was as if a character had wandered on to the wrong set. Platt hadn't been in the script.

'She looks so peaceful, don't she?' the Londoner was saying, making for the bed. He touched her arm, Sammy's bandaged arm, grazing it with the back of his hand. Rebus's fingernails dug into his palms.

Then Platt yawned. 'You know, Rhona, it might not be good manners, but I think I'm about to crash. See you back at the hotel?' She nodded, relieved. Platt picked up the suitcase. As he passed her, his hand went into his trouser pocket, came out with a fold of banknotes.

'Get a cab back, all right?'

'All right, Jackie. See you later.'

'Cheers, pet.' And he squeezed her hand. 'Take care, Mickey. All the best, John.' A huge, face-creasing wink, then he was gone. They waited in silence for a few seconds. Rhona held up her free hand, the one without the wad of notes.

'Not a word, OK?'

'Furthest thing from my mind,' Rebus said, sitting down. ' "Think I'm about to crash". Tactful or what?'

'Come on, Johnny,' Mickey said. Johnny: only Mickey could do that, using the name so that the years fell from both of them. Rebus looked at

his brother and smiled. Mickey was a therapist by profession; he knew the things to say.

'Why the cases?' Rebus asked Rhona.

'What?'

'You're going to a hotel, why not leave them in his car?'

'I thought about staying here. They said I could if I wanted to. Only then I saw her . . . and I changed my mind.' Tears started down her face, smudging already-smudged mascara. Mickey had a handkerchief ready.

'John, what if she . . . ? Oh, Jesus Christ, why did this have to happen?' She was wailing now. Rebus went over to her chair, crouched in front of it, his hands resting on hers. 'She's all we've got, John. She's all we ever had.'

'She's still here, Rhona. She's right here.'

'But why her? Why Samantha?'

'I'll ask him when I find him, Rhona.' He kissed her hair, his eyes on Mickey. 'And believe me, I'm going to find him.'

Later, when Ned Farlowe visited, Rebus took him outside. There was drizzle falling, but the air felt good.

'One of the eyewitnesses,' Rebus said, 'thinks it was deliberate.'

'I don't understand.'

'He thinks the driver meant to hit Sammy.'

'I still don't get it.'

'Look, there are two scenarios. One, he was intent on hitting a pedestrian, and anyone would have done. Two, Sammy was his target. He'd been following her, saw his chance when she crossed the road, only the lights were against him so he had to jump them. Then she was so close to the kerb he had to switch lanes.'

'But why?'

Rebus stared at him. 'This is Sammy's dad and her lover, right? For the purposes of what follows, I want you to stop being a reporter.'

Farlowe stared back, nodded slowly.

'I've had a few run-ins with Tommy Telford,' Rebus said. He was seeing teddy bears: Pa Broon, and the one Telford kept in his car. 'This might have been a message for me.' Telford or Tarawicz: flip a coin. 'Or for you, if you've been asking questions about Telford.'

'You think my book . . .'

'I'm keeping an open mind. I've been working the Lintz case . . . and so have you.'

'Someone warning us off Lintz?'

Rebus thought of Abernethy, shrugged. 'Then there's Sammy's job, working with ex-cons. Maybe one of them had a grudge.'

'Jesus.'

'She hadn't mentioned anyone following her? Nobody odd in the area?' Same question he'd put to the Drinics, only different victim . . .

Farlowe shook his head. 'Look,' he said, 'until five minutes ago I thought this was an accident. Now you're saying it was attempted murder. Are you *sure*?'

'I'm trusting a witness.' But he knew what Bill Pryde thought: a drunk driver, a crazy man. And a grandstand spectator who wore glasses and had read it wrong. He took out the drawing again.

'What's that?'

Rebus handed it over. 'This is what someone saw last night.'

'What kind of car is it?'

'Rover 600, Ford Mondeo, something like that. Dark green. Ring any bells?'

Ned Farlowe shook his head, then looked at Rebus. 'Let me help. I can ask around.'

'One kid in a coma's enough.'

The rest of the office had packed up and gone home. Now there were only Rebus and Sammy's boss, a woman called Mae Crumley. The light from half a dozen desk-lamps illuminated the haphazard office, which was on the top floor of an old four-storey building off Palmerston Place. Rebus knew Palmerston Place: there was a church there where the AA held meetings. He'd been to a couple. He could still taste whisky at the back of his throat. Not that he'd had any so far today, not in daylight hours. But then he hadn't phoned Jack Morton either.

The address might have been posher than Rebus was expecting, but the accommodation was cramped. The office was in the eaves of the building, so that you couldn't stand up in half the available space, which hadn't stopped desks being sited in the most awkward corners.

'Which is hers?' Rebus asked. Mae Crumley pointed to the desk next to her own. There was a computer there somewhere, but only its screen was showing. Loose sheets of paper, books and pamphlets and reports, the whole lot spilled on to the chair and from there down on to the floor.

'She works too hard,' Crumley said. 'We all do.'

Rebus sipped the coffee she'd made him. Cafe Hag.

'When Sammy came here,' she went on, 'the first thing she said was that her father was CID. She never tried to hide it.'

'And you'd no qualms about taking her on?'

'None at all.' Crumley folded her arms. They were big arms; she was a big woman. Her hair was a fiery red, long and frizzy and tied back with a black ribbon. She wore an oatmeal linen shirt with a denim jacket over the top of it. Her eyebrows had been plucked into thin arches over pale grey eyes. Her desk was relatively tidy, but only, as she'd explained to Rebus, because she tended to stay later than anyone else.

'What about her clients?' Rebus asked. 'Could any of them have held a grudge?'

'Against her or against you?'

'Against me *through* her.'

Crumley considered this. 'To the extent that they'd run her over just to make a point? I very much doubt it.'

'I'd be interested to see her client list.'

She shook her head. 'Look ... you shouldn't be doing this. It's too personal, you know that. I mean, who am I talking to here: Sammy's father, or a copper?'

'You think I've a score to settle?'

'Well haven't you?'

Rebus put down the coffee mug. 'Maybe.'

'And that's why you shouldn't be doing this.' She sighed. 'Number one on

my wish list: Sammy back on her feet and back here. But what about if meantime I do a bit of poking around? I stand a better chance of getting them to talk than you do.'

Rebus nodded. 'I'd appreciate that.' He got to his feet. 'Thanks for the coffee.'

Outside, he checked the list the Juice Church had given him. He kept it in his pocket, didn't refer to it often. There was a meeting at Palmerston Place in about an hour and a half. No good. He knew he'd spend the time beforehand in a pub. Jack Morton had introduced him to Al-Anon, but Rebus hadn't really taken to it, though the stories had affected him.

'See,' one man had told the group, 'I had problems at work, problems with my wife, my kids. I had money problems and health problems and everything else. Practically the only problem I didn't have was with the drink. And that's because I was a drunk.'

Rebus lit himself a cigarette and drove home.

He sat in his chair and thought about Rhona. They'd shared so much over so many years . . . and then it had all stopped. He'd chosen his job over his marriage, and that could not be forgiven. Last time he'd seen her had been in London, wearing her new life like armour. Nobody had warned him about Jackie Platt. His phone rang, and he snatched it from the floor.

'Rebus.'

'It's Bill.' Pryde sounded halfway to excited, which was as far as he ever ventured.

'What have you got?'

'Dark green Rover 600 – I think the owner called it "Sherwood Green" – stolen yesterday evening about an hour before the collision.'

'Where from?'

'Metered parking on George Street.'

'What do you reckon?'

'My advice is, keep an open mind. Having said that, at least now we've got a licence plate. Owner reported it at six-forty last night. It hasn't turned up anywhere, so I've upped the alert status.'

'Give me the reg.' Pryde read out the letters and numbers. Rebus thanked him and put down the phone. He was thinking of Danny Simpson, dumped outside Fascination Street around the time Sammy was being hit. Coincidence? Or a double message, Telford and Rebus. Which put Big Ger Cafferty in the frame. He called the hospital, was told there was no change. Farlowe was in visiting. The nurse said he had his laptop with him.

Rebus recalled Sammy growing up – a series of isolated images. He hadn't been there for her. He saw her in a series of fast jerky impressions, as if the film had been spliced. He tried not to think about the hell she had gone through at the hands of Gordon Reeve . . .

He saw good people doing bad things and bad people doing good, and he tried dividing the two into groups. He saw Candice and Tommy Telford and Mr Pink Eyes. And encompassing it all, he saw Edinburgh. He saw the mass of the people just getting on with their lives, and he saluted them. They *knew* things and felt things, things he'd never feel. He used to think he knew things. As a kid, he'd known *everything*. Now he knew differently. The only thing you could be sure of was the inside of your head, and even that could deceive you. I don't even know myself, he thought. So how could he ever hope to know Sammy? And with each year, he understood less.

He thought of the Oxford Bar. Even on the wagon, he'd stayed a regular, drinking cola and mugs of coffee. A pub like the Ox was about so much more than just the hooch. It was therapy and refuge, entertainment and art. He checked his watch, thinking he could head down there now. Just a couple of whiskies and a beer, something to make him feel good about himself until the morning.

The phone rang again. He picked it up.

'Evening, John.'

Rebus smiled, leaned back in his chair. 'Jack, you must be a bloody mind-reader . . .'

14

Mid-morning, Rebus walked through the cemetery. He'd been to the hospital to check on Sammy – no change. Now, he felt he had time to kill . . .

'A bit cooler today, Inspector.' Joseph Lintz rose from his knees and pushed his glasses back up to the bridge of his nose. There were damp patches on his trousers from where he'd been kneeling. He dropped his trowel on to a white polythene bag. Beside the bag stood pots of small green plants.

'Won't the frost get them?' Rebus asked. Lintz shrugged.

'It gets all of us, but we're allowed to bloom for a while.'

Rebus turned away. Today, he wasn't in the mood for games. Warriston Cemetery was vast. In the past, it had been a history lesson to Rebus – headstones telling the story of nineteenth-century Edinburgh – but now he found it a jarring reminder of mortality. They were the only living souls in the place. Lintz had pulled out a handkerchief.

'More questions?' he asked.

'Not exactly.'

'What then?'

'Truth is, Mr Lintz, I've got other things on my mind.'

The old man looked at him. 'Maybe all this archaeology is beginning to bore you, Inspector?'

'I still don't get it, planting things before the first frost?'

'Well, I can't plant very much afterwards, can I? And at my age . . . any day now I could be lying in the ground. I like to think there might be a few flowers surviving above me.' He'd lived in Scotand the best part of half a century, but there was still something lurking beneath the local accent, peculiarities of phrasing and tone that would be with Joseph Lintz until he died, reminders of his far less recent history.

'So,' he said now, 'no questions today?' Rebus shook his head. 'You're right, Inspector, you do seem preoccupied. Is it something I can help with?'

'In what way?'

'I don't really know. But you've come here, questions or no. I take it there's a reason?'

A dog was bounding through the long grass, crunching on the fallen leaves, nose brushing the ground. It was a yellow labrador, short-haired and overweight. Lintz turned towards it and almost growled. Dogs were the enemy.

'I was just wondering,' Rebus was saying, 'what you're capable of.' Lintz looked puzzled. The dog began to paw at the ground. Lintz reached down, picked up a stone, and hurled it. It didn't reach the dog. The labrador's owner was rounding the corner. He was young, crop-haired and skinny.

'That thing should be kept on its lead!' Lintz roared.

'*Jawohl*!' the owner snapped back, clicking his heels. He was laughing as he passed them.

'I am a famous man now,' Lintz reflected, back to his old self after the outburst. 'Thanks to the newspapers.' He looked up at the sky, blinked. 'People send me hate by the Royal Mail. A car was parked outside my home the other night . . . they put a brick through the windscreen. It wasn't my car, but they didn't know that. Now my neighbours keep clear of that spot, just in case.'

He spoke like the old man he was, a little tired, a little defeated.

'This is the worst year of my life.' He stared down at the border he'd been tending. The earth, newly turned, looked dark and rich, like crumbs of chocolate cake. A few worms and wood lice had been disturbed and were still looking for their old homes. 'And it's going to get worse, isn't it?'

Rebus shrugged. His feet were cold, the damp seeping in through his shoes. He was standing on the rough roadway, Lintz six inches above him on the grass. And still Lintz didn't reach his height. A little old man: that's what he was. And Rebus could study him, talk with him, go to his home and see what few photographs remained – according to Lintz – from the old days.

'What did you mean back there?' he said. 'What was it you said? Something about what I was capable of?'

Rebus stared at him. 'It's OK, the dog just showed me.'

'Showed you what?'

'What you're like with the enemy.'

Lintz smiled. 'I don't like dogs, it's true. Don't read too much into it, Inspector. That's the journalists' job.'

'Your life would be easier without dogs, wouldn't it?'

Lintz shrugged. 'Of course.'

'And easier without me, too?'

Lintz frowned. 'If it weren't you, it would be someone else, a boor like your Inspector Abernethy.'

'What do you think he was telling you?'

Lintz blinked. 'I'm not sure. Someone else came to see me. A man called Levy. I refused to talk to him – one privilege still open to me.'

Rebus shuffled his feet, trying to get some warmth into them. 'I have a daughter, did I ever tell you that?'

Lintz looked baffled. 'You might have mentioned it.'

'You know I have a daughter?'

'Yes . . . I mean, I think I knew before today.'

'Well, Mr Lintz, the night before last, someone tried to kill her, or at least do her some serious damage. She's in hospital, still unconscious. And *that* bothers me.'

'I'm so sorry. How did it . . . ? I mean, how do you . . . ?'

'I think maybe someone was trying to send me a message.'

Lintz's eyes widened. 'And you believe *me* capable of such a thing? My God, I thought we had come to understand one another, at least a little.'

Rebus was wondering. He was wondering how easy it would be to put on an act, when you'd spent half a century practising. He was wondering how easy it would be to steel yourself to killing an innocent ... or at least ordering their death. All it took was an order. A few words to someone else who would carry out your bidding. Maybe Lintz had it in him. Maybe it wouldn't be any more difficult than it had been for Josef Linzstek.

'Something you should know,' Rebus said. 'Threats don't scare me off. Quite the opposite.'

'It's good that you are so strong.' Rebus looked for meaning behind the words. 'I'm on my way home. Can I offer you some tea?'

Rebus drove, and then sat in the drawing room while Lintz busied himself in the kitchen. Started flicking through a pile of books on a desk.

'Ancient History, Inspector,' Lintz said, bringing in the tray – he always refused offers of help. 'Another hobby of mine. I'm fascinated by that intersection at which history and fiction meet.' The books were all about Babylonia. 'Babylon is an historical fact, you see, but what about the Tower of Babel?'

'A song by Elton John?' Rebus offered.

'Always making jokes.' Lintz looked up. 'What is it you're afraid of?'

Rebus took one of the cups. 'I've heard of the Gardens of Babylon,' he admitted, putting the book down. 'What other hobbies do you have?'

'Astrology, hauntings, the unknown.'

'Have you ever been haunted?'

Lintz seemed amused. 'No.'

'Would you like to be?'

'By seven hundred French villagers? No, Inspector, I wouldn't like that at all. It was astrology that first brought me to the Chaldeans. They came from Babylonia. Have you ever heard of Babylonian numbers ...?'

Lintz had a way of turning conversations in directions *he* wanted them to take. Rebus wasn't going to be deflected this time. He waited till Lintz had the cup to his lips.

'Did you try to kill my daughter?'

Lintz paused, then sipped, swallowed.

'No, Inspector,' he said quietly.

Which left Telford, Tarawicz and Cafferty. Rebus thought of Telford, surrounded by his Family but wanting to play with the big boys. How different was a gang war from any other kind? You had soldiers, and orders given to them. They had to prove themselves, or lose face, show themselves cowards. Shoot a civilian, run down a pedestrian. Rebus realised that he didn't want the driver as such – he wanted the person who'd *driven* them to do it. Lintz's defence of Linzstek was that the young lieutenant had been under orders, that war itself was the real culprit, as though humans had no say in the matter ...

'Inspector,' the old man was saying, 'do *you* think I'm Linzstek?'

Rebus nodded. 'I know you are.'

A wry smile. 'Then arrest me.'

'Here comes the blue-nose,' Father Conor Leary said. 'Out to steal Ireland's God-given Guinness.' He paused, eyes narrowing. 'Or are you still on that abstention kick?'

'I'm trying,' Rebus said.

'Well, I won't tempt you then.' Leary smiled. 'But you know me, John. I'm not one to judge, but a wee drop never harmed a soul.'

'Problem is, you put lots of wee drops together and you get a bloody big fall.'

Father Leary laughed. 'But aren't we all the fallen? Come away in.'

Father Leary was priest of Our Lady of Perpetual Help. Years back, someone had defaced the board outside to turn 'Help' into 'Hell'. The board had been corrected many times, but Rebus always thought of the place as 'Perpetual Hell': it was what the followers of Knox and Calvin would have believed. Father Leary took him through to the kitchen.

'Here, man, sit yourself down. I haven't seen you in so long, I thought you'd renounced me.' He went to the fridge and lifted out a can of Guinness.

'Are you operating a pharmacy on the side?' Rebus asked. Father Leary looked at him. Rebus nodded towards the fridge. 'The shelves of medicine.'

Father Leary rolled his eyes. 'At my age, you go to the doctor with angina and they dose you for every conceivable ailment. They think it makes old folk feel better.' He brought a glass to the table, placed it next to his can. Rebus felt a hand fall on his shoulder.

'I'm hellish sorry about Sammy.'

'How did you hear?'

'Her name was in one of the rags this morning.' Father Leary sat down. 'Hit and run, they said.'

'Hit and run,' Rebus echoed.

Father Leary shook his head wearily, one hand rubbing slowly over his chest. He was probably in his late-sixties, though he'd never said. Well built, with a thatch of silver hair. Tufts of grey sprouted from his ears, nose and dog-collar. His hand seemed to smother the can of Guinness. But when he poured, he poured gently, almost with reverence.

'It's a terrible thing,' he said quietly. 'Coma, is it?'

'Not until the doctors say so.' Rebus cleared his throat. 'It's only been a day and a half.'

'You know what we believers say,' Father Leary went on. 'When something like this happens, it's a test for all of us. It's a way of making us stronger.' The head on his Guinness was perfect. He took a swallow, licked his lips thoughtfully. 'That's what we *say*; it may not be what we think.' He looked into his drink.

'It didn't make me strong. I went back to the whisky.'

'I can understand that.'

'Until a friend reminded me it was the lazy way out, the cowardly way.'

'And who's to say he's not right?'

' "Faint-Heart and the Sermon",' Rebus said with a smile.

'What's that?'

'A song. But maybe it's us, too.'

'Get away, we're just two old boys having a natter. So how are you holding up, John?'

'I don't know.' He paused. 'I don't think it was an accident. And the man I think is behind it . . . Sammy isn't the first woman he's tried to destroy.' Rebus looked into the priest's eyes. 'I want to kill him.'

'But so far you haven't?'

'I haven't even talked to him.'

'Because you're worried what you might do?'

'Or not do.' Rebus's mobile sounded. He gave a look of apology and switched it on.

'John, it's Bill.'

'Yes, Bill?'

'Green Rover 600.'

'Yes?'

'We've got it.'

The car had been parked illegally on the street outside Piershill Cemetery. There was a parking ticket on its windscreen, dated the previous afternoon. If anyone had checked, they'd have found the driver's-side door unlocked. Maybe someone had: the car was empty, no coins, no map-books or cassettes. The fascia had been removed from the radio/cassette. There were no keys in the ignition. A car transporter had arrived, and the Rover was being winched aboard.

'I called in a favour at Howdenhall,' Bill Pryde was saying, 'they've promised to fingerprint it today.'

Rebus was studying the front passenger side. No dents, nothing to suggest this car had been used as a battering-ram against his daughter.

'I think maybe we need your permission, John.'

'What for?'

'Someone should go to the Infirmary and print Sammy.'

Rebus stared at the front of the car, then got out the drawing. Yes, she'd put out a hand. Her prints might be there, invisible to him.

'Sure,' he said. 'No problem. You think this is it?'

'I'll tell you once we print it.'

'You steal a car,' Rebus said, 'then you hit someone with it, and leave it a couple of miles away.' He looked around. 'Ever been on this street before?' Pryde shook his head. 'Me neither.'

'Someone local?'

'I'm wondering why they stole it in the first place.'

'Stick false plates on and sell it,' Pryde suggested. 'Spot of joyriding maybe.'

'Joyriders don't leave cars looking like this.'

'No, but they'd had a fright. They'd just knocked someone down.'

'And they drove all the way over here before deciding to dump it?'

'Maybe it was stolen for a job, turn over a petrol station. Then they hit Sammy and decide to jump ship. Maybe the job was this side of town.'

'Or Sammy *was* the job.'

Pryde put a hand on his shoulder. 'Let's see what the boffins turn up, eh?'

Rebus looked at him. 'You don't go for it?'

'Look, it's a feeling you've got, and that's fair enough, but right now all you've got is that student's word for it. There were other witnesses, John, and I asked them all again, and they told me the same thing: it looked like the driver lost control, that's all.'

There was an edge of irritation to Pryde's voice. Rebus knew why: long hours.

'Will Howdenhall let you know tonight?'

'They promised. And I'll phone you straight away, OK?'

'On my mobile,' Rebus said. 'I'm going to be on the move.' He looked around. 'There was something about Piershill Cemetery recently, wasn't there?'

'Kids,' Pryde said, nodding. 'They pushed over a load of gravestones.'

Rebus remembered now. 'Just the Jewish headstones, wasn't it?'

'I think so.'

And there, sprayed on the wall near the gates, the same piece of graffiti: Won't Anyone Help?

It was late evening, and Rebus was driving. Not the M90 into Fife: tonight, he was on the M8, heading west, heading for Glasgow. He'd spent half an hour at the hospital, followed by an hour and a half with Rhona and Jackie Platt, their guest for dinner at the Sheraton. He'd worn a fresh suit and shirt. He hadn't smoked. He'd drunk a bottle of Highland Spring.

They were planning yet more tests on Sammy. The neurologist had taken them into his office and talked them through the procedures. There would probably be another operation at the end of it. Rebus could barely remember what the man had said. Rhona had asked for the occasional explanation, but these seemed no more lucid than what had gone before.

Dinner had been a subdued affair. Jackie Platt, it turned out, sold second-hand cars.

'See, John, where I really score is the obituaries. Check the local paper, hare round there and see if they've left a car behind. Quick cash offer.'

'Sammy doesn't drive, sorry,' Rebus had said, causing Rhona to drop her cutlery on to her plate.

At the end of the meal, she'd seen him out to his car, gripped one of his arms hard.

'Get the bastard, John. I want to look him in the face. Just get the bastard who did this to us.' Her eyes were blazing.

He nodded. Stones: 'Just Wanna See His Face'. Rebus wanted it, too.

The M8, which could be a nightmare at rush hour, was a quiet drive in the evenings. Rebus knew he was making good time, and that he would soon see the outline of the Easterhouse estate against the sky. When his phone sounded, he didn't hear it at first: blame Wishbone Ash. As *Argus* finished, he picked up.

'Rebus.'

'John, it's Bill.'

'What've you got?'

'Forensics were good as gold. There are prints all over the car, interior and exterior. Several sets.' He paused, and Rebus thought the connection had gone. 'One good palm and finger set on the front of the bonnet . . .'

'Sammy's?'

'For definite.'

'So we've got our car.'

'The owner's given us a set so we can eliminate him. When we've done that . . .'

'We're still not home and dry, Bill. The car sat unlocked outside that cemetery, we don't know someone didn't clean it out.'

'Owner says the radio/cassette fascia was there when he left it. Also half a dozen tapes, a packet of paracetamol, receipts for petrol and a road map. So someone cleaned it out, whether it's the bastard we want or just some scavenger.'

'At least we know it's the car.'

'I'll check again with Howdenhall tomorrow, collect any other prints and start trying to match them. Plus I'll ask around Piershill, see if anyone saw someone dumping it.'

'Meantime get some sleep, eh?'

'Try and stop me. What about you?'

'Me?' Two cups of espresso after dinner. And with the knowledge of what lay ahead. 'I'll get my head down soon enough, Bill. Talk to you tomorrow.'

On the outskirts of Glasgow, headed for Barlinnie Prison.

He'd phoned ahead, made sure they were expecting him. It was way outside any visiting hours, but Rebus had made up a story about a murder inquiry. 'Follow-up questions,' was what he'd said.

'At this time of night?'

'Lothian and Borders Police, pal. Motto: Justice Never Sleeps.'

Morris Gerald Cafferty probably didn't sleep much either. Rebus imagined him lying awake at night, hands under his head, staring into the darkness.

Scheming.

Running things through his mind: how to keep his empire from falling, how best to combat threats like Tommy Telford. Rebus knew that Cafferty employed a lawyer – a middle-aged pinstripe from the New Town – to carry messages back to his gang in Edinburgh. He thought of Charles Groal, Telford's lawyer. Groal was young and sharp, like his paymaster.

'Strawman.'

He was waiting in the Interview Room, arms folded, chair set well away from the table. And of course his opening gambit was his nickname for Rebus.

'A lovely surprise, two visits in a week. Don't tell me you've another message from the Pole?'

Rebus sat down opposite Cafferty. 'Tarawicz isn't Polish.' He glanced towards the guard who stood by the door, lowered his voice. 'Another of Telford's boys got a doing.'

'How clumsy.'

'He was all but scalped. Are you looking for war?'

Cafferty drew his chair in to the table, leaned across towards Rebus. 'I've never backed down from a fight.'

'My daughter got hurt. Funny that, so soon after we'd had our little chat.'

'Hurt how?'

'Hit and run.'

Cafferty was thoughtful. 'I don't pick on civilians.'

Yes, Rebus thought, but she wasn't a civilian, because *he* had lured her on to the battlefield.

'Convince me,' Rebus said.

'Why should I bother?'

'The conversation we had . . . What you asked me to do.'

'Telford?' A whisper. Cafferty sat back for a moment to consider. When

he leaned forward again, his eyes bored into Rebus's. 'There's something you've forgotten. I lost a son, remember. Think I could do that to another father? I'd do a lot of things, Rebus, but not that, never that.'

Rebus held the stare. 'All right,' he said.

'You want me to find who did it?'

Rebus nodded slowly.

'That's your price?'

Rhona's words: *I want to look him in the face*. Rebus shook his head. 'I want them *delivered* to me. I want you to do that, whatever it takes.'

Cafferty placed his hands on his knees, seemed to take his time positioning them just so. 'You know it's probably Telford?'

'Yes. If it's not you.'

'You'll be going after him then?'

'Any way I can.'

Cafferty smiled. 'But your ways aren't my ways.'

'You might get to him first. I want him *alive*.'

'And meantime, you're my man?'

Rebus stared at him. 'I'm your man,' he said.

15

Rebus got a phone call early the next morning from Leith CID, telling him Joseph Lintz was dead. The bad news was, it looked like murder: the body found hanging from a tree in Warriston Cemetery.

By the time Rebus appeared at the scene, they were cordoning it off, the doctor having concluded that most suicides wouldn't have bothered administering a violent blow to their own head before commencing with operations.

The corpse of Joseph Lintz was being zipped into a body bag. Rebus got a look at the face. He'd seen elderly corpses before, and mostly they'd looked wonderfully at peace, their faces shiny and childlike. But Joseph Lintz looked like he'd suffered. He didn't look to be at rest at all.

'You'll have come to thank us, no doubt,' a man said, walking towards Rebus. His shoulders were hunched inside a navy raincoat and he walked with head bowed, hands in pockets. His hair was thick and silver and wiry, his skin an almost jaundiced yellow – the remains of an autumn holiday tan.

'Hiya, Bobby,' Rebus said.

Bobby Hogan was Leith CID.

'To get back to my initial observation, John . . .'

'What am I supposed to be thanking you for?'

Hogan nodded towards the body bag. 'Taking Mr Lintz off your hands.' 'Don't tell me you were *enjoying* digging into all that?'

'Not exactly.'

'Any idea who might have wanted him dead?'

Rebus puffed out his cheeks. 'Where do you want me to start?'

'I mean, I'm right to rule out the usual, aren't I?' Hogan held up three fingers. 'It wasn't suicide, muggers aren't quite this creative, and it surely wasn't an accident.'

'Someone was making a point, no doubt about it.'

'But what sort of point?'

Scene of Crime officers were busying themselves, filling the *locus* with noise and movement. Rebus gestured for Hogan to walk with him. They were deep in the cemetery, the part Lintz had loved so much. As they walked, the place grew wilder, more overgrown.

'I was here with him yesterday morning,' Rebus said. 'I don't know if he had a routine exactly, but he came here most days.'

'We found a bag of gardening tools.'

'He planted flowers.'

'So if someone knew he'd be coming, they could have been waiting?'

Rebus nodded. 'An assassination.'

Hogan was thoughtful. 'Why hang him?'

'It's what happened at Villefranche. The town elders were strung up in the square.'

'Jesus.' Hogan stopped walking. 'I know you've got other stuff on the go, but can you help out on this, John?'

'Any way I can.'

'A list of possibles would do for a start.'

'How about an old woman living in France, and a Jewish historian who walks with a stick?'

'Is that all you've got?'

'Well, there's always me. Yesterday I as good as accused him of trying to kill my daughter.' Hogan stared at him. 'I don't think he did it.' Rebus paused, thinking of Sammy: he'd called the hospital first thing. She was still unconscious; they still weren't using the word 'coma'. 'One more thing,' he said. 'Special Branch, a guy called Abernethy. He was here talking to Lintz.'

'What's the connection?'

'Abernethy's co-ordinating the various war crimes investigations. He's street-tough, not your typical desk-jockey.'

'A strange choice for the job?' Rebus nodded. 'Which hardly makes him a suspect.'

'I'm doing my best, Bobby. We could check Lintz's house, see if we can turn up any of the hate mail he claimed he'd been getting.'

' "Claimed"?'

Rebus shrugged. 'You were never sure where you were with Lintz. Do you have any idea what happened?'

'From what you've told me, I'd guess he came down here as usual to do his gardening stint – he's certainly dressed for it. Someone was waiting. They smacked him over the head, stuck his neck in a noose, and hauled him up into the tree. The rope was tied around a headstone.'

'Did the hanging kill him?'

'Doctor says yes. Haemorrhages in the eyes. What do you call them?'

'Tardieu spots.'

'That's it. The blow to the head was just to knock him out. Something else – bruising and cuts on the face. Looks like someone kicked him when he was down.'

'Knock him cold, thump him in the face, then string him up.'

'Big-time grudge.'

Rebus looked around. 'Someone with a flair for theatre.'

'And not afraid to take risks. This place might never get exactly crowded, but it's a public space and that tree's in open view. Anyone could have walked past.'

'What time are we talking about?'

'Eight, eight-thirty. I'm guessing Mr Lintz would have wanted to do his digging in daylight.'

'Could have been earlier,' Rebus suggested. 'A pre-arranged meeting.'

'Then why the tools?'

'Because by the time it got light, the meeting would be over.'

Hogan looked doubtful.

'And if it *was* a meeting,' Rebus said, 'there might be some record of it at Lintz's home.'

Hogan looked at him, nodded. 'My car or yours?'

'Better get his keys first.'

They started back up the slope.

'Searching through a dead man's pockets,' Hogan said to himself. 'Why is that never mentioned during recruitment?'

'I was here yesterday,' Rebus said. 'He invited me back for tea.'

'No family?'

'None.'

Hogan looked around the hallway. 'Big place. What happens to the money when it's sold?'

Rebus looked at him. 'We could split it two ways.'

'Or we could just move ourselves in. Basement and ground for me, you can have first and second.'

Hogan smiled, tried one of the doors off the hall. It opened on to an office. 'This could be my bedroom,' he said, going in.

'When I came here before, he always took me upstairs.'

'On you go. We'll take a floor each, then swop.'

Rebus headed up the staircase, running his hand over the varnished banister: not a speck of dust. Cleaning ladies could be invaluable informants.

'If you find a chequebook,' he called down to Hogan, 'look for regular payments to a Mrs Mop.'

Four doors led off the first-floor landing. Two were bedrooms, one a bathroom. The last door led into the huge drawing room, where Rebus had asked his questions and listened to the stories and philosophy that Lintz had used in place of answers.

'Do you think guilt has a genetic component, Inspector?' he'd asked one time. 'Or are we taught it?'

'Does it matter, so long as it's there?' Rebus had said, and Lintz had nodded and smiled, as if the pupil had given some satisfactory answer.

The room was big, not too much furniture. Huge sash windows – recently cleaned – looked down on to the street. There were framed prints and paintings on the walls. They could have been priceless originals or junk-store stuff – Rebus was no expert. He liked one painting. It showed a ragged white-haired man seated on a rock, surrounded by a barren plain. He had a book open on his lap, but was staring skywards in horror or awe as a shining light appeared there, picking him out. It had a Biblical look, but Rebus couldn't quite place it. He knew the look on the man's face though. He'd seen it before when some suspect's carefully crafted alibi had suddenly come tumbling down.

Over the marble fireplace was a large gilt-framed mirror. Rebus studied himself in it. Behind him he could see the room. He knew he didn't fit here.

One bedroom was for guests, the other was Lintz's. A faint smell of embrocation, half a dozen medicine bottles on the bedside table. Books, too, a pile of them. The bed had been made, a dressing-gown draped across it. Lintz was a creature of habit; he'd been in no special hurry this morning.

The next floor up, Rebus found two further bedrooms and a toilet. There was a slight smell of damp in one room, and the ceiling was discoloured. Rebus didn't suppose Lintz got many visitors; no impetus to redecorate. Out on the landing again, he saw that one of the stair-rails was missing. It had been propped against the wall, awaiting repair. A house this size, things would always be going wrong.

He went back downstairs. Hogan was in the basement. The kitchen had a door on to a back garden – stone patio, lawn covered in rotting leaves, an ivy-covered wall giving privacy.

'Look what I found,' Hogan said, coming back from the utility room. He was holding a length of rope, frayed at one end where it had been cut.

'You think it'll match with the noose? That would mean the killer got it from here.'

'Meaning Lintz knew them.'

'Anything in the office?'

'It's going to take a bit of time. There's an address book, lots of entries, but most of them seem to go back a while.'

'How can you tell?'

'Old STD codes.'

'Computer?'

'Not even a typewriter. He used carbons. Lots of letters to his solicitor.'

'Trying to shut the media up?'

'You get a couple of mentions, too. Anything upstairs?'

'Go take a look. I'll check the office.'

Rebus climbed upstairs and stood in the office doorway, looking around. Then he sat down at the desk and imagined the room was his. What did he do here? He conducted his daily business. There were two filing-cabinets, but to get to them he'd have to stand up from the desk. And he was an old man. Say the cabinets were for dead correspondence. More recent stuff would be closer to hand.

He tried the drawers. Found the address book Hogan had mentioned. A few letters. A small snuff-box, its contents turned solid. Lintz hadn't even allowed himself that small vice. In a bottom drawer were some files. Rebus lifted out the one marked 'General/Household'. It comprised bills and guarantees. A large brown envelope was marked BT. Rebus opened it and took out the phone bills. They went back to the beginning of the year. The most recent bill was at the front. Rebus was disappointed to find that it wasn't itemised. Then he noticed that all the other statements *were*. Lintz had been meticulous, placing names beside calls made, double-checking British Telecom's totals at the foot of each page. The whole year was like that ... right up until recently. Frowning, Rebus realised that the penultimate statement was missing. Had Lintz mislaid it? Rebus couldn't see him mislaying anything. A missing bill would have hinted at chaos in his ordered world. No, it had to be somewhere.

But Rebus was damned if he could find it.

Lintz's correspondence was all business, either to lawyers or else to do with local charities and committees. He'd been resigning from his committees. Rebus wondered if pressure had been applied. Edinburgh could be cruel and cold that way.

'Well?' Hogan said, sticking his head round the door.

'I'm just wondering . . .'

'What?'

'Whether to add on a conservatory and knock through from the kitchen.'

'We'd lose some garden space,' Hogan said. He came in, rested against the desk. 'Anything?'

'A missing phone bill, and a sudden change from being itemised.'

'Worth a call,' Hogan admitted. 'I found a chequebook in his bedroom. Stubs show payments of £60 a month to E. Forgan.'

'Where in the bedroom?'

'Marking his place in a book.' Hogan reached into the desk's top drawer, lifted out the address book.

Rebus got up. 'Pretty rich street this. Wonder how many of them do their own dusting.'

Hogan shut the book. 'No listing for an E. Forgan. Think the neighbours will know?'

'Edinburgh neighbours know *everything*. It's just that they most often keep it to themselves.'

16

Joseph Lintz's neighbours: an artist and her husband on one side; a retired advocate and his wife on the other. The artist used a cleaning lady called Ella Forgan. Mrs Forgan lived in East Claremont Street. The artist gave them a telephone number.

Conclusions drawn from the two interviews: shock and horror that Lintz was dead; praise for the quiet, considerate neighbour. A Christmas card every year, and an invitation to drinks one Sunday afternoon each July. Hard to tell when he'd been at home and when he'd been out. He went off on holiday without telling anyone except Mrs Forgan. Visitors to his home had been few – or few had been noticed, which wasn't quite the same thing.

'Men? Women?' Rebus had asked. 'Or a mixture?'

'A mixture, I'd say,' the artist had replied, measuring her words. 'Really, we knew very little about him, to say we've been neighbours these past twenty-odd years . . .'

Ah, and that was Edinburgh for you, too, at least in this price bracket. Wealth was a very private thing in the city. It wasn't brash and colourful. It stayed behind its thick stone walls and was at peace.

Rebus and Hogan held a doorstep conference.

'I'll call the cleaning lady, see if I can meet her, preferably here.' Hogan looked back at Lintz's front door.

'I'd love to know where he got the money to buy this place,' Rebus said.

'That could take some excavating.'

Rebus nodded. 'Solicitor would be the place to start. What about the address book? Worth tracking down some of these elusive friends?'

'I suppose so.' Hogan looked dispirited at the prospect.

'I'll follow up on the phone bills,' Rebus said. 'If that'll help.'

Hogan was nodding. 'And remember to get me copies of your files. Are you busy otherwise?'

'Bobby, if time was money, I'd be in hock to every lender in town.'

Mae Crumley reached Rebus on his mobile.

'I thought you'd forgotten me,' he told Sammy's boss.

'Just being methodical, Inspector. I'm sure you'd want no less.' Rebus stopped at traffic lights. 'I've been in to see Sammy. Is there any news?'

'Nothing much. So you've talked to her clients?'

'Yes, and they all seemed genuinely upset and surprised. Sorry to disappoint you.'

'What makes you think I'm disappointed?'

'Sammy has a good rapport with all her clients. None of them would have wanted her hurt.'

'What about the ones who didn't want to be her clients?'

Crumley hesitated. 'There was one man . . . When he was told Sammy had a police inspector for a father, he'd have nothing to do with her.'

'What's his name?'

'It couldn't have been him though.'

'Why not?'

'Because he killed himself. His name was Gavin Tay. He used to drive an ice-cream van . . .'

Rebus thanked her for her call, and put down the phone. If someone had tried to kill Sammy on purpose, the question was: why? Rebus had been investigating Lintz; Ned Farlowe had been following him. Rebus had twice confronted Telford; Ned was writing a book about organised crime. Then there was Candice . . . Could she have *told* Sammy something, something which might have threatened Telford, or even Mr Pink Eyes? Rebus just didn't know. He knew the most likely culprit – the most vicious – was Tommy Telford. He remembered their first meeting, and the young gangster's words to him: *That's the beauty of games. You can always start again after an accident. Not so easy in real life.* At the time it had sounded like bravado, a performance for the troops. But now it sounded like a plain threat.

And now there was Mr Taystee, connecting Sammy to Telford. Mr Taystee had worked Telford's clubs; Mr Taystee had rejected Sammy. Rebus knew he'd have to talk to the widow.

There was just the one problem. Mr Pink Eyes had intimated that if Telford wasn't left alone, Candice would suffer. He kept seeing images of Candice: torn from home and homeland; used and abused; abusing herself in the hope of respite; clinging to a stranger's legs . . . He recalled Levy's words: *Can time wash away responsibility?* Justice was a fine and noble thing, but revenge . . . revenge was an *emotion*, and so much stronger than an abstract like justice. He wondered if Sammy would want revenge. Probably not. She'd want him to help Candice, which meant yielding to Telford. Rebus didn't think he could do that.

And now there was Lintz's murder, unconnected but resonant.

'I've never felt comfortable with the past, Inspector,' Lintz had said once. Funny, Rebus felt the same way about the present.

Joanne Tay lived in Colinton: a newish three-bedroomed semi with the Merc still parked in the drive.

'It's too big for me,' she explained to Rebus. 'I'll have to sell it.'

He wasn't sure if she meant the house or the car. Having declined her offer of tea, he sat in the busy living room, ornaments on every flat surface. Joanne Tay was still in mourning: black skirt and blouse, dark grooves beneath her eyes. He'd interviewed her back at the start of the inquiry.

'I still don't know why he did it,' she said now, reluctant to see her husband's death as anything other than suicide.

But the pathology and forensic tests had cast this into doubt.

'Have you ever heard,' Rebus asked, 'of a man called Tommy Telford?'

'He runs a nightclub, doesn't he? Gavin took me there once.'

'So Gavin knew him?'

'Seemed to.'

Yes: because no way was Mr Taystee setting up his hot-dog pitch outside Telford's premises without Telford's OK. And Telford's OK almost certainly meant payment of some kind. A percentage maybe ... or a favour.

'The week before Gavin died,' Rebus went on, 'you said he'd been busy?'

'Working all hours.'

'Days as well as nights?' She nodded. 'The weather was lousy that week.'

'I know. I told him: you'll never get them buying ice-cream, a day like this. Pelting down outside. But still he went out.'

Rebus shifted in his chair. 'Did he ever mention SWEEP, Mrs Tay?'

'He had some woman would visit him ... red hair.'

'Mae Crumley?'

She nodded, eyes staring at the coal-effect fire. She asked him again if he wanted some tea. Rebus shook his head and made to leave. Did pretty well: knocked over just the two ornaments on his way to the door.

The hospital was quiet. When he pushed open the door to Sammy's room, he saw that another bed had been added, a middle-aged woman sleeping in it. Her hands lay on the bedcovers, a white identity tag around one wrist. She was hooked up to a machine, and her head was bandaged.

Two women were sitting by Sammy's bed. Rhona, and Patience Aitken. Rebus hadn't seen Patience in a while. The women were sitting close together. Their whispered conversation stopped as he came in. He lifted a chair and placed it beside Patience's. She leaned over and squeezed his hand.

'Hello, John.'

He smiled at her, spoke to Rhona. 'How is she?'

'The specialist says those last tests were very positive.'

'What does that mean?'

'It means there's brain activity. She's not in deep coma.'

'Is that his version?'

'He thinks she'll come out of it, John.' Her eyes were bloodshot. He noticed a handkerchief gripped in one hand.

'That's good,' he said. 'Which doctor was it?'

'Dr Stafford. He's just back from holiday.'

'I can't keep track of them all.' Rebus rubbed his forehead.

'Look,' Patience said, checking her watch, 'I really should be going. I'm sure the two of you ...'

'Stay as long as you like,' Rebus told her.

'I'm already late for an appointment, actually.' She got to her feet. 'Nice to meet you, Rhona.'

'Thanks, Patience.' The two women shook hands a little awkwardly, then Rhona got up and they hugged, and the awkwardness vanished. 'Thanks for coming.'

Patience turned to Rebus. She looked radiant, he decided. Light really seemed to emanate from her skin. She was wearing her usual perfume, and had had her hair restyled.

'Thanks for looking in,' he said.

'She's going to be fine, John.' She took his hands in hers, leaned towards him. A peck on the cheek, a kiss between friends. Rebus saw Rhona watching them.

'John,' she said, 'see Patience out, will you?'

'No, that's all –'

'Of course, yes,' Rebus said.

They left the room together. Walked the first few steps in silence. Patience spoke first.

'She's great, isn't she?'

'Rhona?'

'Yes.'

Rebus was thoughtful. 'She's terrific. Have you met her paramour?'

'He's gone back to London. I've . . . I asked Rhona if she wanted to come stay with me. Hotels can be . . .'

Rebus smiled tiredly. 'Good idea. Then all you'd have to do is invite my brother over and you'd have the whole set.'

Her face cracked into an embarrassed grin. 'I suppose it must look a bit like I'm collecting you all.'

'The perfect hand of Unhappy Families.'

She turned to him. They were at the main doors of the hospital. She touched his shoulder. 'John, I'm really sorry about Sammy. Anything I can do, you've only got to ask.'

'Thanks, Patience.'

'But asking for things has never been your strong point, has it? You just sit in silence and hope they come to you.' She sighed. 'I can't believe I'm saying this, but I miss you. I think that's why I took in Sammy. If I couldn't be close to you, at least I could be close to someone who was. Does that make any sense? Is this where you say something about not deserving me?'

'You've seen the script.' He pulled back a little from her, just so he could look at her face. 'I miss you, too.'

All the nights slumped at the bar, or in his chair at home, the long midnight drives so he could keep his restlessness alive. He'd have the TV and the hi-fi on at the same time, and the flat would still feel empty. Books he tried reading, finding he was ten pages in and couldn't remember anything. Gazing from his window at the darkened flats across the street, imagining lives at rest.

All because he didn't have *her*.

They embraced in silence for a while. 'You're going to be late,' he said.

'God, John, what are we going to do?'

'See one another?'

'That sounds like a start.'

'Tonight? Mario's at eight?' She nodded and they kissed again. He squeezed her hand. Her head was turned to look at him as she pushed open the doors.

Emerson, Lake and Palmer: 'Still . . . You Turn Me On.'

Rebus felt a little giddy as he walked back to Sammy's room. Only it wasn't any more, wasn't 'Sammy's room'. Now there was another patient there. They'd said there was always that possibility – shortage of space, cutbacks. The woman was still asleep or unconscious, breathing noisily. Rebus ignored her and sat where Patience had been sitting.

'I've got a message for you,' Rhona said. 'From Dr Morrison.'

'Who's he when he's at home?'

'I've no idea. All he said was, could he have his T-shirt back?'

The ghoul with the scythe . . . Rebus picked up Pa Broon, turned the bear in his hands. They sat in silence for a while, until Rhona shifted in her chair. 'Patience is really nice.'

'Did the two of you have a good chat?' She nodded. 'And you told her what a perfect husband I'd been?'

'You must be crazy, walking out on her.'

'Sanity's never exactly been my strong point.'

'But you used to know a good thing when you saw it.'

'Trouble is, that's never what I see when I look in the mirror.'

'What do you see?'

He looked at her. 'Sometimes I don't see anything at all.'

Later, they took a coffee-break, went to the machine.

'I lost her, you know,' Rhona said.

'What?'

'Sammy, I lost her. She came back here. She came back to you.'

'We hardly see one another, Rhona.'

'But she's *here*. Don't you get it? It's you she wants, not me.' She turned away from him, fumbled for her handkerchief. He stood close behind her, then couldn't think of anything to say. He was all out of words; every line of sympathy rang hollow to him, just another cliché. He touched the back of her neck, rubbed it. She lowered her head a little, didn't resist. Massage: there'd been a lot of massage early on in their relationship. By the end, he hadn't even given her time for a handshake.

'I don't know why she came back, Rhona,' he said at last. 'But I don't think she was running away, and I don't think it had much to do with seeing me.'

A couple of nurses ran past, urgency in their movements.

'I'd better get back,' Rhona said, rubbing a hand over her face, pulling it into something resembling composure.

Rebus went with her to the room, then said he had to be going. He bent down to kiss Sammy, feeling the breath from her nostrils against his cheek.

'Wake up, Sammy,' he cajoled. 'You can't stay in bed all your life. Time to get up.'

When there was no movement, no response, he turned and left the room.

17

David Levy was no longer in Edinburgh. At least, he wasn't at the Roxburghe Hotel. Rebus could think of only one way of contacting him. Seated at his desk, he called the Holocaust Investigation Bureau in Tel Aviv and asked to speak with Solomon Mayerlink. Mayerlink wasn't available, but Rebus identified himself and said he needed to contact him as a matter of urgency. He got a home telephone number.

'Is there news on Linzstek, Inspector?' Mayerlink's voice was a harsh rasp.

'Of a kind, yes. He's dead.'

Silence on the line, then a slow release of breath. 'That's a pity.'

'It is?'

'People die, a little bit of history dies with them. We would have preferred to see him in court, Inspector. Dead, he's worthless.' Mayerlink paused. 'I take it this ends your inquiry?'

'It changes the nature of the investigation. He was murdered.'

Static on the line; an eight-beat pause. 'How did it happen?'

'He was hung from a tree.'

There was a longer silence on the line. 'I see,' Mayerlink said at last. There was a slight echo on his voice. 'You think the allegations led to his murder?'

'What would you say?'

'I'm not a detective.'

But Rebus knew Mayerlink was lying: detection was *exactly* the role he'd chosen in life. A detective of history.

'I need to talk to David Levy,' Rebus said. 'Do you have his address and phone number?'

'He came to see you?'

'You know he did.'

'It's not that simple with David. He doesn't work for the Bureau. He's self-motivated. I ask him for help occasionally. Sometimes he helps, sometimes he doesn't.'

'But you do have some way of contacting him?'

It took Mayerlink a full minute to come up with the details. An address in Sussex, plus telephone number.

'Is David your number one suspect, Inspector?'

'Why do you ask?'

'I could tell you you're barking up the wrong tree.'

'The same tree Joseph Lintz swung from?'

'Can you really see David Levy as a murderer, Inspector?'

Safari suit, walking-stick. 'It takes all sorts,' Rebus said, putting down the phone.

He tried Levy's number. It rang and rang. He gave it a couple of minutes, drank a coffee, tried again. Still no answer. He called British Telecom instead, explained what he needed, was finally put through to the right person.

'My name's Justine Graham, Inspector. How can I help?'

Rebus gave her Lintz's details. 'He used to get itemised bills, then he switched.'

He heard her fingers hammer a keyboard. 'That's right,' she told him. 'The customer asked for itemised billing to be discontinued.'

'Did he say why?'

'No record of that. You don't need to give an excuse, you know.'

'When was this?'

'A couple of months back. The customer had requested monthly billing several years previously.'

Monthly billing: because he was meticulous, kept his accounts by the month. A couple of months back – September – the Lintz/Linzstek story had blown up in the media. And, suddenly, he hadn't wanted his phone calls to be a matter of record.

'Do you have records of his calls, even the *un*itemised ones?'

'Yes, we should have that information.'

'I'd like to see a list. Everything from the first unitemised call through to this morning.'

'Is that when he died – this morning?'

'Yes.'

She was thoughtful. 'Well, I'll need to check.'

'Please do. But remember, Ms Graham, this is a murder inquiry.'

'Yes, of course.'

'And your information could be absolutely crucial.'

'I'm quite aware of –'

'So if I could have that by the end of today . . .?'

She hesitated. 'I'm not sure I can promise that.'

'And one last thing. The bill for September is missing. I'd like a copy of it. Let me give you the fax number here, speed things up.'

Rebus congratulated himself with another cup of coffee and a cigarette in the car park. She might or might not deliver later in the day, but he was confident she'd be trying her best. Wasn't that all you could ask of anybody?

Another call: Special Branch in London. He asked for Abernethy.

'I'll just put you through.'

Someone picked up: a grunt in place of an acknowledgement.

'Abernethy?' Rebus asked. He heard liquid being swallowed. The voice became clearer.

'He's not here. Can I help?'

'I really need to speak to him.'

'I could have him paged, if it's urgent.'

'My name's DI Rebus, Lothian and Borders Police.'

'Oh, right. Have you lost him or something?'

Rebus's expression turned quizzical. His voice carried a false note of humour. 'You know what Abernethy's like.'

A snort. 'Don't I just.'

'So any help appreciated.'

'Yeah, right. Look, give me your number. I'll get him to call you.'

Have you lost him or something? 'You've no idea where he is then?'

'It's your city, chum. Take your best shot.'

He's up here, Rebus thought. *He's right here.*

'I bet the office is quiet without him.'

Laughter on the line, then the sounds of a cigarette being lit. A long exhalation. 'It's like being on holiday. Keep him as long as you like.'

'So how long have you been without him?'

A pause. As the silence lengthened, Rebus could feel the change of atmosphere.

'What did you say your name was?'

'DI Rebus. I was only asking when he left London.'

'This morning, soon as he heard. So what have I won: the hatchback or the hostess trolley?'

Rebus's turn to laugh. 'Sorry, I'm just nosy.'

'I'll be sure to tell him that.' A single click, then the sound of an open line.

Later that afternoon, Rebus chased up British Telecom, then tried Levy's house again. This time he got through to a woman.

'Hello, Mrs Levy? My name's John Rebus. I was wondering if I could have a word with your husband?'

'You mean my father.'

'I'm sorry. Is your father there?'

'No, he's not.'

'Any idea when . . . ?'

'Absolutely none.' She sounded peeved. 'I'm just his cook and cleaner. Like I don't have a life of my own.' She caught herself. 'Sorry, Mr . . . ?'

'Rebus.'

'It's just that he never says how long he's going to be away.'

'He's away just now?'

'Has been for the best part of a fortnight. He rings two or three times a week, asks if there've been any calls or letters. If I'm lucky, he *might* remember to ask how *I'm* doing.'

'And how are you doing?'

A smile in her voice. 'I know, I know. I sound like I'm his mother or something.'

'Well, you know, fathers . . .' Rebus stared into the middle distance . . . 'if you don't tell them anything's wrong, they're happy to assume the best and hold their peace.'

'You speak from experience?'

'Too much experience.'

She was thoughtful. 'Is it something important?'

'Very.'

'Well, give me your name and number, and next time he calls I'll have him phone you.'

'Thanks.' Rebus reeled off two numbers: home and mobile.

'Got that,' she said. 'Any other message?'

'No, just have him call me.' Rebus thought for a moment. 'Has he had any other calls?'

'You mean, people trying to reach him? Why do you ask?'

'I just ... no real reason.' He didn't want to say he was a policeman; didn't want her spooked. 'No reason,' he repeated.

As he came off the phone, someone handed him another coffee. 'That receiver must be red hot.'

He touched it with the tips of his fingers. It was pretty warm. Then it rang and he picked it up again.

'DI Rebus,' he said.

'John, it's Siobhan.'

'Hiya, how's tricks?'

'John, you remember that guy?' Her tone was warning him of something.

'What guy?' The humour was gone from his voice.

'Danny Simpson.' He of the flappy skull; Telford's lackey.

'What about him?'

'I've just found out he's HIV positive. His GP let the hospital know.'

Blood in Rebus's eyes, his ears, dribbling down his neck ...

'Poor guy,' he said quietly.

'He should have said something at the time.'

'When?'

'When we got him to the hospital.'

'Well, he had other things on his mind, and some of them were in danger of falling off.'

'Christ, John, be serious for a minute!' Her voice was loud enough to have people glance up from their desks. 'You need to get a blood test.'

'Fine, no problem. How is he, by the way?'

'Back home but poorly. And sticking to his story.'

'Do I detect the influence of Telford's lawyer?'

'Charles Groal? That one's so slimy, he's practically primordial.'

'Saves you the cost of a valentine.'

'Look, just phone the hospital. Talk to a Dr Jones. She'll fix an appointment. They can do a test right away. Not that it'll be the last word – there's a three-month incubation.'

'Thanks, Siobhan.'

Rebus put down the receiver, drummed his fingers against it. Wouldn't *that* be a nice irony? Rebus out to get Telford, does the Good Samaritan bit for one of his men, gets AIDS and dies. Rebus stared at the ceiling.

Nice one, Big Man.

The phone rang again. Rebus snatched it up.

'Switchboard,' he said.

'Is that you, John?' Patience Aitken.

'The one and only.'

'Just wanted to check we're still on for tonight.'

'To be honest, Patience, I'm not sure I'll be at my most sparkling.'

'You want to cancel?'

'Absolutely not. But I have something to take care of. At the hospital.'

'Yes, of course.'

'No, I don't think you understand. It's not Sammy this time, it's me.'
'What's wrong?'
So he told her.

She went with him. Same hospital Sammy was in, different department. Last thing he wanted was to bump into Rhona, have to explain everything to her. Possibly HIV-infected: chances were, she'd red-card him from the bedside.

The waiting room was white, clean. Lots of information on the walls. Leaflets on every table, as if paperwork was the real virus.

'I must say, it's very pleasant for a leper colony.'

Patience didn't say anything. They were alone in the room. Someone on reception had dealt with him first, then a nurse had come out and taken some details. Now another door opened.

'Mr Rebus?'

A tall thin woman in a white coat, standing in the doorway: Dr Jones, he presumed. Patience took his arm as they walked towards her. Halfway across the floor, Rebus turned on his heels and bolted.

Patience caught up with him outside, asked what was wrong.

'I don't want to know,' he told her.

'But, John . . .'

'Come on, Patience. All I got was a bit of blood splashed on me.'

She didn't look convinced. 'You need to take the test.'

He looked back towards the building. 'Fine.' Started walking away. 'But some other time, eh?'

It was one in the morning when he drove back into Arden Street. No dinner date with Patience: instead, they'd visited the hospital, sat with Rhona. He'd made a silent pact with the Big Man: bring her back and I'll keep off the booze. He'd driven Patience home. Her last words to him: 'Take that test. Get it over and done with.'

As he locked his car, a figure appeared from nowhere.

'Mr Rebus, long time no see.'

Rebus recognised the face. Pointy chin, misshapen teeth, the breathing a series of small gasps. The Weasel: one of Cafferty's men. He was dressed like a down-and-out, perfect camouflage for his role in life. He was Cafferty's eyes and ears on the street.

'We need to talk, Mr Rebus.' His hands were deep in the pockets of a tweed coat meant for someone eight inches taller. He glanced towards the tenement door.

'Not in my flat,' Rebus stated. Some things were sacrosanct.

'Cold out here.'

Rebus just shook his head, and the Weasel sniffed hard.

'You think it was a hit?' he said.

'Yes,' Rebus answered.

'She was meant to die?'

'I don't know.'

'A pro wouldn't fuck up.'

'Then it was a warning.'

'We could do with seeing your notes.'

'Can't do that.'

The Weasel shrugged. 'Thought you wanted Mr Cafferty's help?'

'I can't give you the notes. What about if I summarise?'

'It'd be a start.'

'Rover 600, stolen from George Street that afternoon. Abandoned on a street by Piershill Cemetery. Radio and some tapes lifted – not necessarily by the same person.'

'Scavengers.'

'Could be.'

The Weasel was thoughtful. 'A warning . . . That would mean a professional driver.'

'Yes,' Rebus said.

'And not one of ours . . . Doesn't leave too many candidates. Rover 600 . . . what colour?'

'Sherwood Green.'

'Parked on George Street?'

Rebus nodded.

'Thanks for that.' The Weasel made to turn away, then paused. 'Nice doing business with you again, Mr Rebus.'

Rebus was about to say something, then remembered he needed the Weasel more than the Weasel needed him. He wondered how much crap he'd take from Cafferty . . . how long he'd have to take it. All his life? Had he made a contract with the devil?

For Sammy, he'd have done much, much worse . . .

In his flat, he stuck on the CD of *Rock 'n' Roll Circus*, skipping to the actual Stones tracks. His answering machine was flashing. Three messages. The first: Hogan.

'Hello, John. Just thought I'd check, see if there's been any word from BT.'

Not by the time Rebus had left the office. Message two: Abernethy.

'Me again, bad penny and all that. Heard you've been trying to catch me. I'll call you tomorrow. Cheers.'

Rebus stared at the machine, willing Abernethy to say more, to give some hint of a location. But the machine was on to the final message. Bill Pryde.

'John, tried you at the office, left a message. But I thought you'd want to know, we've had final word on those prints. If you want to try me at home, I'm on . . .'

Rebus took down the number. Two in the morning, but Bill would understand.

After a minute or so, a woman picked up. She sounded groggy.

'Sorry,' Rebus said. 'Is Bill there?'

'I'll get him.'

He heard background dialogue, then the receiver being hoisted.

'So what's this about prints?' he asked.

'Christ, John, when I said you could call, I didn't mean the middle of the night!'

'It's important.'

'Yes, I know. How's she doing anyway?'

'Still out cold.'

Pryde yawned. 'Well, most of the prints inside the car belong to the owner and his wife. But we found one other set. Problem is, looks like they belong to a kid.'

'What makes you so sure?'

'The size.'

'Plenty of adults around with small hands.'

'I suppose so . . .'

'You sound sceptical.'

'More likely to be one of two scenarios. One, Sammy was hit by a joyrider. I know what you think, but it does happen. Two, the prints belong to whoever rifled the car after it was left at the cemetery.'

'The kid who took the cassette player and tapes?'

'Exactly.'

'No other prints? Not even partials?'

'The car was clean, John.'

'Exterior?'

'Same three sets on the doors, plus Sammy's on the bonnet.' Pryde yawned again. 'So what about your grudge theory?'

'Still holds. A pro would be wearing gloves.'

'That's what I was thinking. Not too many pros out there though.'

'No.' Rebus was thinking of the Weasel: *I'm dealing with slime to catch a slug*. Nothing he hadn't done before, only this time there were personal reasons.

And he didn't think there'd be a trial.

18

Breakfast was on Hogan: bacon rolls in a brown paper bag. They ate them in the CID room at St Leonard's. A Murder Room had been established in Leith, and that's where Hogan should have been.

Only he wanted Rebus's files, and he knew better than to trust Rebus to deliver them.

'Thought I'd save you the hassle,' was what he said.

'You're a gentleman,' Rebus answered, examining the interior of his roll. 'Tell me, are pigs an endangered species?'

'I lifted half a slice from you.' Hogan pulled a string of fat from his mouth, tossed it into a bin. 'Thought I was doing you a favour: cholesterol and all that.'

Rebus put the roll to one side, took a swig from the can of Irn-Bru – Hogan's idea of a morning beverage – and swallowed. What was sugar consumption compared to HIV? 'What did you get from the cleaning lady?'

'Grief. Soon as she heard her employer was dead, the taps were on.' Hogan brushed flour from his fingers: mealtime over. 'She never met any of his friends, never had occasion to answer his telephone, hadn't noticed any change in him recently, and doesn't think he was a mass murderer. Quote: "If he'd killed that many people, I'd have known".'

'What is she, psychic or something?'

Hogan shrugged. 'About all I got from her was a glowing character reference and the fact that as she was paid in advance, she owes his estate a partial refund.'

'There's your motive.'

Hogan smiled. 'Speaking of motives . . .'

'You've got something?'

'Lintz's lawyer has come up with a letter from the deceased's bank.' He handed Rebus a photocopy. 'Seems our man made a cash withdrawal of five grand ten days ago.'

'*Cash?*'

'We found ten quid on his person, and about another thirty bar in the house. No five grand. I'm beginning to think blackmail.'

Rebus nodded. 'What about his address book?'

'Slow work. A lot of old numbers, people who've moved on or died. Plus a few charities, museums . . . an art gallery or two.' Hogan paused. 'What about you?'

Rebus opened his drawer, pulled out the fax sheets. 'Waiting for me this morning. The calls Lintz wanted kept secret.'

Hogan looked down the list. 'Calls plural, or one in particular?'

'I've just started going through them. Best guess: there'll be callers he spoke to regularly. Those numbers will show up on the other statements. We're looking for anomalies, one-offs.'

'Makes sense.' Hogan looked at his watch. 'Anything else I should know?'

'Two things. Remember I told you about the Special Branch interest?'

'Abernethy?'

Rebus nodded. 'I tried calling him yesterday.'

'And?'

'According to his office, he was on his way up here. He'd already heard the news.'

'So I've got Abernethy sniffing around, and you don't trust him? Terrific. What's the other thing?'

'David Levy. I spoke with his daughter. She doesn't know where he is. He could be anywhere.'

'With a grudge against Lintz?'

'It's possible.'

'What's his phone number?'

Rebus patted the topmost file on his desk. 'Ready for you to take away.'

Hogan studied the foot-high pile, looking glum.

'I whittled it down to what's absolutely necessary,' Rebus told him.

'There's a month's reading there.'

Rebus shrugged. 'My case is your case, Bobby.'

With Hogan gone, Rebus went back to the British Telecom list. It was as detailed as could have wished for. Lots of calls to Lintz's solicitor, a few to one of the city's taxi firms. Rebus tried a couple of numbers, found himself connected to charity offices: Lintz would have been phoning to tender his resignation. There were a few calls that stood out from the crowd: the Roxburghe Hotel – duration four minutes; Edinburgh University – twenty-six minutes. The Roxburghe had to mean Levy. Rebus knew Levy had talked to Lintz – Lintz himself had admitted it. Talking to him – being confronted by him – was one thing; calling him at his hotel quite another.

The number for Edinburgh University connected Rebus to the main switchboard. He asked to be put through to Lintz's old department. The secretary was very helpful. She'd been in the job over twenty years, was due to retire. Yes, she remembered Professor Lintz, but he hadn't contacted the department recently.

'Every call that comes through here, I know about it.'

'He might have got straight through to a tutor though?' Rebus suggested.

'No one's mentioned speaking to him. There's nobody here from the Professor's day.'

'He doesn't keep in touch with the department?'

'I haven't spoken to him in years, Inspector. Too many years for me to remember . . .'

So who had he been talking to for over twenty minutes? Rebus thanked the secretary and put down the phone. He went through the other numbers: a couple of restaurants, a wine shop, and the local radio station. Rebus told the receptionist what he was after, and she said she'd do her

best. Then he went back to the restaurants, asked them to check if Lintz had been making a reservation.

Within half an hour, the calls started coming in. First restaurant: a booking for dinner, just the one cover. The radio station: they'd asked Lintz to appear on a programme. He'd said he'd consider it, then had called back to decline. Second restaurant: a lunch reservation, two covers.

'Two?'

'Mr Lintz and one other.'

'Any idea who the "other" might have been?'

'Another gentleman, quite elderly, I think . . . I'm sorry, I don't really remember.'

'Did he walk with a stick?'

'I wish I could help, but it's a madhouse here at lunchtime.'

'You remember Lintz though?'

'Mr Lintz is a regular . . . was a regular.'

'Did he usually eat alone, or with company?'

'Mostly alone. He didn't seem to mind. He'd bring a book with him.'

'Do you happen to recall any of his other guests?'

'I remember a young woman . . . his daughter maybe? Or granddaughter?'

'So when you say "young" . . .?'

'Younger than him.' A pause. 'Maybe much younger.'

'When was this?'

'I really don't remember.' The voice impatient now.

'I appreciate your help, sir. Just one more minute of your time . . . This woman, did he bring her more than once?'

'I'm sorry, Inspector. The kitchen needs me.'

'Well, if you think of anything else . . .'

'Of course. Goodbye.'

Rebus put the phone down, made some notes. Just one number left. He waited for an answer.

'Yeah?' The voice grudging.

'Who's this?'

'This is Malky. Who the fuck are you?'

A voice in the background: 'Tommy says that new machine's fucked.' Rebus put the phone down. His hand was shaking. *That new machine* . . . Tommy Telford on his arcade motorbike. He remembered The Family mugshots: Malky Jordan. Tiny nose and eyes in a balloon of a face. *Joseph Lintz talking to one of Telford's men? Phoning Telford's office??* Rebus found the number of Hogan's mobile.

'Bobby,' he said. 'If you're driving, better slow down right now . . .'

Hogan's notion: five in cash was just Telford's style. Blackmail? But where was the connection? Something else . . .?

Hogan's play: he'd talk to Telford.

Rebus's notion: five was a bit steep for a hit-man. All the same, he wondered about Lintz . . . paying five thou' to Telford to set up the 'accident'. Motive: give Rebus a fright, scare him off? It put Lintz back in the frame, potentially.

Rebus had fixed up another meeting, one he didn't want anyone knowing

about. Haymarket Station was nice and anonymous. The bench on platform one. Ned Farlowe was already waiting. He looked tired: worry over Sammy. They talked about her for a couple of minutes. Then Rebus got down to business.

'You know Lintz has been murdered?'

'I didn't think this was a social call.'

'We're looking at a blackmail angle.'

Farlowe looked interested. 'And he didn't pay up?'

Oh, he paid up all right, Rebus thought. He paid up, and someone still took him out of the game.

'Look, Ned, this is *all* off the record. By rights I should take you in for questioning.'

'Because I followed him for a few days?'

'Yes.'

'And that makes me a suspect?'

'It makes you a possible witness.'

Farlowe thought about it. 'One evening, Lintz left his house, walked down the road, made a call from a phone box, then went straight back home.'

Not wanting to use his home phone . . . afraid it was bugged? Afraid of the number being traced? Telephone bugging: a favourite ploy of Special Branch.

'And something else,' Farlowe was saying. 'He met this woman on his doorstep. Like she was waiting for him. They had a few words. I think she was crying when she left.'

'What did she look like?'

'Tall, short dark hair, well dressed. She had a briefcase with her.'

'Wearing?'

Farlowe shrugged. 'Skirt and jacket . . . matching. Black and white check. You know . . . elegant.'

He was describing Kirstin Mede. Her phone message to Rebus: *I can't do this any more . . .*

'There's something I want to ask you,' Farlowe was saying. 'That girl Candice.'

'What about her?'

'You asked me if anything unusual had happened just before Sammy got hit.'

'Yes?'

'Well, *she* happened, didn't she?' Farlowe's eyes narrowed. 'Does she have anything to do with it?'

Rebus looked at Farlowe, who started nodding.

'Thanks for the confirmation. Who was she?'

'One of Telford's girls.'

Farlowe leaped to his feet, paced the platform. Rebus waited for him to sit down again. When he did, there could be no doubting the fury in his eyes.

'You hid one of Telford's girls with your own *daughter*?'

'I didn't have much choice. Telford knows where I live. I . . .'

'You were using us!' He paused. 'Telford did this, didn't he?'

'I don't know,' Rebus said. Farlowe leaped to his feet again. 'Look, Ned, I don't want you –'

'Quite frankly, *Inspector*, I don't think you're in any position to give advice.' He started walking, and though Rebus called after him, he never once looked back.

As Rebus walked into the Crime Squad office, a paper plane glided past and crashed into the wall. Ormiston had his feet up on the desk. Country and western music was playing softly in the background, its source a tape player on the window ledge behind Claverhouse's desk. Siobhan Clarke had pulled a chair over beside him. They were poring over some report.

'Not exactly the "A-Team" in here, is it?' Rebus retrieved the plane, straightened its crumpled nose, and sent it back to Ormiston, who asked what he was doing there.

'Liaising,' Rebus told him. 'My boss wants a progress report.'

Ormiston glanced towards Claverhouse, who was tipping himself back in his chair, hands behind his head.

'Want to take a guess at the headway we've made?'

Rebus sat down opposite Claverhouse, nodded a greeting to Siobhan.

'How's Sammy?' she asked.

'Just the same,' Rebus answered. Claverhouse looked abashed, and Rebus suddenly realised that he could use Sammy as a lever, play on people's sympathy. Why not? Hadn't he used her in the past? Wasn't Ned Farlowe on the nail there?

'We've pulled the surveillance,' Claverhouse said.

'Why?'

Ormiston snorted, but it was Claverhouse who answered.

'High maintenance, low returns.'

'Orders from above?'

'It isn't as if we were close to getting a result.'

'So we just let him get on with getting on?'

Claverhouse shrugged. Rebus wondered if news would get back to Newcastle. Jake Tarawicz would be happy. He'd think Rebus was fulfilling his part of the bargain. Candice would be safe. Maybe.

'Any news on that nightclub killing?'

'Nothing to link it to your chum Cafferty.'

'He's *not* my chum.'

'Whatever you say. Stick the kettle on, Ormie.' Ormiston glanced towards Clarke, then rose grudgingly from his chair. Rebus had thought the tension in the office was all to do with Telford. Not a bit of it. Claverhouse and Clarke close together, *involved*. Ormiston off on his own, a kid making paper planes, seeking attention. An old Status Quo song: 'Paper Plane'. But the status quo here had been disturbed: Clarke had usurped Ormiston. The office junior was absolved from making the tea.

Rebus could see why Ormiston was pissed off.

'I hear Herr Lintz was a bit of a swinger,' Claverhouse said.

'Now there's a joke I haven't heard before.' Rebus's pager sounded. The display gave him a number to call.

He used Claverhouse's phone. It sounded like he was connected to a payphone. Street sounds, heavy traffic close by.

'Mr Rebus?' Placed the voice at once: the Weasel.

'What is it?'

'A couple of questions. The tape player from the car, any idea of the make?'

'Sony.'

'The front bit detachable?'

'That's right.'

'So all they got was the front bit?'

'Yes.' Claverhouse and Clarke, back at their report, pretending they weren't listening.

'What about the tapes? You said some tapes got stolen?'

'Opera – *The Marriage of Figaro* and Verdi's *Macbeth*.' Rebus squeezed his eyes shut, thinking. 'And another tape with film music on it, famous themes. Plus Roy Orbison's *Greatest Hits*.' This last the wife's. Rebus knew what the Weasel was thinking: whoever took the stuff, they'd try flogging it round the pubs or at a car boot sale. Car boot sales were clearing houses for knock-off. But getting whoever had lifted the stuff from the unlocked car wasn't going to nail the driver . . . Unless the kid – the one who'd lifted the stuff, whose prints were on the car – had *seen* something: been hanging around on the street, watched the car screeching to a stop, a man getting out and hoofing it . . .

An eyewitness, someone who could describe the driver.

'The only prints we got were small, maybe a kid's.'

'That's interesting.'

'Anything else I can do,' Rebus said, 'just let me know.'

The Weasel hung up.

'Sony's a good make,' Claverhouse said, fishing.

'Some stuff lifted from a car,' Rebus told him. 'It might have turned up.'

Ormiston had made the tea. Rebus went to fetch himself a chair, saw someone walk past the open doorway. He dropped the chair and ran into the corridor, grabbed at an arm.

Abernethy spun quickly, saw who it was and relaxed.

'Nice one, son,' he said. 'You almost had knuckles for teeth.' He was working on a piece of chewing gum.

'What are you doing here?'

'Visiting.' Abernethy looked back at the open door, walked towards it. 'What about you?'

'Working.'

Abernethy read the sign on the door. 'Crime Squad,' he said, sounding amused, taking in the office and the people in it. Hands in pockets, he sauntered in, Rebus following.

'Abernethy, Special Branch,' the Londoner said by way of introduction. 'That music's a good idea: play it at interrogations, sap the suspect's will to live.' He was smiling, surveying the premises like he was thinking of moving in. The mug meant for Rebus was on the corner of the desk. Abernethy picked it up and slurped, made a face, started chewing again. The three Crime Squad officers were like a frozen tableau. Suddenly they looked like a unit: it had taken Abernethy to do that.

Had taken him all of ten seconds.

'What you working on?' No one answered. 'Must've got the sign on the door wrong,' Abernethy said. 'Should be Mime Squad.'

'Is there something we can do for you?' Claverhouse asked, his voice level, hostility in his eyes.

'I don't know. It was John pulled me in here.'

'And I'm pulling you out again,' Rebus said, taking his arm. Abernethy shrugged free, bunched his fists. 'A word in the corridor . . . please.'

Abernethy smiled. 'Manners maketh the man, John.'

'What does that maketh you?'

Abernethy turned his head slowly, looked at Siobhan Clarke who'd just spoken.

'I'm just a regular guy with a heart of gold and twelve big inches of ability.' He grinned at her.

'To go with your twelve big points of IQ ,' she said, going back to the report. Ormiston and Claverhouse weren't trying too hard to conceal their laughter as Abernethy stormed out of the room. Rebus hung back long enough to watch Ormiston pat Clarke on the back, then headed off after the Special Branch man.

'What a bitch,' Abernethy said. He was making for the exit.

'She's a friend of mine.'

'And they say you can choose your friends . . .' Abernethy shook his head. 'What brings you back?'

'You have to ask?'

'Lintz is dead. Case closed as far as you're concerned.'

They emerged from the building.

'So?'

'So,' Rebus persisted, 'why come all the way back here? What is there that couldn't be done with a phone or fax?'

Abernethy stopped, turned to face him. 'Loose ends.'

'What loose ends?'

'There aren't any.' Abernethy gave a cheerless smile and took a key from his pocket. As they approached his car, he used the remote to unlock it and disable the alarm.

'What's going on, Abernethy?'

'Nothing to worry your pretty little head about.' He opened the driver's-side door.

'Are you glad he's dead?'

'What?'

'Lintz. How do you feel about him being murdered?'

'I've no feelings either way. He's dead, which means I can cross him off my list.'

'That last time you came up here, you were warning him.'

'Not true.'

'Was his phone bugged?' Abernethy just snorted. 'Did you know he might be killed?'

Abernethy turned on Rebus. 'What's it to you? I'll tell you: nothing. Leith CID are on the murder, and you're out of it. End of story.'

'Is it the Rat Line? Too embarrassing if it all came to light?'

'Christ, what *is* it with you? Just give it a rest.' Abernethy got into the car, closed the door. Rebus didn't move. The engine turned and caught, Abernethy's window slid down. Rebus was ready.

'They sent you four hundred miles just to check there were no loose ends.'

'So?'

'So there's rather a large loose end, isn't there?' Rebus paused. 'Unless you know who Lintz's killer was.'

'I leave that sort of thing to you guys.'

'Heading down to Leith?'

'I have to talk to Hogan.' Abernethy stared at Rebus. 'You're a hard bastard, aren't you? Maybe even a bit selfish.'

'How's that?'

'If I'd a daughter in hospital, police work would be the last thing on my mind.'

As Rebus lunged towards the open window, Abernethy gunned the car. Footsteps behind: Siobhan Clarke.

'Good riddance,' she said, watching the car speed off. A finger appeared from Abernethy's window. She gave a two-fingered reply. 'I didn't want to say anything in the office . . .' she began.

'I took the test yesterday,' Rebus lied.

'It'll be negative.'

'Are you positive?'

She smiled a little longer than the joke merited. 'Ormiston chucked your tea away, said he was going to disinfect the mug.'

'Abernethy has that effect on people.' He looked at her. 'Remember, Ormiston and Claverhouse go back years.'

'I know. I think Claverhouse has a crush on me. It'll pass, but until it does . . .'

'Tread carefully.' They started walking back towards the main entrance. 'And don't let him tempt you into the broom cupboard.'

19

Rebus went back to St Leonard's, saw that the office was coping quite well without him, and headed over to the hospital with Dr Morrison's Iron Maiden T-shirt in a plastic bag. A third bed had been moved into Sammy's room. An elderly woman lay in it. Though awake, she stared fixedly at the ceiling. Rhona was at Sammy's bedside, reading a book.

Rebus stroked his daughter's hair. 'How is she?'

'No change.'

'Any more tests planned?'

'Not that I know of.'

'That's it then? She just stays like this?'

He lifted a chair over, sat down. It had turned into a sort of ritual now, this bedside vigil. It felt almost . . . the word he wanted to use was 'comfortable'. He squeezed Rhona's hand, sat there for twenty minutes, saying almost nothing, then went to find Kirstin Mede.

She was in her office at the French Department, marking scripts. She sat at a big desk in front of the window, but moved from this to a coffee-table with half a dozen chairs arranged around it.

'Sit down,' she said. Rebus sat down.

'I got your message,' he told her.

'Hardly matters now, does it? The man's dead.'

'I know you spoke with him, Kirstin.'

She glanced towards him. 'I'm sorry?'

'You waited for him outside his house. Did the two of you have a nice chat?'

Colour had risen to her cheeks. She crossed her legs, tugged the hem of her skirt towards her knee. 'Yes,' she said at last, 'I went to his house.'

'Why?'

'Because I wanted to see him close up.' Her eyes were on his now, challenging him. 'I thought maybe I could tell from his face . . . the look in his eyes. Maybe something in his tone of voice.'

'And could you?'

She shook her head. 'Not a damned thing. No window to the soul.'

'What did you say to him?'

'I told him who I was.'

'Any reaction?'

'Yes.' She folded her arms. 'His words: "My dear lady, will you kindly piss off".'

'And did you?'

'Yes. Because I knew then. Not whether he was Linzstek or not, but something else.'

'What?'

'That he was at the end of his tether.' She was nodding. 'Absolutely at breaking point.' She looked at Rebus again. 'And capable of anything.'

The problem with the Flint Street surveillance was that it had been so open. A hidden operation – deep cover – that's what was needed. Rebus had decided to scout out the territory.

The tenement flats across the road from Telford's café and arcade were served by a single main door. It was locked, so Rebus chose a buzzer at random – marked HETHERINGTON. Waited, pushed again. An elderly voice came on the intercom.

'Who is it, please?'

'Mrs Hetherington? Detective Inspector Rebus, I'm your Community CID officer. Can I talk to you about home security? There've been a few break-ins around here, especially with elderly victims.'

'Gracious, you'd better come up.'

'Which floor?'

'The first.' The door buzzed, and Rebus pushed it open.

Mrs Hetherington was waiting for him in her doorway. She was tiny and frail-looking, but her eyes were lively and her movements assured. The flat was small, well-maintained. The sitting room was heated by a two-bar electric fire. Rebus wandered over to the window, found himself looking down on to the arcade. Perfect location for a surveillance. He pretended to check her windows.

'These seem fine,' he said. 'Are they always locked?'

'I open them a bit in the summer,' Mrs Hetherington said, 'and when they need washing. But I always lock them again afterwards.'

'One thing I should warn you about, and that's bogus officials. People coming to your door, telling you they're so-and-so. Always ask to see some ID, and don't open up until you're satisfied.'

'How can I see it without opening the door?'

'Ask them to push it through the letterbox.'

'I didn't see *your* identification, did I?'

Rebus smiled. 'No, you didn't.' He took it out and showed her. 'Sometimes the fake stuff can look pretty convincing. If you're unsure, keep the door locked and call the police.' He looked around. 'You have a phone?'

'In the bedroom.'

'Any windows in there?'

'Yes.'

'Can I take a look?'

The bedroom window also looked out on to Flint Street. Rebus noticed travel brochures on the dressing table, a small suitcase standing near the door.

'Off on holiday, eh?' With the flat empty, maybe he could move the surveillance in.

'Just a long weekend,' she said.

'Somewhere nice?'

'Holland. Wrong time of year for the bulb-fields, but I've always wanted to go. It's a nuisance flying from Inverness, but so much cheaper. Since my husband died . . . well, I've done a bit of travelling.'

'Any chance of taking me with you?' Rebus smiled. 'This window's fine, too. I'll just check your door, see if it could do with more locks.' They went into the narrow hall.

'You know,' she said, 'we've always been very lucky here, no break-ins or anything like that.'

Hardly surprising with Tommy Telford as proprietor.

'And with the panic button, of course . . .'

Rebus looked at the wall next to the front door. A large red button. He'd assumed it was for the stairhead lights or something.

'Anyone who calls, anyone at all, I'm supposed to press it.'

Rebus opened the door. 'And do you?'

Two very large men were standing right outside.

'Oh, yes,' Mrs Hetherington said. 'I always do.'

For thugs, they were very polite. Rebus showed them his warrant card and explained the nature of his visit. He asked them who they were, and they told him they were 'representatives of the building's owner'. He knew the faces though: Kenny Houston, Ally Cornwell. Houston – the ugly one – ran Telford's doormen; Cornwell, with his wrestler's bulk, was general muscle. The little charade was carried out with humour and good nature on both sides. They accompanied him downstairs. Across the street, Tommy Telford was standing in the café doorway, wagging his finger. A pedestrian crossed Rebus's line of vision. Too late, Rebus saw who it was. Had his mouth open to shout something, then saw Telford hang his head, hands going to his face. Screeching.

Rebus ran across the road, pulled the pedestrian round: Ned Farlowe. A bottle dropped from Farlowe's hand. Telford's men were closing in. Rebus held tight to Farlowe.

'I'm placing this man under arrest,' he said. 'He's *mine*, understood?'

A dozen faces glaring at him. And Tommy Telford down on his knees.

'Get your boss to the hospital,' Rebus said. 'I'm taking this one to St Leonard's . . .'

Ned Farlowe sat on the ledge in one of the cells. The walls were blue, smeared brown near the toilet-pan. Farlowe was looking pleased with himself.

'Acid?' Rebus said, pacing the cell. '*Acid*? All this research must have gone to your head.'

'It's what he deserved.'

Rebus glared at him. 'You don't know what you've done.'

'I know *exactly* what I've done.'

'He'll kill you.'

Farlowe shrugged. 'Am I under arrest?'

'You'd better believe it, son. I want you kept out of harm's way. If I hadn't been there . . .' But he didn't want to think about that. He looked at Farlowe. Looked at Sammy's lover, who'd just staged a full-frontal assault on Telford, the kind of assault Rebus knew wouldn't work.

Now Rebus would have to redouble his efforts. Because otherwise, Ned Farlowe was a dead man . . . and when Sammy came round, he didn't want news like that to be waiting for her.

He drove back towards Flint Street, parked at a distance from it, and headed there on foot. Telford had the place sewn up, no doubt about it. Letting his flats to old folk might have been a charitable act but he'd made damned sure it served its purpose. Rebus wondered if, given the same circumstances, Cafferty would have been clever enough to think of panic buttons. He suspected not. Cafferty wasn't thick, but most of what he did he did by instinct. Rebus wondered if Tommy Telford had ever made a rash move in his life.

He was staking out Flint Street because he needed an *in*, needed to find the weak link in the chain around Telford. After ten minutes of windchill, he thought of a better idea. On his mobile, he called one of the city's taxi firms. Identified himself and asked if Henry Wilson was on shift. He was. Rebus told the switchboard to put a call out to Henry. It was as simple as that.

Ten minutes later, Wilson turned up. He drank in the Ox occasionally, which was his problem really. Drunk in charge of a taxi-cab. Luckily Rebus had been around to smooth things over, as a result of which Wilson owed him a lifetime of favours. He was tall, heavily built, with short black hair and a long black beard. Ruddy-faced, and he always wore check shirts. Rebus thought of him as 'The Lumberjack'.

'Need a lift?' Wilson said, as Rebus got into the front passenger-seat.

'First thing I need is a blast of the heater.' Wilson obliged. 'Second thing I need is to use your taxi as cover.'

'You mean, sit here?'

'That's what I mean.'

'With the meter running?'

'You've got an engine problem, Henry. Your cab's out of the game for the rest of the afternoon.'

'I'm saving up for Christmas,' Wilson complained. Rebus stared him out. The big man sighed and lifted a newspaper from the side of his seat. 'Help me pick a few winners then,' he said, turning to the racing pages.

They sat for over an hour at the end of Flint Street, and Rebus stayed in the front of the cab. His reasoning: a cab parked with a passenger in the back looked suspicious. A cab parked with two guys in the front, and you'd just think they were on their break, or at shift's end – two cabbies sharing stories and a flask of tea.

Rebus took one sip from the plastic cup and winced. Half a bag of sugar in the flask.

'I've always had a sweet tooth,' Wilson explained. He had a packet of crisps open on his lap: pickled onion flavour.

Finally, Rebus saw two Range Rovers being driven into Flint Street. Sean Haddow – Telford's money man – was driving the lead car. He got out and went into the arcade. On the passenger seat, Rebus could see a huge yellow teddy bear. Haddow was coming out again, bringing Telford with him. Telford: back from the hospital already, hands bandaged, gauze patches on his face like he'd had a particularly ropey shave. But not about

to let a little thing like an acid attack get in the way of business. Haddow held the back door open, and Telford got in.

'This is us, Henry,' Rebus said. 'You're going to be following those two Range Rovers. Stay back as far as you like. Those things are so high off the ground, we'll be able to see them over anything smaller than a double-decker.'

Both Range Rovers headed out of Flint Street. The second car carried three of Telford's 'soldiers'. Rebus recognised Pretty-Boy. The other two were younger recruits, well dressed with groomed hair. One hundred per cent business.

The convoy headed for the city centre, stopped outside a hotel. Telford had a word with his men, but entered the building alone. The cars stayed where they were.

'Are you going in?' Wilson asked.

'I think I'd be noticed,' Rebus said. The drivers of both Range Rovers had got out and were enjoying a smoke, but keeping a keen eye on people entering and leaving the hotel. A couple of prospects looked into the cab, but Wilson shook his head.

'I could be making a mint here,' he muttered. Rebus offered him a Polo. Wilson accepted with a snort.

'Brilliant,' Rebus said. Wilson looked back towards the hotel. A parking warden was talking to Haddow and Pretty-Boy. She had her notebook out. They were tapping their watches, attempting charm. Double-yellow lines kerbside: no parking any time.

Haddow and Pretty-Boy held up their hands in surrender, had a quick confab, then it was back into the Range Rovers. Pretty-Boy made circling motions with one hand, letting his passengers know they were going to circle the block. The warden stood her ground till they'd moved off. Haddow was on his mobile: doubtless letting his boss know the score.

Interesting: they hadn't tried to strongarm the warden, or bribe her, nothing like that. Law-abiding citizens. Telford's rules, no doubt. Again, Rebus couldn't see any of Cafferty's men giving in so quickly.

'You going in then?' Wilson asked.

'Not much point, Henry. Telford will already be in a bedroom or somebody's suite. If he's doing business, it'll be behind closed doors.'

'So that was Tommy Telford?'

'You've heard of him?'

'I'm a taxi driver, we hear things. He's after Big Ger's cab business.' Wilson paused. 'Not that Big Ger *has* a cab business, you understand.'

'Any idea how Telford plans to wrest it away from Cafferty?'

'Scare off the drivers, or get them to switch sides.'

'What about your company, Henry?'

'Honest, legal and decent, Mr Rebus.'

'No approach by Telford?'

'Not yet.'

'Here they come again.' They watched as the two Range Rovers turned back into the street. There was no sign of the warden. A couple of minutes later, Telford emerged from the hotel, bringing with him a Japanese man with spiky hair and a shiny aquamarine suit. He carried a briefcase but didn't look like a businessman. Maybe it was the sunglasses, worn in late-

afternoon twilight; maybe it was the cigarette slouching from the corner of the downturned mouth. Both men got into the back of the lead car. The Japanese leaned forward and ruffled the teddy bear's ears, making some joke. Telford didn't look amused.

'Do we follow them?' Wilson asked. He saw the look on Rebus's face, turned the key in the ignition.

They were heading west out of town. Rebus already had an inkling of their ultimate destination, but he wanted to know what route they'd take. Turned out it was much the same route he'd taken with Candice. She hadn't recognised anything until Juniper Green, but it wasn't as if there were many landmarks. On Slateford Road the back car signalled that it was pulling over.

'What do I do?' Wilson asked.

'Keep going. Make the first left you can, and turn the cab round. We'll wait for them to go past us.'

Haddow had gone into a newspaper shop. Same story as with Candice. Strange, during what was a business trip, that Telford would allow a stop. And what about the building which, according to Candice, he'd seemed so interested in? There it was: an anonymous brick edifice. A warehouse maybe? Rebus could think of reasons why a warehouse might be of interest to Tommy Telford. Haddow stayed in the shop three minutes – Rebus timed him. No one else came out, so it wasn't as if he'd had to queue. Back into the car, and the little convoy set off again. They were heading for Juniper Green, and after that Poyntinghame Country Club. Little point in tagging along: the further they got out of town, the more conspicuous the cab would be. Rebus told Henry to turn around.

He got the cabbie to drop him off at the Oxford Bar. Wilson slid down his window as he was about to move off.

'Are we square now?' he called.

'Till next time, Henry.' Rebus pushed open the door and walked into the pub.

Perched on a stool, daytime TV and Margaret the barmaid for company, Rebus ordered a mug of coffee and a corned beef and beetroot roll. For his main course Margaret suggested a bridie.

'Excellent choice,' Rebus agreed. He was thinking about the Japanese businessman. Who hadn't really looked like a businessman at all. He'd been all sharp edges, chiselled face. Fortified, Rebus walked from the Ox back to the hotel, and kept watch on it from an overpriced bar across the street. He passed the time making calls on his mobile. By the time the battery died, he'd spoken with Hogan, Bill Pryde, Siobhan Clarke, Rhona and Patience, and had been about to call Torphichen cop-shop, see if anyone there could identify the building on Slateford Road. Two hours crawled by. He broke his 'personal best' for slow drinking: two Cokes. The bar wasn't exactly crowded; no one seemed to mind. The music was on a tape-loop. 'Psycho Killer' was coming round for the third time when the Range Rovers stopped outside the hotel. Telford and the Jap shook hands, made slight bows. Telford and his men drove off.

Rebus left the bar, crossed the road, and entered the hotel. The lift doors were closing on Mr Aquamarine. Rebus walked up to reception, showed his ID.

'The guest who just came in, I need his name.'

The receptionist had to check. 'Mr Matsumoto.'

'First name?'

'Takeshi.'

'When did he arrive?'

She checked the register again. 'Yesterday.'

'How long's he staying?'

'Three more days. Look, I should call my supervisor . . .'

Rebus shook his head. 'That's all I needed to know, thanks. Mind if I sit in the lounge for a while?'

She shook her head, so Rebus wandered into the residents' lounge. He settled on a sofa – perfect view of the reception area through the glass double-doors – and picked up a newspaper. Matsumoto was in town on Poyntinghame business, but Rebus had a whiff of something altogether less savoury. Hugh Malahide's story had been that a corporation wanted to buy the club, but Matsumoto didn't look like he worked in any above-board business. When he finally emerged into reception, he'd changed into a white suit, black open-necked shirt, and Burberry trenchcoat, topped off with a woollen tartan scarf. He had a cigarette in his mouth, but didn't light it until he was outside the hotel. With the collar of his coat turned up, he started walking. Rebus followed him for the best part of a mile, and kept checking that no one was following *him*. It was possible, after all, that Telford would want to keep tabs on Matsumoto. But if there was surveillance, it was exceptional. Matsumoto wasn't playing the tourist, wasn't dawdling. He kept his head down, protecting his face from the wind, and seemed to have some destination in mind.

When he disappeared into a building, Rebus paused, studying the glass door behind which stood a flight of red-carpeted stairs. He knew where he was, didn't need the sign above the door to tell him. He was outside the Morvena Casino. The place used to be owned by a local villain called Topper Hamilton and managed by a man called Mandelson. But Hamilton was in retirement, and Mandelson had scarpered. The new owner was still an unknown quantity – or had been till now. Rebus guessed he wouldn't be far wrong if he placed Tommy Telford and his Japanese friends in the frame. He looked around, checking the parked cars: no Range Rovers.

'What the hell,' he said to himself, pushing open the door and starting to climb the stairs.

In the upstairs foyer he was eyeballed by security: two of them looking uncomfortable in their black suits and bowties, white shirts. One skinny – he'd be all about speed and manoeuvres; one a real heavyweight – slow muscle to back up the fast moves. Rebus seemed to pass whatever test they'd just given him. He bought a twenty's worth of chips and walked into the gaming room.

At one time, it would have been the drawing room of a Georgian house. There were two huge bay windows, and ornate cornicing connected the twenty-foot-high cream walls to the pastel-pink ceiling. Now it was home to gaming tables: blackjack, dice, roulette. Hostesses moved between the tables, taking orders for drinks. There was very little noise: the gamblers took their work seriously. Rebus wouldn't have called the place busy, but

what clientele there was comprised a veritable United Nations. Matsumoto's coat had disappeared into the cloakroom, and he was seated at the roulette table. Rebus sat down beside two men at the blackjack table, nodded a greeting. The dealer – young, but obviously sure of himself – smiled. Rebus won with his first hand. Lost with his second and third. Won again with his fourth. There was a voice just behind his right ear.

'Something to drink, sir?'

The hostess had bent forward to speak to him, showing plenty of cleavage.

'Coke,' he told her. 'Ice and lemon.' He pretended to watch her move away. Really, he was scoping the room. He'd sat in on the game quickly: walking around the room would have attracted everyone's interest, and he couldn't be sure if there'd be anyone here who'd know him.

He needn't have worried. The only person he recognised was Matsumoto, rubbing his hands as the croupier pushed chips towards him. Rebus stuck on eighteen. The dealer got twenty. Rebus had never been a great gambler. He'd tried the football pools, sometimes the horses, and now occasionally the lottery. But fruit machines didn't interest him; the poker sessions organised in the office didn't interest him. He had other ways of losing money.

Matsumoto lost and gave what sounded like a curse, a little bit louder than the room liked. The skinny security ape put his head around the door, but Matsumoto ignored him, and when Mr Skinny saw who was making the noise, he retreated fast. Matsumoto laughed: he might not have much English, but he knew he had power in this place. He told everyone something in a stream of Japanese, nodding, trying for eye contact. Then a hostess brought him a big tumbler of whisky and ice. He handed her a couple of chips as a tip. The croupier was telling everyone to place their bets. Matsumoto quietened down and went back to work.

Rebus's drink was a while coming, Coke the unlikely beverage of the high roller. He'd won a couple of hands, felt a bit better. Stood up to accept the drink. The table knew to leave him out of the next deal.

'Where are you from?' he asked the hostess. 'I can't place your accent.'

'I am from Ukraine.'

'You speak good English.'

'Thank you.' She turned away. Conversation was not house policy, it kept the punters away from their games. Ukraine: Rebus wondered if she was another of Tarawicz's imports. Like Candice . . . A few things seemed clear to him. Matsumoto was comfortable here, therefore known. And the staff were wary of him, therefore he had clout, had Telford behind him. Telford wanted him kept sweet. It wasn't much return for all Rebus's work, but it was something.

Then someone walked in. Someone Rebus knew. Dr Colquhoun. He saw Rebus immediately and fear jumped into his face. Colquhoun: with his sick-line to the university; his enforced holiday; no forwarding address. Colquhoun: who'd known Rebus was taking Candice to the Drinics.

Rebus watched him back towards the doors. Watched him turn and run.

Options: go after him, or stay with Matsumoto? Which was the more important to him now, Candice or Telford? Rebus stayed. But now Colquhoun was back in town, he'd track him down.

For definite.

After an hour and a quarter's play, he was considering cashing a cheque for more chips. Twenty quid down in a little over an hour, and Candice fighting for some space in his crowded head. He took a break, moved to a row of fruit machines, but the lights and buttons defeated him. He wasted three nudges and ran out of time on some accumulator. Another two quid gone – this time in a couple of minutes. Little wonder clubs and pubs wanted slot machines. Tommy Telford was in the right business. His hostess came to see him again, asked if he wanted another drink.

'I'm fine,' he said. 'Not much action tonight.'

'It's early,' she told him. 'Wait till after midnight . . .'

No way was he sticking around that long. But Matsumoto surprised him, threw up his hands and came out with another rush of Japanese, nodding and grinning, gathering up his chips. He cashed them and left the casino. Rebus waited all of thirty seconds, then followed. He said a breezy goodnight to the security men, felt their eyes on him all the way back down the stairs.

Matsumoto was buttoning his coat, wrapping the scarf tight around his neck. He was headed back in the direction of the hotel. Rebus, suddenly bone-tired, stopped in his tracks. He was thinking of Sammy and Lintz and the Weasel, thinking of all the time he seemed to be wasting.

'Fuck this for a game of soldiers.'

Turned on his heels and went to collect his car. Ten Years After: 'Goin' Home'.

It was a twenty-minute walk to Flint Street, a lot of it uphill and with the wind doing nobody any favours. The city was quiet: people huddled at bus stops; students munching on baked potatoes, chips with curry sauce. A few souls marching home with the concentrated tread of the sozzled. Rebus stopped, frowned, looked around. This was where he'd left the Saab. He was positive . . . no, not 'positive' – the word had taken on malign overtones. He was *sure*, yes, sure he'd left the Saab right here. Where now a black Ford Sierra was parked, and behind that a Mini. But no sign of Rebus's car.

'Aw, Christ,' he exploded. There were no signs of glass by the roadside, which meant they hadn't taken a brick to one of his windows. Oh, there'd be jokes in the office about this though, whether he got the car back or not. A taxi came along and he flagged it down, then remembered he'd no cash, so waved it off again.

His flat in Arden Street wasn't that far off, but had he been a camel, he'd have been keeping well clear of any straw.

20

He was asleep in his chair by the living-room window, duvet pulled up to his neck, when the buzzer sounded. He couldn't remember setting the alarm. Consciousness brought the dawning realisation that it was his door. He staggered to his feet, found his trousers and put them on.

'All right, all right,' he called, heading for the hall. 'Keep your hair on.'

He opened the door and saw Bill Pryde.

'Jesus, Bill, is this some sort of twisted revenge?' Rebus looked at his watch: two-fifteen.

'Afraid not, John,' Pryde said. His face and voice told Rebus something bad had happened.

Something very bad indeed.

'I've been off the booze for weeks.'

'Sure about that?'

'Definite.' Rebus's eyes burned into those of DCI Gill Templer. They were in her office at St Leonard's. Pryde was there, too. His jacket was off and his sleeves rolled up. Gill Templer looked bleary from interrupted sleep. Rebus was pacing what floor there was, unable to stay seated.

'I've had nothing to drink all day but coffee and Coke.'

'Really?'

Rebus ran his hands through his hair. He felt groggy, and his head was throbbing. But he couldn't ask for paracetamol and water: they'd assume hangover.

'Come on, Gill,' he said, 'I'm being shafted here.'

'Who authorised your surveillance?'

'Nobody. I did it in my own time.'

'How do you work that out?'

'The Chief Super said I could take a bit of time off.'

'He meant so you could visit your daughter.' She paused. 'Is that what this was all about?'

'Maybe.'

'This Mr . . .' she checked her notes '. . . Matsumoto, he was connected to Thomas Telford. And your theory is that Telford was behind the attack on your daughter?'

Rebus thumped the wall with his fists. 'It's a set-up, oldest trick in the book. I've yet to see one perfected. There's got to be something at the scene . . . something out of kilter.' He turned to his colleagues. 'You've got to let me go there, take a look around.'

Templer looked to Bill Pryde. Pryde folded his arms, shrugged assent. But it was Templer's play, she was the senior officer here. She tapped her pen against her teeth, then dropped it on to the desk.

'Will you submit to a blood test?'

Rebus swallowed. 'Why not?' he said at last.

'Come on then,' she said, getting to her feet.

The story was: Matsumoto had been on his way back to his hotel. Crossing the road, he'd been hit by a car travelling at speed. The driver hadn't stopped, not right away. But the car had travelled only another couple of hundred yards before mounting the pavement with its front wheels. It had been abandoned there, driver's door open.

A Saab 900, its identity known to half the Lothian and Borders force.

The interior reeked of whisky, the screw-top from a bottle lying on the passenger seat. No sign of the bottle, no sign of the driver. Just the car, and two hundred yards further back, the body of the Japanese businessman, growing cold by the roadside.

Nobody had seen anything. Nobody had heard anything. Rebus could believe it: never one of the city centre's busier routes, at this hour the place was dead.

'When I followed him from his hotel, he didn't come this way,' Rebus told Templer. She stood with shoulders hunched, hands deep in her coat pockets, keeping out the cold.

'So?' she asked.

'Long way round for a shortcut.'

'Maybe he wanted to see the sights,' Pryde suggested.

'What time's this supposed to have happened?' Rebus asked.

Templer hesitated. 'There's a margin of error.'

'Look, Gill, I know this is awkward. You shouldn't have brought me here, you shouldn't answer my questions. I'm the number one suspect, after all.' Rebus knew how much she had to lose. Over two hundred male chief inspectors in Scotland; only *five* women. Bad odds, and a lot of people waiting for her to fail. He held up his hands. 'Look, if I was blind drunk and I hit somebody, think I'd leave the car at the scene?'

'You might not know you'd hit anyone. You hear a thunk, lose control and mount the kerb, and some survival instinct tells you it's time to get out and walk.'

'Only I hadn't been drinking. I left the car near Flint Street, and that's where they took it from. Any signs it was broken into?'

She didn't say anything.

'I'll guess not,' Rebus went on. 'Because professionals don't leave marks. But to get it started, they must have wired it or got into the steering column. That's what you should be looking for.'

The car had been towed. First thing in the morning, forensics would be all over it.

Rebus laughed, shaking his head. 'It's nice though, isn't it? First they make Sammy look like a hit-and-run, and now they try to pin me for the same thing.'

'Who's "they"?'

'Telford and his men.'

'I thought you said they were doing business with Matsumoto?'

'They're all gangsters, Gill. Gangsters fall out.'

'What about Cafferty?'

Rebus frowned. 'What about him?'

'He's got an old grudge against you. This way, he stitches you up *and* annoys Telford.'

'So you do think I'm being stitched up?'

'I'm giving you the benefit of the doubt.' She paused. 'Not everyone will. What was Matsumoto's business with Telford?'

'Something to do with a country club – on the surface at least. Some Japanese were buying it, and Telford was clearing the way.' He shivered: should have worn a coat over his jacket. He rubbed his arm where the blood sample had been taken to test his alcohol level. 'Of course, a check of the deceased's hotel room might throw up something.'

'We've already been there,' Pryde said. 'Nothing out of the ordinary.'

'Which deadbeat did you send?'

'I went myself,' Gill Templer said, voice as icy as the wind. Rebus bowed his head in apology. She had a point though: Matsumoto and Telford had been doing business. There had been nothing about their farewell to one another to suggest a break-up, and Matsumoto had seemed happy and confident at the casino. What had Telford to gain by bumping him off?

Apart from maybe getting Rebus off his back.

Templer had mentioned Cafferty: was Big Ger capable of such a move? What did *he* stand to gain? Apart from settling a long-held grudge against Rebus, giving Telford a headache, and maybe gaining Poyntinghame and the Japanese deal for himself.

Balance the two – Telford against Cafferty. Cafferty's side tipped, went clunk as it hit the ground.

'Let's get back to the station,' Templer said. 'I'm reaching the early stages of frostbite.'

'Can I go home then?'

'We're not done with you yet, John,' she said, getting into the car. 'Not by a long chalk.'

But eventually they had to let him go. He wasn't being charged, not yet. There was work still to be done. He knew they could make a case against him if they wanted to, knew it only too well. *He'd* followed Matsumoto out of the club. *He* was the one with the grudge against Telford. *He* was the one who'd see poetic justice in sending Telford a message by driving over one of his associates.

He, John Rebus, was firmly in the frame. It was tightly constructed and quite elegant in its way. The scales suddenly tipped back towards Telford again, so much subtler than Cafferty.

Telford.

Rebus visited Farlowe in his cell. The reporter wasn't asleep.

'How long do I have to stay here?' he asked.

'As long as possible.'

'How's Telford?'

'Minor burns. Don't expect him to press charges. He'll want you on the outside.'

'Then you'll have to let me go.'

'Don't bet on it, Ned. *We* can press charges. We don't need Telford.'

Farlowe looked at him. 'You're going to prosecute me?'

'I saw the whole thing. Unwarranted attack on an innocent man.'

Farlowe snorted, then smiled. 'Ironic, isn't it? Charging me for my own good.' He paused. 'I won't be able to see Sammy, will I?'

Rebus shook his head.

'I didn't think of that. Fact is, I didn't *think*.' He looked up from his ledge. 'I just did. And right up until the moment I did it, it felt . . . brilliant.'

'And afterwards?'

Farlowe shrugged. 'What does afterwards matter? It's only the rest of my life.'

Rebus didn't go home, knew he wouldn't sleep. And he'd no car, so he couldn't go driving. Instead, he visited the hospital, sat down by Sammy's bedside. He took her hand, rested it against his face.

When a nurse came in and asked if he wanted anything, he asked if she'd any paracetamol.

'In a hospital?' she said, smiling. 'I'll see what I can do.'

21

Rebus was due for further questioning at St Leonard's at ten o'clock, so when his pager sounded at eight-fifteen, he assumed it was a reminder. But the phone number it wanted him to call was the mortuary down in the Cowgate. He called from the hospital payphone, and was put through to Dr Curt.

'Looks like I've drawn the short straw,' Curt told him.

'You're about to start work on Matsumoto?'

'For my sins. Look, I've heard the stories . . . don't suppose there's any truth in them?'

'I didn't kill him.'

'Glad to hear it, John.' Curt seemed to be struggling to say something. 'There are questions of ethics, of course, so I can't suggest that you come down here . . .'

'There's something you think I should see?'

'That I can't say.' Curt cleared his throat. 'But if you happened to be here . . . and the place is always very quiet this time of the morning . . .'

'I'm on my way.'

The Infirmary to the mortuary: a ten-minute walk. Curt himself was waiting to lead Rebus to the body.

The room was all white tile, bright light and stainless steel. Two of the dissecting-tables lay empty. Matsumoto's naked body lay on the third. Rebus walked around it, stunned by what he saw.

Tattoos.

And not just the kilted piper on a sailor's arm. These were works of art, and they were massive. A scaly green dragon, breathing pink and red fire, covered one shoulder and crept down the arm towards the wrist. Its back legs reached around the body's neck, while its front ones rested on the chest. There were other smaller dragons, and a landscape – Mount Fuji reflected in water. There were Japanese symbols and the visored face of a kendo champion. Curt put on rubber gloves, and had Rebus do the same. Then the two men rolled the body over, displaying a further gallery across Matsumoto's back. A masked actor, something out of a Noh play, and a warrior in full armour. Some delicate flowers. The effect was mesmerising.

'Stunning, aren't they?' Curt said.

'Phenomenal.'

'I've visited Japan a few times, given papers at conferences.'

'So you recognise some of these?'

'A few of the references, yes. Thing is, tattoos – especially on this scale – usually mean you're a gang member.'

'Like the Triads?'

'The Japanese are called Yakuza. Look here.' Curt held up the left hand. The pinkie had been severed at the first joint, the skin healed in a rough crust.

'That's what happens when they screw up, isn't it?' Rebus said, the word 'Yakuza' bouncing around in his head. 'Someone cuts off a finger every time.'

'I think so, yes,' Curt said. 'Just thought you might like to know.'

Rebus nodded, eyes glued to the corpse. 'Anything else?'

'Well, I haven't started on him yet, really. All looks fairly standard: evidence of impact with a moving vehicle. Crushed ribcage, fractures to the arms and legs.' Rebus noticed that a bone was protruding from one calf, obscenely white against the skin. 'There'll be a lot of internal damage. Shock probably killed him.' Curt was thoughtful. 'I must let Professor Gates know. Doubt he'll have seen anything like it.'

'Can I use your phone?' Rebus asked.

He knew one person who might know about the Yakuza – she'd seemed knowledgeable about every other country's criminal gangs. So he spoke to Miriam Kenworthy in Newcastle.

'Tattoos and missing fingers?' she said.

'Bingo.'

'That's Yakuza.'

'Actually, it's only the top bit missing from one little finger. That's done to them when they step out of line, isn't it?'

'Not quite. They do it to *themselves* as a way of saying they're sorry. I'm not sure I know much more than that.' There was the sound of papers being shifted. 'I'm just looking for my notes.'

'What notes?'

'When I was connecting all these gangs, different cultures, I did some research. Might be something on the Yakuza . . . Look, can I call you back?'

'How long?'

'Five minutes.'

Rebus gave her Curt's number, then sat and waited. Curt's room wasn't so much an office as a walk-in cupboard. Files were stacked high on his desk, and a dictaphone lay on top of them, along with a fresh pack of tapes. The room reeked of cigarettes and bad ventilation. On the walls: schedules of meetings, postcards, a couple of framed prints. The place was a bolt-hole, a necessity; Curt spent most of his time elsewhere.

Rebus took out Colquhoun's business card, tried home and office. As far as his secretary was concerned, Dr Colquhoun was still off sick.

Maybe, but he was well enough to visit a casino. One of Telford's casinos. No coincidence surely . . .

Kenworthy was good as gold.

'Yakuza,' she said, sounding like she was lifting from her script. 'Ninety thousand members split into something like two and a half thousand groupings. Utterly ruthless, but also highly intelligent and sophisticated. Very hierarchical structure, almost impenetrable to outsiders. Like a

secret society. They even have a sort of middle management level, called the Sokaiya.'

Rebus was writing it all down. 'How do you spell that?'

She told him. 'Back in Japan they run *pachinko* parlours – that's a sort of gaming thing – and have fingers in most other illegal pies.'

'Unless they've lopped them off. What about outside Japan?'

'Only thing I've got down here is that they ship expensive designer stuff back home to sell on the black market, also stolen art, ship it back to wealthy buyers . . .'

'Wait a minute, you told me Jake Tarawicz started out smuggling icons out of Russia.'

'You're saying Pink Eyes might connect to the Yakuza?'

'Tommy Telford's been chauffeuring them around. There's a warehouse everyone seems interested in, plus a country club.'

'What's in the warehouse?'

'I don't know yet.'

'Maybe you should find out.'

'It's on my list. Something else, these *pachinko* parlours . . . would those be like amusement arcades?'

'Pretty much.'

'Another connection with Telford: he puts gaming machines into half the pubs and clubs on the east coast.'

'You think the Yakuza saw someone they could do a deal with?'

'I don't know.' He tried stifling a yawn.

'Too early in the morning for big questions?'

He smiled. 'Something like that. Thanks for your help, Miriam.'

'No problem. Keep me posted.'

'Sure. Anything new on Tarawicz?'

'Nothing I've heard. No sign of Candice either, sorry.'

'Thanks again.'

'Bye.'

Curt was standing in the doorway. He'd stripped off gown and gloves, and his hands smelled of soap.

'Not much I can do till my assistants get in.' He looked at his watch. 'Fancy a spot of breakfast?'

'You have to appreciate how this looks, John. The media could be all over us. I can think of a few journalists who'd give their drinking-arm to nail you.'

Chief Superintendent Watson was in his element. Seated behind his desk, hands folded, he had the serenity of a large stone Buddha. The occasional crises with which John Rebus presented him had hardened the Farmer to life's lesser knocks and taught him calm acceptance.

'You're going to suspend me,' Rebus stated with conviction – he'd been here before. He finished the coffee his boss had given him, but kept his hands locked around the mug. 'Then you're going to open an investigation.'

'Not straight away,' Watson surprised him by saying. 'What I want first of all is your statement – and I mean a full and frank explanation – of your recent movements, your interest in Mr Matsumoto and Thomas Telford. Bring in anything you want about your daughter's accident, any suspicions

you've had, and above all the *validity* of those suspicions. Telford already has a lawyer asking awkward questions about our Japanese friend's untimely end. The lawyer . . .' Watson looked to Gill Templer, seated by the door, mouth a thin unimpressed line.

'Charles Groal,' she said flatly.

'Groal, yes. He's been asking at the casino. He got a description of a man who came in just after Matsumoto, and left immediately after him. He seems to think it's you.'

'Are you telling him otherwise?' Rebus asked.

'We're telling him nothing, not until our own inquiries have established . . . et cetera. But I can't hold him off for ever, John.'

'Have you asked anyone what Matsumoto was doing here?'

'He works for a firm of management consultants. He was here at a client's behest, finalising the takeover of a country club.'

'With Tommy Telford in tow.'

'John, let's not lose sight of . . .'

'Matsumoto was a member of the Yakuza, sir. The closest I've come to one of those before has been on a TV screen. Now suddenly they're in Edinburgh.' Rebus paused. 'Don't you find that just a *wee* bit curious? I mean, doesn't it worry you at all? I don't know, maybe I'm getting my priorities all wrong, but it seems to me we're splashing about in puddles while a tidal wave's coming in!'

The pressure of his hands around the mug had been increasing by degrees. Now the thing broke, a piece falling to the floor as Rebus winced. He picked one ceramic shard out of his palm. Drops of blood hit the carpet. Gill Templer had come forward, was reaching for his hand.

'Here, let me.'

He spun away from her. 'No!' Way too loud. Fumbling in his pocket for a handkerchief.

'I've got some paper ones in my bag.'

'It's all right.' Blood dripping on to his shoes. Watson was saying something about the mug having a crack; Templer was staring at him. He wrapped white cotton around the wound.

'I'll go wash it,' he said. 'With your permission, sir?'

'On you go, John. Sure you're all right?'

'I'll be fine.'

It wasn't a bad cut. Cold water helped. He dried off with paper towels, which he flushed down the toilet, waiting to see they'd gone. A first aid box next: half a dozen plasters, cover the nick good and proper. He bunched his fist, saw no sign of leakage. Had to be content with that.

Back at his desk, he started on his memoirs – as ordered by Watson. Gill Templer came past, decided he needed a few soft words.

'None of us thinks you did it, John. But something like this . . . questions being asked by the Japanese consul . . . it has to be done by the book.'

'It all comes down to politics in the end, eh?' He was thinking of Joseph Lintz.

At lunchtime he dropped in on Ned Farlowe, asked him if he needed anything. Farlowe wanted sandwiches, books, newspapers, company. He looked drawn, weary of imprisonment. Maybe soon he'd think to ask for a lawyer. A lawyer – any lawyer – would get him out.

Rebus handed his report to Watson's secretary and headed out of the station. He'd gone fifty yards when a car pulled up alongside. Range Rover. Pretty-Boy telling him to get in. Rebus looked into the back of the car.

Telford. Ointment on his blistered face. Looking like a scaled-down Jake Tarawicz . . .

Rebus hesitated. The cop-shop was a short sprint away.

'Get in,' Pretty-Boy repeated. Sucker for a free offer, Rebus got in.

Pretty-Boy turned the car. The giant yellow teddy had been strapped into the passenger seat.

'I don't suppose,' Rebus said, 'it's worth my while asking you to leave Ned Farlowe be?'

Telford's mind was on other things. 'He wants war, he's going to get war.'

'Who?'

'Your boss.'

'I don't work for Cafferty.'

'Don't give me that.'

'I'm the one who put him inside.'

'And you've been snuggling up ever since.'

'I didn't kill Matsumoto.'

Telford looked at him for the first time, and Rebus could see he was itching for violence.

'You know I didn't,' Rebus went on.

'What do you mean?'

'Because you did it, and you want me to –'

Telford's hands were around Rebus's neck. Rebus shrugged them off, tried pinning Telford down. Impossible with the car in motion, cramped in the back seat. Pretty-Boy stopped the car and got out, opened Rebus's door and dragged him on to the pavement. Telford followed, face beetroot-red, eyes bulging.

'You're not going to pin this on me!' he roared. Drivers slowed to watch. Pedestrians crossed the road to safety.

'Who else?' Rebus's voice was shaky.

'Cafferty!' Telford screeched. 'It's you and Cafferty, trying to shut me down!'

'I'm telling you, I didn't do it.'

'Boss,' Pretty-Boy was saying, 'let's screw the head, eh?' He was looking around, nervous of the attention they were attracting. Telford saw his point, let his shoulders relax a little.

'Get in the car,' he said to Rebus. Rebus just stared at him. 'It's OK. Just get in. I want to show you a couple of things.'

Rebus, world's craziest cop, got back in.

There was silence for a couple of minutes, Telford rearranging the dressings on his fingers, which had come loose during the fight.

'I don't think Cafferty wants war,' Rebus said.

'What makes you so sure?'

Because I've done a deal with him – it's me who's going to shut you down. They were heading west. Rebus tried not to think about possible destinations.

'You were in the Army, weren't you?' Telford asked.

Rebus nodded.

'Paratroops, then the SAS.'

'I didn't get past training.' Rebus thinking: he's well informed.

'So you decided to become a cop instead.' Telford was completely calm again. He'd brushed down his suit and checked the knot in his tie. 'Thing is, working for structures like those – Army, cops – you need to obey orders. I hear you're not very good at it. You wouldn't last long with me.' He looked out of the window. 'What's Cafferty planning?'

'No idea.'

'Why were you watching Matsumoto?'

'Because he tied into you.'

'Crime Squad pulled their surveillance.' Rebus said nothing. 'But you kept yours going.' Telford turned towards him. 'Why?'

'Because you tried to kill my daughter.'

Telford stared at him, unblinking. 'Is that what this is about?'

'It's why Ned Farlowe tried to blind you. He's her boyfriend.'

Telford choked out a disbelieving laugh, started to shake his head. 'I'd nothing to do with your daughter. Where's the reason?'

'To get at me. Because she helped me with Candice.'

Telford was thoughtful. 'OK,' he said, nodding, 'I can see your thinking, and I don't suppose my word's going to count for much, but for what it's worth, I know absolutely nothing about your daughter.' He paused. Rebus could hear sirens nearby. 'Is that what took you to Cafferty?'

Rebus said nothing, which seemed, to Telford's mind, to confirm his suspicions. He smiled again.

'Pull over,' Telford said. Pretty-Boy stopped the car. The road ahead was blocked anyway, police diverting traffic down side-streets. Rebus realised he'd been smelling smoke for some time. The tenements had hidden it from view, but now he could see the fire. It was in the lot where Cafferty kept his taxis. The shed used as an office had been reduced to ash. The garage behind, where the cabs were worked on and cleaned up, was about to lose its corrugated roof. A row of vehicles was burning nicely.

'We could have sold tickets,' Pretty-Boy said. Telford turned from the spectacle to Rebus.

'Fire Brigade's going to be stretched. Two of Cafferty's offices are spontaneously combusting . . .' he checked his watch . . . 'right about now, as is that beautiful house of his. Don't worry, we waited till his wife was out shopping. Final ultimatums have been delivered to his men – they can shuffle out of town or off this mortal coil.' He shrugged. 'Makes no odds to me. Go tell Cafferty: he's finished in Edinburgh.'

Rebus licked his lips. 'You've just said I'm wrong about you, that you had nothing to do with my daughter. What if *you're* wrong about Cafferty?'

'Wake up, will you? The stabbing at Megan's, then Danny Simpson . . . Cafferty's not exactly subtle.'

'Did Danny say it was Cafferty's men?'

'He knows, same as I do.' Telford tapped Pretty-Boy's shoulder. 'Back to base.' To Rebus: 'Another little message for you to take to Barlinnie. Here's what I told Cafferty's men – any of them left in this city after midnight are fair game . . . and I don't take prisoners.' He sniffed, seemed pleased with himself, settled back in the seat. 'You won't mind if I drop you at Flint Street? Only I've a business meeting in fifteen minutes.'

'With Matsumoto's bosses?'

'If they want Poyntinghame, they'll keep dealing with me.' He looked at Rebus. 'You should deal with me, too. Think about this: who'd want you pissed off with me? It comes back to Cafferty: hitting your daughter, setting up Matsumoto . . . It *all* comes back to Cafferty. Think it over, then maybe we should talk again.'

After a couple of minutes, Rebus broke the silence.

'You know a man called Joseph Lintz?'

'Bobby Hogan mentioned him.'

'He phoned your office in Flint Street.'

Telford shrugged. 'I'll tell you what I told Hogan. Maybe it was a wrong number. Whatever it was, *I* didn't speak to any old Nazi.'

'You're not the only one uses that office though.' Rebus saw Pretty-Boy watching him in the rearview mirror. 'What about you?'

'Never heard of the cat.'

A car was parked in Flint Street – a huge white limousine with blackened windows. There was a TV aerial on the boot, and the hubcaps were painted pink.

'Christ,' Telford said in amusement, 'look at his latest toy.' He seemed to have forgotten all about Rebus. He was out of the car and loping towards the man who was emerging from the back of the limo. White suit, panama hat, big cigar, and a bright red paisley shirt. None of which stopped you staring at the scarred face and blue-tinted glasses. Telford was commenting on the attire, the car, the audacity, and Mr Pink Eyes was loving it. He put a hand around Telford's shoulder, steering him towards the amusement arcade. But then he stopped, clicked his fingers, turned back to the limo and reached out a hand.

And now a woman was emerging. Short black dress and black tights, fur jacket keeping out the chills. Tarawicz rubbed a hand over her backside; Telford kissed her on the neck. She smiled, eyes slightly glazed. Then Tarawicz and Telford turned towards the Range Rover. They were both staring at Rebus.

'Trip's over, Inspector,' Pretty-Boy said, telling Rebus it was time to get out. He did so, his eyes on Candice. But she wasn't looking at him. She was snuggling into Mr Pink Eyes, head on his chest. He was still rubbing her backside, the dress rising and falling. He was watching Rebus, eyes alight, face pulled into a latex grin. Rebus walked over to them, and now Candice saw him, and looked frightened.

'Inspector,' Tarawicz said, 'good to see you again. Come to whisk the damsel away to safety?'

Rebus ignored him. 'Come on, Candice.' His hand, not quite steady, held out towards her.

She looked at him and shook her head. 'Why would I want that?' she said, and was rewarded with another kiss from Tarawicz.

'You were abducted. You can press charges.'

Tarawicz was laughing, leading her into the café.

'Candice.' Rebus reached for her arm, but she pulled away and followed her master inside.

Two of Telford's men were blocking the door. Pretty-Boy was behind Rebus.

'No cheap heroics?' he asked, making to pass the policeman.

Back at St Leonard's, Rebus took Farlowe his food and newspapers, then hitched a lift in a patrol car to Torphichen. The man he wanted was DI 'Shug' Davidson, and Davidson was in the CID office, looking frazzled.

'Somebody torched a taxi rank,' he told Rebus.

'Any idea who?'

Davidson's eyes narrowed. 'The rank was owned by Jock Scallow. Is there something you're trying to tell me?'

'Who really owned the outfit, Shug?'

'You know damned well.'

'And who's muscling in on Cafferty's patch?'

'I've heard rumours.'

Rebus rested against Davidson's desk. 'Tommy Telford's going into combat, unless we can stop him.'

' "We"?'

'I want you to take me somewhere,' Rebus said.

Shug Davidson was happily married to an understanding wife, and had kids who didn't see as much of him as they deserved. A year back, he'd won forty grand on the Lottery. Everyone in his station got a drink. The rest of the money had been salted away.

Rebus had worked with him before. He wasn't a bad cop, maybe lacking a little in imagination. They had to work their way around the scene of the fire. A further mile and a half on, Rebus told him to stop.

'What is it?' Davidson asked.

'That's what I want you to tell me.' Rebus was looking towards the brick building, the same one which so interested Tommy Telford.

'It's Maclean's,' Davidson said.

'And what's Maclean's when it's at home?'

Davidson smiled. 'You really don't know?' He opened his car door. 'Come on, I'll show you.'

They had to have their identities checked at the main entrance. Rebus noticed a lot of security, albeit subtle: cameras trained down from the corners of the building, catching every angle of approach. A phone call was made, and a man in a white coat came down to sign them in. They pinned visitors' badges to their jackets, and the tour began.

'I've been here before,' Davidson confided. 'If you ask me, it's the best kept secret in the city.'

They climbed steps, walked down passageways. Everywhere there was security: guards checked their badges; doors had to be unlocked; cameras charted their progress. Which puzzled Rebus, for it was such an unassuming building, really. And nothing spectacular was happening.

'What is it, Fort Knox?' he asked. But then their guide handed them white coats to put on, before pushing open the door to a laboratory, and Rebus started to understand.

People were working with chemicals, examining test-tubes, writing notes. There were all sorts of weird and wonderful machines, but in essence it was a school chemistry-lab on a slightly grander scale.

'Welcome,' Davidson said, 'to the world's biggest drugs factory.'

Which wasn't quite correct, for Maclean's was only the world's largest *legal* producer of heroin and cocaine, something the guide explained.

'We're licensed by the government. Back in 1961 there was an international agreement: every country in the world was allowed just one producer, and we're it for Britain.'

'So what do you make?' Rebus was staring at the rows of locked fridges.

'All sorts of things: methadone for heroin addicts, pethidine for women in labour. Diamorphine to ease terminal illnesses and cocaine for use in medical procedures. The company started out supplying laudanum to the Victorians.'

'And these days?'

'We produce about seventy tonnes of opiates a year,' the guide said. 'And around two million pounds' worth of pure cocaine.'

Rebus rubbed his forehead. 'I begin to see the need for security.'

The guide smiled. 'The MoD has asked us for advice – that's how good our security is.'

'No break-ins?'

'A couple of attempts, nothing we couldn't deal with.'

No, Rebus thought, but then you've never had to deal with Tommy Telford and the Yakuza . . . not yet.

Rebus walked around the lab, smiled and nodded at a woman who just seemed to be standing there, not doing anything.

'Who's she?' he asked the guide.

'Our nurse. She's on standby.'

'What for?'

The guide nodded towards where a man was operating one of the machines. 'Etorphine,' he said. 'Forty thousand pounds a kilo, and extremely potent. The nurse has the antidote, just in case.'

'So what's it used for, this etorphine?'

'Knocking out rhinos,' the guide said, like the answer should have been obvious.

The cocaine was produced from coca leaves flown in from Peru. The opium came from plantations in Tasmania and Australia. The pure heroin and cocaine were kept in a strongroom. Each lab had its share of locked safes. The storage warehouse boasted infrared detectors and movement sensors. Five minutes in the place told Rebus *exactly* why Tommy Telford was interested in Maclean's. And he'd brought the Yakuza in on the plan either because he needed their help – which was unlikely – or to brag about the exploit.

Back at the car, Davidson asked the obvious question.

'What's this all about, John?'

Rebus pinched the bridge of his nose. 'I think Telford's planning to hit this place.'

Davidson snorted. 'He'd never get in. Like you said yourself, it's Fort bloody Knox.'

'It's a prestige thing, Shug. If he can empty the place, it'll make his name. He'll have beaten Cafferty hands down.' It was the same with the firebombings: they weren't just a message to Cafferty, but a sort of 'red carpet' for Mr Pink Eyes – welcome to Edinburgh, and look what I can do.

'I'm telling you,' Davidson said, 'there's no way in. Christ, that's cheap!'

Davidson's attention had been diverted by signs on the window of the corner shop. Rebus looked, too. Cut-price cigarettes. Cheap sandwiches and hot rolls. Plus five pence off any morning paper.

'Competition around here must be crippling,' Davidson said. 'Fancy a roll?'

Rebus was watching workers leaving the gates of Maclean's. Afternoon break maybe. Saw them cross the road, dodging traffic. Counting small change from their pockets as they pushed open the door to the shop.

'Yes,' Rebus said quietly, 'why not?'

The small shop was packed out. Davidson got in the queue, while Rebus looked at the rack of papers and magazines. The workers were sharing jokes and gossip. Two staff worked behind the counter – young males, mixing banter with less-than-efficient service.

'What do you fancy, John? Bacon?'

'Fine,' Rebus said. Remembered he hadn't had lunch. 'Make it two.'

Two bacon rolls came in at one pound exactly. They sat in the car to eat.

'You know, Shug, the usual ploy with a shop like that is to take a beating on one or two necessities to get the punters in.' Davidson nodded, attacked his roll. 'But that place looked like Bargain City.' Rebus had stopped eating. 'Do us both a favour: find out the shop's history, who owns it, who those two are behind the counter.'

Davidson's chewing slowed. 'You think ... ?'

'Just check it out, all right?'

22

Back at St Leonard's, his telephone was ringing. He sat down and prised the lid from a beaker of coffee. On the drive back he'd been thinking about Candice. Two swigs of coffee and he lifted the receiver.

'DI Rebus,' he said.

'What the fuck is that little shite up to?' The voice of Big Ger Cafferty.

'Where are you?'

'Where do you think I am?'

'Sounds like a mobile.'

'Amazing the things that find their way into Barlinnie. Now tell me, what is happening over there?'

'You've heard then.'

'He torched my house! My *house*! Am I supposed to let him get away with that?'

'Look, I think I may have found a way to get to him.'

Cafferty calmed a little. 'Tell me?'

'Not yet, I want to –'

'And all my taxis,' Cafferty exploded again. 'The little bastard!'

'Look, the point is: what's he expecting you to do? He's waiting for instant retaliation.'

'And he's going to get it.'

'He'll be ready. Wouldn't it be better to catch him off-guard?'

'That little bastard hasn't been off-guard since he was lifted from the cradle.'

'Shall I tell you why he did it?'

Cafferty's anger ebbed again. 'Why?'

'Because he says you killed Matsumoto.'

'Who?'

'A business acquaintance. Whoever did it made it look like I was behind the wheel.'

'It wasn't me.'

'Try telling Telford that. He thinks you ordered me to do it.'

'We know differently.'

'That's right. *We* know someone was setting me up, trying to get me out of the way.'

'What was his name again, the dead one?'

'Matsumoto.'

'Is that Japanese?'

725

Rebus wished he could see Cafferty's eyes. Even then, it was hard to tell when the man was playing games.

'He was Japanese,' Rebus stated.

'What the hell did he have to do with Telford?'

'Sounds to me like your intelligence has gone to pot.'

There was silence on the line. 'About your daughter . . .'

Rebus froze. 'What about her?'

'A second-hand shop in Porty.' Meaning Portobello. 'The owner bought some stuff from a seller. Including opera tapes and Roy Orbison. Stuck in his mind. They don't naturally go together.'

Rebus's hand tightened on the receiver. 'Which shop? What did the seller look like?'

Cold laughter. 'We're working on it, Strawman, just leave everything to us. Now, about this Japanese fellow . . .?'

'I said *I'd* put Telford out of the game. That was the agreement.'

'I've yet to see any action.'

'I'm working on it!'

'I want to hear about him anyway.'

Rebus paused.

'How is Samantha anyway?' Cafferty asked. 'That's her name, isn't it?'

'She's . . .'

'Because it looks like I'll be fulfilling *my* side of our bargain any day. While you, on the other hand . . .'

'Matsumoto was Yakuza: heard of them?'

A moment's silence. 'I've heard of them.'

'Telford's helping them buy a country club.'

'What in God's name do they want with that?'

'I'm not sure.'

Cafferty was silent again. Rebus almost thought his mobile had died. Then: 'He's got big ideas, hasn't he?' Like there was just a touch of respect there, battling the sense of territorial breach.

'We've both seen people overreach themselves.' An idea formed in Rebus's mind, a sudden notion of where everything was headed.

'Looks like Telford's got plenty of stretch left in him though,' Cafferty was saying. 'And me, I'm not even halfway through *my* stretch.'

'Know something, Cafferty? Every time you start to sound beaten, that's when I know you're just coming to the boil.'

'You know I'm going to have to retaliate, whether I want to or not. A little ritual we have to go through, like shaking hands.'

'How many men have you got?'

'More than enough.'

'Listen, one last thing . . .' Rebus couldn't believe he was telling his arch-enemy this. 'Jake Tarawicz arrived here today. I think the fireworks were meant to impress him.'

'Telford torched my house just so he'd have something to show that ugly Russian bastard?'

Like a kid showing off to his elders, Rebus was thinking. Overreaching himself . . .

'That's it, Strawman!' Cafferty was back to being furious. 'All bets are off. Those two want to get dirty with Morris Gerald Cafferty, I'll give them

both anthrax. I'll infect the pair of them. They'll think they've caught full-blown fucking AIDS by the time I'm finished!'

Which was about as much as Rebus could take. He put down the phone, drank his cold coffee, checked his messages. Patience wondered if he could make it to supper. Rhona said they'd carried out another scan. Bobby Hogan wanted a word.

He called the hospital first. Rhona said something about a new scan to assess the amount of damage done to the brain.

'Then why the hell didn't they give her *that* scan straight away?'

'I don't know.'

'Did you ask?'

'Why don't *you* come down here? Why don't *you* ask? Seems like when I'm not here, you're happy enough spending time with Samantha, even sleeping in the chair. What is it – do I scare you off?'

'Look, Rhona, I'm sorry. It's been a rough day.'

'For you and everyone else.'

'I know. I'm a selfish bastard.'

The rest of their conversation was predictable. It was a relief to say goodbye. He tried Patience, got her answering machine, and told it he'd be happy to accept the invitation. Then he called Bobby Hogan.

'Hiya, Bobby, what've you got?'

'Not much. I had a word with Telford.'

'I know, he told me.'

'You've been speaking to him?'

'Says he never knew Lintz. Did you talk to The Family?'

'The ones who frequent the office. Same story.'

'Did you mention the five thou'?'

'Think I'm stupid? Listen, I thought you might be able to help me.'

'Fire away.'

'Lintz's address book, I found a couple of addresses for a Dr Colquhoun. Thought at first it must be his GP.'

'He's a Slavic Studies lecturer.'

'Only Lintz seems to have been keeping track of him. Three changes of address, going back twenty years. First two addresses have phone numbers with them, but not the most recent. I checked, and Colquhoun's only been at this latest address three years.'

'So?'

'So Lintz didn't have his home phone number. So if he wanted to speak to him . . .'

Rebus twigged. 'He'd phone the university.' The call on Lintz's bill: twenty-odd minutes. Rebus was remembering what Colquhoun had said about Lintz.

I met him at a few social functions . . . our departments weren't that close . . . As I say, we weren't close . . .

'They weren't in the same department,' Rebus said. 'Colquhoun told me they'd barely met . . .'

'So how come Lintz has been keeping up with Colquhoun's various moves around the city?'

'Beats me, Bobby. Have you asked him?'

'No, but I intend to.'

'He's lying low. I've been trying to talk to him for a week.' Last seen at the Morvena: did Colquhoun link Telford to Lintz?

'Well, he's back now.'

'What?'

'I've an appointment with him at his office.'

'Count me in,' Rebus said, getting to his feet.

As Rebus parked in Buccleuch Place – he was in an unmarked Astra, courtesy of St Leonard's – he saw the car in the neighbouring bay make to leave. He waved, but Kirstin Mede didn't see him, and by the time he'd found the horn, she'd pulled away. He wondered how well she knew Colquhoun. After all, she'd been the one to suggest him as a translator . . .

Hogan, standing by the railings, had seen Rebus's attempts at communication.

'Someone you know?'

'Kirstin Mede.'

Hogan placed the name. 'The one who did those translations?'

Rebus looked up at the Slavic Studies building. 'Have you tracked down David Levy?'

'Daughter still hasn't heard from him.'

'How long has that been?'

'Long enough to seem suspicious in itself, only she doesn't seem too bothered.'

'How do you want to play this?' Rebus asked.

'Depends what he's like.'

'You ask your questions. Me, I just want to be there.'

Hogan looked at him, then shrugged and pushed open the door. They started to climb the worn stone steps. 'Hope they haven't put him in the penthouse.'

Colquhoun's name was on a piece of card stuck to a door on the second floor. They pushed it open, and were confronted with a short hallway and another five or six doors. Colquhoun's office was first on the right, and he was already standing in the doorway.

'Thought I heard you. Sound carries in this place. Come in, come in.' He wasn't expecting Hogan to have company. His words dried up when he saw Rebus. He walked back into his office, motioned for both officers to sit, then fussed about moving their chairs around so they'd be facing his desk.

'Terrible muddle,' he said, kicking over a pile of books.

'Know the feeling, sir,' Hogan said.

Colquhoun peered in Rebus's direction. 'My secretary says you used the library.'

'Filling in some of the gaps, sir.' Rebus kept his voice level.

'Yes, Candice . . .' Colquhoun was thoughtful. 'Is she . . . ? I mean, did she . . . ?'

'But today, sir,' Hogan interrupted, 'we want to talk to you about Joseph Lintz.'

Colquhoun sat down heavily in his wooden chair, which creaked under the weight. Then he sprang to his feet again. 'Tea, coffee? You must excuse the mess. Not normally this disorganised . . .'

'Not for us, sir,' Hogan said. 'If you'd just take a seat?'

'Of course, of course.' Again, Colquhoun collapsed on to his chair.

'Joseph Lintz, sir,' Hogan prompted.

'Terrible tragedy ... terrible. They think it's murder, you know.'

'Yes, sir, we do know.'

'Of course you do. Apologies.'

The desk in front of Colquhoun was venerable and spotted with woodworm. The shelves were bowed under the weight of textbooks. There were old framed prints on the walls, and a blackboard with the single word CHARACTER on it. University paperwork was piled on the window ledge, all but blacking out the bottom two panes. The smell in the room was that of intellect gone awry.

'It's just that Mr Lintz had your name in his address book, sir,' Hogan continued. 'And we're talking to all his friends.'

'Friends?' Colquhoun looked up. 'I wouldn't call us "friends" exactly. We were colleagues, but I don't think I met him socially more than three or four times in twenty-odd years.'

'Funny, he seems to have taken an interest in you, sir.' Hogan flipped open his notebook. 'Starting with your address in Warrender Park Terrace.'

'I haven't lived there since the seventies.'

'He also has your telephone number there. After that, it's Currie.'

'I thought I was ready for the rural life ...'

'In Currie?' Hogan sounded sceptical.

Colquhoun tipped his head. 'I eventually realised my mistake.'

'And moved to Duddingston.'

'Not at first. I rented a few properties while I was looking for a place to buy.'

'Mr Lintz has your telephone number in Currie, but not for the Duddingston address.'

'Interesting. I went ex-directory when I moved.'

'Any reason for that, sir?'

Colquhoun swayed in his chair. 'Well, I'm sure it sounds awful ...'

'Try us.'

'I didn't want students bothering me.'

'Did they do that?'

'Oh, yes, phoning to ask questions, advice. Worried about exams or wanting deadlines extended.'

'Do you remember giving Mr Lintz your address, sir?'

'No, I don't.'

'You're sure of that?'

'Yes, but it wouldn't have been hard for him to find out. I mean, he could just have asked one of the secretaries.'

Colquhoun was beginning to look more agitated than ever. The little chair could barely contain him.

'Sir,' Hogan said, 'is there anything you want to tell us about Mr Lintz, anything at all?'

Colquhoun just shook his head, staring at the surface of his desk.

Rebus decided to use their joker. 'Mr Lintz made a phone call to this office. He was talking for over twenty minutes.'

'That's ... simply not true.' Colquhoun mopped his face with a

handkerchief. 'Look, gentlemen, I'd like to help, but the fact is, I barely knew Joseph Lintz.'

'And he didn't phone you?'

'No.'

'And you've no idea why he'd keep note of your Edinburgh addresses for the past three decades?'

'No.'

Hogan sighed theatrically. 'Then we're wasting your time and ours.' He got to his feet. 'Thank you, Dr Colquhoun.'

The look of relief on the old academic's face told both detectives all they needed to know.

They said nothing as they walked back downstairs – like Colquhoun had said, sound could travel. Hogan's car was nearest. They rested against it as they talked.

'He was worried,' Rebus said.

'Hiding something. Think we should go back up?'

Rebus shook his head. 'Let him sweat for a day or so, then hit him.'

'He didn't like the fact you were there.'

'I noticed.'

'That restaurant . . . Lintz dining with an elderly gent.'

'We could tell him we've got a description from the restaurant staff.'

'Without going into specifics?'

Rebus nodded. 'See if it flushes him out.'

'What about the other person Lintz took to lunch, the young woman?'

'No idea.'

'Posh restaurant, old man, young woman . . .'

'A call girl?'

Hogan smiled. 'Do they still call them that?'

Rebus was thoughtful. 'It might explain the phone call to Telford. Only I doubt Telford's daft enough to discuss business like that from his office. Besides, his escort agency runs from another address.'

'Fact is, he called Telford's office.'

'And nobody's owned up to talking to him.'

'Escort agency stuff, could be very innocent. He doesn't want to eat alone, hires some company. Afterwards, a peck on the cheek and separate taxis.' Hogan exhaled. 'This one's running in circles.'

'I know the feeling, Bobby.'

They looked up at the second-floor windows. Saw Colquhoun staring down, handkerchief to his face.

'Let's leave him to it,' Hogan said, unlocking his car.

'I've been meaning to ask: how did you get on with Abernethy?'

'He didn't give me too much trouble.' Hogan avoided Rebus's eyes.

'So he's gone?'

Hogan had disappeared into the driver's seat. 'He's gone. See you, John.'

Leaving Rebus on the pavement, a frown on his face. He waited till Hogan's car had turned the corner, then went back into the stairwell and climbed the steps again.

Colquhoun's office door was open, the old man fidgeting behind his desk. Rebus sat down opposite him, said nothing.

'I've been ill,' Colquhoun said.

'You've been hiding.' Colquhoun started shaking his head. 'You told them where to find Candice.' Head still shaking. 'Then you got worried, so they hid you away, maybe in a room at the casino.' Rebus paused. 'How am I doing?'

'I've no comment to make,' Colquhoun snapped.

'What if I just keep talking then?'

'I want you to leave now. If you don't go, I'll have to call my lawyer.'

'Name of Charles Groal?' Rebus smiled. 'They might have spent the last few days tutoring you, but they can't change what you've done.' Rebus stood up. '*You* sent Candice back to them. *You* did that.' He leaned down over the desk. 'You knew all along who she was, didn't you? That's why you were so nervous. How come you knew who she was, Dr Colquhoun? How come you're so chummy with a turd like Tommy Telford?'

Colquhoun picked up the receiver, his hands shaking so badly he kept missing the digits.

'Don't bother,' Rebus said. 'I'm going. But we'll talk again. And you *will* talk. You'll talk because you're a coward, Dr Colquhoun. And cowards always talk eventually . . .'

23

The Crime Squad office at Fettes: home of country and western; Claverhouse terminating a phone call. No sign of Ormiston and Clarke.

'They're out on a call,' Claverhouse said.

'Any progress on that stabbing?'

'What do you think?'

'I think there's something you should know.' Rebus seated himself behind Siobhan Clarke's desk, admiring its tidy surface. He opened a drawer: it was tidy, too. Compartments, he thought to himself. Clarke was very good at dividing her life into separate compartments. 'Jake Tarawicz is in town. He's got this outrageous white limo, hard to miss.' Rebus paused. 'And he's brought Candice with him.'

'What's he doing here?'

'I think he's here for the show.'

'What show?'

'Cafferty and Telford, fifteen rounds of bare-knuckle and no referee.' Rebus leaned forward, arms on the desk. 'And I've got an idea where it's headed.'

Rebus went home, called Patience and told her he might be late.

'How late?' she asked.

'How late can I be without us falling out?'

She thought about it. 'Half-nine.'

'I'll be there.'

He checked his answering machine: David Levy, saying he could be reached at home.

'Where the hell have you been?' Rebus asked, when Levy's daughter had put her father on.

'I had business elsewhere.'

'You know your daughter's been worried. You might have phoned her.'

'Does this counselling service come free?'

'My fee cancels out when you answer a few questions. You know Lintz is dead?'

'I've heard.'

'Where were you when you *heard*?'

'I've told you, I had business . . . Inspector, am I a suspect?'

'Practically the only one we've got.'

Levy gave a harsh laugh. 'This is preposterous. I'm not a . . .' He couldn't

say the word. Rebus guessed his daughter was within hearing distance. 'Hold on a moment, please.' The receiver was muffled: Levy ordering his daughter out of the room. He came back on, voice lower than before.

'Inspector, for the record, I feel I must let you know how *angry* I felt when I heard the news. Justice may have been done or not done – I can't argue those points just now – but what is absolutely certain is that history has been cheated here!'

'Of the trial?'

'Of course! And the Rat Line, too. With each suspect who dies, we're that much less likely to prove its existence. Lintz isn't the first, you know. One man, the brakes failed on his car. Another fell from an upstairs window. There've been two apparent suicides, six more cases of what look like natural causes.'

'Am I going to get the full conspiracy theory?'

'This isn't a joke, Inspector.'

'Did you hear me laughing? What about you, Mr Levy? When did you leave Edinburgh?'

'Before Lintz died.'

'Did you see him?' Rebus knowing he had, but seeking a lie.

Levy paused. '*Confronted* would be a more apposite term.'

'Just the once?'

'Three times. He wasn't keen to talk about himself, but I stated my case nonetheless.'

'And the phone call?'

Levy paused. 'What phone call?'

'When he called you at the Roxburghe.'

'I wish I'd recorded it for posterity. Rage, Inspector. Foul-mouthed rage. I'm positive he was mad.'

'Mad?'

'You didn't hear him. He's very good at seeming perfectly normal – he must be, or he wouldn't have gone undetected for so long. But the man is . . . was . . . mad. Truly mad.'

Rebus was remembering the crooked little man in the cemetery, and how he'd suddenly let fly at a passing dog. Poise, to rage, to poise again.

'The story he told . . .' Levy sighed.

'Was this in the restaurant?'

'What restaurant?'

'Sorry, I thought the two of you went out to lunch.'

'I can assure you we didn't.'

'So what story is this then?'

'These men, Inspector, they come to justify their actions by blanking them out, or by transference. Transference is the more common.'

'They tell themselves someone else did it?'

'Yes.'

'And that was Lintz's story?'

'Less believable than most. He said it was all a case of mistaken identity.'

'And who did he think you were mistaking him for?'

'A colleague at the university . . . a Dr Colquhoun.'

Rebus called Hogan, gave him the story.

'I told Levy you'd want to speak to him.'

'I'll phone him right now.'

'What do you think?'

'Colquhoun a war criminal?' Hogan snorted.

'Me too,' Rebus said. 'I asked Levy why he didn't think any of this worth telling us.'

'And?'

'He said as he gave it no credence, it was worthless.'

'All the same, we'd better talk to Colquhoun again. Tonight.'

'I've other plans for tonight, Bobby.'

'Fair enough, John. Look, I really appreciate all your help.'

'You're going to talk to him alone?'

'I'll have someone with me.'

Rebus hated being left out. If he cancelled that late supper . . .

'Let me know how you get on.' Rebus put the telephone down. On the hi-fi: Eddie Harris, upbeat and melodic. He went and soaked in a bath, facecloth across his eyes. Everyone, it seemed to him, lived their lives out of little boxes, opening different ones for different occasions. Nobody ever gave their whole self away. Cops were like that, each box a safety mechanism. Most people you met in the course of your life, you never even learned their names. Everybody was boxed off from everybody else. It was called society.

He was wondering about Joseph Lintz, always questioning, turning every conversation into a philosophy lesson. Stuck in his own little box, identity blocked off elsewhere, his past a necessary mystery . . . Joseph Lintz, furious when cornered, possibly clinically mad, driven there by . . . what? Memories? Or the lack of them? Driven there by other people?

The Eddie Harris CD was on its last track by the time he emerged from the bathroom. He put on the clothes he'd be wearing to Patience's. Only he had a couple of stops to make first: check on Sammy at the hospital, and then a meeting at Torphichen.

'The gang's all here,' he said, walking into the CID room.

Shug Davidson, Claverhouse, Ormiston, and Siobhan Clarke, all seated around the one big desk, drinking coffee from identical Rangers mugs. Rebus pulled a chair over.

'Have you filled them in, Shug?'

Davidson nodded.

'What about the shop?'

'I was just getting to that.' Davidson picked up a pen, played with it. 'The last owner went out of business, not enough passing trade. The shop was shut the best part of a year, then suddenly reopened – under new management and with prices that stopped the locals looking elsewhere.'

'And got the workers at Maclean's interested, too,' Rebus added. 'So how long's it been going?'

'Five weeks, selling cut-price everything.'

'No profit motive, you see.' Rebus looked around the table. This was mostly for the benefit of Ormiston and Clarke; he'd given Claverhouse the story already.

'And the owners?' Clarke asked.

'Well, the shop's *run* by a couple of lads called Declan Delaney and Ken Wilkinson. Guess where they come from?'

'Paisley,' Claverhouse said, keen to hurry things on.

'So they're part of Telford's gang?' Ormiston asked.

'Not in so many words, but they're connected to him, no doubt about that.' Davidson blew his nose loudly. 'Of course, Dec and Ken are running the shop, but they don't own it.'

'Telford does,' Rebus stated.

'OK,' Claverhouse said. 'So we've got Telford owning a loss-making business, in the hope of gathering intelligence.'

'I think it goes further than that,' Rebus said. 'I mean, listening in on gossip is one thing, but I don't suppose any of the workers are standing around talking about the various security systems and how to beat them. Dec and Ken are garrulous, perfect for the job Telford's given them. But it's going to look suspicious if they start asking too many questions.'

'So what's Telford looking for?' Ormiston asked. Siobhan Clarke turned to him.

'A mole,' she said.

'Makes sense,' Davidson went on. 'That place *is* well protected, but not impregnable. We all know any break-in's going to be a lot easier with someone on the inside.'

'So what do we do?' Clarke asked.

'We fight Telford's sting with our own,' Rebus explained. 'He wants a man on the inside, *we* give him one.'

'I'm seeing the head of Maclean's later on tonight,' Davidson said.

'I'll come with you,' Claverhouse said, keen not to be left out.

'So we put someone of our own inside the factory.' Clarke was working it out for herself. 'And they shoot their mouth off in the shop, making them an attractive proposition. And we sit and pray that Telford approaches *them* rather than anyone else?'

'The less luck we have to rely on the better,' Claverhouse said. 'Got to do this right.'

'Which is why we work it like this.' Rebus said. 'There's a bookie called Marty Jones. He owes me one big favour. Say our man's just been into Telford's shop. As he's coming out, a car pulls up. Marty and a couple of his men. Marty wants some bets paid off. Big argy-bargy, and a punch in the guts as warning.'

Clarke could see it. 'He stumbles back into the shop, sits down to catch his breath. Dec and Ken ask him what's going on.'

'And he gives them the whole sorry story: gambling debts, broken marriage, whatever.'

'To make him more attractive still,' Davidson said, 'we make him a security guard.'

Ormiston looked at him. 'You think Maclean's will go for it?'

'We'll persuade them,' Claverhouse said quietly.

'More importantly,' Clarke asked, 'will *Telford* go for it?'

'Depends how desperate he is,' Rebus answered.

'A man on the inside ...' Ormiston's eyes were alight. 'Working for Telford – it's what we've always wanted.'

Claverhouse nodded. 'Just one thing.' He looked at Rebus and Davidson. 'Who's it going to be? Telford knows us.'

'We get someone from outside,' Rebus said. 'Someone I've worked with before. Telford won't have heard of him. He's a good man.'

'Is he willing?'

There was silence around the table.

'Depends who's asking,' a voice called from the doorway. A stocky man with thick, well-groomed hair and narrow eyes. Rebus got up, shook Jack Morton's hand, made the introductions.

'I'll need a history,' Morton said, all business. 'John's explained the deal, and I like it. But I'll need a flat, something scruffy and local.'

'First thing tomorrow,' Claverhouse said. 'Look, we need to talk to our bosses about this, make sure it's cleared.' He looked at Morton. 'What did you tell your own boss, Jack?'

'I've got a few days off, didn't think it was worth mentioning.'

Claverhouse nodded. 'I'll talk to him as soon as we get the go-ahead.'

'We need that go-ahead *tonight*,' Rebus said. 'Telford's men may already have lined someone up. If we hang around, we might lose it.'

'Agreed,' Claverhouse said, checking his watch. 'I'll make a few phone calls, interrupt a few post-prandial whiskies.'

'I'll back you up if need be,' Davidson said.

Rebus looked at Jack Morton – his friend – and mouthed the word 'thanks'. Morton shrugged it off. Then Rebus got to his feet.

'I'm going to have to leave you to it,' he told the assembly. 'You've got my pager number and mobile if you need me.'

He was halfway down the hall when Siobhan Clarke caught him.

'I just wanted to say thanks.'

Rebus blinked. 'What for?'

'Ever since you got Claverhouse excited, the tape machine's stayed off.'

24

Supper was fine. He talked to Patience about Sammy, Rhona, his obsession with sixties music, his ignorance of fashion. She talked about work, an experimental cookery class she'd been taking, a trip to Orkney she was thinking of. They ate fresh pasta with a homemade mussel and prawn sauce, and shared a bottle of Highland Spring. Rebus tried his damnedest to forget about the sting operation, Tarawicz, Candice, Lintz . . . She could see at least half his mind was elsewhere; tried not to feel betrayed. She asked him if he was going home.

'Is that an invitation?'

'I'm not sure . . . I suppose so.'

'Let's pretend it wasn't, then I won't feel like complete scum when I turn it down.'

'That sounds reasonable. Things on your mind?'

'I'm surprised you can't see them leaking out of my ears.'

'Do you want to talk about any of it? I mean, you may not have noticed, but we've talked about practically everything tonight except *us*.'

'I don't think talking would help.'

'But bottling it up does?' She threw out an arm. 'Behold the Scottish male, at his happiest when in denial.'

'What am I denying?'

'For a start, you're denying *me* access to your life.'

'Sorry.'

'Christ, John, get the word put on a T-shirt.'

'Thanks, maybe I will.' He got up from the sofa.

'Oh, hell, I'm sorry.' She smiled. 'Look, you've got me at it now.'

'Yes, it's catching, all right.'

She stood up, touched his arm. 'You're worried about taking the test?'

'Right now, believe it or not, that's the least of my worries.'

'It should be. Everything's going to be fine.'

'Hunky-dory.'

'Hunky-dory,' she repeated, smiling again. She pecked him on the cheek. 'You know, I've never quite understood what that meant.'

'*Hunky Dory?*'

She nodded.

'It's a David Bowie album.' He kissed her brow.

He would never know what instinct made him decide on the detour, but he

was glad he'd made it. For there, parked outside the Morvena casino, stood the white stretch limo. The driver leaned against it, smoking a cigarette, looking bored. From time to time he took out a mobile phone and had a short conversation. Rebus stared at the Morvena, thinking: Tommy Telford has a slice of the place; the hostesses come from Eastern Europe, provided by Mr Pink Eyes. Rebus wondered how closely entwined the two empires – Telford's and Tarawicz's – really were. And add a third strand: the Yakuza. Something refused to add up.

What was Tarawicz getting out of it?

Miriam Kenworthy had suggested muscle: Scottish hardmen trained in Telford's organisation then shipped south. But it wasn't *enough* of a trade. There had to be more. Was Mr Pink Eyes due a share of the Maclean's pay-out? Was Telford tempting him with some Yakuza action? What about the theory that Telford was Tarawicz's supplier?

At quarter to midnight, another phone call had the driver springing into action. He flicked his cigarette on to the road, started opening doors. Tarawicz and his entourage breezed out of the casino looking like they owned the world. Candice was wearing a black full-length coat over a shimmering pink dress which didn't quite reach her knees. She was carrying a bottle of champagne. Rebus counted three of Tarawicz's men, remembering them from the scrapyard. Two no-shows: the lawyer, and the Crab. Telford was there, too, with a couple of minders, one of them Pretty-Boy. Pretty-Boy was making sure his jacket hung right, trying to decide whether it would look better buttoned. But his eyes raked the darkened street. Rebus had parked away from the street lights, confident he was invisible. They were piling into the limo. Rebus watched it move off, waited until it had signalled and turned a corner before switching on his own headlamps and starting the engine.

They drove to the same hotel Matsumoto had stayed at. Telford's Range Rover was parked outside. Pedestrians – late-night couples hurrying home from the pub – turned to stare at the limo. Saw the entourage spill out, probably mistook them for pop stars or film people. Rebus as casting director: Candice's starlet being mauled by sleazy producer Tarawicz. Telford a sleek young operator on his way up, looking to learn from the producer before toppling him. The others were bit players, except maybe Pretty-Boy, who was hanging on to his boss's coattails, maybe readying himself for his own big break . . .

If Tarawicz had a suite, there might be room for them all. If not, they'd be in the bar. Rebus parked, followed them inside.

The lights hurt his eyes. The reception area was all mirrors and pine, brass and pot-plants. He tried to look like he'd been left behind by the party. They were settling down in the bar, through a double set of swing-doors with glass panels. Rebus hung back. Sitting target in the empty reception; bigger target in the bar. Retreat to the car? Someone was standing up, shrugging off a long black coat. Candice. Smiling now, saying something to Tarawicz, who was nodding. Took her hand and planted a kiss in the palm. Went further: a slow lick across the palm and up her wrist. Everyone laughing, whistling. Candice looking numb. Tarawicz got to the inside of her elbow and took a bite. She squealed, pulled back, rubbed her arm. Tarawicz had his tongue out, playing to the gallery. Give Tommy Telford credit: he wasn't grinning along with everyone else.

Candice stood there, a stooge to her owner's little act. Then he waved her off with a flick of his hand. Permission granted, she started for the doors. Rebus moved back into a recess where the public telephones sat. She turned right out of the doors, disappeared into the ladies'. At the table, they were busy ordering more champagne – and an orange juice for Pretty-Boy.

Rebus looked around, took a deep breath. Walked into the ladies' toilets like it was the most natural thing in the world.

She was splashing her face with water. A little brown bottle sat next to the sink. Three yellow tablets lying ready. Rebus swept them on to the floor.

'Hey!' She turned, saw him, put a hand to her mouth. She tried backing away, but there was nowhere to go.

'Is this what you want, Karina?' Using her real name as a weapon: friendly fire.

She frowned, shook her head: incomprehension on her face. He grabbed her shoulders, squeezed.

'Sammy,' he hissed. 'Sammy's in hospital. Very ill.' He pointed towards the hotel bar. '*They* tried to kill her.'

The gist got through. Candice shook her head. Tears were smudging her mascara.

'Did you tell Sammy anything?'

She frowned again.

'Anything about Telford or Tarawicz? Did you talk to Sammy about them?'

A slow, determined shake of the head. 'Sammy . . . hospital?'

He nodded. Turned his hands into a steering-wheel, made engine noises, then slammed a fist into his open palm. Candice turned away, grabbed the sink. She was crying, shoulders jerking. She scrabbled for more tablets. Rebus tore them from her hand.

'You want to blank it all out? Forget it.' He threw them on to the floor, crushed them under his heel. She crouched down, licked a finger and dabbed at the powder. Rebus hauled her to her feet. Her knees wouldn't lock; he had to keep holding her upright. She wouldn't look him in the eyes.

'It's funny, we first met in a toilet, remember? You were scared. You hated your life so much you'd slashed your arms.' He touched her scarred wrists. 'That's how much you hated your life. And now you're straight back in it.'

Her face was against his jacket, tears dropping on to his shirt.

'Remember the Japanese?' he cooed. 'Remember Juniper Green, the golf club?'

She drew back, wiped her nose on her bare wrist. 'Juniper Green,' she said.

'That's right. And a big factory . . . the car stopped, and everyone looked at the factory.'

She was nodding.

'Did anyone talk about it? Did they say *anything*?'

She was shaking her head. 'John . . .' Her hands on his lapels. She sniffed, swiped at her nose again. She slid down his jacket, his shirt. She was on her knees, looking up at him, blinking tears, while her damp fingers scored white powder from the tiles. Rebus crouched down in front of her.

'Come with me,' he said. 'I'll help you.' He pointed towards the door, towards the world outside, but she was busy in her own world now, fingers going to her mouth. Someone pushed open the door. Rebus looked up.

A woman: young, drunk, hair falling into her eyes. She stopped and studied the two people on the floor, then smiled and headed for a cubicle.

'Save some for me,' she said, sliding the lock.

'Go, John.' There was powder at the corners of Candice's mouth. A tiny piece of tablet had lodged between her front two teeth. 'Please, go now.'

'I don't want you getting hurt.' He sought her hands, squeezed them.

'I do not hurt any more.'

She got to her feet and turned from him. Checked her face in the mirror, wiped away the powder and dabbed at her mascara. Blew her nose and took a deep breath.

Walked out of the toilets.

Rebus waited a moment, time enough for her to reach the table. Then he opened the door and made his exit. Walked back to his car on legs that seemed to belong to someone else.

Drove home, not quite crying.

But not quite not.

25

Four in the morning, the blessed telephone pulled him out of a nightmare.

Prison-camp prostitutes with teeth filed to points were kneeling in front of him. Jake Tarawicz, in full SS regalia, held him from behind, telling him resistance was useless. Through the barred window, Rebus could see black berets – the *maquis*, busy freeing the camp but leaving his billet till last. Alarm bells ringing, everything telling him that salvation was at hand . . .

. . . alarm becoming his telephone . . . he staggered from his chair, picked it up.

'Yes.'

'John?' The Chief Super's voice: Aberdonian, instantly recognisable.

'Yes, sir?'

'We've got a spot of bother. Get down here.'

'What kind of bother?'

'I'll tell you when you get here. Now *shift*.'

Night-shift, to be precise. The city asleep. St Leonard's was lit up, the tenements around it dark. No sign of the Farmer's 'spot of bother'. The Chief Super's office: the Farmer in conference with Gill Templer.

'Sit down, John. Coffee?'

'No thanks, sir.'

While Templer and the Chief Super were deciding who should speak, Rebus helped them out.

'Tommy Telford's businesses have been hit.'

Templer blinked. 'Telepathy?'

'Cafferty's offices and taxis got firebombed. So did his house.' Rebus shrugged. 'We knew there'd be payback.'

'Did we?'

What could he say? *I did, because Cafferty told me*. He didn't think they'd like that. 'I just put two and two together.'

The Farmer poured himself a mug of coffee. 'So now we've got open war.'

'What got hit?'

'The arcade on Flint Street,' Templer said. 'Not too much damage: the place has a sprinkler system.' She smiled: an amusement arcade with a sprinkler system . . . not that Telford was careful or anything.

'Plus a couple of nightclubs,' the Farmer added. 'And a casino.'

'Which one?'

The Chief Super looked to Templer, who answered: 'The Morvena.'

'Any injuries?'

'The manager and a couple of friends: concussion and bruising.'

'Which they got . . .?'

'Falling over each other as they ran down the stairs.'

Rebus nodded. 'Funny how some people have trouble with stairs.' He sat back. 'So what does all this have to do with me? Don't tell me: having disposed of Telford's Japanese partner, I decided to take up fire-raising?'

'John . . .' The Farmer got up, rested his backside against the desk. 'The three of us, we know you had nothing to do with that. Tell me, we found an untouched half-bottle of malt under your driver's seat . . .'

Rebus nodded. 'It's mine.' Another of his little suicide bombs.

'So why would you be drinking a supermarket blend?'

'Is that what the screw-top was? The cheap bastards.'

'No alcohol in your blood either. Meantime, as you say, Cafferty's in the frame for this. And Cafferty and you . . .'

'You want me to talk to him?'

Gill Templer leaned forward in her chair. 'We don't want war.'

'Takes two to make a ceasefire.'

'I'll talk to Telford,' she said.

'He's a sharp little bugger, watch out for him.'

She nodded. 'Will you talk to Cafferty?'

Rebus didn't want a war. It would take Telford's mind off the Maclean's heist. He'd need all the troops he could get; the shop might even have to close. No, Rebus didn't want a war.

'I'll talk to him,' he said.

Breakfast-time at Barlinnie.

Rebus jangling after the drive, knowing a whisky would smooth out his nerve-endings. Cafferty waiting for him, same room as before.

'Top of the morning, Strawman.' Arms folded, looking pleased with himself.

'You've had a busy night.'

'On the contrary, I slept as well as I ever have done in this place. What about you?'

'I was up at four o'clock, checking damage reports. I could have done without driving all the way here. Maybe if you gave me the number of your mobile . . .?'

Cafferty grinned. 'I hear the nightclubs were gutted.'

'I think your boys are making themselves look good.' Cafferty's grin tightened. 'Telford's premises seem to have state-of-the-art fire prevention. Smoke sensors, sprinklers, fire-doors. The damage was minimal.'

'This is just the start,' Cafferty said. 'I'll have that little arse-wipe.'

'I thought that was supposed to be *my* job?'

'I've seen precious little from you, Strawman.'

'I've got something in the pipeline. If it comes off, you'll like it.'

Cafferty's eyes narrowed. 'Give me details. Make me believe you.'

But Rebus was shaking his head. 'Sometimes, you just have to have faith.' He paused. 'Deal?'

'I must have missed something.'

Rebus spelled it out. 'Back off. Leave Telford to me.'

'We've been through this. He hits me and I do nothing, I look like something you'd step around on the pavement.'

'We're talking to him, warning him off.'

'And meantime I'm supposed to trust you to get the job done?'

'We shook hands on it.'

Cafferty snorted. 'I've shaken hands with a lot of bastards.'

'And now you've met an exception to the rule.'

'You're an exception to a lot of rules, Strawman.' Cafferty looked thoughtful. 'The casino, the clubs, the arcade . . . they weren't badly hit?'

'My guess is the sprinklers will have done as much damage as anything.'

Cafferty's jaw hardened. 'Makes me look even more of a mug.'

Rebus sat in silence, waiting for him to finish whatever chess-game was being played inside his head.

'OK,' the gangster said at last, 'I'll call off the troops. Maybe it's time to do some recruiting anyway.' He looked up at Rebus. 'Time for some fresh blood.'

Which reminded Rebus of another job he'd been putting off.

Danny Simpson lived at home with his mother in a terraced house in Wester Hailes.

This bleak housing-scheme, designed by sadists who'd never had to live anywhere near it, had a heart which had shrivelled but refused to stop pumping. Rebus had a lot of respect for the place. Tommy Smith had grown up here, practising with socks stuffed into the mouth of his sax, so as not to disturb the neighbours through the thin walls of the high-rise. Tommy Smith was one of the best sax players Rebus had ever heard.

In a sense, Wester Hailes existed outside the real world: it wasn't on a route from anywhere to anywhere. Rebus had never had cause to drive *through* it – he only went there if he had business there. The city bypass flew past it, offering many drivers their only encounter with Wester Hailes. They saw: high-rise blocks, terraces, tracts of unused playing field. They didn't see: people. Not so much concrete jungle as concrete vacuum.

Rebus knocked on Danny Simpson's door. He didn't know what he was going to say to the young man. He just wanted to see him again. He wanted to see him without the blood and the pain. Wanted to see him whole and of a piece.

Wanted to see him.

But Danny Simpson wasn't in, and neither was his mother. A neighbour, lacking her top set of dentures, came out and explained the situation.

The situation took Rebus to the Infirmary, where, in a small, gloomy ward not easily found, Danny Simpson lay in bed, head bandaged, sweating like he'd just played a full ninety minutes. He wasn't conscious. His mother sat beside him, stroking his wrist. A nurse explained to Rebus that a hospice would be the best place for Danny, supposing they could find him a bed.

'What happened?'

'We think infection must have set in. When you lose your resistance . . . the world's a lethal place.' She shrugged, looked like she'd been through it all once too often. Danny's mother had seen them talking. Maybe she thought Rebus was a doctor. She got up and came towards him, then just stood there, waiting for him to speak.

'I came to see Danny,' he said.

'Yes?'

'The night he . . . the night of his accident, I was the one who brought him here. I just wondered how he was doing.'

'See for yourself.' Her voice was breaking.

Rebus thought: a five-minute walk from here, he'd be in Sammy's room. He'd thought her situation unique, because it was unique to *him*. Now he saw that within a short radius of Sammy's bed, other parents were crying, and squeezing their children's hands, and asking why.

'I'm really sorry,' he said. 'I wish . . .'

'Me too,' the woman said. 'You know, he's never been a bad laddie. Cheeky, but never bad. His problem was, he was always itching for something new, something to stop him getting bored. We all know where that can lead.'

Rebus nodded, suddenly not wanting to be here, not wanting to hear Danny Simpson's life story. He had enough ghosts to contend with as it was. He squeezed the woman's arm.

'Look,' he said, 'I'm sorry, but I have to go.'

She nodded distractedly, wandered off in the direction of her son's bed. Rebus wanted to curse Danny Simpson for the mere *possibility* that he'd passed on the virus. He realised now that if they'd met on the doorstep, that's the way their conversation would have gone, and maybe Rebus would have gone further.

He wanted to curse him . . . but he couldn't. It would be every bit as efficacious as cursing the Big Man. A waste of time and breath. So instead he went to Sammy's room, to find that she was back on her own. No other patients, no nursing staff, no Rhona. He kissed her forehead. It tasted salty. Sweat: she needed wiping down. There was a smell he hadn't noticed before. Talcum powder. He sat down, took her warm hands in his.

'How are you doing, Sammy? I keep meaning to bring in some Oasis, see if that would bring you round. Your mum sits here listening to classical. I wonder if you can hear it. I don't even know if you like that sort of stuff. Lots of things we've never got round to talking about.'

He saw something. Stood up to be sure. Movement behind her eyelids.

'Sammy? Sammy?'

He hadn't seen her do that before. Pushed the button beside her bed. Waited for a nurse to come. Pushed it again.

'Come on, come on.'

Eyelids fluttering . . . then stopping.

'Sammy!'

Door opening, nurse coming in.

'What is it?'

Rebus: 'I thought I saw . . . she was moving.'

'Moving?'

'Just her eyes, like she was trying to open them.'

'I'll fetch a doctor.'

'Come on, Sammy, try again. Wakey-wakey, sweetheart.' Patting her wrists, then her cheeks.

The doctor arrived. He was the same one Rebus had shouted at that first day. Lifted her eyelids, shone a thin torch into them, pulling it away, checking her pupils.

'If you saw it, I'm sure it was there.'

'Yes, but does it mean anything?'

'Hard to say.'

'Try anyway.' Eyes boring into the doctor's.

'She's asleep. She has dreams. Sometimes when you dream you experience REM: Rapid Eye Movement.'

'So it could be . . .' Rebus sought the word '. . . involuntary?'

'As I say, it's hard to tell. Latest scans show definite improvement.' He paused. '*Minor* improvement, but certainly there.'

Rebus nodding, trembling. The doctor saw it, asked if he needed anything. Rebus shaking his head. The doctor checking his watch, other places to be. The nurse shuffling her feet. Rebus thanked them both and headed out.

HOGAN: You agree to this interview being taped, Dr Colquhoun?

COLQUHOUN: I've no objections.

HOGAN: It's in your interests as well as ours.

COLQUHOUN: I've nothing to hide, Inspector Hogan. (*Coughs.*)

HOGAN: Fine, sir. Maybe we'll just start then?

COLQUHOUN: Might I ask a question? Just for the record, you want to ask me about Joseph Lintz – nothing else?

HOGAN: What else might there be, sir?

COLQUHOUN: I just wanted to check.

HOGAN: You wish to have a solicitor present?

COLQUHOUN: No.

HOGAN: Right you are, sir. Well, if I can begin . . . it's really just a question of your relationship with Professor Joseph Lintz.

COLQUHOUN: Yes.

HOGAN: Only, when we spoke before, you said you didn't know Professor Lintz.

COLQUHOUN: I think I said I didn't know him very well.

HOGAN: OK, sir. If that's what you said . . .

COLQUHOUN: It is, to the best of my recollection.

HOGAN: Only, we've had some new information . . .

COLQUHOUN: Yes?

HOGAN: That you knew Professor Lintz a little better than that.

COLQUHOUN: And this is according to . . .?

HOGAN: New information in our possession. The informant tells us that Joseph Lintz accused you of being a war criminal. Anything to say to that, sir?

COLQUHOUN: Only that it's a lie. An outrageous lie.

HOGAN: He didn't think you were a war criminal?

COLQUHOUN: Oh, he thought it all right! He told me to my face on more than one occasion.

HOGAN: When?

COLQUHOUN: Years back. He got it into his head . . . the man was mad, Inspector. I could see that. Driven by demons.

HOGAN: What did he say exactly?

COLQUHOUN: Hard to remember. This was a long time ago, the early 1970s, I suppose.

HOGAN: It would help us if you could . . .

COLQUHOUN: He came out with it in the middle of a party. I believe it was some function to welcome a visiting professor. Anyway, Joseph insisted on taking me to one side. He looked feverish. Then he came out with it: I was some sort of Nazi, and I'd come to this country by some circuitous route. He kept on about it.

HOGAN: What did you do?

COLQUHOUN: Told him he was drunk, babbling.

HOGAN: And?

COLQUHOUN: And he was. Had to be taken home in a taxi. I said no more about it. In academic circles, one becomes used to a certain amount of . . . eccentric behaviour. We're obsessive people, it can't be helped.

HOGAN: But Lintz persisted?

COLQUHOUN: Not really, no. But every few years . . . there'd . . . he'd say something, allege some atrocity . . .

HOGAN: Did he approach you outside the university?

COLQUHOUN: For a time, he telephoned my home.

HOGAN: You moved?

COLQUHOUN: Yes.

HOGAN: To an unlisted phone number?

COLQUHOUN: Eventually.

HOGAN: To stop him calling you?

COLQUHOUN: I suppose that was part of it.

HOGAN: Did you speak to anyone about Lintz?

COLQUHOUN: You mean the authorities? No, no one. He was a nuisance, nothing more.

HOGAN: And then what happened?

COLQUHOUN: Then these stories started appearing in the papers, saying Joseph might be a Nazi, a war criminal. And suddenly he was on my back again.

HOGAN: He phoned you at your office?

COLQUHOUN: Yes.

HOGAN: You lied to us about that?

COLQUHOUN: I'm sorry. I panicked.

HOGAN: What was there to panic about?

COLQUHOUN: Just . . . I don't know.

HOGAN: So you met him? To straighten things out?

COLQUHOUN: We had lunch together. He seemed . . . lucid. Only what he was saying, it was the stuff of madness. He had a whole history mapped out, only it wasn't mine. I kept saying to him, 'Joseph, when the war ended I wasn't out of my teens.' Besides, I was born and raised here. It's all on record.

HOGAN: What did he say to that?

COLQUHOUN: He said records could be faked.

HOGAN: Faked records . . . one way Josef Linzstek could have gone undetected.

COLQUHOUN: I know.

HOGAN: You think Joseph Lintz was Josef Linzstek?

COLQUHOUN: I don't know. Maybe the stories got to him . . . he started to believe . . . I don't know.

HOGAN: Yes, but these accusations, they began before the media circus – decades before.

COLQUHOUN: That's true.

HOGAN: So he was hounding you. Did he say he would go to the media with his version of events?

COLQUHOUN: He may have . . . I can't remember.

HOGAN: Mmm.

COLQUHOUN: You're looking for a motive, aren't you? You're looking for reasons why I'd want him dead.

HOGAN: Did you kill him, Dr Colquhoun?

COLQUHOUN: Emphatically not.

HOGAN: Any idea who did?

COLQUHOUN: No.

HOGAN: Why didn't you tell us? Why tell lies?

COLQUHOUN: Because I knew this would happen. These suspicions. Stupidly, I thought I could circumvent them.

HOGAN: Circumvent?

COLQUHOUN: Yes.

HOGAN: A young woman was seen dining with Lintz, same restaurant he took you to. Any idea who she might be?

COLQUHOUN: None.

HOGAN: You knew Professor Lintz a long time . . . what did you think were his sexual proclivities?

COLQUHOUN: Never thought about it.

HOGAN: No?

COLQUHOUN: No.

HOGAN: What about yourself, sir?

COLQUHOUN: I don't see what that . . . well, for the record, Inspector, I'm monogamous and heterosexual.

HOGAN: Thank you, sir. I appreciate your frankness.

Rebus switched off the tape.

'I'll bet you did.'

'What do you think?' Bobby Hogan asked.

'I think you mistimed the did-you-do-it. Otherwise, not bad.' Rebus tapped the tape machine. 'Is there much more?'

'Not a lot.'

Rebus switched it back on.

HOGAN: When you met in the restaurant, it was the same routine as before?

COLQUHOUN: Oh, yes. Names, dates . . . countries I was taken through on my way into Britain from the continent.

HOGAN: He told you how this was achieved?

COLQUHOUN: He called it the Rat Line. Said it was operated by the Vatican, if you can believe that. And all the western governments were in cahoots to get the top Nazis – the scientists and intellectuals – away from the Russians. I mean, really . . . it's Ian Fleming meets John Le Carré, isn't it?

HOGAN: But he was very detailed?

COLQUHOUN: Yes, but it can be that way with obsessives.

HOGAN: There have been books written alleging the same thing Professor Lintz was talking about.

COLQUHOUN: Have there?

HOGAN: Nazis smuggled overseas . . . war criminals rescued from the gallows.

COLQUHOUN: Well, yes, but those are just stories. You don't seriously think . . .?

HOGAN: I'm just collecting information, Dr Colquhoun. In my job, we don't throw anything away.

COLQUHOUN: Yes, I can see that. The problem is, sorting out the wheat from the chaff.

HOGAN: You mean the truths from the lies? Yes, that's one problem.

COLQUHOUN: I mean, the stories you hear about Bosnia and Croatia . . . slaughterhouses, mass torture, the guilty being spirited away . . . It's hard to know what's *true*.

HOGAN: Just before we finish . . . any idea what happened to the money?

COLQUHOUN: What money?

HOGAN: The withdrawal Lintz made from his bank. Five thousand pounds in cash.

COLQUHOUN: This is the first I've heard of it. Another motive?

HOGAN: Thank you for your time, Dr Colquhoun. It might be necessary for us to talk again. I'm sorry, but you shouldn't have lied to us, it makes our job that much more difficult.

COLQUHOUN: I'm sorry, Inspector Hogan. I quite understand, but I hope you can comprehend why I did it.

HOGAN: My mum always told me never to lie, sir. Thanks again for your time.

Rebus looked at Hogan. 'Your mum?'

Hogan shrugged. 'Maybe it was my granny.'

Rebus drained his coffee. 'So we know one of Lintz's mealtime companions.'

'And we know he was hounding Colquhoun.'

'Is he a suspect?'

'I'm not exactly snowed under with them.'

'Fair point, but all the same . . .'

'You think he's on the level?'

'I don't know, Bobby. He sounded like he had it rehearsed. And he was relieved at the end.'

'You don't think I got it all? I could bring him in again.'

Rebus was thinking: *stories you hear . . . the guilty being spirited away*. Not stories you *read*, but ones you *hear* . . . Who might he have heard them from? Candice? Jake Tarawicz?

Hogan rubbed the bridge of his nose. 'I need a drink.'

Rebus dropped his beaker into a wastebin. 'Message received and understood. By the way, any word from Abernethy?'

'He's a bloody nuisance,' Hogan said, turning away.

26

'He's in place,' Claverhouse said, when Rebus phoned him to ask about Jack Morton. 'Got him a little one-bedroom shit-hole in Polwarth. Measured him up for his uniform, and he's now officially a member of on-site security.'

'Is anyone else in on it?'

'Just the big boss. His name's Livingstone. We had a long session with him last night.'

'Won't the other security men find it a bit odd, a stranger arriving in their midst?'

'It's down to Jack to put them at ease. He was pretty confident.'

'What's his cover?'

'Secret drinker, open gambler, busted marriage.'

'He doesn't drink.'

'Yes, he told me. Doesn't matter, so long as everyone *thinks* he does.'

'Is he in character?'

'Getting there. He's going to be working double shifts. That way he makes more trips to the shop, some in the evening when the place is quieter. More chance to get to know Ken and Dec. We've no contact with him during the day. Debriefing takes place once he's reached home. Telephone only, can't risk too many meetings.'

'You think they'll watch him?'

'If they're being thorough. And *if* they fall for the plan.'

'Did you talk to Marty Jones?'

'That's set for tomorrow. He'll bring a couple of heavies, but they'll go easy on Jack.'

'Isn't tomorrow a bit soon?'

'Can we afford to wait? They might already have someone in mind.'

'We're asking a lot of him.'

'He was *your* idea.'

'I know.'

'You don't think he's up to it?'

'It's not that ... but he's stepping into a war.'

'Then get the ceasefire sorted out.'

'It is.'

'That's not what I hear ...'

Rebus heard it too, as soon as he got off the phone. He knocked on the Chief Super's door. The Farmer was in conference with Gill Templer.

'Did you talk to him?' the Farmer asked.

'He agreed to a ceasefire,' Rebus said. He was looking at Templer. 'What about you?'

She took a deep breath. 'I spoke to Mr Telford – his solicitor was present throughout. I kept telling him what we wanted, and the lawyer kept telling me I was blackening his client's name.'

'And Telford?'

'Just sat there, arms folded, smiling at the wall.' Colour was creeping up her face. 'I don't think he looked at me once.'

'But you gave him the message?'

'Yes.'

'You said Cafferty would comply?'

She nodded.

'Then what the hell's happening?'

'We can't let it get out of control,' the Farmer said.

'Looks to me like it already is.'

The latest score-line: two of Cafferty's men, their faces mashed to something resembling fruit-pulp.

'Lucky they're not dead,' the Farmer went on.

'You know what's happening?' Rebus said. 'It's Tarawicz, *he's* the problem. Tommy's playing up to him.'

'It's times like this you yearn for independence,' the Farmer agreed. 'Then we could just extradite the bugger.'

'Why don't we?' Rebus suggested. 'Tell him his presence here is no longer acceptable.'

'And if he stays?'

'We shadow him, make sure everyone knows we're doing it. We make *nuisances* of ourselves.'

'You think that would work?' Gill Templer sounded sceptical.

'Probably not,' Rebus agreed, slumping into a chair.

'We've no real leverage,' the Farmer said, glancing at his watch. 'Which isn't going to please the Chief Constable. He wants me in his office in half an hour.' He got on the phone, ordered a car, rose to his feet.

'Look, see if you can thrash something out between you.'

Rebus and Templer exchanged a look.

'I'll be back in an hour or two.' The Farmer looked around, as if he were suddenly lost. 'Lock the door when you leave.' With that and a wave of his hand, he left. There was silence in the room.

'Has to keep his office locked,' Rebus said, 'to stop people stealing the secret of his terrible coffee.'

'Actually, it's been getting better recently.'

'Maybe your taste buds are being corroded. So, Chief Inspector . . .' Rebus turned his chair to face hers. 'What about thrashing it out then, eh?'

She smiled. 'He thinks he's losing it.'

'Is he in for a bollocking?'

'Probably.'

'So it's down to us to come to the rescue?'

'I don't really see us as the Dynamic Duo, do you?'

'No.'

'Then there's always that part of you that says, let them tear each other apart. So long as no civilians get caught in the crossfire.'

Rebus thought of Sammy, of Candice. 'Thing is,' he said, 'they always do.'
She looked at him. 'How are you doing?'
'Same as ever.'
'As bad as that?'
'It's my calling.'
'You're done with Lintz though?'
Rebus shook his head. 'There's half a chance he ties in to Telford.'
'You still think Telford was behind the hit-and-run?'
'Telford or Cafferty.'
'Cafferty?'
'Setting up Telford, the way someone tried to set *me* up for Matsumoto.'
'You know you're not out of the woods?'
He looked at her. 'An internal inquiry? The men with rubber soles?' She
nodded. 'Bring them on.' He sat forward in his chair, rubbed his temples.
'No reason they should be left out of the party.'
'What party?'
'The one inside my head. The party that never stops.' Rebus leaned
across the desk to answer the phone. 'No, he's not here. Can I take a
message? This is DI Rebus.' A pause; he was looking at Gill Templer. 'Yes,
I'm working that case.' He found pen and paper, started writing. 'Mmm, I
see. Yes, sounds like. I'll let him know when he gets back.' Eyes *boring into*
hers. Then the punchline: 'How many did you say were dead?'

Just the one. Another fled the scene, holding his arm, all but severed from
the shoulder. He turned up at a local hospital later, needing surgery and a
huge transfusion of blood.
 In broad daylight. Not in Edinburgh, but Paisley. Telford's hometown,
the town he still ruled. Four men, dressed in council work jackets, like a
road team. But in place of picks and shovels, they'd toted machetes and a
large-calibre revolver. They'd chased two men into a housing scheme. Kids
playing on tricycles; kicking a ball up the street. Women hanging out of
their windows. And grown men itching to hurt one another. A machete
swung overhead, coming down hard. The wounded man kept running. His
friend tried hurdling a fence, wasn't agile enough. Three inches higher and
he'd have made it. As it was, his toe caught, and he fell. He was pushing
himself back up when the barrel of the gun touched the back of his head.
Two shots, a fine drizzle of blood and brain. The children not playing any
more, the women screaming for them to run. But something had been
satisfied by those two shots. The chase was over. The four men turned and
jogged back down the street, towards a waiting van.
 A public execution, in Tommy Telford's heartland.
 The two victims: known money-lenders. The one in hospital was called
'Wee' Stevie Murray, age twenty-two. The one in the mortuary was Donny
Draper – known since childhood as 'Curtains'. They'd be making jokes
about that. Curtains was two weeks shy of his twenty-fifth birthday. Rebus
hoped he'd made the most of his short time on the planet.
 Paisley police knew about Telford's move to Edinburgh, knew there were
some problems there. A courtesy call had been placed to Chief Superin-
tendent Watson.
 The caller said: the men were two of Telford's brightest and best.

The caller said: descriptions of the attackers were vague.

The caller said: the children weren't talking. They were being shielded by their parents, fearful of reprisals. Well, they might not be talking to the *police*, but Rebus doubted they'd be so reticent when Tommy Telford came calling, armed with his own questions and determined to have answers.

This was bad. This was *escalation*. Firebombings and beatings: these could be remedied. But murder . . . murder put the grudge-match on to a much higher plane.

'Is it worth talking to them again?' Gill Templer asked. They were in the canteen, sandwiches untouched in front of them.

'What do you think?'

He knew what she thought. She was talking because she thought talking was better than doing nothing. He could have told her to save her breath.

'They used a machete,' he said.

'Same thing they took to Danny Simpson's scalp.' Rebus nodded. 'I've got to ask . . .' she said.

'What?'

'About Lintz . . . what you said?'

He drained the last inch of his cold coffee. 'Fancy another?'

'John . . .'

He looked at her. 'Lintz had some phone calls he was trying to hide. One of them was to Tommy Telford's office in Flint Street. We don't know how it ties in, but we think it *does* tie in.'

'What could Lintz and Telford have had in common?'

'Maybe Lintz went to him for help. Maybe he rented prossies off him. Like I say, we don't *know*. Which is why we're keeping it under the table.'

'You want Telford very badly, don't you?'

Rebus stared at her, thought about it. 'Not as much as I did. He's not enough any more.'

'You want Cafferty, too?'

'And Tarawicz . . . and the Yakuza . . . and anybody else who's along for the ride.'

She nodded. 'This is the party you were talking about?'

He tapped his head. 'They're all in here, Gill. I've tried kicking them out, but they won't leave.'

'Maybe if you stopped playing their kind of music?'

He smiled tiredly. 'Now there's an idea. What do you reckon: ELP? The Enid? How about a Yes triple album?'

'Your department, not mine, thank God.'

'You don't know what you're missing.'

'Yes I do: I was there first time round.'

Old Scottish proverb: he who has had knuckles rapped will want to rap someone else's. Which is why Rebus found himself back in Watson's office. The Farmer's cheeks were still red from his meeting with the Chief Constable. When Rebus made to sit, Watson told him to get back on his feet.

'You'll sit when you're told and not before.'

'Thank you, sir.'

'What the bloody hell's going on, John?'

'Pardon, sir?'

The Farmer looked at the note Rebus had left on his desk. 'What's this?'

'One dead, one seriously wounded in Paisley, sir. Telford's men. Cafferty's hitting him where it hurts. Probably reckons that Telford's territory's spun a bit thin. Leaves him open to breaches.'

'Paisley.' The Farmer stuffed the note in his drawer. 'Not our problem.'

'It will be, sir. When Telford hits back, it'll be right here.'

'Never mind that, Inspector. Let's talk about Maclean's Pharmaceuticals.'

Rebus blinked, relaxed his shoulders. 'I was going to tell you, sir.'

'But instead I had to hear it from the Chief Constable?'

'Not really my baby, sir. Crime Squad are pushing the pram.'

'But who put the baby *in* the pram?'

'I was going to tell you, sir.'

'Know how it makes me look? I walk into Fettes and I don't know something one of my junior officers knows? I look like a mug.'

'With respect, sir, I'm sure that's not the case.'

'I look like a *mug!*' The Farmer slammed the desk with both palms. 'And it's not as though this was the first time. I've always tried to do my best for you, you know that.'

'Yes, sir.'

'Always been fair.'

'Absolutely, sir.'

'And you pay me back like this?'

'It won't happen again, sir.'

The Farmer stared at him; Rebus held it, returned it.

'I bloody well hope not.' The Farmer leaned back in his chair. He'd calmed down a little. Bollocking as therapy. 'Nothing else you want to tell me, is there, while I've got you here?'

'No, sir. Except ... well ...'

'Go on.' The Farmer sat forward again.

'It's the man in the flat above me, sir,' Rebus said. 'I think he might be Lord Lucan.'

27

Leonard Cohen: 'There Is a War'.

They were waiting for Telford's retaliatory strike. The Chief Constable's idea: 'visible presence as deterrent'. It came as no surprise to Rebus: probably even less so to Telford, who had Charles Groal ready, claiming harassment the minute the patrol cars turned up in Flint Street. How was his client supposed to carry on with his legitimate and substantial business interests, as well as his many community developments, under the pressure of unwarranted and intrusive police surveillance? 'Community developments' meaning the pensioners and their rent-free flats: Telford wouldn't hesitate to use them as pawns. The media would love it.

The patrol cars would be pulled, it was just a matter of time. And afterwards: firework night all over again. That's what everyone was expecting.

Rebus went to the hospital, sat with Rhona. The room, so familiar to him now, was an oasis where calm and order reigned, where each hour of the day brought its comforting rituals.

'They've washed her hair,' he said.

'She's had another scan,' Rhona explained. 'They had to get the gunk off afterwards.' Rebus nodded. 'They said you'd noticed eye movement?'

'I thought I did.'

Rhona touched his arm. 'Jackie says he might manage to come up again at the weekend. Call this fair warning.'

'Received and understood.'

'You look tired.'

He smiled. 'One of these days someone's going to tell me how terrific I'm looking.'

'But not today,' Rhona said.

'Must be all the booze, clubbing and women.'

Thinking: Coke, the Morvena Casino, and Candice.

Thinking: why do I feel like piggy in the middle? Are Cafferty and Telford *both* playing games with me?

Thinking: I hope Jack Morton's OK.

The phone was ringing when he got back to Arden Street. He picked up just as the answering machine was cutting in.

'Hold on till I stop this thing.' Found the right button and hit it.

'Technology, eh, Strawman?'

754

Cafferty.

'What do you want?'

'I've heard about Paisley.'

'You mean you've been talking to yourself?'

'I had nothing to do with it.'

Rebus laughed out loud.

'I'm telling you.'

Rebus fell into his chair. 'And I'm supposed to believe you?' Games, he was thinking.

'Whether you believe me or not, I wanted you to know.'

'Thanks, I'm sure I'll sleep better for that.'

'I'm being set up, Strawman.'

'Telford doesn't *need* to set you up.' Rebus sighed, stretched his neck to left and right. 'Look, have you considered another possibility?'

'What?'

'Your men have lost it. They're going behind your back.'

'I'd know.'

'You'd know what your own lieutenants tell you. What if they're lying? I'm not saying it's the whole gang, could be just two or three gone rogue.'

'I'd know.' The emotion had drained from Cafferty's voice. He was thinking it over.

'Fine, OK, you'd know: who'd be the first to tell you? Cafferty, you're on the other side of the country. You're in *prison*. How hard would it be to keep stuff from you?'

'These are men I'd trust with my life.' Cafferty paused. 'They'd tell me.'

'*If* they knew. *If* they hadn't been warned not to tell you. See what I'm saying?'

'Two or three gone rogue . . .' Cafferty echoed.

'You must have candidates?'

'Jeffries would know.'

'Jeffries? Is that the Weasel's name?'

'Don't let him hear you call him that.'

'Give me his number. I'll talk to him.'

'No, but I'll get him to call you.'

'And if he's part of the breakaway?'

'We don't know there is one.'

'But you admit it makes sense?'

'I admit Tommy Telford's trying to put me in a box.'

Rebus stared from his window. 'You mean literally?'

'I've heard word of a contract.'

'But you've got protection?'

Cafferty chuckled. 'Strawman, you almost sound concerned.'

'You're imagining things.'

'Look, there are only two ways out of this. One, *you* deal with Telford. Two, *I* deal with him. Are we agreed on that? I mean, I'm not the one who went poaching players and territory and putting out frighteners.'

'Maybe he's just more ambitious than you. Maybe he reminds you of the way you used to be.'

'Are you saying I've gone soft?'

'I'm saying it's adapt or die.'

'Have *you* adapted, Strawman?'

'Maybe a little.'

'Aye, a fucking speck, if that.'

'We're not talking about me though.'

'You're as involved as anyone. Remember that, Strawman. And sweet dreams.'

Rebus put down the phone. He felt exhausted, and depressed. The kids across the way were in bed, shutters closed. He looked around the room. Jack Morton had helped him paint it, back when Rebus was thinking of selling. Jack had helped him off the sauce, too . . .

He knew he wouldn't be able to sleep. Got back into the car and headed for Young Street. The Oxford Bar was quiet. A couple of philosophers in the corner, and through in the back room three musicians who'd packed up their fiddles. He drank a couple of cups of black coffee, then drove to Oxford Terrace. Parked the car outside Patience's flat, turned off the ignition and sat there for a while, jazz on the radio. He hit a good streak: Astrid Gilberto, Stan Getz, Art Pepper, Duke Ellington. Told himself he'd wait till a bad record came on, then go knock on Patience's door.

But by then it was too late. He didn't want to turn up unannounced. It would be . . . it wouldn't look right. He didn't mind that it smacked of desperation, but he didn't want her to think he was pushing. He started the engine again and moved off, drove around the New Town and down to Granton. Sat by the edge of the Forth, window down, listening to water and the night-time traffic of HGVs.

Even with eyes closed, he couldn't shut out the world. In fact, in those moments before sleep came, his images were at their most vivid. He wondered what Sammy dreamed about, or even if she dreamed at all. Rhona said that Sammy had come north to be with him. He couldn't think what he'd done to deserve her.

Back into town for an espresso at Gordon's Trattoria, then the hospital: easy to find a parking space this time of night. A taxi was idling outside the entrance. He made his way to Sammy's room, was surprised to see someone there. His first thought: Rhona. The only illumination in the room was that given through the closed curtains. A woman, kneeling by the bed, head resting on the covers. He walked forwards. She heard him, turned, face glistening with tears.

Candice.

Her eyes widened. She stumbled to her feet.

'I wanting see her,' she said quietly.

Rebus nodded. In shadows, she looked even more like Sammy: same build, similar hair and shape to her face. She wore a long red coat, fished in the pocket for a paper hankie.

'I like her,' she said. He nodded again.

'Does Tarawicz know where you are?' he asked.

She shook her head.

'The taxi outside?' he guessed.

She nodded. 'They went casino. I said sore head.' She spoke falteringly, checking each word was right before using it.

'Will he find out you've gone?'

She thought about it, shook her head.

'You sleep in the same room?' Rebus asked.

She shook her head again, smiled. 'Jake not liking women.'

This was news to Rebus. Miriam Kenworthy had said something about him marrying an Englishwoman . . . but put that down to immigration. He remembered the way Tarawicz had pawed Candice, realised now it had been for *Telford's* benefit. He'd been showing Telford that he could control his women. While Telford . . . well, Telford had let her get arrested, then be taken in by the Crime Squad. A small sign of rivalry between the two partners. Something to be exploited?

'Is she . . . will she . . .?'

Rebus shrugged. 'We hope so, Candice.'

She looked down at the floor. 'My name is Karina.'

'Karina,' he echoed.

'Sarajevo was . . .' She looked up at him. 'You know, like *really*. I was escaping . . . lucky. They all said to me: "You lucky, you lucky".' She stabbed at her chest with a finger. 'Lucky. Survivor.' She broke down again, and this time he held her.

The Stones: 'Soul Survivor'. Only sometimes it was the body alone that survived, the soul eaten into, chewed up by experience.

'Karina,' he said, repeating her name, reinforcing her true identity, trying to get through to the one part of her she'd kept hidden since Sarajevo. 'Karina, sshhh. It's going to be all right. Sshhh.' And stroking her hair, her face, his other hand on her back, feeling her tremble. Blinking back his own tears, and watching Sammy's body. The atmosphere in the room crackled like electricity: he wondered if any part of it was reaching Sammy's brain.

'Karina, Karina, Karina . . .'

She pulled away, turned her back on him. He wouldn't let her go. Walked up to her and rested his hands on her shoulders.

'Karina,' he said, 'how did Tarawicz find you?' She seemed not to understand. 'In Anstruther, his men found you.'

'Brian,' she said quietly.

Rebus frowned. 'Brian Summers?' Pretty-Boy . . .

'He tell Jake.'

'He told Tarawicz where you were?' But why not just take her back to Edinburgh? Rebus thought he knew: she was too dangerous; she'd been too close to the police. Best get her out of the way. Not a killing: that would have implicated all of them. But Tarawicz could control her. Mr Pink Eyes bailing out his friend one more time . . .

'He brought you here so he could gloat over Telford.' Rebus was thoughtful. He looked at Candice. What could he do with her? Where would be safe? She seemed to sense his thoughts, squeezed his hand.

'You know I have a . . .' She made a cradling motion with her hands.

'A boy,' Rebus said. She nodded. 'And Tarawicz knows where he is?'

She shook her head. 'The lorries . . . they took him.'

'Tarawicz's refugee lorries?' She nodded again. 'And you don't know where he is?'

'Jake knows. He says his man . . .' she made scuttling motions with her hands '. . . will kill my boy if . . .'

Scuttling motions: the Crab. Something struck Rebus. 'Why isn't the

Crab up here with Tarawicz?' She was looking at him. 'Tarawicz here,' he said, 'Crab in Newcastle. Why?'

She shrugged, looked thoughtful. 'He don't come.' She was remembering some snippet of conversation. 'Danger.'

'Dangerous?' Rebus frowned. 'Who for?'

She shrugged again. Rebus took her hands.

'You can't trust him, Karina. You have to leave him.'

She smiled up at him, eyes glinting. 'I tried.'

They looked at one another, held one another for a while. Afterwards, he walked her back out to her taxi.

28

In the morning he called the hospital, found out how Sammy was doing, then asked to be transferred.

'How's Danny Simpson getting on?'

'I'm sorry, are you family?'

Which told him everything. He identified himself, asked when it had happened.

'In the night,' the nurse said.

Body at its lowest ebb: the dying hours. Rebus called the mother, identified himself again.

'Sorry to hear the news,' he said. 'Is the funeral . . .?'

'Just family, if you don't mind. No flowers. We're asking for donations to be sent to an . . . to a charity. Danny was well thought of, you know.'

'I'm sure.'

Rebus took down details of the charity – an AIDS hospice; the mother couldn't bring herself to say the word. Terminated the call. Got an envelope out and put in ten pounds, plus a note: 'In memory of Danny Simpson'. He wondered about going for that test . . . His phone rang and he picked it up.

'Hello?'

Lots of static and engine noise: car phone, on the move at speed.

'This takes persecution to new levels.' *Telford*.

'What do you mean?' Rebus trying to compose himself.

'Danny Simpson's been dead six hours, and already you're on the phone to his mum.'

'How do you know?'

'I was *there*. Paying my respects.'

'Same reason I phoned then. Know what, Telford? I think *you're* taking persecution complexes to new levels.'

'Yes, and Cafferty's not out to shut me down.'

'He says he didn't have anything to do with Paisley.'

'I bet you believed in the Tooth Fairy when you were a kid.'

'I still do.'

'You'll need more than a good fairy if you side with Cafferty.'

'Is that a threat? Don't tell me: Tarawicz is in the car with you?' Silence. Bingo, Rebus thought. 'You think Tarawicz will respect you because you bad-mouth cops? He's got no respect for you whatsoever – look how he's waving Candice in your face.'

Mixing levity with fury: 'Hey, Rebus, you and Candice in that hotel –

759

what was she like? Jake tells me she's vindaloo.' Background laughter: Mr Pink Eyes, who, according to Candice, had never touched her. For 'laughter' read 'bravado'. Telford and Tarawicz, playing games between themselves, playing games with the world.

Rebus found the tone of voice he wanted. 'I tried to help her. If she's too stupid to know that, she deserves the likes of you and Tarawicz.' Telling them he had no further interest in her. 'Anyway, Tarawicz didn't have any trouble taking her off *your* hands.' Rebus jabbing away, looking for gaps in the armour of the Telford/Tarawicz relationship. 'What if Cafferty wasn't behind Paisley?' he asked into the silence.

'It was his men.'

'Gone rogue.'

'He can't control them, that's his lookout. He's a *joke*, Rebus. He's finished.'

Rebus didn't say anything; listened instead to a muted conversation. Then Telford again: 'Mr Tarawicz wants a word.' The phone was handed over.

'Rebus? I thought we were civilised men?'

'In what way?'

'When we met in Newcastle . . . I thought we came to an understanding?'

The unspoken agreement: leave Telford alone, have nothing more to do with Cafferty, and Candice and her son would be safe. What was Tarawicz getting at?

'I've kept my side.'

A forced chuckle. 'You know what Paisley represents?'

'What?'

'The beginning of the end of Morris Gerald Cafferty.'

'And I bet you'd send flowers to the grave.'

Dead flowers at that.

Rebus went into St Leonard's, got settled in front of his computer screen, and took a look at the Crab.

The Crab: William Andrew Colton. Plenty of form. Rebus decided he'd like to read the files. Phoned in and requested them, backed up the request in writing. Buzzed from downstairs: a man to see him, no name supplied. Description: the Weasel.

Rebus went downstairs.

The Weasel was outside, smoking a cigarette. He was wearing a green waxed jacket, torn at both pockets. A lumberjack hat with its flaps down protected his ears from the wind.

'Let's walk,' Rebus said. The Weasel got into step with him. They wandered through an estate of new flats: satellite dishes and windows picked from Lego boxes. Behind the flats sat Salisbury Crags.

'Don't worry,' Rebus said, 'I'm not in the mood for rock-climbing.'

'I'm in the mood for indoors.' The Weasel tucked his chin into the upturned collar of his coat.

'What's the news on my daughter?'

'We're close, I told you.'

'How close?'

The Weasel measured his response. 'We've got the tapes from the car, the guy who sold them. He says he got them from another party.'

'And he is . . .?'

A sly smile: the Weasel knew he had control over Rebus. He'd play it out as long as possible.

'You're going to be meeting him fairly shortly.'

'Even so ... say the tapes got taken from the car after it was abandoned?'

The Weasel was shaking his head. 'That's not how it was.'

'Then how was it?' He wanted to pull his tormentor down on to the ground and start hammering his skull on the pavement.

'Give us a day or two, we'll have everything you need.' The wind gusted some grit towards them. They turned their faces. Rebus saw a heavy-set man loitering sixty yards behind.

'Don't worry,' the Weasel said, 'he's with me.'

'Getting jittery?'

'After Paisley, Telford's out for blood.'

'What do you know about Paisley?'

The Weasel's eyes became slits. 'Nothing.'

'No? Cafferty's beginning to suspect some of his own men might have gone rogue.' Rebus watched the Weasel shake his head.

'I don't know the first thing about it.'

'Who's your boss's main man?'

'Ask Mr Cafferty.' The Weasel was looking around, as if bored by the conversation. He made a signal to the back-marker, who passed it along. Seconds later, a newish Jaguar – arterial-red paint-job – cruised to a stop beside them. Rebus saw: a driver itching for a less sedentary occupation; cream leather interior; the back-marker jogging forwards, opening the door for the Weasel.

'It's you,' Rebus said. The Weasel: Cafferty's eyes and ears on the street; the man with the look and dress-code of a down-and-out. The Weasel was running the show. All the lieutenants in the various outposts ... all the tailor-made suits ... the collective which, according to police intelligence, ran Cafferty's kingdom in their master's absence ... they were a smokescreen. The hunched man pulling off his lumberjack hat, the man with bad teeth and a blunt razor, *he* was in charge.

Rebus actually laughed. The bodyguard got into the car's passenger seat, having made sure his boss was comfortable in the back. Rebus tapped on the window. The Weasel lowered it.

'Tell me,' Rebus asked, 'have you got the bottle to wrest it away from him?'

'Mr Cafferty trusts me. He knows I'll do right by him.'

'What about Telford?'

The Weasel stared at him. 'Telford's not my concern.'

'Then who is?'

But the window was rising again, and the Weasel – Cafferty had called him Jeffries – had turned his face away, dismissing Rebus from his mind.

He stood there, watching the car drive off. Was Cafferty making a big mistake, putting the Weasel in charge? Was it just that his best men had scarpered or gone over to the other side?

Or was the Weasel every bit as sly, clever and vicious as his namesake?

*

Back at the station, Rebus sought out Bill Pryde. Pryde was shrugging his shoulders even before Rebus had reached his desk.

'Sorry, John, no news.'

'Nothing at all? What about the stolen tapes?' Pryde shook his head. 'That's funny, I've just been talking to someone who claims to know who sold them on, and who *he* got them from.'

Pryde sat back in his chair. 'I wondered why you hadn't been chasing me up. What've you done, hired a private eye?' Blood was rising to his face. 'I've been working my arse off on this, John, you know I have. Now you don't trust me to do the job?'

'It's not like that, Bill.' Rebus suddenly found himself on the defensive.

'Who've you got working for you, John?'

'Just people on the street.'

'Well-connected people by the sound of it.' He paused. 'Are we talking villains?'

'My daughter's in a coma, Bill.'

'I'm well aware of that. Now answer my question!'

People around them were staring. Rebus lowered his voice. 'Just a few of my grasses.'

'Then give me their names.'

'Come on, Bill . . .'

Pryde's hands gripped the table. 'These past days, I've been thinking you'd lost interest. Thinking maybe you didn't *want* an answer.' He was thoughtful. 'You wouldn't go to Telford . . . Cafferty?' His eyes widened. 'Is that it, John?'

Rebus turned his head away.

'Christ, John . . . what's the deal here? He hands over the driver, what do *you* hand *him*?'

'It's not like that.'

'I can't believe you'd trust Cafferty. You put him away, for Christ's sake!'

'It's not a question of trust.'

But Pryde was shaking his head. 'There's a line we don't cross.'

'Get a grip, Bill. There's no line.' Rebus spread his arms. 'If there is, show me it.'

Pryde tapped his forehead. 'It's up here.'

'Then it's a fiction.'

'You really believe that?'

Rebus sought an answer, slumped against the desk, ran his hands over his head. He remembered something Lintz had once said: *when we stop believing in God, we don't suddenly believe in 'nothing' . . . we believe anything.*

'John?' someone called. 'Phone call.'

Rebus stared at Pryde. 'Later,' he said. He walked across to another desk, took the call.

'Rebus here.'

'It's Bobby.' Bobby Hogan.

'What can I do for you, Bobby?'

'For a start, you can help get that Special Branch arsehole off my back.'

'Abernethy?'

'He won't leave me alone.'

'Keeps phoning you?'

'Christ, John, aren't you listening? He's *here*.'

'When did he get in?'

'He never went away.'

'Whoah, hold on.'

'And he's driving me round the twist. He says he knows you from way back, so how about having a word?'

'Are you at Leith?'

'Where else?'

'I'll be there in twenty minutes.'

'I got so pissed off, I went to my boss – and that's something I seldom have to resort to.' Bobby Hogan was drinking coffee like it was something best taken intravenously. The top button of his shirt was undone, tie hanging loose.

'Only,' he went on, '*his* boss had a word with my *boss's* boss, and I ended up with a warning: co-operate or else.'

'Meaning?'

'I wasn't to tell anyone he was still around.'

'Thanks, pal. So what's he actually doing?'

'What *isn't* he doing? He wants to be in on any interviews. He wants copies of tapes and transcripts. He wants to see all the paperwork, wants to know what I'm planning to do next, what I had for breakfast . . .'

'I don't suppose he's managing to be helpful in any shape or form?'

Hogan's look gave Rebus his answer.

'I don't mind him taking an interest, but this verges on the obstructive. He's slowing the case to a dead stop.'

'Maybe that's his plan.'

Hogan looked up from his cup. 'I don't get it.'

'Neither do I. Look, if he's being obstructive, let's put on a show, see how he reacts.'

'What sort of show?'

'What time will he be in?'

Hogan checked his watch. 'Half an hour or so. That's when my work stops for the day, while I fill him in.'

'Half an hour's enough. Mind if I use your phone?'

29

When Abernethy arrived, he didn't manage not to look surprised. The space put aside for the investigation – Hogan's space – now contained three bodies, and they were working at the devil's own pace.

Hogan was on the telephone to a librarian. He was asking for a rundown of books and articles about the 'Rat Line'. Rebus was sorting through paperwork, putting it in order, cross-referencing, laying aside anything he didn't think useful. And Siobhan Clarke was there, too. She appeared to be on the phone to some Jewish organisation, and was asking them about lists of war criminals. Rebus nodded towards Abernethy, but kept on working.

'What's going on?' Abernethy asked, taking off his raincoat.

'Helping out. Bobby's got so many leads to work on . . .' He nodded towards Siobhan. 'And Crime Squad are interested, too.'

'Since when?'

Rebus waved a piece of paper. 'This might be bigger than we think.'

Abernethy looked around. He wanted to speak to Hogan, but Hogan was still on the phone. Rebus was the only one with time to talk.

Which was just the way Rebus had planned it.

He'd only had five minutes in which to brief Siobhan, but she was a born actress, even holding a conversation with the dialling tone. Hogan's fantasy librarian, meantime, was asking him all the right questions. And Abernethy was looking glazed.

'What do you mean?'

'In fact,' Rebus said, putting down a file, 'you might be able to help.'

'How?'

'You're Special Branch, and Special Branch has access to the secret services.' Rebus paused. 'Right?'

Abernethy licked his lips and shrugged.

'See,' Rebus went on, 'we're beginning to wonder something. There could be a dozen reasons why someone would want to kill Joseph Lintz, but the one we've been practically ignoring' (ignoring at Abernethy's suggestion, according to Hogan) 'is the one that just might provide the answer. I'm talking about the Rat Line. What if Lintz's murder had something to do with that?'

'How could it?'

It was Rebus's turn to shrug. 'That's why we need your help. We need any and all information we can get on the Rat Line.'

'But it never existed.'

'Funny, a lot of books seem to say it did.'

'They're wrong.'

'Then there are all these survivors ... except they haven't survived. Suicides, car crashes, a fall from a window. Lintz is just one of a long line of dead men.'

Siobhan Clarke and Bobby Hogan had finished their calls and were listening.

'You're climbing the wrong tree,' Abernethy said.

'Well, you know, if you're in a forest, climbing any tree will give you a better view.'

'There is no Rat Line.'

'You're an expert?'

'I've been collating ...'

'Yes, yes, all the investigations. And how far have you got? Is any one of them going to make it to trial?'

'It's too early to tell.'

'And soon it may be too late. These men aren't getting any younger. I've seen the same thing all around Europe: delay the trial until the defendants are so old they snuff it or go doolally. Result's the same: no trial.'

'Look, this has nothing to do with ...'

'Why are you here, Abernethy? Why did you come up that time to speak to Lintz?'

'Look, Rebus, it's not ...'

'If you can't tell us, talk to your boss. Get *him* to do it. Otherwise, the way we're digging, we're bound to throw up an old bone sooner or later.'

Abernethy stood back a pace. 'I think I get it,' he said. And he began to smile. 'You're trying to stiff me.' He was looking at Hogan. 'That's what this is.'

'Not at all,' Rebus answered. 'What I'm saying is: we'll redouble our efforts. We'll sniff into every little corner. The Rat Line, the Vatican, turning Nazis into Cold War spies for the allies ... it could all count as evidence. The other men on your list, the other suspects ... we'll need to talk to all of them, see if they knew Joseph Lintz. Maybe they met him on the trip over.'

Abernethy was shaking his head. 'I'm not going to let you do that.'

'You're going to obstruct the investigation?'

'That's not what I said.'

'No, but it's what you'll *do*.' Rebus paused. 'If you think we're climbing the wrong tree – and, incidentally, that should be *barking up* – go ahead and prove it. Give us everything you've got on Lintz's past.'

Abernethy's eyes were fierce.

'Or we go on digging and sniffing.' Rebus opened another file, lifted out the first sheet. Hogan picked up his telephone, made another call. Siobhan Clarke looked at a list of numbers and chose one.

'Hello, is that the City Synagogue?' Hogan was saying. 'Yes, it's Detective Inspector Hogan here, Leith CID. Do you by any chance have information on a Joseph Lintz?'

Abernethy grabbed his coat, turned on his heels and left. They waited thirty seconds, then Hogan put the receiver down.

'He looked nettled.'

'That's one Christmas wish I can chalk off,' Siobhan Clarke said.

'Thanks for your time, Siobhan,' Rebus said.

'Happy to oblige. But why did it have to be me?'

'Because he knows you're Crime Squad. I wanted him to think interest was escalating. And because the two of you didn't exactly hit it off last time you met. Antagonism always helps.'

'And what did we accomplish?' Bobby Hogan asked, beginning to gather together the files, half of which belonged to other cases.

'We rattled his cage,' Rebus said. 'He's not up here for the good of his health – or yours, come to that. He's here because Special Branch in London want to know all about the investigation. And to me, that means they're scared of something.'

'The Rat Line?'

'That would be my guess. Abernethy's been keeping an eye on all the new cases nationwide. Someone in London is getting a bit sweaty.'

'They're worried this Rat Line will connect to whoever killed Lintz?'

'I'm not sure it goes that far,' Rebus said.

'Meaning?'

He looked at Clarke. 'Meaning I'm not sure it goes that far.'

'Well,' Hogan said, 'looks like he's off my back for a little while at least, for which I'm grateful.' He got to his feet. 'Get anyone a coffee?'

Clarke checked her watch. 'Go on then.'

Rebus waited till Hogan was gone, then thanked Siobhan again. 'I wasn't sure you'd be able to spare the time.'

'We're giving Jack Morton a wide berth,' she explained. 'Nothing to do but bite our fingernails and wait. What about you, what are you up to?'

'Keeping my nose clean.'

She smiled. 'I'll bet.'

Hogan came back with three coffees. 'Powdered milk, sorry.'

Clarke wrinkled her nose. 'Actually, I've got to be getting back.' She stood up and put on her coat.

'That's one I owe you,' Hogan said, shaking her hand.

'I won't let you forget.' She turned to Rebus. 'See you later.'

'Cheers, Siobhan.'

Hogan put her cup beside his own. 'So we got Abernethy off my back, but did we get anything else?'

'Wait and see, Bobby. I didn't exactly have much time to devise a strategy.'

The phone rang, just as Hogan took a mouthful of scalding coffee. Rebus picked up.

'Hello?'

'Is that you, John?' Country and western twanging in the background: Claverhouse.

'You've just missed her,' Rebus told him.

'It's not Clarke I wanted, it's you.'

'Oh?'

'Something I thought you might be interested in. It's just filtered down from NCIS.' Rebus heard Claverhouse pick up a sheet of paper. 'Sakiji Shoda ... I think I've pronounced that right. Flew into Heathrow from Kansai Airport yesterday. South-East Regional Crime Squad were apprised.'

'Terrific.'

'He didn't hang around, caught a connection to Inverness. Stayed the night in a local hotel, and now I hear he's in Edinburgh.'

Rebus looked out of the window. 'Not exactly golfing weather.'

'I don't think he's up here for the golf. According to the original report, Mr Shoda is a high-ranking member of the . . . can't make it out on the fax. Socky-something.'

'Sokaiya?' Rebus sat up.

'That looks about right.'

'Where is he now?'

'I tried a couple of hotels. He's staying at the Caly. What's the Sokaiya?'

'It's the upper echelons of the Yakuza.'

'How does it read to you?'

'I was going to suggest he's Matsumoto's replacement, but it sounds to me like he's a few grades higher.'

'Matsumoto's boss?'

'Which means he's probably here to find out what happened to his boy.' Rebus tapped a pen against his teeth. Hogan was listening, but not getting any of it. 'Why Inverness? Why not direct to Edinburgh?'

'I've been wondering that.' Claverhouse sneezed. 'How pissed off will he be?'

'Somewhere between "mildly" and "very". More importantly, how are Telford and Mr Pink Eyes going to react?'

'You think Telford will drop Maclean's?'

'On the contrary, I think he'll want to show Mr Shoda that he can do *some* things right.' Rebus thought back to something Claverhouse had said. 'South-East Crime Squad?'

'Yes.'

'Rather than Scotland Yard?'

'Maybe the two are the same?'

'Maybe. Do you have a contact number?'

Claverhouse gave it to him.

'You'll speak to Jack Morton tonight?' Rebus asked.

'Yes.'

'Better tell him about this.'

'Talk to you again.'

Rebus put down the receiver, picked it up again, got an outside line and made the call. Explained his reason for calling and asked if there was anyone who could help him.

He was told to hold.

'Is this to do with Telford?' Hogan asked. Rebus nodded.

'Hey, Bobby, did you ever talk to Telford again?'

'I tried a couple of times. He just kept saying: "It must've been a wrong number".'

'And this was echoed by his staff?'

Hogan nodded, smiled. 'Tell you a funny thing. I walked into Telford's office, and someone was at his desk, back to me. I apologised, said I'd come back when he'd finished with the lady. Well, the "lady" turns, face like fury . . .'

'Pretty-Boy?'

Hogan nodded. 'And pretty fucking angry the last I saw him.' Hogan laughed.

'Putting you through,' the switchboard told Rebus.

'How can I help you?' The voice sounded Welsh.

'My name's DI Rebus, Scottish Crime Squad.' Rebus winked at Hogan: the lie would give him more clout.

'Yes, Inspector?'

'And you are . . .?'

'DI Morgan.'

'We had this message this morning . . .'

'Yes?'

'Concerning Sakiji Shoda.'

'That would be my boss has sent you that.'

'What I'm wondering is, what's your interest?'

'Well, Inspector, I'm more of an expert on *vory v zakone*.'

'That clears things up then.'

Morgan chuckled. ' "Thieves within the code". Meaning *mafiya*.'

'Russian mafia?'

'That's it.'

'You'll have to help me here. What's that got to do with . . .?'

'Why do you want to know?'

Rebus took a sip of coffee. 'We've had a spot of bother with the Yakuza up here. One victim so far. My guess is that Shoda is the victim's boss.'

'And he's up there for a sort of unofficial committal?'

'We don't have the committal stage in Scotland, DI Morgan.'

'Well, pardon me for breathing.'

'Thing is, we've also got a Russian gangster up here. I say he's Russian, word is he's Chechen.'

'Is it Jake Tarawicz?'

'You've heard of him?'

'That's my job, sonny boy.'

'Well, anyway, with the Yakuza and the Chechens in town . . .'

'You've got a nightmare scenario. Understood. Well, look . . . What about if you give me your number there, and I'll call back in five minutes? Need to put some facts together first.'

Rebus gave him the number, then waited ten minutes for the call back. 'You were checking me out,' he told the Welshman.

'Got to be careful. Bit naughty of you to say you were Crime Squad.'

'Let's just say I'm the next best thing. So is there anything you can tell me?'

Morgan took a deep breath. 'We've been chasing a lot of dirty money around the world.'

Rebus couldn't find a clean sheet of paper to write on. Hogan gave him a pad.

'See,' Morgan was saying, 'the old Soviet Asia is now the biggest supplier of raw opium in the world. And wherever there's drugs, there's money needs laundering.'

'And this money makes its way to Britain?'

'On its way elsewhere. Companies in London, private banks in Guernsey . . . the money gets filtered down, getting cleaner all the time. Everyone wants to do business with the Russians.'

'Why?'

'Because they make everyone money. Russia's one giant bazaar. You want weapons, counterfeit goods, money, fake passports, even plastic surgery? You want any of that, it's in Russia. The place has open borders, airports nobody knows exist . . . it's ideal.'

'If you happen to be an international mobster.'

'Exactly. And the *mafiya* have made links with their Sicilian cousins, with the Camorra, the Calabrians . . . I could go on for ever. British villains go shopping there. They all love the Russians.'

'And now they're here?'

'Oh, they're here all right. Running protection and prossies, dealing drugs . . .'

Prostitutes, drugs: Mr Pink Eyes's territory; Telford's territory.

'Any evidence of a hook-up with the Yakuza?'

'Not that I know of.'

'But if they moved into Britain . . .?'

'They'd be trying to control drugs and prostitution. They'd be laundering money.'

Ways to launder money: through legitimate businesses such as country clubs and the like; by swopping dirty money for casino chips at an establishment like the Morvena.

Rebus already knew that the Yakuza liked to smuggle artworks back into Japan. Rebus already knew Mr Pink had made his early money smuggling icons out of Russia. Put the two together.

Then add Tommy Telford to the equation.

Did they need the haul from Maclean's? It didn't sound to Rebus like they did. So why was Tommy Telford doing it? Two possible reasons: one, to show off; two, *because they'd told him to*. Some rite of passage . . . If he wanted to play with the big boys, he had to prove himself. He had to wipe out Cafferty, and pull off what would be the biggest heist in Scottish history.

Something hit Rebus between the eyes.

Telford wasn't meant to succeed. Telford was meant to fail.

Telford was being set up by Tarawicz and the Yakuza.

Because he had something they wanted: a steady supply of drugs; a kingdom waiting to be plucked from his grasp. Miriam Kenworthy had said as much: rumour was, the drugs were going south from Scotland. Which meant Telford had a supply . . . something *nobody* knew about.

With Cafferty out of the way, there'd be no competition. The Yakuza would have their British base – solid, respectable, reliable. The electronics factory would act as perfect cover, maybe even as a laundering operation itself. Every way Rebus looked at it, Telford was unnecessary to the equation, like a zero that could be safely cancelled out.

Which was where Rebus wanted Telford . . . only not at the price being asked.

'Thanks for your help,' he said. He noticed that Hogan had stopped listening and was staring into space. Rebus put the phone down.

'Sorry to have bored you.'

Hogan blinked. 'No, nothing like that. It's just that I thought of something.'

769

'What?'

'Pretty-Boy. I mistook him for a woman.'

'You're probably not the first.'

'Exactly.'

'I'm not sure I follow you?'

'In the restaurant . . . Lintz and a young woman.' Hogan shrugged. 'It's a long shot.'

Rebus saw it. 'Talking business?'

Hogan nodded. 'Pretty-Boy runs Telford's stable.'

'And takes a personal interest in the higher-price models. It's worth a try, Bobby.'

'What do you think – bring him in?'

'Definitely. Beef up the restaurant angle. Say there's a positive ID. See what he says to that.'

'Same gag we pulled with Colquhoun? Pretty-Boy's bound to deny it.'

'Doesn't mean it ain't so.' Rebus patted Hogan on the shoulder.

'What about your call?'

'My call?' Rebus looked at his scrawled notes. Gangsters preparing to carve up Scotland. 'It wasn't the worst news I've ever had.'

'And is that saying much?'

'Afraid not, Bobby,' Rebus said, putting on his jacket. 'Afraid not.'

30

By the end of play, Rebus still hadn't received the files on the Crab, but he had fielded a frank and foul-mouthed call from Abernethy, accusing him of everything from obstruction – which was pretty rich, considering – to racism, which Rebus thought nicely ironic.

They'd given him back his car. Someone had run their finger through the dirt crusted on the boot, creating two messages: TERMINAL CASE, and WASHED BY STEVIE WONDER. The Saab, affronted, started first time and seemed to have shrugged off some of its repertoire of clanks and thunks. On the drive home, Rebus kept the windows open so he wouldn't smell the whisky that had soaked into the upholstery.

The evening had turned out fine, the sky clear, temperature dropping sharply. The low red sun, curse of the city's drivers, had disappeared behind the rooftops. Rebus left his coat unbuttoned as he walked down to the chip shop. He bought a fish supper, two buttered rolls, and a couple of cans of Irn-Bru, then returned to the flat. Nothing on the TV, so he put on a record. Van Morrison: *Astral Weeks*. The record had more scratches than a dog with eczema.

The opening track contained the refrain 'To be born again'. Rebus thought of Father Leary, shored up by a fridge full of medicine. Then he thought of Sammy, crowned with electrodes, machines rising either side of her, like she was being offered to them in sacrifice. Leary often talked of faith, but it was hard to have faith in a human race that never learned, that seemed ready to accept torture, murder, destruction. He opened his newspaper: Kosovo, Zaire, Rwanda. Punishment beatings in Northern Ireland. A young girl found murdered in England, another girl's disappearance termed 'a cause for concern'. The predators were out there, no doubt about it. Strip the veneer, and the world had moved only a couple of steps from the cave.

To be born again ... But sometimes only after a baptism of fire.

Belfast, 1970. A sniper's bullet blew open the skull of a British squaddie. The victim was nineteen, came from Glasgow. Back in the barracks, there'd been little mourning, just an overspill of anger. The assassin would never be caught. He'd slipped back into the shadows of a tower-block, and from there deep into the Catholic housing estate.

Leaving one more newspaper story, one early statistic in the 'Troubles'. And anger.

The ring-leader went by the nickname of 'Mean Machine'. He was a

lance-corporal, came from somewhere in Ayrshire. Cropped blond hair, looked like he'd played rugby, liked to work out, even if it was just press-ups and sit-ups in the barracks. He started the campaign for retribution. It was to be covert – meaning behind the backs of the 'brass'. It was to be a release-valve for the frustration, the pressure that was building in the cramped confines of the barracks. The world outside was enemy terrain, everyone a potential foe. Knowing there was no way to punish the sniper, Mean Machine had decided to hold the entire community to blame: collective responsibility, for which there would be collective justice.

The plan: a raid on a known IRA bar, a place where sympathisers drank and colluded. The pretext: a man with a handgun, chased into the bar, necessitating a search. Maximum harassment, ending with the beating of the local IRA fundraiser.

And Rebus went along with it . . . because it *was* collective. You were either part of the team, or you were dead meat. And Rebus wasn't in the market for pariah status.

But all the same, he knew the line between 'good guys' and 'bad guys' had become blurred. And during the incursion, it disappeared altogether.

Mean Machine went in hardest, teeth bared, eyes ablaze. He swung with his rifle, cracking skulls. Tables flew, pint glasses shattered. Initially the other soldiers seemed shocked by the sudden violence. They looked to each other for guidance. Then one of them lashed out, and the others fell in beside him. A mirror dissolved into glittering stars, stout and lager washed over the wooden floor. Men were shouting, begging, crawling on hands and knees across the glass minefield. Mean Machine had the IRA man pinned to a wall, kneeing him in the groin. He twisted his body, threw him to the floor, then started pummelling him with the rifle-butt. More soldiers were pouring into the drinking-club: armoured cars arriving outside. A chair crashed into the row of optics. The smell of whisky was almost overpowering.

Rebus tried to shut it out, his own teeth bared not in anger but anguish. Then he aimed his rifle at the ceiling and let loose a single shot, and everything froze . . . A final kick to the bloodied figure on the floor and Mean Machine turned and walked out of the club. The others hesitated again, then followed. He'd proved something to the other men: for all his lowly rank, he'd become their leader.

They enjoyed themselves that night in the barracks, chiding Rebus for letting his trigger-finger slip. They cracked open cans of beer and told stories, stories which were already being exaggerated, turning the event into a myth, giving it a grandeur it had lacked.

Turning it into a lie.

A few weeks later, the same IRA man was found shot dead in a stolen car south of the city, on a farm road with a view of hills and grazing land. Protestant paramilitaries took the blame, but Mean Machine, though he admitted nothing, would wink and grin when the incident was mentioned. Bravado or confession – Rebus was never sure. All he knew was that he wanted out, away from Mean Machine's newly minted code of ethics. So he did the one thing he could – applied to join the SAS. Nobody would think him a coward or a turncoat for applying to join the elite.

To be born again.

Side one had finished; Rebus turned the record over, switched off the lights and went to sit in his chair. He felt a chill run through him. Because he *knew* how events like Villefranche could come to be. Because he *knew* how the world's continuing horrors could come to be perpetrated at the cusp of the twentieth century. He knew that mankind's instinct was raw, that every act of bravery and kindness was countered by so many acts of savagery.

And he suspected that if his daughter had been that sniper's victim, he'd have run into the bar with his trigger-finger already working.

Telford's gang ran in a pack, too, trusted their leader. But now *he* wanted to run with an even bigger gang . . .

The phone rang and he picked up.

'John Rebus,' he said.

'John, it's Jack.' Jack Morton. Rebus put down his can.

'Hello, Jack. Where are you?'

'In the poky one-bedroomed flat our friends at Fettes so graciously provided.'

'It has to fit the image.'

'Aye, I suppose so. Got a phone though. Coin job, but you can't have everything.' He paused. 'You OK, John? You sound . . . not all there.'

'That just about sums me up, Jack. What's it like being a security guard?'

'A dawdle, pal. Should have taken it up years ago.'

'Wait till your pension's safe.'

'Aye, right.'

'And it went OK with Marty Jones?'

'Oscars all round. They were just heavy enough. I stumbled back into the shop, said I had to sit down. The Gruesome Twosome were very solicitous, then started asking me all these questions . . . Not very subtle.'

'You don't think they twigged?'

'Like you, I was a bit dubious about setting it up so fast, but I think they fell for it. Whether their boss goes along is a different story.'

'Well, he's under a lot of pressure.'

'With the war going on?'

'I don't think that's the whole story, Jack. I think he's under pressure from his partners.'

'The Russian and the Japs?'

'I think they're setting him up for a fall, and Maclean's is the precipice.'

'Evidence?'

'Gut feeling.'

Jack was thoughtful. 'So where do I stand?'

'Just ca' canny, Jack.'

'I never thought of that.'

Rebus laughed. 'When do you think they'll make contact?'

'They followed me home – that's how desperate they are. They're sitting outside right now.'

'They must think you're a good thing.'

Rebus could see the way it was going. Dec and Ken getting panicky, needing a quick result – feeling vulnerable so far away from Flint Street, not knowing if they'd be Cafferty's next victims. Telford, pressure applied by Tarawicz, and now with the Yakuza boss in town . . . needing a result, something to show he was top dog.

'What about you, John? It's been a while.'

'Yes.'

'How are you holding up?'

'I'm on soft drinks only, if that's what you mean.' And a car doused in whisky ... he could taste it in his lungs.

'Hang on,' Jack said. 'Someone's at the door. I'll call you back.'

'Be careful.'

The phone went dead.

Rebus gave it an hour. When Jack hadn't called, he got on the blower to Claverhouse.

'It's OK,' Claverhouse told him from his mobile. 'Tweedledee and Tweedledum came calling, took him off somewhere.'

'You're watching the flat?'

'Decorator's van parked down the street.'

'So you've no idea where they've taken him?'

'I'd guess he's at Flint Street.'

'With no back-up?'

'That's how we all wanted it.'

'Christ, I don't know ...'

'Thanks for the vote of confidence.'

'It's not you in the firing line. And I'm the one who volunteered him.'

'He knows the score, John.'

'So now you wait for him either to come home or end up on a slab?'

'Christ, John, Calvin was Charlie Chester compared to you.' Claverhouse had lost all patience. Rebus tried to think of a comeback, slammed the phone down instead.

Suddenly he couldn't be doing with Van the Man; put on Bowie instead, *Aladdin Sane*: nicely discordant, Mike Garson's piano in key with his thoughts.

Empty juice cans and a dead pack of cigarettes stared up at him. He didn't know Jack's address. The only person who'd give it to him was Claverhouse, and he didn't want to pick up their conversation. He took Bowie off halfway through side one, substituted *Quadrophenia*. Liner notes: 'Schizophrenic? I'm bleeding Quadrophenic'. Which was just about right.

Quarter past midnight, the phone rang. It was Jack Morton.

'Back home safe and sound?' Rebus asked.

'Right as nails.'

'Have you spoken to Claverhouse?'

'He can wait his turn. I said I'd phone you back.'

'So what did you get?'

'The third degree, basically. Some guy with dyed black hair, frizzy ... tight jeans.'

'Pretty-Boy.'

'Wears mascara.'

'Looks like. So what was the gist?'

'Second hurdle passed. Nobody's mentioned what the job is yet. Tonight was a sort of preface. Wanted to know all about me, told me my money worries could be over. If I could help them with a "little problem" – Pretty-Boy's words.'

'You asked what the problem was?'

'He wasn't saying. If you ask me, he goes to Telford, talks it through. Then there's another meeting, and that's where they tell me the plan.'

'And you'll be miked up?'

'Yes.'

'And if they strip you?'

'Claverhouse has access to some miniaturised stuff, cufflinks and the like.'

'And your character would obviously wear cufflinks.'

'True enough. Maybe fit a transmitter into a bookie's pencil.'

'Now you're thinking.'

'I'm thinking I'm wiped out.'

'What was the mood like?'

'Fraught.'

'Any sign of Tarawicz or Shoda?'

'Nope, just Pretty-Boy and the Gruesome Twosome.'

'Claverhouse calls them Tweedledum and Tweedledee.'

'He's obviously classically educated.' Morton paused. 'You've spoken to him?'

'When you didn't call back.'

'I'm touched. Do you think he's up to it?'

'Claverhouse?' Rebus thought about it. 'I'd feel better if *I* was in charge. But that probably puts me in a minority.'

'I didn't say that.'

'You're a pal, Jack.'

'They're running a check on me. But that's all in place. With luck, I'll pass.'

'What did they say to your sudden arrival at Maclean's?'

'I've been transferred from another plant. If they go looking, I'm in the personnel files.' Morton paused again. 'One thing I want to know . . .'

'What?'

'Pretty-Boy handed me a hundred quid on account: what do I do with it?'

'That's between you and your conscience, Jack. See you soon.'

'Night, John.'

For the first time in a while, Rebus actually made it as far as his bed. His sleep was deep and dreamless.

31

Doctors in white coats were doing things to Sammy when Rebus arrived at the hospital next morning: taking her pulse, shining lights in her eyes. They were setting up another scanner, a nurse trying to untangle the thin coloured leads. Rhona looked like she'd lost some sleep. She jumped up and ran towards him.

'She woke up!'

It took him a second to take it in. Rhona was holding his arms, shaking him.

'She woke *up*, John!'

He pushed his way to the bedside.

'When?'

'Last night.'

'Why didn't you phone me?'

'I tried three, four times. You were engaged. I tried Patience, but there was no answer there.'

'What happened?' To him, Sammy looked the same as ever.

'She just opened her eyes . . . No, first off, it was like she was moving her eyeballs. You know, with her eyelids closed. Then she opened her eyes.'

Rebus could see that the medical personnel were finding their work hampered. Half of him wanted to lash out – *We're her fucking parents!* The other half wanted them to do all they could to bring her round again. He took Rhona by the shoulder and guided her out into the hallway.

'Did she . . . Did she look at you? Did she say anything?'

'She was just staring at the ceiling, where the strip light is. Then I thought she was going to blink, but she closed her eyes again and they stayed shut.' Rhona burst into tears. 'It was like . . . I lost her all over again.'

Rebus took her in his arms. She hugged him back.

'She did it once,' he whispered into her ear, 'she'll do it again.'

'That's what one of the doctors said. He said they're "very hopeful". Oh, John, I wanted to tell you! I wanted to tell *everyone!*'

And he'd been busy with work: Claverhouse, Jack Morton. And he'd got Sammy into all this in the first place. Sammy and Candice – pebbles dropped into a pool. And now the ripples had grown so that he'd all but forgotten about the centre, the starting point. Just like when he was married, work consuming him, becoming an end in itself. And Rhona's words: *You've exploited every relationship you ever had.*

To be born again . . .

'I'm sorry, Rhona,' he said.

'Can you let Ned know?' She started crying again.

'Come on,' he said, 'let's get some breakfast. Have you been here all night?'

'I couldn't leave.'

'I know.' He kissed her cheek.

'The person in the car . . .'

'What?'

She looked at him. 'I don't care any more. I don't care who they were or whether they get caught. All I want is for her to wake up.'

Rebus nodded, told her he understood. Told her breakfast was on him. He kept the talk going, his mind not really on it. Instead, her words bounced around in his head: *I don't care who they were or whether they get caught . . .*

Whichever stress he put on it, he couldn't make it sound like surrender.

At St Leonard's, he broke the news to Ned Farlowe. Farlowe wanted to go to the hospital, but Rebus shook his head. Farlowe was crying as Rebus left his cell. Back at his desk, the files on the Crab were waiting.

The Crab: real name, William Andrew Colton. He had form going back to his teens, celebrated his fortieth birthday on Guy Fawkes Day. Rebus hadn't had many dealings with him during his time in Edinburgh. Looked like the Crab had lived in the city for a couple of years in the early-'80s, and again in the early-'90s. 1982: Rebus gave evidence against him in a conspiracy trial. Charges dropped. 1983: he was in trouble again – a fight in a pub left one man in a coma and his girlfriend needing sixty stitches to her face. Sixty stitches: you could knit a pair of mittens with less.

The Crab had held various jobs: bouncer, bodyguard, general labourer. The Inland Revenue had a go at him in 1986. By '88, he was on the West Coast, which was presumably where Tommy Telford had found him. Knowing good muscle when he saw it, he'd put the Crab on the doors of his club in Paisley. More blood-spilling; more accusations. Nothing came of them. The Crab had lived a charmed life, the sort of life that niggled at cops the world over: witnesses too scared to testify; withdrawing or refusing to give evidence. The Crab didn't often make it to trial. He'd served three adult sentences – a total of twenty-seven months – in a career that was now entering its fourth decade. Rebus went through the paperwork again, picked up the phone and called CID in Paisley. The man he wanted to speak to had been transferred to Motherwell. Rebus made the call, eventually got through to Detective Sergeant Ronnie Hannigan, and explained his interest.

'It's just that reading between the lines, you suspected the Crab of a lot more than ever got put down on paper.'

'You're right.' Hannigan cleared his throat. 'Never got close to proving anything though. You say he's south of the border now?'

'Telford placed him with a gangster in Newcastle.'

'Have criminal tendencies, will travel. Well, let's hope they keep him. He was a one-man reign of terror, and that's no exaggeration. Probably why Telford palmed him off on someone else: the Crab was getting out of

control. My theory is, Telford tried him out as a hit-man. Crab wasn't suitable, so Telford needed to jettison him.'

'What was the hit?'

'Down in Ayr. Must've been ... four years ago? Lot of drugs swilling around, most of them inside a dance-club ... can't remember its name. I don't know what happened: maybe a deal went sour, maybe someone was skimming. Whatever, there was a hit outside the club. Guy got his face half torn off with a carving knife.'

'You put the Crab in the frame?'

'He had an alibi, of course, and the eyewitnesses all seemed to have suffered temporary blindness. Could be a plot for the *X-Files* in that.'

A knife attack outside a nightclub ... Rebus tapped his desk with a pen. 'Any idea how the attacker got away?'

'On a motorbike. The Crab likes bikes. Crash helmet makes a good disguise.'

'We had an almost identical attack recently. Guy on a motorbike went for a drug dealer outside one of Tommy Telford's nightclubs. Killed a bouncer instead.'

And Cafferty denied any involvement ...

'Well, like you say, the Crab's in Newcastle.'

Yes, and staying put ... *scared* to come north. Warned off by Tarawicz. Because Edinburgh was too dangerous ... people might *remember* him.

'Do you know how far away Newcastle is?'

'A couple of hours?'

'No distance at all by bike. Anything else I should know?'

'Well, Telford tried the Crab in the van, but he wasn't much good.'

'What van?'

'The ice-cream van.'

Rebus nearly dropped the phone. 'Explain,' he said.

'Easy: Telford's boys were selling dope from an ice-cream van. The "five-pound special", they called it. You handed over a fiver and got back a cone or wafer with a wee plastic bag tucked inside ...'

Rebus thanked Hannigan and terminated the call. Five-pound specials: Mr Taystee with his clients who ate ice cream in all weathers. His daytime pitches: near schools. His night-time pitches: outside Telford's clubs. Five-pound specials on the menu, Telford taking his cut ... The new Merc: Mr Taystee's big mistake. Telford's moneymen wouldn't have taken long to work out their boy was skimming. Telford would have decided to turn Mr Taystee into a lesson ...

It was coming together. He spun his pen, caught it, and made another call, this time to Newcastle.

'Nice to hear from you,' Miriam Kenworthy said. 'Any sign of your lady friend?'

'She's turned up here.'

'Great.'

'In tow with Mr Pink Eyes.'

'Not so great. I wondered where he'd gone.'

'And he's not here to see the sights.'

'I'll bet he isn't.'

'Which is really why I'm calling.'

'Mmm?'

'I'm just wondering if he's ever been linked to machete attacks.'

'Machetes? Let me think . . .' She was so quiet for so long, he thought the connection had failed. 'You know, that *does* ring a bell. Let me put it up on the screen.' Clackety-clack of her keyboard. Rebus was biting his bottom lip, almost drawing blood.

'God, yes,' she said. 'A year or so back, a battle on an estate. Rival gangs, that was the story, but everyone knew what was behind it: namely, drugs and pitch incursions.'

'And where there's drugs, there's Tarawicz?'

'There was a rumour his men were involved.'

'And they used machetes?'

'One of them did. His name's Patrick Kenneth Moynihan, known to all and sundry as "PK".'

'Can you give me a description?'

'I can fax you his picture. But meantime: tall, heavy build, curly black hair and a black beard.'

He wasn't part of the Tarawicz retinue. Two of Mr Pink's best muscle-men had been left behind in Newcastle. For safety's sake. Rebus put PK down as one of the Paisley attackers – Cafferty again in the clear.

'Thanks, Miriam. Listen, about that rumour . . .'

'Remind me.'

'Telford supplying Tarawicz rather than the other way round: anything to back it up?'

'We tracked Pink Eyes and his men. A couple of jaunts to the continent, only they came back clean.'

'Leading you up the garden path?'

'Which made us start reassessing.'

'Where would Telford be getting the stuff?'

'We didn't reassess that far.'

'Well, thanks again . . .'

'Hey, don't leave me hanging: what's the story?'

'Morning Glory. Cheers, Miriam.'

Rebus went and got a coffee, put sugar in it without realising, had finished half the cup before he noticed. Tarawicz was attacking Telford. Telford was blaming Cafferty. The resulting war would destroy Cafferty and weaken Telford. Then Telford would pull off the Maclean's break-in but be grassed up . . .

And Tarawicz would fill the vacuum. That had been the plan all along. Bluesbreakers: 'Double-Crossing Time'. Christ, it was beautiful: set the two rivals against one another and wait for the carnage to end . . .

The prize: something Rebus didn't yet know. There had to be something big. Tarawicz, the theory went, was sourcing his drugs not from London but from Scotland. From Tommy Telford.

What did Telford know? What was it that made *his* supply so valuable? Did it have something to do with Maclean's? Rebus got another coffee, washed down three paracetamol with it. His head felt ready to explode. Back at his desk, he tried Claverhouse, couldn't get him. Paged him instead, and got an immediate call back.

'I'm in the van,' Claverhouse said.

'I've something to tell you.'

'What?'

Rebus wanted to know what was happening. Wanted in on the action. 'It's got to be face to face. Where are you parked?'

Claverhouse sounded suspicious. 'Down from the shop.'

'White decorator's van?'

'This definitely isn't a good idea ...'

'You want to hear what I've got?'

'Sell me the idea.'

'It clears everything up,' Rebus lied.

Claverhouse waited for more, but Rebus wasn't obliging. Theatrical sigh: life was hard on Claverhouse.

'I'll be there in half an hour,' Rebus said. He put down the phone, looked around the office. 'Anyone got a set of overalls?'

'Nice disguise,' Claverhouse said, as Rebus squeezed into the front seat.

Ormiston was in the driver's seat, plastic piece-box open in front of him. A flask of tea had been opened, steaming up the windscreen. The back of the van was full of paint-tins, brushes and other paraphernalia. A ladder was strapped to the roof, and another was leaning against the wall of the tenement beside which the van had been parked. Claverhouse and Ormiston were in white overalls, daubed with swatches of old paint. The best Rebus could come up with was a blue boiler-suit, tight at the waist and chest. He pulled the first few studs open as he settled in.

'Anything happening?'

'Jack's been in twice this morning.' Claverhouse looked towards the shop. 'Once for ciggies and a paper, once for a can of juice and a filled roll.'

'He doesn't smoke.'

'He does for this operation: perfect excuse to nip to the shop.'

'He hasn't given you any signal?'

'You expecting him to put the flags out?' Ormiston exhaled fish-paste.

'Just asking.' Rebus checked his watch. 'Either of you want a break?'

'We're fine,' Claverhouse said.

'What's Siobhan up to?'

'Paperwork,' Ormiston said with a smile. 'Ever come across a woman house painter?'

'Done much house painting yourself, Ormie?'

This brought a smile from Claverhouse. 'So, John,' he said, 'what is it you've got for us?'

Rebus filled them in quickly, noting Claverhouse's mounting interest.

'So Tarawicz is planning to double-cross Telford?' Ormiston said at the end.

Rebus shrugged. 'That's my guess.'

'Then why the hell are we bothering to set up a sting? Just let them get on with it.'

'That wouldn't give us Tarawicz,' Claverhouse said, his eyes slitted in concentration. 'If he sets up Telford for a fall, *he's* home and dry. Telford gets put away, and all we've done is replace one villain with another.'

'And an altogether nastier species at that,' Rebus said.

'What? And Telford's Robin Hood?'

'No, but at least with him, we know what we're dealing with.'

'And the old dears in his flats love him,' Claverhouse said.

Rebus thought of Mrs Hetherington, readying herself for her trip to Holland. The only drawback: she had to fly from Inverness . . . Sakiji Shoda had flown from London to Inverness . . .

Rebus started laughing.

'What's so funny?'

He shook his head, still laughing, wiping his eyes. It wasn't funny, not really.

'We could let Telford know what we know,' Claverhouse said, studying Rebus. 'Set him against Tarawicz, let them eat each other alive.'

Rebus nodded, took a deep breath. 'That's certainly one option.'

'Give me another.'

'Later,' Rebus said. He opened the door.

'Where are you off to?' Claverhouse asked.

'Got to fly.'

32

But in fact he was driving. A long drive, too. North through Perth and from there into the Highlands, taking a route which could be cut off during the worst of the winter. It wasn't a bad road, but traffic was heavy. He'd get past one slow-moving lorry only to catch up with another. He knew he should be thankful for small mercies: in the summer, caravans could end up fronting mile-long tailbacks.

He did pass a couple of caravans outside Pitlochry. They were from the Netherlands. Mrs Hetherington had said it was out of season for a trip to Holland. Most people her age would go in the spring, ready to fill their senses with the bulb-fields. But not Mrs Hetherington. Telford's offer: go when I say. Telford probably provided spending money, too. Told her to have a good time, not worry about a thing . . .

As he neared Inverness, Rebus hit dual carriageway again. He'd been on the road well over two hours. Sammy might be coming round again; Rhona had his mobile number. Inverness Airport was signposted from the road into town. Rebus parked and got out, stretched his legs and arched his back, feeling the vertebrae pop. He went into the terminal and asked for security. He got a small balding man with glasses and a limp. Rebus introduced himself. The man offered coffee, but Rebus was jumpy enough after the drive. Hungry though: no lunch. He gave the man his story, and eventually they tracked down a representative of Her Majesty's Customs. During his tour of the facilities, Rebus got the impression of a low-key operation. The Customs official was in her early thirties, rosy-cheeked and with black curly hair. There was a purple birthmark, the size of a small coin, in the middle of her forehead, looking for all the world like a third eye.

She took Rebus into the Customs area and found a room they could use for their conversation.

'They've just started direct international flights,' she said, in answer to his question. 'It's shocking really.'

'Why?'

'Because at the same time, they've cut back on manpower.'

'You mean in Customs?'

She nodded.

'You're worried about drugs?'

'Of course.' She paused. 'And everything else.'

'Are there flights to Amsterdam?'

'There will be.'

'But as of now . . . ?'

She shrugged. 'You can fly to London, make the connection there.'

Rebus was thoughtful. 'There was a guy a few days ago, flew from Japan to Heathrow, then got a flight to Inverness.'

'Did he stop off in London?'

Rebus shook his head. 'Caught the first connection.'

'That counts as an international connection.'

'Meaning?'

'His luggage would be put on the plane in Japan, and he wouldn't see it again until Inverness.'

'So you'd be the first Customs point?'

She nodded.

'And if his flight came in at some horrible hour . . .?'

She shrugged again. 'We do what we can, Inspector.'

Yes, Rebus could imagine: a lone, bleary-eyed Customs official, wits not at their sharpest . . .

'So the bags change planes at Heathrow, but no one checks them there?'

'That's about it.'

'And if you were flying from Holland to Inverness via London?'

'Same deal.'

Rebus knew now, knew the brilliance of Tommy Telford's thinking. *He* was supplying drugs for Tarawicz, and Christ knew how many others. His little old ladies and men were bringing them in past early-morning or late-night Customs posts. How difficult would it be to slip something into a piece of luggage? Then Telford's men would be on hand to take everyone back to Edinburgh, carry their luggage upstairs . . . and surreptitiously remove each package.

Old-age pensioners as unwitting drugs couriers. It was stunning.

And Shoda hadn't flown into Inverness so he could check out the local tourist amenities. He'd flown in so he could see how easy it was, what a brilliant route Telford had found, quick and efficient with a minimum of risk. Rebus had to laugh again. The Highlands had its own drugs problem these days: bored teenagers and cash-rich oil-workers. Rebus had smashed one north-east ring back in early summer, only to have Tommy Telford come along . . .

Cafferty would never have thought of it. Cafferty would never have been so daring. But Cafferty would have kept it quiet. He wouldn't have sought to expand, wouldn't have brought partners into the scheme.

Telford was still a kid in some respects. The passenger-seat teddy bear was proof of that.

Rebus thanked the Customs official and went in search of food. Parked in the middle of town and grabbed a burger, sat at a window table and thought it all through. There were still aspects that didn't make sense, but he could cope with that.

He made two calls: one to the hospital; one to Bobby Hogan. Sammy hadn't woken up again. Hogan was interviewing Pretty-Boy at seven o'clock. Rebus said he'd be there.

The weather was kind on the trip south, the traffic manageable. The Saab seemed to enjoy long drives, or maybe it was just that at seventy miles an hour the engine noise disguised all the rattles and bumps.

He drove straight to Leith cop-shop, looked at his watch and found he was quarter of an hour late. Which didn't matter, since they were just starting the interview. Pretty-Boy was there with Charles Groal, all-purpose solicitor. Hogan was sitting with another CID officer, DC James Preston. A tape recorder had been set up. Hogan looked nervous, realising how speculative this whole venture was, especially with a lawyer present. Rebus gave him a reassuring wink and apologised for having been detained. The burger had given him indigestion, and the coffee he'd had with it had done nothing for his frayed nerves. He had to shake his head clear of Inverness and all its implications and concentrate on Pretty-Boy and Joseph Lintz.

Pretty-Boy looked calm. He was wearing a charcoal suit with a yellow T-shirt, black suede winkle-picker boots. He smelt of expensive aftershave. In front of him on the desk: a pair of tortoiseshell Ray-Bans and his car keys. Rebus knew he'd own a Range Rover – it was mandatory for Telford employees – but the key-ring boasted the Porsche marque, and on the street outside Rebus had parked behind a cobalt blue 944. Pretty-Boy showing a touch of individuality . . .

Groal had his briefcase open on the floor beside him. On the desk in front of him: an A4 pad of ruled paper, and a fat black Mont Blanc pen.

Lawyer and client oozed money easily made and just as easily spent. Pretty-Boy used his money to buy class, but Rebus knew his background: working-class Paisley, a granite-hard introduction to life.

Hogan identified those present for the benefit of the tape recorder, then looked at his own notes.

'Mr Summers . . .' Pretty-Boy's real name: Brian Summers. 'Do you know why you're here?'

Pretty-Boy made an O of his glossy lips and stared ceilingwards.

'Mr Summers,' Charles Groal began, 'has informed me that he is willing to co-operate, Inspector Hogan, but that he'd like some indication of the accusations against him and their validity.'

Hogan stared at Groal, didn't blink. 'Who said he's accused of anything?'

'Inspector, Mr Summers works for Thomas Telford, and your police force's harassment of that individual is on record . . .'

'Nothing to do with me, Mr Groal, or this station.' Hogan paused. 'Nothing at all to do with my present inquiries.'

Groal blinked half a dozen times in quick succession. He looked at Pretty-Boy, who was now studying the tips of his boots.

'You want me to say something?' Pretty-Boy asked the lawyer.

'I'm just . . . I'm not sure if . . .'

Pretty-Boy cut him off with a wave of his hand, then looked at Hogan. 'Ask away.'

Hogan made show of studying his notes again. 'Do you know why you're here, Mr Summers?'

'General vilification as part of your witch-hunt against my employer.' He smiled at the three CID men. 'Bet you didn't think I'd know a word like "vilification".' His gaze rested on Rebus, then he turned to Groal.

'DI Rebus isn't based at this station.'

Groal took the hint. 'That's true, Inspector. Might I ask by what authority you've been allowed to sit in on this interview?'

'That will become clear,' Hogan said, '*if* you'll allow us to begin?'

Groal cleared his throat, but said nothing. Hogan let the silence lie for a few moments, then began.

'Mr Summers, do you know a man called Joseph Lintz?'

'No.'

The silence stretched out. Summers recrossed his feet. He looked up at Hogan, and blinked, the blink deteriorating into a momentary twitch of one eye. He sniffed, rubbed at his nose – trying to make out that the twitch meant nothing.

'You've never met him?'

'No.'

'The name means nothing to you?'

'You've asked me about him before. I'll tell you same as I told you then: I never knew the cat.' Summers sat up a bit straighter in his chair.

'You've never spoken to him by telephone?'

Summers looked at Groal.

'Hasn't my client made himself clear, Inspector?'

'I'd like an answer.'

'I don't know him,' Summers said, forcing himself to relax again, 'I've never spoken to him.' He gave Hogan his stare again, and this time held it. There was nothing behind the eyes but naked self-interest. Rebus wondered how anyone could ever think him 'pretty', when his whole outlook on life was so fundamentally ugly.

'He didn't phone you at your . . . business premises?'

'I don't have any business premises.'

'The office you share with your employer.'

Pretty-Boy smiled. He liked those phrases: 'business premises'; 'your employer'. They all knew the truth, yet played this little game . . . and he liked playing games.

'I've already said, I never spoke to him.'

'Funny, the phone company says differently.'

'Maybe they made a mistake.'

'I doubt that, Mr Summers.'

'Look, we've been through this before.' Summers sat forward in his chair. 'Maybe it was a wrong number. Maybe he spoke to one of my associates, and they *told* him he had a wrong number.' He opened his arms. 'This is going nowhere.'

'I agree with my client, Inspector,' Charles Groal said, scribbling something down. 'I mean, is this leading anywhere?'

'It's leading, Mr Groal, to an identification of Mr Summers.'

'Where and by whom?'

'In a restaurant with Mr Lintz. The same Mr Lintz he claims never to have met, never to have spoken to.'

Rebus saw hesitation cross Pretty-Boy's face. *Hesitation*, rather than surprise. He made no immediate denial.

'An identification made by a member of staff at the restaurant,' Hogan continued. 'Corroborated by another diner.'

Groal looked to his client, who wasn't saying anything, but the way he was staring at the table, Rebus wondered a smoking hole didn't start appearing in it.

'Well,' Groal went on, 'this is fairly irregular, Inspector.'

Hogan wasn't interested in the lawyer. It was Pretty-Boy and him now.

'What about it, Mr Summers? Care to revise your version of events? What were you talking about with Mr Lintz? Was he looking for female company? I believe that's your particular area of expertise.'

'Inspector, I must insist . . .'

'Insist away, Mr Groal. It won't change the facts. I'm just wondering what Mr Summers will say in court when he's asked about the phone call, the meeting . . . when the witnesses identify him. I'm sure he's got a fund of stories, but he'll have to find a bloody good one.'

Summers slapped the desk with both palms, half-rose to his feet. There wasn't an ounce of fat on him. Veins stood out on the backs of his hands.

'I told you, I've never met him, never talked to him. Period, end of story, finito. And if you've got witnesses, they're lying. Maybe *you've* told them to lie. And that's all I've got to say.' He sat back down, put his hands in his pockets.

'I've heard,' Rebus said, as though attempting to liven up a flagging conversation between friends, 'that you run the more upmarket girls, the three-figure jobs rather than the gam-and-bam merchants.'

Summers snorted and shook his head.

'Inspector,' Groal said, 'I can't allow these accusations to continue.'

'Was that what Lintz wanted? Did he have expensive tastes?'

Summers continued shaking his head. He seemed about to say something, but caught himself, laughed instead.

'I would like to remind you,' Groal went on, unheeded by anyone, 'that my client has co-operated fully throughout this outrageous . . .'

Rebus caught Pretty-Boy's eyes, held their stare. There was so much he wasn't telling . . . so much he very nearly *wanted* to tell. Rebus thought of the length of rope in Lintz's house.

'He liked to tie them up, didn't he?' Rebus asked quietly.

Groal stood up, yanking Summers to his feet.

'Brian?' Rebus asked.

'Thank you, gentlemen,' Groal said. He was stuffing his notepad into his case, closing its brass locks. 'If you should find yourselves with any questions worth my client's time, we'll be pleased to assist. But otherwise, I'd advise you to . . .'

'Brian?'

DC Preston had turned off the tape recorder and gone to open the door. Summers picked up his car keys, slipped his sunglasses on.

'Gentlemen,' he said, 'it's been educational.'

'S&M,' Rebus persisted, getting in Pretty-Boy's face. 'Did he tie them up?'

Pretty-Boy snorted, shook his head again. He paused as his lawyer led him past Rebus.

'It was for *him*,' he said in an undertone.

It was for him.

Rebus drove to the hospital. Sat with Sammy for twenty minutes. Twenty minutes of meditation and head-clearing. Twenty reviving minutes, at the end of which he squeezed his daughter's hand.

'Thanks for that,' he said.

Back at the flat, he thought of ignoring the answering machine until after he'd had a bath. His shoulders and back were aching from the drive to Inverness. But something made him press the button. Jack Morton's voice: 'I'm on for a meeting with TT. Let's meet after. Half-ten at the Ox. I'll aim for that, but can't promise. Wish me luck.'

He walked in at eleven.

There was folk music in the back room. The front would have been quiet if it weren't for two loud-mouths who looked like they'd been at it since their office closed for the night. They still wore work-suits, newspapers rolled in their pockets. They were drinking G&T.

Rebus asked Jack Morton what he wanted.

'A pint of orange and lemonade.'

'So how did it go?' Rebus ordered the drink. In forty minutes, he'd managed to put away two Cokes, and was now on coffee.

'They seem keen.'

'So who was at the meeting?'

'My sponsors from the shop, plus Telford and a couple of his men.'

'The transmitter worked OK?'

'Sound as a pound.'

'Did they search you?'

Morton shook his head. 'They were sloppy, seemed really sweaty about something. Want to hear the plan?' Rebus nodded. 'Middle of the night, truck arrives at the factory, and I let it through the gates. My story is, I had a phone call from the boss OKing the delivery. So I wasn't suspicious.'

'Only your boss never made the call?'

'That's right. So I was duped by a voice. And that's all I need to tell the police.'

'We'd sweat the truth out of you.'

'Like I say, John, the whole plan's half-baked. I'll give them this though – they did check my background. Seemed satisfied.'

'Who's going to be in the truck?'

'Ten men, armed to the teeth. I'm to get a rough plan of the place to Telford tomorrow, let him know how many people will be around, what the alarm system's like . . .'

'What's in it for you?'

'Five grand. He's judged that right: five gets my debts repaid and puts a wedge in my pocket.'

Five grand: the amount Joseph Lintz had taken out of his bank . . .

'Your story's holding?'

'They've staked out my flat.'

'And they didn't follow you here?'

Morton shook his head, and Rebus filled him in on what he'd learned and what he suspected. While Morton was taking it in, Rebus threw a question at him.

'How does Claverhouse want to play it?'

'The tape evidence is good: Telford talking, me making sure I called him "Mr Telford" and "Tommy" a few times. It's obviously him on the recording. But . . . Claverhouse wants Telford's crew caught red-handed.'

' "Got to do it right".'
'That seems to be his catch-phrase.'
'Is there a date?'
'Saturday, all being well.'
'What's the betting we get a tip-off on Friday?'
'If your theory's right.'
'If I'm right,' he agreed.

33

The tip-off didn't come until Saturday lunchtime, but when it did, Rebus knew his hunch had been right.

Claverhouse was the first to congratulate him, which surprised Rebus, because Claverhouse had a lot on his plate and had acted very casually when the call had come. Pinned to the walls of the Crime Squad office were detailed maps of the drugs plant, along with staff rosters. Coloured stickers showed where personnel would be stationed. During the night, it was security only, unless some big order was demanding overtime. Tonight, the usual security staff would be augmented by Lothian & Borders Police. Twenty people inside the plant, with marksmen stationed on roofs and at certain key windows. A dozen cars and vans as back-up. It was the biggest operation of Claverhouse's career; a lot was expected of him. He kept saying 'it has to be done right'. He said he would leave 'nothing to chance'. Those two phrases had become his mantra.

Rebus had listened to a recording of the snitch call: 'Be at Maclean's factory in Slateford tonight. Two in the morning, it's going to be turned over. Ten men, tooled up, driving a lorry. If you're canny, you can catch all of them.'

Scots accent, but sounding long distance. Rebus smiled, looked at the turning spools, and said 'Hello again, Crab' out loud.

No mention of Telford, which was interesting. Telford's men were loyal: they'd go down without saying a word. And Tarawicz wasn't grassing up Telford. He couldn't know the police already had taped evidence of Telford's involvement. Which meant he was planning on letting Telford go . . . No, think it through. With the plan dead in the water and ten of his best men in custody, Tarawicz didn't *need* Telford under lock and key. He wanted him out in the open and worried, Yakuza breathing down his neck, all his frailties exposed. He could be picked off at any time, or made to hand over *everything*. No blood-letting required; it would be a simple business proposition.

'It has to be . . .'

'Done right,' Rebus said. 'Claverhouse, we *know*, OK?'

Claverhouse lost it. 'You're only here because I tolerate you! So let's get that straight for a start. I snap my fingers and you're out of the game, understood?'

Rebus just stared at him. A line of sweat was running down Claverhouse's left temple. Ormiston was looking up from his desk. Siobhan Clarke, briefing another officer beside a wall-chart, stopped talking.

'I promise I'll be a good boy,' Rebus said quietly, 'if you'll promise to stop with the broken record routine.'

Claverhouse's jaw was working, but eventually he produced a near-smile of apology.

'Let's get on with it then.'

Not that there was much for them to do. Jack Morton was working a double shift, wouldn't start till three o'clock. They'd be watching the place from then on, just in case Telford changed the game-plan. This meant personnel were going to miss the big match: Hibs against Hearts at Easter Road. Rebus had his money on a 3–2 home win.

Ormiston's summing-up: 'Easiest quid you'll ever lose.'

Rebus retired to one of the computers and got back to work. Siobhan Clarke had already come round snooping.

'Writing it up for one of the tabloids?'

'No such luck.'

He tried to keep it simple, and when he was happy with the finished product he printed off two copies. Then he went out to buy a couple of nice, bright folders . . .

He dropped off one of the folders, then returned home, too restless to be much use at Fettes. Three men were waiting in his tenement stairwell. Two more came in behind him, blocking the only escape route. Rebus recognised Jake Tarawicz and one of his muscle-men from the scrapyard. The others were new to him.

'Up the stairs,' Tarawicz ordered. Rebus was a prisoner under escort as they climbed the steps.

'Unlock the door.'

'If I'd known you were coming, I'd have got in some beers,' Rebus said, searching his pockets for keys. He was wondering which was safer: let them in, or keep them out? Tarawicz made the decision for him, nodded some signal. Rebus's arms were grabbed, hands went into his jacket and trousers, found his keys. He kept his face blank, eyes on Tarawicz.

'Big mistake,' he said.

'In,' Tarawicz ordered. They pushed Rebus into the hallway, walked him to the living room.

'Sit.'

Hands pushed Rebus on to the sofa.

'At least let me make a pot of tea,' he said. Inside he was trembling, knowing everything he couldn't afford to give away.

'Nice place,' Mr Pink Eyes was saying. 'Lacks the feminine touch though.' He turned to Rebus. 'Where is she?' Two of the men had peeled off to search the place.

'Who?'

'I mean, who else would she turn to? Not your daughter . . . not now she's in a coma.'

Rebus stared at him. 'What do you know about that?' The two men returned, shook their heads.

'I hear things.' Tarawicz pulled out a dining-chair and sat down. There were two men behind the sofa, two in front.

'Make yourselves at home, lads. Where's the Crab, Jake?' Reasoning: a question he might be expected to ask.

'Down south. What's it to you?'

Rebus shrugged.

'Shame about your daughter. Going to make a recovery, is she?' Rebus didn't answer. Tarawicz smiled. 'National Health Service ... I wouldn't trust it myself.' He paused. 'Where is she, Rebus?'

'Using my finely honed detective's skills, I'll assume you mean Candice.' Meaning she'd done a runner. Trusting to herself for once. Rebus was proud of her.

Tarawicz snapped his fingers. Arms grabbed Rebus from behind, pinning back his shoulders. One man stepped forward and punched him solidly on the jaw. Stepped back again. Second man forward: gut punches. A hand tugged his hair, forcing his eyes up to the ceiling. He didn't see the flat-handed chop aiming for his throat. When it came, he thought he was going to cough out his voice-box. They let him go, and he pitched forward, hands going to his throat, retching for breath. A couple of teeth felt loose, and the skin inside his cheek had burst. He got out a handkerchief, spat blood.

'Unfortunately,' Tarawicz was saying, 'I have no sense of humour. So I hope you'll understand I'm not joking when I say that I'll kill you if I have to.'

Rebus shook his head free of all the secrets he knew, all the power he held over Tarawicz. He told himself: *you don't know anything*.

He told himself: *you're not going to die*.

'Even ... if ... I did know ...' Fighting for breath. 'I wouldn't tell you. If the two of us were standing in a minefield, I wouldn't let you know. Want me ... to tell you why?'

'Sticks and stones, Rebus.'

'It's not because of *who* you are, it's *what* you are. You trade in human beings.' Rebus dabbed at his mouth. 'You're no better than the Nazis.'

Tarawicz put a hand to his chest. 'I'm struck to the quick.'

'Chance would be a fine thing.' Rebus coughed again. 'Tell me, why do you want her back?' Rebus knowing the answer: because he was about to head south, leaving Telford in Shit Street. Because to return to Newcastle without her was a small but palpable defeat. Tarawicz wanted it *all*. He wanted every last crumb on the plate.

'My business,' Tarawicz said. Another signal, and the hands grabbed him again, Rebus resisting this time. Packing-tape was being wound around his mouth.

'Everybody tells me how *genteel* Edinburgh is,' Tarawicz was saying. 'Can't have the neighbours complaining about the screams. Put him on a chair.'

Rebus was lifted up. He struggled. A kidney punch buckled his knees. They forced him down on to a dining-chair. Tarawicz was removing his jacket, undoing gold cufflinks so he could roll up the sleeves of his pink and blue striped shirt. His arms were hairless, thick, and the same mottled colour as his face.

'A skin complaint,' he explained, removing his blue-tinted glasses. 'Some distant cousin of leprosy, they tell me.' He loosened his top button. 'I'm not as pretty as Tommy Telford, but I think you'll find me his master in every other respect.' A smile to his troops, a smile Rebus wasn't supposed to understand. 'We can start anywhere you want, Rebus. And *you* get to

choose when we stop. Just nod your head, tell me where she is, and I walk out of your life for ever.'

He got in close to Rebus, the sheen on his face like a protective seal. His pale blue eyes had tiny black pupils. Rebus thought: consumer as well as pusher. Tarawicz waited for a nod which didn't come, then retreated. Found an anglepoise lamp next to Rebus's chair. Planted both feet on its base and yanked on the mains cable, ripping it free.

'Bring him over here,' he ordered. Two men pulled both Rebus and chair over towards where Tarawicz was checking that the cable was plugged into the wall and that the socket was switched on. Another man closed the curtains: no free show for the kids across the way. Tarawicz was dangling the cable, letting Rebus see the loose wires – the very *live* wires. Two hundred and forty volts just waiting to make his acquaintance.

'Believe me,' Tarawicz said, 'this is nothing. The Serbs had torture down to a fine art. Much of the time, they weren't even looking for a confession. I've helped a few of the more intelligent ones, the ones who knew when it was time to run. There was money to be made in the early days, power for the taking. Now the politicians are moving in, bringing trial-judges with them.' He looked at Rebus. 'The intelligent ones always know when it's time to quit. One last chance, Rebus. Remember, a nod of the head . . .' The wires were inches from his cheek. Tarawicz changed his mind, moved them towards his nostrils, then his eyeballs.

'A nod of the head . . .'

Rebus was twisting, arms holding him down – his legs, arms, shoulders. Hands holding his head, chest. Wait! The shock would pass straight through Tarawicz's men! Rebus saw it for a bluff. His eyes met Tarawicz's, and they both knew. Tarawicz pulled back.

'Tape him to the chair.' Two-inch-wide runs of tape, fixing him in place.

'This time for real, Rebus.' To his men: 'Hold him till I get close. Pull away when I say.'

Rebus thinking: there'd be a split-second after they let go . . . A moment in which to break free. The tape wasn't the strongest he'd seen, but there was plenty of it. Maybe too much. He flexed his chest against it, felt no sign that it would break.

'Here we go,' Tarawicz said. 'First the face . . . then the genitals. You *will* tell me, we both know it. How much bravado you want to show is up to you, but don't think it means anything.'

Rebus said something behind the gag.

'No point talking,' Tarawicz said. 'The only thing I want from you is a nod, understood?'

Rebus nodded.

'Was that a nod?'

Forcing a smile, Rebus shook his head.

Tarawicz didn't look impressed. His mind was on business. That was all Rebus was to him. He aimed the wire at Rebus's cheek.

'Let go!'

The pressure on Rebus fell away. He pushed against his bonds, couldn't budge them. Electricity flashed through his nervous system, and he went rigid. His heart felt like it had doubled in size, his eyeballs bulged, tongue pushing against the gag. Tarawicz lifted the cable away.

'Hold him.'

Arms fell on Rebus again, finding less resistance than before.

'Doesn't even leave a mark,' Tarawicz said. 'And the real beauty is, you end up paying for it from your own electric bill.'

His men laughed. They were beginning to enjoy themselves.

Tarawicz crouched down, face to face. His eyes sought Rebus's.

'For your information, that was a five-second jolt. Things only start to get interesting at the half-minute mark. How's your heart? For your sake, I hope it's in good condition.'

Rebus felt like he'd just mainlined adrenalin. Five seconds: it had seemed much longer. He was changing strategies, trying to think up some new lies Mr Pink might believe, anything to get him out of the flat . . .

'Undo his trousers,' Tarawicz was saying. 'Let's see what a jolt down there will do.'

Behind the gag, Rebus started screaming. His tormentor was looking around the room again.

'Definitely lacks the feminine touch.'

Hands were loosening his trouser-belt. They stopped when a buzzer sounded. There was someone at the main door.

'Just wait,' Tarawicz said quietly. 'They'll go away.'

The buzzer sounded again. Rebus wrestled with his bonds. Silence. Then the buzzer again, more insistent now. One of the men went for the window.

'Don't!' Tarawicz snapped.

Buzzer again. Rebus hoped it would go on for ever. Couldn't think who it might be: Rhona? Patience? A sudden thought . . . what if they persisted, and Tarawicz decided to allow them inside? Rhona or Patience . . .

Time stretched. No more buzzing. They'd gone away. Tarawicz was beginning to relax, focusing his mind on his work once more.

Then there was a knock at the flat door. The person had got into the tenement. Now they were on the landing outside. Knocking again. Lifting the flap of the letterbox.

'Rebus!'

A male voice. Tarawicz looked to his men, nodded another signal. Curtains were opened; Rebus's bonds cut; the tape ripped from his face. Tarawicz rolled down his sleeves, put his jacket back on. Left the flex lying on the floor. One last word to Rebus: 'We'll speak again.' Then he marched his men to the door, opened it.

'Excuse us.'

Rebus was left sitting on the chair. He couldn't move, felt too shaky to stand up.

'Hang on a minute, chief!'

Rebus placed the voice: Abernethy. It didn't sound as if Tarawicz was heeding the Special Branch man.

'What's the score?' Now Abernethy was in the living room, looking around.

'Business meeting,' Rebus croaked.

Abernethy came forward. 'Funny old business where you have to unzip your flies.'

Rebus looked down, started to make repairs.

'Who was that?' Abernethy persisted.

'A Chechen from Newcastle.'

'Likes to travel mob-handed, does he?' Abernethy walked around the room, found the bare flex and tut-tutted, unplugged it at the socket. 'Fun and games,' he said.

'Don't worry,' Rebus told him, 'it's under control.'

Abernethy laughed.

'What do you want anyway?'

'Brought someone to see you.' He nodded towards the doorway. A distinguished-looking man was standing there, dressed in three-quarter-length black woollen coat and white silk scarf. He was completely bald, with a huge dome of a head and cheeks reddened from cold. He had a sniffle, and was wiping his nose with a handkerchief.

'Thought we might pop out somewhere,' the man said, locution impeccable, his eyes everywhere but on Rebus. 'Get a spot to eat, if you're hungry.'

'I'm not,' Rebus said.

'Something to drink then.'

'There's whisky in the kitchen.'

The man looked reluctant.

'Look, pal,' Rebus told him, 'I'm staying right here. You can join me or you can bugger off.'

'I see,' the man said. He put the handkerchief away and stepped forward, stretched out a hand. 'Name's Harris, by the way.'

Rebus took the hand, expecting sparks to leap from his fingertips.

'Mr Harris, let's sit at the dining-table.' Rebus got to his feet. He was shaky, but his knees held till he'd crossed the floor. Abernethy appeared from the kitchen with the bottle and three glasses. Left again, and returned with a milk-jug of water.

Ever the host, Rebus poured, sizing up the trembling in his right arm. He felt disoriented. Adrenalin and electricity coursing through him.

'*Slainte*,' he said, lifting the glass. But he paused with it at his nostrils. Pact with the Big Man: no drinking, and Sammy back. His throat hurt when he swallowed, but he put the glass down untouched. Harris was pouring too much water into his own glass. Even Abernethy looked disapproving.

'So, Mr Harris,' Rebus said, rubbing his throat, 'just who the hell are you?'

Harris affected a smile. He was playing with his glass.

'I'm a member of the intelligence community, Inspector. I know what that probably conjures up in your mind, but I'm afraid the reality is far more prosaic. Intelligence-gathering means just that: lots of paperwork and filing.'

'And you're here because of Joseph Lintz?'

'I'm here because DI Abernethy says you're determined to link the murder of Joseph Lintz with the various accusations which have been made against him.'

'And?'

'And that, of course, is your prerogative. But there are matters not necessarily germane which might prove . . . embarrassing, if brought into the open.'

'Such as that Lintz really was Linzstek, and was brought to this country by the Rat Line, probably with help from the Vatican?'

'As to whether Lintz and Linzstek were the same man . . . I can't tell you. A lot of the documentation was destroyed just after the war.'

'But "Joseph Lintz" was brought to this country by the Allies?'

'Yes.'

'And why did we do that?'

'Lintz was useful to this country, Inspector.'

Rebus poured a fresh whisky for Abernethy. Harris hadn't touched his. 'How useful?'

'He was a reputable academic. As such he was invited to attend conferences and give guest lectures all round the world. During this time, he did some work for us. Translation, intelligence-gathering, recruitment . . .'

'He recruited people in other countries?' Rebus stared at Harris. 'He was a *spy*?'

'He did some dangerous and . . . influential work for this country.'

'And got his reward: the house in Heriot Row?'

'He earned every penny in the early days.'

Harris's tone told Rebus something. 'What happened?'

'He became . . . unreliable.' Harris lifted the glass to his nose, sniffed it, but put it down again untouched.

'Drink it before it evaporates,' Abernethy chided. Harris looked at him, and the Londoner mumbled an apology.

'Define "unreliable",' Rebus said, pushing aside his own glass.

'He began to . . . fantasise.'

'He thought a colleague at the university had been in the Rat Line?'

Harris was nodding. 'He became obsessed with the Rat Line, began to imagine that everyone around him had been involved in it, that we were *all* culpable. Paranoia, Inspector. It affected his work and eventually we had to let him go. This was years back. He hasn't worked for us since.'

'So why the interest? What does it matter if any of this comes out?'

Harris sighed. 'You're right, of course. The problem is not the Rat Line *per se*, or the notion of Vatican involvement or any of the other conspiracy theories.'

'Then what is . . .?' Rebus broke off, realised the truth. 'The problem is the personnel,' he stated. 'The other people brought in by the Rat Line.' He nodded to himself. 'Who are we talking about? Who might be implicated?'

'Senior figures,' Harris admitted. He'd stopped playing with the glass. His hands were flat on the table. He was telling Rebus: this is *serious*.

'Past or present?'

'Past . . . plus people whose children have gone on to achieve positions of power.'

'MPs? Government ministers? Judges?'

Harris was shaking his head. 'I can't tell you, Inspector. I haven't been trusted with that knowledge myself.'

'But you could hazard a guess.'

'I don't deal in guesswork.' He looked at Rebus. There was steel behind the eyes. 'I deal in known quantities. It's a good maxim – one you should try.'

'But whoever killed Lintz did so *because* of his past.'

'Are you sure?'

'It doesn't make sense otherwise.'

'DI Abernethy tells me there's a link with some criminal elements in Edinburgh, perhaps a question of prostitution. It all sounds sordid enough to be believable.'

'And if it's believable, that's good enough for you?'

Harris stood up. 'Thank you for listening.' He blew his nose again, looked to Abernethy. 'Time to go, I believe. DI Hogan is waiting for us.'

'Harris,' Rebus said, 'you said yourself, Lintz had gone loopy, become a liability. Who's to say *you* didn't have him killed?'

Harris shrugged. 'If we'd arranged it, his demise would not have been quite so obvious.'

'Car crash, suicide, falling from a window . . .?'

'Goodbye, Inspector.'

As Harris walked to the door, Abernethy stood up and locked eyes with Rebus. He didn't say anything, but the message was there.

This is deeper water than either of us wants to be in. So do yourself a favour, swim for shore.

Rebus nodded, reached out a hand. The two men shook.

34

Two in the morning.

Frost on the car windscreens. They couldn't clear them: had to blend in with the other cars on the street. Back-up – four units – parked in a builder's yard just round the corner. Bulbs had been removed from street lights, leaving the area in almost total darkness. Maclean's was like a Christmas tree: security lights, every window blazing, same as every other night.

No heating in the unmarked cars: heat would melt the frost; exhaust fumes a dead giveaway.

'This all seems very familiar,' Siobhan Clarke said. The surveillance on Flint Street seemed a lifetime ago to Rebus. Clarke was in the driving seat, Rebus in the back. Two to each car. That way, they had space to duck should anyone come snooping. Not that they expected anyone to do that: the whole heist was half-baked. Telford desperate *and* with his mind on other things. Sakiji Shoda was still in town – a quiet word with the hotel manager had revealed a Monday morning check-out. Rebus was betting Tarawicz and his men had already gone.

'You look pretty snug,' Rebus said, referring to her padded ski-jacket. She brought a hand out of her pocket, showed him what it was holding. It looked like a slim lighter. Rebus lifted it from her palm. It was warm.

'What the hell is it?'

Clarke smiled. 'I got it from one of those catalogues. It's a handwarmer.'

'How does it work?'

'Fuel rods. Each one lasts up to twelve hours.'

'So you've got one warm hand?'

She brought her other hand out, showed him an identical rod. 'I bought two,' she said.

'You might have said.' Rebus closed his fingers around the handwarmer, stuck it deep into his pocket.

'That's not fair.'

'Call it a privilege of rank.'

'Lights,' she warned. They dived for cover, surfaced again when the car had sped past: false alarm.

Rebus checked his watch. Jack Morton had been told to expect the truck some time between one-thirty and two-fifteen. Rebus and Clarke had been in the car since just after midnight. The snipers on the roof, poor bastards, had been in position since one o'clock. Rebus hoped they had a good supply

of fuel rods. He still felt jittery from the afternoon's events. He didn't like that he owed Abernethy such a huge favour; indeed, maybe owed him his life. He knew he could cancel it out by agreeing – along with Hogan – to soft-pedal on the Lintz inquiry. He didn't like the idea, but all the same . . . And the day's silver lining: Candice had made the break from Tarawicz.

Clarke's police radio was silent. They had maintained silence since before midnight. Claverhouse's words: 'The first person to speak will be me, understood? Anyone uses a radio before me, they're in farmyard shit. And I won't utter a sound until the truck's entered the compound. Is that clear?' Nods all around. 'They could be listening in, so this is *important*. We've got to do this *right*.' Averting his eyes from Rebus as he said it. 'I'd wish us all luck, but the less luck's involved the better I'll like it. A few hours from now, if we stick to the plan, we should have broken up Tommy Telford's gang.' He paused. 'Just let that sink in. We'll be heroes.' He swallowed, realising the immensity of the prize.

Rebus couldn't get so excited. The whole enterprise had shown him a simple truth: no vacuum. Where you had society, you had criminals. No belly without an underbelly.

Rebus knew his own criteria came cheaply: his flat, books, music and clapped-out car. And he realised that he had reduced his life to a mere shell in recognition that he had completely failed at the important things: love, relationships, family life. He'd been accused of being in thrall to his career, but that had never been the case. His work sustained him only because it was an easy option. He dealt every day with strangers, with people who didn't mean anything to him in the wider scheme. He could enter their lives, and leave again just as easily. He got to live other people's lives, or at least portions of them, experiencing things at one remove, which wasn't nearly as challenging as the real thing.

Sammy had brought home to him these essential truths: that he was not only a failed father but a failed human being; that police work kept him sane, yet was a substitute for the life he could have had, the kind of life everyone else seemed to lead. And if he became obsessed with his case-work, well, that was no different from being obsessed with train numbers or cigarette cards or rock albums. Obsession came easy – especially to men – because it was a cheap way of achieving *control*, albeit control over something practically worthless. What did it matter if you could reel off the track listing to every '60s Stones album? It didn't matter a damn. What did it matter if Tommy Telford got put away? Tarawicz would take his place, and if he didn't, there was always Big Ger Cafferty. And if not Cafferty, then someone else. The disease was endemic, no cure in sight.

'What are you thinking about?' Clarke asked, switching her rod from left hand to right.

'My next cigarette.' Patience's words: *happiest when in denial* . . .

They heard the truck before they saw it: changing gears noisily. Slid down into their seats, then up again as it made to pull into Maclean's. A wheeze of air-brakes as it jolted to a stop at the gates. A guard came out to talk to the driver. He carried a clip-board.

'Jack really suits a uniform,' Rebus said.

'Clothes maketh the man.'

'You reckon your boss has got it right?' He meant Claverhouse's plan:

when the truck was in the compound, they'd use a megaphone and show the marksmen to whoever was in the driver's cab, tell them to come out. The rest of the men could stay locked in the back of the vehicle. They'd have them toss out any arms and then come out one at a time.

It was either that or wait until they were *all* out of the truck. Merit of this second plan: they'd know what they were dealing with. Merit of the first: most of the gang would be nicely stowed in the truck, and could be dealt with as and when.

Claverhouse had plumped for plan one.

Marked and unmarked cars were to move in as soon as the truck had come to a stop – engine off – in the compound. They would block the exit, then watch from safety while Claverhouse, at a first-floor window with his megaphone, and the marksmen (roof; ground-floor windows) did their stuff. 'Negotiation with force' was how Claverhouse had described it.

'Jack's opening the gates,' Rebus said, peering through the side window.

Engine roar, and the truck jerked forward.

'Driver seems a bit nervous,' Clarke commented.

'Or isn't used to HGVs.'

'OK, they're in.'

Rebus stared at the radio, willing it to burst into life. Clarke had turned the ignition one click away from starting. Jack Morton was watching the truck move into the compound. He turned his head towards the line of cars parked across the way.

'Any second . . .'

The truck's brake lights came on, then went off again. Air-brakes sounded.

The radio fizzed a single word: *'Now!'*

Clarke turned the engine, revved hard. Five other cars did the same. Exhaust smoke billowed suddenly into the night air. The noise was like the start of a stock-car race. Rebus wound his window down, the better to hear Claverhouse's megaphone diplomacy. Clarke's car leaped forward, first to the gates. Both she and Rebus jumped out, keeping their heads down, the car a shield between themselves and the truck.

'Engine's still running,' Rebus hissed.

'What?'

'The truck. Its engine's still running!'

Claverhouse's voice, warbling – partly nerves, partly megaphone quality: 'Armed police. Open the cab doors slowly and come out one at a time, hands held high. I repeat: armed police. Discard weapons before coming out. I repeat: discard weapons.'

'Do it!' Rebus hissed. Then: 'Tell them to switch off the bloody engine!'

Claverhouse: 'The gate is blocked, there's no escape, and we don't want anyone getting hurt.'

'Tell them to throw out the keys.' Cursing, Rebus dived back into the car, grabbed the handset. 'Claverhouse, tell them to ditch the bloody keys!'

Windscreen frosted over; he couldn't see a thing. Heard Clarke's yell: *'Get out!'*

Saw: dim white lights. The truck was reversing. At speed. A roar from its engine, veering crazily but heading for the gates.

Heading straight for him.

An explosion: bricks flying from the factory's front wall.

Rebus dropped the handset, got his arm stuck in the seatbelt. Clarke was screaming as he leaped clear.

A second later, truck and car connected in a rending of metal and smashing of glass. Domino effect: Clarke's car hit the one behind, throwing officers off balance. The road was like a skating rink, the truck pushing one car, two cars, then three cars back on to the highway.

Claverhouse was on the megaphone, choking on dust: 'No shooting! Officers too close! Officers too close!'

Yes, all they needed now was to be pinned down by sniper fire. Men and women were slipping, losing their footing, clambering from their cars. Some of them armed, but dazed. The truck's back doors, buckled by the initial collision, flew open, seven or eight men hit the ground running. Two of them had handguns, and loosed off three or four shots apiece.

Shouts, screams, the megaphone. The glass wall of the gatehouse exploded as a bullet hit it. Rebus couldn't see Jack Morton . . . couldn't see Siobhan. He was lying on his front on a section of grass verge, hands over his head: classic defence/defeat posture and bloody useless with it. The whole area was picked out by floodlights, and one of the gunmen – Declan from the shop – was now aiming at those. Other members of the gang had headed out into the street and were running for it. They carried shotguns, pickaxe handles. Rebus recognised a few more faces: Ally Cornwell, Deek McGrain. The street lights were dead, of course, giving them all the cover they could want. Rebus hoped the back-up cars from the builder's yard were coming.

Yes: turning the corner now, all lights blazing, sirens howling. Tenement curtains were twitching, palms rubbing at windows. And right in front of Rebus, about an inch from his nose, a thickly rimed blade of grass. He could make out each sliver of frost, and the complex patterns which had formed. But he realised it was melting fast as his breath hit it. And his front was growing cold. And the marksmen were running from the building, lit up like a firing-range.

And Siobhan Clarke was safe: he could see her lying beneath a car. Good girl.

And one policewoman, also lying low, had been wounded in the knee. She kept touching it with her hand, then pulling the hand away to stare at the blood.

And there was still no sign of Jack Morton.

The gunmen were returning fire, scattering shots, smashing windscreens. Uniforms were ordered out of the front back-up car. Four of the gang got in.

Second car: uniforms out, three of the gang got in. No windscreens, but they were rolling. Yelling and whooping, waving their weapons. The two remaining gunmen were cool. They were taking a good look round, assessing the situation. Did they want to be here when the marksmen arrived? Maybe they did. Maybe they fancied their chances in that arena, too. Their luck had held *this* far, after all. Claverhouse: *the less luck's involved, the better I'll like it.*

Rebus got on to his knees, then his feet, staying at a crouch. He felt moderately safe. After all, *his* luck had held today, too.

'You OK, Siobhan?' Voice low, eyes on the gunmen. The two getaway cars added up to seven men. Two still left. Where was number ten?

'Fine,' Clarke said. 'What about you?'

'I'm OK.' Rebus left her, worked his way round to the front of the truck. The driver was unconscious behind his wheel, head bleeding where it had connected after the collision. There was some kind of grenade launcher on the seat beside him. It had left a bloody great hole in the wall of Maclean's. Rebus checked the driver for firearms, found none. Then checked the pulse: steady. Recognised the face: one of the arcade regulars; looked about nineteen, twenty. Rebus took out his handcuffs, hooked the driver to the steering-wheel, threw the grenade launcher on to the road.

Then headed for the gatehouse. Jack Morton, in uniform but missing his cap, prone on the floor, covered by a glass shroud. The bullet had pierced his right breast-pocket. Pulse was weak.

'Christ, Jack . . .'

There was a telephone in the booth. Rebus punched 999 and asked for ambulances.

'Police officers down at the Maclean's factory on Slateford Road!' Staring down at his friend.

'Whereabouts on Slateford Road?'

'Believe me, they won't be able to miss it.'

Five marksmen, dressed in black, aimed rifles at Rebus from outside. Saw him on the phone, saw him shake his head, moved on. Saw their targets out on the road, getting into a patrol car. Yelled the order to stop, warning that they would fire.

Response: muzzle-flash. Rebus ducked again. Fire was returned, the noise deafening but momentary.

Shouts from the road: 'Got them!'

A plaintive wail: one of the gunmen wounded. Rebus looked. The other was lying quite still on the road. Marksmen yelling to the wounded man: 'Drop the weapon, turn on to your front, hands behind your back.'

Response: 'I'm shot!'

Rebus to himself: 'Bastard's only wounded. Finish him off.'

Jack Morton unconscious. Rebus knew better than to move him. He could staunch the bleeding, that was all. Removed his jacket, folded it and pressed it to his friend's chest. Must've hurt, but Jack was out of it. Rebus dug the fuel rod out of his own pocket, the tiny canister still warm. Pressed it into Jack's right hand, curled the fingers around it.

'Stick around, pal. Just keep sticking around.'

Siobhan Clarke at the doorway, tears welling in her eyes.

Rebus pushed past her, slid his way across the road to where the Armed Response Team were cuffing the wounded man. Nobody much bothering with his dead partner. A little group of onlookers, keeping their distance. Rebus walked right up to the corpse, prised the handgun from its fingers, walked back around the front of the car. Heard someone call out: 'He's got a gun!'

Rebus bending down until the barrel of the gun touched the back of the wounded man's neck. Declan from the shop: breath coming in short gasps, hair matted with sweat, burrowing his face into the tarmac.

'John . . .'

Claverhouse. No megaphone needed. Standing right behind him. 'You really want to be like them?'

Like them ... Like Mean Machine. Like Telford and Cafferty and Tarawicz. He'd crossed the line before, made several trips forth and back. His foot was on Declan's neck, the gun barrel so hot it was singeing nape-skin.

'Please, no ... oh, Christ, please ... don't ... don't ...'

'Shut up,' Rebus hissed. He felt Claverhouse's hand close over his, flick on the safety.

'My responsibility, John. My fuck-up, don't make it yours, too.'

'Jack ...'

'I know.'

Rebus's vision blurred. 'They're getting away.'

Claverhouse shook his head. 'Road blocks. Back-up are already on it.'

'And Telford?'

Claverhouse checked his watch. 'Ormie will be picking him up right about now.'

Rebus grabbed Claverhouse's lapels. 'Nail him!'

Sirens nearing. Rebus shouted for the drivers to move their cars, make room for the ambulance. Then he ran back to the gatehouse. Siobhan Clarke was kneeling beside Jack, stroking his forehead. Her face was streaked with tears. She looked up at Rebus and shook her head.

'He's gone,' she said.

'No.' But he knew the truth. Which didn't stop him saying the word over and over again.

35

They divided the gang between two different locations – Torphichen and Fettes – and took Telford and a few of his 'lieutenants' to St Leonard's. Result: a logistical nightmare. Claverhouse was washing Pro Plus down with double-strength coffee, part of him wanting to do things right, the other part knowing he was answerable for the blood-bath at Maclean's. One officer dead, six wounded or otherwise injured – one of them seriously. One gunman dead, one wounded – not seriously enough to some people's minds.

The getaway cars had been apprehended and arrests made – shots exchanged but no bloodshed. None of the gang was saying anything, not a single damned word.

Rebus was sitting in an empty Interview Room at St Leonard's, arms on the table, head resting on arms. He'd been sitting there for a while, just thinking about loss, about how suddenly it could strike. A life, a friendship, just snatched away.

Irretrievable.

He hadn't cried, and didn't think he would. Instead, he felt numb, as if his soul had been spiked with novocaine. The world seemed to have slowed, like the mechanism was running down. He wondered if the sun would have the energy to rise again.

And I got him into it.

He had wallowed before in feelings of guilt and inadequacy, but nothing to measure up to this. This was overwhelming. Jack Morton, a copper with a quiet patch in Falkirk ... murdered in Edinburgh because a friend had asked a favour. Jack Morton, who'd brought himself back to life by swearing off cigarettes and booze, getting into shape, eating right, taking *care* of himself ... Lying in the mortuary, deep-body temperature dropping.

And I put him there.

He jumped up suddenly, threw the chair at the wall. Gill Templer walked into the room.

'All right, John?'

He wiped his mouth with the back of his hand.

'Fine.'

'My office is empty if you want to get your head down.'

'No, I'll be fine. Just ...' He looked around. 'Is this place needed?'

She nodded.

'Right. OK.' He picked up the chair. 'Who is it?'

'Brian Summers,' she said.

Pretty-Boy. Rebus straightened his back.

'I can make him talk.'

Templer looked sceptical.

'Honest, Gill.' Hands trembling. 'He doesn't know what I've got on him.'

She folded her arms. 'And what's that?'

'I just need . . .' He checked his watch. 'An hour or so; two hours tops. Bobby Hogan needs to be here. And I want Colquhoun brought in pronto.'

'Who's he?'

Rebus found the business card and handed it over. 'Pronto,' he repeated. He worked at his tie, making himself presentable. Smoothed back his hair. Said nothing.

'John, I'm not sure you're in any state to . . .'

He pointed at her, turned it into a wagging finger. 'Don't presume, Gill. If I say I can break him, I mean it.'

'No one else has said a single word.'

'Summers will be different.' He stared at her. 'Believe me.'

Looking back at him, she believed. 'I'll hold him back till Hogan gets here.'

'Thanks, Gill.'

'And John?'

'Yes?'

'I'm really sorry about Jack Morton. I didn't know him, but I've heard what everyone's saying.'

Rebus nodded.

'They're saying he'd be the last one to blame you.'

Rebus smiled. 'Right at the back of the queue.'

'There's only one person in the queue, John,' she said quietly. 'And you're it.'

Rebus phoned the night-desk at the Caledonian Hotel, learned that Sakiji Shoda had checked out unexpectedly, less than two hours after Rebus had dropped off the green folder which had cost him fifty-five pence at a stationer's on Raeburn Place. Actually, the folders had come in three-packs at one sixty-five. He had the other two in his car, only one of them empty.

Bobby Hogan was on his way. He lived in Portobello. He said to give him half an hour. Bill Pryde came over to Rebus's desk and said how sorry he was about Jack Morton, how he knew the two of them had been old friends.

'Just don't get too close to me, Bill,' Rebus told him. 'The people closest to me tend to lose their health.'

He got a message from reception: someone there to see him. He headed downstairs, found Patience Aitken.

'Patience?'

She had all her clothes on, but not necessarily in the right order, like she'd dressed in a power-cut.

'I heard on the radio,' she said. 'I couldn't sleep, so I had the radio on, and they said about this police raid and how people were dead . . . And you weren't in your flat, so I . . .'

He hugged her. 'I'm OK,' he whispered. 'I should have called you.'

'It's my fault, I . . .' She looked at him. 'You were there, I can see it on your face.' He nodded. 'What happened?'

'I lost a friend.'

'Oh Christ, John.' She hugged him again. She was still warm from the bedclothes. He could smell shampoo on her hair, perfume on her neck. *The people closest to me* . . . He pulled away gently, planted a kiss on her cheek.

'Go get some sleep,' he told her.

'Come for breakfast.'

'I just want to go home and crash.'

'You could sleep at my place. It's Sunday. We could stay in bed.'

'I don't know what time I'll finish here.'

She found his eyes. 'Don't feed on it, John. Don't keep it all inside.'

'OK, Doc.' He pecked her cheek again. 'Now vamoose.'

He managed a smile and a wink: both felt treacherous. He stood at the door and watched her leave. A lot of times while he'd been married, he'd thought of just walking. There were times when all the responsibilities and the shite at work and the pressure and the *need* would make him dream of escape.

He was tempted again now. Push open the door and head off to somewhere that wasn't here, to do something that wasn't this. But that, too, would be treachery. He had scores to settle, and a reason to settle them. He knew Telford was somewhere in the building, probably consulting with Charles Groal, saying nothing to anyone else. He wondered how the team were playing it. When would they let Telford know about the tape? When would they tell him the security guard had been a plant? When would they tell him that same man was now dead?

He hoped they were being clever. He hoped they were rattling Telford's cage.

He couldn't help wondering – and not for the first time – if it was all worth it. Some cops treated it like a game, others like a crusade, and for most of the rest it was neither, just a way of earning their daily bread. He asked himself why he'd invited Jack Morton in. Answers: because he'd wanted a *friend* involved, someone who'd keep *him* in the game; because he'd thought Jack was bored, and would enjoy the challenge; because tactics had demanded an outsider. There were plenty of reasons. Claverhouse had asked if Morton had any family, anyone who should be informed. Rebus had told him: divorced, four kids.

Did Rebus blame Claverhouse? Easy to be wise after the event, but then Claverhouse's reputation had been built on being wise *before* the event. And he'd failed . . . monumentally.

Icy roads: they'd needed the gates closed. The blockade had been too easy to move with the horsepower available to a truck.

Marksmen in the building: fine in the enclosed space of the yard, but they'd failed to keep the truck there, and the marksmen had been ineffectual once the truck had reversed out.

More armed officers *behind* the truck: producing little but a crossfire hazard.

Claverhouse should have got them to turn off the ignition, or – better still – waited for it to be turned off before making his presence known.

Jack Morton should have kept his head down.

And Rebus should have warned him.

Only, a shout would have turned the gunmen's attention towards him. Cowardice: was that what was at the bottom of his feelings? Simple human cowardice. Like in the bar in Belfast, when he hadn't said anything, fearing Mean Machine's wrath, fearing a rifle-butt turned on *him*. Maybe that was why – no, *of course* that was why – Lintz had got beneath Rebus's skin. Because when it came down to it, if Rebus had been in Villefranche ... drunk on failure, the dream of conquest over ... if he'd been under orders, just a lackey with a gun ... if he'd been primed by racism and the loss of comrades ... who was to say what he'd have done?

'Christ, John, how long have you been out here?'

It was Bobby Hogan, touching his face, prising the folder from frozen fingers.

'You're like ice, man, let's get you inside.'

'I'm fine,' Rebus breathed. And it had to be true: how else to explain the sweat on his back and his brow? How else to explain that he only started shivering *after* Bobby led him indoors?

Hogan got two mugs of sweet tea into him. The station was still buzzing: shock, rumour, theories. Rebus filled Hogan in.

'They'll have to let Telford walk, if nobody talks.'

'What about the tape?'

'They'll want to spring that later ... if they're being canny.'

'Who's in with him?'

Rebus shrugged. 'Farmer Watson himself, last time I heard. He was doing a double-act with Bill Pryde, but I saw Bill later, so they've either taken a break or else done a swop.'

Hogan shook his head. 'What a fucking business.'

Rebus stared at his tea. 'I hate sugar.'

'You drank the first mug all right.'

'Did I?' He took a mouthful, squirmed.

'What the hell did you think you were doing out there?'

'Catching a breath.'

'Catching your death more like.' Hogan patted down an unruly clump of hair. 'I had a visit from a man called Harris.'

'What are you going to do?'

Hogan shrugged. 'Let it go, I suppose.'

Rebus stared at him. 'You might not have to.'

36

Colquhoun didn't look happy to be there.

'Thanks for coming in,' Rebus told him.

'I didn't have much choice.' He had a solicitor sitting beside him, a middle-aged man: one of Telford's? Rebus couldn't have cared less.

'You might have to get used to not having choices, Dr Colquhoun. Know who else is in here tonight? Tommy Telford; Brian Summers.'

'Who?'

Rebus shook his head. 'You're getting your script wrong. It's OK for you to know who they are: we talked about them in front of Candice.'

Colquhoun's face flushed.

'You remember Candice, don't you? Her real name's Karina: did I ever tell you that? She's got a son somewhere, only they took him away. Maybe she'll find him one day, maybe not.'

'I don't see what this –'

'Telford and Summers are going to be spending a while behind bars.' Rebus sat back. 'If I want to, I could have a damned good go at putting you in there with them. How would you like that, Dr Colquhoun? Conspiracy to pervert, et cetera.'

Rebus could feel himself relaxing into his work; doing it for Jack.

The solicitor was about to say something, but Colquhoun got in first. 'It was a mistake.'

'A mistake?' Rebus hooted. 'One way of putting it, I suppose.' He sat forward, resting his elbows on the table. 'Time to talk, Dr Colquhoun. You know what they say about confession . . .'

Brian 'Pretty-Boy' Summers looked immaculate.

He had a lawyer with him, too, a senior partner who looked like an undertaker and wasn't taking kindly to being kept waiting. As they settled at the table in the Interview Room, and Hogan slotted tapes into cassette machine and video recorder, the lawyer started the protest he'd spent the past hour or two preparing in his head.

'On behalf of my client, Inspector, I feel duty-bound to say that this is some of the most appalling behaviour I've –'

'You think you've seen appalling behaviour?' Rebus answered. 'In the words of the song, you ain't seen nothing yet.'

'Look, it's clear to me that you –'

Rebus ignored him, slapped the folder down on to the table, slid it towards Pretty-Boy.

'Take a look.'

Pretty-Boy was wearing a charcoal suit and purple shirt, open at the neck. No sunglasses or car-keys. He'd been brought in from his flat in the New Town. Comment from one of the men who'd gone to fetch him: 'Biggest hi-fi I've seen in my life. Bugger was wide awake, listening to Patsy Cline.'

Rebus started whistling 'Crazy': that got Pretty-Boy's attention and a wry smile, but he kept his arms folded.

'I would if I were you,' Rebus said.

'Ready,' Hogan said, meaning he had the tapes running. They went through the formalities: date and time, location, individuals present. Rebus looked towards the lawyer and smiled. He looked pretty expensive. Telford would have ordered the best, same as always.

'Know any Elton John, Brian?' Rebus asked. 'He's got this song: "Someone Saved My Life Tonight". You'll be singing it to me once you've looked inside.' He tapped the folder. 'Go on, you know it makes sense. I'm not playing some trick, and you don't have to say anything. But you really should do yourself a favour . . .'

'I've got nothing to say.'

Rebus shrugged. 'Just open the folder, take a look.'

Pretty-Boy looked to his lawyer, who seemed uncertain.

'Your client won't be incriminating himself,' Rebus explained. 'If you want to read what's in there first, that's fine. It might not mean much to you, but go ahead.'

The lawyer opened the folder, found a dozen sheets of paper.

'Sorry in advance for any mistakes,' Rebus said. 'I typed it in a bit of a rush.'

Pretty-Boy didn't so much as glance towards the material. He kept his eyes on Rebus, while the lawyer sifted through the papers.

'These allegations,' the lawyer finally said, 'you must realise they're worthless?'

'If that's your opinion, fair enough. I'm not asking Mr Summers to admit or deny anything. Like I said, he can do a deaf and dumb routine for all I care, so long as he uses his *eyes*.'

A smile from Pretty-Boy, then a glance towards his lawyer, who shrugged his shoulders, saying there was nothing here to fear. A glance back at Rebus, and Pretty-Boy unfolded his arms, picked up the first sheet, and started reading.

'Just so we have a record for the tape,' Rebus said, 'Mr Summers is now reading a draft report prepared by myself earlier today.' Rebus paused. 'Actually, I mean yesterday, Saturday. He's reading my interpretation of recent events in and around Edinburgh, events concerning his employer, Thomas Telford, a Japanese business consortium – which is really, in my opinion, a Yakuza front – and a gentleman from Newcastle by the name of Jake Tarawicz.'

He paused. The lawyer said: 'Agreed, thus far.' Rebus nodded and continued.

'My version of events is as follows. Jake Tarawicz became an associate of Thomas Telford only because he wanted something Telford had: namely, a slick operation to bring drugs into Britain without raising suspicion. Either that or it was only later on, once their relationship had become established,

that Tarawicz decided he could move in on Telford's turf. To facilitate this, he manufactured a war between Telford and Morris Gerald Cafferty. This was easily accomplished. Telford had moved in aggressively on Cafferty's territory, probably with Tarawicz egging him on. All Tarawicz had to do was make sure things escalated. To this end, he had one of his men attack a drug dealer outside one of Telford's nightclubs, Telford immediately placing the blame on Cafferty. He also had some of his men attack a Telford stronghold in Paisley. Meanwhile, there were attacks on Cafferty's territory and associates, retaliation by Telford for perceived wrongs.'

Rebus cleared his throat, took a sip of tea – a fresh cup, no sugar.

'Does this sound familiar, Mr Summers?' Pretty-Boy said nothing. He was busy reading. 'My guess is that the Japanese were never meant to become involved. In other words, they had no knowledge of what was happening. Telford was showing them around, easing the way for them as they tried to buy a country club. Rest and recreation for their members, plus a good way of laundering money – less suspect than a casino or similar operation, especially when an electronics factory is about to open, so that the Yakuza slip into the country as just a few more Japanese businessmen.

'I think when Tarawicz saw this, he began to worry. He didn't want to get rid of Tommy Telford just to leave the way open for other competitors to muscle in. So he decided they'd have to become part of his plan. He had Matsumoto followed. He had him killed, and in a nice twist made *me* the chief suspect. Why? Two reasons. First, Tommy Telford had me pegged as Cafferty's man, so by fingering me, Tarawicz was fingering Cafferty. Second, he wanted me out of the game, because I'd gone to Newcastle, and had met one of his men, a guy called William 'The Crab' Colton. I knew the Crab of old, and it so happened Tarawicz had used him for the hit on the drug dealer. He didn't want me putting two and two together.'

Rebus paused again. 'How's it sounding, Brian?'

Pretty-Boy had finished reading. His arms were folded again, eyes on Rebus.

'We've yet to see any evidence, Inspector,' the lawyer said.

Rebus shrugged. 'I don't need evidence. See, the same file you've got there, I delivered a copy to a Mr Sakiji Shoda at the Caledonian Hotel.' Rebus watched Pretty-Boy's eyelids flutter. 'Now, the way I see it, Mr Shoda is going to be a bit pissed off. I mean, he's already pissed off, that's why he was here. He'd seen Telford screw up, and wanted to see if he could do anything *right*. I don't suppose the raid on Maclean's will have given him any renewed sense of confidence. But he was also here to find out why one of his men had been killed, and who was responsible. This report tells him Tarawicz was behind it, and if he chooses to believe that, he'll go after Tarawicz. In fact, he checked out of his hotel yesterday evening – seems he was in a bit of a rush. I'm wondering if he was on his way home via Newcastle. Doesn't matter. What matters is that he'll *still* be pissed off at Telford for letting it happen. And meantime Jake Tarawicz is going to be wondering who shopped him to Shoda. The Yakuza are not nice people, Brian. You lot are nursery school by comparison.' Rebus sat back in his chair.

'One last point,' he said. 'Tarawicz's base is Newcastle. I'm betting he had eyes and ears here in Edinburgh. In fact, I know he did. I've just been

having a chat with Dr Colquhoun. You remember him, Brian? You'd heard about him from Lintz. Then when Tarawicz offered East Europeans as working girls, you reckoned maybe Tommy should have a few foreign phrases to hand. Colquhoun did the teaching. You told him stories about Tarawicz, about Bosnia. Catch was, he's the only person round these parts who knew the subject, so when we picked up Candice, we ended up using him, too. Colquhoun sussed straight off what was happening. He wasn't sure if he had anything to fear: he'd never met her, and her answers were reassuringly vague – or he kept them that way. All the same, he came to you. Your solution: ship Candice to Fife, then snatch her, and take Colquhoun out of the game till the heat died.'

Rebus smiled. 'He told *you* about Fife. Yet it was *Tarawicz* who got Candice. I think Tommy will find that a bit odd, don't you? So, here we sit. And I can tell you that the minute you walk out of here, you're going to be a marked man. Could be the Yakuza, could be Cafferty, could be your own boss or Tarawicz himself. You haven't got any friends, and nowhere's safe any more.' Rebus paused. 'Unless *we* help you. I've talked to Chief Superintendent Watson, and he's agreeing to witness protection, new identity, whatever you want. There may be a short sentence to serve – just so it looks right – but it'll be a soft option, room of your own, no other prisoners allowed near. And afterwards, you'll be home and dry. That's a big commitment on our part, and we'll need a big commitment from *you*. We'll want everything.' Rebus counted off on his fingers. 'The drug shipments, the war with Cafferty, the Newcastle connection, the Yakuza, the prostitutes.' He paused again, drained his tea. 'Tall order, I know. Your boss had a meteoric rise, Brian, and he nearly made it. But that's all over. Best thing you can do now is talk. It's either that or spend the rest of your days waiting for the bullet or the machete to strike . . .'

The lawyer started to protest. Rebus held up a hand.

'We'll need all of it, Brian. Including Lintz.'

'Lintz,' Pretty-Boy said dismissively. 'Lintz is nothing.'

'So where's the harm?'

The look in Pretty-Boy's eyes was a mix of anger, fear and disorientation. Rebus stood up.

'I need something else to drink. What about you gentlemen?'

'Coffee,' the lawyer said, 'black, no sugar.'

Pretty-Boy hesitated, then said, 'Get me a Coke.' And at that point – for the very first time – Rebus knew a deal might be done. He stopped the interview, Hogan switched off the tapes, and both men left the room. Hogan patted him on the back.

Farmer Watson was coming along the corridor towards them. Rebus moved to meet him, leading them away from the door.

'I think we might be in with a shout, sir,' Rebus said. 'He'll try to twist the deal, give us less than we want, but I think there's a chance.'

Watson beamed a smile, as Rebus leaned against the wall, eyes closed. 'I feel about a hundred years old.'

'Experience tells,' Hogan said.

Rebus growled at him, then they went to fetch the drinks.

'Mr Summers,' the lawyer said, as Rebus handed him his cup, 'would like to

tell you the story of his relationship with Joseph Lintz. But first we'll need some assurances.'

'What about everything else I mentioned?'

'These can be negotiated.'

Rebus stared at Pretty-Boy. 'You don't trust me?'

Pretty-Boy picked up his can, said 'No', and drank.

'Fine.' Rebus walked over to the far wall. 'In that case, you're free to go.' He checked his watch. 'Soon as you've finished your drinks, I want you out of here. Interview Rooms are at a premium tonight. DI Hogan, mark up the tapes, will you?'

Hogan ejected both cassettes. Rebus sat down beside him and they started discussing work, as though Pretty-Boy had been dismissed from their minds. Hogan examined a sheet of paper, checking who was due to be interviewed next.

From the corner of his eye, Rebus saw Pretty-Boy leaning in towards his lawyer, whispering something. He turned on them.

'Can you do that outside, please? We need to vacate this room.'

Pretty-Boy *knew* Rebus was bluffing ... knew the policeman needed him. But he realised, too, that Rebus was *not* bluffing about giving the file to Shoda, and he was far too intelligent not to be scared. He didn't move from the chair, and held his lawyer's arm so he had to stay and listen. Eventually the lawyer cleared his throat.

'Inspector, Mr Summers is willing to answer your questions.'

'*All* my questions?'

The lawyer nodded. 'But I must insist on hearing more of the "deal" you're proposing.'

Rebus looked at Hogan. 'Go get the Chief Super.'

Rebus left the room, stood in the hallway while Hogan was away. Cadged a cigarette off a passing uniform. He'd just got it lit when Farmer Watson came barrelling towards him, Hogan behind as though attached to Watson by an invisible leash.

'No smoking, John, you know that.'

'Yes, sir,' Rebus said, crimping the tip. 'I was just holding it for Inspector Hogan.'

Watson nodded towards the door. 'What do they want?'

'We've been talking possible immunity from prosecution. At the very least, he'll want a soft sentence, and a safe one, plus new ID afterwards.'

Watson was thoughtful. 'We haven't had a cheep out of any of them. Not that it matters greatly. There's the gang we caught red-handed, plus Telford on the audio tape ...'

'Summers is a real insider, knows Telford's organisation.'

'So how come he's willing to spill?'

'Because he's scared, and his fear is overwhelming his loyalty. I'm not saying we'll get every last detail out of him, but we'll probably get enough to start pressing the other members. Once they know someone's yapping, they'll all want a trade.'

'What's his lawyer like?'

'Expensive.'

'No point shilly-shallying then.'

'I couldn't have put it better myself, sir.'

The Chief Super pinned back his shoulders. 'All right, let's do a deal.'

'When did you first meet Joseph Lintz?'

Pretty-Boy's arms were no longer folded. He was resting them on the desk, head in his hands. His hair flopped forward, making him look younger than ever.

'About six months ago. We'd spoken on the phone before that.'

'He was a punter?'

'Yes.'

'Meaning what exactly?'

Pretty-Boy looked at the turning spools. 'You want me to explain for all our listeners?'

'That's right.'

'Joseph Lintz was a client of the escort service for which I worked.'

'Come on, Brian, you were a bit more than a flunkey. You ran it, didn't you?'

'If you say so.'

'Anytime you want to walk, Brian . . .'

Eyes burning. 'OK, I *ran* it for my employer.'

'And Mr Lintz phoned wanting an escort?'

'He wanted one of our girls to go to his home.'

'And?'

'And that was it. He'd sit there opposite her and just stare for half an hour.'

'Both of them fully clothed?'

'Yes.'

'Nothing else?'

'Not at first.'

'Ah.' Rebus paused. 'You must have been curious.'

Pretty-Boy shrugged. 'Takes all sorts, doesn't it?'

'I suppose it does. So how did your business relationship progress?'

'Well, on a gig like that, there's always a chaperone.'

'Yourself?'

'Yes.'

'You didn't have better things to do?'

Another shrug. 'I was curious.'

'About what?'

'The address: Heriot Row.'

'Mr Lintz had . . . class?'

'Coming out his ears. I mean, I've met plenty fat cats, corporate types looking for a shag in their hotel, but Lintz was a long way from that.'

'He just wanted to look at the girls.'

'That's right. And this huge house he had . . .'

'You went in? You didn't just wait in the car?'

'Told him it was company policy.' A smile. 'Really, all I wanted was to snoop.'

'Did you talk to him?'

'Later, yes.'

'You became friends?'

'Not really . . . maybe. He knew things, had a real brain on him.'

'You were impressed.'

Pretty-Boy nodded. Yes, Rebus could imagine. His previous role model had always been Tommy Telford, but Pretty-Boy had aspirations. He *wanted* class. He wanted people to acknowledge him for his mind. Rebus knew how seductive Lintz's storytelling could be. How much more seductive would Pretty-Boy have found it?

'Then what happened?'

Pretty-Boy shifted. 'His tastes changed.'

'Or his real tastes started to emerge?'

'That's what I wondered.'

'So what did he want?'

'He wanted the girls . . . he had this length of rope . . . he'd made it into a noose.' Pretty-Boy swallowed. His lawyer had stopped writing, was listening intently. 'He wanted the girls to slip it over their heads, then lie down like they were dead.'

'Dressed or naked?'

'Naked.'

'And?'

'And he'd . . . he'd sit on his chair and get off. Some of the girls wouldn't go along. He wanted the works: bulging eyes, tongue sticking out, neck twisted . . .' Pretty-Boy rubbed his hands through his hair.

'Did you ever talk about it?'

'With him? No, never.'

'So what did you talk about?'

'All sorts of things.' Pretty-Boy looked up at the ceiling, laughed. 'He told me once, he believed in God. Said the problem was, he wasn't sure God believed in him. That seemed clever at the time . . . he always managed to get me thinking. And this was the same guy who tossed himself off over bodies with ropes round their necks.'

'All this personal attention you were giving him,' Rebus said, 'you were sizing him up, weren't you?'

Pretty-Boy looked into his lap, nodded.

'For the tape, please.'

'Tommy always wanted to know if a punter was worth squeezing.'

'And . . . ?'

Pretty-Boy shrugged. 'We found out about the Nazi stuff, realised we couldn't hurt him any more than he was already being hurt. Turned into a bit of a joke. There we were, thinking of threatening him with exposure as a perv, and at the same time the papers were saying he was a mass murderer.' He laughed again.

'So you dropped that idea?'

'Yes.'

'But he paid you five grand?' Rebus fishing.

Pretty-Boy licked his lips. 'He'd tried topping himself. He told me that. Tying the rope to the top of his banister and jumping off. Only it didn't work. Banister snapped and he fell half a flight.'

Rebus remembering: the broken stair-rail.

Rebus remembering: Lintz with a scarf around his neck, his voice hoarse. Telling Rebus he had a throat bug.

'He told you this?'

'He phoned the office, said we had to meet. That was unusual. In the past, he'd always used phone boxes and got me on my mobile. Safe old bugger, I'd always thought. Then he calls from home, right to the office.'

'Where did you meet?'

'In a restaurant. He bought me lunch.' The young woman . . . 'Told me he'd tried killing himself and couldn't do it. He kept saying he'd proved himself a "moral coward", whatever that means.'

'So what did he want?'

Pretty-Boy stared up at Rebus. 'He needed someone to help him.'

'You?'

Pretty-Boy shrugged.

'And the price was right?'

'No haggling necessary. He wanted it done in Warriston Cemetery.'

'Did you ask him why?'

'I knew he liked the place. We met at his house, really early. I drove him down there. He seemed the same as ever, except he kept thanking me for my "resolve". I wasn't sure what he meant by that. To me, Resolve is something you take after a hard night.'

Rebus smiled, as was expected. 'Go on,' he said.

'Not much more to tell, is there? *He* put the noose over his head. *He* told me to pull on the rope. I had a last go at talking him out of it, but the bugger was determined. It's not murder, is it? Assisted suicide: a lot of places, it's legal.'

'How did the dunt get on his head?'

'He was heavier than I thought. First time I hauled him up, the rope slipped and he fell, thumped himself on the ground.'

Bobby Hogan cleared his throat. 'Brian, did he say anything . . . right at the end?'

'Famous last words and all that?' Pretty-Boy shook his head. 'All he said was "thank you". Poor old sod. One thing: he wrote it all down.'

'What?'

'About me helping him. A sort of insurance, in case anyone ever linked us. Letter says he paid me, begged me to help.'

'Where is this?'

'In a safe. I can get it for you.'

Rebus nodded, stretched his back. 'Did you ever talk about Villefranche?'

'A little bit, mostly about the way the papers and TV were hounding him, how difficult it made it when he wanted . . . company.'

'But not the massacre itself?'

Pretty-Boy shook his head. 'Know something else? Even if he *had* told me, I wouldn't tell you.'

Rebus tapped his pen against the desk. He knew the Lintz story was as closed as it was ever going to be. Bobby Hogan knew it, too. They had the secret at last, the story of how Lintz had died. They knew he'd been helped by the Rat Line, but they'd never know whether he'd been Josef Linzstek or not. The circumstantial evidence was overwhelming, but so was the evidence that Lintz had been hounded to death. He'd started putting the escorts into nooses only *after* the accusations had been made.

Hogan caught Rebus's eye and shrugged, as if to say: what does it matter? Rebus nodded back. Part of him wanted to take a break, but now that Pretty-Boy was rolling it was important to keep up the steam.

'Thanks for that, Mr Summers. We may come back to Mr Lintz if we think of any more questions. But meantime, let's move on to the relationship between Thomas Telford and Jake Tarawicz.'

Pretty-Boy shifted, as if trying to get comfortable. 'This could take a while,' he said.

'Take as long as you like,' Rebus told him.

37

They got it all, in time.

Pretty-Boy had to rest, and so did they. Other teams came in, worked on different areas. The tapes were filling up, being listened to elsewhere, notes and transcripts made. Back-up questions were forwarded to the Interview Room. Telford wasn't talking. Rebus went and took a look at him, sat across from him. Telford didn't blink once. He sat ramrod-straight, hands on knees. And all the while, Pretty-Boy's confession was being used to squeeze other gang members – without letting slip who was singing.

The ranks broke, slowly at first and then in a cataract of accusation, self-defence and denial. And they got it all.

Telford and Tarawicz: European prostitutes heading north; muscle and dope heading south.

Mr Taystee: taking more than his fair share; dealt with accordingly.

The Japanese: using Telford as their introduction to Scotland, finding it a good base of operations.

Only now Rebus had scuppered that. In his folder to Shoda he'd warned the gangster to leave Poyntinghame alone, or he'd be 'implicated in ongoing criminal investigations'. The Yakuza weren't stupid. He doubted they'd be back . . . for a while at least.

His last trip of the night: Rebus went down to the cells, unlocked one of the doors and told Ned Farlowe he was free. Told him he had nothing to fear . . .

Unlike Mr Pink Eyes. The Yakuza had a score to settle. And it didn't stay unsettled long. He was found in his car-crusher, seatbelt welded shut. His men had started running.

Some of them were running still.

Rebus sat in his living room, staring at the door Jack Morton had stripped and varnished. He was thinking about the funeral, about how the Juice Church would be there in force. He wondered if they'd blame him. Jack's kids would be there, too. Rebus had never met them; didn't think he wanted to see them.

Wednesday morning, he was back in Inverness, meeting Mrs Hethering-ton off her flight. She'd been delayed in Holland, answering Customs questions. They'd laid a little trap, caught a man called De Gier – a known trafficker – planting the kilo package of heroin in Mrs Hetherington's

luggage: a secret compartment in her suitcase, the suitcase itself a gift from her landlord. Several of Telford's other elderly tenants were enjoying short breaks in Belgium. They'd be questioned by local police.

Home again, Rebus telephoned David Levy.

'Lintz committed suicide,' he told him.

'That's your conclusion?'

'It's the truth. No conspiracy, no cover-up.'

A sigh. 'It's of little consequence, Inspector. What matters is that we've lost another one.'

'Villefranche doesn't mean a thing to you, does it? The Rat Line, that's all you care about.'

'There's nothing we can do about Villefranche.'

Rebus took a deep breath. 'A man called Harris came to see me. He works for British Intelligence. They're protecting some big names, high-level people. Rat Line survivors, maybe their children. Tell Mayerlink to keep digging.'

There was silence for a moment. 'Thank you, Inspector.'

Rebus was in a car. It was the Weasel's Jag. The Weasel was in the back with him. Their driver was missing a big chunk of his left ear. The shape made him resemble a pixie – but only from the side, and you wouldn't want to tell him to his face.

'You did well,' the Weasel was saying. 'Mr Cafferty's pleased.'

'How long have you been holding him?'

The Weasel smiled. 'Nothing gets past you, Rebus.'

'Rangers have offered me a trial in goal. How long have you had him?'

'A few days. Had to be sure we had the right one, didn't we?'

'And now you're sure?'

'Absolutely positive.'

Rebus looked out of the window at the passing parade of shops, pedestrians, buses. The car was heading down towards Newhaven and Granton. 'You wouldn't be setting up some loser to take the blame?'

'He's genuine.'

'You could have spent the past few days making sure he was going to say the right things.'

The Weasel seemed amused. 'Such as?'

'Such as that he was in Telford's pay.'

'Rather than Mr Cafferty's, you mean?' Rebus glared at the Weasel, who laughed. 'I think you'll find him a pretty convincing candidate.'

The way he said it made Rebus shiver. 'He's still alive, isn't he?'

'Oh yes. How long he remains so is entirely up to you.'

'You think I want him dead?'

'I know you do. You didn't go to Mr Cafferty because you wanted justice. You went out of *revenge*.'

Rebus stared at the Weasel. 'You don't sound like yourself.'

'You mean I don't sound like my persona – different thing entirely.'

'And do many people get behind the persona?' The Who: 'Can You See the Real Me?'

The Weasel smiled again. 'I thought you deserved it, after all the trouble you've gone to.'

'I didn't break Telford just to please your boss.'

'Nevertheless . . .' The Weasel slid across his seat towards Rebus. 'How's Sammy, by the way?'

'She's fine.'

'Recuperating?'

'Yes.'

'That's good news. Mr Cafferty will be pleased. He's disappointed you haven't been to see him.'

Rebus took a newspaper from his pocket. It was folded at a story: FATAL STABBING AT JAIL.

'Your boss?' he said, handing the paper over.

The Weasel made show of reading it. ' "Aged twenty-six, from Govan . . . stabbed through the heart in his cell . . . no witnesses, no weapon recovered despite a thorough search." ' He tutted. 'Bit careless.'

'He'd taken up the contract on Cafferty?'

'Had he?' The Weasel looked amazed.

'Fuck off,' Rebus said, turning back to his window.

'By the way, Rebus, if you decide not to go to trial with the driver . . .' The Weasel was holding something out. A homemade screwdriver, filed to a point, grip covered in packing-tape. Rebus looked at it in disgust.

'I washed the blood off,' the Weasel assured him. Then he laughed again. Rebus felt like he was being ferried straight to hell. In front of him he could see the grey expanse of the Firth of Forth, and Fife beyond it. They were coming into an area of docks, gas-plant and warehouses. It had been earmarked for a development spill-over from Leith. The whole city was changing. Traffic routes and priorities were altered overnight, cranes were kept busy on building-sites, and the council, who always complained about being broke, had all manner of schemes under way to further alter the shape and scope of his chosen home.

'Nearly there,' the Weasel said.

Rebus wondered if there'd be any turning back.

They stopped at the gates to a warehouse complex. The driver undid the padlock, pulled the chain free. The gates swung open. In they went. The Weasel ordered the driver to park around the back. There was a plain white van there, more rust than metal. Its back windows had been painted over, turning it into a suitable hearse should occasion demand.

They got out into a salt wind. The Weasel shuffled over towards a door and banged once. The door was pushed open from within. They stepped inside.

A huge open space, filled with only a few packing cases, a couple of pieces of machinery covered with oil-cloth. And two men: the one who'd let them in, and another at the far end. This man was standing in front of a wooden chair. There was a figure tied to the chair, half-hidden by the man. The Weasel led the procession. Rebus tried to control his breathing, which was growing painfully shallow. His heart was racing, nerves jangling. He pushed back the anger, wasn't sure he could hold it.

When they were eight feet from the chair, the Weasel nodded and the man stood away, revealing to Rebus the terrified figure of a kid.

A boy.

Nine or ten, no older.

One black eye, nose caked with blood, both cheeks bruised and a graze on his chin. Burst lip beginning to heal, trousers torn at the knees, one shoe missing.

And a smell, as if he'd wet himself, maybe even worse.

'What the hell is this?' Rebus asked.

'This,' the Weasel said, 'is the little bastard who stole the car. This is the little bastard who lost his nerve at a red light and gunned through it, losing control of the pedals because he could barely reach them. This . . .' The Weasel stepped forward, planted a hand on the kid's shoulder. 'This is the culprit.'

Rebus looked at the faces around him. 'Is this your idea of a joke?'

'No joke, Rebus.'

He looked at the boy. Dried tear-tracks. Eyes bloodshot from crying. Shoulders trembling. They'd tied his arms behind him. Tied his ankles to the chair-legs.

'Puh-please, mister . . .' Dry, cracked voice. 'I . . . help me, puh-please . . .'

'Nicked the car,' the Weasel recited, 'then did the hit-and-run, got scared, and dumped the car near where he lives. Took the cassette and the tapes. He wanted the car for a race. That's what they do, race cars around the schemes. This little runt can start an engine in ten seconds flat.' He rubbed his hands together. 'So . . . here we all are.'

'Help me . . .'

Rebus recalling the city's graffiti: Won't Anyone Help? The Weasel nodding towards one of his men, the man producing a pickaxe-handle.

'Or the screwdriver,' the Weasel said. 'Or whatever you like, really. We are at your command.' And he gave a little bow.

Rebus could hardly speak. 'Cut the ropes.'

Silence in the warehouse.

'*Cut those fucking ropes!*'

A sniff from the Weasel. 'You heard the man, Tony.'

Ca-chink of a flick-knife opening. Ropes severed like cutting through butter. Rebus walked to within inches of the boy.

'What's your name?'

'J-Jordan.'

'Is that your first name or your second?'

The boy looked at him. 'First.'

'OK, Jordan.' Rebus leaned down. The boy flinched, but did not resist as Rebus picked him up. He weighed almost nothing. Rebus started walking with him.

'What now, Rebus?' the Weasel asked. But Rebus didn't answer. He carried the boy to the threshold, kicked open the door, stepped out into sunshine.

'I'm . . . I'm really sorry.' The boy had a hand across his eyes, unused to the light. He was starting to cry.

'You know what you did?'

Jordan nodded. 'I've been . . . ever since that night. I knew it was bad . . .' Now the tears came.

'Did they say who I was?'

'Please don't kill me.'

'I'm not going to kill you, Jordan.'

The boy blinked, trying to clear tears from his eyes, the better to know whether he was being lied to.

'I think you've been through enough, pal,' Rebus said. Then added: 'I think we both have.'

So after everything, it had come to this. Bob Dylan: 'Simple Twist of Fate'. Segue to Leonard Cohen: 'Is This What You Wanted?'

Rebus didn't know the answer to that.

38

Clean and sober, he went to the hospital. An open ward this time, set hours for visitors. No more darkened vigils. No return visit by Candice, though nurses spoke of regular phone calls by someone foreign-sounding. No way of knowing where she was. Maybe out there searching for her son. It didn't matter, so long as she was safe. So long as she was in control.

When he reached the ward's far end, two women rose from their chairs so he could kiss them: Rhona and Patience. He had a carrier bag with him, magazines and grapes. Sammy was sitting up, supported by three pillows, Pa Broon propped beside her. Her hair had been washed and brushed, and she was smiling at him.

'Women's magazines,' he said, shaking his head. 'They should be on the top shelf.'

'I need a few fantasies to sustain me in here,' Sammy said. Rebus beamed at her, said hello, then bent down and kissed his daughter.

The sun was shining as they walked through The Meadows – a rare day off for both. They held hands and watched people sunbathing and playing football. He knew Rhona was excited, and thought he knew why. But he wasn't going to spoil things with speculation.

'If you had a daughter, what would you call her?' she asked.

He shrugged. 'Haven't really thought about it.'

'What about a son?'

'I quite like Sam.'

'Sam?'

'When I was a kid, I had a bear called Sam. My mum knitted it for me.'

'Sam . . .' She tried the name out. 'It would work both ways, wouldn't it?'

He stopped, circled his arms around her waist. 'How do you mean?'

'Well, it could be Samuel or Samantha. You don't get many of those – names that work both ways.'

'I suppose not. Rhona, is there . . .?'

She put a finger to his lips, then kissed him. They walked on. There didn't seem to be a cloud in the whole damned sky.

Afterword

My fictional French village of Villefranche d'Albarede owes its existence to the real village of Oradour-sur-Glâne, which was the subject of an attack by the 3rd Company of the SS 'Der Führer' regiment.

On the afternoon of Saturday 10 June 1944, 3rd Company – known as 'Das Reich' – entered the village and rounded up everyone. The women and children were herded into the church, while the men were split into groups and marched to various barns and other buildings around the village. Then the slaughter began.

Some 642 victims have been accounted for, but the estimate is that up to a thousand people may have perished that day. Only fifty-three corpses were ever identified. One boy from Lorraine, having first-hand knowledge of SS atrocities, managed to flee when the troops entered the village. Five men escaped the massacre in Laudy's barn. Wounded, they were able to crawl from the burning building and hide until the next day. One woman escaped from the church, climbing out of a window after playing dead beside the corpse of her child.

Soldiers went from house to house, finding villagers too sick or elderly to leave their beds. These people were shot and their houses set alight. Some of the bodies were hidden in mass graves, or dumped down wells and in bread ovens.

General Lammerding was the commanding officer. On 9 June he'd ordered the deaths of ninety-nine hostages in Tulle. He also gave the order for the Oradour massacre. Later on in the war, Lammerding was captured by the British, who refused his extradition to France. Instead, he was returned to Düsseldorf, where he ran a successful company until his death in 1971.

In the general euphoria of the Normandy landings, the tragedy at Oradour went almost unnoticed. Eventually, in January 1953, the trial opened in Bordeaux of sixty-five men identified as having been involved in the massacre. Of these sixty-five, only twenty-one were present: seven Germans, and fourteen natives of French Alsace. None of the men was of officer rank.

Every individual found guilty at the Bordeaux trial left court a free man. A special Act of Amnesty had been passed, in the interests of national unity. (People in Alsace were disgruntled that their countrymen had been picked out for condemnation.) Meantime, the Germans were said to have already served their terms.

823

As a result, Oradour broke off all relations with the French state, a rupture which lasted seventeen years.

In May 1983, a man stood trial in East Berlin, charged with having been a lieutenant in 'Das Reich' during the Oradour massacre. He admitted everything, and was sentenced to life imprisonment.

In June 1996, it was reported that around 12,000 foreign volunteers to the Waffen SS are still receiving pensions from the Federal German government. One of these pensioners, a former Obersturmbannführer, was a participant at Oradour . . .

Oradour still stands as a shrine. The village has been left just the way it was on that day in June 1944.